* *

THE BEDSIDE BOOK OF

FAMOUS BRITISH

STORIES

* *

Edited by

BENNETT A. CERF

Editor of the Modern Library

and

HENRY C. MORIARTY

of The Harvard Co-operative Society

With an Introduction by

BLISS PERRY

Francis Lee Higginson Professor
of English Literature, Emeritus
in Harvard University

* *

THE LITERARY GUILD OF AMERICA, INC.   NEW YORK

THE BEDSIDE BOOK OF

FAMOUS BRITISH

STORIES

Edited by

BENNETT A. CERF

Editor of the Modern Library

and

HENRY C. MORIARTY

of The Harvard Co-operative Society

With an Introduction by

BLISS PERRY

Francis Lee Higginson Professor
of English Literature, Emeritus
in Harvard University

To

George Ellsworth Cole
This book is dedicated
with respect and affection

★ *Contents* ★

CONTENTS

⋆ *Acknowledgments* ⋆

A COLLECTION of so many famous stories as this, by authors known the world over, is made possible only by the gracious permissions extended by the authors themselves, their publishers, representatives, or holders of the copyrights listed below. In several instances they allowed the editors to reprint stories that have never before appeared in an anthology. The concluding group of stories, in particular, are unfamiliar additions to a collection of this kind; they end the volume, in the opinion of the editors, on a note of cynicism and perplexity that is only too characteristic of the day in which we are living.

The editors also gratefully acknowledge valuable suggestions from Professor Bliss Perry, Professor Charles Townsend Copeland, Montague Barry Piper, Ralph Brown, Herbert A. Wise and Terence Holliday.

Permissions:

D. APPLETON-CENTURY COMPANY, INC.: for *Rivers of Damascus* by Donn Byrne, Copyright, 1931.

EDWARD ARNOLD: for *The Mezzotint* by Montague Rhodes James.

THE ESTATE OF ARNOLD BENNETT: for *Mary with the High Hand* by Arnold Bennett.

BORISWOOD LIMITED: for *The Eyes* by Thomas Owen Beachcroft.

JOHN BUCHAN: for *The Kings of Orion* by John Buchan.

JONATHAN CAPE LIMITED: for *The Higgler* by A. E. Coppard; *The Old Hunter* by Liam O'Flaherty.

COWARD-McCANN, INC.: for *The Clerk's Quest* by George Moore.

xi

CURTIS BROWN, LIMITED: for *The Stranger in the Village* by Sir Philip Gibbs, Copyright, 1923; *The Cavalier of the Streets* by Michael Arlen, Copyright, 1923.

ANDREW DAKERS LIMITED: for *The Higgler* by A. E. Coppard; *A Day in a Woman's Life* by Sheila Kaye-Smith; *The Old Hunter* by Liam O'Flaherty.

DODD, MEAD AND COMPANY: for *Malachi's Cove* by Anthony Trollope; *The Story of Dr. MacLure,* from *A Doctor of the Old School* by John Watson, Copyright, 1895; *The Adventure of the Kind Mr. Smith,* from *Far Away Stories* by William J. Locke, Copyright, 1919; *The Monkey's Paw,* from *The Lady of the Barge* by W. W. Jacobs, Copyright, 1902; *The Happy Hypocrite* by Max Beerbohm, Copyright, 1896; *The Hammer of God,* from *The Innocence of Father Brown* by G. K. Chesterton, Copyright, 1910.

DOUBLEDAY DORAN AND COMPANY: for *Youth* by Joseph Conrad, Copyright, 1903, 1925; *The Drums of the Fore and Aft,* Copyright, 1899, 1927, and *The Man Who Would Be King,* Copyright, 1899, 1927, by Rudyard Kipling; *Action* by C. E. Montague, Copyright, 1929; *Red* by W. Somerset Maugham, Copyright, 1921; *Jeeves and the Song of Songs* by P. G. Wodehouse, Copyright, 1929, 1930; *Mr. Oddy* by Sir Hugh Walpole, Copyright, 1903.

E. P. DUTTON AND COMPANY: for *The Doll in the Pink Silk Dress* from *A Chair on the Boulevard* by Leonard Merrick, Copyright, 1921; *The Valley of the Beasts* from *The Wolves of God and Other Fey Stories* by Algernon Blackwood, Copyright, 1921; *The Trapper's Mates* from *The Old Stag* by Henry Williamson, Copyright, 1927.

HARPER AND BROTHERS: for *The Three Strangers* by Thomas Hardy; *The Adventure of the Speckled Band,* by A. Conan Doyle, Copyright, 1892; *The Gioconda Smile* by Aldous Huxley, Copyright, 1921, 1922.

HOUGHTON MIFFLIN COMPANY: for *Fish Are Such Liars* by Roland Pertwee.

ALFRED A. KNOPF, INC.: for *Story of a Piebald Horse* by W. H. Hudson, Copyright, 1916; *The Derelict* by H. M. Tomlinson, Copyright, 1920; *The Celestial Omnibus* by E. M. Forster; *Life of Ma Parker* by Katherine Mansfield, Copyright, 1922.

JOHN LANE THE BODLEY HEAD LIMITED: for *The Eyes* by Thomas Owen Beachcroft.

MRS. FREDA LAWRENCE: for *The Prussian Officer* by D. H. Lawrence.

LONGMANS, GREEN AND COMPANY LIMITED: for *Philippa's Fox-Hunt* by E. Somerville and Martin Ross.

JOHN LUCE AND COMPANY: for *The Sword of Welleran* by Lord Dunsany.

THE MACMILLAN COMPANY: for *The Pardoner's Tale* by Geoffrey Chaucer, from *The Modern Reader's Chaucer* by Tatlock and MacKaye, Copyright, 1912; *The Babus of Nayanjore* by Sir Rabindranath Tagore, from *The Hungry Stones and Other Stories,* Copyright, 1916; *"Hey Diddle Diddle, the Cat . . ."* by Eden Phillpotts, from *Up Hill, Down Dale; Red Hanrahan* by William Butler Yeats, from *Early Poems and Stories,* Copyright 1906, 1914, 1925; *The Western Islands* by John Masefield, from *A Mainsail Haul,* Copyright, 1913; *Three Lovers Who Lost* by James Stephens, from *Here Are Ladies,* Copyright, 1913; *A Source of Irritation* by Stacy Aumonier, from *The Golden Windmill and Other Stories,* Copyright, 1921.

MATSON AND DUGGAN: for *Bella Fleace Gave a Party,* from *Mr. Loveday's Little Outing* by Evelyn Waugh, Copyright, 1936.

ROBERT M. McBRIDE AND COMPANY: for *The Chink and the Child* by Thomas Burke, Copyright, 1917, 1926.

THE MODERN LIBRARY, INC.: for *That Brute Simmons* by Arthur Morrison.

RANDOM HOUSE, INC.: for *The Forty-Third Division* by Ralph Bates, Copyright, 1939.

CHARLES SCRIBNER'S SONS: for *The Punishment of Shahpesh, the Persian, on Khipil, the Builder,* from *The Shaving of Shagpat* by George Meredith, Copyright, 1898; *Sire de Malétroit's Door* and *A Lodging for the Night,* from *New Arabian Nights* by Robert Louis Stevenson; *The Courting of T'nowhead's Bell,* from *Auld Licht Idylls* by Sir James Matthew Barrie; *The Apple-Tree* by John Galsworthy, Copyright, 1916.

FREDERICK A. STOKES COMPANY: for *The Log of the "Evening Star"* by Alfred Noyes, Copyright, 1918.

THE VIKING PRESS, INC.: for *Faith* by R. Cunninghame Graham, Copyright, 1929; *Mrs. Packletide's Tiger* by Saki, Copyright, 1930; *The Dead* by James Joyce.

IVES WASHBURN: for *A Sleeping Draft* by Weston Martyr, Copyright, 1930.

ANN WATKINS, INC.: for *A Busman's Holiday* by Francis Brett Young, Copyright, 1933.

A. P. WATT AND SON: for *The Adventure of the Speckled Band* by A. Conan Doyle; *The Drums of the Fore and Aft* and *The Man Who Would Be King* from *Wee Willie Winkie* by Rudyard Kipling.

H. G. WELLS: for *The Country of the Blind* by H. G. Wells.

✶ Introduction ✶

By BLISS PERRY

THIS is a Bedside Book in more senses than one. Besides all of the famous stories by Britain's greatest writers, it contains a number of tales, equally fine, by comparative unknowns, and these, for the most part, were discovered during a long illness of Mr. Henry C. Moriarty, whose fame has spread far beyond his den in the Harvard "Coop." Mr. Bennett Cerf, of Random House, who had edited, in collaboration with Angus Burrell, a bedside book of American stories a few years before, heard from Mr. Moriarty himself and from a score of Harvard-bred booklovers, of the collection of stories he had made. When Mr. Cerf decided, therefore, to publish a companion volume to the American selection, he headed straight for Cambridge to consult Mr. Moriarty. Together, these two gentlemen chose the final contents for the book, and I must say that I find the result an eminently satisfactory one.

Of course there will never be any unanimous agreement as to the choice of stories for bedside reading. I recall an unlucky selection of my own, some thirty years ago. I wanted something to read aloud, one evening, to a very young lady who was convalescing from typhoid fever in Brussels. The only books in English at the best discoverable bookshop were *John Halifax, Gentleman,* some plays by Oscar Wilde, Upton Sinclair's *Jungle,* and a book of short stories by A. Conan Doyle. I purchased the latter, and returning to the young lady, opened to a story which I had never happened to read, *The Adventure of the Speckled Band.* It ornaments the present volume, but it made the anxious parent in Brussels dream all night long of snakes, while the terrified convalescent never slept at all! *John Halifax, Gentleman* would have been a more soporific choice, although I wish we might have had the then unwritten story of *Jeeves and the Song of Songs* or W. J. Locke's delightful *The Adventure of the Kind Mr. Smith.*

It is a truism that different persons want different things, and also

xv

that the same persons want one kind of reading at one time and another kind at other times. John Masefield has recently reminded us of the general purpose of reading, which is, in his expert opinion, to seek "recreation and cheer, guidance, counsel and consolation." These are desirable aims, no doubt, although the Poet Laureate seems to forget the needs of those unfortunate bedtime readers who crave primarily something that will send them to sleep. George Borrow deals surprisingly with these insomniacs in chapter XXII of *The Romany Rye*. It was Wordsworth's *Excursion*, on that occasion, that did the trick. Yet all prescriptions have their drawbacks. We agree as to the necessity of having the proper vitamins in one's diet, but precisely what vitamins are to be recommended to a given patient? Was not Anatole France essentially right when he affirmed that every masterpiece of literature is a different book to every reader of it, and a different book to the same reader in different moods or at different ages? Take for example Roland Pertwee's delectable story, *Fish are Such Liars*. Many an angler would prefer to re-read it on a winter's night when all fishing is but a memory and a hope, rather than on a June evening when he is wearied by a long day on the river. The words may be the same, but in June it will not be the same story.

The editors of this collection, I suspect, have troubled themselves very little with definitions of the short story and with discussions of origins and influences and periods and changing techniques. There are dozens of books about all that. Mr. Somerset Maugham, who has just been discussing the craftsmanship of tellers of tales, is right enough when he selects Poe's famous criticism of Hawthorne's *Twice Told Tales* in 1842, as the true starting-point of modern disquisitions upon the art of the short story. Poe made that hole in one, nearly a hundred years ago, and his record stands. Yet we may be tempted to ask how many real critics there are among, say, each hundred thousand addicts of the short story? What effect upon these average readers have all the analyses of craftsmanship actually wrought? I confess that a perusal of these eighty British stories has simplified, at least for me, the essential factors in this business of spinning a yarn.

Turn to any one of the stories. Here, precisely as in a play, are certain persons doing certain things in certain circumstances, and the spinner of the yarn is telling us who the persons are and what they are doing or trying to do under those conditions of time and place which provide the "setting," the environment or atmosphere of the tale. Said Robert Louis Stevenson to Graham Balfour long ago: "There are, so far as I know, three ways only, of writing a story. You may take a plot and fit characters to it, or you may take a character and choose incidents and situations to develop it, or lastly—you must bear with me while I try to make this clear—(here he made a gesture with his hand as if he were trying to shape something and give it outline and form) —you may take a certain atmosphere and get action and persons to express and realize it. I'll give you an example—*The Merry Men.*" But only a few years later Rudyard Kipling was asserting with equally infectious dogmatism:

> *"There are nine and sixty ways of*
> *constructing tribal lays,*
> *And every single one of them is right!"*

It may be immaterial whether we vote personally for one of the three ways or for any of the sixty-nine ways. Yet it is fairly clear that the man who is spinning a particular yarn may seem to be chiefly interested in the persons whom he is depicting, or in the events in which they are involved, or in what Stevenson called the "atmosphere" surrounding and affecting the persons and the plot. The "atmosphere" does not mean merely the wind on the heath, a rainy day or a tropical hurricane, but all the environing circumstances that mold the incidents and situations of the story: let us say poverty in Ireland, thrift in Scotland, fox-hunting, totalitarianism, or a civil war in Spain. According to the stress of the writer's preoccupation with one or another of the factors in his tale, we may think of Yeats's *Red Hanrahan* as chiefly a "character" story, of Eden Phillpotts' *Hey, Diddle Diddle, the Cat . . ."* as a "plot" story, and of Somerset Maugham's *Red* as a study of the "atmosphere," physical and moral, of a South Sea Island. Yet we are aware, at the same time, that none of the factors can really be isolated from the others; the degenerative influences of residence in a South Sea Island are observable, not on a weather chart, but in the actions of men and women. And all labelling seems crude and futile while we are reading such unforgettable stories as Hardy's *The Three Strangers,* Kipling's *The Man Who Would be King,* Galsworthy's *The Apple-Tree,* and Sheila Kaye-Smith's *A Day in a Woman's Life.* Under the spell of such tales as these one forgets to analyse and classify. Here, assuredly, are human characters and credible incidents and enveloping background, but these various elements are blended into indissoluble unity. We perceive a consummate balance of qualities, as in poetry. The spell is unbroken by any disbelief.

To explain the story-teller's instinct is not easy. Why should one boy or girl in a family have the knack of writing a good letter—in spite of all the misspelled words—when the other brothers and sisters lack it and can never learn it? Fenimore Cooper, who is derided today by many clever novelists, used to speak of Leather-Stocking's "gift," by which he meant eye and ear and nose for following a trail, and a mind that sought back from consequence to cause. The born story-teller has that "gift." Neither Henry James nor Joseph Conrad, eminent artists as they became, were not, in my judgment, such "natural" story-tellers as W. J. Locke and Leonard Merrick. Even Thackeray made many a false start, for the excellent fooling of *Sultan Stork* represents but a slender segment of Thackeray's real power. Yet Stevenson's first published story, *A Lodging for the Night,* remains one of his best, and *The Pickwick Papers* were written by a cub reporter, a boy who, very luckily, never grew up. In ordinary life, we know a good story-teller from a poor one by the former's instinct for sticking to the point—that is to say, his "theme," his "idea" or what Poe called "the one pre-established design." His finds and follows the trail. The club bore cannot do that, nor the garrulous stranger in the Pullman smoker. Yet the born story-teller seems to be taking his time and spinning this particular yarn by choice from a hundred others that await his fancy. His affluence is like that of George Meredith's Khipil the Builder sitting on a slab of marble and reciting to his smiling workmen "adventures interspersed with anecdotes and recitations and poetic instances, as was his wont."

But whether the teller be Khipil or Chaucer, Defoe or Wodehouse, we can never be quite sure where he gets his "stuff." Is it borrowed or his own? "There is no thief like the Warwickshire thief." Is it experience or dream? Some of the stuff from which the yarn is spun is obviously and immemorially old—folk-tales, myths, legends, nightmares of the cave-men or happy fables of wise beasts. Precisely where did Chaucer pick up that story of the fatal quarrel among thieves, which the rascally Pardoner relates for the moral edification of the pilgrims? The most learned Chaucerians are not sure. What Chaucer certainly did not borrow was his own delight in colored, singing words, the humor and satire and pleasing wit, the endless curiosity about human nature. Or where did the good knight Sir Thomas Malory find that story about the sword thrust into the stone, moveless until the one right person drew it forth? The yarn was told again only the other day, though a little differently, by an equally veracious chronicler, Mr.

T. H. White, in *The Sword in the Stone*. May not both of the chron-
iclers have been remembering a still older tale, and the germ of the
Arthurian legend be the exploit of the war-worn Ulysses, returning in
time to draw that old bow of his which none of the suitors could bend?
And who told first that story to which W. W. Jacobs gave the title of
The Monkey's Paw, and which turns upon the eternal human inability
to know what to wish for? There is an ancient Persian proverb: "What
will you have? quoth God. *Pay for it,* and take it." But the essential
tragedy of *The Monkey's Paw* is far older than Persia.

Nor is this question of origins always simple, even if we take the
apparently straightforward statements of the matter-of-fact men, the
observers and recorders of everyday experience. Defoe, a master in this
school, is called by one of his admiring biographers "a liar, a very great
liar, perhaps the greatest liar that ever lived;" which is almost precisely what the old Duchess of Marlborough said when she first read
Gulliver's Travels. A couple of generations ago we were assured that
The Apparition of Mrs. Veal was pure invention, made credible by
Defoe's devices of verisimilitude, corroborative detail and anticipation
of every objection to the evidence. Nowadays, however, the Defoe
specialists are convinced that he invented next to nothing, but simply
repeated a short story current in London at the time. On either theory,
what an artist! And one cannot say how much the young James Barrie
really saw from that *Window in Thrums* or Arnold Bennett in *Mary
with the High Hand* or Cunninghame Graham in *Faith* or Katherine
Mansfield in *The Life of Ma Parker.* Of the nine and sixty ways, none
is apparently more convincing than the way of the writer who ostensibly is telling us what his own eyes have seen. Yet the exact ratio between first-hand experience and reconstructive imagination may be unknown even to the writer himself. Since there is nothing in any story
except what some man or woman has put there, we cannot dodge the
factor of personality, even in the most objective and dispassionate of
tales. Every Hardy story is saturated with Thomas Hardy, and every
"Father Brown" story reveals the familiar features of G. K. Chesterton.
Whether a writer has been amused, saddened or ennobled by the
human spectacle will betray itself upon the printed page.

The editors of this collection have shown hospitality to some stories
of another type—dreams, fantasies, the unseen world that surrounds
and shrouds, for a moment at least, the things that are tangible and
visible. The Irish and the Scotch notoriously, and many a hard-headed
Saxon as well, have this gift of second sight, a glimpse of something

beyond the veil of the senses. Do you believe in ghosts, in spells, in enchantments? Perhaps not at nine o'clock in the morning of a brisk October day, but turn that very night to Dunsany's *The Sword of Welleran*, E. M. Forster's *The Celestial Omnibus*, Bulwer-Lytton's *The House and the Brain* and M. R. James's *The Mezzotint*. If then, whether by nature or by professional habit, you are sceptically unable to suspend your disbelief, there is nothing to do about it except to turn out the light and go to sleep. But remember that there will be plenty of other readers who will lie awake in the dark—and listen.

Trevelyan's *History of England* takes pains to remind us that there is no spot in that tight little island more than seventy miles distant from salt water. The sea is in the blood of most of the poets of England, and of many of her story-writers. Conrad, although born in Poland and never touching English soil until he was twenty-one, makes Marlowe say in *Youth:* "Wasn't that the best time, when we were young at sea. . . . . Oh, youth! The strength of it, the faith of it, the imagination of it!" And over his own name Conrad writes in *Some Reminiscences:* "I have tried with an almost filial regard to render the vibration of life in the great world of waters, in the hearts of the simple men who have for ages traversed its solitudes, and also that something sentient which seems to dwell in ships—the creatures of their hands and the objects of their care." If one wishes to feel the vibration of life in the great world of waters, the present volume contains not only the incomparable *Youth*, but also such stories as Quiller-Couch's *The Roll-Call of the Reef*, Morley Roberts's *The Captain of the "Ullswater,"* Tomlinson's *The Derelict*, Masefield's *The Western Islands*, and Alfred Noyes's *The Log of the "Evening Star."*

Very British, likewise, is the romance of far-away places, as in John Buchan's *The Kings of Orion*, Kipling's *The Drums of the Fore and Aft*, H. G. Wells's *The Country of the Blind*, or Philip Gibbs's *The Stranger in the Village*. Of the relatively few war stories in this book, Stacy Aumonier's *A Source of Irritation* seems to me the most original and D. H. Lawrence's *The Prussian Officer* the most morbidly poignant, as Ralph Bates's *The Forty-third Division* is assuredly the most up to date.

Yet whether being up to date is really an asset or a liability few contemporaries can judge. There are some critics who hold that if a story was a good story one hundred years ago it is a good story still. Perhaps; but the case calls for closer definition and a more accurate survey of literary fashions than is possible here. Surely *The Pardoner's Tale* has been a good story for five hundred years, and certain Greek and He-brew narratives for twenty-five hundred. I should call Sir Walter Scott's *The Two Drovers* and Dr. John Brown's *Rab and His Friends* and Dickens's *A Christmas Carol* very good stories indeed, in spite of what seems now their old-fashioned mechanism. Many of us cherish affec-tionate memories of the original T-model Ford, though it had to be cranked before starting. It is much easier to push the button of a 1940 car, but do we have any greater real fun in motoring? I admit that I like to watch Sir Walter Scott cranking his car. The process is slow and a bit ludicrous, but once that engine is started, Sir Walter knows how to drive.

Even the "Oriental" tales of the eighteenth century, like Addison's *The Vision of Mirza* and Goldsmith's *Asem,* which are really moral es-says in fictional disguise, gave pleasure to several generations whose literary taste was more exacting than our own. Victorian three-decker novelists like Anthony Trollope proved occasionally that they could sail smaller craft with skill. Read Trollope's *Malachi's Cove.* They lacked, it is true, the speed, the vividness, the slickness which we admire in magazine stories of today.

Each generation, after all, knows what it likes, and it is only the anthologists and the historians who concern themselves very deeply with what the public used to like. But these stories which Mr. Cerf and Mr. Moriarty have gathered afford a wide outlook over the British scene and character. You may go fox-hunting with Philippa in County Cork, brood over Dublin tragedy with James Joyce, or attend Dr. MacLure's funeral in Scotland. You may watch the self-conscious stylists like Oscar Wilde and George Moore, or turn to the unaffected and beautiful prose of W. H. Hudson and Henry Williamson and Tagore. You can study the steady advance in the life-like rendering of dialogue—although I think that our American short story writers of the last ten years still lead in that field. You can amuse yourself by tracing here and there the influence of non-British models like Poe and De Maupassant and Chekhov. Freudian psychology and Marxian theory are noticeably absent, though they have run wild in American fiction for a score of years. You can discover in a few of the stories the Post-War disillusion and cynicism. Or better still, you can lose yourself and forget the day's job and ignore all "sources" and "influences" and "periods" in such tales as Donn Byrne's *Rivers of Damascus,* L. A. G. Strong's *The White Cottage,* May Edginton's *Purple and Fine Linen,* Francis Brett Young's *A Busman's Holiday,* or—to climb the Alps and the invisible summits of free will a little higher than you are ever likely to go by yourself—in C. E. Montague's triumphant story entitled *Action.*

For what we have here, after all is said, is a book by some eighty writers, each with an individual mind. Each has his own experience and memories, his personal insight—whether superficial or profound —into the puzzlements of human character and conduct. Each has his own instinct for the significance of situation and action, each his own sensitiveness—acute or dulled—to the various aspects and pressures of the visible world. Each writer is limited, naturally, by the range of his own daylight vision and by the wing-power of his imagination in the twilight. Each must perforce be something of an artist in words, for words are the only permissible colors upon the writer's canvas, the only notes allowable in the music or discord of his prose. No one writes, even in a short story, as well as he ought. He is fortunate if he has written as well as he could. Nevertheless these eighty stories, told as they are by Britons who, like the Wife of Bath, have had their world as in their time, provide a fascinating composite picture of the British mind. Considered *sub specie aeternitatis,* this book—like most books and, for that matter, most Empires—may be such stuff as dreams are made of. But dreams go well with bedtime.

THE BEDSIDE BOOK OF
FAMOUS BRITISH
STORIES

The Pardoner's Tale

BY GEOFFREY CHAUCER

WHILOM there dwelt in Flanders a company of young folk who followed after folly, as riotous living and gaming in stews and taverns, where with harps, lutes and citterns they danced and played at dice day and night, and ate and drank inordinately. Thus they did service to the Devil in cursed fashion within those Devil's temples by abominable superfluity. Their oaths were so great and so damnable that it was grisly to hear them swear; they rent our blessed Lord's body in pieces anew (as if the Jews had not rent him enough!), and each laughed at the others' sins. And anon came dancing girls, graceful and slim young fruit-wenches, singers with harps, bawds and confectioners, who are all very officers of the Devil to kindle and blow that fire of lust that is near allied to gluttony. I take Holy Writ to witness that in wine and drunkenness are excess and lust. Lo, how drunken Lot sinned against nature, not knowing what he did; he was so drunk he knew not what he wrought. Herod (let any one look up the history), when he was full of wine at his feast, gave command at his own table to slay the Baptist John, guiltless. Seneca also of a surety says a good word; he says he can find no difference betwixt a man that is out of his mind and him who is drunken, except that madness, when it attacks an ill-conditioned fellow, endures longer than drunkenness. Oh cursed gluttony, first cause of our undoing, origin of our damnation, until Christ redeemed us with His blood! Only think how dearly was this cursed sin paid for; this whole world was ruined by gluttony! Our father Adam and his wife in verity were driven from Paradise to labor and woe for that vice. For whilst Adam fasted I read that he was in Paradise, and when he ate of the forbidden fruit of the tree, he was cast out to woe and pain. O gluttony, well may we accuse thee! If a man but knew how

3

many maladies follow from gluttony and excess, he would be more moderate of his diet as he sits at table. Alas! for the tender mouth and the short throat, east and west and south and north men labor in the earth and air and water to get dainty meat and drink for a glutton. On this, O Paul, well canst thou discourse. "Meat unto belly and belly unto meat,—God shall destroy both," as Paul says. Alas! foul is it to say, by my faith, but fouler is the act, when a man drinks so of the white and red that he makes a jakes of his throat through this accursed excess. The apostle, weeping, says piteously, "There walk many of whom I have told you, and I say it now weeping and with a piteous voice, they are enemies of the cross of Christ, their end is death, their god is their belly." O belly, foul bag, full of corruption! what labor and cost to provide for thee! How these cooks pound and strain and grind, and turn substance into accident, to satisfy all thy greedy taste! Out of the hard bones they knock the marrow, and cast away naught that may go through the gullet soft and sweet. Of spicery and bark, root and leaf, is made the glutton's delicious sauce, to get him ever a new appetite. But he that follows after such delights, certes, is dead whilst he lives in those vices.

Wine is a lecherous thing, and drunkenness is full of wretchedness and contention. O drunken man, thy face is disfigured, thy breath is sour, thou art foul to clasp in arms, and the sound through thy drunken nose seems as if thou saidest ever, "Sam-soun, Sam-soun!" And yet Samson drank never wine, God wot. Thou fallest like a stuck pig, thy tongue is lost and all thy care for honest things, for drunkenness is the very sepulchre of man's wit and discretion. He over whom drink has dominion can keep no counsel, of a surety. Now keep you from the wine white and red, and chiefly from the white wine of Lepe for sale in Fish Street, or Cheapside. This Spanish wine subtly creeps through other wines growing hard by, and such fumes arise therefrom that after two or three draughts, though a man deem himself to be at home in Cheapside, he is even at the town of Lepe in Spain, not at Rochelle nor at Bordeaux; and then he will say, "Sam-soun, Sam-soun!"

But hearken to one word, I pray you, lordings all; the supreme acts of victory in the Old Testament, I dare be bound, were done through the help of the true omnipotent God in prayer and abstinence. Look into the Bible and there you may see it. Look too at Attila, the great conqueror, who died in shame and disgrace, bleeding at his nose in a drunken sleep. A great captain should live soberly. And moreover, consider right carefully what was commanded to Lemuel,—not Samuel, I say, but Lemuel; read the Bible and find it expressly set down as to giving wine to them that have oversight of justice. But no more now, for this may suffice.

Now that I have spoken of gluttony, I will forbid you gaming, which is the very mother of lies, deceit, and cursed forswearing, of blaphemy of Christ, manslaughter and waste of money and of time; and furthermore, it is a disgrace and against all honor to be known as a common gamester. And ever the higher a man's estate, the more abandoned he is held to be. If a prince practise hazard, by all temperance and public policy common opinion will hold him the lower in reputation. Stilbon, the wise ambassador, was sent to Corinth in great pomp from Lacedaemon to make an alliance; and when he came he chanced to find all the greatest men of that land playing at hazard. Wherefore, as soon as might be, he stole home again to his country and said, "I will not lose my good name there, nor will I take on me such a shame as to ally you to gamblers. Send other wise ambassadors; for by my troth I would rather die than ally you with gamesters. For you who be so glorious in honors shall not be allied with gamesters by my will, or treaty of my making." Thus spake this wise philosopher. Look also how the king of the Parthians, as the book tells us, sent in scorn a set of golden dice to King Demetrius because he had practised gambling; wherefore he held at no value his glory and renown. Lords may find other kinds of virtuous diversion to pass the day with.

Now I will speak a word or two of false and great oaths that old books treat of. Violent swearing is an abominable thing, and false swearing is yet more to be blamed. The high God, as witness Matthew, forbade swearing at all; but especially the holy Jeremy says of swearing, "Thou shalt say thine oaths in sooth, and not lie, and swear in righteousness and judgment." But idle swearing is a cursedness. Behold how in the first table of the high God's glorious commandments the second commandment is, "Take not my name amiss or in vain." Lo, He forbids such swearing earlier than He forbids homicide or many other cursed things. I say that it stands in this order, as any one knows who knows the commandments, how that is the second commandment. And moreover I tell you flatly that vengeance will not depart from the house of him who is too outrageous of his oaths. "By God's precious heart and by the nails of his cross, by the blood of Christ in the abbey of Hales, my chance is seven; yours is five and three. By God's arms, if you play falsely, this dagger shall go through your heart!" This is the fruit that comes of the two dice-bones, forswearing, ire, falseness, murder. Now for the love of Christ Who died for us, forsake your oaths, great and small. But, sirs, I now will tell on my tale.

These three rioters of whom I speak, long before any bell had rung for prime, were set down in a tavern to drink. And as they sat, they heard a bell tinkle that was carried before a corpse to his grave. One of them called to his boy, "Off with you, and ask straightway what corpse it is passing by; and see you report his name aright."

"Sir," quoth the boy, "it needs not. It was told me two hours before you came here; he was an old fellow of yours, perdy, and he was slain suddenly in the night, as he sat very drunk on his bench. A privy thief men call Death, that slays all the people in this country-side, came with his spear and smote his heart in two, and went his way without a word. He has slain a thousand in this pestilence; and master, ere you come before him, methinks you were best be warned of such an adversary. Be ready to meet him ever; thus my mother taught me, I can say no more."

"The child speaks truth, by St. Mary," said the taverner, "for over a mile hence, in a large village, he has slain both woman, child, churl and knave. I trow his habitation be there. It were great wisdom, a man to be on his guard lest he do him a hurt."

"Yea, God's arms!" quoth this reveller, "is it such peril to meet with him? I vow to God's bones I will seek him in the highways and the byways. Hearken, fellows, we are all as one; let each of us hold up his hand and become the others' brother, and slay this false traitor Death. He shall be slain ere night that slays so many, by God's dignity!"

These three plighted their troth together, each to live and die for the rest as he were their sworn brother, and up they all started in this drunken fury, and forth they went toward that village of which the taverner had spoken; and many a grisly oath they swore, and Christ's blessed body they rent to pieces,—"Death shall be dead if they can but catch him."

When they had gone but a little way, even as they were treading over a stile, an old man and poor met them, and greeted them full meekly, and said, "Now, lordings, God be with you!"

The proudest of these three revellers answered, "What, churl, bad luck to you! Why are you all wrapped up save your face? Why live you so long and so decrepit?"

This old man began to peer into his visage, and said, "Because I cannot find a man, though I walked from hence to India, in hamlet or in city, who will exchange his youth for mine age. And therefore I must keep mine old age as long as it is God's will. Alas, death will not take me! Thus I walk, a restless caitiff, and thus morn and night I knock with my staff upon the ground, which is my mother's gate, and say, 'Dear mother, let me in. Lo, how I vanish away, flesh and skin and blood! Alas, when shall my bones be at peace? Mother, I would exchange my chest with you, which has been long time in my chamber, yea, for an hair-cloth shroud to wrap me in!' But still she will not do me that favor; wherefore my face is full pale and withered.—But sirs, it is not a courteous thing to speak churlishly to an old man, unless he trespass in act or word. You may read yourselves in Holy Writ, 'Before an old hoary-head man ye shall arise;' wherefore I counsel you, do no harm now to an old man, no more than you would that it were done to you in your old age, if you abide so long. And now God be with you, wherever you go or be; I must go whither I have to go."

"Nay, old churl, not so fast, by God," said this second gamester straightway. "By St. John, you part not so lightly! You spoke even now of that traitor Death who slays all our friends in this country-side, By my troth, you are his spy! Tell where he is, or by God and the Holy Sacrament you shall pay for it. Truly you are of his consent to slay us young folk, false thief."

"Now sirs," quoth he, "if you are so fain to find Death, turn up this crooked path; for by my faith I left him in that grove under a tree, and there he will tarry, nor for all your bluster will he hide him. See you that oak? There you shall find him. May God, Who redeemed mankind, save you and amend you!" Thus spoke this old wight.

And each of these revellers ran till he came to that tree, and there they found wellnigh eight bushels, as it seemed to them, of florins coined of fine round gold. No longer sought they then after Death, but each was so glad at the sight of the precious hoard that they sat them down by the fair shining of florins. The worst of them spoke the first word. "Brethren," he said, "heed what I say; though I jest oft and make sport, I have a pretty headpiece. Now Fortune has given us this treasure that we may live the rest of our lives in mirth and jollity, and lightly as it comes, so we will spend it. Eh! God's precious dignity! Who would have weened to-day that we should have so fair a grace! Could this gold be but carried hence to my house or else to yours,—for you know well all this gold is ours,—then were we in high felicity. But truly it may not be done by day. Folk would call us sturdy thieves and hang us for our own treasure. It must be carried by night, as wisely and slyly as may be. Therefore I advise that we draw cuts amongst us all, and he that draws the shortest shall run with a blithe heart to the town and that forthwith, and privily bring us wine and bread. And two of us shall cunningly guard this treasure, and at night, if he delay us not, we will carry it where we all agree is safest."

One of them brought the cuts in his fist and bade them look where the lot should fall. It fell to the youngest of them and he straightway went forth toward the town. So soon as he was gone, the second said to the third, "You well know you are my sworn brother, and now I will tell you somewhat to your advantage. Here is gold great plenty, to divide amongst the three of us; and you know well our fellow is gone. Now if I can shape it so that it be divided amongst the two of us, had I not done you a friendly turn?"

"I wot not how that may be," the other answered, "he knows the gold is left with us two. What shall we do? What shall we say to him?"

"Shall it be a secret?" said the first villain. "I shall tell you in few words what we shall do to bring it about."

"I assent," said the other, "not to betray you, by my troth."

"Now," quoth the first, "you know well we be two and that two shall be stronger than one. Look when he is set down; do you arise and scuffle with him as in sport, and I will rive him through the two sides, and look that you do the same with your dagger. And then shall all this gold be shared betwixt you and me, dear friend. Then may we both fulfill all our lusts, and play at dice at our own pleasure." And thus were these two villains accorded to slay the third as I have said.

The youngest, going to the town, revolved full often in his heart the beauty of those bright new florins. "O Lord," quoth he, "if so be I could have all this treasure to myself, no man living under God's throne should live so merry as I!" And at last the fiend, our enemy, put it into his thought to buy poison with which to slay his two fellows; for the fiend found him in such a way of life that he had leave to bring him to perdition, for utterly his full purpose was to slay them both and never to repent. And forth he went without delay into the town to an apothecary, and prayed him to sell him some poison that he might kill his rats; and eke there was a pole-cat in his yard, he said, which had killed his capons, and he would fain wreak him upon the vermin that ruined him by night. "And you shall have such a thing," answered the apothecary, "that, so may God save my soul, no creature in all this world can eat or drink of this compound the amount of a grain of wheat, but he shall die anon. Yea, he shall die the death, and that in less time than you can walk a mile, this poison is so violent."

This cursed man gripped the box of poison in his hand, and then ran into the next street to a shop and borrowed three large bottles. Into two of them he poured his poison, but the third he kept clean for his own drink, for he planned to labor all night long carrying away the gold. And when this reveller, the Devil take him!, had filled his three great bottles with wine, he repaired again to his fellows.

What need to discourse about it more? For as they had planned his death, even so they slew him, and that anon. When this was done, one of the two said, "Now let us sit and drink and make merry, and then we will bury his body." And with that word he chanced to take one of the bottles where the poison was, and he drank and gave his fellow to drink also. Wherefore anon they both died. And certes Avicenna wrote never in any canon or any chapter more wondrous signs of empoisoning than these two wretches showed ere they died. Thus ended these two murderers, and eke the false poisoner also.

O cursed sin, full of cursedness! O treacherous homicide! O gluttony, lust and gaming! Thou blasphemer of Christ with insult and great oaths habitual and proud! Alas mankind, how may it be that to thy Creator Who made thee, and redeemed thee with His precious heart's blood, thou art so false and unkind, alas!

Now, good men, God forgive you your trespasses and guard you from the sin of avarice. My holy pardon will cure you all, so you offer nobles and other sterling coin, or else silver rings, brooches, spoons. Bow your heads, bow them under this holy bull! Come up, wives, offer of your yarn! See, I enter your name here in my roll; you shall enter into heaven's bliss; I assoil you by mine high power, you that will make offerings, as clear and clean as when you were born—(lo sirs, thus I preach). And may Jesu Christ, our soul's physician, grant you to receive His pardon; for that is better than mine, I will not deceive you.

But sirs, one word I have forgot to say. Here in my wallet I have relics and indulgences as fair as any man's in Britain, that were given me by the pope's own hand. If any of you of devotion will make an offering and have mine absolution, come forth now and kneel down here and take meekly my pardon; or else take pardons all new and fresh as you go along, at every town's end, so you ever anew offer nobles and pence which be good and sound. It is an honor to every wight here to have a competent pardoner to absolve you as you ride through the lonely country, in case of misadventure which might befall. Peradventure one or two may fall down off their horses and break their necks in two. Look what a security it is to you all that I fell into your company, who may assoil you all, high and low, when the soul shall pass from the body! I counsel that our Host here be the first, for he is most enveloped in sin. Come forth, Sir Host, and offer first, and you shall kiss all the relics, yea, for a groat; straightway unbuckle your purse!

"Nay, nay, may I have Christ's malison if I do," quoth he. "Let be; it shall not be, on my soul. You would make me kiss your old breech and swear it were a saint's relic, be it never so foul! But by the holy cross and St. Helen, I would I had your guts in my hand instead of relics or halidom; pull them out, I will help you carry them. They shall be shrined in a hog's belly!"

This Pardoner answered not a word; so wroth he was, he would not speak.

"Now," quoth our Host, "I will not talk with you longer, nor with any other angry man."

But anon when the worthy Knight saw all the people laughing, he said, "Enough, no more of this. Sir Pardoner, be of merry cheer, and I pray you, Sir Host, that are so dear to me, kiss the Pardoner. And Pardoner, I pray you draw near again, and let us laugh and make sport as we did before." And forthwith they kissed and rode on.

Here is ended the Pardoner's Tale.

2

The Marvellous Adventure of the Sword

BY SIR THOMAS MALORY

AND at the vigil of Pentecost, when all the fellowship of the Round Table were come unto Camelot, and there heard their service, and the tables were set ready to the meat, right so entered into the hall a full fair gentlewoman on horseback, that had ridden full fast, for her horse was all besweat. Then she there alighted, and came before the King, and saluted him; and then he said, Damsel, God thee bless! Sir, said she, I pray you say me where Sir Launcelot is? Yonder ye may see him, said the King. Then she went unto Launcelot and said, Sir Launcelot, I salute you on King Pelles' behalf, and I require you to come on with me hereby into a forest. Then Sir Launcelot asked her with whom she dwelt. I dwell, said she, with King Pelles. What will ye with me? said Sir Launcelot. Ye shall know, said she, when ye come thither. Well, said he, I will gladly go with you. So Sir Launcelot bade his squire saddle his horse and bring his arms; and in all haste he did his commandment. Then came the Queen unto Launcelot and said, Will ye leave us at this high feast? Madam, said the gentlewoman, wit ye well he shall be with you to-morrow by dinner-time. If I wist, said the Queen, that he should not be with us here to-morrow morn, he should not go with you by my good will.

Right so departed Sir Launcelot with the gentlewoman, and rode until that he came into a forest, and into a great valley, where they saw an abbey of nuns; and there was a squire ready, and opened the gates; and so they entered, and descended off their horses, and there came a fair fellowship about Sir Launcelot and welcomed him, and were passing glad of his coming. And then they led him into the Abbess's chamber, and unarmed him, and right so he was ware upon a bed lying two of his cousins, Sir Bors and Sir Lionel, and then he waked them, and when they saw him they made great joy. Sir, said Sir Bors unto Sir Launcelot, what adventure hath brought thee hither, for we thought to-morrow to have found you at Camelot? Truly, said Sir Launcelot, a gentlewoman brought me hither, but I know not the cause. In the meanwhile, as they stood thus talking together, there came twelve nuns which brought with them Galahad, the which was passing fair and well made, that scarcely in the world men might not find his match; and all those ladies wept. Sir, said the ladies, we bring you here this child, the which we have nourished, and we pray you to make him a knight; for of a more worthier man's hand may he not receive the order of knighthood. Sir Launcelot beheld that young squire, and saw him seemly and demure as a dove, with all manner of good features, that he thought of his age never to have seen so fair a man of form. Then said Sir Launcelot, Cometh this desire of himself? He and all they said, Yea. Then shall he, said Sir Launcelot, receive the high order of knighthood as to-morrow at the reverence of the high feast. That night Sir Launcelot had passing good cheer, and on the morn at the hour of prime, at Galahad's desire, he made him knight, and said, God make him a good man. For beauty faileth you not as any that liveth.

Now, fair sir, said Sir Launcelot, will ye come with me unto the Court of King Arthur? Nay, said he, I will not go with you as at this time. Then he departed from them and took his two cousins with him, and so they came unto Camelot by the hour of undorne[1] on Whitsunday. By that time the King and the Queen were gone to the minister to head their service: then the King and the Queen were passing glad of Sir Bors and Sir Lionel, and so was all the fellowship. So when the King and all the knights were come from service, the barons espied in the sieges of the Round Table, all about written with gold letters. Here ought to sit he, and he ought to sit here. And thus they went so long until that they came to the siege perilous, where they found letters newly written of gold, that said: Four hundred winters and fifty-four accomplished after the passion of our Lord Jesu Christ ought this siege to be fulfilled. Then all they said, This is a marvellous thing, and an adventurous. In the name of God, said Sir Launcelot; and then he accounted the term of the writing, from the birth of our Lord unto that day. It seemeth me, said Sir Launcelot, this siege ought to be fulfilled this same day, for this is the feast of Pentecost after the four hundred and four and fifty year; and if it would please all parties, I would none of these letters were seen this day, till he be come that ought to

---

[1] Nine in the morning.

achieve this adventure. Then made they to ordain a cloth of silk for to cover these letters in the siege perilous. Then the King bade haste unto dinner. Sir, said Sir Kay the steward, if ye go now unto your meat, ye shall break your old custom of your Court. For ye have not used on this day to sit at your meat or that ye have seen some adventure. Ye say sooth, said the King, but I had so great joy of Sir Launcelot and of his cousins, which be come to the Court whole and sound, that I bethought me not of my old custom. So as they stood speaking, in came a squire, and said unto the King, Sir, I bring unto you marvellous tidings. What be they? said the King. Sir, there is here beneath at the river a great stone, which I saw float above the water, and therein saw I sticking a sword. The King said, I will see that marvel. So all the knights went with him, and when they came unto the river, they found there a stone floating, as it were of red marble, and therein stuck a fair and rich sword, and in the pommel thereof were precious stones, wrought with subtle letters of gold. Then the barons read the letters, which said in this wise: Never shall man take me hence but only he by whose side I ought to hang, and he shall be the best knight of the world. When the King had seen these letters, he said unto Sir Launcelot, Fair sir, this sword ought to be yours, for I am sure ye be the best knight of the world. Then Sir Launcelot answered full soberly: Certes, sir, it is not my sword: also, sir, wit ye well I have no hardiness to set my hand to, for it longed not to hang at my side. Also who that assayeth to take that sword, and faileth of it, he shall receive a wound by that sword, that he shall not be whole long after. And I will that ye wit that this same day will the adventures of the Sancgreal, that is called the holy vessel, begin.

Now, fair nephew, said the King unto Sir Gawaine, assay ye for my love. Sir, he said, save your good grace, I shall not do that. Sir, said the King, assay to take the sword, and at my commandment. Sir, said Gawaine, your commandment I will obey. And therewith he took up the sword by the handles, but he might not stir it. I thank you, said the King to Sir Gawaine. My lord Sir Gawaine, said Sir Launcelot, now wit ye well, this sword shall touch you so sore that ye shall will ye had never set your hand thereto, for the best castle of this realm. Sir, he said, I might not withsay mine uncle's will and commandment. But when the King heard this, he repented it much, and said unto Sir Percivale that he should assay for his love. And he said, Gladly, for to bear Sir Gawaine fellowship. And therewith he set his hand on the sword, and drew it strongly, but he might not move it. Then were there more that durst be so hardy to set their hands thereto. Now may ye go to your dinner, said Sir Kay unto the King, for a marvellous adventure have ye seen. So the King and all went unto the Court, and every knight knew his own place, and set him therein, and young men that were knights served them. So when they were served, and all sieges fulfilled, save only the siege perilous, anon there befell a marvellous adventure, that all the doors and the windows of the place shut by themselves. Not for then the hall was not greatly darkened, and therewith they abashed both one and other. Then King Arthur spake first, and said, Fair fellows and lords, we have seen this day great marvels, but or night I suppose we shall see greater marvels. In the mean while came in a good old man, and an ancient, clothed all in white, and there was no knight knew from whence he came. And with him he brought a young knight, both on foot, in red arms, without sword or shield, save a scabbard hanging by his side. And these words he said, Peace be with you, fair lords. Then the old man said unto Arthur, Sir, I bring here a young knight the which is of king's lineage, and of the kindred of Joseph of Arimathie, whereby the marvels of this Court and of strange realms shall be fully accomplished.

The King was right glad of his words, and said unto the good man, Sir, ye be right welcome, and the young knight with you. Then the old man made the young man to unarm him; and he was in a coat of red sendel, and bare a mantle upon his shoulder that was furred with ermine, and put that upon him. And the old knight said unto the young knight, Sir, follow me. And anon he led him unto the siege perilous, where beside sat Sir Launcelot, and the good man lift up the cloth, and found there letters that said thus: This is the siege of Galahad the haut prince. Sir, said the old knight, wit ye well that place is yours. And then he set him down surely in that siege. And then he said to the old man, Sir, ye may now go your way, for well have ye done that ye were commanded to do. And recommend me unto my grandsire King Pelles, and unto my lord Petchere, and say them on my behalf, I shall come and see them as soon as ever I may. So the good man departed, and there met him twenty noble squires, and so took their horses and went their way. Then all the knights of the Table Round marvelled them greatly of Sir Galahad, that he durst sit there in that siege perilous, and was so tender of age, and wist not from whence he came, but all only by God, and said, This is he by whom the Sancgreal shall be achieved, for there sat never none but he, but he were mischieved. Then Sir Launcelot beheld his son, and had great joy of him. Then Sir Bors told his fellows, Upon pain of my life this young knight shall come unto great worship. This noise was great in all the Court, so that it came to the Queen. Then she had marvel what knight it might be that durst adventure him to sit in the siege perilous. Many said unto the Queen, he resembled much unto Sir Launcelot. I may well suppose, said the

Queen, that he is son of Sir Launcelot and King Pelles' daughter, and his name is Galahad. I would fain see him, said the Queen, for he must needs be a noble man, for so is his father; I report me unto all the Table Round. So when the meat was done, that the King and all were risen, the King went unto the siege perilous, and lift up the cloth, and found there the name of Galahad, and then he showed it unto Sir Gawaine, and said, Fair nephew, now have we among us Sir Galahad the good knight, that shall worship us all, and upon pain of my life he shall achieve the Sancgreal, right so as Sir Launcelot hath done us to understand. Then came King Arthur unto Galahad, and said, Sir, ye be welcome, for ye shall move many good knights to the quest of the Sancgreal, and ye shall achieve that never knights might bring to an end. Then the King took him by the hand, and went down from the palace to show Galahad the adventures of the stone.

The Queen heard thereof, and came after with many ladies, and showed them the stone where it hoved on the water. Sir, said the King unto Sir Galahad, here is a great marvel as ever I saw, and right good knights have assayed and failed. Sir, said Galahad, that is no marvel, for this adventure is not theirs, but mine, and for the surety of this sword I brought none with me; for here by my side hangeth the scabbard. And anon he laid his hand on the sword, and lightly drew it out of the stone, and put in the sheath, and said unto the King, Now it goeth better than it did aforehand.

3

The Apparition of Mrs. Veal

BY DANIEL DEFOE

THIS thing is so rare in all its circumstances and on so good authority, that my reading and conversation has not given me anything like it. It is fit to gratify the most ingenious and serious inquirer.

Mrs. Bargrave is the person to whom Mrs. Veal appeared after her death; she is my intimate friend, and I can avouch for her reputation for these last fifteen or sixteen years, on my own knowledge; and I can confirm the good character she had from her youth to the time of my acquaintance; though since this relation she is calumniated by some people that are friends to the brother of Mrs. Veal who appeared, who think the relation of this appearance to be a reflection, and endeavor what they can to blast Mrs. Bargrave's reputation and to laugh the story out of countenance. But by the circumstances thereof, and the cheerful disposition of Mrs. Bargrave, notwithstanding the unheard-of ill-usage of a very wicked husband, there is not the least sign of dejection in her face; nor did I ever hear her let fall a desponding or murmuring expression; nay, not when actually under her husband's barbarity, which I have been witness to, and several other persons of undoubted reputation.

Now, you must know Mrs. Veal was a maiden gentlewoman of about thirty years of age, and for some years last past had been troubled with fits, which were perceived coming on her by her going off from her discourse very abruptly to some impertinence.

She was maintained by an only brother, and kept his house in Dover. She was a very pious woman, and her brother a very sober man, to all appearance; but now he does all he can to null or quash the story.

Mrs. Veal was intimately acquainted with Mrs. Bargrave from her childhood. Mrs. Veal's circumstances were then mean. Her father did not take care of his children as he ought, so that they were exposed to hardships; and Mrs. Bargrave in those days had as unkind a father, though she wanted neither for food nor clothing, while Mrs. Veal wanted for both; so that it was in the power of Mrs. Bargrave to be very much her friend in several instances, which mightily endeared Mrs. Veal; insomuch that she would often say:

"Mrs. Bargrave, you are not only the best, but the only friend I have in the world; and no circumstance in life shall ever dissolve my friendship."

They would often condole each other's adverse fortune, and read together "Drelincourt Upon Death," and other good books; and so, like two Christian friends, they comforted each other under their sorrow.

Some time after, Mr. Veal's friends got him a place in the customhouse at Dover, which occasioned Mrs. Veal, by little and little, to fall off from her intimacy with Mrs. Bargrave, though there was never any such thing as a quarrel; but an indifferency came on by degrees, till at last Mrs. Bargrave had not seen her in two years and a half; though above a twelvemonth of the time Mrs. Bargrave had been absent from Dover, and this last half-year had been in Canterbury about two months of the time, dwelling in a house of her own.

In this house, on the 8th of September last (1705), she was sitting alone, in the forenoon, thinking over her unfortunate life, and arguing herself into a due resignation to Providence, though her condition seemed hard.

"And," said she, "I have been provided for hitherto, and doubt not but I shall be still; and am well satisfied that my affliction shall end when it is most fit for me;" and then took up her sewing-work, which she had no sooner done but she hears a knocking at the door.

She went to see who it was there, and this proved to be Mrs. Veal, her old friend, who was in a riding-habit. At that moment of time the clock struck twelve at noon.

"Madam," says Mrs. Bargrave, "I am surprised to see you, you have been so long a stranger;" but told her she was glad to see her, and offered to salute her, which Mrs. Veal complied with, till their lips almost touched; and then Mrs. Veal drew her hand across her own eyes and said: "I am not very well," and so waived it. She told Mrs. Bargrave she was going a journey, and had a great mind to see her first.

"But," says Mrs. Bargrave, "how came you to take a journey alone? I am amazed at it, because I know you have so fond a brother."

"Oh," says Mrs. Veal, "I gave my brother the slip, and came away, because I had so great a desire to see you before I took my journey."

So Mrs. Bargrave went in with her into another room within the first, and Mrs. Veal set her down in an elbow-chair, in which Mrs. Bargrave was sitting when she heard Mrs. Veal knock. Then says Mrs. Veal:

"My dear friend, I am come to renew our old friendship again, and beg your pardon for my breach of it; and if you can forgive me, you are one of the best of women."

"Oh," says Mrs. Bargrave, "don't mention such a thing; I have not had an uneasy thought about it; I can easily forgive it."

"What did you think of me?" said Mrs. Veal.

Says Mrs. Bargrave: "I thought you were like the rest of the world, and that prosperity had made you forget yourself and me."

Then Mrs. Veal reminded Mrs. Bargrave of the many friendly offices she did her in former days, and much of the conversation they had with each other in the time of their adversity; what books they read, and what comfort in particular they received from Drelincourt's "Book of Death," which was the best, she said, on that subject ever wrote. She also mentioned Dr. Sherlock, and two Dutch books which were translated, wrote upon death, and several others; but Drelincourt, she said, had the clearest notions of death and of the future state of any who had handled that subject. Then she asked Mrs. Bargrave whether she had Drelincourt.

She said: "Yes."

Says Mrs. Veal: "Fetch it."

And so Mrs. Bargrave goes up-stairs and brings the book down. Says Mrs. Veal:

"Dear Mrs. Bargrave, if the eyes of our faith were as open as the eyes of our body, we should see numbers of angels about us for our guard. The notions we have of heaven now are nothing like what it is, as Drelincourt says. Therefore, be comforted under your afflictions, and believe that the Almighty has a particular regard to you, and that your afflictions are marks of God's favor; and when they have done the business they are sent for, they shall be removed from you. And believe me, my dear friend, believe what I say to you, one minute of future happiness will infinitely reward you for all your sufferings; for I can never believe"—and claps her hand upon her knee with great earnestness, which indeed ran through most of her discourse—"that ever God will suffer you to spend all your days in this afflicted state; but be assured that your afflictions shall leave you, or you them in a short time."

She spake in that pathetical and heavenly manner, that Mrs. Bargrave wept several times, she was so deeply affected with it.

Then Mrs. Veal mentioned Dr. Horneck's "Ascetick," at the end of

4

which he gives an account of the lives of the primitive Christians. Their pattern she recommended to our imitation, and said their conversation was not like this of our age; "for now," says she, "there is nothing but frothy, vain discourse, which is far different from theirs. Theirs was to edification, and to build one another up in faith; so that they were not as we are, nor are we as they were; but," said she, "we might do as they did. There was a hearty friendship among them; but where is it now to be found?"

Says Mrs. Bargrave: "'Tis hard indeed to find a true friend in these days."

Says Mrs. Veal: "Mr. Norris has a fine copy of verses, called 'Friendship in Perfection,' which I wonderfully admire. Have you seen the books?" says Mrs. Veal.

"No," says Mrs. Bargrave, "but I have the verses of my own writing out."

"Have you?" says Mrs. Veal; "then fetch them."

Which she did from above-stairs, and offered them to Mrs. Veal to read, who refused, and waived the thing, saying, holding down her head would make it ache; and then desired Mrs. Bargrave to read them to her, which she did. As they were admiring "Friendship" Mrs. Veal said:

"Dear Mrs. Bargrave, I shall love you forever."

In the verses there is twice used the word Elysian.

"Ah!" says Mrs. Veal, "these poets have such names for heaven!" She would often draw her hand across her own eyes and say: "Mrs. Bargrave, don't you think I am mightily impaired by my fits?"

"No," says Mrs. Bargrave, "I think you look as well as ever I knew you."

After all this discourse, which the apparition put in words much finer than Mrs. Bargrave said she could pretend to, and was much more than she can remember—for it cannot be thought that an hour and three-quarters' conversation could all be retained, though the main of it she thinks she does—she said to Mrs. Bargrave she would have her write a letter to her brother, and tell him she would have him give rings to such and such, and that there was a purse of gold in her cabinet, and that she would have two broad pieces given to her cousin Watson.

Talking at this rate, Mrs. Bargrave thought that a fit was coming upon her, and so placed herself in a chair just before her knees, to keep her from falling to the ground, if her fit should occasion it—for the elbow-chair, she thought, would keep her from falling on either side; and to divert Mrs. Veal, as she thought, she took hold of her gown-

sleeve several times and commended it. Mrs. Veal told her it was a
scoured silk, and newly made up. But for all this, Mrs. Veal persisted
in her request, and told Mrs. Bargrave she must not deny her; and she
would have her tell her brother all their conversation when she had
an opportunity.

"Dear Mrs. Veal," said Mrs. Bargrave, "this seems so impertinent
that I cannot tell how to comply with it; and what a mortifying story
will our conversation be to a young gentleman!"

"Well," says Mrs. Veal, "I must not be denied."

"Why," says Mrs. Bargrave, " 'tis much better, methinks, to do it
yourself."

"No," says Mrs. Veal, "though it seems impertinent to you now,
you will see more reason for it hereafter."

Mrs. Bargrave then, to satisfy her importunity, was going to fetch
a pen and ink; but Mrs. Veal said:

"Let it alone now, and do it when I am gone; but you must be sure
to do it;" which was one of the last things she enjoined her at parting;
and so she promised her.

Then Mrs. Veal asked for Mrs. Bargrave's daughter. She said she
was not at home: "but if you have a mind to see her," says Mrs. Bargrave, "I'll send for her."

"Do," says Mrs. Veal.

On which she left her, and went to a neighbor's to send for her;
and by the time Mrs. Bargrave was returning, Mrs. Veal was got without the door in the street, in the face of the beast-market, on a Saturday
(which is market-day), and stood ready to part as soon as Mrs. Bargrave came to her. She asked her why she was in such haste. She said
she must be going, though perhaps she might not go her journey until
Monday; and told Mrs. Bargrave she hoped she should see her again
at her cousin Watson's before she went whither she was a going. Then
she said she would take her leave of her, and walked from Mrs. Bargrave in her view, till a turning interrupted the sight of her, which
was three-quarters after one in the afternoon.

Mrs. Veal died the 7th of September, at twelve o'clock at noon, of her
fits, and had not above four hours' senses before death, in which time
she received the sacrament.

The next day after Mrs. Veal's appearance, being Sunday, Mrs. Bargrave was mightily indisposed with a cold and a sore throat, that she
could not go out that day; but on Monday morning she sends a person
to Captain Watson's to know if Mrs. Veal were there. They wondered
at Mrs. Bargrave's inquiry, and sent her word that she was not there,
nor was expected.

At this answer, Mrs. Bargrave told the maid she had certainly mistook the name, or made some blunder. And though she was ill, she put on her hood, and went herself to Captain Watson's, though she knew none of the family, to see if Mrs. Veal was there or not. They said they wondered at her asking, for that she had not been in town; they were sure, if she had, she would have been there.

Says Mrs. Bargrave: "I am sure she was with me on Saturday almost two hours."

They said it was impossible; for they must have seen her, if she had. In comes Captain Watson while they are in dispute, and said that Mrs. Veal was certainly dead, and her escutcheons were making. This strangely surprised Mrs. Bargrave, who went to the person immediately who had the care of them, and found it true. Then she related the whole story to Captain Watson's family, and what gown she had on, and how striped, and that Mrs. Veal told her it was scoured.

Then Mrs. Watson cried out: "You have seen her indeed, for none knew but Mrs. Veal and myself that the gown was scoured." And Mrs. Watson owned that she described the gown exactly; "for," she said, "I helped her to make it up."

This Mrs. Watson blazed all about the town, and avouched the demonstration of the truth of Mrs. Bargrave's seeing Mrs. Veal's apparition; and Captain Watson carried two gentlemen immediately to Mrs. Bargrave's house to hear the relation from her own mouth. And then it spread so fast that gentlemen and persons of quality, the judicious and skeptical part of the world, flocked in upon her, which at last became such a task that she was forced to go out of the way; for they were in general extremely satisfied of the truth of the thing, and plainly saw that Mrs. Bargrave was no hypochondriac, for she always appears with such a cheerful air and pleasing mien, that she has gained the favor and esteem of all the gentry, and 'tis thought a great favor if they can but get the relation from her own mouth.

I should have told you before that Mrs. Veal told Mrs. Bargrave that her sister and brother-in-law were just come down from London to see her.

Says Mrs. Bargrave: "How came you to order matters so strangely?"

"It could not be helped," says Mrs. Veal.

And her sister and brother did come to see her, and entered the town of Dover just as Mrs. Veal was expiring.

Mrs. Bargrave asked her whether she would drink some tea.

Says Mrs. Veal: "I do not care if I do; but I'll warrant this mad fellow"—meaning Mrs. Bargrave's husband—"has broke all your trinkets."

"But," says Mrs. Bargrave, "I'll get something to drink in for all that."

But Mrs. Veal waived it, and said: "It is no matter; let it alone;" and so it passed.

All the time I sat with Mrs. Bargrave, which was some hours, she recollected fresh sayings of Mrs. Veal. And one material thing more she told Mrs. Bargrave—that old Mr. Breton allowed Mrs. Veal ten pounds a year, which was a secret, and unknown to Mrs. Bargrave till Mrs. Veal told it her.

Mrs. Bargrave never varies in her story, which puzzles those who doubt of the truth, or are unwilling to believe it. A servant in a neighbor's yard adjoining to Mrs. Bargrave's house heard her talking to somebody an hour of the time Mrs. Veal was with her. Mrs. Bargrave went out to her next neighbor's the very moment she parted with Mrs. Veal, and told what ravishing conversation she had with an old friend, and told the whole of it.

Drelincourt's "Book of Death" is, since this happened, bought up strangely. And it is to be observed that, nowithstanding all this trouble and fatigue Mrs. Bargrave has undergone upon this account, she never took the value of a farthing, nor suffered her daughter to take anything of anybody, and therefore can have no interest in telling the story.

Mrs. Veal's often drawing her hand over her eyes, and asking Mrs. Bargrave whether her fits had not impaired her, looks to me as if she did it on purpose to remind Mrs. Bargrave of her fits, to prepare her not to think it strange that she should put her upon writing to her brother to dispose of rings and gold, which looked so much like a dying person's request; and it took accordingly with Mrs. Bargrave, as the effects of her fits coming upon her; and was one of the many instances of her wonderful love to her, and care of her, that she should not be affrighted; which indeed appears in her whole management, particularly in her coming to her in the daytime, waiving the salutation, and when she was alone; and then the manner of her parting, to prevent a second attempt to salute her.

Now, why Mr. Veal should think this relation a reflection—as 'tis plain he does by his endeavoring to stifle it—I can't imagine, because the generality believe her to be a good spirit, her discourse was so heavenly. Her two great errands were to comfort Mrs. Bargrave in her affliction, and to ask her forgiveness for her breach of friendship, and with a pious discourse to encourage her. So that, after all, to suppose that Mrs. Bargrave could hatch such an invention as this from Friday noon till Saturday noon (supposing that she knew of Mrs. Veal's death the very first moment), without jumbling circumstances, and without any interest, too, she must be more witty, fortunate, and wicked, too, than any indifferent person, I dare say, will allow.

I asked Mrs. Bargrave several times if she was sure she felt the gown. She answered modestly: "If my senses be to be relied on, I am sure of it."

I asked her if she heard a sound when she clapped her hand upon her knee. She said she did not remember she did; and she said: "She appeared to be as much a substance as I did, who talked with her; and I may," said she, "be as soon persuaded that your apparition is talking to me now as that I did not really see her; for I was under no manner of fear; I received her as a friend, and parted with her as such. I would not," says she, "give one farthing to make any one believe it; I have no interest in it. Nothing but trouble is entailed upon me for a long time, for aught I know; and had it not come to light by accident, it would never have been made public."

But now she says she will make her own private use of it, and keep herself out of the way as much as she can; and so she has done since. She says she had a gentleman who came thirty miles to her to hear the relation, and that she had told it to a room full of people at a time. Several particular gentlemen have had the story from Mrs. Bargrave's own mouth.

This thing has very much affected me, and I am as well satisfied as I am of the best grounded matter of fact. And why we should dispute matter of fact because we cannot solve things of which we have no certain or demonstrative notions, seems strange to me. Mrs. Bargrave's authority and sincerity alone would have been undoubted in any other case.

The Vision of Mirzah

BY JOSEPH ADDISON

WHEN I was at Grand Cairo, I picked up several Oriental manuscripts, which I have still by me. Among others I met with one entitled, *The Visions of Mirzah,* which I have read over with great pleasure. I intend to give it to the public when I have no other entertainment for them; and shall begin with the first vision, which I have translated word for word as follows:

"On the fifth day of the moon, which according to the custom of my forefathers I always keep holy, after having washed myself, and offered up my morning devotions, I ascended the high hills of Bagdat, in order to pass the rest of the day in meditation and prayer. As I was here airing myself on the tops of the mountains, I fell into a profound contemplation on the vanity of human life; and passing from one thought to another, Surely, said I, man is but a shadow and life a dream. Whilst I was thus musing, I cast my eyes towards the summit of a rock that was not far from me, where I discovered one in the habit of a shepherd, with a little musical instrument in his hand. As I looked upon him he applied it to his lips, and began to play upon it. The sound of it was exceeding sweet, and wrought into a variety of tunes that were inexpressibly melodious, and altogether different from anything I had ever heard: they put me in mind of those heavenly airs that are played to the departed souls of good men upon their first arrival in Paradise, to wear out the impressions of their last agonies, and qualify them for the pleasures of that happy place. My heart melted away in secret raptures.

"I had been often told that the rock before me was the haunt of a Genius; and that several had been entertained with music who had passed by it, but never heard that the musician had before made himself visible. When he had raised my thoughts by those transporting airs

24

which he played, to taste the pleasures of his conversation, as I looked upon him like one astonished, he beckoned to me, and by the waving of his hand directed me to approach the place where he sat. I drew near with that reverence which is due to a superior nature; and as my heart was entirely subdued by the captivating strains I had heard, I fell down at his feet and wept. The Genius smiled upon me with a look of compassion and affability that familiarised him to my imagination, and at once dispelled all the fears and apprehensions with which I approached him. He lifted me from the ground, and taking me by the hand, Mirzah, said he, I have heard thee in thy soliloquies; follow me.

"He then led me to the highest pinnacle of the rock, and placed me on the top of it. Cast thy eyes eastward, said he, and tell me what thou seest. I see, said I, a huge valley, and a prodigious tide of water rolling through it. The valley that thou seest, said he, is the vale of misery, and the tide of water that thou seest is part of the great tide of eternity. What is the reason, said I, that the tide I see rises out of a thick mist at one end, and again loses itself in a thick mist at the other? What thou seest, said he, is that portion of eternity which is called time, measured out by the sun, and reaching from the beginning of the world to its consummation. Examine now, said he, this sea that is bounded with darkness at both ends, and tell me what thou discoverest in it. I see a bridge, said I, standing in the midst of the tide. The bridge thou seest, said he, is human life, consider it attentively. Upon a more leisurely survey of it, I found that it consisted of threescore and ten entire arches, with several broken arches, which added to those that were entire, made up the number about a hundred. As I was counting the arches, the Genius told me that this bridge consisted at first of a thousand arches; but that a great flood swept away the rest, and left the bridge in the ruinous condition I now beheld it: But tell me further, said he, what thou discoverest on it. I see multitudes of people passing over it, said I, and a black cloud hanging on each end of it. As I looked more attentively, I saw several of the passengers dropping through the bridge, into the great tide that flowed underneath it; and upon further examination, perceived there were innumerable trapdoors that lay concealed in the bridge, which the passengers no sooner trod upon, but they fell through them into the tide and immediately disappeared. These hidden pitfalls were set very thick at the entrance of the bridge, so that the throngs of people no sooner broke through the cloud, but many of them fell into them. They grew thinner towards the middle, but multiplied and lay closer together towards the end of the arches that were entire.

"There were indeed some persons, but their number was very small, that continued a kind of hobbling march on the broken arches, but fell through one after another, being quite tired and spent after so long a walk.

"I passed some time in the contemplation of this wonderful structure, and the great variety of objects which it presented. My heart was filled with a deep melancholy to see several dropping unexpectedly in the midst of mirth and jollity, and catching at everything that stood by them to save themselves. Some were looking up towards the heavens in a thoughtful posture, and in the midst of a speculation stumbled and fell out of sight. Multitudes were very busy in the pursuit of bubbles that glittered in their eyes and danced before them; but often when they thought themselves within the reach of them their footing failed and down they sunk. In this confusion of objects, I observed some with scimitars in their hands, who ran to and fro upon the bridge, thrusting several persons on trap-doors which did not seem to lie in their way, and which they might have escaped, had they not been thus forced upon them.

"The Genius seeing me indulge myself in this melancholy prospect, told me I had dwelt long enough upon it: Take thine eyes off the bridge, said he, and tell me if thou yet seest anything thou dost not comprehend. Upon looking up, What mean, said I, those great flights of birds that are perpetually hovering about the bridge, and settling upon it from time to time? I see vultures, harpies, ravens, cormorants, and among many other feathered creatures several little winged boys, that perch in great numbers upon the middle arches. These, said the Genius, are Envy, Avarice, Superstition, Despair, Love, with the like cares and passions that infest human life.

"I here fetched a deep sigh; Alas, said I, man was made in vain! How is he given away to misery and mortality! tortured in life, and swallowed up in death! The Genius, being moved with compassion towards me, bid me quit so uncomfortable a prospect; Look no more, said he, on man in the first stage of his existence, in his setting out for eternity; but cast thine eye on that thick mist into which the tide bears the several generations of mortals that fall into it. I directed my sight as I was ordered, and (whether or no the good Genius strengthened it with any supernatural force, or dissipated part of the mist that was before too thick for the eye to penetrate) I saw the valley opening at the farther end, and spreading forth into an immense ocean, that had a huge rock of adamant running through the midst of it, and dividing it into two equal parts. The clouds still rested on one half of it, insomuch that I could discover nothing in it: but the other appeared to me a vast ocean planted with innumerable islands, that were covered with fruits and flowers, and interwoven with a thousand little shining seas that ran among them. I could see persons dressed in glorious habits with garlands upon their heads, passing among the trees, lying down by the sides of fountains, or resting on beds of flowers; and could hear a confused harmony of singing birds, falling waters, human voices, and musical instruments. Gladness grew in me upon the discovery of so delightful a scene. I wished for the wings of an eagle, that I might fly away to those happy seats; but the Genius told me there was no passage to them, except through the gates of death that I saw opening every moment upon the bridge. The islands, said he, that lie so fresh and green before thee, and with which the whole face of the ocean appears spotted as far as thou canst see, are more in number than the sands on the sea-shore; there are myriads of islands behind those which thou here discoverest, reaching farther than thine eye, or even thine imagination can extend itself. These are the mansions of good men after death, who, according to the degree and kinds of virtue in which they excelled, are distributed among these several islands, which abound with pleasures of different kinds and degrees, suitable to the relishes and perfections of those who are settled in them; every island is a paradise accommodated to its respective inhabitants. Are not these, O Mirzah, habitations worth contending for? Does life appear miserable, that gives thee opportunities of earning such a reward? Is death to be feared, that will convey thee to so happy an existence? Think not man was made in vain, who has such an eternity reserved for him. I gazed with inexpressible pleasure on these happy islands. At length, said I, show me now, I beseech thee, the secrets that lie hid under those dark clouds which cover the ocean on the other side of the rock of adamant. The Genius making me no answer, I turned about to address myself to him a second time, but I found that he had left me; I then turned again to the vision which I had been so long contemplating; but instead of the rolling tide, the arched bridge, and the happy islands, I saw nothing but the long hollow valley of Bagdat, with oxen, sheep, and camels grazing upon the sides of it."

5

Asem

AN EASTERN TALE

BY OLIVER GOLDSMITH

WHERE Tauris lifts its head above the storm, and presents nothing to the sight of the distant traveller but a prospect of nodding rocks, falling torrents, and all the variety of tremendous nature; on the bleak bosom of this frightful mountain, secluded from society, and detesting the ways of men, lived Asem the Man-Hater.

Asem had spent his youth with men, had shared in their amusements, and had been taught to love his fellow-creatures with the most ardent affection; but, from the tenderness of his disposition, he exhausted all his fortune in relieving the wants of the distressed. The petitioner never sued in vain; the weary traveller never passed his door; he only desisted from doing good when he had no longer the power of relieving.

For a fortune thus spent in benevolence he expected a grateful return from those he had formerly relieved, and made his application with confidence of redress: the ungrateful world soon grew weary of his importunity; for pity is but a short-lived passion. He soon, therefore, began to view mankind in a very different light from that in which he had before beheld them: he perceived a thousand vices he had never before suspected to exist; wherever he turned, ingratitude, dissimulation, and treachery, contributed to increase his detestation of them. Resolved, therefore, to continue no longer in a world which he hated, and which repaid his detestation with contempt, he retired to this region of sterility, in order to brood over his resentment in solitude, and converse with the only honest heart he knew—namely, with his own.

A cave was his only shelter from the inclemency of the weather;

fruits, gathered with difficulty from the mountain's side, his only food; and his drink was fetched, with danger and toil, from the headlong torrent. In this manner he lived, sequestered from society, passing the hours in meditation, and sometimes exulting that he was able to live independent of his fellow-creatures.

At the foot of the mountain an extensive lake displayed its glassy bosom, reflecting on its broad surface the impending horrors of the mountain. To this capacious mirror he would sometimes descend, and, reclining on its steep banks, cast an eager look on the smooth expanse that lay before him. "How beautiful," he often cried, "is Nature! how lovely even in her wildest scenes! How finely contrasted is the level plain that lies beneath me with yon awful pile that hides its tremendous head in clouds! But the beauty of these scenes is no way comparable with their utility; hence an hundred rivers are supplied, which distribute health and verdure to the various countries through which they flow. Every part of the universe is beautiful, just, and wise; but man, vile man, is a solecism in nature, the only monster in the creation. Tempests and whirlwinds have their use; but vicious, ungrateful man is a blot in the fair page of universal beauty. Why was I born of that detested species, whose vices are almost a reproach to the wisdom of the divine Creator? Were men entirely free from vice, all would be uniformity, harmony, and order. A world of moral rectitude should be the result of a perfect moral agent. Why, why then, O Alla! must I be thus confined in darkness, doubt, and despair?"

Just as he uttered the word despair, he was going to plunge into the lake beneath him, at once to satisfy his doubts, and put a period to his anxiety, when he perceived a most majestic being walking on the surface of the water, and approaching the bank on which he stood. So unexpected an object at once checked his purpose; he stopped, contemplated, and fancied he saw something awful and divine in his aspect.

"Son of Adam," cried the Genius, "stop thy rash purpose; the Father of the Faithful has seen thy justice, thy integrity, thy miseries, and hath sent me to afford and administer relief. Give me thine hand, and follow without trembling wherever I shall lead: in me behold the Genius of Conviction, kept by the great Prophet, to turn from their errors those who go astray, not from curiosity, but a rectitude of intention. Follow me and be wise."

Asem immediately descended upon the lake, and his guide conducted him along the surface of the water, till, coming near the centre of the lake, they both began to sink; the waters closed over their heads; they descended several hundred fathoms, till Asem, just ready to give up his life as inevitably lost, found himself, with his celestial guide, in another world, at the bottom of the waters, where human foot had never trod before. His astonishment was beyond description, when he saw a sun like that he had left, a serene sky over his head, and blooming verdure under his feet.

"I plainly perceive your amazement," said the Genius; "but suspend it for a while. This world was formed by Alla, at the request, and under the inspection, of our great Prophet, who once entertained the same doubts which filled your mind when I found you, and from the consequence of which you were so lately rescued. The rational inhabitants of this world are formed agreeable to your own ideas; they are absolutely without vice. In other respects it resembles your earth, but differs from it in being wholly inhabited by men who never do wrong. If you find this world more agreeable than that you so lately left, you have free permission to spend the remainder of your days in it; but permit me for some time to attend you, that I may silence your doubts, and make you better acquainted with your company and your new habitation."

"A world without vice! Rational beings without immorality!" cried Asem, in a rapture; "I thank thee, O Alla! who hast at length heard my petitions: this, this indeed will produce happiness, ecstasy, and ease. Oh, for an immortality, to spend it among men who are incapable of ingratitude, injustice, fraud, violence, and a thousand other crimes that render society miserable!"

"Cease thine exclamations," replied the Genius. "Look around thee: reflect on every object and action before us, and communicate to me the result of thine observations. Lead wherever you think proper, I shall be your attendant and instructor." Asem and his companion travelled on in silence for some time, the former being entirely lost in astonishment; but at last recovering his former serenity, he could not help observing, that the face of the country bore a near resemblance to that he had left, except that this subterranean world still seemed to retain its primeval wildness.

"Here," cried Asem, "I perceive animals of prey and others that seem only designed for their subsistence; it is the very same in the world over our heads. But had I been permitted to instruct our Prophet, I would have removed this defect, and formed no voracious or destructive animals, which only prey on the other parts of the creation."

—"Your tenderness for inferior animals is, I find, remarkable," said the Genius, smiling. "But, with regard to meaner creatures, this world exactly resembles the other, and, indeed, for obvious reasons; for the earth can support a more considerable number of animals by their thus becoming food for each other, than if they had lived entirely on her vegetable productions. So that animals of different natures thus formed, instead of lessening their multitude, subsist in the greatest number possible. But let us hasten on to the inhabited country before us, and see what that offers for instruction."

They soon gained the utmost verge of the forest, and entered the country inhabited by men without vice; and Asem anticipated in idea the rational delight he hoped to experience in such an innocent society. But they had scarcely left the confines of the wood, when they beheld one of the inhabitants flying with hasty steps, and terror in his countenance, from an army of squirrels, that closely pursued him. "Heavens!" cried Asem, "why does he fly? What can he fear from animals so contemptible?" He had scarcely spoken, when he perceived two dogs pursuing another of the human species, who with equal terror and haste attempted to avoid them. "This," cried Asem to his guide, "is truly surprising; nor can I conceive the reason for so strange an action."—"Every species of animals," replied the Genius, "has of late grown very powerful in this country; for the inhabitants, at first, thinking it unjust to use either fraud or force in destroying them, they have insensibly increased, and now frequently ravage their harmless frontiers."—"But they should have been destroyed," cried Asem; "you see the consequence of such neglect."—"Where is, then, that tenderness you so lately expressed for subordinate animals?" replied the Genius, smiling; "you seem to have forgot that branch of justice."—"I must acknowledge my mistake," returned Asem; "I am now convinced that we must be guilty of tyranny and injustice to the brute creation, if we would enjoy the world ourselves. But let us no longer observe the duty of man to these irrational creatures, but survey their connections with one another."

As they walked farther up the country, the more he was surprised to see no vestiges of handsome houses, no cities, nor any mark of elegant design. His conductor, perceiving his surprise, observed, that the inhabitants of this new world were perfectly content with their ancient simplicity; each had a house, which, though homely, was sufficient to lodge his little family; they were too good to build houses, which could only increase their own pride, and the envy of the spectator: what they built was for convenience, and not for show. "At least, then," said Asem, "they have neither architects, painters, nor statuaries, in their society; but these are idle arts, and may be spared. However, before I spend much more time here, you should have my thanks for introducing me into the society of some of their wisest men: there is scarce any pleasure to me equal to a refined conversation; there is nothing of which I am so much enamoured as wisdom."—"Wisdom!" replied his instructor; "how ridiculous! We have no wisdom here, for we have no occasion for it; true wisdom is only a knowledge of our own duty, and the duty of others to us; but of what use is such wisdom here? each intuitively performs what is right in himself, and expects the same from others. If by wisdom you should mean vain curiosity and empty speculation, as such pleasures have their origin in vanity, luxury, or avarice, we are too good to pursue them."—"All this may be right," says Asem: "but methinks I observe a solitary disposition prevail among the people; each family keeps separately within their own precincts, without society, or without intercourse."—"That indeed, is true," replied the other; "here is no established society, nor should there be any; all societies are made either through fear or friendship: the people we are among are too good to fear each other; and there are no motives to private friendship, where all are equally meritorious."—"Well, then," said the sceptic, "as I am to spend my time here, if I am to have neither the polite arts, nor wisdom, nor friendship, in such a world, I should be glad at least of an easy companion, who may tell me his thoughts, and to whom I may communicate mine."—"And to what purpose should either do this?" says the Genius: "flattery or curiosity are vicious motives, and never allowed of here; and wisdom is out of the question."

"Still, however," said Asem, "the inhabitants must be happy; each is contented with his own possessions, nor avariciously endeavours to heap up more than is necessary for his own subsistence; each has therefore leisure for pitying those that stand in need of his compassion." He had scarce spoken, when his ears were assaulted with the lamentations of a wretch who sat by the way-side, and in the most deplorable distress seemed gently to murmur at his own misery. Asem immediately ran to his relief, and found him in the last stage of a consumption. "Strange," cried the son of Adam, "that men who are free from vice should thus suffer so much misery without relief!"—"Be not surprised," said the wretch who was dying: "would it not be the utmost injustice for beings who have only just sufficient to support themselves, and are content with a bare subsistence, to take it from their own mouths to put it into mine? They never are possessed of a single meal more than is necessary, and what is barely necessary cannot be dispensed with."—"They should have been supplied with more than is necessary," cried Asem—"and yet I contradict my own opinion but a moment before—all is doubt, perplexity, and confusion. Even the want of ingratitude is no virtue here, since they never received a favour. They have, however, another excellence yet behind; the love of their country is still, I hope, one of their darling virtues."—"Peace, Asem," replied the Guardian, with a countenance not less severe than beautiful; "nor forfeit all thy pretensions to wisdom: the same selfish motives by which we prefer our own interests to that of others, induce us to regard our country preferably to that of another. Nothing less than universal benevolence is free from vice, and that you see is prac-tised here."—"Strange!" cries the disappointed pilgrim, in an agony of distress; "what sort of a world am I now introduced to? There is scarce a single virtue, but that of temperance, which they practise: and in that they are no way superior to the very brute creation. There is scarce an amusement which they enjoy; fortitude, liberality, friend-ship, wisdom, conversation, and love of country, all are virtues entirely unknown here: thus it seems that to be unacquainted with vice is not to know virtue. Take me, O my Genius, back to that very world which I have despised: a world which has Alla for its contriver is much more wisely formed than that which has been projected by Mahomet. In-gratitude, contempt, and hatred, I can now suffer, for perhaps I have deserved them. When I arraigned the wisdom of Providence, I only showed my own ignorance; henceforth let me keep from vice myself, and pity it in others."

He had scarce ended, when the Genius, assuming an air of terrible complacency, called all his thunders around him, and vanished in a whirlwind. Asem, astonished at the terror of the scene, looked for his imaginary world; when, casting his eyes around, he perceived himself in the very situation, and in the very place, where he first began to repine and despair; his right foot had been just advanced to take the fatal plunge, nor had it been yet withdrawn; so instantly did Provi-dence strike the series of truths just imprinted on his soul. He now departed from the water-side in tranquillity; and leaving his horrid mansion, travelled to Segestan, his native city, where he diligently ap-plied himself to commerce, and put in practice that wisdom he had learned in solitude. The frugality of a few years soon produced opu-lence; the number of his domestics increased; his friends came to him from every part of the city; nor did he receive them with disdain; and a youth of misery was concluded with an old age of elegance, affluence, and ease.

6

The Two Drovers

BY SIR WALTER SCOTT

IT WAS the day after Doune
Fair when my story commences. It had been a brisk market; several
dealers had attended from the northern and midland counties in England, and English money had flown so merrily about as to gladden
the hearts of the Highland farmers. Many large droves were about to
set off for England, under the protection of their owners, or of the
tops-men whom they employed in the tedious, laborious, and responsible office of driving the cattle for many hundred miles, from the
market where they had been purchased, to the fields or farm-yards
where they were to be fattened for the shambles.

The Highlanders, in particular, are masters of this difficult trade of
driving, which seems to suit them as well as the trade of war. It affords
exercise for all their habits of patient endurance and active exertion.
They are required to know perfectly the drove-roads, which lie over
the wildest tracks of the country, and to avoid as much as possible the
highways, which distress the feet of the bullocks, and the turnpikes,
which annoy the spirit of the drover; whereas on the broad green or
gray track, which leads across the pathless moor, the herd not only move
at ease and without taxation, but, if they mind their business, may pick
up a mouthful of food by the way. At night, the drovers usually sleep
along with their cattle, let the weather be what it will; and many of
these hardy men do not once rest under a roof during a journey on foot
from Lochaber to Lincolnshire. They are paid very highly, for the
trust reposed is of the last importance, as it depends on their prudence,
vigilance, and honesty, whether the cattle reach the final market in
good order, and afford a profit to the grazier. But as they maintain
themselves at their own expense, they are especially economical in that
particular. At the period we speak of, a Highland drover was victualled

for his long and toilsome journey with a few handfuls of oatmeal, and two or three onions, renewed from time to time, and a ram's horn filled with whiskey, which he used regularly but sparingly, every night and morning. His dirk, or *skene-dhu* (*i.e.,* black-knife), so worn as to be concealed beneath the arm, or by the folds of the plaid, was his only weapon, excepting the cudgel with which he directed the movements of the cattle. A Highlander was never so happy as on these occasions. There was a variety in the whole journey, which exercised the Celt's natural curiosity and love of motion; there were the constant change of place and scene, the petty adventures incidental to the traffic, and the intercourse with the various farmers, graziers, and traders, intermingled with occasional merrymakings, not the less acceptable to Donald that they were void of expense;—and there was the consciousness of superior skill; for the Highlander, a child amongst flocks, is a prince amongst herds, and his natural habits induce him to disdain the shepherd's slothful life, so that he feels himself nowhere more at home than when following a gallant drove of his country cattle in the character of their guardian.

Of the number who left Doune in the morning, and with the purpose we described, not a *Glunamie* of them all cocked his bonnet more briskly, or gartered his tartan hose under knee over a pair of more promising *spiogs* (legs), than did Robin Oig, that is, Young, or the Lesser, Robin. Though small of stature, as the epithet Oig implies, and not very strongly limbed, he was light and alert as one of the deer of the mountains. He had an elasticity of step, which, in the course of a long march, made many a stout fellow envy him; and the manner in which he busked his plaid and adjusted his bonnet, argued a consciousness that so smart a John Highlandman as himself would not pass unnoticed among the Lowland lasses. The ruddy cheek, red lips, and white teeth, set off a countenance which had gained by exposure to the weather a healthful and hardy rather than a rugged hue. If Robin Oig did not laugh, or even smile frequently, as indeed is not the practice among his countrymen, his bright eyes usually gleamed from under his bonnet with an expression of cheerfulness ready to be turned into mirth.

The departure of Robin Oig was an incident in the little town, in and near which he had many friends, male and female.

He was a topping person in his way, transacted considerable business on his own behalf, and was intrusted by the best farmers in the Highlands, in preference to any other drover in that district. He might have increased his business to any extent had he condescended to manage it by deputy; but except a lad or two, sister's sons of his own, Robin rejected the idea of assistance, conscious, perhaps, how much his reputation depended upon his attending in person to the practical discharge of his duty in every instance. He remained, therefore, contented with the highest premium given to persons of his description, and comforted himself with the hopes that a few journeys to England might enable him to conduct business on his own account, in a manner becoming his birth. For Robin Oig's father, Lachlan M'Combich (or *son of my friend,* his actual clan-surname being M'Gregor), had been so called by the celebrated Rob Roy, because of the particular friendship which had subsisted between the grandsire of Robin and that renowned cateran. Some people even say, that Robin Oig derived his Christian name from one as renowned in the wilds of Loch Lomond as ever was his namesake Robin Hood in the precincts of merry Sherwood. "Of such ancestry," as James Boswell says, "who would not be proud?" Robin Oig was proud accordingly; but his frequent visits to England and to the Lowlands had given him tact enough to know that pretensions, which still gave him a little right to distinction in his own lonely glen, might be both obnoxious and ridiculous if preferred elsewhere. The pride of birth, therefore, was like the miser's treasure, the secret subject of his contemplation, but never exhibited to strangers as a subject of boasting.

Many were the words of gratulation and good luck which were bestowed on Robin Oig. The judges commended his drove, especially Robin's own property, which were the best of them. Some thrust out their snuff-mulls for the parting pinch—others tendered the *doch-an-dorrach,* or parting cup. All cried—"Good-luck travel out with you and come home with you.—Give you luck in the Saxon market—brave notes in the *leabhardhu"* (black pocketbook), "and plenty of English gold in the *sporan"* (pouch of goat-skin).

The bonny lasses made their adieus more modestly, and more than one, it was said, would have given her best brooch to be certain that it was upon her that his eye last rested as he turned towards the road.

Robin Oig had just given the preliminary *"Hoo-hoo!"* to urge forward the loiterers of the drove, when there was a cry behind him.

"Stay, Robin—bide a blink. Here is Janet of Tomahourich—auld Janet, your father's sister."

"Plague on her, for an auld Highland witch and spaewife," said a farmer from the carse of Stirling; "she'll cast some of her cantrips on the cattle."

"She canna do that," said another sapient of the same profession— "Robin Oig is no the lad to leave any of them without tying Saint Mungo's knot on their tails, and that will put to her speed the best witch that ever flew over Dimayet upon a broomstick."

It may not be indifferent to the reader to know, that the Highland cattle are peculiarly liable to be *taken*, or infected, by spells and witch-craft; which judicious people guard against, by knitting knots of pe-culiar complexity on the tuft of hair which terminates the animal's tail.

But the old woman who was the object of the farmer's suspicion, seemed only busied about the drover, without paying any attention to the drove. Robin, on the contrary, appeared rather impatient of her presence.

"What auld-world fancy," he said, "has brought you so early from the ingle-side this morning, Muhme? I am sure I bid you good-even, and had your God-speed, last night."

"And left me more siller than the useless old woman will use till you come back again, bird of my bosom," said the sibyl. "But it is little that I would care for the food that nourishes me, or the fire that warms me, or for God's blessed sun itself, if aught but weel should happen to the grandson of my father. So let me walk the *deasil* round you, that you may go safe out into the foreign land, and come safe home."

Robin Oig stopped, half embarrassed, half laughing, and signing to those near that he only complied with the old woman to soothe her humour. In the mean time, she traced around him, with wavering steps, the propitiation, which some have thought has been derived from the Druidical mythology. It consists, as is well known, in the person who makes the *deasil* walking three times round the person who is the object of the ceremony, taking care to move according to the course of the sun. At once, however, she stopped short, and exclaimed, in a voice of alarm and horror, "Grandson of my father, there is blood on your hand."

"Hush, for God's sake, aunt," said Robin Oig; "you will bring more trouble on yourself with this *taishataragh*" (second sight) "than you will be able to get out of for many a day."

The old woman only repeated with a ghastly look, "There is blood on your hand, and it is English blood. The blood of the Gael is richer and redder. Let us see—let us——"

Ere Robin Oig could prevent her, which, indeed, could only have been done by positive violence, so hasty and peremptory were her pro-ceedings, she had drawn from his side the dirk which lodged in the folds of his plaid, and held it up, exclaiming, although the weapon gleamed clear and bright in the sun, "Blood, blood—Saxon blood again. Robin Oig M'Combich, go not this day to England!"

"Prutt trutt," answered Robin Oig, "that will never do neither—it would be next thing to running the country. For shame, Muhme—give me the dirk. You cannot tell by the color the difference betwixt the blood of a black bullock and a white one, and you speak of knowing Saxon from Gaelic blood. All men have their blood from Adam,

Muhme. Give me my skene-dhu, and let me go on my road. I should have been half-way to Stirling Brig by this time.—Give me my dirk, and let me go."

"Never will I give it to you," said the old woman—"Never will I quit my hold on your plaid, unless you promise me not to wear that unhappy weapon."

The women around him urged him also, saying few of his aunt's words fell to the ground; and as the Lowland farmers continued to look moodily on the scene, Robin Oig determined to close it at any sacrifice.

"Well, then," said the young drover, giving the scabbard of the weapon to Hugh Morrison, "you Lowlanders care nothing for these freats. Keep my dirk for me. I cannot give it to you, because it was my father's; but your drove follows ours, and I am content it should be in your keeping, not in mine.—Will this do, Muhme?"

"It must," said the old woman,—"that is, if the Lowlander is mad enough to carry the knife."

The strong westlandman laughed aloud.

"Goodwife," said he, "I am Hugh Morrison from Glenae, come of the Manly Morrisons of auld langsyne, that never took short weapon against a man in their lives. And neither needed they. They had their broadswords, and I have this bit supple," showing a formidable cudgel —"for dirking ower the board, I leave that to John Highlandman—Ye needna snort, none of you Highlanders, and you in especial, Robin. I'll keep the bit knife, if you are feared for the auld spaewife's tale, and give it back to you whenever you want it."

Robin was not particularly pleased with some part of Hugh Morrison's speech; but he had learned in his travels more patience than belonged to his Highland constitution originally and he accepted the service of the descendant of the Manly Morrisons without finding fault with the rather depreciating manner in which it was offered.

"If he had not had his morning in his head, and been but a Dumfriesshire hog into the boot, he would have spoken more like a gentleman. But you cannot have more of a sow than a grumph. It's shame my father's knife should ever slash a haggis for the like of him."

Thus saying (but saying it in Gaelic), Robin drove on his cattle, and waved farewell to all behind him. He was in the greater haste, because he expected to join at Falkirk, a comrade and brother in profession, with whom he proposed to travel in company.

Robin Oig's chosen friend was a young Englishman, Harry Wakefield by name, well known at every northern market, and in his way as much famed and honored as our Highland driver of bullocks. He was nearly six feet high, gallantly formed to keep the rounds at Smithfield, or maintain the ring at a wrestling match; and although he might have been overmatched perhaps, among the regular professors of the Fancy, yet, as a yokel, or rustic, or a chance customer, he was able to give a bellyful to any amateur of the pugilistic art. Doncaster races saw him in his glory, betting his guinea, and generally successfully; nor was there a main fought in Yorkshire, the feeders being persons of celebrity, at which he was not to be seen if business permitted. But though a *sprack* lad, and fond of pleasure and its haunts, Harry Wakefield was steady, and not the cautious Robin Oig M'Combich himself was more attentive to the main chance. His holidays were holidays indeed; but his days of work were dedicated to steady and persevering labor. In countenance and temper, Wakefield was the model of old England's merry yeomen, whose clothyard shafts, in so many hundred battles, asserted her superiority over the nations, and whose good sabres, in our own time, are her cheapest and most assured defence. His mirth was readily excited; for, strong in limb and constitution, and fortunate in circumstances, he was disposed to be pleased with everything about him; and such difficulties as he might occasionally encounter, were, to a man of his energy, rather matter of amusement than serious annoyance. With all the merits of a sanguine temper, our young English drover was not without his defects. He was irascible, sometimes to the verge of being quarrelsome; and perhaps not the less inclined to bring his disputes to a pugilistic decision, because he found few antagonists able to stand up to him in the boxing ring.

It is difficult to say how Harry Wakefield and Robin Oig first became intimates; but it is certain a close acquaintance had taken place betwixt them, although they had apparently few common subjects of conversation or of interest, so soon as their talk ceased to be of bullocks. Robin Oig, indeed, spoke the English language rather imperfectly upon any other topics but stots and kyloes, and Harry Wakefield could never bring his broad Yorkshire tongue to utter a single word of Gaelic. It was in vain Robin spent a whole morning, during a walk over Minch Moor, in attempting to teach his companion to utter, with true precision, the shibboleth *Llhu,* which is the Gaelic for a calf. From Traquair to Murder-cairn, the hill rang with the discordant attempts of the Saxon upon the unmanageable monosyllable, and the heartfelt laugh which followed at every failure. They had, however, better modes of awakening the echoes; for Wakefield could sing many a ditty to the praise of Moll, Susan, and Cicely, and Robin Oig had a particular gift at whistling interminable pibrochs through all their involutions, and what was more agreeable to his companion's southern ear, knew many of the northern airs, both lively and pathetic, to which Wakefield learned to pipe a bass. Thus, though Robin could hardly have comprehended his companion's stories about horse-racing, and cock-fighting, or fox-hunting, and although his own legends of clan-fights and *creaghs,* varied with talk of Highland goblins and fairy folk, would have been caviare to his companion, they contrived nevertheless to find a degree of pleasure in each other's company, which had for three years back induced them to join company and travel together, when the direction of their journey permitted. Each, indeed, found his advantage in this companionship; for where could the Englishman have found a guide through the Western Highlands like Robin Oig M'Combich? And when they were on what Harry called the *right* side of the border, his patronage, which was extensive, and his purse, which was heavy, were at all times at the service of his Highland friend, and on many occasions his liberality did him genuine yeoman's service.

II

Were ever two such loving friends!—
How could they disagree?
Oh, thus it was, he loved him dear,
And thought how to requite him,
And having no friend left but he,
He did resolve to fight him.

DUKE UPON DUKE

The pair of friends had traversed with their usual cordiality the grassy wilds of Liddesdale, and crossed the opposite part of Cumberland, emphatically called The Waste. In these solitary regions, the cattle under the charge of our drovers derived their subsistence chiefly by picking their food as they went along the drove road, or sometimes by the tempting opportunity of a *start and owerloup,* or invasion of the neighboring pasture, where an occasion presented itself. But now the scene changed before them; they were descending towards a fertile and enclosed country, where no such liberties could be taken with impunity, or without a previous arrangement and bargain with the possessors of the ground. This was more especially the case, as a great northern fair was upon the eve of taking place, where both the Scotch and English drover expected to dispose of a part of their cattle, which it was desirable to produce in the market rested and in good order. Fields were therefore difficult to be obtained, and only upon high terms. This necessity occasioned a temporary separation betwixt the two friends, who went to bargain, each as he could, for the separate accommodation of his herd. Unhappily it chanced that both of them, unknown to each other, thought of bargaining for the ground they wanted on the property of a country gentleman of some fortune, whose estate lay in the neighborhood. The English drover applied to the bailiff on the property, who was known to him. It chanced that the Cumbrian Squire, who had entertained some suspicions of his manager's honesty, was taking occasional measures to ascertain how far they were well founded, and had desired that any inquiries about his enclosures, with a view to occupy them for a temporary purpose, should be referred to himself. As, however, Mr. Ireby had gone the day before upon a journey of some miles' distance to the northward, the bailiff chose to consider the check upon his full powers as for the time removed, and concluded that he should best consult his master's interest, and perhaps his own, in making an agreement with Harry Wakefield. Meanwhile, ignorant of what his comrade was doing, Robin Oig, on his side, chanced to be overtaken by a good-looking smart little man upon a pony, most knowingly bogged and cropped, as was then the fashion, the rider wearing tight leather breeches, and long-necked bright spurs. This cavalier asked one or two pertinent questions about markets and the price of stock. So Robin, seeing him a well-judging civil gentleman, took the freedom to ask him whether he could let him know if there was any grass land to be let in that neighborhood, for the temporary accommodation of his drove. He could not have put the question to more willing ears. The gentleman of the buckskin was the proprietor, with whose bailiff Harry Wakefield had dealt, or was in the act of dealing.

"Thou art in good luck, my canny Scot," said Mr. Ireby, "to have spoken to me, for I see thy cattle have done their day's work, and I have at my disposal the only field within three miles that is to be let in these parts."

"The drove can pe gang two, three, four miles very pratty weel indeed," said the cautious Highlander; "put what would his honor be axing for the peasts pe the head, if she was to tak the park for two or three days?"

"We don't differ, Sawney, if you let me have six stots for winterers, in the way of reason."

"And which peasts wad your honor pe for having?"

"Why—let me see—the two black—the dun one—yon doddy—him with the twisted horn—the brocket——How much by the head?"

"Ah," said Robin, "your honor is a shudge—a real shudge—I couldna have set off the pest six peasts better mysell, me that ken them as if they were my pairns, puir things."

"Well, how much per head, Sawney?" continued Mr. Ireby.

"It was high markets at Doune and Falkirk," answered Robin.

And thus the conversation proceeded, until they had agreed on the *prix juste* for the bullocks, the Squire throwing in the temporary accommodation of the enclosure for the cattle into the boot, and Robin making, as he thought, a very good bargain, provided the grass was but tolerable. The Squire walked his pony alongside of the drove, partly to show him the way, and see him put into possession of the field, and partly to learn the latest news of the northern markets.

They arrived at the field, and the pasture seemed excellent. But what was their surprise when they saw the bailiff quietly inducting the cattle of Harry Wakefield into the grassy Goshen which had just been assigned to those of Robin Oig M'Combich by the proprietor himself! Squire Ireby set spurs to his horse, dashed up to his servant, and learning what had passed between the parties, briefly informed the English drover that his bailiff had let the ground without his authority, and that he might seek grass for his cattle wherever he would, since he was to get none there. At the same time he rebuked his servant severely for having transgressed his commands, and ordered him instantly to assist in ejecting the hungry and weary cattle of Harry Wakefield, which were just beginning to enjoy a meal of unusual plenty, and to introduce those of his comrade, whom the English drover now began to consider as a rival.

The feelings which arose in Wakefield's mind would have induced him to resist Mr. Ireby's decision; but every Englishman has a tolerably accurate sense of law and justice, and John Fleecebumpkin, the bailiff, having acknowledged that he had exceeded his commission, Wakefield saw nothing else for it than to collect his hungry and disappointed charges, and drive them on to seek quarters elsewhere. Robin Oig saw what had happened with regret, and hastened to offer his English friend to share with him the disputed possession. But Wakefield's pride was severely hurt, and he answered disdainfully, "Take it all, man—take it all—never make two bites of a cherry—thou canst talk over the gentry, and blear a plain man's eye—Out upon you, man—I would not kiss any man's dirty latchets for leave to bake in his oven."

Robin Oig, sorry but not surprised at his comrade's displeasure, hastened to entreat his friend to wait but an hour till he had gone to the Squire's house to receive payment for the cattle he had sold, and he would come back and help him to drive the cattle into some convenient place of rest, and explain to him the whole mistake they had both of them fallen into. But the Englishman continued indignant: "Thou hast been selling, hast thou? Ay, ay—thou is a cunning lad for kenning the hours of bargaining. Go to the devil with thyself, for I will ne'er see thy fause loon's visage again—thou should be ashamed to look me in the face."

"I am ashamed to look no man in the face," said Robin Oig, something moved; "and, moreover, I will look you in the face this blessed day, if you will bide at the clachan down yonder."

"Mayhap you had as well keep away," said his comrade; and, turning his back on his former friend, he collected his unwilling associates, assisted by the bailiff, who took some real and affected interest in seeing Wakefield accommodated.

After spending some time in negotiating with more than one of the neighboring farmers, who could not, or would not, afford the accommodation desired, Harry Wakefield at last, and in his necessity, accomplished his point by means of the landlord of the alehouse at which Robin Oig and he had agreed to pass the night, when they first separated from each other. Mine host was content to let him turn his cattle on a piece of barren moor, at a price little less than the bailiff had asked for the disputed enclosure; and the wretchedness of the pasture, as well as the price paid for it, were set down as exaggerations of the breach of faith and friendship of his Scottish crony. This turn of Wakefield's passions was encouraged by the bailiff (who had his own reasons for being offended against poor Robin, as having been the unwitting cause of his falling into disgrace with his master), as well as by the innkeeper, and two or three chance guests, who stimulated the drover in his resentment against his quondam associate—some from the ancient grudge against the Scots, which, when it exists anywhere, is to be found lurking in the Border counties, and some from the general love of mischief, which characterizes mankind in all ranks of life, to the honor of Adam's children be it spoken. Good John Barleycorn also, who always heightens and exaggerates the prevailing passions, be they angry or kindly, was not wanting in his offices on this occasion; and confusion to false friends and hard masters was pledged in more than one tankard.

In the meanwhile Mr. Ireby found some amusement in detaining the northern drover at his ancient hall. He caused a cold round of beef to be placed before the Scot in the butler's pantry, together with a foaming tankard of home-brewed, and took pleasure in seeing the hearty appetite with which these unwonted edibles were discussed by Robin Oig M'Combich. The Squire himself, lighting his pipe, compounded between his patrician dignity and his love of agricultural gossip, by walking up and down while he conversed with his guest.

"I passed another drove," said the Squire, "with one of your countrymen behind them—they were something less beasts than your drove, doddies most of them—a big man was with them—none of your kilts though, but a decent pair of breeches—D'ye know who he may be?"

"Hout ay—that might, could, and would be Hughie Morrison—I didna think he could hae peen sae weel up. He has made a day on us;

but his Argyleshires will have wearied shanks. How far was he pe-
hind?"

"I think about six or seven miles," answered the Squire, "for I passed
them at the Christenbury Crag, and I overtook you at the Hollan Bush.
If his beasts be leg-weary, he may be selling bargains."

"Na, na, Hughie Morrison is no the man for pargains—ye maun
come to some Highland body like Robin Oig hersell for the like of
these—put I maun pe wishing you goot-night, and twenty of them let
alane ane, and I maun down to the clachan to see if the lad Harry
Waakfelt is out of his humdudgeons yet."

The party at the alehouse were still in full talk, and the treachery
of Robin Oig still the theme of conversation, when the supposed culprit
entered the apartment. His arrival, as usually happens in such a case,
put an instant stop to the discussion of which he had furnished the
subject, and he was received by the company assembled with that chilling silence, which, more than a thousand exclamations, tells an intruder that he is unwelcome. Surprised and offended, but not appalled
by the reception which he experienced, Robin entered with an un-
daunted and even a haughty air, attempted no greeting, as he saw he
was received with none, and placed himself by the side of the fire, a
little apart from a table at which Harry Wakefield, the bailiff, and two
or three other persons, were seated. The ample Cumbrian kitchen
would have afforded plenty of room even for a larger separation.

Robin, thus, seated, proceeded to light his pipe, and call for a pint of
twopenny.

"We have no twopence ale," answered Robert Heskett, the landlord;
"but as thou find'st thy own tobacco, it's like thou may'st find thy own
liquor too—it's the wont of thy country, I wot."

"Shame, goodman," said the landlady, a blithe bustling housewife,
hasting herself to supply the guest with liquor—"Thou knowest well
enow what the strange man wants, and it's thy trade to be civil, man.
Thou shouldst know, that if the Scot likes a small pot, he pays a sure
penny."

Without taking any notice of this nuptial dialogue, the Highlander
took the flagon in his hand, and addressing the company generally,
drank the interesting toast of "Good Markets," to the party assembled.

"The better, that the wind blew fewer dealers from the north," said
one of the farmers, "and fewer Highland runts to eat up the English
meadows."

"Saul of my pody, put you are wrang there, my friend," answered
Robin, with composure; "it is your fat Englishmen that eat up our
Scots cattle, puir things."

"I wish there was a summat to eat up their drovers," said another;

"a plain Englishman canna make bread within a kenning of them."

"Or an honest servant keep his master's favor, but they will come sliding in between him and the sunshine," said the bailiff.

"If these pe jokes," said Oig, with the same composure, "there is ower mony jokes upon one man."

"It is no joke, but downright earnest," said the bailiff. "Harkye, Mr. Robin Ogg, or whatever is your name, it's right we should tell you that we are all of one opinion, and that is, that you, Mr. Robin Ogg, have behaved to our friend, Mr. Harry Wakefield here, like a raff and a blackguard."

"Nae doubt, nae doubt," answered Robin with great composure; "and you are a set of very pretty judges, for whose prains or pehavior I wad not give a pinch of sneeshing. If Mr. Harry Waakfelt kens where he is wranged, he kens where he may be righted."

"He speaks truth," said Wakefield, who had listened to what passed, divided between the offence which he had taken at Robin's late behavior, and the revival of his habitual feelings of regard.

He now arose, and went towards Robin, who got up from his seat as he approached, and held out his hand.

"That's right, Harry—go it—serve him out," resounded on all sides— "tip him the nailer—show him the mill."

"Hold your peace all of you, and be ——," said Wakefield; and then addressing his comrade, he took him by the extended hand, with something alike of respect and defiance. "Robin," he said, "thou hast used me ill enough this day; but if you mean, like a frank fellow, to shake hands, and make a tussel for love on the sod, why I'll forgie thee, man, and we shall be better friends than ever."

"And would it not pe petter to pe cood friends without more of the matter?" said Robin; "we will be much petter friendships with our panes hale than proken."

Harry Wakefield dropped the hand of his friend, or rather threw it from him.

"I did not think I had been keeping company for three years with a coward."

"Coward pelongs to none of my name," said Robin, whose eyes began to kindle, but keeping the command of his temper. "It was no coward's legs or hands, Harry Waakfelt, that drew you out of the fords of Frew, when you was drifting ower the plack rock, and every eel in the river expected his share of you."

"And that is true enough, too," said the Englishman, struck by the appeal.

"Adzooks!" exclaimed the bailiff—"sure Harry Wakefield, the nattiest lad at Whitson Tryste, Wooler Fair, Carlisle Sands, or Stagshaw

Bank, is not going to show white feather? Ah, this comes of living so long with kilts and bonnets—men forget the use of their daddles."

"I may teach you, Master Fleecebumpkin, that I have not lost the use of mine," said Wakefield, and then went on. "This will never do, Robin. We must have a turn-up, or we shall be the talk of the country-side. I'll be d——d if I hurt thee—I'll put on the gloves gin thou like. Come, stand forward like a man."

"To pe peaten like a dog," said Robin; "is there any reason in that? If you think I have done you wrong, I'll go before your shudge, though I neither know his law nor his language."

A general cry of "No, no—no law, no lawyer! a bellyful and be friends," was echoed by the bystanders.

"But," continued Robin, "if I am to fight, I've no skill to fight like a jackanapes, with hands and nails."

"How would you fight then?" said his antagonist; "though I am thinking it would be hard to bring you to the scratch any how."

"I would fight with proadswords, and sink points on the first plood drawn—like a gentlemans."

A loud shout of laughter followed the proposal, which indeed had rather escaped from poor Robin's swelling heart, than been the dictate of his sober judgment.

"Gentleman, quotha!" was echoed on all sides, with a shout of un-extinguishable laughter; "a very pretty gentleman, God wot—Canst get two swords for the gentlemen to fight with, Ralph Heskett?"

"No, but I can send to the armory at Carlisle, and lend them two forks, to be making shift with in the mean time."

"Tush, man," said another, "the bonny Scots come into the world with the blue bonnet on their heads, and dirk and pistol at their belt."

"Best send post," said Mr. Fleecebumpkin, "to the Squire of Corby Castle, to come and stand second to the *gentleman.*"

In the midst of this torrent of general ridicule, the Highlander in-stinctively gripped beneath the folds of his plaid.

"But it's better not," he said in his own language. "A hundred curses on the swine-eaters, who know neither decency nor civility!"

"Make room, the pack of you," he said, advancing to the door.

But his former friend interposed his sturdy bulk, and opposed his leaving the house; and when Robin Oig attempted to make his way by force, he hit him down on the floor, with as much ease as a boy bowls down a nine-pin.

"A ring, a ring!" was now shouted until the dark rafters, and the hams that hung on them, trembled again, and the very platters on the *bink* clattered against each other. "Well done, Harry,"—"Give it him home, Harry,"—"take care of him now,—he sees his own blood!"

Such were the exclamations, while the Highlander, starting from the ground, all his coldness and caution lost in frantic rage, sprung at his antagonist with the fury, the activity, and the vindictive purpose, of an incensed tiger-cat. But when could rage encounter science and temper? Robin Oig again went down in the unequal contest; and as the blow was a severe one, he lay motionless on the floor of the kitchen. The landlady ran to offer some aid, but Mr. Fleecebumpkin would not permit her to approach.

"Let him alone," he said, "he will come to within time, and come up to the scratch again. He has not got half his broth yet."

"He has got all I mean to give him, though," said his antagonist, whose heart began to relent towards his old associate; "and I would rather by half give the rest to yourself, Mr. Fleecebumpkin, for you pretend to know a thing or two, and Robin had not art enough even to peel before setting to, but fought with his plaid dangling about him— Stand up, Robin, my man! all friends now; and let me hear the man that will speak a word against you or your country for your sake."

Robin Oig was still under the dominion of his passion, and eager to renew the onset; but being withheld on the one side by the peacemaking Dame Heskett, and on the other, aware that Wakefield no longer meant to renew the combat, his fury sunk into gloomy sullenness.

"Come, come, never grudge so much at it, man," said the brave-spirited Englishman, with the placability of his country; "shake hands, and we will be better friends than ever."

"Friends!" exclaimed Robin Oig, with strong emphasis—"friends!— Never. Look to yourself, Harry Waakfelt."

"Then the curse of Cromwell on your proud Scots stomach, as the man says in the play, and you may do your worst, and be d——d! for one man can say nothing more to another after a tussle, than that he is sorry for it."

On these terms the friends parted; Robin Oig drew out, in silence, a piece of money, threw it on the table, and then left the alehouse. But turning at the door, he shook his hand at Wakefield, pointing with his forefinger upwards, in a manner which might imply either a threat or a caution. He then disappeared in the moonlight.

Some words passed after his departure, between the bailiff, who piqued himself on being a little of a bully, and Harry Wakefield, who, with generous inconsistency, was now not indisposed to begin a new combat in defence of Robin Oig's reputation, "although he could not use his daddles like an Englishman, as it did not come natural to him." But Dame Heskett prevented his second quarrel from coming to a head by her peremptory interference. "There should be no more fighting in this house," she said; "there had been too much already.—And you, Mr. Wakefield, may live to learn," she added, "what it is to make a deadly enemy out of a good friend."

"Pshaw, dame! Robin Oig is an honest fellow, and will never keep malice."

"Do not trust to that—you do not know the dour temper of the Scots, though you have dealt with them so often. I have a right to know them, my mother being a Scot."

"And so is well seen on her daughter," said Ralph Heskett.

This nuptial sarcasm gave the discourse another turn; fresh customers entered the tap-room or kitchen, and others left it. The conversation turned on the expected markets, and the report of prices from different parts both of Scotland and England—treaties were commenced, and Harry Wakefield was lucky enough to find a chap for a part of his drove, and at a very considerable profit; an event of consequence more than sufficient to blot out all remembrances of the unpleasant scuffle in the earlier part of the day. But there remained one party from whose mind that recollection could not have been wiped away by the possession of every head of cattle betwixt Esk and Eden.

This was Robin Oig M'Combich—"That I should have had no weapon," he said, "and for the first time in my life!—Blighted be the tongue that bids the Highlander part with the dirk—the dirk—ha! the English blood!—My Muhme's word—when did her word fall to the ground?"

The recollection of the fatal prophecy confirmed the deadly intention which instantly sprung up in his mind.

"Ha! Morrison cannot be many miles behind; and if it were a hundred, what then?"

His impetuous spirit had now a fixed purpose and motive of action, and he turned the light foot of his country towards the wilds, through which he knew, by Mr. Ireby's report, that Morrison was advancing. His mind was wholly engrossed by the sense of injury—injury sustained from a friend; and by the desire of vengeance on one whom he now accounted his most bitter enemy. The treasured ideas of self-importance and self-opinion—of ideal birth and quality, had become more precious to him, like the hoard to the miser, because he could only enjoy them in secret. But that hoard was pillaged, the idols which he had secretly worshipped had been desecrated and profaned. Insulted, abused, and beaten, he was no longer worthy, in his own opinion, of the name he bore, or the lineage which he belonged to—nothing was left to him —nothing but revenge; and, as the reflection added a galling spur to every step, he determined it should be as sudden and signal as the offence.

When Robin Oig left the door of the alehouse, seven or eight English miles at least lay betwixt Morrison and him. The advance of the former was slow, limited by the sluggish pace of his cattle; the last left behind him stubble-field and hedgerow, crag and dark heath, all glittering with frost-rime in the broad November moonlight, at the rate of six miles an hour. And now the distant lowing of Morrison's cattle is heard; and now they are seen creeping like moles in size and slowness of motion on the broad face of the moor; and now he meets them—passes them, and stops their conductor.

"May good betide us," said the Southlander—"Is this you, Robin M'Combich, or your wraith?"

"It is Robin Oig M'Combich," answered the Highlander, "and it is not.—But never mind that, put pe giving me the skene-dhu."

"What! you are for back to the Highlands—The devil!—have you selt all off before the fair? This beats all for quick markets!"

"I have not sold—I am not going north—May pe I will never go north again.—Give me pack my dirk, Hugh Morrison, or there will pe words petween us."

"Indeed, Robin, I'll be better advised before I gie it back to you—it is a wanchancy weapon in a Highlandman's hand, and I am thinking you will be about some barn's-breaking."

"Prutt, trutt! let me have my weapon," said Robin Oig, impatiently.

"Hooly and fairly," said his well-meaning friend. "I'll tell you what will do better than these dirking doings—Ye ken Highlander, and Lowlander, and Border-men, are a' ae man's bairns when you are over the Scots dyke. See, the Eskdale callants, and fighting Charlie of Liddesdale, and the Lockerby lads, and the four Dandies of Lustruther, and a wheen mair gray plaids, are coming up behind, and if you are wranged, there is the hand of a Manly Morrison, we'll see you righted, if Carlisle and Stanwix baith took up the feud."

"To tell you the truth," said Robin Oig, desirous of eluding the suspicions of his friend, "I have enlisted with a party of the Black Watch, and must march off to-morrow morning."

"Enlisted! Were you mad or drunk?—You must buy yourself off—I can lend you twenty notes, and twenty to that, if the drove sell."

"I thank you—thank ye, Hughie; but I go with good will the gate that I am going,—so the dirk—the dirk!"

"There it is for you then, since less wunna serve. But think on what I was saying.—Waes me, it will be sair news in the Braes of Balquidder, that Robin Oig M'Combich should have run an ill gate, and ta'en on."

"Ill news in Balquidder, indeed!" echoed poor Robin. "But Cot speed you, Hughie, and send you good marcats. Ye winna meet with Robin Oig again, either at tryste or fair."

So saying, he shook hastily the hand of his acquaintance, and set out in the direction from which he had advanced, with the spirit of his former pace.

"There is something wrang with the lad," muttered the Morrison to himself; "but we'll maybe see better into it the morn's morning."

But long ere the morning dawned, the catastrophe of our tale had taken place. It was two or three hours after the affray had happened, and it was totally forgotten by almost every one, when Robin Oig returned to Heskett's inn. The place was filled at once by various sorts of men, and with noises corresponding to their character. There were the grave low sounds of men engaged in busy traffic, with the laugh, the song, and the riotous jest of those who had nothing to do but to enjoy themselves. Among the last was Harry Wakefield, who, amidst a grinning group of smock-frocks, hobnailed shoes, and jolly English physiognomies, was trolling forth the old ditty.

"What though my name be Roger,
Who drives the plough and cart"—

when he was interrupted by a well-known voice saying in a high and stern tone, marked by the sharp Highland accent, "Harry Waakfelt— if you be a man, stand up!"

"What is the matter?—what is it?" the guests demanded of each other.

"It is only a d——d Scotsman," said Fleecebumpkin, who was by this time very drunk, "whom Harry Wakefield helped to his broth the day, who is now come to have *his cauld kail* het again."

"Harry Waakfelt," repeated the same ominous summons, "stand up, if you be a man!"

There is something in the tone of deep and concentrated passion, which attracts attention and imposes awe, even by the very sound. The guests shrunk back on every side, and gazed at the Highlander as he stood in the middle of them, his brows bent and his features rigid with resolution.

"I will stand up with all my heart, Robin, my boy, but it shall be to shake hands with you, and drink down all unkindness. It is not the fault of your heart, man, that you don't know how to clench your hands."

By this time he stood opposite to his antagonist; his open and unsuspecting look strangely contrasted with the stern purpose, which gleamed wild, dark, and vindictive in the eyes of the Highlander.

"'T is not thy fault, man, that, not having the luck to be an Englishman, thou canst not fight more than a school-girl."

"I *can* fight," answered Robin Oig sternly, but calmly, "and you shall know it. You, Harry Waakfelt, showed me to-day how the Saxon churls fight—I show you now how the Highland Dunniè-wassel fights."

He seconded the word with the action, and plunged the dagger, which he suddenly displayed, into the broad breast of the English yeoman, with such fatal certainty and force, that the hilt made a hollow sound against the breast-bone, and the double-edged point split the very heart of his victim. Harry Wakefield fell and expired with a single groan. His assassin next seized the bailiff by the collar, and offered the bloody poniard to his throat, whilst dread and surprise rendered the man incapable of defence.

"It were very just to lay you beside him," he said, "but the blood of a base pick-thank shall never mix on my father's dirk with that of a brave man."

As he spoke, he cast the man from him with so much force that he fell on the floor, while Robin, with his other hand, threw the fatal weapon into the blazing turf-fire.

"There," he said, "take me who likes—and let fire cleanse blood if it can."

The pause of astonishment still continuing, Robin Oig asked for a peace-officer, and a constable having stepped out, he surrendered himself to his custody.

"A bloody night's work you have made of it," said the constable.

"Your own fault," said the Highlander. "Had you kept his hands off me twa hours since he would have been now as well and merry as he was twa minutes since."

"It must be sorely answered," said the peace-officer.

"Never you mind that—death pays all debts; it will pay that too."

The horror of the bystanders began now to give way to indignation; and the sight of a favorite companion murdered in the midst of them, the provocation being, in their opinion, so utterly inadequate to the excess of vengeance, might have induced them to kill the perpetrator of the deed even upon the very spot. The constable, however, did his duty on this occasion, and, with the assistance of some of the more reasonable persons present, procured horses to guard the prisoner to Carlisle, to abide his doom at the next assizes. While the escort was preparing, the prisoner neither expressed the least interest nor attempted the slightest reply. Only before he was carried from the fatal apartment, he desired to look at the dead body, which, raised from the floor, had been deposited upon the large table (at the head of which Harry Wakefield had presided but a few minutes before, full of life, vigor and animation) until the surgeons should examine the mortal wound. The face of the corpse was decently covered with a napkin. To the surprise and horror of the bystanders, which displayed itself in a general *Ah!* drawn through clenched teeth and half-shut lips, Robin Oig removed the cloth, and gazed with a mournful but steady eye on the lifeless visage, which had been so lately animated, that the smile of good-humoured confidence in his own strength, of conciliation at once, and contempt towards his enemy, still curled his lip. While those present expected that the wound, which had so lately flooded the apartment with gore, would send forth fresh streams at the touch of the homicide, Robin Oig replaced the covering, with the brief exclamation, "He was a pretty man!"

My story is nearly ended. The unfortunate Highlander stood his trial at Carlisle. I was myself present, and as a young Scottish lawyer, or barrister at least, and reputed a man of some quality, the politeness of the Sheriff of Cumberland offered me a place on the bench. The facts of the case were proved in the manner I have related them; and whatever might be at first the prejudice of the audience against a crime so un-English as that of assassination from revenge, yet when the rooted national prejudices of the prisoner had been explained, which made him consider himself as stained with indelible dishonor, when subjected to personal violence; when his previous patience, moderation, and endurance, were considered, the generosity of the English audience was inclined to regard his crime as the wayward aberration of a false idea of honor rather than as flowing from a heart naturally savage, or perverted by habitual vice. I shall never forget the charge of the venerable Judge to the jury, although not at that time liable to be much affected either by that which was eloquent or pathetic.

"We have had," he said, "in the previous part of our duty" (alluding to some former trials), "to discuss crimes which infer disgust and abhorrence, while they call down the well-merited vengeance of the law. It is now our still more melancholy task to apply its salutary though severe enactments to a case of a very singular character, in which the crime (for a crime it is, and a deep one) arose less out of the malevolence of the heart, than the error of the understanding—less from any idea of committing wrong, than from an unhappily perverted notion of that which is right. Here we have two men, highly esteemed, it has been stated, in their rank of life, and attached, it seems, to each other as friends, one of whose lives has been already sacrificed to a punctilio, and the other is about to prove the vengeance of the offended laws; and yet both may claim our commiseration at least, as men acting in ignorance of each other's national prejudices, and unhappily misguided rather than voluntarily erring from the path of right conduct.

"In the original cause of the misunderstanding, we must in justice give the right to the prisoner at the bar. He had acquired possession of the enclosure, which was the object of competition, by a legal contract with the proprietor, Mr. Ireby; and yet, when accosted with reproaches undeserved in themselves, and galling doubtless to a temper at least sufficiently susceptible of passion, he offered notwithstanding to yield up half his acquisition, for the sake of peace and good neighborhood, and his amicable proposal was rejected with scorn. Then follows the scene at Mr. Heskett the publican's, and you will observe how the stranger was treated by the deceased, and, I am sorry to observe, by those around, who seem to have urged him in a manner which was aggravating in the highest degree. While he asked for peace and for composition, and offered submission to a magistrate, or to a mutual arbiter, the prisoner was insulted by a whole company, who seem on this occasion to have forgotten the national maxim of 'fair play'; and while attempting to escape from the place in peace, he was intercepted, struck down, and beaten to the effusion of his blood.

"Gentlemen of the Jury, it was with some impatience that I heard my learned brother, who opened the case for the crown, give an unfavorable turn to the prisoner's conduct on this occasion. He said the prisoner was afraid to encounter his antagonist in fair fight, or to submit to the laws of the ring; and that, therefore, like a cowardly Italian, he had recourse to his fatal stiletto, to murder the man whom he dared not meet in manly encounter. I observed the prisoner shrink from this part of the accusation with the abhorrence natural to a brave man; and as I would wish to make my words impressive, when I point his real crime, I must secure his opinion of my impartiality, by rebutting everything that seems to me a false accusation. There can be no doubt that the prisoner is a man of resolution—too much resolution—I wish to Heaven that he had less, or rather that he had had a better education to regulate it.

"Gentlemen, as to the laws my brother talks of, they may be known in the Bull-ring, or the Bear-garden, or the Cockpit, but they are not known here. Or, if they should be so far admitted as furnishing a species of proof that no malice was intended in this sort of combat, from which fatal accidents do sometimes arise, it can only be so admitted when both parties are *in pari casu,* equally acquainted with, and equally willing to refer themselves to, that species of arbitrament. But will it be contended that a man of superior rank and education is to be subjected, or is obliged to subject himself, to this coarse and brutal strife, perhaps in opposition to a younger, stronger, or more skilful opponent? Certainly even the pugilistic code, if founded upon the fair play of Merry Old England, as my brother alleges it to be, can contain nothing so preposterous. And, gentlemen of the jury, if the laws would support an English gentleman, wearing, we will suppose, his sword, in defending himself by force against a violent personal aggression of the nature offered to this prisoner, they will not less protect a foreigner and a stranger, involved in the same unpleasing circumstances. If, therefore, gentlemen of the jury, when thus pressed by a *vis major,* the object of obloquy to a whole company, and of direct violence from one at least, and, as he might reasonably apprehend, from more, the panel had produced the weapon which his countrymen, as we are informed generally carry about their persons, and the same unhappy circumstances had ensued which you have heard detailed in evidence, I could not in my conscience have asked from you a verdict of murder. The prisoner's personal defence might, indeed, even in that case, have gone more or less beyond the *Moderamen inculpatæ tutelæ,* spoken of by lawyers, but the punishment incurred would have been that of manslaughter, not of murder. I beg leave to add, that I should have thought this milder species of charge was demanded in the case supposed, notwithstanding the statute of James I. cap. 8, which takes the case of slaughter by stabbing with a short weapon, even without malice prepense, out of the benefit of clergy. For this statute of stabbing, as it is termed, arose out of a temporary cause; and as the real guilt is the same, whether the slaughter be committed by the dagger, or by sword or pistol, the benignity of the modern law places them all on the same, or nearly the same footing.

"But, gentlemen of the jury, the pinch of the case lies in the interval of two hours interposed betwixt the reception of the injury and the fatal retaliation. In the heat of affray and *chaude mêlée,* law, compassionating the infirmities of humanity, makes allowance for the passions which rule such a stormy moment, . . . for the sense of present pain, for the apprehension of farther injury, for the difficulty of ascertaining with due accuracy the precise degree of violence which is necessary to protect the person of the individual, without annoying or injuring the assailant more than is absolutely requisite. But the time necessary to walk twelve miles, however speedily performed, was sufficient for the prisoner to have recollected himself; and the violence with which he carried his purpose into effect, with so many circumstances of deliberate determination, could neither be induced by the passion of anger, nor that of fear. It was the purpose and the act of predetermined revenge, for which law neither can, will, nor ought, to have sympathy or allowance.

"It is true, we may repeat to ourselves, in alleviation of this poor man's unhappy action, that his case is a very peculiar one. The country which he inhabits was, in the days of many now alive, inaccessible to the laws, not only of England, which have not even yet penetrated thither, but to those to which our neighbors of Scotland are subjected, and which must be supposed to be, and no doubt actually are, founded upon the general principles of justice and equity which pervade every civilized country. Amongst their mountains, as among the North American Indians, the various tribes were wont to make war upon each other, so that each man was obliged to go armed for his own protection. These men, from the ideas which they entertained of their own descent and of their own consequence, regarded themselves as so many cavaliers or men-at-arms, rather than as the peasantry of a peaceful country. Those laws of the ring, as my brother terms them, were unknown to the race of warlike mountaineers; that decision of quarrels by no other weapons than those which nature has given every man, must to them have seemed as vulgar and as preposterous as to the Noblesse of France. Revenge, on the other hand, must have been as familiar to their habits of society as to those of the Cherokees or Mohawks. It is indeed, as described by Bacon, at bottom, a kind of wild untutored justice; for the fear of retaliation must withhold the hands of the oppressor where there is no regular law to check daring violence. But though all this may be granted, and though we may allow that, such having been the case of the Highlands in the days of the prisoner's fathers, many of the opinions and sentiments must still continue to influence the present generation, it cannot, and ought not, even in this most painful case, to alter the administration of the law, either in your hands, gentlemen of the jury, or in mine. The first object of civilization is to place the general protection of the law, equally administered, in the room of that wild justice, which every man cut and carved for himself, according to the length of his sword and the strength of his arm. The law says to the subjects, with a voice only inferior to that of the Deity, 'Vengeance is mine.' The instant that there is time for passion to cool, and reason to interpose, an injured party must become aware, that the law assumes the exclusive cognizance of the right and wrong betwixt the parties, and opposes her inviolable buckler to every attempt of the private party to right himself. I repeat, that this unhappy man ought personally to be the object rather of our pity than our abhorrence, for he failed in his ignorance, and from mistaken notions of honor. But his crime is not the less that of murder, gentlemen, and in your high and important office, it is your duty so to find. Englishmen have their angry passions as well as Scots; and should this man's action remain unpunished you may unsheath, under various pretences, a thousand daggers betwixt the Land's-end and the Orkneys."

The venerable judge thus ended what, to judge by his apparent emotion, and by the tears which filled his eyes, was really a painful task. The jury, according to his instructions, brought in a verdict of Guilty; and Robin Oig M'Combich, *alias* M'Gregor, was sentenced to death, and left for execution, which took place accordingly. He met his fate with great firmness, and acknowledged the justice of his sentence. But he repelled indignantly the observations of those who accused him of attacking an unarmed man. "I give a life for the life I took," he said, "and what can I do more?"

The Iron Shroud

BY WILLIAM MUDFORD

THE CASTLE of the Prince of Tolfi was built on the summit of the towering and precipitous rock of Scylla, and commanded a magnificent view of Sicily in all its grandeur. Here, during the wars of the Middle Ages, when the fertile plains of Italy were devastated by hostile factions, those prisoners were confined, for whose ransom a costly price was demanded. Here, too, in a dungeon, excavated deep in the solid rock, the miserable victim was immured, whom revenge pursued—the dark, fierce, and unpitying revenge of an Italian heart.

Vivenzio—the noble and the generous, the fearless in battle, and the pride of Naples in her sunny hours of peace—the young, the brave, the proud Vivenzio, fell beneath this subtle and remorseless spirit. He was the prisoner of Tolfi, and he languished in that rock-encircled dungeon, which stood alone, and whose portals never opened twice upon a living captive.

It had the semblance of a vast cage, for the roof and floor and sides were of iron, solidly wrought and spaciously constructed. High above there ran a range of seven grated windows, guarded with massy bars of the same metal, which admitted light and air.

Save these, and the tall folding doors beneath them which occupied the center, no chink or chasm or projection broke the smooth black surface of the walls. An iron bedstead, littered with straw, stood in one corner; and beside it, a vessel with water and a coarse dish filled with coarser food.

Even the intrepid soul of Vivenzio shrank with dismay as he entered this abode, and heard the ponderous doors triple-locked by the silent ruffians who conducted him to it. Their silence seemed prophetic of his fate, of the living grave that had been prepared for him.

57

His menaces and his entreaties, his indignant appeals for justice, and his questioning of their intentions were alike vain. They listened, but spoke not. Fit ministers of a crime that should have no tongue!

How dismal was the sound of their retiring steps! And, as their faint echoes died along the winding passages, a fearful presage grew within him that never more the face or voice or tread of man would greet his senses.

He had seen human beings for the last time! And he had looked his last upon the bright sky, and upon the smiling earth, and upon a beautiful world he loved and whose minion he had been! Here he was to end his life—a life he had just begun to revel in!

And by what means? By secret poison or by murderous assault? No —for then it had been needless to bring him hither. Famine perhaps —a thousand deaths in one!

It was terrible to think of it; but it was yet more terrible to picture long, long years of captivity, in a solitude so appalling, a loneliness so dreary, that thought, for want of fellowship, would lose itself in madness or stagnate into idiocy.

He could not hope to escape, unless he had the power of rending asunder, with his bare hands, the solid iron walls of his prison. He could not hope for liberty from the relenting mercies of his enemy.

His instant death, under any form of refined cruelty, was not the object of Tolfi, for he might have inflicted it, and he had not. It was too evident, therefore, he was reserved for some premeditated scheme of subtle vengeance; and what vengeance could transcend in fiendish malice either the slow death of famine or the still slower one of solitary incarceration, till the last lingering spark of life expired or till reason fled, and nothing should remain to perish but the brute functions of the body?

It was evening when Vivenzio entered his dungeon, and the approaching shades of night wrapped it in total darkness, as he paced up and down, revolving in his mind these horrible forebodings.

No tolling bell from the castle, or from any neighboring church or convent, struck upon his ear to tell how the hours passed. Frequently he would stop and listen for some sound that might betoken the vicinity of man; but the solitude of the desert, the silence of the tomb, are not so still and deep as the oppressive desolation by which he was encompassed.

His heart sank within him, and he threw himself dejectedly down upon his couch of straw. Here sleep gradually obliterated the consciousness of misery, and bland dreams wafted his delighted spirit to scenes which were once glowing realities for him, in whose ravishing illusions he soon lost the remembrance that he was Tolfi's prisoner.

When he awoke it was daylight, but how long he had slept he knew not. It might be early morning or it might be sultry noon.

He had been so happy in his sleep, amid friends who loved him, and the sweeter endearments of those who loved him as friends could not, that, in the first moments of waking, his startled mind seemed to admit the knowledge of his situation as if it had burst upon it for the first time, fresh in all its appalling horrors.

He gazed around with an air of doubt and amazement, and took up a handful of the straw upon which he lay, as though he would ask himself what it meant. But memory, too faithful to her office, soon unveiled the melancholy past, while reason, shuddering at the task, flashed before his eyes the tremendous future.

The contrast overpowered him. He remained for some time lamenting, like a truth, the bright visions that had vanished, and recoiling from the present, which clung to him as a poisoned garment.

When he grew more calm he surveyed his gloomy dungeon. Alas! the stronger light of day only served to confirm what the gloomy indistinctness of the preceding evening had partially disclosed, the utter impossibility of escape. As, however, his eyes wandered round and round, and from place to place, he noticed two circumstances which excited his surprise and curiosity.

The one, he thought, might be fancy, but the other was positive. His pitcher of water and the dish which contained his food had been removed from his side while he slept, and now stood near the door.

Were he even inclined to doubt this, by supposing he had mistaken the spot where he saw them overnight, he could not, for the pitcher now in his dungeon was neither of the same form nor color as the other, while the food was changed for some other of better quality. He had been visited, therefore, during the night. But how had the person obtained entrance? Could he have slept so soundly that the unlocking and opening of those ponderous portals were effected without waking him?

He would have said this was not possible, but that in doing so he must admit a greater difficulty—an entrance by other means—of which he was convinced there existed none.

It was not intended, then, that he should be left to perish from hunger. But the secret and mysterious mode of supplying him with food seemed to indicate he was to have no opportunity of communicating with a human being.

The other circumstance which had attracted his notice was the disappearance, as he believed, of one of the seven grated windows that ran along the top of his prison.

He felt confident that he had observed and counted them; for he was rather surprised at their number, and there was something peculiar in their form, as well as in the manner of their arrangement, at unequal distances.

It was much easier, however, to suppose he was mistaken than that a portion of the solid iron, which formed the walls, could have escaped from its position, and he dismissed the thought from his mind.

Vivenzio partook of the food that was before him without apprehension. It might be poisoned; but if it were, he knew he could not escape death should such be the design of Tolfi, and the quickest death would be the speediest release.

The day passed wearily and gloomily, though not without a faint hope that, by keeping watch at night, he might observe when the person came again to bring him food, which he supposed he would do in the same way as before.

The mere thought of being approached by a living creature, and the opportunity it might present of learning the doom prepared, or preparing, for him, imparted some comfort. Besides, if he came alone, might be not in a furious onset overpower him? Or he might be accessible to pity, or the influence of such munificent rewards as he could bestow if once more at liberty and master of himself. Say he were armed. The worst that could befall, if not bribe, nor prayers, nor force prevailed, was a friendly blow, which, though dealt in a damned cause, might work a desired end. There was no chance so desperate but it looked lovely in Vivenzio's eyes.

The night came, and Vivenzio watched. Morning came, and Vivenzio was confounded! He must have slumbered without knowing it. Sleep must have stolen over him when exhausted by fatigue, and in that interval of feverish repose he had been baffled; for there stood his replenished pitcher of water, and there his day's meal!

Nor was this all. Casting his looks toward the windows of his dungeon, he counted but *five!*

Here was no deception; and he was now convinced there had been none the day before. But what did all this portend? Into what strange and mysterious den had he been cast?

He gazed till his eyes ached; he could discover nothing to explain the mystery. That it was so, he knew. Why it was so, he racked his imagination in vain to conjecture. He examined the doors. A simple circumstance convinced him that they had not been opened.

A wisp of straw, which he had carelessly thrown against them the preceding day, as he paced to and fro, remained where he had cast it, though it must have been displaced by the slightest motion of either of the doors. This was evidence that could not be disputed; and it followed there must be some secret machinery in the walls by which a person could enter.

He inspected them closely. They appeared to him one solid and compact mass of iron; or joined, if joined they were, with such nice art that no mark of division was perceptible.

Again and again he surveyed them—and the floor—and the roof—and that range of visionary windows, as he was now almost tempted to consider them: he could discover nothing, absolutely nothing, to relieve his doubts or satisfy his curiosity.

Sometimes he fancied that altogether the dungeon had a more contracted appearance—that it looked smaller; but this he ascribed to fancy, and the impression naturally produced upon his mind by the undeniable disappearance of two of the windows.

With intense anxiety, Vivenzio looked forward to the return of night; and as it approached, he resolved that no treacherous sleep should again betray him.

Instead of seeking his bed of straw, he continued to walk up and down his dungeon till daylight, straining his eyes in every direction through the darkness, to watch for any appearances that might explain these mysteries.

While thus engaged, and as nearly as he could judge—by the time that afterward elapsed before morning came in—about two o'clock, there was a slight tremulous motion of the floors.

The motion lasted nearly a minute, but it was so extremely gentle that he almost doubted whether it was real or only imaginary. He listened. Not a sound could be heard.

Presently, however, he felt a rush of cold air blow upon him, and dashing toward the quarter whence it seemed to proceed, he stumbled over something which he judged to be the water-ewer. The rush of cold air was no longer perceptible, and as Vivenzio stretched out his hands he found himself close to the walls. He remained motionless for a considerable time, but nothing occurred during the remainder of the night to excite his attention, though he watched with unabated vigilance.

The first approaches of the morning were visible through the grated windows, breaking, with faint divisions of light, the darkness that still pervaded every other part, long before Vivenzio was enabled to distingush any object in his dungeon.

Instinctively and fearfully he turned his eyes, hot and inflamed with watching, toward them. There were *four!* He could see only four; but it might be that some intervening object prevented the fifth from

becoming perceptible, and he waited impatiently to ascertain if it were
so.

As the light strengthened, however, and penetrated every corner of
the cell, other objects of amazement struck his sight. On the ground
lay the broken fragments of the pitcher he had used the day before,
and at a small distance from them, nearer to the wall, stood the one he
had noticed the first night.

He was now certain that, by some mechanical contrivance, an opening was obtained through the iron wall, and that through this opening
the current of air had found entrance. But how noiselessly! For had a
feather almost waved at the time, he must have heard it.

Again he examined that part of the wall, but, both to sight and
touch, it appeared one even and uniform surface, while, to repeated
and violent blows, there was no reverberating sound indicative of hol-
lowness.

This perplexing mystery had for a time withdrawn his thoughts
from the windows; but now, directing his eyes toward them, he saw
that the fifth had disappeared in the same manner as the preceding
two, without the least distinguishable alteration of external appearances.

The remaining four looked as the seven had originally looked; that
is, occupying, at irregular distances, the top of the wall on that side of
the dungeon. The tall folding door, too, still seemed to stand beneath,
in the center of these four, as it had at first stood in the center of the
seven.

But he could no longer doubt what, on the preceding day, he fancied
might be the effect of visual deception. The dungeon *was* smaller. The
roof had lowered—and the opposite ends had contracted the intermediate distance by a space equal, he thought, to that over which the three
windows had extended.

He was bewildered in vain imaginings to account for these things.
Some frightful purpose—some devilish torture of mind or body—
some unheard-of device for producing exquisite misery, lurked, he
was sure, in what had taken place.

Oppressed with this belief, and distracted more by the dreadful uncertainty of whatever fate impended than he could be dismayed, he
thought, by the knowledge of the worst, he sat ruminating, hour after
hour, yielding his fears in succession to every haggard fancy.

At last a horrible suspicion flashed across his mind, and he started
up with a frantic air.

"Yes!" he exclaimed, looking wildly round his dungeon, and shuddering as he spoke, "yes, it must be so! I see it! I feel the maddening

truth like scorching flames upon my brain! Eternal God! support me, it must be so! Yes, yes, *that* is to be my fate! Yon roof will descend! —these walls will hem me round—and slowly, slowly crush me in their iron arms! Lord God! look down upon me, and in mercy strike me with instant death! O fiend! O devil! Is this your revenge?"

He dashed himself upon the ground in agony—tears burst from him, and the sweat stood in large drops upon his face—he sobbed aloud—he tore his hair—he rolled about like one suffering intolerable anguish of body, and would have bitten the iron floor beneath him —he breathed fearful curses upon Tolfi, and the next moment passionate prayers to heaven for immediate death.

Then the violence of his grief became exhausted, and he lay still, weeping as a child would weep. The twilight of departing day shed its gloom around him ere he rose from that posture of utter and hopeless sorrow.

He had taken no food. Not one drop of water had cooled the fever of his parched lips. Sleep had not visited his eyes for six-and-thirty hours. He was faint with hunger; weary with watching, and with the excess of his emotions.

He tasted of his food; he drank with avidity of the water; and, reeling like a drunken man in his straw, cast himself upon it to brood again over the appalling image that had fastened itself upon his almost frenzied thoughts.

He slept. But his slumbers were not tranquil. He resisted as long as he could their approach; and when, at last, enfeebled nature yielded to their influence, he found no oblivion from his cares.

Terrible dreams haunted him—ghastly visions harrowed up his imagination—he shouted and screamed, as if he already felt the dungeon's ponderous roof descending on him—he breathed hard and thick, as though writhing between its iron walls.

Then would he spring up—stare wildly about him—stretch forth his hands, to be sure he yet had space enough to live—and, muttering some incoherent words, sink down again, to pass through the same fierce vicissitudes of delirious sleep.

The morning of the fourth day dawned upon Vivenzio. But it was high noon before his mind shook off its stupor.

And what a fixed energy of despair sat upon his pale features as he cast his eye upward, and gazed upon the *three* windows that now alone remained!

The three!—there were no more—and they seemed to number his own allotted days. Slowly and calmly he next surveyed the top and sides, and comprehended all the meaning of the diminished height of the former, as well as of the gradual approximation of the latter.

The contracted dimensions of his mysterious prison were now too gross and palpable to be the juggle of his heated imagination. Still lost in wonder at the means, Vivenzio could put no cheat upon his reason as to the end.

By what horrible ingenuity it was contrived that walls and roof and windows should thus silently and imperceptibly, without noise, and without motion, almost, fold, as it were, within each other, he knew not. He only knew they did so; and he vainly strove to persuade himself it was the intention of the contriver to rack the miserable wretch who might be immured there with anticipation merely of a fate from which, in the very crisis of his agony, he was to be reprieved.

Gladly would he have clung even to this possibility, if his heart would have let him; but he felt a dreadful assurance of its fallacy. And what matchless inhumanity it was to doom the sufferer to such lingering torments—to lead him day by day to so appalling a death, unsupported by the consolations of religion, unvisited by any human being, abandoned to himself, deserted of all, and denied even the sad privilege of knowing that his destiny would awaken pity! Alone he was to perish—alone he was to wait a slow-coming torture, whose most exquisite pangs would be inflicted by that very solitude and that tardy coming!

"It is not death I fear," he exclaimed, "but the death I must prepare for! Methinks, too, I could meet even that—all-horrible and revolting as it is—if it might overtake me now. But where shall I find fortitude to tarry till it comes? How can I outlive the three long days and nights I have to live? There is no power within me to bid the hideous specter hence—none to make it familiar to my thoughts, or myself patient of its errand. My thought, rather, will flee from me, and I will grow mad in looking at it. Oh! for a deep sleep to fall upon me! That so, in death's likeness, I might embrace death itself, and drink no more of the cup that is presented to me than my fainting spirit has already tasted!"

In the midst of these lamentations, Vivenzio noticed that his accustomed meal, with the pitcher of water, had been conveyed, as before, into his dungeon.

But this circumstance no longer excited his surprise. His mind was overwhelmed with others of a far greater magnitude. It suggested, however, a feeble hope of deliverance.

He resolved to watch, during the ensuing night, for the signs he had before observed; and should he again feel the gentle tremulous motion of the floor, or the current of air, to seize that moment for giving audible expression to his misery.

Some person must be near him, and within reach of his voice, at the instant when his food was supplied; some one, perhaps, susceptible of pity. Or if not, to be told even that his apprehensions were just, and that his fate *was* to be what he foreboded, would be preferable to a suspense which hung upon the possibility of his worst fears being visionary.

The night came, and as the hour approached when Vivenzio imagined he might expect the signs, he stood fixed and silent as a statue. He feared to breathe, almost, lest he might lose any sound which would warn him of their coming.

While thus listening, with every faculty of mind and body strained to an agony of attention, it occurred to him he should be more sensible of motion, probably, if he stretched himself along the iron floor. He accordingly laid himself softly down, and had not been long in that position when—yes, he was certain of it—the floor moved under him! He sprang up and, in a voice nearly suffocated with emotion, called aloud.

He paused—the motion ceased—he felt no stream of air—all was hushed—no voice answered to his—he burst into tears, and as he sank to the ground, in renewed anguish, exclaimed: "O, my God! my God! You alone have power to save me now, or strengthen me for the trial you permit!"

Another morning dawned upon the wretched captive, and the fatal index of his doom met his eyes. Two windows!—and *two* days—and all would be over! Fresh food—fresh water! The mysterious visit had been paid, though he had implored in vain.

But how awfully was his prayer answered in what he now saw! The roof of the dungeon was within a foot of his head. The two ends were so near that in six paces he trod the space between them.

Vivenzio shuddered as he gazed, and as his steps traversed the narrowed area. But his feelings no longer vented themselves in frantic wailings. With folded arms and clenched teeth, with eyes that were bloodshot from much watching, and fixed with a vacant glare upon the ground, with a hard quick breathing and a hurried walk, he strode backward and forward in silent musing for several hours.

What mind shall conceive, what tongue utter, or what pen describe the dark and terrible character of his thoughts? Like the fate that molded them, they had no similitude in the wide range of this world's agony for man. Suddenly he stopped, and his eyes were riveted upon that part of the wall which was over his bed. Words are inscribed there! A human language, traced by a human hand! He rushes toward them; but his blood freezes as he reads:

I, Ludovico Sforza, tempted by the gold of the prince of Tolfi, spent three years in contriving and executing this accursed triumph of my art. When it was completed, the perfidious Tolfi, more devil than man, who conducted me hither one morning, to be witness, as he said, of its perfection, doomed me to be the first victim of my own pernicious skill; lest, as he declared, I should divulge the secret, or repeat the effort of my ingenuity. May God pardon him, as I hope He will me, that ministered to his unhallowed purpose. Miserable wretch, whoe'er thou art, that readest these lines, fall on thy knees, and invoke, as I have done, His sustaining mercy alone can nerve thee to meet the vengeance of Tolfi—armed with this tremendous engine, which, in a few hours, must crush you, as it will the needy wretch who made it.

A deep groan burst from Vivenzio. He stood like one transfixed, with dilated eyes, expanded nostrils, and quivering lips, gazing at this fatal inscription. It was as if a voice from the sepulcher had sounded in his ears, "Prepare!"

Hope forsook him. There was his sentence, recorded in those dismal words. The future stood unveiled before him, ghastly and appalling!

His brain already feels the descending horror—his bones seem to crack and crumble in the mighty grasp of the iron walls! Unknowing what it is he does, he fumbles in his garment for some weapon of self-destruction. He clenches his throat in his convulsive gripe, as though he would strangle himself at once. He stares upon the walls, and his warring spirit demands, "Will they not anticipate their office if I dash my head against them?" An hysterical laugh chokes him as he exclaims, "Why should I? He was but a man who died first in their fierce embrace; and I should be less than man not to be able to do as much!"

The evening sun was descending, and Vivenzio beheld its golden beams streaming through one of the windows. What a thrill of joy shot through his soul at the sight! It was a precious link that united him, for the moment, with the world beyond. There was ecstasy in the thought.

As he gazed, long and earnestly, it seemed as if the windows had lowered sufficiently for him to reach them. With one bound he was beneath them—with one wild spring he clung to the bars. Whether it was so contrived purposely to madden with delight the wretch who looked, he knew not; but, at the extremity of a long vista, cut through the solid rocks, the ocean, the sky, the setting sun, olive-groves, shady walks, and, in the farthest distance, delicious glimpses of magnificent Sicily, burst upon his sight.

How he gazed and panted, and still clung to his hold, sometimes hanging by one hand, sometimes by the other, and then grasping the bars with both, as loath to quit the smiling paradise outstretched before him; till exhausted, and his hands swollen and benumbed, he dropped helpless down, and lay stunned for a considerable time by the fall.

When he recovered the glorious vision had vanished. He was in darkness. He doubted whether it was not a dream that had passed before his sleeping fancy; but gradually his scattered thoughts returned, and with them came remembrance.

Yes! he had looked once again upon the gorgeous splendor of nature! Once again his eyes had trembled beneath their veiled lids, at the sun's radiance, and sought repose in the soft verdure of the olive-tree, or the gentle swell of undulating waves. Oh, that he were a mariner exposed upon those waves to the worst fury of storm and tempest; or a very wretch, loathsome with disease, plague-stricken, and his body one leprous contagion from crown to sole, hunted forth to gasp out the remnant of infectious life beneath those verdant trees.

Vain thoughts like these would steal over his mind from time to time, in spite of himself; but they scarcely moved it from that stupor into which it had sunk, and which kept him during the whole night like one who had been drugged with opium.

He remained on the ground, sometimes sitting, sometimes lying; at intervals, sleeping heavily; and when not sleeping, silently brooding over what was to come, or talking aloud, in disordered speech, of his wrongs, of his friends, of his home, and of those he loved, with a confused mingling of all.

In this pitiable condition the sixth and last morning dawned upon Vivenzio—if dawn it might be called—the dim, obscure light which faintly struggled through the *one solitary* window of his dungeon.

He could hardly be said to notice the melancholy token. And yet he did notice it, for, as he raised his eyes and saw the portentous sign, there was a slight convulsive distortion of his countenance.

But what did attract his notice, and at the sight of which his agitation was excessive, was the change his iron bed had undergone.

It was a bed no longer. It stood before him, the visible semblance of a funeral couch or bier! When he beheld this, he started from the ground; and in raising himself, suddenly struck his head against the roof, which was now so low that he could no longer stand upright.

"God's will be done!" was all he said, as he crouched his body and placed his hand upon the bier, for such it was. The iron bedstead had been so contrived, by the mechanical art of Ludovico Sforza that, as the advancing walls came in contact with its head and feet, a pressure was produced upon concealed springs, which, when made to play, set in motion a very simple though ingeniously contrived machinery, that effected the transformation.

The object was, of course, to heighten, in the closing scene of this horrible drama, all the feelings of despair and anguish which the preceding ones had aroused. For the same reason, the last window was so made as to admit only a shadowy kind of gloom rather than light, that the wretched captive might be surrounded, as it were, with every seeming preparation for approaching death.

Vivenzio seated himself on his bier. Then he knelt and prayed fervently; and sometimes tears would gush from him.

His wasted spirits and oppressed mind no longer struggled within him. He was past hope, and fear shook him no more. Happy if revenge had thus struck its final blow, for he would have fallen beneath it almost unconscious of a pang.

But such a lethargy of the soul, after such an excitement of its passions, had entered into the diabolical calculations of Tolfi, and the artificer of his designs had imagined a counteracting device.

The tolling of an enormous bell struck upon the ears of Vivenzio! He started.

It beat but once. The sound was so close and stunning that it seemed to shatter his very brain, while it echoed through the rocky passages like reverberating peals of thunder.

This was followed by a sudden crash of the roof and walls, as if they were about to fall upon and close around him at once. Vivenzio screamed, and instinctively spread forth his arms, as though he had a giant's strength to hold them back. They had moved nearer to him, and were now motionless.

Vivenzio looked up, and saw the roof almost touching his head, even as he sat cowering beneath it; and he felt that a farther contraction of but a few inches only must commence the frightful operation.

Roused as he had been, he now gasped for breath. His body shook violently—he was bent nearly double. His hands rested upon either wall, and his feet were drawn under him to avoid the pressure in front.

Thus he remained for an hour, when that deafening bell beat again, and again there came the crash of horrid death.

But the concussion was now so great that it struck Vivenzio down.

As he lay gathered up in lessened bulk, the bell beat loud and frequent —crash succeeded crash—and on, and on, and on came the mysterious engine of death, till Vivenzio's smothered groans were heard no more! He was horribly crushed by the ponderous roof and collapsing sides— and the flattened bier was his *Iron Shroud*.

8

The Gridiron

BY SAMUEL LOVER

A CERTAIN old gentleman in the west of Ireland, whose love of the ridiculous quite equalled his taste for claret and fox-hunting, was wont, upon festive occasions, to amuse his friends by drawing out one of his servants, exceedingly fond of what he termed his "thravels," and in whom a good deal of whim, some queer stories, and long and faithful services had established a right of loquacity. He was one of those few trusty and privileged domestics, who, if his master unheedingly uttered a rash thing in a fit of passion, would venture to set him right. If the squire said, "I'll turn that rascal off," my friend Pat would say, "Throth you won't, sir"; and Pat was always right.

But I am digressing: on such merry meetings as I have alluded to, the master, after making certain "approaches," as a military man would say, as the preparatory steps in laying siege to some extravaganza of his servant, might, perchance, assail Pat thus: "By the by, Sir John (addressing a distinguished guest), Pat has a very curious story, which something you told me today reminds me of. You remember, Pat (turning to the man, evidently pleased at the notice thus paid to himself), you remember that queer adventure you had in France?"

"Throth I do, sir," grins forth Pat.

"What!" exclaims Sir John, in feigned surprise, "was Pat ever in France?"

"Indeed he was," cries mine host; and Pat adds, "Ay, and farther, plaze your honor."

"I assure you, Sir John," continues my host, "Pat told me a story once that surprised me very much, respecting the ignorance of the French."

"Indeed!" rejoined the baronet; "really, I always supposed the French to be a most accomplished people."

"Throth, then, they're not, sir," interrupts Pat.

"O, by no means," adds mine host, shaking his head emphatically.

"I believe, Pat, 'twas when you were crossing the Atlantic?" says the master, turning to Pat with a seductive air, and leading into the "full and true account"—(for Pat had thought fit to visit North Amerikay, for "a raison he had," in the autumn of the year ninety-eight).

"Yes, sir," says Pat, "the broad Atlantic"—a favorite phrase of his which he gave with a brogue as broad as the Atlantic itself.

"It was the time I was lost in crassin' the broad Atlantic, a comin' home," began Pat, decoyed into the recital; "whin the winds began to blow, and the sae to rowl, that you'd think the *Colleen Dhas* (that was her name) would not have a mast left but what would rowl out of her.

"Well, sure enough, the masts went by the board, at last, and the pumps were choked (divil choke them for that same) and av coorse the water gained an us; and throth, to be filled with water is neither good for man or baste; and she was sinkin' fast, settlin' down, as the sailors call it; and faith I never was good at settlin' down in my life, and I liked it then less nor ever.

"Accordingly we prepared for the worst and put out the boat and got a sack o' bishkits and a cask o' pork, and a kag o' wather, and a thrifle o' rum aboord, and any other little matthers we could think iv in the mortial hurry we wor in—and faith there was no time to be lost, for, my darlint, the *Colleen Dhas* went down like a lump o' lead, afore we wor many sthrokes o' the oar away from her.

"Well, we dhrifted away all that night, and next mornin' we put up a blanket an the end av a pole as well as we could, and then we sailed iligant; for we daren't show a stitch o' canvas the night before, bekase it was blowin' like bloody murther, savin' your presence, and sure it's the wondher of the world we worn't swally'd alive by the ragin' sae.

"Well, away we wint, for more nor a week, and nothin' before our two good-lookin' eyes but the canophy iv heaven, and the wide ocean —the broad Atlantic—not a thing was to be seen but the sae and the sky; and though the sae and the sky is mighty purty things in themselves, throth they're no great things when you've nothin' else to look at for a week together. And then, soon enough, throth, our provisions began to run low, the bishkits, and the wather, and the rum— throth *that* was gone first of all—God help uz—and oh! it was thin that starvation began to stare us in the face—'O, murther, murther, Captain darlint,' says I, 'I wish we could land anywhere,' says I.

" 'More power to your elbow, Paddy, my boy,' says he, 'for sitch a good wish, and throth it's myself wishes the same.'

" 'Och,' says I, 'that it may plaze you, sweet queen iv heaven, supposing it was only a *dissolute* island,' says I, 'inhabited wid Turks, sure they wouldn't be such bad Christians as to refuse us a bit and a sup.'

" 'Whisht, whisht, Paddy,' says the captain, 'don't be talking bad of any one,' says he; 'you don't know how soon you may want a good word put in for yourself, if you should be called to quarthers in th' other world all of a suddint,' says he.

" 'Thrue for you, Captain darlint,' says I—I made free with him, you see, bekase disthress makes us all equal—'thrue for you, Captain jewel —God betune uz and harm, I owe no man any spite—and throth that was only thruth. Well, the last bishkit was sarved out, and by gor the *wather itself* was all gone at last, and we passed the night mighty cowld; well, at the brake o' day the sun riz most beautifully out o' the waves, that was as bright as silver and as clear as crystal. But it was only the more cruel upon us, for we wor beginnin' to feel *terrible* hungry; when all at wanst I thought I spied the land—by gor, I thought I felt my heart up in my throat in a minit, and 'Thunder an' turf, Captain,' says I, 'look to leeward,' says I.

" 'What for?' says he.

" 'I think I see the land,' says I. So he ups with his bring-'em-near (that's what the sailors call a spy-glass, sir) and looks out, and, sure enough, it was.

" 'Hurra!' says he, 'we're all right now; pull away, my boys,' says he.

" 'Then, whereabouts in the wide world are we, Captain?' says I; 'maybe it id be in Roosia, or Proosia, or the Garmant Oceant,' says I.

" 'Tut, you fool,' says he, for he had that consaited way wid him— thinkin' himself cleverer nor any one else—'tut, you fool,' says he, 'that's France.'

" 'Tare an ouns,' says I, 'do you tell me so? and how do you know it's France it is, Captain dear,' says I.

" 'Bekase this is the Bay o' Bishky we're in now,' says he.

"Well, with that, my heart began to grow light; and when I seen my life was safe, I began to grow twice hungrier nor ever—so, says I, 'Captain jewel, I wish we had a gridiron.'

" 'Why, then,' says he, 'thunder and turf,' says he, 'what puts a gridiron into your head?'

" 'Bekase I'm starvin' with the hunger,' says I.

" 'And sure, bad luck to you,' says he, 'you couldn't eat a gridiron,' says he, 'barrin' you were a pelican o' the wildherness,' says he.

" 'Ate a gridiron,' says I, 'och, in throth, I'm not such a *gommoch* all out as that, anyhow. But sure, if we had a gridiron, we could dress a beefstake?' says I.

" 'Arrah! but where's the beefstake?' says he.

" 'Sure, couldn't we cut a slice aff the pork,' says I.

" 'Be gor, I never thought o' that,' says the captain. 'You're a clever fellow, Paddy,' says he, laughin'.

" 'Well, then,' says I, 'if you put me ashore there beyant' (for we were nearin' the land all the time) 'and sure I can ax them for to lind me the loan of a gridiron,' says I.

" 'O, by gor, the butther's comin' out o' the stirabout in airnest now,' says he, 'you gommoch,' says he, 'sure I told you before that's France —and sure they're all furriners there,' says the captain.

" 'Well,' says I, 'and how do you know but I'm as good a furriner myself as any o' thim?'

" 'What do you mane?' says he.

" 'I mane,' says I, 'what I towld you, that I'm as good a furriner myself as any o' thim.'

" 'Make me sinsible,' says he.

" 'By dad, maybe that's more nor me, or greater nor me, could do,' says I—and we all began to laugh at him, for I thought I would pay him off for his bit o' consait about the Garmant Oceant.

" 'Lave aff your humbuggin',' says he, 'I bid you, and tell me what it is you mane, at all at all.'

" '*Parly voo frongsay*,' says I.

" 'O, your humble sarvant,' says he; 'why, by gor, you're a scholar, Paddy,' says he.

" 'Throth, you may say that,' says I.

" 'Why, you're a clever fellow, Paddy,' says the captain.

" 'You're not the first that said that,' says I, 'whether you joke or no.'

" 'O, but I'm in airnest,' says the captain; 'and do you tell me, Paddy,' says he, 'that you spake Frinch?'

" '*Parly voo frongsay*,' says I.

" 'By gor, that bangs Banagher, and all the world knows Banagher bangs the divil—I never met the likes o' you, Paddy,' says he—'pull away, boys, and put Paddy ashore.'

"So, with that, it wos no sooner said nor done—they pulled away, and got close in to shore in less than no time, and run the boat up in a little creek. Out I got—and it's stiff enough in the limbs I was, afther bein' cramped up in the boat, and perished with the cowld and hunger, but I conthrived to scramble on, one way or t' other, tow'rds a little bit iv a wood that was close to the shore, and the smoke curlin' out iv it, quite timptin' like.

"'By the powdhers o' war, I'm all right,' says I, 'there's a house there'—and sure enough there was, and a parcel of men, women and childher, ating their dinner round a table, quite convanient. And so I wint up to the door, and I thought I'd be very civil to them, as I heerd the French was always mighty p'lite intirely—and I thought I'd show them I knew what good manners was.

"So I took off my hat, and, making a low bow, says I, 'God save all here,' says I.

"Well, to be sure, they all stapt eating at wanst, and began to stare at me, and faith they almost looked me out of countenance—and I thought to myself, it was not good manners at all, more betoken from furriners which they call so mighty p'lite; but I never minded that, in regard o' wantin' the gridiron; and so says I, 'I beg your pardon,' says I, 'for the liberty I take, but it's only bein' in disthress in regard of ating, says I, 'that I made bowld to throuble yez, and if you could lind me the loan of a gridiron,' says I, 'I'd be entirely obleeged to ye.'

"By gor, they all stared at me twice worse nor before—and with that, says I (knowing what was in their minds), 'Indeed it's thrue for you,' says I, 'I'm tathered to pieces, and God knows I look quare enough—but it's by raison of the storm,' says I, 'which dhruv us ashore here below, and we're all starvin',' says I.

"So then they began to look at each other again; and myself, seeing at once dirty thoughts was in their heads, says I, 'O, not at all,' says I, 'by no manes—we have plenty of mate ourselves there below, and we'll dhress it,' says I, 'if you would be plased to lind us the loan of a gridiron,' says I, makin' a low bow.

"Well, sir, with that, throth, they stared at me twice worse nor ever, and faith I began to think that maybe the captain was wrong, and that it was not France at all at all; and so says I, 'I beg pardon, sir,' says I, to a fine ould man, with a head of hair as white as silver—'maybe I'm under a mistake,' says I, 'but I thought I was in France, sir: aren't you furriners?' says I—'Parlay voo frongsay?'

"'We, munseer,' says he.

"'Then would you lind me the loan of a gridiron!' says I.

"Well, sir, the ould chap began to munseer me; but the devil a bit of a gridiron he'd gi' me; and so I began to think they wor all neygars, for all their fine manners; and throth my blood begun to rise, and says I, 'By my sowl, if it was you was in distress,' says I, 'and if it was to ould Ireland you kem, it's not only the gridiron they'd give you, if you axed it, but something to put an it, too, and the drop o' dhrink into the bargain, and *cead mile failte.*'

"Well, the word *cead mile failte* seemed to sthreck his heart, and the ould chap cocked his ear, and so I thought I'd give him another offer, and so says I, wanst more, quite slow, '*Parlay—voo—frongsay?*'

" 'We munseer,' says he.

" 'Then lind me the loan of a gridiron,' says I, 'and bad scram to you.'

"Well, what would you think, but he shook his old noddle as much as to say he wouldn't; and so, says I, 'Bad cess to the likes o' that I ever seen—throth if you wor in my counthry it's not that away they'd use you. The curse o' the crows an you, you ould sinner,' says I.

"So he seen I was vexed, and I thought I seen him begin to relint, and that his conscience throubled him; and says I, turnin' back, 'Well, I'll give you one chance more—you ould thief—are you a Chrishthan at all?' says I. 'Bad luck to you, do you understand your own language? —*Parly voo frongsay?*'

" 'We, munseer,' says he.

" 'Then, thunder an' turf,' says I, 'will you lind me the loan of a gridiron?'

"Well, sir, the divil resave the bit of it he'd gi' me—and so, with that, the 'curse o' the hungry an you, you ould negarly villain,' says I; 'the back o' my hand and the sowl o' my foot to you, that you may want a gridiron yourself yit,' says I; and with that I left them there, sir, and kem away—and, in throth, it's often sinse that I thought that it was remarkable."

9

The House and the Brain

BY E. BULWER-LYTTON

A FRIEND of mine, who is a man of letters and a philosopher, said to me one day, as if between jest and earnest, "Fancy! since we last met I have discovered a haunted house in the midst of London."

"Really haunted? and by what—ghosts?"

"Well, I can't answer these questions; all I know is this: six weeks ago I and my wife were in search of a furnished apartment. Passing a quiet street, we saw on the window of one of the houses a bill, 'Apartments Furnished.' The situation suited us; we entered the house, liked the rooms, engaged them by the week, and left them the third day. No power on earth could have reconciled my wife to stay longer; and I don't wonder at it."

"What did you see?"

"Excuse me; I have no desire to be ridiculed as a superstitious dreamer, nor, on the other hand, could I ask you to accept on my affirmation what you would hold to be incredible, without the evidence of your own senses. Let me only say this: it was not so much what we saw or heard (in which you might fairly suppose that we were the dupes of our own excited fancy, or the victims of imposture in others) that drove us away, as it was an undefinable terror which seized both of us whenever we passed by the door of a certain unfurnished room, in which we neither saw nor heard anything; and the strangest marvel of all was that for once in my life I agreed with my wife, silly woman though she be, and allowed after the third night that it was impossible to stay a fourth in that house.

"Accordingly, on the fourth morning I summoned the woman who kept the house and attended on us, and told her that the rooms did not quite suit us, and we would not stay out our week. She said dryly:

"'I know why; you have stayed longer than any other lodger. Few ever stayed a second night; none before you a third. But I take it that they have been very kind to you.'

"'They—who?' I asked, affecting a smile.

"'Why, they who haunt the house, whoever they are; I don't mind them; I remember them many years ago, when I lived in this house not as a servant; but I know they will be the death of me some day. I don't care—I'm old and must die soon anyhow; and then I shall be with them, and in this house still.'

"The woman spoke with so dreary a calmness that really it was a sort of awe that prevented my conversing with her further. I paid for my week, and too happy were I and my wife to get off so cheaply."

"You excite my curiosity," said I; "nothing I should like better than to sleep in a haunted house. Pray give me the address of the one which you left so ignominiously."

My friend gave me the address; and when we parted I walked straight toward the house thus indicated.

It is situated on the north side of Oxford Street, in a dull but respectable thoroughfare. I found the house shut up; no bill on the window, and no response to my knock. As I was turning away, a beer-boy, collecting pewter pots at the neighboring areas, said to me, "Do you want any one at that house, sir?"

"Yes; I heard it was to be let."

"Let! Why, the woman who kept it is dead; has been dead these three weeks; and no one can be found to stay there, though Mr. J—— offered ever so much. He offered mother, who chars for him, one pound a week just to open and shut the windows, and she would not."

"Would not! and why?"

"The house is haunted; and the old woman who kept it was found dead in her bed with her eyes wide open. They say the devil strangled her."

"Pooh! You speak of Mr. J——. Is he the owner of the house?"

"Yes."

"Where does he live?"

"In G—— Street, No. —."

"What is he—in any business?"

"No, sir, nothing particular; a single gentleman."

I gave the pot-boy the gratuity earned by his liberal information, and proceeded to Mr. J—— in G—— Street, which was close by the street that boasted the haunted house. I was lucky enough to find Mr. J—— at home; an elderly man with intelligent countenance and prepossessing manners.

I communicated my name and my business frankly. I said I heard the house was considered to be haunted; that I had a strong desire to examine a house with so equivocal a reputation; that I should be greatly obliged if he would allow me to hire it, though only for a night. I was willing to pay for that privilege whatever he might be inclined to ask.

"Sir," said Mr. J——, with great courtesy, "the house is at your service for as short or as long a time as you please. Rent is out of the question; the obligation will be on my side, should you be able to discover the cause of the strange phenomena which at present deprive it of all value. I cannot let it, for I cannot even get a servant to keep it in order or answer the door.

"Unluckily, the house is haunted, if I may use that expression, not only by night but by day; though at night the disturbances are of a more unpleasant and sometimes of a more alarming character. The poor old woman who died in it three weeks ago was a pauper whom I took out of a workhouse; for in her childhood she had been known to some of my family, and had once been in such good circumstances that she had rented that house of my uncle. She was a woman of superior education and strong mind, and was the only person I could ever induce to remain in the house. Indeed, since her death, which was sudden, and the coroner's inquest, which gave it a notoriety in the neighborhood, I have so despaired of finding any person to take charge of it, much more a tenant, that I would most willingly let it rent free for a year to any one who would pay its rates and taxes."

"How long ago did the house acquire this character?"

"That I can scarcely tell you, but many years since; the old woman I spoke of said it was haunted when she rented it, between thirty and forty years ago. The fact is that my life has been spent in the East Indies, and in the civil service of the East India Company.

"I returned to England last year, on inheriting the fortune of an uncle, among whose possessions was the house in question. I found it shut up and uninhabited. I was told that it was haunted, and no one would inhabit it. I smiled at what seemed to me so idle a story.

"I spent some money in repainting and roofing it, added to its old-fashioned furniture a few modern articles, advertised it, and obtained a lodger for a year. He was a colonel retired on half pay. He came in with his family, a son and a daughter, and four or five servants; they all left the house the next day; and although they deponed that they had all seen something different, that something was equally terrible to all. I really could not in conscience sue, or even blame, the colonel for breach of agreement.

"Then I put in the old woman I have spoken of, and she was empowered to let the house in apartments. I never had one lodger who stayed more than three days. I do not tell you their stories; to no two lodgers have exactly the same phenomena been repeated. It is better that you should judge for yourself than enter the house with an imagination influenced by previous narratives; only be prepared to see and to hear something or other, and take whatever precautions you yourself please."

"Have you never had a curiosity yourself to pass a night in that house?"

"Yes; I passed, not a night, but three hours in broad daylight alone in that house. My curiosity is not satisfied, but it is quenched. I have no desire to renew the experiment. You cannot complain, you see, sir, that I am not sufficiently candid; and unless your interest be exceedingly eager and your nerves unusually strong, I honestly add that I advise you *not* to pass a night in that house."

"My interest *is* exceedingly keen," said I; "and though only a coward will boast of his nerves in situations wholly unfamiliar to him, yet my nerves have been seasoned in such variety of danger that I have the right to rely on them, even in a haunted house."

Mr. J—— said very little more; he took the keys of the house out of his bureau, and gave them to me; and, thanking him cordially for his frankness and his urbane concession to my wish, I carried off my prize.

Impatient for the experiment, as soon as I reached home I summoned my confidential servant—a young man of gay spirits, fearless temper, and as free from superstitious prejudice as any one I could think of.

"F——," said I, "you remember in Germany how disappointed we were at not finding a ghost in that old castle which was said to be haunted by a headless apparition? Well, I have heard of a house in London which, I have reason to hope, is decidedly haunted. I mean to sleep there to-night. From what I hear, there is no doubt that something will allow itself to be seen or to be heard—something perhaps excessively horrible. Do you think, if I take you with me, I may rely on your presence of mind, whatever may happen?"

"Oh, sir; pray trust me!" said he, grinning with delight.

"Very well, then, here are the keys of the house; this is the address. Go now, select for me any bedroom you please; and since the house has not been inhabited for weeks, make up a good fire, air the bed well; see, of course, that there are candles as well as fuel. Take with you my revolver and my dagger—so much for my weapons—arm yourself equally well; and if we are not a match for a dozen ghosts, we shall be but a sorry couple of Englishmen."

I was engaged for the rest of the day on business so urgent that I had not leisure to think much on the nocturnal adventure to which I had plighted my honor. I dined alone and very late, and while dining read, as is my habit. The volume I selected was one of Macaulay's essays. I thought to myself that I would take the book with me; there was so much of healthfulness in the style, and practical life in the subjects, that it would serve as an antidote against the influences of superstitious fancy.

Accordingly, about half-past nine I put the book into my pocket and strolled leisurely toward the haunted house. I took with me a favorite dog—an exceedingly sharp, bold, and vigilant bull-terrier, a dog fond of prowling about strange ghostly corners and passages at night in search of rats, a dog of dogs for a ghost.

It was a summer night, but chilly, the sky somewhat gloomy and overcast; still there was a moon—faint and sickly, but still a moon—and if the clouds permitted, after midnight it would be brighter.

I reached the house, knocked, and my servant opened with a cheerful smile.

"All right, sir, and very comfortable."

"Oh!" said I, rather disappointed; "have you not seen nor heard anything remarkable?"

"Well, sir, I must own that I have heard something queer."

"What?—what?"

"The sound of feet pattering behind me; and once or twice small noises like whispers close at my ear; nothing more."

"You are not at all frightened?"

"I! Not a bit of it, sir!"

And the man's bold look reassured me on one point, namely, that, happen what might, he would not desert me.

We were in the hall, the street-door closed, and my attention as now drawn to my dog. He had at first run in eagerly enough, but had sneaked back to the door, and was scratching and whining to get out. After I had patted him on the head and encouraged him gently, the dog seemed to reconcile himself to the situation, and followed me and F—— through the house, but keeping close at my heels, instead of hurrying inquisitively in advance, which was his usual and normal habit in all strange places.

We first visited the subterranean apartments, the kitchen and other offices, and especially the cellars, in which last were two or three bottles of wine still left in a bin, covered with cobwebs, and evidently, by their appearance, undisturbed for many years. It was clear that the ghosts were not wine-bibbers.

For the rest, we discovered nothing of interest. There was a gloomy little back-yard, with very high walls. The stones of this yard were very damp; and what with the damp and what with the dust and smoke-grime on the pavement, our feet left a slight impression where we passed.

And now appeared the first strange phenomenon witnessed by myself in this strange abode.

I saw, just before me, the print of a foot suddenly form itself, as it were. I stopped, caught hold of my servant, and pointed to it. In advance of that footprint as suddenly dropped another. We both saw it. I advanced quickly to the place; the footprint kept advancing before me; a small footprint—the foot of a child; the impression was too faint thoroughly to distinguish the shape, but it seemed to us both that it was the print of a naked foot.

This phenomenon ceased when we arrived at the opposite wall, nor did it repeat itself when we returned. We remounted the stairs and entered the rooms on the ground floor—a dining-parlor, a small back-parlor, and a still smaller third room that had probably been appropriated to a footman—all still as death.

We then visited the drawing-rooms, which seemed fresh and new. In the front room I seated myself in an arm-chair. F—— placed on the table the candlestick with which he had lighted us. I told him to shut the door. As he turned to do so, a chair opposite to me moved from the wall quickly and noiselessly, and dropped itself about a yard from my own chair, immediately fronting it.

"Why, this is better than the turning-tables," said I laughing; and as I laughed, my dog put back his head and howled.

F——, coming back, had not observed the movement of the chair. He employed himself now in stilling the dog. I continued to gaze on the chair, and fancied I saw on it a pale, blue, misty outline of a human figure; but an outline so indistinct that I could only distrust my own vision. The dog was now quiet.

"Put back the chair opposite to me," said I to F——; "put it back to the wall."

F—— obeyed.

"Was that you, sir?" said he, turning abruptly.

"I—what?"

"Why, something struck me. I felt it sharply on the shoulder, just here."

"No," said I; "but we have jugglers present, and though we may not discover their tricks, we shall catch *them* before they frighten *us*."

We did not stay long in the drawing-rooms; in fact, they felt so damp and so chilly that I was glad to get to the fire up-stairs. We locked the doors of the drawing-rooms—a precaution which, I should observe, we had taken with all the rooms we had searched below.

The bedroom my servant had selected for me was the best on the floor; a large one, with two windows fronting the street. The four-posted bedstead, which took up no inconsiderable space, was opposite to the fire, which burned clear and bright; a door in the wall to the left, between the bed and the window, communicated with the room which my servant appropriated to himself. This last was a small room with a sofa-bed, and had no communication with the landing-place; no other door but that which conducted to the bedroom I was to occupy.

On either side of my fireplace was a cupboard, without locks, flush with the wall, and covered with the same dull-brown paper. We examined these cupboards; only hooks to suspend female dresses—nothing else. We sounded the walls; evidently solid—the outer walls of the building.

Having finished the survey of these apartments, warmed myself a few moments, and lighted my cigar, I then, still accompanied by F——, went forth to complete my reconnoiter. In the landing-place there was another door; it was closed firmly.

"Sir," said my servant in surprise, "I unlocked this door with all the others when I first came in; it cannot have got locked from the inside, for it is a——"

Before he had finished his sentence, the door, which neither of us was then touching, opened quietly of itself. We looked at each other a single instant. The same thought seized both: some human agency might be detected here. I rushed in first, my servant followed. A small, blank, dreary room without furniture, a few empty boxes and hampers in a corner, a small window, the shutters closed—not even a fireplace—no other door but that by which we had entered, no carpet on the floor, and the floor seemed very old, uneven, worm-eaten, mended here and there, as was shown by the whiter patches on the wood; but no living being, and no visible place in which a living being could have hidden.

As we stood gazing round, the door by which we had entered closed as quietly as it had before opened; we were imprisoned.

For the first time I felt a creep of undefinable horror. Not so my servant.

"Why, they don't think to trap us, sir; I could break that trumpery door with a kick of my foot."

"Try first if it will open to your hand," said I, shaking off the vague apprehension that had seized me, "while I open the shutters and see what is without."

I unbarred the shutters; the window looked on the little back-yard I have before described; there was no ledge without, nothing but sheer descent. No man getting out of that window would have found any footing till he had fallen on the stones below.

F—— meanwhile was vainly attempting to open the door. He now turned round to me and asked my permission to use force. And I should here state, in justice to the servant, that, far from evincing any superstitious terror, his nerve, composure, and even gaiety amid circumstances so extraordinary, compelled my admiration and made me congratulate myself on having secured a companion in every way fitted to the occasion. I willingly gave him the permission he required. But, though he was a remarkably strong man, his force was as idle as his milder efforts; the door did not even shake to his stoutest kick.

Breathless and panting, he desisted. I then tried the door myself, equally in vain. As I ceased from the effort, again that creep of horror came over me; but this time it was more cold and stubborn. I felt as if some strange and ghastly exhalation were rising from the chinks of that rugged floor and filling the atmosphere with a venomous influence hostile to human life.

The door now very slowly and quietly opened as of its own accord. We precipitated ourselves onto the landing-place. We both saw a large, pale light—as large as the human figure, but shapeless and unsubstantial—move before us and ascend the stairs that led from the landing into the attics.

I followed the light, and my servant followed me. It entered, to the right of the landing, a small garret, of which the door stood open. I entered in the same instant. The light then collapsed into a small globule, exceedingly brilliant and vivid; rested a moment on a bed in the corner, quivered, and vanished.

We approached the bed and examined it—a half-tester, such as is commonly found in attics devoted to servants. On the drawers that stood near it we perceived an old faded silk kerchief, with the needle still left in the rent half repaired. The kerchief was covered with dust; probably it had belonged to the old woman who had last died there, and this might have been her sleeping-room.

I had sufficient curiosity to open the drawers; there were a few odds and ends of female dress, and two letters tied round with a narrow ribbon of faded yellow. I took the liberty to possess myself of the letters. We found nothing else in the room worth noticing, nor did the light reappear; but we distinctly heard, as we turned to go, a pattering footfall on the floor just before us.

We went through the other attics (in all four), the footfall still preceding us. Nothing to be seen, nothing but the footfall heard. I had the letters in my hand; just as I was descending the stairs I distinctly felt my wrist seized, and a faint, soft effort made to draw the letters from my clasp. I only held them the more tightly, and the effort ceased.

We regained the bedchamber appropriated to myself, and I then remarked that my dog had not followed us when we had left it. He was thrusting himself close to the fire and trembling. I was impatient to examine the letters; and while I read them my servant opened a little box in which he had deposited the weapons I had ordered him to bring, took them out, placed them on a table close at my bed-head, and then occupied himself in soothing the dog, who, however, seemed to heed him very little.

The letters were short; they were dated—the dates exactly thirty-five years ago. They were evidently from a lover to his mistress, or a husband to some young wife. Not only the terms of expression, but a distinct reference to a former voyage indicated the writer to have been a seafarer. The spelling and handwriting were those of a man imperfectly educated; but still the language itself was forcible. In the expressions of endearment there was a kind of rough, wild love; but here and there were dark, unintelligible hints at some secret not of love—some secret that seemed of crime.

"We ought to love each other," was one of the sentences I remember, "for how every one else would execrate us if all was known."

Again: "Don't let any one be in the same room with you at night— you talk in your sleep."

And again: "What's done can't be undone; and I tell you there's nothing against us, unless the dead should come to life."

Here was interlined, in a better handwriting (a female's), "They do!"

At the end of the letter latest in date the same female hand had written these words:

"Lost at sea the 4th of June, the same day as——"

I put down the letters, and began to muse over their contents.

Fearing, however, that the train of thought into which I fell might unsteady my nerves, I fully determined to keep my mind in a fit state to cope with whatever of the marvelous the advancing night might bring forth. I roused myself, laid the letters on the table, stirred up the fire, which was still bright and cheering, and opened my volume of Macaulay.

I read quietly enough till about half-past eleven. I then threw myself dressed upon the bed, and told my servant he might retire to his own room, but must keep himself awake. I bade him leave open the doors between the two rooms. Thus alone I kept two candles burning on the table by my bed-head. I placed my watch beside the weapons, and calmly resumed my Macaulay. Opposite to me the fire burned clear, and on the hearth-rug, seemingly asleep, lay the dog. In about twenty minutes I felt an exceedingly cold air pass by my cheek, like a sudden draft. I fancied the door to my right, communicating with the landing-place, must have got open; but no, it was closed.

I then turned my glance to the left, and saw the flames of the candles violently swayed as by a wind. At the same moment the watch beside the revolver softly slid from the table—softly, softly—no visible hand—it was gone. I sprang up, seizing the revolver with the one hand, the dagger with the other: I was not willing that my weapons should share the fate of the watch.

Thus armed, I looked round the floor: no sign of the watch. Three slow, loud, distinct knocks were now heard at the bed-head; my servant called out:

"Is that you, sir?"

"No; be on your guard."

The dog now roused himself and sat on his haunches, his ears moving quickly backward and forward. He kept his eyes fixed on me with a look so strange that he concentered all my attention on himself. Slowly he rose, all his air bristling, and stood perfectly rigid, and with the same wild stare.

I had no time, however, to examine the dog. Presently my servant emerged from his room; and if I ever saw horror in the human face, it was then. I should not have recognized him had we met in the streets, so altered was every lineament. He passed by me quickly, saying, in a whisper that seemed scarcely to come from his lips:

"Run! run! It is after me!"

He gained the door to the landing, pulled it open, and rushed forth. I followed him into the landing involuntarily, calling him to stop; but, without heeding me, he bounded down the stairs, clinging to the balusters and taking several steps at a time. I heard, where I stood, the street-door open, heard it again clap to.

I was left alone in the haunted house.

It was but for a moment that I remained undecided whether or not to follow my servant; pride and curiosity alike forbade so dastardly a flight. I re-entered my room, closing the door after me, and proceeded cautiously into the interior chamber. I encountered nothing to justify my servant's terror.

I again carefully examined the walls, to see if there were any concealed door. I could find no trace of one—not even a seam in the dull-brown paper with which the room was hung. How then had the THING, whatever it was, which had so scared him, obtained ingress, except through my own chamber?

I returned to my room, shut and locked the door that opened upon the interior one, and stood on the hearth, expectant and prepared.

I now perceived that the dog had slunk into an angle of the wall, and was pressing close against it, as if literally striving to force his way into it. I approached the animal and spoke to it; the poor brute was evidently beside itself with terror. It showed all its teeth, the slaver dropping from its jaws, and would certainly have bitten me if I had touched it. It did not seem to recognize me. Whoever has seen at the Zoological Gardens a rabbit fascinated by a serpent, cowering in a corner, may form some idea of the anguish which the dog exhibited.

Finding all efforts to soothe the animal in vain, and fearing that his bite might be as venomous in that state as if in the madness of hydrophobia, I left him alone, placed my weapons on the table beside the fire, seated myself, and recommenced my Macaulay.

Perhaps, in order not to appear seeking credit for a courage, or rather a coolness, which the reader may conceive I exaggerate, I may be pardoned if I pause to indulge in one or two egotistical remarks.

As I hold presence of mind, or what is called courage, to be precisely proportioned to familiarity with the circumstances that lead to it, so I should say that I had been long sufficiently familiar with all experiments that appertain to the marvelous. I had witnessed many very extraordinary phenomena in various parts of the world—phenomena that would be either totally disbelieved if I stated them, or ascribed to supernatural agencies.

Now, my theory is that the supernatural is the impossible, and that what is called supernatural is only a something in the laws of nature of which we have been hitherto ignorant. Therefore, if a ghost rise before me, I have not the right to say, "So, then, the supernatural is possible," but rather, "So, then, the apparition of a ghost is, contrary to received opinion, within the laws of nature, namely, not supernatural."

Now, in all that I had hitherto witnessed, and indeed in all the wonders which the amateurs of mystery in our age record as facts, a material living agency is always required. On the Continent you will still find magicians who assert that they can raise spirits. Assume for a moment that they assert truly, still the living material form of the magician is present; he is the material agency by which, from some constitutional peculiarities, certain strange phenomena are represented to your natural senses.

Accept, again, as truthful the tales of spirit manifestation in America —musical or other sounds, writings on paper, produced by no discernible hand, articles of furniture moved without apparent human agency, or the actual sight and touch of hands, to which no bodies seem to belong—still there must be found the medium, or living being, with constitutional peculiarities capable of obtaining these signs.

In fine, in all such marvels, supposing even that there is no imposture, there must be a human being like ourselves, by whom or through whom the effects presented to human beings are produced. It is so with the now familiar phenomena of mesmerism or electro-biology; the mind of the person operated on is affected through a material living agent.

Nor, supposing it true that a mesmerized patient can respond to the will or passes of a mesmerizer a hundred miles distant, is the response less occasioned by a material being. It may be through a material fluid, call it Electric, call it Odic, call it what you will, which has the power of traversing space and passing obstacles, that the material effect is communicated from one to the other.

Hence, all that I had hitherto witnessed, or expected to witness, in this strange house, I believed to be occasioned through some agency or medium as mortal as myself; and this idea necessarily prevented the awe with which those who regard as supernatural things that are not within the ordinary operations of nature might have been impressed by the adventures of that memorable night.

As, then, it was my conjecture that all that was presented, or would be presented, to my senses, must originate in some human being gifted by constitution with the power so to present them, and having some motive so to do, I felt an interest in my theory which, in its way, was rather philosophical than superstitious. And I can sincerely say that I was in as tranquil a temper for observation as any practical experimentalist could be in awaiting the effects of some rare though perhaps perilous chemical combination. Of course, the more I kept my mind detached from fancy the more the temper fitted for observation would be obtained; and I therefore riveted eye and thought on the strong daylight sense in the page of my Macaulay.

I now became aware that something interposed between the page and the light: the page was overshadowed. I looked up and saw what I shall find very difficult, perhaps impossible, to describe.

It was a darkness shaping itself out of the air in very undefined outline. I cannot say it was of a human form, and yet it had more of a resemblance to a human form, or rather shadow, than anything else. As it stood, wholly apart and distinct from the air and the light around it, its dimensions seemed gigantic; the summit nearly touched the ceiling.

While I gazed, a feeling of intense cold seized me. An iceberg before me could not more have chilled me; nor could the cold of an iceberg have been more purely physical. I feel convinced that it was not the cold caused by fear. As I continued to gaze, I thought—but this I cannot say with precision—that I distinguished two eyes looking down on me from the height. One moment I seemed to distinguish them clearly, the next they seemed gone; but two rays of a pale, blue light frequently shot through the darkness, as from the height on which I half believed, half doubted, that I had encountered the eyes.

I strove to speak; my voice utterly failed me. I could only think to myself, "Is this fear? it is *not* fear!" I strove to rise, in vain; I felt as weighed down by an irresistible force. Indeed, my impression was that of an immense and overwhelming power opposed to my volition; that sense of utter inadequacy to cope with a force beyond man's, which one may feel *physically* in a storm at sea, in a conflagration, or when confronting some terrible wild beast, or rather, perhaps, the shark of the ocean, I felt *morally*. Opposed to my will was another will, as far superior to its strength as storm, fire, and shark are superior in material force to the force of man.

And now, as this impression grew on me, now came, at last, horror —horror to a degree that no words can convey. Still I retained pride, if not courage; and in my own mind I said, "This is horror, but it is not fear, unless I fear I cannot be harmed; my reason rejects this thing; it is an illusion, I do not fear."

With a violent effort I succeeded at last in stretching out my hand toward the weapon on the table; as I did so, on the arm and shoulder I received a strange shock, and my arm fell to my side powerless. And now, to add to my horror, the light began slowly to wane from the candles; they were not, as it were, extinguished, but their flame seemed very gradually withdrawn; it was the same with the fire, the light was extracted from the fuel; in a few minutes the room was in utter darkness.

The dread that came over me to be thus in the dark with that dark thing, whose power was so intensely felt, brought a reaction of nerve. In fact, terror had reached that climax that either my senses must have deserted me, or I must have burst through the spell.

I did burst through it.

I found voice, though the voice was a shriek. I remember that I broke forth with words like these, "I do not fear, my soul does not fear"; and at the same time I found strength to rise.

Still in that profound gloom, I rushed to one of the windows, tore aside the curtain, flung open the shutters; my first thought was, LIGHT.

And when I saw the moon, high, clear, and calm, I felt a joy that almost compensated for the previous terror. There was the moon, there was also the light from the gas-lamps in the deserted, slumberous street. I turned to look back into the room; the moon penetrated its shadow very palely and partially, but still there was light. The dark thing, whatever it might be, was gone; except that I could yet see a dim shadow, which seemed the shadow of that shade, against the opposite wall.

My eye now rested on the table, and from under the table (which was without cloth or cover, an old mahogany round table) rose a hand, visible as far as the wrist. It was a hand, seemingly, as much of flesh and blood as my own, but the hand of an aged person, lean, wrinkled, small too, a woman's hand. That hand very softly closed on the two letters that lay on the table; hand and letters both vanished. Then came the same three loud measured knocks I had heard at the bed-head before this extraordinary drama had commenced.

As these sounds slowly ceased, I felt the whole room vibrate sensibly; and at the far end rose, as from the floor, sparks or globules like bubbles of light, many-colored—green, yellow, fire-red, azure—up and down, to and fro, hither, thither, as tiny will-o'-the-wisps the sparks moved, slow or swift, each at its own caprice. A chair (as in the drawing-room below) was now advanced from the wall without apparent agency, and placed at the opposite side of the table.

Suddenly, as forth from the chair, grew a shape, a woman's shape. It was distinct as a shape of life, ghastly as a shape of death. The face was that of youth, with a strange, mournful beauty; the throat and shoulders were bare, the rest of the form in a loose robe of cloudy white.

It began sleeking its long yellow hair, which fell over its shoulders; its eyes were not turned toward me, but to the door; it seemed listening, watching, waiting. The shadow of the shade in the background grew darker, and again I thought I beheld the eyes gleaming out from the summit of the shadow, eyes fixed upon that shape.

As if from the door, though it did not open, grew out another shape, equally distinct, equally ghastly—a man's shape, a young man's. It was in the dress of the last century, or rather in a likeness of such dress; for both the male shape and the female, though defined, were evidently unsubstantial, impalpable—simulacre, fantasms; and there was something incongruous, grotesque, yet fearful, in the contrast between the elaborate finery, the courtly precision of that old-fashioned garb, with its ruffles and lace and buckles, and the corpse-like aspect and ghost-like stillness of the flitting wearer. Just as the male shape approached the female, the dark shadow darted from the wall, all three for a moment wrapped in darkness.

When the pale light returned, the two fantoms were as if in the grasp of the shadow that towered between them, and there was a blood-stain on the breast of the female; and the fantom male was leaning on its fantom sword, and blood seemed trickling fast from the ruffles, from the lace; and the darkness of the intermediate shadow swallowed them up—they were gone. And again the bubbles of light shot, and sailed, and undulated, growing thicker and thicker and more wildly confused in their movements.

The closet door to the right of the fire-place now opened, and from the aperture came the form of a woman, aged. In her hand she held letters—the very letters over which I had seen *the* hand close; and behind her I heard a footstep. She turned round as if to listen, and then she opened the letters and seemed to read: and over her shoulder I saw a livid face, the face as of a man long drowned—bloated, bleached, sea-weed tangled in its dripping hair; and at her feet lay a form as of a corpse, and beside the corpse cowered a child, a miserable squalid child, with famine in its cheeks and fear in its eyes. As I looked in the old woman's face, the wrinkles and lines vanished, and it became a face of youth—hard-eyed, stony, but still youth; and the shadow darted forth and darkened over these fantoms, as it had darkened over the last.

Nothing now was left but the shadow, and on that my eyes were intently fixed, till again eyes grew out of the shadow—malignant, serpent eyes. And the bubbles of light again rose and fell, and in their disordered, irregular, turbulent maze mingled with the wan moonlight. And now from these globules themselves, as from the shell of an egg, monstrous things burst out; the air grew filled with them; larvæ so bloodless and so hideous that I can in no way describe them except to remind the reader of the swarming life which the solar microscope brings before his eyes in a drop of water—things transparent, supple, agile, chasing each other, devouring each other—forms like naught ever beheld by the naked eye.

As the shapes were without symmetry, so their movements were without order. In their very vagrancies there was no sport; they came round me and round, thicker and faster and swifter, swarming over my head, crawling over my right arm, which was outstretched in involuntary command against all evil beings.

Sometimes I felt myself touched, but not by them; invisible hands touched me. Once I felt the clutch as of cold, soft fingers at my throat. I was still equally conscious that if I gave way to fear I should be in bodily peril, and I concentered all my faculties in the single focus of resisting, stubborn will. And I turned my sight from the shadow, above all from those strange serpent eyes—eyes that had now become distinctly visible. For there, though in naught else around me, I was aware that there was a will, and a will of intense, creative, working evil, which might crush down my own.

The pale atmosphere in the room began now to redden as if in the air of some near conflagration. The larvæ grew lurid as things that live in fire. Again the room vibrated; again were heard the three measured knocks; and again all things were swallowed up in the darkness of the dark shadow, as if out of that darkness all had come, into that darkness all returned.

As the gloom receded, the shadow was wholly gone. Slowly as it had been withdrawn, the flame grew again into the candles on the table, again into the fuel in the grate. The whole room came once more calmly, healthfully into sight.

The two doors were still closed, the door communicating with the servant's room still locked. In the corner of the wall, into which he had convulsively niched himself, lay the dog. I called to him—no movement; I approached—the animal was dead; his eyes protruded, his tongue out of his mouth, the froth gathered round his jaws. I took him in my arms; I brought him to the fire; I felt acute grief for the loss of my poor favorite, acute self-reproach; I accused myself of his death; I imagined he had died of fright. But what was my surprise on finding that his neck was actually broken—actually twisted out of the vertebræ. Had this been done in the dark? Must it not have been done by a hand human as mine? Must there not have been a human agency all the while in that room? Good cause to suspect it. I cannot tell. I cannot do more than state the fact fairly; the reader may draw his own inference.

Another surprising circumstance—my watch was restored to the table from which it had been so mysteriously withdrawn; but it had stopped at the very moment it was so withdrawn; nor, despite all the skill of the watchmaker, has it ever gone since—that is, it will go in a strange, erratic way for a few hours, and then come to a dead stop; it is worthless.

Nothing more chanced for the rest of the night; nor, indeed, had I long to wait before the dawn broke. Not till it was broad daylight did I quit the haunted house. Before I did so I revisited the little blind room in which my servant and I had been for a time imprisoned.

I had a strong impression, for which I could not account, that from that room had originated the mechanism of the phenomena, if I may use the term, which had been experienced in my chamber; and though I entered it now in the clear day, with the sun peering through the filmy window, I still felt, as I stood on its floor, the creep of the horror which I had first experienced there the night before, and which had been so aggravated by what had passed in my own chamber.

I could not, indeed, bear to stay more than half a minute within those walls. I descended the stairs, and again I heard the footfall before me;

and when I opened the street-door I thought I could distinguish a very low laugh. I gained my own home, expecting to find my run-away servant there. But he had not presented himself; nor did I hear more of him for three days, when I received a letter from him, dated from Liverpool, to this effect:

> HONORED SIR—*I humbly entreat your pardon, though I can scarcely hope that you will think I deserve it, unless—which heaven forbid!—you saw what I did. I feel that it will be years before I can recover myself; and as to being fit for service, it is out of the question. I am therefore going to my brother-in-law at Melbourne. The ship sails to-morrow. Perhaps the long voyage may set me up. I do nothing now but start and tremble, and fancy it is behind me. I humbly beg you, honored sir, to order my clothes, and whatever wages are due to me, to be sent to my mother's, at Walworth: John knows her address.*

The letter ended with additional apologies, somewhat incoherent, and explanatory details as to effects that had been under the writer's charge.

This flight may perhaps warrant a suspicion that the man wished to go to Australia, and had been somehow or other fraudulently mixed up with the events of the night. I say nothing in refutation of that conjecture; rather, I suggest it as one that would seem to many persons the most probable solution of improbable occurrences.

My own theory remained unshaken. I returned in the evening to the house, to bring away in a hack cab the things I had left there, with my poor dog's body. In this task I was not disturbed, nor did any incident worth note befall me, except that still, on ascending and descending the stairs, I heard the same footfall in advance. On leaving the house, I went to Mr. J——'s. He was at home. I returned him the keys, told him that my curiosity was sufficiently gratified, and was about to relate quickly what had passed, when he stopped me and said, though with much politeness, that he had no longer any interest in a mystery which none had ever solved.

I determined at least to tell him of the two letters I had read, as well as of the extraordinary manner in which they had disappeared; and I then inquired if he thought they had been addressed to the woman who had died in the house, and if there were anything in her early history which could possibly confirm the dark suspicions to which the letters gave rise.

Mr. J—— seemed startled, and after musing a few moments, answered:

"I know but little of the woman's earlier history, except, as I before told you, that her family were known to mine. But you revive some vague reminiscences to her prejudice. I will make inquiries, and inform you of their result. Still, even if we could admit the popular superstition that a person who had been either the perpetrator or the victim of dark crimes in life could revisit, as a restless spirit, the scene in which those crimes had been committed, I should observe that the house was infested by strange sights and sounds before the old woman died. You smile; what would you say?"

"I would say this: that I am convinced, if we could get to the bottom of these mysteries, we should find a living, human agency."

"What! you believe it is all an imposture? For what object?"

"Not an imposture, in the ordinary sense of the word. If suddenly I were to sink into a deep sleep, from which you could not awake me, but in that deep sleep could answer questions with an accuracy which I could not pretend to when awake—tell you what money you had in your pocket, nay, describe your very thoughts—it is not necessarily an imposture, any more than it is necessarily supernatural. I should be, unconsciously to myself, under a mesmeric influence, conveyed to me from a distance by a human being who had acquired power over me by previous *rapport*."

"Granting mesmerism, so far carried, to be a fact, you are right. And you would infer from this that a mesmerizer might produce the extraordinary effects you and others have witnessed over inanimate objects— fill the air with sights and sounds?"

"Or impress our senses with the belief in them, we never having been *en rapport* with the person acting on us? No. What is commonly called mesmerism could not do this; but there may be a power akin to mesmerism and superior to it—the power that in the old days was called magic. That such a power may extend to all inanimate objects of matter, I do not say; but if so, it would not be against nature, only a rare power in nature, which might be given to constitutions with certain peculiarities, and cultivated by practice to an extraordinary degree.

"That such a power might extend over the dead—that is, over certain thoughts and memories that the dead may still retain—and compel, not that which ought properly to be called the soul, and which is far beyond human reach, but rather a fantom of what has been most earth-stained on earth, to make itself apparent to our senses—is a very ancient though obsolete theory, upon which I will hazard no opinion. But I do not conceive the power would be supernatural.

"Let me illustrate what I mean, from an experiment which Paracelsus describes as not difficult, and which the author of the 'Curiosities of Literature' cites as credible: A flower perishes; you burn it. Whatever were the elements of that flower while it lived are gone, dispersed, you know not whither; you can never discover nor re-collect them. But you can, by chemistry, out of the burnt dust of that flower, raise a spectrum of the flower, just as it seemed in life.

"It may be the same with a human being. The soul has as much escaped you as the essence or elements of the flower. Still you may make a spectrum of it. And this fantom, though in the popular superstition it is held to be the soul of the departed, must not be confounded with the true soul; it is but the eidolon of the dead form.

"Hence, like the best-attested stories of ghosts or spirits, the thing that most strikes us is the absence of what we hold to be soul—that is, of superior, emancipated intelligence. They come for little or no object; they seldom speak, if they do come; they utter no ideas above those of an ordinary person on earth. These American spirit-seers have published volumes of communications in prose and verse, which they assert to be given in the names of the most illustrious dead—Shakespeare, Bacon, heaven knows whom.

"Those communications, taking the best, are certainly not of a whit higher order than would be communications from living persons of fair talent and education; they are wondrously inferior to what Bacon, Shakespeare, and Plato said and wrote when on earth. Nor, what is more notable, do they ever contain an idea that was not on the earth before.

"Wonderful, therefore, as such phenomena may be (granting them to be truthful), I see much that philosophy may question, nothing that it is incumbent on philosophy to deny, namely, nothing supernatural. They are but ideas conveyed somehow or other (we have not yet discovered the means) from one mortal brain to another. Whether in so doing tables walk of their own accord, or fiend-like shapes appear in a magic circle, or bodiless hands rise and remove material objects, or a thing of darkness, such as presented itself to me, freeze our blood— still am I persuaded that these are but agencies conveyed, as by electric wires, to my own brain from the brain of another.

"In some constitutions there is a natural chemistry, and these may produce chemic wonders; in others a natural fluid, call it electricity, and these produce electric wonders. But they differ in this from normal science: they are alike objectless, purposeless, puerile, frivolous. They lead on to no grand results, and therefore the world does not heed, and true sages have not cultivated them. But sure I am, that of all I saw or heard, a man, human as myself, was the remote originator; and, I believe, unconsciously to himself as to the exact effects produced, for this reason: no two persons, you say, have ever told you that they experienced exactly the same thing; well, observe, no two persons ever experience exactly the same dream.

"If this were an ordinary imposture, the machinery would be

arranged for results that would but little vary; if it were a supernatural agency permitted by the Almighty, it would surely be for some definite end. These phenomena belong to neither class. My persuasion is that they originate in some brain now far distant; that that brain had no distinct volition in anything that occurred; that what does occur reflects but its devious, motley, ever-shifting, half-formed thoughts; in short, that it has been but the dreams of such a brain put into action and invested with a semi-substance.

"That this brain is of immense power, that it can set matter into movement, that it is malignant and destructive, I believe. Some material force must have killed my dog; it might, for aught I know, have sufficed to kill myself, had I been as subjugated by terror as the dog—had my intellect or my spirit given me no countervailing resistance in my will."

"It killed your dog! That is fearful! Indeed, it is strange that no animal can be induced to stay in that house; not even a cat. Rats and mice are never found in it."

"The instincts of the brute creation detect influences deadly to their existence. Man's reason has a sense less subtle, because it has a resisting power more supreme. But enough; do you comprehend my theory?"

"Yes, though imperfectly; and I accept any crotchet (pardon the word), however odd, rather than embrace at once the notion of ghosts and hobgoblins we imbibed in our nurseries. Still, to my unfortunate house the evil is the same. What on earth can I do with the house?"

"I will tell you what I would do. I am convinced from my own internal feelings that the small unfurnished room, at right angles to the door of the bedroom which I occupied, forms a starting-point or receptacle for the influences which haunt the house; and I strongly advise you to have the walls opened, the floor removed, nay, the whole room pulled down. I observe that it is detached from the body of the house, built over the small back-yard, and could be removed without injury to the rest of the building."

"And you think that if I did that——"

"You would cut off the telegraph-wires. Try it. I am so persuaded that I am right that I will pay half the expense if you will allow me to direct the operations."

"Nay, I am well able to afford the cost; for the rest, allow me to write to you."

About ten days afterwards I received a letter from Mr. J——, telling me that he had visited the house since I had seen him; that he had found the two letters I had described replaced in the drawer from which I had taken them; that he had read them with misgivings like my own; that he had instituted a cautious inquiry about the woman to whom I rightly conjectured they had been written.

It seemed that thirty-six years ago (a year before the date of the letters) she had married, against the wish of her relatives, an American of very suspicious character; in fact, he was generally believed to have been a pirate. She herself was the daughter of very respectable trades-people, and had served in the capacity of nursery governess before her marriage. She had a brother, a widower, who was considered wealthy, and who had one child about six years old. A month after the marriage the body of this brother was found in the Thames, near London Bridge; there seemed some marks of violence about his throat, but they were not deemed sufficient to warrant the inquest in any other verdict than that of "found drowned."

The American and his wife took charge of the little boy, the deceased brother having by his will left his sister the guardian of his only child, and in the event of the child's death the sister inherited. The child died about six months afterward; it was supposed to have been neglected and ill-treated. The neighbors deposed to have heard it shriek at night.

The surgeon who had examined it after death said that it was emaciated as if from want of nourishment, and the body was covered with livid bruises. It seemed that one winter night the child had sought to escape; had crept out into the back-yard, tried to scale the wall, fallen back exhausted, and had been found at morning on the stones in a dying state.

But though there was some evidence of cruelty, there was none of murder; and the aunt and her husband had sought to palliate cruelty by alleging the exceeding stubbornness and perversity of the child, who was declared to be half-witted. Be that as it may, at the orphan's death the aunt inherited her brother's fortune.

Before the first wedded year was out, the American quitted England abruptly, and never returned to it. He obtained a cruising vessel, which was lost in the Atlantic two years afterward. The widow was left in affluence; but reverses of various kinds had befallen her; a bank broke, an investment failed, she went into a small business and became insolvent, then she entered into service, sinking lower and lower, from housekeeper down to maid-of-all-work, never long retaining a place, though nothing peculiar against her character was ever alleged.

She was considered sober, honest, and peculiarly quiet in her ways; still nothing prospered with her. And so she had dropped into the work-house, from which Mr. J—— had taken her, to be placed in charge of the very house which she had rented as mistress in the first year of her wedded life.

Mr. J—— added that he had passed an hour alone in the unfurnished room which I had urged him to destroy, and that his impressions of dread while there were so great, though he had neither heard nor seen anything, that he was eager to have the walls bared and the floors removed, as I had suggested. He had engaged persons for the work, and would commence any day I would name.

The day was accordingly fixed. I repaired to the haunted house; we went into the blind, dreary room, took up the skirting and then the floors. Under the rafters, covered with rubbish, was found a trap-door, quite large enough to admit a man. It was closely nailed down with clamps and rivets of iron. On removing these we descended into a room below, the existence of which had never been suspected.

In this room there had been a window and a flue, but they had been bricked over, evidently for many years. By the help of candles we examined this place; it still retained some moldering furniture—three chairs, an oak settee, a table—all of the fashion of about eighty years ago.

There was a chest of drawers against the wall, in which we found, half rotted away, old-fashioned articles of a man's dress, such as might have been worn eighty or a hundred years ago, by a gentleman of some rank; costly steel buckles and buttons, like those yet worn in court-dresses, a handsome court-sword; in a waistcoat which had once been rich with gold-lace, but which was now blackened and foul with damp, we found five guineas, a few silver coins, and an ivory ticket, probably for some place of entertainment long since passed away.

But our main discovery was in a kind of iron safe fixed to the wall, the lock of which it cost us much trouble to get picked.

In this safe were three shelves and two small drawers. Ranged on the shelves were several small bottles of crystal, hermetically stopped. They contained colorless volatile essences, of what nature I shall say no more than that they were not poisons; phosphor and ammonia entered into some of them. There were also some very curious glass tubes, and a small pointed rod of iron, with a large lump of rock crystal, and another of amber, also a lodestone of great power.

In one of the drawers we found a miniature portrait set in gold, and retaining the freshness of its colors most remarkably, considering the length of time it had probably been there. The portrait was that of a man who might be somewhat advanced in middle life, perhaps forty-seven or forty-eight.

It was a most peculiar face, a most impressive face. If you could fancy some mighty serpent transformed into man, preserving in the human lineaments the old serpent type, you would have a better idea of that countenance than long descriptions can convey; the width and flatness of frontal, the tapering elegance of contour, disguising the strength of the deadly jaw; the long, large, terrible eye, glittering and green as the emerald, and withal a certain ruthless calm, as if from the consciousness of an immense power.

The strange thing was this: the instant I saw the miniature I recognized a startling likeness to one of the rarest portraits in the world; the portrait of a man of rank only below that of royalty, who in his own day had made a considerable noise. History says little or nothing of him; but search the correspondence of his contemporaries, and you find reference to his wild daring, his bold profligacy, his restless spirit, his taste for the occult sciences.

While still in the meridian of life he died and was buried, so say the chronicles, in a foreign land. He died in time to escape the grasp of the law; for he was accused of crimes which would have given him to the headsman. After his death the portraits of him, which had been numerous, for he had been a munificent encourager of art, were bought up and destroyed, it was supposed by his heirs, who might have been glad could they have razed his very name from their splendid line.

He had enjoyed vast wealth; a large portion of this was believed to have been embezzled by a favorite astrologer or soothsayer; at all events, it had unaccountably vanished at the time of his death. One portrait alone of him was supposed to have escaped the general destruction; I had seen it in the house of a collector some months before. It had made on me a wonderful impression, as it does on all who behold it—a face never to be forgotten; and there was that face in the miniature that lay within my hand. True that in the miniature the man was a few years older than in the portrait I had seen, or than the original was even at the time of his death. But a few years!—why, between the date in which flourished that direful noble and the date in which the miniature was evidently painted there was an interval of more than two centuries. While I was thus gazing, silent and wondering, Mr. J——said:

"But is it possible? I have known this man."

"How? where?" cried I.

"In India. He was high in the confidence of the Rajah of ——, and well-nigh drew him into a revolt which would have lost the Rajah his dominions. The man was a Frenchman; his name De V——; clever, bold, lawless; we insisted on his dismissal and banishment. It must be the same man, no two faces like his, yet this miniature seems nearly a hundred years old."

Mechanically I turned round the miniature to examine the back of it, and on the back was engraved a pentacle; in the middle of the pentacle a ladder, and the third step of the ladder was formed by the date 1765. Examining still more minutely, I detected a spring; this, on being pressed, opened the back of the miniature as a lid.

Within-side the lid were engraved: "Mariana, to thee. Be faithful in life and in death to ——."

Here follows a name that I will not mention, but it was not unfamiliar to me. I had heard it spoken of by old men in my childhood as the name borne by a dazzling charlatan, who had made a great sensation in London for a year or so, and had fled the country on the charge of a double murder within his own house—that of his mistress and his rival. I said nothing of this to Mr. J——, to whom reluctantly I resigned the miniature.

We had found no difficulty in opening the first drawer within the iron safe; we found great difficulty in opening the second: it was not locked, but it resisted all efforts, till we inserted in the chinks the edge of a chisel. When we had thus drawn it forth we found a very singular apparatus, in the nicest order.

. Upon a small, thin book, or rather tablet, was placed a saucer of crystal; this saucer was filled with a clear liquid; on that liquid floated a kind of compass, with a needle shifting rapidly round; but instead of the usual points of a compass, were seven strange characters, not very unlike those used by astrologers to denote the planets.

A very peculiar, but not strong nor displeasing odor came from this drawer, which was lined with a wood that we afterward discovered to be hazel. Whatever the cause of this odor, it produced a material effect on the nerves. We all felt it, even the two workmen who were in the room; a creeping, tingling sensation, from the tips of the fingers to the roots of the hair.

Impatient to examine the tablet, I removed the saucer. As I did so, the needle of the compass went round and round with exceeding swiftness, and I felt a shock that ran through my whole frame, so that I dropped the saucer on the floor. The liquid was spilt, the saucer was broken, the compass rolled to the end of the room, and at that instant the walls shook to and fro as if a giant had swayed and rocked them.

The two workmen were so frightened that they ran up the ladder by which we had descended from the trapdoor; but, seeing that nothing more happened, they were easily induced to return.

Meanwhile I had opened the tablet; it was bound in plain red leather, with a silver clasp; it contained but one sheet of thick vellum, and on that sheet were inscribed, within a double pentacle, words in old monkish Latin, which are literally to be translated thus:

On all that it can reach within these walls, sentient or inanimate,

*living or dead, as moves the needle, so works my will! Accursed be
the house, and restless the dwellers therein.*

We found no more. Mr. J—— burned the tablet and its anathema.
He razed to the foundation the part of the building containing the
secret room, with the chamber over it. He had then the courage to
inhabit the house himself for a month, and a quieter, better conditioned
house could not be found in all London. Subsequently he let it to
advantage, and his tenant has made no complaints.

But my story is not yet done. A few days after Mr. J—— had removed
into the house, I paid him a visit. We were standing by the open
window and conversing. A van containing some articles of furniture
which he was moving from his former house was at the door.

I had just urged on him my theory that all those phenomena regarded
as supermundane had emanated from a human brain; adducing the
charm, or rather curse we had found and destroyed, in support of my
theory.

Mr. J—— was observing in reply, "that even if mesmerism, or whatever analogous power it might be called, could really thus work in
the absence of the operator, and produce effects so extraordinary, still
could those effects continue when the operator himself was dead?
and if the spell had been wrought, and, indeed, the room walled up,
more than seventy years ago, the probability was that the operator had
long since departed this life"—Mr. J——, I say, was thus answering,
when I caught hold of his arm and pointed to the street below.

A well-dressed man had crossed from the opposite side, and was
accosting the carrier in charge of the van. His face, as he stood, was
exactly fronting our window. It was the face of the miniature we had
discovered; it was the face of the portrait of the noble three centuries
ago.

"Good heavens!" cried Mr. J——, "that is the face of De V——, and
scarcely a day older than when I saw it in the Rajah's court in my
youth!"

Seized by the same thought, we both hastened down-stairs; I was
first in the street, but the man had already gone. I caught sight of
him, however, not many yards in advance, and in another moment I
was by his side.

I had resolved to speak to him, but when I looked into his face I felt
as if it were impossible to do so. That eye—the eye of the serpent—fixed
and held me spellbound. And withal, about the man's whole person
there was a dignity, an air of pride and station and superiority that
would have made any one, habituated to the usages of the world, hesitate long before venturing upon a liberty or impertinence.

And what could I say? What was it I could ask?

Thus ashamed of my first impulse, I fell a few paces back, still, however, following the stranger, undecided what else to do. Meanwhile he turned the corner of the street; a plain carriage was in waiting with a servant out of livery, dressed like a *valet de place,* at the carriage door. In another moment he had stepped into the carriage, and it drove off. I returned to the house.

Mr. J—— was still at the street-door. He had asked the carrier what the stranger had said to him.

"Merely asked whom that house now belonged to."

The same evening I happened to go with a friend to a place in town called the Cosmopolitan Club, a place open to men of all countries, all opinions, all degrees. One orders one's coffee, smokes one's cigar. One is always sure to meet agreeable, sometimes remarkable persons.

I had not been two minutes in the room before I beheld at table, conversing with an acquaintance of mine, whom I will designate by the initial G——, the man, the original of the miniature. He was now without his hat, and the likeness was yet more startling, only I observed that while he was conversing there was less severity in the countenance; there was even a smile, though a very quiet and very cold one. The dignity of mien I had acknowledged in the street was also more strik- ing; a dignity akin to that which invests some prince of the East, conveying the idea of supreme indifference and habitual, indisputable, indolent but resistless power.

G—— soon after left the stranger, who then took up a scientific journal, which seemed to absorb his attention.

I drew G—— aside.

"Who and what is that gentleman?"

"That? Oh, a very remarkable man indeed! I met him last year amid the caves of Petra, the Scriptural Edom. He is the best Oriental scholar I know. We joined company, had an adventure with robbers, in which he showed a coolness that saved our lives; afterward he invited me to spend a day with him in a house he had bought at Damascus, buried among almond-blossoms and roses—the most beautiful thing! He had lived there for some time, quite as an Oriental, in grand style.

"I half suspect he is a renegade, immensely rich, very odd; by the by, a great mesmerizer. I have seen him with my own eyes produce an effect on inanimate things. If you take a letter from your pocket and throw it to the other end of the room, he will order it to come to his feet, and you will see the letter wriggle itself along the floor till it has obeyed his command. 'Pon my honor 'tis true; I have seen him affect even the weather, disperse or collect clouds by means of a glass tube or wand. But he does not like talking of these matters to strangers. He has only just arrived in England; says he has not been here for a great many years; let me introduce him to you."

"Certainly! He is English, then? What is his name?"

"Oh! a very homely one—Richards."

"And what is his birth—his family?"

"How do I know? What does it signify? No doubt some *parvenue;* but rich, so infernally rich!"

G—— drew me up to the stranger, and the introduction was effected. The manners of Mr. Richards were not those of an adventurous traveler. Travelers are in general gifted with high animal spirits; they are talkative, eager, imperious. Mr. Richards was calm and subdued in tone, with manners which were made distant by the loftiness of punctilious courtesy, the manners of a former age.

I observed that the English he spoke was not exactly of our day. I should even have said that the accent was slightly foreign. But then Mr. Richards remarked that he had been little in the habit for years of speaking in his native tongue.

The conversation fell upon the changes in the aspect of London since he had last visited our metropolis. G—— then glanced off to the moral changes—literary, social, political—the great men who were removed from the stage within the last twenty years; the new great men who were coming on.

In all this Mr. Richards evinced no interest. He had evidently read none of our living authors, and seemed scarcely acquainted by name with our younger statesmen. Once, and only once, he laughed; it was when G—— asked him whether he had any thoughts of getting into Parliament; and the laugh was inward, sarcastic, sinister—a sneer raised into a laugh.

After a few minutes, G—— left us to talk to some other acquaintances who had just lounged into the room, and I then said, quietly:

"I have seen a miniature of you, Mr. Richards, in the house you once inhabited, and perhaps built—if not wholly, at least in part—in Oxford Street. You passed by that house this morning."

Not till I had finished did I raise my eyes to his, and then he fixed my gaze so steadfastly that I could not withdraw it—those fascinating serpent-eyes. But involuntarily, and as if the words that translated my thought were dragged from me, I added, in a low whisper, "I have been a student in the mysteries of life and nature; of those mysteries I have known the occult professors. I have the right to speak to you thus." And I uttered a certain password.

"Well, I concede the right. What would you ask?"

"To what extent human will in certain temperaments can extend?"

"To what extent can thought extend? Think, and before you draw breath you are in China!"

"True; but my thought has no power in China."

"Give it expression, and it may have. You may write down a thought which, sooner or later, may alter the whole condition of China. What is a law but a thought? Therefore thought is infinite. Therefore thought has power; not in proportion to its value—a bad thought may make a bad law as potent as a good thought can make a good one."

"Yes; what you say confirms my own theory. Through invisible currents one human brain may transmit its ideas to other human brains, with the same rapidity as a thought promulgated by visible means. And as thought is imperishable, as it leaves its stamp behind it in the natural world, even when the thinker has passed out of this world, so the thought of the living may have power to rouse up and revive the thoughts of the dead, such as those thoughts *were in life,* though the thought of the living cannot reach the thoughts which the dead *now* may entertain. Is it not so?"

"I decline to answer, if in my judgment thought has the limit you would fix to it. But proceed; you have a special question you wish to put."

"Intense malignity in an intense will, engendered in a peculiar temperament, and aided by natural means within the reach of science, may produce effects like those ascribed of old to evil magic. It might thus haunt the walls of a human habitation with spectral revivals of all guilty thoughts and guilty deeds once conceived and done within those walls; all, in short, with which the evil will claims *rapport* and affinity—imperfect, incoherent, fragmentary snatches at the old dramas acted therein years ago.

"Thoughts thus crossing each other haphazard, as in the nightmare of a vision, growing up into fantom sights and sounds, and all serving to create horror; not because those sights and sounds are really visitations from a world without, but that they are ghastly, monstrous renewals of what have been in this world itself, set into malignant play by a malignant mortal. And it is through the material agency of that human brain that these things would acquire even a human power; would strike as with the shock of electricity, and might kill, if the thought of the person assailed did not rise superior to the dignity of the original assailer; might kill the most powerful animal, if unnerved by fear, but not injure the feeblest man, if, while his flesh crept, his mind stood out fearless.

"Thus when in old stories we read of a magician rent to pieces by the fiends he had invoked, or still more, in Eastern legends, that one magician succeeds by arts in destroying another, there may be so far truth, that a material being has clothed, from his own evil propensities, certain elements and fluids, usually quiescent or harmless, with awful shapes and terrific force; just as the lightning, that had lain hidden and innocent in the cloud, becomes by natural law suddenly visible, takes a distinct shape to the eye, and can strike destruction on the object to which it is attracted."

"You are not without glimpses of a mighty secret," said Mr. Richards, composedly. "According to your view, could a mortal obtain the power you speak of, he would necessarily be a malignant and evil being."

"If the power were exercised, as I have said, most malignant and most evil; though I believe in the ancient traditions that he could not injure the good. His will could only injure those with whom it has established an affinity, or over whom it forces unresisted sway. I will now imagine an example that may be within the laws of nature, yet seem wild as the fables of a bewildered monk.

"You will remember that Albertus Magnus, after describing minutely the process by which the spirits may be invoked and commanded, adds emphatically that the process will instruct and avail only to the few; that *a man must be born a magician!*—that is, born with a peculiar physical temperament, as a man is born a poet.

"Rarely are men in whose constitutions lurks this occult power of the highest order of intellect; usually in the intellect there is some twist, perversity, or disease. But on the other hand, they must possess, to an astonishing degree, the faculty to concentrate thought on a single object —the energic faculty that we call WILL. Therefore, though their intellect be not sound, it is exceedingly forcible for the attainment of what it desires. I will imagine such a person, preeminently gifted with this constitution and its concomitant forces. I will place him in the loftier grades of society.

"I will suppose his desires emphatically those of the sensualist; he has, therefore, a strong love of life. He is an absolute egotist; his will is concentered in himself; he has fierce passions; he knows no enduring, no holy affections, but he can covet eagerly what for the moment he desires; he can hate implacably what opposes itself to his objects; he can commit fearful crimes, yet feel small remorse; he resorts rather to curses upon others than to penitence for his misdeeds. Circumstances to which his constitution guides him, lead him to a rare knowledge of the natural secrets which may serve his egotism. He is a close observer where his passions encourage observation; he is a minute calculator, not from love of truth, but where love of self sharpens his faculties; therefore he can be a man of science.

"I suppose such a being, having by experience learned the power of his arts over others, trying what may be the power of will over his own frame, and studying all that in natural philosophy may increase that power. He loves life, he dreads death; *he wills to live on.* He cannot restore himself to youth; he cannot entirely stay the progress of death; he cannot make himself immortal in the flesh and blood. But he may arrest, for a time so long as to appear incredible if I said it, that hardening of the parts which constitutes old age.

"A year may age him no more than an hour ages another. His intense will, scientifically trained into system, operates, in short, over the wear and tear of his own frame. He lives on. That he may not seem a portent and a miracle, he *dies,* from time to time, seemingly, to certain persons. Having schemed the transfer of a wealth that suffices to his wants, he disappears from one corner of the world, and contrives that his obsequies shall be celebrated.

"He reappears at another corner of the world, where he resides undetected, and does not visit the scenes of his former career till all who could remember his features are no more. He would be profoundly miserable if he had affections; he has none but for himself. No good man would accept his longevity; and to no man, good or bad, would he or could he communicate its true secret.

"Such a man might exist; such a man as I have described I see now before me—Duke of ——, in the court of ——, dividing time between lust and brawl, alchemists and wizards; again, in the last century, charlatan and criminal, with name less noble, domiciled in the house at which you gazed to-day, and flying from the law you had outraged, none knew whither; traveler once more revisiting London with the same earthly passion which filled your heart when races now no more walked through yonder streets; outlaw from the school of all the nobler and diviner mysteries. Execrable image of life in death and death in life, I warn you back from the cities and homes of healthful men! back to the ruins of departed empires! back to the deserts of nature unredeemed!"

There answered me a whisper so musical, so potently musical, that it seemed to enter into my whole being and subdue me despite myself. Thus it said:

"I have sought one like you for the last hundred years. Now I have found you, we part not till I know what I desire. The vision that sees through the past and cleaves through the veil of the future is in you at this hour—never before, never to come again. The vision of no puling, fantastic girl, of no sick-bed somnambule, but of a strong man with a vigorous brain. Soar, and look forth!"

As he spoke, I felt as if I rose out of myself upon eagle wings. All the weight seemed gone from air, roofless the room, roofless the dome of space. I was not in the body—where, I knew not; but aloft over time, over earth.

Again I heard the melodious whiper:

"You say right. I have mastered great secrets by the power of will. True, by will and by science I can retard the process of years, but death comes not by age alone. Can I frustrate the accidents which bring death upon the young?"

"No; every accident is a providence. Before a providence snaps every human will."

"Shall I die at last, ages and ages hence, by the slow though inevitable growth of time, or by the cause that I call accident?"

"By a cause you call accident."

"Is not the end still remote?" asked the whisper, with a slight tremor.

"Regarded as my life regards time, it is still remote."

"And shall I, before then, mix with the world of men as I did ere I learned these secrets; resume eager interest in their strife and their trouble; battle with ambition, and use the power of the sage to win the power that belongs to kings?"

"You will yet play a part on the earth that will fill earth with commotion and amaze. For wondrous designs have you, a wonder yourself, been permitted to live on through the centuries. All the secrets you have stored will then have their uses; all that now makes you a stranger amid the generations will contribute then to make you their lord. As the trees and the straws are drawn into a whirlpool, as they spin round, are sucked to the deep, and again tossed aloft by the eddies, so shall races and thrones be drawn into your vortex. Awful destroyer! but in destroying, made, against your own will, a constructor."

"And that date, too, is far off?"

"Far off; when it comes, think your end in this world is at hand!"

"How and what is the end? Look east, west, south, and north."

"In the north, where you never yet trod, toward the point whence your instincts have warned you, there a specter will seize you. 'Tis Death! I see a ship; it is haunted; 'tis chased! it sails on. Baffled navies sail after that ship. It enters the region of ice. It passes a sky red with meteors. Two moons stand on high, over ice-reefs. I see the ship locked between white defiles; they are ice-rocks. I see the dead strew the decks, stark and livid, green mold on their limbs. All are dead but one man— it is you! But years, though so slowly they come, have then scathed you. There is the coming of age on your brow, and the will is relaxed in the cells of the brain. Still that will, though enfeebled, exceeds all that man knew before you; through the will you live on, gnawed with famine. And nature no longer obeys you in that death-spreading region;

the sky is a sky of iron, and the air has iron clamps, and the ice-rocks wedge in the ship. Hark how it cracks and groans! Ice will imbed it as amber imbeds a straw. And a man has gone forth, living yet, from the ship and its dead; and he has clambered up the spikes of an iceberg, and the two moons gaze down on his form. That man is yourself, and terror is on you—terror; and terror has swallowed up your will.

"And I see, swarming up the steep ice-rock, gray, grizzly things. The bears of the North have scented their quarry; they come nearer and nearer, shambling, and rolling their bulk. In that day every moment shall seem to you longer than the centuries through which you have passed. Heed this: after life, moments continued make the bliss or the hell of eternity."

"Hush!" said the whisper. "But the day, you assure me, is far off, very far! I go back to the almond and rose of Damascus! Sleep!"

The room swam before my eyes. I became insensible. When I recovered, I found G—— holding my hand and smiling. He said, "You, who have always declared yourself proof against mesmerism, have succumbed at last to my friend Richards."

"Where is Mr. Richards?"

"Gone, when you passed into a trance, saying quietly to me, 'Your friend will not wake for an hour.'"

I asked, as collectedly as I could, where Mr. Richards lodged.

"At the Trafalgar Hotel."

"Give me your arm," said I to G——. "Let us call on him; I have something to say."

When we arrived at the hotel we were told that Mr. Richards had returned twenty minutes before, paid his bill, left directions with his servant (a Greek) to pack his effects, and proceed to Malta by the steamer that should leave Southampton the next day. Mr. Richards had merely said of his own movements that he had visits to pay in the neighborhood of London, and it was uncertain whether he should be able to reach Southampton in time for that steamer; if not, he should follow in the next one.

The waiter asked me my name. On my informing him, he gave me a note that Mr. Richards had left for me in case I called.

The note was as follows:

I wished you to utter what was in your mind. You obeyed. I have therefore established power over you. For three months from this day you can communicate to no living man what has passed between us. You cannot even show this note to the friend by your side. During three months silence complete as to me and mine. Do you doubt my power to lay on you this command? Try to disobey me. At the

end of the third month the spell is raised. For the rest, I spare you.
I shall visit your grave a year and a day after it has received you.

So ends this strange story, which I ask no one to believe. I write it
down exactly three months after I received the above note. I could not
write it before, nor could I show to G——, in spite of his urgent
request, the note which I read under the gas-lamp by his side.

10

Con Cregan's Legacy

BY CHARLES LEVER

I WAS born in a little cabin on the borders of Meath and King's County; it stood on a small triangular bit of ground, beside a cross-road; and although the place was surveyed every ten years or so, they were never able to say to which county we belonged; there being just the same number of arguments for one side as for the other—a circumstance, many believed, that decided my father in his original choice of the residence; for while, under the "disputed boundary question," he paid no rates or county cess, he always made a point of voting at both county elections. This may seem to indicate that my parent was of a naturally acute habit; and, indeed, the way he became possessed of the bit of ground will confirm that impression.

There was nobody of the rank of gentry in the parish, not even "squireen"; the richest being a farmer, a snug old fellow, one Harry McCabe, that had two sons, who were always fighting between themselves which was to have the old man's money. Peter, the elder, doing everything to injure Mat, and Mat never backward in paying off the obligation. At last Mat, tired out in the struggle, resolved he would bear no more. He took leave of his father one night, and next day set off for Dublin, and listed in the "Buffs." Three weeks after he sailed for India; and the old man, overwhelmed by grief, took to his bed, and never arose from it after. Not that his death was in any way sudden, for he lingered on for months long; Peter always teasing him to make his will, and be revenged on "the dirty spalpeen" that disgraced the family, but old Harry as stoutly resisting, and declaring that whatever he owned should be fairly divided between them. These disputes between them were well known in the neighbourhood. Few of the country people passing the house at night but had overheard the old man's weak, reedy voice, and Peter's deep hoarse one, in altercation. When, at last—it was on a Sunday night—all was still and quiet in the house; not a word, not a footstep could be heard, no more than if it were uninhabited, the neighbours looked knowingly at each other, and wondered if the old man was worse—if he were dead!

It was a little after midnight that a knock came to the door of our cabin. I heard it first, for I used to sleep in a little snug basket near the fire; but I didn't speak, for I was frightened. It was repeated still louder, and then came a cry—

"Con Cregan! Con, I say! open the door! I want you."

I knew the voice well, it was Peter McCabe's; but I pretended to be fast asleep, and snored loudly. At last my father unbolted the door, and I heard him say—

"Oh, Mr. Peter, what's the matter? is the ould man worse?"

"Faix! that's what he is, for he's dead!"

"Glory be his bed! when did it happen?"

"About an hour ago," said Peter, in a voice that even I from my corner could perceive was greatly agitated. "He died like an ould hay-then, Con, and never made a will!"

"That's bad," said my father; for he was always a polite man, and said whatever was pleasing to the company.

"It is bad," said Peter; "but it would be worse if we couldn't help it. Listen to me now, Conny, I want ye to help me in this business; and here's five guineas in goold, if ye do what I bid ye. You know that ye were always reckoned the image of my father, and before he took ill ye were mistaken for each other every day of the week."

"Anan!" said my father; for he was getting frightened at the notion, without well knowing why.

"Well, what I want is, for ye to come over to the house and get into the bed."

"Not beside the corpse?" said my father, trembling.

"By no means; but by yourself; and you're to pretend to be my father, and that ye want to make yer will before ye die; and then I'll send for the neighbours, and Billy Scanlan the schoolmaster, and ye'll tell him what to write, laving all the farm and everything to me—ye understand. And as the neighbours will see ye and hear yer voice, it will never be believed but it was himself that did it."

"The room must be very dark," says my father.

"To be sure it will, but have no fear! Nobody will dare to come nigh the bed; and ye'll only have to make a cross with your pen under the name."

"And the priest?" said my father.

"My father quarrelled with him last week about the Easter dues, and Father Tom said he'd not give him the 'rites'; and that's lucky now! Come along now, quick, for we've no time to lose; it must be all finished before the day breaks."

My father did not lose much time at his toilet, for he just wrapped his big coat 'round him, and slipping on his brogues, left the house. I sat up in the basket and listened till they were gone some minutes; and then, in a costume light as my parent's, set out after them, to watch the course of the adventure. I thought to take a short cut and be before them; but by bad luck I fell into a bog-hole, and only escaped being drowned by a chance. As it was, when I reached the house the performance had already begun. I think I see the whole scene this instant before my eyes, as I sat on a little window with one pane, and that a broken one, and surveyed the proceeding. It was a large room, at one end of which was a bed, and beside it a table, with physic-bottles, and spoons, and tea-cups; a little farther off was another table, at which sat Billy Scanlan, with all manner of writing materials before him. The country people sat two, sometimes three deep round the walls, all intently eager and anxious for the coming event. Peter himself went from place to place, trying to smother his grief, and occasionally helping the company to whisky—which was supplied with more than accustomed liberality. All my consciousness of the deceit and trickery could not deprive the scene of a certain solemnity. The misty distance of the half-lighted room; the highly-wrought expression of the country people's faces, never more intensely excited than at some moment of this kind; the low, deep-drawn breathings, unbroken save by a sigh or a sob—the tribute of some affectionate sorrow to some lost friend, whose memory was thus forcibly brought back; these, I repeat it, were all so real that, as I looked, a thrilling sense of awe stole over me, and I actually shook with fear.

A low, faint cough, from the dark corner where the bed stood, seemed to cause even a deeper stillness; and then in a silence where the buzzing of a fly would have been heard, my father said—

"Where's Billy Scanlan? I want to make my will!"

"He's here, father!" said Peter, taking Billy by the hand and leading him to the bedside.

"Write what I bid ye, Billy, and be quick, for I hav'n't a long time before me here. I die a good Catholic, though Father O'Rafferty won't give me the 'rites'!"

A general chorus of "Oh, musha, musha," was now heard through the room; but whether in grief over the sad fate of the dying man, or the unflinching severity of the priest, is hard to say.

"I die in peace with all my neighbours and all mankind!"

Another chorus of the company seemed to approve these charitable expressions.

"I bequeath unto my son, Peter—and never was there a better son, or a decenter boy!—have you that down? I bequeath unto my son, Peter, the whole of my two farms of Killimundoonery and Knocksheboorn, with the fallow meadows behind Lynch's house; the forge, and the right of turf on the Dooran bog. I give him, and much good may it do him, Lanty Cassarn's acre, and the Luary field, with the lime-kiln—and that reminds me that my mouth is just as dry; let me taste what ye have in the jug."

Here the dying man took a very hearty pull, and seemed considerably refreshed by it.

"Where was I, Billy Scanlan?" says he; "oh, I remember, at the lime-kiln; I leave him—that's Peter, I mean—the two potato-gardens at Noonan's Well; and it is the elegant fine crops grows there."

"An't you gettin' wake, father, darlin'?" says Peter, who began to be afraid of my father's loquaciousness; for, to say the truth, the punch got into his head, and he was greatly disposed to talk.

"I am, Peter, my son," says he, "I am getting wake; just touch my lips again with the jug. Ah, Peter, Peter, you watered the drink!"

"No, indeed, father, but it's the taste is leavin' you," says Peter; and again a low chorus of compassionate pity murmured through the cabin.

"Well, I'm nearly done now," says my father; "there's only one little plot of ground remaining, and I put it on you, Peter—as ye wish to live a good man, and die with the same asy heart I do now—that ye mind my last words to ye here. Are ye listening? Are the neighbours listening? Is Billy Scanlan listening?"

"Yes, sir. Yes, father. We're all minding," chorused the audience.

"Well, then, it's my last will and testament, and may—give me over the jug"—here he took a long drink—"and may that blessed liquor be poison to me if I'm not as eager about this as every other part of my will; I say, then, I bequeath the little plot at the cross-roads to poor Con Cregan; for he has a heavy charge, and is as honest and as hard-working a man as ever I knew. Be a friend to him, Peter dear; never let him want while ye have it yerself; think of me on my deathbed whenever he asks ye for any trifle. Is it down, Billy Scanlan? the two acres at the cross to Con Cregan and his heirs, in *secla seclorum*. Ah, blessed be the saints! but I feel my heart lighter after that," says he; "a good work makes an easy conscience; and now I'll drink all the company's good health, and many happy returns——"

What he was going to add there's no saying; but Peter, who was now terribly frightened at the lively tone the sick man was assuming, hurried all the people away into another room, to let his father die in peace. When they were all gone Peter slipped back to my father, who was putting on his brogues in a corner.

"Con," says he, "ye did it all well; but sure that was a joke about the two acres at the cross."

"Of course it was," says he; "sure it was all a joke for the matter of that; won't I make the neighbours laugh hearty to-morrow when I tell them all about it!"

"You wouldn't be mean enough to betray me?" says Peter, trembling with fright.

"Sure ye wouldn't be mean enough to go against yer father's dying words?" says my father; "the last sentence ever he spoke;" and here he gave a low, wicked laugh that made me shake with fear.

"Very well, Con!" says Peter, holding out his hand; "a bargain's a bargain; yer a deep fellow, that's all!" and so it ended; and my father slipped quietly home over the bog, mighty well satisfied with the legacy he left himself. And thus we became the owners of the little spot known to this day as Con's Acre.

11

Rab and His Friends

BY JOHN BROWN

FOUR-AND-THIRTY years ago, Bob Ainslie and I were coming up Infirmary Street from the High School, our heads together, and our arms inter-twisted as only lovers and boys know how or why.

When we got to the top of the street and turned north we espied a crowd at the Tron Church. "A dog-fight!" shouted Bob, and was off; and so was I, both of us all but praying that it might not be over before we got up! And is not this boy-nature, and human nature, too? And don't we all wish a house on fire not to be out before we see it? Dogs like fighting; old Isaac says they "delight" in it, and for the best of all reasons; and boys are not cruel because they like to see the fight. They see three of the great cardinal virtues of dog or man—courage, endurance, and skill—in intense action. This is very different from a love of making dogs fight, and aggravating and making gain by their pluck. A boy—be he ever so fond himself of fighting, if he be a good boy, hates and despises all this, but he would have run off with Bob and me fast enough; it is a natural, and a not wicked, interest that all boys and men have in witnessing intense energy in action.

Does any curious and finely ignorant woman wish to know how Bob's eye at a glance announced a dog-fight to his brain? He did not—he could not—see the dogs fighting; it was a flash of an inference, a rapid induction. The crowd round a couple of dogs fighting is a crowd masculine mainly, with an occasional active, compassionate woman fluttering wildly round the outside and using her tongue and her hands freely upon the men, as so many "brutes"; it is a crowd annular, compact, and mobile; a crowd centripetal, having its eyes and its heads all bent downward and inward to one common focus.

Well, Bob and I are up, and find it is not over; a small thoroughbred,

114

white bull-terrier is busy throttling a large shepherd's dog, unaccustomed to war but not to be trifled with. They are hard at it; the scientific little fellow doing his work in great style, his pastoral enemy fighting wildly, but with the sharpest of teeth and a great courage. Science and breeding, however, soon had their own; the Game Chicken, as the premature Bob called him, working his way up, took his final grip of poor Yarrow's throat—and he lay gasping and done for. His master, a brown, handsome, big, young shepherd from Tweedsmuir, would have liked to have knocked down any man, would "drink up Esil, or eat a crocodile," for that part, if he had a chance; it was no use kicking the little dog; that would only make him hold the closer. Many were the means shouted out in mouthfuls of the best possible ways of ending it. "Water!" but there was none near, and many cried for it who might have got it from the well at Blackfriar's Wynd. "Bite the tail!" and a large, vague, benevolent, middle-aged man, more desirous than wise, with some struggle got the bushy end of Yarrow's tail into his ample mouth and bit it with all his might. This was more than enough for the much-enduring, much-perspiring shepherd, who, with a gleam of joy over his broad visage, delivered a terrific facer upon our large, vague, benevolent, middle-aged friend, who went down like a shot.

Still the Chicken holds; death not far off. "Snuff! a pinch of snuff!" observed a calm, highly dressed young buck with an eye-glass in his eye. "Snuff, indeed!" growled the angry crowd, affronted and glaring. "Snuff! a pinch of snuff!" again observes the buck, but with more urgency; whereon were produced several open boxes, and from a mull which may have been at Culloden he took a pinch, knelt down, and presented it to the nose of the Chicken. The laws of physiology and of snuff take their course; the Chicken sneezes, and Yarrow is free!

The young pastoral giant stalks off with Yarrow in his arms—comforting him.

But the bull-terrier's blood is up, and his soul unsatisfied; he grips the first dog he meets, and, discovering she is not a dog, in Homeric phrase, he makes a brief sort of *amende* and is off. The boys, with Bob and me at their head, are after him: down Niddry Street he goes, bent on mischief; up the Cowgate like an arrow—Bob and I, and our small men, panting behind.

There, under the single arch of the South Bridge, is a huge mastiff, sauntering down the middle of the causeway, as if with his hands in his pockets; he is old, brindled, as big as a little Highland bull, and has the Shakespearean dewlaps shaking as he goes.

The Chicken makes straight at him, and fastens on his throat. To our astonishment, the great creature does nothing but stand still, hold himself up, and roar—yes, roar, a long, serious, remonstrative roar. How is

this? Bob and I are up to them. *He is muzzled!* The bailies had proclaimed a general muzzling, and his master, studying strength and
economy mainly, had encompassed his huge jaws in a home-made apparatus constructed out of the leather of some ancient *brcechin.* His
mouth was open as far as it could; his lips curled up in rage—a sort of
terrible grin; his teeth gleaming, ready, from out the darkness; the strap
across his mouth tense as a bowstring; his whole frame stiff with indignation and surprise; his roar asking us all round, "Did you ever see
the like of this?" He looked a statue of anger and astonishment done in
Aberdeen granite.

We soon had a crowd; the Chicken held on. "A knife!" cried Bob;
and a cobbler gave him his knife; you know the kind of knife, worn
obliquely to a point and always keen. I put its edge to the tense leather;
it ran before it; and then!—one sudden jerk of that enormous head, a
sort of dirty mist about his mouth, no noise, and the bright and fierce
little fellow is dropped, limp and dead. A solemn pause; this was more
than any of us had bargained for. I turned the little fellow over, and saw
he was quite dead: the mastiff had taken him by the small of the back
like a rat and broken it.

He looked down at his victim appeased, ashamed, and amazed;
sniffed him all over, stared at him, and, taking a sudden thought, turned
round and trotted off. Bob took the dead dog up, and said, "John, we'll
bury him after tea." "Yes," said I, and was off after the mastiff. He made
up the Cowgate at a rapid swing; he had forgotten some engagement.
He turned up the Candlemaker Row, and stopped at the Harrow Inn.

There was a carrier's cart ready to start, and a keen, thin, impatient,
black-a-vised little man, his hand at his gray horse's head, looking about
angrily for something. "Rab, ye thief!" said he, aiming a kick at my
great friend, who drew cringing up, and, avoiding the heavy shoe with
more agility than dignity and watching his master's eye, slunk dismayed
under the cart—his ears down, and as much as he had of tail down, too.

What a man this must be—thought I—to whom my tremendous hero
turns tail! The carrier saw the muzzle hanging, cut and useless, from
his neck, and I eagerly told him the story, which Bob and I always
thought, and still think, Homer, or King David, or Sir Walter alone
were worthy to rehearse. The severe little man was mitigated, and condescended to say, "Rab, ma man—puir Rabbie," whereupon the stump
of a tail rose up, the ears were cocked, the eyes filled and were comforted; the two friends were reconciled. "Hupp!" and a stroke of the
whip were given to Jess, and off went the three.

Bob and I buried the Game Chicken that night (we had not much
of a tea) in the back-green of his house, in Melville Street, No. 17, with

considerable gravity and silence; and being at the time in the *Iliad,* and, like all boys, Trojans, we of course called him Hector.

Six years have passed—a long time for a boy and a dog; Bob Ainslie is off to the wars; I am a medical student, and clerk at Minto House Hospital.

Rab I saw almost every week, on the Wednesday, and we had much pleasant intimacy. I found the way to his heart by frequent scratching of his huge head and an occasional bone. When I did not notice him he would plant himself straight before me and stand wagging that bud of a tail, and looking up, with his head a little to the one side. His master I occasionally saw; he used to call me "Maister John," but was laconic as any Spartan.

One fine October afternoon I was leaving the hospital, when I saw the large gate open, and in walked Rab, with that great and easy saunter of his. He looked as if taking possession of the place, like the Duke of Wellington entering a subdued city, satiated with victory and peace. After him came Jess, now white from age, with her cart; and in it a woman carefully wrapped up—the carrier leading the horse anxiously and looking back. When he saw me, James (for his name was James Noble) made a curt and grotesque "boo," and said, "Maister John, this is the mistress; she's got a trouble in her breest—some kind o' an income, we're thinkin'."

By this time I saw the woman's face; she was sitting on a sack filled with straw, with her husband's plaid round her, and his big-coat, with its large, white metal buttons, over her feet.

I never saw a more unforgettable face—pale, serious, *lonely,* delicate, sweet, without being at all what we call fine. She looked sixty, and had on a mutch, white as snow, with its black ribbon; her silvery, smooth hair setting off her dark-gray eyes—eyes such as one sees only twice or thrice in a lifetime, full of suffering, full also of the overcoming of it; her eyebrows black and delicate, and her mouth firm, patient, and contented, which few mouths ever are.

As I have said, I never saw a more beautiful countenance, or one more subdued to settled quiet. "Ailie," said James, "this is Maister John, the young doctor; Rab's friend, ye ken. We often speak aboot you, doctor." She smiled and made a movement, but said nothing, and prepared to come down, putting her plaid aside and rising. Had Solomon, in all his glory, been handing down the Queen of Sheba at his palace gate, he could not have done it more daintily, more tenderly, more like a gentleman than James, the Howland carrier, when he lifted down Ailie, his wife. The contrast of his small, swarthy, weather-beaten, keen, worldly face to hers—pale, subdued, and beautiful—was something wonderful.

Rab looked on concerned and puzzled, but ready for anything that might turn up, were it to strangle the nurse, the porter, or even me. Ailie and he seemed great friends.

"As I was sayin', she's got a kind o' trouble in her breest, doctor; wull ye tak' a look at it?" We walked into the consulting-room, all four; Rab, grim and comic, willing to be happy and confidential if cause should be shown, willing also to be the reverse on the same terms. Ailie sat down, undid her open gown and her lawn handkerchief round her neck, and, without a word, showed me her right breast. I looked at it and examined it carefully, she and James watching me, and Rab eying all three. What could I say? There it was, that had once been so soft, so shapely, so white, so gracious and bountiful, so "full of all blessed condition," hard as a stone, a centre of horrid pain, making that pale face, with its gray, lucid, reasonable eyes, and its sweet, resolved mouth, express the full measure of suffering overcome. Why was that gentle, modest, sweet woman, clean and lovable, condemned by God to bear such a burden?

I got her away to bed. "May Rab and me bide?" said James. "*You* may; and Rab, if he will behave himself." "I'se warrant he's do that, doctor." And in slunk the faithful beast. There are no such dogs now. He belonged to a lost tribe. As I have said, he was brindled, and gray like Rubislaw granite; his hair short, hard, and close, like a lion's; his body thick-set, like a little bull—a sort of compressed Hercules of a dog. He must have been ninety pounds' weight, at the least; he had a large, blunt head; his muzzle black as night; his mouth blacker than any night; a tooth or two—being all he had—gleaming out of his jaws of darkness. His head was scarred with the records of old wounds, a sort of series of fields of battles all over it; one eye out, one ear cropped as close as was Archbishop Leighton's father's; the remaining eye had the power of two; and above it, and in constant communication with it, was a tattered rag of an ear, which was forever unfurling itself, like an old flag; and then that bud of a tail, about one inch long, if it could in any sense be said to be long, being as broad as long—the mobility, the instantaneousness of that bud were very funny and surprising, and its expressive twinklings and winkings, the intercommunications between the eye, the ear, and it, were of the oddest and swiftest.

Rab had the dignity and simplicity of great size; and, having fought his way all along the road to absolute supremacy, he was as mighty in his own line as Julius Cæsar or the Duke of Wellington, and had the gravity of all great fighters.

You must have often observed the likeness of certain men to certain animals, and of certain dogs to men. Now, I never looked at Rab without thinking of the great Baptist preacher, Andrew Fuller. The same large, heavy, menacing, combative, sombre, honest countenance, the same deep, inevitable eye; the same look, as of thunder asleep, but ready—neither a dog nor a man to be trifled with.

Next day my master, the surgeon, examined Ailie. There could be no doubt it must kill her, and soon. If it could be removed—it might never return—it would give her speedy relief—she should have it done. She curtsied, looked at James, and said, "When?" "To-morrow," said the kind surgeon—a man of few words. She and James and Rab and I retired. I noticed that he and she spoke little, but seemed to anticipate everything in each other. The following day, at noon, the students came in, hurrying up the great stair. At the first landing-place, on a small, well-known blackboard, was a bit of paper fastened by wafers, and many remains of old wafers beside it. On the paper were the words:

"*An operation to-day.—J. B.,* CLERK."

Up ran the youths, eager to secure good places; in they crowded, full of interest and talk. "What's the case?" "Which side is it?"

Don't think them heartless; they are neither better nor worse than you or I; they get over their professional horrors, and into their proper work; and in them pity, as an *emotion,* ending in itself or at best in tears and a long-drawn breath, lessens, while pity, as a *motive,* is quickened, and gains power and purpose. It is well for poor human nature that it is so.

The operating-theatre is crowded; much talk and fun, and all the cordiality and stir of youth. The surgeon with his staff of assistants is there. In comes Ailie; one look at her quiets and abates the eager students. That beautiful old woman is too much for them; they sit down, and are dumb, and gaze at her. These rough boys feel the power of her presence. She walks in quietly, but without haste; dressed in her mutch, her neckerchief, her white dimity short-gown, her black bombazeen petticoat, showing her white worsted stockings and her carpet shoes. Behind her was James with Rab. James sat down in the distance, and took that huge and noble head between his knees. Rab looked perplexed and dangerous—forever cocking his ear and dropping it as fast.

Ailie stepped up on a seat, and laid herself on the table, as her friend the surgeon told her; arranged herself, gave a rapid look at James, shut her eyes, rested herself on me, and took my hand. The operation was at once begun; it was necessarily slow; and chloroform—one of God's best gifts to his suffering children—was then unknown. The surgeon did his work. The pale face showed its pain, but was still and silent. Rab's soul was working within him; he saw something strange was going on, blood flowing from his mistress, and she suffering; his

ragged ear was up and importunate; he growled and gave now and
then a sharp, impatient yelp; he would have liked to have done something to that man. But James had him firm, and gave him a *glower*
from time to time, and an intimation of a possible kick; all the better
for James—it kept his eye and his mind off Ailie.

It is over; she is dressed, steps gently and decently down from the
table, looks for James; then turning to the surgeon and the students,
she curtsies, and in a low, clear voice, begs their pardon if she has behaved ill. The students—all of us—wept like children; the surgeon
wrapped her up carefully, and, resting on James and me, Ailie went
to her room, and Rab followed. We put her to bed. James took off his
heavy shoes, crammed with tackets, heel-capped and toe-capped, and
put them carefully under the table, saying: "Maister John, I'm for
nane o' yer strynge nurse bodies for Ailie. I'll be her nurse, and I'll gang
aboot on my stockin' soles as canny as pussy." And so he did; and
handy and clever, and swift and tender as any woman was that horny-
handed, snell, peremptory little man. Everything she got he gave her;
he seldom slept; and often I saw his small, shrewd eyes out of the
darkness, fixed on her. As before, they spoke little.

Rab behaved well, never moving, showing us how meek and gentle
he could be, and occasionally, in his sleep, letting us know that he was
demolishing some adversary. He took a walk with me every day, generally to the Candlemaker Row; but he was sombre and mild; declined
doing battle, though some fit cases offered, and indeed submitted to
sundry indignities; and was always very ready to turn, and came faster
back, and trotted up the stair with much lightness, and went straight
to that door.

Jess, the mare, had been sent, with her weather-beaten cart, to Howgate, and had doubtless her own dim and placid meditations and con-
fusions on the absence of her master and Rab and her unnatural freedom from the road and her cart.

For some days Ailie did well. The wound healed "by the first intention"; for as James said, "Oor Ailie's skin's ower clean to beil." The
students came in quiet and anxious, and surrounded her bed. She said
she liked to see their young, honest faces. The surgeon dressed her,
and spoke to her in his own short, kind way, pitying her through his
eyes, Rab and James outside the circle—Rab being now reconciled, and
even cordial, and having made up his mind that as yet nobody required
worrying, but, as you may suppose, *semper paratus*.

So far well; but, four days after the operation, my patient had a
sudden and long shivering, a "groosin," as she called it. I saw her soon
after; her eyes were too bright, her cheek colored; she was restless, and
ashamed of being so; the balance was lost; mischief had begun. On

looking at the wound, a blush of red told the secret; her pulse was rapid, her breathing anxious and quick; she wasn't herself, as she said, and was vexed at her restlessness. We tried what we could. James did everything, was everywhere, never in the way, never out of it; Rab subsided under the table into a dark place, and was motionless, all but his eye, which followed every one. Ailie got worse; began to wander in her mind, gently; was more demonstrative in her ways to James, rapid in her questions, and sharp at times. He was vexed, and said, "She was never that way afore, no, never." For a time she knew her head was wrong, and was always asking our pardon—the dear, gentle old woman; then delirium set in strong, without pause. Her brain gave way, and then came that terrible spectacle,

> *"The intellectual power, through words and things,*
> *Went sounding on, a dim and perilous way";*

she sang bits of old songs and Psalms, stopping suddenly, mingling the Psalms of David and the diviner words of his Son and Lord with homely odds and ends of ballads.

Nothing more touching, or in a sense more strangely beautiful, did I ever witness. Her tremulous, rapid, affectionate, eager, Scotch voice—the swift, aimless, bewildered mind, the baffled utterance, the bright and perilous eye; some wild words, some household cares, something for James, the names of the dead, Rab called rapidly and in a "fremyt" voice, and he starting up, surprised, and slinking off as if he were to blame somehow, or had been dreaming he heard. Many eager questions and beseechings which James and I could make nothing of, and on which she seemed to set her all, and then sink back ununderstood. It was very sad, but better than many things that are not called sad. James hovered about, put out and miserable, but active and exact as ever; read to her, when there was a lull, short bits from the Psalms, prose and metre, chanting the latter in his own rude and serious way, showing great knowledge of the fit words, bearing up like a man, and doating over her as his "ain Ailie." "Ailie, ma woman!" "Ma ain bonnie wee dawtie!"

The end was drawing on; the golden bowl was breaking; the silver cord was fast being loosed—that *animula, blandula, vagula, hospes, comesque,* was about to flee. The body and the soul—companions for sixty years—were being sundered and taking leave. She was walking, alone, through the valley of that shadow into which one day we must all enter—and yet she was not alone, for we know whose rod and staff were comforting her.

One night she had fallen quiet, and, as we hoped, asleep; her eyes were shut. We put down the gas, and sat watching her. Suddenly she sat up in bed, and, taking a bed-gown which was lying on it rolled up, she held it eagerly to her breast—to the right side. We could see her eyes bright with a surprising tenderness and joy, bending over this bundle of clothes. She held it as a woman holds her sucking child; opening out her night-gown impatiently, and holding it close and brooding over it and murmuring foolish little words, as over one whom his mother comforteth, and who sucks and is satisfied. It was pitiful and strange to see her wasted, dying look, keen and yet vague —her immense love.

"Preserve me!" groaned James, giving way. And then she rocked back and forward, as if to make it sleep, hushing it, and wasting on it her infinite fondness. "Wae's me, doctor; I declare she's thinkin' it's that bairn." "What bairn?" "The only bairn we ever had; our wee Mysie, and she's in the Kingdom forty years and mair." It was plainly true; the pain in the breast, telling its urgent story to a bewildered, ruined brain, was misread and mistaken; it suggested to her the un-easiness of a breast full of milk, and then the child; and so again once more they were together, and she had her ain wee Mysie on her bosom.

This was the close. She sank rapidly; the delirium left her; but, as she whispered, she was "clean silly"; it was the lightening before the final darkness. After having for some time lain still, her eyes shut, she said, "James!" He came close to her, and, lifting up her calm, clear, beautiful eyes, she gave him a long look, turned to me kindly but shortly, looked for Rab but could not see him, then turned to her hus-band again, as if she would never leave off looking, shut her eyes, and composed herself. She lay for some time breathing quick, and passed away so gently that, when we thought she was gone, James, in his old-fashioned way, held the mirror to her face. After a long pause, one small spot of dimness was breathed out; it vanished away, and never returned, leaving the blank, clear darkness without a stain. "What is our life? It is even as a vapor, which appeareth for a little time, and then vanisheth away."

Rab all this time had been full awake and motionless; he came for-ward beside us; Ailie's hand, which James had held, was hanging down; it was soaked with his tears; Rab licked it all over carefully, looked at her, and returned to his place under the table.

James and I sat, I don't know how long, but for some time. Saying nothing, he started up abruptly, and with some noise went to the table, and, putting his right fore and middle fingers each into a shoe, pulled them out and put them on, breaking one of the leather latchets, and muttering in anger, "I never did the like o' that afore!"

I believe he never did; nor after either. "Rab!" he said, roughly, and, pointing with his thumb to the bottom of the bed. Rab leaped up and settled himself, his head and eye to the dead face. "Maister John, ye'll wait for me," said the carrier; and disappeared in the darkness, thundering down-stairs in his heavy shoes. I ran to a front window; there he was, already round the house and out at the gate, fleeing like a shadow.

I was afraid about him, and yet not afraid; so I sat down beside Rab, and, being wearied, fell asleep. I awoke from a sudden noise outside. It was November, and there had been a heavy fall of snow. Rab was *in statu quo;* he heard the noise, too, and plainly knew it, but never moved. I looked out; and there, at the gate, in the dim morning—for the sun was not up—was Jess and the cart, a cloud of steam rising from the old mare. I did not see James; he was already at the door, and came up the stairs and met me. It was less than three hours since he left, and he must have posted out—who knows how?—to Howgate, full nine miles off, yoked Jess, and driven her astonished into town. He had an armful of blankets, and was streaming with perspiration. He nodded to me, and spread out on the floor two pairs of clean old blankets having at their corners, "A. G., 1794," in large letters in red worsted. These were the initials of Alison Graeme, and James may have looked in at her from without—himself unseen but not unthought of—when he was "wat, wat, and weary," and, after having walked many a mile over the hills, may have seen her sitting, while "a' the lave were sleeping," and by the firelight working her name on the blankets for her ain James's bed.

He motioned Rab down, and, taking his wife in his arms, laid her in the blankets, and happed her carefully and firmly up, leaving the face uncovered; and then, lifting her, he nodded again sharply to me, and with a resolved but utterly miserable face strode along the passage and down-stairs, followed by Rab. I followed with a light; but he didn't need it. I went out, holding stupidly the candle in my hand in the calm, frosty air; we were soon at the gate. I could have helped him, but I saw he was not to be meddled with, and he was strong, and did not need it. He laid her down as tenderly, as safely, as he had lifted her out ten days before—as tenderly as when he had her first in his arms when she was only "A. G."—sorted her, leaving that beautiful sealed face open to the heavens; and then, taking Jess by the head, he moved away. He did not notice me, neither did Rab, who presided behind the cart.

I stood till they passed through the long shadow of the College and turned up Nicolson Street. I heard the solitary cart sound through the streets, and die away and come again; and I returned, thinking of that company going up Libberton Brae, then along Roslin Muir, the morning light touching the Pentlands, and making them like onlooking ghosts; then down the hill through Auchindinny woods, past "haunted Woodhouselee"; and as daybreak came sweeping up the bleak Lammermuirs, and fell on his own door, the company would stop, and James would take the key, and lift Ailie up again, laying her on her own bed, and, having put Jess up, would return with Rab and shut the door.

James buried his wife, with his neighbors mourning, Rab watching the proceedings from a distance. It was snow, and that black, ragged hole would look strange in the midst of the swelling, spotless cushion of white. James looked after everything; then rather suddenly fell ill, and took to bed; was insensible when the doctor came, and soon died. A sort of low fever was prevailing in the village, and his want of sleep, his exhaustion, and his misery made him apt to take it. The grave was not difficult to reopen. A fresh fall of snow had again made all things white and smooth; Rab once more looked on, and slunk home to the stable.

And what of Rab? I asked for him next week at the new carrier who got the good-will of James's business and was now master of Jess and her cart. "How's Rab?" He put me off, and said, rather rudely, "What's *your* business wi' the dowg?" I was not to be so put off. "Where's Rab?" He, getting confused and red, and intermeddling with his hair, said, "'Deed, sir, Rab's deid." "Dead! What did he die of?" "Weel, sir," said he, getting redder, "he didna' exactly dee; he was killed. I had to brain him wi' a rack-pin; there was nae doin' wi' him. He lay in the treviss wi' the mear, and wadna come oot. I tempit him wi' kail and meat, but he wad tak naething, and keepit me frae feeding the beast, and he was aye gurrin', and grup, gruppin' me by the legs. I was laith to mak' awa' wi' the auld dowg, his like wasna atween this and Thornhill—but, 'deed, sir, I could do naething else." I believed him. Fit end for Rab, quick and complete. His teeth and his friends gone, why should he keep the peace and be civil?

He was buried in the braeface, near the burn, the children of the village, his companions, who used to make very free with him and sit on his ample stomach as he lay half asleep at the door in the sun, watching the solemnity.

12

The Half-Brothers

BY ELIZABETH C. GASKELL

MY mother was twice married.
She never spoke of her first husband, and it is only from other people
that I have learnt what little I know about him. I believe she was
scarcely seventeen when she was married to him: and he was barely
one-and-twenty. He rented a small farm up in Cumberland, somewhere
towards the sea-coast; but he was perhaps too young and inexperienced
to have the charge of land and cattle; anyhow, his affairs did not
prosper, and he fell into ill-health, and died of consumption before they
had been three years man and wife, leaving my mother a young widow
of twenty, with a little child only just able to walk, and the farm on her
hands for four years more by the lease, with half the stock on it dead,
or sold off one by one to pay the more pressing debts, and with no
money to purchase more, or even to buy the provisions needed for the
small consumption of every day. There was another child coming, too;
and sad and sorry, I believe, she was to think of it. A dreary winter
she must have had in her lonesome dwelling with never another near
it for miles around; her sister came to bear her company, and they two
planned and plotted how to make every penny they could raise go as
far as possible. I can't tell you how it happened that my little sister,
whom I never saw, came to sicken and die; but, as if my poor mother's
cup was not full enough, only a fortnight before Gregory was born
the little girl took ill of scarlet fever, and in a week she lay dead. My
mother was, I believe, just stunned with this last blow. My aunt has
told me that she did not cry; Aunt Fanny would have been thankful if
she had; but she sat holding the poor wee lassie's hand, and looking
in her pretty, pale, dead face, without so much as shedding a tear.
And it was all the same, when they had to take her away to be buried.

She just kissed the child, and sat her down in the window-seat to watch the little black train of people (neighbours—my aunt, and one far-off cousin, who were all the friends they could muster) go winding away amongst the snow, which had fallen thinly over the country the night before. When my aunt came back from the funeral, she found my mother in the same place, and as dry-eyed as ever. So she continued until after Gregory was born; and, somehow, his coming seemed to loosen the tears, and she cried day and night, till my aunt and the other watcher looked at each other in dismay, and would fain have stopped her if they had but known how. But she bade them let her alone, and not be over-anxious, for every drop she shed eased her brain, which had been in a terrible state before for want of the power to cry. She seemed after that to think of nothing but her new little baby; she had hardly appeared to remember either her husband or her little daughter that lay dead in Brigham churchyard—at least so Aunt Fanny said; but she was a great talker, and my mother was very silent by nature, and I think Aunt Fanny may have been mistaken in believing that my mother never thought of her husband and child just because she never spoke about them. Aunt Fanny was older than my mother, and had a way of treating her like a child; but, for all that, she was a kind, warm-hearted creature, who thought more of her sister's welfare than she did of her own; and it was on her bit of money that they principally lived, and on what the two could earn by work-ing for the great Glasgow sewing merchants. But by-and-by my mother's eyesight began to fail. It was not that she was exactly blind, for she could see well enough to guide herself about the house, and to do a good deal of domestic work; but she could no longer do fine sew-ing and earn money. It must have been with the heavy crying she had had in her day, for she was but a young creature at this time, and as pretty a young woman, I have heard people say, as any on the country side. She took it sadly to heart that she could no longer gain anything towards the keep of herself and her child. My Aunt Fanny would fain have persuaded her that she had enough to do in managing their cot-tage and minding Gregory; but my mother knew that they were pinched, and that Aunt Fanny herself had not as much to eat, even of the commonest kind of food, as she could have done with; and as for Gregory, he was not a strong lad, and needed, not more food—for he always had enough, whoever went short—but better nourishment, and more flesh meat. One day—it was Aunt Fanny who told me all this about my poor mother, long after her death—as the sisters were sitting together, Aunt Fanny working, and my mother hushing Greg-ory to sleep, William Preston, who was afterwards my father, came in. He was reckoned an old bachelor; I suppose he was long past forty, and he was one of the wealthiest farmers thereabouts, and had known my grandfather well, and my mother and my aunt in their more prosperous days. He sat down, and began to twirl his hat by way of being agreeable; my Aunt Fanny talked, and he listened and looked at my mother. But he said very little, either on that visit, or on many another that he paid before he spoke out what had been the real purpose of his calling so often all along, and from the very first time he came to their house. One Sunday, however, my Aunt Fanny stayed away from church, and took care of the child, and my mother went alone. When she came back, she ran straight upstairs, without going into the kitchen to look at Gregory or speak any word to her sister, and Aunt Fanny heard her cry as if her heart was breaking; so she went up and scolded her right well through the bolted door, till at last she got her to open it. And then she threw herself on my aunt's neck, and told her that William Preston had asked her to marry him, and had promised to take good charge of her boy, and to let him want for nothing, neither in the way of keep nor of education, and that she had consented. Aunt Fanny was a good deal shocked at this; for, as I have said, she had often thought that my mother had forgotten her first husband very quickly, and now here was proof positive of it, if she could so soon think of marrying again. Besides, as Aunt Fanny used to say, she herself would have been a far more suitable match for a man of William Preston's age than Helen, who, though she was a widow, had not seen her four-and-twentieth summer. However, as Aunt Fanny said, they had not asked her advice; and there was much to be said on the other side of the question. Helen's eyesight would never be good for much again, and as William Preston's wife she would never need to do anything, if she chose to sit with her hands before her; and a boy was a great charge to a widowed mother; and now there would be a decent steady man to see after him. So, by-and-by, Aunt Fanny seemed to take a brighter view of the marriage than did my mother herself, who hardly ever looked up, and never smiled after the day when she promised William Preston to be his wife. But much as she had loved Gregory before, she seemed to love him more now. She was continually talking to him when they were alone, though he was far too young to understand her moaning words, or give her any comfort, except by his caresses.

At last William Preston and she were wed; and she went to be mistress of a well-stocked house, not above half an hour's walk from where Aunt Fanny lived. I believe she did all that she could to please my father; and a more dutiful wife, I have heard him himself say, could never have been. But she did not love him, and he soon found it out. She loved Gregory, and she did not love him. Perhaps, love would have come in time, if he had been patient enough to wait; but it just turned him sour to see how her eye brightened and her colour came at the sight of that little child, while for him who had given her so much she had only gentle words as cold as ice. He got to taunt her with the difference in her manner, as if that would bring love; and he took a positive dislike to Gregory—he was so jealous of the ready love that always gushed out like a spring of fresh water when he came near. He wanted her to love him more, and perhaps that was all well and good, but he wanted her to love her child less, and that was an evil wish. One day he gave way to his temper, and cursed and swore at Gregory, who had got into some mischief, as children will; my mother made some excuse for him; my father said it was hard enough to have to keep another man's child without having it perpetually held up in its naughtiness by his wife, who ought to be always in the same mind as he was; and so from little they got to more; and the end of it was, that my mother took to her bed before her time, and I was born that very day. My father was glad, and proud, and sorry, all in a breath; glad and proud that a son was born to him; and sorry for his poor wife's state, and to think how his angry words had brought it on. But he was a man who liked better to be angry than sorry, so he soon found out that it was all Gregory's fault, and owed him an additional grudge for having hastened my birth. He had another grudge against him before long. My mother began to sink the day after I was born. My father sent to Carlisle for doctors, and would have coined his heart's blood into gold to save her, if that could have been; but it could not. My Aunt Fanny used to say sometimes, that she thought that Helen did not wish to live, and so just let herself die away without trying to take hold on life; but when I questioned her, she owned that my mother did all the doctors bade her do, with the same sort of uncomplaining patience with which she had acted through life. One of her last requests was to have Gregory laid in her bed by my side, and then she made him take hold of my little hand. Her husband came in while she was looking at us so, and when he bent tenderly over her to ask her how she felt now, and seemed to gaze on us two little half-brothers, with a grave sort of kindliness, she looked up in his face and smiled, almost her first smile at him; and such a sweet smile! as more besides Aunt Fanny have said. In an hour she was dead. Aunt Fanny came to live with us. It was the best thing that could be done. My father would have been glad to return to his old mode of bachelor life, but what could he do with two little children? He needed a woman to take care of him, and who so fitting as his wife's elder sister? So she had the charge of me from my birth; and for a time I was weakly, as was but natural, and she was always beside me, night and day watching over me, and my father nearly as anxious as she. For his land had come down from father to son for more than three hundred years, and he would have cared for me merely as his flesh and blood that was to inherit the land after him. But he needed something to love, for all that, to most people, he was a stern, hard man, and he took to me as, I fancy, he had taken to no human being before—as he might have taken to my mother, if she had had no former life for him to be jealous of. I loved him back again right heartily. I loved all around me, I believe, for everybody was kind to me. After a time, I overcame my original weakliness of constitution, and was just a bonny, strong-looking lad whom every passer-by noticed, when my father took me with him to the nearest town.

At home I was the darling of my aunt, the tenderly-beloved of my father, the pet and plaything of the old domestics, the "young master" of the farm-labourers, before whom I played many a lordly antic, assuming a sort of authority which sat oddly enough, I doubt not, on such a baby as I was.

Gregory was three years older than I. Aunt Fanny was always kind to him in deed and in action, but she did not often think about him, she had fallen so completely into the habit of being engrossed by me, from the fact of my having come into her charge as a delicate baby. My father never got over his grudging dislike to his step-son, who had so innocently wrestled with him for the possession of my mother's heart. I mistrust me, too, that my father always considered him as the cause of my mother's death and my early delicacy; and utterly unreasonable as this may seem, I believe my father rather cherished his feeling of alienation to my brother as a duty, than strove to repress it. Yet not for the world would my father have grudged him anything that money could purchase. That was, as it were, in the bond when he had wedded my mother. Gregory was lumpish and loutish, awkward and ungainly, marring whatever he meddled in, and many a hard word and sharp scolding did he get from the people about the farm, who hardly waited till my father's back was turned before they rated the step-son. I am ashamed—my heart is sore to think how I fell into the fashion of the family, and slighted my poor orphan step-brother. I don't think I ever scouted him, or was wilfully ill-natured to him; but the habit of being considered in all things, and being treated as something uncommon and superior, made me insolent in my prosperity, and I exacted more than Gregory was always willing to grant, and then, irritated, I sometimes repeated the disparaging words I had heard others use with regard to him, without fully understanding their meaning. Whether he did or not I cannot tell. I am afraid he did. He used to turn silent and quiet—sullen and sulky, my father thought it: stupid

Aunt Fanny used to call it. But every one said he was stupid and dull,
and this stupidity and dulness grew upon him. He would sit without
speaking a word, sometimes, for hours; then my father would bid him
rise and do some piece of work, may be, about the farm. And he would
take three or four tellings before he would go. When we were sent to
school, it was all the same. He could never be made to remember his
lessons; the schoolmaster grew weary of scolding and flogging, and
at last advised my father just to take him away, and set him to some
farm-work that might not be above his comprehension. I think he was
more gloomy and stupid than ever after this, yet he was not a cross
lad; he was patient and good-natured, and would try to do a kind turn
for anyone, even if they had been scolding or cuffing him not a minute
before. But very often his attempts at kindness ended in some mischief
to the very people he was trying to serve, owing to his awkward, ungainly ways. I suppose I was a clever lad; at any rate, I always got
plenty of praise; and was, as we called it, the cock of the school. The
schoolmaster said I could learn anything I chose, but my father, who
had no great learning himself, saw little use in much for me, and took
me away betimes, and kept me with him about the farm. Gregory was
made into a kind of shepherd, receiving his training under old Adam,
who was nearly past his work. I think old Adam was almost the first
person who had a good opinion of Gregory. He stood to it that my
brother had good parts, though he did not rightly know how to bring
them out; and, for knowing the bearings of the Fells, he said he had
never seen a lad like him. My father would try to bring Adam round
to speak of Gregory's faults and shortcomings; but, instead of that,
he would praise him twice as much, as soon as he found out what was
my father's object.

   One winter-time, when I was about sixteen and Gregory nineteen,
I was sent by my father on an errand to a place about seven miles distant by the road, but only about four by the Fells. He bade me return
by the road whichever way I took in going, for the evenings closed in
early, and were often thick and misty; besides which, old Adam, now
paralytic and bed-ridden, foretold a downfall of snow before long.
I soon got to my journey's end, and soon had done my business; earlier
by an hour, I thought, than my father had expected, so I took the
decision of the way by which I would return into my own hands, and set
off back again over the Fells, just as the first shades of evening began
to fall. It looked dark and gloomy enough; but everything was so still
that I thought I should have plenty of time to get home before the
snow came down. Off I set at a pretty quick pace. But night came on
quicker. The right path was clear enough in the daytime, although at

several points two or three exactly similar diverged from the same place; but when there was a good light, the traveller was guided by the sight of distant objects—a piece of rock—a fall in the ground— which were quite invisible to me now. I plucked up a brave heart, however, and took what seemed to me the right road. It was wrong, nevertheless, and led me whither I knew not, but to some wild boggy moor where the solitude seemed painful, intense, as if never footfall of man had come thither to break the silence. I tried to shout—with the dimmest possible hope of being heard—rather to reassure myself by the sound of my own voice; but my voice came husky and short, and yet it dismayed me; it seemed so weird and strange, in that noiseless expanse of black darkness. Suddenly the air was filled thick with dusky flakes, my face and hands were wet with snow. It cut me off from the slightest knowledge of where I was, for I lost every idea of the direction from which I had come, so that I could not even retrace my steps; it hemmed me in, thicker, thicker, with a darkness that might be felt. The boggy soil on which I stood quaked under me if I remained long in one place, and yet I dared not move far. All my youthful hardiness seemed to leave me at once. I was on the point of crying, and only very shame seemed to keep it down. To save myself from shedding tears, I shouted—terrible, wild shouts for bare life they were. I turned sick as I paused to listen; no answering sound came but the unfeeling echoes. Only the noiseless, pitiless snow kept falling thicker, thicker—faster, faster! I was growing numb and sleepy. I tried to move about, but I dared not go far, for fear of the precipices which, I knew, abounded in certain places on the Fells. Now and then I stood still and shouted again; but my voice was getting choked with tears, as I thought of the desolate helpless death I was to die, and how little they at home, sitting round the warm, red, bright fire, wotted what was become of me—and how my poor father would grieve for me— it would surely kill him—it would break his heart, poor old man! Aunt Fanny too—was this to be the end of all her cares for me? I began to review my life in a strange kind of vivid dream, in which the various scenes of my few boyish years passed before me like visions. In a pang of agony, caused by such remembrance of my short life, I gathered up my strength and called out once more, a long, despairing, wailing cry, to which I had no hope of obtaining any answer, save from the echoes around, dulled as the sound might be by the thickened air. To my surprise I heard a cry—almost as long, as wild as mine—so wild, that it seemed unearthly, and I almost thought it must be the voice of some of the mocking spirits of the Fells, about whom I had heard so many tales. My heart suddenly began to beat fast and loud. I could not reply for a minute or two. I nearly fancied I had lost the power of utterance. Just at this moment a dog barked. Was it Lassie's bark—my brother's collie?—an ugly enough brute, with a white, ill-looking face, that my father always kicked whenever he saw it, partly for its own demerits, partly because it belonged to my brother. On such occasions Gregory would whistle Lassie away, and go off and sit with her in some out-house. My father had once or twice been ashamed of himself, when the poor collie had yowled out with the suddenness of the pain, and had relieved himself of his self-reproach by blaming my brother, who, he said, had no notion of training a dog, and was enough to ruin any collie in Christendom with his stupid way of allowing them to lie by the kitchen fire. To all which Gregory would answer nothing, nor even seem to hear, but go on looking absent and moody.

Yes! there again! It was Lassie's bark! Now or never! I lifted up my voice and shouted "Lassie! Lassie! For God's sake, Lassie!" Another moment, and the great white-faced Lassie was curving and gambolling with delight round my feet and legs, looking, however, up in my face with her intelligent, apprehensive eyes, as if fearing lest I might greet her with a blow, as I had done oftentimes before. But I cried with glad-ness, as I stooped down and patted her. My mind was sharing in my body's weakness, and I could not reason, but I knew that help was at hand. A grey figure came more and more distinctly out of the thick, close-pressing darkness. It was Gregory wrapped in his maud.

"Oh, Gregory!" said I, and I fell upon his neck, unable to speak an-other word. He never spoke much, and made me no answer for some little time. Then he told me we must move, we must walk for the dear life—we must find our road home, if possible; but we must move, or we should be frozen to death.

"Don't you know the way home?" I asked.

"I thought I did when I set out, but I am doubtful now. The snow blinds me, and I am feared that in moving about just now, I have lost the right gait homewards."

He had his shepherd's staff with him, and by dint of plunging it before us at every step we took—clinging close to each other, we went on safely enough, as far as not falling down any of the steep rocks, but it was slow, dreary work. My brother, I saw, was more guided by Lassie and the way she took than anything else, trusting to her instinct. It was too dark to see far before us; but he called her back continually, and noted from what quarter she returned, and shaped our slow steps accordingly. But the tedious motion scarcely kept my very blood from freezing. Every bone, every fibre in my body seemed first to ache, and then to swell, and then to turn numb with the intense cold. My brother bore it better than I, from having been more out upon the hills. He did not speak, except to call Lassie. I strove to be brave, and not complain; but now I felt the deadly fatal sleep stealing over me.

"I can go no farther," I said, in a drowsy tone. I remember I suddenly became dogged and resolved. Sleep I would, were it only for five minutes. If death were to be the consequence, sleep I would. Gregory stood still. I suppose, he recognized the peculiar phase of suffering to which I had been brought by the cold.

"It is of no use," said he, as if to himself. "We are no nearer home than we were when we started, as far as I can tell. Our only chance is in Lassie. Here! roll thee in my maud, lad, and lay thee down on this sheltered side of this bit of rock. Creep close under it, lad, and I'll lie by thee, and strive to keep the warmth in us. Stay! hast gotten aught about thee they'll know at home?"

I felt him unkind thus to keep me from slumber, but on his repeating the question, I pulled out my pocket-handkerchief, of some showy pattern, which Aunt Fanny had hemmed for me. Gregory took it, and tied it round Lassie's neck.

"Hie thee, Lassie, hie thee home!" And the white-faced ill-favoured brute was off like a shot in the darkness. Now I might lie down—now I might sleep. In my drowsy stupor, I felt that I was being tenderly covered up by my brother; but what with I neither knew nor cared—I was too dull, too selfish, too numb to think and reason, or I might have known that in that bleak bare place there was naught to wrap me in, save what was taken off another. I was glad enough when he ceased his cares and lay down by me. I took his hand.

"Thou canst not remember, lad, how we lay together thus by our dying mother. She put thy small, wee hand in mine—I reckon she sees us now; and belike we shall soon be with her. Anyhow, God's will be done."

"Dear Gregory," I muttered, and crept nearer to him for warmth. He was talking still, and again about our mother, when I fell asleep. In an instant—or so it seemed—there were many voices about me— many faces hovering round me—the sweet luxury of warmth was stealing into every part of me. I was in my own little bed at home. I am thankful to say, my first word was "Gregory?"

A look passed from one to another—my father's stern old face strove in vain to keep its sternness; his mouth quivered, his eyes filled with unwonted tears.

"I would have given him half my land—I would have blessed him as my son—Oh God! I would have knelt at his feet, and asked him to forgive my hardness of heart."

I heard no more. A whirl came through my brain, catching me back to death.

I came slowly to my consciousness, weeks afterwards. My father's hair was white when I recovered, and his hands shook as he looked into my face.

We spoke no more of Gregory. We could not speak of him; but he was strangely in our thoughts. Lassie came and went with never a word of blame; nay, my father would try to stroke her, but she shrank away; and he, as if reproved by the poor dumb beast, would sigh, and be silent and abstracted for a time.

Aunt Fanny—always a talker—told me all. How, on that fatal night, my father, irritated by my prolonged absence, and probably more anxious than he cared to show, had been fierce and imperious, even beyond his wont, to Gregory; had upbraided him with his father's poverty, his own stupidity which made his services good for nothing —for so, in spite of the old shepherd, my father always chose to consider them. At last, Gregory had risen up, and whistled Lassie out with him—poor Lassie crouching underneath his chair for fear of a kick or a blow. Some time before, there had been some talk between my father and my aunt respecting my return; and when Aunt Fanny told me all this, she said she fancied that Gregory might have noticed the coming storm, and gone out silently to meet me. Three hours afterwards, when all were running about in wild alarm, not knowing whither to go in search of me—not even missing Gregory, or heeding his absence, poor fellow—poor, poor fellow!—Lassie came home, with my handkerchief tied round her neck. They knew and understood, and the whole strength of the farm was turned out to follow her, with wraps, and blankets, and brandy, and everything that could be thought of. I lay in chilly sleep, but still alive, beneath the rock that Lassie guided them to. I was covered over with my brother's plaid, and his thick shepherd's coat was carefully wrapped round my feet. He was in his shirt-sleeves—his arm thrown over me—a quiet smile (he had hardly ever smiled in life) upon his still, cold face.

My father's last words were, "God forgive me my hardness of heart towards the fatherless child!"

And what marked the depth of his feeling of repentance, perhaps more than all, considering the passionate love he bore my mother, was this: we found a paper of directions after his death, in which he desired that he might lie at the foot of the grave in which, by his desire, poor Gregory had been laid with OUR MOTHER.

13

Sultan Stork

BEING
THE ONE THOUSAND AND SECOND NIGHT

Translated from the Persian

By Major G. O'G. Gahagan, H.E.I.C.S.

BY WILLIAM MAKEPEACE THACKERAY

I. THE MAGIC POWDER

"AFTER those long wars," began Scheherazade, as soon as her husband had given the accustomed signal, "after those long wars in Persia, which ended in the destruction of the ancient and monstrous Ghebir, or fire-worship, in that country, and the triumph of our holy religion: for though, my lord, the Persians are Soonies by creed, and not followers of Omar, as every true believer in the Prophet ought to be, nevertheless——"

"A truce to you nevertheless, madam," interrupted the Sultan. "I want to hear a story, and not a controversy."

"Well, sir, after the expulsion of the Ahrimanians, King Abdulraman governed Persia worthily until he died after a surfeit of peaches, and left his throne to his son Mushook, or the Beautiful—a title, by the way," remarked Scheherazade, blushing, and casting down her lovely eyes, "which ought at present to belong to Your Majesty."

Although the Sultan only muttered, "Stuff and nonsense, get along with you," it was evident, by the blush in the royal countenance, and the smile which lightened up the black waves of the imperial beard, as a sunbeam does the sea, that His Majesty was pleased, and that the storm was about to disappear. Scheherazade continued:

135

"Mushook, ascending the throne, passed honourably the first year of his reign in perfecting the work so happily begun by his royal father. He caused a general slaughter of all the Ghebirs in his land to take place, not only of the royal family, but of the common sort; nor of the latter did there remain any unkilled (if I may coin such a word) or unconverted; and, as to the former, they were extirpated root and branch, with the exception of one most dogged enchanter and Ahrimanian, Ghuzroo by name, who, with his son Ameen-Adhawb, managed to escape out of Persia, and fled to India, where still existed some remnants of their miserably superstitious race. But Bombay is a long way from Persia, and at the former place it was that Ghuzroo and his son took refuge, giving themselves up to their diabolical enchantments and worship, and calling themselves King and Prince of Persia. For them, however, their plans and their pretensions, King Mushook little cared, often singing, in allusion to them, those well-known verses of Hafiz:

" 'Buldoo says that he is the rightful owner of the rice-field,
  And declares that the lamb is his undisputed property.
  Brag, O Buldoo, about your rights and your possessions;
  But the lamb and rice are his who dines on the pilau.' "

The Sultan could hardly contain himself for laughing at this admirable epigram, and, without further interruption, Scheherazade continued her story:

"King Mushook was then firmly established on his throne, and had for his Vizier that famous and worthy statesman, Munsoor; one of the ugliest and oldest, but also one of the wisest of men, and attached beyond everything to the Mushook dynasty, though his teeth had been knocked out by the royal slipper."

"And, no doubt, Mushook served him right," observed the Sultan.

"Though his teeth had been knocked out, yet wisdom and persuasion ever hung on his lips; though one of his eyes, in a fit of royal indignation, had been closed for ever, yet no two eyes in all the empire were as keen as his remaining ball; he was, in a word, the very best and honestest of Viziers, as fat and merry, too, as he was wise and faithful.

"One day as Shah Mushook was seated after dinner in his beautiful garden-pavilion at Tehran, sick of political affairs, which is no wonder —sick even of the beautiful houris who had been dancing before him to the sound of lutes and mandolins—tired of the jokes and antics of his buffoons and story-tellers—let me say at once dyspeptic, and in a shocking ill-humour; old Munsoor (who had already had the royal pipe and slippers flung half a dozen times at his head), willing by any means to dissipate his master's ill-will, lighted in the outer courts of the palace, as he was hieing disconsolately home, upon an old pedlar-woman, who was displaying her wares to a crowd of wondering persons and palace servants, and making them die with laughing at her jokes.

"The Vizier drew near, heard her jokes[1] and examined her wares, which were extraordinarily beautiful, and determined to conduct her into the august presence of the King.

"Mushook was so pleased with her stock in trade that, like a royal and generous prince, he determined to purchase her whole pack, box, trinkets, and all; giving her own price for them. So she yielded up her box, only taking out of one of the drawers a little bottle, surrounded by a paper, not much bigger than an ordinary bottle of Macassar oil."

"Macassar oil! Here's an anachronism!" thought the Sultan. But he suffered his wife to proceed with her tale.

"The old woman was putting this bottle away into her pocket, when the Sultan's eye lighted upon it, and he asked her, in a fury, why she was making off with his property?

"She said she had sold him the whole pack, with the exception of that bottle; and that it could be of no good to him, as it was only a common old crystal bottle, a family piece, of no sort of use to any but the owner.

" 'What is there in the bottle?' exclaimed the keen and astute Vizier.

"At this the old woman blushed as far as her weazened old face could blush, hemmed, ha'd, stuttered, and showed evident signs of confusion. She said it was only a common bottle—that there was nothing in it—that is, only a powder—a little rhubarb.

" 'It's poison!' roared Mushook; 'I'm sure it's poison!' And he forthwith seized the old hag by the throat, and would have strangled her, if the Vizier had not wisely interposed, remarking, that if the woman were strangled there could be no means of knowing what the bottle contained.

" 'To show you, sire, that it is not poison,' cried the old creature to the King, who by this time had wrenched the bottle out of her pocket, and held it in his hand, 'I will take a little of the powder it contains.' Whereupon His Majesty called for a teaspoon, determined to administer the powder to her himself. The chief of the eunuchs brought the teaspoon, the King emptied a little of the powder into it, and bidding the old wretch open her great, black, gaping, ruinous mouth, put a little of the powder on her tongue; when, to his astonishment, and as true as I sit here, her old hooked beak of a nose (which, by way of precaution, he was holding in his fingers) slipped from between them;

---

[1] These, as they have no sort of point except for the Persian scholar, are here entirely omitted.—G. O'G. G.

the old, black tongue, on which he placed the teaspoon, disappeared from under it; and not only the nose and the tongue, but the whole old woman vanished away entirely, and His Majesty stood there with his two hands extended—the one looking as if it pulled an imaginary nose, the other holding an empty teaspoon; and he himself staring wildly at vacancy!"

"Scheherazade," said the Sultan gravely, "you are drawing the long-bow a little too strongly. In the thousand and one nights that we have passed together, I have given credit to every syllable you uttered. But this tale about the old woman, my love, is, upon my honour, too mon-strous."

"Not a whit, sir; and I assure Your Majesty that it is as true as the Koran itself. It is a fact perfectly well authenticated, and written after-wards, by King Mushook's orders, in the Persian annals. The old woman vanished altogether; the King was left standing there with the bottle and spoon; the Vizier was dumb with wonder; and the only thing seen to quit the room was a little canary-bird, that suddenly started up before the King's face, and chirping out 'kikiriki,' flew out of the open window, skimmed over the ponds and plane trees in the garden, and was last seen wheeling round and round the minaret of the great mosque of Tehran."

"Mashallah!" exclaimed the Sultan. "Heaven is great; but I never should have credited the tale, had not you, my love, vouched for it. Go on, madam, and tell us what became of the bottle and Sultan Mushook."

"Sir, when the King had recovered from his astonishment, he fell, as his custom was, into a fury, and could only be calmed by the argu-ments and persuasions of the Grand Vizier.

"'It is evident, sire,' observed that dignitary, 'that the powder which you have just administered possesses some magic property, either to make the persons taking it invisible, or else to cause them to change into the form of some bird or other animal; and very possibly the canary-bird which so suddenly appeared and disappeared just now, was the very old woman with whom Your Majesty was talking. We can easily see whether the powder creates invisibility, by trying its effects upon someone—the chief of the eunuchs, for example.' And ac-cordingly Hudge Gudge, the chief of the eunuchs, against whom the Vizier had an old grudge, was compelled, with many wry faces, to taste the mixture.

"'Thou art so ugly, Hudge Gudge,' exclaimed the Vizier with a grin, "that to render thee invisible will only be conferring a benefit upon thee.' But, strange to say, though the eunuch was made to swallow a large dose, the powder had no sort of effect upon him, and he stood before His Majesty and the Prime Minister as ugly and as visible as ever.

"They now thought of looking at the paper in which the bottle was wrapped, and the King, not knowing how to read himself, bade the Grand Vizier explain to him the meaning of the writing which appeared upon the paper.

"But the Vizier confessed, after examining the document, that he could not understand it; and though it was presented at the divan that day, to all the councillors, mollahs, and men learned in the law, not one of them could understand a syllable of the strange characters written on the paper. The council broke up in consternation; for His Majesty swore that if the paper was not translated before the next day at noon, he would bastinado every one of the privy council, beginning with His Excellency the Grand Vizier.

"'Who has such a sharp wit as necessity?' touchingly exclaims the poet Sadee, and so, in corroboration of the words of that divine songster, the next day at noon, sure enough, a man was found—a most ancient, learned, and holy dervish, who knew all the languages under the sun, and, by consequence, that in which the paper was written.

"It was in the most secret Sanscrit tongue; and when the dervish read it, he requested that he might communicate its contents privately to His Majesty, or at least only in the presence of his first minister.

"Retiring then to the private apartments with the Vizier, His Majesty bade the dervish interpret the meaning of the writing round the bottle.

"'The meaning, sire, is this,' said the learned dervish. 'Whoever, after bowing his head three times to the east——'

"'The old woman waggled hers,' cried the King. 'I remarked it, but thought it was only palsy.'

"'Whoever, after bowing his head three times to the east, swallows a grain of this powder, may change himself into whatever animal he please: be it beast, or insect, or bird. Likewise, when he is so changed, he will know the language of beasts, insects, and birds, and be able to answer each after his kind. And when the person so transformed desires to be restored to his own shape, he has only to utter the name of the god "Budgaroo," who himself appeared upon earth in the shape of beasts, birds, ay, and fishes,[1] and he will instantly resume his proper figure. But let the person using this precious powder especially beware, that during the course of his metamorphosis he do not give way to laughter; for should he indulge in any such unholy mirth, his memory will infallibly forsake him, and not being able to recall the talismanic word, he will remain in the shape into which he has changed himself.'

---

[1] In Professor Schwam's *Sankritische Alterthumskunde,* is a learned account of the transmutations of this Indian divinity.—G. O'G. G.

"When this strange document had been communicated to His Majesty, he caused the dervish's mouth to be filled with sugar-candy, gave him a purse of gold, and bade him depart with every honour.

" 'You had better at least have waited,' said the shrewd Vizier, 'to see if the interpretation be correct, for who can tell whether this dervish is deceiving us or no?'

"King Mushook rejoined that that point should be put at rest at once, and, grimly smiling, ordered the Vizier to take a pinch of powder and change himself into whatever animal he pleased.

"Munsoor had nothing for it but to wish himself a dog; he turned to the east, nodded his head thrice, swallowed the powder, and lo! there he was—a poodle—an old, fat, lame, one-eyed poodle, whose appearance made his master laugh inordinately, though Munsoor himself, remembering the prohibition and penalty, was far too wise to indulge in any such cachinnation.

"Having satisfied his royal master by his antics, the old Vizier uttered the requisite word, and was speedily restored to his former shape.

"And now I might tell how the King of Persia and his faithful attendant indulged themselves in all sorts of transformations by the use of the powder; how they frequented the society of all manner of beasts, and gathered a deal of wisdom from their conversation; how, perching on this house-top in the likeness of sparrows, they peered into all the family secrets of the proprietors; how, buzzing into that harem window in the likeness of bluebottle flies, they surveyed at their leisure the beauties within, and enjoyed the confusion of the emirs and noblemen, when they described to them at divan every particular regarding the shape, and features, and dress of the ladies they kept so secretly in the anderoon. One of these freaks had like to have cost the King dear; for sitting on Hassan Ebu Suneebee's wall, looking at Bulkous, his wife, and lost in admiration of that moon of beauty, a spider issued out from a crevice, and had as nearly as possible gobbled up the King of Persia. This event was a lesson to him, therefore; and he was so frightened by it, that he did not care for the future to be too curious about other people's affairs, or at least to take upon himself the form of such a fragile thing as a bluebottle fly.

"One morning—indeed I believe on my conscience that His Majesty and the Vizier had been gadding all night, or they never could have been abroad so early—they were passing those large swampy grounds, which everybody knows are in the neighbourhood of Tehran, and where the Persian lords are in the habit of hunting herons with the hawk. The two gentlemen were disguised, I don't know how; but seeing a stork by the side of the pool, stretching its long neck and tossing about its legs very queerly, King Mushook felt suddenly a longing to know what these motions of the animal meant, and taking upon themselves likewise the likeness of storks (the Vizier's dumpy nose stretched out into a very strange bill, I promise you), they both advanced to the bird at the pool and greeted it in the true storkish language.

" 'Good morning, Mr. Long Bill,' said the stork (a female), curtsying politely, 'you are abroad early to-day; and the sharp air, no doubt, makes you hungry; here is half an eel which I beg you to try, or a frog, which you will find very fat and tender.' But the royal stork was not inclined to eat frogs, being no Frank."

"Have a care, Scheherazade," here interposed the Sultan. "Do you mean to tell me that there are any people, even among the unbelievers, who are such filthy wretches as to eat frogs?—Bah! I can't believe it!"

Scheherazade did not vouch for the fact, but continued. "The King declined the proffered breakfast, and presently, falling into conversation with the young female stork, bantered her gaily about her presence in such a place of a morning, and without her mamma, praised her figure and the slimness of her legs (which made the young stork blush till she was almost as red as a flamingo), and paid her a thousand compliments that made her think the stranger one of the most delightful creatures she had ever met.

" 'Sir,' said she, 'we live in some reeds hard by; and as my mamma, one of the best mothers in the world, who fed us children with her own blood when we had nothing else for dinner, is no more, my papa, who is always lazy, has bidden us to look out for ourselves. You were pleased just now to compliment my l—— my *limbs,*' says the stork, turning her eyes to the ground; 'and the fact is, that I wish to profit, sir, by those graces with which nature endowed me, and am learning to dance. I came out here to practise a little step that I am to perform before some friends this morning, and here, sir, you have my history.'

" 'I do pray and beseech you to let us see the rehearsal of the step,' said the King, quite amused; on which the young stork, stretching out her scraggy neck, and giving him an ogle with her fish-like eyes, fell to dancing and capering in such a ridiculous way that the King and Vizier could restrain their gravity no longer, but burst out into an immoderate fit of laughter. I do not know that Munsoor would have laughed of his own accord, for he was a man of no sort of humour; but he made it a point whenever his master laughed always to roar too; and in this instance his servility cost him dear.

"The young female stork, as they were laughing, flew away in a huff, and thought them, no doubt, the most ill-mannered brutes in the world. When they were restored to decent gravity, the King voted that they should resume their shapes again and hie home to breakfast.

So he turned himself round to the east, bobbed his head three times according to the receipt, and——

"'Vizier,' said he, 'what the deuce is the word? Hudge, kudge, fudge. What is it?'

"The Vizier had forgotten too; and then the condition annexed to the charm came over these wretched men, and they felt they were storks for ever. In vain they racked their poor brains to discover the word—they were no wiser at the close of the day than at the beginning, and at nightfall were fain to take wing from the lonely morass where they had passed so many miserable hours and seek for shelter somewhere."

II. THE ENCHANTED PRINCESS

"After flying about for some time the poor storks perched upon the palace, where it was evident that all was in consternation. 'Ah!' said the King, with a sigh, 'why, O cursed Vizier, didst thou ever bring that beggar-woman into my presence? Here it is an hour after sunset, and at this hour I should have been seated at a comfortable supper but for thy odious officiousness and my own fatal curiosity.'

"What His Majesty said was true; and, having eaten nothing all day (for they could not make up their stomachs to subsist upon raw frogs and fish), he saw, to his inexpressible mortification, his own supper brought into the royal closet at the usual hour, taken away from thence, and the greater part of it eaten up by the servants as they carried it back to the kitchen.

"For three days longer, as they lingered about Tehran, that city was in evident dismay and sorrow. On the first day a council was held, and a great deal of discussion took place between the mollahs and emirs; on the second day another council was held, and all the mollahs and emirs swore eternal fidelity to King Mushook; on the third day a third council was held, and they voted to a man that all faithful Persians had long desired the return of their rightful sovereign and worship, and proclaimed Ghuzroo Sultan of Persia. Ghuzroo and his son, Ameen Adawb, entered the divan. What a thrill passed through the bosom of Mushook (who was perched on a window of the hall) when he saw Ghuzroo walk up and take possession of his august throne, and beheld in the countenance of that unbeliever the traits of the very old woman who had sold him the box!

"It would be tedious to describe to Your Majesty the numberless voyages and the long dreary flights which the unhappy Sultan and Vizier now took. There is hardly a mosque in all Persia or Arabia on which they did not light; and as for frogs and fishes, they speedily learned to be so little particular as to swallow them raw with considerable satisfaction, and, I do believe, tried every pond and river in Asia.

"At last they came to India; and being then somewhere in the neighbourhood of Agra, they went to take their evening meal at a lake in a wood: the moon was shining on it, and there was upon one of the trees an owl hooting and screaming in the most melancholy manner.

"The two wanderers were discussing their victuals, and it did not at first come into their heads to listen to the owl's bewailings; but as they were satisfied, they began presently to hearken to the complaints of the bird of night that sate on a mango tree, its great round, white face shining in the moon. The owl sung a little elegy, which may be rendered in the following manner:

" 'Too—too—too—oo *long have I been in imprisonment;*
Who—o—o—o *is coming to deliver me?*
In the darkness of the night I look out, and see not my deliverer;
I make the grove resound with my strains, but no one hears me.

I look out at the moon—my face was once as fair as hers:
She is the queen of night, and I was a princess as celebrated.
I sit under the cypress trees, and was once as thin as they are:
Could their dark leaves compare to my raven tresses?

I was a princess once, and my talents were everywhere sung of;
I was indebted for my popularity not only to beauty but to whit;
Ah, where is the destined prince that is to come to liberate, and to
who—o?' "

"Cut the verses short, Scheherazade," said the Sultan. And the obedient Princess instantly resumed her story in prose.

" 'What!' said King Mushook, stepping up to the owl. 'Are you the victim of enchantment?'

" 'Alas! kind stranger, of whatever feather you be—for the moon is so bright that I cannot see you in the least,—I was a princess, as I have just announced in my poem; and famous, I may say, for my beauty all over India. Rotu Muckun is my name, and my father is King of Hindostan. A monster from Bombay, an idolater and practiser of enchantments, came to my court and asked my hand for his son; but because I spurned the wretch, he, under the disguise of an old woman ——'

" 'With a box of trinkets,' broke out the Vizier.

" 'Of no such thing,' said the owl, or rather the disguised Princess Rotu Muckun; 'with a basket of peaches, of which I was known to be fond, entered the palace garden one evening as I was seated there with my maidens, and offered me a peach, of which I partook, and was that instant turned into an owl. My attendants fled, screaming at the metamorphosis; and as the old woman went away, she clenched her fist at me and laughed, and said, "Now, Princess, you will remember the vengeance of Ghuzroo."'

" 'This *is* indeed marvellous!' exclaimed the King of Persia. 'Know, madam, that the humble individual who now addresses you was a year since no other than Persia's king.'

" 'Heavens!' said the Princess, trembling, and rustling all her feathers; 'can you be the famous and beautiful Mushook who disappeared from Tehran with his Grand Vizier?'

" 'No other, madam,' said the King, laying his claw on his breast; 'and the most devoted of your servants.'

" 'Heigho!' said she; 'I would that you had resumed your former shape, and that what you said were true; but you men, I have always heard, are sad, sad deceivers!'

"Being pressed farther to explain the meaning of her wish, the Princess said that she never could resume her former appearance until she could find someone who would marry her under her present form; and what was more, she said, an old Brahmin had made a prophecy concerning her, that she should be saved from destruction by a stork.

" 'This speech,' said the Vizier, drawing His Majesty aside, 'is the sheerest and most immodest piece of fiction on the part of Madam Owl that ever I heard. What is the upshot of it? The hideous old wretch, pining for a husband, and not being able on account of her age and ugliness, doubtless, to procure one among birds of her own degree, sees us two slim, elegant, fashionable fellows pass, and trumps up instantly a story about her being a princess, and the deuce knows what. Even suppose she be a princess, let Your Majesty remember what the poet Ferooz observes:

> *"Women are not all beautiful—for one moon-eyed,*
> *Nine hundred and ninety-nine are as ugly as Shaitan."*

Let us have a care, then, how we listen to her stories.'

" 'Vizier,' answered His Majesty, 'I have remarked that you are always talking about ugliness; and, by my beard, you are the ugliest man in my dominions. Be she handsome or hideous, I am sure that there is something in the story of the Princess mysteriously connected with our fate. Do you not remember that extraordinary dream which I had in my youth, and which declared that I too should be saved from danger by an owl? Had you not also such a dream on the self-same night? Let us not, therefore, disregard the warnings of Fate:—the risk shall be run; the Princess shall be married, or my name's not Mushook.'

" 'Well, sir,' said the Vizier, with a shrug, 'if you insist upon marrying her, I cannot, of course, give any objection to the royal will: and Your Majesty must remember that I wash my hands of the business altogether.'

" '*I* marry her!' screamed the King in a rage. 'Vizier, are you a fool? Do you suppose me such a fool as to buy a pig in a poke, as they say in Bagdad?'

" 'I was sure Your Majesty would not be so imprudent,' said the Vizier in a soothing tone.

" 'Of course I wouldn't; no, Vizier, my old and tried servant, *you* shall marry the Princess Rotu Muckun, and incur the risk of this adventure.'

"The poor Vizier knew he had only to obey were his master to bid him to bite off his own nose; so he promised compliance in this instance with as good a grace as he could muster. But the gentlemen, in the course of this little dispute, had not taken into consideration that the owl had wings as well as they, and had followed them into the dark brake where the colloquy took place, and could see them perfectly and hear every word that passed.

" 'Tut-tut-tut-too!' shrieked out the owl, in a shrill voice,—'my lord of Persia, and you, Grand Vizier, do you suppose that I, the Princess of Hindostan, am to be cast about from one person to another like a shuttlecock? Do you suppose that I, the loveliest woman in the universe, am tamely to listen to doubts regarding my beauty, and finally to yield up my charms to an ugly, old, decrepit monster like your Grand Vizier?'

" 'Madam——' interposed the King of Persia.

" 'Tut-tut-too! Don't madam me, sir,' said the Princess in a fluster, —'Mademoiselle, if you please; and mademoiselle to remain, rather than be insulted so. Talk about buying a pig in a poke, indeed! Here is a pretty gentlemanlike phrase for a monarch who has been used to good society!—pig in a poke, indeed! I'll tell you what, my lord, I have a great mind to make you carry your pigs to another market. And as for my poor person, I will see,' cried the owl, sobbing, 'if some noble-hearted person be not more favourable to-to-to to-*it*-to-oo-oo-oo-oo!' Here she set up such an hysterical howling that His Majesty the King of Persia thought she would have dropped off her perch.

"He was a good-natured sovereign, and could not bear to see the tears of a woman."

"What a fool!" said the Sultan. But Scheherazade took no notice.

"And having his heart melted by her sorrows, said to her, 'Cheer up, madam, it shall never be said that Mushook deserted a lady in distress. I swear to you by the ninth book of the Koran that you shall have my hand as soon as I get it back myself; in the meanwhile accept my claw, and with it the heart of the King of Persia.'

" 'Oh, sir!' said the owl, 'this is too great joy—too much honour—I cannot,' said she, in a faint voice, 'bear it!—Oh, heavens!—Maidens, unlace me!—Some water—some water—a jug-jug-jug——'

"Here what the King had formerly feared actually took place, and the owl, in an excess of emotion, actually tumbled off the branch in a fainting fit, and fell into the thicket below.

"The Vizier and His Majesty ran like mad to the lake for water; but ah! what a scene met their view on coming back!

"Forth there came to meet them the loveliest damsel that ever greeted the eyes of monarch or vizier. Fancy, sir, a pair of eyes——"

"Cut the description short, Scheherazade," interrupted the Sultan; "your eyes, my dear, are quite pretty enough for me."

"In short, sir, she was the most lovely woman in the world of her time; and the poor old Vizier, as he beheld her, was mad to think what a prize he had lost. The King of Persia flung himself at her feet, and vowed himself to be the happiest of men."

"Happiest of men!" roared out the Sultan. "Why, woman, he is a stork; how did he get back to his shape, I want to know?"

"Why, sir, it must be confessed that when the Princess of Hindostan, now restored to her pristine beauty, saw that no sort of change had taken place in her affianced husband, she felt a little ashamed of the connection, and more than once in their journey from Agra to the court of her father at Delhi, she thought of giving her companion the slip; 'For how,' said she, 'am I to marry a stork?' However, the King would never leave her for a moment out of his sight, or, when His Majesty slept, the Vizier kept his eye upon her; and so at last they walked and walked until they came near to Delhi on the banks of the Jumna.

"A magnificent barge was floating down the river, pulled by a hundred men with gilded oars, and dressed in liveries of cloth of gold. The prow of the barge was shaped like a peacock, and formed of precious stones and enamel; and at the stern of the vessel was an awning of crimson silk, supported by pillars of silver, under which, in a yellow satin robe, covered with diamonds of intolerable brightness, there sat an old gentleman smoking, and dissolved, seemingly, in grief.

" 'Heavens!' cried the Princess, ' 'tis my father!' and straightway she began flapping her pocket-handkerchief, and crying at the top of her voice, 'Father, father, 'tis your Rotu Muckun calls!'

"When the old gentleman, who was smoking in yellow satin, heard that voice, he started up wildly, let drop his hookah, shouted hoarsely to the rowers to pull to the shore, and the next minute tumbled backwards in a fainting fit. The next minute but one he was in the arms of his beloved girl, the proudest and happiest of fathers.

"The Princess, at the moment of meeting, and in the hurry of running into the boat, had, it must be confessed, quite forgotten her two storks; and as these made an effort to follow her, one of the rowers, with his gilded oar, gave the Grand Vizier a crack over the leg, which caused that poor functionary to limp for many years after. But our wanderers were not to be put off so. Taking wing, they flew right under the awning of the boat, and perched down on the sofa close by the King of Hindostan and his daughter.

" 'What, in Heaven's name,' said Hindostan, 'are these filthy birds that smell so horribly of fish? Faugh! turn them out.'

" 'Filthy yourself, sir, my 'brother,' answered the King of Persia. 'The smell of fish is not much worse than that of tobacco, I warrant. Heigho! I have not had a pipe for many a long day!'

"Here Rotu Muckun, seeing her father's wonder that a stork should talk his language, and his anger at the bird's impudence, interposed, and related to His Majesty all the circumstances attending the happy change that had taken place.

"While she was speaking (and her story was a pretty long one), the King of Persia flung himself back in an easy attitude on one of the sofas, crossing his long legs, and folding his wings over his chest. He was, to tell the truth, rather piqued at the reception which his brother of Hindostan had given him. Old Munsoor stood moodily at a little distance, holding up his game leg.

"His master, however, was determined to show that he was perfectly at his ease. 'Hindostan, my old buck,' said he, 'what a deuced comfortable sofa this is; and, egad, what a neat turn-out of a barge.'

"The old gentleman, who was a stickler for ceremony, said dryly, 'I am glad Your Majesty finds the sofa comfortable, and the barge to your liking. Here we don't call it a barge, but a BUDGEROW.'

"As he spoke this word, the King of Persia bounced off his seat as if he had been shot, and upset the hookah over the King of Hindostan's legs; the moody old Grand Vizier clapped his wings and screamed for joy; the Princess shrieked for astonishment; and the whole boat's crew were in wonder, as they saw the two birds turn towards the east, bob their long bills three times, and call out 'Budgerow!'

"At that word the birds disappeared, and in their place, before the astonished sovereign of Hindostan, there stood two gentlemen in the

Persian habit. One of them was fat, old and one-eyed, of a yellow complexion, and limping on a leg—'twas Munsoor, the Vizier. The other —ah, what a thrill passed through Rotu Muckun's heart as she beheld him!—had a dark countenance, a dark flashing eye, a royal black beard, a high forehead, on which a little Persian cap was jauntily placed. A pelisse of cashmere and sables covered his broad chest, and showed off his excessively slim waist to advantage; his little feet were encased in yellow slippers; when he spoke, his cornelian lips displayed thirty-two pearly teeth; in his girdle was his sword, and on the hilt of it that famous diamond, worth one hundred and forty-three millions of tomauns.

"When the King of Hindostan saw that diamond, he at once knew that Mushook could be no impostor, and taking him heartily by the hand, the good-natured monarch ordered servants to pick up the pieces of the chillum, and to bring fresh ones for the King of Persia and himself.

"'You say it is a long time since you smoked a pipe,' said Hindostan waggishly; 'there is a lady here that I dare swear will fill one for you.' With this and other sallies the royal party passed on to Delhi, where Munsoor was accommodated with diaculum and surgical aid, and where the marriage was celebrated between the King of Persia and the Princess of Hindostan."

"And did the King of Persia ever get his kingdom back again?" asked the Sultan.

"Of course he did, sir," replied Scheherazade, "for where did you ever hear of a king who had been kept out of his just rights by a wicked enchanter that did not regain his possessions at the end of a story? No, sir, at the last page of a tale, wicked enchanters are always punished, and suffering virtue always rewarded; and though I have my doubts whether in real life——"

"Be hanged to your prate, madam, and let me know at once *how* King Mushook got back his kingdom, and what he did to Ghuzroo and his son, Ameen Adawb?"

"Why, sir, marching with five hundred thousand men, whom his father-in-law placed under his command, King Mushook went, via Caubul and Affghanistan, into Persia; he defeated the usurping Ghuzroo upon the plains of Tehran, and caused that idolatrous monarch to be bastinadoed to death. As for his son, Ameen Adawb, as that young Prince had not taken any part in his father's rebellion, Mushook, who was a merciful sovereign, only ordered him to take a certain quantity of the powder, and to wish himself to be a stork. Then he put him into a cage, and hung him outside the palace wall. This done, Mushook and his Princess swayed magnificently the sceptre of Persia, lived happily, were blest by their subjects, had an infinite number of children, and ate pilau and rice every day.

"Now, sir, it happened, after several years' captivity in the cage, that the Prince Ameen Adawb——"

Here Scheherazade paused; for, looking at her royal husband, she saw that His Majesty was fast asleep, and deferred the history of Prince Ameen Adawb until another occasion.

14

A Christmas Carol

BY CHARLES DICKENS

STAVE ONE: MARLEY'S GHOST

MARLEY was dead, to begin with. There is no doubt whatever about that. The register of his burial was signed by the clergyman, the clerk, the undertaker, and the chief mourner. Scrooge signed it. And Scrooge's name was good upon 'Change for anything he chose to put his hand to.

Old Marley was as dead as a doornail.

Scrooge knew he was dead? Of course he did. How could it be otherwise? Scrooge and he were partners for I don't know how many years. Scrooge was his sole executor, his sole administrator, his sole assign, his sole residuary legatee, his sole friend, his sole mourner.

Scrooge never painted out old Marley's name, however. There it yet stood, years afterward, above the warehouse door—Scrooge and Marley. The firm was known as Scrooge and Marley. Sometimes people new to the business called Scrooge Scrooge, and sometimes Marley. He answered to both names. It was all the same to him.

Oh! But he was a tight-fisted hand at the grindstone, was Scrooge! a squeezing, wrenching, grasping, scraping, clutching, covetous old sinner! External heat and cold had little influence on him. No warmth could warm, no cold could chill him. No wind that blew was bitterer than he, no falling snow was more intent upon its purpose, no pelting rain less open to entreaty. Foul weather didn't know where to have him. The heaviest rain and snow and hail and sleet could boast of the advantage over him in only one respect—they often "came down" handsomely, and Scrooge never did.

Nobody ever stopped him in the street to say, with gladsome looks, "My dear Scrooge, how are you? When will you come to see me?"

No beggars implored him to bestow a trifle, no children asked him what it was o'clock, no man or woman ever once in all his life inquired the way to such and such a place of Scrooge. Even the blind men's dogs appeared to know him; and when they saw him coming on, would tug their owners into doorways and up courts; and then would wag their tails as though they said, "No eye at all is better than evil eye, dark master!"

But what did Scrooge care! It was the very thing he liked. To edge his way along the crowded paths of life, warning all human sympathy to keep its distance, was what the knowing ones call "nuts" to Scrooge.

Once upon a time—of all the good days in the year, upon a Christmas eve—old Scrooge sat busy in his counting-house. It was cold, bleak, biting, foggy weather; and the city clocks had only just gone three, but it was quite dark already.

The door of Scrooge's counting-house was open, that he might keep his eye upon his clerk, who, in a dismal little cell beyond, a sort of tank, was copying letters. Scrooge had a very small fire, but the clerk's fire was so very much smaller that it looked like one coal. But he couldn't replenish it, for Scrooge kept the coal-box in his own room; and so surely as the clerk came in with the shovel the master predicted that it would be necessary for them to part. Wherefore the clerk put on his white comforter, and tried to warm himself at the candle; in which effort, not being a man of a strong imagination, he failed.

"A merry Christmas, uncle! God save you!" cried a cheerful voice. It was the voice of Scrooge's nephew, who came upon him so quickly that this was the first intimation Scrooge had of his approach.

"Bah!" said Scrooge; "humbug!"

"Christmas a humbug, uncle! You don't mean that, I am sure?"

"I do. Out upon merry Christmas! What's Christmas-time to you but a time for paying bills without money; a time for finding yourself a year older, and not an hour richer; a time for balancing your books and having every item in 'em through a round dozen of months presented dead against you? If I had my will, every idiot who goes about with 'Merry Christmas' on his lips should be boiled with his own pudding, and buried with a stake of holly through his heart! He should!"

"Uncle!"

"Nephew, keep Christmas in your own way, and let me keep it in mine."

"Keep it! But you don't keep it."

"Let me leave it alone, then. Much good may it do you! Much good it has ever done you!"

"There are many things from which I might have derived good, by which I have not profited, I dare say, Christmas among the rest. But I am sure I have always thought of Christmas-time, when it has come round—apart from the veneration due to its sacred origin, if anything belonging to it *can* be apart from that—as a good time; a kind, forgiving, charitable, pleasant time; the only time I know of, in the long calendar of the year, when men and women seem by one consent to open their shut-up hearts freely, and to think of people below them as if they really were fellow travelers to the grave, and not another race of creatures bound on other journeys. And therefore, uncle, though it has never put a scrap of gold or silver in my pocket, I believe that it *has* done me good, and *will* do me good; and I say, God bless it!"

The clerk in the tank involuntarily applauded.

"Let me hear another sound from *you*," said Scrooge, "and you'll keep your Christmas by losing your situation! You're quite a powerful speaker, sir," he added, turning to his nephew. "I wonder you don't go into Parliament."

"Don't be angry, uncle. Come! Dine with us to-morrow."

Scrooge said that he would see him—yes, indeed he did. He went the whole length of the expression, and said that he would see him in that extremity first.

"But why?" cried Scrooge's nephew. "Why?"

"Why did you get married?"

"Because I fell in love."

"Because you fell in love!" growled Scrooge, as if that were the only one thing in the world more ridiculous than a merry Christmas. "Good afternoon!"

"Nay, uncle, but you never came to see me before that happened. Why give it as a reason for not coming now?"

"Good afternoon."

"I want nothing from you; I ask nothing of you; why cannot we be friends?"

"Good afternoon."

"I am sorry, with all my heart, to find you so resolute. We have never had any quarrel, to which I have been a party. But I have made the trial in homage to Christmas, and I'll keep my Christmas humor to the last. So A Merry Christmas, uncle!"

"Good afternoon!"

"And A Happy New Year!"

"Good afternoon!"

His nephew left the room without an angry word, notwithstanding. The clerk, in letting Scrooge's nephew out, had let two other people in. They were portly gentlemen, pleasant to behold, and now stood, with their hats off, in Scrooge's office. They had books and papers in their hands, and bowed to him.

"Scrooge and Marley's, I believe?" said one of the gentlemen, referring to his list. "Have I the pleasure of addressing Mr. Scrooge, or Mr. Marley?"

"Mr. Marley has been dead these seven years. He died seven years ago, this very night."

"At this festive season of the year, Mr. Scrooge," said the gentleman, taking up a pen, "it is more than usually desirable that we should make some slight provision for the poor and destitute, who suffer greatly at the present time. Many thousands are in want of common necessaries; hundreds of thousands are in want of common comforts, sir."

"Are there no prisons?"

"Plenty of prisons. But under the impression that they scarcely furnish Christian cheer of mind or body to the unoffending multitude, a few of us are endeavoring to raise a fund to buy the poor some meat and drink, and means of warmth. We choose this time, because it is a time of all others when Want is keenly felt and Abundance rejoices. What shall I put you down for?"

"Nothing!"

"You wish to be anonymous?"

"I wish to be left alone. Since you ask me what I wish, gentlemen, that is my answer. I don't make merry myself at Christmas, and I can't afford to make idle people merry. I help to support the prisons and the workhouses—they cost enough—and those who are badly off must go there."

"Many can't go there; and many would rather die."

"If they would rather die, they had better do it, and decrease the surplus population."

At length the hour of shutting up the counting-house arrived. With an ill will Scrooge, dismounting from his stool, tacitly admitted the fact to the expectant clerk in the Tank, who instantly snuffed his candle out, and put on his hat.

"You'll want all day to-morrow, I suppose?"

"If quite convenient, sir."

"It's not convenient, and it's not fair. If I was to stop half a crown for it, you'd think yourself mightily ill-used, I'll be bound?"

"Yes, sir."

"And yet you don't think *me* ill-used, when I pay a day's wages for no work."

"It's only once a year, sir."

"A poor excuse for picking a man's pocket every twenty-fifth of December! But I suppose you must have the whole day. Be here all the earlier *next* morning."

The clerk promised that he would; and Scrooge walked out with a growl. The office was closed in a twinkling, and the clerk, with the long ends of his white comforter dangling below his waist (for he boasted no great-coat), went down a slide, at the end of a lane of boys, twenty times, in honor of its being Christmas eve, and then ran home as hard as he could pelt, to play at blind man's buff.

Scrooge took his melancholy dinner in his usual melancholy tavern; and having read all the newspapers, and beguiled the rest of the evening with his banker's book, went home to bed. He lived in chambers which had once belonged to his deceased partner. They were a gloomy suite of rooms, in a lowering pile of building up a yard. The building was old enough now, and dreary enough; for nobody lived in it but Scrooge, the other rooms being all let out as offices.

Now it is a fact, that there was nothing at all particular about the knocker on the door of this house, except that it was very large; also, that Scrooge had seen it, night and morning, during his whole residence in that place; also, that Scrooge had as little of what is called fancy about him as any man in the city of London. And yet Scrooge, having his key in the lock of the door, saw in the knocker, without its undergoing any intermediate process of change, not a knocker, but Marley's face.

Marley's face, with a dismal light about it, like a bad lobster in a dark cellar. It was not angry or ferocious, but it looked at Scrooge as Marley used to look—with ghostly spectacles turned up upon its ghostly forehead.

As Scrooge looked fixedly at this phenomenon, it was a knocker again. He said, "Pooh, pooh!" and closed the door with a bang.

The sound resounded through the house like thunder. Every room above, and every cask in the wine-merchant's cellars below, appeared to have a separate peal of echoes of its own. Scrooge was not a man to be frightened by echoes. He fastened the door, and walked across the hall, and up the stairs. Slowly, too, trimming his candle as he went.

Up Scrooge went, not caring a button for its being very dark. Darkness is cheap, and Scrooge liked it. But before he shut his heavy door, he walked through his rooms to see that all was right. He had just enough recollection of the face to desire to do that.

Sitting-room, bedroom, lumber-room, all as they should be. Nobody under the table, nobody under the sofa; a small fire in the grate; spoon and basin ready; and the little saucepan of gruel (Scrooge had a cold in his head) upon the hob. Nobody under the bed; nobody in the closet; nobody in his dressing-gown, which was hanging up in a suspicious attitude against the wall. Lumber-room as usual. Old fire-guard, old shoes, two fish-baskets, washing-stand on three legs, and a poker.

Quite satisfied, he closed his door, and locked himself in; double-locked himself in, which was not his custom. Thus secured against surprise, he took off his cravat, put on his dressing-gown and slippers and his nightcap, and sat down before the very low fire to take his gruel.

As he threw his head back in the chair, his glance happened to rest upon a bell, a disused bell, that hung in the room, and communicated, for some purpose now forgotten, with a chamber in the highest story of the building. It was with great astonishment, and with a strange, inexplicable dread, that, as he looked, he saw this bell begin to swing. Soon it rang out loudly, and so did every bell in the house.

This was succeeded by a clanking noise, deep down below, as if some person were dragging a heavy chain over the casks in the wine-merchant's cellar.

Then he heard the noise much louder, on the floors below; then coming up the stairs; then coming straight toward his door.

It came on through the heavy door, and a specter passed into the room before his eyes. And upon its coming in, the dying flame leaped up, as though it cried, "I know him! Marley's ghost!"

The same face, the very same. Marley in his pigtail, usual waistcoat, tights, and boots. His body was transparent; so that Scrooge, observing him, and looking through his waistcoat, could see the two buttons on his coat behind.

Scrooge had often heard it said that Marley had no bowels, but he had never believed it until now.

No, nor did he believe it even now. Though he looked the fantom through and through, and saw it standing before him—though he felt the chilling influence of its death-cold eyes, and noticed the very texture of the folded kerchief bound about its head and chin—he was still incredulous.

"How now!" said Scrooge, caustic and cold as ever. "What do you want with me?"

"Much!"—Marley's voice, no doubt about it.

"Who are you?"

"Ask me who I *was*."

"Who *were* you, then?"

"In life I was your partner, Jacob Marley."

"Can you—can you sit down?"

"I can."

"Do it, then."

Scrooge asked the question because he didn't know whether a ghost so transparent might find himself in a condition to take a chair; and felt that, in the event of its being impossible, it might involve the necessity of an embarrassing explanation. But the ghost sat down on the opposite side of the fireplace, as if he were quite used to it.

"You don't believe in me."

"I don't."

"What evidence would you have of my reality beyond that of your senses?"

"I don't know."

"Why do you doubt your senses?"

"Because a little thing affects them. A slight disorder of the stomach makes them cheats. You may be an undigested bit of beef, a blot of mustard, a crumb of cheese, a fragment of an underdone potato. There's more of gravy than of grave about you, whatever you are!"

Scrooge was not much in the habit of cracking jokes, nor did he feel in his heart by any means waggish then. The truth is, that he tried to be smart, as a means of distracting his own attention, and keeping down his horror.

But how much greater was his horror when, the fantom taking off the bandage round its head, as if it were too warm to wear indoors, its lower jaw dropped down upon its breast!

"Mercy! Dreadful apparition, why do you trouble me? Why do spirits walk the earth, and why do they come to me?"

"It is required of every man, that the spirit within him should walk abroad among his fellow men, and travel far and wide; and if that spirit goes not forth in life, it is condemned to do so after death. I cannot tell you all I would. A very little more is permitted to me. I cannot rest, I cannot stay, I cannot linger anywhere. My spirit never walked beyond our counting-house—mark me!—in life my spirit never roved beyond the narrow limits of our money-changing hole; and weary journeys lie before me!"

"Seven years dead. And traveling all the time? You travel fast?"

"On the wings of the wind."

"You might have got over a great quantity of ground in seven years."

"O blind man, blind man! not to know that ages of incessant labor by immortal creatures for this earth must pass into eternity before the good of which it is susceptible is all developed. Not to know that any Christian spirit working kindly in its little sphere, whatever it may be, will find its mortal life too short for its vast means of usefulness. Not to know that no space of regret can make amends for one life's opportunities misused! Yet I was like this man; I once was like this man!"

"But you were always a good man of business, Jacob," faltered Scrooge, who now began to apply this to himself.

"Business!" cried the Ghost, wringing his hands again. "Mankind was my business. The common welfare was my business; charity, mercy, forbearance, benevolence, were all my business. The dealings of my trade were but a drop of water in the comprehensive ocean of my business."

Scrooge was very much dismayed to hear the specter going on at this rate, and began to quake exceedingly.

"Hear me! My time is nearly gone."

"I will. But don't be hard upon me! Don't be flowery, Jacob! Pray!"

"I am here to-night to warn you that you have yet a chance and hope of escaping my fate. A chance and a hope of my procuring, Ebenezer."

"You were always a good friend to me. Thank'ee!"

"You will be haunted by Three Spirits."

"Is that the chance and hope you mentioned, Jacob? I—I think I'd rather not."

"Without their visits you cannot hope to shun the path I tread. Expect the first to-morrow night, when the bell tolls One. Expect the second on the next night at the same hour. The third, upon the next night, when the last stroke of Twelve has ceased to vibrate. Look to see me no more; and look that, for your own sake, you remember what has passed between us!"

It walked backward from him; and at every step it took, the window raised itself a little, so that, when the apparition reached it, it was wide open.

Scrooge closed the window, and examined the door by which the Ghost had entered. It was double-locked, as he had locked it with his own hands, and the bolts were undisturbed. Scrooge tried to say "Humbug!" but stopped at the first syllable. And being, from the emotion he had undergone, or the fatigues of the day, or his glimpse of the invisible world, or the dull conversation of the Ghost, or the lateness of the hour, much in need of repose, he went straight to bed, without undressing, and fell asleep on the instant.

STAVE TWO: THE FIRST OF THE THREE SPIRITS

When Scrooge awoke it was so dark that, looking out of bed, he could scarcely distinguish the transparent window from the opaque walls of his chamber, until suddenly the church clock tolled a deep, dull, hollow, melancholy ONE.

Light flashed up in the room upon the instant, and the curtains of his bed were drawn aside by a strange figure—like a child: yet not so like a child as like an old man, viewed through some supernatural medium, which gave him the appearance of having receded from the view, and being diminished to a child's proportions. Its hair, which hung about its neck and down its back, was white as if with age; and yet the face had not a wrinkle in it, and the tenderest bloom was on the skin. It held a branch of fresh green holly in its hand; and, in singular contradiction of that wintry emblem, had its dress trimmed with summer flowers. But the strangest thing about it was, that from the crown of its head there sprung a bright clear jet of light, by which all this was visible; and which was doubtless the occasion of its using, in its duller moments, a great extinguisher for a cap, which it now held under its arm.

"Are you the Spirit, sir, whose coming was foretold to me?"

"I am!"

"Who and what are you?"

"I am the Ghost of Christmas Past."

"Long past?"

"No. Your past. The things that you will see with me are shadows of the things that have been; they will have no consciousness of us."

Scrooge then made bold to inquire what business brought him there.

"Your welfare. Rise, and walk with me!"

It would have been in vain for Scrooge to plead that the weather and the hour were not adapted to pedestrian purposes; that the bed was warm, and the thermometer a long way below freezing; that he was clad but lightly in his slippers, dressing-gown, and nightcap; and that he had a cold upon him at that time. The grasp, though gentle as a woman's hand, was not to be resisted. He rose; but, finding that the Spirit made toward the window, clasped its robe in supplication.

"I am a mortal, and liable to fall."

"Bear but a touch of my hand *there*," said the Spirit, laying it upon his heart, "and you shall be upheld in more than this!"

As the words were spoken, they passed through the wall, and stood in the busy thoroughfares of a city. It was made plain enough by the dressing of the shops that here, too, it was Christmas-time.

The Ghost stopped at a certain warehouse door, and asked Scrooge if he knew it.

"Know it? Was I apprenticed here!"

They went in. At sight of an old gentleman in a Welsh wig, sitting behind such a high desk that, if he had been two inches taller, he must have knocked his head against the ceiling, Scrooge cried in great excitement, "Why, it's old Fezziwig! Bless his heart, it's Fezziwig, alive again!"

Old Fezziwig laid down his pen, and looked up at the clock, which pointed to the hour of seven. He rubbed his hands; adjusted his capacious waistcoat; laughed all over himself, from his shoes to his organ of benevolence; and called out in a comfortable, oily, rich, fat, jovial voice, "Yo ho, there! Ebenezer! Dick!"

A living and moving picture of Scrooge's former self, a young man, came briskly in, accompanied by his fellow 'prentice.

"Dick Wilkins, to be sure!" said Scrooge to the Ghost. "My old fellow 'prentice, bless me, yes. There he is. He was very much attached to me, was Dick. Poor Dick! Dear, dear!"

"Yo ho, my boys!" said Fezziwig. "No more work to-night. Christmas eve, Dick. Christmas, Ebenezer! Let's have the shutters up before a man can say Jack Robinson! Clear away, my lads, and let's have lots of room here!"

Clear away! There was nothing they wouldn't have cleared away, or couldn't have cleared away, with old Fezziwig looking on. It was done in a minute. Every movable was packed off, as if it were dismissed from public life forevermore; the floor was swept and watered, the lamps were trimmed, fuel was heaped upon the fire; and the warehouse was as snug and warm and dry and bright a ballroom as you would desire to see upon a winter's night.

In came a fiddler with a music-book, and went up to the lofty desk, and made an orchestra of it, and tuned like fifty stomach-aches. In came Mrs. Fezziwig, one vast substantial smile. In came the three Miss Fezziwigs, beaming and lovable. In came the six young followers whose hearts they broke. In came all the young men and women employed in the business. In came the housemaid, with her cousin the baker. In came the cook, with her brother's particular friend the milkman.

In they all came one after another; some shyly, some boldly, some gracefully, some awkwardly, some pushing, some pulling; in they all came, anyhow and everyhow. Away they all went, twenty couples at once; hands half round and back again the other way; down the middle and up again; round and round in various stages of affectionate grouping; old top couple always turning up in the wrong place; new top couple starting off again, as soon as they got there; all top couples at last, and not a bottom one to help them. When this result was brought about, old Fezziwig, clapping his hands to stop the dance, cried out, "Well done!" and the fiddler plunged his hot face into a pot of porter especially provided for that purpose.

There were more dances, and there were forfeits, and more dances, and there was cake, and there was negus, and there was a great piece of Cold Roast, and there was a great piece of Cold Boiled, and there were mince-pies and plenty of beer. But the great effect of the evening came after the Roast and Boiled, when the fiddler struck up "Sir Roger de Coverley." Then old Fezziwig stood out to dance with Mrs. Fezziwig. Top couple, too; with a good stiff piece of work cut out for them; three or four and twenty pairs of partners; people who were not to be trifled with; people who *would* dance, and had no notion of walking.

But if they had been twice as many—four times—old Fezziwig would have been a match for them, and so would Mrs. Fezziwig. As to *her,* she was worthy to be his partner in every sense of the term. A positive light appeared to issue from Fezziwig's calves. They shone in every part of the dance. You couldn't have predicted, at any given time, what would become of 'em next. And when old Fezziwig and Mrs. Fezziwig had gone all through the dance—advance and retire, turn your partner, bow and courtesy, corkscrew, thread the needle, and back again to your place—Fezziwig "cut"—cut so deftly, that he appeared to wink with his legs.

When the clock struck eleven this domestic ball broke up. Mr. and Mrs. Fezziwig took their stations, one on either side the door, and, shaking hands with every person individually as he or she went out, wished him or her a Merry Christmas. When everybody had retired but the two 'prentices, they did the same to them; and thus the cheerful voices died away, and the lads were left to their beds, which were under a counter in the back shop.

"A small matter," said the Ghost, "to make these silly folks so full of gratitude. He has spent but a few pounds of your mortal money— three or four perhaps. Is that so much that he deserves this praise?"

"It isn't that," said Scrooge, heated by the remark, and speaking unconsciously like his former, not his latter self—"it isn't that, Spirit. He has the power to render us happy or unhappy; to make our service light or burdensome, a pleasure or a toil. Say that his power lies in words and looks; in things so slight and insignificant that it is impossible to add and count 'em up: what then? The happiness he gives is quite as great as if it cost a fortune."

He felt the Spirit's glance, and stopped.

"What is the matter?"

"Nothing particular."

"Something, I think?"

"No, no. I should like to be able to say a word or two to my clerk just now. That's all."

"My time grows short," observed the Spirit. "Quick!"

This was not addressed to Scrooge, or to any one whom he could see, but it produced an immediate effect. For again he saw himself. He was older now; a man in the prime of life.

He was not alone, but sat by the side of a fair young girl in a black dress, in whose eyes there were tears.

"It matters little," she said softly to Scrooge's former self. "To you, very little. Another idol has displaced me; and if it can comfort you in time to come, as I would have tried to do, I have no just cause to grieve."

"What Idol has displaced you?"

"A golden one. You fear the world too much. I have seen your nobler aspirations fall off one by one, until the master-passion, Gain, engrosses you. Have I not?"

"What then? Even if I have grown so much wiser, what then? I am not changed toward you. Have I ever sought release from our engagement?"

"In words, no. Never."

"In what, then?"

"In a changed nature; in an altered spirit; in another atmosphere of life; another Hope as its great end. If you were free to-day, to-morrow, yesterday, can even I believe that you would choose a dowerless girl; or, choosing her, do I not know that your repentance and regret would surely follow? I do; and I release you. With a full heart, for the love of him you once were."

"Spirit! remove me from this place."

"I told you these were shadows of the things that have been," said the Ghost. "That they are what they are, do not blame me!"

"Remove me!" Scrooge exclaimed. "I cannot bear it! Leave me! Take me back. Haunt me no longer!"

As he struggled with the Spirit he was conscious of being exhausted, and overcome by an irresistible drowsiness; and, further, of being in his own bedroom. He had barely time to reel to bed before he sank into a heavy sleep.

STAVE THREE: THE SECOND OF THE THREE SPIRITS

Scrooge awoke in his own bedroom. There was no doubt about that. But it and his own adjoining sitting-room, into which he shuffled in his slippers, attracted by a great light there, had undergone a surprising transformation. The walls and ceiling were so hung with living green, that it looked a perfect grove. The leaves of holly, mistletoe, and ivy reflected back the light, as if so many little mirrors had been scattered there; and such a mighty blaze went roaring up the chimney, as that petrifaction of a hearth had never known in Scrooge's time, or Marley's, or for many and many a winter season gone.

Heaped upon the floor, to form a kind of throne, were turkeys, geese, game, brawn, great joints of meat, sucking-pigs, long wreaths of sausages, mince-pies, plum-puddings, barrels of oysters, red-hot chestnuts, cherry-cheeked apples, juicy oranges, luscious pears, immense twelfth-cakes, and great bowls of punch. In easy state upon this couch there sat a Giant glorious to see; who bore a glowing torch, in shape not unlike Plenty's horn, and who raised it high to shed its light on Scrooge as he came peeping round the door.

"Come in; come in! and know me better, man! I am the Ghost of Christmas Present. Look upon me! You have never seen the like of me before!"

"Never."

"Have never walked forth with the younger members of my family; meaning (for I am very young) my elder brothers born in these later years?" pursued the Fantom.

"I don't think I have, I am afraid I have not. Have you had many brothers, Spirit?"

"More than eighteen hundred."

"A tremendous family to provide for! Spirit, conduct me where you will. I went forth last night on compulsion, and I learned a lesson which is working now. To-night, if you have aught to teach me, let me profit by it."

"Touch my robe!"

Scrooge did as he was told, and held it fast.

The room and its contents all vanished instantly, and they stood in the city streets upon a snowy Christmas morning.

Scrooge and the Ghost passed on, invisible, straight to Scrooge's clerk's; and on the threshold of the door the Spirit smiled, and stopped to bless Bob Cratchit's dwelling with the sprinklings of his torch. Think of that! Bob had but fifteen "Bob" a week himself; he pocketed on Saturdays but fifteen copies of his Christian name; and yet the Ghost of Christmas Present blessed his four-roomed house!

Then up rose Mrs. Cratchit, Cratchit's wife, dressed out but poorly in a twice-turned gown, but brave in ribbons, which are cheap and make a goodly show for sixpence; and she laid the cloth, assisted by Belinda Cratchit, second of her daughters, also brave in ribbon; while Master Peter Cratchit plunged a fork into the saucepan of potatoes, and, getting the corners of his monstrous shirt-collar (Bob's private property, conferred upon his son and heir in honor of the day) into his mouth, rejoiced to find himself so gallantly attired, and yearned to show his linen in the fashionable Parks.

And now two smaller Cratchits, boy and girl, came tearing in, screaming that outside the baker's they had smelled the goose, and known it for their own; and, basking in luxurious thoughts of sage and onion, these young Cratchits danced about the table, and exalted Master Peter Cratchit to the skies, while he (not proud, although his collars nearly choked him) blew the fire, until the slow potatoes, bubbling up, knocked loudly at the saucepan-lid to be let out and peeled.

"What has ever got your precious father, then?" said Mrs. Cratchit. "And your brother Tiny Tim? And Martha warn't as late last Christmas day by half an hour!"

"Here's Martha, mother!" said a girl, appearing as she spoke.

"Here's Martha, mother!" cried the two young Cratchits. "Hurrah! There's *such* a goose, Martha!"

"Why, bless your heart alive, my dear, how late you are!" said Mrs. Cratchit, kissing her a dozen times, and taking off her shawl and bonnet for her.

"We'd a deal of work to finish up last night," replied the girl, "and had to clear away this morning, mother!"

"Well! Never mind so long as you are come," said Mrs. Cratchit. "Sit ye down before the fire, my dear, and have a warm, Lord bless ye!"

"No, no! There's father coming," cried the two young Cratchits, who were everywhere at once. "Hide, Martha, hide!"

So Martha hid herself, and in came little Bob, the father, with at least three feet of comforter, exclusive of the fringe, hanging down before him; and his threadbare clothes darned up and brushed, to look seasonable; and Tiny Tim upon his shoulder. Alas for Tiny Tim, he bore a little crutch, and had his limbs supported by an iron frame!

"Why, where's our Martha?" cried Bob Cratchit, looking round.

"Not coming," said Mrs. Cratchit.

"Not coming?" said Bob, with a sudden declension in his high spirits; for he had been Tim's blood-horse all the way from church, and had come home rampant—"not coming upon Christmas day?"

Martha didn't like to see him disappointed, if it were only in joke; so she came out prematurely from behind the closet door, and ran into his arms, while the two young Cratchits hustled Tiny Tim, and bore him off into the wash-house that he might hear the pudding singing in the copper.

"And how did little Tim behave?" asked Mrs. Cratchit, when she had rallied Bob on his credulity, and Bob had hugged his daughter to his heart's content.

"As good as gold," said Bob, "and better. Somehow he gets thoughtful, sitting by himself so much, and thinks the strangest things you ever heard. He told me, coming home, that he hoped the people saw him in the church, because he was a cripple, and it might be pleasant to them to remember, upon Christmas day, who made lame beggars walk and blind men see."

Bob's voice was tremulous when he told them this, and trembled more when he said that Tiny Tim was growing strong and hearty.

His active little crutch was heard upon the floor, and back came Tiny Tim before another word was spoken, escorted by his brother and sister to his stool beside the fire; and while Bob, turning up his cuffs —as if, poor fellow, they were capable of being made more shabby— compounded some hot mixture in a jug with gin and lemons, and stirred it round and round and put it on the hob to simmer, Master Peter and the two ubiquitous young Cratchits went to fetch the goose, with which they soon returned in high procession.

Mrs. Cratchit made the gravy (ready beforehand in a little sauce-pan) hissing hot; Master Peter mashed the potatoes with incredible vigor; Miss Belinda sweetened up the apple-sauce; Martha dusted the hot plates; Bob took Tiny Tim beside him in a tiny corner at the table; the two young Cratchits set chairs for everybody, not forgetting them-selves, and mounting guard upon their posts, crammed spoons into their mouths, lest they should shriek for goose before their turn came to be helped.

At last the dishes were set on, and grace was said. It was succeeded by a breathless pause, as Mrs. Cratchit, looking slowly all along the carving-knife, prepared to plunge it in the breast; but when she did, and when the long-expected gush of stuffing issued forth, one murmur of delight arose all round the board, and even Tiny Tim, excited by the two young Cratchits, beat on the table with the handle of his knife, and feebly cried, Hurrah!

There never was such a goose. Bob said he didn't believe there ever was such a goose cooked. Its tenderness and flavor, size and cheapness, were the themes of universal admiration. Eked out by apple-sauce and mashed potatoes, it was a sufficient dinner for the whole family; indeed, as Mrs. Cratchit said with great delight (surveying one small atom of a bone upon the dish), they hadn't ate it all at last!

Yet every one had had enough, and the youngest Cratchits in par-ticular were steeped in sage and onion to the eyebrows! But now, the plates being changed by Miss Belinda, Mrs. Cratchit left the room alone—too nervous to bear witnesses—to take the pudding up, and bring it in.

Suppose it should not be done enough! Suppose it should break in turning out! Suppose somebody should have got over the wall of the back yard, and stolen it, while they were merry with the goose—a supposition at which the two young Cratchits became livid! All sorts of horrors were supposed.

Hallo! A great deal of steam! The pudding was out of the copper. A smell like a washing-day! That was the cloth. A smell like an eating-house and a pastry-cook's next door to each other, with a laundress's next door to that! That was the pudding! In half a minute Mrs. Cratchit entered—flushed but smiling proudly—with the pudding, like a speckled cannon-ball, so hard and firm, blazing in half of half a quartern of ignited brandy, and bedight with Christmas holly stuck into the top.

Oh, a wonderful pudding! Bob Cratchit said, and calmly, too, that he regarded it as the greatest success achieved by Mrs. Cratchit since their marriage. Mrs. Cratchit said that now the weight was off her mind, she would confess she had had her doubts about the quantity of flour. Everybody had something to say about it, but nobody said or thought it was at all a small pudding for a large family. Any Cratchit would have blushed to hint at such a thing.

At last the dinner was all done, the cloth was cleared, the hearth swept, and the fire made up. The compound in the jug being tasted and considered perfect, apples and oranges were put upon the table, and a shovelful of chestnuts on the fire.

Then all the Cratchit family drew round the hearth, in what Bob Cratchit called a circle, and at Bob Cratchit's elbow stood the family display of glass—two tumblers, and a custard-cup without a handle.

These held the hot stuff from the jug, however, as well as golden goblets would have done; and Bob served it out with beaming looks, while the chestnuts on the fire sputtered and crackled noisily. Then Bob proposed:

"A merry Christmas to us all, my dears. God bless us!"

Which all the family reechoed.

"God bless us every one!" said Tiny Tim, the last of all.

He sat very close to his father's side, upon his little stool. Bob held his withered little hand in his, as if he loved the child, and wished to keep him by his side, and dreaded that he might be taken from him.

Scrooge raised his head speedily, on hearing his own name.

"Mr. Scrooge!" said Bob; "I'll give you Mr. Scrooge, the Founder of the Feast!"

"The Founder of the Feast, indeed!" cried Mrs. Cratchit, reddening. "I wish I had him here. I'd give him a piece of my mind to feast upon, and I hope he'd have a good appetite for it."

"My dear," said Bob, "the children! Christmas day."

"It should be Christmas day, I am sure," said she, "on which one drinks the health of such an odious, stingy, hard, unfeeling man as Mr. Scrooge. You know he is, Robert! Nobody knows it better than you do, poor fellow!"

"My dear," was Bob's mild answer, "Christmas day."

"I'll drink his health for your sake and the day's," said Mrs. Cratchit, "not for his. Long life to him! A merry Christmas and a happy New Year! He'll be very merry and very happy, I have no doubt!"

The children drank the toast after her. It was the first of their proceedings which had no heartiness in it. Tiny Tim drank it last of all, but he didn't care twopence for it. Scrooge was the Ogre of the family. The mention of his name cast a dark shadow on the party, which was not dispelled for full five minutes.

After it had passed away, they were ten times merrier than before, from the mere relief of Scrooge the Baleful being done with. Bob Cratchit told them how he had a situation in his eye for Master Peter, which would bring in, if obtained, full five and sixpence weekly. The two young Cratchits laughed tremendously at the idea of Peter's being a man of business; and Peter himself looked thoughtfully at the fire from between his collars, as if he were deliberating what particular investments he should favor when he came into the receipt of that bewildering income.

Martha, who was a poor apprentice at a milliner's then told them what kind of work she had to do, and how many hours she worked at a stretch, and how she meant to lie abed to-morrow morning for a good long rest; to-morrow being a holiday she passed at home. Also how she had seen a countess and a lord some days before, and how the lord "was much about as tall as Peter"; at which Peter pulled up his collars so high that you couldn't have seen his head if you had been there. All this time the chestnuts and the jug went round and round; and by and by they had a song, about a lost child traveling in the snow, from Tiny Tim, who had a plaintive little voice, and sang it very well indeed.

There was nothing of high mark in this. They were not a handsome family; they were not well dressed; their shoes were far from being water-proof; their clothes were scanty; and Peter might have known, and very likely did, the inside of a pawnbroker's. But they were happy, grateful, pleased with one another, and contented with the time; and when they faded, and looked happier yet in the bright sprinklings of the Spirit's torch at parting, Scrooge had his eye upon them, and especially on Tiny Tim, until the last.

It was a great surprise to Scrooge, as this scene vanished, to hear a hearty laugh. It was a much greater surprise to Scrooge to recognize it as his own nephew's, and to find himself in a bright, dry, gleaming room, with the Spirit standing smiling by his side, and looking at that same nephew.

It is a fair, even-handed, noble adjustment of things, that while there is infection in disease and sorrow, there is nothing in the world so irresistibly contagious as laughter and good-humor. When Scrooge's nephew laughed, Scrooge's niece by marriage laughed as heartily as he. And their assembled friends, being not a bit behindhand, laughed out lustily.

"He said that Christmas was a humbug, as I live!" cried Scrooge's nephew. "He believed it, too!"

"More shame for him, Fred!" said Scrooge's niece, indignantly. Bless those women! they never do anything by halves. They are always in earnest.

She was very pretty, exceedingly pretty. With a dimpled, surprised-looking, capital face; a ripe little mouth that seemed made to be kissed —as no doubt it was; all kinds of good little dots about her chin, that melted into one another when she laughed; and the sunniest pair of eyes you ever saw in any little creature's head. Altogether she was what you would have called provoking, but satisfactory, too. Oh, perfectly satisfactory!

"He's a comical old fellow," said Scrooge's nephew, "that's the truth; and not so pleasant as he might be. However, his offenses carry their own punishment, and I have nothing to say against him. Who suffers by his ill whims? Himself, always. Here he takes it into his head to dislike us, and he won't come and dine with us. What's the consequence? He doesn't lose much of a dinner."

"Indeed, I think he loses a very good dinner," interrupted Scrooge's niece. Everybody else said the same, and they must be allowed to have been competent judges, because they had just had dinner; and, with the dessert upon the table, were clustered round the fire, by lamplight.

"Well, I am very glad to hear it," said Scrooge's nephew, "because I haven't any great faith in these young housekeepers. What do *you* say, Topper?"

Topper clearly had his eye on one of Scrooge's niece's sisters, for he answered that a bachelor was a wretched outcast, who had no right to express an opinion on the subject. Whereat Scrooge's niece's sister —the plump one with the lace tucker, not the one with the roses— blushed.

After tea they had some music. For they were a musical family, and knew what they were about when they sung a Glee or Catch, I can assure you—especially Topper, who could growl away in the bass like a good one, and never swell the large veins in his forehead, or get red in the face over it.

But they didn't devote the whole evening to music. After a while they played at forfeits; for it is good to be children sometimes, and never better than at Christmas, when its mighty Founder was a child himself. There was first a game at blind man's buff, though. And I no more believe Topper was really blinded than I believe he had eyes in his boots. Because the way in which he went after that plump sister in the lace tucker was an outrage on the credulity of human nature. Knocking down the fire-irons, tumbling over the chairs, bumping up against the piano, smothering himself among the curtains, wherever she went there went he!

He always knew where the plump sister was. He wouldn't catch anybody else. If you had fallen up against him, as some of them did, and stood there, he would have made a feint of endeavoring to seize you, which would have been an affront to your understanding, and would instantly have sidled off in the direction of the plump sister.

"Here is a new game," said Scrooge. "One half-hour, Spirit, only one!"

It was a Game called Yes and No, where Scrooge's nephew had to think of something, and the rest must find out what; he only answering to their questions yes or no, as the case was. The fire of questioning to which he was exposed elicited from him that he was thinking of an animal, a live animal, rather a disagreeable animal, a savage animal, an animal that growled and grunted sometimes, and talked sometimes, and lived in London, and walked about the streets, and wasn't made a show of, and wasn't led by anybody, and didn't live in a menagerie, and was never killed in a market, and was not a horse, or an ass, or a cow, or a bull, or a tiger, or a dog, or a pig, or a cat, or a bear.

At every new question put to him, this nephew burst into a fresh roar of laughter; and was so inexpressibly tickled, that he was obliged to get up off the sofa and stamp. At last the plump sister cried out:

"I have found it out! I know what it is, Fred! I know what it is!"

"What is it?" cried Fred.

"It's your uncle Scro-o-o-o-oge!"

Which it certainly was. Admiration was the universal sentiment, though some objected that the reply to "Is it a bear?" ought to have been "Yes."

Uncle Scrooge had imperceptibly become so gay and light of heart, that he would have drank to the unconscious company in an inaudible speech. But the whole scene passed off in the breath of the last word spoken by his nephew; and he and the Spirit were again upon their travels.

Much they saw, and far they went, and many homes they visited, but always with a happy end. The Spirit stood beside sick-beds, and they were cheerful; on foreign lands, and they were close at home; by struggling men, and they were patient in their greater hope; by poverty, and it was rich. In almshouse, hospital, and jail, in misery's every refuge, where vain man in his little brief authority had not made fast the door, and barred the Spirit out, he left his blessing, and taught Scrooge his precepts. Suddenly, as they stood together in an open place, the bell struck twelve.

Scrooge looked about him for the Ghost, and saw it no more. As the last stroke ceased to vibrate, he remembered the prediction of old Jacob Marley, and, lifting up his eyes, beheld a solemn Fantom, draped and hooded, coming like a mist along the ground toward him.

STAVE FOUR: THE LAST OF THE SPIRITS

The Fantom slowly, gravely, silently approached. When it came near him, Scrooge bent down upon his knee; for in the air through which this Spirit moved it seemed to scatter gloom and mystery.

It was shrouded in a deep black garment, which concealed its head, its face, its form, and left nothing of it visible save one outstretched hand. He knew no more, for the Spirit neither spoke nor moved.

"I am in the presence of the Ghost of Christmas Yet To Come? Ghost of the Future! I fear you more than any specter I have seen. But as I know your purpose is to do me good, and as I hope to live to be another man from what I was, I am prepared to bear you company, and do it with a thankful heart. Will you not speak to me?"

It gave him no reply. The hand was pointed straight before them.

"Lead on! Lead on! The night is waning fast, and it is precious time to me, I know. Lead on, Spirit!"

They scarcely seemed to enter the city; for the city rather seemed to spring up about them. But there they were in the heart of it; on 'Change, among the merchants.

The Spirit stopped beside one little knot of business men. Observing that the hand was pointed to them, Scrooge advanced to listen to their talk.

"No," said a great fat man with a monstrous chin, "I don't know much about it either way. I only know he's dead."

"When did he die?" inquired another.

"Last night, I believe."

"Why, what was the matter with him? I thought he'd never die."

"God knows," said the first, with a yawn.

"What has he done with his money?" asked a red-faced gentleman.

"I haven't heard," said the man with the large chin. "Company, perhaps. He hasn't left it to me. That's all I know. By, by!"

Scrooge was at first inclined to be surprised that the Spirit should attach importance to conversation apparently so trivial; but feeling assured that it must have some hidden purpose, he set himself to consider what it was likely to be. It could scarcely be supposed to have any bearing on the death of Jacob, his old partner, for that was Past, and this Ghost's province was the Future.

He looked about in that very place for his own image; but another man stood in his accustomed corner, and though the clock pointed to his usual time of day for being there, he saw no likeness of himself among the multitudes that poured in through the Porch. It gave him little surprise, however; for he had been revolving in his mind a change of life, and he thought and hoped he saw his new-born resolutions carried out in this.

They left this busy scene, and went into an obscure part of the town, to a low shop where iron, old rags, bottles, bones, and greasy offal were bought. A gray-haired rascal, of great age, sat smoking his pipe.

Scrooge and the Fantom came into the presence of this man, just as a woman with a heavy bundle slunk into the shop. But she had scarcely entered, when another woman, similarly laden, came in, too; and she was closely followed by a man in faded black. After a short period of blank astonishment, in which the old man with the pipe had joined them, they all three burst into a laugh.

"Let the charwoman alone to be the first!" cried she who had entered first. "Let the laundress alone to be the second; and let the undertaker's man alone to be the third. Look here, old Joe, here's a chance! If we haven't all three met here without meaning it!"

"You couldn't have met in a better place. You were made free of it long ago, you know; and the other two ain't strangers. What have you got to sell? What have you got to sell?"

"Half a minute's patience, Joe, and you shall see."

"What odds, then! What odds, Mrs. Dilber?" said the woman. "Every person has a right to take care of themselves. *He* always did! Who's the worse for the loss of a few things like these? Not a dead man, I suppose."

Mrs. Dilber, whose manner was remarkable for general propitiation, said, "No, indeed, ma'am."

"If he wanted to keep 'em after he was dead, a wicked old screw, why wasn't he natural in his lifetime? If he had been, he'd have had somebody to look after him when he was struck with Death, instead of lying gasping out his last there, alone by himself."

"It's the truest word that ever was spoke; it's a judgment on him."

"I wish it was a little heavier judgment, and it should have been, you may depend upon it, if I could have laid my hands on anything else. Open that bundle, old Joe, and let me know the value of it. Speak out plain. I'm not afraid to be the first, nor afraid for them to see it."

Joe went down on his knees for the greater convenience of opening the bundle, and dragged out a large and heavy roll of some dark stuff.

"What do you call this? Bed-curtains!"

"Ah! Bed-curtains! Don't drop that oil upon the blankets, now."

"*His* blankets?"

"Whose else's, do you think? He isn't likely to take cold without 'em, I dare say. Ah! You may look through that shirt till your eyes ache; but you won't find a hole in it, nor a threadbare place. It's the best he had, and a fine one, too. They'd have wasted it by dressing him up in it, if it hadn't been for me."

Scrooge listened to this dialogue in horror.

"Spirit! I see, I see. The case of this unhappy man might be my own. My life tends that way now. Merciful Heaven, what is this?"

The scene had changed, and now he almost touched a bare, uncurtained bed. A pale light, rising in the outer air, fell straight upon this bed; and on it, unwatched, unwept, uncared for, was the body of this plundered unknown man.

"Spirit, let me see some tenderness connected with a death, or this dark chamber, Spirit, will be forever present to me."

The Ghost conducted him to poor Bob Cratchit's house—the dwelling he had visited before—and found the mother and the children seated round the fire.

Quiet. Very quiet. The noisy little Cratchits were as still as statues in one corner, and sat looking up at Peter, who had a book before him. The mother and her daughters were engaged in needlework. But surely they were very quiet!

" 'And He took a child, and set him in the midst of them.' "

Where had Scrooge heard those words? He had not dreamed them. The boy must have read them out, as he and the Spirit crossed the threshold. Why did he not go on?

The mother laid her work upon the table, and put her hand up to her face.

"The color hurts my eyes," she said.

The color? Ah, poor Tiny Tim!

"They're better now again. It makes them weak by candle-light; and I wouldn't show weak eyes to your father when he comes home, for the world. It must be near his time."

"Past it, rather," Peter answered, shutting up his book. "But I think he has walked a little slower than he used, these few last evenings, mother."

"I have known him walk with—I have known him walk with Tiny Tim upon his shoulder, very fast indeed."

"And so have I," cried Peter. "Often."

"And so have I," exclaimed another. So had all.

"But he was very light to carry, and his father loved him so, that it was no trouble—no trouble. And there is your father at the door!"

She hurried out to meet him; and little Bob in his comforter—he had need of it, poor fellow—came in. His tea was ready for him on the hob, and they all tried who should help him to it most. Then the two young Cratchits got upon his knees and laid, each child, a little cheek against his face, as if they said, "Don't mind it, father. Don't be grieved!"

Bob was very cheerful with them, and spoke pleasantly to all the family. He looked at the work upon the table, and praised the industry and speed of Mrs. Cratchit and the girls. They would be done long before Sunday, he said.

"Sunday! You went to-day, then, Robert?"

"Yes, my dear," returned Bob. "I wish you could have gone. It would have done you good to see how green a place it is. But you'll see it often. I promised him that I would walk there on a Sunday. My little, little child! My little child!"

He broke down all at once. He couldn't help it. If he could have helped it, he and his child would have been farther apart, perhaps, than they were.

"Specter," said Scrooge, "something informs me that our parting moment is at hand. I know it, but I know not how. Tell me what man that was, with the covered face, whom we saw lying dead?"

The Ghost of Christmas Yet To Come conveyed him to a dismal, wretched, ruinous churchyard.

The Spirit stood among the graves, and pointed down to One.

"Before I draw nearer to that stone to which you point, answer me one question. Are these the shadows of the things that Will be, or are they shadows of the things that May be only?"

Still the Ghost pointed downward to the grave by which it stood.

"Men's courses will foreshadow certain ends, to which, if persevered in, they must lead. But if the courses be departed from, the ends will change. Say it is thus with what you show me!"

The Spirit was immovable as ever.

Scrooge crept toward it, trembling as he went; and, following the finger, read upon the stone of the neglected grave his own name— EBENEZER SCROOGE.

"Am _I_ that man who lay upon the bed? No, Spirit! Oh, no, no! Spirit! hear me! I am not the man I was. I will not be the man I must have been but for this intercourse. Why show me this, if I am past all hope? Assure me that I yet may change these shadows you have shown me by an altered life."

For the first time the kind hand faltered.

"I will honor Christmas in my heart, and try to keep it all the year. I will live in the Past, the Present, and the Future. The Spirits of all three shall strive within me. I will not shut out the lessons that they teach. Oh, tell me I may sponge away the writing on this stone!"

Holding up his hands in one last prayer to have his fate reversed, he saw an alteration in the Fantom's hood and dress. It shrunk, collapsed, and dwindled down into a bedpost.

Yes, and the bedpost was his own. The bed was his own, the room was his own. Best and happiest of all, the Time before him was his own, to make amends in!

He was checked in his transports by the churches ringing out the lustiest peals he had ever heard.

Running to the window, he opened it, and put out his head. No fog, no mist, no night; clear, bright, stirring, golden day.

"What's to-day?" cried Scrooge, calling downward to a boy in Sunday clothes, who perhaps had loitered in to look about him.

"EH?"

"What's to-day, my fine fellow?"

"To-day! Why, CHRISTMAS DAY."

"It's Christmas day! I haven't missed it. Hallo, my fine fellow!"

"Hallo!"

"Do you know the Poulterer's, in the next street but one, at the corner?"

"I should hope I did."

"An intelligent boy! A remarkable boy! Do you know whether they've sold the prize Turkey that was hanging up there? Not the little prize Turkey—the big one?"

"What, the one as big as me?"

"What a delightful boy! It's a pleasure to talk to him. Yes, my buck!"

"It's hanging there now."

"Is it? Go and buy it."

"Walk-ER!" exclaimed the boy.

"No, no, I am in earnest. Go and buy it, and tell 'em to bring it here, that I may give them the direction where to take it. Come back with the man, and I'll give you a shilling. Come back with him in less than five minutes, and I'll give you half a crown!"

The boy was off like a shot.

"I'll send it to Bob Cratchit's! He sha'n't know who sends it. It's twice the size of Tiny Tim. Joe Miller never made such a joke as sending it to Bob's will be!"

The hand in which he wrote the address was not a steady one; but write it he did, somehow, and went down-stairs to open the street door, ready for the coming of the poulterer's man.

It *was* a Turkey! He never could have stood upon his legs, that bird. He would have snapped 'em short off in a minute, like sticks of sealing-wax.

Scrooge dressed himself "all in his best," and at last got out into the streets. The people were by this time pouring forth, as he had seen them with the Ghost of Christmas Present; and, walking with his hands behind him, Scrooge regarded every one with a delighted smile. He looked so irresistibly pleasant, in a word, that three or four good-humored fellows said, "Good morning, sir! A merry Christmas to you!" And Scrooge said often afterward, that, of all the blithe sounds he had ever heard, those were the blithest in his ears.

In the afternoon, he turned his steps toward his nephew's house. He passed the door a dozen times, before he had the courage to go up and knock. But he made a dash, and did it.

"Is your master at home, my dear?" said Scrooge to the girl. Nice girl! Very.

"Yes, sir."

"Where is he, my love?"

"He's in the dining-room, sir, along with mistress."

"He knows me," said Scrooge, with his hand already on the dining-room lock. "I'll go in here, my dear."

"Fred!"

"Why, bless my soul!" cried Fred, "who's that?"

"It's I. Your Uncle Scrooge. I have come to dinner. Will you let me in, Fred?"

Let him in! It is a mercy he didn't shake his arm off. He was at home in five minutes. Nothing could be heartier. His niece looked just the same. So did Topper when *he* came. So did the plump sister when *she* came. So did every one when *they* came. Wonderful party, wonderful games, wonderful unanimity, won-der-ful happiness!

But he was early at the office next morning. Oh, he was early there! If he could only be there first, and catch Bob Cratchit coming late! That was the thing he had set his heart upon.

And he did it. The clock struck nine. No Bob. A quarter past. No Bob. Bob was full eighteen minutes and a half behind his time. Scrooge sat with his door wide open, that he might see him come into the Tank.

Bob's hat was off before he opened the door; his comforter, too. He was on his stool in a jiffy; driving away with his pen, as if he were trying to overtake nine o'clock.

"Hallo!" growled Scrooge in his accustomed voice, as near as he could feign it. "What do you mean by coming here at this time of day?"

"I am very sorry, sir. I *am* behind my time."

"You are? Yes. I think you are. Step this way, if you please."

"It's only once a year, sir. It shall not be repeated. I was making rather merry yesterday, sir."

"Now, I'll tell you what, my friend. I am not going to stand this sort of thing any longer. And therefore," Scrooge continued, leaping from his stool, and giving Bob such a dig in the waistcoat that he staggered back into the Tank again—"and therefore I am about to raise your salary!"

Bob trembled, and got a little nearer to the ruler.

"A merry Christmas, Bob!" said Scrooge, with an earnestness that could not be mistaken, as he clapped him on the back. "A merrier Christmas, Bob, my good fellow, than I have given you for many a year! I'll raise your salary, and endeavor to assist your struggling family, and we will discuss your affairs this very afternoon, over a Christmas bowl of smoking bishop, Bob! Make up the fires, and buy a second coal-scuttle before you dot another i, Bob Cratchit!"

Scrooge was better than his word. He did it all, and infinitely more; and to Tiny Tim, who did NOT die, he was a second father. He became as good a friend, as good a master, and as good a man as the good old city knew, or any other good old city, town, or borough in the good old world. Some people laughed to see the alteration in him; but his own heart laughed, and that was quite enough for him.

He had no further intercourse with spirits, but lived in that respect upon the total-abstinence principle ever afterward; and it was always said of him, that he knew how to keep Christmas well, if any man alive possessed the knowledge. May that be truly said of us, and all of us! And so, as Tiny Tim observed, God bless us, every one!

15

Malachi's Cove

BY ANTHONY TROLLOPE

ON the northern coast of Cornwall, between Tintagel and Bossiney, down on the very margin of the sea, there lived not long since an old man who got his living by saving seaweed from the waves, and selling it for manure. The cliffs there are bold and fine, and the sea beats in upon them from the north with a grand violence. I doubt whether it be not the finest morsel of cliff scenery in England, though it is beaten by many portions of the west coast of Ireland, and perhaps also by spots in Wales and Scotland. Cliffs should be nearly precipitous, they should be broken in their outlines, and should barely admit here and there of an insecure passage from their summit to the sand at their feet. The sea should come, if not up to them, at least very near to them, and then, above all things, the water below them should be blue, and not of that dead leaden colour which is so familiar to us in England. At Tintagel all these requisites are there, except that bright blue colour which is so lovely. But the cliffs themselves are bold and well broken, and the margin of sand at high water is very narrow—so narrow that at spring-tides there is barely a footing there.

Close upon this margin was the cottage, or hovel, of Malachi Trenglos, the old man of whom I have spoken. But Malachi, or old Glos, as he was commonly called by the people around him, had not built his house absolutely upon the sand. There was a fissure in the rock so great that at the top it formed a narrow ravine, and so complete from the summit to the base that it afforded an opening for a steep and rugged track from the top of the rock to the bottom. This fissure was so wide at the bottom that it had afforded space for Trenglos to fix his habitation on a foundation of rock, and here he had lived for many years. It was told of him that in the early days of his trade he had always carried the weed in a basket on his back to the top, but latterly he had been possessed of a donkey which had been trained to go up and down the steep track with a single pannier over his loins, for the rocks would not admit of panniers hanging by his side; and for this assistant he had built a shed adjoining his own, and almost as large as that in which he himself resided.

But, as years went on, old Glos procured other assistance than that of the donkey, or, as I should rather say, Providence supplied him with other help; and, indeed, had it not been so, the old man must have given up his cabin and his independence and gone into the workhouse at Camelford. For rheumatism had afflicted him, old age had bowed him till he was nearly double, and by degrees he became unable to attend the donkey on its upward passage to the world above, or even to assist in rescuing the coveted weed from the waves.

At the time to which our story refers, Trenglos had not been up the cliff for twelve months, and for the last six months he had done nothing towards the furtherance of his trade, except to take the money and keep it, if any of it was kept, and occasionally to shake down a bundle of fodder for the donkey. The real work of the business was done altogether by Mahala Trenglos, his granddaughter.

Mally Trenglos was known to all the farmers round the coast, and to all the small tradespeople in Camelford. She was a wild-looking, almost unearthly creature, with wild-flowing, black, uncombed hair, small in stature, with small hands and bright, black eyes; but people said that she was very strong, and the children around declared that she worked day and night, and knew nothing of fatigue. As to her age there were many doubts. Some said she was ten, and others five-and-twenty, but the reader may be allowed to know that at this time she had in truth passed her twentieth birthday. The old people spoke well of Mally, because she was so good to her grandfather; and it was said of her that though she carried to him a little gin and tobacco almost daily, she bought nothing for herself;—and as to the gin, no one who looked at her would accuse her of meddling with that. But she had no friends, and but few acquaintances among people of her own age. They said that she was fierce and ill-natured, that she had not a good word for anyone, and that she was, complete at all points, a thorough little vixen. The young men did not care for her; for, as regards dress, all days were alike with her. She never made herself smart on Sundays. She was generally without stockings, and seemed to care not at all to exercise any of those feminine attractions which might have been hers had she studied to attain them. All days were the same to her in regard to dress; and, indeed, till lately, all days had, I fear, been the same to her in other respects. Old Malachi had never been seen inside a place of worship since he had taken to live under the cliff.

But within the last two years Mally had submitted herself to the teaching of the clergyman at Tintagel, and had appeared at church on Sundays, if not absolutely with punctuality, at any rate so often that no one who knew the peculiarity of her residence was disposed to quarrel with her on that subject. But she made no difference in her dress on these occasions. She took her place on a low stone seat just inside the church door, clothed as usual in her thick, red serge petticoat and loose, brown serge jacket, such being the apparel which she had found to be best adapted for her hard and perilous work among the waters. She had pleaded to the clergyman when he attacked her on the subject of church attendance with vigour that she had got no church-going clothes. He had explained to her that she would be received there without distinction to her clothing. Mally had taken him at his word, and had gone, with a courage which certainly deserved admiration, though I doubt whether there was not mingled with it an obstinacy which was less admirable.

For people said that old Glos was rich, and that Mally might have proper clothes if she chose to buy them. Mr. Polwarth, the clergyman, who, as the old man could not come to him, went down the rocks to the old man, did make some hint on the matter in Mally's absence. But old Glos, who had been patient with him on other matters, turned upon him so angrily when he made an allusion to money, that Mr. Polwarth found himself obliged to give that matter up, and Mally continued to sit upon the stone bench in her short serge petticoat, with her long hair streaming down her face. She did so far sacrifice to decency as on such occasions to tie up her back hair with an old shoe-string. So tied it would remain through the Monday and Tuesday, but by Wednesday afternoon Mally's hair had generally managed to escape.

As to Mally's indefatigable industry there could be no manner of doubt, for the quantity of seaweed which she and the donkey amassed between them was very surprising. Old Glos, it was declared, had never collected half what Mally gathered together; but then the article was becoming cheaper, and it was necessary that the exertion should be greater. So Mally and the donkey toiled and toiled, and the seaweed came up in heaps which surprised those who looked at her little hands and light form. Was there not someone who helped her at nights, some fairy, or demon, or the like? Mally was so snappish in her answers to people that she had no right to be surprised if ill-natured things were said of her.

No one ever heard Mally Trenglos complain of her work, but about this time she was heard to make great and loud complaints of the treatment she received from some of her neighbours. It was known that she went with her plaints to Mr. Polwarth; and when he could not help her, or did not give her such instant help as she needed, she went—ah, so foolishly! to the office of a certain attorney at Camelford, who was not likely to prove himself a better friend than Mr. Polwarth.

Now the nature of her injury was as follows: The place in which she collected her seaweed was a little cove; the people had come to call it Malachi's Cove from the name of the old man who lived there; —which was so formed, that the margin of the sea therein could only be reached by the passage from the top down to Trenglos's hut. The breadth of the cove when the sea was out might perhaps be two hundred yards, and on each side the rocks ran out in such a way that both from north and south the domain of Trenglos was guarded from intruders. And this locality had been well chosen for its intended purpose.

There was a rush of the sea into the cove, which carried there large, drifting masses of seaweed, leaving them among the rocks when the tide was out. During the equinoctial winds of the spring and autumn the supply would never fail; and even when the sea was calm, the long, soft, salt-bedewed, trailing masses of the weed could be gathered there when they could not be found elsewhere for miles along the coast. The task of getting the weed from the breakers was often difficult and dangerous—so difficult that much of it was left to be carried away by the next incoming tide.

Mally doubtless did not gather half the crop that was there at her feet. What was taken by the returning waves she did not regret; but when interlopers came upon her cove, and gathered her wealth,—her grandfather's wealth, beneath her eyes, then her heart was broken. It was this interloping, this intrusion, that drove poor Mally to the Camelford attorney. But, alas, though the Camelford attorney took Mally's money, he could do nothing for her, and her heart was broken!

She had an idea, in which no doubt her grandfather shared, that the path to the cove was, at any rate, their property. When she was told that the cove, and sea running into the cove, were not the freeholds of her grandfather, she understood that the statement might be true. But what then as to the use of the path? Who had made the path what it was? Had she not painfully, wearily, with exceeding toil, carried up bits of rock with her own little hands, that her grandfather's donkey might have footing for his feet? Had she not scraped together crumbs of earth along the face of the cliff that she might make easier to

the animal the track of that rugged way? And now, when she saw
big farmers' lads coming down with other donkeys,—and, indeed,
there was one who came with a pony; no boy, but a young man, old
enough to know better than rob a poor old man and a young girl,—
she reviled the whole human race, and swore that the Camelford
attorney was a fool.

Any attempt to explain to her that there was still weed enough for
her was worse than useless. Was it not all hers and his, or, at any rate,
was not the sole way to it his and hers? And was not her trade stopped
and impeded? Had she not been forced to back her laden donkey
down, twenty yards she said, but it had, in truth, been five, because
Farmer Gunliffe's son had been in the way with his thieving pony?
Farmer Gunliffe had wanted to buy her weed at his own price, and
because she had refused he had set on his thieving son to destroy her
in this wicked way.

"I'll hamstring the beast the next time as he's down here!" said Mally
to old Glos, while the angry fire literally streamed from her eyes.

Farmer Gunliffe's small homestead—he held about fifty acres of land
—was close by the village of Tintagel, and not a mile from the cliff.
The sea-wrack, as they call it, was pretty well the only manure within
his reach, and no doubt he thought it hard that he should be kept from
using it by Mally Trenglos and her obstinacy.

"There's heaps of other coves, Barty," said Mally to Barty Gunliffe,
the farmer's son.

"But none so nigh, Mally, nor yet none that fills 'emselves as this
place."

Then he explained to her that he would not take the weed that came
up close to hand. He was bigger than she was, and stronger, and
would get it from the outer rocks, with which she never meddled.
Then, with scorn in her eye, she swore that she could get it where
he durst not venture, and repeated her threat of hamstringing the
pony. Barty laughed at her wrath, jeered her because of her wild hair,
and called her a mermaid.

"I'll mermaid you!" she cried. "Mermaid, indeed! I wouldn't be a
man to come and rob a poor girl and an old cripple. But you're no man,
Barty Gunliffe! You're not half a man."

Nevertheless, Bartholomew Gunliffe was a very fine young fellow,
as far as the eye went. He was about five feet eight inches high, with
strong arms and legs, with light, curly brown hair and blue eyes. His
father was but in a small way as a farmer, but, nevertheless, Barty
Gunliffe was well thought of among the girls around. Everybody liked
Barty—excepting only Mally Trenglos, and she hated him like poison.

Barty, when he was asked why so good-natured a lad as he perse-
cuted a poor girl and an old man, threw himself upon the justice of
the thing. It wouldn't do at all, according to his view, that any single
person should take upon himself to own that which God Almighty
sent as the common property of all. He would do Mally no harm,
and so he had told her. But Mally was a vixen—a wicked little vixen;
and she must be taught to have a civil tongue in her head. When once
Mally would speak him civil as he went for weed, he would get his
father to pay the old man some sort of toll for the use of the path.

"Speak him civil?" said Mally. "Never; not while I have a tongue
in my mouth!" And I fear old Glos encouraged her rather than otherwise in her view of the matter.

But her grandfather did not encourage her to hamstring the pony.
Hamstringing a pony would be a serious thing, and old Glos thought
it might be very awkward for both of them if Mally were put into
prison. He suggested, therefore, that all manner of impediments
should be put in the way of the pony's feet, surmising that the well-
trained donkey might be able to work in spite of them. And Barty
Gunliffe, on his next descent, did find the passage very awkward when
he came near to Malachi's hut, but he made his way down, and poor
Mally saw the lumps of rock at which she had laboured so hard pushed
on one side or rolled out of the way with a steady persistency of injury
towards herself that almost drove her frantic.

"Well, Barty, you're a nice boy," said old Glos, sitting in the doorway
of the hut, as he watched the intruder.

"I ain't a-doing no harm to none as doesn't harm me," said Barty.
"The sea's free to all, Malachi."

"And the sky's free to all, but I mustn't get up on the top of your
big barn to look at it," said Mally, who was standing among the rocks
with a long hook in her hand. The long hook was the tool with which
she worked in dragging the weed from the waves. "But you ain't got
no justice nor yet no spirit, or you wouldn't come here to vex an old
man like he."

"I didn't want to vex him, nor yet to vex you, Mally. You let me be
for a while, and we'll be friends yet."

"Friends!" exclaimed Mally. "Who'd have the likes of you for a
friend? What are you moving them stones for? Them stones belongs to
grandfather." And in her wrath she made a movement as though she
were going to fly at him.

"Let him be, Mally," said the old man; "let him be. He'll get his
punishment. He'll come to be drowned some day if he comes down
here when the wind is in shore."

"That he may be drowned then!" said Mally, in her anger. "If he was in the big hole there among the rocks, and the sea running in at half tide, I wouldn't lift a hand to help him out."

"Yes, you would, Mally; you'd fish me up with your hook like a big stick of seaweed."

She turned from him with scorn as he said this, and went into the hut. It was time for her to get ready for her work, and one of the great injuries done her lay in this,—that such a one as Barty Gunliffe should come and look at her during her toil among the breakers.

It was an afternoon in April, and the hour was something after four o'clock. There had been a heavy wind from the north-west all the morning, with gusts of rain, and the sea-gulls had been in and out of the cove all the day, which was a sure sign to Mally that the incoming tide would cover the rocks with weed.

The quick waves were now returning with wonderful celerity over the low reefs, and the time had come at which the treasure must be seized, if it was to be garnered on that day. By seven o'clock it would be growing dark, at nine it would be high water, and before daylight the crop would be carried out again if not collected. All this Mally understood very well, and some of this Barty was beginning to understand also.

As Mally came down with her bare feet, bearing her long hook in her hand, she saw Barty's pony standing patiently on the sand, and in her heart she longed to attack the brute. Barty at this moment, with a common three-pronged fork in his hand, was standing down on a large rock, gazing forth towards the waters. He had declared that he would gather the weed only at places which were inaccessible to Mally, and he was looking out that he might settle where he would begin.

"Let 'un be, let 'un be," shouted the old man to Mally, as he saw her take a step towards the beast, which she hated almost as much as she hated the man.

Hearing her grandfather's voice through the wind, she desisted from her purpose, if any purpose she had had, and went forth to her work. As she passed down the cove, and scrambled in among the rocks, she saw Barty still standing on his perch; out beyond, the white-curling waves were cresting and breaking themselves with violence, and the wind was howling among the caverns and abutments of the cliff.

Every now and then there came a squall of rain, and though there was sufficient light, the heavens were black with clouds. A scene more beautiful might hardly be found by those who love the glories of the coast. The light for such objects was perfect. Nothing could exceed the grandeur of the colours,—the blue of the open sea, the white of the breaking waves, the yellow sands, or the streaks of red and brown which gave such richness to the cliff.

But neither Mally nor Barty were thinking of such things as these. Indeed, they were hardly thinking of their trade after its ordinary forms. Barty was meditating how he might best accomplish his purpose of working beyond the reach of Mally's feminine powers, and Mally was resolving that wherever Barty went she would go farther.

And, in many respects, Mally had the advantage. She knew every rock in the spot, and was sure of those which gave a good foothold, and sure also of those which did not. And then her activity had been made perfect by practice for the purpose to which it was to be devoted. Barty, no doubt, was stronger than she, and quite as active. But Barty could not jump among the waves from one stone to another as she could do, nor was he as yet able to get aid in his work from the very force of the water as she could get it. She had been hunting seaweed in that cove since she had been an urchin of six years old, and she knew every hole and corner and every spot of vantage. The waves were her friends, and she could use them. She could measure their strength, and knew when and where it would cease.

Mally was great down in the salt pools of her own cove,—great, and very fearless. As she watched Barty make his way forward from rock to rock, she told herself, gleefully, that he was going astray. The curl of the wind as it blew into the cove would not carry the weed up to the northern buttresses of the cove; and then there was the great hole just there—the great hole of which she had spoken when she wished him evil.

And now she went to work, hooking up the dishevelled hairs of the ocean, and landing many a cargo on the extreme margin of the sand, from whence she would be able in the evening to drag it back before the invading waters would return to reclaim the spoil.

And on his side also Barty made his heap up against the northern buttresses of which I have spoken. Barty's heap became big and still bigger, so that he knew, let the pony work as he might, he could not take it all up that evening. But still it was not as large as Mally's heap. Mally's hook was better than his fork, and Mally's skill was better than his strength. And when he failed in some haul Mally would jeer him with a wild, weird laughter, and shriek to him through the wind that he was not half a man. At first he answered her with laughing words, but before long, as she boasted of her success and pointed to his failure, he became angry, and then he answered her no more. He became angry with himself, in that he missed so much of the plunder before him.

The broken sea was full of the long straggling growth which the waves had torn up from the bottom of the ocean, but the masses were carried past him, away from him,—nay, once or twice over him; and then Mally's weird voice would sound in his ear, jeering him. The gloom among the rocks was now becoming thicker and thicker, the tide was beating in with increased strength, and the gusts of wind came with quicker and greater violence. But still he worked on. While Mally worked he would work, and he would work for some time after she was driven in. He would not be beaten by a girl.

The great hole was now full of water, but of water which seemed to be boiling as though in a pot. And the pot was full of floating masses,—large treasures of seaweed which were thrown to and fro upon its surface, but lying there so thick that one would seem almost able to rest upon it without sinking.

Mally knew well how useless it was to attempt to rescue aught from the fury of that boiling cauldron. The hole went in under the rocks, and the side of it towards the shore lay high, slippery, and steep. The hole, even at low water, was never empty; and Mally believed that there was no bottom to it. Fish thrown in there could escape out to the ocean, miles away,—so Mally in her softer moods would tell the visitors to the cove. She knew the hole well. Poulnadioul she was accustomed to call it; which was supposed, when translated, to mean that this was the hole of the Evil One. Never did Mally attempt to make her own the weed which had found its way into that pot.

But Barty Gunliffe knew no better, and she watched him as he endeavoured to steady himself on the treacherously slippery edge of the pool. He fixed himself there and made a haul, with some small success. How he managed it she hardly knew, but she stood still for a while watching him anxiously, and then she saw him slip. He slipped, and recovered himself;—slipped again, and again recovered himself.

"Barty, you fool!" she screamed; "if you get yourself pitched in there, you'll never come out no more."

Whether she simply wished to frighten him, or whether her heart relented and she had thought of his danger with dismay, who shall say? She could not have told herself. She hated him as much as ever,—but she could hardly have wished to see him drowned before her eyes.

"You go on, and don't mind me," said he, speaking in a hoarse, angry tone.

"Mind you!—who minds you?" retorted the girl. And then she again prepared herself for her work.

But as she went down over the rocks with her long hook balanced in her hands, she suddenly heard a splash, and, turning quickly round, saw the body of her enemy tumbling amidst the eddying waves in the pool. The tide had now come up so far that every succeeding wave washed into it and over it from the side nearest to the sea, and then ran down again back from the rocks, as the rolling wave receded, with a noise like the fall of a cataract. And then, when the surplus water had retreated for a moment, the surface of the pool would be partly calm, though the fretting bubbles would still boil up and down, and there was ever a simmer on the surface, as though, in truth, the cauldron were heated. But this time of comparative rest was but a moment, for the succeeding breaker would come up almost as soon as the foam of the preceding one had gone, and then again the waters would be dashed upon the rocks, and the sides would echo with the roar of the angry wave.

Instantly Mally hurried across to the edge of the pool, crouching down upon her hands and knees for security as she did so. As a wave receded, Barty's head and face was carried round near to her, and she could see that his forehead was covered with blood. Whether he were alive or dead she did not know. She had seen nothing but his blood, and the light-coloured hair of his head lying amidst the foam. Then his body was drawn along by the suction of the retreating wave; but the mass of water that escaped was not on this occasion large enough to carry the man out with it.

Instantly Mally was at work with her hook, and getting it fixed into his coat, dragged him towards the spot on which she was kneeling. During the half minute of repose she got him so close that she could touch his shoulder. Straining herself down, laying herself over the long bending handle of the hook, she strove to grasp him with her right hand. But she could not do it; she could only touch him.

Then came the next breaker, forcing itself on with a roar, looking to Mally as though it must certainly knock her from her resting-place, and destroy them both. But she had nothing for it but to kneel, and hold by her hook.

What prayer passed through her mind at that moment for herself or for him, or for that old man who was sitting unconsciously up at the cabin, who can say? The great wave came and rushed over her as she lay almost prostrate, and when the water was gone from her eyes, and the tumult of the foam, and the violence of the roaring breaker had passed by her, she found herself at her length upon the rock, while his body had been lifted up, free from her hook, and was lying upon the slippery ledge, half in the water and half out of it. As she looked at him, in that instant, she could see that his eyes were open and that he was struggling with his hands.

"Hold by the hook, Barty," she cried, pushing the stick of it before him, while she seized the collar of his coat in her hands.

Had he been her brother, her lover, her father, she could not have

clung to him with more of the energy of despair. He did contrive to
hold by the stick which she had given him, and when the succeeding
wave had passed by, he was still on the ledge. In the next moment she
was seated a yard or two above the hole, in comparative safety, while
Barty lay upon the rocks with his still bleeding head resting upon her
lap.

What could she do now? She could not carry him; and in fifteen
minutes the sea would be up where she was sitting. He was quite insensible and very pale, and the blood was coming slowly,—very slowly,
—from the wound on his forehead. Ever so gently she put her hand
upon his hair to move it back from his face; and then she bent over
his mouth to see if he breathed, and as she looked at him she knew
that he was beautiful.

What would she not give that he might live? Nothing now was so
precious to her as his life,—as this life which she had so far rescued
from the waters. But what could she do? Her grandfather could
scarcely get himself down over the rocks, if indeed he could succeed
in doing so much as that. Could she drag the wounded man backwards, if it were only a few feet, so that he might lie above the reach
of the waves till further assistance could be procured?

She set herself to work and she moved him, almost lifting him. As she
did so she wondered at her own strength, but she was very strong at
that moment. Slowly, tenderly, falling on the rocks herself so that he
might fall on her, she got him back to the margin of the sand, to a spot
which the waters would not reach for the next two hours.

Here her grandfather met them, having seen at last what had happened from the door.

"Dada," she said, "he fell into the pool yonder, and was battered
against the rocks. See there at his forehead."

"Mally, I'm thinking that he's dead already," said old Glos, peering
down over the body.

"No, dada; he is not dead; but mayhap he's dying. But I'll go at
once up to the farm."

"Mally," said the old man, "look at his head. They'll say we murdered him."

"Who'll say so? Who'll lie like that? Didn't I pull him out of the
hole?"

"What matters that? His father'll say we killed him."

It was manifest to Mally that whatever anyone mght say hereafter,
her present course was plain before her. She must run up the path to
Gunliffe's farm and get necessary assistance. If the world were as bad
as her grandfather said, it would be so bad that she would not care to

live longer in it. But be that as it might, there was no doubt as to what she must do now.

So away she went as fast as her naked feet could carry her up the cliff. When at the top she looked round to see if any person might be within ken, but she saw no one. So she ran with all her speed along the headland of the corn-field which led in the direction of old Gunliffe's house, and as she drew near to the homestead she saw that Barty's mother was leaning on the gate. As she approached, she attempted to call, but her breath failed her for any purpose of loud speech, so she ran on till she was able to grasp Mrs. Gunliffe by the arm.

"Where's himself?" she said, holding her hand upon her beating heart that she might husband her breath.

"Who is it you mean?" said Mrs. Gunliffe, who participated in the family feud against Trenglos and his granddaughter. "What does the girl clutch me for in that way?"

"He's dying then, that's all."

"Who is dying? Is it old Malachi? If the old man's bad, we'll send someone down."

"It ain't dada, it's Barty! Where's himself? Where's the master?"

But by this time Mrs. Gunliffe was in an agony of despair, and was calling out for assistance lustily. Happily Gunliffe, the father, was at hand, and with him a man from the neighbouring village.

"Will you not send for the doctor?" said Mally. "Oh, man, you should send for the doctor!"

Whether any orders were given for the doctor she did not know, but in a very few minutes she was hurrying across the field again towards the path to the cove, and Gunliffe with the other man and his wife were following her.

As Mally went along she recovered her voice, for their step was not so quick as hers, and that which to them was a hurried movement, allowed her to get her breath again. And as she went she tried to explain to the father what had happened, saying but little, however, of her own doings in the matter. The wife hung behind listening, exclaiming every now and again that her boy was killed, and then asking wild questions as to his being yet alive. The father, as he went, said little. He was known as a silent, sober man, well spoken of for diligence and general conduct, but supposed to be stern and very hard when angered.

As they drew near to the top of the path, the other man whispered something to him, and then he turned round upon Mally and stopped her.

"If he has come by his death between you, your blood shall be taken for his," said he.

Then the wife shrieked out that her child had been murdered, and Mally, looking round into the faces of the three, saw that her grandfather's words had come true. They suspected her of having taken the life, in saving which she had nearly lost her own.

She looked round at them with awe in her face, and then, without saying a word, preceded them down the path. What had she to answer when such a charge as that was made against her? If they chose to say that she pushed him into the pool, and hit him with her hook as he lay amidst the waters, how could she show that it was not so?

Poor Mally knew little of the law of evidence, and it seemed to her that she was in their hands. But as she went down the steep track with a hurried step,—a step so quick that they could not keep up with her,— her heart was very full,—very full and very high. She had striven for the man's life as though he had been her brother. The blood was yet not dry on her own legs and arms, where she had torn them in his service. At one moment she had felt sure that she would die with him in that pool. And now they said that she had murdered him! It may be that he was not dead, and what would he say if ever he should speak again? Then she thought of that moment when his eyes had opened, and he had seemed to see her. She had no fear for herself, for her heart was very high. But it was full also,—full of scorn, disdain, and wrath.

When she had reached the bottom, she stood close to the door of the hut waiting for them, so that they might precede her to the other group, which was there in front of them, at a little distance on the sand.

"He is there, and dada is with him. Go and look at him," said Mally.

The father and mother ran on stumbling over the stones, but Mally remained behind by the door of the hut.

Barty Gunliffe was lying on the sand where Mally had left him, and old Malachi Trenglos was standing over him, resting himself with difficulty upon a stick.

"Not a move he's moved since she left him," said he, "not a move. I put his head on the old rug as you see, and I tried 'un with a drop of gin, but he wouldn't take it,—he wouldn't take it."

"Oh, my boy! my boy!" said the mother, throwing herself beside her son upon the sand.

"Haud your tongue, woman," said the father, kneeling down slowly by the lad's head, "whimpering that way will do 'un no good."

Then having gazed for a minute or two upon the pale face beneath him, he looked up sternly into that of Malachi Trenglos.

The old man hardly knew how to bear this terrible inquisition.

"He would come," said Malachi; "he brought it all upon hisself."

"Who was it struck him?" said the father.

"Sure he struck hisself, as he fell among the breakers."

"Liar!" said the father, looking up at the old man.

"They have murdered him!—They have murdered him!" shrieked the mother.

"Haud your peace, woman!" said the husband again. "They shall give us blood for blood."

Mally, leaning against the corner of the hovel, heard it all, but did not stir. They might say what they liked. They might make it out to be murder. They might drag her and her grandfather to Camelford Gaol, and then to Bodmin, and the gallows; but they could not take from her the conscious feeling that was her own. She had done her best to save him,—her very best. And she had saved him!

She remembered her threat to him before they had gone down on the rocks together, and her evil wish. Those words had been very wicked; but since that she had risked her life to save his. They might say what they pleased of her, and do what they pleased. She knew what she knew.

Then the father raised his son's head and shoulders in his arms, and called on the others to assist him in carrying Barty towards the path. They raised him between them carefully and tenderly, and lifted their burden on towards the spot at which Mally was standing. She never moved, but watched them at their work; and the old man followed them, hobbling after them with his crutch.

When they had reached the end of the hut she looked upon Barty's face, and saw that it was very pale. There was no longer blood upon the forehead, but the great gash was to be seen there plainly, with its jagged cut, and the skin livid and blue round the orifice. His light brown hair was hanging back, as she had made it to hang when she had gathered it with her hand after the big wave had passed over them. Ah, how beautiful he was in Mally's eyes with that pale face, and the sad scar upon his brow! She turned her face away, that they might not see her tears; but she did not move, nor did she speak.

But now, when they had passed the end of the hut, shuffling along with their burden, she heard a sound which stirred her. She roused herself quickly from her leaning posture, and stretched forth her head as though to listen; then she moved to follow them. Yes, they had stopped at the bottom of the path, and had again laid the body on the rocks. She heard that sound again, as of a long, long sigh, and then, regardless of any of them, she ran to the wounded man's head.

"He is not dead," she said. "There; he is not dead."

As she spoke Barty's eyes opened, and he looked about him.

"Barty, my boy, speak to me," said the mother.

Barty turned his face upon his mother, smiled, and then stared about him wildly.

"How is it with thee, lad?" said his father.

Then Barty turned his face again to the latter voice, and as he did so his eyes fell upon Mally.

"Mally!" he said. "Mally!"

It could have wanted nothing further to any of those present to teach them that, according to Barty's own view of the case, Mally had not been his enemy; and, in truth, Mally herself wanted no further triumph. That word had vindicated her, and she withdrew back to the hut.

"Dada," she said, "Barty is not dead, and I'm thinking they won't say anything more about our hurting him."

Old Glos shook his head. He was glad the lad hadn't met his death there; he didn't want the young man's blood, but he knew what folk would say. The poorer he was the more sure the world would be to trample on him. Mally said what she could to comfort him, being full of comfort herself.

She would have crept up to the farm if she dared, to ask how Barty was. But her courage failed her when she thought of that, so she went to work again, dragging back the weed she had saved to the spot at which on the morrow she would load the donkey. As she did this she saw Barty's pony still standing patiently under the rock, so she got a lock of fodder and threw it down before the beast.

It had become dark down in the cove, but she was still dragging back the seaweed, when she saw the glimmer of a lantern coming down the pathway. It was a most unusual sight, for lanterns were not common down in Malachi's Cove. Down came the lantern rather slowly, —much more slowly than she was in the habit of descending, and then through the gloom she saw the figure of a man standing at the bottom of the path. She went up to him, and saw that it was Mr. Gunliffe, the father.

"Is that Mally?" said Gunliffe.

"Yes, it is Mally; and how is Barty, Mr. Gunliffe?"

"You must come to 'un yourself, now at once," said the farmer. "He won't sleep a wink till he's seed you. You must not say but you'll come."

"Sure I'll come if I'm wanted," said Mally.

Gunliffe waited a moment, thinking that Mally might have to prepare herself, but Mally needed no preparation. She was dripping with salt water from the weed which she had been dragging, and her elfin locks were streaming wildly from her head; but, such as she was, she was ready.

"Dada's in bed," she said, "and I can go now if you please."

Then Gunliffe turned round and followed her up the path, wondering at the life which this girl led so far away from all her sex. It was now dark night, and he had found her working at the very edge of the rolling waves by herself, in the darkness, while the only human being who might seem to be her protector had already gone to his bed.

When they were at the top of the cliff Gunliffe took her by her hand, and led her along. She did not comprehend this, but she made no attempt to take her hand from his. Something he said about falling on the cliffs, but it was muttered so lowly that Mally hardly understood him. But, in truth, the man knew that she had saved his boy's life, and that he had injured her instead of thanking her. He was now taking her to his heart, and as words were wanting to him, he was showing his love after this silent fashion. He held her by the hand as though she were a child, and Mally tripped along at his side asking him no questions.

When they were at the farm-yard gate, he stopped for a moment.

"Mally, my girl," he said, "he'll not be content till he sees thee, but thou must not stay long wi' him, lass. Doctor says he's weak like, and wants sleep badly."

Mally merely nodded her head, and then they entered the house. Mally had never been within it before, and looked about with wondering eyes at the furniture of the big kitchen. Did any idea of her future destiny flash upon her then, I wonder? But she did not pause here a moment, but was led up to the bedroom above stairs, where Barty was lying on his mother's bed.

"Is it Mally herself?" said the voice of the weak youth.

"It's Mally herself," said the mother, "so now you can say what you please."

"Mally," said he, "Mally, it's along of you that I'm alive this moment."

"I'll not forget it on her," said the father, with his eyes turned away from her. "I'll never forget it on her."

"We hadn't a one but only him," said the mother, with her apron up to her face.

"Mally, you'll be friends with me now?" said Barty.

To have been made lady of the manor of the cove for ever, Mally couldn't have spoken a word now. It was not only that the words and presence of the people there cowed her and made her speechless, but the big bed, and the looking-glass, and the unheard-of wonders of the chamber, made her feel her own insignificance. But she crept up to Barty's side, and put her hand upon his.

"I'll come and get the weed, Mally; but it shall all be for you," said Barty.

"Indeed, you won't then, Barty dear," said the mother; "you'll never go near the awesome place again. What would we do if you were took from us?"

"He mustn't go near the hole if he does," said Mally, speaking at last in a solemn voice, and imparting the knowledge which she had kept to herself while Barty was her enemy; " 'specially not if the wind's any way from the nor'ard."

"She'd better go down now," said the father.

Barty kissed the hand which he held, and Mally, looking at him as he did so, thought that he was like an angel.

"You'll come and see us to-morrow, Mally," said he.

To this she made no answer, but followed Mrs. Gunliffe out of the room. When they were down in the kitchen, the mother had tea for her, and thick milk, and a hot cake,—all the delicacies which the farm could afford. I don't know that Mally cared much for the eating and drinking that night, but she began to think that the Gunliffes were good people,—very good people. It was better thus, at any rate, than being accused of murder and carried off to Camelford prison.

"I'll never forget it on her—never," the father had said.

Those words stuck to her from that moment, and seemed to sound in her ears all the night. How glad she was that Barty had come down to the cove,—oh, yes, how glad! There was no question of his dying now, and as for the blow on his forehead, what harm was that to a lad like him?

"But father shall go with you," said Mrs. Gunliffe, when Mally prepared to start for the cove by herself.

Mally, however, would not hear of this. She could find her way to the cove whether it was light or dark.

"Mally, thou art my child now, and I shall think of thee so," said the mother, as the girl went off by herself.

Mally thought of this, too, as she walked home. How could she become Mrs. Gunliffe's child; ah, how?

I need not, I think, tell the tale any further. That Mally did become Mrs. Gunliffe's child, and how she became so the reader will understand; and in process of time the big kitchen and all the wonders of the farmhouse were her own. The people said that Barty Gunliffe had married a mermaid out of the sea; but when it was said in Mally's hearing I doubt whether she liked it; and when Barty himself would call her a mermaid she would frown at him, and throw about her black hair, and pretend to cuff him with her little hand.

Old Glos was brought up to the top of the cliff, and lived his few remaining days under the roof of Mr. Gunliffe's house; and as for the cove and the right of seaweed, from that time forth all that has been supposed to attach itself to Gunliffe's farm, and I do not know that any of the neighbours are prepared to dispute the right.

16

The Punishment of Shahpesh, the Persian, on Khipil, the Builder

BY GEORGE MEREDITH

THEY relate that Shahpesh, the Persian, commanded the building of a palace, and Khipil was his builder. The work lingered from the first year of the reign of Shahpesh even to his fourth. One day Shahpesh went to the river-side where it stood, to inspect it. Khipil was sitting on a marble slab among the stones and blocks; round him stretched lazily the masons and stone-cutters and slaves of burden; and they with the curve of humorous enjoyment on their lips, for he was reciting to them adventures, interspersed with anecdotes and recitations and poetic instances, as was his wont. They were like pleased flocks whom the shepherd hath led to a pasture freshened with brooks, there to feed indolently; he, the shepherd, in the midst.

Now, the King said to him, "O Khipil, show me my palace where it standeth, for I desire to gratify my sight with its fairness."

Khipil abased himself before Shahpesh, and answered, " 'Tis even here, O King of the age, where thou delightest the earth with thy foot and the ear of thy slave with sweetness. Surely a site of vantage, one that dominateth earth, air, and water, which is the builder's first and chief requisition for a noble palace, a palace to fill foreign kings and sultans with the distraction of envy; and it is, O Sovereign of the time, a site, this site I have chosen, to occupy the tongues of travellers and awaken the flights of poets!"

Shahpesh smiled and said, "The site is good! I laud the site! Likewise I laud the wisdom of Ebn Busrac, where he exclaims:

"Be sure, where Virtue faileth to appear,
For her a gorgeous mansion men will rear;
And day and night her praises will be heard,
Where never yet she spake a single word."

Then said he, "O Khipil, my builder, there was once a farm-servant that, having neglected in the seed-time to sow, took to singing the richness of his soil when it was harvest, in proof of which he displayed the abundance of weeds that coloured the land everywhere. Discover to me now the completeness of my halls and apartments, I pray thee, O Khipil, and be the excellence of thy construction made visible to me!"

Quoth Khipil, "To hear is to obey."

He conducted Shahpesh among the unfinished saloons and imperfect courts and roofless rooms, and by half-erected obelisks, and columns pierced and chipped, of the palace of his building. And he was bewildered at the words spoken by Shahpesh; but now the King exalted him, and admired the perfection of his craft, the greatness of his labour, the speediness of his construction, his assiduity; feigning not to behold his negligence.

Presently they went up winding balusters to a marble terrace, and the King said, "Such is thy devotion and constancy in toil, O Khipil, that thou shalt walk before me here."

He then commanded Khipil to precede him, and Khipil was heightened with the honour. When Khipil had paraded a short space he stopped quickly, and said to Shahpesh, "Here is, as it chanceth, a gap, O King! and we can go no further this way."

Shahpesh said, "All is perfect, and it is my will thou delay not to advance."

Khipil cried, "The gap is wide, O mighty King, and manifest, and it is an incomplete part of thy palace."

Then said Shahpesh, "O Khipil, I see no distinction between one part and another; excellent are all parts in beauty and proportion, and there can be no part incomplete in this palace that occupieth the builder four years in its building: so advance, do my bidding."

Khipil yet hesitated, for the gap was of many strides, and at the bottom of the gap was a deep water, and he one that knew not the motion of swimming. But Shahpesh ordered his guard to point their arrows in the direction of Khipil, and Khipil stepped forward hurriedly, and fell in the gap, and was swallowed by the water below. When he rose the second time, succour reached him, and he was drawn to land trembling, his teeth chattering. And Shahpesh praised him, and said, "This is an apt contrivance for a bath, Khipil O my builder!

well conceived; one that taketh by surprise; and it shall be thy reward daily when much talking hath fatigued thee."

Then he bade Khipil lead him to the hall of state. And when they were there Shahpesh said, "For a privilege, and as a mark of my approbation, I give thee permission to sit in the marble chair of yonder throne, even in my presence, O Khipil."

Khipil said, "Surely, O King, the chair is not yet executed."

And Shahpesh exclaimed, "If this be so, thou art but the length of thy measure on the ground, O talkative one!"

Khipil said, "Nay, 'tis not so, O King of splendours! blind that I am! yonder 's indeed the chair."

And Khipil feared the King, and went to the place where the chair should be, and bent his body in a sitting posture, eyeing the King, and made pretence to sit in the chair of Shahpesh, as in conspiracy to amuse his master.

Then said Shahpesh, "For a token that I approve thy execution of the chair, thou shalt be honoured by remaining seated in it up to the hour of noon; but move thou to the right or to the left, showing thy soul insensible of the honour done thee, transfixed thou shalt be with twenty arrows and five."

The King then left him with a guard of twenty-five of his bodyguard; and they stood around him with bent bows, so that Khipil dared not move from his sitting posture. And the masons and the people crowded to see Khipil sitting on his master's chair, for it became rumoured about. When they beheld him sitting upon nothing, and he trembling to stir for fear of the loosening of the arrows, they laughed so that they rolled upon the floor of the hall, and the echoes of laughter were a thousand-fold. Surely the arrows of the guards swayed with the laughter that shook them.

Now, when the time had expired for his sitting in the chair, Shahpesh returned to him, and he was cramped, pitiable to see; and Shahpesh said, "Thou hast been exalted above men, O Khipil! for that thou didst execute for thy master has been found fitting for thee."

Then he bade Khipil lead the way to the noble gardens of dalliance and pleasure that he had planted and contrived. And Khipil went in that state described by the poet, when we go draggingly, with remonstrating members,

> *Knowing a dreadful strength behind,*
> *And a dark fate before.*

They came to the gardens, and behold, these were full of weeds and nettles, the fountains dry, no tree to be seen—a desert. And Shahpesh cried, "This is indeed of admirable design, O Khipil! Feelest thou not the coolness of the fountains?—their refreshingness? Truly I am grateful to thee! And these flowers, pluck me now a handful, and tell me of their perfume."

Khipil plucked a handful of the nettles that were there in the place of flowers, and put his nose to them before Shahpesh, till his nose was reddened; and desire to rub it waxed in him, and possessed him, and became a passion, so that he could scarce refrain from rubbing it even in the King's presence. And the King encouraged him to sniff and enjoy their fragrance, repeating the poet's words:

> Methinks I am a lover and a child,
> A little child and happy lover, both!
> When by the breath of flowers I am beguiled
> From sense of pain, and lulled in odorous sloth.
> So I adore them, that no mistress sweet
> Seems worthier of the love which they awake:
> In innocence and beauty more complete,
> Was never maiden cheek in morning lake.
> Oh, while I live, surround me with fresh flowers,
> Oh, when I die, then bury me in their bowers!

And the King said, "What sayest thou, O my builder? that is a fair quotation, applicable to thy feelings, one that expresseth them?"

Khipil answered, " 'Tis eloquent, O great King! comprehensiveness would be its portion, but that it alludeth not to the delight of chafing."

Then Shahpesh laughed, and cried, "Chafe not! it is an ill thing and a hideous! This nosegay, O Khipil, it is for thee to present to thy mistress. Truly she will receive thee well after its presentation! I will have it now sent in thy name, with word that thou followest quickly. And for thy nettled nose, surely if the whim seize thee that thou desirest its chafing, to thy neighbour is permitted what to thy hand is refused.'

The King set a guard upon Khipil to see that his orders were executed, and appointed a time for him to return to the gardens.

At the hour indicated Khipil stood before Shahpesh again. He was pale, saddened; his tongue drooped like the tongue of a heavy bell, that when it soundeth giveth forth mournful sounds only: he had also the look of one battered with many beatings. So the King said, "How of the presentation of the flowers of thy culture, O Khipil?"

He answered, "Surely, O King, she received me with wrath, and I am shamed by her."

And the King said, "How of my clemency in the matter of the chafing?"

Khipil answered, "O King of splendours! I made petition to my neighbours whom I met, accosting them civilly and with imploring, for I ached to chafe, and it was the very raging thirst of desire to chafe that was mine, devouring eagerness for solace of chafing. And they chafed me, O King; yet not in those parts which throbbed for the chafing, but in those which abhorred it."

Then Shahpesh smiled and said, " 'Tis certain that the magnanimity of monarchs is as the rain that falleth, the sun that shineth: and in this spot it fertilizeth richness; in that encourageth rankness. So art thou but a weed, O Khipil! and my grace is thy chastisement."

Now, the King ceased not persecuting Khipil, under pretence of doing him honour and heaping favours on him. Three days and three nights was Khipil gasping without water, compelled to drink the drought of the fountain, as an honour at the hands of the King. And he was seven days and seven nights made to stand with stretched arms, as they were the branches of a tree, in each hand a pomegranate. And Shahpesh brought the people of his court to regard the wondrous pomegranate-shoot planted by Khipil, very wondrous, and a new sort, worthy the gardens of a King. So the wisdom of the King was applauded, and men wotted he knew how to punish offences in coin, by the punishment inflicted on Khipil the builder. Before that time his affairs had languished, and the currents of business instead of flowing had become stagnant pools. It was the fashion to do as did Khipil, and fancy the tongue a constructor rather than a commentator; and there is a doom upon that people and that man which runneth to seed in gabble, as the poet says in his wisdom:

> *If thou wouldst be famous, and rich in splendid fruits,*
> *Leave to bloom the flower of things, and dig among the roots.*

Truly after Khipil's punishment there were few in the dominions of Shahpesh who sought to win the honours bestowed by him on gabblers and idlers: as again the poet:

> *When to loquacious fools with patience rare*
> *I listen, I have thoughts of Khipil's chair:*
> *His bath, his nosegay, and his fount I see,—*
> *Himself stretch'd out as a pomegranate-tree.*
> *And that I am not Shahpesh I regret,*
> *So to inmesh the babbler in his net.*
> *Well is that wisdom worthy to be sung,*
> *Which raised the Palace of the Wagging Tongue!*

And whoso is punished after the fashion of Shahpesh, the Persian, on Khipil the Builder, is said to be one "in the Palace of the Wagging Tongue" to this time.

17

The Three Strangers

BY THOMAS HARDY

Among the few features of agricultural England which retain an appearance but little modified by the lapse of centuries may be reckoned the high, grassy and furzy downs, coombs, or ewe-leases, as they are indifferently called, that fill a large area of certain counties in the south and southwest. If any mark of human occupation is met with hereon, it usually takes the form of the solitary cottage of some shepherd.

Fifty years ago such a lonely cottage stood on such a down, and may possibly be standing there now. In spite of its loneliness, however, the spot, by actual measurement, was not more than five miles from a county-town. Yet that affected it little. Five miles of irregular upland, during the long inimical seasons, with their sleets, snows, rains, and mists, afford withdrawing space enough to isolate a Timon or a Nebuchadnezzar; much less, in fair weather, to please that less repellent tribe, the poets, philosophers, artists, and others who "conceive and meditate of pleasant things."

Some old earthern camp or barrow, some clump of trees, at least some starved fragment of ancient hedge is usually taken advantage of in the erection of these forlorn dwellings. But, in the present case, such a kind of shelter had been disregarded. Higher Crowstairs, as the house was called, stood quite detached and undefended. The only reason for its precise situation seemed to be the crossing of two footpaths at right angles hard by, which may have crossed there and thus for a good five hundred years. Hence the house was exposed to the elements on all sides. But, though the wind up here blew unmistakably when it did blow, and the rain hit hard whenever it fell, the various weathers of the winter season were not quite so formidable on the coomb as they were imagined to be by dwellers on low ground. The raw rimes were not so pernicious as in the hollows, and the frosts were scarcely so severe. When the shepherd and his family who tenanted the house were pitied for their sufferings from the exposure, they said that upon the whole they were less inconvenienced by "wuzzes and flames" (hoarses and phlegms) than when they had lived by the stream of a snug neighbouring valley.

The night of March 28, 182—, was precisely one of the nights that were wont to call forth these expressions of commiseration. The level rainstorm smote walls, slopes, and hedges like the clothyard shafts of Senlac and Crecy. Such sheep and outdoor animals as had no shelter stood with their buttocks to the winds; while the tails of little birds trying to roost on some scraggy thorn were blown inside-out like umbrellas. The gable-end of the cottage was stained with wet, and the eavesdroppings flapped against the wall. Yet never was commiseration for the shepherd more misplaced. For that cheerful rustic was entertaining a large party in glorification of the christening of his second girl.

The guests had arrived before the rain began to fall, and they were all now assembled in the chief or living room of the dwelling. A glance into the apartment at eight o'clock on this eventful evening would have resulted in the opinion that it was as cosy and comfortable a nook as could be wished for in boisterous weather. The calling of its inhabitant was proclaimed by a number of highly polished sheep crooks without stems that were hung ornamentally over the fireplace, the curl of each shining crook varying from the antiquated type engraved in the patriarchal pictures of old family Bibles to the most approved fashion of the last local sheep-fair. The room was lighted by half a dozen candles having wicks only a trifle smaller than the grease which enveloped them, in candlesticks that were never used but at high-days, holy-days, and family feasts. The lights were scattered about the room, two of them standing on the chimney piece. This position of candles was in itself significant. Candles on the chimney piece always meant a party.

On the hearth, in front of a back-brand to give substance, blazed a fire of thorns, that crackled "like the laughter of the fool."

Nineteen persons were gathered here. Of these, five women, wearing gowns of various bright hues, sat in chairs along the wall; girls shy and not shy filled the window-bench; four men, including Charley Jake the hedge-carpenter, Elijah New the parish-clerk, and John Pitcher, a neighboring dairyman, the shepherd's father-in-law, lolled in the settle; a young man and maid, who were blushing over tentative *pourparlers* on a life-companionship, sat beneath the corner-cupboard; and an elderly engaged man of fifty or upward moved restlessly about from spots where his betrothed was not to the spot where she was. Enjoyment was pretty general, and so much the more prevailed in being unhampered by conventional restrictions. Absolute confidence in each other's good opinion begat perfect ease, while the finishing stroke of manner, amounting to a truly princely serenity, was lent to the majority by the absence of any expression or trait denoting that they wished to get on in the world, enlarge their minds, or do any eclipsing thing whatever—which nowadays so generally nips the bloom and *bonhomie* of all except the two extremes of the social scale.

Shepherd Fennel had married well, his wife being a dairyman's daughter from a vale at a distance, who brought fifty guineas in her pocket—and kept them there, till they should be required for ministering to the needs of a coming family. This frugal woman had been somewhat exercised as to the character that should be given to the gathering. A sit-still party had its advantages; but an undisturbed position of ease in chairs and settles was apt to lead on the men to such an unconscionable deal of toping that they would sometimes fairly drink the house dry. A dancing-party was the alternative; but this, while avoiding the foregoing objection on the score of good drink, had a counterbalancing disadvantage in the matter of good victuals, the ravenous appetites engendered by the exercise causing immense havoc in the buttery. Shepherdess Fennel fell back upon the intermediate plan of mingling short dances with short periods of talk and singing, so as to hinder any ungovernable rage in either. But this scheme was entirely confined to her own gentle mind: the shepherd himself was in the mood to exhibit the most reckless phases of hospitality.

The fiddler was a boy of those parts, about twelve years of age, who had a wonderful dexterity in jigs and reels, though his fingers were so small and short as to necessitate a constant shifting for the high notes, from which he scrambled back to the first position with sounds not of unmixed purity of tone. At seven the shrill tweedle-dee of this youngster had begun, accompanied by a booming ground-bass from Elijah New, the parish-clerk, who had thoughtfully brought with him his favorite musical instrument, the serpent. Dancing was instantaneous, Mrs. Fennel privately enjoining the players on no account to let the dance exceed the length of a quarter of an hour.

But Elijah and the boy, in the excitement of their position, quite forgot the injunction. Moreover, Oliver Giles, a man of seventeen, one of the dancers, who was enamored of his partner, a fair girl of thirty-three rolling years, had recklessly handed a new crown-piece to the musicians, as a bribe to keep going as long as they had muscle and wind. Mrs. Fennel, seeing the steam begin to generate on the countenances of her guests, crossed over and touched the fiddler's elbow and put her hand on the serpent's mouth. But they took no notice, and fearing she might lose her character of genial hostess if she were to interfere too markedly, she retired and sat down helpless. And so the dance whizzed on with cumulative fury, the performers moving in their planet-like courses, direct and retrograde, from apogee to perigee, till the hand of the well-kicked clock at the bottom of the room had traveled over the circumference of an hour.

While these cheerful events were in course of enactment within Fennel's pastoral dwelling, an incident having considerable bearing on the party had occurred in the gloomy night without. Mrs. Fennel's concern about the growing fierceness of the dance corresponded in point of time with the ascent of a human figure to the solitary hill of Higher Crowstairs from the direction of the distant town. This personage strode on through the rain without a pause, following the little-worn path which, further on in its course, skirted the shepherd's cottage.

It was nearly the time of full moon, and on this account, though the sky was lined with a uniform sheet of dripping cloud, ordinary objects out of doors were readily visible. The sad, wan light revealed the lonely pedestrian to be a man of supple frame; his gait suggested that he had somewhat passed the period of perfect and instinctive agility, though not so far as to be otherwise than rapid of motion when occasion required. At a rough guess, he might have been about forty years of age. He appeared tall, but a recruiting sergeant, or other person accustomed to the judging of men's heights by the eye, would have discerned that this was chiefly owing to his gauntness, and that he was not more than five-feet-eight or nine.

Notwithstanding the regularity of his tread, there was caution in it, as in that of one who mentally feels his way; and despite the fact that it was not a black coat nor a dark garment of any sort that he wore, there was something about him which suggested that he naturally belonged to the black-coated tribes of men. His clothes were of fustian, and his boots hobnailed, yet in his progress he showed not the mud-accustomed bearing of hobnailed and fustianed peasantry.

By the time that he had arrived abreast of the shepherd's premises the rain came down, or rather came along, with yet more determined violence. The outskirts of the little settlement partially broke the force of wind and rain, and this induced him to stand still. The most salient of the shepherd's domestic erections was an empty sty at the forward corner of his hedgeless garden, for in these latitudes the principle of masking the homelier features of your establishment by a conventional frontage was unknown. The traveler's eye was attracted to this small building by the pallid shine of the wet slates that covered it. He turned aside, and, finding it empty, stood under the pent-roof for shelter.

While he stood, the boom of the serpent within the adjacent house, and the lesser strains of the fiddler, reached the spot as an accompaniment to the surging hiss of the flying rain on the sod, its louder beating on the cabbage-leaves of the garden, on the eight or ten beehives just discernible by the path, and its dripping from the eaves into a row of buckets and pans that had been placed under the walls of the cottage. For at Higher Crowstairs, as at all such elevated domiciles, the grand difficulty of housekeeping was an insufficiency of water; and a casual rainfall was utilized by turning out, as catchers, every utensil that the house contained. Some queer stories might be told of the contrivances for economy in suds and dishwaters that are absolutely necessitated in upland habitations during the droughts of summer. But at this season there were no such exigencies; a mere acceptance of what the skies bestowed was sufficient for an abundant store.

At last the notes of the serpent ceased and the house was silent. This cessation of activity aroused the solitary pedestrian from the reverie into which he had elapsed, and, emerging from the shed, with an apparently new intention, he walked up the path to the house-door. Arrived here, his first act was to kneel down on a large stone beside the row of vessels, and to drink a copious draught from one of them. Having quenched his thirst, he rose and lifted his hand to knock, but paused with his eye upon the panel. Since the dark surface of the wood revealed absolutely nothing, it was evident that he must be mentally looking through the door, as if he wished to measure thereby all the possibilities that a house of this sort might include, and how they might bear upon the question of his entry.

In his indecision he turned and surveyed the scene around. Not a soul was anywhere visible. The garden path stretched downward from his feet, gleaming like the track of a snail; the roof of the little well (mostly dry), the well-cover, the top rail of the garden-gate, were varnished with the same dull liquid glaze; while, far away in the vale, a faint whiteness of more than usual extent showed that the rivers were high in the meads. Beyond all this winked a few bleared lamplights through the beating drops—lights that denoted the situation of the county-town from which he had appeared to come. The absence of all notes of life in that direction seemed to clinch his intentions, and he knocked at the door.

Within, a desultory chat had taken the place of movement and musical sound. The hedge-carpenter was suggesting a song to the company, which nobody just then was inclined to undertake, so that the knock afforded a not unwelcome diversion.

"Walk in!" said the shepherd, promptly.

The latch clicked upward, and out of the night our pedestrian appeared upon the door-mat. The shepherd arose, snuffed two of the nearest candles, and turned to look at him.

Their light disclosed that the stranger was dark in complexion and not unprepossessing as to feature. His hat, which for a moment he did not remove, hung low over his eyes, without concealing that they were large, open, and determined, moving with a flash rather than a glance round the room. He seemed pleased with his survey, and, baring his shaggy head, said, in a rich, deep voice: "The rain is so heavy, friends, that I ask leave to come in and rest awhile."

"To be sure, Stranger," said the shepherd. "And faith, you've been lucky in choosing your time, for we are having a bit of a fling for a glad cause—though, to be sure, a man could hardly wish that glad cause to happen more than once a year."

"Nor less," spoke up a woman. "For 'tis best to get your family over and done with, as soon as you can, so as to be all the earlier out of the fag o't."

"And what may be this glad cause?" asked the stranger.

"A birth and christening," said the shepherd.

The stranger hoped his host might not be made unhappy either by too many or too few of such episodes and, being invited by a gesture to a pull at the mug, he readily acquiesced. His manner, which, before entering, had been so dubious, was now altogether that of a careless and candid man.

"Late to be traipsing athwart this coomb—hey?" said the engaged man of fifty.

"Late it is, Master, as you say.—I'll take a seat in the chimney corner, if you have nothing to urge against it, Ma'am; for I am a little moist on the side that was next the rain."

Mrs. Shepherd Fennel assented, and made room for the self-invited comer, who, having got completely inside the chimney corner, stretched out his legs and arms with the expansiveness of a person quite at home.

"Yes, I am rather cracked in the vamp," he said freely, seeing that the eyes of the shepherd's wife fell upon his boots, "and I am not well fitted either. I have had some rough times lately, and have been forced to pick up what I can get in the way of wearing, but I must find a suit better fit for working-days when I reach home."

"One of hereabouts?" she inquired.

"Not quite that—further up the country."

"I thought so. And so be I; and by your tongue you come from my neighborhood."

"But you would hardly have heard of me," he said quickly. "My time would be long before yours, Ma'am, you see."

This testimony to the youthfulness of his hostess had the effect of stopping her cross-examination.

"There is only one thing more wanted to make me happy," continued the newcomer, "and that is a little baccy, which I am sorry to say I am out of."

"I'll fill your pipe," said the shepherd.

"I must ask you to lend me a pipe likewise."

"A smoker, and no pipe about 'ee?"

"I have dropped it somewhere on the road."

The shepherd filled and handed him a new clay pipe, saying, as he did so, "Hand me your baccy-box—I'll fill that too, now I am about it."

The man went through the movement of searching his pockets.

"Lost that too?" said his entertainer, with some surprise.

"I am afraid so," said the man with some confusion. "Give it to me in a screw of paper." Lighting his pipe at the candle with a suction that drew the whole flame into the bowl, he resettled himself in the corner and bent his looks upon the faint steam from his damp legs, as if he wished to say no more.

Meanwhile the general body of guests had been taking little notice of this visitor by reason of an absorbing discussion in which they were engaged with the band about a tune for the next dance. The matter being settled, they were about to stand up when an interruption came in the shape of another knock at the door.

At sound of the same the man in the chimney corner took up the poker and began stirring the brands as if doing it thoroughly were the one aim of his existence; and a second time the shepherd said, "Walk in!" In a moment another man stood upon the straw-woven door-mat. He too was a stranger.

This individual was one of a type radically different from the first. There was more of the commonplace in his manner, and a certain jovial cosmopolitanism sat upon his features. He was several years older than the first arrival, his hair being slightly frosted, his eyebrows bristly, and his whiskers cut back from his cheeks. His face was rather full and flabby, and yet it was not altogether a face without power. A few grog-blossoms marked the neighborhood of his nose. He flung back his long drab greatcoat, revealing that beneath it he wore a suit of cinder-gray shade throughout, large heavy seals, of some metal or other that would take a polish, dangling from his fob as his only personal ornament. Shaking the water drops from his low-crowned glazed hat, he said, "I must ask for a few minutes' shelter, comrades, or I shall be wetted to my skin before I get to Casterbridge."

"Make yourself at home, Master," said the shepherd, perhaps a trifle less heartily than on the first occasion. Not that Fennel had the least tinge of niggardliness in his composition; but the room was far from large, spare chairs were not numerous, and damp companions were not altogether desirable at close quarters for the women and girls in their bright-colored gowns.

However, the second comer, after taking off his greatcoat, and hanging his hat on a nail in one of the ceiling-beams as if he had been specially invited to put it there, advanced and sat down at the table. This had been pushed so closely into the chimney corner, to give all available room to the dancers, that its inner edge grazed the elbow of the man who had ensconced himself by the fire; and thus the two strangers were brought into close companionship. They nodded to each other by way of breaking the ice of unacquaintance, and the first stranger handed his neighbor the family mug—a huge vessel of brown ware, having its upper edge worn away like a threshold by the rub of whole generations of thirsty lips that had gone the way of all flesh, and bearing the following inscription burnt upon its rotund side in yellow letters:

THERE IS NO FUN
UNTIL i CUM.

The other man, nothing loth, raised the mug to his lips, and drank on, and on, and on—till a curious blueness overspread the countenance of the shepherd's wife, who had regarded with no little surprise the first stranger's free offer to the second of what did not belong to him to dispense.

"I knew it!" said the toper to the shepherd with much satisfaction. "When I walked up your garden before coming in, and saw the hives all of a row, I said to myself, 'Where there's bees there's honey, and where there's honey there's mead.' But mead of such a truly comfortable sort as this I really didn't expect to meet in my older days." He took yet another pull at the mug, till it assumed an ominous elevation.

"Glad you enjoy it!" said the shepherd warmly.

"It is goodish mead," assented Mrs. Fennel, with an absence of enthusiasm which seemed to say that it was possible to buy praise for one's cellar at too heavy a price. "It is trouble enough to make—and really I hardly think we shall make any more. For honey sells well, and we ourselves can make shift with a drop o' small mead and metheglin for common use from the comb-washings."

"Oh, but you'll never have the heart!" reproachfully cried the stranger in cinder-gray, after taking up the mug a third time and setting it down empty. "I love mead, when 'tis old like this, as I love to go to church o' Sundays, or to relieve the needy any day of the week."

"Ha, ha, ha!" said the man in the chimney corner, who, in spite of the taciturnity induced by the pipe of tobacco, could not or would not refrain from this slight testimony to his comrade's humor.

Now the old mead of those days, brewed of the purest first-year or maiden honey, four pounds to the gallon—with its due complement of white of eggs, cinnamon, ginger, cloves, mace, rosemary, yeast, and processes of working, bottling, and cellaring—tasted remarkably strong; but it did not taste so strong as it actually was. Hence, presently, the stranger in cinder-gray at the table, moved by its creeping influence, unbuttoned his waistcoat, threw himself back in his chair, spread his legs, and made his presence felt in various ways.

"Well, well, as I say," he resumed, "I am going to Casterbridge, and to Casterbridge I must go. I should have been almost there by this time; but the rain drove me into your dwelling, and I'm not sorry for it."

"You don't live in Casterbridge?" said the shepherd.

"Not as yet; though I shortly mean to move there."

"Going to set up in trade, perhaps?"

"No, no," said the shepherd's wife. "It is easy to see that the gentleman is rich, and don't want to work at anything."

The cinder-gray stranger paused, as if to consider whether he would accept that definition of himself. He presently rejected it by answering, "Rich is not quite the word for me, Dame. I do work, and I must work. And even if I only get to Casterbridge by midnight I must begin work there at eight tomorrow morning. Yes, het or wet, blow or snow, famine or sword, my day's work tomorrow must be done."

"Poor man! Then, in spite o' seeming, you be worse off than we," replied the shepherd's wife.

" 'Tis the nature of my trade, men and maidens. 'Tis the nature of my trade more than my poverty. . . . But really and truly I must up and off, or I shan't get a lodging in the town." However, the speaker did not move, and directly added, "There's time for one more draught of friendship before I go; and I'd perform it at once if the mug were not dry."

"Here's a mug o' small," said Mrs. Fennel. "Small, we call it, though to be sure 'tis only the first wash o' the combs."

"No," said the stranger, disdainfully. "I won't spoil your first kindness by partaking o' your second."

"Certainly not," broke in Fennel. "We don't increase and multiply every day, and I'll fill the mug again." He went away to the dark place under the stairs where the barrel stood. The shepherdess followed him.

"Why should you do this?" she said, reproachfully, as soon as they were alone. "He's emptied it once, though it held enough for ten people; and now he's not contented wi' the small, but must needs call for more o' the strong! And a stranger unbeknown to any of us. For my part, I don't like the look o' the man at all."

"But he's in the house, my honey; and 'tis a wet night, and a christening. Daze it, what's a cup of mead more or less? There'll be plenty more next bee-burning."

"Very well—this time, then," she answered, looking wistfully at the barrel. "But what is the man's calling, and where is he one of, that he should come in and join us like this?"

"I don't know. I'll ask him again."

The catastrophe of having the mug drained dry at one pull by the stranger in cinder-gray was effectually guarded against this time by Mrs. Fennel. She poured out his allowance in a small cup, keeping the large one at a discreet distance from him. When he had tossed off his portion the shepherd renewed his inquiry about the stranger's occupation.

The latter did not immediately reply, and the man in the chimney corner, with sudden demonstrativeness, said, "Anybody may know my trade—I'm a wheelwright."

"A very good trade for these parts," said the shepherd.

"And anybody may know mine—if they've the sense to find it out," said the stranger in cinder-gray.

"You may generally tell what a man is by his claws," observed the hedge-carpenter, looking at his own hands. "My fingers be as full of thorns as an old pincushion is of pins."

The hands of the man in the chimney corner instinctively sought the shade, and he gazed into the fire as he resumed his pipe. The man at the table took up the hedge-carpenter's remark, and added smartly, "True; but the oddity of my trade is that, instead of setting a mark upon me, it sets a mark upon my customers."

No observation being offered by anybody in elucidation of this enigma, the shepherd's wife once more called for a song. The same obstacles presented themselves as at the former time—one had no voice, another had forgotten the first verse. The stranger at the table, whose soul had now risen to a good working temperature, relieved the difficulty by exclaiming that, to start the company, he would sing himself. Thrusting one thumb into the armhole of his waistcoat, he waved the other hand in the air, and, with an extemporizing gaze at the shining sheep-crooks above the mantelpiece, began:

> *O my trade it is the rarest one,*
>   *Simple shepherds all—*
> *My trade is a sight to see;*

For my customers I tie, and take them up on high,
And waft 'em to a far countree!

The room was silent when he had finished the verse—with one exception, that of the man in the chimney corner, who at the singer's word, "Chorus!" joined him in a deep bass voice of musical relish:

And waft 'em to a far countree!

Oliver Giles, John Pitcher the dairyman, the parish-clerk, the engaged man of fifty, the row of young women against the wall, seemed lost in thought not of the gayest kind. The shepherd looked meditatively on the ground, the shepherdess gazed keenly at the singer, and with some suspicion; she was doubting whether this stranger were merely singing an old song from recollection, or was composing one there and then for the occasion. All were as perplexed at the obscure revelation as the guests at Belshazzar's Feast, except the man in the chimney corner, who quietly said, "Second verse, stranger," and smoked on.

The singer thoroughly moistened himself from his lips inward, and went on with the next stanza as requested:

My tools are but common ones,
            Simple shepherds all—
My tools are no sight to see:
A little hempen string, and a post whereon to swing,
Are implements enough for me!

Shepherd Fennel glanced round. There was no longer any doubt that the stranger was answering his question rhythmically. The guests one and all started back with suppressed exclamations. The young woman engaged to the man of fifty fainted halfway, and would have proceeded, but finding him wanting in alacrity for catching her she sat down trembling.

"Oh, he's the——!" whispered the people in the background, mentioning the name of an ominous public officer. "He's come to do it! 'Tis to be at Casterbridge jail tomorrow—the man for sheep-stealing —the poor clockmaker we heard of, who used to live away at Shottsford and had no work to do—Timothy Summers, whose family were astarving, and so he went out of Shottsford by the highroad, and took a sheep in open daylight, defying the farmer and the farmer's wife and the farmer's lad, and every man jack among 'em. He" (and they nodded toward the stranger of the deadly trade) "is come from up the country to do it because there's not enough to do in his own county-town, and he's got the place here now our own county-man's dead; he's going to live in the same cottage under the prison wall."

The stranger in cinder-gray took no notice of this whispered string of observations, but again wetted his lips. Seeing that his friend in the chimney corner was the only one who reciprocated his joviality in any way, he held out his cup toward that appreciative comrade, who also held out his own. They clinked together, the eyes of the rest of the room hanging upon the singer's actions. He parted his lips for the third verse; but at that moment another knock was audible upon the door. This time the knock was faint and hesitating.

The company seemed scared; the shepherd looked with consternation toward the entrance, and it was with some effort that he resisted his alarmed wife's deprecatory glance, and uttered for the third time the welcoming words, "Walk in!"

The door was gently opened, and another man stood upon the mat. He, like those who had preceded him, was a stranger. This time it was a short, small personage, of fair complexion, and dressed in a decent suit of dark clothes.

"Can you tell me the way to——?" he began: when, gazing round the room to observe the nature of the company among whom he had fallen, his eyes lighted on the stranger in cinder-gray. It was just at the instant when the latter, who had thrown his mind into his song with such a will that he scarcely heeded the interruption, silenced all whispers and inquiries by bursting into his third verse:

> Tomorrow is my working day,
> > Simple shepherds all—
> Tomorrow is a working day for me:
> For the farmer's sheep is slain, and the lad who did it ta'en,
> And on his soul may God ha' merc-y!

The stranger in the chimney corner, waving cups with the singer so heartily that his mead splashed over on the hearth, repeated in his bass voice as before:

> And on his soul may God ha' merc-y!

All this time the third stranger had been standing in the doorway. Finding now that he did not come forward or go on speaking, the guests particularly regarded him. They noticed to their surprise that he stood before them the picture of abject terror—his knees trembling, his hand shaking so violently that the door-latch by which he supported himself rattled audibly: his white lips were parted, and his eyes fixed on the merry officer of justice in the middle of the room. A moment more and he had turned, closed the door, and fled.

"What a man can it be?" said the shepherd.

The rest, between the awfulness of their late discovery and the odd conduct of this third visitor, looked as if they knew not what to think, and said nothing. Instinctively they withdrew further and further from the grim gentleman in their midst, whom some of them seemed to take for the Prince of Darkness himself, till they formed a remote circle, an empty space of floor being left between them and him—

. . . *circulas, cujus centrum diabolus.*

The room was so silent—though there were more than twenty people in it—that nothing could be heard but the patter of the rain against the window-shutters, accompanied by the occasional hiss of a stray drop that fell down the chimney into the fire, and the steady puffing of the man in the corner, who had now resumed his pipe of long clay.

The stillness was unexpectedly broken. The distant sound of a gun reverberated through the air—apparently from the direction of the county-town.

"Be jiggered!" cried the stranger who had sung the song, jumping up.

"What does that mean?" asked several.

"A prisoner escaped from the jail—that's what it means."

All listened. The sound was repeated, and none of them spoke but the man in the chimney corner, who said quietly, "I've often been told that in this county they fire a gun at such times; but I never heard it till now."

"I wonder if it is *my* man?" murmured the personage in cinder-gray.

"Surely it is!" said the shepherd involuntarily. "And surely we've zeed him! That little man who looked in at the door by now, and quivered like a leaf when he zeed ye and heard your song!"

"His teeth chattered, and the breath went out of his body," said the dairyman.

"And his heart seemed to sink within him like a stone," said Oliver Giles.

"And he bolted as if he'd been shot at," said the hedge-carpenter.

"True—his teeth chattered, and his heart seemed to sink; and he bolted as if he'd been shot at," slowly summed up the man in the chimney corner.

"I didn't notice it," remarked the hangman.

"We were all awondering what made him run off in such a fright," faltered one of the women against the wall, "and now 'tis explained!"

The firing of the alarm-gun went on at intervals, low and sullenly, and their suspicions became a certainty. The sinister gentleman in cinder-gray roused himself. "Is there a constable here?" he asked, in thick tones. "If so, let him step forward."

The engaged man of fifty stepped quavering out from the wall, his betrothed beginning to sob on the back of the chair.

"You are a sworn constable?"

"I be, Sir."

"Then pursue the criminal at once, with assistance, and bring him back here. He can't have gone far."

"I will, Sir, I will—when I've got my staff. I'll go home and get it, and come sharp here, and start in a body."

"Staff!—never mind your staff; the man'll be gone!"

"But I can't do nothing without my staff—can I, William, and John, and Charles Jake? No; for there's the king's royal crown apainted on en in yaller and gold, and the lion and the unicorn, so as when I raise en up and hit my prisoner, 'tis made a lawful blow thereby. I wouldn't 'tempt to take up a man without my staff—no, not I. If I hadn't the law to gie me courage, why, instead o' my taking up him he might take up me!"

"Now, I'm a king's man myself, and can give you authority enough for this," said the formidable officer in gray. "Now then, all of ye, be ready. Have ye any lanterns?"

"Yes—have ye any lanterns?—I demand it!" said the constable.

"And the rest of you able-bodied——"

"Able-bodied men—yes—the rest of ye!" said the constable.

"Have you some good stout staves and pitchforks——"

"Staves and pitchforks—in the name o' the law! And take 'em in yer hands and go in quest, and do as we in authority tell ye!"

Thus aroused, the men prepared to give chase. The evidence was, indeed, though circumstantial, so convincing, that but little argument was needed to show the shepherd's guests that after what they had seen it would look very much like connivance if they did not instantly pursue the unhappy third stranger, who could not as yet have gone more than a few hundred yards over such uneven country.

A shepherd is always well provided with lanterns; and, lighting these hastily, and with hurdle-staves in their hands, they poured out of the door, taking a direction along the crest of the hill, away from the town, the rain having fortunately a little abated.

Disturbed by the noise, or possibly by unpleasant dreams of her baptism, the child who had been christened began to cry heart-brokenly in the room overhead. These notes of grief came down through the chinks of the floor to the ears of the women below, who jumped up one by one, and seemed glad of the excuse to ascend and comfort the baby, for the incidents of the last half-hour greatly oppressed them. Thus in the space of two or three minutes the room on the ground-floor was deserted quite.

But it was not for long. Hardly had the sound of footsteps died away when a man returned round the corner of the house from the direction the pursuers had taken. Peeping in at the door, and seeing nobody there, he entered leisurely. It was the stranger of the chimney corner, who had gone out with the rest. The motive of his return was shown by his helping himself to a cut piece of skimmer-cake that lay on a ledge beside where he had sat, and which he had apparently forgotten to take with him. He also poured out half a cup more mead from the quantity that remained, ravenously eating and drinking these as he stood. He had not finished when another figure came in just as quietly—his friend in cinder-gray.

"Oh—you here?" said the latter, smiling. "I thought you had gone to help in the capture." And this speaker also revealed the object of his return by looking solicitously round for the fascinating mug of old mead.

"And I thought you had gone," said the other, continuing his skimmer-cake with some effort.

"Well, on second thoughts, I felt there were enough without me," said the first confidentially, "and such a night as it is, too. Besides, 'tis the business o' the Government to take care of its criminals—not mine."

"True; so it is. And I felt as you did, that there were enough without me."

"I don't want to break my limbs running over the humps and hollows of this wild country."

"Nor I neither, between you and me."

"These shepherd-people are used to it—simple-minded souls, you know, stirred up to anything in a moment. They'll have him ready for me before the morning, and no trouble to me at all."

"They'll have him, and we shall have saved ourselves all labor in the matter."

"True, true. Well, my way is to Casterbridge; and 'tis as much as my legs will do to take me that far. Going the same way?"

"No, I am sorry to say! I have to get home over there" (he nodded indefinitely to the right), "and I feel as you do, that it is quite enough for my legs to do before bedtime."

The other had by this time finished the mead in the mug, after which, shaking hands heartily at the door, and wishing each other well, they went their several ways.

In the meantime the company of pursuers had reached the end of the hog's-back elevation which dominated this part of the down. They had decided on no particular plan of action; and, finding that the man of the baleful trade was no longer in their company, they seemed quite unable to form any such plan now. They descended in all directions down the hill, and straightway several of the party fell into the snare set by Nature for all misguided midnight ramblers over this part of the cretaceous formation. The "lanchets," or flint slopes, which belted the escarpment at intervals of a dozen yards, took the less cautious ones unawares, and losing their footing on the rubbly steep they slid sharply downward, the lanterns rolling from their hands to the bottom, and there lying on their sides till the horn was scorched through.

When they had again gathered themselves together, the shepherd, as the man who knew the country best, took the lead, and guided them round these treacherous inclines. The lanterns, which seemed rather to dazzle their eyes and warn the fugitive than to assist them in the exploration, were extinguished, due silence was observed; and in this more rational order they plunged into the vale. It was a grassy, briery, moist defile, affording some shelter to any person who had sought it; but the party perambulated it in vain, and ascended on the other side. Here they wandered apart, and after an interval closed together again to report progress. At the second time of closing in they found themselves near a lonely ash, the single tree on this part of the coomb, probably sown there by a passing bird some fifty years before. And here, standing a little to one side of the trunk, as motionless as the trunk itself appeared the man they were in quest of, his outline being well defined against the sky beyond. The band noiselessly drew up and faced him.

"Your money or your life!" said the constable sternly to the still figure.

"No, no," whispered John Pitcher. "'Tisn't our side ought to say that. That's the doctrine of vagabonds like him, and we be on the side of the law."

"Well, well," replied the constable, impatiently; "I must say something, mustn't I? and if you had all the weight o' this undertaking upon your mind, perhaps you'd say the wrong thing, too!—Prisoner at the bar, surrender in the name of the Father—the Crown, I mane!"

The man under the tree seemed now to notice them for the first time, and, giving them no opportunity whatever for exhibiting their courage, he strolled slowly toward them. He was, indeed, the little man, the third stranger; but his trepidation had in a great measure gone.

"Well, travelers," he said, "did I hear you speak to me?"

"You did; you've got to come and be our prisoner at once!" said the constable. "We arrest 'ee on the charge of not biding in Casterbridge jail in a decent proper manner to be hung tomorrow morning. Neighbors, do your duty, and seize the culpet!"

On hearing the charge, the man seemed enlightened, and, saying not another word, resigned himself with preternatural civility to the search-party, who, with their staves in their hands, surrounded him on all sides, and marched him back toward the shepherd's cottage.

It was eleven o'clock by the time they arrived. The light shining from the open door, a sound of men's voices within, proclaimed to them as they approached the house that some new events had arisen in their absence. On entering they discovered the shepherd's living-room to be invaded by two officers from Casterbridge jail, and a well-known magistrate who lived at the nearest country-seat, intelligence of the escape having become generally circulated.

"Gentlemen," said the constable, "I have brought back your man—not without risk and danger; but every one must do his duty! He is inside this circle of able-bodied persons, who have lent me useful aid, considering their ignorance of Crown work.—Men, bring forward your prisoner!" And the third stranger was led to the light.

"Who is this?" said one of the officials.

"The man," said the constable.

"Certainly not," said the turnkey; and the first corroborated his statement.

"But how can it be otherwise?" asked the constable. "Or why was he so terrified at sight o' the singing instrument of the law who sat there?" Here he related the strange behavior of the third stranger on entering the house during the hangman's song.

"Can't understand it," said the officer coolly. "All I know is that it is not the condemned man. He's quite a different character from this one; a gauntish fellow, with dark hair and eyes, rather good-looking, and with a musical bass voice that if you heard it once you'd never mistake as long as you lived."

"Why, souls—'twas the man in the chimney corner!"

"Hey—what?" said the magistrate, coming forward after inquiring particulars from the shepherd in the background. "Haven't you got the man after all?"

"Well, Sir," said the constable, "he's the man we were in search of, that's true; and yet he's not the man we were in search of. For the man we were in search of was not the man we wanted, Sir, if you understand my everyday way; for 'twas the man in the chimney corner!"

"A pretty kettle of fish altogether!" said the magistrate. "You had better start for the other man at once."

The prisoner now spoke for the first time. The mention of the man in the chimney corner seemed to have moved him as nothing else could do. "Sir," he said, stepping forward to the magistrate, "take no more trouble about me. The time is come when I may as well speak. I have done nothing; my crime is that the condemned man is my brother. Early this afternoon I left home at Shottsford to tramp it all the way to Casterbridge jail to bid him farewell. I was benighted, and called here to rest and ask the way. When I opened the door I saw before me the very man, my brother, that I thought to see in the condemned cell at Casterbridge. He was in this chimney corner; and jammed close to him, so that he could not have got out if he had tried, was the executioner who'd come to take his life, singing a song about it and not knowing that it was his victim who was close by, joining in to save appearances. My brother looked a glance of agony at me, and I know he meant, 'Don't reveal what you see; my life depends on it.' I was so terror-struck that I could hardly stand, and, not knowing what I did, I turned and hurried away."

The narrator's manner and tone had the stamp of truth, and his story made a great impression on all around. "And do you know where your brother is at the present time?" asked the magistrate.

"I do not. I have never seen him since I closed this door."

"I can testify to that, for we've been between ye ever since," said the constable.

"Where does he think to fly to?—what is his occupation?"

"He's a watch-and-clock-maker, Sir."

"'A said 'a was a wheelwright—a wicked rogue," said the constable.

"The wheels of clocks and watches he meant, no doubt," said Shepherd Fennel. "I thought his hands were palish for's trade."

"Well, it appears to me that nothing can be gained by retaining this poor man in custody," said the magistrate; "your business lies with the other, unquestionably."

And so the little man was released off-hand; but he looked nothing the less sad on that account, it being beyond the power of magistrate or constable to raze out the written troubles in his brain, for they concerned another whom he regarded with more solicitude than himself. When this was done, and the man had gone his way, the night was found to be so far advanced that it was deemed useless to renew the search before the next morning.

Next day, accordingly, the quest for the clever sheep-stealer became general and keen, to all appearance at least. But the intended punishment was cruelly disproportioned to the transgression, and the sympathy of a great many country-folk in that district was strongly on the side of the fugitive. Moreover, his marvelous coolness and daring in hob-and-nobbing with the hangman, under the unprecedented circumstances of the shepherd's party, won their admiration. So that it may be questioned if all those who ostensibly made themselves so busy in exploring woods and fields and lanes were quite so thorough when it came to the private examination of their own lofts and outhouses.

Stories were afloat of a mysterious figure being occasionally seen in some old overgrown trackway or other, remote from turnpike roads, but when a search was instituted in any of these suspected quarters nobody was found. Thus the days and weeks passed without tidings.

In brief, the bass-voiced man of the chimney corner was never re-captured. Some said that he went across the sea, others that he did not, but buried himself in the depths of a populous city. At any rate, the gentleman in cinder-gray never did his morning's work at Caster-bridge, nor met anywhere at all, for business purposes, the genial comrade with whom he had passed an hour of relaxation in the lonely house on the coomb.

The grass has long been green on the graves of Shepherd Fennel and his frugal wife; the guests who made up the christening party have mainly followed their entertainers to the tomb; the baby in whose honor they all had met is a matron in the sere and yellow leaf. But the arrival of the three strangers at the shepherd's that night, and the details connected therewith, is a story as well-known as ever in the country about Higher Crowstairs.

18

Story of a Piebald Horse

BY W. H. HUDSON

THIS is all about a piebald. People there are like birds that come down in flocks, hop about chattering, gobble up their seed, then fly away, forgetting what they have swallowed. I love not to scatter grain for such as these. With you, friend, it is different. Others may laugh if they like at the old man of many stories, who puts all things into his copper memory. I can laugh, too, knowing that all things are ordered by destiny; otherwise I might sit down and cry.

The things I have seen! There was the piebald that died long ago; I could take you to the very spot where his bones used to lie bleaching in the sun. There is a nettle growing on the spot. I saw it yesterday. What important things are these to remember and talk about! Bones of a dead horse and a nettle; a young bird that falls from its nest in the night and is found dead in the morning; puff-balls blown about by the wind; a little lamb left behind by the flock bleating at night amongst the thorns and thistles, where only the fox or wild dog can hear it! Small matters are these, and our lives, what are they? And the people we have known, the men and women who have spoken to us and touched us with warm hands—the bright eyes and red lips! Can we cast these things like dead leaves on the fire? Can we lie down full of heaviness because of them, and sleep and rise in the morning without them? Ah, friend!

Let us to the story of the piebald. There was a cattle-marking at neighbor Sotelo's estancia, and out of a herd of three thousand head we had to part all the yearlings to be branded. After that, dinner and a dance. At sunrise we gathered, about thirty of us; all friends and neighbors, to do the work. Only with us came one person nobody knew.

He joined us when we were on our way to the cattle; a young man, slender, well-formed, of pleasing countenance and dressed as few could dress in those days. His horse also shone with silver trappings. And what an animal! Many horses have I seen in this life, but never one with such a presence as this stranger's piebald.

Arrived at the herd, we began to separate the young animals, the men riding in couples through the cattle, so that each calf when singled out could be driven by two horsemen, one on each side, to prevent it from doubling back. I happened to be mounted on a demon with a fiery mouth—there was no making him work, so I had to leave the parters and stand with little to do, watching the yearlings already parted, to keep them from returning to the herd.

Presently neighbor Chapaco rode up to me. He was a good-hearted man, well-spoken, half Indian and half Christian; but he also had another half, and that was devil.

"What! neighbor Lucero, are you riding on a donkey or a goat, that you remain here doing boy's work?"

I began telling him about my horse, but he did not listen; he was looking at the parters. "Who is that young stranger?" he asked.

"I see him today," I replied, "and if I see him again tomorrow then I shall have seen him twice."

"And in what country of which I have never heard did he learn cattle-parting?" said he.

"He rides," I answered, "like one presuming on a good horse. But he is safe, his fellow-worker has all the danger."

"I believe you," said Chapaco. "He charges furiously and hurls the heifer before his comrade, who has all the work to keep it from doubling, and all the danger, for at any moment his horse may go over it and fall. This our young stranger does knowingly, thinking that no one here will resent it. No, Lucero, he is presuming more on his long knife than on his good horse."

Even while we spoke, the two we were watching rode up to us. Chapaco saluted the young man, taking off his hat, and said—"Will you take me for a partner, friend?"

"Yes; why not, friend?" returned the other; and together the two rode back.

Now I shall watch them, said I to myself, to see what this Indian devil intends doing. Soon they came out of the herd driving a very small animal. Then I knew what was coming. "May your guardian angel be with you to avert a calamity, young stranger!" I exclaimed. Whip and spur those two came towards me like men riding a race and not parting cattle. Chapaco kept close to the calf, so that he had the advantage, for his horse was well trained. At length he got a little ahead, then, quick as lightning, he forced the calf round square before the other. The piebald struck it full in the middle, and fell because it had to fall. But, Saints in Heaven! why did not the rider save himself? Those who were watching saw him throw up his feet to tread the horse's neck and leap away; nevertheless man, horse and calf came down together. They ploughed the ground for some distance, so great had been their speed, and the man was under. When we picked him up he was senseless, the blood flowing from his mouth. Next morning, when the sun rose and God's light fell on the earth, he expired.

Of course there was no dancing that night. Some of the people, after eating, went away; others remained sitting about all night, talking in low tones, waiting for the end. A few of us were at his bedside watching his white face and closed eyes. He breathed, and that was all. When the sunlight came over the world he opened his eyes, and Sotelo asked him how he did. He took no notice, but presently his lips began to move, though they seemed to utter no sound. Sotelo bent his ear down to listen. "Where does she live?" he asked. He could not answer—he was dead.

"He seemed to be saying many things," Sotelo told us, "but I understood only this—'Tell her to forgive me . . . I was wrong. She loved him from the first. . . . I was jealous and hated him. . . . Tell Elaria not to grieve—Anacleto will be good to her.' Alas! my friends, where shall I find his relations to deliver this dying message to them?"

The Alcalde came that day and made a list of the dead man's possessions, and bade Sotelo take charge of them till the relations could be found. Then, calling all the people together, he bade each person cut on his whip-handle and on the sheath of his knife the mark branded on the flank of the piebald, which was in shape like a horse-shoe with a cross inside, so that it might be shown to all strangers, and made known through the country until the dead man's relations should hear of it.

When a year had gone by, the Alcalde told Sotelo that, all inquiries having failed, he could now take the horse and the silver trappings for himself. Sotelo would not listen to this, for he was a devout man and coveted no person's property, dead or alive. The horse and things, however, still remained in his charge.

Three years later I was one afternoon sitting with Sotelo, taking maté, when his herd of dun mares were driven up. They came galloping and neighing to the corral and ahead of them, looking like a wild horse, was the piebald, for no person ever mounted him.

"Never do I look on that horse," I remarked, "without remember-ing the fatal marking, when its master met his death."

"Now you speak of it," said he, "let me inform you that I am about to try a new plan. That noble piebald and all those silver trappings hanging in my room are always reproaching my conscience. Let us not forget the young stranger we put under ground. I have had many masses said for his soul's repose, but that does not quite satisfy me. Somewhere there is a place where he is not forgotten. Hands there are, perhaps, that gather wild flowers to place them with lighted can-dles before the image of the Blessed Virgin; eyes there are that weep and watch for his coming. You know how many travelers and cattle-drovers going to Buenos Ayres from the south call for refreshment at the *pulpería*. I intend taking the piebald and tying him every day at the gate there. No person calling will fail to notice the horse, and some day perhaps some traveler will recognize the brand on its flank and will be able to tell us what department and what estancia it comes from."

Next morning the piebald was tied up at the gate of the *pulpería,* at the road side, only to be released again when night came, and this was repeated every day for a long time. So fine an animal did not fail to attract the attention of all strangers passing that way, still several weeks went by and nothing was discovered. At length, one evening, just when the sun was setting, there appeared a troop of cattle driven by eight men. It had come a great distance, for the troop was a large one—about nine hundred head—and they moved slowly, like cattle that had been many days on the road. Some of the men came in for refreshments; then the store-keeper noticed that one remained outside leaning on the gate.

"What is the capatas doing that he remains outside?" said one of the men.

"Evidently he has fallen in love with that piebald," said another, "for he cannot take his eyes off it."

At length the capatas, a young man of good presence, came in and sat down on a bench. The others were talking and laughing about the strange things they had all been doing the day before; for they had been many days and nights on the road, only nodding a little in their saddles, and at length becoming delirious from want of sleep, they had begun to act like men that are half-crazed.

"Enough of the delusions of yesterday," said the capatas, who had been silently listening to them, "but tell me, boys, am I in the same condition today?"

"Surely not!" they replied. "Thanks to those horned devils being so tired and footsore, we all had some sleep last night."

"Very well then," said he, "now you have finished eating and drinking, go back to the troop, but before you leave look well at that piebald tied at the gate. He that is not a cattle-drover may ask, 'How can my eyes deceive me?' but I know that a crazy brain makes us see many strange things when the drowsy eyes can only be held open with the fingers."

The men did as they were told, and when they had looked well at the piebald, they all shouted out, "He has the brand of the estancia de Silva on his flank, and no counter-brand—claim the horse, capatas, for he is yours." And after that they rode away to the herd.

"My friend," said the capatas to the storekeeper, "will you explain how you came possessed of this piebald horse?"

Then the other told him everything, even the dying words of the young stranger, for he knew all.

The capatas bent down his head, and covering his face shed tears. Then he said, "And you died thus, Torcuato, amongst strangers! From my heart I have forgiven you the wrong you did me. Heaven rest your soul, Torcuato; I cannot forget that we were once brothers. I, friend, am that Anacleto of whom he spoke with his last breath."

Sotelo was then sent for, and when he arrived and the *pulpería* was closed for the night, the capatas told his story, which I will give you in his own words, for I was also present to hear him. This is what he told us:

I was born on the southern frontier. My parents died when I was very small, but Heaven had compassion on me and raised up one to shelter me in my orphanhood. Don Loreto Silva took me to his estancia on the Sarandi, a stream half a day's journey from Tandil, toward the setting sun. He treated me like one of his own children, and I took the name of Silva. He had two other children, Torcuato, who was about the same age as myself, and his daughter, Elaria, who was younger. He was a widower when he took charge of me, and died when I was still a youth. After his death we moved to Tandil, where we had a house close to the little town; for we were all minors, and the property had been left to be equally divided between us when we should be of age. For four years we lived happily together; then when we were of age we preferred to keep the property undivided. I proposed that we should go and live on the estancia, but Torcuato would not consent, liking the place where we were living best. Finally, not being able to persuade him, I resolved to go and attend to the estancia myself. He said that I could please myself and that he should stay where he was with Elaria. It was only when I told Elaria of these things that

I knew how much I loved her. She wept and implored me not to leave her.

"Why do you shed tears, Elaria?" I said; "is it because you love me? Know then, that I also love you with all my heart, and if you will be mine, nothing can ever make us unhappy. Do not think that my absence at the estancia will deprive me of this feeling which has ever been growing up in me."

"I do love you, Anacleto," she replied, "and I have also known of your love for a long time. But there is something in my heart which I cannot impart to you; only I ask you, for the love you bear me, do not leave me, and do not ask me why I say this to you."

After this appeal I could not leave her, nor did I ask her to tell me her secret. Torcuato and I were friendly, but not as we had been before this difference. I had no evil thoughts of him; I loved him and was with him continually; but from the moment I announced to him that I had changed my mind about going to the estancia, and was silent when he demanded the reason, there was a something in him which made it different between us. I could not open my heart to him about Elaria, and sometimes I thought that he also had a secret which he had no intention of sharing with me. This coldness did not, however, distress me very much, so great was the happiness I now experienced, knowing that I possessed Elaria's love. He was much away from the house, being fond of amusements, and he had also begun to gamble. About three months passed in this way, when one morning Torcuato, who was saddling his horse to go out, said, "Will you come with me, today, Anacleto?"

"I do not care to go," I answered.

"Look, Anacleto," said he; "once you were always ready to accompany me to a race or dance or cattle-marking. Why have you ceased to care for these things? Are you growing devout before your time, or does my company no longer please you?"

"It is best to tell him everything and have done with secrets," said I to myself, and so replied—

"Since you ask me, Torcuato, I will answer you frankly. It is true that I now take less pleasure than formerly in these pastimes; but you have not guessed the reason."

"What then is this reason of which you speak?"

"Since you cannot guess it," I replied, "know that it is love."

"Love for whom?" he asked quickly and turning very pale.

"Do you need ask? Elaria," I replied.

I had scarcely uttered the name before he turned on me full of rage. "Elaria!" he exclaimed. "Do you dare tell me of love for Elaria!

But you are only a blind fool, and do not know that I am going to marry her myself."

"Are you mad, Torcuato, to talk of marrying your sister?"

"She is no more my sister than you are my brother," he returned. "I," he continued, striking his breast passionately, "am the only child of my father, Loreto Silva. Elaria, whose mother died in giving her birth, was adopted by my parents. And because she is going to be my wife, I am willing that she should have a share of the property; but you, a miserable foundling, why were you lifted up so high? Was it not enough that you were clothed and fed till you came to man's estate? Not a hand's-breadth of the estancia land should be yours, and now you presume to speak of love for Elaria."

My blood was on fire with so many insults, but I remembered all the benefits I had received from his father, and did not raise my hand against him. Without more words he left me. I then hastened to Elaria and told her what had passed.

"This," I said, "is the secret you would not impart to me. Why, when you knew these things, was I kept in ignorance?"

"Have pity on me, Anacleto," she replied, crying. "Did I not see that you two were no longer friends and brothers, and this without knowing of each other's love? I dared not open my lips to you or to him. It is always a woman's part to suffer in silence. God intended us to be poor, Anacleto, for we were both born of poor parents, and had this property never come to us, how happy we might have been!"

"Why do you say such things, Elaria? Since we love each other, we cannot be unhappy, rich or poor."

"Is it a little matter," she replied, "that Torcuato must be our bitter enemy? But you do not know every thing. Before Torcuato's father died, he said he wished his son to marry me when we came of age. When he spoke about it we were sitting together by him."

"And what did you say, Elaria?" I asked, full of concern.

"Torcuato promised to marry me. I only covered my face, and was silent, for I loved you best even then, though I was almost a child, and my heart was filled with grief at his words. After we came here, Torcuato reminded me of his father's words. I answered that I did not wish to marry him, that he was only a brother to me. Then he said that we were young and he could wait until I was of another mind. This is all I have to say; but how shall we three live together any longer? I cannot bear to part from you, and every moment I tremble to think what may happen when you two are together."

"Fear nothing," I said. "Tomorrow morning you can go to spend a week at some friend's house in the town; then I will speak to Torcuato, and tell him that since we cannot live in peace together we must separate. Even if he answers with insults I shall do nothing to grieve you, and if he refuses to listen to me, I shall send some person we both respect to arrange all things between us."

This satisfied her, but as evening approached she grew paler, and I knew she feared Torcuato's return. He did not, however, come back that night. Early next morning she was ready to leave. It was an easy walk to the town, but the dew was heavy on the grass, and I saddled a horse for her to ride. I had just lifted her to the saddle when Torcuato appeared. He came at great speed, and throwing himself off his horse, advanced to us. Elaria trembled and seemed ready to sink upon the earth to hide herself like a partridge that has seen the hawk. I prepared myself for insults and perhaps violence. He never looked at me; he only spoke to her.

"Elaria," he said, "something has happened—something that obliges me to leave this house and neighborhood at once. Remember when I am away that my father, who cherished you and enriched you with his bounty, and who also cherished and enriched this ingrate, spoke to us from his dying bed and made me promise to marry you. Think what his love was; do not forget that his last wish is sacred, and that Anacleto has acted a base, treacherous part in trying to steal you from me. He was lifted out of the mire to be my brother and equal in everything except this. He has got a third part of my inheritance—let that satisfy him; your own heart, Elaria, will tell you that a marriage with him would be a crime before God and man. Look not for my return tomorrow nor for many days. But if you two begin to laugh at my father's dying wishes, look for me, for then I shall not delay to come back to you, Elaria, and to you, Anacleto. I have spoken."

He then mounted his horse and rode away. Very soon we learned the cause of his sudden departure. He had quarrelled over his cards and in a struggle that followed had stabbed his adversary to the heart. He had fled to escape the penalty. We did not believe that he would remain long absent; for Torcuato was very young, well off, and much liked, and this was, moreover, his first offence against the law. But time went on and he did not return, nor did any message from him reach us, and we at last concluded that he had left the country. Only now after four years have I accidentally discovered his fate through seeing his piebald horse.

After he had been absent from home for over a year, I asked Elaria to become my wife. "We cannot marry till Torcuato returns," she said. "For if we take the property that ought to have been all his, and at the same time disobey his father's dying wish, we shall be doing an evil thing. Let us take care of the property till he returns to receive it all back from us; then, Anacleto, we shall be free to marry."

I consented, for she was more to me than lands and cattle. I put the estancia in order and leaving a trustworthy person in charge of everything I invested my money in fat bullocks to resell in Buenos Ayres, and in this business I have been employed ever since. From the estancia I have taken nothing, and now it must all come back to us—his inheritance and ours. This is a bitter thing and will give Elaria great grief.

Thus ended Anacleto's story, and when he had finished speaking and still seemed greatly troubled in his mind, Sotelo said to him, "Friend, let me advise you what to do. You will now shortly be married to the woman you love and probably some day a son will be born to you. Let him be named Torcuato, and let Torcuato's inheritance be kept for him. And if God gives you no son, remember what was done for you and for the girl you are going to marry, when you were orphans and friendless, and look out for some unhappy child in the same condition, to protect and enrich him as you were enriched."

"You have spoken well," said Anacleto. "I will report your words to Elaria, and whatever she wishes done that will I do."

So ends my story, friend. The cattle-drover left us that night and we saw no more of him. Only before going he gave the piebald and the silver trapping to Sotelo. Six months after his visit, Sotelo also received a letter from him to say that his marriage with Elaria had taken place; and the letter was accompanied with a present of seven cream-colored horses with black manes and hoofs.

19

Sire de Malétroit's Door

BY ROBERT LOUIS STEVENSON

DENIS DE BEAULIEU was not yet two-and-twenty, but he counted himself a grown man, and a very accomplished cavalier into the bargain. Lads were early formed in that rough, warfaring epoch; and when one has been in a pitched battle and a dozen raids, has killed one's man in an honourable fashion, and knows a thing or two of strategy and mankind, a certain swagger in the gait is surely to be pardoned. He had put up his horse with due care, and supped with due deliberation; and then, in a very agreeable frame of mind, went out to pay a visit in the grey of the evening. It was not a very wise proceeding on the young man's part. He would have done better to remain beside the fire or go decently to bed. For the town was full of the troops of Burgundy and England under a mixed command; and though Denis was there on safe-conduct, his safe-conduct was like to serve him little on a chance encounter.

It was September, 1429; the weather had fallen sharp; a flighty piping wind, laden with showers, beat about the township; and the dead leaves ran riot along the streets. Here and there a window was already lighted up; and the noise of men-at-arms making merry over supper within, came forth in fits and was swallowed up and carried away by the wind. The night fell swiftly; the flag of England, fluttering on the spire-top, grew ever fainter and fainter against the flying clouds —a black speck like a swallow in the tumultuous, leaden chaos of the sky. As the night fell the wind rose, and began to hoot under archways and roar amid the tree-tops in the valley below the town.

Denis de Beaulieu walked fast and was soon knocking at his friend's door; but though he promised himself to stay only a little while and make an early return, his welcome was so pleasant, and he found so much to delay him, that it was already long past midnight before he said good-bye upon the threshold. The wind had fallen again in the meanwhile; the night was as black as the grave; not a star, nor a glimmer of moonshine, slipped through the canopy of cloud. Denis was ill-acquainted with the intricate lanes of Chateau Landon; even by daylight he had found some trouble in picking his way; and in this absolute darkness he soon lost it altogether. He was certain of one thing only—to keep mounting the hill; for his friend's house lay at the lower end, or tail, of Chateau Landon, while the inn was up at the head, under the great church spire. With this clue to go upon he stumbled and groped forward, now breathing more freely in open places where there was a good slice of sky overhead, now feeling along the wall in stifling closes. It is an eerie and mysterious position to be thus submerged in opaque blackness in an almost unknown town. The silence is terrifying in its possibilities. The touch of cold window bars to the exploring hand startles the man like the touch of a toad; the inequalities of the pavement shake his heart into his mouth; a piece of denser darkness threatens an ambuscade or a chasm in the pathway; and where the air is brighter, the houses put on strange and bewildering appearances, as if to lead him farther from his way. For Denis, who had to regain his inn without attracting notice, there was real danger as well as mere discomfort in the walk; and he went warily and boldly at once, and at every corner paused to make an observation.

He had been for some time threading a lane so narrow that he could touch a wall with either hand, when it began to open out and go sharply downward. Plainly this lay no longer in the direction of his inn; but the hope of a little more light tempted him forward to reconnoitre. The lane ended in a terrace with a bartizan wall, which gave an outlook between high houses, as out of an embrasure, into the valley lying dark and formless several hundred feet below. Denis looked down, and could discern a few tree-tops waving and a single speck of brightness where the river ran across a weir. The weather was clearing up, and the sky had lightened, so as to show the outline of the heavier clouds and the dark margin of the hills. By the uncertain glimmer, the house on his left hand should be a place of some pretensions; it was surmounted by several pinnacles and turret-tops; the round stern of a chapel, with a fringe of flying buttresses, projected boldly from the main block; and the door was sheltered under a deep porch carved with figures and overhung by two long gargoyles. The windows of the chapel gleamed through their intricate tracery with a light as of many tapers, and threw out the buttresses and the peaked roof in a more intense blackness against the sky. It was plainly the hotel of some great family of the neighbourhood; and as it reminded Denis of a town house of his own at Bourges, he stood for some time gazing up at it and mentally gauging the skill of the architects and the consideration of the two families.

There seemed to be no issue to the terrace but the lane by which he had reached it; he could only retrace his steps, but he had gained some notion of his whereabouts, and hoped by this means to hit the main thoroughfare and speedily regain the inn. He was reckoning without that chapter of accidents which was to make this night memorable above all others in his career; for he had not gone back above a hundred yards before he saw a light coming to meet him, and heard loud voices speaking together in the echoing narrows of the lane. It was a party of men-at-arms going the night round with torches. Denis assured himself that they had all been making free with the wine-bowl, and were in no mood to be particular about safe-conducts or the niceties of chivalrous war. It was as like as not that they would kill him like a dog and leave him where he fell. The situation was inspiriting but nervous. Their own torches would conceal him from sight, he reflected; and he hoped that they would drown the noise of his footsteps with their own empty voices. If he were but fleet and silent, he might evade their notice altogether.

Unfortunately, as he turned to beat a retreat, his foot rolled upon a pebble; he fell against the wall with an ejaculation, and his sword rang loudly on the stones. Two or three voices demanded who went there —some in French, some in English; but Denis made no reply, and ran faster down the lane. Once upon the terrace, he paused to look back. They still kept calling after him, and just then began to double the pace in pursuit, with a considerable clank of armour, and great tossing of the torchlight to and fro in the narrow jaws of the passage.

Denis cast a look around and darted into the porch. There he might escape observation, or—if that were too much to expect—was in a capital posture whether for parley or defense. So thinking, he drew his sword and tried to set his back against the door. To his surprise, it yielded behind his weight; and though he turned in a moment, continued to swing back on oiled and noiseless hinges, until it stood wide open on a black interior. When things fall out opportunely for the person concerned, he is not apt to be critical about the how or why, his own immediate personal convenience seeming a sufficient reason for the strangest oddities and revolutions in our sublunary things; and so Denis, without a moment's hesitation, stepped within and partly closed the door behind him to conceal his place of refuge. Nothing was further from his thoughts than to close it altogether; but for some inexplicable reason—perhaps by a spring or a weight—the ponderous mass of oak whipped itself out of his fingers and clanked to, with a formidable rumble and a noise like the falling of an automatic bar.

The round, at that very moment, debouched upon the terrace and proceeded to summon him with shouts and curses. He heard them ferreting in the dark corners; the stock of a lance even rattled along the outer surface of the door behind which he stood; but these gentlemen were in too high a humour to be long delayed, and soon made on down a corkscrew pathway which had escaped Denis' observation, and passed out of sight and hearing along the battlements of the town.

Denis breathed again. He gave them a few minutes' grace for fear of accidents, and then groped about for some means of opening the door and slipping forth again. The inner surface was quite smooth, not a handle, not a moulding, not a projection of any sort. He got his finger-nails round the edges and pulled, but the mass was immovable. He shook it, it was as firm as a rock. Denis de Beaulieu frowned and gave vent to a little noiseless whistle. What ailed the door? he wondered. Why was it open? How came it to shut so easily and so effectually after him? There was something obscure and underhand about all this, that was little to the young man's fancy. It looked like a snare; and yet who could suppose a snare in such a quiet by-street and in a house of so prosperous and even noble an exterior? And yet—snare or no snare, intentionally or unintentionally—here he was, prettily trapped; and for the life of him he could see no way out of it again. The darkness began to weigh upon him. He gave ear; all was silent without, but within and close by he seemed to catch a faint sighing, a faint sobbing rustle, a little stealthy creak—as though many persons were at his side, holding themselves quite still, and governing even their respiration with the extreme of slyness. The idea went to his vitals with a shock, and he faced about suddenly as if to defend his life. Then, for the first time, he became aware of a light about the level of his eyes and at some distance in the interior of the house—a vertical thread of light, widening towards the bottom, such as might escape between two wings of arras over a doorway. To see anything was a relief to Denis; it was like a piece of solid ground to a man labouring in a morass; his mind seized upon it with avidity; and he stood staring at it and trying to piece together some logical conception of his surroundings. Plainly there was a flight of steps ascending from his own level to that of the illuminated doorway; and indeed he thought he could make out another thread of light, as fine as a needle and as faint as phosphorescence, which might very well be reflected along the polished wood of a handrail. Since he had begun to suspect that he was not alone, his heart had continued to beat with smothering violence, and an intolerable desire for action of any sort had possessed itself of his spirit. He was in deadly peril, he believed. What could be more natural than to mount the staircase, lift the curtain, and confront his difficulty at once? At least he would be dealing with something tangible; at least he would be no longer in the dark. He stepped slowly forward with outstretched hands, until his foot struck the bottom step; then he rapidly scaled the stairs, stood for a moment to compose his expression, lifted the arras and went in.

He found himself in a large apartment of polished stone. There were three doors; one on each of three sides; all similarly curtained with tapestry. The fourth side was occupied by two large windows and a great stone chimney-piece, carved with the arms of the Malétroits. Denis recognized the bearings, and was gratified to find himself in such good hands. The room was strongly illuminated; but it contained little furniture except a heavy table and a chair or two, the hearth was innocent of fire, and the pavement was but sparsely strewn with rushes clearly many days old.

On a high chair beside the chimney, and directly facing Denis as he entered, sat a little old gentleman in a fur tippet. He sat with his legs crossed and his hands folded, and a cup of spiced wine stood by his elbow on a bracket on the wall. His countenance had a strongly masculine cast; not properly human, but such as we see in the bull, the goat, or the domestic boar, something equivocal and wheedling, something greedy, brutal, and dangerous. The upper lip was inordinately full, as though swollen by a blow or a toothache; and the smile, the peaked eyebrows, and the small, strong eyes were quaintly and almost comically evil in expression. Beautiful white hair hung straight all round his head, like a saint's, and fell in a single curl upon the tippet. His beard and moustache were the pink of venerable sweetness. Age, probably in consequence of inordinate precautions, had left no mark upon his hands; and the Malétroit hand was famous. It would be difficult to imagine anything at once so fleshy and so delicate in design; the taper, sensual fingers were like those of one of Leonardo's women; the fork of the thumb made a dimpled protuberance when closed; the nails were perfectly shaped, and of a dead, surprising whiteness. It rendered his aspect tenfold more redoubtable, that a man with hands like these should keep them devoutly folded in his lap like a virgin martyr—that a man with so intense and startling an expression of face should sit patiently on his seat and contemplate people with an unwinking stare, like a god, or a god's statue. His quiescence seemed ironical and treacherous, it fitted so poorly with his looks.

Such was Alain, Sire de Malétroit.

Denis and he looked silently at each other for a second or two.

"Pray step in," said the Sire de Malétroit. "I have been expecting you all the evening."

He had not risen, but he accompanied his words with a smile and a slight but courteous inclination of the head. Partly from the smile, partly from the strange musical murmur with which the Sire prefaced his observation, Denis felt a strong shudder of disgust go through his marrow. And what with disgust and honest confusion of mind, he could scarcely get words together in reply.

"I fear," he said, "that this is a double accident. I am not the person you suppose me. It seems you were looking for a visit; but for my part, nothing was further from my thoughts—nothing could be more contrary to my wishes—than this intrusion."

"Well, well," replied the old gentleman indulgently, "here you are, which is the main point. Seat yourself, my friend, and put yourself entirely at your ease. We shall arrange our little affairs presently."

Denis perceived that the matter was still complicated with some misconception, and he hastened to continue his explanation.

"Your door . . ." he began.

"About my door?" asked the other, raising his peaked eyebrows. "A little piece of ingenuity." And he shrugged his shoulders. "A hospitable fancy! By your own account, you were not desirous of making my acquaintance. We old people look for such reluctance now and then; and when it touches our honours, we cast about until we find some way of overcoming it. You arrive uninvited, but believe me, very welcome."

"You persist in error, sir," said Denis. "There can be no question between you and me. I am a stranger in this countryside. My name is Denis, damoiseau de Beaulieu. If you see me in your house, it is only ——."

"My found friend," interrupted the other, "you will permit me to have my own ideas on that subject. They probably differ from yours at the present moment," he added with a leer, "but time will show which of us is in the right."

Denis was convinced he had to do with a lunatic. He seated himself with a shrug, content to wait the upshot; and a pause ensued, during which he thought he could distinguish a hurried gabbling as of prayer from behind the arras immediately opposite him. Sometimes there seemed to be but one person engaged, sometimes two; and the vehemence of the voice, low as it was, seemed to indicate either great haste or an agony of spirit. It occurred to him that this piece of tapestry covered the entrance to the chapel he had noticed from without.

The old gentleman meanwhile surveyed Denis from head to foot with a smile, and from time to time emitted little noises like a bird or a mouse, which seemed to indicate a high degree of satisfaction. This state of matters became rapidly insupportable; and Denis, to put an end to it, remarked politely that the wind had gone down.

The old gentleman fell into a fit of silent laughter, so prolonged and violent that he became quite red in the face. Denis got upon his feet at once, and put on his hat with a flourish.

"Sir," he said, "if you are in your wits, you have affronted me grossly. If you are out of them, I flatter myself I can find better employment for my brains than to talk with lunatics. My conscience is clear; you have made a fool of me from the first moment; you have refused to hear my explanations; and now there is no power under God will make me stay here any longer; and if I cannot make my way out in a more decent fashion, I will hack your door in pieces with my sword."

The Sire de Malétroit raised his right hand and wagged it at Denis with the fore and little fingers extended.

"My dear nephew," he said, "sit down."

"Nephew!" retorted Denis, "you lie in your throat"; and he snapped his fingers in his face.

"Sit down, you rogue!" cried the old gentleman, in a sudden, harsh voice, like the barking of a dog. "Do you fancy," he went on, "that when I had made my little contrivance for the door I had stopped short with that? If you prefer to be bound hand and foot till your bones ache, rise and try to go away. If you choose to remain a free young buck, agreeably conversing with an old gentleman—why, sit where you are in peace, and God be with you."

"Do you mean I am a prisoner?" demanded Denis.

"I state the facts," replied the other. "I would rather leave the conclusion to yourself."

Denis sat down again. Externally he managed to keep pretty calm; but within, he was now boiling with anger, now chilled with apprehension. He no longer felt convinced that he was dealing with a madman. And if the old gentleman was sane, what, in God's name, had he to look for? What absurd or tragical adventure had befallen him? What countenance was he to assume?

While he was thus unpleasantly reflecting, the arras that overhung the chapel door was raised, and a tall priest in his robes came forth and, giving a long, keen stare at Denis, said something in an undertone to Sire de Malétroit.

"She is in a better frame of spirit?" asked the latter.

"She is more resigned, messire," replied the priest.

"Now the Lord help her, she is hard to please!" sneered the old gentleman. "A likely stripling—not ill-born—and of her own choosing, too? Why, what more would the jade have?"

"The situation is not usual for a young damsel," said the other, "and somewhat trying to her blushes."

"She should have thought of that before she began the dance. It was none of my choosing, God knows that: but since she is in it, by our Lady, she shall carry it to the end." And then addressing Denis, "Monsieur de Beaulieu," he asked, "may I present you to my niece? she has been waiting your arrival, I may say, with even greater impatience than myself."

Denis had resigned himself with a good grace—all he desired was to know the worst of it as speedily as possible; so he rose at once, and bowed in acquiescence. The Sire de Malétroit followed his example and limped, with the assistance of the chaplain's arm, towards the chapel door. The priest pulled aside the arras, and all three entered. The building had considerable architectural pretensions. A light groining sprang from six stout columns, and hung down in two rich pendants from the centre of the vault. The place terminated behind the altar in a round end, embossed and honeycombed with a superfluity of ornament in relief, and pierced by many little windows shaped like stars, trefoils, or wheels. These windows were imperfectly glazed, so that the night air circulated freely in the chapel. The tapers, of which there must have been half a hundred burning on the altar, were unmercifully blown about; and the light went through many different phases of brilliancy and semi-eclipse. On the steps in front of the altar knelt a young girl richly attired as a bride. A chill settled over Denis as he observed her costume; he fought with desperate energy against the conclusion that was being thrust upon his mind; it could not—it should not—be as he feared.

"Blanche," said the Sire, in his most flute-like tones, "I have brought a friend to see you, my little girl; turn round and give him your pretty hand. It is good to be devout; but it is necessary to be polite, my niece."

The girl rose to her feet and turned towards the newcomer. She moved all of a piece; and shame and exhaustion were expressed in every line of her fresh young body; and she held her head down and kept her eyes upon the pavement, as she came slowly forward. In the course of her advance, her eyes fell upon Denis de Beaulieu's feet— feet of which he was justly vain, be it remarked, and wore in the most elegant accoutrement even while traveling. She paused—started, as if his yellow boots had conveyed some shocking meaning—and glanced suddenly up into the wearer's countenance. Their eyes met; shame gave place to horror and terror in her looks; the blood left her lips; with a piercing scream she covered her face with her hands and sank upon the chapel floor.

"That is not the man!" she cried. "My uncle, that is not the man!"

The Sire de Malétroit chirped agreeably. "Of course not," he said; "I expected as much. It was so unfortunate you could not remember his name."

"Indeed," she cried, "indeed, I have never seen this person till this moment—I have never so much as set eyes upon him—I never wish to see him again. Sir," she said, turning to Denis, "if you are a gentleman, you will bear me out. Have I ever seen you—have you ever seen me—before this accursed hour?"

"To speak for myself, I have never had that pleasure," answered the young man. "This is the first time, messire, that I have met with your engaging niece."

The old gentleman shrugged his shoulders.

"I am distressed to hear it," he said. "But it is never too late to begin. I had little more acquaintance with my own late lady ere I married her; which proves," he added with a grimace, "that these impromptu marriages may often produce an excellent understanding in the long-run. As the bridegroom is to have a voice in the matter, I will give him two hours to make up for lost time before we proceed with the ceremony." And he turned towards the door, followed by the clergyman.

The girl was on her feet in a moment. "My uncle, you cannot be in earnest," she said. "I declare before God I will stab myself rather than be forced on that young man. The heart rises at it; God forbids such marriages; you dishonour your white hair. Oh, my uncle, pity me! There is not a woman in all the world but would prefer death to such a nuptial. Is it possible," she added, faltering—"is it possible that you do not believe me—that you still think this"—and she pointed at Denis with a tremor of anger and contempt—"that you still think *this* to be the man?"

"Frankly," said the old gentleman, pausing on the threshold, "I do. But let me explain to you once for all, Blanche de Malétroit, my way of thinking about this affair. When you took it into your head to dishonour my family and the name that I have borne, in peace and war, for more than three-score years, you forfeited, not only the right to question my designs, but that of looking me in the face. If your father had been alive, he would have spat on you and turned you out of doors. His was the hand of iron. You may bless your God you have only to deal with the hand of velvet, mademoiselle. It was my duty to get you married without delay. Out of pure goodwill, I have tried to find your own gallant for you. And I believe I have succeeded. But before God and all the holy angels, Blanche de Malétroit, if I have not, I care not one jack-straw. So let me recommend you to be polite to our young friend; for upon my word, your next groom may be less appetizing."

And with that he went out, with the chaplain at his heels; and the arras fell behind the pair.

The girl turned upon Denis with flashing eyes.

"And what, sir," she demanded, "may be the meaning of all this?"

"God knows," returned Denis gloomily. "I am a prisoner in this house, which seems full of mad people. More I know not; and nothing do I understand."

"And pray how came you here?" she asked.

He told her as briefly as he could. "For the rest," he added, "perhaps you will follow my example, and tell me the answer to all these riddles, and what, in God's name, is like to be the end of it."

She stood silent for a little, and he could see her lips tremble and her tearless eyes burn with a feverish lustre. Then she pressed her forehead in both hands.

"Alas, how my head aches!" she said wearily—"to say nothing of my poor heart! But it is due to you to know my story, unmaidenly as it must seem. I am called Blanche de Malétroit; I have been without father or mother for—oh! for as long as I can recollect, and indeed I have been most unhappy all my life. Three months ago a young captain began to stand near me every day in church. I could see that I pleased him; I am much to blame, but I was so glad that any one should love me; and when he passed me a letter, I took it home with me and read it with great pleasure. Since that time he has written many. He was so anxious to speak with me, poor fellow! and kept asking me to leave the door open some evening that we might have two words upon the stair. For he knew how much my uncle trusted me." She gave something like a sob at that, and it was a moment before she could go on. "My uncle is a hard man, but he is very shrewd," she said at last. "He has performed many feats in war, and was a great person at court, and much trusted by Queen Isabeau in old days. How he came to suspect me I cannot tell; but it is hard to keep anything from his knowledge; and this morning, as we came from mass, he took my hand in his, forced it open, and read my little billet, walking by my side all the while. When he had finished, he gave it back to me with great politeness. It contained another request to have the door left open; and this has been the ruin of us all. My uncle kept me strictly in my room until evening, and then ordered me to dress myself as you see me—a hard mockery for a young girl, do you not think so? I suppose, when he could not prevail with me to tell him the young captain's name, he must have laid a trap for him: into which, alas! you have fallen in the anger of God. I looked for much confusion; for how could I tell whether he was willing to take me for his wife on these sharp terms? He might have been trifling with me from the first; or I might have made myself too cheap in his eyes. But truly I had not looked for such a shameful punishment as this. I could not think that God would let a girl be so disgraced before a young man. And now I have told you all; and I can scarcely hope that you will not despise me."

Denis made her a respectful inclination.

"Madam," he said, "you have honoured me by your confidence. It remains for me to prove that I am not unworthy of the honour. Is Messire de Malétroit at hand?"

"I believe he is writing in the salle without," she answered.

"May I lead you thither, madam?" asked Denis, offering his hand with his most courtly bearing.

She accepted it; and the pair passed out of the chapel, Blanche in a very drooping and shamefaced condition, but Denis strutting and ruffling in the consciousness of a mission, and the boyish certainty of accomplishing it with honour.

The Sire de Malétroit rose to meet them with an ironical obeisance.

"Sir," said Denis, with the grandest possible air, "I believe I am to have some say in the matter of this marriage; and let me tell you at once, I will be no party to forcing the inclination of this young lady. Had it been freely offered to me, I should have been proud to accept her hand, for I perceive she is as good as she is beautiful; but as things are, I have now the honour, messire, of refusing."

Blanche looked at him with gratitude in her eyes; but the old gentleman only smiled and smiled, until his smile grew positively sickening to Denis.

"I am afraid," he said, "Monsieur de Beaulieu, that you do not perfectly understand the choice I have to offer you. Follow me, I beseech you, to this window." And he led the way to one of the large windows which stood open on the night. "You observe," he went on, "there is an iron ring in the upper masonry, and reeved through that, a very efficacious rope. Now, mark my words: if you should find your disinclination to my niece's person insurmountable, I shall have you hanged out of this window before sunrise. I shall only proceed to such an extremity with the greatest regret, you may believe me. For it is not at all your death that I desire, but my niece's establishment in life. At the same time, it must come to that if you prove obstinate. Your family, Monsieur de Beaulieu, is very well in its way; but if you sprang from Charlemagne, you should not refuse the hand of a Malétroit with impunity—not if she had been as common as the Paris road—not if she were as hideous as the gargoyle over my door. Neither my niece nor you, nor my own private feelings, move me at all in this matter. The honour of my house has been compromised; I believe you to be the guilty person; at least you are now in the secret; and you can hardly wonder if I request you to wipe out the stain. If you will not, your blood be on your own head! It will be no great satisfaction to me to have your interesting relics kicking their heels in the breeze below my windows; but half a loaf is better than no bread, and if I cannot cure the dishonour, I shall at least stop the scandal."

There was a pause.

"I believe there are other ways of settling such imbroglios among gentlemen," said Denis. "You wear a sword, and I hear you have used it with distinction."

The Sire de Malétroit made a signal to the chaplain, who crossed the room with long silent strides and raised the arras over the third of the three doors. It was only a moment before he let it fall again; but Denis had time to see a dusky passage full of armed men.

"When I was a little younger, I should have been delighted to honour you, Monsieur de Beaulieu," said Sire Alain; "but I am now too old. Faithful retainers are the sinews of age, and I must employ the strength I have. This is one of the hardest things to swallow as a man grows up in years; but with a little patience, even this becomes habitual. You and the lady seem to prefer the salle for what remains of your two hours; and as I have no desire to cross your preference, I shall resign it to your use with all the pleasure in the world. No haste!" he added, holding up his hand, as he saw a dangerous look come into Denis de Beaulieu's face. "If your mind revolts against hanging, it will be time enough two hours hence to throw yourself out of the window or upon the pikes of my retainers. Two hours of life are always two hours. A great many things may turn up in even as little a while as that. And besides, if I understand her appearance, my niece has still something to say to you. You will not disfigure your last hours by a want of politeness to a lady?"

Denis looked at Blanche, and she made him an imploring gesture.

It is likely that the old gentleman was hugely pleased at this symptom of an understanding; for he smiled on both, and added sweetly: "If you will give me your word of honour, Monsieur de Beaulieu, to await my return at the end of the two hours before attempting anything desperate, I shall withdraw my retainers, and let you speak in greater privacy with mademoiselle."

Denis again glanced at the girl, who seemed to beseech him to agree. "I give you my word of honour," he said.

Messire de Malétroit bowed, and proceeded to limp about the apartment, clearing his throat the while with that odd musical chirp which had already grown so irritating in the ears of Denis de Beaulieu. He first possessed himself of some papers which lay upon the table; then he went to the mouth of the passage and appeared to give an order to the men behind the arras; and lastly he hobbled out through the door by which Denis had come in, turning upon the threshold to address a last smiling bow to the young couple, and followed by the chaplain with a hand-lamp.

No sooner were they alone than Blanche advanced towards Denis with her hands extended. Her face was flushed and excited, and her eyes shone with tears.

"You shall not die!" she cried, "you shall marry me after all."

"You seem to think, madam," replied Denis, "that I stand much in fear of death."

"Oh, no, no," she said, "I see you are no poltroon. It is for my own sake—I could not bear to have you slain for such a scruple."

"I am afraid," returned Denis, "that you underrate the difficulty, madam. What you may be too generous to refuse, I may be too proud to accept. In a moment of noble feeling towards me, you forget what you perhaps owe to others."

He had the decency to keep his eyes upon the floor as he said this, and after he had finished, so as not to spy upon her confusion. She stood silent for a moment, then walked suddenly away, and falling on her uncle's chair, fairly burst out sobbing. Denis was in the acme of embarrassment. He looked round, as if to seek for inspiration, and seeing a stool, plumped down upon it for something to do. There he sat, playing with the guard of his rapier, and wishing himself dead a thousand times over, and buried in the nastiest kitchen-heap in France. His eyes wandered round the apartment but found nothing to arrest them. There were such wide spaces between the furniture, the light fell so badly and cheerlessly over all, the dark outside air looked in so coldly through the windows, that he thought he had never seen a church so vast, nor a tomb so melancholy. The regular sobs of Blanche de Malétroit measured out the time like the ticking of a clock. He read the device upon the shield over and over again, until his eyes became obscured; he stared into shadowy corners until he imagined they were swarming with horrible animals; and every now and again he awoke with a start, to remember that his last two hours were running and death was on the march.

Oftener and oftener, as the time went on, did his glance settle on the girl herself. Her face was bowed forward and covered with her hands, and she was shaken at intervals by the convulsive hiccup of grief. Even thus she was not an unpleasant object to dwell upon, so plump and yet so fine, with a warm brown skin, and the most beautiful hair, Denis thought, in the whole world of womankind. Her hands were like her uncle's; but they were more in place at the end of her young arms, and looked infinitely soft and caressing. He remembered how her blue eyes had shone upon him, full of anger, pity, and innocence. And the more he dwelt on her perfections, the uglier death looked, and the more deeply was he smitten with penitence at her continued tears. Now he felt that no man could have the courage to leave a world which contained so beautiful a creature; and now he would have given forty minutes of his last hour to have unsaid his cruel speech.

Suddenly a hoarse and ragged peal of cockcrow rose to their ears from the dark valley below the windows. And this shattering noise in the silence all around was like a light in a dark place, and shook them both out of their reflections.

"Alas, can I do nothing to help you?" she said, looking up.

"Madam," replied Denis, with a fine irrelevancy, "if I have said anything to wound you, believe me, it was for your own sake and not for mine."

She thanked him with a tearful look.

"I feel your position cruelly," he went on. "The world has been bitter hard on you. Your uncle is a disgrace to mankind. Believe me, madam, there is no young gentleman in all France but would be glad of my opportunity, to die in doing you a momentary service."

"I know already that you can be very brave and generous," she answered. "What I *want* to know is whether I can serve you—now or afterwards," she added, with a quaver.

"Most certainly," he answered with a smile. "Let me sit beside you as if I were a friend, instead of a foolish intruder; try to forget how awkwardly we are placed to one another; make my last moments go pleasantly; and you will do me the chief service possible."

"You are very gallant," she added, with a yet deeper sadness . . . "very gallant . . . and it somehow pains me. But draw nearer, if you please, and if you find anything to say to me, you will at least make certain of a very friendly listener. Ah! Monsieur de Beaulieu, how can I look you in the face?" And she fell to weeping again with a renewed effusion.

"Madam," said Denis, taking her hand in both of his, "reflect on the little time I have before me, and the great bitterness into which I am cast by the sight of your distress. Spare me, in my last moments, the spectacle of what I cannot cure even with the sacrifice of my life."

"I am very selfish," answered Blanche. "I will be braver, Monsieur de Beaulieu, for your sake. But think if I can do you no kindness in the future—if you have no friends to whom I could carry your adieux. Charge me as heavily as you can; every burden will lighten, by so little, the invaluable gratitude I owe you. Put it in my power to do something more for you than weep."

"My mother is married again, and has a young family to care for. My brother Guichard will inherit my fiefs; and if I am not in error, that will content him amply for my death. Life is a little vapour that passeth away, as we are told by those in holy orders. When a man is in a fair way and sees all life open in front of him, he seems to himself to make a very important figure in the world. His horse whinnies to him; the trumpets blow and the girls look out of windows as he rides into town before his company; he receives many assurances of trust and regard—sometimes by express in a letter—sometimes face to face, with persons of great consequence falling on his neck. It is not wonderful if his head is turned for a time. But once he is dead, were he as brave as Hercules or as wise as Solomon, he is soon forgotten. It is not ten years since my father fell, with many other knights around him, in a very fierce encounter, and I do not think that any one of them, nor so much as the name of the fight, is now remembered. No, no, madam, the nearer you come to it, you see that death is a dark and dusty corner, where a man gets into his tomb and has the door shut after him till the judgment day. I have few friends just now, and once I am dead I shall have none."

"Ah, Monsieur de Beaulieu!" she exclaimed, "you forget Blanche de Malétroit."

"You have a sweet nature, madam, and you are pleased to estimate a little service far beyond its worth."

"It is not that," she answered. "You mistake me if you think I am so easily touched by my own concerns. I say so, because you are the noblest man I have ever met; because I recognise in you a spirit that would have made even a common person famous in the land."

"And yet here I die in a mouse-trap—with no more noise about it than my own speaking," answered he.

A look of pain crossed her face, and she was silent for a little while. Then a light came into her eyes, and with a smile she spoke again.

"I cannot have my champion think meanly of himself. Any one who gives his life for another will be met in Paradise by all the heralds and angels of the Lord God. And you have no such cause to hang your head. For . . . . Pray, do you think me beautiful?" she asked, with a deep flush.

"Indeed, madam, I do," he said.

"I am glad of that," she answered, heartily. "Do you think there are many men in France who have been asked in marriage by a beautiful maiden—with her own lips—and who have refused her to her face? I know you men would half despise such a triumph; but believe me, we women know more of what is precious in love. There is nothing that should set a person higher in his own esteem; and we women would prize nothing more dearly."

"You are very good," he said; "but you cannot make me forget that I was asked in pity and not for love."

"I am not so sure of that," she replied, holding down her head. "Hear me to an end, Monsieur de Beaulieu. I know how you must despise me; I feel you are right to do so; I am too poor a creature to occupy one thought of your mind, although, alas! you must die for me this morning. But when I asked you to marry me, indeed, and indeed, it was because I respected and admired you, and loved you with my whole soul, from the very moment that you took my part against my uncle. If you had seen yourself, and how noble you looked, you would pity rather than despise me. And now," she went on, hurriedly checking him with her hand, "although I have laid aside all reserve and told you so much, remember that I know your sentiments towards me already. I would not, believe me, being nobly born, weary you with importunities into consent. I too have a pride of my own: and I declare before the holy mother of God, if you should now go back from your word already given, I would no more marry you than I would marry my uncle's groom."

Denis smiled a little bitterly.

"It is a small love," he said, "that shies at a little pride."

She made no answer, although she probably had her own thought.

"Come hither to the window," he said, with a sigh. "Here is the dawn."

And indeed the dawn was already beginning. The hollow of the sky was full of essential daylight, colourless and clean; and the valley underneath was flooded with a grey reflection. A few thin vapors clung in the coves of the forest or lay along the winding course of the river. The scene disengaged a surprising effect of stillness, which was hardly interrupted when the cocks began once more to crow among the steadings. Perhaps the same fellow who had made so horrid a clangour in the darkness not half an hour before, now sent up the merriest cheer to greet the coming day. A little wind went bustling and eddying among the tree-tops underneath the windows. And still the daylight kept flooding insensibly out of the east, which was soon to grow incandescent and cast up that red-hot cannon-ball, the rising sun.

Denis looked out over all this with a bit of a shiver. He had taken her hand and retained it in his almost unconsciously.

"Has the day begun already?" she said; and then, illogically enough: "the night has been so long! Alas! what shall we say to my uncle when he returns?"

"What you will," said Denis, and he pressed her fingers in his.

She was silent.

"Blanche," he said, with a swift, uncertain, passionate utterance, "you have seen whether I fear death. You must know well enough that I would as gladly leap out of the window into the empty air as to lay a finger on you without your free and full consent. But if you care for me at all do not let me lose my life in a misapprehension; for I love you better than the whole world; and though I will die for you blithely, it would be like all the joys of Paradise to live on and spend my life in your service."

As he stopped speaking, a bell began to ring loudly in the interior of the house, and a clatter of armour in the corridor showed that the retainers were returning to their post, and the two hours were at an end.

"After all that you have heard?" she whispered, leaning towards him with her lips and eyes.

"I have heard nothing," he replied.

"The captain's name was Florimond de Champdivers," she said in his ear.

"I did not hear it," he answered, taking her supple body in his arms and covering her wet face with kisses.

A melodious chirping was audible behind, followed by a beautiful chuckle, and the voice of Messire de Malétroit wished his new nephew a good morning.

A Lodging for the Night

BY ROBERT LOUIS STEVENSON

IT was late in November, 1456. The snow fell over Paris with rigourous, relentless persistence; sometimes the wind made a sally and scattered it in flying vortices; sometimes there was a lull, and flake after flake descended out of the black night air, silent, circuitous, interminable. To poor people, looking up under moist eyebrows, it seemed a wonder where it all came from. Master Francis Villon had propounded an alternative that afternoon at a tavern window: was it only Pagan Jupiter plucking geese upon Olympus? or were the holy angels moulting? He was only a poor Master of Arts, he went on; and as the question somewhat touched upon divinity, he durst not venture to conclude. A silly old priest from Montargis, who was among the company, treated the young rascal to a bottle of wine in honor of the jest and grimaces with which it was accompanied, and swore on his own white beard that he had been just such another irreverent dog when he was Villon's age.

The air was raw and pointed, but not far below freezing; and the flakes were large, damp, and adhesive. The whole city was sheeted up. An army might have marched from end to end and not a footfall given the alarm. If there were any belated birds in heaven, they saw the island like a large white patch, and the bridges like slim white spars, on the black ground of the river. High up overhead the snow settled among the tracery of the cathedral towers. Many a niche was drifted full; many a statue wore a long white bonnet on its grotesque or sainted head. The gargoyles had been transformed into great false noses, drooping towards the point. The crockets were like upright pillows swollen on one side. In the intervals of the wind, there was a dull sound of dripping about the precincts of the church.

The cemetery of St. John had taken its own share of the snow. All the graves were decently covered; tall white housetops stood around in grave array; worthy burghers were long ago in bed, be-nightcapped like their domiciles; there was no light in all the neighborhood but a little peep from a lamp that hung swinging in the church choir, and tossed the shadows to and fro in time to its oscillations. The clock was hard on ten when the patrol went by with halberds and a lantern, beating their hands; and they saw nothing suspicious about the cemetery of St. John.

Yet there was a small house, backed up against the cemetery wall, which was still awake, and awake to evil purpose, in that snoring district. There was not much to betray it from without; only a stream of warm vapor from the chimney-top, a patch where the snow melted on the roof, and a few half-obliterated footprints at the door. But within, behind the shuttered windows, Master Francis Villon the poet, and some of the thievish crew with whom he consorted, were keeping the night alive and passing round the bottle.

A great pile of living embers diffused a strong and ruddy glow from the arched chimney. Before this straddled Dom Nicolas, the Picardy monk, with his skirts picked up and his fat legs bared to the comfortable warmth. His dilated shadow cut the room in half; and the firelight only escaped on either side of his broad person, and in a little pool between his outspread feet. His face had the beery, bruised appearance of the continual drinker's; it was covered with a network of congested veins, purple in ordinary circumstances, but now pale violet, for even with his back to the fire the cold pinched him on the other side. His cowl had half fallen back, and made a strange excrescence on either side of his bull neck. So he straddled, grumbling, and cut the room in half with the shadow of his portly frame.

On the right, Villon and Guy Tabary were huddled together over a scrap of parchment; Villon making a ballade which he was to call the "Ballade of Roast Fish," and Tabary spluttering admiration at his shoulder. The poet was a rag of a man, dark, little, and lean, with hollow cheeks and thin black locks. He carried his four-and-twenty years with feverish animation. Greed had made folds about his eyes, evil smiles had puckered his mouth. The wolf and pig struggled together in his face. It was an eloquent, sharp, ugly, earthly countenance. His hands were small and prehensile, with fingers knotted like a cord; and they were continually flickering in front of him in violent and expressive pantomime. As for Tabary, a broad, complacent, admiring imbecility breathed from his squash nose and slobbering lips: he had become a thief, just as he might have become the most decent of burgesses, by the imperious chance that rules the lives of human geese and human donkeys.

At the monk's other hand, Montigny and Thevenin Pensete played a game of chance. About the first there clung some flavour of good birth and training, as about a fallen angel; something long, lithe, and courtly in the person; something aquiline and darkling in the face. Thevenin, poor soul, was in great feather: he had done a good stroke of knavery that afternoon in the Faubourg St. Jacques, and all night he had been gaining from Montigny. A flat smile illuminated his face; his bald head shone rosily in a garland of red curls; his little protuberant stomach shook with silent chucklings as he swept in his gains.

"Doubles or quits?" said Thevenin.

Montigny nodded grimly.

"*Some may prefer to dine in state,*" wrote Villon, "*on bread and cheese on silver plate.* Or, or—help me out, Guido!"

Tabary giggled.

"*Or parsley on a golden dish,*" scribbled the poet.

The wind was freshening without; it drove the snow before it, and sometimes raised its voice in a victorious whoop, and made sepulchral grumblings in the chimney. The cold was growing sharper as the night went on. Villon, protruding his lips, imitated the gust with something between a whistle and a groan. It was an eerie, uncomfortable talent of the poet's, much detested by the Picardy monk.

"Can't you hear it rattle in the gibbet?" said Villon. "They are all dancing the devil's jig on nothing, up there. You may dance, my gallants, you'll be none the warmer! Whew! what a gust! Down went somebody just now! A medlar the fewer on the three-legged medlar-tree!—I say, Dom Nicolas, it'll be cold to-night on the St. Denis Road?" he asked.

Dom Nicolas winked both his big eyes, and seemed to choke upon his Adam's apple. Montfaucon, the great grisly Paris gibbet, stood hard by the St. Denis Road, and the pleasantry touched him on the raw. As for Tabary, he laughed immoderately over the medlars; he had never heard anything more light-hearted; and he held his sides and crowed. Villon fetched him a fillip on the nose, which turned his mirth into an attack of coughing.

"Oh, stop that row," said Villon, "and think of rhymes to 'fish.'"

"Doubles or quits," said Montigny doggedly.

"With all my heart," quoth Thevenin.

"Is there any more in that bottle?" asked the monk.

"Open another," said Villon. "How do you ever hope to fill that big hogshead, your body, with little things like bottles? And how do you expect to get to heaven? How many angels, do you fancy, can be spared to carry up a single monk from Picardy? Or do you think yourself another Elias—and they'll send the coach for you?"

"*Hominibus impossibile*," replied the monk as he filled his glass. Tabary was in ecstasies.

Villon filliped his nose again.

"Laugh at my jokes, if you like," he said.

"It was very good," objected Tabary.

Villon made a face at him. "Think of rhymes to 'fish,'" he said. "What have you to do with Latin? You'll wish you knew none of it at the great assizes, when the devil calls for Guido Tabary, clericus— the devil with the hump-back and red-hot finger-nails. Talking of the devil," he added in a whisper, "look at Montigny!"

All three peered covertly at the gamester. He did not seem to be enjoying his luck. His mouth was a little to a side; one nostril nearly shut, and the other much inflated. The black dog was on his back, as people say, in terrifying nursery metaphor; and he breathed hard under the gruesome burden.

"He looks as if he could knife him," whispered Tabary, with round eyes.

The monk shuddered, and turned his face and spread his open hands to the red embers. It was the cold that thus affected Dom Nicolas, and not any excess of moral sensibility.

"Come now," said Villon—"about this ballade. How does it run so far?" And beating time with his hand, he read it aloud to Tabary.

They were interrupted at the fourth rhyme by a brief and fatal movement among the gamesters. The round was completed, and Thevenin was just opening his mouth to claim another victory, when Montigny leaped up, swift as an adder, and stabbed him to the heart. The blow took effect before he had time to utter a cry, before he had time to move. A tremor or two convulsed his frame; his hands opened and shut, his heels rattled on the floor; then his head rolled backward over one shoulder with the eyes wide open, and Thevenin Pensete's spirit had returned to Him who made it.

Everyone sprang to his feet; but the business was over in two two's. The four living fellows looked at each other in rather a ghastly fashion; the dead man contemplating a corner of the roof with a singular and ugly leer.

"My God!" said Tabary; and he began to pray in Latin.

Villon broke out into hysterical laughter. He came a step forward and ducked a ridiculous bow at Thevenin, and laughed still louder. Then he sat down suddenly, all of a heap, upon a stool, and continued laughing bitterly as though he would shake himself to pieces.

Montigny recovered his composure first.

"Let's see what he has about him," he remarked, and he picked the dead man's pockets with a practised hand, and divided the money into four equal portions on the table. "There's for you," he said.

The monk received his share with a deep sigh, and a single stealthy glance at the dead Thevenin, who was beginning to sink into himself and topple sideways off the chair.

"We're all in for it," cried Villon, swallowing his mirth. "It's a hanging job for every man jack of us that's here—not to speak of those who aren't." He made a shocking gesture in the air with his raised right hand, and put out his tongue and threw his head on one side, so as to counterfeit the appearance of one who has been hanged. Then he pocketed his share of the spoil, and executed a shuffle with his feet as if to restore the circulation.

Tabary was the last to help himself; he made a dash at the money, and retired to the other end of the apartment.

Montigny stuck Thevenin upright in the chair, and drew out the dagger, which was followed by a jet of blood.

"You fellows had better be moving," he said, as he wiped the blade on his victim's doublet.

"I think we had," returned Villon, with a gulp. "Damn his fat head!" he broke out. "It sticks in my throat like phlegm. What right has a man to have red hair when he is dead?" And he fell all of a heap again upon the stool, and fairly covered his face with his hands.

Montigny and Dom Nicolas laughed aloud, even Tabary feebly chiming in.

"Cry-baby," said the monk.

"I always said he was a woman," added Montigny, with a sneer. "Sit up, can't you?" he went on, giving another shake to the murdered body. "Tread out that fire, Nick!"

But Nick was better employed; he was quietly taking Villon's purse, as the poet sat limp and trembling on the stool where he had been making a ballade not three minutes before. Montigny and Tabary dumbly demanded a share of the booty, which the monk silently promised as he passed the little bag into the bosom of his gown. In many ways an artistic nature unfits a man for practical existence.

No sooner had the theft been accomplished than Villon shook himself, jumped to his feet, and began helping to scatter and extinguish the embers. Meanwhile Montigny opened the door and cautiously peered into the street. The coast was clear; there was no meddlesome patrol in sight. Still it was judged wiser to slip out severally; and as Villon was himself in a hurry to escape from the neighbourhood of the dead Thevenin, and the rest were in a still greater hurry to get rid of him before he should discover the loss of his money, he was the first by general consent to issue forth into the street.

The wind had triumphed and swept all the clouds from heaven. Only a few vapours, as thin as moonlight, fleeted rapidly across the stars. It was bitter cold; and by a common optical effect, things seemed almost more definite than in the broadest daylight. The sleeping city was absolutely still; a company of white hoods, a field full of little alps, below the twinkling stars. Villon cursed his fortune. Would it were still snowing! Now, wherever he went, he left an indelible trail behind him on the glittering streets; wherever he went he was still tethered to the house by the cemetery of St. John; wherever he went he must weave, with his own plodding feet, the rope that bound him to the crime and would bind him to the gallows. The leer of the dead man came back to him with a new significance. He snapped his fingers as if to pluck up his own spirits, and choosing a street at random, stepped boldly forward in the snow.

Two things preoccupied him as he went; the aspect of the gallows at Montfaucon in this bright, windy phase of the night's existence, for one; and for another, the look of the dead man with his bald head and garland of red curls. Both struck cold upon his heart, and he kept quickening his pace as if he could escape from unpleasant thoughts by mere fleetness of foot. Sometimes he looked back over his shoulder with a sudden nervous jerk; but he was the only moving thing in the white streets, except when the wind swooped round a corner and threw up the snow, which was beginning to freeze, in spouts of glittering dust.

Suddenly he saw, a long way before him, a black clump and a couple of lanterns. The clump was in motion, and the lanterns swung as though carried by men walking. It was a patrol. And though it was merely crossing his line of march he judged it wiser to get out of eyeshot as speedily as he could. He was not in the humour to be challenged, and he was conscious of making a very conspicuous mark upon the snow. Just on his left hand there stood a great hotel, with some turrets and a large porch before the door; it was half-ruinous, he remembered, and had long stood empty; and so he made three steps of it, and jumped into the shelter of the porch. It was pretty dark inside, after the glimmer of the snowy streets, and he was groping forward with outspread hands, when he stumbled over some substance which offered an indescribable mixture of resistances, hard and soft, firm and loose. His heart gave a leap, and he sprang two steps back and stared dreadfully at the obstacle. Then he gave a little laugh of relief. It was only a woman, and she dead. He knelt beside her to make sure upon this latter point. She was freezing cold, and rigid like a stick. A little ragged finery fluttered in the wind about her hair and her cheeks had been heavily rouged that same afternoon. Her pockets were quite empty; but in her stocking, underneath the garter, Villon found two of the small coins that went by the name of whites. It was little enough; but it was always something; and the poet was moved with a deep sense of pathos that she should have died before she had spent her money. That seemed to him a dark and pitiable mystery; and he looked from the coins in his hand to the dead woman, and back again to the coins, shaking his head over the riddle of man's life. Henry V. of England, dying at Vincennes just after he had conquered France, and this poor jade cut off by a cold draught in a great man's doorway, before she had time to spend her couple of whites—it seemed a cruel way to carry on the world. Two whites would have taken such a little while to squander; and yet it would have been one more good taste in the mouth, one more smack of the lips, before the devil got the soul, and the body was left to birds and vermin. He would like to use all his tallow before the light was blown out and the lantern broken.

While these thoughts were passing through his mind, he was feeling, half mechanically, for his purse. Suddenly his heart stopped beating; a feeling of cold scales passed up the back of his legs, and a cold blow seemed to fall upon his scalp. He stood petrified for a moment; then he felt again with one feverish movement; and then his loss burst upon him, and he was covered at once with perspiration. To spendthrifts money is so living and actual—it is such a thin veil between them and their pleasures! There is only one limit to their fortune—that of time; and a spendthrift with only a few crowns is the Emperor of Rome until they are spent. For such a person to lose his money is to suffer the most shocking reverse, and fall from heaven to hell, from all to nothing, in a breath. And all the more if he has put his head in the halter for it; if he may be hanged to-morrow for that same purse, so dearly earned, so foolishly departed! Villon stood and cursed; he threw the two whites into the street; he shook his fist at heaven; he stamped, and was not horrified to find himself trampling the poor corpse. Then he began rapidly to retrace his steps towards the house beside the cemetery. He had forgotten all fear of the patrol, which was long gone by at any rate, and had no idea but that of his lost purse. It was in vain that he looked right and left upon the snow; nothing was to be seen. He had not dropped it in the streets. Had it fallen in the house? He would have liked dearly to go in and see; but the idea of the grisly occupant unmanned him. And he saw besides, as he drew near, that their efforts to put out the fire had been unsuccessful; on the contrary, it had broken into a blaze, and a changeful light played in the chinks of door and window, and revived his terror for the authorities and Paris gibbet.

He returned to the hotel with the porch, and groped about upon the snow for the money he had thrown away in his childish passion. But he could only find one white; the other had probably struck sideways and sunk deeply in. With a single white in his pocket, all his projects for a rousing night in some wild tavern vanished utterly away. And it was not only pleasure that fled laughing from his grasp; positive discomfort, positive pain, attacked him as he stood ruefully before the porch. His perspiration had dried upon him; and although the wind had now fallen, a binding frost was setting in stronger with every hour, and he felt benumbed and sick at heart. What was to be done? Late as was the hour, improbable as was success, he would try the house of his adopted father, the chaplain of St. Benoît.

He ran there all the way, and knocked timidly. There was no answer. He knocked again and again, taking heart with every stroke; and at last steps were heard approaching from within. A barred wicket fell open in the iron-studded door, and emitted a gush of yellow light.

"Hold up your face to the wicket," said the chaplain from within.

"It's only me," whimpered Villon.

"Oh, it's only you, is it?" returned the chaplain; and he cursed him with foul unpriestly oaths for disturbing him at such an hour, and bade him be off to hell, where he came from.

"My hands are blue to the wrist," pleaded Villon; "my feet are dead and full of twinges; my nose aches with the sharp air; the cold lies at my heart. I may be dead before morning. Only this once, father, and before God, I will never ask again!"

"You should have come earlier," said the ecclesiastic coolly. "Young men require a lesson now and then." He shut the wicket and retired deliberately into the interior of the house.

Villon was beside himself; he beat upon the door with his hands and feet, and shouted hoarsely after the chaplain.

"Wormy old fox!" he cried. "If I had my hand under your twist, I would send you flying headlong into the bottomless pit."

A door shut in the interior, faintly audible to the poet down long passages. He passed his hand over his mouth with an oath. And then the humour of the situation struck him, and he laughed and looked lightly up to heaven, where the stars seemed to be winking over his discomfiture.

What was to be done? It looked very like a night in the frosty streets. The idea of the dead woman popped into his imagination, and gave him a hearty fright; what had happened to her in the early night might very well happen to him before morning. And he so young! and with such immense possibilities of disorderly amusement before him! He felt quite pathetic over the notion of his own fate, as if it had been some one else's, and made a little imaginative vignette of the scene in the morning when they should find his body.

He passed all his chances under review, turning the white between his thumb and forefinger. Unfortunately he was on bad terms with some old friends who would once have taken pity on him in such a plight. He had lampooned them in verses; he had beaten and cheated them; and yet now, when he was in so close a pinch, he thought there was at least one who might perhaps relent. It was a chance. It was worth trying at least, and he would go and see.

On the way, two little accidents happened to him which coloured his musings in a very different manner. For, first, he fell in with the track of a patrol, and walked in it for some hundred yards, although it lay out of his direction. And this spirited him up; at least he had confused his trail; for he was still possessed with the idea of people tracking him all about Paris over the snow, and collaring him next morning before he was awake. The other matter affected him quite differently. He passed a street corner, where, not so long before, a woman and her child had been devoured by wolves. This was just the kind of weather, he reflected, when wolves might take it into their heads to enter Paris again; and a lone man in these deserted streets would run the chance of something worse than a mere scare. He stopped and looked upon the place with an unpleasant interest—it was the centre where several lanes intersected each other; and he looked down them all, one after another, and held his breath to listen, lest he should detect some galloping black things on the snow or hear the sound of howling between him and the river. He remembered his mother telling him the story and pointing out the spot, while he was yet a child. His mother! If he only knew where she lived, he might make sure at least of shelter. He determined he would inquire upon the morrow; nay, he would go and see her, too, poor old girl! So thinking, he arrived at his destination—his last hope for the night.

The house was quite dark, like its neighbors; and yet after a few taps, he heard a movement overhead, a door opening, and a cautious voice asking who was there. The poet named himself in a loud whisper, and waited, not without some trepidation, the result. Nor had he to wait long. A window was suddenly opened, and a pailful of slops splashed down upon the doorstep. Villon had not been unprepared for something of the sort, and had put himself as much in shelter as the nature of the porch admitted; but for all that, he was deplorably drenched below the waist. His hose began to freeze almost at once. Death from cold and exposure stared him in the face; he remembered he was of phthisical tendency, and began coughing tentatively. But the gravity of the danger steadied his nerves. He stopped a few hundred yards from the door where he had been so rudely used, and reflected with his finger to his nose. He could only see one way of getting a lodging and that was to take it. He had noticed a house not far away, which looked as if it might be easily broken into, and thither he betook himself promptly, entertaining himself on the way with the idea of a room still hot, with a table still loaded with the remains of supper, where he might pass the rest of the black hours and whence he should issue, on the morrow, with an armful of valuable plate. He even considered on what viands and what wines he should prefer; and as he was calling the roll of his favourite dainties, roast fish presented itself to his mind with an odd mixture of amusement and horror.

"I shall never finish that ballade," he thought to himself; and then, with another shudder at the recollection, "Oh, damn his fat head!" he repeated fervently, and spat upon the snow.

The house in question looked dark at first sight; but as Villon made a preliminary inspection in search of the handiest point of attack, a little twinkle of light caught his eye from behind a curtained window.

"The devil!" he thought. "People awake! Some student or some saint, confound the crew. Can't they get drunk and lie in bed snoring like their neighbors! What's the good of curfew, and poor devils of bell-ringers jumping at a rope's end in bell-towers? What's the use of day, if people sit up all night? The gripes to them!" He grinned as he saw where his logic was leading him. "Every man to his business, after all," added he, "and if they're awake, by the Lord, I may come by a supper honestly for once, and cheat the devil."

He went boldly to the door and knocked with an assured hand. On both previous occasions, he had knocked timidly and with some dread of attracting notice; but now when he had just discarded the thought of a burglarious entry, knocking at a door seemed a mighty simple and innocent proceeding. The sound of his blows echoed through the house with thin, phantasmal reverberations, as though it were quite empty; but these had scarcely died away before a measured tread drew near, a couple of bolts were withdrawn, and one wing was opened broadly, as though no guile or fear of guile were known to those within. A tall figure of a man, muscular and spare, but a little bent, confronted Villon. The head was massive in bulk, but finely sculptured; the nose blunt at the bottom, but refining upward to where it joined a pair of strong and honest eyebrows; the mouth and eyes surrounded with delicate markings, and the whole face based upon a thick white beard, boldly and squarely trimmed. Seen as it was by the light of a flickering hand-lamp, it looked perhaps nobler than it had a right to do; but it was a fine face, honourable, rather than intelligent, strong, simple, and righteous.

"You knock late, sir," said the old man in resonant, courteous tones.

Villon cringed, and brought up many servile words of apology; at a crisis of this sort, the beggar was uppermost in him, and the man of genius hid his head with confusion.

"You are cold," repeated the old man, "and hungry? Well, step in." And he ordered him into the house with a noble enough gesture.

"Some great seigneur," thought Villon, as his host, setting down the lamp on the flagged pavement of the entry, shot the bolts once more into their places.

"You will pardon me if I go in front," he said, when this was done; and he preceded the poet up-stairs into a large apartment, warmed with a pan of charcoal and lit by a great lamp hanging from the roof. It was very bare of furniture: only some gold plate on a sideboard; some folios; and a stand of armour between the windows. Some smart tapestry hung upon the walls, representing the crucifixion of our Lord in one piece, and in another a scene of shepherds and shepherdesses by a running stream. Over the chimney was a shield of arms.

"Will you seat yourself," said the old man, "and forgive me if I leave you? I am alone in my house to-night, and if you are to eat I must forage for you myself."

No sooner was his host gone than Villon leaped from the chair on which he had just seated himself, and began examining the room, with the stealth and passion of a cat. He weighed the gold flagons in his hand, opened all the folios, and investigated the arms upon the shield, and the stuff with which the seats were lined. He raised the window curtains, and saw that the windows were set with rich stained glass in figures, so far as he could see, of martial import. Then he stood in the middle of the room, drew a long breath and retaining it with puffed cheeks, looked round and round him, turning on his heels, as if to impress every feature of the apartment on his memory.

"Seven pieces of plate," he said. "If there had been ten, I would have risked it. A fine house, and a fine old master, so help me all the saints!"

And just then, hearing the old man's tread returning along the corridor, he stole back to his chair, and began humbly toasting his wet legs before the charcoal pan.

His entertainer had a plate of meat in one hand and a jug of wine in the other. He sat down the plate upon the table, motioning Villon to draw in his chair, and going to the sideboard, brought back two goblets, which he filled.

"I drink to your better fortune," he said gravely touching Villon's cup with his own.

"To our better acquaintance," said the poet, growing bold. A mere man of the people would have been awed by the courtesy of the old seigneur, but Villon was hardened in that matter; he had made mirth for great lords before now, and found them as black rascals as himself. And so he devoted himself to the viands with a ravenous gusto, while the old man, leaning backward, watched him with steady, curious eyes.

"You have blood on your shoulder, my man," he said.

Montigny must have laid his wet hand upon him as he left the house. He cursed Montigny in his heart.

"It was none of my shedding," he stammered.

"I had not supposed so," returned his host quietly. "A brawl?"

"Well, something of that sort," Villon admitted with a quaver.

"Perhaps a fellow murdered?"

"Oh, no, not murdered," said the poet, more and more confused. "It was all fair play—murdered by accident. I had no hand in it, God strike me dead!" he added fervently.

"One rogue the fewer, I dare say," observed the master of the house.

"You may dare to say that," agreed Villon, infinitely relieved. "As big a rogue as there is between here and Jerusalem. He turned up his toes like a lamb. But it was a nasty thing to look at. I dare say you've seen dead men in your time, my lord?" he added, glancing at the armour.

"Many," said the old man. "I have followed the wars, as you imagine."

Villon laid down his knife and fork, which he had just taken up again.

"Were any of them bald?" he asked.

"Oh, yes; and with hair as white as mine."

"I don't think I should mind the white so much," said Villon. "His was red." And he had a return of his shuddering and tendency to laughter, which he drowned with a great draught of wine. "I'm a little put out when I think of it," he went on. "I knew him—damn him! And then the cold gives a man fancies—or the fancies give a man cold, I don't know which."

"Have you any money?" asked the old man.

"I have one white," returned the poet, laughing. "I got it out of a dead jade's stocking in a porch. She was as dead as Cæsar, poor wench, and as cold as a church, with bits of ribbon sticking in her hair. This is a hard world in winter for wolves and wenches and poor rogues like me."

"I," said the old man, "am Enguerrand de la Feuillèe, seigneur de Brisetout, bailly du Patatrac. Who and what may you be?"

Villon rose and made a suitable reverence. "I am called Francis Villon," he said, "a poor Master of Arts of this university. I know some Latin, and a deal of vice. I can make chansons, ballades, lais, virelais, and roundels, and I am very fond of wine. I was born in a garret, and I shall not improbably die upon the gallows. I may add, my lord, that from this night forward I am your lordship's very obsequious servant to command."

"No servant of mine," said the knight; "my guest for this evening, and no more."

"A very grateful guest," said Villon politely, and he drank in dumb show to his entertainer.

"You are shrewd," began the old man, tapping his forehead, "very shrewd; you have learning; you are a clerk; and yet you take a small piece of money off a dead woman in the street. Is it not a kind of theft?"

"It is a kind of theft much practised in the wars, my lord."

"The wars are the field of honour," returned the old man proudly. "There a man plays his life upon the cast; he fights in the name of his lord the king, his Lord God, and all their lordships the holy saints and angels."

"Put it," said Villon, "that I were really a thief, should I not play my life also, and against heavier odds?"

"For gain but not for honour."

"Gain?" repeated Villon with a shrug. "Gain! The poor fellow wants supper, and takes it. So does the soldier in a campaign. Why, what are all these requisitions we hear so much about? If they are not gain to those who take them, they are loss enough to the others. The men-at-arms drink by a good fire, while the burgher bites his nails to buy them wine and wood. I have seen a good many ploughmen swinging on trees about the country; ay, I have seen thirty to one elm, and a very poor figure they made; and when I asked someone how all these came to be hanged, I was told it was because they could not scrape together enough crowns to satisfy the men-at-arms."

"These things are a necessity of war, which the low-born must endure with constancy. It is true that some captains drive overhard; there are spirits in every rank not easily moved by pity; and, indeed, many follow arms who are no better than brigands."

"You see," said the poet, "you cannot separate the soldier from the brigand; and what is a thief but an isolated brigand with circumspect manners? I steal a couple of mutton chops, without so much as disturbing people's sleep; the farmer grumbles a bit, but sups none the less wholesomely on what remains. You come up blowing gloriously on a trumpet, take away the whole sheep, and beat the farmer pitifully into the bargain. I have no trumpet; I am only Tom, Dick, or Harry; I am a rogue and a dog, and hanging's too good for me—with all my heart; but just ask the farmer which of us he prefers, just find out which of us he lies awake to curse on cold nights."

"Look at us two," said his lordship. "I am old, strong, and honoured. If I were turned from my house tomorrow, hundreds would be proud to shelter me. Poor people would go out and pass the night in the streets with their children, if I merely hinted that I wished to be alone. And I find you up, wandering homeless, and picking farthings off dead women by the wayside! I fear no man and nothing; I have seen you tremble and lose countenance at a word. I wait God's summons contentedly in my own house, or, if it please the king to call me out again, upon the field of battle. You look for the gallows; a rough, swift death, without hope or honour. Is there no difference between these two?"

"As far as to the moon," Villon acquiesced. "But if I had been born lord of Brisetout, and you have been the poor scholar Francis, would the difference have been any the less? Should not I have been warming my knees at this charcoal pan, and would not you have been groping for farthings in the snow? Should not I have been the soldier, and you the thief?"

"A thief?" cried the old man. "I a thief! If you understood your words, you would repent them."

Villon turned out his hands with a gesture of inimitable impudence. "If your lordship had done me the honour to follow my argument!" he said.

"I do you too much honour in submitting to your presence," said the knight. "Learn to curb your tongue when you speak with old and honourable men, or some one hastier than I may reprove you in a sharper fashion." And he rose and paced the lower end of the apartment, struggling with anger and antipathy. Villon surreptitiously refilled his cup, and settled himself more comfortably in the chair, crossing his knees and leaning his head upon one hand and the elbow against the back of the chair. He was now replete and warm, and he was in no-wise frightened for his host, having gauged him as justly as was possible between two such different characters. The night was far spent, and in a very comfortable fashion after all; and he felt morally certain of a safe departure on the morrow.

"Tell me one thing," said the old man, pausing in his walk. "Are you really a thief?"

"I claim the sacred right of hospitality," returned the poet. "My lord, I am."

"You are very young," the knight continued.

"I should never have been so old," replied Villon, showing his fingers, "if I had not helped myself with these ten talents. They have been my nursing mothers and my nursing fathers."

"You may still repent and change."

"I repent daily," said the poet. "There are few people more given to repentance than poor Francis. As for change, let somebody change my circumstances. A man must continue to eat, if it were only that he may continue to repent."

"The change must begin in the heart," returned the old man solemnly.

"My dear lord," answered Villon, "do you really fancy that I steal for pleasure? I hate stealing, like any other piece of work or of danger. My teeth chatter when I see a gallows. But I must eat, I must drink, I must mix in society of some sort. What the devil! Man is not a solitary animal—*Cui Deus fœminam tradit*. Make me king's pantler—make me abbot of St. Denis; make me bailly of the Patatrac; and then I shall be changed indeed. But as long as you leave me the poor scholar Francis Villon, without a farthing, why, of course, I remain the same."

"The Grace of God is all-powerful."

"I should be a heretic to question it," said Francis. "It has made you lord of Brisetout and bailly of the Patatrac; it has given me nothing but the quick wits under my hat and these ten toes upon my hands. May I help myself to wine? I thank you respectfully. By God's grace, you have a very superior vintage."

The lord of Brisetout walked to and fro with his hands behind his back. Perhaps he was not yet quite settled in his mind about the parallel between thieves and soldiers; perhaps Villon had interested him by some cross-thread of sympathy; perhaps his wits were simply muddled by so much unfamiliar reasoning; but whatever the cause, he somehow yearned to convert the young man to a better way of thinking, and could not make up his mind to drive him forth again into the street.

"There is something more than I can understand in this," he said at length. "Your mouth is full of subtleties, and the devil has led you very far astray; but the devil is only a very weak spirit before God's truth, and all his subtleties vanish at a word of true honour, like darkness at morning. Listen to me once more. I learned long ago that a gentleman should live chivalrously and lovingly to God, and the king, and his lady; and though I have seen many strange things done, I have still striven to command my ways upon that rule. It is not only written in all noble histories, but in every man's heart if he will take care to read. You speak of food and wine, and I know very well that hunger is a difficult trial to endure; but you do not speak of other wants; you say nothing of honour, of faith to God and other men, of courtesy, of love without reproach. It may be that I am not very wise—and yet I think I am—but you seem to me like one who has lost his way and made a great error in life. You are attending to the little wants, and you have totally forgotten the great and only real ones, like a man who should be doctoring toothache on the Judgment Day. For such things as honour and love and faith are not only nobler than food and drink, but indeed I think we desire them more, and suffer more sharply for their absence. I speak to you as I think you will most easily understand me. Are you not, while careful to fill your belly, disregarding another appetite in your heart, which spoils the pleasure of your life and keeps you continually wretched?"

Villon was sensibly nettled under all this sermonizing.

"You think I have no sense of honour!" he cried. "I'm poor enough, God knows! It's hard to see rich people with their gloves, and you blowing in your hands. An empty belly is a bitter thing, although you speak so lightly of it. If you had had as many as I, perhaps you would change your tune. Any way I'm a thief—make the most of that—but I'm not a devil from hell, God strike me dead. I would have you to know I've an honour of my own, as good as yours, though I don't prate about it all day long, as if it was a God's miracle to have any. It seems quite natural to me; I keep it in its box till it's wanted. Why now, look you here, how long have I been in this room with you? Did you not tell me you were alone in the house? Look at your gold plate! You're strong, if you like, but you're old and unarmed, and I have my knife. What did I want but a jerk of the elbow and here would have been you with the cold steel in your bowels, and there would have been me, linking in the streets, with an armful of golden cups! Did you suppose I hadn't wit enough to see that? And I scorned the action. There are your damned goblets, as safe as in a church; there are you, with your heart ticking as good as new; and here am I, ready to go out again as poor as I came in, with my one white that you threw in my teeth! And you think I have no sense of honour—God strike me dead!"

The old man stretched out his right arm. "I will tell you what you are," he said. "You are a rogue, my man, an impudent and black-hearted rogue and vagabond. I have passed an hour with you. Oh! believe me, I feel myself disgraced! And you have eaten and drunk at my table. But now I am sick of your presence; the day has come, and the night-bird should be off to his roost. Will you go before, or after?"

"Which you please," returned the poet, rising. "I believe you to be strictly honourable." He thoughtfully emptied his cup. "I wish I could add you were intelligent," he went on, knocking on his head with his nuckles. "Age! age! the brains stiff and rheumatic."

The old man preceded him from a point of self-respect; Villon followed, whistling, with his thumbs in his girdle.

"God pity you," said the lord of Brisetout at the door.

"Good-bye, papa," returned Villon with a yawn. "Many thanks for the cold mutton."

The door closed behind him. The dawn was breaking over the white roofs. A chill, uncomfortable morning ushered in the day. Villon stood and heartily stretched himself in the middle of the road.

"A very dull old gentleman," he thought. "I wonder what his goblets may be worth."

21

The Story of Dr. MacLure

BY JOHN WATSON (Ian Maclaren)

I.—THE DOCTOR'S LAST JOURNEY

IT was a bitter December Sabbath, and the fathers were settling the affairs of the parish ankle deep in snow, when MacLure's old housekeeper told Drumsheugh that the doctor was not able to rise, and wished to see him in the afternoon.

"Aye, aye," said Hillocks, shaking his head, and that day Drumsheugh omitted four pews with the ladle, while Jamie was so vicious on the way home that none could endure him.

Janet had lit a fire in the unused grate, and hung a plaid (shawl) by the window to break the power of the cruel north wind, but the bare room, with its half a dozen bits of furniture and a worn strip of carpet, and the outlook upon the snow drifted up to the second pane of the window and the black firs laden with their icy burden, sent a chill to Drumsheugh's heart.

The doctor had weakened sadly, and could hardly lift his head, but his face lit up at the sight of his visitor, and the big hand, which was now quite refined in its whiteness, came out from the bed-clothes with the old warm grip.

"Come in by, man, and sit doon. It's an awfu' day tae bring ye sae far, but a' kent ye wudna grudge the traivel. A' wesna sure till last nicht, an' then a' felt it wudna be lang, an' a' took a wearyin' this morn- in' tae see ye. We've been freends sin' we were laddies at the auld schule in the firs, an' a' wud like ye tae be wi' me at the end. Ye 'ill stay the nicht, Paitrick, for auld lang syne."

Drumsheugh was much shaken, and the sound of the Christian name, which he had not heard since his mother's death, gave him a "grue" (shiver), as if one had spoken from the other world.

"It's maist awfu' tae hear ye speakin' aboot deein'. Weelum; a' canna bear it. We 'ill hae the Muirtown doctor up, an' ye 'ill be aboot again in nae time. Ye hevna ony sair tribble; ye're juist trachled (worn out) wi' hard wark an' needin' a rest. Dinna say ye're gaein' tae leave us, Weelum; we canna dae withoot ye in Drumtochty;" and Drumsheugh looked wistfully for some word of hope.

"Na, na, Paitrick, naething can be dune, an' it's ower late tae send for ony doctor. There's a knock that canna be mista'en, an' a' heard it last night. A've focht deith for ither fouk mair than forty year, but ma ain time hes come at laist. A've nae tribble worth mentionin'—a bit titch o' bronchitis—an' a've hed a graund constitution; but a'm fair worn oot, Paitrick; that's ma complaint, an' it's past curin'."

Drumsheugh went over to the fireplace, and for a while did nothing but break up the smoldering peats, whose smoke powerfully affected his nose and eyes.

"When ye're ready, Paitrick, there's twa or three little trokes (trifles) a' wud like ye tae look aifter, an' a'll tell ye aboot them as lang's ma head's clear. A' didna keep buiks, as ye ken, for a' ay hed a guid memory, so naebody 'ill be harried for money aifter ma deith, and ye 'ill hae nae accoonts tae collect. But the fouk are honest in Drumtochty, and they 'ill be offerin' ye siller, an' a'll gie ye ma mind aboot it. Gin (if) it be a puir body, tell her tae keep and get a bit plaidie (shawl) wi' the money, and she 'ill maybe think o' her auld doctor at a time. Gin it be a bien (well-to-do) man, tak half of what he offers, for a Drum-tochty man wud scorn to be mean in sic circumstances; and if onybody needs a doctor an' canna pay for him, see he's no left tae dee when a'm oot o' the road."

"Nae fear o' that as lang as a'm livin', Weelum. But what 'ill become o's when ye're no here tae gie a hand in time o' need? We 'ill take ill wi' a stranger that disna ken ane o's frae anither."

"It's a' for the best, Paitrick, an' ye 'ill see that in a whilie. A've kent fine (known well) that ma day wes ower, an' that ye sud hae a younger man. A' did what a' cud tae keep up wi' the new medicine, but a' hed little time for readin', an' nane for traivelin'. A'm the last o' the auld schule, an' a' ken as weel as onybody thet a' wesna sae dainty an' fine-mannered as the town doctors. Ye took me as a' wes, an' naebody ever cuist up tae me that a' wes a plain man. Na, na; ye'be been rael kind an' conseederate a' thae years."

"Weelum, gin ye cairry on sic nonsense ony langer," interrupted Drumsheugh huskily, "a'll leave the hoose; a' canna stand it."

"It's the truth, Paitrick, but we 'ill gae on wi' oor wark, for a'm failin' fast. Gie Janet ony sticks of furniture she needs tae furnish a hoose, and sell a' thing else tae pay the wricht (undertaker) an' bedrel (grave-digger). If the new doctor be a young laddie and no verra rich, ye micht let him hae the buiks an' instruments; it 'ill aye be a help. But a' wudna like ye tae sell Jess, for she's been a faithfu' servant, an' a freend, tae. There's a note or twa in that drawer a' savit, an' if ye kent ony man that wud gie her a bite o' grass and a sta' in his stable till she followed her maister——"

"Confoond ye, Weelum," broke out Drumsheugh; "it's doonricht cruel o' ye to speak like this tae me. Whar wud Jess gang but tae Drumsheugh? She 'ill hae her run o' heck an' manger sae lang as she lives; the Glen wudna like tae see anither man on Jess, and nae man 'ill ever touch the auld mare."

"Dinna mind me, Paitrick, for a' expeckit this; but ye ken we're no verra gleg (quick) wi' oor tongues in Drumtochty, an' dinna tell a' that's in oor hearts. Weel, that's a' that a' mind, an' the rest a' leave tae yersel. A've neither kith nor kin tae bury me, sae you an' the neeburs 'ill need tae lat me doon; but gin Tammas Mitchell or Saunders be stannin' near and lookin' as if they wud like a cord, gie't tae them, Paitrick. They're baith dour chiels (hard men), and haena muckle (much) tae say, but Tammas hes a graund hert, and there's waur (worse) fouk in the Glen than Saunders.

"A'm gettin' drowsy, an' a'll no be able tae follow ye sune, a' doot; wud ye read a bit tae me afore a' fa' ower? Ye 'ill find ma mither's Bible on the drawers' heid, but ye 'ill need tae come close tae the bed, for a'm no hearin' or seein' sae weel as a' wes when ye cam."

Drumsheugh put on his spectacles and searched for a comfortable Scripture, while the light of the lamp fell on his shaking hands and the doctor's face, where the shadow was now settling.

"Ma mither aye wantit this read tae her when she was sober (weak);" and Drumsheugh began, " 'In my Father's house are many mansions,' " but MacLure stopped him.

"It's a bonnie word, and yir mither wes a sanct; but it's no for the like o' me. It's ower gude; a' dourna tak it. Shut the buik an' let it open itsel, an' ye 'ill get a bit a've been readin' every nicht the laist month."

Then Drumsheugh found the parable wherein the Master tells us what God thinks of a Pharisee and of a penitent sinner, till he came to the words:

"And the publican, standing afar off, would not lift up so much as his eyes to heaven, but smote upon his breast, saying, God be merciful to me a sinner."

"That micht hae been written for me, Paitrick, or ony ither auld sinner that hes feenished his life, an' hes naething tae say for himsel. It wesna easy for me tae get tae kirk, but a' cud hae managed wi' a stretch, an' a' used langidge a' sudna, an' a' micht hae been gentler, and no been so short in the temper. A' see't a' noo. It's ower late tae mend, but ye 'ill maybe juist say to the fouk that I wes sorry, an' a'm houpin' that the Almichty 'ill hae mercy on me. Cud ye—pit up a bit prayer, Paitrick?"

"A haena the words," said Drumsheugh in great distress; "wud ye like's tae send for the minister?"

"It's no the time for that noo, an' a' wud rather hae yersel—juist what's in yir heart, Paitrick; the Almichty 'ill ken the lave (rest) Himsel'."

So Drumsheugh knelt and prayed, with many pauses:

"Almichty God—dinna be hard on Weelum MacLure, for he's no been hard wi' onybody in Drumtochty. Be kind tae him as he's been tae us a' for forty year. We're a' sinners afore Thee. Forgive him what he's dune wrang, an' dinna cuist it up tae him. Mind the fouk he's helpit —the weemen an' bairnies—an' gie him a welcome hame, for he's sair needin't after a' his wark. Amen."

"Thank ye, Paitrick, and gude nicht tae ye. Ma ain true freend, gie's yir hand, for a'll maybe no ken ye again. Noo a'll say ma mither's prayer and hae a sleep, but ye 'ill no leave me till a' is ower."

Then he repeated, as he had done every night of his life:

This night I lay me down to sleep,
I pray the Lord my soul to keep,
And if I die before I wake,
I pray the Lord my soul to take.

He was sleeping quietly when the wind drove the snow against the window with a sudden swish; and he instantly awoke, so to say, in his sleep. Some one needed him.

"Are ye frae Glen Urtach?" and an unheard voice seemed to have answered him. "Worse is she, an' sufferin' awfu'; that's no lichtsome; ye did richt tae come. The front door's drifted up; gang roond tae the back, an' ye 'ill get intae the kitchen; a'll be ready in a meenut. Gie's a hand wi' the lantern when a'm saiddling Jess, an' ye needna come on till daylicht; a' ken the road."

Then he was away in his sleep on some errand of mercy, and struggling through the storm.

"It's a coorse nicht, Jess, an' heavy traivelin'. Can ye see afore ye, lass? For a'm clean confused wi' the snow; bide a wee till a' find the diveesion o' the roads; it's aboot here back or forrit.

"Steady, lass, steady, dinna plunge; it's a drift we're in, but ye're no sinkin'; up noo—there ye are on the road again.

"Eh, it's deep the nicht, an' hard on us baith, but there's a puir wumman micht dee if we didna warstle through. That's it; ye ken fine what a'm sayin'.

"We 'ill hae tae leave the road here, an' tak tae the muir. Sandie 'ill no can leave the wife alane tae meet us; feel for yersel, lass, and keep oot o' the holes.

"Yon's the hoose, black in the snaw. Sandie, man, ye frichtened us; a' didna see ye ahint the dyke; hoo's the wife?"

After a while he began again:

"Ye're fair dune, Jess, and so a' am masel; we're baith gettin' auld, an' dinna tak sae weel wi' the nicht wark.

"We 'ill sune be hame noo; this is the black wood, an' it's no lang aifter that; we're ready for oor beds, Jess.

"Yon's the licht in the kitchen window; nae wonder ye're nickering (neighing). It's been a stiff journey; a'm tired, lass—a'm tired tae deith," and the voice died into silence.

Drumsheugh held his friend's hand, which now and again tightened in his, and as he watched, a change came over the face on the pillow beside him. The lines of weariness disappeared, as if God's hand had passed over it; and peace began to gather round the closed eyes.

The doctor has forgotten the toil of later years, and has gone back to his boyhood.

"The Lord's my Shepherd, I'll not want,"

he repeated, till he came to the last verse, and then he hesitated.

Goodness and mercy all my life
Shall surely follow me.

"Follow me—and—and—what's next? Mither said I wes tae head ready when she cam. 'A'll come afore ye gang tae sleep, Wullie, but ye 'ill no get yir kiss unless ye can feenish the psalm.

"And—in God's house—for evermore my—hoo dis it rin? A' canna mind the next word. My, my——

"It's ower dark noo tae read it, an' mither 'ill sune be comin'."

Drumsheugh, in an agony, whispered into his ear, "'My dwelling-place,' Weelum."

"That's it, that's it a' noo. Wha said it?

"And in God's house for evermore
My dwelling-place shall be.

"A'm ready noo, an' a'll get ma kiss when mither comes; a' wish she wud come, for a'm tired an' wantin' tae sleep.

"Yon's her step—an' she's carryin' a licht in her hand; a' see it through the door. Mither! A' kent ye wudna forget yir laddie, for ye promised tae come, and' a've feenished ma psalm.

"And in God's house for evermore
My dwelling-place shall be.

"Gie me the kiss, mither, for a've been waitin' for ye, an' a'll sune be asleep."

The gray morning light fell on Drumsheugh, still holding his friend's cold hand, and staring at a hearth where the fire had died down into white ashes; but the peace on the doctor's face was of one who rested from his labors.

II.—THE MOURNING OF THE GLEN

Dr. MacLure was buried during the great snow-storm, which is still spoken of, and will remain the standard of snowfall in Drumtochty for the century. The snow was deep on the Monday, and the men that gave notice of his funeral had hard work to reach the doctor's distant patients. On Tuesday morning it began to fall again in heavy, fleecy flakes, and continued till Thursday; and then on Thursday the north wind rose and swept the snow into the hollows of the roads that went to the upland farms, and built it into a huge bank at the mouth of Glen Urtach, and laid it across our main road in drifts of every size and the most lovely shapes, and filled up crevices in the hills to the depth of fifty feet.

On Friday morning the wind had sunk to passing gusts that powdered your coat with white, and the sun was shining on one of those winter landscapes no townsman can imagine and no countryman ever forgets. The Glen, from end to end and side to side, was clothed in a glistering mantle white as no fuller on earth could white it, that flung its skirts over the clumps of trees and scattered farmhouses, and was only divided where the Tochty ran with black, swollen stream. The great moor rose and fell in swelling billows of snow that arched themselves over the burns, running deep in the mossy ground, and hid the black peat-bogs with a thin, treacherous crust. Beyond, the hills northward and westward stood high in white majesty, save where the black crags of Glen Urtach broke the line, and, above our lower Grampians, we caught glimpses of the distant peaks that lifted their heads in holiness unto God.

It seemed to me a fitting day for William MacLure's funeral, rather than summer-time, with its flowers and golden corn. He had not been a soft man, nor had he lived an easy life, and now he was to be laid to rest amid the austere majesty of winter, yet in the shining of the sun. Jamie Soutar, with whom I toiled across the Glen, did not think with me, but was gravely concerned.

"Nae doot it's a graund sicht; the like o't is no gien tae us twice in a generation, an' nae king was ever carried tae his tomb in sic a cathedral. But it's the fouk a'm conseederin', an' hoo they 'ill win through; it's hard eneuch for them 'at's on the road, an' it's clean impossible for the lave. They 'ill dae their best, every man o' them, ye may depend on that, an' hed it been open weather there wudna hev been six able-bodied men missin'.

"A' wes mad at them, because they never said onything when he wae leevin,' but they felt for a' that what he hed dune, an', a' think, he kent it afore he deed. He hed juist ae one faut, tae ma thinkin', for a' never jidged the waur o' him for his titch of rochness—guid trees hae gnarled bark—but he thocht ower little o' himsel. Noo, gin a' hed asked him hoo mony fouk wud come tae his beerial, he wud hae said, 'They 'ill be Drumsheugh an' yersel,' an' maybe twa or three neeburs besides the minister,' an' the fact is that nae man in oor time wud hae sic a githerin' if it werena for the storm.

"Ye see," said Jamie, who had been counting heads all morning, "there's six shepherds in Glen Urtach—they're shut up fast; an' there micht hae been a gude half-dizen frae Dunleith wy, an' a'm telt there's nae road; an' there's the heich (high) Glen, nae man cud cross the muir the day, an' its aucht (eight) mile roond"; and Jamie proceeded to review the Glen in every detail of age, driftiness of road, and strength of body, till we arrived at the doctor's cottage, when he had settled on a reduction of fifty through stress of weather.

Drumsheugh was acknowledged as chief mourner by the Glen, and received us at the gate with a labored attempt at every-day manners.

"Ye've hed heavy traivelin', a doot, an' ye 'ill be cauld. There wes nae use trying tae dig oot the front door yestreen, for it wud hae been drifted up again before morning. We've cleared awa the snow at the back for the prayer; ye 'ill get in at the kitchen door. There's a puckle (few) Dunleith men——"

"Wha?" cried Jamie in an instant.

"Dunleith men," said Drumheugh.

"Div (do) ye mean they're here? Whar are they?"

"Drying themselves at the fire, an' no withoot need; ane of them gaed ower the head in a drift, and his neeburs had tae pu' him oot. It took them a gude fower oors tae get across, an' it wes coorse wark; they likit him weel doon that wy, an', Jamie man"—here Drumsheugh's voice changed its note, and his public manner disappeared—"what div ye think o' this? Every man o' them hes on his blacks (Sunday suit)."

"It's mair than cud be expeckit," said Jamie; "but whar dae yon men come frae, Drumsheugh?"

Two men in plaids were descending the hill behind the doctor's cottage, taking three feet at a stride, and carrying long staffs in their hands.

"They're Glen Urtach men, Jamie, for ane o' them wes at Kildrummie fair wi' sheep, but hoo they've wun doon passes me."

"It canna be, Drumsheugh," said Jamie, greatly excited. "Glen Urtach's steikit (closed) up wi' sna like a locked door. Ye're no surely frae the Glen, lads?" as the men leaped the dyke and crossed to the back door, the snow falling from their plaids as they walked.

"We're that an' nae mistak, but a' thocht we wud be lickit (beaten) ae place, eh, Charlie? A'm no sae weel acquant wi' the hill on this side, an' there wes some kittle (hazardous) drifts."

"It wes grand o' ye tae mak the attempt," said Drumsheugh, "an' a'm gled ye're safe."

"He cam through as bad himsel tae help ma wife," was Charlie's reply.

"They're three mair Urtach shepherds 'ill come in by sune; they're frae Upper Urtach, an' we saw them fording the river, ma certes (on my word), it took them a' their time, for it wes up tae their waists and rinnin' like a mill-lade (mill-stream), but they jined hands and cam ower fine." And the Urtach men went in to the fire.

The Glen began to arrive in twos and threes, and Jamie, from a point of vantage at the gate, and under an appearance of utter indifference, checked his roll till even he was satisfied.

"Weelum MacLure 'ill hae the beerial he deserves in spite o' sna and drifts; it passes a' tae see hoo they've githered frae far an' near. A'm thinkin' ye can colleck them for the minister noo, Drumsheugh. A'body's here except the heich Glen, an' we maunna luke for them."

"Dinna be sae sure o' that, Jamie. Yon's terrible like them on the road, wi' Whinnie at their head"; and so it was, twelve in all, only old Adam Ross absent, detained by force, being eighty-two years of age.

"It wud hae been temptin' Providence tae cross the muir," Whinnie explained, "and it's a fell stap (long step) roond; a' doot we're laist."

"See, Jamie," said Drumsheugh, as he went to the house, "gin there be ony antern body (any one else) in sicht afore we begin; we maun mak allooances the day wi' twa feet o' sna on the grund, tae say naethin' o' drifts."

"There's something at the turnin', an' it's no fouk; it's a machine o' some kind or ither—maybe a bread-cart that's focht its wy up."

"Na, it's no that; there's twa horses, ane afore the ither; if it's no a dog-cairt wi' twa men in the front; they 'ill be comin' tae the beerial."

"What wud ye sae, Jamie," Hillocks suggested, "but it might be some o' thae Muirtown doctors? They were awfu' chief (friendly) wi' Mac-Lure."

"It's nae Muirtown doctors," cried Jamie, in great exultation, "nor ony ither doctors. A' ken thae horses, and wha's ahint them. Quick, man Hillocks, stop the fouk, and tell Drumsheugh tae come oot, for Lord Kilspindie hes come up frae Muirtown Castle!"

Jamie himself slipped behind, and did not wish to be seen.

"It's the respeck he's gettin' the day frae high an' low!" was Jamie's husky apology. "Tae think o' them fechtin their wy doon frae Glen Urtach, and toiling roond frae the heich Glen, an' his lordship driving through the drifts a' the road frae Muirtown, juist tae honor Weelum MacLure's beerial! It's nae ceremony the day, ye may lippen tae (depend on) it; it's the hert brocht the fouk, an' ye can see it in their faces; ilka man hes his ain reason, an' he's thinkin' on't, though he's speakin' o' naethin' but the storm; he's mindin' the day Weelum pu'ed him oot frae the jaws o' death, or the nicht he savit the gude wife in her oor o' tribble. That's why they pit on their blacks this mornin' afore it wes licht, and wrastled through the snadrifts at risk o' life. Drumtochty fouk canna say muckle, it's an awfu' peety, and they 'ill dae their best tae show naethin', but a' can read it a' in their een.

"But wae's me"—and Jamie broke down utterly behind a fir-tree, so tender a thing is a cynic's heart—"that fouk 'ill tak a man's best wark a' his days withoot a word, an' no dae him honor till he dees. Oh, if they hed only githered like this juist aince when he wes livin', an' lat him see he hedna labored in vain! His reward hes come ower late, ower late."

During Jamie's vain regret, the castle trap, bearing the marks of a wild passage in the snow-covered wheels, a broken shaft tied with rope, a twisted lamp, and the panting horses, pulled up between two rows of farmers, and Drumsheugh received his lordship with evident emotion.

"Ma lord—we never thocht o' this—an' sic a road!"

"How are you, Drumsheugh? And how are you all this wintry day? That's how I'm half an hour late; it took us four hours' stiff work for sixteen miles, mostly in the drifts, of course."

"It wes gude o' yir lordship tae mak sic an effort, an' the hale Glen wull be gratefu' tae ye, for ony kindness tae him is kindness tae us."

"You make too much of it, Drumsheugh," and the clear, firm voice was heard of all; "it would have taken more than a few snow-drifts to keep me from showing my respect to William MacLure's memory."

When all had gathered in a half-circle before the kitchen door, Lord Kilspindie came out—every man noticed he had left his overcoat, and was in black, like the Glen—and took a place in the middle with Drum-sheugh and Burnbrae, his two chief tenants, on the right and left, and as the minister appeared every man bared his head. The doctor looked on the company—a hundred men such as for strength and gravity you could hardly have matched in Scotland—standing out in picturesque relief against the white background, and he said:

"It's a bitter day, friends, and some of you are old; perhaps it might be wise to cover your heads before I begin to pray."

Lord Kilspindie, standing erect and gray-headed between the two old men, replied:

"We thank you, Dr. Davidson, for your thoughtfulness; but he endured many a storm in our service, and we are not afraid of a few minutes' cold at his funeral."

A look flashed round the stern faces, and was reflected from the minister, who seemed to stand higher.

His prayer, we noticed with critical appreciation, was composed for the occasion, and the first part was a thanksgiving to God for the life-work of our doctor, wherein each clause was a reference to his services and sacrifices. No one moved or said "Amen"—it had been strange with us—but when every man had heard the gratitude of his dumb heart offered to Heaven, there was a great sigh.

After which the minister prayed that we might have grace to live as this man had done from youth to old age, not for himself, but for others, and that we might be followed to our grave by somewhat of "that love wherewith we mourn this day Thy servant departed." Again the same sigh, and the minister said "Amen."

The wricht (undertaker) stood in the doorway without speaking, and four stalwart men came forward. They were the volunteers that would lift the coffin and carry it for the first stage. One was Tammas, Annie Mitchell's man; and another was Saunders Baxter, for whose life MacLure had a great fight with death; and the third was the Glen Urtach shepherd for whose wife's sake MacLure suffered a broken leg and three fractured ribs in a drift; and the fourth, a Dunleith man, had his own reasons of remembrance.

"He's far lichter than ye wud expeck for sae big a man—there wesna muckle left o' him, ye see—but the road is heavy, and a'll change ye aifter the first half-mile."

"Ye needna tribble yersel, wricht," said the man from Glen Urtach; "the'll be nae change in the cairryin' the day"; and Tammas was thankful some one had saved him speaking.

Surely no funeral is like unto that of a doctor for pathos, and a peculiar sadness fell on that company as his body was carried out who

for nearly half a century had been their help in sickness, and had
beaten back death time after time from their door. Death after all was
victor, for the man that saved them had not been able to save himself.

The black thread wound itself along the whiteness of the Glen, the
coffin first, with his lordship and Drumsheugh behind, and the others as
they pleased, but in closer ranks than usual, because the snow on either
side was deep, and because this was not as other funerals. They could
see the women standing at the door of every house on the hillside, and
weeping, for each family had some good reason, in forty years, to remember MacLure. When Bell Baxter saw Saunders alive, and the coffin
of the doctor that saved him on her man's shoulder, she bowed her
head on the dyke, and the bairns in the village made such a wail for
him they loved that the men nearly disgraced themselves.

"A'm gled we're through that, at ony rate," said Hillocks; "he was
awfu' taen up wi' the bairns, conseederin' he hed nane o' his ain."

There was only one drift on the road between his cottage and the
kirkyard, and it had been cut early that morning.

Before daybreak Saunders had roused the lads in the bothy (laborers'
lodging-house), and they had set to work by the light of lanterns with
such good-will that, when Drumsheugh came down to engineer a cir-
cuit for the funeral, there was a fair passage, with walls of snow twelve
feet high on either side.

"Man, Saunders," he said, "this wes a kind thocht, and rael weel
dune."

But Saunders's only reply was this:

"Mony a time he's hed tae gang roond; he micht as weel hae an open
road for his last traivel."

When the coffin was laid down at the mouth of the grave, the only
blackness in the white kirkyard, Tammas Mitchell did the most beautiful thing in all his life. He knelt down and carefully wiped off the snow
the wind had blown upon the coffin, and which had covered the name;
and when he had done this he disappeared behind the others, so that
Drumsheugh could hardly find him to take a cord. For these were the
eight that buried Dr. MacLure—Lord Kilspindie at the head as landlord, and Drumsheugh at the feet as his friend; the two ministers of
the parish came first on the right and left; then Burnbrae and Hillocks
of the farmers, and Saunders and Tammas for the plowmen. So the
Glen he loved laid him to rest.

When the bedrel (grave-digger) had finished his work and the turf
had been spread, Lord Kilspindie spoke:

"Friends of Drumtochty, it would not be right that we should part in
silence and no man say what is in every heart. We have buried the
remains of one that served this Glen with a devotion that has known

no reserve, and a kindliness that never failed, for more than forty years. I have seen many brave men in my day, but no man in the trenches of Sebastopol carried himself more knightly than William MacLure. You will never have heard from his lips what I may tell you to-day, that my father secured for him a valuable post in his younger days, and he preferred to work among his own people; and I wished to do many things for him when he was old, but he would have nothing for himself. He will never be forgotten while one of us lives, and I pray that all doctors everywhere may share his spirit. If it be your pleasure, I shall erect a cross above his grave, and shall ask my old friend and companion, Dr. Davidson, your minister, to choose the text to be inscribed."

"We thank you, Lord Kilspindie," said the doctor, "for your presence with us in our sorrow and your tribute to the memory of William Mac-Lure, and I choose this for his text: 'Greater love hath no man than this, that a man lay down his life for his friends.' "

Milton was, at that time, held in the bonds of a very bitter theology, and his indignation was stirred by this unqualified eulogium.

"No doubt Dr. MacLure hed mony natural virtues, an' he did his wark weel, but it wes a peety he didna mak mair profession o' re-leegion."

"When William MacLure appears before the Judge, Milton," said Lachlan Campbell, who that day spoke his last words in public, and they were in defense of charity, "He will not be asking him about his professions, for the doctor's judgment hass been ready long ago; and it iss a good judgment, and you and I will be happy men if we get the like of it. It iss written in the Gospel, but it iss William MacLure that will not be expecting it."

"What it's, Lachlan?" asked Jamie Soutar eagerly.

The old man, now very feeble, stood in the middle of the road, and his face, once so hard, was softened into a winsome tenderness.

" 'Come, ye blessed of My Father—I was sick, and ye visited Me.' "

22

Faith

BY R. CUNNINGHAME GRAHAM

"I TOLD you," said Hamed-el-Angeri, "of how once on a time all beasts could speak and of how Allah, in his might, and for his glory, and no doubt for some wise cause, rendered them dumb, or at least caused them to lose their Arabic. Now will I tell you of a legend of the Praised One who sleepeth in Medina, and whom alone Allah has pardoned of all men."

He paused, and the hot sun streamed through the branches of the carob tree under whose shade we sat upon a rug, during the hottest hours, and threw his shadow on the sandy soil, drawing him, long of limb, and lithe of pose, like John the Baptist revealed by Donatello in red clay.

Our horses hung their heads, and from the plain a mist of heat arose, dancing and shivering in the air, as the flame dances waveringly from a broken gas-pipe lighted by workmen in a street. Grasshoppers twittered, raising their pandean pipe of praise to Allah for his heat, and now and then a locust whirred across the sky, falling again into the hard dry grass, just as a flying-fish falls out of sight into the sea. "They say," Hamed again began, "that in Medina, or in Mecca, in the blessed days when God spake to his Prophet, and he composed his book, making his laws, and laying down his rules of conduct for men's lives, that many wondered that no nook or corner in all Paradise was set apart for those who bore us, or whose milk we sucked, when they had passed their prime."

Besides the Perfect Four, women there were who, with the light that Allah gave them, strove to be faithful, just, and loving, and to do their duty as it seemed to them, throughout their lives.

One there was, Rahma, a widow, who had borne four stalwart sons, all slain in battle, and who, since their deaths, had kept herself in honour and repute, labouring all day with distaff and with loom.

Seated in a lost duar in the hills, she marvelled much that the wise son of Ámina, he to whom the word of God had been vouchsafed, and who himself had owed his fortune to a woman, could be unjust. Long did she ponder in her hut beyond Medina, and at last resolved to take her ass, and set forth, even to Mecca, and there speak with God's messenger, and hear from him the why and wherefore of the case. She set her house in order, leaving directions to the boy who watched her goats to tend them diligently, and upon the lucky day of all the week, that Friday upon which the faithful all assemble to give praise, she took her way.

The people of the village thought her mad, as men in every age have always thought all those demented who have determined upon any course which has not entered into their own dull brains. Wrinkled and withered like a mummy, draped in her shroud-like haik, she sat upon her ass. A bag of dates, with one of barley, and a small waterskin her luggage, and in her heart that foolish, generous, undoubting Arab faith, powerful enough to move the most stupendous mountain chain of facts which weigh down European souls, she journeyed on.

Rising before the dawn, in the cold chill of desert nights, she fed her beast from her small store of corn, shivering and waiting for the sun to warm the world. Then, as the first faint flush of pink made palm trees look like ghosts and half revealed the mountain tops floating above a sea of mist, she turned towards the town, wherein he dwelt who denied Paradise to all but girls, and prayed. Then, drawing out her bag of dates, she ate, with the content of those to whom both appetite and food are not perennial gifts.

As the day broke, and the fierce sun rose, as it seemed with his full power, the enemy of those who travel in those wilds, she clambered stiffly to her seat on her straw pillion and with a suddra thorn urged on her ass to a fast stumbling walk, his feet seeming but scarce to leave the ground as he bent forward his meek head as if he bore the sins of all mankind upon his back.

The dew lay thickly on the scant mimosa scrub and camel-thorn, bringing out aromatic odours, and filling the interstices of spiders' webs as snow fills up the skeletons of leaves. The colocynths growing between the stones seemed frosted with the moisture of the dawn, and for a brief half-hour nature was cool, and the sun shone in vain. Then, as by magic, all the dew disappeared, and the fierce sunlight heated the stones, and turned the sand to fire.

Green lizards, with kaleidoscopic tints, squattered across the track, and hairy spiders waddled in and out the stones. Scorpions and centipedes revived, and prowled about like sharks or tigers looking for their prey, whilst beetles, rolling balls of camels' dung, strove to as little purpose as do men, who, struggling in the dung of business, pass their lives, like beetles, with their eyes fixed upon the ground.

As the sun gradually gained strength, the pilgrim drew her tattered haik about her face, and sat, a bundle of white rags, head crouched on her breast and motionless, except the hand holding the reins, which half mechanically moved up and down, as she urged on the ass into a shuffling trot.

The hot hours caught her under a solitary palm tree, by a half-stagnant stream, in which great tortoises put up their heads, and then sank out of sight as noiselessly as they had risen, leaving a trail of bubbles on the slimy pool. Some red flamingoes lazily took flight, and then with outstretched wings descended further off, and stood expectant, patient as fishers, and wrapt in contemplation during the mysteries of their gentle craft.

Then the full silence of the desert noontide fell upon the scene, as the old woman, after having tied her ass's feet with a thin goat's-hair cord, sat down to rest. Long did she listen to her ass munching his scanty feed of corn, and then the cricket's chirp and the faint rustling of the lone palm-trees' leaves lulled her to sleep.

Slumbering, she dreamed of her past life—for dreams are but the shadow of the past, reflected on the mirror of the brain—and saw herself, a girl, watching her goats, happy to lie beneath a bush all day, eating her bread dipped in the brook at noon, and playing on a reed; then, evening come, driving her charges home, to sleep on the hard ground upon a sheepskin, in the corner of the tent. She saw herself a maiden, not wondering overmuch at the new view of life which age had brought, accepting in the same way as did her goats, that she too must come under the law of nature, and in pain bear sons. Next, marriage, with its brief feasting, and eternal round of grinding corn, broken alone by childbirth once a year, during the period of her youth. Then came the one brief day of joy since she kept goats a child upon the hills, the morning when she bore a son, one who would be a man, and ride, and fill his father's place upon the earth.

She saw her sons grow up, her husband die, and then her children follow him, herself once more alone, and keeping goats upon the hill, only brown, bent and wrinkled, instead of round, upright and rosy, as when she was a child. Still, with the resignation of her race, a resignation as of rocks to rain, she did not murmur, but took it all just as her goats bore all things, yielding their necks, almost, as it were, cheerfully,

to her blunt knife, upon the rare occasions when she found herself
constrained to kill one for her food.

Waking and dozing, she passed through the hottest hours when even
palm trees drooped, and the tired earth appears to groan under the
fury of the sun.

Then rising up refreshed, she led her ass to water at the stream,
watching him drink amongst the stones, whitened with the salt scum,
which in dry seasons floats upon all rivers in that land.

Mounting, she struck into the sandy deep-worn track which, fringed
with feathery tamarisks, led out into the plain. Like a faint cloud on
the horizon rose the white city where the Prophet dwelt, and as the ass
shuffled along, travellers from many paths passed by, and the road
grew plainer as she advanced upon her way.

Horsemen, seated high above their horses in their chair saddles,
ambled along, their spears held sloping backwards or trailing in the
dust. Meeting each other on the way, they whirled and charged, drawing up short when near and going through the evolutions of the "Jerid,"
and then with a brief "Peace," again becoming grave and silent, they
ambled on, their straight sharp spurs pressed to their horses' sides.

Camels with bales of goods, covered with sheepskin or with striped
cloth, swayed onward in long lines, their heads moving alternately
about, as if they were engaged in some strange dance. Asses, with piles
of brushwood covering them to their ears, slid past like animated hay-
stacks and men on foot veiled to the eyes, barefooted, with their slippers in their hands, or wearing sandals, tramped along the road. Pack-
mules, with bundles of chopped straw packed hard in nets, or carrying
loads of fresh-cut barley or of grass, passed by, their riders sitting sideways on the loads, or, running at their tails with one hand on their
quarters, seemed to push on their beasts, as with the curses, without
which no mule will move, they whiled away the time. A fine red dust
enveloped everything as in a sand storm, turning burnouses and haiks
brown, and caking thickly on the sweaty faces of the men.

Nearing the city gates the crush grew thicker, till at last a constant
stream of people blocked the way, jostling and pushing, but good-
humouredly, after the way of those to whom time is the chiefest
property they own.

Dark rose the crenellated walls, and the white gate made a strange
blot of light in the surrounding brown of plain and roads and mud-
built houses of the town.

Entering upon the cobbled causeway, she passed through the gate,
and in a corner, squatting on the ground, saw the scribes writing, the
spearmen lounging in the twisted passage with their spears stacked

against the wall. Then the great rush of travellers bore her as on a wave into the precincts of the town.

She rode by heaps of rubbish, on which lay chickens and dead dogs, with scraps of leather, camels' bones, and all the jetsam of a hundred years, burned by the sun till they became innocuous, but yet sending out odours which are indeed the very perfumes of Araby the blest.

Huts made of canes, near which grew castor-oil plants, fringed the edge of the high dunghill of the town, and round it curs, lean, mangy, and as wild as jackals, slept with a bloodshot eye half open, ready to rush and bark at anyone who ventured to infringe upon the limits of their sphere of influence.

She passed the sandy horse-market, where auctioneers, standing up in their stirrups with a switch between their teeth, circled and wheeled their horses as a seagull turns upon the wing, or, starting them full speed, stopped them with open mouth and foam-flecked bit, turned suddenly to statues, just at the feet of the impassive bystanders, who showed their admiration but by a guttural "Wah," or gravely inter-jected "Allah," as they endeavoured to press home some lie, too gross to pass upon its merits, even in that bright atmosphere of truth which in all lands encompasses the horse.

A second gate she passed, in which more tribesmen lounged, their horses hobbled, and themselves stretched out on mats, and the tired pilgrim found herself in a long cobbled street, on which her ass skated and slipped about, being accustomed to the desert sands. In it the dyers plied their craft, their arms stained blue or red, as they plunged hanks of wool into their vats, from which a thick dark steam rose, filling the air with vapours as from a solfatara, or such as rises from those islands in the west, known to those daring men "who ride that huge unwieldy beast, the sea, like fools, trembling upon its waves in hollow logs," and braving death upon that element which Allah has not given to his faithful to subdue. Smiths and artificers in brass and those who ply the bellows, sweating and keeping up a coil, unfit for council, but by whose labour and the wasting of whose frames cities are rendered stable, and states who cherish them set their foundations like wise builders on a rock, she passed.

Stopping, the pilgrim asked from a white-bearded man where in the city did the Prophet sit, and if the faithful, even the faithful such as she, had easy access to the person of the man whom God had chosen as his vicegerent upon earth.

Stroking his beard, the elder made reply: "Praise be to God, the One, our Lord Mohammed keeps no state. He sits within the mosque which we of Mecca call Masjida n'Nabi, with his companions, talking and teaching, and at times is silent, as his friends think, communing with the Lord. All can approach him, and if thou hast anything to ask, tether thine ass at the mosque door and go in boldly, and thou wilt be received."

The pilgrim gave "the Peace," and passed along in the dense crowd, in which camels and mules, with horses, negroes, tribesmen, sellers of sweetmeats, beggars, and watercarriers, all swelled the press.

Again she entered into streets, streets, and more streets. She threaded through bazaars where saddle-makers wrought, bending the camels' shoulder bones to form the trees, and stretching unshrunk mare's hide over all. Crouched in their booths, they sat like josses in a Chinese temple, sewing elaborate patterns, plaiting stirrup leathers, and cutting out long Arab reins which dangle almost to the ground. Before their booths stood wild-eyed Bedouins, their hair worn long and greased with mutton fat till it shone glossy as a raven's wing. They chaffered long for everything they bought. Spurs, reins, or saddle-cloths were all important to them, therefore they took each piece up separately, appraised it to its disadvantage, and often made pretence to go away calling down maledictions on the head of him who for his goods wished to be paid in life's blood of the poor. Yet they returned, and, after much expenditure of eloquence, bore off their purchase, as if they feared that robbers would deprive them of their prize, hiding it cautiously under the folds of their brown goat's-hair cloaks, or stowed in the recesses of their saddle-bags.

A smell of spices showed the tired wanderer that she approached the Kaiseria, wherein dwell those who deal in saffron, pepper, anise, and cummin, asafœtida, cloves, nutmegs, cinnamon, sugar and all the merchandise which is brought over sea by ship to Yembo, and then conveyed to Mecca and Medina upon camels' backs.

Stopping an instant where a Jaui had his wares displayed, she bought an ounce of semsin, knowing Abdallah's son had three things specially in which he took delight, women, scents, and meat, but not knowing that of the first two, as his wife Ayesha said in years to come, he had had his fill, but never of the third. The Kaiseria left behind, she felt her heart beat as she neared the mosque.

Simple it stood on a bare space of sand, all made of palm trees hewn foursquare, the walls of cane and of mud, the roof of palm leaves over the mihráb—simple and only seven cubits high, and yet a fane in which the pæan to the God of Battles echoed so loudly that its last blast was heard in Aquitaine, in farthest Hind, Irac, in China, and by the marshy shores of the Lake Chad.

As she drew near the mosque not knowing (as a woman) how to pray, she yet continued muttering something which, whilst no doubt strengthening her soul, was to the full as acceptable to the One God as it were framed after the strictest canon of the Moslem law. Then, sliding to the ground, she tied her ass's feet with a palmetto cord, and taking in her hand her ounce of semsin as an offering, passed into the court.

Under the orange trees a marble fountain played, stained here and there by time, murmuring its never-ending prayer, gladdening the souls of men with its faint music, and serving as a drinking-place to countless birds, who, after drinking, washed, and then, flying back to the trees, chanted their praises to the giver of their lives.

A little while she lingered, and then, after the fashion of her race, which, desert born, cannot pass running water, even if they are being led to death, without a draught, she stopped and drank. Then, lifting up her eyes, she saw a group seated beneath a palm tree, and at once felt her eyes had been considered worthy to behold the man whom, of all men, his Maker in his life had pardoned and set His seal upon his shoulder as a memorial of His grace.

As she drew near she marked the Prophet, the Promised, the Blessed One, who in the middle of his friends sat silently as they discussed or prayed.

Of middle height he was and strongly made, his colour fair, his hair worn long and parted, neither exactly curling nor yet smooth, his beard well shaped and flecked with silver here and there, clipped close upon his upper lip; and about the whole man an air of neatness and of cleanliness. His dress was simple, for, hanging to the middle of his calf, appeared his undershirt, and over it he wore, as it fell out upon that day, a fine striped mantle from the Yemen, which he wrapped round about him tightly after the fashion of a coat; his shoes, which lay beside him, were of the fashion of the Hadhramút, with thongs and clouted; his staff lay near to them, and as he spoke, he beat with his left hand upon the right, and often smiled so that his teeth appeared as white as hailstones, new fallen on the grass after an April storm.

Advancing to the group, the pilgrim gave "the Peace," and then tendering her offering, stood silent in the sight of all the company. Fear sealed her lips, and sweat ran down her cheeks as she gazed on the face of him to whom the Lord of Hosts had spoken, giving him power both to unloose and bind.

Gently he spoke, and lifting up his hand, said: "Mother, what is it you seek, and why this offering?"

Then courage came to her, and words which all the Arabs have at their command, and she poured forth her troubles, telling the prophet of her loneliness, her goats, her hut, of her lost husband and her sons all slain in battle, in the service of the Lord. She asked him why her sex was barred from Paradise, and if the prophet would exclude Ámina, she who bore him, from the regions of the blessed. With the direct and homely logic of her race, she pressed her claims.

Well did she set out woman's life, how she bore children in sore suffering, reared them in trouble and anxiety, moulded and formed their minds in childhood, as she had moulded and formed their bodies in the womb.

When she had finished she stood silent, anxiously waiting a reply, whilst on the faces of the fellowship there came a look as if they too remembered those who in tents and duars on the plains had nurtured them, but no one spoke, for the respect they bore to him who, simply clad as they, was yet superior to all created men.

Long did he muse, no doubt remembering Kadija, and how she clave to him in evil and in good report, when all men scoffed, and then opening his lips he gave his judgment on the pilgrim's statement of the case.

"Allah," he said, "has willed it that no old woman enter Paradise, therefore depart, and go in peace, and trouble not the prophet of the Lord."

Tears rose to Rahma's eyes, and she stood turned to stone, and through the company there ran a murmur of compassion for her suffering. Then stretching out his hand, Mohammed smiled and said: "Mother, Allah has willed it as I declared to you, but as his power is infinite, at the last day, it may be he will make you young again, and you shall enter into the regions of the blessed, and sit beside the Perfect Ones, the four, who of all women have found favour in his sight."

He ceased, and opening the offered packet, took the semsin in his hand, and eagerly inhaled the scent, and Rahma, having thanked him, stooped down and kissed the fringes of his striped Yemen mantle, then straightening herself as she had been a girl, passed through the court-yard, mounted on her ass and struck into the plain.

23

The Clerk's Quest

BY GEORGE MOORE

FOR thirty years Edward Dempsey had worked low down in the list of clerks in the firm of Quin and Wee. He did his work so well that he seemed born to do it, and it was felt that any change in which Dempsey was concerned would be unlucky. Managers had looked at Dempsey doubtingly and had left him in his habits. New partners had come into the business, but Dempsey showed no sign of interest. He was interested only in his desk. There it was by the dim window, there were his pens, there was his penwiper, there was the ruler, there was the blotting-pad. Dempsey was always the first to arrive and the last to leave. Once in thirty years of service he had accepted a holiday. It had been a topic of conversation all the morning, and the clerks tittered when he came into the bank in the afternoon saying he had been looking into the shop windows all the morning, and had come down to the bank to see how they were getting on.

An obscure, clandestine, taciturn little man, occupying in life only the space necessary to bend over a desk, and whose conical head leaned to one side as if in token of his humility.

It seemed that Dempsey had no other ambition than to be allowed to stagnate at a desk to the end of his life, and this modest ambition would have been realised had it not been for a slight accident—the single accident that had found its way into Dempsey's well-ordered and closely guarded life. One summer's day, the heat of the areas arose and filled the open window, and Dempsey's somnolescent senses were moved by a soft and suave perfume. At first he was puzzled to say whence it came; then he perceived that it had come from the bundle of cheques which he held in his hand; and then that the odoriferous paper was a pale pink cheque in the middle of the bundle. He had hardly seen a flower for thirty years, and could not determine whether the odour was that of mignonette, or honeysuckle, or violet. But at that moment the cheques were called for; he handed them to his superior, and with cool hand and clear brain continued to make entries in the ledger until the bank closed.

But that night, just as he was falling asleep, a remembrance of the insinuating perfume returned to him. He wondered whose cheque it was, and regretted not having looked at the signature, and many times during the succeeding weeks he paused as he was making entries in the ledger to think if the haunting perfume were rose, lavender, or mignonette. It was not the scent of rose, he was sure of that. And a vague swaying of hope began. Dreams that had died or had never been born floated up like things from the depths of the sea, and many old things that he had dreamed about or had never dreamed at all drifted about. Out of the depths of life a hope that he had never known, or that the severe rule of his daily life had checked long ago, began its struggle for life; and when the same sweet odour came again—he knew now it was the scent of heliotrope—his heart was lifted and he was overcome in a sweet possessive trouble. He sought for the cheque amid the bundle of cheques and, finding it, he pressed the paper to his face. The cheque was written in a thin, feminine handwriting, and was signed "Henrietta Brown," and the name and handwriting were pregnant with occult significance in Dempsey's disturbed mind. His hand paused amid the entries, and he grew suddenly aware of some dim, shadowy form, gracile and sweet-smelling as the spring—moist shadow of wandering cloud, emanation of earth, or woman herself? Dempsey pondered, and his absentmindedness was noticed, and occasioned comment among the clerks.

For the first time in his life he was glad when the office hours were over. He wanted to be alone, he wanted to think, he felt he must abandon himself to the new influence that had so suddenly and unexpectedly entered his life. Henrietta Brown! the name persisted in his mind like a half-forgotten, half-remembered tune; and in his efforts to realise her beauty he stopped before the photographic displays in the shop windows; but none of the famous or the infamous celebrities there helped him in the least. He could only realise Henrietta Brown by turning his thoughts from without and seeking the intimate sense of her perfumed cheques. The end of every month brought a cheque from Henrietta Brown, and for a few moments the clerk was transported and lived beyond himself.

An idea had fixed itself in his mind. He knew not if Henrietta Brown was young or old, pretty or ugly, married or single; the perfume and the name were sufficient, and could no longer be separated from the idea, now forcing its way through the fissures in the failing brain of this poor little bachelor clerk—that idea of light and love and grace so inherent in man, but which rigorous circumstances had compelled Dempsey to banish from his life.

Dempsey had had a mother to support for many years, and had found it impossible to economise. But since her death he had laid by about one hundred and fifty pounds. He thought of this money with awe, and awed by his good fortune he wondered how much more he might save before he was forced to leave his employment; and to have touched a penny of his savings would have seemed to him a sin near to sacrilege. Yet he did not hesitate to send Henrietta Brown, whose address he had been able to obtain through the bank books, a diamond brooch which had cost twenty pounds. He omitted to say whence it had come, and for days he lived in a warm wonderment, satisfied in the thought that she was wearing something that he had seen and touched.

His ideal was now by him and always, and its dominion was so complete that he neglected his duties at the bank, and was censured by the amazed manager. The change of his condition was so obvious that it became the subject for gossip, and jokes were now beginning to pass into serious conjecturing. Dempsey took no notice, and his plans matured amid jokes and theories. The desire to write and reveal himself to his beloved had become imperative; and after some very slight hesitation—for he was moved more by instinct than by reason—he wrote a letter urging the fatality of the circumstances that separated them, and explaining rather than excusing this revelation of his identity. His letter was full of deference, but at the same time it left no doubt as to the nature of his attachments and hopes. The answer to this letter was a polite note begging him not to persist in this correspondence, and warning him that if he did it would become necessary to write to the manager of the bank. But the return of his brooch did not dissuade Dempsey from the pursuit of his ideal; and as time went by it became more and more impossible for him to refrain from writing love letters, and sending occasional presents of jewellery. When the letters and the jewellery were returned to him he put them away carelessly, and he bought the first sparkle of diamonds that caught his fancy, and forwarded ring, bracelet, and ear-ring, with whatever word of rapturous love that came to his mind.

One day he was called into the manager's room, severely reprimanded, and eventually pardoned in consideration of his long and faithful service. But the reprimands of his employers were of no use and he continued to write to Henrietta Brown, growing more and more careless of his secret. He dropped brooches about the office, and his letters. At last the story was whispered from desk to desk. Dempsey's dismissal was the only course open to the firm; and it was with much regret that the partners told their old servant that his services were no longer required.

To their surprise Dempsey seemed quite unaffected by his dismissal; he even seemed relieved, and left the bank smiling, thinking of Henrietta, bestowing no thought on his want of means. He did not even think of providing himself with money by the sale of some of the jewellery he had about him, nor of his going to his lodging and packing up his clothes, he did not think how he should get to Edinburgh—it was there that she lived. He thought of her even to the exclusion of the simplest means of reaching her, and was content to walk about the streets in happy mood, waiting for glimpses of some evanescent phantom at the wood's edge wearing a star on her forehead, or catching sight in the wood's depth of a glistening shoulder and feet flying towards the reeds. Full of happy aspiration he wandered seeking the country through the many straggling villages that hang like children round the skirts of Dublin, and was passing through one of these at nightfall, and, feeling tired, he turned into the bar of the inn, and asked for bread and cheese.

"Come a long way, governor?" said one of two rough fellows.

"I am going a long way," replied Dempsey; "I am going north—very far north."

"And what may yer be going north for, if I may make bold to ask?"

"I am going to the lady I love, and I am taking her beautiful presents of jewellery."

The two rough fellows exchanged glances; and it is easy to imagine how Dempsey was induced to let them have his diamonds, so that inquiries might be made of a friend round the corner regarding their value. After waiting a little while, Dempsey paid for his bread and cheese, and went in search of the thieves. But the face of Henrietta Brown obliterated all remembrance of thieves and diamonds, and he wandered for a few days, sustained by his dream and the crusts that his appearance drew from the pitiful. At last he even neglected to ask for a crust, and, foodless, followed the beckoning vision, from sunrise to sundown.

It was a soft, quiet summer's night when Dempsey lay down to sleep for the last time. He was very tired, he had been wandering all day, and threw himself on the grass by the roadside. He lay there looking up at the stars, thinking of Henrietta, knowing that everything was slipping away, and he passing into a diviner sense. Henrietta seemed to be coming nearer to him and revealing herself more clearly; and when the word of death was in his throat, and his eyes opened for the last time, it seemed to him that one of the stars came down from the sky and laid its bright face upon his shoulder.

24

The Birthday of the Infanta

BY OSCAR WILDE

IT was the birthday of the Infanta. She was just twelve years of age, and the sun was shining brightly in the gardens of the palace.

Although she was a real Princess and the Infanta of Spain, she had only one birthday every year, just like the children of quite poor people, so it was naturally a matter of great importance to the whole country that she should have a really fine day for the occasion. And a really fine day it certainly was. The tall striped tulips stood straight up upon their stalks, like long rows of soldiers, and looked defiantly across the grass at the roses, and said: "We are quite as splendid as you are now." The purple butterflies fluttered about with gold dust on their wings, visiting each flower in turn; the little lizards crept out of the crevices of the wall, and lay basking in the white glare; and the pomegranates split and cracked with the heat, and showed their bleeding red hearts. Even the pale yellow lemons, that hung in such profusion from the mouldering trellis and along the dim arcades, seemed to have caught a richer colour from the wonderful sunlight, and the magnolia trees opened their great globe-like blossoms of folded ivory, and filled the air with a sweet heavy perfume.

The little Princess herself walked up and down the terrace with her companions, and played at hide and seek round the stone vases and the old moss-grown statues. On ordinary days she was only allowed to play with children of her own rank, so she had always to play alone, but her birthday was an exception, and the King had given orders that she was to invite any of her young friends whom she liked to come and amuse themselves with her. There was a stately grace about these slim Spanish children as they glided about, the boys with their large-plumed hats and short fluttering cloaks, the girls holding up the trains of their long brocaded gowns, and shielding the sun from their eyes with huge fans of black and silver. But the Infanta was the most graceful of all, and the most tastefully attired, after the somewhat cumbrous fashion of the day. Her robe was of grey satin, the skirt and the wide puffed sleeves heavily embroidered with silver, and the stiff corset studded with rows of fine pearls. Two tiny slippers with big pink rosettes peeped out beneath her dress as she walked. Pink and pearl was her great gauze fan, and in her hair, which like an aureole of faded gold stood out stiffly round her pale little face, she had a beautiful white rose.

From a window in the palace the sad melancholy King watched them. Behind him stood his brother, Don Pedro of Aragon, whom he hated, and his confessor, the Grand Inquisitor of Granada, sat by his side. Sadder even than usual was the King, for as he looked at the Infanta bowing with childish gravity to the assembling courtiers, or laughing behind her fan at the grim Duchess of Albuquerque who always accompanied her, he thought of the young Queen, her mother, who but a short time before—so it seemed to him—had come from the gay country of France, and had withered away in the sombre splendour of the Spanish court, dying just six months after the birth of her child, and before she had seen the almonds blossom twice in the orchard, or plucked the second year's fruit from the old gnarled fig-tree that stood in the centre of the now grass-grown courtyard. So great had been his love for her that he had not suffered even the grave to hide her from him. She had been embalmed by a Moorish physician, who in return for this service had been granted his life, which for heresy and suspicion of magical practices had been already forfeited, men said, to the Holy Office, and her body was still lying on its tapestried bier in the black marble chapel of the Palace, just as the monks had borne her in on that windy March day nearly twelve years before. Once every month the King, wrapped in a dark cloak and with a muffled lantern in his hand, went in and knelt by her side, calling out, *"Mi reina! Mi reina!"* and sometimes breaking through the formal etiquette that in Spain governs every separate action of life, and sets limits even to the sorrow of a King, he would clutch at the pale jewelled hands in a wild agony of grief, and try to wake by his mad kisses the cold painted face.

To-day he seemed to see her again, as he had seen her first at the Castle of Fontainebleau, when he was but fifteen years of age, and she still younger. They had been formally betrothed on that occasion by the Papal Nuncio in the presence of the French King and all the Court, and he had returned to the Escurial bearing with him a little ringlet of yellow hair, and the memory of two childish lips bending down to kiss his hand as he stepped into his carriage. Later on had followed the marriage, hastily performed at Burgos, a small town on the frontier between the two countries, and the grand public entry into Madrid with the customary celebration of high mass at the Church of La Atocha, and a more than usually solemn *auto-da-fé,* in which nearly three hundred heretics, amongst whom were many Englishmen, had been delivered over to the secular arm to be burned.

Certainly he had loved her madly, and to the ruin, many thought, of his country, then at war with England for the possession of the empire of the New World. He had hardly ever permitted her to be out of his sight; for her, he had forgotten, or seemed to have forgotten, all grave affairs of State; and, with that terrible blindness that passion brings upon its servants, he had failed to notice that the elaborate ceremonies by which he sought to please her did but aggravate the strange malady from which she suffered. When she died he was, for a time, like one bereft of reason. Indeed, there is no doubt but that he would have formally abdicated and retired to the great Trappist monastery at Granada, of which he was already titular Prior, had he not been afraid to leave the little Infanta at the mercy of his brother, whose cruelty, even in Spain, was notorious, and who was suspected by many of having caused the Queen's death by means of a pair of poisoned gloves that he had presented to her on the occasion of her visiting his castle in Aragon. Even after the expiration of the three years of public mourning that he had ordained throughout his whole dominions by royal edict, he would never suffer his ministers to speak about any new alliance, and when the Emperor himself sent to him, and offered him the hand of the lovely Archduchess of Bohemia, his niece, in marriage, he bade the ambassadors tell their master that the King of Spain was already wedded to Sorrow, and that though she was but a barren bride he loved her better than Beauty; an answer that cost his crown the rich provinces of the Netherlands, which soon after, at the Emperor's instigation, revolted against him under the leadership of some fanatics of the Reformed Church.

His whole married life, with its fierce, fiery-coloured joys and the terrible agony of its sudden ending, seemed to come back to him to-day as he watched the Infanta playing on the terrace. She had all the Queen's pretty petulance of manner, the same wilful way of tossing her head, the same proud, curved beautiful mouth, the same wonderful smile—*vrai sourire de France* indeed—as she glanced up now and then at the window, or stretched out her little hand for the stately Spanish gentleman to kiss. But the shrill laughter of the children grated on his ears, and the bright, pitiless sunlight mocked his sorrow, and a dull odour of strange spices, spices such as embalmers use, seemed to taint

—or was it fancy?—the clear morning air. He buried his face in his hands, and when the Infanta looked up again the curtains had been drawn, and the King had retired.

She made a little *moue* of disappointment, and shrugged her shoulders. Surely he might have stayed with her on her birthday. What did the stupid State-affairs matter? Or had he gone to that gloomy chapel, where the candles were always burning, and where she was never allowed to enter? How silly of him, when the sun was shining so brightly, and everybody was so happy! Besides, he would miss the sham bull-fight for which the trumpet was already sounding, to say nothing of the puppet show and the other wonderful things. Her uncle and the Grand Inquisitor were much more sensible. They had come out on the terrace, and paid her nice compliments. So she tossed her pretty head, and taking Don Pedro by the hand, she walked slowly down the steps towards a long pavilion of purple silk that had been erected at the end of the garden, the other children following in strict order of precedence, those who had the longest names going first.

A procession of noble boys, fantastically dressed as toreadors came out to meet her, and the young Count of Tierra-Nueva, a wonderfully handsome lad of about fourteen years of age, uncovering his head with all the grace of a born hidalgo and grandee of Spain, led her solemnly in to a little gilt and ivory chair that was placed on a raised daïs above the arena. The children grouped themselves all around, fluttering their big fans and whispering to each other, and Don Pedro and the Grand Inquisitor stood laughing at the entrance. Even the Duchess—the Camerera-Mayor as she was called—a thin, hard-featured woman with a yellow ruff, did not look quite so bad-tempered as usual, and something like a chill smile flitted across her wrinkled face and twitched her thin, bloodless lips.

It certainly was a marvelous bull-fight, and much nicer, the Infanta thought, than the real bull-fight that she had been brought to see at Seville, on the occasion of the visit of the Duke of Parma to her father. Some of the boys pranced about on richly-caparisoned hobby-horses brandishing long javelins with gay streamers of bright ribands attached to them; others went on foot waving their scarlet cloaks before the bull, and vaulting lightly over the barrier when he charged them; and as for the bull himself he was just like a live bull, though he was only made of wicker-work and stretched hide, and sometimes insisted on running round the arena on his hind legs, which no live bull ever dreams of doing. He made a splendid fight of it, too, and the children got so excited that they stood up upon the benches, and waved their lace handkerchiefs and cried out: *Bravo toro! Bravo toro!* just as sensibly as if they had been grown-up people. At last, however, after a prolonged combat, during which several of the hobby-horses were gored through and through, and their riders dismounted, the young Count of Tierra-Nueva brought the bull to his knees, and having obtained permission from the Infanta to give the *coup de grâce,* he plunged his wooden sword into the neck of the animal with such violence that the head came right off, and disclosed the laughing face of little Monsieur de Lorraine, the son of the French Ambassador at Madrid.

The arena was then cleared amidst much applause, and the dead hobby-horses dragged solemnly away by two Moorish pages in yellow and black liveries, and after a short interlude, during which a French posture-master performed upon the tight rope, some Italian puppets appeared in the semi-classical tragedy of *Sophonisba* on the stage of a small theatre that had been built up for the purpose. They acted so well, and their gestures were so extremely natural, that at the close of the play the eyes of the Infanta were quite dim with tears. Indeed some of the children really cried, and had to be comforted with sweetmeats, and the Grand Inquisitor himself was so affected that he could not help saying to Don Pedro that it seemed to him intolerable that things made simply out of wood and coloured wax, and worked mechanically by wires, should be so unhappy and meet with such terrible misfortunes.

An African juggler followed, who brought in a large flat basket covered with a red cloth, and having placed it in the centre of the arena, he took from his turban a curious reed pipe, and blew through it. In a few moments the cloth began to move, and as the pipe grew shriller and shriller two green and gold snakes put out their strange wedge-shaped heads and rose slowly up, swaying to and fro with the music as a plant sways in the water. The children, however, were rather frightened at their spotted hoods and quick darting tongues, and were much more pleased when the juggler made a tiny orange-tree grow out of the sand and bear pretty white blossoms and clusters of real fruit; and when he took the fan of the little daughter of the Marquess de Las Torres, and changed it into a blue bird that flew all round the pavilion and sang, their delight and amazement knew no bounds. The solemn minuet, too, performed by the dancing boys from the church of Neustra Señora Del Pilar, was charming. The Infanta had never before seen this wonderful ceremony which takes place every year at May-time in front of the high altar of the Virgin, and in her honour; and, indeed, none of the royal family of Spain had entered the great cathedral of Saragossa since a mad priest, supposed by many to have been in the pay of Elizabeth of England, had tried to administer a poisoned wafer to the Prince of the Asturias. So she had known only by hearsay of "Our Lady's Dance," as it was called, and it certainly was a beautiful sight. The boys wore old-fashioned court dresses of white velvet, and their curious three-cornered hats were fringed with silver and surmounted with huge plumes of ostrich feathers, the dazzling whiteness of their costumes, as they moved about in the sunlight, being still more accentuated by their swarthy faces and long black hair. Everybody was fascinated by the grave dignity with which they moved through the intricate figures of the dance, and by the elaborate grace of their slow gestures, and stately bows, and when they had finished their performance and doffed their great plumed hats to the Infanta, she acknowledged their reverence with much courtesy, and made a vow that she would send a large wax candle to the shrine of Our Lady of Pilar in return for the pleasure that she had given her.

A troop of handsome Egyptians—as the gipsies were termed in those days—then advanced into the arena, and sitting down cross-legs, in a circle, began to play softly upon their zithers, moving their bodies to the tune, and humming, almost below their breath, a low, dreamy air. When they caught sight of Don Pedro they scowled at him, and some of them looked terrified, for only a few weeks before he had had two of their tribe hanged for sorcery in the marketplace at Seville, but the pretty Infanta charmed them as she leaned back peeping over her fan with her great blue eyes, and they felt sure that one so lovely as she was could never be cruel to anybody. So they played on very gently and just touching the cords of the zithers with their long pointed nails, and their heads began to nod as though they were falling asleep. Suddenly, with a cry so shrill that all the children were startled and Don Pedro's hand clutched at the agate pommel of his dagger, they leapt to their feet and whirled madly round the enclosure beating their tambourines, and chanting some wild love-song in their strange guttural language. Then at another signal they all flung themselves again to the ground and lay there quite still, the dull strumming of the zithers being the only sound that broke the silence. After they had done this several times, they disappeared for a moment and came back leading a brown shaggy bear by a chain, and carrying on their shoulders some little Barbary apes. The bear stood upon his head with the utmost gravity, and the wizened apes played all kinds of amusing tricks with two gipsy boys who seemed to be their masters, and fought with tiny swords, and fired off guns, and went through a regular soldier's drill just like the King's own bodyguard. In fact the gipsies were a great success.

But the funniest part of the whole morning's entertainment was undoubtedly the dancing of the little Dwarf. When he stumbled into the arena, waddling on his crooked legs and wagging his huge, misshapen head from side to side, the children went off into a loud shout of delight, and the Infanta herself laughed so much that the Camerera was obliged to remind her that although there were many precedents in Spain for a King's daughter weeping before her equals, there were none for a Princess of the blood royal making so merry before those who were her inferiors in birth. The Dwarf, however, was really quite irresistible, and even at the Spanish Court, always noted for its cultivated passion for the horrible, so fantastic a little monster had never been seen. It was his first appearance, too. He had been discovered only the day before, running wild through the forest, by two of the nobles who happened to have been hunting in a remote part of the great cork-wood that surrounded the town, and had been carried off by them to the Palace as a surprise for the Infanta; his father, who was a poor charcoal-burner, being but too well pleased to get rid of so ugly and useless a child. Perhaps the most amusing thing about him was his complete unconsciousness of his own grotesque appearance. Indeed, he seemed quite happy and full of the highest spirits. When the children laughed, he laughed as freely and as joyously as any of them, and at the close of each dance he made them each the funniest of bows, smiling and nodding at them just as if he was really one of themselves, and not a little misshapen thing that Nature, in some humorous mood, had fashioned for others to mock at. As for the Infanta, she absolutely fascinated him. He could not keep his eyes off her, and seemed to dance for her alone, and when at the close of the performance, remembering how she had seen the great ladies of the Court throw bouquets to Caffarelli the famous Italian treble, whom the Pope had sent from his own chapel to Madrid that he might cure the King's melancholy by the sweetness of his voice, she took out of her hair the beautiful white rose, and partly for a jest and partly to tease the Camerera, threw it to him across the arena with her sweetest smile; he took the whole matter quite seriously, and pressing the flower to his rough, coarse lips he put his hand upon his heart, and sank on one knee before her, grinning from ear to ear, and with his little bright eyes sparkling with pleasure.

This so upset the gravity of the Infanta that she kept on laughing long after the little Dwarf had run out of the arena, and expressed a desire to her uncle that the dance should be immediately repeated. The Camerera, however, on the plea that the sun was too hot, decided that it would be better that her Highness should return without delay to the Palace, where a wonderful feast had been already prepared for her, including a real birthday cake with her own initials worked all over it in painted sugar and a lovely silver flag waving from the top. The Infanta accordingly rose up with much dignity, and having given orders that the little Dwarf was to dance again for her after the hour of siesta, and conveyed her thanks to the young Count of Tierra-Nueva for his

charming reception, she went back to her apartments, the children following in the same order in which they had entered.

Now when the little Dwarf heard that he was to dance a second time
before the Infanta, and by her own express command, he was so proud
that he ran out into the garden, kissing the white rose in an absurd
ecstasy of pleasure, and making the most uncouth and clumsy gestures
of delight.

The Flowers were quite indignant at his daring to intrude into their
beautiful home, and when they saw him capering up and down the
walks, and waving his arms above his head in such a ridiculous manner, they could not restrain their feelings any longer.

"He is really far too ugly to be allowed to play in any place where
we are," cried the Tulips.

"He should drink poppy-juice, and go to sleep for a thousand years,"
said the great scarlet Lilies, and they grew quite hot and angry.

"He is a perfect horror!" screamed the Cactus. "Why, he is twisted
and stumpy, and his head is completely out of proportion with his legs.
Really he makes me feel prickly all over, and if he comes near me I
will sting him with my thorns."

"And he has actually got one of my best blooms!" exclaimed the
White Rose-Tree. "I gave it to the Infanta this morning myself, as a
birthday present, and he has stolen it from her." And she called out:
"Thief, thief, thief!" at the top of her voice.

Even the red Geraniums, who did not usually give themselves airs,
and were known to have a great many poor relations themselves,
curled up in disgust when they saw him, and when the Violets meekly
remarked that though he was certainly extremely plain, still he could
not help it, they retorted with a good deal of justice that that was his
chief defect, and that there was no reason why one should admire a
person because he was incurable; and, indeed, some of the Violets
themselves felt that the ugliness of the little Dwarf was almost osten-
tatious, and that he would have shown much better taste if he had
looked sad, or at least pensive, instead of jumping about merrily, and
throwing himself into such grotesque and silly attitudes.

As for the old Sundial, who was an extremely remarkable individual,
and had once told the time of day to no less a person than the Emperor
Charles V. himself, he was so taken aback by the little Dwarf's appearance, that he almost forgot to mark two whole minutes with his long
shadowy finger, and could not help saying to the great milk-white
Peacock, who was sunning herself on the balustrade, that everyone
knew that the children of Kings were Kings, and that the children
of charcoal-burners were charcoal-burners, and that it was absurd to

pretend that it wasn't so; a statement with which the Peacock entirely agreed, and indeed screamed out, "Certainly, certainly," in such a loud, harsh voice, that the gold-fish who lived in the basin of the cool splashing fountain put their heads out of the water and asked the huge stone Tritons what on earth was the matter.

But somehow the Birds liked him. They had seen him often in the forest, dancing about like an elf after the eddying leaves, or crouched up in the hollow of some old oak-tree, sharing his nuts with the squirrels. They did not mind his being ugly, a bit. Why, even the nightingale herself, who sang so sweetly in the orange groves at night that sometimes the Moon leaned down to listen, was not much to look at after all; and, besides, he had been kind to them, and during that terribly bitter winter, when there were no berries on the trees, and the ground was as hard as iron, and the wolves had come down to the very gates of the city to look for food, he had never forgotten them, but had always given them crumbs out of his little hunch of black bread, and divided with them whatever poor breakfast he had.

So they flew round and round him, just touching his cheek with their wings as they passed, and chattered to each other, and the little Dwarf was so pleased that he could not help showing them the beautiful white rose, and telling them that the Infanta herself had given it to him because she loved him.

They did not understand a single word of what he was saying, but that made no matter, for they put their heads on one side, and looked wise, which is quite as good as understanding a thing, and very much easier.

The Lizards also took an immense fancy to him, and when he grew tired of running about and flung himself down on the grass to rest, they played and romped all over him, and tried to amuse him in the best way they could. "Every one cannot be as beautiful as a lizard," they cried; "that would be too much to expect. And, though it sounds absurd to say so, he is really not so ugly after all, provided, of course, that one shuts one's eyes, and does not look at him." The Lizards were extremely philosophical by nature, and often sat thinking for hours and hours together, when there was nothing else to do, or when the weather was too rainy for them to go out.

The flowers, however, were excessively annoyed at their behaviour, and at the behaviour of the birds. "It only shows," they said, "what a vulgarising effect this incessant rushing and flying about has. Well-bred people always stay exactly in the same place, as we do. No one ever saw us hopping up and down the walks, or galloping madly through the grass after dragonflies. When we do want change of air, we send for the gardener, and he carries us to another bed. This is dignified, and as it should be. But birds and lizards have no sense of repose, and, indeed, birds have not even a permanent address. They are mere vagrants like the gipsies, and should be treated in exactly the same manner." So they put their noses in the air, and looked very haughty, and were quite delighted when after some time they saw the little Dwarf scramble up from the grass, and make his way across the terrace to the palace.

"He should certainly be kept indoors for the rest of his natural life," they said. "Look at his hunched back, and his crooked legs," and they began to titter.

But the little Dwarf knew nothing of all this. He liked the birds and the lizards immensely, and thought that the flowers were the most marvellous things in the whole world, except, of course, the Infanta, but then she had given him the beautiful white rose, and she loved him, and that made a great difference. How he wished that he had gone back with her! She would have put him on her right hand, and smiled at him, and he would have never left her side, but would have made her his playmate, and taught her all kinds of delightful tricks. For though he had never been in a palace before, he knew a great many wonderful things. He could make little cages out of rushes for the grasshoppers to sing in, and fashion the long-jointed bamboo into the pipe that Pan loves to hear. He knew the cry of every bird, and could call the starlings from the tree-top, or the heron from the mere. He knew the trail of every animal, and could track the hare by its delicate footprints, and the boar by the trampled leaves. All the wind-dances he knew, the mad dance in red raiment with the autumn, the light dance in blue sandals over the corn, the dance with white snow-wreaths in winter, and the blossom-dance through the orchards in spring. He knew where the wood-pigeons built their nests, and once when a fowler had snared the parent birds, he had brought up the young ones himself, and had built a little dovecot for them in the cleft of a pollard elm. They were quite tame, and used to feed out of his hands every morning. She would like them, and the rabbits that scurried about in the long fern, and the jays with their steely feathers and black bills, and the hedgehogs that could curl themselves up into prickly balls, and the great wise tortoises that crawled slowly about, shaking their heads and nibbling at the young leaves. Yes, she must certainly come to the forest and play with him. He would give her his own little bed, and would watch outside the window till dawn, to see that the wild horned cattle did not harm her, nor the gaunt wolves creep too near the hut. And at dawn he would tap at the shutters and wake her, and they would go out and dance together all the day long. It was really not a bit lonely in the forest. Sometimes a Bishop rode through on his white mule, reading out of a painted book. Sometimes in their green velvet caps, and their jerkins of tanned deerskin, the falconers passed by, with wooded hawks on their wrists. At vintage time came the grape-treaders, with purple hands and feet, wreathed with glossy ivy and carrying dripping skins of wine; and the charcoal-burners sat round their huge braziers at night, watching the dry logs charring slowly in the fire, and roasting chestnuts in the ashes, and the robbers came out of their caves and made merry with them. Once, too, he had seen a beautiful procession winding up the long dusty road to Toledo. The monks went in front singing sweetly, and carrying bright banners and crosses of gold, and then, in silver armour, with match-locks and pikes came the soldiers, and in their midst walked three barefooted men, in strange yellow dresses painted all over with won-derful figures, and carrying lighted candles in their hands. Certainly there was a great deal to look at in the forest, and when she was tired he would find a soft bank of moss for her, or carry her in his arms, for he was very strong, though he knew that he was not tall. He would make her a necklace of red bryony berries, that would be quite as pretty as the white berries that she wore on her dress, and when she was tired of them, she could throw them away, and he would find her others. He would bring her acorn-cups and dew-drenched anemones, and tiny glow-worms to be stars in the pale gold of her hair.

But where was she? He asked the white rose, and it made him no answer. The whole palace seemed asleep, and even where the shutters had not been closed, heavy curtains had been drawn across the win-dows to keep out the glare. He wandered all round looking for some place through which he might gain an entrance, and at last he caught sight of a little private door that was lying open. He slipped through, and found himself in a splendid hall, far more splendid, he feared, than the forest, there was so much gilding everywhere, and even the floor was made of great coloured stones, fitted together into a sort of geometrical pattern. But the little Infanta was not there, only some wonderful white statues that looked down on him from their jasper pedestals, with sad blank eyes and strangely smiling lips.

At the end of the hall hung a richly embroidered curtain of black velvet, powdered with suns and stars, the King's favourite devices, and broidered on the colour he loved best. Perhaps she was hiding behind that? He would try at any rate.

So he stole quietly across, and drew it aside. No; there was only another room, though a prettier room, he thought, than the one he had just left. The walls were hung with a many-figured green arras of needle-wrought tapestry representing a hunt, the work of some Flem-ish artists who had spent more than seven years in its composition.

It had once been the chamber of *Jean le Fou,* as he was called, that mad King who was so enamoured of the chase, that he had often tried in his delirium to mount the huge rearing horses, and to drag down the stag on which the great hounds were leaping, sounding his hunting horn, and stabbing with his dagger at the pale flying deer. It was now used as the council-room, and on the centre table were lying the red portfolios of the ministers, stamped with the gold tulips of Spain, and with the arms and emblems of the house of Hapsburg.

The little Dwarf looked in wonder all round him, and was half-afraid to go on. The strange silent horsemen that galloped so swiftly through the long glades without making any noise, seemed to him like those terrible phantoms of whom he had heard the charcoal burners speaking—the Comprachos, who hunt only at night, and if they meet a man, turn him into a hind, and chase him. But he thought of the pretty Infanta, and took courage. He wanted to find her alone, and to tell her that he, too, loved her. Perhaps she was in the room beyond.

He ran across the soft Moorish carpets, and opened the door. No! She was not here either. The room was quite empty.

It was a throne-room, used for the reception of foreign ambassadors, when the King, which of late had not been often, consented to give them a personal audience; the same room in which, many years before, envoys had appeared from England to make arrangements for the marriage of their Queen, then one of the Catholic sovereigns of Europe, with the Emperor's eldest son. The hangings were of gilt Cordovan leather, and a heavy gilt chandelier with branches for three hundred wax lights hung down from the black and white ceiling. Underneath a great canopy of gold cloth, on which the lions and towers of Castile were broidered in seed pearls, stood the throne itself, covered with a rich pall of black velvet studded with silver tulips and elaborately fringed with silver and pearls. On the second step of the throne was placed the kneeling-stool of the Infanta, with its cushion of cloth of silver tissue, and below that again, and beyond the limit of the canopy, stood the chair for the Papal Nuncio, who alone had the right to be seated in the King's presence on the occasion of any public ceremonial, and whose Cardinal's hat, with its tangled scarlet tassels, lay on a purple tabouret in front. On the wall, facing the throne, hung a life-sized portrait of Charles V. in hunting dress, with a great mastiff by his side, and a picture of Philip II. receiving the homage of the Netherlands occupied the centre of the other wall. Between the windows stood a black ebony cabinet, inlaid with plates of ivory, on which the figures from Holbein's Dance of Death had been graved—by the hand, some said, of that famous master himself.

But the little Dwarf cared nothing for all this magnificence. He would not have given his rose for all the pearls on the canopy, nor one white petal of his rose for the throne itself. What he wanted was to see the Infanta before she went down to the pavilion, and to ask her to come away with him when he had finished his dance. Here, in the Palace, the air was close and heavy, but in the forest the wind blew free, and the sunlight with wandering hands of gold moved the tremulous leaves aside. There were flowers, too, in the forest, not so splendid, perhaps, as the flowers in the garden, but more sweetly scented for all that; hyacinths in early spring that flooded with waving purple the cool glens, and grassy knolls; yellow primroses that nestled in little clumps round the gnarled roots of the oak-trees; bright celandine, and blue speedwell, and irises lilac and gold. There were grey catkins on the hazels, and the fox-gloves drooped with the weight of their dappled bee-haunted cells. The chestnut had its spires of white stars, and the hawthorn its pallid moons of beauty. Yes: surely she would come if he could only find her! She would come with him to the fair forest, and all day long he would dance for her delight. A smile lit up his eyes at the thought, and he passed into the next room.

Of all the rooms this was the brightest and the most beautiful. The walls were covered with a pink-flowered Lucca damask, patterned with birds and dotted with dainty blossoms of silver; the furniture was of massive silver, festooned with florid wreaths, and swinging Cupids; in front of the two large fire-places stood great screens broidered with parrots and peacocks, and the floor, which was of sea-green onyx, seemed to stretch far away into the distance. Nor was he alone. Standing under the shadow of the doorway, at the extreme end of the room, he saw a little figure watching him. His heart trembled, a cry of joy broke from his lips, and he moved out into the sunlight. As he did so, the figure moved out also, and he saw it plainly.

The Infanta! It was a monster, the most grotesque monster he had ever beheld. Not properly shaped, as all other people were, but hunchbacked, and crooked-limbed, with huge lolling head and mane of black hair. The little Dwarf frowned, and the monster frowned also. He laughed, and it laughed with him, and held its hands to its sides, just as he himself was doing. He made it a mocking bow, and it returned him a low reverence. He went towards it, and it came to meet him, copying each step that he made, and stopping when he stopped himself. He shouted with amusement, and ran forward, and reached out his hand, and the hand of the monster touched his, and it was as cold as ice. He grew afraid, and moved his hand across, and the monster's hand followed it quickly. He tried to press on, but something smooth and hard stopped him. The face of the monster was now close to his own, and seemed full of terror. He brushed his hair off his eyes. It imitated him. He struck at it, and it returned blow for blow. He loathed it, and it made hideous faces at him. He drew back, and it retreated.

What is it? He thought for a moment, and looked round at the rest of the room. It was strange, but everything seemed to have its double in this invisible wall of clear water. Yes, picture for picture was repeated, and couch for couch. The sleeping Faun that lay in the alcove by the doorway had its twin brother that slumbered, and the silver Venus that stood in the sunlight held out her arms to a Venus as lovely as herself.

Was it Echo? He had called to her once in the valley, and she had answered him word for word. Could she mock the eye, as she mocked the voice? Could she make a mimic world just like the real world? Could the shadows of things have colour and life and movement? Could it be that—?

He started, and taking from his breast the beautiful white rose, he turned round, and kissed it. The monster had a rose of its own, petal for petal the same! It kissed it with like kisses, and pressed it to its heart with horrible gestures.

When the truth dawned upon him, he gave a wild cry of despair, and fell sobbing to the ground. So it was he who was misshapen and hunchbacked, foul to look at and grotesque. He himself was the monster, and it was at him that all the children had been laughing, and the little Princess who he thought loved him—she, too, had been merely mocking at his ugliness, and making merry over his twisted limbs. Why had they not left him in the forest, where there was no mirror to tell him how loathsome he was? Why had his father not killed him, rather than sell him to his shame? The hot tears poured down his cheeks, and he tore the white rose to pieces. The sprawling monster did the same, and scattered the faint petals in the air. It grovelled on the ground, and, when he looked at it, it watched him with a face drawn with pain. He crept away, lest he should see it, and covered his eyes with his hands. He crawled, like some wounded thing, into the shadow, and lay there moaning.

And at that moment the Infanta herself came in with her companions through the open window and, when they saw the ugly little dwarf lying on the ground and beating the floor with his clenched hands, in the most fantastic and exaggerated manner, they went off into shouts of happy laughter, and stood all round him and watched him.

"His dancing was funny," said the Infanta; "but his acting is funnier still. Indeed he is almost as good as the puppets, only, of course, not quite so natural." And she fluttered her big fan, and applauded.

But the little Dwarf never looked up, and his sobs grew fainter and fainter, and suddenly he gave a curious gasp, and clutched his side. And then he fell back again, and lay quite still.

"That is capital," said the Infanta, after a pause; "but now you must dance for me."

"Yes," cried all the children, "you must get up and dance, for you are as clever as the Barbary apes, and much more ridiculous."

But the little Dwarf made no answer.

And the Infanta stamped her foot, and called out to her uncle, who was walking on the terrace with the Chamberlain, reading some despatches that had just arrived from Mexico where the Holy Office had recently been established. "My funny little dwarf is sulking," she cried, "you must wake him up, and tell him to dance for me."

They smiled at each other, and sauntered in, and Don Pedro stooped down, and slapped the Dwarf on the cheek with his embroidered glove. "You must dance," he said, *"petit monstre*. You must dance. The Infanta of Spain and the Indies wishes to be amused."

But the little Dwarf never moved.

"A whipping master should be sent for," said Don Pedro wearily, and he went back to the terrace. But the Chamberlain looked grave, and he knelt beside the little dwarf, and put his hand upon his heart. And after a few moments he shrugged his shoulders, and rose up, and having made a low bow to the Infanta, he said:

"*Mi bella Princesa,* your funny little dwarf will never dance again. It is a pity, for he is so ugly that he might have made the King smile."

"But why will he not dance again?" asked the Infanta, laughing.

"Because his heart is broken," answered the Chamberlain.

And the Infanta frowned, and her dainty rose-leaf lips curled in pretty disdain. "For the future let those who come to play with me have no hearts," she cried, and she ran out into the garden.

25

Youth

BY JOSEPH CONRAD

THIS could have occurred nowhere but in England, where men and sea interpenetrate, so to speak—the sea entering into the life of most men, and the men knowing something or everything about the sea, in the way of amusement, of travel, or of bread-winning.

We were sitting round a mahogany table that reflected the bottle, the claret-glasses, and our faces as we leaned on our elbows. There was a director of companies, an accountant, a lawyer, Marlow, and myself. The director had been a Conway boy, the accountant had served four years at sea, the lawyer—a fine crusted Tory, High Churchman, the best of old fellows, the soul of honour—had been chief officer in the P. & O. service in the good old days when mail-boats were square-rigged at least on two masts, and used to come down the China Sea before a fair monsoon with stun'-sails set alow and aloft. We all began life in the merchant service. Between the five of us there was the strong bond of the sea, and also the fellowship of the craft, which no amount of enthusiasm for yachting, cruising, and so on can give, since one is only the amusement of life and the other is life itself.

Marlow (at least I think that is how he spelt his name) told the story, or rather the chronicle, of a voyage:—

"Yes, I have seen a little of the Eastern seas; but what I remember best is my first voyage there. You fellows know there are those voyages that seem ordered for the illustration of life, that might stand for a symbol of existence. You fight, work, sweat, nearly kill yourself, sometimes do kill yourself, trying to accomplish something—and you can't. Not from any fault of yours. You simply can do nothing, neither great nor little—not a thing in the world—not even marry an old maid, or get a wretched 600-ton cargo of coal to its port of destination.

"It was altogether a memorable affair. It was my first voyage to the East, and my first voyage as second mate; it was also my skipper's first command. You'll admit it was time. He was sixty if a day; a little man, with a broad, not very straight back, with bowed shoulders and one leg more bandy than the other, he had that queer twisted-about appearance you see so often in men who work in the fields. He had a nut-cracker face—chin and nose trying to come together over a sunken mouth—and it was framed in iron-gray fluffy hair, that looked like a chin-strap of cotton-wool sprinkled with coal-dust. And he had blue eyes in that old face of his, which were amazingly like a boy's, with that candid expression some quite common men preserve to the end of their days by a rare internal gift of simplicity of heart and rectitude of soul. What induced him to accept me was a wonder. I had come out of a crack Australian clipper, where I had been third officer, and he seemed to have a prejudice against crack clippers as aristocratic and high-toned. He said to me, 'You know, in this ship you will have to work.' I said I had to work in every ship I had ever been in. 'Ah, but this is different, and you gentlemen out of them big ships; . . . but there! I dare say you will do. Join to-morrow.'

"I joined to-morrow. It was twenty-two years ago; and I was just twenty. How time passes! It was one of the happiest days of my life. Fancy! Second mate for the first time—a really responsible officer! I wouldn't have thrown up my new billet for a fortune. The mate looked me over carefully. He was also an old chap, but of another stamp. He had a Roman nose, a snow-white, long beard, and his name was Mahon, but he insisted that it should be pronounced Mann. He was well connected; yet there was something wrong with his luck, and he had never got on.

"As to the captain, he had been for years in coasters, then in the Mediterranean, and last in the West Indian trade. He had never been round the Capes. He could just write a kind of sketchy hand, and didn't care for writing at all. Both were thorough good seamen of course, and between those two old chaps I felt like a small boy between two grandfathers.

"The ship also was old. Her name was the *Judea*. Queer name, isn't it? She belonged to a man Wilmer, Wilcox—some name like that; but he has been bankrupt and dead these twenty years or more, and his name don't matter. She had been laid up in Shadwell basin for ever so long. You may imagine her state. She was all rust, dust, grime—soot aloft, dirt on deck. To me it was like coming out of a palace into a ruined cottage. She was about 400 tons, had a primitive windlass, wooden latches to the doors, not a bit of brass about her, and a big square stern. There was on it, below her name in big letters, a lot of scrollwork, with the gilt off, and some sort of a coat of arms, with the motto 'Do or Die' underneath. I remember it took my fancy immensely. There was a touch of romance in it, something that made me love the old thing—something that appealed to my youth!

"We left London in ballast—sand ballast—to load a cargo of coal in a northern port of Bankok. Bankok! I thrilled. I had been six years at sea, but had only seen Melbourne and Sydney, very good places, charming places in their way—but Bankok!

"We worked out of the Thames under canvas, with a North Sea pilot on board. His name was Jermyn, and he dodged all day long about the galley drying his handkerchief before the stove. Apparently he never slept. He was a dismal man, with a perpetual tear sparkling at the end of his nose, who either had been in trouble, or was in trouble, or expected to be in trouble—couldn't be happy unless something went wrong. He mistrusted my youth, my common-sense, and my seamanship, and made a point of showing it in a hundred little ways. I dare say he was right. It seems to me I knew very little then, and I know not much more now; but I cherish a hate for that Jermyn to this day.

"We were a week working up as far as Yarmouth Roads, and then we got into a gale—the famous October gale of twenty-two years ago. It was wind, lightning, sleet, snow, and a terrific sea. We were flying light, and you may imagine how bad it was when I tell you we had smashed bulwarks and a flooded deck. On the second night she shifted her ballast into the lee bow, and by that time we had been blown off somewhere on the Dogger Bank. There was nothing for it but go below with shovels and try to right her, and there we were in that vast hold, gloomy like a cavern, the tallow dips stuck and flickering on the beams, the gale howling above, the ship tossing about like mad on her side; there we all were, Jermyn, the captain, every one, hardly able to keep our feet, engaged on that gravedigger's work, and trying to toss shovel-fuls of wet sand up to windward. At every tumble of the ship you could see vaguely in the dim light men falling down with a great flourish of shovels. One of the ship's boys (we had two), impressed by the weirdness of the scene, wept as if his heart would break. We could hear him blubbering somewhere in the shadows.

"On the third day the gale died out, and by and by a north-country tug picked us up. We took sixteen days in all to get from London to the Tyne! When we got into dock we had lost our turn for loading, and they hauled us off to a tier where we remained for a month. Mrs. Beard (the captain's name was Beard) came from Colchester to see the old man. She lived on board. The crew of runners had left, and there remained only the officers, one boy and the steward, a mulatto who answered to the name of Abraham. Mrs. Beard was an old woman, with a face all wrinkled and ruddy like a winter apple, and the figure of a young girl. She caught sight of me once, sewing on a button, and insisted on having my shirts to repair. This was something different from the captains' wives I had known on board crack clippers. When I brought her the shirts, she said: 'And the socks? They want mending, I am sure, and John's—Captain Beard's—things are all in order now. I would be glad of something to do.' Bless the old woman. She overhauled my outfit for me, and meantime I read for the first time *Sartor Resartus* and Burnaby's *Ride to Khiva*. I didn't understand much of the first then; but I remember I preferred the soldier to the philosopher at the time; a preference which life has only confirmed. One was a man, and the other was either more—or less. However, they are both dead and Mrs. Beard is dead, and youth, strength, genius, thoughts, achievements, simple hearts—all die. . . . No matter.

"They loaded us at last. We shipped a crew. Eight able seamen and two boys. We hauled off one evening to the buoys at the dock-gates, ready to go out, and with a fair prospect of beginning the voyage next day. Mrs. Beard was to start for home by a late train. When the ship was fast we went to tea. We sat rather silent through the meal—Mahon, the old couple, and I. I finished first, and slipped away for a smoke, my cabin being in a deck-house just against the poop. It was high water, blowing fresh with a drizzle; the double dock-gates were opened, and the steam-colliers were going in and out in the darkness with their lights burning bright, a great plashing of propellers, rattling of winches, and a lot of hailing on the pier-heads. I watched the procession of head-lights gliding high and of green lights gliding low in the night, when suddenly a red gleam flashed at me, vanished, came into view again, and remained. The fore-end of a steamer loomed up close. I shouted down the cabin, 'Come up, quick!' and then heard a startled voice saying afar in the dark, 'Stop her, sir.' A bell jingled. Another voice cried warningly, 'We are going right into that barque, sir.' The answer to this was a gruff 'All right,' and the next thing was a heavy crash as the steamer struck a glancing blow with the bluff of her bow about our fore-rigging. There was a moment of confusion, yelling, and running about. Steam roared. Then somebody was heard saying, 'All clear, sir.' . . . 'Are you all right?' asked the gruff voice. I had jumped forward to see the damage, and hailed back, 'I think so.' 'Easy astern,' said the gruff voice. A bell jingled. 'What steamer is that?' screamed Mahon. By that time she was no more to us than a bulky shadow manœuvring a little way off. They shouted at us some name—a woman's name, Miranda or Melissa—or some such thing. 'This means another month in this beastly hole,' said Mahon to me, as we peered with lamps about the splintered bulwarks and broken braces. 'But where's the captain?'

"We had not heard or seen anything of him all that time. We went aft to look. A doleful voice arose hailing somewhere in the middle of the dock, '*Judea* ahoy!' . . . How the devil did he get there? . . . 'Hallo!' we shouted. 'I am adrift in our boat without oars,' he cried. A belated water-man offered his services, and Mahon struck a bargain with him for half-a-crown to tow our skipper alongside; but it was Mrs. Beard that came up the ladder first. They had been floating about the dock in that mizzly cold rain for nearly an hour. I was never so surprised in my life.

"It appears that when he heard my shout 'Come up' he understood at once what was the matter, caught up his wife, ran on deck, and across, and down into our boat, which was fast to the ladder. Not bad for a sixty-year-old. Just imagine that old fellow saving heroically in his arms that old woman—the woman of his life. He set her down on a thwart, and was ready to climb back on board when the painter came adrift somehow, and away they went together. Of course in the confusion we did not hear him shouting. He looked abashed. She said cheerfully, 'I suppose it does not matter my losing the train now?' 'No, Jenny—you go below and get warm,' he growled. Then to us: 'A sailor has no business with a wife—I say. There I was, out of the ship. Well, no harm done this time. Let's go and look at what that fool of a steamer smashed.'

"It wasn't much, but it delayed us three weeks. At the end of that time, the captain being engaged with his agents, I carried Mrs. Beard's bag to the railway-station and put her all comfy into a third-class carriage. She lowered the window to say, 'You are a good young man. If you see John—Captain Beard—without his muffler at night, just remind him from me to keep his throat well wrapped up.' 'Certainly, Mrs. Beard,' I said. 'You are a good young man; I noticed how attentive you are to John—to Captain——' The train pulled out suddenly; I took my cap off to the old woman: I never saw her again. . . . Pass the bottle.

"We went to sea next day. When we made that start for Bankok we had been already three months out of London. We had expected to be a fortnight or so—at the outside.

"It was January, and the weather was beautiful—the beautiful sunny winter weather that has more charm than in the summer-time, because it is unexpected, and crisp, and you know it won't, it can't, last long. It's like a windfall, like a godsend, like an unexpected piece of luck.

"It lasted all down the North Sea, all down Channel; and it lasted till we were three hundred miles or so to the westward of the Lizards: then the wind went round to the sou'west and began to pipe up. In two days it blew a gale. The *Judea,* hove to, wallowed on the Atlantic like an old candle-box. It blew day after day: it blew with spite, without interval, without mercy, without rest. The world was nothing but an immensity of great foaming waves rushing at us, under a sky low enough to touch with the hand and dirty like a smoked ceiling. In the stormy space surrounding us there was as much flying spray as air. Day after day and night after night there was nothing round the ship but the howl of the wind, the tumult of the sea, the noise of water pouring over her deck. There was no rest for her and no rest for us. She tossed, she pitched, she stood on her head, she sat on her tail, she rolled, she groaned, and we had to hold on while on deck and cling to our bunks when below, in a constant effort of body and worry of mind.

"One night Mahon spoke through the small window of my berth. It opened right into my very bed, and I was lying there sleepless, in my boots, feeling as though I had not slept for years, and could not if I tried. He said excitedly——

"'You got the sounding-rod in here, Marlow? I can't get the pumps to suck. By God! it's no child's play.'

"I gave him the sounding-rod and lay down again, trying to think of various things—but I thought only of the pumps. When I came on deck they were still at it, and my watch relieved at the pumps. By the light of the lantern brought on deck to examine the sounding-rod I caught a glimpse of their weary, serious faces. We pumped all the four hours. We pumped all night, all day, all the week—watch and watch. She was working herself loose, and leaked badly—not enough to drown us at once, but enough to kill us with the work at the pumps. And while we pumped the ship was going from us piecemeal: the bulwarks went, the stanchions were torn out, the ventilators smashed, the cabin-door burst in. There was not a dry spot in the ship. She was being gutted bit by bit. The long-boat changed, as if by magic, into matchwood where she stood in her gripes. I had lashed her myself, and was rather proud of my handiwork, which had withstood so long the malice of the sea. And we pumped. And there was no break in the weather. The sea was white like a sheet of foam, like a caldron of boiling milk; there was not a break in the clouds, no—not the size of a man's hand—no, not for so much as ten seconds. There was for us no sky, there were for us no stars, no sun, no universe—nothing but angry clouds and an infuriated sea. We pumped watch and watch, for dear life; and it seemed to last for months, for years, for all eternity, as though we had been dead and gone to a hell for sailors. We forgot the day of the week, the name of the month, what year it was, and whether we had ever been ashore. The sails blew away, she lay broadside on under a weather-cloth, the ocean poured over her, and we did not care. We turned those handles, and had the eyes of idiots. As soon as we had crawled on deck I used to take a round turn with a rope about the men, the pumps, and the mainmast, and we turned, we turned incessantly, with the water to our waists, to our necks, over our heads. It was all one. We had forgotten how it felt to be dry.

"And there was somewhere in me the thought: By Jove! this is the deuce of an adventure—something you read about; and it is my first voyage as second mate—and I am only twenty—and here I am lasting it out as well as any of these men, and keeping my chaps up to the mark. I was pleased. I would not have given up the experience for worlds. I had moments of exultation. Whenever the old dismantled craft pitched heavily with her counter high in the air, she seemed to me to throw up, like an appeal, like a defiance, like a cry to the clouds without mercy, the words written on her stern: '*Judea,* London. Do or Die.'

"O youth! The strength of it, the faith of it, the imagination of it! To me she was not an old rattle-trap carting about the world a lot of coal for a freight—to me she was the endeavour, the test, the trial of life. I think of her with pleasure, with affection, with regret—as you would think of someone dead you have loved. I shall never forget her. . . . Pass the bottle.

"One night when tied to the mast, as I explained, we were pumping on, deafened with the wind, and without spirit enough in us to wish ourselves dead, a heavy sea crashed aboard and swept clean over us. As soon as I got my breath I shouted, as in duty bound, 'Keep on, boys!' when suddenly I felt something hard floating on deck strike the calf of my leg. I made a grab at it and missed. It was so dark we could not see each other's faces within a foot—you understand.

"After that thump the ship kept quiet for a while, and the thing, whatever it was, struck my leg again. This time I caught it—and it was a saucepan. At first, being stupid with fatigue and thinking of nothing but the pumps, I did not understand what I had in my hand. Suddenly it dawned upon me, and I shouted, 'Boys, the house on deck is gone. Leave this, and let's look for the cook.'

"There was a deck-house forward, which contained the galley, the cook's berth, and the quarters of the crew. As we had expected for days to see it swept away, the hands had been ordered to sleep in the cabin—the only safe place in the ship. The steward, Abraham, however, persisted in clinging to his berth, stupidly, like a mule—from sheer fright I believe, like an animal that won't leave a stable falling in an earthquake. So we went to look for him. It was chancing death, since once out of our lashings we were as exposed as if on a raft. But we went. The house was shattered as if a shell had exploded inside. Most of it had gone overboard—stove, men's quarters, and their property, all was gone; but two posts, holding a portion of the bulkhead to which Abraham's bunk was attached, remained as if by a miracle. We groped in the ruins and came upon this, and there he was, sitting in his bunk, surrounded by foam and wreckage, jabbering cheerfully to himself. He was out of his mind; completely and forever mad, with this sudden shock coming upon the fag-end of his endurance. We snatched him up, lugged him aft, and pitched him head-first down the cabin companion. You understand there was no time to carry him down with infinite precautions and wait to see how he got on. Those below would pick him up at the bottom of the stairs all right. We were in a hurry to go back to the pumps. That business could not wait. A bad leak is an inhuman thing.

"One would think that the sole purpose of that fiendish gale had been to make a lunatic of that poor devil of a mulatto. It eased before morning, and next day the sky cleared, and as the sea went down the leak took up. When it came to bending a fresh set of sails the crew demanded to put back—and really there was nothing else to do. Boats gone, decks swept clean, cabin gutted, men without a stitch but what they stood in, stores spoiled, ship strained. We put her head for home, and—would you believe it? The wind came east right in our teeth. It blew fresh, it blew continuously. We had to beat up every inch of the way, but she did not leak so badly, the water keeping comparatively smooth. Two hours' pumping in every four is no joke—but it kept her afloat as far as Falmouth.

"The good people there live on casualties of the sea, and no doubt were glad to see us. A hungry crowd of shipwrights sharpened their chisels at the sight of that carcass of a ship. And, by Jove! they had pretty pickings off us before they were done. I fancy the owner was already in a tight place. There were delays. Then it was decided to take part of the cargo out and caulk her topsides. This was done, the repairs finished, cargo reshipped; a new crew came on board, and we went out —for Bankok. At the end of a week we were back again. The crew said they weren't going to Bankok—a hundred and fifty days' passage —in a something hooker that wanted pumping eight hours out of the twenty-four; and the nautical papers inserted again the little paragraph: 'Judea. Barque. Tyne to Bankok; coals; put back to Falmouth leaky and with crew refusing duty.'

"There were more delays—more tinkering. The owner came down for a day, and said she was as right as a little fiddle. Poor old Captain Beard looked like the ghost of a Geordie skipper—through the worry and humiliation of it. Remember he was sixty, and it was his first command. Mahon said it was a foolish business, and would end badly. I loved the ship more than ever, and wanted awfully to get to Bankok.

To Bankok! Magic name, blessed name. Mesopotamia wasn't a patch on it. Remember I was twenty, and it was my first second-mate's billet, and the East was waiting for me.

"We went out and anchored in the outer roads with a fresh crew— the third. She leaked worse than ever. It was as if those confounded ship-wrights had actually made a hole in her. This time we did not even go outside. The crew simply refused to man the windlass.

"They towed us back to the inner harbour, and we became a fixture, a feature, an institution of the place. People pointed us out to visitors as 'that 'ere barque that's going to Bankok—has been here six months —put back three times.' On holidays the small boys pulling about in boats would hail, '*Judea,* ahoy!' and if a head showed above the rail shouted, 'Where you bound to?—Bankok?' and jeered. We were only three on board. The poor old skipper mooned in the cabin. Mahon un-dertook the cooking, and unexpectedly developed all a Frenchman's genius for preparing nice little messes. I looked languidly after the rig-ging. We became citizens of Falmouth. Every shopkeeper knew us. At the barber's or tobacconist's they asked familiarly, 'Do you think you will ever get to Bankok?' Meantime the owner, the underwriters, and the charterers squabbled amongst themselves in London, and our pay went on. . . . Pass the bottle.

"It was horrid. Morally it was worse than pumping for life. It seemed as though we had been forgotten by the world, belonged to nobody, would get nowhere; it seemed that, as if bewitched, we would have to live for ever and ever in that inner harbour, a derision and a by-word to generations of long-shore loafers and dishonest boatmen. I obtained three months' pay and a five days' leave, and made a rush for London. It took me a day to get there and pretty well another to come back— but three months' pay went all the same. I don't know what I did with it. I went to a music-hall, I believe, lunched, dined, and supped in a swell place in Regent Street, and was back to time, with nothing but a complete set of Byron's works and a new railway rug to show for three months' work. The boat-man who pulled me off to the ship said: 'Hallo! I thought you had left the old thing. *She* will never get to Bankok.' 'That's all *you* know about it,' I said scornfully—but I didn't like that prophecy at all.

"Suddenly a man, some kind of agent to somebody, appeared with full powers. He had grog-blossoms all over his face, an indomitable energy, and was a jolly soul. We leaped into life again. A hulk came alongside, took our cargo, and then we went into dry dock to get our copper stripped. No wonder she leaked. The poor thing, strained be-yond endurance by the gale, had, as if in disgust, spat out all the oakum of her lower seams. She was recaulked, new coppered, and made as tight as a bottle. We went back to the hulk and reshipped our cargo.

"Then, on a fine moonlight night, all the rats left the ship.

"We had been infested with them. They had destroyed our sails, consumed more stores than the crew, affably shared our beds and our dangers, and now, when the ship was made seaworthy, concluded to clear out. I called Mahon to enjoy the spectacle. Rat after rat appeared on our rail, took a last look over his shoulder, and leaped with a hollow thud into the empty hulk. We tried to count them, but soon lost the tale. Mahon said: 'Well, well! don't talk to me about the intelligence of rats. They ought to have left before, when we had that narrow squeak from foundering. There you have the proof how silly is the superstition about them. They leave a good ship for an old rotten hulk, where there is nothing to eat, too, the fools! . . . I don't believe they know what is safe or what is good for them, any more than you or I.'

"And after some more talk we agreed that the wisdom of rats had been grossly overrated, being in fact no greater than that of men.

"The story of the ship was known, by this, all up the Channel from Land's End to the Forelands, and we could get no crew on the south coast. They sent us one all complete from Liverpool, and we left once more—for Bankok.

"We had fair breezes, smooth water right into the tropics, and the old *Judea* lumbered along in the sunshine. When she went eight knots everything cracked aloft, and we tied our caps to our heads; but mostly she strolled on at the rate of three miles an hour. What could you expect? She was tired—that old ship. Her youth was where mine is— where yours is—you fellows who listen to this yarn; and what friend would throw your years and your weariness in your face? We didn't grumble at her. To us aft, at least, it seemed as though we had been born in her, reared in her, had lived in her for ages, had never known any other ship. I would just as soon have abused the old village church at home for not being a cathedral.

"And for me there was also my youth to make me patient. There was all the East before me, and all life, and the thought that I had been tried in that ship and had come out pretty well. And I thought of men of old who, centuries ago, went that road in ships that sailed no better, to the land of palms, and spices, and yellow sands, and of brown nations ruled by kings more cruel than Nero the Roman, and more splendid than Solomon the Jew. The old bark lumbered on, heavy with her age and the burden of her cargo, while I lived the life of youth in ignorance and hope. She lumbered on through an interminable procession of days; and the fresh gilding flashed back at the setting sun, seemed to cry out over the darkening sea the words painted on her stern, 'Judea, London. Do or Die.'

"Then we entered the Indian Ocean and steered northerly for Java Head. The winds were light. Weeks slipped by. She crawled on, do or die, and people at home began to think of posting us as overdue.

"One Saturday evening, I being off duty, the men asked me to give them an extra bucket of water or so—for washing clothes. As I did not wish to screw on the fresh-water pump so late, I went forward whistling, and with a key in my hand to unlock the forepeak scuttle, intending to serve the water out of a spare tank we kept there.

"The smell down below was as unexpected as it was frightful. One would have thought hundreds of paraffin-lamps had been flaring and smoking in that hole for days. I was glad to get out. The man with me coughed and said, 'Funny smell, sir.' I answered negligently, 'It's good for the health they say,' and walked aft.

"The first thing I did was to put my head down the square of the midship ventilator. As I lifted the lid a visible breath, something like a thin fog, a puff of faint haze, rose from the opening. The ascending air was hot, and had a heavy, sooty, paraffiny smell. I gave one sniff, and put down the lid gently. It was no use choking myself. The cargo was on fire.

"Next day she began to smoke in earnest. You see it was to be expected, for though the coal was of a safe kind, that cargo had been so handled, so broken up with handling, that it looked more like smithy coal than anything else. Then it had been wetted—more than once. It rained all the time we were taking it back from the hulk, and now with this long passage it got heated, and there was another case of spontaneous combustion.

"The captain called us into the cabin. He had a chart spread on the table, and looked unhappy. He said, 'The coast of West Australia is near, but I mean to proceed to our destination. It is the hurricane month, too; but we will just keep her head for Bankok, and fight the fire. No more putting back anywhere, if we all get roasted. We will try first to stifle this 'ere damned combustion by want of air.'

"We tried. We battened down everything, and still she smoked. The smoke kept coming out through imperceptible crevices; it forced itself through bulkheads and covers; it oozed here and there and everywhere in slender threads, in an invisible film, in an incomprehensible manner. It made its way into the cabin, into the forecastle; it poisoned the sheltered places on the deck, it could be sniffed as high as the mainyard. It was clear that if the smoke came out the air came in. This was disheartening. This combustion refused to be stifled.

"We resolved to try water, and took the hatches off. Enormous volumes of smoke, whitish, yellowish, thick, greasy, misty, choking, ascended as high as the trucks. All hands cleared out aft. Then the poisonous cloud blew away, and we went back to work in a smoke that was no thicker now than that of an ordinary factory chimney.

"We rigged the force-pump, got the hose along, and by and by it burst. Well, it was as old as the ship—a prehistoric hose, and past repair. Then we pumped with the feeble head-pump, drew water with buckets, and in this way managed in time to pour lots of Indian Ocean into the main hatch. The bright stream flashed in sunshine, fell into a layer of white crawling smoke, and vanished on the black surface of coal. Steam ascended mingling with the smoke. We poured salt water as into a barrel without a bottom. It was our fate to pump in that ship, to pump out of her, to pump into her; and after keeping water out of her to save ourselves from being drowned, we frantically poured water into her to save ourselves from being burnt.

"And she crawled on, do or die, in the serene weather. The sky was a miracle of purity, a miracle of azure. The sea was polished, was blue, was pellucid, was sparkling like a precious stone, extending on all sides, all round to the horizon—as if the whole terrestrial globe had been one jewel, one colossal sapphire, a single gem fashioned into a planet. And on the lustre of the great calm waters the *Judea* glided imperceptibly, enveloped in languid and unclean vapours, in a lazy cloud that drifted to leeward, light and slow; a pestiferous cloud defiling the splendour of sea and sky.

"All this time of course we saw no fire. The cargo smouldered at the bottom somewhere. Once Mahon, as we were working side by side, said to me with a queer smile: 'Now, if she only would spring a tidy leak—like that time when we first left the Channel—it would put a stopper on this fire. Wouldn't it?' I remarked irrelevantly, 'Do you remember the rats?'

"We fought the fire and sailed the ship too as carefully as though nothing had been the matter. The steward cooked and attended on us. Of the other twelve men, eight worked while four rested. Everyone took his turn, captain included. There was equality, and if not exactly fraternity, then a deal of good feeling. Sometimes a man, as he dashed a bucketful of water down the hatchway, would yell out, 'Hurrah for Bankok!' and the rest laughed. But generally we were taciturn and serious—and thirsty. Oh! how thirsty! And we had to be careful with the water. Strict allowance. The ship smoked, the sun blazed. . . . Pass the bottle.

"We tried everything. We even made an attempt to dig down to the fire. No good, of course. No man could remain more than a minute below. Mahon, who went first, fainted there, and the man who went to fetch him out did likewise. We lugged them out on deck. Then I leaped down to show how easily it could be done. They had learned wisdom by that time, and contented themselves by fishing for me with a chain-hook tied to a broom-handle, I believe. I did not offer to go and fetch up my shovel, which was left down below.

"Things began to look bad. We put the long-boat into the water. The second boat was ready to swing out. We had also another, a 14-foot thing, on davits aft, where it was quite safe.

"Then, behold, the smoke suddenly decreased. We redoubled our efforts to flood the bottom of the ship. In two days there was no smoke at all. Everybody was on the broad grin. This was on a Friday. On Saturday no work, but sailing the ship of course, was done. The men washed their clothes and their faces for the first time in a fortnight, and had a special dinner given them. They spoke of spontaneous combustion with contempt, and implied *they* were the boys to put out combustions. Somehow we all felt as though we each had inherited a large fortune. But a beastly smell of burning hung about the ship. Captain Beard had hollow eyes and sunken cheeks. I had never noticed so much before how twisted and bowed he was. He and Mahon prowled soberly about hatches and ventilators, sniffing. It struck me suddenly poor Mahon was a very, very old chap. As to me, I was as pleased and proud as though I had helped to win a great naval battle. O! Youth!

"The night was fine. In the morning a homeward-bound ship passed us hull down—the first we had seen for months; but we were nearing the land at last, Java Head being about 190 miles off, and nearly due north.

"Next day it was my watch on deck from eight to twelve. At breakfast the captain observed, 'It's wonderful how that smell hangs about the cabin.' About ten, the mate being on the poop, I stepped down on the main-deck for a moment. The carpenter's bench stood abaft the mainmast: I leaned against it sucking at my pipe, and the carpenter, a young chap, came to talk to me. He remarked, 'I think we have done very well, haven't we?' and then I perceived with annoyance the fool was trying to tilt the bench. I said curtly, 'Don't, Chips,' and immediately became aware of a queer sensation, of an absurd delusion,—I seemed somehow to be in the air. I heard all round me like a pent-up breath released—as if a thousand giants simultaneously had said Phoo! —and felt a dull concussion which made my ribs ache suddenly. No doubt about it—I was in the air, and my body was describing a short parabola. But short as it was, I had the time to think several thoughts in, as far as I can remember, the following order: 'This can't be the carpenter—What is it?—Some accident—Submarine volcano?—Coals, gas!—By Jove! we are being blown up—Everybody's dead—I am fall-ing into the after-hatch—I see fire in it.'

"The coal-dust suspended in the air of the hold had glowed dull-red at the moment of the explosion. In the twinkling of an eye, in an infin-itesimal fraction of a second since the first tilt of the bench, I was sprawl-ing full length on the cargo. I picked myself up and scrambled out. It was quick like a rebound. The deck was a wilderness of smashed tim-ber, lying crosswise like trees in a wood after a hurricane; an immense curtain of soiled rags waved gently before me—it was the mainsail blown to strips. I thought, The masts will be toppling over directly; and to get out of the way bolted on all-fours towards the poop-ladder. The first person I saw was Mahon, with eyes like saucers, his mouth open, and the long white hair standing straight on end round his head like a silver halo. He was just about to go down when the sight of the main-deck stirring, heaving up, and changing into splinters before his eyes, petrified him on the top step. I stared at him in unbelief, and he stared at me with a queer kind of shocked curiosity. I did not know that I had no hair, no eyebrows, no eyelashes, that my young mustache was burnt off, that my face was black, one cheek laid open, my nose cut, and my chin bleeding. I had lost my cap, one of my slippers, and my shirt was torn to rags. Of all this I was not aware. I was amazed to see the ship still afloat, the poop-deck whole—and, most of all, to see anybody alive. Also the peace of the sky and the serenity of the sea were distinctly surprising. I suppose I expected to see them convulsed with horror. . . . Pass the bottle.

"There was a voice hailing the ship from somewhere—in the air, in the sky—I couldn't tell. Presently I saw the captain—and he was mad. He asked me eagerly, 'Where's the cabin-table?' and to hear such a question was a frightful shock. I had just been blown up, you under-stand, and vibrated with that experience,—I wasn't quite sure whether I was alive. Mahon began to stamp with both feet and yelled at him, 'Good God! don't you see the deck's blown out of her?' I found my voice, and stammered out as if conscious of some gross neglect of duty, 'I don't know where the cabin-table is.' It was like an absurd dream.

"Do you know what he wanted next? Well, he wanted to trim the yards. Very placidly, and as if lost in thought, he insisted on having the foreyard squared. 'I don't know if there's anybody alive,' said Ma-hon, almost tearfully. 'Surely,' he said, gently, 'there will be enough left to square the foreyard.'

"The old chap, it seems, was in his own berth winding up the chronometers, when the shock sent him spinning. Immediately it oc-curred to him—as he said afterwards—that the ship had struck some-thing, and he ran out into the cabin. There, he saw, the cabin-table had vanished somewhere. The deck being blown up, it had fallen down into the lazarette of course. Where we had our breakfast that morning he saw only a great hole in the floor. This appeared to him so awfully mysterious, and impressed him so immensely, that what he saw and heard after he got on deck were mere trifles in comparison. And, mark, he noticed directly the wheel deserted and his barque off her course— and his only thought was to get that miserable, stripped, undecked, smouldering shell of a ship back again with her head pointing at her port of destination. Bankok! That's what he was after. I tell you this quiet, bowed, bandy-legged, almost deformed little man was immense in the singleness of his idea and in his placid ignorance of our agitation. He motioned us forward with a commanding gesture, and went to take the wheel himself.

"Yes; that was the first thing we did—trim the yards of that wreck! No one was killed, or even disabled, but everyone was more or less hurt. You should have seen them! Some were in rags, with black faces, like coal-heavers, like sweeps, and had bullet heads that seemed closely cropped, but were in fact singed to the skin. Others, of the watch below, awakened by being shot out from their collapsing bunks, shivered incessantly, and kept on groaning even as we went about our work. But they all worked. That crew of Liverpool hard cases had in them the right stuff. It's my experience they always have. It is the sea that gives it—the vastness, the loneliness surrounding their dark stolid souls. Ah! Well! we stumbled, we crept, we fell, we barked our shins on the wreckage, we hauled. The masts stood, but we did not know how much they might be charred down below. It was nearly calm, but a long swell ran from the west and made her roll. They might go at any moment. We looked at them with apprehension. One could not foresee which way they would fall.

"Then we retreated aft and looked about us. The deck was a tangle of planks on edge, of planks on end, of splinters, of ruined woodwork. The masts rose from that chaos like big trees above a matted undergrowth. The interstices of that mass of wreckage were full of something whitish, sluggish, stirring—of something that was like a greasy fog. The smoke of the invisible fire was coming up again, was trailing, like a poisonous thick mist in some valley choked with dead wood. Already lazy wisps were beginning to curl upwards amongst the mass of splinters. Here and there a piece of timber, stuck upright, resembled a post. Half of a fife-rail had been shot through the foresail, and the sky made a patch of glorious blue in the ignobly soiled canvas. A portion of several boards holding together had fallen across the rail, and one end protruded overboard, like a gangway leading upon nothing, like a gangway leading over the deep sea, leading to death—as if inviting us to walk the plank at once and be done with our ridiculous troubles. And still the air, the sky—a ghost, something invisible was hailing the ship.

"Someone had the sense to look over, and there was the helmsman, who had impulsively jumped overboard, anxious to come back. He yelled and swam lustily like a merman, keeping up with the ship. We threw him a rope, and presently he stood amongst us streaming with water and very crestfallen. The captain had surrendered the wheel, and apart, elbow on rail and chin in hand, gazed at the sea wistfully. We asked ourselves, What next? I thought, Now, this is something like. This is great. I wonder what will happen. O youth!

"Suddenly Mahon sighted a steamer far astern. Captain Beard said, 'We may do something with her yet.' We hoisted two flags, which said in the international language of the sea, 'On fire. Want immediate assistance.' The steamer grew bigger rapidly, and by and by spoke with two flags on her foremast, 'I am coming to your assistance.'

"In half an hour she was abreast, to windward, within hail, and rolling slightly, with her engines stopped. We lost our composure, and yelled all together with excitement, 'We've been blown up.' A man in a white helmet, on the bridge, cried, 'Yes! All right! all right!' and he nodded his head, and smiled, and made soothing motions with his hand as though at a lot of frightened children. One of the boats dropped in the water, and walked towards us upon the sea with her long oars. Four Calashes pulled a swinging stroke. This was my first sight of Malay seamen. I've known them since, but what struck me then was their unconcern: they came alongside, and even the bowman standing up and holding to our main-chains with the boat-hook did not deign to lift his head for a glance. I thought people who had been blown up deserved more attention.

"A little man, dry like a chip and agile like a monkey, clambered up. It was the mate of the steamer. He gave one look, and cried, 'O boys—you had better quit.'

"We were silent. He talked apart with the captain for a time,—seemed to argue with him. Then they went away together to the steamer.

"When our skipper came back we learned that the steamer was the *Somerville*, Captain Nash, from West Australia to Singapore *via* Batavia with mails, and that the agreement was she should tow us to Anjer or Batavia, if possible, where we could extinguish the fire by scuttling, and then proceed on our voyage—to Bankok! The old man seemed excited. 'We will do it yet,' he said to Mahon, fiercely. He shook his fist at the sky. Nobody else said a word.

"At noon the steamer began to tow. She went ahead slim and high, and what was left of the *Judea* followed at the end of seventy fathom of tow-rope,—followed her swiftly like a cloud of smoke with mast-heads protruding above. We went aloft to furl the sails. We coughed on the yards, and were careful about the bunts. Do you see the lot of us there, putting a neat furl on the sails of that ship doomed to arrive nowhere? There was not a man who didn't think that at any moment the masts would topple over. From aloft we could not see the ship for smoke, and they worked carefully, passing the gaskets with even turns. 'Harbour furl—aloft there!' cried Mahon from below.

"You understand this? I don't think one of those chaps expected to get down in the usual way. When we did I heard them saying to each other, 'Well, I thought we would come down overboard, in a lump—sticks and all—blame me if I didn't.' 'That's what I was thinking to myself,' would answer wearily another battered and bandaged scarescrow. And, mind, these were men without the drilled-in habit of obedience. To an onlooker they would be a lot of profane scallywags without a redeeming point. What made them do it—what made them obey me when I, thinking consciously how fine it was, made them drop the bunt of the foresail twice to try and do it better? What? They had no professional reputation—no examples, no praise. It wasn't a sense of duty; they all knew well enough how to shirk, and laze, and dodge—when they had a mind to it—and mostly they had. Was it the two pounds ten a-month that sent them there? They didn't think their pay half good enough. No; it was something in them, something inborn and subtle and everlasting. I don't say positively that the crew of a French or German merchantman wouldn't have done it, but I doubt whether it would have been done in the same way. There was a completeness in it, something solid like a principle, and masterful like an instinct—a disclosure of something secret—of that hidden something, that gift of good or evil that makes racial difference, that shapes the fate of nations.

"It was that night at ten that, for the first time since we had been fighting it, we saw the fire. The speed of the towing had fanned the smouldering destruction. A blue gleam appeared forward, shining below the wreck of the deck. It wavered in patches, it seemed to stir and creep like the light of a glowworm. I saw it first, and told Mahon. 'Then the game's up,' he said. 'We had better stop this towing, or she will burst out suddenly fore and aft before we can clear out.' We set up a yell; rang bells to attract their attention; they towed on. At last Mahon and I had to crawl forward and cut the rope with an axe. There was no time to cast off the lashings. Red tongues could be seen licking the wilderness of splinters under our feet as we made our way back to the poop.

"Of course they very soon found out in the steamer that the rope was gone. She gave a loud blast of her whistle, her lights were seen sweeping in a wide circle, she came up ranging close along-side, and stopped. We were all in a tight group on the poop looking at her. Every man had saved a little bundle or a bag. Suddenly a conical flame with a twisted top shot up forward and threw upon the black sea a circle of light, with the two vessels side by side and heaving gently in its centre. Captain Beard had been sitting on the gratings still and mute for hours, but now he rose slowly and advanced in front of us, to the mizzen-shrouds. Captain Nash hailed: 'Come along! Look sharp. I have mail-bags on board. I will take you and your boats to Singapore.'

" 'Thank you! No!' said our skipper. 'We must see the last of the ship.'

" 'I can't stand by any longer,' shouted the other. 'Mails—you know.'

" 'Ay! ay! We are all right.'

" 'Very well! I'll report you in Singapore. . . . Good-bye!'

"He waved his hand. Our men dropped their bundles quietly. The steamer moved ahead, and passing out of the circle of light, vanished at once from our sight, dazzled by the fire which burned fiercely. And then I knew that I would see the East first as commander of a small boat. I thought it fine; and the fidelity to the old ship was fine. We should see the last of her. Oh, the glamour of youth! Oh, the fire of it, more dazzling than the flames of the burning ship, throwing a magic light on the wide earth, leaping audaciously to the sky, presently to be quenched by time, more cruel, more pitiless, more bitter than the sea —and like the flames of the burning ship surrounded by an impenetrable night.

"The old man warned us in his gentle and inflexible way that it was part of our duty to save for the underwriters as much as we could of the ship's gear. Accordingly we went to work aft, while she blazed forward to give us plenty of light. We lugged out a lot of rubbish. What didn't we save? An old barometer fixed with an absurd quantity of screws nearly cost me my life: a sudden rush of smoke came upon me, and I just got away in time. There were various stores, bolts of canvas, coils of rope; the poop looked like a marine bazaar, and the boats were lumbered to the gunwales. One would have thought the old man wanted to take as much as he could of his first command with him. He was very, very quiet, but off his balance evidently. Would you believe it? He wanted to take a length of old stream-cable and a kedge-anchor with him in the long-boat. We said, 'Ay, ay, sir,' deferentially, and on the quiet let the things slip overboard. The heavy medicine-chest went that way, two bags of green coffee, tins of paint—

fancy, paint!—a whole lot of things. Then I was ordered with two hands into the boats to make a stowage and get them ready against the time it would be proper for us to leave the ship.

"We put everything straight, stepped the long-boat's mast for our skipper, who was to take charge of her, and I was not sorry to sit down for a moment. My face felt raw, every limb ached as if broken, I was aware of all my ribs, and would have sworn to a twist in the back-bone. The boats, fast astern, lay in a deep shadow, and all around I could see the circle of the sea lighted by the fire. A gigantic flame arose forward straight and clear. It flared fierce, with noises like the whirr of wings, with rumbles as of thunder. There were cracks, detonations, and from the cone of flame the sparks flew upwards, as man is born to trouble, to leaky ships, and to ships that burn.

"What bothered me was that the ship, lying broadside to the swell and to such wind as there was—a mere breath—the boats would not keep astern where they were safe, but persisted, in a pig-headed way boats have, in getting under the counter and then swinging alongside. They were knocking about dangerously and coming near the flame, while the ship rolled on them, and, of course, there was always the danger of the masts going over the side at any moment. I and my two boat-keepers kept them off as best we could, with oars and boat-hooks; but to be constantly at it became exasperating, since there was no reason why we should not leave at once. We could not see those on board, nor could we imagine what caused the delay. The boat-keepers were swearing feebly, and I had not only my share of the work but also had to keep at it two men who showed a constant inclination to lay themselves down and let things slide.

"At last I hailed, 'On deck there,' and someone looked over. 'We're ready here,' I said. The head disappeared, and very soon popped up again. 'The captain says, All right, sir, and to keep the boats well clear of the ship.'

"Half an hour passed. Suddenly there was a frightful racket, rattle, clanking of chain, hiss of water, and millions of sparks flew up into the shivering column of smoke that stood leaning slightly above the ship. The cat-heads had burned away, and the two red-hot anchors had gone to the bottom, tearing out after them two hundred fathom of red-hot chain. The ship trembled, the mass of flame swayed as if ready to collapse, and the fore top-gallant-mast fell. It darted down like an arrow of fire, shot under, and instantly leaping up within an oar's-length of the boats, floated quietly, very black on the luminous sea. I hailed the deck again. After some time a man in an unexpectedly cheerful but also muffled tone, as though he had been trying to speak with his mouth shut, informed me, 'Coming directly, sir,' and vanished. For a long time I heard nothing but the whirr and roar of the fire. There were also whistling sounds. The boats jumped, tugged at the painters, ran at each other playfully, knocked their sides together, or, do what we would, swung in a bunch against the ship's side. I couldn't stand it any longer, and swarming up a rope, clambered aboard over the stern.

"It was as bright as day. Coming up like this, the sheet of fire facing me was a terrifying sight, and the heat seemed hardly bearable at first. On a settee cushion dragged out of the cabin Captain Beard, his legs drawn up and one arm under his head, slept with the light playing on him. Do you know what the rest were busy about? They were sitting on deck right aft, round an open case, eating bread and cheese and drinking bottled stout.

"On the background of flames twisting in fierce tongues above their heads they seemed at home like salamanders, and looked like a band of desperate pirates. The fire sparkled in the whites of their eyes, gleamed on patches of white skin seen through the torn shirts. Each had the marks as of a battle about him—bandaged heads, tied-up arms, a strip of dirty rag round a knee—and each man had a bottle between his legs and a chunk of cheese in his hand. Mahon got up. With his handsome and disreputable head, his hooked profile, his long white beard, and with an uncorked bottle in his hand, he resembled one of those reckless sea-robbers of old making merry amidst violence and disaster. 'The last meal on board,' he explained solemnly. 'We had nothing to eat all day, and it was no use leaving all this.' He flourished the bottle and indicated the sleeping skipper. 'He said he couldn't swallow anything, so I got him to lie down,' he went on; and as I stared, 'I don't know whether you are aware, young fellow, the man had no sleep to speak of for days—and there will be dam' little sleep in the boats.' 'There will be no boats by-and-by if you fool about much longer,' I said, indignantly. I walked up to the skipper and shook him by the shoulder. At last he opened his eyes, but did not move. 'Time to leave her, sir,' I said quietly.

"He got up painfully, looked at the flames, at the sea sparkling round the ship, and black, black as ink farther away; he looked at the stars shining dim through a thin veil of smoke in a sky black, black as Erebus.

"'Youngest first,' he said.

"And the ordinary seaman, wiping his mouth with the back of his hand, got up, clambered over the taffrail, and vanished. Others followed. One, on the point of going over, stopped short to drain his bottle, and with a great swing of his arm flung it at the fire. 'Take this!' he cried.

"The skipper lingered disconsolately, and we left him to commune alone for a while with his first command. Then I went up again and brought him away at last. It was time. The ironwork on the poop was hot to the touch.

"Then the painter of the long-boat was cut, and the three boats, tied together, drifted clear of the ship. It was just sixteen hours after the explosion when we abandoned her. Mahon had charge of the second boat, and I had the smallest—the 14-foot thing. The long-boat would have taken the lot of us; but the skipper said we must save as much property as we could—for the underwriters—and so I got my first command. I had two men with me, a bag of biscuits, a few tins of meat, and a breaker of water. I was ordered to keep close to the long-boat, that in case of bad weather we might be taken into her.

"And do you know what I thought? I thought I would part company as soon as I could. I wanted to have my first command all to myself. I wasn't going to sail in a squadron if there were a chance for independent cruising. I would make land by myself. I would beat the other boats. Youth! All youth! The silly, charming, beautiful youth.

"But we did not make a start at once. We must see the last of the ship. And so the boats drifted about that night, heaving and setting on the swell. The men dozed, waked, sighed, groaned. I looked at the burning ship.

"Between the darkness of earth and heaven she was burning fiercely upon a disc of purple sea shot by the blood-red play of gleams; upon a disc of water glittering and sinister. A high, clear flame, an immense and lonely flame, ascended from the ocean, and from its summit the black smoke poured continuously at the sky. She burned furiously; mournful and imposing like a funeral pile kindled in the night, surrounded by the sea, watched over by the stars. A magnificent death had come like a grace, like a gift, like a reward to that old ship at the end of her laborious days. The surrender of her weary ghost to the keeping of stars and sea was stirring like the sight of a glorious triumph. The masts fell just before daybreak, and for a moment there was a burst and turmoil of sparks that seemed to fill with flying fire the night patient and watchful, the vast night lying silent upon the sea. At daylight she was only a charred shell, floating still under a cloud of smoke and bearing a glowing mass of coal within.

"Then the oars were got out, and the boats forming in a line moved round her remains as if in procession—the long-boat leading. As we pulled across her stern a slim dart of fire shot out viciously at us, and suddenly she went down, head first, in a great hiss of steam. The unconsumed stern was the last to sink; but the paint had gone, had cracked, had peeled off, and there were no letters, there was no word, no stubborn device that was like her soul, to flash at the rising sun her creed and her name.

"We made our way north. A breeze sprang up, and about noon all the boats came together for the last time. I had no mast or sail in mine, but I made a mast out of a spare oar and hoisted a boat-awning for a sail, with a boat-hook for a yard. She was certainly over-masted, but I had the satisfaction of knowing that with the wind aft I could beat the other two. I had to wait for them. Then we all had a look at the captain's chart, and, after a sociable meal of hard bread and water, got our last instructions. These were simple: steer north, and keep together as much as possible. 'Be careful with that jury-rig, Marlow,' said the captain; and Mahon, as I sailed proudly past his boat, wrinkled his curved nose and hailed, 'You will sail that ship of yours under water, if you don't look out, young fellow.' He was a malicious old man— and may the deep sea where he sleeps now rock him gently, rock him tenderly to the end of time!

"Before sunset a thick rain-squall passed over the boats, which were far astern, and that was the last I saw of them for a time. Next day I sat steering my cockle-shell—my first command—with nothing but water and sky around me. I did sight in the afternoon the upper sails of a ship far away, but said nothing, and my men did not notice her. You see I was afraid she might be homeward bound, and I had no mind to turn back from the portals of the East. I was steering for Java— another blessed name—like Bankok, you know. I steered many days.

"I need not tell you what it is to be knocking about in an open boat. I remember nights and days of calm, when we pulled, we pulled, and the boat seemed to stand still, as if bewitched within the circle of the sea horizon. I remember the heat, the deluge of rain-squalls that kept us baling for dear life (but filled our water-cask), and I remember sixteen hours on end with a mouth dry as a cinder and a steering-oar over the stern to keep my first command head on to a breaking sea. I did not know how good a man I was till then. I remember the drawn faces, the dejected figures of my two men, and I remember my youth and the feeling that will never come back any more—the feeling that I could last for ever, outlast the sea, the earth, and all men; the deceitful feeling that lures us on to joys, to perils, to love, to vain effort—to death; the triumphant conviction of strength, the heat of life in the handful of dust, the glow in the heart that with every year grows dim, grows cold, grows small, and expires—and expires, too soon, too soon—before life itself.

"And this is how I see the East. I have seen its secret places and have looked into its very soul; but now I see it always from a small boat, a high outline of mountains, blue and afar in the morning; like a faint

mist at noon; a jagged wall of purple at sunset. I have the feel of the
oar in my hand, the vision of a scorching blue sea in my eyes. And I see
a bay, a wide bay, smooth as glass and polished like ice, shimmering in
the dark. A red light burns far off upon the gloom of the land, and the
night is soft and warm. We drag at the oars with aching arms, and suddenly a puff of wind, a puff faint and tepid and laden with strange
odours of blossoms, of aromatic wood, comes out of the still night—
the first sigh of the East on my face. That I can never forget. It was
impalpable and enslaving, like a charm, like a whispered promise of
mysterious delight.

"We had been pulling this finishing spell for eleven hours. Two
pulled, and he whose turn it was to rest sat at the tiller. We had made
out the red light in that bay and steered for it, guessing it must mark
some small coasting port. We passed two vessels, outlandish and high-
sterned, sleeping at anchor, and, approaching the light, now very dim,
ran the boat's nose against the end of a jutting wharf. We were blind
with fatigue. My men dropped the oars and fell off the thwarts as if
dead. I made fast to a pile. A current rippled softly. The scented obscurity of the shore was grouped into vast masses, a density of colossal
clumps of vegetation, probably—mute and fantastic shapes. And at their
foot the semicircle of a beach gleamed faintly, like an illusion. There
was not a light, not a stir, not a sound. The mysterious East faced me,
perfumed like a flower, silent like death, dark like a grave.

"And I sat weary beyond expression, exulting like a conqueror, sleepless and entranced as if before a profound, a fateful enigma.

"A splashing of oars, a measured dip reverberating on the level of
water, intensified by the silence of the shore into loud claps, made me
jump up. A boat, a European boat, was coming in. I invoked the name
of the dead; I hailed: *Judea* ahoy! A thin shout answered.

"It was the captain. I had beaten the flagship by three hours, and I
was glad to hear the old man's voice again, tremulous and tired. 'Is it
you, Marlow?' 'Mind the end of that jetty, sir,' I cried.

"He approached cautiously, and brought up with the deep-sea lead-
line which we had saved—for the underwriters. I eased my painter and
fell alongside. He sat, a broken figure at the stern, wet with dew, his
hands clasped in his lap. His men were asleep already. 'I had a terrible
time of it,' he murmured. 'Mahon is behind—not very far.' We conversed in whispers, in low whispers, as if afraid to wake up the land.
Guns, thunder, earthquakes would not have awakened the men just
then.

"Looking round as we talked, I saw away at sea a bright light travelling in the night. 'There's a steamer passing the bay,' I said. She was not
passing, she was entering, and she even came close and anchored. 'I

wish,' said the old man, 'you would find out whether she is English. Perhaps they could give us a passage somewhere.' He seemed nervously anxious. So by dint of punching and kicking I started one of my men into a state of somnambulism, and giving him an oar, took another and pulled towards the lights of the steamer.

"There was a murmur of voices in her, metallic hollow clangs of the engine-room, footsteps on the deck. Her ports shone, round like dilated eyes. Shapes moved about, and there was a shadowy man high up on the bridge. He heard my oars.

"And then, before I could open my lips, the East spoke to me, but it was in a Western voice. A torrent of words was poured into the enigmatical, the fateful silence; outlandish, angry words, mixed with words and even whole sentences of good English, less strange but even more surprising. The voice swore and cursed violently; it riddled the solemn peace of the bay by a volley of abuse. It began by calling me Pig, and from that went crescendo into unmentionable adjectives—in English. The man up there raged aloud in two languages, and with a sincerity in his fury that almost convinced me I had, in some way, sinned against the harmony of the universe. I could hardly see him, but began to think he would work himself into a fit.

"Suddenly he ceased, and I could hear him snorting and blowing like a porpoise. I said—

" 'What steamer is this, pray?'

" 'Eh? What's this? And who are you?'

" 'Castaway crew of an English barque burnt at sea. We came here to-night. I am the second mate. The captain is in the long-boat, and wishes to know if you would give us a passage somewhere.'

" 'Oh, my goodness! I say. . . . This is the *Celestial* from Singapore on her return trip. I'll arrange with your captain in the morning, . . . and, . . . I say, . . . did you hear me just now?'

" 'I should think the whole bay heard you.'

" 'I thought you were a shore-boat. Now, look here—this infernal lazy scoundrel of a caretaker has gone to sleep again—curse him. The light is out, and I nearly ran foul of the end of this damned jetty. This is the third time he plays me this trick. Now, I ask you, can anybody stand this kind of thing? It's enough to drive a man out of his mind. I'll report him. . . . I'll get the Assistant Resident to give him the sack, by . . . ! See—there's no light. It's out, isn't it? I take you to witness the light's out. There should be a light, you know. A red light on the ——'

" 'There was a light,' I said, mildly.

" 'But it's out, man! What's the use of talking like this? You can see for yourself it's out—don't you? If you had to take a valuable steamer along this God-forsaken coast you would want a light, too. I'll kick him from end to end of his miserable wharf. You'll see if I don't. I will ——'

"'So I may tell my captain you'll take us?' I broke in.

"'Yes, I'll take you. Good-night,' he said, brusquely.

"I pulled back, made fast again to the jetty, and then went to sleep at last. I had faced the silence of the East. I had heard some of its language. But when I opened my eyes again the silence was as complete as though it had never been broken. I was lying in a flood of light, and the sky had never looked so far, so high, before. I opened my eyes and lay without moving.

"And then I saw the men of the East—they were looking at me. The whole length of the jetty was full of people. I saw brown, bronze, yellow faces, the black eyes, the glitter, the colour of an Eastern crowd. And all these beings stared without a murmur, without a sigh, without a movement. They stared down at the boats, at the sleeping men who at night had come to them from the sea. Nothing moved. The fronds of palms stood still against the sky. Not a branch stirred along the shore, and the brown roofs of hidden houses peeped through the green foliage, through the big leaves that hung shining and still like leaves forged of heavy metal. This was the East of the ancient navigators, so old, so mysterious, resplendent and sombre, living and unchanged, full of danger and promise. And these were the men. I sat up suddenly. A wave of movement passed through the crowd from end to end, passed along the heads, swayed the bodies, ran along the jetty like a ripple on the water, like a breath of wind on a field—and all was still again. I see it now—the wide sweep of the bay, the glittering sands, the wealth of green infinite and varied, the sea blue like the sea of a dream, the crowd of attentive faces, the blaze of vivid colour—the water reflecting it all, the curve of the shore, the jetty, the high-sterned outlandish craft floating still, and the three boats with the tired men from the West sleeping, unconscious of the land and the people and of the violence of sunshine. They slept thrown across the thwarts, curled on bottom-boards, in the careless attitudes of death. The head of the old skipper, leaning back in the stern of the long-boat, had fallen on his breast, and he looked as though he would never wake. Farther out old Mahon's face was upturned to the sky, with the long white beard spread out on his breast, as though he had been shot where he sat at the tiller; and a man, all in a heap in the bows of the boat, slept with both arms embracing the stem-head and with his cheek laid on the gunwhale. The East looked at them without a sound.

"I have known its fascination since; I have seen the mysterious shores, the still water, the lands of brown nations, where a stealthy Nemesis lies in wait, pursues, overtakes so many of the conquering race, who are proud of their wisdom, of their knowledge, of their strength. But for me all the East is contained in that vision of my youth. It is all in that moment when I opened my young eyes on it. I came upon it from a tussle with the sea—and I was young—and I saw it looking at me. And this is all that is left of it! Only a moment; a moment of strength, of romance, of glamour—of youth! . . . A flick of sunshine upon a strange shore, the time to remember, the time for a sigh, and—good-bye—Night —Good-bye . . . !"

He drank.

"Ah! The good old time—the good old time. Youth and the sea. Glamour and the sea! The good, strong sea, the salt, bitter sea, that could whisper to you and roar at you and knock your breath out of you."

He drank again.

"By all that's wonderful it is the sea, I believe, the sea itself—or is it youth alone? Who can tell? But you here—you all had something out of life: money, love—whatever one gets on shore—and, tell me, wasn't that the best time, that time when we were young at sea; young and had nothing, on the sea that gives nothing, except hard knocks—and sometimes a chance to feel your strength—that only—what you all regret?"

And we all nodded at him: the man of finance, the man of accounts, the man of law, we all nodded at him over the polished table that like a still sheet of brown water reflected our faces, lined, wrinkled; our faces marked by toil, by deceptions, by success, by love; our weary eyes looking still, looking always, looking anxiously for something out of life, that while it is expected is already gone—has passed unseen, in a sigh, in a flash—together with the youth, with the strength, with the romance of illusions.

26

The Captain of the "Ullswater"

BY MORLEY ROBERTS

THERE were enemies of Captain Amos Brown who said that he was a liar. He certainly had a vivid imagination, or a memory for a more romantic career than falls to the lot of most at sea or ashore.

"By the time we make Callao,[1] Mr. Wardle," said the skipper to his new mate, as they lay in Prince's Dock, Liverpool, "I expect to be able to tell you something of my life, which has been a very remarkable one."

"You don't say so, sir," said Mr. Wardle, who, as it happened, had heard nothing about the skipper, and was innocently prepared to swallow quite a deal. "You don't say so, sir."

"I do say so," replied the skipper. "It has been a most remarkable career from first to last. Wonders happen to me, Mr. Wardle, so that when I am at sea I just know that something will occur that is strange. I have a collection of binoculars, with inscriptions on them for saving lives at sea, that would surprise you. They have been given me by almost every Government of any importance under the sun."

"That must be very gratifyin', sir," said the mate.

"It gets monotonous," said the skipper with a yawn. "At times I wish foreign Governments had more imagination. They never seem to think two pairs of glasses enough for any man. And the silver-mounted sextants I possess are difficult to stow away in my house. If you don't mind the inscription to me on it, I'll give you a sextant presented to me by France, Mr. Wardle, if I can remember to bring it with me from home next time."

Mr. Wardle said he should be delighted to own it, and said, further, that the inscription would naturally give it an added interest. At this the skipper yawned again, and said that he was tired of inscriptions.

[1] The chief port of Peru.

"The next lot I pick up I'll request not to give my name," he said. "My wife, Mr. Wardle, gets tired of keeping a servant specially to polish 'to Captain Brown,' with a lot of complimentary jaw to follow that makes her tired. She knows what I am, Mr. Wardle, and doesn't require to be reminded of it by falling over a gold-mounted sextant every time she turns round. A woman even of a greedy mind can easily get palled with sextants, and a woman sees no particular use in them when they take up room that she wants to devote to heirlooms in her family. Before we get to Callao I'll tell you all about my wife, and how I came to marry her. It is a romantic story. She belongs to a noble family. She is the most beautiful woman that you ever set eyes on. I'll tell you all about it before we get to Callao. I've always been a very attractive man to the other sex, Mr. Wardle. She's rather jealous, too, though she belongs to a noble family. I understand in noble families it isn't good taste to be jealous, but she is. However, I must write to her now, or I shall have a letter from her at Callao that would surprise you, if by that time I know you well enough to show it to you. And now, what were you saying about those three cases marked P. D., and consigned to Manuel Garcia?"

Mr. Wardle told him what he had been saying about the cases marked P. D., and consigned to Manuel Garcia, and it was settled what was to be done with them. The skipper said that he wished they were full of his binoculars and diamond-mounted sextants, and also his gold watches with fulsome inscriptions on them, and that they were consigned to Davy Jones.

"And this is a letter for you, sir," said the mate. The skipper opened it.

"From my wife," he said, and then he swore.

"Another pair of binoculars from the Swedish Government," he groaned. "I shall write and say that I would rather have a suit of clothes, and that if there must be an inscription on them will they put it where it can't be seen. The German Government once did that for me, but they put the inscription in good English on the collar, and I found it very inconvenient, for strangers would come and breathe in my neck while they read it."

Mr. Wardle went away to ask the second mate what he thought of the skipper. He sighed, and the second mate laughed. The second mate was an unbelieving dog and a merry one. When it came six o'clock they had a wash, and put on clean clothes, and went up town together, and had a friendly drink at a well-known public-house which was a great resort for mates and second mates, though a skipper rarely put his nose inside it.

"I wonder what kind of a chap the skipper is, after all," said Humphries the second mate. "It seems to me, sir, that he is a holy terror of a liar, and no mistake."

"Oh, I shouldn't like to say that," replied Wardle. "I do, however, think he exaggerates and puts it on a bit thick. That isn't bein' a liar. I daresay he has saved life at sea. He wouldn't have offered me a silver-mounted sextant if he hadn't several."

"I shall believe you will get it when I see you with it," said Jack Humphries. "In my opinion, Captain Amos Brown is a first-class liar."

Perhaps he spoke a little too loudly for a public place, though that public place was a billiard-room with four second mates playing a four-handed game, and making as much row over it as if they were picking up the bunt of the foresail in a gale of wind. He was overheard by the only old man in the room.

"Did I hear you mention someone called Amos Brown?" asked the old chap sitting next to him.

"I did, sir," said the second mate of the *Ullswater*. "Do you know him?"

"I had an Amos Brown as an apprentice with me when I commanded the *Samuel Plimsoll*," replied the old gentleman, "and he was a very remarkable lad. I think I heard you say that this one was a liar?"

"I did," said Humphries; "though perhaps I shouldn't have done so, as I'm second mate with him now, sir."

The old boy shook his head.

"I won't tell him. But it surely must be the same. The Brown I knew was an awful liar, and I've seen many in my time, gentlemen."

He asked them to drink with him, and they did it willingly. To know the one-time skipper of the old *Samuel Plimsoll* was something worth while, seeing that she had once held the record for a day's run. And if his Brown was theirs it was a chance not to be missed. They took their drinks, and asked him to tell them all about Amos Brown.

"He went overboard in a gale of wind and saved another boy who couldn't swim," said the stranger, "and when we got them back on board, and he could speak, the very first thing he said was that he had seventeen medals from the Royal Humane Society for saving other lives. Does that sound like your man?"

Wardle told him about the binoculars and gold watches and silver-mounted sextants.

"Ah, he's the man," said the old skipper. "Don't you think because he gasses that he hasn't pluck. I'd not be surprised to hear that there is some truth in what he says. I've known one man with four pairs of inscribed binoculars. I daresay Captain Brown has a pair or two. When you see him, tell him that you met Captain Gleeson, who used to com-

~nand the *Samuel Plimsoll*. And as I'm goin' now, I don't mind owning
that I'm the man that has the four pairs of binoculars, gentlemen."

He bade them good-night, and Humphries said when he had gone
that he was probably as big a liar as the skipper, and had never seen
the *Samuel Plimsoll*.

"And as for Brown bein' a hero," added the second mate, "I simply
don't believe it. A liar can't be brave."

This was a large and youthful saying, and Wardle, who was not so
young as his subordinate, had his doubts of it.

"I rather think the captain is all right," he said. "I'll ask him to-
morrow if he was ever in the *Samuel Plimsoll*."

They were at sea before he got a chance to do so.

"The *Samuel Plimsoll*? well, I should say so!" said the skipper. "And
you actually met dear old Gleeson! Why, Mr. Wardle, he was the man
that set me on makin' this collection of inscribed articles. Bar myself
he is the one man in the whole merchant service with more than he
can do with. His native town has a department in its museum especially
devoted to what he has given them in that way. His wife refused to give
them house-room, and I don't blame her. I saved most of the crew in
that dear old hooker at one time or another, went overboard after them
in gales of wind. They got to rely on me and grew very careless. I often
told them that I wouldn't go after any more, but when you see a poor
chap drownin' it is difficult to stay in the dry and let him."

"Ah," said Wardle, "he did speak about your savin' one."

The skipper cast a quick look at him, and then laughed.

"One, indeed," he said contemptuously. "Why, I saved the whole of
the mate's watch, the mate included; and on three other occasions I
was hauled out of my bunk to go after one of the starboard watch. The
only thing I have against old Gleeson is that he was jealous when he
saw I was likely to knock his collection of medals and binoculars into
a cocked hat. One, indeed! I've saved seventy men, boys, and women,
by goin' in after 'em myself; and somethin' like forty-five crews by
skilful seamanship in the face of unparalleled difficulties. I wish I could
have a talk with Gleeson."

"He said you were one of the bravest lads he ever met, sir," said
Wardle.

The skipper's face softened.

"Did he now? Well, that was nice of him, but I think he might have
told you about more than one I saved."

"And he said he had only four pairs of binoculars given him by foreign Governments," added Wardle.

"That is his false modesty," said Captain Brown. "He has an idea that if he told the truth he would not be believed. I don't care who doesn't believe me, Mr. Wardle. If surprisin' things occur to a man why should he not relate them? There's my wife, for instance, one of the nobility, a knight's daughter! I know men that wouldn't mention it for fear of not bein' believed they had married so far above them. She is the most beautiful woman in the three kingdoms, to say nothin' of Europe. I know men that it would seem like braggin' to say that, but when you get to know me, and know that speakin' the truth isn't out of gear with my natural modesty, you will see why I mention it so freely."

In the course of the next few days Captain Amos Brown mentioned a good many things freely that redounded to the credit of himself and his family, and he did it so nicely, with such an engaging air of innocent and delightful candour, that poor Wardle did not know whether he was shipmates with the most wonderful man on earth or the most magnificent liar.

"I don't know where I am," he confided in his junior.

"I know where *I* am," said the graceless second greaser. "I am with a skipper with as much jaw as a sheep's head, and if he said it was raining I should take off my oilskins. He's the biggest braggart and liar I ever met, sir."

"I cannot listen to you sayin' such things," said the mate.

"I beg your pardon for doin' so," replied Humphries, "but the 'old man' is a scorcher, and I can't help seein' it."

To a less prejudiced observer it must have been obvious that there were many fine qualities in Captain Amos Brown. He inspected the cooking of the men's food at intervals, which annoyed the cook and kept him up to his work. When he went his rounds he saw that things were shipshape even in the deck-house. The men for'ard said he might be a notorious liar, as they heard from the steward, but they said he looked like a man and a seaman. Mr. Wardle found him as smart a navigator as he had ever sailed with, and before long was learning mathematics from him.

"No officer need be shamed of takin' a wrinkle from me, Mr. Wardle," said the skipper, after giving him a lesson in star observations that made the mate sit up. "The Astronomer Royal himself owned to me that I could give him pounds and a beating at a great deal of mathematics. I love it, there is something so fine and free about it. I go sailin' over the sea of the calculus with both sheets aft. He is goin' to publish some observations of mine about the imperfections of the sextant. They were brought to my notice by my series of silver-mounted ones. I'm inventin' a new one compensated for all different temperatures."

And yet it was quite true that, as far as Wardle went with him, a better and clearer-headed teacher could not be found.

"I shall end in believing every word he says," thought the mate.

And if the mate found him his master in navigation, Humphries found that there wasn't a trick of practical seamanship that wasn't at his finger-ends, from cutting out a jib to a double Matthew Walker on a four-stranded rope, which the skipper could almost do with his eyes shut.

"Everything is all the same to me, Mr. Humphries," said the skipper calmly. "I'm a born pilot, and I can handle every rig as easy as if I'd been born in 'em. I can sail a scow or a schooner, and every kind of sailing-boat from a catamaran to an Arab dhow. And at steam I'm just as good."

Humphries did not believe a word of it, and used to read up old-fashioned seamanship in order to pose him. He never did, and the most out-of-date sea-riddle was to the skipper as easy as slinging a nun buoy.

"He beats me, I own," said the second mate. "He's the best at all-round sailorizin' that I ever sailed with."

The men for'ard said the same. And the bo'son, who was a very crusty beast from Newcastle, was of opinion that what the "old man" did not know about ships was not worth knowing.

"I'm goin' to believe 'im hif so be e's bin to the moon," said one cockney. "But for hall we knows the 'old man' may not show hup and shine as 'e does now w'en it's 'ard weather. I was ship-met wiv a skipper once that was wonderful gassy so lon's it was topmast stuns'l weather, but when it blew a gale 'e crawled into 'is bunk like a sick stooard, and there 'e stayed till the sun shone."

They soon had a chance of seeing whether the skipper was a fair-weather sailor or not. They had taken an almighty time to get to the south'ard of the Bay of Biscay, for it had been almost as calm as a pond all the way from the Tuscar. Now the barometer began to fall in a steady, business-like way that looked as if it meant work, while a heavy swell came rolling up from the south. The dawn next morning was what ladies would have called beautiful, for it was full of wonderful colour, and reached in a strange glory right to the zenith. It afforded no joy, artistic or otherwise, to anyone on board the *Ullswater,* as she rolled in the swell with too little wind to steady her. The watch below came out before breakfast, and looked at the scarlet and gold uneasily. There was a tremendously dark cloud on the horizon, and the high dawn above it was alone a threat of wind. The clouds, that were lighted by the hidden sun, were hard and oily; they had no loose edges, the colour was brilliant but opaque. To anyone who could read the book of the sky the signs were as easy as the south cone. They meant "very

heavy weather from the south and west." The skipper looked a deal
more happy than he had done before. His eyes were clear and bright;
there was a ring in his voice which encouraged everybody; he walked
the poop rubbing his hands as if he was enjoying himself, as he undoubtedly was. He shortened the *Ullswater* down in good time, but
set his three t'gallan's'ls over the reefed topsails, and hung on to them
until squalls began to come out of the south which threatened to save
all trouble of furling them. By noon the sun was out of sight under a
heavy grey pall, and the sea got up rapidly as the wind veered into the
west of south. An hour later it was blowing enough to make it hard
to hear anyone speak, and he roared the most dreadful and awe-inspiring lies into the ear of his mate.

"This is going to be quite a breeze, Mr. Wardle," he shouted joyously, "but I don't think the weather nowadays is ever what it was
when I was young. I've been hove to in the Bay for three weeks at a
time. And once we were on our beam ends for a fortnight, and all we
ate all that time was one biscuit each. I was so thin at the finish that I
had to carry weights in my pocket to keep myself from bein' blown
overboard. Oh, this is nothin'! We can hang on to this till the wind is
sou'-west, and then maybe we'll heave to."

By the middle of the afternoon watch the *Ullswater* was hanging on
to a gale on the port-tack with her main-hatch awash, and the crowd
for'ard had come to the conclusion that for carrying sail the "old man"
beat any American Scotchman they had ever heard of. When he at
last condescended to heave her to, all hands, after wearing her, had a
job with the fore and mizzen-topsails that almost knocked the stuffing
out of them, as they phrased it. The skipper, however, told them that
they had done very well, and told the steward to serve out grog. As
the owners of the *Ullswater* were teetotallers, and about as economical
as owners are made, this grog was at the skipper's own expense. When
they had got it down, the entire crowd said that they would believe
anything the skipper said henceforth. They went for'ard and enjoyed
themselves, while the old hooker lay to with a grummet on her wheel,
and the great south-wester howled across the Bay. If the main-topsail
hadn't been as strong as the grog and the skipper's yarns, it would
have been blown out of the bolt-ropes before dark, for the way the
wind blew then made the "old man" own at supper-time that it re-
reminded him of the days of his youth.

"But you never will catch me heavin' to under anythin' so measly as
a tarpaulin' in the rigging," said Captain Amos Brown, with his mouth
full of beef and his leg round the leg of the table, as the *Ullswater*
climbed the rising seas and dived again like a swooping frigate-bird.
"I like to have my ship under some kind of command however it blows.

One can never tell, Mr. Humphries, when one may need to make sail to save some of our fellow-creatures. As yet neither of you two gentlemen have got as much as the cheapest pair of binoculars out of our own Board of Trade or a foreign Government. With me you'll have your chance to go home to your girl and chuck somethin' of that sort into her lap, and make her cry with joy. I saved my own wife, who is the most beautiful woman in the world, and weighs eleven stone, and has for years, and I got a sextant and a nobleman's daughter at one fell swoop. Oh, I've been a lucky man."

"How did you save your wife, sir?" asked Humphries, who was almost beginning to believe what the skipper said.

"You may well ask, and I can't tell," replied the skipper proudly. "I hardly remember how it was, for when I get excited I do things which kind friends of mine say are heroic, and I can't remember 'em. But so far as I can recall it, I swam near a mile in a sea like this, and took command of a dismasted barque with most of the crew disabled through havin' their left legs broke, a most remarkable fact. There wasn't a sound left leg in the whole crowd except my wife's, and the only thing out of order was that the captain's left leg was broke in two places. I took charge of her, and put splints on their legs, and we were picked up by a tug from Queenstown and towed in there, and the doctors all said I was the neatest hand with splints they had ever seen. And I married my wife then and there with a special licence, and I've never regretted it from that day to this. By Jove, though, doesn't it blow!"

How the "nobleman's" daughter came to be on board the dismasted barque he did not explain, and he shortly afterwards turned in, leaving orders to be called if it blew much harder.

"And when I say much harder, Mr. Wardle, I mean much harder. Please don't disturb me for a potty squall."

As a result of these orders he was not called till the early dawn, when it was blowing nearly hard enough to unship the main capstan. Even then Wardle would not have ventured to rouse him if he had not fancied that he saw some dismasted vessel far to leeward in the mirk and smother of the storm.

"I think I saw a vessel just now down to loo'ard," screamed the mate as the skipper made a bolt for him under the weather cloth on the mizzen rigging. "Dismasted I think, sir."

He saw the "old man's" eye brighten and snap.

"Where did you say?" he roared; and before he could hear they had to wait till a singing squall went over.

"To loo'ard," said the mate again; and the next moment the skipper saw what he looked for.

"Not dismasted, on her beam ends," he shouted. And in a few more minutes, as the grey dawn poured across the waste of howling seas, Wardle saw that the "old man" was right.

"Poor devils," he said, "it's all over with them."

The word that there was a vessel in difficulties soon brought out the watch on deck, who were taking shelter in the deckhouse. As it was close on four o'clock the watch below soon joined them, and presently Humphries came up on the poop.

"Ah!" said the second mate, "they are done for, poor chaps."

This the skipper heard, and he turned round sharply and roared, "What, with me here? Oh, not much!"

He turned to Wardle.

"Here's your chance for a pair of inscribed binoculars," he said. "I believe she's French, and the French Government have generous minds in the way of fittings and inscriptions, Mr. Wardle."

"But in this sea, sir?" stammered the mate. "Why, a boat couldn't live in it for a second, even if we launched one safe, sir."

"I've launched boats in seas to which this was a mere calm," said the skipper ardently. "And if I can't get you or Humphries to go I shall go myself."

"You don't mean it, sir," said the mate; and then the skipper swore many powerful oaths that he did mean it.

"In the meantime we're drifting down to her," said Captain Brown, "for she is light and high out of the water and we are as deep as we can be."

It soon got all over the ship that the "old man" meant to attempt a rescue of those in distress, and there was a furious argument for'ard as to whether it could be done, and whether any captain was justified in asking his crew to man a boat in such a sea. The unanimous opinion of all the older men was that it couldn't be done. The equally unanimous opinion of all the younger ones was that if the skipper said it could be done he would go in the first boat himself rather than be beaten.

"Well, it will be a case for volunteers," said one old fo'c'sle man, "and when I volunteer to drown my wife's husband I'll let all you chaps know."

And that was very much the opinion of Wardle, who was a married man too. As for Humphries, he was naturally reckless, and was now ready to do almost anything the skipper asked.

"He may be a liar," said the second mate, "but I think he's all right, and I like him."

Now it was broad daylight, and the vessel was within a mile of them. Sometimes she was quite hidden, and sometimes she was flung up high on the crest of a wave. Heavy green seas broke over her as she lay with her starboard yardarms dipping. She had been running under a heavy press of canvas when she broached to, and went over on her beam ends, for even yet the sheets of the upper main-topsail were out to the lower yardarm, and though the starboard half of the sail had blown out of the bolt ropes the upper or port yardarm still was sound and as tight as a drum with the wind.

"If she hasn't sunk yet she'll swim a while longer," said the skipper of the *Ullswater,* as the day grew lighter and lighter still. "Show the British ensign, Mr. Humphries, and cheer them up if they're alive. I wish I could tell them that I am here. I'll bet they know me. I'm famous with the French from Dunkirk to Toulon. At Marseilles they call me Mounseer Binoculaire, and stand in rows to see me pass."

The lies that he told now no one had any ears for. Wardle owned afterwards that he was afraid that the "old man" would ask him to go in command of a boat, and, like the old fo'c'sle man, he was thinking a good deal of his wife's husband. But all the while Captain Amos Brown was telling whackers that would have done credit to Baron Munchausen, he was really thinking of how he was to save those whose passage to a port not named in any bills of lading looked almost certain. By this time the foreigner was not far to leeward of them.

"No one could blame us if he let 'em go," shrieked the "old man" in his mate's ear as the wind lulled for one brief moment. "But I never think of what other men would do, Mr. Wardle. I remember once in a cyclone in the Formosa Channel——"

What dreadful deed of inspired heroism he had performed in a cyclone in the Formosa Channel Wardle never knew, for the wind cut the words from the skipper's lips, and sent them in a howling shower of spray far to loo'ard. But his last words became audible.

"I was insensible for the best part of a month after it," screamed Amos Brown. "The usual . . . silver-mounted . . . sickened . . . wife as I said."

Then he caught the mate by the arm.

"We'll stand by 'em, Mr. Wardle. If I get another sextant, as I suspect, I must put up with it. Get the lifeboat ready, Mr. Wardle, and get all the empty small casks and oil-drums that you can and lash them under the thwarts fore and aft. Make her so that she can't sink and I'll go in her myself."

"That's my job, sir," he said shortly, for he forgot all about his wife's husband at that moment.

"I know it," said the skipper, "but with your permission I'll take it on myself, as I've had so much experience in this sort of thing and you've had none. And I tell you you'll have to handle the *Ullswater* so as to pick us up as we go to loo'ard, and it will be a job for a seaman and no fatal error."

The mate swore softly and went away and did as he was told. The men hung back a little when he told them to get the boat ready for launching, though they followed him when they saw him begin to cast off the gear by which she was made fast. But the old fo'c'sle man had something to say.

"The captain ain't goin' to put a boat over the side in a sea like this, is he, sir?"

Wardle snorted.

"You had better ask him," he replied savagely, and then there was no more talk. He went back to the poop and reported that the boat was ready. He also reported that the men were very unlikely to volunteer.

"They'll volunteer fast enough when they know I'm goin' to ask nothin' of them that I don't ask of myself," said the captain. "I really think the wind is takin' off a little, Mr. Wardle."

Perhaps it was, but if so the sea was a trifle worse. But it seemed to the skipper and the two mates that the French vessel was lower in the water than she had been. She was getting a pounding that nothing built by human hands could stand for long.

"There's not much time to lose," said the skipper.

Captain Amos Brown apparently knew his business, and knew it, as far as boats were concerned, in a way to make half the merchant skippers at sea blush for their ignorance of one of the finest points of seamanship. The skipper had the crew aft under the break of the poop, and came down to them himself. They huddled in the space between the two poop-ladders and looked very uneasy.

"Do any of you volunteer to try and save those poor fellows to loo-ard of us?" asked the "old man." And no one said a word. They looked at the sea and at each other with shifty eyes, but not at him.

"Why, sir, 'tis our opinion that no boat can't live in this sea," said the bo'son.

"I think it can," said the captain, "and I'm goin' to try. Do any of you volunteer to come with your captain? I ask no man to do what I won't do myself."

There was something very fine about the liar of the *Ullswater* as he spoke, and everyone knew that now at least he was telling no lies.

"I'm wiv you, sir," said a young cockney, who was the foulest mouthed young ruffian in the ship, and had been talked to very severely by his mates on that very point. It is not good form for a youngster to use worse language than his elders at sea. Some of the others looked at him angrily, as if they felt that they had to go now. A redheaded Irishman followed the cockney, just as he had followed him into horrid dens down by Tiger Bay.[1]

[1] An unsavoury quarter of Cardiff.

"I'm with ye, too, sorr," said Mike.

"I'm only askin' for six," said the skipper. Then the old fo'c'sle man, who had been so anxious about his wife's husband, hooked a black quid out of his black teeth and threw it overboard.

"I'll come, sir."

But now all the other young men spoke together. The skipper had his choice, and he took the unmarried ones.

He gave his orders now to the mate without a touch of braggadocio. "We'll run her off before the wind, Mr. Wardle, and then quarter the sea and lower away on the lee quarter. See that there is a man on the weather quarter with oil, so as to give us all the smooth you can. When we are afloat give us your lee to work in all you can, and hang her up in the wind to windward of the wreck all you know. While you are there don't spare oil; let it come down to her and us. It is possible that we may not be able to get a line to the wreck, but we'll go under her stern and try. With all her yards and gear in the sea it won't be possible to get right in her lee, so we may have to call to them to jump. My reckonin' is that we may pick up some that way before we get too far to loo'ard. When we get down close to her, fire the signal-gun to rouse them up to try and help us. When you see us well to loo'ard of the wreck, put your helm up, and run down and give us your lee again. If we miss her and have to try again, we must beat to windward once more. But that's anticipatin', ain't it? You can put your helm up now, Mr. Wardle. Shake hands."

And they shook hands. Then the skipper and his men took to the boat, which was ready to lower in patent gear, with Humphries in charge of it, and the *Ullswater* went off before the wind. Then at a nod from the captain she came up a little, till she quartered the sea with very little way on her.

"Now, Mr. Humphries," said the skipper. In ten seconds they hit the water fair and the hooks disengaged. The oil that was being poured over on the weather quarter helped them for a moment, and even when they got beyond its immediate influence they kept some of the lee of the ship. They drifted down upon the wreck, and rode the seas by pulling ahead or giving her sternway till they were within half a cable's length of the doomed vessel. At that moment they fired the signal-gun on board the *Ullswater,* and they saw some of the poor chaps to loo'ard of them show their heads above the rail. Then the full sweep of the storm struck them. But the liar of the *Ullswater,* who had saved more crews in worse circumstances than he could count, actually whistled as he sat in the stern-sheets with a steering oar in his hands.

To handle a boat in a heavy sea, with the wind blowing a real gale, is a thing that mighty few deepwater seamen are good at. But the skip-

per of the *Ullswater* knew his business even then as if he had been a
Deal puntman, a North Sea trawler, or a Grand Bank fisherman all his
life. The boat in which he made his desperate and humane venture was
double-ended like a whale-boat, and she rode the seas for the most part
like a cork. In such a situation the great thing is to avoid a sea breaking
inboard, and sometimes they pulled ahead, and sometimes backed
astern, so that when a heavy sea did break it did so to windward or to
loo'ard of them. And yet a hundred times in the dreadful full minutes
that it took them to get down to the wreck there were moments when
those in the boat and those in the *Ullswater* thought that it was all over
with them. Once a sea that no one could have avoided broke over
them, and it was desperate work to bale her out. And the roar of the
wind deafened them; the seas raced and hissed; they pulled or backed
water with their teeth clenched. Some of them thought of nothing;
others were sorry they had volunteered, and looked at the captain furiously while he whistled through his clenched teeth. One cockney swore
at him horribly in a thin piping scream, and called him horrid names.
For this is the strange nature of man. But he pulled as well as the others,
and the skipper smiled at him as his blasphemies cut the wind. For the
skipper saw a head over the rail of the wreck, and he knew that there
was work to be done and that he was doing it, and that the brave fool
that cursed him was a man and was doing his best. The words he spoke
were such as come out of a desperate mind, and out of a man that can
do things. They towed an oil-bag to windward, but there was no oil
to calm the movements of the soul at such a time.

"Oh, damn you, pull!" said Amos Brown. He ceased to whistle, and
cursed with a sudden and tremendous frenzy that was appalling. The
cursing cockney looked up at him with open mouth.

By the "old man's" side in the stern-sheets there was a coil of rope
attached to a little grapnel. If the men still alive on board the French
barque were capable of motion they might be able to make a rope fast,
but after hours of such a storm, while they were lashed under the
weather bulwarks, it was possible that they were almost numb and helpless. Now the boat came sweeping down by the stern of the barque;
they saw her smashed rudder beating to and fro, and heard the batter-
ing-ram of the south-west seas strike on her weather side.

"Back-water!" roared the skipper, for astern of them a big sea roared,
and began to lift a dreadful lip. They held the boat, and the "old man"
kept it straight on the roaring crest, and at that moment they were lifted
high, and saw beyond the hull of the barque the white waste of driven
seas. Then they went down, down, down; and when they were flung
up again the skipper screamed to those on board, and as he screamed
he threw the grapnel at the gear of the spanker, and as they surged past

her stern the hooks caught in the bight of her loosened vangs. For all her gear was in a coil and tangle, and the topping lifts of the gaff had parted. The men backed water hard, and the boat hung half in the lee of the wreck, but dangerously near the wreck of the mizzen-topmast, which had gone at the cap and swayed in the swash of the seas. Now they saw the seamen whom they had come to save, and no man of the boat's crew could hereafter agree as to what happened or the order of events. The skipper called to the poor wretches, and one cut himself adrift and slid down the sloping deck and struck the lower rail with horrible force. They heard him squeal, and then a sea washed him over to them. He was insensible, and that was lucky, for his leg was broken. Then they made out that one of the survivors was the captain, and they saw that he was speaking, though they heard nothing. There were, it seemed, no more than ten of the crew left, for they counted ten with the one man that they had. But it seemed that they moved slow, and the sea was worse than ever. It boiled over the weather-rail and then came over green, and all the men in the boat yelled filthy oaths at the poor numb wretches, and called them horrible names. The Irishman prayed aloud to heaven and to all the saints and to the Virgin, and then cursed so awfully that the others fell into silence.

"Jump, jump!" screamed the skipper, and another man slid down the deck and came overboard for them. He went under and got his head cut open on a swaying block, and knew nothing of it till he was dragged on board. Then he wiped the blood from his eyes and fell to weeping, whereon the swearing cockney, who had been oddly silent since his eyes had met the skipper's, cuffed him hard on the side of the head, and said, " 'Old your row, you bleedin' 'owler!" And then three of his mates laughed as they watched their boat and fended it off the wreck of the mizzen-mast with deadly and preoccupied energy. The cockney took out a foul handkerchief and dabbed it on the bleeding man's head, and then threw the rag at him with an oath, saying that a little blood was nothing, and that he was a blasted Dago, and, further, he'd feel sorry for him when he was on board the *Ullswater*. Then another man jumped and was swept under and past them, and just as he was going the skipper reached over and, grabbing him by the hair, got him on board in a state of unconsciousness. Then three of the poor fellows jumped at once, two being saved and the third never showing above the water again.

"As well now as wiv the rest of hus," said the cockney, who had given the Dago his "wipe," and he snivelled a little. "Hif I gets hout of this I'm for stayin' in Rovver'ive all the rest of my life."

Then they got another, and there were only the French skipper and one more man left. It was probably his mate, but he had a broken arm and moved slow. The French captain got a rope round him and slid him down to loo'ard. But when he was halfway down the old chap (he was at anyrate white-haired) lost his own hold, and came down into the swash of the lee scuppers with a run. He fell overboard, and the Irishman got him by the collar. He was lugged on board with difficulty, and lay down on the bottom boards absolutely done for. The other man didn't show up, and the men said that he must be dead. They began talking all at once, and the skipper, who was now up at the bows of the boat, turned suddenly and cuffed the Irishman hard, whereupon Mike drew his sheath-knife, saying in a squeal, "You swine, I'll kill you!" But the bo'son struck him with the loom of his oar under the jaw, and nearly broke it. He snatched his knife from him and threw it overboard.

Now they saw the *Ullswater* right to windward of the sinking barque, and some oil that they poured into the sea came down to them, so that the hiss of the sea was so much less that it seemed as if silence fell on them. They heard the Irishman say with difficulty as he held his jaw:

"All right, my puggy, I'll have your blood."

He had lost his oar, and the other men were wild with him. What they might have said no one knows, but the skipper turned to them, saying that he would go on board after the last man. They all said at once that he shouldn't. They gave him orders not to do it, and their eyes were wild and fierce, for they were strained and tired, and fear got hold of them, making them feel chilly in the fierce wind. They clung to the captain in their minds. If he did not come back they would never be saved, for now the boat was heavily laden. They opened their mouths and said, "Oh please, sir," and then he jumped overboard and went hand over hand along the grapnel line and the tangle of the vangs. They groaned, and the Irishman wagged his head savagely, though no one knew what he meant, least of all himself. They saw the "old man" clamber on board as a big sea broke over her, and they lost sight of him in the smother of it. They sat in the heaving boat as if they were turned into stone, and then the Irishman saw something in the sea and grabbed for it. He hauled hard, and they cried out that the skipper mustn't try it again. But as the drowning man came to the surface they saw that it was not the skipper after all, but the French mate, and they said, "Oh, hell!" being of half a mind to let him go. But the bo'son screamed out something, and they hung on to a dead man's legs, for to the dead man's hands the skipper was clinging. They got him on board not quite insensible, and the Irishman fell to weeping over him.

"Oh, it's the brave bhoy you are," he said; and then the skipper came to and vomited some water.

"Hold on, what are you doin'?" he asked, as he saw the two cockneys trying to heave the dead man back in the sea. They said that he was dead. The bo'son said that the deader had only half a head, and couldn't be alive in that condition. So they let the body go, and the skipper woke right up and was a man again. They hauled up to the grapnel or near it, for they were strained enough to do foolish things. Then they saw it was silly and cut the line. They drifted to loo'ard fast, and got out into the full force of the gale, which howled horribly. They saw the *Ullswater* lying to under her sturdy old maintopsail, and as soon as they saw her they were seen by the second mate, who was up aloft with his coat half torn off him. To get her off before the wind quick they showed the head of the foretopmast-staysail, which was promptly blown out of the bolt-ropes with a report they heard in the boat like the dull sound of a far-off gun. She squared away and came to the nor'-east, and presently was to windward of them, and in her lee they felt very warm and almost safe, though they went up to the sky like a lark and then down as if into a grave. And then they saw their shipmates' faces, and the skipper laughed oddly. The strain had told on him, as it had on all of them, not least perhaps on some of those who had not faced the greater risks. And it seemed to the skipper that there was something very absurd in Wardle's whiskers as the wind caught them and wrapped them in a kind of hairy smear across one weather-beaten cheek. All those in the boat were now quite calm; the excitement was on board the *Ullswater,* and when the gale let them catch a word of what the mate said, as he stood on the rail with his arm about a backstay, they caught the quality of strain.

"Ould Wardle is as fidgety as a fool," said Mike the Irishman, as he still held on to his jaw. "He'll be givin' someone the oncivil word for knockin' the oar out o' me hand."

He sat with one hand to his face, with the other, as he had turned round, he helped the bo'son.

"What about your pullin' your knife on the captain?" asked the bo'son.

Then Micky shook his head.

"Did I now? And he struck me, and he's a brave lad," he said simply. But the hook of the davit tackle dangled overhead as they were flung skyward on a sea. There were davit ropes fitted, and one slapped the Irishman across the face.

"It's in the wars I am," he said; and then there was a wind flurry that bore the *Ullswater* almost over on them. The way was nearly off her, and in another minute she would be drifting and coming down on them.

"Now!" screamed the skipper, and they hooked on and were hauled out and up.

"Holy mother," said Mike, "and I'm not drowned this trip!"

The boat was hauled on board, and when the skipper's foot touched the deck he reeled. Humphries caught him.

"Oh, steady, sir," said Humphries, as Mike came up to them.

The captain stared at him, for he did not remember striking him.

"It's the brrave man you are," said Mike simply; "and you're the firrst man that I've tuk a blow from since I was the length of my arm. Oh, bhoys, it's the brrave man the skipper is."

The second mate pushed him away, and he went like a child and lent a hand to help the poor "divils of Dagoes," as he called those who had been saved. The mate came and shook hands with the captain. The tears ran down Wardle's hairy face, and he could not speak.

"I shall have another pair of binoculars over this," said Captain Amos Brown with quivering lips.

"You are a hero," bawled the mate as the wind roared again in a blinding squall with rain in it. The skipper flushed.

"Oh, it's nothin', this," he said. "Now in the Bay of Bengal——"

The wind took that story to loo'ard, and no one heard it. But they heard him wind up with "gold-mounted binoculars."

A year later he got a pair from the great French Republic. They were the first he ever got.

27

The Adventure of the Speckled Band

BY A. CONAN DOYLE

IN glancing over my notes of the seventy-odd cases in which I have during the last eight years studied the methods of my friend Sherlock Holmes, I find many tragic, some comic, a large number merely strange, but none commonplace; for, working as he did rather for the love of his art than for the acquirement of wealth, he refused to associate himself with any investigation which did not tend toward the unusual, and even the fantastic. Of all these varied cases, however, I cannot recall any which presented more singular features than that which was associated with the well-known Surrey family of the Roylotts of Stoke Moran. The events in question occurred in the early days of my association with Holmes, when we were sharing rooms as bachelors in Baker Street. It is possible that I might have placed them upon record before, but a promise of secrecy was made at the time, from which I have only been freed during the last month by the untimely death of the lady to whom the pledge was given. It is perhaps as well that the facts should now come to light, for I have reasons to know that there are wide-spread rumors as to the death of Dr. Grimesby Roylott which tend to make the matter even more terrible than the truth.

It was early in April in the year '83 that I woke one morning to find Sherlock Holmes standing, fully dressed, by the side of my bed. He was a late riser as a rule, and as the clock on the mantel-piece showed me that it was only a quarter past seven, I blinked up at him in some surprise, and perhaps just a little resentment, for I was myself regular in my habits.

"Very sorry to knock you up, Watson," said he, "but it's the common lot this morning. Mrs. Hudson has been knocked up, she retorted upon me, and I on you."

"What is it, then—a fire?"

"No; a client. It seems that a young lady has arrived in a considerable state of excitement, who insists upon seeing me. She is waiting now in the sitting-room. Now, when young ladies wander about the metropolis at this hour of the morning, and knock sleepy people up out of their beds, I presume that it is something very pressing which they have to communicate. Should it prove to be an interesting case, you would, I am sure, wish to follow it from the outset. I thought, at any rate, that I should call you and give you the chance."

"My dear fellow, I would not miss it for anything."

I had no keener pleasure than in following Holmes in his professional investigations, and in admiring the rapid deductions, as swift as intuitions, and yet always founded on a logical basis, with which he unravelled the problems which were submitted to him. I rapidly threw on my clothes, and was ready in a few minutes to accompany my friend down to the sitting-room. A lady dressed in black and heavily veiled, who had been sitting in the window, rose as we entered.

"Good-morning, madam," said Holmes, cheerily. "My name is Sherlock Holmes. This is my intimate friend and associate, Dr. Watson, before whom you can speak as freely as before myself. Ha! I am glad to see that Mrs. Hudson has had the good sense to light the fire. Pray draw up to it, and I shall order you a cup of hot coffee, for I observe that you are shivering."

"It is not cold which makes me shiver," said the woman, in a low voice, changing her seat as requested.

"What, then?"

"It is fear, Mr. Holmes. It is terror." She raised her veil as she spoke, and we could see that she was indeed in a pitiable state of agitation, her face all drawn and gray, with restless, frightened eyes, like those of some hunted animal. Her features and figure were those of a woman of thirty, but her hair was shot with premature gray, and her expression was weary and haggard. Sherlock Holmes ran her over with one of his quick, all-comprehensive glances.

"You must not fear," said he, soothingly, bending forward and patting her forearm. "We shall soon set matters right, I have no doubt. You have come in by train this morning, I see."

"You know me, then?"

"No, but I observe the second half of a return ticket in the palm of your left glove. You must have started early, and yet you had a good drive in a dog-cart, along heavy roads, before you reached the station."

The lady gave a violent start, and stared in bewilderment at my companion.

"There is no mystery, my dear madam," said he, smiling. "The left arm of your jacket is spattered with mud in no less than seven places. The marks are perfectly fresh. There is no vehicle save a dog-cart which throws up mud in that way, and then only when you sit on the left-hand side of the driver."

"Whatever your reasons may be, you are perfectly correct," said she. "I started from home before six, reached Leatherhead at twenty past, and came in by the first train to Waterloo. Sir, I can stand this strain no longer; I shall go mad if it continues. I have no one to turn to—none, save only one, who cares for me, and he, poor fellow, can be of little aid. I have heard of you, Mr. Holmes; I have heard of you from Mrs. Farintosh, whom you helped in the hour of her sore need. It was from her that I had your address. Oh, sir, do you not think that you could help me, too, and at least throw a little light through the dense darkness which surrounds me? At present it is out of my power to reward you for your services, but in a month or six weeks I shall be married, with the control of my own income, and then at least you shall not find me ungrateful."

Holmes turned to his desk, and unlocking it, drew out a small case-book, which he consulted.

"Farintosh," said he. "Ah yes, I recall the case; it was concerned with an opal tiara. I think it was before your time, Watson. I can only say, madam, that I shall be happy to devote the same care to your case as I did to that of your friend. As to reward, my profession is its own reward; but you are at liberty to defray whatever expenses I may be put to, at the time which suits you best. And now I beg that you will lay before us everything that may help us in forming an opinion upon the matter."

"Alas!" replied our visitor, "the very horror of my situation lies in the fact that my fears are so vague, and my suspicions depend so entirely upon small points, which might seem trivial to another, that even he to whom of all others I have a right to look for help and advice looks upon all that I tell him about it as the fancies of a nervous woman. He does not say so, but I can read it from his soothing answers and averted eyes. But I have heard, Mr. Holmes, that you can see deeply into the manifold wickedness of the human heart. You may advise me how to walk amid the dangers which encompass me."

"I am all attention, madam."

"My name is Helen Stoner, and I am living with my step-father, who is the last survivor of one of the oldest Saxon families in England, the Roylotts of Stoke Moran, on the western border of Surrey."

Holmes nodded his head. "The name is familiar to me," said he.

"The family was at one time among the richest in England, and the estates extended over the borders into Berkshire in the north and Hampshire in the west. In the last century, however, four successive heirs were of a dissolute and wasteful disposition, and the family ruin was eventually completed by a gambler in the days of the Regency. Nothing was left save a few acres of ground, and the two-hundred-year-old house, which is itself crushed under a heavy mortgage. The last squire dragged out his existence there, living the horrible life of an aristocratic pauper; but his only son, my step-father, seeing that he must adapt himself to the new conditions, obtained an advance from a relative, which enabled him to take a medical degree, and went out to Calcutta, where, by his professional skill and his force of character, he established a large practice. In a fit of anger, however, caused by some robberies which had been perpetrated in the house, he beat his native butler to death, and narrowly escaped a capital sentence. As it was, he suffered a long term of imprisonment, and afterward returned to England a morose and disappointed man.

"When Dr. Roylott was in India he married my mother, Mrs. Stoner, the young widow of Major-General Stoner, of the Bengal Artillery. My sister Julia and I were twins, and we were only two years old at the time of my mother's remarriage. She had a considerable sum of money —not less than £1000 a year—and this she bequeathed to Dr. Roylott entirely while we resided with him, with a provision that a certain annual sum should be allowed to each of us in the event of our marriage. Shortly after our return to England my mother died—she was killed eight years ago in a railway accident near Crewe. Dr. Roylott then abandoned his attempts to establish himself in practice in London, and took us to live with him in the old ancestral house at Stoke Moran. The money which my mother had left was enough for all our wants, and there seemed to be no obstacle to our happiness.

"But a terrible change came over our step-father about this time. Instead of making friends and exchanging visits with our neighbors, who had at first been overjoyed to see a Roylott of Stoke Moran back in the old family seat, he shut himself up in his house, and seldom came out save to indulge in ferocious quarrels with whoever might cross his path. Violence of temper approaching to mania has been hereditary in the men of the family, and in my step-father's case it had, I believe, been intensified by his long residence in the tropics. A series of disgraceful brawls took place, two of which ended in the police-court, until at last he became the terror of the village, and the folks would fly at his approach, for he is a man of immense strength, and absolutely uncontrollable in his anger.

"Last week he hurled the local blacksmith over a parapet into a stream, and it was only by paying over all the money which I could gather together that I was able to avert another public exposure. He had no friends at all save the wandering gypsies, and he would give these vagabonds leave to encamp upon the few acres of bramble-covered land which represent the family estate, and would accept in return the hospitality of their tents, wandering away with them sometimes for weeks on end. He has a passion also for Indian animals, which are sent over to him by a correspondent, and he has at this moment a cheetah and a baboon, which wander freely over his grounds, and are feared by the villagers almost as much as their master.

"You can imagine from what I say that my poor sister Julia and I had no great pleasure in our lives. No servant would stay with us, and for a long time we did all the work of the house. She was but thirty at the time of her death, and yet her hair had already begun to whiten, even as mine has."

"Your sister is dead, then?"

"She died just two years ago, and it is of her death that I wish to speak to you. You can understand that, living the life which I have described, we were little likely to see any one of our own age and position. We had, however, an aunt, my mother's maiden sister, Miss Honoria Westphail, who lives near Harrow, and we were occasionally allowed to pay short visits at this lady's house. Julia went there at Christmas two years ago, and met there a half-pay major of marines, to whom she became engaged. My step-father learned of the engagement when my sister returned, and offered no objection to the marriage; but within a fortnight of the day which had been fixed for the wedding, the terrible event occurred which has deprived me of my only companion."

Sherlock Holmes had been leaning back in his chair with his eyes closed and his head sunk in a cushion, but he half opened his lids now and glanced across at his visitor.

"Pray be precise as to details," said he.

"It is easy for me to be so, for every event of that dreadful time is seared into my memory. The manor-house is, as I have already said, very old, and only one wing is now inhabited. The bedrooms in this wing are on the ground floor, the sitting-rooms being in the central block of the buildings. Of these bedrooms the first is Dr. Roylott's, the second my sister's, and the third my own. There is no communication between them, but they all open out into the same corridor. Do I make myself plain?"

"Perfectly so."

"The windows of the three rooms open out upon the lawn. That fatal night Dr. Roylott had gone to his room early, though we knew that he had not retired to rest, for my sister was troubled by the smell of the strong Indian cigars which it was his custom to smoke. She left her room, therefore, and came into mine, where she sat for some time, chatting about her approaching wedding. At eleven o'clock she rose to leave me, but she paused at the door and looked back.

" 'Tell me, Helen,' said she, 'have you ever heard any one whistle in the dead of the night?'

" 'Never,' said I.

" 'I suppose that you could not possibly whistle, yourself, in your sleep?'

" 'Certainly not. But why?'

" 'Because during the last few nights I have always, about three in the morning, heard a low, clear whistle. I am a light sleeper, and it has awakened me. I cannot tell where it came from—perhaps from the next room, perhaps from the lawn. I thought that I would just ask you whether you had heard it.'

" 'No, I have not. It must be those wretched gypsies in the plantation.'

" 'Very likely. And yet if it were on the lawn, I wonder that you did not hear it also.'

" 'Ah, but I sleep more heavily than you.'

" 'Well, it is of no great consequence, at any rate.' She smiled back at me, closed my door, and a few moments later I heard her key turn in the lock."

"Indeed," said Holmes. "Was it your custom always to lock yourselves in at night?"

"Always."

"And why?"

"I think that I mentioned to you that the doctor kept a cheetah and a baboon. We had no feeling of security unless our doors were locked."

"Quite so. Pray proceed with your statement."

"I could not sleep that night. A vague feeling of impending misfortune impressed me. My sister and I, you will recollect, were twins, and you know how subtle are the links which bind two souls which are so closely allied. It was a wild night. The wind was howling outside, and the rain was beating and splashing against the windows. Suddenly, amid all the hubbub of the gale, there burst forth the wild scream of a terrified woman. I knew that it was my sister's voice. I sprang from my bed, wrapped a shawl round me, and rushed into the corridor. As I opened my door I seemed to hear a low whistle, such as my sister described, and a few moments later a clanging sound, as if a mass of metal had fallen. As I ran down the passage my sister's door was unlocked, and revolved slowly upon its hinges. I stared at it horror-stricken, not knowing what was about to issue from it. By the light of the corridor-lamp I saw my sister appear at the opening, her face blanched with terror, her hands groping for help, her whole figure swaying to and fro like that of a drunkard. I ran to her and threw my arms round her, but at that moment her knees seemed to give way and she fell to the ground. She writhed as one who is in terrible pain, and her limbs were dreadfully convulsed. At first I thought that she had not recognized me, but as I bent over her she suddenly shrieked out, in a voice which I shall never forget: 'Oh, my God! Helen! It was the band! The speckled band!' There was something else which she would fain have said, and she stabbed with her finger into the air in the direction of the doctor's room, but a fresh convulsion seized her and choked her words. I rushed out, calling loudly for my step-father, and I met him hastening from his room in his dressing-gown. When he reached my sister's side she was unconscious, and though he poured brandy down her throat and sent for medical aid from the village, all efforts were in vain, for she slowly sank and died without having recovered her consciousness. Such was the dreadful end of my beloved sister."

"One moment," said Holmes; "are you sure about this whistle and metallic sound? Could you swear to it?"

"That was what the county coroner asked me at the inquiry. It is my strong impression that I heard it, and yet, among the crash of the gale and the creaking of an old house, I may possibly have been deceived."

"Was your sister dressed?"

"No, she was in her night-dress. In her right hand was found the charred stump of a match, and in her left a match-box."

"Showing that she had struck a light and looked about her when the alarm took place. That is important. And what conclusions did the coroner come to?"

"He investigated the case with great care, for Dr. Roylott's conduct had long been notorious in the county, but he was unable to find any satisfactory cause of death. My evidence showed that the door had been fastened upon the inner side, and the windows were blocked by old-fashioned shutters with broad iron bars, which were secured every night. The walls were carefully sounded, and were shown to be quite solid all round, and the flooring was also thoroughly examined, with the same result. The chimney is wide, but is barred up by four large staples. It is certain, therefore, that my sister was quite alone when she met her end. Besides, there were no marks of any violence upon her."

"How about poison?"

"The doctors examined her for it, but without success."

"What do you think that this unfortunate lady died of, then?"

"It is my belief that she died of pure fear and nervous shock, though what it was that frightened her I cannot imagine."

"Were there gypsies in the plantation at the time?"

"Yes, there are nearly always some there."

"Ah, and what did you gather from this allusion to a band—a speckled band?"

"Sometimes I have thought that it was merely the wild talk of delirium, sometimes that it may have referred to some band of people, perhaps to these very gypsies in the plantation. I do not know whether the spotted handkerchiefs which so many of them wear over their heads might have suggested the strange adjective which she used."

Holmes shook his head like a man who is far from being satisfied.

"These are very deep waters," said he; "pray go on with your narrative."

"Two years have passed since then, and my life has been until lately lonelier than ever. A month ago, however, a dear friend, whom I have known for many years, has done me the honor to ask my hand in marriage. His name is Armitage—Percy Armitage—the second son of Mr. Armitage, of Crane Water, near Reading. My step-father has offered no opposition to the match, and we are to be married in the course of the spring. Two days ago some repairs were started in the west wing of the building, and my bedroom wall has been pierced, so that I have had to move into the chamber in which my sister died, and to sleep in the very bed in which she slept. Imagine, then, my thrill of terror when last night, as I lay awake, thinking over her terrible fate, I suddenly heard in the silence of the night the low whistle which had been the herald of her own death. I sprang up and lit the lamp, but nothing was to be seen in the room. I was too shaken to go to bed again, however, so I dressed, and as soon as it was daylight I slipped down, got a dog-cart at the 'Crown Inn,' which is opposite, and drove to Leatherhead, from whence I have come on this morning with the one object of seeing you and asking your advice."

"You have done wisely," said my friend. "But have you told me all?"

"Yes, all."

"Miss Roylott, you have not. You are screening your step-father."

"Why, what do you mean?"

For answer Holmes pushed back the frill of black lace which fringed the hand that lay upon our visitor's knee. Five little livid spots, the marks of four fingers and a thumb, were printed upon the white wrist.

"You have been cruelly used," said Holmes.

The lady colored deeply and covered over her injured wrist. "He is a hard man," she said, "and perhaps he hardly knows his own strength."

There was a long silence, during which Holmes leaned his chin upon his hands and stared into the crackling fire.

"This is a very deep business," he said, at last. "There are a thousand details which I should desire to know before I decide upon our course of action. Yet we have not a moment to lose. If we were to come to Stoke Moran to-day, would it be possible for us to see over these rooms without the knowledge of your step-father?"

"As it happens, he spoke of coming into town to-day upon some most important business. It is probable that he will be away all day, and that there would be nothing to disturb you. We have a housekeeper now, but she is old and foolish, and I could easily get her out of the way."

"Excellent. You are not averse to this trip, Watson?"

"By no mean."

"Then we shall both come. What are you going to do yourself?"

"I have one or two things which I would wish to do now that I am in town. But I shall return by the twelve-o'clock train, so as to be there in time for your coming."

"And you may expect us early in the afternoon. I have myself some small business matters to attend to. Will you not wait and breakfast?"

"No, I must go. My heart is lightened already since I have confided my trouble to you. I shall look forward to seeing you again this afternoon." She dropped her thick black veil over her face and glided from the room.

"And what do you think of it all, Watson?" asked Sherlock Holmes, leaning back in his chair.

"It seems to me to be a most dark and sinister business."

"Dark enough and sinister enough."

"Yet if the lady is correct in saying that the flooring and walls are sound, and that the door, window, and chimney are impassable, then her sister must have been undoubtedly alone when she met her mysterious end."

"What becomes, then, of these nocturnal whistles, and what of the very peculiar words of the dying woman?"

"I cannot think."

"When you combine the ideas of whistles at night, the presence of a band of gypsies who are on intimate terms with this old doctor, the fact that we have every reason to believe that the doctor has an interest in preventing his step-daughter's marriage, the dying allusion to a band, and, finally, the fact that Miss Helen Stoner heard a metallic clang, which might have been caused by one of those metal bars which secured the shutters falling back into its place, I think that there is good ground to think that the mystery may be cleared along those lines."

"But what, then, did the gypsies do?"

"I cannot imagine."

"I see many objections to any such theory."

"And so do I. It is precisely for that reason that we are going to Stoke Moran this day. I want to see whether the objections are fatal, or if they may be explained away. But what in the name of the devil!"

The ejaculation had been drawn from my companion by the fact that our door had been suddenly dashed open, and that a huge man had framed himself in the aperture. His costume was a peculiar mixture of the professional and of the agricultural, having a black top-hat, a long frock-coat, and a pair of high gaiters, with a hunting-crop swinging in his hand. So tall was he that his hat actually brushed the cross-bar of the doorway, and his breadth seemed to span it across from side to side. A large face, seared with a thousand wrinkles, burned yellow with the sun, and marked with every evil passion, was turned from one to the other of us, while his deep-set, bile-shot eyes, and his high, thin, flesh-less nose, gave him somewhat the resemblance to a fierce old bird of prey.

"Which of you is Holmes?" asked this apparition.

"My name, sir; but you have the advantage of me," said my companion, quietly.

"I am Dr. Grimesby Roylott, of Stoke Moran."

"Indeed, doctor," said Holmes, blandly. "Pray take a seat."

"I will do nothing of the kind. My step-daughter has been here. I have traced her. What has she been saying to you?"

"It is a little cold for the time of the year," said Holmes.

"What has she been saying to you?" screamed the old man, furiously.

"But I have heard that the crocuses promise well," continued my companion, imperturbably.

"Ha! You put me off, do you?" said our new visitor, taking a step forward and shaking his hunting-crop. "I know you, you scoundrel! I have heard of you before. You are Holmes, the meddler."

My friend smiled.

"Holmes, the busybody!"

His smile broadened.

"Holmes, the Scotland-yard Jack-in-office!"

Holmes chuckled heartily. "Your conversation is most entertaining," said he. "When you go out close the door, for there is a decided draught."

"I will go when I have said my say. Don't you dare to meddle with my affairs. I know that Miss Stoner has been here. I traced her! I am a dangerous man to fall foul of! See here." He stepped swiftly forward, seized the poker, and bent it into a curve with his huge brown hands.

"See that you keep yourself out of my grip," he snarled; and hurling the twisted poker into the fireplace, he strode out of the room.

"He seems a very amiable person," said Holmes, laughing. "I am not quite so bulky, but if he had remained I might have shown him that my grip was not much more feeble than his own." As he spoke he picked up the steel poker, and with a sudden effort straightened it out again.

"Fancy his having the insolence to confound me with the official detective force! This incident gives zest to our investigation, however, and I only trust that our little friend will not suffer from her imprudence in allowing this brute to trace her. And now, Watson, we shall order breakfast, and afterward I shall walk down to Doctors' Commons, where I hope to get some data which may help us in this matter."

It was nearly one o'clock when Sherlock Holmes returned from his excursion. He held in his hand a sheet of blue paper, scrawled over with notes and figures.

"I have seen the will of the deceased wife," said he. "To determine its exact meaning I have been obliged to work out the present prices of the investments with which it is concerned. The total income, which at the time of the wife's death was little short of £1100, is now, through the fall in agricultural prices, not more than £750. Each daughter can claim an income of £250, in case of marriage. It is evident, therefore, that if both girls had married, this beauty would have had a mere pittance, while even one of them would cripple him to a very serious extent. My morning's work has not been wasted, since it has proved that he has the very strongest motives for standing in the way of anything of the sort. And now, Watson, this is too serious for dawdling, especially as the old man is aware that we are interesting ourselves in his affairs; so if you are ready, we shall call a cab and drive to Waterloo. I should be very much obliged if you would slip your revolver into your pocket. An Eley's No. 2 is an excellent argument with gentlemen who can twist steel pokers into knots. That and a tooth-brush are, I think, all that we need."

At Waterloo we were fortunate in catching a train for Leatherhead, where we hired a trap at the station inn, and drove for four or five miles through the lovely Surrey lanes. It was a perfect day, with a bright sun and a few fleecy clouds in the heavens. The trees and wayside hedges were just throwing out their first green shoots, and the air was full of the pleasant smell of the moist earth. To me at least there was a strange contrast between the sweet promise of the spring and this sinister quest upon which we were engaged. My companion sat in front of the trap, his arms folded, his hat pulled down over his eyes, and his chin sunk upon his breast, buried in the deepest thought. Suddenly, however, he started, tapped me on the shoulder, and pointed over the meadows.

"Look there!" said he.

A heavily timbered park stretched up in a gentle slope, thickening into a grove at the highest point. From amid the branches there jutted out the gray gables and high roof-tree of a very old mansion.

"Stoke Moran?" said he.

"Yes, sir, that be the house of Dr. Grimesby Roylott," remarked the driver.

"There is some building going on there," said Holmes; "that is where we are going."

"There's the village," said the driver, pointing to a cluster of roofs some distance to the left; "but if you want to get to the house, you'll find it shorter to get over this stile, and so by the foot-path over the fields. There it is, where the lady is walking."

"And the lady, I fancy, is Miss Stoner," observed Holmes, shading his eyes. "Yes, I think we had better do as you suggest."

We got off, paid our fare, and the trap rattled back on its way to Leatherhead.

"I thought it as well," said Holmes, as we climbed the stile, "that this fellow should think we had come here as architects or on some definite business. It may stop his gossip. Good-afternoon, Miss Stoner. You see that we have been as good as our word."

Our client of the morning had hurried forward to meet us with a face which spoke her joy. "I have been waiting so eagerly for you!" she cried, shaking hands with us warmly. "All has turned out splendidly. Dr. Roylott has gone to town, and it is unlikely that he will be back before evening."

"We have had the pleasure of making the doctor's acquaintance," said Holmes, and in a few words he sketched out what had occurred. Miss Stoner turned white to the lips as she listened.

"Good heavens!" she cried, "he has followed me, then."

"So it appears."

"He is so cunning that I never know when I am safe from him. What will he say when he returns?"

"He must guard himself, for he may find that there is some one more cunning than himself upon his track. You must lock yourself up from him to-night. If he is violent, we shall take you away to your aunt's at Harrow. Now, we must make the best use of our time, so kindly take us at once to the rooms which we are to examine."

The building was of gray, lichen-blotched stone, with a high central portion, and two curving wings, like the claws of a crab, thrown out on each side. In one of these wings the windows were broken, and blocked with wooden boards, while the roof was partly caved in, a picture of ruin. The central portion was in little better repair, but the right-hand block was comparatively modern, and the blinds in the windows, with the blue smoke curling up from the chimneys, showed that this was where the family resided. Some scaffolding had been erected against the end wall, and the stone-work had been broken into, but there were no signs of any workmen at the moment of our visit. Holmes walked slowly up and down the ill-trimmed lawn, and examined with deep attention the outsides of the windows.

"This, I take it, belongs to the room in which you used to sleep, the centre one to your sister's, and the one next to the main building to Dr. Roylott's chamber?"

"Exactly so. But I am now sleeping in the middle one."

"Pending the alterations, as I understand. By-the-way, there does not seem to be any very pressing need for repairs at that end wall."

"There were none. I believe that it was an excuse to move me from my room."

"Ah! that is suggestive. Now, on the other side of this narrow wing runs the corridor from which these three rooms open. There are windows in it, of course?"

"Yes, but very small ones. Too narrow for any one to pass through."

"As you both locked your doors at night, your rooms were unapproachable from that side. Now, would you have the kindness to go into your room and bar your shutters."

Miss Stoner did so, and Holmes, after a careful examination through the open window, endeavored in every way to force the shutter open, but without success. There was no slit through which a knife could be passed to raise the bar. Then with his lens he tested the hinges, but they were of solid iron, built firmly into the massive masonry. "Hum!" said he, scratching his chin in some perplexity; "my theory certainly presents some difficulties. No one could pass these shutters if they were bolted. Well, we shall see if the inside throws any light upon the matter."

A small side door led into the whitewashed corridor from which the three bedrooms opened. Holmes refused to examine the third chamber, so we passed at once to the second, that in which Miss Stoner was now sleeping, and in which her sister had met with her fate. It was a homely little room, with a low ceiling and a gaping fireplace, after the fashion of old country-houses. A brown chest of drawers stood in one corner, a narrow white-counterpaned bed in another, and a dressing-table on the left-hand side of the window. These articles, with two small wicker-work chairs, made up all the furniture in the room, save for a square of Wilton carpet in the centre. The boards round and the panelling of the walls were of brown, worm-eaten oak, so old and discolored that it may have dated from the original building of the house. Holmes drew one of the chairs into a corner and sat silent, while his eyes travelled round and round and up and down, taking in every detail of the apartment.

"Where does that bell communicate with?" he asked, at last, pointing to a thick bell-rope which hung down beside the bed, the tassel actually lying upon the pillow.

"It goes to the housekeeper's room."

"It looks newer than the other things?"

"Yes, it was only put there a couple of years ago."

"Your sister asked for it, I suppose?"

"No, I never heard of her using it. We used always to get what we wanted for ourselves."

"Indeed, it seemed unnecessary to put so nice a bell-pull there. You will excuse me for a few minutes while I satisfy myself as to this floor." He threw himself down upon his face with his lens in his hand, and crawled swiftly backward and forward, examining minutely the cracks between the boards. Then he did the same with the woodwork with which the chamber was panelled. Finally he walked over to the bed, and spent some time in staring at it, and in running his eye up and down the wall. Finally he took the bell-rope in his hand and gave it a brisk tug.

"Why, it's a dummy," said he.

"Won't it ring?"

"No, it is not even attached to a wire. This is very interesting. You can see now that it is fastened to a hook just above where the little opening for the ventilator is."

"How very absurd! I never noticed that before."

"Very strange!" muttered Holmes, pulling at the rope. "There are one or two very singular points about this room. For example, what a fool a builder must be to open a ventilator into another room, when, with the same trouble, he might have communicated with the outside air!"

"That is also quite modern," said the lady.

"Done about the same time as the bell-rope?" remarked Holmes.

"Yes, there were several little changes carried out about that time."

"They seem to have been of a most interesting character—dummy bell-ropes, and ventilators which do not ventilate. With your permission, Miss Stoner, we shall now carry our researches into the inner apartment."

Dr. Grimesby Roylott's chamber was larger than that of his step-daughter, but was as plainly furnished. A camp-bed, a small wooden shelf full of books, mostly of a technical character, an arm-chair beside the bed, a plain wooden chair against the wall, a round table, and a large iron safe were the principal things which met the eye. Holmes walked slowly round and examined each and all of them with the keenest interest.

"What's in here?" he asked, tapping the safe.

"My step-father's business papers."

"Oh! you have seen inside, then?"

"Only once, some years ago. I remember that it was full of papers."

"There isn't a cat in it, for example?"

"No. What a strange idea!"

"Well, look at this!" He stook up a small saucer of milk which stood on the top of it."

"No; we don't keep a cat. But there is a cheetah and a baboon."

"Ah, yes, of course! Well, a cheetah is just a big cat, and yet a saucer of milk does not go very far in satisfying its wants, I dare say. There is one point which I should wish to determine." He squatted down in front of the wooden chair, and examined the seat of it with the greatest attention.

"Thank you. That is quite settled," said he, rising and putting his lens in his pocket. "Hello! Here is something interesting!"

The object which had caught his eye was a small dog-lash hung on one corner of the bed. The lash, however, was curled upon itself, and tied so as to make a loop of whip-cord.

"What do you make of that, Watson?"

"It's a common enough lash. But I don't know why it should be tied."

"That is not quite so common, is it? Ah, me! it's a wicked world, and when a clever man turns his brains to crime it is the worst of all. I think that I have seen enough now, Miss Stoner, and with your permission we shall walk out upon the lawn."

I had never seen my friend's face so grim or his brow so dark as it was when we turned from the scene of this investigation. We had walked several times up and down the lawn, neither Miss Stoner nor myself liking to break in upon his thoughts before he roused himself from his reverie.

"It is very essential, Miss Stoner," said he, "that you should absolutely follow my advice in every respect."

"I shall most certainly do so."

"The matter is too serious for any hesitation. Your life may depend upon your compliance."

"I assure you that I am in your hands."

"In the first place, both my friend and I must spend the night in your room."

Both Miss Stoner and I gazed at him in astonishment.

"Yes, it must be so. Let me explain. I believe that that is the village inn over there?"

"Yes, that is the 'Crown.'"

"Very good. Your windows would be visible from there?"

"Certainly."

"You must confine yourself to your room, on pretence of a headache, when your step-father comes back. Then when you hear him retire for the night, you must open the shutters of your window, undo the hasp, put your lamp there as a signal to us, and then withdraw quietly with everything which you are likely to want into the room which you used to occupy. I have no doubt that, in spite of the repairs, you could manage there for one night."

"Oh yes, easily."

"The rest you will leave in our hands."

"But what will you do?"

"We shall spend the night in your room, and we shall investigate the cause of this noise which has disturbed you."

"I believe, Mr. Holmes, that you have already made up your mind," said Miss Stoner, laying her hand upon my companion's sleeve.

"Perhaps I have."

"Then, for pity's sake, tell me what was the cause of my sister's death."

"I should prefer to have clearer proofs before I speak."

"You can at least tell me whether my own thought is correct, and if she died from some sudden fright."

"No, I do not think so. I think that there was probably some more tangible cause. And now, Miss Stoner, we must leave you, for if Dr. Roylott returned and saw us, our journey would be in vain. Good-bye, and be brave, for if you will do what I have told you, you may rest assured that we shall soon drive away the dangers that threaten you."

Sherlock Holmes and I had no difficulty in engaging a bedroom and sitting-room at the "Crown Inn." They were on the upper floor, and from our window we could command a view of the avenue gate, and of the inhabited wing of Stoke Moran Manor-House. At dusk we saw Dr. Grimesby Roylott drive past, his huge form looming up beside the little figure of the lad who drove him. The boy had some slight difficulty in undoing the heavy iron gates, and we heard the hoarse roar of the doctor's voice, and saw the fury with which he shook his clinched fists at him. The trap drove on, and a few minutes later we saw a sudden light spring up among the trees as the lamp was lit in one of the sitting-rooms.

"Do you know, Watson," said Holmes, as we sat together in the gathering darkness, "I have really some scruples as to taking you to-night. There is a distinct element of danger."

"Can I be of assistance?"

"Your presence might be invaluable."

"Then I shall certainly come."

"It is very kind of you."

"You speak of danger. You have evidently seen more in these rooms than was visible to me."

"No, but I fancy that I may have deduced a little more. I imagine that you saw all that I did."

"I saw nothing remarkable save the bell-rope, and what purpose that could answer I confess is more than I can imagine."

"You saw the ventilator, too?"

"Yes, but I do not think that it is such a very unusual thing to have a small opening between two rooms. It was so small that a rat could hardly pass through."

"I knew that we should find a ventilator before ever we came to Stoke Moran."

"My dear Holmes!"

"Oh yes, I did. You remember in her statement she said that her sister could smell Dr. Roylott's cigar. Now, of course that suggested at once that there must be a communication between the two rooms. It could only be a small one, or it would have been remarked upon at the coroner's inquiry. I deduced a ventilator."

"But what harm can there be in that?"

"Well, there is at least a curious coincidence of dates. A ventilator is made, a cord is hung, and a lady who sleeps in the bed dies. Does not that strike you?"

"I cannot as yet see any connection."

"Did you observe anything very peculiar about that bed?"

"No."

"It was clamped to the floor. Did you ever see a bed fastened like that before?"

"I cannot say that I have."

"The lady could not move her bed. It must always be in the same relative position to the ventilator and to the rope—for so we may call it, since it was clearly never meant for a bell-pull."

"Holmes," I cried, "I seem to see dimly what you are hinting at! We are only just in time to prevent some subtle and horrible crime."

"Subtle enough and horrible enough. When a doctor does go wrong, he is the first of criminals. He has nerve and he has knowledge. Palmer and Pritchard were among the heads of their profession. This man strikes even deeper; but I think, Watson, that we shall be able to strike deeper still. But we shall have horrors enough before the night is over; for goodness' sake let us have a quiet pipe, and turn our minds for a few hours to something more cheerful."

About nine o'clock the light among the trees was extinguished, and all was dark in the direction of the Manor-House. Two hours passed slowly away, and then, suddenly, just at the stroke of eleven, a single bright light shone out in front of us.

"That is our signal," said Holmes, springing to his feet; "it comes from the middle window."

As we passed out he exchanged a few words with the landlord, explaining that we were going on a late visit to an acquaintance, and that it was possible that we might spend the night there. A moment later we were out on the dark road, a chill wind blowing in our faces, and one yellow light twinkling in front of us through the gloom to guide us on our sombre errand.

There was little difficulty in entering the grounds, for unrepaired breaches gaped in the old park wall. Making our way among the trees, we reached the lawn, crossed it, and were about to enter through the window, when out from a clump of laurel-bushes there darted what seemed to be a hideous and distorted child, who threw itself upon the grass with writhing limbs, and then ran swiftly across the lawn into the darkness.

"My God!" I whispered; "did you see it?"

Holmes was for the moment as startled as I. His hand closed like a vise upon my wrist in his agitation. Then he broke into a low laugh, and put his lips to my ear.

"It is a nice household," he murmured. "That is the baboon."

I had forgotten the strange pets which the doctor affected. There was a cheetah, too; perhaps we might find it upon our shoulders at any moment. I confess that I felt easier in my mind when, after following Holmes's example and slipping off my shoes, I found myself inside the bedroom. My companion noiselessly closed the shutters, moved the lamp onto the table, and cast his eyes round the room. All was as we had seen it in the daytime. Then creeping up to me and making a trumpet of his hand, he whispered into my ear again so gently that it was all that I could do to distinguish the words:

"The least sound would be fatal to our plans."

I nodded to show that I had heard.

"We must sit without light. He would see it through the ventilator."

I nodded again.

"Do not go asleep; your very life may depend upon it. Have your pistol ready in case we should need it. I will sit on the side of the bed, and you in that chair."

I took out my revolver and laid it on the corner of the table.

Holmes had brought up a long, thin cane, and this he placed upon the bed beside him. By it he laid the box of matches and the stump of a candle. Then he turned down the lamp, and we were left in darkness.

How shall I ever forget that dreadful vigil? I could not hear a sound, not even the drawing of a breath, and yet I knew that my companion sat open-eyed, within a few feet of me, in the same state of nervous tension in which I was myself. The shutters cut off the least ray of light, and we waited in absolute darkness. From outside came the occasional cry of a night-bird, and once at our very window a long-drawn, cat-like whine, which told us that the cheetah was indeed at liberty. Far away we could hear the deep tones of the parish clock, which boomed out every quarter of an hour. How long they seemed, those quarters! Twelve struck, and one and two and three, and still we sat waiting silently for whatever might befall.

Suddenly there was the momentary gleam of a light up in the direction of the ventilator, which vanished immediately, but was succeeded by a strong smell of burning oil and heated metal. Some one in the next room had lit a dark-lantern. I heard a gentle sound of movement, and then all was silent once more, though the smell grew stronger. For half an hour I sat with straining ears. Then suddenly another sound became audible—a very gentle, soothing sound, like that of a small jet of steam escaping continually from a kettle. The instant that we heard it, Holmes sprang from the bed, struck a match, and lashed furiously with his cane at the bell-pull.

"You see it, Watson?" he yelled. "You see it?"

But I saw nothing. At the moment when Holmes struck the light I heard a low, clear whistle, but the sudden glare flashing into my weary eyes made it impossible for me to tell what it was at which my friend lashed so savagely. I could, however, see that his face was deadly pale, and filled with horror and loathing.

He had ceased to strike, and was gazing up at the ventilator, when suddenly there broke from the silence of the night the most horrible cry to which I have ever listened. It swelled up louder and louder, a hoarse yell of pain and fear and anger all mingled in the one dreadful shriek. They say that away down in the village, and even in the distant parsonage, that cry raised the sleepers from their beds. It struck cold to our hearts, and I stood gazing at Holmes, and he at me, until the last echoes of it had died away into the silence from which it rose.

"What can it mean?" I gasped.

"It means that it is all over," Holmes answered. "And perhaps, after all, it is for the best. Take your pistol, and we will enter Dr. Roylott's room."

With a grave face he lit the lamp and led the way down the corridor. Twice he struck at the chamber door without any reply from within. Then he turned the handle and entered, I at his heels, with the cocked pistol in my hand.

It was a singular sight which met our eyes. On the table stood a dark-lantern with the shutter half open, throwing a brilliant beam of light upon the iron safe, the door of which was ajar. Beside this table, on the wooden chair, sat Dr. Grimesby Roylott, clad in a long gray dressing-gown, his bare ankles protruding beneath, and his feet thrust into red heelless Turkish slippers. Across his lap lay the short stock with the long lash which we had noticed during the day. His chin was cocked upward and his eyes were fixed in a dreadful, rigid stare at the corner of the ceiling. Round his brow he had a peculiar yellow band, with brownish speckles, which seemed to be bound tightly round his head. As we entered he made neither sound nor motion.

"The band! the speckled band!" whispered Holmes.

I took a step forward. In an instant his strange head-gear began to move, and there reared itself from among his hair the squat diamond-shaped head and puffed neck of a loathsome serpent.

"It is a swamp adder!" cried Holmes; "the deadliest snake in India. He has died within ten seconds of being bitten. Violence does, in truth, recoil upon the violent, and the schemer falls into the pit which he digs for another. Let us thrust this creature back into its den, and we can then remove Miss Stoner to some place of shelter, and let the county police know what has happened."

As he spoke he drew the dog-whip swiftly from the dead man's lap, and throwing the noose round the reptile's neck, he drew it from its horrid perch, and carrying it at arm's-length, threw it into the iron safe, which he closed upon it.

Such are the true facts of the death of Dr. Grimesby Roylott, of Stoke Moran. It is not necessary that I should prolong a narrative which has already run to too great a length, by telling how we broke the sad news to the terrified girl, how we conveyed her by the morning train to the care of her good aunt at Harrow, of how the slow process of official inquiry came to the conclusion that the doctor met his fate while indiscreetly playing with a dangerous pet. The little which I had yet to learn of the case was told me by Sherlock Holmes as we travelled back next day.

"I had," said he, "come to an entirely erroneous conclusion, which shows, my dear Watson, how dangerous it always is to reason from insufficient data. The presence of the gypsies, and the use of the word 'band,' which was used by the poor girl, no doubt to explain the appearance which she had caught a hurried glimpse of by the light of her match, were sufficient to put me upon an entirely wrong scent. I can only claim the merit that I instantly reconsidered my position when, however, it became clear to me that whatever danger threatened an occupant of the room could not come either from the window or the door. My attention was speedily drawn, as I have already remarked to you, to this ventilator, and to the bell-rope which hung down to the bed. The discovery that this was a dummy, and that the bed was clamped to the floor, instantly gave rise to the suspicion that the rope was there as bridge for something passing through the hole and coming to the bed. The idea of a snake instantly occurred to me, and when I coupled it with my knowledge that the doctor was furnished with a supply of creatures from India, I felt that I was probably on the right track. The idea of using a form of poison which could not possibly be discovered by any chemical test was just such a one as would occur to a clever and ruthless man who had had an Eastern training. The rapidity with which such a poison would take effect would also, from his point of view, be an advantage. It would be a sharp-eyed coroner, indeed, who could distinguish the two little dark punctures which would show where the poison fangs had done their work. Then I thought of the whistle. Of course he must recall the snake before the morning light revealed it to the victim. He had trained it, probably by the use of the milk which we saw, to return to him when summoned. He would put it through this ventilator at the hour that he thought best, with the certainty that it would crawl down the rope and land on the bed. It might or might not bite the occupant, perhaps she might escape every night for a week, but sooner or later she must fall a victim.

"I had come to these conclusions before ever I had entered his room. An inspection of his chair showed me that he had been in the habit of standing on it, which of course would be necessary in order that he should reach the ventilator. The sight of the safe, the saucer of milk, and the loop of whip-cord were enough to finally dispel any doubts which may have remained. The metallic clang heard by Miss Stoner was obviously caused by her step-father hastily closing the door of his safe upon its terrible occupant. Having once made up my mind, you know the steps which I took in order to put the matter to the proof. I heard the creature hiss, as I have no doubt that you did also, and I instantly lit the light and attacked it."

"With the result of driving it through the ventilator."

"And also with the result of causing it to turn upon its master at the other side. Some of the blows of my cane came home, and roused its snakish temper, so that it flew upon the first person it saw. In this way I am no doubt indirectly responsible for Dr. Grimesby Roylott's death, and I cannot say that it is likely to weigh very heavily upon my conscience."

28

The Courting of T'nowhead's Bell

BY SIR JAMES MATTHEW BARRIE

FOR two years it had been notorious in the square that Sam'l Dickie was thinking of courting T'nowhead's Bell, and that if little Sanders Elshioner (which is the Thrums pronunciation of Alexander Alexander) went in for her, he might prove a formidable rival. Sam'l was a weaver in the Tenements, and Sanders a coal-carter, whose trade-mark was a bell on his horse's neck that told when coal was coming. Being something of a public man, Sanders had not, perhaps, so high a social position as Sam'l, but he had succeeded his father on the coal-cart, while the weaver had already tried several trades. It had always been against Sam'l, too, that once when the kirk was vacant he had advised the selection of the third minister who preached for it on the ground that it came expensive to pay a large number of candidates. The scandal of the thing was hushed up, out of respect for his father, who was a God-fearing man, but Sam'l was known by it in Lang Tammas' circle. The coal-carter was called Little Sanders to distinguish him from his father, who was not much more than half his size. He had grown up with the name, and its inapplicability now came home to nobody. Sam'l's mother had been more far-seeing than Sanders'. Her man had been called Sammy all his life because it was the name he got as a boy, so when their eldest son was born she spoke of him as Sam'l while still in the cradle. The neighbors imitated her, and thus the young man had a better start in life than had been granted to Sammy, his father.

It was Saturday evening—the night in the week when Auld Licht young men fell in love. Sam'l Dickie, wearing a blue glengarry bonnet with a red ball on the top, came to the door of a one-story house in the Tenements, and stood there wriggling, for he was in a suit of tweed for the first time that week, and did not feel at one with them. When his

365

feeling of being a stranger to himself wore off, he looked up and down the road, which straggles between houses and gardens, and then, picking his way over the puddles, crossed to his father's hen-house and sat down on it. He was now on his way to the square.

Eppie Fargus was sitting on an adjoining dyke knitting stockings, and Sam'l looked at her for a time.

"Is't yersel, Eppie?" he said at last.

"It's a' that," said Eppie.

"Hoo's a' wi' ye?" asked Sam'l.

"We're juist aff an' on," replied Eppie, cautiously.

There was not much more to say, but as Sam'l sidled off the hen-house, he murmured politely, "Ay, ay." In another minute he would have been fairly started, but Eppie resumed the conversation.

"Sam'l," she said, with a twinkle in her eye, "ye can tell Lisbeth Fargus I'll likely be drappin' in on her aboot Mununday or Teisday."

Lisbeth was sister to Eppie, and wife of Tammas McQuhatty, better known as T'nowhead, which was the name of his farm. She was thus Bell's mistress.

Sam'l leaned against the hen-house as if all his desire to depart had gone.

"Hoo d'ye kin I'll be at the T'nowhead the nicht?" he asked, grinning in anticipation.

"Ou, I'se warrant ye'll be after Bell," said Eppie.

"Am no sae sure o' that," said Sam'l, trying to leer. He was enjoying himself now.

"Am no sure o' that," he repeated, for Eppie seemed lost in stitches.

"Sam'l!"

"Ay."

"Ye'll be speirin' her sune noo, I dinna doot?"

This took Sam'l, who had only been courting Bell for a year or two, a little aback.

"Hoo d'ye mean, Eppie?" he asked.

"Maybe ye'll do't the nicht."

"Na, there's nae hurry," said Sam'l.

"Weel, we're a' coontin' on't, Sam'l."

"Gae wa wi' ye."

"What for no?"

"Gae wa wi' ye," said Sam'l again.

"Bell's gei an' fond o' ye, Sam'l."

"Ay," said Sam'l.

"But am dootin' ye're a fell billy wi' the lasses."

"Ay, oh, I d'na kin, moderate, moderate," said Sam'l in high delight.

"I saw ye," said Eppie, speaking with a wire in her mouth, "gae'in on terr'ble wi' Mysy Haggart at the pump last Saturday."

"We was juist amoosin' oorsels," said Sam'l.

"It'll be nae amoosement to Mysy," said Eppie, "gin ye brak her heart."

"Losh, Eppie," said Sam'l, "I didna think o' that."

"Ye maun kin weel, Sam'l, 'at there's mony a lass wid jump at ye."

"Ou, weel," said Sam'l, implying that a man must take these things as they come.

"For ye're a dainty child to look at, Sam'l."

"Do ye think so, Eppie? Ay, ay; oh, I d'na kin am onything by the ordinar."

"Ye mayna be," said Eppie, "but lasses doesna do to be ower partikler."

Sam'l resented this, and prepared to depart again.

"Ye'll no tell Bell that?" he asked anxiously.

"Tell her what?"

"Aboot me an' Mysy."

"We'll see hoo ye behave yersel, Sam'l."

"No 'at I care, Eppie; ye can tell her gin ye like. I widna think twice o' tellin' her mysel."

"The Lord forgie ye for leein', Sam'l," said Eppie, as he disappeared down Tammy Tosh's close. Here he came upon Henders Webster.

"Ye're late, Sam'l," said Henders.

"What for?"

"Ou, I was thinkin' ye wid be gaen the length o' T'nowhead the nicht, an' I saw Sanders Elshioner makkin's wy there an oor syne."

"Did ye?" cried Sam'l, adding craftily, "but it's naething to me."

"Tod, lad," said Henders, "gin ye dinna buckle to, Sanders'll be carryin' her off."

Sam'l flung back his head and passed on.

"Sam'l!" cried Henders after him.

"Ay," said Sam'l, wheeling round.

"Gie Bell a kiss frae me."

The full force of this joke struck neither all at once. Sam'l began to smile at it as he turned down the school-wynd, and it came upon Henders while he was in his garden feeding his ferret. Then he slapped his legs gleefully, and explained the conceit to Will'um Byars, who went into the house and thought it over.

There were twelve or twenty little groups of men in the square, which was lit by a flare of oil suspended over a cadger's cart. Now and again a staid young woman passed through the square with a basket on her arm, and if she had lingered long enough to give them time, some of the idlers would have addressed her. As it was, they gazed after her, and then grinned to each other.

"Ay, Sam'l," said two or three young men, as Sam'l joined them beneath the town-clock.

"Ay, Davit," replied Sam'l.

This group was composed of some of the sharpest wits in Thrums, and it was not to be expected that they would let this opportunity pass. Perhaps when Sam'l joined them he knew what was in store for him.

"Was ye lookin' for T'nowhead's Bell, Sam'l?" asked one.

"Or mebbe ye was wantin' the minister?" suggested another, the same who had walked out twice with Chirsty Duff and not married her after all.

Sam'l could not think of a good reply at the moment, so he laughed good-naturedly.

"Ondootedly she's a snod bit crittur," said Davit, archly.

"An' michty clever wi' her fingers," added Jamie Deuchars.

"Man, I've thocht o' makkin' up to Bell mysel," said Pete Ogle. "Wid there be ony chance, think ye, Sam'l?"

"I'm thinkin' she widna hae ye for her first, Pete," replied Sam'l, in one of those happy flashes that come to some men, "but there's nae sayin' but what she micht tak ye to finish up wi'."

The unexpectedness of this sally startled every one. Though Sam'l did not set up for a wit, however, like Davit, it was notorious that he could say a cutting thing once in a way.

"Did ye ever see Bell reddin' up?" asked Pete, recovering from his overthrow. He was a man who bore no malice.

"It's a sicht," said Sam'l, solemnly.

"Hoo will that be?" asked Jamie Deuchars.

"It's weel worth yer while," said Pete, "to ging atower to the T'nowhead an' see. Ye'll mind the closed-in beds i' the kitchen? Ay, weel, they're a fell spoilt crew, T'nowhead's litlins, an' no that aisy to manage. Th' ither lasses Lisbeth's hae'n had a michty trouble wi' them. When they war i' the middle o' their reddin' up the bairns wid come tumlin' about the floor, but, sal, I assure ye, Bell didna fash lang wi' them. Did she, Sam'l?"

"She did not," said Sam'l, dropping into a fine mode of speech to add emphasis to his remark.

"I'll tell ye what she did," said Pete to the others. "She juist lifted up the litlins, twa at a time, an' flung them into the coffin-beds. Syne she snibbit the doors on them an' keepit them there till the floor was dry."

"Ay, man, did she so?" said Davit, admiringly.

"I've seen her do't mysel," said Sam'l.

"There's no a lassie maks better bannocks this side o' Fetter Lums," continued Pete.

"Her mither tocht her that," said Sam'l; "she was a gran' han' at the bakin', Kitty Ogilvy."

"I've heard say," remarked Jamie, putting it this way so as not to tie himself down to anything, " 'at Bell's scones is equal to Mag Lunan's."

"So they are," said Sam'l, almost fiercely.

"I kin she's a neat han' at singein' a hen," said Pete.

"An' wi't a'," said Davit, "she's a snod, canty bit stocky in her Sabbath claes."

"If onything, thick in the waist," suggested Jamie.

"I dinna see that," said Sam'l.

"I d'na care for her hair either," continued Jamie, who was very nice in his tastes; "something mair yallowchy wid be an improvement."

"A'body kins," growled Sam'l, " 'at black hair's the bonniest."

The others chuckled.

"Puir Sam'l!" Pete said.

Sam'l not being certain whether this should be received with a smile or a frown, opened his mouth wide as a kind of compromise. This was position one with him for thinking things over.

Few Auld Lichts, as I have said, went the length of choosing a helpmate for themselves. One day a young man's friends would see him mending the washing-tub of a maiden's mother. They kept the joke until Saturday night, and then he learned from them what he had been after. It dazed him for a time, but in a year or so he grew accustomed to the idea, and they were then married. With a little help he fell in love just like other people.

Sam'l was going the way of the others, but he found it difficult to come to the point. He only went courting once a week, and he could never take up the running at the place where he left off the Saturday before. Thus he had not, so far, made great headway. His method of making up to Bell had been to drop in at T'nowhead on Saturday nights and talk with the farmer about the rinderpest.

The farm kitchen was Bell's testimonial. Its chairs, tables, and stools were scoured by her to the whiteness of Rob Angus' saw-mill boards, and the muslin blind on the window was starched like a child's pinafore. Bell was brave, too, as well as energetic. Once Thrums had been overrun with thieves. It is now thought that there may have been only one, but he had the wicked cleverness of a gang. Such was his repute that there were weavers who spoke of locking their doors when they went from home. He was not very skilful, however, being generally caught, and when they said they knew he was a robber, he gave them their things back and went away. If they had given him time there is no doubt that he would have gone off with his plunder. One night he went to T'nowhead, and Bell, who slept in the kitchen, was awakened by the noise. She knew who it would be, so she rose and dressed herself, and went to look for him with a candle. The thief had not known what to do when he got in, and as it was very lonely he was glad to see Bell. She told him he ought to be ashamed of himself, and would not let him out by the door until he had taken off his boots so as not to soil the carpet.

On this Saturday evening Sam'l stood his ground in the square, until by and by he found himself alone. There were other groups there still, but his circle had melted away. They went separately, and no one said good-night. Each took himself off slowly, backing out of the group until he was fairly started.

Sam'l looked about him, and then, seeing that the others had gone, walked round the town-house into the darkness of the brae that leads down and then up to the farm of T'nowhead.

To get into the good graces of Lisbeth Fargus you had to know her ways and humor them. Sam'l, who was a student of women, knew this, and so, instead of pushing the door open and walking in, he went through the rather ridiculous ceremony of knocking. Sanders Elshioner was also aware of this weakness of Lisbeth's, but though he often made up his mind to knock, the absurdity of the thing prevented his doing so when he reached the door. T'nowhead himself had never got used to his wife's refined notions, and when any one knocked he always started to his feet, thinking there must be something wrong.

Lisbeth came to the door, her expansive figure blocking the way in.

"Sam'l," she said.

"Lisbeth," said Sam'l.

He shook hands with the farmer's wife, knowing that she liked it, but only said, "Ay, Bell," to his sweetheart, "Ay, T'nowhead," to McQuhatty, and "It's yersel, Sanders," to his rival.

They were all sitting round the fire; T'nowhead, with his feet on the ribs, wondering why he felt so warm, and Bell darned a stocking, while Lisbeth kept an eye on a goblet full of potatoes.

"Sit into the fire, Sam'l," said the farmer, not, however, making way for him.

"Na, na," said Sam'l; "I'm to bide nae time." Then he sat into the fire. His face was turned away from Bell, and when she spoke he answered her without looking round. Sam'l felt a little anxious. Sanders Elshioner, who had one leg shorter than the other, but looked well when sitting, seemed suspiciously at home. He asked Bell questions out of his own head, which was beyond Sam'l, and once he said something to her in such a low voice that the others could not catch it. T'now-head asked curiously what it was, and Sanders explained that he had only said, "Ay, Bell, the morn's the Sabbath." There was nothing star-tling in this, but Sam'l did not like it. He began to wonder if he were too late, and had he seen his opportunity would have told Bell of a nasty rumor that Sanders intended to go over to the Free Church if they would make him kirk-officer.

Sam'l had the good-will of T'nowhead's wife, who liked a polite man. Sanders did his best, but from want of practice he constantly made mis-takes. To-night, for instance, he wore his hat in the house because he did not like to put up his hand and take it off. T'nowhead had not taken his off either, but that was because he meant to go out by and by and lock the byre door. It was impossible to say which of her lovers Bell preferred. The proper course with an Auld Licht lassie was to prefer the man who proposed to her.

"Ye'll bide a wee, an' hae something to eat?" Lisbeth asked Sam'l, with her eyes on the goblet.

"No, I thank ye," said Sam'l, with true gentility.

"Ye'll better."

"I dinna think it."

"Hoots aye; what's to hender ye?"

"Weel, since ye're sae pressin', I'll bide."

No one asked Sanders to stay. Bell could not, for she was but the servant, and T'nowhead knew that the kick his wife had given him meant that he was not to do so either. Sanders whistled to show that he was not uncomfortable.

"Ay, then, I'll be stappin' ower the brae," he said at last.

He did not go, however. There was sufficient pride in him to get him off his chair, but only slowly, for he had to get accustomed to the no-tion of going. At intervals of two or three minutes he remarked that he must now be going. In the same circumstances Sam'l would have acted similarly. For a Thrums man, it is one of the hardest things in life to get away from anywhere.

At last Lisbeth saw that something must be done. The potatoes were burning, and T'nowhead had an invitation on his tongue.

"Yes, I'll hae to be movin'," said Sanders, hopelessly, for the fifth time.

"Guid nicht to ye, then, Sanders," said Lisbeth. "Gie the door a fling-to, ahent ye."

Sanders, with a mighty effort, pulled himself together. He looked boldly at Bell, and then took off his hat carefully. Sam'l saw with mis-givings that there was somethng in it which was not a handkerchief. It was a paper bag glittering with gold braid, and contained such an assortment of sweets as lads bought for their lasses on the Muckle Friday.

"Hae, Bell," said Sanders, handing the bag to Bell in an off-hand way as if it were but a trifle. Nevertheless he was a little excited, for he went off without saying good-night.

No one spoke. Bell's face was crimson. T'nowhead fidgeted on his chair, and Lisbeth looked at Sam'l. The weaver was strangely calm and collected, though he would have liked to know whether this was a proposal.

"Sit in by to the table, Sam'l," said Lisbeth, trying to look as if things were as they had been before.

She put a saucerful of butter, salt, and pepper near the fire to melt, for melted butter is the shoeing-horn that helps over a meal of potatoes. Sam'l, however, saw what the hour required, and jumping up, he seized his bonnet.

"Hing the tatties higher up the joist, Lisbeth," he said with dignity; "I'se be back in ten meenits."

He hurried out of the house, leaving the others looking at each other.

"What do ye think?" asked Lisbeth.

"I d'na kin," faltered Bell.

"Thae tatties is lang o' comin' to the boil," said T'nowhead.

In some circles a lover who behaved like Sam'l would have been suspected of intent upon his rival's life, but neither Bell nor Lisbeth did the weaver that injustice. In a case of this kind it does not much matter what T'nowhead thought.

The ten minutes had barely passed when Sam'l was back in the farm kitchen. He was too flurried to knock this time, and, indeed, Lisbeth did not expect it of him.

"Bell, hae!" he cried, handing his sweetheart a tinsel bag twice the size of Sanders' gift.

"Losh preserve's!" exclaimed Lisbeth; "I'se warrant there's a shillin's worth."

"There's a' that, Lisbeth—an' mair," said Sam'l firmly.

"I thank ye, Sam'l," said Bell, feeling an unwonted elation as she gazed at the two paper bags in her lap.

"Ye're ower extravegint, Sam'l," Lisbeth said.

"Not at all," said Sam'l; "not at all. But I widna advise ye to eat thae ither anes, Bell—they're second quality."

Bell drew back a step from Sam'l.

"How do ye kin?" asked the farmer shortly, for he liked Sanders.

"I speired i' the shop," said Sam'l.

The goblet was placed on a broken plate on the table with the saucer beside it, and Sam'l, like the others, helped himself. What he did was to take potatoes from the pot with his fingers, peel off their coats, and then dip them into the butter. Lisbeth would have liked to provide knives and forks, but she knew that beyond a certain point T'nowhead was master in his own house. As for Sam'l, he felt victory in his hands, and began to think that he had gone too far.

In the mean time Sanders, little witting that Sam'l had trumped his trick, was sauntering along the kirk-wynd with his hat on the side of his head. Fortunately he did not meet the minister.

The courting of T'nowhead's Bell reached its crisis one Sabbath about a month after the events above recorded. The minister was in great force that day, but it is no part of mine to tell how he bore himself. I was there, and am not likely to forget the scene. It was a fateful Sabbath for T'nowhead's Bell and her swains, and destined to be remembered for the painful scandal which they perpetrated in their passion.

Bell was not in the kirk. There being an infant of six months in the house it was a question of either Lisbeth or the lassie's staying at home with him, and though Lisbeth was unselfish in a general way, she could not resist the delight of going to church. She had nine children besides the baby, and being but a woman, it was the pride of her life to march them into the T'nowhead pew, so well watched that they dared not misbehave, and so tightly packed that they could not fall. The congregation looked at that pew, the mothers enviously, when they sang the lines—

> "Jerusalem like a city is
> Compactly built together."

The first half of the service had been gone through on this particular Sunday without anything remarkable happening. It was at the end of the psalm which preceded the sermon that Sanders Elshioner, who sat near the door, lowered his head until it was no higher than the pews, and in that attitude, looking almost like a four-footed animal, slipped out of the church. In their eagerness to be at the sermon many of the congregation did not notice him, and those who did put the matter by in their minds for future investigation. Sam'l, however, could not take it so coolly. From his seat in the gallery he saw Sanders disappear, and his mind misgave him. With the true lover's instinct he understood it all. Sanders had been struck by the fine turn-out in the T'nowhead pew. Bell was alone at the farm. What an opportunity to work one's way up to a proposal! T'nowhead was so overrun with children that such a chance seldom occurred, except on a Sabbath. Sanders, doubtless, was off to propose, and he, Sam'l, was left behind.

The suspense was terrible. Sam'l and Sanders had both known all along that Bell would take the first of the two who asked her. Even those who thought her proud admitted that she was modest. Bitterly the weaver repented having waited so long. Now it was too late. In ten minutes Sanders would be at T'nowhead; in an hour all would be over. Sam'l rose to his feet in a daze. His mother pulled him down by the coat-tail, and his father shook him, thinking he was walking in his sleep. He tottered past them, however, hurried up the aisle, which was so narrow that Dan'l Ross could only reach his seat by walking sideways, and was gone before the minister could do more than stop in the middle of a whirl and gape in horror after him.

A number of the congregation felt that day the advantage of sitting in the laft. What was a mystery to those downstairs was revealed to them. From the gallery windows they had a fine open view to the south; and as Sam'l took the common, which was a short cut through a steep ascent, to T'nowhead, he was never out of their line of vision. Sanders was not to be seen, but they guessed rightly the reason why. Thinking he had ample time, he had gone round by the main road to save his boots—perhaps a little scared by what was coming. Sam'l's design was to forestall him by taking the shorter path over the burn and up the commonty.

It was a race for a wife, and several onlookers in the gallery braved the minister's displeasure to see who won. Those who favored Sam'l's suit exultingly saw him leap the stream, while the friends of Sanders fixed their eyes on the top of the common where it ran into the road. Sanders must come into sight there, and the one who reached this point first would get Bell.

As Auld Lichts do not walk abroad on the Sabbath, Sanders would probably not be delayed. The chances were in his favor. Had it been any other day in the week Sam'l might have run. So some of the congregation in the gallery were thinking, when suddenly they saw him bend low and then take to his heels. He had caught sight of Sanders' head bobbing over the hedge that separated the road from the common, and feared that Sanders might see him. The congregation who could crane their necks sufficiently saw a black object, which they guessed to be the carter's hat, crawling along the hedge-top. For a moment it was motionless, and then it shot ahead. The rivals had seen each other. It was now a hot race. Sam'l, dissembling no longer, clattered up the common, becoming smaller and smaller to the on-lookers as he neared the top. More than one person in the gallery almost rose to their feet in their excitement. Sam'l had it. No, Sanders was in front. Then the two figures disappeared from view. They seemed to run into each other at the top of the brae, and no one could say who was first. The congregation looked at one another. Some of them perspired. But the minister held on his course.

Sam'l had just been in time to cut Sanders out. It was the weaver's saving that Sanders saw this when his rival turned the corner; for Sam'l was sadly blown. Sanders took in the situation and gave in at once. The last hundred yards of the distance he covered at his leisure, and when he arrived at his destination he did not go in. It was a fine afternoon for the time of year, and he went round to have a look at the pig, about which T'nowhead was a little sinfully puffed up.

"Ay," said Sanders, digging his fingers critically into the grunting animal; "quite so."

"Grumph," said the pig, getting reluctantly to his feet.

"Ou, ay; yes," said Sanders, thoughtfully.

Then he sat down on the edge of the sty, and looked long and silently at an empty bucket. But whether his thoughts were of T'nowhead's Bell, whom he had lost forever, or of the food the farmer fed his pig on, is not known.

"Lord preserve's! Are ye no at the kirk?" cried Bell, nearly dropping the baby as Sam'l broke into the room.

"Bell!" cried Sam'l.

Then T'nowhead's Bell knew that her hour had come.

"Sam'l," she faltered.

"Will ye hae's, Bell?" demanded Sam'l, glaring at her sheepishly.

"Ay," answered Bell.

Sam'l fell into a chair.

"Bring's a drink o' water, Bell," he said. But Bell thought the occasion required milk, and there was none in the kitchen. She went out to the byre, still with the baby in her arms, and saw Sanders Elshioner sitting gloomily on the pig-sty.

"Weel, Bell," said Sanders.

"I thocht ye'd been at the kirk, Sanders," said Bell.

Then there was a silence between them.

"Has Sam'l speired ye, Bell?" asked Sanders stolidly.

"Ay," said Bell again, and this time there was a tear in her eye. Sanders was little better than an "orra man," and Sam'l was a weaver, and yet—— But it was too late now. Sanders gave the pig a vicious poke with a stick, and when it had ceased to grunt, Bell was back in the kitchen. She had forgotten about the milk, however, and Sam'l only got water after all.

In after days, when the story of Bell's wooing was told, there were some who held that the circumstances would have almost justified the lassie in giving Sam'l the go-by. But these perhaps forgot that her other lover was in the same predicament as the accepted one—that of the two, indeed, he was the more to blame, for he set off to T'nowhead on the Sabbath of his own accord, while Sam'l only ran after him. And then there is no one to say for certain whether Bell heard of her suitors' delinquencies until Lisbeth's return from the kirk. Sam'l could never remember whether he told her, and Bell was not sure whether, if he did, she took it in. Sanders was greatly in demand for weeks after to tell what he knew of the affair, but though he was twice asked to tea to the manse among the trees, and subjected thereafter to ministerial cross-examinations, this is all he told. He remained at the pig-sty until Sam'l left the farm, when he joined him at the top of the brae, and they went home together.

"It's yersel, Sanders," said Sam'l.

"It is so, Sam'l," said Sanders.

"Very cauld," said Sam'l.

"Blawy," assented Sanders.

After a pause—

"Sam'l," said Sanders.

"Ay."

"I'm hearin' ye're to be mairit."

"Ay."

"Weel, Sam'l, she's a snod bit lassie."

"Thank ye," said Sam'l.

"I had ance a kin' o' notion o' Bell mysel," continued Sanders.

"Ye had?"

"Yes, Sam'l; but I thocht better o't."

"Hoo d'ye mean?" asked Sam'l, a little anxiously.

"Weel, Sam'l, mairitch is a terrible responsibeelity."

"It is so," said Sam'l, wincing.

"An' no the thing to tak up withoot conseederation."

"But it's a blessed and honorable state, Sanders; ye've heard the minister on't."

"They say," continued the relentless Sanders, " 'at the minister doesna get on sair wi' the wife himsel."

"So they do," cried Sam'l, with a sinking at the heart.

"I've been telt," Sanders went on, " 'at gin ye can get the upper han' o' the wife for a while at first, there's the mair chance o' a harmonious exeestence."

"Bell's no the lassie," said Sam'l appealingly, "to thwart her man." Sanders smiled.

"D'ye think she is, Sanders?"

"Weel, Sam'l, I d'na want to fluster ye, but she's been ower lang wi' Lisbeth Fargus no to hae learnt her ways, An a'body kins what a life T'nowhead has wi' her."

"Guid sake, Sanders, hoo did ye no speak o' this afore?"

"I thocht ye kent o't, Sam'l."

They had now reached the square, and the U. P. kirk was coming out. The Auld Licht kirk would be half an hour yet.

"But, Sanders," said Sam'l, brightening up, "ye was on yer wy to spier her yersel."

"I was, Sam'l," said Sanders, "and I canna but be thankfu' ye was ower quick for's."

"Gin't hadna been you," said Sam'l, "I wid never hae thocht o't."

"I'm sayin' naething agin Bell," pursued the other, "but, man Sam'l, a body should be mair deleeberate in a thing o' the kind."

"It was michty hurried," said Sam'l, wofully.

"It's a serious thing to spier a lassie," said Sanders.

"It's an awfu' thing," said Sam'l.

"But we'll hope for the best," added Sanders in a hopeless voice.

They were close to the Tenements now, and Sam'l looked as if he were on his way to be hanged.

"Sam'l!"

"Ay, Sanders."

"Did ye—did ye kiss her, Sam'l"?

"Na."

"Hoo?"

"There's was varra little time, Sanders."

"Half an 'oor," said Sanders.

"Was there? Man Sanders, to tell ye the truth, I never thocht o't."

Then the soul of Sanders Elshioner was filled with contempt for Sam'l Dickie.

The scandal blew over. At first it was expected that the minister would interfere to prevent the union, but beyond intimating from the pulpit that the souls of Sabbath-breakers were beyond praying for, and then praying for Sam'l and Sanders at great length, with a word thrown in for Bell, he let things take their course. Some said it was because he was always frightened lest his young men should intermarry with other denominations, but Sanders explained it differently to Sam'l.

"I hav'na a word to say agin the minister," he said; "they're gran' prayers, but, Sam'l, he's a mairit man himsel."

"He's a' the better for that, Sanders, isna he?"

"Do ye no see," asked Sanders compassionately, "'at he's tryin' to mak the best o't?"

"Oh, Sanders, man!" said Sam'l.

"Cheer up, Sam'l," said Sanders, "it'll sune be ower."

Their having been rival suitors had not interfered with their friendship. On the contrary, while they had hitherto been mere acquaintances, they became inseparables as the wedding-day drew near. It was noticed that they had much to say to each other, and that when they could not get a room to themselves they wandered about together in the churchyard. When Sam'l had anything to tell Bell he sent Sanders to tell it, and Sanders did as he was bid. There was nothing that he would not have done for Sam'l.

The more obliging Sanders was, however, the sadder Sam'l grew. He never laughed now on Saturdays, and sometimes his loom was silent half the day. Sam'l felt that Sanders' was the kindness of a friend for a dying man.

It was to be a penny wedding, and Lisbeth Fargus said it was delicacy that made Sam'l superintend the fitting-up of the barn by deputy. Once he came to see it in person, but he looked so ill that Sanders had to see him home. This was on the Thursday afternoon, and the wedding was fixed for Friday.

"Sanders, Sanders," said Sam'l, in a voice strangely unlike his own, "it'll a' be ower by this time the morn."

"It will," said Sanders.

"If I had only kent her langer," continued Sam'l.

"It wid hae been safer," said Sanders.

"Did ye see the yellow floor in Bell's bonnet?" asked the accepted swain.

"Ay," said Sanders reluctantly.

"I'm dootin'—I'm sair dootin' she's but a flichty, light-hearted crittur after a'."

"I had ay my suspeecions o't," said Sanders.

"Ye hae kent her langer than me," said Sam'l.

"Yes," said Sanders, "but there's nae gettin' at the heart o' women. Man, Sam'l, they're desperate cunnin'."

"I'm dootin't; I'm sair dootin't."

"It'll be a warnin' to ye, Sam'l, no to be in sic a hurry i' the futur," said Sanders.

Sam'l groaned.

"Ye'll be gaein up to the manse to arrange wi' the minister the morn's mornin'," continued Sanders, in a subdued voice.

Sam'l looked wistfully at his friend.

"I canna do't, Sanders," he said, "I canna do't."

"Ye, maun," said Sanders.

"It's aisy to speak," retorted Sam'l bitterly.

"We have a' oor troubles, Sam'l," said Sanders soothingly, "an' every man maun bear his ain burdens. Johnny Davie's wife's dead, an' he's no repinin'."

"Ay," said Sam'l, "but a death's no a mairitch. We hae haen deaths in our family too."

"It may a' be for the best," added Sanders, "an' there wid be a michty talk o' the hale country-side gin ye didna ging to the minister like a man."

"I maun hae langer to think o't," said Sam'l.

"Bell's mairitch is the morn," said Sanders decisively.

Sam'l glanced up with a wild look in his eyes.

"Sanders!" he cried.

"Sam'l!"

"Ye hae been a guid friend to me, Sanders, in this sair affliction."

"Nothing ava," said Sanders; "dount mention'd."

"But, Sanders, ye canna deny but what your rinnin oot o' the kirk that awfu' day was at the bottom o'd a'."

"It was so," said Sanders bravely.

"An' ye used to be fond o' Bell, Sanders."

"I dinna deny't."

"Sanders, laddie," said Sam'l, bending forward and speaking in a wheedling voice, "I aye thocht it was you she likit."

"I had some sic idea mysel," said Sanders.

"Sanders, I canna think to pairt twa fowk sae weel suited to ane anither as you an' Bell."

"Canna ye, Sam'l?"

"She wid make ye a guid wife, Sanders. I hae studied her weel, and she's a thrifty, douce, clever lassie. Sanders, there's no the like o' her. Mony a time, Sanders, I hae said to mysel, 'There's a lass ony man micht be prood to tak.' A'body says the same, Sanders. There's nae risk ava, man: nane to speak o'. Tak her, laddie, tak her, Sanders; it's a grand chance, Sanders. She's yours for the spierin'. I'll gie her up, Sanders."

"Will ye, though?" said Sanders.

"What d'ye think?" asked Sam'l.

"If ye wid rayther," said Sanders politely.

"There's my han' on't," said Sam'l. "Bless ye, Sanders; ye've been a true frien' to me."

Then they shook hands for the first time in their lives; and soon afterward Sanders struck up the brae to T'nowhead.

Next morning Sanders Elshioner, who had been very busy the night before, put on his Sabbath clothes and strolled up to the manse.

"But—but where is Sam'l?" asked the minister; "I must see himself."

"It's a new arrangement," said Sanders.

"What do you mean, Sanders?"

"Bell's to marry me," explained Sanders.

"But—but what does Sam'l say?"

"He's willin'," said Sanders.

"And Bell?"

"She's willin', too. She prefers't."

"It is unusual," said the minister.

"It's a' richt," said Sanders.

"Well, you know best," said the minister.

"You see the hoose was taen, at ony rate," continued Sanders. "An' I'll juist ging in til't instead o' Sam'l."

"Quite so."

"An' I cudna think to disappoint the lassie."

"Your sentiments do you credit, Sanders," said the minister; "but I hope you do not enter upon the blessed state of matrimony without full consideration of its responsibilities. It is a serious business, marriage."

"It's a' that," said Sanders, "but I'm willin' to stan' the risk."

So, as soon as it could be done, Sanders Elshioner took to wife T'nowhead's Bell, and I remember seeing Sam'l Dickie trying to dance at the penny wedding.

Years afterward it was said in Thrums that Sam'l had treated Bell badly, but he was never sure about it himself.

"It was a near thing—a michty near thing," he admitted in the square.

"They say," some other weaver would remark, " 'at it was you Bell liked best."

"I d'na kin," Sam'l would reply, "but there's nae doot the lassie was fell fond o' me. Ou, a mere passin' fancy's ye micht say."

29

The Babus of Nayanjore

BY SIR RABINDRANATH TAGORE

ONCE upon a time the Babus of Nayanjore were famous landholders. They were noted for their princely extravagance. They would tear off the rough border of their Dacca muslin, because it rubbed against their skin. They could spend many thousands of rupees over the wedding of a kitten. On a certain grand occasion it is alleged that in order to turn night into day they lighted numberless lamps and showered silver threads from the sky to imitate sunlight. Those were the days before the flood. The flood came. The line of succession among these old-world Babus, with their lordly habits, could not continue for long. Like a lamp with too many wicks burning, the oil flared away quickly, and the light went out.

Kailas Babu, our neighbour, is the last relic of this extinct magnificence. Before he grew up, his family had very nearly reached its lowest ebb. When his father died, there was one dazzling outburst of funeral extravagance, and then insolvency. The property was sold to liquidate the debt. What little ready money was left over was altogether insufficient to keep up the past ancestral splendours.

Kailas Babu left Nayanjore, and came to Calcutta. His son did not remain long in this world of faded glory. He died, leaving behind him an only daughter.

In Calcutta we are Kailas Babu's neighbours. Curiously enough our own family history is just the opposite to his. My father got his money by his own exertions, and prided himself on never spending a penny more than was needed. His clothes were those of a working man, and his hands also. He never had any inclination to earn the title of Babu by extravagant display, and I myself his only son, owe him gratitude for that. He gave me the very best education, and I was able to make my way in the world. I am not ashamed of the fact that I am a self-made man. Crisp bank-notes in my safe are dearer to me than a long pedigree in an empty family chest.

I believe this was why I disliked seeing Kailas Babu drawing his heavy cheques on the public credit from the bankrupt bank of his ancient Babu reputation. I used to fancy that he looked down on me, because my father had earned money with his own hands.

I ought to have noticed that no one showed any vexation towards Kailas Babu except myself. Indeed it would have been difficult to find an old man who did less harm than he. He was always ready with his kindly little acts of courtesy in times of sorrow and joy. He would join in all the ceremonies and religious observances of his neighbours. His familiar smile would greet young and old alike. His politeness in asking details about domestic affairs was untiring. The friends who met him in the street were perforce ready to be button-holed, while a long string of questions of this kind followed one another from his lips:

"My dear friend, I am delighted to see you. Are you quite well? How is Shashi? and Dada—is he all right? Do you know, I've only just heard that Madhu's son has got fever. How is he? Have you heard? And Hari Charan Babu—I have not seen him for a long time—I hope he is not ill. What's the matter with Rakkhal? And, er—er, how are the ladies of your family?"

Kailas Babu was spotlessly neat in his dress on all occasions, though his supply of clothes was sorely limited. Every day he used to air his shirts and vests and coats and trousers carefully, and put them out in the sun, along with his bed-quilt, his pillow-case, and the small carpet on which he always sat. After airing them he would shake them, and brush them, and put them on the rock. His little bits of furniture made his small room decent, and hinted that there was more in reserve if needed. Very often, for want of a servant, he would shut up his house for a while. Then he would iron out his shirts and linen with his own hands, and do other little menial tasks. After this he would open his door and receive his friends again.

Though Kailas Babu, as I have said, had lost all his landed property, he had still some family heirlooms left. There was a silver cruet for sprinkling scented water, a filigree box for otto-of-roses, a small gold salver, a costly ancient shawl, and the old-fashioned ceremonial dress and ancestral turban. These he had rescued with the greatest difficulty from the money-lenders' clutches. On every suitable occasion he would bring them out in state, and thus try to save the world-famed dignity of the Babus of Nayanjore. At heart the most modest of men, in his daily speech he regarded it as a sacred duty, owed to his rank, to give free play to his family pride. His friends would encourage this trait in his character with kindly good-humour, and it gave them great amusement.

The neighbourhood soon learnt to call him their Thakur Dada.[1] They would flock to his house, and sit with him for hours together. To prevent his incurring any expense, one or other of his friends would bring him tobacco, and say: "Thakur Dada, this morning some tobacco was sent to me from Gaya. Do take it, and see how you like it."

Thakur Dada would take it, and say it was excellent. He would then go on to tell of a certain exquisite tobacco which they once smoked in the old days at Nayanjore at the cost of a guinea an ounce.

"I wonder," he used to say, "I wonder if any one would like to try it now. I have some left, and can get it at once."

Every one knew that, if they asked for it, then somehow or other the key of the cupboard would be missing; or else Ganesh, his old family servant, had put it away somewhere.

"You never can be sure," he would add, "where things go to when servants are about. Now, this Ganesh of mine,—I can't tell you what a fool he is, but I haven't the heart to dismiss him."

Ganesh, for the credit of the family, was quite ready to bear all the blame without a word.

One of the company usually said at this point: "Never mind, Thakur Dada. Please don't trouble to look for it. This tobacco we're smoking will do quite well. The other would be too strong."

Then Thakur Dada would be relieved, and settle down again, and the talk would go on.

When his guests got up to go away, Thakur Dada would accompany them to the door, and say to them on the door-step: "Oh, by the way, when are you all coming to dine with me?"

One or other of us would answer: "Not just yet, Thakur Dada, not just yet. We'll fix a day later."

"Quite right," he would answer. "Quite right. We had much better wait till the rains come. It's too hot now. And a grand rich dinner such as I should want to give you would upset us in weather like this."

But when the rains did come, every one was very careful not to remind him of his promise. If the subject was brought up, some friend would suggest gently that it was very inconvenient to get about when the rains were so severe, that it would be much better to wait till they were over. And so the game went on.

His poor lodging was much too small for his position, and we used to condole with him about it. His friends would assure him they quite understood his difficulties: it was next to impossible to get a decent house in Calcutta. Indeed, they had all been loking out for years for a

---

[1] Grandfather.

house to suit him, but, I need hardly add, no friend had been foolish enough to find one. Thakur Dada used to say, after a long sigh of resignation: "Well, well, I suppose I shall have to put up with this house after all." Then he would add with a genial smile: "But, you know, I could never bear to be away from my friends. I must be near you. That really compensates for everything."

Somehow I felt all this very deeply indeed. I suppose the real reason was, that when a man is young stupidity appears to him the worst of crimes. Kailas Babu was not really stupid. In ordinary business matters every one was ready to consult him. But with regard to Nayanjore his utterances were certainly void of common sense. Because, out of amused affection for him, no one contradicted his impossible statements, he refused to keep them in bounds. When people recounted in his hearing the glorious history of Nayanjore with absurd exaggerations he would accept all they said with the utmost gravity, and never doubted, even in his dreams, that any one could disbelieve it.

When I sit down and try to analyse the thoughts and feelings that I had towards Kailas Babu I see that there was a still deeper reason for my dislike. I will now explain.

Though I am the son of a rich man, and might have wasted time at college, my industry was such that I took my M.A. degree in Calcutta University when quite young. My moral character was flawless. In addition, my outward appearance was so handsome, that if I were to call myself beautiful, it might be thought a mark of self-estimation, but could not be considered an untruth.

There could be no question that among the young men of Bengal I was regarded by parents generally as a very eligible match. I was myself quite clear on the point, and had determined to obtain my full value in the marriage market. When I pictured my choice, I had before my mind's eye a wealthy father's only daughter, extremely beautiful and highly educated. Proposals came pouring in to me from far and near; large sums in cash were offered. I weighed these offers with rigid impartiality, in the delicate scales of my own estimation. But there was no one fit to be my partner. I became convinced, with the poet Bhabavuti, that

> In this world's endless time and boundless space
> One may be born at last to match my sovereign grace.

But in this puny modern age, and this contracted space of modern Bengal, it was doubtful if the peerless creature existed as yet.

Meanwhile my praises were sung in many tunes, and in different metres, by designing parents.

Whether I was pleased with their daughters or not, this worship which they offered was never unpleasing. I used to regard it as my proper due, because I was so good. We are told that when the gods withhold their boons from mortals they still expect their worshippers to pay them fervent honour, and are angry if it is withheld. I had that divine expectance strongly developed in myself.

I have already mentioned that Thakur Dada had an only granddaughter. I had seen her many times, but had never mistaken her for beautiful. No thought had ever entered my mind that she would be a possible partner for myself. All the same, it seemed quite certain to me that some day or other Kailas Babu would offer her, with all due worship, as an oblation at my shrine. Indeed—this was the secret of my dislike—I was thoroughly annoyed that he had not done it already.

I heard he had told his friends that the Babus of Nayanjore never craved a boon. Even if the girl remained unmarried, he would not break the family tradition. It was this arrogance of his that made me angry. My indignation smouldered for some time. But I remained perfectly silent, and bore it with the utmost patience, because I was so good.

As lightning accompanies thunder, so in my character a flash of humour was mingled with the mutterings of my wrath. It was, of course, impossible for me to punish the old man merely to give vent to my rage; and for a long time I did nothing at all. But suddenly one day such an amusing plan came into my head, that I could not resist the temptation of carrying it into effect.

I have already said that many of Kailas Babu's friends used to flatter the old man's vanity to the full. One, who was a retired Government servant, had told him that whenever he saw the Chota Lord Sahib he always asked for the latest news about the Babus of Nayanjore, and the Chota Lord had been heard to say that in all Bengal the only really respectable families were those of the Maharaja of Burdwan and the Babus of Nayanjore. When this monstrous falsehood was told to Kailas Babu he was extremely gratified, and often repeated the story. And whereever after that he met this Government servant in company he would ask, along with other questions:

"Oh! er—by the way, how is the Chota Lord Sahib? Quite well, did you say? Ah, yes, I am so delighted to hear it! And the dear Mem Sahib, is she quite well too? Ah, yes! and the little children—are they quite well also? Ah, yes! that's very good news! Be sure and give them my compliments when you see them."

Kailas Babu would constantly express his intention of going some day and paying a visit to the Sahib. But it may be taken for granted that many Chota Lords and Burra Lords also would come and go, and much water would pass down the Hoogly, before the family coach of Nayan-jore would be furnished up to pay a visit to Government House.

One day I took Kailas Babu aside, and told him in a whisper: "Tha-kur Dada, I was at the Levee yesterday, and the Chota Lord happened to mention the Babus of Nayanjore. I told him that Kailas Babu had come to town. Do you know, he was terribly hurt because you hadn't called. He told me he was going to put etiquette on one side, and pay you a private visit himself this very afternoon."

Anybody else could have seen through this plot of mine in a moment. And, if it had been directed against another person, Kailas Babu would have understood the joke. But after all he had heard from his friend the Government servant, and after all his own exaggerations, a visit from the Lieutenant-Governor seemed the most natural thing in the world. He became highly nervous and excited at my news. Each detail of the coming visit exercised him greatly—most of all his own ignorance of English. How on earth was that difficulty to be met? I told him there was no difficulty at all: it was aristocratic not to know English: and, besides, the Lieutenant-Governor always brought an interpreter with him, and he had expressly mentioned that this visit was to be private.

About mid-day, when most of our neighbours are at work, and the rest are asleep, a carriage and pair stopped before the lodging of Kailas Babu. Two flunkeys in livery came up the stairs, and announced in a loud voice, "The Chota Lord Sahib has arrived." Kailas Babu was ready, waiting for him, in his old-fashioned ceremonial robes and an-cestral turban, and Ganesh was by his side, dressed in his master's best suit of clothes for the occasion. When the Chota Lord Sahib was an-nounced, Kailas Babu ran panting and puffing and trembling to the door, and led in a friend of mine, in disguise, with repeated salaams, bowing low at each step, and walking backward as best he could. He had his old family shawl spread over a hard wooden chair, and he asked the Lord Sahib to be seated. He then made a high-flown speech in Urdu, the ancient Court language of the Sahibs, and presented on the golden salver a string of gold *mohurs,* the last relics of his broken fortune. The old family servant Ganesh, with an expression of awe bordering on terror, stood behind with the scent-sprinkler, drenching the Lord Sahib, touching him gingerly from time to time with the attar-of-roses from the filigree box.

Kailas Babu repeatedly expressed his regret at not being able to re-ceive His Honour Bahadur with all the ancestral magnificence of his own family estate at Nayanjore. There he could have welcomed him properly with due ceremonial. But in Calcutta he was a mere stranger and sojourner—in fact a fish out of water.

My friend, with his tall silk hat on, very gravely nodded. I need hardly say that according to English custom the hat ought to have been removed inside the room. But my friend did not dare to take it off for fear of detection; and Kailas Babu and his old servant Ganesh were sublimely unconscious of the breach of etiquette.

After a ten minutes' interview, which consisted chiefly of nodding the head, my friend rose to his feet and departed. The two flunkeys in livery, as had been planned beforehand, carried off in state the string of gold *mohurs,* the gold salver, the old ancestral shawl, the silver scent-sprinkler, and the attar-of-roses filigree box; they placed them ceremoniously in the carriage. Kailas Babu regarded this as the usual habit of Chota Lord Sahibs.

I was watching all the while from the next room. My sides were aching with suppressed laughter. When I could hold myself in no longer, I rushed into a further room, suddenly to discover, in a corner, a young girl sobbing as if her heart would break. When she saw my uproarious laughter she stood upright in passion, flashing the lightning of her big dark eyes in mine, and said with a tear-choked voice: "Tell me! What harm has my grandfather done to you? Why have you come to deceive him? Why have you come here? Why——"

She could say no more. She covered her face with her hands, and broke into sobs.

My laughter vanished in a moment. It had never occurred to me that there was anything but a supremely funny joke in this act of mine, and here I discovered that I had given the cruelest pain to this tenderest little heart. All the ugliness of my cruelty rose up to condemn me. I slunk out of the room in silence, like a kicked dog.

Hitherto I had only looked upon Kusum, the grand-daughter of Kailas Babu, as a somewhat worthless commodity in the marriage market, waiting in vain to attract a husband. But now I found, with a shock of surprise, that in the corner of that room a human heart was beating.

The whole night through I had very little sleep. My mind was in a tumult. On the next day, very early in the morning, I took all those stolen goods back to Kailas Babu's lodgings, wishing to hand them over in secret to the servant Ganesh. I waited outside the door, and, not finding any one, went upstairs to Kailas Babu's room. I heard from the passage Kusum asking her grandfather in the most winning voice: "Dada, dearest, do tell me all that the Chota Lord Sahib said to you yesterday. Don't leave out a single word. I am dying to hear it all over again."

And Dada needed no encouragement. His face beamed over with pride as he related all manner of praises, which the Lord Sahib had been good enough to utter concerning the ancient families of Nayanjore.

The girl was seated before him, looking up into his face, and listening with rapt attention. She was determined, out of love for the old man, to play her part to the full.

My heart was deeply touched, and tears came to my eyes. I stood there in silence in the passage, while Thakur Dada finished all his embellishments of the Chota Lord Sahib's wonderful visit. When he left the room at last, I took the stolen goods and laid them at the feet of the girl and came away without a word.

Later in the day I called again to see Kailas Babu himself. According to our ugly modern custom, I had been in the habit of making no greeting at all to this old man when I came into the room. But on this day I made a low bow, and touched his feet. I am convinced the old man thought that the coming of the Chota Lord Sahib to his house was the cause of my new politeness. He was highly gratified by it, and an air of benign severity shone from his eyes. His friends had flocked in, and he had already begun to tell again at full length the story of the Lieutenant-Governor's visit with still further adornments of a most fantastic kind. The interview was already becoming an epic, both in quality and in length.

When the other visitors had taken their leave, I made my proposal to the old man in a humble manner. I told him that, "though I could never for a moment hope to be worthy of marriage connection with such an illustrious family, yet . . . etc. etc."

When I made clear my proposal of marriage, the old man embraced me, and broke out in a tumult of joy: "I am a poor man, and could never have expected such great good fortune."

That was the first and last time in his life that Kailas Babu confessed to being poor. It was also the first and last time in his life that he forgot, if only for a single moment, the ancestral dignity that belongs to the Babus of Nayanjore.

30

Philippa's Fox-Hunt

BY E. SOMERVILLE and MARTIN ROSS

No ONE can accuse Philippa and me of having married in haste. As a matter of fact, it was but little under five years from that autumn evening on the river when I had said what is called in Ireland "the hard word," to the day in August when I was led to the altar by my best man, and was subsequently led away from it by Mrs. Sinclair Yeates. About two years out of the five had been spent by me at Shreelane in ceaseless warfare with drains, eaveshoots, chimneys, pumps; all those fundamentals, in short, that the ingenuous and improving tenant expects to find established as a basis from which to rise to higher things. As far as rising to higher things went, frequent ascents to the roof to search for leaks summed up my achievements; in fact, I suffered so general a shrinkage of my ideals that the triumph of making the hall-door bell ring blinded me to the fact that the rat-holes in the hall floor were nailed up with pieces of tin biscuit boxes, and that the casual visitor could, instead of leaving a card, have easily written his name in the damp on the walls.

Philippa, however, proved adorably callous to these and similar shortcomings. She regarded Shreelane and its floundering, foundering ménage of incapables in the light of a gigantic picnic in a foreign land; she held long conversations daily with Mrs. Cadogan, in order, as she informed me, to acquire the language; without any ulterior domestic intention she engaged kitchen-maids because of the beauty of their eyes, and housemaids because they had such delightfully picturesque old mothers, and she declined to correct the phraseology of the parlor-maid, whose painful habit it was to whisper "Do ye choose cherry or clarry?" when proffering the wine. Fast-days, perhaps, afforded my wife her first insight into the sterner realities of Irish house-keeping. Philippa had what are known as High Church proclivities, and took the matter seriously.

"I don't know how we are to manage for the servants' dinner to-morrow, Sinclair," she said, coming in to my office on Thursday morning; "Julia says she 'promised God this long time that she wouldn't eat an egg on a fast-day,' and the kitchen-maid says she won't eat herrings 'without they're fried with onions,' and Mrs. Cadogan says she will 'not go to them extremes for servants.' "

"I should let Mrs. Cadogan settle the menu herself," I suggested.

"I asked her to do that," replied Philippa, "and she only said she 'thanked God *she* had no appetite!' "

The lady of the house here fell away into unseasonable laughter.

I made the demoralizing suggestion that, as we were going away for a couple of nights, we might safely leave them to fight it out, and the problem was abandoned.

Philippa had been much called on by the neighborhood in all its shades and grades, and daily she and her trousseau frocks presented themselves at hall-doors of varying dimensions in due acknowledgment of civilities. In Ireland, it may be noted, the process known in England as "summering and wintering" a new-comer does not obtain; sociability and curiosity alike forbid delay. The visit to which we owed our escape from the intricacies of the fast-day was to the Knoxes of Castle Knox, relations in some remote and tribal way of my landlord, Mr. Flurry of that ilk. It involved a short journey by train, and my wife's longest basket-trunk; it also, which was more serious, involved my being lent a horse to go out cubbing the following morning.

At Castle Knox we sank into an almost forgotten environment of draft proof windows and doors, of deep carpets, of silent servants instead of clattering belligerents. Philippa told me afterwards that it had only been by an effort that she had restrained herself from snatching up the train of her wedding-gown as she paced across the wide hall on little Sir Valentine's arm. After three weeks at Shreelane she found it difficult to remember that the floor was neither damp nor dusty.

I had the good fortune to be of the limited number of those who got on with Lady Knox, chiefly, I imagine, because I was as a worm before her, and thankfully permitted her to do all the talking.

"Your wife is extremely pretty," she pronounced autocratically, surveying Philippa between the candle-shades; "does she ride?"

Lady Knox was a short square lady, with a weather-beaten face, and an eye decisive from long habit of taking her own line across country and elsewhere. She would have made a very imposing little coachman, and would have caused her stable helpers to rue the day they had the presumption to be born; it struck me that Sir Valentine sometimes did so.

"I'm glad you like her looks," I replied, "as I fear you will find her thoroughly despicable otherwise; for one thing, she not only can't ride, but she believes that I can!"

"Oh, come, you're not as bad as all that!" my hostess was good enough to say; "I'm going to put you up on Sorcerer to-morrow, and we'll see you at the top of the hunt—if there is one. That young Knox hasn't a notion how to draw these woods."

"Well, the best run we had last year out of this place was with Flurry's hounds," struck in Miss Sally, sole daughter of Sir Valentine's house and home, from her place half-way down the table. It was not difficult to see that she and her mother held different views on the subject of Mr. Flurry Knox.

"I call it a criminal thing in any one's great-great-grandfather to rear up a preposterous troup of sons and plant them all out in his own country," Lady Knox said to me with apparent irrelevance. "I detest collaterals. Blood may be thicker than water, but it is also a great deal nastier. In this country I find that fifteenth cousins consider themselves near relations if they live within twenty miles of one!"

Having before now taken in the position with regard to Flurry Knox, I took care to accept these remarks as generalities, and turned the conversation to other themes.

"I see Mrs. Yeates is doing wonders with Mr. Hamilton," said Lady Knox presently, following the direction of my eyes, which had strayed away to where Philippa was beaming upon her left-hand neighbor, a mildewed-looking old clergyman, who was delivering a long dissertation, the purport of which we were happily unable to catch.

"She has always had a gift for the Church," I said.

"Not curates?" said Lady Knox, in her deep voice.

I made haste to reply that it was the elders of the Church who were venerated by my wife.

"Well, she has her fancy in old Eustace Hamilton; he's elderly enough!" said Lady Knox. "I wonder if she'd venerate him as much if she knew that he had fought with his sister-in-law, and they haven't spoken for thirty years! though for the matter of that," she added, "I think it shows his good sense!"

"Mrs. Knox is rather a friend of mine," I ventured.

"Is she? H'm! Well, she's not one of mine!" replied my hostess, with her usual definiteness. "I'll say one thing for her, I believe she's always been a sportswoman. She's very rich, you know, and they say she only married old Badger Knox to save his hounds from being sold to pay his debts, and then she took the horn from him and hunted them herself. Has she been rude to your wife yet? No? Oh, well, she will. It's a mere question of time. She hates all English people. You know the story they tell of her? She was coming home from London, and when she was getting her ticket the man asked if she had said a ticket for York. 'No, thank God, Cork!' says Mrs. Knox."

"Well, I rather agree with her!" said I; "but why did she fight with Mr. Hamilton?"

"Oh, nobody knows. I don't believe they know themselves! Whatever it was, the old lady drives five miles to Fortwilliam every Sunday, rather than go to his church, just outside her own back gates," Lady Knox said with a laugh like a terrier's bark. "I wish I'd fought with him myself," she said; "he gives us forty minutes every Sunday."

As I struggled into my boots the following morning, I felt that Sir Valentine's acid confidences on cub-hunting, bestowed on me at midnight, did credit to his judgment. "A very moderate amusement, my dear Major," he had said, in his dry little voice; "you should stick to shooting. No one expects you to shoot before daybreak."

It was six o'clock as I crept down-stairs, and found Lady Knox and Miss Sally at breakfast, with two lamps on the table, and a foggy daylight oozing in from under the half-raised blinds. Philippa was already in the hall, pumping up her bicycle, in a state of excitement at the prospect of her first experience of hunting that would have been more comprehensible to me had she been going to ride a strange horse, as I was. As I bolted my food I saw the horses being led past the windows, and a faint twang of a horn told that Flurry Knox and his hounds were not far off.

Miss Sally jumped up.

"If I'm not on the Cockatoo before the hounds come up, I shall never get there!" she said, hobbling out of the room in the toils of her safety habit. Her small, alert face looked very childish under her riding-hat; the lamplight struck sparks out of her thick coil of golden-red hair: I wondered how I had ever thought her like her prim little father.

She was already on her white cob when I got to the hall-door, and Flurry Knox was riding over the glistening wet grass with his hounds, while his whip, Dr. Jerome Hickey, was having a stirring time with the young entry and the rabbit-holes. They moved on without stopping, up a back avenue, under tall and dripping trees, to a thick laurel covert, at some little distance from the house. Into this the hounds were thrown, and the usual period of fidgety inaction set in for the riders, of whom, all told, there were about half-a-dozen. Lady Knox, square and solid, on her big, confidential iron-gray, was near me, and her eyes were on me and my mount; with her rubicund face and white collar she was more than ever like a coachman.

"Sorcerer looks as if he suited you well," she said, after a few minutes of silence, during which the hounds rustled and crackled steadily through the laurels; "he's a little high on the leg, and so are you, you know, so you show each other off."

Sorcerer was standing like a rock, with his good-looking head in the air and his eyes fastened on the covert. His manners, so far, had been those of a perfect gentleman, and were in marked contrast to those of Miss Sally's cob, who was sidling, hopping, and snatching unappeasably at his bit. Philippa had disappeared from view down the avenue ahead. The fog was melting, and the sun threw long blades of light through the trees; everything was quiet, and in the distance the curtained windows of the house marked the warm repose of Sir Valentine, and those of the party who shared his opinion of cubbing.

"Hark! hark to cry there!"

It was Flurry's voice, away at the other side of the covert. The rustling and brushing through the laurels became more vehement, then passed out of hearing.

"He never will leave his hounds alone," said Lady Knox disapprovingly.

Miss Sally and the Cockatoo moved away in a series of heraldic capers toward the end of the laurel plantation, and at the same moment I saw Philippa on her bicycle shoot into view on the drive ahead of us.

"I've seen a fox!" she screamed, white with what I believe to have been personal terror, though she says it was excitement; "it passed quite close to me!"

"What way did he go?" bellowed a voice which I recognized as Dr. Hickey's, somewhere in the deep of the laurels.

"Down the drive!" returned Philippa, with a pea-hen quality in her tones with which I was quite unacquainted.

An electrifying screech of "Gone away!" was projected from the laurels by Dr. Hickey.

"Gone away!" chanted Flurry's horn at the top of the covert.

"This is what he calls cubbing!" said Lady Knox, "a mere farce!" but none the less she loosed her sedate monster into a canter.

Sorcerer got his hind-legs under him, and hardened his crest against the bit, as we all hustled along the drive after the flying figure of my wife. I knew very little about horses, but I realized that even with the hounds tumbling hysterically out of the covert, and the Cockatoo kicking the gravel into his face, Sorcerer comported himself with the manners of the best society. Up a side road I saw Flurry Knox opening half of a gate and cramming through it; in a moment we also had crammed through, and the turf of a pasture field was under our feet. Dr. Hickey leaned forward and took hold of his horse; I did likewise, with the trifling difference that my horse took hold of me, and I steered for Flurry Knox with a single-hearted purpose, the hounds, already a field ahead, being merely an exciting and noisy accompaniment of this endeavor. A heavy stone wall was the first occurrence of note. Flurry chose a place where the top was loose, and his clumsy-looking brown mare changed feet on the rattling stones like a fairy. Sorcerer came at it, tense and collected as a bow at full stretch, and sailed steeply into the air; I saw the wall far beneath me, with an unsuspected ditch on the far side, and I felt my hat following me at the full stretch of its guard as we swept over it, then, with a long slant, we descended to earth some sixteen feet from where we had left it, and I was possessor of the gratifying fact that I had achieved a good-sized "fly," and had not perceptibly moved in my saddle. Subsequent disillusioning experience has taught me that but few horses jump like Sorcerer, so gallantly, so sympathetically, and with such supreme mastery of the subject; but none the less the enthusiasm that he imparted to me has never been extinguished, and that October morning ride revealed to me the unsuspected intoxication of fox-hunting.

Behind me I heard the scrabbling of the Cockatoo's little hoofs among the loose stones, and Lady Knox, galloping on my left, jerked a maternal chin over her shoulder to mark her daughter's progress. For my part, had there been an entire circus behind me, I was far too much occupied with ramming on my hat and trying to hold Sorcerer, to have looked round, and all my spare faculties were devoted to steering for Flurry, who had taken a right-handed turn, and was at that moment surmounting a bank of uncertain and briary aspect. I surmounted it also, with the swiftness and simplicity for which the Quaker's methods of bank-jumping had not prepared me, and two or three fields, traversed at the same steeplechase pace, brought us to a road and to an abrupt check. There, suddenly, were the hounds, scrambling in baffled silence down into the road from the opposite bank, to look for the line they had overrun, and there, amazingly, was Philippa, engaged in excited converse with several men with spades over their shoulders.

"Did ye see the fox, boys?" shouted Flurry, addressing the group.

"We did! we did!" cried my wife and her friends in chorus; "he ran up the road!"

"We'd be badly off without Mrs. Yeates!" said Flurry, as he whirled his mare round and clattered up the road with a hustle of hounds after him.

It occurred to me as forcibly as any mere earthly thing can occur to those who are wrapped in the sublimities of a run, that, for a young woman who had never before seen a fox out of a cage at the Zoo, Philippa was taking to hunting very kindly. Her cheeks were a most brilliant pink, her blue eyes shone.

"Oh, Sinclair!" she exclaimed, "they say he's going for Aussolas, and there's a road I can ride all the way!"

"Ye can, Miss! Sure we'll show you!" chorused her *cortège*.

Her foot was on the pedal ready to mount. Decidedly my wife was in no need of assistance from me.

Up the road a hound gave a yelp of discovery, and flung himself over a stile into the fields; the rest of the pack went squealing and jostling after him, and I followed Flurry over one of those infinitely varied erections, pleasantly termed "gaps" in Ireland. On this occasion the gap was made of three razor-edged slabs of slate leaning against an iron bar, and Sorcerer conveyed to me his thorough knowledge of the matter by a lift of his hind-quarters that made me feel as if I were being skilfully kicked down-stairs. To what extent I looked it, I can not say, nor providentially can Philippa, as she had already started. I only know that undeserved good luck restored to me my stirrup before Sorcerer got away with me in the next field.

What followed was, I am told, a very fast fifteen minutes; for me time was not; the empty fields rushed past uncounted, fences came and went in a flash, while the wind sang in my ears, and the dazzle of the early sun was in my eyes. I saw the hounds occasionally, sometimes pouring over a green bank, as the charging breaker lifts and flings itself, sometimes driving across a field, as the white tongues of foam slide racing over the sand; and always ahead of me was Flurry Knox, going as a man goes who knows his country, who knows his horse, and whose heart is wholly and absolutely in the right place.

Do what I would, Sorcerer's implacable stride carried me closer and closer to the brown mare, till, as I thundered down the slope of a long field, I was not twenty yards behind Flurry. Sorcerer had stiffened his neck to iron, and to slow him down was beyond me; but I fought his head away to the right, and found myself coming hard and steady at a stone-faced bank with broken ground in front of it. Flurry bore away to the left, shouting something that I did not understand. That Sorcerer shortened his stride at the right moment was entirely due to his own judgment; standing well away from the jump, he rose like a stag out of the tussocky ground, and as he swung my twelve-stone six into the air the obstacle revealed itself to him and me as consisting not of one bank but of two, and between the two lay a deep grassy lane, half choked with furze. I have often been asked to state the width of the bohereen, and can only reply that in my opinion it was at least eighteen feet; Flurry Knox and Dr. Hickey, who did not jump it, say that it is not more than five. What Sorcerer did with it, I cannot say; the sensation was of a towering flight with a kick back in it, a biggish drop, and a landing on cee-springs, still on the down-hill grade. That was how one of the best horses in Ireland took one of Ireland's most ignorant riders over a very nasty place.

A somber line of fir-wood lay ahead, rimmed with a gray wall, and in another couple of minutes we had pulled up on the Aussolas road, and were watching the hounds struggling over the wall into Aussolas demesne.

"No hurry now," said Flurry, turning in his saddle to watch the Cockatoo jump into the road; "he's to ground in the big earth inside. Well, Major, it's well for you that's a big-jumped horse. I thought you were a dead man a while ago when you faced him at the bohereen!"

I was disclaiming intention in the matter when Lady Knox and the others joined us.

"I thought you told me your wife was no sportswoman," she said to me, critically scanning Sorcerer's legs for cuts the while, "but when I saw her a minute ago she had abandoned her bicycle and was running across country like——"

"Look at her now!" interrupted Miss Sally. "Oh!—oh!" In the interval between these exclamations my incredulous eyes beheld my wife in mid-air, hand in hand with a couple of stalwart country boys, with whom she was leaping in unison from the top of a bank on to the road.

Every one, even the saturnine Dr. Hickey, began to laugh; I rode back to Philippa, who was exchanging compliments and congratulations with her escort.

"Oh, Sinclair!" she cried, "wasn't it splendid? I saw you jumping, and everything! Where are they going now?"

"My dear girl," I said, with marital disapproval, "you're killing yourself. Where's your bicycle?"

"Oh, it's punctured in a sort of lane, back there. It's all right; and then they"—she breathlessly waved her hand at her attendants—"they showed me the way."

"Begor! you proved very good, Miss!" said a grinning cavalier.

"Faith she did!" said another, polishing his shining brow with his white-flannel coat-sleeve, "she lepped like a haarse!"

"And may I ask how you propose to go home?" said I.

"I don't know and I don't care! I'm not going home!" She cast an entirely disobedient eye at me. "And your eye-glass is hanging down your back and your tie is bulging out over your waistcoat!"

The little group of riders had begun to move away.

"We're going on into Aussolas," called out Flurry; "come on, and make my grandmother give you some breakfast, Mrs. Yeates; she always has it at eight o'clock."

The front gates were close at hand, and we turned in under the tall beech-trees, with the unswept leaves rustling round the horses' feet, and the lovely blue of the October morning sky filling the spaces between smooth gray branches and golden leaves. The woods rang with the voices of the hounds, enjoying an untrammeled rabbit hunt, while the Master and the Whip, both on foot, strolled along unconcernedly with their bridles over their arms, making themselves agreeable to my wife, an occasional touch of Flurry's horn, or a crack of Dr. Hickey's whip, just indicating to the pack that the authorities still took a friendly interest in their doings.

Down a grassy glade in the wood a party of old Mrs. Knox's young horses suddenly swept into view, headed by an old mare, who, with her tail over her back, stampeded ponderously past our cavalcade, shaking and swinging her handsome old head, while her youthful friends bucked and kicked and snapped at each other round her with the ferocious humor of their kind.

"Here, Jerome, take the horn," said Flurry to Dr. Hickey; "I'm going to see Mrs. Yeates up to the house, the way these tomfools won't gallop on top of her."

From this point it seems to me that Philippa's adventures are more worthy of record than mine, and as she has favored me with a full account of them, I venture to think my version may be relied on.

Mrs. Knox was already at breakfast when Philippa was led, quaking, into her formidable presence. My wife's acquaintance with Mrs. Knox was, so far, limited to a state visit on either side, and she found but little comfort in Flurry's assurances that his grandmother wouldn't mind if he brought all the hounds in to breakfast, coupled with the statement that she would put her eyes on sticks for the Major.

Whatever the truth of this may have been, Mrs. Knox received her guest with an equanimity quite unshaken by the fact that her boots were in the fender instead of on her feet, and that a couple of shawls of varying dimensions and degrees of age did not conceal the inner presence of a magenta flannel dressing-jacket. She installed Philippa at the table and plied her with food, oblivious as to whether the needful implements with which to eat it were forthcoming or no. She told Flurry where a vixen had reared her family, and she watched him ride away, with some biting comments on his mare's hocks screamed after him from the window.

The dining-room at Aussolas Castle is one of the many rooms in Ireland in which Cromwell is said to have stabled his horse (and probably no one would have objected less than Mrs. Knox had she been consulted in the matter). Philippa questions if the room had ever been tidied up since, and she indorses Flurry's observation that "there wasn't a day in the year you wouldn't get feeding for a hen and chickens on the floor." Opposite to Philippa, on a Louis Quinze chair, sat Mrs. Knox's woolly dog, its suspicious little eyes peering at her out of their setting of pink lids and dirty white wool. A couple of young horses outside the windows tore at the matted creepers on the walls, or thrust faces that were half-shy, half-impudent, into the room. Portly pigeons waddled to and fro on the broad window-sill, sometimes flying in to perch on the picture-frames, while they kept up incessantly a hoarse and pompous cooing.

Animals and children are, as a rule, alike destructive to conversation; but Mrs. Knox, when she chose, *bien entendu,* could have made herself agreeable in a Noah's ark, and Philippa has a gift of sympathetic attention that personal experience has taught me to regard with distrust as well as respect, while it has often made me realize the worldly wisdom of Kingsley's injunction:

Be good, sweet maid, and let who will be clever.

Family prayers, declaimed by Mrs. Knox with alarming austerity, followed close on breakfast, Philippa and a vinegar-faced henchwoman forming the family. The prayers were long, and through the open window as they progressed came distantly a whoop or two; the declamatory tones staggered a little, and then continued at a distinctly higher rate of speed.

"Ma'am! Ma'am!" whispered a small voice at the window.

Mrs. Knox made a repressive gesture and held on her way. A sudden outcry of hounds followed, and the owner of the whisper, a small boy with a face freckled like a turkey's egg, darted from the window and dragged a donkey and bath-chair into view. Philippa admits to having lost the thread of the discourse, but she thinks that the "Amen" that immediately ensued can hardly have come in its usual place. Mrs. Knox shut the book abruptly, scrambled up from her knees, and said, "They've found!"

In a surprisingly short space of time she had added to her attire her boots, a fur cape, and a garden hat, and was in the bath-chair, the small boy stimulating the donkey with the success peculiar to his class, while Philippa hung on behind.

The woods of Aussolas are hilly and extensive, and on that particular morning it seemed that they held as many foxes as hounds. In vain was the horn blown and the whips cracked, small rejoicing parties of hounds, each with a fox of its own, scoured to and fro: every laborer in the vicinity had left his work, and was sedulously heading every fox with yells that would have befitted a tiger hunt, and sticks and stones when occasion served.

"Will I pull out as far as the big rosy-dandhrum, ma'am?" inquired the small boy; "I see three of the dogs go in it, and they yowling."

"You will," said Mrs. Knox, thumping the donkey on the back with her umbrella; "here! Jeremiah Regan! Come down out of that with that pitchfork! Do you want to kill the fox, you fool?"

"I do not, your honor, ma'am," responded Jeremiah Regan, a tall young countryman, emerging from a bramble brake.

"Did you see him?" said Mrs. Knox eagerly.

"I seen himself and his ten pups drinking below at the lake ere yesterday, your honor, ma'am, and he as big as a chestnut horse!" said Jeremiah.

"Faugh! Yesterday!" snorted Mrs. Knox; "go on to the rhododendrons, Johnny!"

The party, reenforced by Jeremiah and the pitchfork, progressed at a high rate of speed along the shrubbery path, encountering *en route* Lady Knox, stooping on to her horse's neck under the sweeping branches of the laurels.

"Your horse is too high for my coverts, Lady Knox," said the Lady of the Manor, with a malicious eye at Lady Knox's flushed face and dinged hat; "I'm afraid you will be left behind like Absalom when the hounds go away!"

"As they never do anything here but hunt rabbits," retorted her ladyship, "I don't think that's likely."

Mrs. Knox gave her donkey another whack, and passed on.

"Rabbits, my dear!" she said scornfully to Philippa. "That's all she knows about it. I declare, it disgusts me to see a woman of that age making such a Judy of herself! Rabbits indeed!"

Down in the thicket of rhododendron everything was very quiet for a time. Philippa strained her eyes in vain to see any of the riders; the horn blowing and the whip cracking passed on almost out of hearing. Once or twice a hound worked through the rhododendrons, glanced at the party, and hurried on, immersed in business. All at once Johnny, the donkey-boy, whispered excitedly:

"Look at he! Look at he!" and pointed to a boulder of gray rock that stood out among the dark evergreens. A big yellow cub was crouching on it; he instantly slid into the shelter of the bushes, and the irrepressible Jeremiah, uttering a rending shriek, plunged into the thicket after him. Two or three hounds came rushing at the sound, and after this Philippa says she finds some difficulty in recalling the proper order of events; chiefly, she confesses, because of the wholly ridiculous tears of excitement that blurred her eyes.

"We ran," she said, "we simply tore, and the donkey galloped, and as for that old Mrs. Knox, she was giving cracked screams to the hounds all the time, and they were screaming too; and then somehow we were all out on the road!"

What seems to have occurred was that three couple of hounds, Jeremiah Regan, and Mrs. Knox's equipage, among them somehow hustled the cub out of Aussolas demesne and up on to a hill on the farther side of the road. Jeremiah was sent back by this mistress to fetch Flurry, and the rest of the party pursued a thrilling course along the road, parallel with that of the hounds, who were hunting slowly through the gorse on the hillside.

"Upon my honor and word, Mrs. Yeates, my dear, we have the hunt to ourselves!" said Mrs. Knox to the panting Philippa, as they pounde. along the road. "Johnny, d'ye see the fox?"

"I do, ma'am!" shrieked Johnny, who possessed the usual field-glass vision bestowed upon his kind. "Look at him over-right us on the hill above! Hi! The spotty dog have him! No, he's gone from him! *Gwan out o' that!*" This to the donkey, with blows that sounded like the beating of carpets, and produced rather more dust.

They had left Aussolas some half a mile behind, when, from a strip of wood on their right, the fox suddenly slipped over the bank on to the road just ahead of them, ran up it for a few yards and whisked in at a small entrance gate, with the three couple of hounds yelling on a red-hot scent, not thirty yards behind. The bath-chair party whirled in at their heels, Philippa and the donkey considerably blown, Johnny scarlet through his freckles, but as fresh as paint, the old lady blind and deaf to all things save the chase. The hounds went raging through the shrubs beside the drive, and away down a grassy slope toward a shallow glen, in the bottom of which ran a little stream, and after them over the grass bumped the bath-chair. At the stream they turned sharply and ran up the glen toward the avenue, which crossed it by means of a rough stone viaduct.

"'Pon me conscience, he's into the old culvert!" exclaimed Mrs. Knox; "there was one of my hounds choked there once, long ago! Beat on the donkey, Johnny!"

At this juncture Philippa's narrative again becomes incoherent, not to say breathless. She is, however, positive that it was somewhere about here that the upset of the bath-chair occurred, but she cannot be clear as to whether she picked up the donkey or Mrs. Knox, or whether she herself was picked up by Johnny while Mrs. Knox picked up the donkey. From my knowledge of Mrs. Knox I should say she picked up herself and no one else. At all events, the next salient point is the palpitating moment when Mrs. Knox, Johnny, and Philippa successively applying an eye to the opening of the culvert by which the stream trickled under the viaduct, while five dripping hounds bayed and leaped around them, discovered by more senses than that of sight that the fox was in it, and furthermore that one of the hounds was in it, too.

"There's a sthrong grating before him at the far end," said Johnny, his head in at the mouth of the hole, his voice sounding as if he were talking into a jug, "the two of them's fighting in it; they'll be choked surely!"

"Then don't stand gabbling there, you little fool, but get in and pull the hound out!" exclaimed Mrs. Knox, who was balancing herself on a stone in the stream.

"I'd be in dread, ma'am," whined Johnny.

"Balderdash!" said the implacable Mrs. Knox. "In with you!"

I understand that Philippa assisted Johnny into the culvert, and presume it was in so doing that she acquired the two Robinson Crusoe bare footprints which decorated her jacket when I next met her.

"Have you got hold of him yet, Johnny?" cried Mrs. Knox up the culvert.

"I have, ma'am, by the tail," responded Johnny's voice, sepulchral in the depths.

"Can you stir him, Johnny?"

"I cannot, ma'am, and the wather is rising in it."

"Well, please God, they'll not open the mill dam!" remarked Mrs. Knox philosophically to Philippa, as she caught hold of Johnny's dirty ankles. "Hold on to the tail, Johnny!"

She hauled, with, as might be expected, no appreciable result. "Run, my dear, and look for somebody, and we'll have that fox yet!"

Philippa ran, whither she knew not, pursued by fearful visions of bursting mill dams, and maddened foxes at bay. As she sped up the avenue she heard voices, robust male voices, in a shrubbery, and made for them. Advancing along an embowered walk toward her was what she took for one wild instant to be a funeral; a second glance showed her that it was a party of clergymen of all ages, walking by twos and threes in the dappled shade of the over-arching trees. Obviously she had intruded her sacrilegious presence into a Clerical Meeting. She acknowledges that at this awe-inspiring spectacle she faltered, but the thought of Johnny, the hound, and the fox, suffocating, possibly drowning together in the culvert, nerved her. She does not remember what she said or how she said it, but I fancy she must have conveyed to them the impression that old Mrs. Knox was being drowned, as she immediately found herself heading a charge of the Irish Church toward the scene of disaster.

Fate has not always used me well, but on this occasion it was mercifully decreed that I and the other members of the hunt should be privileged to arrive in time to see my wife and her rescue party precipitating themselves down the glen.

"Holy Biddy!" ejaculated Flurry, "is she running a paper-chase with all the parsons? But look! For pity's sake will you look at my grandmother and my Uncle Eustace?"

Mrs. Knox and her sworn enemy the old clergyman, whom I had met at dinner the night before, were standing, apparently in the stream, tugging at two bare legs that projected from a hole in the viaduct, and arguing at the top of their voices. The bath-chair lay on its side with the donkey grazing beside it, on the bank a stout Archdeacon was tendering advice, and the hounds danced and howled round the entire group.

"I tell you, Eliza, you had better let the Archdeacon try," thundered Mr. Hamilton.

"Then I tell you I will not!" vociferated Mrs. Knox, with a tug at the end of the sentence that elicited a subterranean lament from Johnny. "Now who was right about the second grating? I told you so twenty years ago!"

Exactly as Philippa and her rescue party arrived, the efforts of Mrs. Knox and her brother-in-law triumphed. The struggling, sopping form of Johnny was slowly drawn from the hole, drenched, speechless, but clinging to the stern of a hound, who, in its turn, had its jaws fast in the hindquarters of a limp, yellow cub.

"Oh, it's dead!" wailed Philippa, "I *did* think I should have been in time to save it!"

"Well, if that doesn't beat all!" said Dr. Hickey.

31

The Mezzotint

BY MONTAGUE RHODES JAMES

SOME time ago I believe I had the pleasure of telling you the story of an adventure which happened to a friend of mine by the name of Dennistoun, during his pursuit of objects of art for the museum at Cambridge.

He did not publish his experiences very widely upon his return to England; but they could not fail to become known to a good many of his friends, and among others to the gentleman who at that time presided over an art museum at another University. It was to be expected that the story should make a considerable impression on the mind of a man whose vocation lay in lines similar to Dennistoun's, and that he should be eager to catch at any explanation of the matter which tended to make it seem improbable that he should ever be called upon to deal with so agitating an emergency. It was, indeed, somewhat consoling to him to reflect that he was not expected to acquire ancient MSS. for his institution; that was the business of the Shelburnian Library. The authorities of that institution might, if they pleased, ransack obscure corners of the Continent for such matters. He was glad to be obliged at the moment to confine his attention to enlarging the already unsurpassed collection of English topographical drawings and engravings possessed by his museum. Yet, as it turned out, even a department so homely and familiar as this may have its dark corners, and to one of these Mr. Williams was unexpectedly introduced.

Those who have taken even the most limited interest in the acquisition of topographical pictures are aware that there is one London dealer whose aid is indispensable to their researches. Mr. J. W. Britnell publishes at short intervals very admirable catalogues of a large and constantly changing stock of engravings, plans, and old sketches of mansions, churches, and towns in England and Wales. These catalogues were, of course, the ABC of his subject to Mr. Williams: but as his museum already contained an enormous accumulation of topographical pictures, he was a regular, rather than a copious, buyer; and he rather looked to Mr. Britnell to fill up gaps in the rank and file of his collection than to supply him with rarities.

Now, in February of last year there appeared upon Mr. Williams's desk at the museum a catalogue from Mr. Britnell's emporium, and accompanying it was a typewritten communication from the dealer himself. This latter ran as follows:

> *Dear Sir,*
>   *We beg to call your attention to No. 978 in our accompanying catalogue, which we shall be glad to send on approval.*
>   *Yours faithfully,*
>   *J. W. Britnell.*

To turn to No. 978 in the accompanying catalogue was with Mr. Williams (as he observed to himself) the work of a moment, and in the place indicated he found the following entry:

> *978.—Unknown. Interesting mezzotint: View of a manor-house, early part of the century. 15 by 10 inches; black frame. £2 2s.*

It was not specially exciting, and the price seemed high. However, as Mr. Britnell, who knew his business and his customer, seemed to set store by it, Mr. Williams wrote a postcard asking for the article to be sent on approval, along with some other engravings and sketches which appeared in the same catalogue. And so he passed without much excitement of anticipation to the ordinary labours of the day.

A parcel of any kind always arrives a day later than you expect it, and that of Mr. Britnell proved, as I believe the right phrase goes, no exception to the rule. It was delivered at the museum by the afternoon post of Saturday, after Mr. Williams had left his work, and it was accordingly brought round to his rooms in college by the attendant, in order that he might not have to wait over Sunday before looking through it and returning such of the contents as he did not propose to keep. And here he found it when he came in to tea, with a friend.

The only item with which I am concerned was the rather large, black-framed mezzotint of which I have already quoted the short description given in Mr. Britnell's catalogue. Some more details of it will have to be given, though I cannot hope to put before you the look of the picture as clearly as it is present to my own eye. Very nearly the exact duplicate of it may be seen in a good many old inn parlours, or in the passages of undisturbed country mansions at the present moment. It was a rather indifferent mezzotint, and an indifferent mezzotint is, perhaps, the worst form of engraving known. It presented a full-face view of a not very large manor-house of the last century, with three rows of plain sashed windows with rusticated masonry about them, a parapet with balls or vases at the angles, and a small portico in the centre. On either side were trees, and in front a considerable expanse of lawn. The legend "A. W. F. sculpsit" was engraved on the narrow margin; and there was no further inscription. The whole thing gave the impression that it was the work of an amateur. What in the world Mr. Britnell could mean by affixing the price of £2 2s. to such an object was more than Mr. Williams could imagine. He turned it over with a good deal of contempt; upon the back was a paper label, the left-hand half of which had been torn off. All that remained were the ends of two lines of writing: the first had the letters—*ngley Hall;* the second,—*ssex.*

It would, perhaps, be just worth while to identify the place represented, which he could easily do with the help of a gazetteer, and then he would send it back to Mr. Britnell, with some remarks reflecting upon the judgment of that gentleman.

He lighted the candles, for it was now dark, made the tea, and supplied the friend with whom he had been playing golf (for I believe the authorities of the University I write of indulge in that pursuit by way of relaxation); and tea was taken to the accompaniment of a discussion which golfing persons can imagine for themselves, but which the conscientious writer has no right to inflict upon any non-golfing persons.

The conclusion arrived at was that certain strokes might have been better, and that in certain emergencies neither player had experienced that amount of luck which a human being has a right to expect. It was now that the friend—let us call him Professor Binks—took up the framed engraving, and said:

"What's this place, Williams?"

"Just what I am going to try to find out," said Williams, going to the shelf for a gazetteer. "Look at the back. Somethingley Hall, either in Sussex or Essex. Half the name's gone, you see. You don't happen to know it, I suppose?"

"It's from that man Britnell, I suppose, isn't it?" said Binks. "Is it for the museum?"

"Well, I think I should buy it if the price was five shillings," said Williams; "but for some unearthly reason he wants two guineas for it. I can't conceive why. It's a wretched engraving, and there aren't even any figures to give it life."

"It's not worth two guineas, I should think," said Binks; "but I don't think it's so badly done. The moonlight seems rather good to me; and I should have thought there *were* figures, or at least a figure, just on the edge in front."

"Let's look," said Williams. "Well, it's true the light is rather cleverly given. Where's your figure? Oh, yes! Just the head, in the very front of the picture."

And indeed there was—hardly more than a black blot on the extreme edge of the engraving—the head of a man or woman, a good deal muffled up, the back turned to the spectator, and looking towards the house.

Williams had not noticed it before.

"Still," he said, "though it's a cleverer thing than I thought, I can't spend two guineas of museum money on a picture of a place I don't know."

Professor Binks had his work to do, and soon went; and very nearly up to Hall time Williams was engaged in a vain attempt to identify the subject of his picture. "If the vowel before the *ng* had only been left, it would have been easy enough," he thought; "but as it is, the name may be anything from Guestingley to Langley, and there are many more names ending like this than I thought; and this rotten book has no index of terminations."

Hall in Mr. Williams's college was at seven. It need not be dwelt upon; the less so as he met there colleagues who had been playing golf during the afternoon, and words with which we have no concern were freely bandied across the table—merely golfing words, I would hasten to explain.

I suppose an hour or more to have been spent in what is called common-room after dinner. Later in the evening some few retired to Williams's rooms, and I have little doubt that whist was played and tobacco smoked. During a lull in these operations Williams picked up the mezzotint from the table without looking at it, and handed it to a person mildly interested in art, telling him where it had come from, and the other particulars which we already know.

The gentleman took it carelessly, looked at it, then said, in a tone of some interest:

"It's really a very good piece of work, Williams; it has quite a feeling of the romantic period. The light is admirably managed, it seems to me, and the figure, though it's rather too grotesque, is somehow very impressive."

"Yes, isn't it?" said Williams, who was just then busy giving whisky-and-soda to others of the company, and was unable to come across the room to look at the view again.

It was by this time rather late in the evening, and the visitors were on the move. After they went Williams was obliged to write a letter or two and clear up some odd bits of work. At last, some time past midnight, he was disposed to turn in, and he put out his lamp after lighting his bedroom candle. The picture lay face upwards on the table where the last man who looked at it had put it, and it caught his eye as he turned the lamp down. What he saw made him very nearly drop the candle on the floor, and he declares now that if he had been left in the dark at that moment he would have had a fit. But, as that did not happen, he was able to put down the light on the table and take a good look at the picture. It was indubitable—rankly impossible, no doubt, but absolutely certain. In the middle of the lawn in front of the unknown house there was a figure where no figure had been at five o'clock that afternoon. It was crawling on all-fours towards the house, and it was muffled in a strange black garment with a white cross on the back.

I do not know what is the ideal course to pursue in a situation of this kind. I can only tell you what Mr. Williams did. He took the picture by one corner and carried it across the passage to a second set of rooms which he possessed. There he locked it up in a drawer, sported the doors of both sets of rooms, and retired to bed; but first he wrote out and signed an account of the extraordinary change which the picture had undergone since it had come into his possession.

Sleep visited him rather late; but it was consoling to reflect that the behaviour of the picture did not depend upon his own unsupported testimony. Evidently the man who had looked at it the night before had seen something of the same kind as he had, otherwise he might have been tempted to think that something gravely wrong was happening either to his eyes or his mind. This possibility being fortunately precluded, two matters awaited him on the morrow. He must take stock of the picture very carefully, and call in a witness for the purpose, and he must make a determined effort to ascertain what house it was that was represented. He would therefore ask his neighbour Nisbet to breakfast with him, and he would subsequently spend a morning over the gazetteer.

Nisbet was disengaged, and arrived about 9.30. His host was not quite dressed, I am sorry to say, even at this late hour. During breakfast nothing was said about the mezzotint by Williams, save that he had a picture on which he wished for Nisbet's opinion. But those who are familiar with University life can picture for themselves the wide and delightful range of subjects over which the conversation of two Fellows of Canterbury College is likely to extend during a Sunday morning breakfast. Hardly a topic was left unchallenged, from golf to lawn-tennis. Yet I am bound to say that Williams was rather distraught;

for his interest naturally centred in that very strange picture which was now reposing, face downwards, in the drawer in the room opposite.

The morning pipe was at last lighted, and the moment had arrived for which he looked. With very considerable—almost tremulous—excitement, he ran across, unlocked the drawer, and, extracting the picture—still face downwards—ran back, and put it into Nisbet's hands.

"Now," he said, "Nisbet, I want you to tell me exactly what you see in that picture. Describe it, if you don't mind, rather minutely. I'll tell you why afterwards."

"Well," said Nisbet, "I have here a view of a country-house—English, I presume—by moonlight."

"Moonlight? You're sure of that?"

"Certainly. The moon appears to be on the wane, if you wish for details, and there are clouds in the sky."

"All right. Go on. I'll swear," added Williams in an aside, "there was no moon when I saw it first."

"Well, there's not much more to be said," Nisbet continued. "The house has one—two—three rows of windows, five in each row, except at the bottom, where there's a porch instead of the middle one, and——"

"But what about figures?" said Williams, with marked interest.

"There aren't any," said Nisbet; "but——"

"What! No figure on the grass in front?"

"Not a thing."

"You'll swear to that?"

"Certainly I will. But there's just one other thing."

"What?"

"Why, one of the windows on the ground-floor—left of the door—is open."

"Is it really so? My goodness! he must have got in," said Williams, with great excitement; and he hurried to the back of the sofa on which Nisbet was sitting, and, catching the picture from him, verified the matter for himself.

It was quite true. There was no figure, and there was the open window. Williams, after a moment of speechless surprise, went to the writing-table and scribbled for a short time. Then he brought two papers to Nisbet, and asked him first to sign one—it was his own description of the picture, which you have just heard—and then to read the other which was Williams's statement written the night before.

"What can it all mean?" said Nisbet.

"Exactly," said Williams. "Well, one thing I must do—or three things, now I think of it. I must find out from Garwood"—this was his last night's visitor—"what he saw, and then I must get the thing photographed before it goes further, and then I must find out what the place is."

"I can do the photographing myself," said Nisbet, "and I will. But, you know, it looks very much as if we were assisting at the working out of a tragedy somewhere. The question is, Has it happened already, or is it going to come off? You must find out what the place is. Yes," he said, looking at the picture again, "I expect you're right: he has got in. And if I don't mistake there'll be the devil to pay in one of the rooms upstairs."

"I'll tell you what," said Williams: "I'll take the picture across to old Green" (this was the senior Fellow of the College, who had been Bursar for many years). "It's quite likely he'll know it. We have property in Essex and Sussex, and he must have been over the two counties a lot in his time."

"Quite likely he will," said Nisbet; "but just let me take my photograph first. But look here, I rather think Green isn't up to-day. He wasn't in Hall last night, and I think I heard him say he was going down for the Sunday."

"That's true, too," said Williams; "I know he's gone to Brighton. Well, if you'll photograph it now, I'll go across to Garwood and get his statement, and you keep an eye on it while I'm gone. I'm beginning to think two guineas is not a very exorbitant price for it now."

In a short time he had returned, and brought Mr. Garwood with him. Garwood's statement was to the effect that the figure, when he had seen it, was clear of the edge of the picture, but had not got far across the lawn. He remembered a white mark on the back of its drapery, but could not have been sure it was a cross. A document to this effect was then drawn up and signed, and Nisbet proceeded to photograph the picture.

"Now what do you mean to do?" he said. "Are you going to sit and watch it all day?"

"Well, no, I think not," said Williams. "I rather imagine we're meant to see the whole thing. You see, between the time I saw it last night and this morning there was time for lots of things to happen, but the creature only got into the house. It could easily have got through its business in the time and gone to its own place again; but the fact of the window being open, I think, must mean that it's in there now. So I feel quite easy about leaving it. And besides, I have a kind of idea that it wouldn't change much, if at all, in the daytime. We might go out for a walk this afternoon, and come in to tea, or whenever it gets dark. I shall leave it out on the table here, and sport the door. My skip can get in, but no one else."

The three agreed that this would be a good plan; and, further, that if they spent the afternoon together they would be less likely to talk about the business to other people; for any rumour of such a transaction as was going on would bring the whole of the Phasmatological Society about their ears.

We may give them a respite until five o'clock.

At or near that hour the three were entering Williams's staircase. They were at first slightly annoyed to see that the door of his rooms was unsported; but in a moment it was remembered that on Sunday the skips came for orders an hour or so earlier than on week-days. However, a surprise was awaiting them. The first thing they saw was the picture leaning up against a pile of books on the table, as it had been left, and the next thing was Williams's skip, seated on a chair opposite, gazing at it with undisguised horror. How was this? Mr. Filcher (the name is not my own invention) was a servant of considerable standing, and set the standard of etiquette to all his own college and to several neighbouring ones, and nothing could be more alien to his practice than to be found sitting on his master's chair, or appearing to take any particular notice of his master's furniture or pictures. Indeed, he seemed to feel this himself. He started violently when the three men were in the room, and got up with a marked effort. Then he said:

"I ask your pardon, sir, for taking such a freedom as to set down."

"Not at all, Robert," interposed Mr. Williams. "I was meaning to ask you some time what you thought of that picture."

"Well, sir, of course I don't set up my opinion again yours, but it ain't the pictur I should 'ang where my little girl could see it, sir."

"Wouldn't you, Robert? Why not?"

"No, sir. Why, the pore child, I recollect once she see a Door Bible, with pictures not 'alf what that is, and we 'ad to set up with her three or four nights afterwards, if you'll believe me; and if she was to ketch a sight of this skelinton here, or whatever it is, carrying off the pore baby, she would be in a taking. You know 'ow it is with children; 'ow nervish they git with a little thing and all. But what I should say, it don't seem a right pictur to be laying about, sir, not where anyone that's liable to be startled could come on it. Should you be wanting anything this evening, sir? Thank you, sir."

With these words the excellent man went to continue the round of his masters, and you may be sure the gentlemen whom he left lost no time in gathering round the engraving. There was the house, as before, under the waning moon and the drifting clouds. The window that had been open was shut, and the figure was once more on the lawn: but not this time crawling cautiously on hands and knees. Now it was erect and stepping swiftly, with long strides, towards the front of the picture. The moon was behind it, and the black drapery hung down over its face so that only hints of that could be seen, and what was visible made the spectators profoundly thankful that they could see no more than a white dome-like forehead and a few straggling hairs. The head was bent down, and the arms were tightly clasped over an object which could be dimly seen and identified as a child, whether dead or living it was not possible to say. The legs of the appearance alone could be plainly discerned, and they were horribly thin.

From five to seven the three companions sat and watched the picture by turns. But it never changed. They agreed at last that it would be safe to leave it, and that they would return after Hall and await further developments.

When they assembled again, at the earliest possible moment, the engraving was there, but the figure was gone, and the house was quiet under the moonbeams. There was nothing for it but to spend the evening over gazetteers and guide-books. Williams was the lucky one at last, and perhaps he deserved it. At 11.30 p.m. he read from Murray's *Guide to Essex* the following lines:

16½ miles, Anningley. The church has been an interesting building of Norman date, but was extensively classicized in the last century. It contains the tomb of the family of Francis, whose mansion, Anningley Hall, a solid Queen Anne house, stands immediately beyond the churchyard in a park of about 80 acres. The family is now extinct, the last heir having disappeared mysteriously in infancy in the year 1802. The father, Mr. Arthur Francis, was locally known as a talented amateur engraver in mezzotint. After his son's disappearance he lived in complete retirement at the Hall, and was found dead in his studio on the third anniversary of the disaster, having just completed an engraving of the house, impressions of which are of considerable rarity.

This looked like business, and, indeed, Mr. Green on his return at once identified the house as Anningley Hall.

"Is there any kind of explanation of the figure, Green?" was the question which Williams naturally asked.

"I don't know, I'm sure, Williams. What used to be said in the place when I first knew it, which was before I came up here, was just this: old Francis was always very much down on these poaching fellows, and whenever he got a chance he used to get a man whom he suspected of it turned off the estate, and by degrees he got rid of them all but one. Squires could do a lot of things then that they daren't think of now. Well, this man that was left was what you find pretty often in that country—the last remains of a very old family. I believe they were Lords of the Manor at one time. I recollect just the same thing in my own parish."

"What, like the man in *Tess o' the Durbervilles*," Williams put in.

"Yes, I dare say; it's not a book I could ever read myself. But this fellow could show a row of tombs in the church there that belonged to his ancestors, and all that went to sour him a bit; but Francis, they said, could never get at him—he always kept just on the right side of the law—until one night the keepers found him at it in a wood right at the end of the estate. I could show you the place now; it marches with some land that used to belong to an uncle of mine. And you can imagine there was a row; and this man Gawdy (that was the name, to be sure —Gawdy; I thought I should get it—Gawdy), he was unlucky enough, poor chap! to shoot a keeper. Well, that was what Francis wanted, and grand juries—you know what they would have been then—and poor Gawdy was strung up in double-quick time; and I've been shown the place he was buried in, on the north side of the church—you know the way in that part of the world: anyone that's been hanged or made away with themselves, they bury them that side. And the idea was that some friend of Gawdy's—not a relation, because he had none, poor devil! he was the last of his line: kind of *spes ultima gentis*—must have planned to get hold of Francis's boy and put an end to *his* line, too. I don't know —it's rather an out-of-the-way thing for an Essex poacher to think of —but, you know, I should say now it looks more as if old Gawdy had managed the job himself. Booh! I hate to think of it! have some whisky, Williams!"

The facts were communicated by Williams to Dennistoun, and by him to a mixed company, of which I was one, and the Sadducean Professor of Ophiology another. I am sorry to say that the latter when asked what he thought of it, only remarked: "Oh, those Bridgeford people will say anything"—a sentiment which met with the reception it deserved.

I have only to add that the picture is now in the Ashleian Museum; that it has been treated with a view to discovering whether sympathetic ink has been used in it, but without effect; that Mr. Britnell knew nothing of it save that he was sure it was uncommon; and that, though carefully watched, it has never been known to change again.

32

"Hey Diddle Diddle, the Cat . . ."

BY EDEN PHILLPOTTS

WHEN you be done larning, you might so well stop living, and for my part, though I'm sixty-five, I thank God as I can still gather useful knowledge when it comes my way.

For example, but four years ago, I had my eyes opened about a matter on which I'd thought wrong for more than half a century. I never could understand man or woman who loved a beast; and when I see an old maid dote on her cat, or an old bachelor share the best off his own plate with his dog, I scorned 'em. And when the creatures came to a bad end, as pets so often will, and their owners weren't above shedding a tear for 'em, I said, in my ignorance, they did ought to be ashamed, and called 'em weak-minded zanies to let a dumb animal reign over 'em in such a fashion. But I don't put on no airs and graces now when I see anybody fretting for a sick or dead creature; because I be in the same boat myself.

As a widow man and pretty well-to-do, I be one of them that count at Ponsworthy, and have always tried to keep up the dignity of the village and be a good neighbour and help on the welfare of us all in my small way. And being addicted to childer, though never blessed or cursed with none, I made friends with the young things and stood well in their opinion.

So it came about that, as I minded their birthdays pretty often, a sharp little maid axed me when mine might be; and I told her, doubting not that she'd forget again. Daisy Bird she was called, the youngest daughter of my particular friend, Martin Bird, of the all-sorts shop.

Well, Daisy remembered, and on my birthday she brought me a kitten just old enough to leave his mother. 'Twas a cat of a well-known mother, but the father was wrapped in mystery, as fathers too often are.

413

The kitling weren't nothing to praise, nor yet to blame—just a very every day young cat, with a piebald face and a bit of yellow and black dabbed about over a white ground. His eyes were doubtful and Daisy promised me as they'd turn a nice green when he'd growed a bit, same as his mother's; and if you'd looked my gift-cat in the mouth, you'd have seen 'twas pink as a rose, with just the beginning of small, pearly teeth coming. No tail to name; but there again Daisy came to the rescue and solemnly vowed that he had the promise of a very fine tail, if I'd only be patient about it.

'Twas to be called "Sunny Jim," and she much hoped I'd take to it and be a kind friend to it; and if I did not, it had got to be drowned.

I paused at that, for I had meant to beg Daisy to carry it home and let me take the kind will for the deed. But when I see the little thing so trustful and so wishful to please, and so well satisfied with me from the first; and when I understood it was a choice between life along with me and death in the river, I hesitated.

Daisy picked him up and put him in my hand; and if he'd showed any sauce, or turned against me, it would have been "good-bye." But he knew 'twas touch and go; and whenever does a cat do a thing that makes against its own prosperity? He looked up in my face and purred, with the little gruff purr as young cats have, and rubbed his small carcass against my waistcoat, as if he'd found the very person he was wanting. So there it stood; I kept him and let him have his run and his fill, and watched him grow into a very ugly cat in other eyes, but not ugly to me—never to me.

I always say that it's a beautiful thing to see the contentment of animals. No doubt it only happens because they've got no wits and no power to compare their lot with any other; but whatever it be—horse or donkey, dog or cat, only let him know he's welcome and have got a man or woman friend, and he'll cleave to the lowliest lot and be just so cheerful and good-hearted and faithful along with a tinker as a king. They'll fit in, make themselves part of the home, feel 'tis the one place in the world that matters, however poor and humble, and go about the troublesome business of being alive, with such pluck and patience and good appetite that they be often a lesson to us grumbling grizzling humans.

No dog or cat will ever look on the dark side of things. Nature have made 'em hopeful. They be quick to scent pleasure, and though there's a good and bad among 'em and some more easily cast down than others, they be prone to welcome life and give of their best in exchange for small mercies.

My Sunny Jim was a very well-named cat. He had what you might call a reasonable mind, and if he'd lacked the many virtues that came out to him, still I'd have been bound in common justice to rate him as a very worthy chap—along of his amazing affection for me. He seemed to know from the first as I had no use for domestic animals, and he said to himself: "Then I'll break you in and make you properly mad about me and conquer your hard heart."

He went about it very cunning, too. He knew I was a terrible clean old man and liked my house to be so spick and span as myself; and so he began by showing me what cleanliness really was; and a more fussy cat from his youth up I have never met. His father must have been a gentleman for sartain. You felt the cat had good blood in him, he was so nice. Never a hair out of place you might say, and he'd lick himself and wash his chops sometimes after a sup and bite till I'd shout at him to let be. Mud was his abomination, and if he come in with a speck on his pads, he'd bite and fidget, as if he was pulling off a pair of gloves; and he never thanked me more grateful nor purred louder than when I gave him his brush and comb. But, to tell truth, I humoured him in that matter, and finding what a godsend it was to him to have a rub from time to time, I met him there and kept an old brush a' purpose.

At six months I knew he'd got me, and I was a lot too fond of the cat; and on his birthday, which Daisy Bird remembered, us gave Sunny Jim a party, and Daisy and half a score of childer agreed to come. 'Twas a great success. Us provided him with three sardines and a drop of cream, and long after the party was over and the childer gone, he sat polishing up. Then, when he felt perfection inside and out, he just give a sigh of satisfaction, and tucked in his paws and sat quite silent thinking over the day's fine doings.

As for mice, he was a very fine performer, but my house never had no mice in it as he soon found, so he went down three doors to Mrs. Wilkinson's, where there were scores of dozens, and he never drawed a blank there. Not that he'd often eat a mouse; but he was a mighty hunter of 'em—a proper mouse-tiger, you might say—though not much a one for birds. He seldom went afield and never laid a paw to fur or feathers, like many a hard-bitten poacher of a cat, as makes a shameful end soon or late on gamekeeper's gallows.

He slept along with me, at my bed-foot, and I'd trained him to come in for his supper an hour or so after dark. But he liked the evening hour and the moth time. Then he'd sit on the party wall and take the air, or join in a cat chorus perhaps, but all like a gentleman; and he never went too far, or done anything to be ashamed of. A wife or two he may have had, but all well within honour; and he wouldn't fight nor nothing like that, for the good reason that he weighed about five pounds heavier than any cat at Ponsworthy, and no other tom in his right senses would have took him on for a moment.

He supped with me, and by ten o'clock we was both to bed. Then when he was stretched at my feet and the candle out, I'd bid him say his prayers, and he'd purr gentle and steady; and for a good few years the last sound I have heard, as I closed my eyes, was Sunny Jim saying his prayers.

Mrs. Wilkinson warned me, strangely enough, just a week before the crash came.

"You be putting that tortoiseshell tom afore your God, Peter Blount," she said to me, "and 'tis terrible dangerous, for the Almighty's jealous as the grave, and you may get a nasty awakener."

A proper prophet the woman was, for seven nights later, just afore the hour when the cat was due—a moony night in autumn, bright and peaceful, with the owls calling each other in Western Wood—I heard a harsh, sharp sound which I knowed for a heavy air-gun; and not liking it none too well at that late hour, I went in my garden instanter to call Sunny Jim.

The back side of my house gave on waste land that ran up to furze brakes, and I was going to give a look over the wall and see who it might be prowling round, when my cat crawled up to me on three legs. I picked him up and took him in to the lamp; and then I found as he'd got his shoulder all smashed by a bullet.

I kept my head and ministered to the poor soul, and he fixed his eyes upon me and seemed to ask if it was to be a fatal matter. For a time I thought he was sinking, for he lay cruel still with his eyes shut, breathing hard; but then, seeing he weren't in no immediate danger of death, I offered him water, which he lapped, and after that I picked him up so tender as I might, put him in a big vegetable basket, with a bit of blanket in the bottom, and carried him over to see Billy Blades.

Billy weren't a man I liked, being a doubtful customer in many ways, and said to have shortened his wife's life by unkindness; but he was a very clever vet., and properly renowned for his knowledge of four-footed creatures. He was a great dog-fancier without a doubt, and though 'twas whispered he fancied other people's dogs a thought too often, yet the skill was there; so I took Sunny Jim to see the man, and he was home by good luck and gave me all his attention. The cat knew perfectly well what his doctor was up to, and behaved like a Christian under the search.

"His shoulder blade be smashed to pieces," said Billy, "and if the ball had took him an inch lower, it would have gone through the creature and slain him. The man who done this made a bad shot, I reckon, and when he found he'd only winged the cat, he ran for it, knowing the creature would have strength to get home and give the show away."

"But why should any mortal man want for to kill my cat?" I asked.

"For his skin," explained Billy Blades. "Cat and coney be worth money nowadays. A skin like this here will die black and be worth fifteen shillings, or a pound, to any man; and that's why a good few cats have failed to come home lately. But I bain't going to say he won't live. I think he may. He's in good health and in his prime by the look of him, and he's got a patient sort of nature. You see how he bears up. If all goes well and there's no fatal poison in the wound, he'll very likely make a good recovery. Us can't tell yet; but if, as may happen, the wound gets ugly in a few days, then I'll give him a whiff of chloroform and see into the evil and find if the bullet's there."

"I can take hope, then?" I asked.

"You can," he said, "but not too much. He's hard hit."

So all was dreadful suspense, and nought could be done for a time till the extent of the danger showed.

I took Sunny Jim home, and, to my great thanksgiving, he ate a bit of raw mutton, as I cut off a leg and minced for him. Not much, but enough to keep up his strength; and he got a little sleep also off and on, though I did not; and in the morning, I carried him down, and he just lay, patient and resigned, on his little mat by the kitchen fire, while I swallowed my breakfast.

But my rage knew no bounds, and if I could have catched the anointed devil as done it, I'd have choked his breath out of him between my hands. I never did feel so properly hard to any fellow-creature before; and to this day when I see the vision of thicky cat crawling home on three legs, with the moonlight on his poor, terrified eyes, I feel a thrill of hate and passion.

Next morning it was round the village like a flame of fire that Sunny Jim had been shot and might die of it, and a proper rally of neighbors —women, children, and men—streamed along to see him and say how cruel vexed they was on my account, and to hope that Sunny Jim might be spared. 'Twas the general opinion that no neighbour could have sunk to such a crime, for none was known to bear me a grudge, nor yet him.

Billy Blades came morning and evening to view the patient. And then he gave me a ray of hope, for, in a week, he believed the wound was clean and wouldn't get no worse. In fact, it began to heal very nice outside, and now the danger was whether Sunny Jim's sinews would join up too, or whether they would not. And much depended upon that. He couldn't put his paw down yet, of course, but Job never beat him for patience. He didn't like me out of his sight, however, and wouldn't let down his victuals for anybody but me.

And then in my wrath I issued an advertisement, for I was death on bringing the sinner to justice and felt if a man had done the crime he must be had up and disgraced afore the magistrates; while if it was only a wicked, hard-hearted boy, then the least they could do to him, for his own salvation and my satisfaction, would be a damned good hiding.

And I wrote with my own hand six advertisements offering £5 reward for the name of the man, or boy, as had shot my famous cat. One I stuck on my front gate, one on the guide post at the cross roads outside Ponsworthy, one in Martin Bird's shop window, one in the post office, one by the upping-stock, outside "The Green Man" public house, and the other in the bar of the same.

People marvelled at the sight of such big money, and they said, behind my back, as I must be a millionaire, or else going weak in my head; but it was a fortnight afore any response reached me, and then I had the surprise of my life on hearing the sinner's name.

I learnt it of a Friday, when Billy Blades dropped in for a look at Sunny Jim, and he said he was very pleased indeed with the cat's progress, and now felt it was safe to assure me he'd make a recovery and was out of danger.

"The ligaments be joined up beautiful," said Billy, "and the bone have growed together. You see how he can use his leg and trust it again; and he could trust it more than he do, only he's nervous yet. But, though he may go a thought lame for life, it will be nothing to interfere with his pleasure. And in time even the lameness may wear off altogether, when the muscles and sinews get used to the change."

Then I thanked Blades with all my heart and shook his hand and told him I thought he was a very clever man and must send in his account.

"And now 'tis all over," he said, "I'll tell you another thing about this here cat, and that's the name of the party as tried to shoot him and failed."

"You know!" I cried out. "Then I thank Providence, Billy; and never shall I part from a five-pound note with better will."

"No you won't," he answered. "You'll hate to part, Peter; but life's life and cats are cats, and a fiver is a fiver, so just you keep your nerve and take it as it comes. I shot your cat. I was poking about in the furzes with a new air-gun, and seeing the beggar airing himself, I thought a quid for his skin was worth while, me being harder up than usual. So I fired to drop him, but he moved and so was saved alive. Then he was gone like a streak; and so was I, because I knowed you'd fetch him along to me so soon as you could, if he weren't done for. But I'm right down glad to have saved him and be nearly so fond of the chap now as you are yourself."

"You God-forgotten villain!" I cried to the wretch, trembling with white rage.

"I know," he answered. "That's all right, and you can lay it on so thick as you please and cuss till you're winded. But you understand the situation, don't you? You summons me, and I get a dressing down and a caution and a fine. And the fine will be ten shillings and sixpence; and time don't stand still and the matter will soon be forgot; and I get your five pounds."

"Hookem snivey beast!" I said to him. "That ban't all, I promise you! My five pound you may have; but I'll ruin your business and set every honest man and woman against you, and hound you out of Ponsworthy. By God's light I will!"

He laughed his hateful, coarse laugh, and his sharp nose grew sharper than ever.

"You do your worstest and welcome, Peter Blount," he said. "I ban't much afraid. There ain't no other vet. within ten miles that I know about, and the farmers don't care how wicked a man may be, so long as he knows how to cure their things. So you give me my fiver, and then have me up for trying to shoot your cat. And always remember that I'm terrible glad I missed his vitals—though how I failed I can't guess, for 'twas bright moonlight and I was as sober as I am now."

I blazed up at that and ordered him out of my house, and he went; and I bided awake three parts of the night thinking on the awful ways of human nature and the hateful surprises that may be hid in your next-door neighbour and familiar friend. In fact I cussed Billy to hell and raged against him something furious; and first thing next morning I went up to Martin Bird and catched him taking down his shutters, and told him the monstrous tale.

It interested him a lot, and he seemed to think it funny in a way, though for my part I didn't see nothing funny to it.

"To give the traitor as shot Sunny Jim four pound ten shilling for his trouble, be a bit of a joke sure enough," said Martin Bird. "Of course, you'll have the satisfaction of getting him up afore the Justices and turning public opinion against him; but after all, as he very truly said, a cat's only a cat—masterpiece though your cat is known to be—and the law must hold an even balance between man and man; and when you think of the dark crimes that human nature will do at a pinch, the law have to keep a bit up its sleeve for the murderers and such like. And so, no doubt, ten and six for a cat be about the justice of it."

"I don't want no vengeance like that," I told Martin. "We all know vengeance be the Lord's; and to speak plain, I'm a lot more set now on keeping my five-pound note than on having that beastly toad afore the beaks. It ain't money, but the shame; for he'll have the laugh against me to my dying day if he gets the cash."

"He will," admitted Martin. "Billy Blades is an artful item best of times, and it would hit him much harder to withhold your money than have him up."

"But how can it be done in honesty?" I asked. "There it is in plain black and white. I offer five pounds to know who shot my cat; and he told me."

Martin Bird said it was a very pretty problem, but he didn't give up all hope of solving it. He was a clever man, as them with a barrow-load of children must be, if they want to keep their young and themselves out of the workhouse, and he promised me he'd look in during the evening if any light struck upon the subject.

"Anyway, 'tis Saturday, and you can well leave his claim unsettled till you decide whether to summon him," said Bird to me.

So I went home to Sunny Jim, and couldn't help feeling that anything less than the law against Billy would be treachery to my cat. And yet again, there was no doubt that Billy had been wondrous clever with the animal, and so healed his shoulder that he was to have the blessing of his leg. For what be the fulness of life to a cat on three legs? Billy had, in fact, made good his own evil work in a manner of speaking, and I was bound to admit that, once the cat was in his hands, he might have finished the murder, and I shouldn't have been none the wiser.

I couldn't see my duty all day, and the more I thought on Billy Blades the more I detested him, for he'd played a devilish part, and not been ashamed to confess it for blood money. So, when Martin strolled in, after he'd shut up his shop, and asked for a spot of whisky, I weren't no forwarder than in the morn. But, if anything, I hated worse than ever the thought of handing my five pounds to the assassin.

Martin stroked Sunny Jim for a bit and watched him walk, and said that by the look of it he was making a very brave recovery.

"The bone be joined up and the sinews going on fine," I told Bird, "and I shall leave him to nature now, for I won't have that cat-murderer in my house no more."

"Well," answered Martin, "I believe I see the way out for you. It come to me, like the Light to Paul, while I was cutting off a pound of bacon. If you want to diddle Billy Blades, it can be done, and you've only to say the word."

"I do," I said. "I never felt to want nothing so much."

"Right," he answered. "Say no more, Peter, but just go about your business and leave the rest to me."

'Twas a very puzzling direction, and I asked Martin to speak a thought plainer; but he refused.

"See what happens o' Monday morning," was all he would answer. And so, full of wonder and quite in the dark, I had to leave it at that.

Then Bird went his way after a lot of whisky, but he explained that I needn't grudge it, because he was going to take a tidy bit of trouble on my account. And when he was gone, me and Sunny Jim toddled off to bed. He couldn't quite get upstairs yet, so I had to carry him; and I reckoned that the poor hero had lost about three of his nine lives by this fearful adventure.

Nought happened Sunday, though, as I found afterwards, Martin had been so busy as a bee on my account; and when Monday came, afore I'd done my breakfast, and while the cat was washing his face after his, the mystery began to unfold. But when I say "washing his face" I must tell you that Sunny Jim could only polish up one side as yet, for his right front paw couldn't work to perfection so far; and 'twas among his greatest griefs, while he was recovering, that the right side of his head and his right whisker and right ear had to go untended. I done what I could, but nought to satisfy him.

Then who should come in but Andy White, the water-keeper, a very knowledgeable man with the rare gift to see in the dark.

"Well, White," I axed, "and what might you want?"

"Five pounds," he said. "I know who 'twas tried to slay your cat."

I leapt out of my chair as if I was sitting on fire.

"Guy Fawkes and angels!" I cried. "D'you tell me you done it, Andy?"

"Me done it!" he said. "No, Peter Blount, I ban't a cat shooter as ever I heard tell about. And I'm sorry you think I'd so demean myself. 'Twas Neddy Tutt, that young rip from Falcon Farm. He's got an air-gun and the deed was his."

Well, for the life of me I couldn't see even yet what was afoot, and after Andy had said he'd be round with proofs for his money a bit later, and had gone to work, I sat marvelling at his news.

And then, just as Mrs. Bassett come in to tidy up for me and see after one thing and another, which she performed regular for half-a-crown a week, who should knock at the door but Willie Stockman, the shoe-smith.

"Hullo, Willie, and what can I do for you?" I asked the young man. He was rather a favourite of mine, for he had a kind heart and kept his widowed mother.

"Ban't what you can do for me, master, but what I can do for you," he answered. "Come in the garden and I'll tell you something you be wishful to know."

So I stepped out, and Sunny Jim, he stepped out with me. You'd have thought the blessed cat was in the know, for he sat and looked at Willie without winking while he spoke.

" 'Tis no less a job than the business of this poor creature," said Stockman. "I happened to be going home in the moonlight with my young woman, and just as us came through the furze brakes up over, I marked a chap with a gun. He lifted it and let fly, and then he was sloking off, but he came full upon us, Peter, and gave us 'Good night'. And 'twas that poaching rascal, Timothy Bamsey, from Lower Town. So now you know what you want to know. And I may say your five pounds be going to push on our wedding. There's no hurry, however till you've got the proofs of the crime."

Of course, I thanked him very grateful; and when he was gone I beginned slow and sure to see the terrible cunning of Martin Bird. In fact, I'd never have given the man credit for such amazing stratagems; and even that weren't all, for an hour later, as I was digging a few potatoes in the sun, and the cat was practising his game leg gentle, and seeing if he could clean his claws on the stem of my lilac bush according to his daily use, if Timothy Bamsey himself didn't heave up the road! A hugeous young man—six foot three inches of wickedness, by all accounts. I knew him by sight, no more, and I also knew he'd only escaped clink by the skin of his teeth after a row over the pheasants down to Squire Mannering's preserves. But there he was, and he stopped at the gate and asked in a big voice if I could tell him where I lived.

"Do'e know the man round about here what had his cat shot long ago?" said Timothy Bamsey to me, and I left my fork sticking in the ground and went down to him.

"I'm the man," I said, "and what about it?" For I felt sure he was come to own the felony and claim the fiver, same as Billy Blades had done. I felt fierce, I admit, for I was getting in a miz-maze along of all this plotting. I'd almost forgot Billy, and for the moment I felt as if I stood face to face with the real, living villain at last.

But he soon undeceived me.

"Well, I know who shot your cat, master. By chance I was going home along behind these here houses on the night, and just as I came down, I see a man in the moonlight lift a gun and fire—an air-gun it was, for there weren't no explosion, but just a whizz and a jolt, like what air-guns make. Then he runned forward to take up his prey; but he found nought. He cussed something terrible, and was just making off, when he very near ran into me and tried to hide his face. But I see him so plain as I see you this minute."

"And who was the man, Timothy Bamsey?" I asked, so stern as I could.

"Willie Stockman, the shoesmith," he answered. "There ain't no manner of doubt about it, I assure you. And I'll have my fiver, if it's all one, Mr. Blount."

Well, my head was spinning now till I thought it would roll off in the road.

"Us'll talk about this another time," I said to the man. "There's a mystery here, and I must seek my friends afore I do ought in such a dark matter. I'm very much obliged to you, and you'll hear of me again presently; but I don't part with no five-pound notes for the minute, for it begins to look as if I should have to summon half the parish afore I get to the bitter truth."

"I've told 'e the truth," he says, "and you owe me five pounds."

"I may, or I may not; but be sure justice shall be done," I said. And with that he went off, leaving me in a proper confusion of brain till the evening come. Then Martin Bird dropped in to hear the result of his work. And when he did hear it he was terrible pleased.

"Now," he said, "you stand in a firm position, for here be a cloud of witnesses, Peter, and one man's word is as good as another's, and better for that matter. Because everybody knows Billy Blades is a liar, and nobody would take his word against t'others. So all you need to say is that you don't know who the deuce to believe among 'em, which is true. And then you keep your money in your pocket!"

"A masterpiece of politics, Martin!" I said. "And gratefully I thank you for it, but while Sunny Jim's living, it's always in the power of a wicked man to have the last word and lay him out. Don't you forget that."

"I haven't," answered Bird, who fairly staggered me with his wondrous brain power. "I haven't overlooked the future, and what I advise you to do be this, Peter; Ax the whole crew of 'em in to supper one night, and give 'em a tidy feed and a bit of baccy to each, and a bottle of whisky also. Do 'em a treat; then they'll all be your friends for life."

"And Blades also?" I asked.

"Certainly Blades. He's the one that matters most. 'Cause we know he done it in reality. Then, when they be got together and their bellies filled and their pipes drawing suent and their glasses topped up, you can tell 'em, amiable like, that they be a pack of bare-faced liars, and you find such a lot of men shot your cat that you ain't going to make no distinctions, but trust to the goodwill and gentlemanly feeling of 'em all never to do it no more. It will run you in a pound or so, but you're a snug man and won't be none the worse.

"You've took the lead in this matter," I said, "and I'll go through with it according as you direct. All I ask is that you come to the feed with the rest."

Which Martin Bird did do; and, God's my Judge, I never want to spend a pleasanter evening. They all obeyed my invite; and they all laughed fit to die when I told 'em they was a set of low-down, lying blackguards; and Billy Blades had to be seen home after, for he was blind afore the finish, singing shameful songs, as be long gone out of print, thank the watching Lord.

Sunny Jim, he much enjoyed his evening, also, and got nothing but kind words. And rabbit pie being very near his favourite food, he done himself so well as any of us. But the merriment tired him, and you can't blame the dear chap for not seeing the joke quite so clear as Billy and Timothy and Martin and Andy and Neddy and Willie saw it.

'Twas a good night, however, and me and Sunny Jim felt very glad to get to bed when the boys had gone.

And this I can say: no hand was ever lifted to my cat again. He walked on his way rejoicing, and though I ban't going to pretend he was ever quite the same light-hearted, high-spirited party as of old, yet his higher qualities still shine out of him; and he's all the world to me.

Billy Blades was round only a night ago, and he thought as Sunny Jim ought to live a good five year yet. So I be contented in my mind about him; and while there's a purr left in him, I shall be his very willing servant and faithful friend.

But never again! Life be a cloudy and difficult business enough at best without mixing yourself up with the dumb things and letting a creature without a soul into your heart. I won't love nought on four feet no more. They get too terrible a grip upon your vitals—specially if you're a lonely old blid, without much else to set store by, same as me.

33

The Adventure of the Kind Mr. Smith

BY WILLIAM J. LOCKE

ARISTIDE PUJOL started life
on his own account as a *chasseur* in a Nice *café*—one of those luckless
children tightly encased in bottle-green cloth by means of brass buttons,
who earn a sketchy livelihood by enduring with cherubic smiles the continuous maledictions of the establishment. There he soothed his hours
of servitude by dreams of vast ambitions. He would become the manager of a great hotel—not a contemptible hostelry where commercial
travellers and seedy Germans were indifferently bedded, but one of
those white palaces where milords (English) and millionaires (American) paid a thousand francs a night for a bedroom and five louis for a
glass of beer. Now, in order to derive such profit from the Anglo-Saxon
a knowledge of English was indispensable. He resolved to learn the
language. How he did so, except by sheer effrontery, taking linguistic
toll of frequenters of the *café,* would be a mystery to anyone unacquainted with Aristide. But to his friends his mastery of the English
tongue in such circumstances is comprehensible. To Aristide the impossible was ever the one thing easy of attainment; the possible the one
thing he never could achieve. That was the paradoxical nature of the
man. Before his days of hunted-little-devildom were over he had acquired sufficient knowledge of English to carry him, a few years later,
through various vicissitudes in England, until, fired by new social ambitions and self-educated in a haphazard way, he found himself appointed Professor of French in an academy for young ladies.

One of these days, when I can pin my dragonfly friend down to a
plain, unvarnished autobiography, I may be able to trace some chrono-
logical sequence in the kaleidoscopic changes in his career. But hitherto,
in his talks with me, he flits about from any one date to any other during a couple of decades, in a manner so confusing that for the present I

abandon such an attempt. All I know of the date of the episode I am about to chronicle is that it occurred immediately after the termination of his engagement at the academy just mentioned. Somehow, Aristide's history is a category of terminations.

If the head mistress of the academy had herself played dragon at his classes, all would have gone well. He would have made his pupils conjugate irregular verbs, rendered them adepts in the mysteries of the past participle and the subjunctive mood, and turned them out quite innocent of the idiomatic quaintnesses of the French tongue. But *dis aliter visum.* The gods always saw wrong-headedly otherwise in the case of Aristide. A weak-minded governess—and in a governess a sense of humour and of novelty is always a sign of a weak mind—played dragon during Aristide's lessons. She appreciated his method, which was colloquial. The colloquial Aristide was jocular. His lessons therefore were a giggling joy from beginning to end. He imparted to his pupils delicious knowledge. *En avez-vous des-z-homards? Oh, les sales bêtes, elles ont du poil aux pattes,* which, being translated, is: "Have you any lobsters? Oh, the dirty animals, they have hair on their feet"—a catch phrase which, some years ago, added greatly to the gaiety of Paris, but in which I must confess to seeing no gleam of wit—became the historic property of the school. He recited to them, till they were word-perfect, a music-hall ditty of the early eighties, *Sur le bi, sur le banc, sur le bi du bout du banc,* and delighted them with dissertations on Mme. Yvette Guilbert's earlier *répertoire.* But for him they would have gone to their lives' end without knowing that *pognon* meant money; *rouspétance,* assaulting the police; *thune,* a five-franc piece; and *bouffer,* to take nourishment. He made (according to his own statement) French a living language. There was never a school in Great Britain, the Colonies, or America on which the Parisian accent was so electrically impressed. The retort, *Eh! ta sœur,* was the purest Montmartre; also *Fich'-moi la paix, mon petit,* and *Tu as un toupet, toi;* and the delectable locution, *Allons étrangler un perroquet* (let us strangle a parrot), employed by Apaches when inviting each other to drink a glass of absinthe, soon became current French in the school for invitations to surreptitious cocoa-parties.

The progress that academy made in a real grip of the French language was miraculous; but the knowledge it gained in French grammar and syntax was deplorable. A certain mid-term examination—the paper being set by a neighbouring vicar—produced awful results. The phrase, "How do you do, dear?" which ought, by all the rules of Stratford-atte-Bowe, to be translated by *Comment vous portez-vous, ma chère?* was rendered by most of the senior scholars *Eh, ma vieille, ça boulotte?* One innocent and anachronistic damsel, writing on the execution of Charles I, declared that he *cracha dans le panier* in 1649, thereby mystifying the good vicar, who was unaware that "to spit into the basket" is to be guillotined. This wealth of vocabulary was discounted by abject poverty in other branches of the language. No one could give a list of the words in *al* that took *s* in the plural, no one knew anything at all about the defective verb *échoir,* and the orthography of the school would have disgraced a kindergarten. The head mistress suspected a lack of method in the teaching of M. Pujol, and one day paid his class a surprise visit.

The sight that met her eyes petrified her. The class, including the governess, bubbled and gurgled and shrieked with laughter. M. Pujol, his bright eyes agleam with merriment and his arms moving in frantic gestures, danced about the platform. He was telling them a story—and when Aristide told a story, he told it with the eloquence of his entire frame. He bent himself double and threw out his hands.

"Il était saoûl comme un porc," he shouted.

And then came the hush of death. The rest of the artless tale about the man as drunk as a pig was never told. The head mistress, indignant majesty, strode up the room.

"M. Pujol, you have a strange way of giving French lessons."

"I believe, madame," said he, with a polite bow, "in interesting my pupils in their studies."

"Pupils have to be taught, not interested," said the head mistress. "Will you kindly put the class through some irregular verbs?"

So for the remainder of the lesson Aristide, under the freezing eyes of the head mistress, put his sorrowful class through irregular verbs, of which his own knowledge was singularly inexact, and at the end received his dismissal. In vain he argued. Outraged Minerva was implacable. Go he must.

We find him, then, one miserable December evening, standing on the arrival platform of Euston Station (the academy was near Manchester), an unwonted statue of dubiety. At his feet lay his meagre valise; in his hand was an enormous bouquet, a useful tribute of esteem from his disconsolate pupils; around him luggage-laden porters and passengers hurried; in front were drawn up the long line of cabs, their drivers' waterproofs glistening with wet; and in his pocket rattled the few paltry coins that, for Heaven knew how long, were to keep him from starvation. Should he commit the extravagance of taking a cab or should he go forth, valise in hand, into the pouring rain? He hesitated.

"Sacré mille cochons! Quel chien de climat!" he muttered.

A smart footman standing by turned quickly and touched his hat.

"Beg pardon, sir; I'm from Mr. Smith."

"I'm glad to hear it, my friend," said Aristide.

"You're the French gentleman from Manchester?"

"Decidedly," said Aristide.

"Then, sir, Mr. Smith has sent the carriage for you."

"That's very kind of him," said Aristide.

The footman picked up the valise and darted down the platform. Aristide followed. The footman held invitingly open the door of a cosy brougham. Aristide paused for the fraction of a second. Who was this hospitable Mr. Smith?

"Bah!" said he to himself, "the best way of finding out is to go and see."

He entered the carriage, sank back luxuriously on the soft cushions, and inhaled the warm smell of leather. They started, and soon the pelting rain beat harmlessly against the windows. Aristide looked out at the streaming streets, and, hugging himself comfortably, thanked Providence and Mr. Smith. But who was Mr. Smith? *Tiens,* thought he, there were two little Miss Smiths at the academy; he had pitied them because they had chilblains, freckles, and perpetual colds in their heads; possibly this was their kind papa. But, after all, what did it matter whose papa he was? He was expecting him. He had sent the carriage for him. Evidently a well-bred and attentive person. And *tiens!* there was even a hot-water can on the floor of the brougham. "He thinks of everything, that man," said Aristide. "I feel I am going to like him."

The carriage stopped at a house in Hampstead, standing, as far as he could see in the darkness, in its own grounds. The footman opened the door for him to alight and escorted him up the front steps. A neat parlourmaid received him in a comfortably furnished hall and took his hat and great-coat and magnificent bouquet.

"Mr. Smith hasn't come back yet from the City, sir; but Miss Christabel is in the drawing-room."

"Ah!" said Aristide. "Please give me back my bouquet."

The maid showed him into the drawing-room. A pretty girl of three-and-twenty rose from a fender-stool and advanced smilingly to meet him.

"Good afternoon, M. le Baron. I was wondering whether Thomas would spot you. I'm so glad he did. You see, neither Father nor I could give him any description, for we had never seen you."

This fitted in with his theory. But why Baron? After all, why not? The English loved titles.

"He seems to be an intelligent fellow, mademoiselle."

There was a span of silence. The girl looked at the bouquet, then at Aristide, who looked at the girl, then at the bouquet, then at the girl again.

"Mademoiselle," said he, "will you deign to accept these flowers as a token of my respectful homage?"

Miss Christabel took the flowers and blushed prettily. She had dark hair and eyes and a fascinating, upturned little nose, and the kindest little mouth in the world.

"An Englishman would not have thought of that," she said.

Aristide smiled in his roguish way and raised a deprecating hand.

"Oh, yes, he would. But he would not have had—what you call the cheek to do it."

Miss Christabel laughed merrily, invited him to a seat by the fire, and comforted him with tea and hot muffins. The frank charm of his girl-hostess captivated Aristide and drove from his mind the riddle of his adventure. Besides, think of the Arabian Nights' enchantment of the change from his lonely and shabby bed-sitting-room in the Rusholme Road to this fragrant palace with princess and all to keep him company! He watched the firelight dancing through her hair, the dainty play of laughter over her face, and decided that the brougham had transported him to Bagdad instead of Hampstead.

"You have the air of a veritable princess," said he.

"I once met a princess—at a charity bazaar—and she was a most matter-of-fact businesslike person."

"Bah!" said Aristide. "A princess of a charity bazaar! I was talking of the princess in a fairy-tale. They are the only real ones."

"Do you know," said Miss Christabel, "that when men pay such compliments to English girls they are apt to get laughed at?"

"Englishmen, yes," replied Aristide, "because they think over a compliment for a week, so that by the time they pay it, it is addled, like a bad egg. But we of Provence pay tribute to beauty straight out of our hearts. It is true. It is sincere. And what comes out of the heart is not ridiculous."

Again the girl coloured and laughed. "I've always heard that a Frenchman makes love to every woman he meets."

"Naturally," said Aristide. "If they are pretty. What else are pretty women for? Otherwise they might as well be hideous."

"Oh!" said the girl, to whom this Provençal point of view had not occurred.

"So, if I make love to you, it is but your due."

"I wonder what my fiancé would say if he heard you?"

"Your——?"

"My fiancé! There's his photograph on the table beside you. He is six foot one, and so jealous!" she laughed again.

"The Turk!" cried Aristide, his swiftly conceived romance crumbling into dust. Then he brightened up. "But when this six feet of muscle and egotism is absent, surely other poor mortals can glean a smile?"

"You will observe that I'm not frowning," said Miss Christabel. "But you must not call my fiancé a Turk, for he's a very charming fellow whom I hope you'll like very much."

Aristide sighed. "And the name of this thrice-blessed mortal?"

Miss Christabel told his name—one Harry Ralston—and not only his name, but, such was the peculiar, childlike charm of Aristide Pujol, also many other things about him. He was the Honourable Harry Ralston, the heir to a great brewery peerage, and very wealthy. He was a member of Parliament, and but for Parliamentary duties would have dined there that evening; but he was to come in later, as soon as he could leave the House. He also had a house in Hampshire, full of the most beautiful works of art. It was through their common hobby that her father and Harry had first made acquaintance.

"We're supposed to have a very fine collection here," she said, with a motion of her hand.

Aristide looked round the walls and saw them hung with pictures in gold frames. In those days he had not acquired an extensive culture. Besides, who having before him the firelight gleaming through Miss Christabel's hair could waste his time over painted canvas? She noted his cursory glance.

"I thought you were a connoisseur?"

"I am," said Aristide, his bright eyes fixed on her in frank admiration. She blushed again; but this time she rose.

"I must go and dress for dinner. Perhaps you would like to be shown your room?"

He hung his head on one side.

"Have I been too bold, Mademoiselle?"

"I don't know," she said. "You see, I've never met a Frenchman before."

"Then a world of undreamed-of homage is at your feet," said he.

A servant ushered him up broad, carpeted staircases into a bedroom such as he had never seen in his life before. It was all curtains and hangings and rugs and soft couches and satin quilts and dainty writing-tables and subdued lights, and a great fire glowed red and cheerful, and before it hung a clean shirt. His poor little toilet apparatus was laid on the dressing-table, and (with a tact which he did not appreciate, for he had, sad to tell, no dress-suit) the servant had spread his precious frock-coat and spare pair of trousers on the bed. On the pillow lay his night-shirt, neatly folded.

"Evidently," said Aristide, impressed by these preparations, "it is expected that I wash myself now and change my clothes, and that I sleep here for the night. And for all that the ravishing Miss Christabel is engaged to her Honourable Harry, this is none the less a corner of Paradise."

So Aristide attired himself in his best, which included a white tie and a pair of nearly new brown boots—a long task, as he found that his valise had been spirited away and its contents, including the white tie of ceremony (he had but one), hidden in unexpected drawers and wardrobes—and eventually went downstairs into the drawing-room. There he found Miss Christabel and, warming himself on the hearthrug, a bald-headed, beefy-faced Briton, with little pig's eyes and a hearty manner, attired in a dinner-suit.

"My dear fellow," said this personage, with outstretched hand, "I'm delighted to have you here. I've heard so much about you; and my little girl has been singing your praises."

"Mademoiselle is too kind," said Aristide.

"You must take us as you find us," said Mr. Smith. "We're just ordinary folk, but I can give you a good bottle of wine and a good cigar— it's only in England, you know, that you can get champagne fit to drink and cigars fit to smoke—and I can give you a glimpse of a modest English home. I believe you haven't a word for it in French."

"*Ma foi,* no," said Aristide, who had once or twice before heard this lunatic charge brought against his country. "In France the men all live in *cafés,* the children are all put out to nurse, and the women, saving the respect of mademoiselle—well, the less said about them the better."

"England is the only place, isn't it?" Mr. Smith declared, heartily. "I don't say that Paris hasn't its points. But after all—the Moulin Rouge and the Folies Bergères and that sort of thing soon pall, you know— soon pall."

"Yet Paris has its serious side," argued Aristide. "There is always the tomb of Napoleon."

"Papa will never take me to Paris," sighed the girl.

"You shall go there on your honeymoon," said Mr. Smith.

Dinner was announced. Aristide gave his arm to Miss Christabel, and proud not only of his partner, but also of his frock-coat, white tie, and shiny brown boots, strutted into the dining-room. The host sat at the end of the beautifully set table, his daughter on his right, Aristide on his left. The meal began gaily. The kind Mr. Smith was in the best of humours.

"And how is our dear old friend, Jules Dancourt?" he asked.

"*Tiens!*" said Aristide, to himself, "we have a dear friend Jules Dancourt. Wonderfully well," he replied at a venture, "but he suffers terribly at times from the gout."

"So do I, confound it!" said Mr. Smith, drinking sherry.

"You and the good Jules were always sympathetic," said Aristide. "Ah! he has spoken to me so often about you, the tears in his eyes."

"Men cry, my dear, in France," Mr. Smith explained. "They also kiss each other."

"*Ah, mais c'est un beau pays, mademoiselle!*" cried Aristide, and he began to talk of France and to draw pictures of his country which set the girl's eyes dancing. After that he told some of the funny little stories which had brought him disaster at the academy. Mr. Smith, with jovial magnanimity, declared that he was the first Frenchman he had ever met with a sense of humour.

"But I thought, Baron," said he, "that you lived all your life shut up in that old château of yours?"

"*Tiens!*" thought Aristide. "I am still a Baron, and I have an old château."

"Tell us about the château. Has it a fosse and a drawbridge and a Gothic chapel?" asked Miss Christabel.

"Which one do you mean?" inquired Aristide, airily. "For I have two."

When relating to me this Arabian Nights' adventure, he drew my special attention to his astuteness.

His host's eye quivered in a wink. "The one in Languedoc," said he.

Languedoc! Almost Pujol's own country! With entire lack of morality, but with picturesque imagination, Aristide plunged into a description of that non-existent baronial hall. Fosse, drawbridge, Gothic chapel were but insignificant features. It had tourelles, emblazoned gateways, bastions, donjons, barbicans; it had innumerable rooms; in the *salle des chevaliers* two hundred men-at-arms had his ancestors fed at a sitting. There was the room in which François Premier had slept, and one in which Joan of Arc had almost been assassinated. What the name of himself or of his ancestors was supposed to be Aristide had no ghost of an idea. But as he proceeded with the erection of his airy palace he gradually began to believe in it. He invested the place with a living atmosphere; conjured up a staff of family retainers, notably one Marie-Joseph Loufoque, the wizened old major-domo, with his long white whiskers and blue and silver livery. There were also Madeline Mioulles the cook, and Bernadet the groom, and La Petite Fripette the goose girl. Ah! they should see La Petite Fripette! And he kept dogs and horses and cows and ducks and hens—and there was a great pond whence frogs were drawn to be fed for the consumption of the household.

Miss Christabel shivered. "I should not like to eat frogs."

"They also eat snails," said her father.

"I have a snail farm," said Aristide. "You never saw such interesting little animals. They are so intelligent. If you're kind to them they come and eat out of your hand."

"You've forgotten the pictures," said Mr. Smith.

"Ah! the pictures," cried Aristide, with a wide sweep of his arms. "Galleries full of them. Raphael, Michael Angelo, Wiertz, Reynolds ——"

He paused, not in order to produce the effect of a dramatic aposiopesis, but because he could not for the moment remember other names of painters.

"It is a truly historical château," said he.

"I should love to see it," said the girl.

Aristide threw out his arms across the table. "It is yours, mademoiselle, for your honeymoon," said he.

Dinner came to an end. Miss Christabel left the gentlemen to their wine, an excellent port whose English qualities were vaunted by the host. Aristide, full of food and drink and the mellow glories of the castle in Languedoc, and smoking an enormous cigar, felt at ease with all the world. He knew he should like the kind Mr. Smith, hospitable though somewhat insular man. He could stay with him for a week—or a month—why not a year?

After coffee and liqueurs had been served Mr. Smith rose and switched on a powerful electric light at the end of the large room, showing a picture on an easel covered by a curtain. He beckoned to Aristide to join him and, drawing the curtain, disclosed the picture.

"There!" said he. "Isn't it a stunner?"

It was a picture all grey skies and grey water and grey feathery trees, and a little man in the foreground wore a red cap.

"It is beautiful, but indeed it is magnificent!" cried Aristide, always impressionable to things of beauty.

"Genuine Corot, isn't it?"

"Without doubt," said Aristide.

His host poked him in the ribs. "I thought I'd astonish you. You wouldn't believe Gottschalk could have done it. There it is—as large as life and twice as natural. If you or anyone else can tell it from a genuine Corot I'll eat my hat. And all for eight pounds."

Aristide looked at the beefy face and caught a look of cunning in the little pig's eyes.

"Now are you satisfied?" asked Mr. Smith.

"More than satisfied," said Aristide, though what he was to be satisfied about passed, for the moment, his comprehension.

"If it was a copy of an existing picture, you know—one might have understood it—that, of course, would be dangerous—but for a man to go and get bits out of various Corots and stick them together like this is miraculous. If it hadn't been for a matter of business principle I'd have given the fellow eight guineas instead of pounds—hanged if I wouldn't! He deserves it."

"He does indeed," said Aristide Pujol.

"And now that you've seen it with your own eyes, what do you think you might ask me for it? I suggested something between two and three thousand—shall we say three? You're the owner, you know." Again the process of rib-digging. "Came out of that historic château of yours. My eye! you're a holy terror when you begin to talk. You almost persuaded me it was real."

"*Tiens!*" said Aristide to himself. "I don't seem to have a château after all."

"Certainly three thousand," said he, with a grave face.

"That young man thinks he knows a lot, but he doesn't," said Mr. Smith.

"Ah!" said Aristide, with singular laconicism.

"Not a blooming thing," continued his host. "But he'll pay three thousand, which is the principal, isn't it? He's partner in the show, you know, Ralston, Wiggins, and Wix's Brewery"—Aristide pricked up his ears—"and when his doddering old father dies he'll be Lord Ranelagh and come into a million of money."

"Has he seen the picture?" asked Aristide.

"Oh, yes. Regards it as a masterpiece. Didn't Brauneberger tell you of the Lancret we planted on the American?" Mr. Smith rubbed hearty hands at the memory of the iniquity. "Same old game. Always easy. I have nothing to do with the bargaining or the sale. Just an old friend of the ruined French nobleman with the historic château and family treasures. He comes along and fixes the price. I told our friend Harry——"

"Good," thought Aristide. "This is the same Honourable Harry, M.P., who is engaged to the ravishing Miss Christabel."

"I told him," said Mr. Smith, "that it might come to three or four thousand. He jibbed a bit—so when I wrote to you I said two or three. But you might try him with three to begin with."

Aristide went back to the table and poured himself out a fresh glass of his kind host's 1865 brandy and drank it off.

"Exquisite, my dear fellow," said he. "I've none finer in my historic château."

"Don't suppose you have," grinned the host, joining him. He slapped him on the back. "Well," said he, with a shifty look in his little pig's eyes, "let us talk business. What do you think would be your fair commission? You see, all the trouble and invention have been mine. What do you say to four hundred pounds?"

"Five," said Aristide, promptly.

A sudden gleam came into the little pig's eyes.

"Done!" said Mr. Smith, who had imagined that the other would demand a thousand and was prepared to pay eight hundred. "Done!" said he again.

They shook hands to seal the bargain and drank another glass of old brandy. At that moment, a servant, entering, took the host aside.

"Please excuse me a moment," said he, and went with the servant out of the room.

Aristide, left alone, lighted another of his kind host's fat cigars and threw himself in a great leathern armchair by the fire, and surrendered himself deliciously to the soothing charm of the moment. Now and then he laughed, finding a certain comicality in his position. And what a charming father-in-law, this kind Mr. Smith!

His cheerful reflections were soon disturbed by the sudden irruption of his host and a grizzled, elderly, foxy-faced gentleman with a white moustache, wearing the ribbon of the Legion of Honour in the buttonhole of his overcoat.

"Here, you!" cried the kind Mr. Smith, striding up to Aristide, with a very red face. "Will you have the kindness to tell me who the devil you are?"

Aristide rose, and, putting his hands behind the tails of his frockcoat, stood smiling radiantly on the hearthrug. A wit much less alert than my irresponsible friend's would have instantly appreciated the fact that the real Simon Pure had arrived on the scene.

"I, my dear friend," said he, "am the Baron de Je ne Sais Plus."

"You're a confounded impostor," spluttered Mr. Smith.

"And this gentleman here to whom I have not had the pleasure of being introduced?" asked Aristide, blandly.

"I am M. Poiron, monsieur, the agent of Messrs. Brauneberger and Compagnie, art dealers, of the Rue Notre-Dame des Petits Champs of Paris," said the newcomer, with an air of defiance.

"Ah, I thought you were the Baron," said Aristide.

"There's no blooming Baron at all about it!" screamed Mr. Smith. "Are you Poiron, or is he?"

"I would not have a name like Poiron for anything in the world," said Aristide. "My name is Aristide Pujol, soldier of fortune, at your service."

"How the blazes did you get here?"

"Your servant asked me if I was a French gentleman from Manchester. I was. He said that Mr. Smith had sent his carriage for me. I thought it hospitable of the kind Mr. Smith. I entered the carriage— *et voilà!*"

"Then clear out of here this very minute," said Mr. Smith, reaching forward his hand to the bell-push.

Aristide checked his impulsive action.

"Pardon me, dear host," said he. "It is raining dogs and cats outside. I am very comfortable in your luxurious home. I am here, and here I stay."

"I'm shot if you do," said the kind Mr. Smith, his face growing redder and uglier. "Now, will you go out, or will you be thrown out?"

Aristide, who had no desire whatever to be ejected from this snug nest into the welter of the wet and friendless world, puffed at his cigar, and looked at his host with the irresistible drollery of his eyes.

"You forget, *mon cher ami,*" said he, "that neither the beautiful Miss Christabel nor her affianced, the Honourable Harry, M.P., would care to know that the talented Gottschalk got only eight pounds, not even guineas, for painting that three-thousand-pound picture."

"So it's blackmail, eh?"

"Precisely," said Aristide, "and I don't blush at it."

"You infernal little blackguard!"

"I seem to be in congenial company," said Aristide. "I don't think our friend M. Poiron has more scruples than he has right to the ribbon of the Legion of Honour which he is wearing."

"How much will you take to go out? I have a cheque-book handy."

Mr. Smith moved a few steps from the hearthrug. Aristide sat down in the armchair. An engaging, fantastic impudence was one of the charms of Aristide Pujol.

"I'll take five hundred pounds," said he, "to stay in."

"Stay in?" Mr. Smith grew apoplectic.

"Yes," said Aristide. "You can't do without me. Your daughter and your servants know me as M. le Baron—by the way, what is my name? And where is my historic château in Languedoc?"

"Mireilles," said M. Poiron, who was sitting grim and taciturn on one of the dining-room chairs. "And the place is the same, near Montpellier."

"I like to meet an intelligent man," said Aristide.

"I should like to wring your infernal neck," said the kind Mr. Smith. "But, by George, if we do let you in you'll have to sign me a receipt implicating yourself up to the hilt. I'm not going to be put into the cart by you, you can bet your life."

"Anything you like," said Aristide, "so long as we all swing together."

Now, when Aristide Pujol arrived at this point in his narrative, I, his chronicler, who am nothing if not an eminently respectable, law-abiding Briton, took him warmly to task for his sheer absence of moral sense. His eyes, as they sometimes did, assumed a luminous pathos.

"My dear friend," said he, "have you ever faced the world in a foreign country in December with no character and fifteen pounds five and threepence in your pocket? Five hundred pounds was a fortune. It is one now. And to be gained just by lending oneself to a good farce, which didn't hurt anybody. You and your British morals! Bah!" said he, with a fine flourish.

Aristide, after much parleying, was finally admitted into the nefarious brotherhood. He was to retain his rank as the Baron de Mireilles, and play the part of the pecuniarily inconvenienced nobleman forced to sell some of his rare collection. Mr. Smith had heard of the Corot through their dear old common friend, Jules Dancourt of Rheims, had mentioned it alluringly to the Honourable Harry, had arranged for the Baron, who was visiting England, to bring it over and dispatch it to Mr. Smith's house, and on his return from Manchester to pay a visit to Mr. Smith, so that he could meet the Honourable Harry in person. In whatever transaction ensued Mr. Smith, so far as his prospective son-in-law was concerned, was to be the purely disinterested friend. It was Aristide's wit which invented a part for the supplanted M. Poiron. He should be the eminent Parisian expert who, chancing to be in London, had been telephoned for by the kind Mr. Smith.

"It would not be wise for M. Poiron," said Aristide, chuckling inwardly with puckish glee, "to stay here for the night—or for two or three days—or a week—like myself. He must go back to his hotel when the business is concluded."

"*Mais, pardon!*" cried M. Poiron, who had been formally invited, and had arrived late solely because he had missed his train at Manchester, and come on by the next one. "I cannot go out into the wet, and I have no hotel to go to."

Aristide appealed to his host. "But he is unreasonable, *cher ami*. He must play his *rôle*. M. Poiron has been telephoned for. He can't possibly stay here. Surely five hundred pounds is worth one little night of discomfort? And there are a legion of hotels in London."

"Five hundred pounds!" exclaimed M. Poiron. "*Qu'est-ce que vous chantez là?* I want more than five hundred pounds."

"Then you're jolly well not going to get it," cried Mr. Smith, in a rage. "And as for you"—he turned on Aristide—"I'll wring your infernal neck yet."

"Calm yourself, calm yourself!" smiled Aristide, who was enjoying himself hugely.

At this moment the door opened and Miss Christabel appeared. On seeing the decorated stranger she started with a little "Oh!" of surprise. "I beg your pardon."

Mr. Smith's angry face wreathed itself in smiles.

"This, my darling, is M. Poiron, the eminent Paris expert, who has been good enough to come and give us his opinion on the picture."

M. Poiron bowed. Aristide advanced.

"Mademoiselle, your appearance is like a mirage in a desert."

She smiled indulgently and turned to her father. "I've been wondering what had become of you. Harry has been here for the last half-hour."

"Bring him in, dear child, bring him in!" said Mr. Smith, with all the heartiness of the fine old English gentleman. "Our good friends are dying to meet him."

The girl flickered out of the room like a sunbeam (the phrase is Aristide's), and the three precious rascals put their heads together in a hurried and earnest colloquy. Presently Miss Christabel returned, and with her came the Honourable Harry Ralston, a tall, soldierly fellow, with close-cropped fair curly hair and a fair moustache, and frank blue eyes that, even in Parliament, had seen no harm in his fellow-creatures. Aristide's magical vision caught him wincing ever so little at Mr. Smith's effusive greeting and overdone introductions. He shook Aristide warmly by the hand.

"You have a beauty there, Baron, a perfect beauty," said he, with the insane ingenuousness of youth. "I wonder how you can manage to part with it."

"Ma foi," said Aristide, with his back against the end of the dining-table and gazing at the masterpiece. "I have so many at the Château de Mireilles. When one begins to collect, you know—and when one's grandfather and father have had also the divine mania——"

"You were saying, M. le Baron," said M. Poiron of Paris, "that your respected grandfather bought this direct from Corot himself."

"A commission," said Aristide. "My grandfather was a patron of Corot."

"Do you like it, dear?" asked the Honourable Harry.

"Oh, yes!" replied the girl, fervently. "It is beautiful. I feel like Harry about it." She turned to Aristide. "How can you part with it? Were you really in earnest when you said you would like me to come and see your collection?"

"For me," said Aristide, "it would be a visit of enchantment."

"You must take me, then," she whispered to Harry. "The Baron has been telling us about his lovely old château."

"Will you come, monsieur?" asked Aristide.

"Since I'm going to rob you of your picture," said the young man, with smiling courtesy, "the least I can do is to pay you a visit of apology. Lovely!" said he, going up to the Corot.

Aristide took Miss Christabel, now more bewitching than ever with the glow of young love in her eyes and a flush on her cheek, a step or two aside and whispered:

"But he is charming, your fiancé! He almost deserves his good fortune."

"Why almost?" she laughed, shyly.

"It is not a man, but a demi-god, that would deserve you, mademoiselle."

M. Poiron's harsh voice broke out.

"You see, it is painted in the beginning of Corot's later manner—it is 1864. There is the mystery which, when he was quite an old man, became a trick. If you were to put it up to auction at Christie's it would fetch, I am sure, five thousand pounds."

"That's more than I can afford to give," said the young man, with a laugh. "Mr. Smith mentioned something between three and four thousand pounds. I don't think I can go above three."

"I have nothing to do with it, my dear boy, nothing whatever," said Mr. Smith, rubbing his hands. "You wanted a Corot. I said I thought I could put you on to one. It's for the Baron here to mention his price. I retire now and for ever."

"Well, Baron?" said the young man, cheerfully. "What's your idea?"

Aristide came forward and resumed his place at the end of the table. The picture was in front of him beneath the strong electric light; on his left stood Mr. Smith and Poiron, on his right Miss Christabel and the Honourable Harry.

"I'll not take three thousand pounds for it," said Aristide. "A picture like that! Never!"

"I assure you it would be a fair price," said Poiron.

"You mentioned that figure yourself only just now," said Mr. Smith, with an ugly glitter in his little pig's eyes.

"I presume, gentlemen," said Aristide, "that this picture is my own property." He turned engagingly to his host. "Is it not, *cher ami?*"

"Of course it is. Who said it wasn't?"

"And you, M. Poiron, acknowledge formally that it is mine?" he asked, in French.

"*Sans aucun doute.*"

"*Eh bien,*" said Aristide, throwing open his arms and gazing round sweetly. "I have changed my mind. I do not sell the picture at all."

"Not sell it? What the—what do you mean?" asked Mr. Smith, striving to mellow the gathering thunder on his brow.

"I do not sell," said Aristide. "Listen, my dear friends!" He was in the seventh heaven of happiness—the principal man, the star, taking the centre of the stage. "I have an announcement to make to you. I have fallen desperately in love with mademoiselle."

There was a general gasp. Mr. Smith looked at him, red-faced and open-mouthed. Miss Christabel blushed furiously and emitted a sound half between a laugh and a scream. Harry Ralston's eyes flashed.

"My dear sir——" he began.

"Pardon," said Aristide, disarming him with the merry splendour of his glance. "I do not wish to take mademoiselle from you. My love is hopeless! I know it. But it will feed me to my dying day. In return for the joy of this hopeless passion I will not sell you the picture—I give it to you as a wedding present."

He stood, with the air of a hero, both arms extended towards the amazed pair of lovers.

"I give it to you," said he. "It is mine. I have no wish but for your happiness. In my Château de Mireilles there are a hundred others."

"This is madness!" said Mr. Smith, bursting with suppressed indignation, so that his bald head grew scarlet.

"My dear fellow!" said Mr. Harry Ralston. "It is unheard-of generosity on your part. But we can't accept it."

"Then," said Aristide, advancing dramatically to the picture, "I take it under my arm, I put it in a hansom cab, and I go with it back to Languedoc."

Mr. Smith caught him by the wrist and dragged him out of the room.

"You little brute! Do you want your neck broken?"

"Do you want the marriage of your daughter with the rich and Honourable Harry broken?" asked Aristide.

"Oh, damn! Oh, damn! Oh, damn!" cried Mr. Smith, stamping about helplessly and half weeping.

Aristide entered the dining-room and beamed on the company.

"The kind Mr. Smith has consented. Mr. Honourable Harry and Miss Christabel, there is your Corot. And now, may I be permitted?" He rang the bell. A servant appeared.

"Some champagne to drink to the health of the fiancés," he cried. "Lots of champagne."

Mr. Smith looked at him almost admiringly.

"By Jove!" he muttered. "You *have* got a nerve."

"*Voilà!*" said Aristide, when he had finished the story.

"And did they accept the Corot?" I asked.

"Of course. It is hanging now in the big house in Hampshire. I stayed with the kind Mr. Smith for six weeks," he added, doubling himself up in his chair and hugging himself with mirth, "and we became very good friends. And I was at the wedding."

"And what about their honeymoon visit to Languedoc?"

"Alas!" said Aristide. "The morning before the wedding I had a telegram—it was from my old father at Aigues-Mortes—to tell me that the historic Château de Mireilles, with my priceless collection of pictures, had been burned to the ground."

34

The Roll-Call of the Reef

BY SIR ARTHUR T. QUILLER-COUCH

"YES, sir," said my host the quarryman, reaching down the relics from their hook in the wall over the chimney-piece; "they've hung there all my time, and most of my father's. The women won't touch 'em; they're afraid of the story. So here they'll dangle, and gather dust and smoke, till another tenant comes and tosses 'em out o' doors for rubbish. Whew! 'tis coarse weather."

He went to the door, opened it, and stood studying the gale that beat upon his cottage-front, straight from the Manacle Reef. The rain drove past him into the kitchen, aslant like threads of gold silk in the shine of the wreckwood fire. Meanwhile by the same firelight I examined the relics on my knee. The metal of each was tarnished out of knowledge. But the trumpet was evidently an old cavalry trumpet, and the threads of its parti-coloured sling, though frayed and dusty, still hung together. Around the side-drum, beneath its cracked brown varnish, I could hardly trace a royal coat-of-arms, and a legend running—*Per Mare per Terram*—the motto of the Marines. Its parchment, though coloured and scented with wood-smoke, was limp and mildewed; and I began to tighten up the straps—under which the drumsticks had been loosely thrust—with the idle purpose of trying if some music might be got out of the old drum yet.

But as I turned it on my knee, I found the drum attached to the trumpet-sling by a curious barrel-shaped padlock, and paused to examine this. The body of the lock was composed of half a dozen brass rings, set accurately edge to edge; and, rubbing the brass with my thumb, I saw that each of the six had a series of letters engraved around it.

I knew the trick of it, I thought. Here was one of those word-padlocks, once so common; only to be opened by getting the rings to spell a certain word, which the dealer confides to you.

My host shut and barred the door, and came back to the hearth.

" 'Twas just such a wind—east by south—that brought in what you've got between your hands. Back in the year 'nine it was; my father has told me the tale a score o' times. You're twisting round the rings, I see. But you'll never guess the word. Parson Kendall, he made the word, and locked down a couple o' ghosts in their graves with it; and when his time came, he went to his own grave and took the word with him."

"Whose ghosts, Matthew?"

"You want the story, I see, sir. My father could tell it better than I can. He was a young man in the year 'nine, unmarried at the time, and living in this very cottage just as I be. That's how he came to get mixed up with the tale."

He took a chair, lit a short pipe, and unfolded the story in a low musing voice, with his eyes fixed on the dancing violet flames.

"Yes, he'd ha' been about thirty year old in January, of the year 'nine. The storm got up in the night o' the twenty-first o' that month. My father was dressed and out long before daylight; he never was one to 'bide in bed, let be that the gale by this time was pretty near lifting the thatch over his head. Besides which, he'd fenced a small 'taty-patch that winter, down by Lowland Point, and he wanted to see if it stood the night's work. He took the path across Gunner's Meadow—where they buried most of the bodies afterwards. The wind was right in his teeth at the time, and once on the way (he's told me this often) a great strip of ore-weed came flying through the darkness and fetched him a slap on the cheek like a cold hand. But he made shift pretty well till he got to Lowland, and then had to drop upon his hands and knees and crawl, digging his fingers every now and then into the shingle to hold on, for he declared to me that the stones, some of them as big as a man's head, kept rolling and driving past till it seemed the whole foreshore was moving westward under him. The fence was gone, of course; not a stick left to show where it stood; so that, when first he came to the place, he thought he must have missed his bearings. My father, sir, was a very religious man; and if he reckoned the end of the world was at hand—there in the great wind and night, among the moving stones— you may believe he was certain of it when he heard a gun fired, and, with the same, saw a flame shoot up out of the darkness to windward, making a sudden fierce light in all the place about. All he could find to think or say was, 'The Second Coming—The Second Coming! The Bridegroom cometh, and the wicked He will toss like a ball into a large country!' and being already upon his knees, he just bowed his head and 'bided, saying this over and over.

"But by'm-by, between two squalls, he made bold to lift his head and look, and then by the light—a bluish colour 'twas—he saw all the coast clear away to Manacle Point, and off the Manacles, in the thick of the weather, a sloop-of-war with top-gallants housed, driving stern foremost towards the reef. It was she, of course, that was burning the flare. My father could see the white streak and the ports of her quite plain as she rose to it, a little outside the breakers, and he guessed easy enough that her captain had just managed to wear ship, and was trying to force her nose to the sea with the help of her small bower anchor and the scrap or two of canvas that hadn't yet been blown out of her. But while he looked, she fell off, giving her broadside to it foot by foot, and drifting back on the breakers around Carn dû and the Varses. The rocks lie so thick thereabouts, that 'twas a toss up which she struck first; at any rate, my father couldn't tell at the time, for just then the flare died down and went out.

"Well, sir, he turned then in the dark and started back for Coverack to cry the dismal tidings—though well knowing ship and crew to be past any hope; and as he turned, the wind lifted him and tossed him forward 'like a ball,' as he'd been saying, and homeward along the foreshore. As you know, 'tis ugly work, even by daylight, picking your way among the stones there, and my father was prettily knocked about at first in the dark. But by this 'twas nearer seven than six o'clock, and the day spreading. By the time he reached North Corner, a man could see to read print; hows'ever, he looked neither out to sea nor towards Coverack, but headed straight for the first cottage—the same that stands above North Corner to-day. A man named Billy Ede lived there then, and when my father burst into the kitchen bawling, 'Wreck! wreck!' he saw Billy Ede's wife, Ann, standing there in her clogs, with a shawl over her head, and her clothes wringing wet.

" 'Save the chap!' says Billy Ede's wife, Ann. 'What d' 'ee mean by crying stale fish at that rate?'

" 'But 'tis a wreck, I tell 'ee. I've a-zeed 'n!'

" 'Why, so 'tis,' says she, 'and I've a-zeed 'n too; and so has everyone with an eye in his head.'

"And with that she pointed straight over my father's shoulder, and he turned; and there, close under Dolor Point, at the end of Coverack town, he saw *another* wreck washing, and the point black with people, like emmets, running to and fro in the morning light. While he stood staring at her, he heard a trumpet sounded on board, the notes coming in little jerks, like a bird rising against the wind; but faintly, of course, because of the distance and the gale blowing—though this had dropped a little.

" 'She's a transport,' said Billy Ede's wife, Ann, 'and full of horse soldiers, fine long men. When she struck they must ha' pitched the hosses over first to lighten the ship, for a score of dead hosses had washed in afore I left, half an hour back. An' three or four soldiers, too—fine long corpses in white breeches and jackets of blue and gold. I held the lantern to one. Such a straight young man!'

"My father asked her about the trumpeting.

"'That's the queerest bit of all. She was burnin' a light when me an' my man joined the crowd down there. All her masts had gone; whether they carried away, or were cut away to ease her, I don't rightly know. Anyway, there she lay 'pon the rocks with her decks bare. Her keelson was broke under her and her bottom sagged and stove, and she had just settled down like a sitting hen—just the leastest list to starboard; but a man could stand there easy. They had rigged up ropes across her, from bulwark to bulwark, an' beside these the men were mustered, holding on like grim death whenever the sea made a clean breach over them, an' standing up like heroes as soon as it passed. The captain an' the officers were clinging to the rail of the quarter-deck, all in their golden uniforms, waiting for the end as if 'twas King George they expected. There was no way to help, for she lay right beyond cast of line, though our folk tried it fifty times. And beside them clung a trumpeter, a whacking big man, an' between the heavy seas he would lift his trumpet with one hand, and blow a call; and every time he blew, the men gave a cheer. There' (she says) '—hark 'ee now—there he goes agen! But you won't hear no cheering any more, for few are left to cheer, and their voices weak. Bitter cold the wind is, and I reckon it numbs their grip o' the ropes, for they were dropping off fast with every sea when my man sent me home to get his breakfast. *Another* wreck, you say? Well, there's no hope for the tender dears, if 'tis the Manacles. You'd better run down and help yonder; though 'tis little help that any man can give. Not one came in alive while I was there. The tide's flowing, an' she won't hold together another hour, they say.'

"Well, sure enough, the end was coming fast when my father got down to the point. Six men had been cast up alive, or just breathing—a seaman and five troopers. The seaman was the only one that had breath to speak; and while they were carrying him into the town, the word went round that the ship's name was the *Despatch,* transport, homeward bound from Corunna, with a detachment of the 7th Hussars, that had been fighting out there with Sir John Moore. The seas had rolled her farther over by this time, and given her decks a pretty sharp slope; but a dozen men still held on, seven by the ropes near the ship's waist, a couple near the break of the poop, and three on the quarter-deck. Of these three my father made out one to be the skipper; close by him clung an officer in full regimentals—his name, they heard after, was Captain Duncanfield; and last came the tall trumpeter; and if you'll believe me, the fellow was making shift there, at the very last, to blow *God Save the King*. What's more, he got to *Send us victorious* before an extra big sea came bursting across and washed them off the deck— every man but one of the pair beneath the poop—and *he* dropped his hold before the next wave; being stunned, I reckon. The others went out of sight at once, but the trumpeter—being, as I said, a powerful man as well as a tough swimmer—rose like a duck, rode out a couple of breakers, and came in on the crest of the third. The folks looked to see him broke like an egg at their feet; but when the smother cleared, there he was, lying face downward on a ledge below them; and one of the men that happened to have a rope round him—I forget the fellow's name, if I ever heard it—jumped down and grabbed him by the ankle as he began to slip back. Before the next big sea, the pair were hauled high enough to be out of harm, and another heave brought them up to grass. Quick work; but master trumpeter wasn't quite dead; nothing worse than a cracked head and three staved ribs. In twenty minutes or so they had him in bed, with the doctor to tend him.

"Now was the time—nothing being left alive upon the transport— for my father to tell of the sloop he'd seen driving upon the Manacles. And when he got a hearing, though the most were set upon salvage, and believed a wreck in the hand, so to say, to be worth half a dozen they couldn't see, a good few volunteered to start off with him and have a look. They crossed Lowland Point; no ship to be seen on the Manacles, nor anywhere upon the sea. One or two was for calling my father a liar. 'Wait till we come to Dean Point,' said he. Sure enough, on the far side of Dean Point, they found the sloop's mainmast washing about with half a dozen men lashed to it—men in red jackets—every mother's son drowned and staring; and a little farther on, just under the Dean, three or four bodies cast up on the shore, one of them a small drummer-boy, side-drum and all; and, near by, part of a ship's gig, with 'H.M.S. *Primrose*' cut on the stern-board. From this point on, the shore was littered thick with wreckage and dead bodies—the most of them Marines in uniform; and in Godrevy Cove, in particular, a heap of furniture from the captain's cabin, and amongst it a water-tight box, not much damaged, and full of papers; by which, when it came to be examined next day, the wreck was easily made out to be the *Primrose,* of eighteen guns, outward bound from Portsmouth, with a fleet of transports for the Spanish War—thirty sail, I've heard, but I've never heard what became of them. Being handled by merchant skippers, no doubt they rode out the gale and reached the Tagus safe and sound.

Not but what the captain of the *Primrose* (Mein was his name) did quite right to try and club-haul his vessel when he found himself under the land: only he never ought to have got there if he took proper soundings. But it's easy talking.

"The *Primrose,* sir, was a handsome vessel—for her size, one of the handsomest in the King's service—and newly fitted out at Plymouth Dock. So the boys had brave pickings from her in the way of brass-work, ship's instruments, and the like, let alone some barrels of stores not much spoiled. They loaded themselves with as much as they could carry, and started for home, meaning to make a second journey before the preventive men got wind of their doings and came to spoil the fun. But as my father was passing back under the Dean, he happened to take a look over his shoulder at the bodies there. 'Hullo,' says he, and dropped his gear: 'I do believe there's a leg moving!' And, running fore, he stooped over the small drummer-boy that I told you about. The poor little chap was lying there, with his face a mass of bruises and his eyes closed: but he had shifted one leg an inch or two, and was still breathing. So my father pulled out a knife and cut him free from his drum—that was lashed on to him with a double turn of Manilla rope—and took him up and carried him along here, to this very room that we're sitting in. He lost a good deal by this, for when he went back to fetch his bundle the preventive men had got hold of it, and were thick as thieves along the foreshore; so that 'twas only by paying one or two to look the other way that he picked up anything worth carrying off: which you'll allow to be hard, seeing that he was the first man to give news of the wreck.

"Well, the inquiry was held, of course, and my father gave evidence; and for the rest they had to trust to the sloop's papers: for not a soul was saved besides the drummer-boy, and he was raving in a fever, brought on by the cold and the fright. And the seamen and the five troopers gave evidence about the loss of the *Despatch.* The tall trumpeter, too, whose ribs were healing, came forward and kissed the Book; but somehow his head been hurt in coming ashore, and he talked foolish-like, and 'twas easy seen he would never be a proper man again. The others were taken up to Plymouth, and so went their ways; but the trumpeter stayed on in Coverack; and King George, finding he was fit for nothing, sent him down a trifle of a pension after a while—enough to keep him in board and lodging, with a bit of tobacco over.

"Now the first time that this man—William Tallifer, he called himself—met with the drummer-boy, was about a fortnight after the little chap had bettered enough to be allowed a short walk out of doors, which he took, if you please, in full regimentals. There never was a soldier so proud of his dress. His own suit had shrunk a brave bit with the salt water; but into ordinary frock an' corduroys he declared he would not get—not if he had to go naked the rest of his life; so my father, being a good-natured man and handy with the needle, turned to and repaired damages with a piece or two of scarlet cloth cut from the jacket of one of the drowned Marines. Well, the poor little chap chanced to be standing, in this rig-out, down by the gate of Gunner's Meadow, where they had buried two score and over of his comrades. The morning was a fine one, early in March month; and along came the cracked trumpeter, likewise taking a stroll.

" 'Hullo!' says he; 'good mornin'! And what might you be doin' here?'

" 'I was a-wishin',' says the boy, 'I had a pair o' drum-sticks. Our lads were buried yonder without so much as a drum tapped or a musket fired; and that's not Christian burial for British soldiers.'

" 'Phut!' says the trumpeter, and spat on the ground; 'a parcel of Marines!'

"The boy eyed him a second or so, and answered up: 'If I'd a tab of turf handy, I'd bung it at your mouth, you greasy cavalryman, and learn you to speak respectful of your betters. The Marines are the handiest body of men in the service.'

"The trumpeter looked down on him from the height of six foot two, and asked: 'Did they die well?'

" 'They died very well. There was a lot of running to and fro at first, and some of the men began to cry, and a few to strip off their clothes. But when the ship fell off for the last time, Captain Mein turned and said something to Major Griffiths, the commanding officer on board, and the Major called out to me to beat to quarters. It might have been for a wedding, he sang it out so cheerful. We'd had word already that 'twas to be parade order, and the men fell in as trim and decent as if they were going to church. One or two even tried to shave at the last moment. The Major wore his medals. One of the seamen, seeing I had hard work to keep the drum steady—the sling being a bit loose for me and the wind what you remember—lashed it tight with a piece of rope; and that saved my life afterwards, a drum being as good as a cork until 'tis stove. I kept beating away until every man was on deck; and then the Major formed them up and told them to die like British soldiers, and the chaplain read a prayer or two—the boys standin' all the while like rocks, each man's courage keeping up the others'. The chaplain was in the middle of a prayer when she struck. In ten minutes she was gone. That was how they died, cavalryman.'

" 'And that was very well done, drummer of the Marines. What's your name?'

" 'John Christian.'

" 'Mine is William George Tallifer, trumpeter, of the 7th Light Dragoons—the Queen's Own. I played *God Save the King* while our men were drowning. Captain Duncanfield told me to sound a call or two, to put them in heart; but that matter of *God Save the King* was a notion of my own. I won't say anything to hurt the feelings of a Marine, even if he's not much over five-foot tall; but the Queen's Own Hussars is a tearin' fine regiment. As between horse and foot, 'tis a question o' which gets the chance. All the way from Sahagun to Corunna 'twas we that took and gave the knocks—at Mayorga and Rueda, and Bennyventy.' (The reason, sir, I can speak the names so pat is that my father learnt 'em by heart afterwards from the trumpeter, who was always talking about Mayorga and Rueda and Bennyventy.) 'We made the rear-guard, under General Paget, and drove the French every time; and all the infantry did was to sit about in wine-shops till we whipped 'em out, an' steal an' straggle an' play the tom-fool in general. And when it came to a stand-up fight at Corunna, 'twas the horse, or the best part of it, that had to stay sea-sick aboard the transports, an' watch the infantry in the thick o' the caper. Very well they behaved, too; 'specially the 4th Regiment, an' the 42nd Highlanders an' the Dirty Half-Hundred. Oh, ay; they're decent regiments, all three. But the Queen's Own Hussars is a tearin' fine regiment. So you played on your drum when the ship was goin' down? Drummer John Christian, I'll have to get you a new pair o' drum-sticks for that.'

"Well, sir, it appears that the very next day the trumpeter marched into Helston, and got a carpenter there to turn him a pair of box-wood drum-sticks for the boy. And this was the beginning of one of the most curious friendships you ever heard tell of. Nothing delighted the pair more than to borrow a boat off my father and pull out to the rocks where the *Primrose* and the *Despatch* had struck and sunk; and on still days 'twas pretty to hear them out there off the Manacles, the drummer playing his tattoo—for they always took their music with them— and the trumpeter practising calls, and making his trumpet speak like an angel. But if the weather turned roughish, they'd be walking together and talking; leastwise, the youngster listened while the other discoursed about Sir John's campaign in Spain and Portugal, telling how each little skirmish befell; and of Sir John himself, and General Baird and General Paget, and Colonel Vivian, his own commanding officer, and what kind of men they were; and of the last bloody stand-up at Corunna, and so forth, as if neither could have enough.

"But all this had to come to an end in the late summer; for the boy, John Christian, being now well and strong again, must go up to Plymouth to report himself. 'Twas his own wish (for I believe King George had forgotten all about him), but his friend wouldn't hold him back. As for the trumpeter, my father had made an arrangement to take him on as a lodger as soon as the boy left; and on the morning fixed for the start, he was up at the door here by five o'clock, with his trumpet slung by his side, and all the rest of his kit in a small valise. A Monday morning it was, and after breakfast he had fixed to walk with the boy some way on the road towards Helston, where the coach started. My father left them at breakfast together, and went out to meat the pig, and do a few odd morning jobs of that sort. When he came back, the boy was still at table, and the trumpeter standing here by the chimney-place with the drum and trumpet in his hands, hitched together just as they be at this moment.

" 'Look at this,' he says to my father, showing him the lock; 'I picked it up off a starving brass-worker in Lisbon, and it is not one of your common locks that one word of six letters will open at any time. There's *janius* in this lock; for you've only to make the rings spell any six-letter word you please, and snap down the lock upon that, and never a soul can open it—not the maker, even—until somebody comes along that knows the word you snapped it on. Now, Johnny here's goin', and he leaves his drum behind him; for, though he can make pretty music on it, the parchment sags in wet weather, by reason of the sea-water getting at it; an' if he carries it to Plymouth, they'll only condemn it and give him another. And, as for me, I shan't have the heart to put lip to the trumpet any more when Johnny's gone. So we've chosen a word together, and locked 'em together upon that; and, by your leave, I'll hang 'em here together on the hook over your fireplace. Maybe Johnny'll come back; maybe not. Maybe, if he comes, I'll be dead an' gone, an' he'll take 'em apart an' try their music for old sake's sake. But if he never comes, nobody can separate 'em; for nobody beside knows the word. And if you marry and have sons, you can tell 'em that here are tied together the souls of Johnny Christian, drummer of the Marines, and William George Tallifer, once trumpeter of the Queen's Own Hussars. Amen.'

"With that he hung the two instruments 'pon the hook there; and the boy stood up and thanked my father and shook hands; and the pair went forth of the door, towards Helston.

"Somewhere on the road they took leave of one another; but nobody saw the parting, nor heard what was said between them. About three in the afternoon the trumpeter came walking back over the hill; and by the time my father came home from the fishing, the cottage was tidied up and the tea ready, and the whole place shining like a new pin. From that time for five years he lodged here with my father, looking after the house and tilling the garden; and all the while he was steadily failing, the hurt in his head spreading, in a manner, to his limbs. My father watched the feebleness growing on him, but said nothing. And from first to last neither spake a word about the drummer, John Christian; nor did any letter reach them, nor word of his doings.

"The rest of the tale you'm free to believe, sir, or not, as you please. It stands upon my father's words, and he always declared he was ready to kiss the Book upon it before judge and jury. He said, too, that he never had the wit to make up such a yarn; and he defied anyone to explain about the lock, in particular, by any other tale. But you shall judge for yourself.

"My father said that about three o'clock in the morning, April fourteenth of the year 'fourteen, he and William Tallifer were sitting here, just as you and I, sir, are sitting now. My father had put on his clothes a few minutes before, and was mending his spiller by the light of the horn lantern, meaning to set off before daylight to haul the trammel. The trumpeter hadn't been to bed at all. Towards the last he mostly spent his nights (and his days, too) dozing in the elbow-chair where you sit at this minute. He was dozing then (my father said), with his chin dropped forward on his chest, when a knock sounded upon the door, and the door opened, and in walked an upright young man in scarlet regimentals.

"He had grown a brave bit, and his face was the colour of wood-ashes; but it was the drummer, John Christian. Only his uniform was different from the one he used to wear, and the figures '38' shone in brass upon his collar.

"The drummer walked past my father as if he never saw him, and stood by the elbow-chair and said:

" 'Trumpeter, trumpeter, are you one with me?'

"And the trumpeter just lifted the lids of his eyes, and answered, 'How should I not be one with you, drummer Johnny—Johnny boy? The men are patient. 'Till you come, I count; while you march, I mark time; until the discharge comes.'

" 'The discharge has come to-night,' said the drummer, 'and the word is Corunna no longer'; and stepping to the chimney-place, he unhooked the drum and trumpet, and began to twist the brass rings of the lock, spelling the word aloud, so—C-O-R-U-N-A. When he had fixed the last letter, the padlock opened in his hand.

" 'Did you know, trumpeter, that when I came to Plymouth they put me into a line regiment?'

" 'The 38th is a good regiment,' answered the old Hussar, still in his dull voice. 'I went back with them from Sahagun to Corunna. At Corunna they stood in General Fraser's division, on the right. They behaved well.'

" 'But I'd fain see the Marines again,' says the drummer, handing him the trumpet; 'and you—you shall call once more for the Queen's Own. Matthew,' he says, suddenly, turning on my father—and when he turned, my father saw for the first time that his scarlet jacket had a round hole by the breast-bone, and that the blood was welling there— 'Matthew, we shall want your boat.'

"Then my father rose on his legs like a man in a dream, while they two slung on, the one his drum, and t'other his trumpet. He took the lantern, and went quaking before them down to the shore, and they breathed heavily behind him; and they stepped into his boat, and my father pushed off.

" 'Row you first for Dolor Point,' says the drummer. So my father rowed them out past the white houses of Coverack to Dolor Point, and there, at a word, lay on his oars. And the trumpeter, William Tallifer, put his trumpet to his mouth and sounded the *Revelly*. The music of it was like rivers running.

" 'They will follow,' said the drummer. 'Matthew, pull you now for the Manacles.'

"So my father pulled for the Manacles, and came to an easy close outside Carn dû. And the drummer took his sticks and beat a tattoo, there by the edge of the reef; and the music of it was like a rolling chariot.

" 'That will do,' says he, breaking off; 'they will follow. Pull now for the shore under Gunner's Meadow.'

"Then my father pulled for the shore, and ran his boat in under Gunner's Meadow. And they stepped out, all three, and walked up to the meadow. By the gate the drummer halted and began his tattoo again, looking out towards the darkness over the sea.

"And while the drum beat, and my father held his breath, there came up out of the sea and the darkness a troop of many men, horse and foot, and formed up among the graves; and others rose out of the graves and formed up—drowned Marines with bleached faces, and pale Hussars riding their horses, all lean and shadowy. There was no clatter of hoofs or accoutrements, my father said, but a soft sound all the while, like the beating of a bird's wing, and a black shadow lying like a pool about the feet of all. The drummer stood upon a little knoll just inside the gate, and beside him the tall trumpeter, with hand on hip, watching them gather; and behind them both my father, clinging to the gate. When no more came, the drummer stopped playing, and said, 'Call the roll.'

"Then the trumpeter stepped towards the end man of the rank and called, 'Troop-Sergeant-Major Thomas Irons!' and the man in a thin voice answered 'Here!'

" 'Troop-Sergeant-Major Thomas Irons, how is it with you?'

"The man answered, 'How should it be with me? When I was young, I betrayed a girl; and when I was grown, I betrayed a friend; and for these things I must pay. But I died as a man ought. God save the King!'

"The trumpeter called to the next man, 'Trooper Henry Buckingham!' and the next man answered, 'Here!'

" 'Trooper Henry Buckingham, how is it with you?'

" 'How should it be with me? I was a drunkard, and I stole, and in Lugo, in a wine-shop, I knifed a man. But I died as a man should. God save the King!'

"So the trumpeter went down the line; and when he had finished, the drummer took it up, hailing the dead Marines in their order. Each man answered to his name, and each man ended with 'God save the King!' When all were hailed, the drummer stepped back to his mound, and called:

" 'It is well. You are content, and we are content to join you. Wait yet a little while.'

"With this he turned and ordered my father to pick up the lantern, and lead the way back. As my father picked it up, he heard the ranks of dead men cheer and call, 'God save the King!' all together, and saw them waver and fade back into the dark, like a breath fading off a pane.

"But when they came back here to the kitchen, and my father set the lantern down, it seemed they'd both forgot about him. For the drummer turned in the lantern-light—and my father could see the blood still welling out of the hole in his breast—and took the trumpet-sling from around the other's neck, and locked drum and trumpet together again, choosing the letters on the lock very carefully. While he did this he said:

" 'The word is no more Corunna, but Bayonne. As you left out an "n" in Corunna, so must I leave out an "n" in Bayonne.' And before snapping the padlock, he spelt out the word slowly—'B-A-Y-O-N-E.' After that, he used no more speech; but turned and hung the two instruments back on the hook; and then took the trumpeter by the arm; and the pair walked out into the darkness, glancing neither to right nor left.

"My father was on the point of following, when he heard a sort of sigh behind him; and there, sitting in the elbow-chair, was the very trumpeter he had just seen walk out by the door! If my father's heart jumped before, you may believe it jumped quicker now. But after a bit, he went up to the man asleep in the chair, and put a hand upon him. It was the trumpeter in flesh and blood that he touched; but though the flesh was warm, the trumpeter was dead.

"Well, sir, they buried him three days after; and at first my father was minded to say nothing about his dream (as he thought it). But the day after the funeral, he met Parson Kendall coming from Helston market: and the parson called out: 'Have 'ee heard the news the coach brought down this mornin'?' 'What news?' says my father. 'Why, that peace is agreed upon.' 'None too soon,' says my father. 'Not soon enough for our poor lads at Bayonne,' the parson answered. 'Bayonne!' cries my father, with a jump. 'Why, yes'; and the parson told him all about a great sally the French had made on the night of April 13th. 'Do you happen to know if the 38th Regiment was engaged?' my father asked. 'Come, now,' said Parson Kendall, 'I didn't know you was so well up in the campaign. But, as it happens, I *do* know that the 38th was engaged, for 'twas they that held a cottage and stopped the French advance.'

"Still my father held his tongue; and when, a week later, he walked into Helston and bought a *Mercury* off the Sherborne rider, and got the landlord of the 'Angel' to spell out the list of killed and wounded, sure enough, there among the killed was Drummer John Christian, of the 38th Foot.

"After this, there was nothing for a religious man but to make a clean breast. So my father went up to Parson Kendall and told the whole story. The parson listened, and put a question or two, and then asked:

" 'Have you tried to open the lock since that night?'

" 'I han't dared to touch it,' says my father.

" 'Then come along and try.' When the parson came to the cottage here, he took the things off the hook and tried the lock. 'Did he say "Bayonne"? The word has seven letters.'

" 'Not if you spell it with one "n" as *he* did,' says my father.

"The parson spelt it out—B-A-Y-O-N-E. 'Whew!' says he, for the lock had fallen open in his hand.

"He stood considering it a moment, and then he says, 'I tell you what. I shouldn't blab this all round the parish, if I was you. You won't get no credit for truth-telling, and a miracle's wasted on a set of fools. But if you like, I'll shut down the lock again upon a holy word that no one but me shall know, and neither drummer nor trumpeter, dead nor alive, shall frighten the secret out of me.'

" 'I wish to gracious you would, parson,' said my father.

"The parson chose the holy word there and then, and shut the lock back upon it, and hung the drum and trumpet back in their place. He is gone long since, taking the word with him. And till the lock is broken by force, nobody will ever separate those twain."

35

That Brute Simmons

BY ARTHUR MORRISON

SIMMONS'S infamous behavior toward his wife is still matter for profound wonderment among the neighbors. The other women had all along regarded him as a model husband, and certainly Mrs. Simmons was a most conscientious wife. She toiled and slaved for that man, as any woman in the whole street would have maintained, far more than any husband had a right to expect. And now this was what she got for it. Perhaps he had suddenly gone mad.

Before she married Simmons, Mrs. Simmons had been the widowed Mrs. Ford. Ford had got a berth as donkey-man on a tramp steamer, and that steamer had gone down with all hands off the cape—a judgment, the widow woman feared, for long years of contumacy which had culminated in the wickedness of taking to the sea, and taking to it as a donkey-man, an immeasurable fall for a capable engine-fitter. Twelve years as Mrs. Ford had left her still childless, and childless she remained as Mrs. Simmons.

As for Simmons, he, it was held, was fortunate in that capable wife. He was a moderately good carpenter and joiner, but no man of the world, and he wanted to be one. Nobody could tell what might not have happened to Tommy Simmons if there had been no Mrs. Simmons to take care of him. He was a meek and quiet man, with a boyish face and sparse, limp whiskers. He had no vices (even his pipe departed him after his marriage), and Mrs. Simmons had ingrafted on him divers exotic virtues. He went solemnly to chapel every Sunday, under a tall hat, and put a penny—one returned to him for the purpose out of his week's wages—in plate. Then, Mrs. Simmons overseeing, he took off his best clothes and brushed them with solicitude and pains. On Saturday afternoons, he cleaned the knives, the forks, the boots, the kettles and the windows, patiently and conscientiously. On Tuesday evenings he took the clothes to the mangling. And on Saturday nights he attended Mrs. Simmons in her marketing, to carry the parcels.

Mrs. Simmons's own virtues were native and numerous. She was a wonderful manager. Every penny of Tommy's thirty-six or thirty-eight shillings a week was bestowed to the greatest advantage, and Tommy never ventured to guess how much of it she saved. Her cleanliness in housewifery was distracting to behold. She met Simmons at the front door whenever he came home, and then there he changed his boots for slippers, balancing himself painfully on alternate feet on the cold flags. This was because she scrubbed the passage and doorstep turn about with the wife of the downstairs family, and because the stair-carpet was her own. She vigilantly supervised her husband all through the process of "cleaning himself" after work, so as to come between her walls and the possibility of random splashes; and if, in spite of her diligence, a spot remained to tell the tale, she was at pains to impress the fact on Simmons's memory, and to set forth at length all the circumstances of his ungrateful selfishness. In the beginning she had always escorted him to the ready-made clothes shop, and had selected and paid for his clothes—for the reason that men are such perfect fools, and shopkeepers do as they like with them. But she presently improved on that. She found a man selling cheap remnants at a street corner, and straightway she conceived the idea of making Simmons's clothes herself. Decision was one of her virtues, and a suit of uproarious check tweeds was begun that afternoon from the pattern furnished by an old one. More: it was finished by Sunday, when Simmons, overcome by astonishment at the feat, was indued in it, and pushed off to chapel ere he could recover his senses. The things were not altogether comfortable, he found; the trousers clung tight against his shins, but hung loose behind his heels; and when he sat, it was on a wilderness of hard folds and seams. Also his waistcoat collar tickled his nape, but his coat collar went straining across from shoulder to shoulder, while the main garment bagged generously below his waist. Use made a habit of his discomfort, but it never reconciled him to the chaff of his shopmates; for as Mrs. Simmons elaborated successive suits, each one modeled on the last, the primal accidents of her design developed into principles, and grew even bolder and more hideously pronounced. It was vain for Simmons to hint —as hint he did—that he shouldn't like her to overwork herself, tailoring being bad for the eyes, and there was a new tailor's in the Mile End Road, very cheap, where . . . "Ho yus," she retorted, "you're very consid'rit I dessay sittin' there actin' a livin' lie before your own wife, Thomas Simmons, as though I couldn't see through you like a book; a lot you care about overworkin' me as long as *your* turn's served throw-in' away money like dirt in the street on a lot o' swindling tailors an' me workin' an' slavin' 'ere to save a 'apenny an' this is my return for it; any one 'ud think you could pick up money in the 'orseroad an' I b'lieve I'd be thought better of if I laid in bed all day like some would, that I do." So that Thomas Simmons avoided the subject, nor even murmured when she resolved to cut his hair.

So his placid fortune endured for years. Then there came a golden summer evening when Mrs. Simmons betook herself with a basket to do some small shopping, and Simmons was left at home. He washed and put away the tea-things, and then he fell to meditating on a new pair of trousers, finished that day and hanging behind the parlor door. There they hung, in all their decent innocence of shape in the seat, and they were shorter of leg, longer of waist, and wilder of pattern than he had ever worn before. And as he looked on them the small devil of original sin awoke and clamored in his breast. He was ashamed of it, of course, for well he knew the gratitude he owed his wife for those same trousers, among other blessings. Still, there the small devil was, and the small devil was fertile in base suggestions, and could not be kept from hinting at the new crop of workshop gibes that would spring at Tommy's first public appearance in such things.

"Pitch 'em in the dust-bin!" said the small devil, at last; "it's all they're fit for."

Simmons turned away in sheer horror of his wicked self, and for a moment thought of washing the tea-things over again by way of discipline. Then he made for the back room, but saw from the landing that the front door was standing open, probably by the fault of the child downstairs. Now, a front door standing open was a thing that Mrs. Simmons would *not* abide; it looked low. So Simmons went down, that she might not be wroth with him for the thing when she came back; and, as he shut the door, he looked forth into the street.

A man was loitering on the pavement, and prying curiously about the door. His face was tanned, his hands were deep in the pockets of his unbraced blue trousers, and well back on his head he wore the high-crowned peaked cap topped with a knob of wool, which is affected by Jack ashore about the docks. He lurched a step nearer to the door, and: "Mrs. Ford ain't in, is she?" he said.

Simmons stared at him for a matter of five seconds, and then said: "Eh?"

"Mrs. Ford as was, then—Simmons now, ain't it?"

He said this with a furtive leer that Simmons neither liked nor understood.

"No," said Simmons, "she ain't in now."

"You ain't her 'usband, are ye?"

"Yus."

The man took his pipe from his mouth, and grinned silently and long. "Blimy," he said, at length, "you look the sort o' bloke she'd like." And with that he grinned again. Then, seeing that Simmons made ready to shut the door, he put a foot on the sill and a hand against the panel. "Don't be in a 'urry, matey," he said; "I come 'ere t'ave a little talk with you, man to man, d'ye see?" And he frowned fiercely.

Tommy Simmons felt uncomfortable, but the door would not shut, so he parleyed. "Wotjer want?" he asked. "I dunno you."

"Then if you'll excuse the liberty, I'll interdooce meself, in a manner of speaking." He touched his cap with a bob of mock humility. "I'm Bob Ford," he said, "come back out o' kingdom-come, so to say. Me as went down with the *Mooltan*—safe dead five years gone. I come to see my wife."

During this speech Thomas Simmons's jaw was dropping lower and lower. At the end of it he poked his fingers up through his hair, looked down at the mat, then up at the fanlight, then out into the street, then hard at his visitor. But he found nothing to say.

"Come to see my wife," the man repeated. "So now we can talk it over—as man to man."

Simmons slowly shut his mouth, and led the way upstairs mechanically, his fingers still in his hair. A sense of the state of affairs sunk gradually into his brain, and the small devil woke again. Suppose this man *was* Ford? Suppose he did claim his wife? Would it be a knockdown blow? Would it hit him out?—or not? He thought of the trousers, the tea-things, the mangling, the knives, the kettles and the windows; and he thought of them in the way of a backslider.

On the landing Ford clutched at his arm, and asked, in a hoarse whisper: " 'Ow long 'fore she's back?"

" 'Bout a hour, I expect," Simmons replied, having first of all repeated the question in his own mind. And then he opened the parlor door.

"Ah," said Ford, looking about him, "you've bin pretty comf'table. Them chairs an' things"—jerking his pipe toward them—"was hers— mine, that is to say, speaking straight, and man to man." He sat down, puffing meditatively at his pipe, and presently: "Well," he continued, " 'ere I am agin, ol' Bob Ford dead an' done for—gawn down in the *Mooltan*. On'y I *ain't* done for, see?"—and he pointed the stem of his pipe at Simmons's waistcoat—"I ain't done for, 'cause why? Cons- 'kence o' bein' picked up by a ol' German sailin'-'utch an' took to 'Frisco 'fore the mast. I've 'ad a few years o' knockin' about since then, an' now"—looking hard at Simmons—"I've come back to see my wife."

"She—she don't like smoke in 'ere," said Simmons, as it were, at random.

"No, I bet she don't," Ford answered, taking his pipe from his mouth, and holding it low in his hand. "I know 'Anner. 'Ow d'you find 'er? Do she make ye clean the winders?"

"Well," Simmons admitted, uneasily, "I—I do 'elp 'er sometimes, o' course."

"Ah! An' the knives too, I bet, an' the bloomin' kittles. I know. Wy"—he rose and bent to look behind Simmons's head—"s'elp me, I b'lieve she cuts yer 'air! Well, I'm damned! Jes' wot she would do, too."

He inspected the blushing Simmons from divers points of vantage. Then he lifted a leg of the trousers hanging behind the door. "I'd bet a trifle," he said, "she made these 'ere trucks. Nobody else 'ud do 'em like that. Damme—they're wuss'n wot you're got on."

The small devil began to have the argument all its own way. If this man took his wife back, perhaps he'd have to wear those trousers.

"Ah!" Ford pursued, "she ain't got no milder. An', my davy, wot a jore!"

Simmons began to feel that this was no longer his business. Plainly, 'Anner was this other man's wife, and he was bound in honor to acknowledge the fact. The small devil put it to him as a matter of duty.

"Well," said Ford, suddenly, "time's short, an' this ain't business. I won't be 'ard on you, matey. I ought prop'ly to stand on my rights, but seein' as you're a well-meanin' young man, so to speak, an' all settled an' a-livin' 'ere quiet an' matrimonual, I'll"—this with a burst of generosity—"damme, yus, I'll compound the felony, an' take me 'ook. Come, I'll name a figure, as man to man, fust an' last, no less an' no more. Five pound does it."

Simmons hadn't five pounds—he hadn't even five pence—and he said so. "An' I wouldn't think for to come between a man an' 'is wife," he added, "not on no account. It may be rough on me, but it's a dooty. I'll 'ook it."

"No," said Ford, hastily, clutching Simmons by the arm, "don't do that. I'll make it a bit cheaper. Say three quid—come, that's reasonable, ain't it? Three quid ain't much compensation for me goin' away forever—where the stormy winds do blow, so to say—an' never as much as seein' me own wife again for better nor wuss. Between man an' man now—three quid; an' I'll shunt. That's fair, ain't it?"

"Of course it's fair," Simmons replied, effusively. "It's more'n fair; it's noble—downright noble, I call it. But I ain't goin' to take a mean advantage o' your good-heartedness, Mr. Ford. She's your wife, an' I oughtn't to 'a' come between you. I apologize. You stop an' 'ave yer proper rights. It's me as ought to shunt, an' I will." And he made a step toward the door.

" 'Old on," quoth Ford, and got between Simmons and the door;

"don't do things rash. Look wot a loss it'll be to you with no 'ome to go to, an' nobody to look after ye, an' all that. It'll be dreadful. Say a couple—there, we won't quarrel, jest a single quid, between man an' man, an' I'll stand a pot o' the money. You can easy raise a quid—the clock 'ud pretty nigh do it. A quid does it; an' I'll——"

There was a loud double-knock at the front door. In the East End a double-knock is always for the upstairs lodgers.

"Oo's that?" asked Bob Ford, apprehensively.

"I'll see," said Thomas Simmons in reply, and he made a rush for the staircase.

Bob Ford heard him open the front door. Then he went to the window, and just below him, he saw the crown of a bonnet. It vanished, and borne to him from within the door there fell upon his ear the sound of a well-remembered female voice.

"Where ye goin' now with no 'at?" asked the voice, sharply.

"Awright, 'Anner—there's—there's somebody upstairs to see you," Simmons answered. And, as Bob Ford could see, a man went scuttling down the street in the gathering dusk. And behold, it was Thomas Simmons.

Ford reached the landing in three strides. His wife was still at the front door, staring after Simmons. He flung into the back room, threw open the window, dropped from the wash-house roof into the back-yard, scrambled desperately over the fence, and disappeared into the gloom. He was seen by no living soul. And that is why Simmons's base desertion—under his wife's very eyes, too—is still an astonishment to the neighbors.

The Monkey's Paw

BY W. W. JACOBS

WITHOUT, the night was cold and wet, but in the small parlor of Lakesnam Villa the blinds were drawn and the fire burned brightly. Father and son were at chess, the former, who possessed ideas about the game involving radical changes, putting his king into such sharp and unnecessary perils that it even provoked comment from the white-haired old lady knitting placidly by the fire.

"Hark at the wind," said Mr. White, who, having seen a fatal mistake after it was too late, was amiably desirous of preventing his son from seeing it.

"I'm listening," said the latter, grimly surveying the board as he stretched out his hand. "Check."

"I should hardly think that he'd come tonight," said his father, with his hand poised over the board.

"Mate," replied the son.

"That's the worst of living so far out," bawled Mr. White, with sudden and unlooked-for violence; "of all the beastly, slushy, out-of-the-way places to live in, this is the worst. Pathway's a bog, and the road's a torrent. I don't know what people are thinking about. I suppose because only two houses on the road are let, they think it doesn't matter."

"Never mind, dear," said his wife soothingly; "perhaps you'll win the next one."

Mr. White looked up sharply, just in time to intercept a knowing glance between mother and son. The words died away on his lips, and he hid a guilty grin in his thin gray beard.

"There he is," said Herbert White, as the gate banged to loudly and heavy footsteps came toward the door.

462

The old man rose with hospitable haste, and opening the door, was heard condoling with the new arrival. The new arrival also condoled with himself, so that Mrs. White said, "Tut, tut!" and coughed gently as her husband entered the room, followed by a tall burly man, beady of eye and rubicund of visage.

"Sergeant-Major Morris," he said, introducing him.

The sergeant-major shook hands, and taking the proffered seat by the fire, watched contentedly while his host got out whisky and tumblers and stood a small copper kettle on the fire.

At the third glass his eyes got brighter, and he began to talk, the little family circle regarding with eager interest this visitor from distant parts, as he squared his broad shoulders in the chair and spoke of strange scenes and doughty deeds, of wars and plagues and strange peoples.

"Twenty-one years of it," said Mr. White, nodding at his wife and son. "When he went away he was a slip of a youth in the warehouse. Now look at him."

"He don't look to have taken much harm," said Mrs. White politely.

"I'd like to go to India myself," said the old man, "just to look round a bit, you know."

"Better where you are," said the sergeant-major, shaking his head. He put down the empty glass and, sighing softly, shook it again.

"I should like to see those old temples and fakirs and jugglers," said the old man. "What was that you started telling me the other day about a monkey's paw or something, Morris?"

"Nothing," said the soldier hastily. "Leastways, nothing worth hearing."

"Monkey's paw?" said Mrs. White curiously.

"Well, it's just a bit of what you might call magic, perhaps," said the sergeant-major off-handedly.

His three listeners leaned forward eagerly. The visitor absent-mindedly put his empty glass to his lips and then set it down again. His host filled it for him.

"To look at," said the sergeant-major, fumbling in his pocket, "it's just an ordinary little paw, dried to a mummy."

He took something out of his pocket and proffered it. Mrs. White drew back with a grimace, but her son, taking it, examined it curiously.

"And what is there special about it?" inquired Mr. White, as he took it from his son and, having examined it, placed it upon the table.

"It had a spell put on it by an old fakir," said the sergeant-major, "a very holy man. He wanted to show that fate ruled people's lives, and that those who interfered with it did so to their sorrow. He put a spell on it so that three separate men could each have three wishes from it."

His manner was so impressive that his hearers were conscious that their light laughter jarred somewhat.

"Well, why don't you have three, sir?" said Herbert White cleverly.

The soldier regarded him in the way that middle age is wont to regard presumptuous youth. "I have," he said quietly, and his blotchy face whitened.

"And did you really have the three wishes granted?" asked Mrs. White.

"I did," said the sergeant-major, and his glass tapped against his strong teeth.

"And has anybody else wished?" inquired the old lady.

"The first man had his three wishes, yes," was the reply. "I don't know what the first two were, but the third was for death. That's how I got the paw."

His tones were so grave that a hush fell upon the group.

"If you've had your three wishes, it's no good to you now, then, Morris," said the old man at last. "What do you keep it for?"

The soldier shook his head. "Fancy, I suppose," he said slowly. "I did have some idea of selling it, but I don't think I will. It has caused enough mischief already. Besides, people won't buy. They think it's a fairy tale, some of them, and those who do think anything of it want to try it first and pay me afterward."

"If you could have another three wishes," said the old man, eyeing him keenly, "would you have them?"

"I don't know," said the other. "I don't know."

He took the paw, and dangling it between his front finger and thumb, suddenly threw it upon the fire. White, with a slight cry, stooped down and snatched it off.

"Better let it burn," said the soldier solemnly.

"If you don't want it, Morris," said the old man, "give it to me."

"I won't," said his friend doggedly. "I threw it on the fire. If you keep it, don't blame me for what happens. Pitch it on the fire again, like a sensible man."

The other shook his head and examined his new possession closely. "How do you do it?" he inquired.

"Hold it up in your right hand and wish aloud," said the sergeant-major, "but I warn you of the consequences."

"Sounds like the *Arabian Nights*," said Mrs. White, as she rose and began to set the supper. "Don't you think you might wish for four pairs of hands for me?"

Her husband drew the talisman from his pocket and then all three burst into laughter as the sergeant-major, with a look of alarm on his face, caught him by the arm.

"If you must wish," he said gruffly, "wish for something sensible."

Mr. White dropped it back into his pocket, and placing chairs, motioned his friend to the table. In the business of supper the talisman was partly forgotten, and afterward the three sat listening in an enthralled fashion to a second installment of the soldier's adventures in India.

"If the tale about the monkey paw is not more truthful than those he has been telling us," said Herbert, as the door closed behind their guest, just in time for him to catch the last train, "we shan't make much out of it."

"Did you give him anything for it, father?" inquired Mrs. White, regarding her husband closely.

"A trifle," said he, coloring slightly. "He didn't want it, but I made him take it. And he pressed me again to throw it away."

"Likely," said Herbert, with pretended horror. "Why, we're going to be rich, and famous, and happy. Wish to be an emperor, father, to begin with; then you can't be henpecked."

He darted round the table, pursued by the maligned Mrs. White armed with an antimacassar.

Mr. White took the paw from his pocket and eyed it dubiously. "I don't know what to wish for, and that's a fact," he said slowly. "It seems to me I've got all I want."

"If you only cleared the house, you'd be quite happy, wouldn't you?" said Herbert, with his hand on his shoulder. "Well, wish for two hundred pounds, then; that'll just do it."

His father, smiling shamefacedly at his own credulity, held up the talisman, as his son, with a solemn face somewhat marred by a wink at his mother, sat down at the piano and struck a few impressive chords.

"I wish for two hundred pounds," said the old man distinctly.

A fine crash from the piano greeted the words, interrupted by a shuddering cry from the old man. His wife and son ran toward him.

"It moved," he cried, with a glance of disgust at the object as it lay on the floor. "As I wished it twisted in my hands like a snake."

"Well, I don't see the money," said his son, as he picked it up and placed it on the table, "and I bet I never shall."

"It must have been your fancy, father," said his wife, regarding him anxiously.

He shook his head. "Never mind, though; there's no harm done, but it gave me a shock all the same."

They sat down by the fire again while the two men finished their pipes. Outside, the wind was higher than ever, and the old man started nervously at the sound of a door banging upstairs. A silence unsual and depressing settled upon all three, which lasted until the old couple rose to retire for the night.

"I expect you'll find the cash tied up in a big bag in the middle of your bed," said Herbert, as he bade them good night, "and something horrible squatting up on top of the wardrobe watching you as you pocket your ill-gotten gains."

II

In the brightness of the wintry sun next morning as it streamed over the breakfast table Herbert laughed at his fears. There was an air of prosaic wholesomeness about the room which it had lacked on the previous night, and the dirty, shriveled little paw was pitched on the sideboard with a carelessness which betokened no great belief in its virtues.

"I suppose all old soldiers are the same," said Mrs. White. "The idea of our listening to such nonsense! How could wishes be granted in these days? And if they could, how could two hundred pounds hurt you, father?"

"Might drop on his head from the sky," said the frivolous Herbert.

"Morris said the things happened so naturally," said his father, "that you might if you so wished attribute it to coincidence."

"Well, don't break into the money before I come back," said Herbert, as he rose from the table. "I'm afraid it'll turn you into a mean, avaricious man, and we shall have to disown you."

His mother laughed, and following him to the door, watched him down the road, and returning to the breakfast table, was very happy at the expense of her husband's credulity. All of which did not prevent her from scurrying to the door at the postman's knock, nor prevent her from referring somewhat shortly to retired sergeant-majors of bibulous habits when she found that the post brought a tailor's bill.

"Herbert will have some more of his funny remarks, I expect, when he comes home," she said, as they sat at dinner.

"I dare say," said Mr. White, pouring himself out some beer; "but for all that, the thing moved in my hand; that I'll swear to."

"You thought it did," said the old lady soothingly.

"I say it did," replied the other. "There was no thought about it; I had just—What's the matter?"

His wife made no reply. She was watching the mysterious movements of a man outside, who, peering in an undecided fashion at the house, appeared to be trying to make up his mind to enter. In mental connection with the two hundred pounds, she noticed that the stranger was well dressed and wore a silk hat of glossy newness. Three times he paused at the gate, and then walked on again. The fourth time he stood with his hand upon it, and then with sudden resolution flung it open and walked up the path. Mrs. White at the same moment placed her hands behind her, and hurriedly unfastening the strings of her apron, put that useful article of apparel beneath the cushion of her chair.

She brought the stranger, who seemed ill at ease, into the room. He gazed furtively at Mrs. White, and listened in a preoccupied fashion as the old lady apologized for the appearance of the room, and her husband's coat, a garment which he usually reserved for the garden. She then waited as patiently as her sex would permit for him to broach his business, but he was at first strangely silent.

"I—was asked to call," he said at last, and stooped and picked a piece of cotton from his trousers. "I come from Maw and Meggins."

The old lady started. "Is anything the matter?" she asked breathlessly. "Has anything happened to Herbert? What is it? What is it?"

Her husband interposed. "There, there, mother," he said hastily. "Sit down, and don't jump to conclusions. You've not brought bad news, I'm sure, sir," and he eyed the other wistfully.

"I'm sorry——" began the visitor.

"Is he hurt?" demanded the mother.

The visitor bowed in assent. "Badly hurt," he said quietly, "but he is not in any pain."

"Oh, thank God!" said the old woman, clasping her hands. "Thank God for that! Thank——"

She broke off suddenly as the sinister meaning of the assurance dawned upon her and she saw the awful confirmation of her fears in the other's averted face. She caught her breath, and turning to her slower-witted husband, laid her trembling old hand upon his. There was a long silence.

"He was caught in the machinery," said the visitor at length, in a low voice.

"Caught in the machinery," repeated Mr. White, in a dazed fashion, "yes."

He sat staring blankly out at the window, and taking his wife's hand between his own, pressed it as he had been wont to do in their old courting days nearly forty years before.

"He was the only one left to us," he said, turning gently to the visitor. "It is hard."

The other coughed, and rising, walked slowly to the window. "The firm wished me to convey their sincere sympathy with you in your great loss," he said, without looking round. "I beg that you will understand I am only their servant and merely obeying orders."

There was no reply; the old woman's face was white, her eyes staring, and her breath inaudible; on the husband's face was a look such as his friend the sergeant might have carried into his first action.

"I was to say that Maw and Meggins disclaim all responsibility," continued the other. "They admit no liability at all, but in consideration of your son's services they wish to present you with a certain sum as compensation."

Mr. White dropped his wife's hand, and rising to his feet, gazed with a look of horror at his visitor. His dry lips shaped the words, "How much?"

"Two hundred pounds," was the answer.

Unconscious of his wife's shriek, the old man smiled faintly, put out his hands like a sightless man, and dropped, a senseless heap, to the floor.

III

In the huge new cemetery, some two miles distant, the old people buried their dead, and came back to a house steeped in shadow and silence. It was all over so quickly that at first they could hardly realize it, and remained in a state of expectation as though of something else to happen—something else which was to lighten this load, too heavy for old hearts to bear. But the days passed, and expectation gave place to resignation—the hopeless resignation of the old, sometimes miscalled apathy. Sometimes they hardly exchanged a word, for now they had nothing to talk about, and their days were long to weariness.

It was about a week after that that the old man, waking suddenly in the night, stretched out his hand and found himself alone. The room was in darkness, and the sound of subdued weeping came from the window. He raised himself in bed and listened.

"Come back," he said tenderly. "You will be cold."

"It is colder for my son," said the old woman, and wept afresh.

The sound of her sobs died away on his ears. The bed was warm, and his eyes heavy with sleep. He dozed fitfully, and then slept until a sudden wild cry from his wife awoke him with a start.

"The monkey's paw!" she cried wildly. "The monkey's paw!"

He started up in alarm. "Where? Where is it? What's the matter?"

She came stumbling across the room toward him. "I want it," she said quietly. "You've not destroyed it?"

"It's in the parlor, on the bracket," he replied, marveling. "Why?"

She cried and laughed together, and bending over, kissed his cheek.

"I only just thought of it," she said hysterically. "Why didn't I think of it before? Why didn't you think of it?"

"Think of what?" he questioned.

"The other two wishes," she replied rapidly. "We've only had one."

"Was not that enough?" he demanded fiercely.

"No," she cried triumphantly; "we'll have one more. Go down and get it quickly, and wish our boy alive again."

The man sat up in bed and flung the bedclothes from his quaking limbs. "Good God, you are mad!" he cried, aghast.

"Get it," she panted; "get it quickly, and wish—Oh, my boy, my boy!"

Her husband struck a match and lit the candle. "Get back to bed," he said unsteadily. "You don't know what you are saying."

"We had the first wish granted," said the old woman feverishly; "why not the second?"

"A coincidence," stammered the old man.

"Go and get it and wish," cried the old woman, and dragged him toward the door.

He went down in the darkness, and felt his way to the parlor, and then to the mantelpiece. The talisman was in its place, and a horrible fear that the unspoken wish might bring his mutilated son before him ere he could escape from the room seized upon him, and he caught his breath as he found that he had lost the direction of the door. His brow cold with sweat, he felt his way round the table, and groped along the wall until he found himself in the small passage with the unwholesome thing in his hand.

Even his wife's face seemed changed as he entered the room. It was white and expectant, and to his fears seemed to have an unnatural look upon it. He was afraid of her.

"Wish!" she cried, in a strong voice.

"It is foolish and wicked," he faltered.

"Wish!" repeated his wife.

He raised his hand. "I wish my son alive again."

The talisman fell to the floor, and he regarded it shudderingly. Then he sank trembling into a chair as the old woman, with burning eyes, walked to the window and raised the blind.

He sat until he was chilled with the cold, glancing occasionally at the figure of the old woman peering through the window. The candle end, which had burnt below the rim of the china candlestick, was throwing pulsating shadows on the ceiling and walls, until, with a flicker larger than the rest, it expired. The old man, with an unspeakable sense of relief at the failure of the talisman, crept back to his bed, and a minute or two afterward the old woman came silently and apathetically beside him.

Neither spoke, but both lay silently listening to the ticking of the clock. A stair creaked, and a squeaky mouse scurried noisily through the wall. The darkness was oppressive, and after lying for some time screwing up his courage, the husband took the box of matches, and striking one, went downstairs for a candle.

At the foot of the stairs the match went out, and he paused to strike another, and at the same moment a knock, so quiet and stealthy as to be scarcely audible, sounded on the front door.

The matches fell from his hand. He stood motionless, his breath suspended until the knock was repeated. Then he turned and fled swiftly back to his room, and closed the door behind him. A third knock sounded through the house.

"*What's that?*" cried the old woman, starting up.

"A rat," said the old man, in shaking tones—"a rat. It passed me on the stairs."

His wife sat up in bed listening. A loud knock resounded through the house.

"It's Herbert!" she screamed. "It's Herbert!"

She ran to the door, but her husband was before her, and catching her by the arm, held her tightly.

"What are you going to do?" he whispered hoarsely.

"It's my boy; it's Herbert!" she cried, struggling mechanically. "I forgot it was two miles away. What are you holding me for? Let go. I must open the door."

"For God's sake don't let it in," cried the old man, trembling.

"You're afraid of your own son," she cried, struggling. "Let me go. I'm coming, Herbert; I'm coming."

There was another knock, and another. The old woman with a sudden wrench broke free and ran from the room. Her husband followed to the landing, and called after her appealingly as she hurried downstairs. He heard the chain rattle back and the bottom bolt drawn slowly and stiffly from the socket. Then the old woman's voice, strained and panting.

"The bolt," she cried loudly. "Come down. I can't reach it."

But her husband was on his hands and knees groping wildly on the floor in search of the paw. If he could only find it before the thing outside got in. A perfect fusillade of knocks reverberated though the house, and he heard the scraping of a chair as his wife put it down in the passage against the door. He heard the creaking of the bolt as it came slowly back, and at the same moment, he found the monkey's paw, and frantically breathed his third and last wish.

The knocking ceased suddenly, although the echoes of it were still in the house. He heard the chair drawn back and the door opened. A cold wind rushed up the staircase, and a long loud wail of disappointment and misery from his wife gave him courage to run down to her side, and then to the gate beyond. The street lamp flickering opposite shone on a quiet and deserted road.

37

The Doll in the Pink Silk Dress

BY LEONARD MERRICK

HOW can I write the fourth Act with this ridiculous thing posed among my papers? What thing? It is a doll in a pink silk dress—an elaborate doll that walks, and talks, and warbles snatches from the operas. A terrible lot it cost! Why does an old dramatist keep a doll on his study table? I do not keep it there. It came in a box from the Boulevard an hour ago, and I took it from its wrappings to admire its accomplishments again—and ever since it has been reminding me that women are strange beings.

Yes, women are strange, and this toy sets me thinking of one woman in particular: that woman who sued, supplicated for my help, and then, when she had all my interest—— Confound the doll; here is the incident, just as it happened!

It happened when all Paris flocked to see my plays and "Paul de Varenne" was a name to conjure with. Fashions change. To-day I am a little out of the running, perhaps; younger men have shot forward. In those days I was still supreme, I was master of the Stage.

Listen! It was a spring morning, and I was lolling at my study window, scenting the lilac in the air. Maximin, my secretary, came in and said:

"Mademoiselle Jeanne Laurent asks if she can see you, monsieur."

"Who is mademoiselle Jeanne Laurent?" I inquired.

"She is an actress begging for an engagement, monsieur."

"I regret that I am exceedingly busy. Tell her to write."

"The lady has already written a thousand times," he mentioned, going. " 'Jeanne Laurent' has been one of the most constant contributors to our waste-paper basket."

"Then tell her that I regret I can do nothing for her. Mon Dieu! is it imagined that I have no other occupation than to interview nonentities? By the way, how is it you have bothered me about her, why this unusual embassy? I suppose she is pretty, hein?"

"Yes, monsieur."

"And young?"

"Yes, monsieur."

I wavered. Let us say my sympathy was stirred. But perhaps the lilac was responsible—lilac and a pretty girl seem to me a natural combination, like coffee and a cigarette. "Send her in!" I said.

I sat at the table and picked up a pen.

"Monsieur de Varenne——" She paused nervously on the threshold.

Maximin was a fool, she was not "pretty"; she was either plain, or beautiful. To my mind, she had beauty, and if she hadn't been an actress come to pester me for a part I should have foreseen a very pleasant quarter of an hour. "I can spare you only a moment, mademoiselle," I said, ruffling blank paper.

"It is most kind of you to spare me that."

I liked her voice too. "Be seated," I said more graciously.

"Monsieur, I have come to implore you to do something for me. I am breaking my heart in the profession for want of a helping hand. Will you be generous and give me a chance?"

"My dear mademoiselle—er—Laurent," I said, "I sympathize with your difficulties, and I thoroughly understand them, but I have no engagement to offer you—I am not a manager."

She smiled bitterly. "You are de Varenne—a word from you would 'make' me!"

I was wondering what her age was. About eight - and - twenty, I thought, but alternately she looked much younger and much older.

"You exaggerate my influence—like every other artist that I consent to see. Hundreds have sat in that chair and cried that I could 'make' them. It is all bosh. Be reasonable! I cannot 'make' anybody."

"You could cast me for a part in Paris. You are 'not a manager,' but any manager will engage a woman that you recommend. Oh, I know that hundreds appeal to you, I know that I am only one of a crowd; but, monsieur, think what it means to me! Without help, I shall go on knocking at the stage doors of Paris and never get inside; I shall go on writing to the Paris managers and never get an answer. Without help I shall go on eating my heart out in the provinces till I am old and tired and done for!"

Her earnestness touched me. I had heard the same tale so often that I was sick of hearing it, but this woman's earnestness touched me. If I had had a small part vacant, I would have tried her in it.

"Again," I said, "as a dramatist I fully understand the difficulties of an actress's career; but you, as an actress, do not understand a drama-tist's. There is no piece of mine going into rehearsal now, therefore I have no opening for you, myself; and it is impossible for me to write to a manager or a brother author, advising him to entrust a part, even the humblest, to a lady of whose capabilities I know nothing."

"I am not applying for a humble part," she answered quietly.

"Hein?"

"My line is lead."

I stared at her pale face, speechless; the audacity of the reply took my breath away.

"You are mad," I said, rising.

"I sound so to you, monsieur?"

"Stark, staring mad. You bewail that you are at the foot of the lad-der, and at the same instant you stipulate that I shall lift you at a bound to the top. Either you are a lunatic, or you are an amateur."

She, too, rose—resigned to her dismissal, it seemed. Then, suddenly, with a gesture that was a veritable abandonment of despair, she laughed.

"That's it, I am an amateur!" she rejoined passionately. "I will tell you the kind of 'amateur' I am, monsieur de Varenne! I was learning my business in a fit-up when I was six years old—yes, I was playing parts on the road when happier children were playing games in nur-series. I was thrust on for lead when I was a gawk of fifteen, and had to wrestle with half a dozen rôles in a week, and was beaten if I failed to make my points. I have supered to stars, not to earn the few francs I got by it, for by that time the fit-ups paid me better, but that I might observe, and improve my method. I have waited in the rain, for hours, at the doors of the milliners and modistes, that I might note how great ladies stepped from their carriages and spoke to their footmen—and when I snatched a lesson from their aristocratic tones I was in heaven, though my feet ached and the rain soaked my wretched clothes. I have played good women and bad women, beggars and queens, ingénues and hags. I was born and bred on the stage, have suffered and starved on it. It is my life and my destiny." She sobbed. "An 'amateur'!"

I could not let her go like that. She interested me strongly; somehow I believed in her. I strode to and fro, considering.

"Sit down again," I said. "I will do this for you: I will go to the country to see your performance. When is your next show?"

"I have nothing in view."

"Bigre! Well, the next time you are playing, write to me."

"You will have forgotten all about me," she urged feverishly, "or your interest will have faded, or Fate will prevent your coming."

"Why do you say so?"

"Something tells me. You will help me now, or you will never help me—my chance is to-day! Monsieur, I entreat you——"

"To-day I can do nothing at all, because I have not seen you act."

"I could recite to you."

"Zut!"

"I could rehearse on trial."

"And if you made a mess of it? A nice fool I should look, after fighting to get you in!"

A servant interrupted us to tell me that my old friend de Lavardens was downstairs. And now I did a foolish thing. When I intimated to mademoiselle Jeanne Laurent that our interview must conclude, she begged so hard to be allowed to speak to me again after my visitor went, that I consented to her waiting. Why? I had already said all that I had to say, and infinitely more than I had contemplated. Perhaps she impressed me more powerfully than I realised; perhaps it was sheer compassion, for she had an invincible instinct that if I sent her away at this juncture, she would never hear from me any more. I had her shown into the next room, and received General de Lavardens in the study.

Since his retirement from the Army, de Lavardens had lived in his château at St. Wandrille, in the neighbourhood of Caudebec-en-Caux, and we had met infrequently of late. But we had been at college together; I had entered on my military service in the same regiment as he; and we had once been comrades. I was glad to see him.

"How are you, my dear fellow? I didn't know you were in Paris."

"I have been here twenty-four hours," he said. "I have looked you up at the first opportunity. Now am I a nuisance? Be frank! I told the servant that if you were at work you weren't to be disturbed. Don't humbug about it; if I am in the way, say so!"

"You are not in the way a bit," I declared. "Put your hat and cane down. What's the news? How is Georges?"

"Georges" was Captain de Lavardens, his son, a young man with good looks, and brains, an officer for whom people predicted a brilliant future.

"Georges is all right," he said hesitatingly. "He is dining with me to-night. I want you to come, too, if you can. Are you free?"

"To-night? Yes, certainly; I shall be delighted."

"That was one of the reasons I came round—to ask you to join us." He glanced towards the table again. "Are you sure you are not in a hurry to get back to that?"

"Have a cigar, and don't be a fool. What have you got to say for yourself! Why are you on the spree here?"

"I came up to see Georges," he said. "As a matter of fact, my dear chap, I am devilish worried."

"Not about Georges?" I asked, surprised.

He grunted. "About Georges."

"Really? I'm very sorry."

"Yes. I wanted to talk to you about it. You may be able to give me a tip. Georges—the boy I hoped so much for"—his gruff voice quivered —"is infatuated with an actress."

"Georges?"

"What do you say to that?"

"Are you certain it is true?"

"True? He makes no secret of it. That isn't all. The idiot wants to marry her!"

"Georges wants to marry an actress?"

"*Voilà!*"

"My dear old friend!" I stammered.

"Isn't it amazing? One thinks one knows the character of one's own son, hein? And then, suddenly, a boy—a boy? A man! Georges will soon be thirty—a man one is proud of, who is distinguishing himself in his profession, he loses his head about some creature of the theatre and proposes to mar his whole career."

"As for that, it might not mar it," I said.

"We are not in England, in France gentlemen do not choose their wives from the stage! I can speak freely to you; you move among these people because your writing has taken you among them, but you are not of their breed."

"Have you reasoned with him?"

"Reasoned? Yes."

"What did he say?"

"Prepare to be amused. He said that 'unfortunately, the lady did not love him'!"

"What? Then there is no danger?"

"Do you mean to say that it takes you in? You may be sure her 're-luctance' is policy, she thinks it wise to disguise her eagerness to hook him. He told me plainly that he would not rest till he had won her. It is a nice position! The honour of the family is safe only till this adven-turess consents, *consents* to accept his hand! What can I do? I can re-tard the marriage by refusing my permission, but I cannot prevent it, if he summons me. . . . Of course, if I could arrange matters with her, I would do it like a shot—at any price!"

"Who is she?"

"A nobody; he tells me she is quite obscure. I don't suppose you have ever heard of her. But I thought you might make inquiries for me, that you might ascertain whether she is the sort of woman we could settle with?"

"I will do all I can, you may depend. Where is she—in Paris?"

"Yes, just now."

"What's her name?"

"Jeanne Laurent."

My mouth fell open: "Hein?"

"Do you know her?"

"She is there!"

"What?"

"In the next room. She just called on business."

"*Mon Dieu!* That's queer!"

"It's lucky. It was the first time I had ever met her."

"What's she like?"

"Have you never seen her? You shall do so in a minute. She came to beg me to advance her professionally, she wants my help. This ought to save you some money, my friend. We'll have her in! I shall tell her who you are."

"How shall I talk to her?"

"Leave it to me."

I crossed the landing, and opened the salon door. The room was littered with the illustrated journals, but she was not diverting herself with any of them—she was sitting before a copy of *La Joconde,* striving to reproduce on her own face the enigma of the smile: I had discovered an actress who never missed an opportunity.

"Please come here."

She followed me back, and my friend stood scowling at her.

"This gentleman is General de Lavardens," I said.

She bowed—slightly, perfectly. That bow acknowledged de Lavardens' presence, and rebuked the manner of my introduction, with all the dignity of the patricians whom she had studied in the rain.

"Mademoiselle, when my servant announced that the General was downstairs you heard the name. You did not tell me that you knew his son."

" 'Dame, non, monsieur!" she murmured.

"And when you implored me to assist you, you did not tell me that you aspired to a marriage that would compel you to leave the stage. I never waste my influence. Good-morning!"

"I do not aspire to the marriage," she faltered, pale as death.

"Rubbish, I know all about it. Of course, it is your aim to marry him sooner or later, and of course he will make it a condition that you cease to act. Well, I have no time to help a woman who is playing the fool! That's all about it. I needn't detain you."

"I have refused to marry him," she gasped. "On my honour! You can ask him. It is a fact."

"But you see him still," broke in de Lavardens wrathfully; "he is with you every day! That is a fact, too, isn't it? If your refusal is sincere, why are you not consistent? why do you want him at your side?"

"Because, monsieur," she answered, "I am weak enough to miss him when he goes."

"Ah! you admit it. You profess to be in love with him?"

"No, monsieur," she dissented thoughtfully, "I am not in love with him—and my refusal has been quite sincere, incredible as it may seem that a woman like myself rejects a man like him. I could never make a marriage that would mean death to my ambition. I could not sacrifice my art—the stage is too dear to me for that. So it is evident that I am not in love with him, for when a woman loves, the man is dearer to her than all else."

De Lavardens grunted. I knew his grunts: there was some apology in this one.

"The position is not fair to my son," he demurred. "You show good sense in what you say—you are an artist, you are quite right to devote yourself to your career; but you reject and encourage him at the same time. If he married you it would be disastrous—to you, and to him; you would ruin his life, and spoil your own. *Enfin,* give him a chance to forget you! Send him away. What do you want to keep seeing him for?"

She sighed. "It is wrong of me, I own!"

"It is highly unnatural," said I.

"No, monsieur; it is far from being unnatural, and I will tell you why—he is the only man I have ever known, in all my vagabond life, who realised that a struggling actress might have the soul of a gentlewoman. Before I met him, I had never heard a man speak to me with courtesy, excepting on the stage; I had never known a man to take my hand respectfully when he was not performing behind the footlights. . . . I met him first in the country; I was playing the Queen in *Ruy Blas,* and the manager brought him to me in the wings. In everything he said and did he was different from others. We were friends for months before he told me that he loved me. His friendship has been the gift of God, to brighten my miserable lot. Never to see him any more would be awful to me!"

I perceived that if she was not in love with him she was so dangerously near to it that a trifle might turn the scale. De Lavardens had the same thought. His glance at me was apprehensive.

"However, you acknowledge that you are behaving badly!" I exclaimed. "It is all right for *you,* friendship is enough for you, and you pursue your career. But for *him,* it is different; he seeks your love, and he neglects his duties. For him to spend his life sighing for you would be monstrous, and for him to marry you would be fatal. If you like him so much, be just to him, set him free! Tell him that he is not to visit you any more."

"He does not visit me; he has never been inside my lodging."

"Well, that he is not to write there—that there are to be no more dinners, drives, bouquets!"

"And I do not let him squander money on me. I am not that kind of woman."

"We do not accuse you, mademoiselle. On the contrary, we appeal to your good heart. Be considerate, be brave! Say good-bye to him!"

"You are asking me to suffer cruelly," she moaned.

"It is for your friend's benefit. Also, the more you suffer, the better you will act. Every actress should suffer."

"Monsieur, I have served my apprenticeship to pain."

"There are other things than friendship—you have your prospects to think about."

"What prospects?" she flashed back.

"Well, I cannot speak definitely to-day, as you know; but you would not find me unappreciative."

De Lavardens grunted again—emotionally, this time. I checked him with a frown.

"What use would it be for me to refuse to see him?" she objected chokily. "When I am playing anywhere, *he* can always see *me*. I cannot kill his love by denying myself his companionship. Besides, he would not accept the dismissal. One night, when I left the theatre, I should find him waiting there again."

This was unpalatably true.

"If a clever woman desires to dismiss a man, she can dismiss him thoroughly, especially a clever actress," I said. "You could talk to him in such a fashion that he would have no wish to meet you again. Such things have been done."

"What? You want me to teach him to despise me?"

"Much better if he did!"

"To turn his esteem to scorn, hein?"

"It would be a generous action."

"To falsify and degrade myself?"

"For your hero's good!"

"I will not do it!" she flamed. "You demand too much. What have *you* done for *me* that I should sacrifice myself to please you? I entreat your help, and you give me empty phrases; I cry that I despair this morning, and you answer that by-and-by, some time, in the vague future, you will remember that I exist. I shall not do this for you—I keep my friend!"

"Your rhetoric has no weight with me," I said. "I do not pretend that I have a claim on you. In such circumstances a noble woman would take the course I suggest, not for my sake, not for the sake of General de Lavardens, but for the sake of the man himself. You will 'keep your friend'? *Bien!* But you will do so because you are indifferent to his welfare and too selfish to release him."

She covered her face. There were tears on it. The General and I exchanged glances again.

I went on:

"You charge me with giving you only empty phrases. That is undeserved. I said all that was possible, and I meant what I said. I could not pledge myself to put you into anything without knowing what you are capable of doing; but, if you retain my good will, I repeat that I will attend your next performance."

"And then?" she queried.

"Then—if I think well of it—you shall have a good part."

"Lead?"

"*Bigre!* I cannot say that. A good part, in Paris!"

"It is a promise?"

"Emphatically—if I think well of your performance."

"Of my next—the very next part I play?"

"Of the very next part you play."

She paused, reflecting. The pause lasted so long that it began to seem to my suspense as if none of us would ever speak again. I took a cigarette, and offered the box, in silence, to de Lavardens. He shook his head without turning it to me, his gaze was riveted on the woman.

"All right," she groaned, "I agree!"

"Ah! good girl!"

"All you require is that Captain de Lavardens shall no longer seek me for his wife. Is that it?"

"That's it."

"Very well. I know what would repel him—it shall be done to-night. But you, gentlemen, will have to make the opportunity for me; you will have to bring him to my place—both of you. You can find some reason for proposing it? To-night at nine o'clock. He knows the address."

She moved weakly to the door.

De Lavardens took three strides and grasped her hands. "Mademoiselle," he stuttered, "I have no words to speak my gratitude. I am a father, and I love my son, but—*mon Dieu!* if—if things had been different, upon my soul, I should have been proud to call you my daughter-in-law!"

Oh, how she could bow, that woman—the eloquence of her ill-fed form!

"Au revoir, gentlemen," she said.

Phew! We dropped into chairs.

"Paul," he grunted at me, "we have been a pair of brutes!"

"I know it. But you feel much relieved?"

"I feel another man. What is she going to say to him? I wish it were over. *I* should find it devilish difficult to propose going to see her, you know! It will have to be *your* suggestion. And supposing he won't take us?"

"He will take us right enough," I declared, "and rejoice at the chance. Hourra! hourra! hourra!" I sprang up and clapped him on the back. "My friend, if that woman had thrown herself away on Georges it might have been a national calamity."

"What?" he roared, purpling.

"Oh, no slight to Georges! I think—I think—I am afraid to say what I think, I am afraid to think it!" I paced the room, struggling to control myself. "Only, once in a blue moon, Jules, there is a woman born of the People with a gift that is a blessing, and a curse—and her genius makes an epoch, and her name makes theatrical history. And if a lover of the stage like me discovers such a woman, you stodgy old soldier, and blazes her genius in his work, he feels like Cheops, Chephrenus, and Asychis rearing the Pyramids for immortality!"

My excitement startled him. "You believe she is a genius? Really?"

"I dare not believe," I panted. "I refuse to let myself believe, for I have never seen blue moons. But—but—I wonder!"

We dined at Voisin's. It had been arranged that he should make some allusion to the courtship; and I said to Georges, "I hope you don't mind your father having mentioned the subject to me—we are old friends, you know?" The topic was led up to very easily. It was apparent that Georges thought the world of her. I admired the way he spoke. It was quiet and earnest. As I feigned partial sympathy with his matrimonial hopes, I own that I felt a Judas.

"I, too, am an artist," I said. "To me social distinctions naturally seem somewhat less important than they do to your father."

"Indeed, monsieur," he answered gravely, "mademoiselle Laurent is worthy of homage. If she were willing to accept me, every man who knew her character would think me fortunate. Her education has not qualified her to debate with professors, and she has no knowledge of society small-talk, but she is intelligent, and refined, and good."

It was child's play. A sudden notion, over the liqueurs: "Take us to see her! Come along, *mon ami!*" Astonishment (amateurish); persuasion (masterly); Georges's diffidence to intrude, but his obvious delight at the thought of the favourable impression she would create. He had "never called there yet—it would be very unconventional at such an hour?" "Zut, among artists! My card will be a passport, I assure you." Poor fellow, the trap made short work of him! At half-past eight we were all rattling to the left bank in a cab.

The cab stopped before a dilapidated house in an unsavoury street. I knew that the aspect of her home went to his heart. "Mademoiselle Laurent has won no prize in her profession," he observed, "and she is an honest girl." Well said! In the dim passage a neglected child directed us to the fourth floor. On the fourth floor a slattern, who replied at last to our persistent tapping, told us shortly that mademoiselle was out. I realised that we had committed the error of being before our time; and the woman, evidently unprepared for our visit, did not suggest our going in. It seemed bad stage-management.

"Will it be long before mademoiselle is back?" I inquired, annoyed.

"Mais non."

"We will wait," I said, and we were admitted sulkily to a room, of which the conspicuous features were a malodorous lamp, and a brandy-bottle. I had taken the old drab for a landlady rather the worse for liquor, but, more amiably, she remarked now: "It's a pity Jeanne didn't know you were coming."

At the familiar "Jeanne" I saw Georges start.

"Mademoiselle is a friend of yours?" I asked, dismayed.

"A friend? She is my daughter." She sat down.

By design the girl was out! The thought flashed on me. It flashed on me that she had plotted for her lover to learn what a mother-in-law he would have. The revelation must appal him. I stole a look—his face was blanched. The General drew a deep breath, and nodded to himself. The nod said plainly, "He is saved. Thank God!"

"Will you take a little drop while you are waiting, gentlemen?"

"Nothing for us, thank you."

She drank alone, and seemed to forget that we were present. None of us spoke. I began to wonder if we need remain. Then, drinking, she grew garrulous. It was of Jeanne she talked. She gave us her maternal views, and incidentally betrayed infamies of her own career. I am a man of the world, but I shuddered at that woman. The suitor who could have risked making her child his wife would have been demented, or sublime. And while she maundered on, gulping from her glass, and chuckling at her jests, the ghastliness of it was that, in the gutter face before us, I could trace a likeness to Jeanne; I think Georges must have traced it, too. The menace of heredity was horrible. We were listening to Jeanne wrecked, Jeanne thirty years older—Jeanne as she might become!

Ciel! To choose a bride with this blood in her—a bride from the dregs!

"Let us go, Georges," I murmured. "Courage! You will forget her. We'll be off."

He was livid. I saw that he could bear no more.

But the creature overheard, and in those bleary eyes intelligence awoke.

"What? Hold on!" she stammered. "Is one of you the toff that wants to marry her? Ah! . . . I've been letting on finely, haven't I? It was a plant, was it? You've come here ferreting and spying?" She turned towards me in a fury: "You!"

Certainly I had made a comment from time to time, but I could not see why she should single me out for her attack. She lurched towards me savagely. Her face was thrust into mine. And then, so low that only I could hear, and like another woman, she breathed a question:

"Can I act?"

Jeanne herself! Every nerve in me jumped. The next instant she was back in her part, railing at Georges.

I took a card from my case, and scribbled six words.

"When your daughter comes in, give her that!" I said. I had scribbled: "I write you a star rôle!"

She gathered the message at a glance, and I swear that the moroseness of her gaze was not lightened by so much as a gleam. She was representing a character; the actress sustained the character even while she read words that were to raise her from privation to renown.

"Not that I care if I *have* queered her chance," she snarled. "A good job, too, the selfish cat! I've got nothing to thank her for. Serve her right if you do give her the go-by, my Jackanapes, *I* don't blame you!"

"Madame Laurent," Georges answered sternly, and his answer vibrated through the room, "I have never admired, pitied, or loved Jeanne so much as now that I know that she has been—motherless."

All three of us stood stone-still. The first to move was she. I saw what was going to happen. She burst out crying.

"It's I, Jeanne!—I love you! I thought I loved the theatre best—I was wrong." Instinctively she let my card fall to the ground. "Forgive me—I did it for your sake, too. It was cruel, I am ashamed. Oh, my own, if my love will not disgrace you, take me for your wife! In all the world there is no woman who will love you better—in all my heart there is no room for anything but you!"

They were in each other's arms. De Lavardens, whom the proclamation of identity had electrified, dragged me outside. The big fool was blubbering with sentiment.

"This is frightful," he grunted.

"Atrocious!" said I.

"But she is a woman in a million."

"She is a great actress," I said reverently.

"I could never approve the marriage," he faltered. "What do you think?"

"Out of the question! I have no sympathy with either of them."

"You humbug! Why, there is a tear running down your nose!"

"There are two running down yours," I snapped; "a General should know better."

And why has the doll in the pink silk dress recalled this to me? Well, you see, to-morrow will be New Year's Day and the doll is a gift for my godchild—and the name of my godchild's mother is "Jeanne de Lavardens." Oh, I have nothing to say against her as a mother, the children idolise her! I admit that she has conquered the General, and that Georges is the proudest husband in France. But when I think of the parts I could have written for her, of the lustre the stage has lost, when I reflect that, just to be divinely happy, the woman deliberately declined a world-wide fame—*Morbleu!* I can never forgive her for it, never—the darling!

38

The Drums of the Fore and Aft

BY RUDYARD KIPLING

IN the army list they still stand as "The Fore and Fit Princess Hohenzollern-Sigmaringen-Anspach's Merther-Tydfilshire Own Royal Loyal Light Infantry, Regimental District 329 A," but the army, through all its barracks and canteens, knows them now as "The Fore and Aft." They may in time do something that shall make their new title honorable, but at present they are bitterly ashamed, and the man who calls them "Fore and Aft" does so at the risk of the head which is on his shoulders.

Two words breathed into the stables of a certain cavalry regiment will bring the men out into the streets with belts and mops and bad language; but a whisper of "Fore and Aft" will bring out this regiment with rifles.

Their one excuse is that they came again and did their best to finish the job in style. But for a time all their world knows that they were openly beaten, whipped, dumbcowed, shaking, and afraid. The men know it; their officers know it; the Horse Guards know it, and when the next war comes the enemy will know it also. There are two or three regiments of the line that have a black mark against their names which they will then wipe out; and it will be excessively inconvenient for the troops upon whom they do their wiping.

The courage of the British soldier is officially supposed to be above proof, and, as a general rule, it is so. The exceptions are decently shoveled out of sight, only to be referred to in the freshest of unguarded talk that occasionally swamps a mess-table at midnight. Then one hears strange and horrible stories of men not following their officers, of orders being given by those who had no right to give them, and of disgrace that, but for the standing luck of the British army, might have ended in brilliant disaster. These are unpleasant stories to listen to, and the messes tell them under their breath, sitting by the big wood-fires, and the young officer bows his head and thinks to himself that, please God, his men shall never behave unhandily.

The British soldier is not altogether to be blamed for occasional lapses; but this verdict he should not know. A moderately intelligent general will waste six months in mastering the craft of the particular war that he may be waging; a colonel may utterly misunderstand the capacity of his regiment for three months after it has taken the field, and even a company commander may err and be deceived as to the temper and temperament of his own handful: wherefore the soldier, and the soldier of to-day more particularly, should not be blamed for falling back. He should be shot or hanged afterward—to encourage the others; but he should not be vilified in newspapers, for that is want of tact and waste of space.

He has, let us say, been in the service of the empress for, perhaps, four years. He will leave in another two years. He has no inherited morals, and four years are not sufficient to drive toughness into his fiber, or to teach him how holy a thing is his regiment. He wants to drink, he wants to enjoy himself—in India he wants to save money—and he does not in the least like getting hurt. He has received just sufficient education to make him understand half the purport of the orders he receives, and to speculate on the nature of clean, incised, and shattering wounds. Thus, if he is told to deploy under fire preparatory to an attack, he knows that he runs a very great risk of being killed while he is deploying, and suspects that he is being thrown away to gain ten minutes' time. He may either deploy with desperate swiftness, or he may shuffle, or bunch, or break, according to the discipline under which he has lain for four years.

Armed with imperfect knowledge, cursed with the rudiments of an imagination, hampered by the intense selfishness of the lower classes, and unsupported by any regimental associations, this young man is suddenly introduced to an enemy who in Eastern lands is always ugly, generally tall and hairy, and frequently noisy. If he looks to the right and the left and sees old soldiers—men of twelve years' service, who, he knows, know what they are about—taking a charge, rush, or demonstration without embarrassment, he is consoled and applies his shoulder to the butt of his rifle with a stout heart. His peace is the greater if he hears a senior, who has taught him his soldiering and broken his head on occasion, whispering: "They'll shout and carry on like this for five minutes. Then they'll rush in, and then we've got 'em by the short hairs!"

But, on the other hand, if he sees only men of his own term of service, turning white and playing with their triggers and saying, "What the hell's up now?" while the company commanders are sweating into their sword-hilts and shouting: "Front rank, fix bayonets. Steady there —steady! Sight for three hundred—no, for five! Lie down, all! Steady! Front rank kneel!" and so forth, he becomes unhappy, and grows acutely miserable when he hears a comrade turn over with the rattle of fire-irons falling into the fender, and the grunt of a pole-axed ox. If he can be moved about a little and allowed to watch the effect of his own fire on the enemy, he feels merrier, and may be then worked up to the blind passion of fighting, which is, contrary to general belief, controlled by a chilly devil and shakes men like ague. If he is not moved about, and begins to feel cold at the pit of the stomach, and in that crisis is badly mauled and hears orders that were never given, he will break, and he will break badly; and of all things under the light of the sun there is nothing more terrible than a broken British regiment. When the worst comes to the worst and the panic is really epidemic, the men must be e'en let go, and the company commanders had better escape to the enemy and stay there for safety's sake. If they can be made to come again they are not pleasant men to meet; because they will not break twice.

About thirty years from this date, when we have succeeded in half-educating everything that wears trousers, our army will be a beautifully unreliable machine. It will know too much and it will do too little. Later still, when all men are at the mental level of the officer of to-day, it will sweep the earth. Speaking roughly, you must employ either black-guards or gentlemen, or, best of all, blackguards commanded by gentlemen, to do butcher's work with efficiency and despatch. The ideal soldier should, of course, think for himself—the "Pocketbook" says so. Unfortunately, to attain this virtue, he has to pass through the phase of thinking of himself, and that is misdirected genius. A blackguard may be slow to think for himself, but he is genuinely anxious to kill, and a little punishment teaches him how to guard his own skin and perforate another's. A powerfully prayerful Highland regiment, officered by rank Presbyterians, is, perhaps, one degree more terrible in action than a hard-bitten thousand of irresponsible Irish ruffians led by most improper young unbelievers. But these things prove the rule—which is that the midway men are not to be trusted alone. They have ideas about the value of life and an upbringing that has not taught them to go on and take the chances. They are carefully unprovided with a backing of comrades who have been shot over, and until that backing is reintroduced, as a great many regimental commanders intend it shall be, they are more liable to disgrace themselves than the size of the empire or the dignity of the army allows. Their officers are as good as can be, because their training begins early, and God has arranged that a clean-run youth of the British middle classes shall, in the matter of backbone, brains, and bowels, surpass all other youths. For this reason a child of eighteen will stand up, doing nothing, with a tin sword in his hand and joy in his heart until he is dropped. If he dies, he dies like a gentleman. If he lives, he writes home that he has been "potted," "sniped," "chipped," or "cut over," and sits down to besiege government for a wound gratuity until the next little war breaks out, when he perjures himself before a medical board, blarneys his colonel, burns incense round his adjutant, and is allowed to go to the front once more.

Which homily brings me directly to a brace of the most finished little fiends that ever banged drum or tootled fife in the band of a British regiment. They ended their sinful career by open and flagrant mutiny, and were shot for it. Their names were Jakin and Lew—Piggy Lew— and they were bold, bad drummer-boys, both of them frequently birched by the drum-major of the Fore and Aft.

Jakin was a stunted child of fourteen, and Lew was about the same age. When not looked after, they smoked and drank. They swore habitually after the manner of the barrack-room, which is cold swearing and comes from between clenched teeth, and they fought religiously once a week. Jakin had sprung from some London gutter and may or may not have passed through Dr. Barnardo's hands ere he arrived at the dignity of drummer-boy. Lew could remember nothing except the regiment and the delight of listening to the band from his earliest years. He hid somewhere in his grimy little soul a genuine love for music, and was most mistakenly furnished with the head of a cherub: insomuch that beautiful ladies who watched the regiment in church were wont to speak of him as a "darling." They never heard his vitriolic comments on their manners and morals as he walked back to barracks with the band and matured fresh causes of offense against Jakin.

The other drummer-boys hated both lads on account of their illogical conduct. Jakin might be pounding Lew, or Lew might be rubbing Jakin's head in the dirt, but any attempt at aggression on the part of an outsider was met by the combined forces of Lew and Jakin; and the consequences were painful. The boys were the Ishmaels of the corps, but wealthy Ishmaels, for they sold battles in alternate weeks for the sport of the barracks when they were not pitted against other boys; and thus amassed money.

On this particular day there was dissension in the camp. They had just been convicted afresh of smoking, which is bad for little boys who use plug tobacco, and Lew's contention was that Jakin had "stunk so 'orrid bad from keepin' the pipe in pocket," that he and he alone was responsible for the birching they were both tingling under.

"I tell you I 'id the pipe back o' barracks," said Jakin, pacifically.

"You're a bloomin' liar," said Lew, without heat.

"You're a bloomin' little barstard," said Jakin, strong in the knowledge that his own ancestry was unknown.

Now there is one word in the extended vocabulary of barrack-room abuse that cannot pass without comment. You may call a man a thief and risk nothing. You may even call him a coward without finding more than a boot whiz past your ear; but you must not call a man a bastard unless you are prepared to prove it on his front teeth.

"You might ha' kep' that till I wasn't so sore," said Lew, sorrowfully, dodging around Jakin's guard.

"I'll make you sorer," said Jakin, genially, and got home on Lew's alabaster forehead. All would have gone well, and this story, as the books say, would never have been written, had not his evil fate prompted the bazaar-sergeant's son, a long, employless man of five and twenty, to put in an appearance after the first round. He was eternally in need of money, and knew that the boys had silver.

"Fighting again," said he. "I'll report you to my father, and he'll report you to the color-sergeant."

"What's that to you?" said Jakin, with an unpleasant dilation of the nostrils.

"Oh! nothing to *me*. You'll get into trouble, and you've been up too often to afford that."

"What the hell do you know about what we've done?" asked Lew the Seraph. "*You* aren't in the army, you lousy, cadging civilian."

He closed in on the man's left flank.

"Jes' 'cause you find two gentlemen settlin' their diff'rences with their fists, you stick in your ugly nose where you aren't wanted. Run 'ome to your 'arf-caste slut of a ma—or we'll give you what for," said Jakin.

The man attempted reprisals by knocking the boys' heads together. The scheme would have succeeded had not Jakin punched him vehemently in the stomach, or had Lew refrained from kicking his shins. They fought together, bleeding and breathless, for half an hour, and, after heavy punishment, triumphantly pulled down their opponent as terriers pull down a jackal.

"Now," gasped Jakin, "I'll give you what for." He proceeded to pound the man's features while Lew stamped on the outlying portions of his anatomy. Chivalry is not a strong point in the composition of the average drummer-boy. He fights, as do his betters, to make his mark.

Ghastly was the ruin that escaped, and awful was the wrath of the bazaar-sergeant. Awful too was the scene in orderly-room when the two reprobates appeared to answer the charge of half murdering a "civilian." The bazaar sergeant thirsted for a criminal action, and his son lied. The boys stood to attention while the black clouds of evidence accumulated.

"You little devils are more trouble than the rest of the regiment put together," said the colonel angrily. "One might as well admonish thistle-down, and I can't well put you in cells or under stoppages. You must be birched again."

"Beg y' pardon, sir. Can't we say nothin' in our own defense, sir?" shrilled Jakin.

"Hey! What? Are you going to argue with *me?*" said the colonel.

"No, sir," said Lew. "But if a man come to you, sir, and said he was going to report you, sir, for 'aving a bit of a turn-up with a friend, sir, an' wanted to get money out of *you,* sir——"

The orderly-room exploded in a roar of laughter. "Well?" said the colonel.

"That was what that measly *jarnwar* there did, sir, and 'e'd 'a' *done* it, sir, if we 'adn't prevented 'im. We didn't 'it 'im much, sir. 'E 'adn't no manner o' right to interfere with us, sir. I don't mind bein' birched by the drum-major, sir, nor yet reported by *any* corp'ral, but I'm—but I don't think it's fair, sir, for a civilian to come an' talk over a man in the army."

A second shout of laughter shook the orderly-room, but the colonel was grave.

"What sort of characters have these boys?" he asked of the regimental sergeant-major.

"Accordin' to the bandmaster, sir," returned that revered official—the only soul in the regiment whom the boys feared—"they do everything *but* lie, sir."

"Is it like we'd go for that man for fun, sir?" said Lew, pointing to the plaintiff.

"Oh, admonished! admonished!" said the colonel testily, and when the boys had gone he read the bazaar sergeant's son a lecture on the sin of unprofitable meddling, and gave orders that the bandmaster should keep the drums in better discipline.

"If either of you come to practise again with so much as a scratch on your two ugly little faces," thundered the bandmaster, "I'll tell the drum-major to take the skin off your backs. Understand that, you young devils."

Then he repented of his speech for just the length of time that Lew, looking like a seraph in red worsted embellishments took the place of one of the trumpets—in hospital—and rendered the echo of a battle-piece. Lew certainly was a musician, and had often in his more exalted moments expressed a yearning to master every instrument of the band.

"There's nothing to prevent your becoming a bandmaster, Lew," said the bandmaster, who had composed waltzes of his own, and worked day and night in the interests of the band.

"What did he say?" demanded Jakin after practise.

"Said I might be a bloomin' bandmaster, an' be asked in to 'ave a glass o' sherry wine on mess nights."

"Ho! Said you might be a bloomin' non-combatant, did 'e! That's just what 'e would say. When I've put in my boy's service—it's a bloomin' shame that doesn't count for pension—I'll take on as a privit. Then I'll be a lance in a year—knowin' what I know about the ins and outs o' things. In three years I'll be a bloomin' sergeant. I won't marry, then, not I! I'll 'old on and learn the orf'cers' ways an' apply for exchange into a reg'ment that doesn't know all about me. Then I'll be a bloomin' orf'cer. Then I'll ask you to 'ave a glass o' sherry wine, *Mister* Lew, an' you'll bloomin well 'ave to stay in the hantyroom while the mess sergeant brings it to your dirty 'ands."

" 'S'pose I'm going to be a bandmaster? Not I, quite. I'll be an orf'cer, too. There's nothin' like takin' to a thing an' stickin' to it, the schoolmaster says. The reg'ment don't go 'ome for another seven years. I'll be a lance then, or near to."

Thus the boys discussed their futures, and conducted themselves piously for a week. That is to say, Lew started a flirtation with the color-sergeant's daughter, aged thirteen—"not," as he explained to Jakin, "with any intention o' matrimony, but by way o' keepin' my 'and in." And the black-haired Cris Delighan enjoyed that flirtation more than previous ones, and the other drummer-boys raged furiously together, and Jakin preached sermons on the dangers of "bein' tangled along o' petticoats."

But neither love nor virtue would have held Lew long in the paths of propriety had not the rumor gone abroad that the regiment was to be sent on active service, to take part in a war which, for the sake of brevity, we will call "The War of the Lost Tribes."

The barracks had the rumor almost before the mess-room, and of all the nine hundred men in barracks, not ten had seen a shot fired in anger. The colonel had, twenty years ago, assisted at a frontier expedition; one of the majors had seen service at the Cape; a confirmed deserter in E company had helped to clear streets in Ireland; but that was all. The regiment had been put by for many years. The overwhelming mass of its rank and file had from three to four years' service; the non-commissioned officers were under thirty years old; and men and sergeants alike had forgotten to speak of the stories written in brief upon the colors—the new colors that had been formally blessed by an archbishop in England ere the regiment came away.

They wanted to go to the front—they were enthusiastically anxious to go—but they had no knowledge of what war meant, and there was none to tell them. They were an educated regiment, the percentage of school certificates in their ranks was high, and most of the men could do more than read and write. They had been recruited in loyal observance of the territorial idea; but they themselves had no notion of that idea. They were made up of drafts from an overpopulated manufacturing district. The system had put flesh and muscle upon their small bones, but it could not put heart into the sons of those who for generations had done overmuch work for overscanty pay, had sweated in drying-rooms, stooped over looms, coughed among white lead, and shivered on lime barges. The men had found food and rest in the army, and now they were going to fight "niggers"—people who ran away if you shook a stick at them. Wherefore they cheered lustily when the rumor ran, and the shrewd, clerkly non-commissioned officers speculated on the chances of batta and of saving their pay. At headquarters men said: "The Fore and Fit have never been under fire within the last generation. Let us, therefore, break them in easily by setting them to guard lines of communication." And this would have been done but for the fact that British regiments were wanted—badly wanted—at the front, and there were doubtful native regiments that could fill the minor duties. "Brigade 'em with two strong regiments," said headquarters. "They may be knocked about a bit, but they'll learn their business before they come through. Nothing like a night alarm and a little cutting up of stragglers to make a regiment smart in the field. Wait till they've had half a dozen sentries' throats cut."

The colonel wrote with delight that the temper of his men was excellent, that the regiment was all that could be wished, and as sound as a bell. The majors smiled with a sober joy, and the subalterns waltzed in pairs down the mess-room after dinner, and nearly shot themselves at revolver practise. But there was consternation in the hearts of Jakin and Lew. What was to be done with the drums? Would the band go to the front? How many of the drums would accompany the regiment?

They took council together, sitting in a tree and smoking.

"It's more than a bloomin' toss up they'll leave us be'ind at the depot with the women. You'll like that," said Jakin sarcastically.

" 'Cause o' Cris, y' mean? Wot's a woman, or a 'ole bloomin' depot o' women, 'longside o' the chanst o' field service? You know I'm as keen on goin' as you," said Lew.

"Wish I was a bloomin' bugler," said Jakin sadly. "They'll take Tom Kidd along, that I can plaster a wall with, an' like as not they won't take us."

"Then let's go an' make Tom Kidd so bloomin' sick 'e can't bugle no more. You 'old 'is 'ands an' I'll kick him," said Lew, wriggling on the branch.

"That ain't no good neither. We ain't the sort o' characters to presoom on our rep'tations—they're bad. If they have the band at the depot we don't go, and no error *there*. If they take the band we may get cast for medical unfitness. Are you medical fit, Piggy?" said Jakin, digging Lew in the ribs with force.

"Yus," said Lew, with an oath. "The doctor says your 'eart's weak through smokin' on an empty stummick. Throw a chest an' I'll try yer."

Jakin threw out his chest, which Lew smote with all his might. Jakin turned very pale, gasped, crowed, screwed up his eyes and said, "That's all right."

"You'll do," said Lew. "I've 'eard o' men dying when you 'it 'em fair on the breastbone."

"Don't bring us no nearer goin', though," said Jakin. "Do you know where we're ordered?"

"Gawd knows, an' 'E won't split on a pal. Somewheres up to the front to kill Paythans—hairy, big beggars that turn you inside out if they get 'old o' you. They say their women are good-looking, too."

"Any loot?" asked the abandoned Jakin.

"Not a bloomin' anna, they say, unless you dig up the ground an' see what the niggers 'ave 'id. They're a poor lot." Jakin stood upright on the branch and gazed across the plain.

"Lew," said he, "there's the colonel comin'. Colonel's a good old beggar. Let's go an' talk to 'im."

Lew nearly fell out of the tree at the audacity of the suggestion. Like Jakin, he feared not God, neither regarded he man, but there are limits even to the audacity of a drummer-boy, and to speak to a colonel was——

But Jakin had slid down the trunk and doubled in the direction of the colonel. That officer was walking wrapped in thought and visions of a C. B.—yes, even a K.C.B., for had he not at command one of the best regiments of the line, the Fore and Fit? And he was aware of two small boys charging down upon him. Once before it had been solemnly reported to him that "the drums were in a state of mutiny," Jakin and Lew being the ringleaders. This looked like an organized conspiracy.

The boys halted at twenty yards, walked to the regulation four paces, and saluted together, each as well set up as a ramrod and little taller.

The colonel was in a genial mood; the boys appeared very forlorn and unprotected on the desolate plain, and one of them was handsome.

"Well!" said the colonel, recognizing them. "Are you going to pull

me down in the open? I'm sure I never interfere with you, even though"
—he sniffed suspiciously—"you have been smoking."

It was time to strike while the iron was hot. Their hearts beat tumultuously.

"Beg y' pardon, sir," began Jakin. "The reg'ment's ordered on active service, sir?"

"So I believe," said the colonel courteously.

"Is the band goin', sir?" said both together. Then, without pause, "We're goin', sir, ain't we?"

"You!" said the colonel, stepping back the more fully to take in the two small figures. "You! You'd die in the first march."

"No, we wouldn't, sir. We can march with the reg'ment anywheres —p'rade and anywhere else," said Jakin.

"If Tom Kidd goes 'e'll shut up like a claspknife," said Lew. "Tom 'as very-close veins in both 'is legs, sir."

"Very how much?"

"Very-close veins, sir. That's why they swells after long p'rade, sir. If 'e can go, we can go, sir."

Again the colonel looked at them long and intently.

"Yes, the band is going," he said, as gravely as though he had been addressing a brother officer. "Have you any parents, either of you two?"

"No, sir," rejoicingly from Lew and Jakin. "We're both orphans, sir. There's no one to be considered of on our account, sir."

"You poor little sprats, and you want to go up to the front with the regiment, do you? Why?"

"I've wore the queen's uniform for two years," said Jakin. "It's very 'ard, sir, that a man don't get no recompense for doin' of his dooty, sir."

"An'—an' if I don't go, sir," interrupted Lew, "the bandmaster says 'e'll catch and make a bloo—a blessed musician o' me, sir. Before I've seen any service, sir."

The colonel made no answer for a long time. Then he said quietly: "If you're passed by the doctor, I dare say you can go. I shouldn't smoke if I were you."

The boys saluted and disappeared. The colonel walked home and told the story to his wife, who nearly cried over it. The colonel was well pleased. If that was the temper of the children, what would not the men do?

Jakin and Lew entered the boys' barrack-room with great stateliness, and refused to hold any conversation with their comrades for at least ten minutes. Then, bursting with pride, Jakin drawled: "I've bin intervooin' the colonel. Good old beggar is the colonel. Says I to 'im, 'Colonel,' says I, 'let me go to the front, along o' the reg'ment.' 'To the front you shall go,' says 'e, 'an' I only wish there was more like you among the dirty little devils that bang the bloomin' drums.' Kidd, if you throw your 'courterments at me for telling you the truth to your own advantage, your legs'll swell."

None the less there was a battle royal in the barrack-room, for the boys were consumed with envy and hate, and neither Jakin nor Lew behaved in conciliatory wise.

"I'm goin' out to say adoo to my girl," said Lew, to cap the climax. "Don't none o' you touch my kit, because it's wanted for active service; me bein' specially invited to go by the colonel."

He strolled forth and whistled in the clump of trees at the back of the married quarters till Cris came to him, and, the preliminary kisses being given and taken, Lew began to explain the situation.

"I'm going to the front with the reg'ment," he said valiantly.

"Piggy, you're a little liar," said Cris, but her heart misgave her, for Lew was not in the habit of lying.

"Liar yourself, Cris," said Lew, slipping an arm around her. "I'm goin'. When the reg'ment marches out, you'll see me with them, all galliant and gay. Give us another kiss, Cris, on the strength of it."

"If you'd on'y a stayed at the depot—where you *ought* ha' bin—you could get as many of 'em as—as you dam please," whimpered Cris, putting up her mouth.

"It's 'ard, Cris. I grant you it's 'ard. But what's a man to do? If I'd stayed at the depot, you wouldn't think anything of me."

"Like as not, but I'd 'ave you with me, Piggy. An' all the thinkin' in the world isn't like kissin'."

"And all the kissin' in the world isn't like 'avin' a medal to wear on the front of your coat."

"*You* won't get no medal."

"Oh, yus, I shall, though. Me an' Jakin are the only acting drummers that'll be took along. All the rest is full men, an' we'll get our medals with them."

"They might ha' taken anybody but you, Piggy. You'll get killed—you're so venturesome. Stay with me, Piggy darlin', down at the depot, an' I'll love you true, forever."

"Ain't you goin' to do that *now*, Cris? You said you was."

"O' course I am, but th' other's more comfortable. Wait till you've growed a bit, Piggy. You aren't no taller than me now."

"I've bin in the army for two years, an' I'm not goin' to get out of a chanst o' seein' service, an' don't you try to make me do so. I'll come back, Cris, an' when I take on as a man I'll marry you—marry you when I'm a lance."

"Promise, Piggy?"

Lew reflected on the future as arranged by Jakin a short time previously, but Cris's mouth was very near to his own.

"I promise, s'elp me, Gawd!" said he.

Cris slid an arm round his neck.

"I won't 'old you back no more, Piggy. Go away an' get your medal, an' I'll make you a new button-bag as nice as I know how," she whispered.

"Put some o' your 'air into it, Cris, an' I'll keep it in my pocket so long's I'm alive."

Then Cris wept anew, and the interview ended. Public feeling among the drummer-boys rose to fever pitch, and the lives of Jakin and Lew became unenviable. Not only had they been permitted to enlist two years before the regulation boy's age—fourteen—but, by virtue, it seemed, of their extreme youth, they were allowed to go to the front— which thing had not happened to acting drummers within the knowledge of boy. The band, which was to accompany the regiment, had been cut down to the regulation twenty men, the surplus returning to the ranks. Jakin and Lew were attached to the band as supernumeraries, though they would much have preferred being company buglers.

"Don't matter much," said Jakin, after the medical inspection. "Be thankful that we're 'lowed to go at all. The doctor 'e said that if we could stand what we took from the bazaar sergeant's son we'd stand pretty nigh anything."

"Which we will," said Lew, looking tenderly at the ragged and ill-made house-wife that Cris had given him, with a lock of her hair worked into a sprawling "L" upon the cover.

"It was the best that I could do," she sobbed. "I wouldn't let mother nor the sergeant's tailor 'elp me. Keep it always, Piggy, an' remember I love you true."

They marched to the railway station, nine hundred and sixty strong, and every soul in cantonments turned out to see them go. The drummers gnashed their teeth at Jakin and Lew marching with the band, the married women wept upon the platform, and the regiment cheered its noble self black in the face.

"A nice, level lot," said the colonel to the second in command, as they watched the first four companies entraining.

"Fit to do anything," said the second in command, enthusiastically. "But it seems to me they're a thought too young and tender for the work in hand. It's bitter cold up at the front now."

"They're sound enough," said the colonel. "We must take our chance of sick casualties."

So they went northward, ever northward, past droves and droves of camels, armies of camp-followers, and legions of laden mules, the throng thickening day by day, till with a shriek the train pulled up at a hopelessly congested junction where six lines of temporary track accommodated six forty-wagon trains, where whistles blew, Babus sweated, and commissariat officers swore from dawn till far into the night amid the wind-driven chaff of the fodder bales and the lowing of a thousand steers.

"Hurry up—you're badly wanted at the front," was the message that greeted the Fore and Aft, and the occupants of the Red Cross carriages told the same tale.

" 'Tisn't so much the bloomin' fightin'," gasped a headbound trooper of Hussars to a knot of admiring Fore and Afts. " 'Tisn't so much the bloomin' fightin', though there's enough of that. It's the bloomin' food an' the bloomin' climate. Frost all night 'cept when it hails, and bilin' sun all day, and the water stinks fit to knock you down. I got my 'ead chipped like a egg; I've got pneumonia, too, an' my guts is all out o' order. 'Tain't no bloomin' picnic in those parts, I can tell you."

"Wot are the niggers like?" demanded a private.

"There's some prisoners in that train yonder. Go an' look at 'em. They're the aristocracy o' the country. The common folk are a dashed sight uglier. If you want to know what they fight with, reach under my seat an' pull out the long knife that's there."

They dragged out and beheld for the first time the grim, bonehandled, triangular Afghan knife. It was almost as long as Lew.

"That's the thing to jint ye," said the trooper feebly. "It can take off a man's arm at the shoulder as easy as slicing butter. I halved the beggar that used that 'un, but there's more of his likes up above. They don't understand thrustin', but they're devils to slice."

The men strolled across the tracks to inspect the Afghan prisoners. They were unlike any "niggers" that the Fore and Aft had ever met— these huge, black-haired, scowling sons of the Beni-Israel. As the men stared the Afghans spat freely and muttered one to another with lowered eyes.

"My eyes! Wot awful swine!" said Jakin, who was in the rear of the procession. "Say, old man, how you got *puckrowed,* eh? *Kiswasti* you wasn't hanged for your ugly face, hey?"

The tallest of the company turned, his leg irons clanking at the movement, and stared at the boy. "See!" he cried to his fellows in Pushto. "They send children against us. What a people, and what fools!"

"*Hya!*" said Jakin, nodding his head cheerily. "You go down country. *Khana* get, *peenikapanee* get—live like a bloomin' rajah *ke marfik*. That's a better *bandobust* than baynit get it in your innards. Goodby, ole man. Take care o' your beautiful figure 'ed, an' try to look *kushy*."

The men laughed and fell in for their first march, when they began to realize that a soldier's life was not all beer and skittles. They were much impressed with the size and bestial ferocity of the niggers whom they had now learned to call "Paythans," and more with the exceeding discomfort of their own surroundings. Twenty old soldiers in the corps would have taught them how to make themselves moderately snug at night, but they had no old soldiers, and, as the troops on the line of march said, "they lived like pigs." They learned the heart-breaking cussedness of camp kitchens and camels, and the depravity of an E.P. tent and a wither-wrung mule. They studied animalculæ in water, and developed a few cases of dysentery in their study.

At the end of their third march they were disagreeably surprised by the arrival in their camp of a hammered iron slug, which, fired from a steady rest at seven hundred yards, flicked out the brains of a private seated by the fire. This robbed them of their peace for a night, and was the beginning of a long-range fire carefully calculated to that end. In the daytime they saw nothing except an unpleasant puff of smoke from a crag above the line of march. At night there were distant spurts of flame and occasional casualties, which set the whole camp blazing into the gloom and, occasionally, into opposite tents. Then they swore vehemently and vowed that this was magnificent, but not war.

Indeed it was not. The regiment could not halt for reprisals against the sharpshooters of the countryside. Its duty was to go forward and make connection with the Scotch and Gurkha troops with which it was brigaded. The Afghans knew this, and knew, too, after their first tentative shots, that they were dealing with a raw regiment. Thereafter they devoted themselves to the task of keeping the Fore and Aft on the strain. Not for anything would they have taken equal liberties with a seasoned corps—with the wicked little Gurkhas, whose delight it was to lie out in the open on a dark night and stalk their stalkers—with the terrible, big men dressed in women's clothes, who could be heard praying to their God in the night-watches, and whose peace of mind no amount of "sniping" could shake—or with those vile Sikhs, who marched so ostentatiously unprepared and who dealt out such grim reward to those who tried to profit by that unpreparedness. This white regiment was different—quite different. It slept like a hog, and, like a hog, charged in every direction when it was roused. Its sentries walked with a footfall that could be heard for a quarter of a mile; would fire at anything that moved—even a driven donkey—and, when they had once fired, could be scientifically "rushed" and laid out a horror and an offense against the morning sun. Then there were camp-followers who straggled and could be cut up without fear. Their shrieks would disturb the white boys, and the loss of their services would inconvenience them sorely.

Thus, at every march, the hidden enemy became bolder, and the regiment writhed and twisted under attacks it could not avenge. The crowning triumph was a sudden night-rush ending in the cutting of many tent-ropes, the collapse of the sodden canvas, and a glorious knifing of the men who struggled and kicked below. It was a great deed, neatly carried out, and it shook the already shaken nerves of the Fore and Aft. All the courage that they had been required to exercise up to this point was the "two o'clock in the morning courage"; and, so far, they had only succeeded in shooting their comrades and losing their sleep.

Sullen, discontented, cold, savage, sick, with their uniforms dulled and unclean, the Fore and Aft joined their brigade.

"I hear you had a tough time of it coming up," said the brigadier. But when he saw the hospital sheets his face fell.

"This is bad," said he to himself. "They're as rotten as sheep." And aloud to the colonel: "I'm afraid we can't spare you just yet. We want all we have, else I should have given you ten days to recover in."

The colonel winced. "On my honor, sir," he returned, "there is not the least necessity to think of sparing us. My men have been rather mauled and upset without a fair return. They only want to go in somewhere where they can see what's before them."

"Can't say I think much of the Fore and Fit," said the brigadier in confidence to his brigade major. "They've lost all their soldiering, and, by the trim of them, might have marched through the country from the other side. A more fagged-out set of men I never put eyes on."

"Oh, they'll improve as the work goes on. The parade gloss has been rubbed off a little, but they'll put on field polish before long," said the brigade major. "They've been mauled, and they don't quite understand it."

They did not. All the hitting was on one side, and it was cruelly hard hitting with accessories that made them sick. There was also the real sickness that laid hold of a strong man and dragged him howling to the grave. Worst of all, their officers knew just as little of the country as the men themselves, and looked as if they did. The Fore and Aft were in a thoroughly unsatisfactory condition, but they believed that all would be well if they could once get a fair go-in at the enemy. Pot shots up and down the valleys were unsatisfactory, and the bayonet never seemed to get a chance. Perhaps it was as well, for a long-limbed Afghan with a knife had a reach of eight feet and could carry away lead that would disable three Englishmen.

The Fore and Aft would like some rifle-practise at the enemy—all seven hundred rifles blazing together. That wish showed the mood of the men.

The Gurkhas walked into their camp, and in broken, barrack-room English strove to fraternize with them; offered them pipes of tobacco and stood them treat at the canteen. But the Fore and Aft, not knowing much of the nature of the Gurkhas, treated them as they would treat any other "niggers," and the little men in green trotted back to their firm friends the Highlanders, and with many grins confided to them: "That dam white regiment no dam use. Sulky—ugh! Dirty—ugh! Hya, any tot for Johnny?" Whereat the Highlanders smote the Gurkhas as to the head, and told them not to vilify a British regiment, and the Gurkhas grinned cavernously, for the Highlanders were their elder brothers and entitled to the privileges of kinship. The common soldier who touches a Gurkha is more than likely to have his head sliced open.

Three days later the brigadier arranged a battle according to the rules of war and the peculiarity of the Afghan temperament. The enemy was massing in inconvenient strength among the hills, and the moving of many green standards warned him that the tribes were "up" in aid of the Afghan regular troops. A squadron and a half of Bengal Lancers represented the available cavalry, and the two screw guns, borrowed from a column thirty miles away, the artillery at the general's disposal.

"If they stand, as I've a very strong notion that they will, I fancy we shall see an infantry fight that will be worth watching," said the brigadier. "We'll do it in style. Each regiment shall be played into action by its band, and we'll hold the cavalry in reserve."

"For *all* the reserve?" somebody asked.

"For all the reserve; because we're going to crumple them up," said the brigadier, who was an extraordinary brigadier, and did not believe in the value of a reserve when dealing with Asiatics. Indeed, when you come to think of it, had the British army consistently waited for reserves in all its little affairs, the boundaries of our empire would have stopped at Brighton beach.

That battle was to be a glorious battle.

The three regiments debouching from three separate gorges, after duly crowning the heights above, were to converge from the center, left, and right upon what we will call the Afghan army, then stationed toward the lower extremity of a flat-bottomed valley. Thus it will be seen that three sides of the valley practically belonged to the English, while the fourth was strictly Afghan property. In the event of defeat the Afghans had the rocky hills to fly to, where the fire from the guerrilla tribes in aid would cover their retreat. In the event of victory these same tribes would rush down and lend their weight to the rout of the British.

The screw guns were to shell the head of each Afghan rush that was made in close formation, and the cavalry, held in reserve in the right

valley, were to stimulate gently the break-up which would follow on
the combined attack. The brigadier, sitting upon a rock overlooking
the valley, would watch the battle unrolled at his feet. The Fore and
Aft would debouch from the central gorge, the Gurkhas from the left,
and the Highlanders from the right, for the reason that the left flank
of the enemy seemed as though it required the most hammering. It was
not every day that an Afghan force would take ground in the open, and
the brigadier was resolved to make the most of it.

"If we only had a few more men," he said plaintively, "we could sur-
round the creatures and crumple 'em up thoroughly. As it is, I'm afraid
we can only cut them up as they run. It's a great pity."

The Fore and Aft had enjoyed unbroken peace for five days, and were
beginning, in spite of dysentery, to recover their nerve. But they were
not happy, for they did not know the work in hand, and had they
known, would not have known how to do it. Throughout those five
days in which old soldiers might have taught them the craft of the
game, they discussed together their misadventures in the past—how
such an one was alive at dawn and dead ere the dusk, and with what
shrieks and struggles such another had given up his soul under the
Afghan knife. Death was a new and horrible thing to the sons of me-
chanics who were used to die decently of zymotic disease; and their
careful conservation in barracks had done nothing to make them look
upon it with less dread.

Very early in the dawn the bugles began to blow, and the Fore and
Aft, filled with a misguided enthusiasm, turned out without waiting
for a cup of coffee and a biscuit; and were rewarded by being kept
under arms in the cold while the other regiments leisurely prepared for
the fray. All the world knows that it is ill taking the breeks off a Highlander. It is much iller to try to make him stir unless he is convinced of
the necessity for haste.

The Fore and Aft waited, leaning upon their rifles and listening to
the protests of their empty stomachs. The colonel did his best to remedy
the default of lining as soon as it was borne in upon him that the affair
would not begin at once, and so well did he succeed that the coffee was
just ready when—the men moved off, their band leading. Even then
there had been a mistake in time, and the Fore and Aft came out into
the valley ten minutes before the proper hour. Their band wheeled to
the right after reaching the open, and retired behind a little rocky knoll,
still playing while the regiment went past.

It was not a pleasant sight that opened on the uninstructed view, for
the lower end of the valley appeared to be filled by an army in position
—real and actual regiments attired in red coats, and—of this there was
no doubt—firing Martini-Henri bullets which cut up the ground a hun-

dred yards in front of the leading company. Over that pock-marked ground the regiment had to pass, and it opened the ball with a general and profound courtesy to the piping pickets—ducking in perfect time, as though it had been brazed on a rod. Being half-capable of thinking for itself, it fired a volley by the simple process of pitching its rifle into its shoulder and pulling the trigger. The bullets may have accounted for some of the watchers on the hillside, but they certainly did not affect the mass of enemy in front, while the noise of the rifles drowned any orders that might have been given.

"Good God!" said the brigadier, sitting on the rock high above all. "That regiment has spoilt the whole show. Hurry up the others, and let the screw guns get off."

But the screw guns in working round the heights had stumbled upon a wasp's nest of a small mud fort, which they incontinently shelled at eight hundred yards, to the huge discomfort of the occupants, who were unaccustomed to weapons of such devilish precision.

The Fore and Aft continued to go forward, but with shortened stride. Where were the other regiments, and why did these niggers use Martinis? They took open order instinctively, lying down and firing at random, rushing a few paces forward and lying down again, according to the regulations. Once in this formation, each man felt himself desperately alone, and edged in toward his fellow for comfort's sake.

Then the crack of his neighbor's rifle at his ear led him to fire as rapidly as he could—again for the sake of the comfort of the noise. The reward was not long delayed. Five volleys plunged the files in banked smoke impenetrable to the eye, and the bullets began to take ground twenty or thirty yards in front of the firers, as the weight of the bayonet dragged down and to the right arms wearied with holding the kick of the leaping Martini. The company commanders peered helplessly through the smoke, the more nervous mechanically trying to fan it away with their helmets.

"High and to the left!" bawled a captain till he was hoarse. "No good! Cease firing, and let it drift away a bit."

Three and four times the bugles shrieked the order, and when it was obeyed the Fore and Aft looked that their foe should be lying before them in mown swaths of men. A light wind drove the smoke to leeward, and showed the enemy still in position and apparently unaffected. A quarter of a ton of lead had been buried a furlong in front of them, as the ragged earth attested.

That was not demoralizing to the Afghans, who have not European nerves. They were waiting for the mad riot to die down, and were firing quietly into the heart of the smoke. A private of the Fore and Aft spun up his company shrieking with agony, another was kicking the earth and gasping, and a third, ripped through the lower intestines by a jagged bullet, was calling aloud on his comrades to put him out of his pain. These were the casualties, and they were not soothing to hear or see. The smoke cleared to a dull haze.

Then the foe began to shout with a great shouting, and a mass—a black mass—detached itself from the main body, and rolled over the ground at horrid speed. It was composed of, perhaps, three hundred men, who would shout and fire and slash if the rush of their fifty comrades who were determined to die carried home. The fifty were Ghazis, half-maddened with drugs and wholly mad with religious fanaticism. When they rushed the British fire ceased, and in the lull the order was given to close ranks and meet them with the bayonet.

Any one who knew the business could have told the Fore and Aft that the only way of dealing with a Ghazi rush is by volleys at long ranges; because a man who means to die, who desires to die, who will gain heaven by dying, must, in nine cases out of ten, kill a man who has a lingering prejudice in favor of life. Where they should have closed and gone forward, the Fore and Aft opened out and skirmished; and where they should have opened out and fired, they closed and waited.

A man dragged from his blankets half-awake and unfed is never in a pleasant frame of mind. Nor does his happiness increase when he watches the whites of the eyes of three hundred six-foot fiends upon whose beards the foam is lying, upon whose tongues is a roar of wrath, and in whose hands are yard-long knives.

The Fore and Aft heard the Gurkha bugles bringing that regiment forward at the double, while the neighing of the Highland pipes came from the left. They strove to stay where they were, though the bayonets wavered down the line like the oars of a ragged boat. Then they felt body to body the amazing physical strength of their foes; a shriek of pain ended the rush, and the knives fell amid scenes not to be told. The men clubbed together and smote blindly—as often as not at their own fellows. Their front crumpled like paper, and the fifty Ghazis passed on —their backers, now drunk with success, fighting as madly as they.

Then the rear ranks were bidden to close up, and the subalterns dashed into the stew—alone. For the rear ranks had heard the clamor in front, the yells and the howls of pain, and had seen the dark stale blood that makes afraid. They were not going to stay. It was the rushing of the camps over again. Let their officers go to hell, if they chose; they would get away from the knives.

"Come on!" shrieked the subalterns, and their men, cursing them, drew back, each closing into his neighbor and wheeling round.

Charteris and Devlin, subalterns of the last company, faced their death alone in the belief that their men would follow.

"You've killed me, you cowards," sobbed Devlin, and dropped, cut from the shoulder-strap to the center of the chest, and a fresh detachment of his men retreating, always retreating, trampled him under foot as they made for the pass whence they had emerged.

> *I kissed her in the kitchen and I kissed her in the hall,*
>   *Child'un, child'un, follow me!*
> "Oh, Golly," said the cook, "is he gwine to kiss us all?
>   *Halla—Halla—Halla—Halleluiah!"*

The Gurkhas were pouring through the left gorge and over the heights at the double to the invitation of their regimental quickstep. The black rocks were crowned with dark-green spiders as the bugles gave tongue jubilantly:

> *In the morning! In the morning by the bright light!*
> *When Gabriel blows his trumpet in the morning!*

The Gurkha rear companies tripped and blundered over loose stones. The front files halted for a moment to take stock of the valley and to settle stray boot-laces. Then a happy little sigh of contentment soughed down the ranks, and it was as though the land smiled, for behold there below was the enemy, and it was to meet them that the Gurkhas had doubled so hastily. There was much enemy. There would be amusement. The little men hitched their *kukris* well to hand, and gaped expectantly at their officers as terriers grin ere the stone is cast for them to fetch. The Gurkhas' ground sloped downward to the valley, and they enjoyed a fair view of the proceedings. They sat upon the boulders to watch, for their officers were not going to waste their wind in assisting to repulse a Ghazi rush more than half a mile away. Let the white men look to their own front.

"Hi yi!" said the subahdar major, who was sweating profusely. "Dam fools yonder, stand close order! This is no time for close order; it is the time for volleys. Ugh!"

Horrified, amused, and indignant, the Gurkhas beheld the retirement of the Fore and Aft with a running chorus of oaths and commentaries.

"They run! The white men run! Colonel Sahib, may *we* also do a little running?" murmured Runbir Thappa, the senior jemidar.

But the colonel would have none of it. "Let the beggars be cut up a little," said he wrathfully. "Serves 'em right. They'll be prodded into facing round in a minute." He looked through his field-glasses, and caught the glint of an officer's sword.

"Beating 'em with the flat—damned conscripts! How the Ghazis are walking into them!" said he.

The Fore and Aft, heading back, bore with them their officers. The narrowness of the pass forced the mob into solid formation, and the rear ranks delivered some sort of a wavering volley. The Ghazis drew off, for they did not know what reserve the gorge might hide. Moreover, it was never wise to chase white men too far. They returned as wolves return to cover, satisfied with the slaughter that they had done, and only stopping to slash at the wounded on the ground. A quarter of a mile had the Fore and Aft retreated, and now, jammed in the pass, was quivering with pain, shaken and demoralized with fear, while the officers, maddened beyond control, smote the men with the hilts and the flats of their swords.

"Get back! Get back, you cowards—you women! Right about face— column of companies, form—you hounds!" shouted the colonel, and the subalterns swore aloud. But the regiment wanted to go—to go anywhere out of the range of those merciless knives. It swayed to and fro irresolutely with shouts and outcries, while from the right the Gurkhas dropped volley after volley of cripple-stopper Snider bullets at long range into the mob of the Ghazis returning to their own troops.

The Fore and Aft band, though protected from direct fire by the rocky knoll under which it had sat down, fled at the first rush. Jakin and Lew would have fled also, but their short legs left them fifty yards in the rear, and by the time the band had mixed with the regiment they were painfully aware that they would have to close in alone and unsupported.

"Get back to that rock," gasped Jakin. "They won't see us there."

And they returned to the scattered instruments of the band, their hearts nearly bursting their ribs.

"Here's a nice show for *us*," said Jakin, throwing himself full length on the ground. "A bloomin' fine show for British infantry! Oh, the devils! They've gone an' left us alone here! Wot'll we do?"

Lew took possession of a cast-off water-bottle, which naturally was full of canteen rum, and drank till he coughed again.

"Drink," said he, shortly. "They'll come back in a minute or two— you see."

Jakin drank, but there was no sign of the regiment's return. They could hear a dull clamor from the head of the valley of retreat, and saw the Ghazis slink back, quickening their pace as the Gurkhas fired at them.

"We're all that's left of the band, an' we'll be cut up as sure as death," said Jakin.

"I'll die game then," said Lew thickly, fumbling with his tiny drummer's sword. The drink was working on his brain as it was on Jakin's.

" 'Old on! I know something better than fightin'," said Jakin, stung by the splendor of a sudden thought due chiefly to rum. "Tip our bloomin' cowards yonder the word to come back. The Paythan beggars are well away. Come on, Lew! We won't get hurt. Take the fife an' give me the drum. The old step for all your bloomin' guts are worth! There's a few of our men coming back now. Stand up, ye drunken little defaulter. By your right—quick march!"

He slipped the drum-sling over his shoulder, thrust the fife into Lew's hand, and the two boys marched out of the cover of the rock into the open, making a hideous hash of the first bars of the "British Grenadiers."

As Lew had said, a few of the Fore and Aft were coming back sullenly and shamefacedly under the stimulus of blows and abuse; their red coats shone at the head of the valley, and behind them were wavering bayonets. But between this shattered line and the enemy, who with Afghan suspicion feared that the hasty retreat meant an ambush, and had not moved therefore, lay half a mile of level ground dotted only by the wounded.

The tune settled into full swing, and the boys kept shoulder to shoulder, Jakin banging the drum as one possessed. The one fife made a thin and pitiful squeaking, but the tune carried far, even to the Gurkhas.

"Come on, you dogs!" muttered Jakin to himself. "Are we to play forhever?" Lew was staring straight in front of him and marching more stiffly than ever he had done on parade.

And in bitter mockery of the distant mob, the old tune of the old line shrilled and rattled—

> *Some talk of Alexander,*
> *And some of Hercules;*
> *Of Hector and Lysander,*
> *And such great names as these!*

There was a far-off clapping of hands from the Gurkhas, and a roar from the Highlanders in the distance, but never a shot was fired by British or Afghan. The two little red dots moved forward in the open, parallel to the enemy's front.

> *But of all the world's great heroes*
> *There's none that can compare,*
> *With a tow-row-row-row-row-row,*
> *To the British Grenadier.*

The men of the Fore and Aft were gathering thick at the entrance into the plain. The brigadier on the heights far above was speechless with rage. Still no movement from the enemy. The day stayed to watch the children.

Jakin halted and beat the long roll of the assembly, while the fife squealed despairingly.

"Right about face! Hold up, Lew, you're drunk," said Jakin. They wheeled and marched back—

> *Those heroes of antiquity*
> *Ne'er saw a cannon-ball,*
> *Nor knew the force o' powder,*

"Here they come!" said Jakin. "Go on, Lew"—

> *To scare their foes withal!*

The Fore and Aft were pouring out of the valley. What officers had said to men in that time of shame and humiliation will never be known; for neither officers nor men speak of it now.

"They are coming anew!" shouted a priest among the Afghans. "Do not kill the boys! Take them alive, and they shall be of our faith."

But the first volley had been fired, and Lew dropped on his face. Jakin stood for a minute, spun round, and collapsed, as the Fore and Aft came forward, the curses of their officers in their ears, and in their hearts the shame of open shame.

Half the men had seen the drummers die, and they made no sign. They did not even shout. They doubled out straight across the plain in open order, and they did not fire.

"This," said the colonel of the Gurkhas softly, "is the real attack, as it should have been delivered. Come on, my children."

"Ulu-lu-lu-lu!" squealed the Gurkhas, and came down with a joyful clicking of *kukris*—those vicious Gurkha knives.

On the right there was no rush. The Highlanders, cannily commending their souls to God (for it matters as much to a dead man whether he has been shot in a Border scuffle or at Waterloo), opened out and fired according to their custom—that is to say, without heat and without intervals—while the screw guns, having disposed of the impertinent mud fort afore-mentioned, dropped shell after shell into the clusters round the flickering green standards on the heights.

"Charrging is an unfortunate necessity," murmured the color-sergeant of the right company of the Highlanders. "It makes the men sweer so, but I am thinkin' that it will come to a charrge if these black devils stand much longer. Stewartt, man, you're firing into the eye of the sun, and he'll not take any harm for government ammuneetion. A foot lower and a great deal slower! What are the English doing? They're very quiet there in the center. Running again?"

The English were not running. They were hacking and hewing and stabbing, for though one white man is seldom physically a match for

an Afghan in a sheepskin or wadded coat, yet, through the pressure of
many white men behind, and a certain thirst for revenge in his heart,
he becomes capable of doing much with both ends of his rifle. The Fore
and Aft held their fire till one bullet could drive through five or six
men, and the front of the Afghan force gave on the volley. They then
selected their men, and slew them with deep gasps and short, hacking
coughs, and groanings of leather belts against strained bodies, and realized for the first time that an Afghan attacked is far less formidable
than an Afghan attacking; which fact old soldiers might have told
them.

But they had no old soldiers in their ranks.

The Gurkhas' stall at the bazaar was the noisiest, for the men were
engaged—to a nasty noise as of beef being cut on the block—with the
kukri, which they preferred to the bayonet, well knowing how the
Afghan hates the half-moon blade.

As the Afghans wavered, the green standards on the mountain moved
down to assist them in a last rally. This was unwise. The Lancers chafing in the right gorge had thrice despatched their only subaltern as
galloper to report on the progress of affairs. On the third occasion he
returned, with a bullet graze on his knee, swearing strange oaths in
Hindustani, and saying that all things were ready. So that squadron
swung round the right of the Highlanders with a wicked whistling of
wind in the pennons of its lances, and fell upon the remnant just when,
according to all the rules of war, it should have waited for the foe to
show more signs of wavering.

But it was a dainty charge, deftly delivered, and it ended by the cavalry finding itself at the head of the pass by which the Afghans intended
to retreat; and down the track that the lances had made streamed two
companies of the Highlanders, which was never intended by the brigadier. The new development was successful. It detached the enemy
from his base as a sponge is torn from a rock, and left him ringed about
with fire in that pitiless plain. And as a sponge is chased round the bath-
tub by the hand of the bather, so were the Afghans chased till they
broke into little detachments much more difficult to dispose of than
large masses.

"See!" quoth the brigadier. "Everything has come as I arranged.
We've cut their base, and now we'll bucket 'em to pieces."

A direct hammering was all that the brigadier had dared to hope for,
considering the size of the force at his disposal; but men who stand or
fall by the errors of their opponents may be forgiven for turning chance
into design. The bucketing went forward merrily. The Afghan forces
were upon the run—the run of wearied wolves who snarl and bite over
their shoulders. The red lances dipped by twos and threes, and, with a

shriek, uprose the lance butt, like a spar on a stormy sea, as the trooper, cantering forward, cleared his point. The Lancers kept between their prey and the steep hills, for all who could were trying to escape from the valley of death. The Highlanders gave the fugitives two hundred yards' law, and then brought them down, gasping and choking ere they could reach the protection of the boulders above. The Gurkhas followed suit; but the Fore and Aft were killing on their own account, for they had penned a mass of men between their bayonets and a wall of rock, and the flash of the rifles was lighting the wadded coats.

"We cannot hold them, Captain Sahib!" panted a Ressaidar of Lancers. "Let us try the carbine. The lance is good, but it wastes time."

They tried the carbine, and still the enemy melted away—fled up the hills by hundreds when there were only twenty bullets to stop them. On the heights the screw guns ceased firing—they had run out of ammunition—and the brigadier groaned, for the musketry fire could not sufficiently smash the retreat. Long before the last volleys were fired, the doolies were out in force looking for the wounded. The battle was over, and, but for want of fresh troops, the Afghans would have been wiped off the earth. As it was, they counted their dead by hundreds, and nowhere were the dead thicker than in the track of the Fore and Aft.

But the regiment did not cheer with the Highlanders, nor did they dance uncouth dances with the Gurkhas among the dead. They looked under their brows at the colonel, as they leaned upon their rifles and panted.

"Get back to camp, you! Haven't you disgraced yourself enough for one day! Go and look to the wounded. It's all you're fit for," said the colonel. Yet for the past hour the Fore and Aft had been doing all that mortal commander could expect. They had lost heavily because they did not know how to set about their business with proper skill, but they had borne themselves gallantly, and this was their reward.

A young and sprightly color-sergeant, who had begun to imagine himself a hero, offered his water-bottle to a Highlander, whose tongue was black with thirst. "I drink with no cowards," answered the youngster, huskily, and, turning to a Gurkha, said: "Hya, Johnny! Drink water got it?" The Gurkha grinned and passed his bottle. The Fore and Aft said no word.

They went back to camp when the field of strife had been a little mopped up and made presentable, and the brigadier, who saw himself a knight in three months, was the only soul who was complimentary to them. The colonel was heart-broken, and the officers were savage and sullen.

"Well," said the brigadier, "they are young troops, of course, and it was not unnatural that they should retire in disorder for a bit."

"Oh, my only Aunt Maria!" murmured a junior staff officer. "Retire in disorder! It was a bally run!"

"But they came again, as we all know," cooed the brigadier, the colonel's ashy-white face before him, "and they behaved as well as could possibly be expected. Behaved beautifully, indeed. I was watching them. It is not a matter to take to heart, colonel. As some German general said of his men, they wanted to be shooted over a little, that was all." To himself he said: "Now they're blooded I can give 'em responsible work. It's as well that they got what they did. Teach 'em more than half a dozen rifle flirtations, that will—later—run alone and bite. Poor old colonel, though."

All that afternoon the heliograph winked and flickered on the hills, striving to tell the good news to a mountain forty miles away. And in the evening there arrived, dusty, sweating, and sore, a misguided correspondent who had gone out to assist at a trumpery village burning, and who had read off the message from afar, cursing his luck the while.

"Let's have the details somehow—as full as ever you can, please. It's the first time I've ever been left this campaign," said the correspondent to the brigadier, and the brigadier, nothing loath, told him how an army of communication had been crumpled up, destroyed, and all but annihilated by the craft, strategy, wisdom, and foresight of the brigadier.

But some say, and among these be the Gurkhas who watched on the hillside, that that battle was won by Jakin and Lew, whose little bodies were borne up just in time to fit two gaps at the head of the big ditch-grave for the dead under the heights of Jagai.

39

The Man Who Would Be King

BY RUDYARD KIPLING

"Brother to a Prince and fellow to a beggar if he be found worthy."

THE LAW, as quoted, lays down a fair conduct of life, and one not easy to follow. I have been fellow to a beggar again and again under circumstances which prevented either of us finding out whether the other was worthy. I have still to be brother to a Prince, though I once came near to kinship with what might have been a veritable King and was promised the reversion of a Kingdom— army, law-courts, revenue and policy all complete. But, to-day, I greatly fear that my King is dead, and if I want a crown I must go and hunt it for myself.

The beginning of everything was in a railway train upon the road to Mhow from Ajmir. There had been a Deficit in the Budget, which necessitated traveling, not Second-class, which is only half as dear as First-class, but by Intermediate, which is very awful indeed. There are no cushions in the Intermediate class, and the population are either Intermediate, which is Eurasian, or native, which for a long night journey is nasty, or Loafer, which is amusing though intoxicated. Intermediates do not patronize refreshment-rooms. They carry their food in bundles and pots, and buy sweets from the native sweet-meat-sellers, and drink the roadside water. That is why in the hot weather Intermediates are taken out of the carriages dead, and in all weathers are most properly looked down upon.

My particular Intermediate happened to be empty till I reached Nasirabad, when a huge gentleman in shirt-sleeves entered, and, following the custom of Intermediates, passed the time of day. He was a wanderer and a vagabond like myself, but with an educated taste for whiskey. He told tales of things he had seen and done, of out-of-the-way corners of the Empire into which he had penetrated, and of adventures in which he risked his life for a few days' food. "If India was filled with men like you and me, not knowing more than the crows where they'd get their next day's rations, it isn't seventy millions of revenue the land would be paying—it's seven hundred millions," said he; and as I looked at his mouth and chin I was disposed to agree with him. We talked politics—the politics of Loaferdom that sees things from the underside where the lath and plaster is not smoothed off—and we talked postal arrangements because my friend wanted to send a telegram back from the next station to Ajmir, which is the turning-off place from the Bombay to the Mhow line as you travel westward. My friend had no money beyond eight annas which he wanted for dinner, and I had no money at all, owing to the hitch in the Budget before mentioned. Further, I was going into a wilderness where, though I should resume touch with the Treasury, there were no telegraph offices. I was, therefore, unable to help him in any way.

"We might threaten a Station-master, and make him send a wire on tick," said my friend, "but that'd mean inquiries for you and for me, and I've got my hands full these days. Did you say you are traveling back along this line within any days?"

"Within ten," I said.

"Can't you make it eight?" said he. "Mine is rather urgent business."

"I can send your telegram within ten days if that will serve you," I said.

"I couldn't trust the wire to fetch him now I think of it. It's this way. He leaves Delhi on the 23d for Bombay. That means he'll be running through Ajmir about the night of the 23d."

"But I am going into the Indian Desert," I explained.

"Well and good," said he. "You'll be changing at Marwar Junction to get into Jodhpore territory—you must do that—and he'll be coming through Marwar Junction in the early morning of the 24th by the Bombay Mail. Can you be at Marwar Junction on that time? 'Twon't be inconveniencing you because I know that there's precious few pickings to be got out of these Central India States—even though you pretend to be correspondent of the *Backwoodsman*."

"Have you ever tried that trick?" I asked.

"Again and again, but the Residents find you out, and then you get escorted to the Border before you've time to get your knife into them. But about my friend here. I *must* give him a word o'mouth to tell him what's come to me or else he won't know where to go. I would take it more than kind of you if you was to come out of Central India in time to catch him at Marwar Junction, and say to him:—'He has gone South

for the week.' He'll know what that means. He's a big man with a red
beard, and a great swell he is. You'll find him sleeping like a gentleman
with all his luggage round him in a Second-class compartment. But
don't you be afraid. Slip down the window, and say:—'He has gone
South for the week,' and he'll tumble. It's only cutting your time of stay
in those parts by two days. I ask you as a stranger—going to the West,"
he said, with emphasis.

"Where have *you* come from?" said I.

"From the East," said he, "and I am hoping that you will give him the
message on the Square—for the sake of my Mother as well as your
own."

Englishmen are not usually softened by appeals to the memory of
their mothers, but for certain reasons, which will be fully apparent, I
saw fit to agree.

"It's more than a little matter," said he, "and that's why I ask you to
do it—and now I know that I can depend on you doing it. A Second-
class carriage at Marwar Junction, and a red-haired man asleep in it.
You'll be sure to remember. I get out at the next station, and I must
hold on there till he comes or sends me what I want."

"I'll give the message if I catch him," I said, "and for the sake of your
Mother as well as mine I'll give you a word of advice. Don't try to run
the Central India States just now as the correspondent of the *Backwoodsman*. There's a real one knocking about here, and it might lead
to trouble."

"Thank you," said he, simply, "and when will the swine be gone? I
can't starve because he's ruining my work. I wanted to get hold of the
Degumber Rajah down here about his father's widow, and give him a
jump."

"What did he do to his father's widow, then?"

"Filled her up with red pepper and slippered her to death as she hung
from a beam. I found that out myself and I'm the only man that would
dare going into the State to get hush-money for it. They'll try to poison
me, same as they did in Chortumna when I went on the loot there. But
you'll give the man at Marwar Junction my message?"

He got out at a little roadside station, and I reflected. I had heard,
more than once, of men personating correspondents of newspapers and
bleeding small Native States with threats of exposure, but I had never
met any of the caste before. They lead a hard life, and generally die
with great suddenness. The Native States have a wholesome horror of
English newspapers, which may throw light on their peculiar methods
of government, and do their best to choke correspondence with champagne, or drive them out of their mind with four-in-hand barouches.
They do not understand that nobody cares a straw for the internal ad-

ministration of Native States so long as oppression and crime are kept within decent limits, and the ruler is not drugged, drunk, or diseased from one end of the year to the other. Native States were created by Providence in order to supply picturesque scenery, tigers, and tall-writing. They are the dark places of the earth, full of unimaginable cruelty, touching the Railway and the Telegraph on one side, and, on the other, the days of Harun-al-Raschid. When I left the train I did business with divers Kings, and in eight days passed through many changes of life. Sometimes I wore dress-clothes and consorted with Princes and Politicals, drinking from crystal and eating from silver. Sometimes I lay out upon the ground and devoured what I could get, from a plate made of a flapjack, and drank the running water, and slept under the same rug as my servant. It was all in the day's work.

Then I headed for the Great Indian Desert upon the proper date, as I had promised, and the Night Mail set me down at Marwar Junction, where a funny little, happy-go-lucky, native-managed railway runs to Jodhpore. The Bombay Mail from Delhi makes a short halt at Marwar. She arrived as I got in, and I had just time to hurry to her platform and go down the carriages. There was only one Second-class on the train. I slipped the window and looked down upon a flaming red beard, half covered by a railway rug. That was my man, fast asleep, and I dug him gently in the ribs. He woke with a grunt and I saw his face in the light of the lamps. It was a great and shining face.

"Tickets again?" said he.

"No," said I. "I am to tell you that he is gone South for the week. He is gone South for the week!"

The train had begun to move out. The red man rubbed his eyes. "He has gone South for the week," he repeated. "Now that's just like his impidence. Did he say that I was to give you anything?—'Cause I won't."

"He didn't," I said, and dropped away, and watched the red lights die out in the dark. It was horribly cold because the wind was blowing off the sands. I climbed into my own train—not an Intermediate Carriage this time—and went to sleep.

If the man with the beard had given me a rupee I should have kept it as a memento of a rather curious affair. But the consciousness of having done my duty was my only reward.

Later on I reflected that two gentlemen like my friends could not do any good if they foregathered and personated correspondents of newspapers, and might, if they "stuck up" one of the little rat-trap states of Central India or Southern Rajputana, get themselves into serious difficulties. I therefore took some trouble to describe them as accurately as I could remember to people who would be interested in deporting them:

and succeeded, so I was later informed, in having them headed back from the Degumber border.

Then I became respectable, and returned to an Office where there were no Kings and no incidents except the daily manufacture of a newspaper. A newspaper office seems to attract every conceivable sort of person, to the prejudice of discipline. Zenana-mission ladies arrive, and beg that the Editor will instantly abandon all his duties to describe a Christian prize-giving in a back-slum of a perfectly inaccessible village; Colonels who have been over-passed for commands sit down and sketch the outline of a series of ten, twelve, or twenty-four leading articles on Seniority *versus* Selection; missionaries wish to know why they have not been permitted to escape from their regular vehicles of abuse and swear at a brother-missionary under special patronage of the editorial We; stranded theatrical companies troop up to explain that they cannot pay for their advertisements, but on their return from New Zealand or Tahiti will do so with interest; inventors of patent punkah-pulling machines, carriage couplings and unbreakable swords and axle-trees call with specifications in their pockets and hours at their disposal; tea-companies enter and elaborate their prospectuses with the office pens; secretaries of ball-committees clamor to have the glories of their last dance more fully expounded; strange ladies rustle in and say:—"I want a hundred lady's cards printed *at once*, please," which is manifestly part of an Editor's duty; and every dissolute ruffian that ever tramped the Grand Trunk Road makes it his business to ask for employment as a proof-reader. And, all the time, the telephone-bell is ringing madly, and Kings are being killed on the Continent, and Empires are saying—"You're another," and Mister Gladstone is calling down brimstone upon the British Dominions, and the little black copy-boys are whining, *"kaa-pi chay-ha-yeh"* (copy wanted) like tired bees, and most of the paper is as blank as Modred's shield.

But that is the amusing part of the year. There are other six months wherein none ever come to call, and the thermometer walks inch by inch up to the top of the glass, and the office is darkened to just above reading-light, and the press machines are red-hot of touch, and nobody writes anything but accounts of amusements in the Hill-stations or obituary notices. Then the telephone becomes a tinkling terror, because it tells you of the sudden deaths of men and women that you knew intimately, and the prickly-heat covers you as with a garment, and you sit down and write:—"A slight increase of sickness is reported from the Khuda Janta Khan District. The outbreak is purely sporadic in its nature, and, thanks to the energetic efforts of the District authorities, is now almost at an end. It is, however, with deep regret we record the death, etc."

Then the sickness really breaks out, and the less recording and report-
ing the better for the peace of the subscribers. But the Empires and the
Kings continue to divert themselves as selfishly as before, and the Fore-
man thinks that a daily paper really ought to come out once in twenty-
four hours, and all the people at the Hill-stations in the middle of their
amusements say:—"Good gracious! Why can't the paper be sparkling?
I'm sure there's plenty going on up here."

That is the dark half of the moon, and, as the advertisements say,
"must be experienced to be appreciated."

It was in that season, and a remarkably evil season, that the paper began running the last issue of the week on Saturday night, which is to
say Sunday morning, after the custom of a London paper. This was a
great convenience, for immediately after the paper was put to bed, the
dawn would lower the thermometer from 96° to almost 84° for half an
hour, and in that chill—you have no idea how cold is 84° on the grass
until you begin to pray for it—a very tired man could set off to sleep ere
the heat roused him.

One Saturday night it was my pleasant duty to put the paper to bed
alone. A King or courtier or a courtesan or a community was going to
die or get a new Constitution, or do something that was important on
the other side of the world, and the paper was to be held open till the
latest possible minute in order to catch the telegram. It was a pitchy
black night, as stifling as a June night can be, and the *loo,* the red-hot
wind from the westward, was booming among the tinder-dry trees and
pretending that the rain was on its heels. Now and again a spot of almost boiling water would fall on the dust with the flop of a frog, but all
our weary world knew that was only pretence. It was a shade cooler
in the press-room than the office, so I sat there, while the type ticked and
clicked, and the night-jars hooted at the windows, and the all but naked
compositors wiped the sweat from their foreheads and called for water.
The thing that was keeping us back, whatever it was, would not come
off, though the *loo* dropped and the last type was set, and the whole
round earth stood still in the choking heat, with its finger on its lip,
to wait the event. I drowsed, and wondered whether the telegraph was a
blessing, and whether this dying man, or struggling people, was aware
of the inconvenience the delay was causing. There was no special reason
beyond the heat and worry to make tension, but, as the clock hands
crept up to three o'clock and the machines spun their fly-wheels two and
three times to see that all was in order, before I said the word that would
set them off, I could have shrieked aloud.

Then the roar and rattle of the wheels shivered the quiet into little
bits. I rose to go away, but two men in white clothes stood in front of

me. The first one said:—"It's him!" The second said:—"So it is!" And they both laughed almost as loudly as the machinery roared, and mopped their foreheads. "We see there was a light burning across the road and we were sleeping in that ditch there for coolness, and I said to my friend here, The office is open. Let's come along and speak to him as turned us back from the Degumber State," said the smaller of the two. He was the man I had met in the Mhow train, and his fellow was the red-bearded man of Marwar Junction. There was no mistaking the eyebrows of the one or the beard of the other.

I was not pleased, because I wished to go to sleep, not to squabble with loafers. "What do you want?" I asked.

"Half an hour's talk with you cool and comfortable, in the office," said the red-bearded man. "We'd *like* some drink—the Contrack doesn't begin yet, Peachey, so you needn't look—but what we really want is advice. We don't want money. We ask you as a favor, because you did us a bad turn about Degumber."

I led from the press-room to the stifling office with the maps on the walls, and the red-haired man rubbed his hands. "That's something like," said he. "This was the proper shop to come to. Now, Sir, let me introduce to you Brother Peachey Carnehan, that's him, and Brother Daniel Dravot, that is *me,* and the less said about our professions the better, for we have been most things in our time. Soldier, sailor, compositor, photographer, proof-reader, street-preacher, and correspondents of the *Backwoodsman* when we thought the paper wanted one. Carnehan is sober, and so am I. Look at us first and see that's sure. It will save you cutting into my talk. We'll take one of your cigars apiece, and you shall see us light."

I watched the test. The men were absolutely sober, so I gave them each a tepid peg.

"Well *and* good," said Carnehan of the eyebrows, wiping the froth from his moustache. "Let me talk now, Dan. We have been all over India, mostly on foot. We have been boiler-fitters, engine-drivers, petty contractors, and all that, and we have decided that India isn't big enough for such as us."

They certainly were too big for the office. Dravot's beard seemed to fill half the room and Carnehan's shoulders the other half, as they sat on the big table. Carnehan continued:—"The country isn't half worked out because they that governs it won't let you touch it. They spend all their blessed time in governing it, and you can't lift a spade, nor chip a rock, nor look for oil, nor anything like that without all the Government saying—'Leave it alone and let us govern.' Therefore, such as it is, we will let it alone, and go away to some other place where a man isn't crowded and can come to his own. We are not little men, and there is nothing that we are afraid of except Drink, and we have signed a Contrack on that. *Therefore,* we are going away to be Kings."

"Kings in our own right," muttered Dravot.

"Yes, of course," I said. "You've been tramping in the sun, and it's a very warm night, and hadn't you better sleep over the notion? Come to-morrow."

"Neither drunk nor sunstruck," said Dravot. "We have slept over the notion half a year, and require to see Books and Atlases, and we have decided that there is only one place now in the world that two strong men can Sar-a-*whack*. They call it Kafiristan. By my reckoning it's the top right-hand corner of Afghanistan, not more than three hundred miles from Peshawur. They have two and thirty heathen idols there, and we'll be the thirty-third. It's a mountainous country, and the women of those parts are very beautiful."

"But that is provided against in the Contrack," said Carnehan. "Neither Women nor Liqu-or, Daniel."

"And that's all we know, except that no one has gone there, and they fight, and in any place where they fight a man who knows how to drill men can always be a King. We shall go to those parts and say to any King we find—'D' you want to vanquish your foes?' and we will show him how to drill men; for that we know better than anything else. Then we will subvert that King and seize his Throne and establish a Dynasty."

"You'll be cut to pieces before you're fifty miles across the Border," I said. "You have to travel through Afghanistan to get to that country. It's one mass of mountains and peaks and glaciers, and no Englishman has been through it. The people are utter brutes, and even if you reached them you couldn't do anything."

"That's more like," said Carnehan. "If you could think us a little more mad we would be more pleased. We have come to you to know about this country, to read a book about it, and to be shown maps. We want you to tell us that we are fools and to show us your books." He turned to the bookcases.

"Are you at all in earnest?" I said.

"A little," said Dravot, sweetly. "As big a map as you have got, even if it's all blank where Kafiristan is, and any books you've got. We can read, though we aren't very educated."

I uncased the big thirty-two-miles-to-the-inch-map of India, and two smaller Frontier maps, hauled down volume INFKAN of the *Encyclopædia Britannica,* and the men consulted them.

"See here!" said Dravot, his thumb on the map. "Up to Jagdallak, Peachey and me know the road. We was there with Roberts's Army.

We'll have to turn off to the right at Jagdallak through Laghmann territory. Then we get among the hills—fourteen thousand feet—fifteen thousand—it will be cold work there, but it don't look very far on the map."

I handed him Wood on the *Sources of the Oxus.* Carnehan was deep in the *Encyclopædia.*

"They're a mixed lot," said Dravot, reflectively; "and it won't help us to know the names of their tribes. The more tribes the more they'll fight, and the better for us. From Jagdallak to Ashang. H'mm!"

"But all the information about the country is as sketchy and inaccurate as can be," I protested. "No one knows anything about it really. Here's the file of the *United Services' Institute.* Read what Bellew says."

"Blow Bellew!" said Carnehan. "Dan, they're an all-fired lot of heathens, but this book here says they think they're related to us English."

I smoked while the men pored over *Raverty, Wood,* the maps and the *Encyclopædia.*

"There is no use your waiting," said Dravot, politely. "It's about four o'clock now. We'll go before six o'clock if you want to sleep, and we won't steal any of the papers. Don't you sit up. We're two harmless lunatics, and if you come, to-morrow evening, down to the Serai we'll say good-bye to you."

"You *are* two fools," I answered. "You'll be turned back at the Frontier or cut up the minute you set foot in Afghanistan. Do you want any money or a recommendation down-country? I can help you to the chance of work next week."

"Next week we shall be hard at work ourselves, thank you," said Dravot. "It isn't so easy being a King as it looks. When we've got our Kingdom in going order we'll let you know, and you can come up and help us to govern it."

"Would two lunatics make a Contrack like that?" said Carnehan, with subdued pride, showing me a greasy half-sheet of note-paper on which was written the following. I copied it, then and there, as a curiosity:

This Contrack between me and you persuing witnesseth in the name of God—Amen and so forth.

(*One*)   *That me and you will settle this matter together: i.e., to be Kings of Kafiristan.*

(*Two*)   *That you and me will not, while this matter is being settled, look at any Liquor, nor any Woman, black, white or brown, so as to get mixed up with one or the other harmful.*

*(Three) That we conduct ourselves with dignity and discretion, and
    if one of us gets into trouble the other will stay by him.
Signed by you and me this day.*
            Peachey Taliaferro Carnehan.
            Daniel Dravot.
            Both Gentlemen at Large.

"There was no need for the last article," said Carnehan, blushing
modestly; "but it looks regular. Now you know the sort of men that
loafers are—we *are* loafers, Dan, until we get out of India—and *do* you
think that we would sign a Contrack like that unless we was in earnest?
We have kept away from the two things that make life worth having."

"You won't enjoy your lives much longer if you are going to try this
idiotic adventure. Don't set the office on fire," I said, "and go away before nine o'clock."

I left them still poring over the maps and making notes on the back
of the "Contrack." "Be sure to come down to the Serai to-morrow,"
were their parting words.

The Kumharsen Serai is the great four-square sink of humanity
where the strings of camels and horses from the North load and unload.
All the nationalities of Central Asia may be found there, and most of
the folk of India proper. Balkh and Bokhara there meet Bengal and
Bombay, and try to draw eye-teeth. You can buy ponies, turquoises,
Persian pussy-cats, saddle-bags, fat-tailed sheep and musk in the Kumharsen Serai, and get many strange things for nothing. In the afternoon
I went down there to see whether my friends intended to keep their
word or were lying about drunk.

A priest attired in fragments of ribbons and rags stalked up to me,
gravely twisting a child's paper whirligig. Behind him was his servant
bending under the load of a crate of mud toys. The two were loading
up two camels, and the inhabitants of the Serai watched them with
shrieks of laughter.

"The priest is mad," said a horse-dealer to me. "He is going up to
Kabul to sell toys to the Amir. He will either be raised to honor or have
his head cut off. He came in here this morning and has been behaving
madly ever since."

"The witless are under the protection of God," stammered a flat-
cheeked Usbeg in broken Hindi. "They foretell future events."

"Would they could have foretold that my caravan would have been
cut up by the Shinwaris almost within shadow of the Pass!" grunted the
Eusufzai agent of a Rajputana trading-house whose goods had been
feloniously diverted into the hands of other robbers just across the Border, and whose misfortunes were the laughing-stock of the bazar. "Ohé,
priest, whence come you and whither do you go?"

"From Roum have I come," shouted the priest, waving his whirligig; "from Roum, blown by the breath of a hundred devils across the sea! O thieves, robbers, liars, the blessing of Pir Khan on pigs, dogs, and perjurers! Who will take the Protected of God to the North to sell charms that are never still to the Amir? The camels shall not gall, the sons shall not fall sick, and the wives shall remain faithful while they are away, of the men who give me place in their caravan. Who will assist me to slipper the King of the Roos with a golden slipper with a silver heel? The protection of Pir Khan be upon his labors!" He spread out the skirts of his gaberdine and pirouetted between the lines of tethered horses.

"There starts a caravan from Peshawur to Kabul in twenty days, *Huzrut,*" said the Eusufzai trader. "My camels go therewith. Do thou also go and bring us good-luck."

"I will go even now!" shouted the priest. "I will depart upon my winged camels, and be at Pashawur in a day! Ho! Hazar Mir Khan," he yelled to his servant, "drive out the camels, but let me first mount my own."

He leaped on the back of his beast as it knelt, and, turning round to me, cried:—"Come thou also, Sahib, a little along the road and I will sell thee a charm—an amulet that shall make thee King of Kafiristan."

Then the light broke upon me and I followed the two camels out of the Serai till we reached open road and the priest halted.

"What d' you think o' that?" said he in English. "Carnehan can't talk their patter, so I've made him my servant. He makes a handsome servant. 'Tisn't for nothing that I've been knocking about the country for fourteen years. Didn't I do that talk neat? We'll hitch on to a caravan at Peshawur till we get to Jagdallak, and then we'll see if we can get donkeys for our camels, and strike into Kafiristan. Whirligigs for the Amir, O Lor! Put your hand under the camel-bags and tell me what you feel."

I felt the butt of a Martini, and another and another.

"Twenty of 'em," said Dravot, placidly. "Twenty of 'em, and ammunition to correspond, under the whirligigs and the mud dolls."

"Heaven help you if you are caught with those things!" I said. "A Martini is worth her weight in silver among the Pathans."

"Fifteen hundred rupees of capital—every rupee we could beg, borrow, or steal—are invested on these two camels," said Dravot. "We won't get caught. We're going through the Khaiber with a regular caravan. Who'd touch a poor mad priest?"

"Have you got everything you want?" I asked, overcome with astonishment.

"Not yet, but we shall soon. Give us a memento of your kindness,

Brother. You did me a service yesterday, and that time in Marwar. Half my Kingdom shall you have, as the saying is." I slipped a small charm compass from my watch-chain and handed it up to the priest.

"Good-bye," said Dravot, giving me a hand cautiously. "It's the last time we'll shake hands with an Englishman these many days. Shake hands with him, Carnehan," he cried, as the second camel passed me.

Carnehan leaned down and shook hands. Then the camels passed away along the dusty road, and I was left alone to wonder. My eye could detect no failure in the disguises. The scene in Serai attested that they were complete to the native mind. There was just the chance, therefore, that Carnehan and Dravot would be able to wander through Afghanistan without detection. But, beyond, they would find death, certain and awful death.

Ten days later a native friend of mine, giving me the news of the day from Peshawur, wound up his letter with:—"There has been much laughter here on account of a certain mad priest who is going in his estimation to sell petty gauds and insignificant trinkets which he ascribes as great charms to H. H. the Amir of Bokhara. He passed through Peshawur and associated himself to the Second Summer caravan that goes to Kabul. The merchants are pleased because through superstition they imagine that such mad fellows bring good-fortune."

The two, then, were beyond the Border. I would have prayed for them, but, that night, a real King died in Europe and demanded an obituary notice.

The wheel of the world swings through the same phases again and again. Summer passed and winter thereafter, and came and passed again. The daily paper continued and I with it, and upon the third summer there fell a hot night, a night-issue, and a strained waiting for something to be telegraphed from the other side of the world, exactly as had happened before. A few great men had died in the past two years, the machines worked with more clatter, and some of the trees in the Office garden were a few feet taller. But that was all the difference.

I passed over to the press-room, and went through just such a scene as I have already described. The nervous tension was stronger than it had been two years before, and I felt the heat more acutely. At three o'clock I cried, "Print off," and turned to go, when there crept to my chair what was left of a man. He was bent into a circle, his head was sunk between his shoulders, and he moved his feet one over the other like a bear. I could hardly see whether he walked or crawled—this ragwrapped, whining cripple who addressed me by name, crying that he was come back, "Can you give me a drink?" he whimpered. "For the Lord's sake, give me a drink!"

I went back to the office, the man following with groans of pain, and I turned up the lamp.

"Don't you know me?" he gasped, dropping into a chair, and he turned his drawn face, surmounted by a shock of grey hair, to the light.

I looked at him intently. Once before had I seen eyebrows that met over the nose in an inch-broad black band, but for the life of me I could not tell where.

"I don't know you," I said, handing him the whiskey. "What can I do for you?"

He took a gulp of the spirit raw, and shivered in spite of the suffocating heat.

"I've come back," he repeated; "and I was the King of Kafiristan— me and Dravot—crowned Kings we was! In this office we settled it— you setting there and giving us the books. I am Peachey—Peachey Taliaferro Carnehan, and you've been setting here ever since—O Lord!"

I was more than a little astonished, and expressed my feelings accordingly.

"It's true," said Carnehan, with a dry cackle, nursing his feet, which were wrapped in rags. "True as gospel. Kings we were, with crowns upon our heads—me and Dravot—poor Dan—oh, poor, poor Dan, that would never take advice, not though I begged of him!"

"Take the whiskey," I said, "and take your own time. Tell me all you can recollect of everything from beginning to end. You got across the border on your camels, Dravot dressed as a mad priest and you his servant. Do you remember that?"

"I ain't mad—yet, but I shall be that way soon. Of course I remember. Keep looking at me, or maybe my words will go all to pieces. Keep looking at me in my eyes and don't say anything."

I leaned forward and looked into his face as steadily as I could. He dropped one hand upon the table and I grasped it by the wrist. It was twisted like a bird's claw, and upon the back was a ragged, red, diamond-shaped scar.

"No, don't look there. Look at *me*," said Carnehan.

"That comes afterward, but for the Lord's sake don't distrack me. We left with that caravan, me and Dravot playing all sorts of antics to amuse the people we were with. Dravot used to make us laugh in the evenings when all the people were cooking their dinners—cooking their dinners, and . . . what did they do then? They lit little fires with sparks that went into Dravot's beard, and we all laughed—fit to die. Little red fires they was, going into Dravot's big red beard—so funny." His eyes left mine and he smiled foolishly.

"You went as far as Jagdallak with that caravan," I said, at a venture, "after you had lit those fires. To Jagdallak, where you turned off to try to get into Kafiristan."

"No, we didn't neither. What are you talking about? We turned off before Jagdallak, because we heard the roads was good. But they wasn't good enough for our two camels—mine and Dravot's. When we left the caravan, Dravot took off all his clothes and mine too, and said we would be heathen, because the Kafirs didn't allow Mohammedans to talk to them. So we dressed betwixt and between, and such a sight as Daniel Dravot I never saw yet nor expect to see again. He burned half his beard, and slung a sheep-skin over his shoulder, and shaved his head into patterns. He shaved mine, too, and made me wear outrageous things to look like a heathen. That was in a most mountainous country, and our camels couldn't go along any more because of the mountains. They were tall and black, and coming home I saw them fight like wild goats—there are lots of goats in Kafiristan. And these mountains, they never keep still, no more than the goats. Always fighting they are, and don't let you sleep at night."

"Take some more whiskey," I said, very slowly. "What did you and Daniel Dravot do when the camels could go no further because of the rough roads that led into Kafiristan?"

"What did which do? There was a party called Peachey Taliaferro Carnehan that was with Dravot. Shall I tell you about him? He died out there in the cold. Slap from the bridge fell old Peachey, turning and twisting in the air like a penny whirligig that you can sell to the Amir. —No; they was two for three ha'pence, those whirligigs, or I am much mistaken and woful sore. And then these camels were no use, and Peachey said to Dravot—'For the Lord's sake, let's get out of this before our heads are chopped off,' and with that they killed the camels all among the mountains, not having anything in particular to eat, but first they took off the boxes with the guns and the ammunition, till two men came along driving four mules. Dravot up and dances in front of them, singing,—'Sell me four mules.' Says the first man,—'If you are rich enough to buy, you are rich enough to rob'; but before ever he could put his hand to his knife, Dravot breaks his neck over his knee, and the other party runs away. So Carnehan loaded the mules with the rifles that was taken off the camels, and together we starts forward into those bitter cold mountainous parts, and never a road broader than the back of your hand."

He paused for a moment, while I asked him if he could remember the nature of the country through which he had journeyed.

"I am telling you as straight as I can, but my head isn't as good as it might be. They drove nails through it to make me hear better how Dravot died. The country was mountainous and the mules were most contrary, and the inhabitants was dispersed and solitary. They went up and up, and down and down, and that other party, Carnehan, was imploring of Dravot not to sing and whistle so loud, for fear of bringing down the tremenjus avalanches. But Dravot says that if a King couldn't sing it wasn't worth being King, and whacked the mules over the rump, and never took no heed for ten cold days. We came to a big level valley all among the mountains, and the mules were near dead, so we killed them, not having anything in special for them or us to eat. We sat upon the boxes, and played odds and even with the cartridges that was jolted out.

"Then ten men with bows and arrows ran down that valley, chasing twenty men with bows and arrows, and the row was tremenjus. They was fair men—fairer than you or me—with yellow hair and remarkable well built. Says Dravot, unpacking the guns—'This is the beginning of the business. We'll fight for the ten men,' and with that he fires two rifles at the twenty men, and drops one of them at two hundred yards from the rock where we was sitting. The other men began to run but Carnehan and Dravot sits on the boxes picking them off at all ranges, up and down the valley. Then we goes up to the ten men that had run across the snow too, and they fires a footy little arrow at us. Dravot he shoots above their heads and they all falls down flat. Then he walks over them and kicks them, and then he lifts them up and shakes hands all round to make them friendly like. He calls them and gives them the boxes to carry, and waves his hand for all the world as though he was King already. They takes the boxes and him across the valley and up the hill into a pine wood on the top, where there was half a dozen big stone idols. Dravot he goes to the biggest—a fellow they call Imbra—and lays a rifle and cartridge at his feet, rubbing his nose respectful with his own nose, patting him on the head, and saluting in front of it. He turns round to the men and nods his head, and says,—'That's all right. I'm in the know too, and all these old jim-jams are my friends.' Then he opens his mouth and points down it, and when the first man brings him food, he says—'No'; and when the second man brings him food, he says 'No'; but when one of the old priests and the boss of the village brings him food, he says—'Yes'; very haughty, and eats it slow. That was how we came to our first village, without any trouble, just as though we had tumbled from the skies. But we tumbled from one of those damned rope-bridges, you see, and you couldn't expect a man to laugh much after that."

"Take some more whiskey and go on," I said. "That was the first village you came into. How did you get to be King?"

"I wasn't King," said Carnehan. "Dravot he was the King, and a handsome man he looked with the gold crown on his head and all.

Him and the other party stayed in that village, and every morning Dravot sat by the side of old Imbra, and the people came and worshipped. That was Dravot's order. Then a lot of men came into the valley, and Carnehan and Dravot picks them off with the rifles before they knew where they was, and runs down into the valley and up again the other side, and finds another village, same as the first one, and the people all falls down flat on their faces, and Dravot says,—'Now what is the trouble between you two villages?' and the people points to a woman, as fair as you or me, that was carried off, and Dravot takes her back to the first village and counts up the dead—eight there was. For each dead man Dravot pours a little milk on the ground and waves his arms like a whirligig and 'That's all right,' says he. Then he and Carnehan takes the big boss of each village by the arm and walks them down into the valley, and shows them how to scratch a line with a spear right down the valley, and gives each a sod of turf from both sides o' the line. Then all the people comes down and shouts like the devil and all, and Dravot says,—'Go and dig the land, and be fruitful and multiply,' which they did, though they didn't understand. Then we asks the names of things in their lingo—bread and water and fire and idols and such, and Dravot leads the priest of each village up to the idol, and says he must sit there and judge the people, and if anything goes wrong he is to be shot.

"Next week they was all turning up the land in the valley as quiet as bees and much prettier, and the priests heard all the complaints and told Dravot in dumb show what it was about. 'That's just the beginning,' said Dravot. 'They think we're Gods.' He and Carnehan picks out twenty good men and shows them how to click off a rifle, and form fours, and advance in line, and they was very pleased to do so, and clever to see the hang of it. Then he takes out his pipe and his baccy-pouch and leaves one at one village and one at the other, and off we two goes to see what was to be done in the next valley. That was all rock, and there was a little village there, and Carnehan says,—'Send 'em to the old valley to plant,' and takes 'em there and gives 'em some land that wasn't took before. They were a poor lot, and we blooded 'em with a kid before letting 'em into the new Kingdom. That was to impress the people, and then they settled down quiet, and Carnehan went back to Dravot who had got into another valley, all snow and ice and most mountainous. There was no people there and the Army got afraid, so Dravot shoots one of them, and goes on till he finds some people in a village, and the Army explains that unless the people wants to be killed they had better not shoot their little matchlocks; for they had matchlocks. We make friends with the priest and I stays there alone with two of the Army, teaching the men how to drill, and a thundering big Chief comes across the snow with kettle-drums and horns twanging, because he heard there was a new God kicking about. Carnehan sights for the brown of the men half a mile across the snow and wings one of them. Then he sends a message to the Chief that, unless he wished to be killed, he must come and shake hands with me and leave his arms behind. The chief comes alone first, and Carnehan shakes hands with him and whirls his arms about, same as Dravot used, and very much surprised that Chief was, and strokes my eyebrows. Then Carnehan goes alone to the Chief, and asks him in dumb show if he had an enemy he hated. 'I have,' says the Chief. So Carnehan weeds out the pick of his men, and sets the two of the Army to show them drill and at the end of two weeks the men can manœuvre about as well as Volunteers. So he marches with the Chief to a great big plain on the top of a mountain, and the Chief's men rushes into a village and takes it; we three Martinis firing into the brown of the enemy. So we took that village too, and I gives the Chief a rag from my coat and says, 'Occupy till I come': which was scriptural. By way of a reminder, when me and the Army was eighteen hundred yards away, I drops a bullet near him standing on the snow, and all the people falls flat on their faces. Then I sends a letter to Dravot, wherever he be by land or by sea."

At the risk of throwing the creature out of train I interrupted, "How could you write a letter up yonder?"

"The letter? Oh!—The letter! Keep looking at me between the eyes, please. It was a string-talk letter, that we'd learned the way of it from a blind beggar in the Punjab."

I remember that there had once come to the office a blind man with a knotted twig and a piece of string which he wound round the twig according to some cypher of his own. He could, after the lapse of days or hours, repeat the sentence which he had reeled up. He had reduced the alphabet to eleven primitive sounds; and tried to teach me his method, but failed.

"I sent that letter to Dravot," said Carnehan; "and told him to come back because this Kingdom was growing too big for me to handle, and then I struck for the first valley, to see how the priests were working. They called the village we took along with the Chief, Bashkai, and the first village we took, Er-Heb. The priests at Er-Heb were doing all right, but they had a lot of pending cases about land to show me, and some men from another village had been firing arrows at night. I went out and looked for that village and fired four rounds at it from a thousand yards. That used all the cartridges I cared to spend, and I waited for Dravot, who had been away two or three months, and I kept my people quiet.

"One morning I heard the devil's own noise of drums and horns, and Dan Dravot marches down the hill with his Army and a tail of hundreds of men, and, which was the most amazing—a great gold crown on his head. 'My Gord, Carnehan,' says Daniel, 'this is a tremendjus business, and we've got the whole country as far as it's worth having. I am the son of Alexander by Queen Semiramis, and you're my younger brother and a God too! It's the biggest thing we've ever seen. I've been marching and fighting for six weeks with the Army, and every footy little village for fifty miles has come in rejoiceful; and more than that, I've got the key of the whole show, as you'll see, and I've got a crown for you! I told 'em to make two of 'em at a place called Shu, where the gold lies in the rock like suet in mutton. Gold I've seen, and turquoise I've kicked out of the cliffs, and there's garnets in the sands of the river, and here's a chunk of amber that a man brought me. Call up all the priests and, here, take your crown.'

"One of the men opens a black hair bag and I slips the crown on. It was too small and too heavy, but I wore it for the glory. Hammered gold it was—five pound weight, like a hoop of a barrel.

" 'Peachey,' says Dravot, 'we don't want to fight no more. The Craft's the trick so help me!' and he brings forward that same Chief that I left at Bashkai—Billy Fish we called him afterward, because he was so like Billy Fish that drove the big tank-engine at Mach on the Bolan in the old days. 'Shake hands with him,' says Dravot, and I shook hands and nearly dropped, for Billy Fish gave me the Grip. I said nothing, but tried him with the Fellow Craft Grip. He answers, all right, and I tried the Master's Grip, but that was a slip. 'A Fellow Craft he is!' I says to Dan. 'Does he know the word?' 'He does,' says Dan, 'and all the priests know. It's a miracle! The Chiefs and the priests can work a Fellow Craft Lodge in a way that's very like ours, and they've cut the marks on the rocks, but they don't know the Third Degree, and they've come to find out. It's Gord's Truth. I've known these long years that the Afghans knew up to the Fellow Craft Degree, but this is a miracle. A God and a Grand-Master of the Craft am I, and a Lodge in the Third Degree I will open, and we'll raise the head priests and the Chiefs of the villages.'

" 'It's against all the law,' I says, 'holding a Lodge without warrant from any one; and we never held office in any Lodge.'

" 'It's a master-stroke of policy,' says Dravot. 'It means running the country as easy as a four-wheeled bogy on a down grade. We can't stop to inquire now, or they'll turn against us. I've forty Chiefs at my heel, and passed and raised according to their merit they shall be. Billet these men on the villages and see that we run up a Lodge of some kind. The temple of Imbra will do for the Lodge-room. The women must make aprons as you show them. I'll hold a levee of Chiefs to-night and Lodge to-morrow."

"I was fair run off my legs, but I wasn't such a fool as not to see what a pull this Craft business gave us. I showed the priests' families how to make aprons of the degrees, but for Dravot's apron the blue border and marks was made of turquoise lumps on white hide, not cloth. We took a great square stone in the temple for the Master's chair, and little stones for the officers' chairs, and painted the black pavement with white squares, and did what we could to make things regular.

"At the levee which was held that night on the hillside with big bonfires, Dravot gives out that him and me were Gods and sons of Alexander, and Past Grand-Masters in the Craft, and was come to make Kafiristan a country where every man should eat in peace and drink in quiet, and specially obey us. Then the Chiefs come round to shake hands, and they was so hairy and white and fair it was just shaking hands with old friends. We gave them names according as they was like men we had known in India—Billy Fish, Holly Dilworth, Pikky Kergan that was Bazar-master when I was at Mhow, and so on and so on.

"The *most* amazing miracle was at Lodge next night. One of the old priests was watching us continuous, and I felt uneasy, for I knew we'd have to fudge the Ritual, and I didn't know what the men knew. The old priest was a stranger come in from beyond the village of Bashkai. The minute Dravot puts on the Master's apron that the girls had made for him, the priest fetches a whoop and a howl, and tries to overturn the stone that Dravot was sitting on. 'It's all up now,' I says. 'That comes of meddling with the Craft without warrant!' Dravot never winked an eye, not when ten priests took and tilted over the Grand-Master's chair—which was to say the stone of Imbra. The priest begins rubbing the bottom end of it to clear away the black dirt, and presently he shows all the other priests the Master's Mark, same as was on Dravot's apron, cut into the stone. Not even the priests of the temple of Imbra knew it was there. The old chap falls flat on his face at Dravot's feet and kisses 'em. 'Luck again,' says Dravot, across the Lodge to me, 'they say it's the missing Mark that no one could understand the why of. We're more than safe now.' Then he bangs the butt of his gun for a gavel and says:—'By virtue of the authority vested in me by my own right hand and the help of Peachey, I declare myself Grand-Master of all Freemasonry in Kafiristan in this the Mother Lodge o' the country, and King of Kafiristan equally with Peachey!' At that he puts on his crown and I puts on mine—I was doing Senior Warden— and we opens the Lodge in most ample form. It was an amazing miracle! The priests moved in Lodge through the first two degrees almost without telling, as if the memory was coming back to them.

After that, Peachey and Dravot raised such as was worthy—high priests and Chiefs of far-off villages. Billy Fish was the first, and I can tell you we scared the soul out of him. It was not in any way according to Ritual, but it served our turn. We didn't raise more than ten of the biggest men because we didn't want to make the Degree common. And they was clamoring to be raised.

" 'In another six months,' says Dravot, 'we'll hold another Communication and see how you are working.' Then he asks them about their villages, and learns that they was fighting one against the other and were fair sick and tired of it. And when they wasn't doing that they was fighting with the Mohammedans. 'You can fight those when they come into our country,' says Dravot. 'Tell off every tenth man of your tribes for a Frontier guard, and send two hundred at a time to this valley to be drilled. Nobody is going to be shot or speared any more so long as he does well, and I know that you won't cheat me because you're white people—sons of Alexander—and not like common, black Mohammedans. You are *my* people and by God,' says he, running off into English at the end—'I'll make a damned fine Nation of you, or I'll die in the making!'

"I can't tell all we did for the next six months because Dravot did a lot I couldn't see the hang of, and, he learned their lingo in a way I never could. My work was to help the people plough, and now and again go out with some of the Army and see what the other villages were doing, and make 'em throw rope-bridges across the ravines which cut up the country horrid. Dravot was very kind to me, but when he walked up and down in the pine wood pulling that bloody red beard of his with both fists I knew he was thinking plans I could not advise him about, and I just waited for orders.

"But Dravot never showed me disrespect before the people. They were afraid of me and the Army, but they loved Dan. He was the best of friends with the priests and the Chiefs; but any one could come across the hills with a complaint and Dravot would hear him out fair, and call four priests together and say what was to be done. He used to call in Billy Fish from Bashkai, and Pikky Kergan from Shu, and an old Chief we called Kafuzelum—it was like enough to his real name—and hold councils with 'em when there was any fighting to be done in small villages. That was his Council of War, and the four priests of Bashkai, Shu, Khawak, and Madora was his Privy Council. Between the lot of 'em they send me, with forty men and twenty rifles, and sixty men carrying turquoises, into the Ghorband country to buy those hand-made Martini rifles, that come out of the Amir's workshops at Kabul, from one of the Amir's Herati regiments that would have sold the very teeth out of their mouths for turquoises.

"I stayed in Ghorband a month, and gave the Governor there the pick of my baskets for hush-money, and bribed the Colonel of the regiment some more, and, between the two and the tribes-people, we got more than a hundred hand-made Martinis, a hundred good Kohat Jezails, that'll throw to six hundred yards, and forty man-loads of very bad ammunition for the rifles. I came back with what I had, and distributed 'em among the men that the Chiefs sent to me to drill. Dravot was too busy to attend to those things, but the old Army that we first made helped me, and we turned out five hundred men that could drill, and two hundred that knew how to hold arms pretty straight. Even those cork-screwed, hand-made guns was a miracle to them. Dravot talked big about powder-shops and factories, walking up and down in the pine wood when the winter was coming on.

" 'I won't make a Nation,' says he, 'I'll make an Empire! These men aren't niggers; they're English! Look at their eyes—look at their mouths. Look at the way they stand up. They sit on chairs in their own houses. They're the Lost Tribes, or something like it, and they've grown to be English. I'll take a census in the spring if the priests don't get frightened. There must be a fair two million of 'em in these hills. The villages are full o' little children. Two million people—two hundred and fifty thousand fighting men—and all English! They only want the rifles and a little drilling. Two hundred and fifty thousand men, ready to cut in on Russia's right flank when she tries for India! Peachey, man,' he says, chewing his beard in great hunks, 'we shall be Emperors —Emperors of the Earth! Rajah Brooke will be a suckling to us. I'll treat with the Viceroy on equal terms. I'll ask him to send me twelve picked English—twelve that I know of—to help us govern a bit. There's Mackray, Sergeant-pensioner at Segowli—many's the good dinner he's given me, and his wife a pair of trousers. There's Donkin, the Warder of Tounghoo Jail; there's hundreds that I could lay my hand on if I was in India. The Viceroy shall do it for me. I'll send a man through in the spring for those men, and I'll write for a dispensation from the Grand Lodge for what I've done as Grand-Master. That—and all the Sniders that'll be thrown out when the native troops in India take up the Martini. They'll be worn smooth, but they'll do for fighting in these hills. Twelve English, a hundred thousand Sniders run through the Amir's country in driblets—I'd be content with twenty thousand in one year—and we'd be an Empire. When everything was shipshape, I'd hand over the crown—this crown I'm wearing now—to Queen Victoria on my knees, and she'd say: "Rise up, Sir Daniel Dravot." Oh, it's big! It's big, I tell you! But there's so much to be done in every place—Bashkai, Khawak, Shu, and everywhere else.'

" 'What is it?' I says. 'There are no more men coming in to be drilled this autumn. Look at those fat, black clouds. They're bringing the snow.'

" 'It isn't that,' says Daniel, putting his hand very hard on my shoulder; 'and I don't wish to say anything that's against you, for no other living man would have followed me and made me what I am as you have done. You're a first-class Commander-in-Chief, and the people know you; but—it's a big country, and somehow you can't help me, Peachey, in the way I want to be helped.'

" 'Go to your blasted priests then!' I said, and I was sorry when I made that remark, but it did hurt me sore to find Daniel talking so superior when I'd drilled all the men, and done all he told me.

" 'Don't let's quarrel, Peachey,' says Daniel, without cursing. 'You're a King too, and the half of this Kingdom is yours; but can't you see, Peachey, we want cleverer men than us now—three or four of 'em, that we can scatter about for our Deputies. It's a hugeous great State, and I can't always tell the right thing to do, and I haven't time for all I want to do, and here's the winter coming on and all.' He put half his beard into his mouth, and it was as red as the gold of his crown.

" 'I'm sorry, Daniel,' says I. 'I've done all I could. I've drilled the men and shown the people how to stack their oats better; and I've brought in those tinware rifles from Ghorband—but I know what you're driving at. I take it Kings always feel oppressed that way.'

" 'There's another thing too,' says Dravot, walking up and down. 'The winter's coming and these people won't be giving much trouble, and if they do we can't move about. I want a wife.'

" 'For God's sake leave the women alone!' I says. 'We've both got all the work we can, though I *am* a fool. Remember the Contrack, and keep clear o' women.'

" 'The Contrack only lasted till such time as we was Kings; and Kings we have been these months past,' says Dravot, weighing his crown in his hand. 'You go get a wife too, Peachey—a nice, strappin', plump girl that'll keep you warm in the winter. They're prettier than English girls, and we can take the pick of 'em. Boil 'em once or twice in hot water, and they'll come as fair as chicken and ham.'

" 'Don't tempt me!' I says. 'I will not have any dealings with a woman not till we are a dam' side more settled than we are now. I've been doing the work o' two men, and you've been doing the work o' three. Let's lie off a bit, and see if we can get some better tobacco from Afghan country and run in some good liquor; but no women.'

" 'Who's talking o' *women*?' says Dravot. 'I said *wife*—a Queen to breed a King's son for the King. A Queen out of the strongest tribe, that'll make them your blood-brothers, and that'll lie by your side and tell you all the people thinks about you and their own affairs. That's what I want.'

" 'Do you remember that Bengali woman I kept at Mogul Serai when I was a plate-layer?' says I. 'A fat lot o' good she was to me. She taught me the lingo and one or two other things; but what happened? She ran away with the Station Master's servant and half my month's pay. Then she turned up at Dadur Junction in tow of a half-caste, and had the impidence to say I was her husband—all among the drivers in the running-shed!'

" 'We've done with that,' says Dravot. 'These women are whiter than you or me, and a Queen I will have for the winter months.'

" 'For the last time o' asking, Dan, do *not*,' I says. 'It'll only bring us harm. The Bible says that Kings ain't to waste their strength on women, 'specially when they've got a new raw Kingdom to work over.'

" 'For the last time of answering I will,' said Dravot, and he went away through the pine-trees looking like a big red devil. The low sun hit his crown and beard on one side and the two blazed like hot coals.

"But getting a wife was not as easy as Dan thought. He put it before the Council, and there was no answer till Billy Fish said that he'd better ask the girls. Dravot damned them all round. 'What's wrong with me?' he shouts, standing by the idol Imbra. 'Am I a dog or am I not enough of a man for your wenches? Haven't I put the shadow of my hand over this country? Who stopped the last Afghan raid?' It was me really, but Dravot was too angry to remember. 'Who brought your guns? Who repaired the bridges? Who's the Grand-Master of the sign cut in the stone?' and he thumped his hand on the block that he used to sit on in Lodge, and at Council, which opened like Lodge always. Billy Fish said nothing and no more did the others. 'Keep your hair on, Dan,' said I; 'and ask the girls. That's how it's done at Home, and these people are quite English.'

" 'The marriage of the King is a matter of State,' says Dan, in a white-hot rage, for he could feel, I hope, that he was going against his better mind. He walked out of the Council-room, and the others sat still, looking at the ground.

" 'Billy Fish,' says I to the Chief of Bashkai, 'what's the difficulty here? A straight answer to a true friend.' 'You know,' says Billy Fish. 'How should a man tell you who knows everything? How can daughters of men marry Gods or Devils? It's not proper.'

"I remember something like that in the Bible; but, if, after seeing us as long as they had they still believed we were Gods, it wasn't for me to undeceive them.

" 'A God can do anything,' says I. 'If the King is fond of a girl he'll not let her die.' 'She'll have to,' said Billy Fish. 'There are all sorts of Gods and Devils in these mountains, and now and again a girl marries one of them and isn't seen any more. Besides, you two know the Mark cut in the stone. Only the Gods know that. We thought you were men till you showed the sign of the Master.'

"I wished then that we had explained about the loss of the genuine secrets of a Master-Mason at the first go-off; but I said nothing. All that night there was a blowing of horns in a little dark temple half-way down the hill, and I heard a girl crying fit to die. One of the priests told us that she was being prepared to marry the King.

" 'I'll have no nonsense of that kind,' says Dan. 'I don't want to interfere with your customs, but I'll take my own wife.' 'The girl's a little bit afraid,' says the priest. 'She thinks she's going to die, and they are a-heartening of her up down in the temple.'

" 'Hearten her very tender, then,' says Dravot, 'or I'll hearten you with the butt of a gun so that you'll never want to be heartened again.' He licked his lips, did Dan, and stayed up walking about more than half the night, thinking of the wife that he was going to get in the morning. I wasn't any means comfortable, for I knew that dealings with a woman in foreign parts, though you was a crowned King twenty times over, could not but be risky. I got up very early in the morning while Dravot was asleep, and I saw the priests talking together in whispers, and the Chiefs talking together too, and they looked at me out of the corners of their eyes.

" 'What is up, Fish?' I says to the Bashkai man, who was wrapped up in his furs and looking splendid to behold.

" 'I can't rightly say,' says he; 'but if you can induce the King to drop all this nonsense about marriage, you'll be doing him and me and yourself a great service.'

" 'That I do believe,' says I. 'But sure, you know, Billy, as well as me, having fought against and for us, that the King and me are nothing more than two of the finest men that God Almighty ever made. Nothing more, I do assure you.'

" 'That may be,' says Billy Fish, 'and yet I should be sorry if it was.' He sinks his head upon his great fur cloak for a minute and thinks. 'King,' says he, 'be you man or God or Devil, I'll stick by you to-day. I have twenty of my men with me, and they will follow me. We'll go to Bashkai until the storm blows over.'

"A little snow had fallen in the night, and everything was white except the greasy fat clouds that blew down and down from the north. Dravot came out with his crown on his head, swinging his arms and stamping his feet, and looking more pleased than Punch.

" 'For the last time, drop it, Dan,' says I, in a whisper. 'Billy Fish here says that there will be a row.'

" 'A row among my people!' says Dravot. 'Not much. Peachey, you're a fool not to get a wife too. Where's the girl?' says he, with a voice as loud as the braying of a jackass. 'Call up all the Chiefs and priests, and let the Emperor see if his wife suits him.'

"There was no need to call any one. They were all there leaning on their guns and spears round the clearing in the centre of the pine wood. A deputation of priests went down to the little temple to bring up the girl, and the horns blew up fit to wake the dead. Billy Fish saunters round and gets as close to Daniel as he could, and behind him stood his twenty men with matchlocks. Not a man of them under six feet. I was next to Dravot, and behind me was twenty men of the regular Army. Up comes the girl, and a strapping wench she was, covered with silver and turquoises but white as death, and looking back every minute at the priests.

" 'She'll do,' said Dan, looking her over. 'What's to be afraid of, lass? Come and kiss me.' He puts his arm round her. She shuts her eyes, gives a bit of a squeak, and down goes her face in the side of Dan's flaming red beard.

" 'The slut's bitten me!' says he, clapping his hand to his neck, and, sure enough, his hand was red with blood. Billy Fish and two of his matchlock-men catches hold of Dan by the shoulders and drags him into the Bashkai lot, while the priests howls in their lingo,—'Neither God nor Devil but a man!' I was all taken aback, for a priest cut at me in front, and the Army behind began firing into the Bashkai men.

" 'God A-mighty!' says Dan. 'What is the meaning o' this?'

" 'Come back! Come away!' says Billy Fish. 'Ruin and Mutiny is the matter. We'll break for Bashkai if we can.'

"I tried to give some sort of orders to my men—the men o' the regular Army—but it was no use, so I fired into the brown of 'em with an English Martini and drilled three beggars in a line. The valley was full of shouting, howling creatures, and every soul was shrieking, 'Not a God nor a Devil but only a man!' The Bashkai troops stuck to Billy Fish all they were worth, but their matchlocks wasn't half as good as the Kabul breach-loaders, and four of them dropped. Dan was bellowing like a bull, for he was very wrathy; and Billy Fish had a hard job to prevent him running out at the crowd.

" 'We can't stand,' says Billy Fish. 'Make a run for it down the valley! The whole place is against us.' The matchlock-men ran, and we went down the valley in spite of Dravot's protestations. He was swearing horribly and crying out that he was a King. The priests rolled great stones on us, and the regular Army fired hard, and there wasn't more than six men, not counting Dan, Billy Fish, and Me, that came down to the bottom of the valley alive.

"Then they stopped firing and the horns in the temple blew again. 'Come away—for Gord's sake come away!' says Billy Fish. 'They'll send runners out to all the villages before ever we get to Bashkai. I can protect you there, but I can't do anything now.'

"My own notion is that Dan began to go mad in his head from that hour. He stared up and down like a stuck pig. Then he was all for walking back alone and killing the priests with his bare hands; which he could have done. 'An Emperor am I,' says Daniel, 'and next year I shall be a Knight of the Queen.'

" 'All right, Dan,' says I; 'but come along now while there's time.'

" 'It's your fault,' says he, 'for not looking after your Army better. There was mutiny in the midst, and you didn't know—you damned engine-driving, plate-laying, missionary's-pass-hunting hound!' He sat upon a rock and called me every foul name he could lay tongue to. I was too heart-sick to care, though it was all his foolishness that brought the smash.

" 'I'm sorry, Dan,' says I, 'but there's no accounting for natives. This business is our Fifty-Seven. Maybe we'll make something out of it yet, when we've got to Bashkai.'

" 'Let's get to Bashkai, then,' says Dan, 'and, by God, when I come back here again I'll sweep the valley so there isn't a bug in a blanket left!'

"We walked all that day, and all that night Dan was stumping up and down on the snow, chewing his beard and muttering to himself.

" 'There's no hope o' getting clear,' said Billy Fish. 'The priests will have sent runners to the villages to say that you are only men. Why didn't you stick on as Gods till things was more settled? I'm a dead man,' says Billy Fish, and he throws himself down on the snow and begins to pray to his Gods.

"Next morning we was in a cruel bad country—all up and down, no level ground at all, and no food either. The six Bashkai men looked at Billy Fish hungry-wise as if they wanted to ask something, but they said never a word. At noon we came to the top of a flat mountain all covered with snow, and when we climbed up into it, behold, there was an Army in position waiting in the middle!

" 'The runners have been very quick,' says Billy Fish, with a little bit of a laugh. 'They are waiting for us.'

"Three or four men began to fire from the enemy's side, and a chance shot took Daniel in the calf of the leg. That brought him to his senses. He looks across the snow at the Army, and sees the rifles that we had brought into the country.

" 'We're done for,' says he. 'They are Englishmen, these people,—and it's my blasted nonsense that has brought you to this. Get back, Billy Fish, and take your men away; you've done what you could, and now cut for it. Carnehan,' says he, 'shake hands with me and go along with Billy. Maybe they won't kill you. I'll go and meet 'em alone. It's me that did it. Me, the King!'

" 'Go!' says I. 'Go to Hell, Dan. I'm with you here. Billy Fish, you clear out, and we two will meet those folk.'

" 'I'm a Chief,' says Billy Fish, quite quiet. 'I stay with you. My men can go.'

"The Bashkai fellows didn't wait for a second word but ran off, and Dan and Me and Billy Fish walked across to where the drums were drumming and the horns were horning. It was cold—awful cold. I've got that cold in the back of my head now. There's a lump of it there."

The punkah-coolies had gone to sleep. Two kerosene lamps were blazing in the office, and the perspiration poured down my face and splashed on the blotter as I leaned forward. Carnehan was shivering, and I feared that his mind might go. I wiped my face, took a fresh grip of the piteously mangled hands, and said:—"What happened after that?"

The momentary shift of my eyes had broken the clear current.

"What was you pleased to say?" whined Carnehan. "They took them without any sound. Not a little whisper all along the snow, not though the King knocked down the first man that set hand on him—not though old Peachey fired his last cartridge into the brown of 'em. Not a single solitary sound did those swines make. They just closed up tight, and I tell you their furs stunk. There was a man called Billy Fish, a good friend of us all, and they cut his throat, Sir, then and there, like a pig; and the King kicks up the bloody snow and says: 'We've had a dashed fine run for our money. What's coming next?' But Peachey, Peachey Taliaferro, I tell you, Sir, in confidence as betwixt two friends, he lost his head, Sir. No, he didn't neither. The King lost his head, so he did, all along o' one of those cunning rope-bridges. Kindly let me have the paper-cutter, Sir. It tilted this way. They marched him a mile across that snow to a rope-bridge over a ravine with a river at the bottom. You may have seen such. They prodded him behind like an ox. 'Damn your eyes!' says the King. 'D'you suppose I can't die like a gentleman?' He turns to Peachey—Peachey that was crying like a child. 'I've brought you to this, Peachey,' says he. 'Brought you out of your happy life to be killed in Kafiristan, where you was late Commander-in-Chief of the Emperor's forces. Say you forgive me, Peachey.' 'I do,' says Peachey. 'Fully and freely do I forgive you, Dan.' 'Shake hands,

Peachey,' says he. 'I'm going now.' Out he goes, looking neither right nor left, and when he was plumb in the middle of those dizzy dancing ropes, 'Cut, you beggars,' he shouts; and they cut, and old Dan fell, turning round and round and round twenty thousand miles, for he took half an hour to fall till he struck the water, and I could see his body caught on a rock with the gold crown close beside.

"But do you know what they did to Peachey between two pine trees? They crucified him, Sir, as Peachey's hand will show. They used wooden pegs for his hands and his feet; and he didn't die. He hung there and screamed, and they took him down next day, and said it was a miracle that he wasn't dead. They took him down—poor old Peachey that hadn't done them any harm—that hadn't done them any. . . ."

He rocked to and fro and wept bitterly, wiping his eyes with the back of his scarred hands and moaning like a child for some ten minutes.

"They were cruel enough to feed him up in the temple, because they said he was more of a God than old Daniel that was a man. Then they turned him out on the snow, and told him to go home, and Peachey came home in about a year, begging along the roads quite safe; for Daniel Dravot he walked before and said:—'Come along, Peachey. It's a big thing we're doing.' The mountains they danced at night, and the mountains they tried to fall on Peachey's head, but Dan he held up his hand, and Peachey came along bent double. He never let go of Dan's hand, and he never let go of Dan's head. They gave it to him as a present in the temple, to remind him not to come again, and though the crown was pure gold, and Peachey was starving, never would Peachey sell the same. You knew Dravot, Sir! You knew Right Worshipful Brother Dravot! Look at him now!"

He fumbled in the mass of rags round his bent waist; brought out a black horsehair bag embroidered with silver thread; and shook therefrom on to my table—the dried, withered head of Daniel Dravot! The morning sun that had long been paling the lamps struck the red beard and blind sunken eyes; struck, too, a heavy circlet of gold studded with raw turquoises, that Carnehan placed tenderly on the battered temples.

"You behold now," said Carnehan, "the Emperor in his habit as he lived—the King of Kafiristan with his crown upon his head. Poor old Daniel that was a monarch once!"

I shuddered, for, in spite of defacements manifold, I recognized the head of the man of Marwar Junction. Carnehan rose to go. I attempted to stop him. He was not fit to walk abroad. "Let me take away the whiskey and give me a little money," he gasped. "I was a King once. I'll go to the Deputy Commissioner and ask to set in the Poorhouse till I get my health. No, thank you, I can't wait till you get a carriage for me. I've urgent private affairs—in the south—at Marwar."

He shambled out of the office and departed in the direction of the Deputy Commissioner's house. That day at noon I had occasion to go down the blinding hot Mall, and I saw a crooked man crawling along the white dust of the roadside, his hat in his hand, quavering dolorously after the fashion of street-singers at Home. There was not a soul in sight and he was out of all possible earshot of the houses. And he sang through his nose, turning his head from right to left:

> *The Son of Man goes forth to war,*
> *A golden crown to gain;*
> *His blood-red banner streams afar—*
> *Who follows in his train?*

I waited to hear no more, but put the poor wretch into my carriage and drove him off to the nearest missionary for eventual transfer to the Asylum. He repeated the hymn twice while he was with me whom he did not in the least recognize, and I left him singing it to the missionary.

Two days later I inquired after his welfare of the Superintendent of the Asylum.

"He was admitted suffering from sun-stroke. He died early yesterday morning," said the Superintendent. "Is it true that he was half an hour bareheaded in the sun at midday?"

"Yes," said I, "but do you happen to know if he had anything upon him by any chance when he died!"

"Not to my knowledge," said the Superintendent.

And there the matter rests.

40

Red Hanrahan

BY WILLIAM BUTLER YEATS

HANRAHAN, the hedge school-master, a tall, strong, red-haired young man, came into the barn where some of the men of the village were sitting on Samhain Eve. It had been a dwelling-house, and when the man that owned it had built a better one, he had put the two rooms together, and kept it for a place to store one thing or another. There was a fire on the old hearth, and there were dip candles stuck in bottles, and there was a black quart bottle upon some boards that had been put across two barrels to make a table. Most of the men were sitting beside the fire, and one of them was singing a long wandering song, about a Munster man and a Connaught man that were quarrelling about their two provinces.

Hanrahan went to the man of the house and said, "I got your message"; but when he had said that, he stopped, for an old mountainy man that had a shirt and trousers of unbleached flannel, and that was sitting by himself near the door, was looking at him, and moving an old pack of cards about in his hands and muttering. "Don't mind him," said the man of the house; "he is only some stranger came in awhile ago, and we bade him welcome, it being Samhain night, but I think he is not in his right wits. Listen to him now and you will hear what he is saying."

They listened then, and they could hear the old man muttering to himself as he turned the cards, "Spades and Diamonds, Courage and Power; Clubs and Hearts, Knowledge and Pleasure."

"That is the kind of talk he has been going on with for the last hour," said the man of the house, and Hanrahan turned his eyes from the old man as if he did not like to be looking at him.

"I got your message," Hanrahan said then; " 'he is in the barn with his three first cousins from Gilchreist,' the messenger said, 'and there are some of the neighbours with them.'"

"It is my cousin over there is wanting to see you," said the man of the house, and he called over a young frieze-coated man, who was listening to the song, and said, "This is Red Hanrahan you have the message for."

"It is a kind message, indeed," said the young man, "for it comes from your sweetheart, Mary Lavelle."

"How would you get a message from her, and what do you know of her?"

"I don't know her, indeed, but I was in Loughrea yesterday, and a neighbour of hers that had some dealings with me was saying that she bade him send you word, if he met any one from this side in the market, that her mother has died from her, and if you have a mind yet to join with herself, she is willing to keep her word to you."

"I will go to her indeed," said Hanrahan.

"And she bade you make no delay, for if she has not a man in the house before the month is out, it is likely the little bit of land will be given to another."

When Hanrahan heard that, he rose up from the bench he had sat down on. "I will make no delay indeed," he said, "there is a full moon, and if I get as far as Gilchreist to-night, I will reach to her before the setting of the sun to-morrow."

When the others heard that, they began to laugh at him for being in such haste to go to his sweetheart, and one asked him if he would leave his school in the old lime-kiln, where he was giving the children such good learning. But he said the children would be glad enough in the morning to find the place empty, and no one to keep them at their task; and as for his school he could set it up again in any place, having as he had his little inkpot hanging from his neck by a chain, and his big Virgil and his primer in the skirt of his coat.

Some of them asked him to drink a glass before he went, and a young man caught hold of his coat, and said he must not leave them without singing the song he had made in praise of Venus and of Mary Lavelle. He drank a glass of whisky, but he said he would not stop but would set out on his journey.

"There's time enough, Red Hanrahan," said the man of the house. "It will be time enough for you to give up sport when you are after your marriage, and it might be a long time before we will see you again."

"I will not stop," said Hanrahan; "my mind would be on the roads all the time, bringing me to the woman that sent for me, and she lonesome and watching till I come."

Some of the others came about him, pressing him that had been such a pleasant comrade, so full of songs and every kind of trick and fun, not to leave them till the night would be over, but he refused them all, and shook them off, and went to the door. But as he put his foot over the threshold, the strange old man stood up and put his hand that was thin and withered like a bird's claw on Hanrahan's hand, and said: "It is not Hanrahan, the learned man and the great songmaker, that should go out from a gathering like this, on a Samhain night. And stop here, now," he said, "and play a hand with me; and here is an old pack of cards has done its work many a night before this, and old as it is, there has been much of the riches of the world lost and won over it."

One of the young men said, "It isn't much of the riches of the world has stopped with yourself, old man," and he looked at the old man's bare feet, and they all laughed. But Hanrahan did not laugh, but he sat down very quietly, without a word. Then one of them said, "So you will stop with us after all, Hanrahan"; and the old man said: "He will stop indeed, did you not hear me asking him?"

They all looked at the old man then as if wondering where he came from. "It is far I am come," he said, "through France I have come, and through Spain, and by Lough Greine of the hidden mouth, and none has refused me anything." And then he was silent and nobody liked to question him, and they began to play. There were six men at the boards playing, and the others were looking on behind. They played two or three games for nothing, and then the old man took a fourpenny bit, worn very thin and smooth, out from his pocket, and he called to the rest to put something on the game. Then they all put down something on the boards, and little as it was it looked much, from the way it was shoved from one to another, first one man winning it and then his neighbour. And sometimes the luck would go against a man and he would have nothing left, and then one or another would lend him something, and he would pay it again out of his winnings, for neither good nor bad luck stopped long with any one.

And once Hanrahan said as a man would say in a dream, "It is time for me to be going the road"; but just then a good card came to him, and he played it out, and all the money began to come to him. And once he thought of Mary Lavelle, and he sighed; and that time his luck went from him, and he forgot her again.

But at last the luck went to the old man and it stayed with him, and all they had flowed into him, and he began to laugh little laughs to himself, and to sing over and over to himself, "Spades and Diamonds, Courage and Power," and so on, as if it was a verse of a song.

And after a while any one looking at the men, and seeing the way their bodies were rocking to and fro, and the way they kept their eyes on the old man's hands, would think they had drink taken, or that the whole store they had in the world was put on the cards; but that was not so, for the quart bottle had not been disturbed since the game began, and was nearly full yet, and all that was on the game was a few sixpenny bits and shillings, and maybe a handful of coppers.

"You are good men to win and good men to lose," said the old man, "you have play in your hearts." He began then to shuffle the cards and to mix them, very quick and fast, till at last they could not see them to be cards at all, but you would think him to be making rings of fire in the air, as little lads would make them with whirling a lighted stick; and after that it seemed to them that all the room was dark, and they could see nothing but his hands and the cards.

And all in a minute a hare made a leap out from between his hands, and whether it was one of the cards that took that shape, or whether it was made out of nothing in the palms of his hands, nobody knew, but there it was running on the floor of the barn, as quick as any hare that ever lived.

Some looked at the hare, but more kept their eyes on the old man, and while they were looking at him a hound made a leap out between his hands, the same way as the hare did, and after that another hound and another, till there was a whole pack of them following the hare round and round the barn.

The players were all standing up now, with their backs to the boards, shrinking from the hounds, and nearly deafened with the noise of their yelping, but as quick as the hounds were they could not overtake the hare, but it went round, till at the last it seemed as if a blast of wind burst open the barn door, and the hare doubled and made a leap over the boards where the men had been playing, and went out of the door and away through the night, and the hounds over the boards and through the door after it.

Then the old man called out, "Follow the hounds, follow the hounds, and it is a great hunt you will see to-night," and he went out after them. But used as the men were to go hunting after hares, and ready as they were for any sport, they were in dread to go out into the night, and it was only Hanrahan that rose up and that said, "I will follow, I will follow on."

"You had best stop here, Hanrahan," the young man that was nearest him said, "for you might be going into some great danger." But Hanrahan said, "I will see fair play, I will see fair play," and he went stumbling out of the door like a man in a dream, and the door shut after him as he went.

He thought he saw the old man in front of him, but it was only his own shadow that the full moon cast on the road before him, but he could hear the hounds crying after the hare over the wide green fields of Granagh, and he followed them very fast for there was nothing to stop him; and after a while he came to smaller fields that had little walls of loose stones around them, and he threw the stones down as he crossed them, and did not wait to put them up again; and he passed by the place where the river goes under ground at Ballylee, and he could hear the hounds going before him up towards the head of the river. Soon he found it harder to run, for it was uphill he was going, and clouds came over the moon, and it was hard for him to see his way, and once he left the path to take a short cut, but his foot slipped into bog-hole and he had to come back to it. And how long he was going he did not know, or what way he went, but at last he was up the bare mountain, with nothing but the rough heather about him, and he could neither hear the hounds nor any other thing. But their cry began to come to him again, at first far off and then very near, and when it came quite close to him, it went up all of a sudden into the air, and there was the sound of hunting over his head; then it went away northward till he could hear nothing at all. "That's not fair," he said, "that's not fair." And he could walk no longer, but sat down on the heather where he was, in the heart of Slieve Echtge, for all the strength had gone from him, with the dint of the long journey he had made.

And after a while he took notice that there was a door close to him, and a light coming from it, and he wondered that being so close to him he had not seen it before. And he rose up, and tired as he was he went in at the door, and although it was night time outside, it was daylight he found within. And presently he met with an old man that had been gathering summer thyme and yellow flag-flowers, and it seemed as if all the sweet smells of the summer were with them. And the old man said: "It is a long time you have been coming to us, Hanrahan the learned man and the great songmaker."

And with that he brought him into a very big shining house, and every grand thing Hanrahan had ever heard of, and every colour he had ever seen, were in it. There was a high place at the end of the house, and on it there was sitting in a high chair a woman, the most beautiful the world ever saw, having a long pale face and flowers about it, but she had the tired look of one that had been long waiting. And there was sitting on the step below her chair four grey old women, and the one of them was holding a great cauldron in her lap; and another a great stone on her knees, and heavy as it was it seemed light to her; and another of them had a very long spear that was made of pointed wood; and the last of them had a sword that was without a scabbard.

Hanrahan stood looking at them for a long time, but none of them spoke any word to him or looked at him at all. And he had it in his mind to ask who that woman in the chair was, that was like a queen, and what she was waiting for; but ready as he was with his tongue and afraid of no person, he was in dread now to speak to so beautiful a woman, and in so grand a place. And then he thought to ask what were the four things the four grey old women were holding like great treasures, but he could not think of the right words to bring out.

Then the first of the old women rose up, holding the cauldron between her two hands, and she said "Pleasure," and Hanrahan said no word. Then the second old woman rose up with the stone in her hands, and she said "Power"; and the third old woman rose up with the spear in her hand, and she said "Courage"; and the last of the old women rose up having the sword in her hands, and she said "Knowledge." And every one, after she had spoken, waited as if for Hanrahan to question her, but he said nothing at all. And then the four old women went out of the door, bringing their four treasures with them, and as they went out one of them said, "He has no wish for us"; and another said, "He is weak, he is weak"; and another said, "He is afraid"; and the last said, "His wits are gone from him." And then they all said, "Echtge, daughter of the Silver Hand, must stay in her sleep. It is a pity, it is a great pity."

And then the woman that was like a queen gave a very sad sigh, and it seemed to Hanrahan as if the sigh had the sound in it of hidden streams; and if the place he was in had been ten times grander and more shining than it was, he could not have hindered sleep from coming on him; and he staggered like a drunken man and lay down there and then.

When Hanrahan awoke, the sun was shining on his face, but there was white frost on the grass around him, and there was ice on the edge of the stream he was lying by, and that goes running on through Dairecaol and Druim-da-rod. He knew by the shape of the hills and by the shining of Lough Greine in the distance that he was upon one of the hills of Slieve Echtge, but he was not sure how he came there; for all that had happened in the barn had gone from him, and all of his journey but the soreness of his feet and the stiffness in his bones.

It was a year after that, there were men of the village of Cappaghtagle sitting by the fire in a house on the roadside, and Red Hanrahan that was now very thin and worn and his hair very long and wild, came to the half-door and asked leave to come in and rest himself; and they bid him welcome because it was Samhain night. He sat down with them, and they gave him a glass of whisky out of a quart bottle; and they saw the little inkpot hanging about his neck, and knew he was a scholar, and asked for stories about the Greeks.

He took the Virgil out of the big pocket of his coat, but the cover was very black and swollen with the wet, and the page when he opened it was very yellow, but that was no great matter, for he looked at it like a man that had never learned to read. Some young man that was there began to laugh at him then, and to ask why did he carry so heavy a book with him when he was not able to read it.

It vexed Hanrahan to hear that, and he put the Virgil back in his pocket and asked if they had a pack of cards among them, for cards were better than books. When they brought out the cards he took them and began to shuffle them, and while he was shuffling them something seemed to come into his mind, and he put his hand to his face like one that is trying to remember, and he said: "Was I ever here before, or where was I on a night like this?" and then of a sudden he stood up and let the cards fall to the floor, and he said, "Who was it brought me a message from Mary Lavelle?"

"We never saw you before now, and we never heard of Mary Lavelle," said the man of the house. "And who is she," he said, "and what is it you are talking about?"

"It was this night a year ago, I was in a barn, and there were men playing cards, and there was money on the table, they were pushing it from one to another here and there—and I got a message, and I was going out of the door to look for my sweetheart that wanted me, Mary Lavelle." And then Hanrahan called out very loud: "Where have I been since then? Where was I for the whole year?"

"It is hard to say where you might have been in that time," said the oldest of the men, "or what part of the world you may have travelled; and it is like enough you have the dust of many roads on your feet; for there are many go wandering and forgetting like that," he said, "when once they have been given the touch."

"That is true," said another of the men. "I knew a woman went wandering like that through the length of seven years; she came back after, and she told her friends she had often been glad enough to eat the food that was put in the pig's trough. And it is best for you to go to the priest now," he said, "and let him take off you what ever may have been put upon you."

"It is to my sweetheart I will go, to Mary Lavelle," said Hanrahan; "it is too long I have delayed, how do I know what might have happened her in the length of a year?"

He was going out of the door then, but they all told him it was best for him to stop the night, and to get strength for the journey; and indeed he wanted that, for he was very weak, and when they gave him food he ate it like a man that had never seen food before, and one of them said, "He is eating as if he had trodden on the hungry grass." It was in the white light of the morning he set out, and the time seemed long to him till he could get to Mary Lavelle's house. But when he came to it, he found the door broken, and the thatch dropping from the roof, and no living person to be seen. And when he asked the neighbours what had happened her, all they could say was that she had been put out of the house, and had married some labouring man, and they had gone looking for work to London or Liverpool or some big place. And whether she found a worse place or a better he never knew, but anyway he never met with her or with news of her again.

41

The Country of the Blind

BY H. G. WELLS

THREE hundred miles and more from Chimborazo, one hundred from the snows of Cotopaxi, in the wildest wastes of Ecuador's Andes, there lies that mysterious mountain valley, cut off from the world of men, the Country of the Blind. Long years ago that valley lay so far open to the world that men might come at last throught frightful gorges and over an icy pass into its equable meadows; and thither indeed men came, a family or so of Peruvian half-breeds fleeing from the lust and tyranny of an evil Spanish ruler. Then came the stupendous outbreak of Mindobamba, when it was night in Quito for seventeen days, and the water was boiling at Yaguachi and all the fish floating dying even as far as Guayaquil; everywhere along the Pacific slopes there were landslips and swift thawings and sudden floods, and one whole side of the old Arauca crest slipped and came down in thunder, and cut off the Country of the Blind for ever from the exploring feet of men. But one of these early settlers had chanced to be on the hither side of the gorges when the world had so terribly shaken itself, and he perforce had to forget his wife and his child and all the friends and possessions he had left up there, and start life over again in the lower world. He started it again but ill, blindness overtook him, and he died of punishment in the mines; but the story he told begot a legend that lingers along the length of the Cordilleras of the Andes to this day.

He told of his reason for venturing back from that fastness, into which he had first been carried lashed to a llama, beside a vast bale of gear, when he was a child. The valley, he said, had in it all that the heart of man could desire—sweet water, pasture, and even climate, slopes of rich brown soil with tangles of a shrub that bore an excellent fruit, and on one side great hanging forests of pine that held the avalanches high. Far overhead, on three sides, vast cliffs of grey-green rock were capped by cliffs of ice; but the glacier stream came not to them but flowed away by the farther slopes, and only now and then huge ice masses fell on the valley side. In this valley it neither rained nor snowed, but the abundant springs gave a rich green pasture, that irrigation would spread over all the valley space. The settlers did well indeed there. Their beasts did well and multiplied, and but one thing marred their happiness. Yet it was enough to mar it greatly. A strange disease had come upon them, and had made all the children born to them there—and indeed, several older children also—blind. It was to seek some charm or antidote against this plague of blindness that he had with fatigue and danger and difficulty returned down the gorge. In those days, in such cases, men did not think of germs and infections but of sins; and it seemed to him that the reason of this affliction must lie in the negligence of these priestless immigrants to set up a shrine so soon as they entered the valley. He wanted a shrine—a handsome, cheap, effectual shrine—to be erected in the valley; he wanted relics and such-like potent things of faith, blessed objects and mysterious medals and prayers. In his wallet he had a bar of native silver for which he would not account; he insisted there was none in the valley with something of the insistence of an inexpert liar. They had all clubbed their money and ornaments together, having little need for such treasure up there, he said, to buy them holy help against their ill. I figure this dim-eyed young mountaineer, sunburnt, gaunt, and anxious, hat-brim clutched feverishly, a man all unused to the ways of the lower world, telling this story to some keen-eyed, attentive priest before the great convulsion; I can picture him presently seeking to return with pious and infallible remedies against that trouble, and the infinite dismay with which he must have faced the tumbled vastness where the gorge had once come out. But the rest of his story of mischances is lost to me, save that I know of his evil death after several years. Poor stray from that remoteness! The stream that had once made the gorge now bursts from the mouth of a rocky cave, and the legend his poor, ill-told story set going developed into the legend of a race of blind men somewhere "over there" one may still hear to-day.

And amidst the little population of that now isolated and forgotten valley the disease ran its course. The old became groping and purblind, the young saw but dimly, and the children that were born to them saw never at all. But life was very easy in that snow-rimmed basin, lost to all the world, with neither thorns nor briars, with no evil insects nor any beasts save the gentle breed of llamas they had lugged and thrust and followed up the beds of the shrunken rivers in the gorges up which they had come. The seeing had become purblind so gradually that they scarcely noted their loss. They guided the sightless youngsters hither and thither until they knew the whole valley marvellously, and when at last sight died out among them the race lived on. They had even time to adapt themselves to the blind control of fire, which they made carefully in stoves of stone. They were a simple strain of people at the first, unlettered, only slightly touched with the Spanish civilisation, but with something of a tradition of the arts of old Peru and of its lost philosophy. Generation followed generation. They forgot many things; they devised many things. Their tradition of the greater world they came from became mythical in colour and uncertain. In all things save sight they were strong and able; and presently the chance of birth and heredity sent one who had an original mind and who could talk and persuade among them, and then afterwards another. These two passed, leaving their effects, and the little community grew in numbers and in understanding, and met and settled social and economic problems that arose. Generation followed generation. Generation followed generation. There came a time when a child was born who was fifteen generations from that ancestor who went out of the valley with a bar of silver to seek God's aid, and who never returned. Thereabouts it chanced that a man came into this community from the outer world. And this is the story of that man.

He was a mountaineer from the country near Quito, a man who had been down to the sea and had seen the world, a reader of books in an original way, an acute and enterprising man, and he was taken on by a party of Englishmen who had come out to Ecuador to climb mountains, to replace one of their three Swiss guides who had fallen ill. He climbed here and he climbed there, and then came the attempt on Parascotopetl, the Matterhorn of the Andes, in which he was lost to the outer world. The story of the accident has been written a dozen times. Pointer's narrative is the best. He tells how the party worked their difficult and almost vertical way up to the very foot of the last and greatest precipice, and how they built a night shelter amidst the snow upon a little shelf of rock, and, with a touch of real dramatic power, how presently they found Nunez had gone from them. They shouted, and there was no reply; shouted and whistled, and for the rest of that night they slept no more.

As the morning broke they saw the traces of his fall. It seems impossible he could have uttered a sound. He had slipped eastward towards the unknown side of the mountain; far below he had struck a steep slope of snow, and ploughed his way down it in the midst of a snow avalanche. His track went straight to the edge of a frightful precipice, and beyond that everything was hidden. Far, far below, and hazy with distance, they could see trees rising out of a narrow, shut-in valley—the lost Country of the Blind. But they did not know it was the lost Country of the Blind, nor distinguish it in any way from any other narrow streak of upland valley. Unnerved by this disaster, they abandoned their attempt in the afternoon, and Pointer was called away to the war before he could make another attack. To this day Parascotopetl lifts an unconquered crest, and Pointer's shelter crumbles unvisited amidst the snows.

And the man who fell survived.

At the end of the slope he fell a thousand feet, and came down in the midst of a cloud of snow upon a snow slope even steeper than the one above. Down this he was whirled, stunned and insensible, but without a bone broken in his body; and then at last came to gentler slopes, and at last rolled out and lay still, buried amidst a softening heap of the white masses that had accompanied and saved him. He came to himself with a dim fancy that he was ill in bed; then realised his position with a mountaineer's intelligence, and worked himself loose and, after a rest or so, out until he saw the stars. He rested flat upon his chest for a space, wondering where he was and what had happened to him. He explored his limbs, and discovered that several of his buttons were gone and his coat turned over his head. His knife had gone from his pocket and his hat was lost, though he had tied it under his chin. He recalled that he had been lookng for loose stones to raise his piece of the shelter wall. His ice-axe had disappeared.

He decided he must have fallen, and looked up to see, exaggerated by the ghastly light of the rising moon, the tremendous flight he had taken. For a while he lay, gazing blankly at that vast pale cliff towering above, rising moment by moment out of a subsiding tide of darkness. Its phantasmal, mysterious beauty held him for a space, and then he was seized with a paroxysm of sobbing laughter. . . .

After a great interval of time he became aware that he was near the lower edge of the snow. Below, down what was now a moonlit and practicable slope, he saw the dark and broken appearance of rock-strewn turf. He struggled to his feet, aching in every joint and limb, got down painfully from the heaped loose snow about him, went downward until he was on the turf, and there dropped rather than lay beside a boulder, drank deep from the flask in his inner pocket, and instantly fell asleep.

He was awakened by the singing of birds in the trees far below.

He sat up and perceived he was on a little alp at the foot of a vast precipice, that was grooved by the gully down which he and his snow had come. Over against him another wall of rock reared itself against the sky. The gorge between these precipices ran east and west and was full of the morning sunlight, which lit to the westward the mass of fallen mountain that closed the descending gorge. Below him it seemed there was a precipice equally steep, but behind the snow in the gully he found a sort of chimney-cleft dripping with snow-water down which a desperate man might venture. He found it easier than it seemed, and came at last to another desolate alp, and then after a rock climb of no particular difficulty to a steep slope of trees. He took his bearings and turned his face up the gorge, for he saw it opened out above upon green meadows, among which he now glimpsed quite distinctly a cluster of stone huts of unfamiliar fashion. At times his progress was like clambering along the face of a wall, and after a time the rising sun ceased to strike along the gorge, the voices of the singing birds died away, and the air grew cold and dark about him. But the distant valley with its houses was all the brighter for that. He came presently to talus, and among the rocks he noted—for he was an observant man—an unfamiliar fern that seemed to clutch out of the crevices with intense green hands. He picked a frond or so and gnawed its stalk and found it helpful.

About midday he came at last out of the throat of the gorge into the plain and the sunlight. He was stiff and weary; he sat down in the shadow of a rock, filled up his flask with water from a spring and drank it down, and remained for a time resting before he went on to the houses.

They were very strange to his eyes, and indeed the whole aspect of that valley became, as he regarded it, queerer and more unfamiliar. The greater part of its surface was lush green meadow, starred with many beautiful flowers, irrigated with extraordinary care, and bearing evidence of systematic cropping piece by piece. High up and ringing the valley about was a wall, and what appeared to be a circumferential water-channel, from which the little trickles of water that fed the meadow plants came, and on the higher slopes above this flocks of llamas cropped the scanty herbage. Sheds, apparently shelters or feeding-places for the llamas, stood against the boundary wall here and there. The irrigation streams ran together into a main channel down the centre of the valley, and this was enclosed on either side by a wall breast high. This gave a singularly urban quality to this secluded place, a quality that was greatly enhanced by the fact that a number of paths paved with black and white stones, and each with a curious little kerb at the side, ran hither and thither in an orderly manner. The houses of the central village were quite unlike the casual and higgledy-piggledy agglomeration of the mountain villages he knew; they stood in a continuous row on either side of a central street of astonishing cleanness; here and there their parti-coloured façade was pierced by a door, and not a solitary window broke their even frontage. They were parti-coloured with extraordinary irregularity; smeared with a sort of plaster that was sometimes grey, sometimes drab, sometimes slate-coloured or dark brown; and it was the sight of this wild plastering first brought the word "blind" into the thoughts of the explorer. "The good man who did that," he thought, "must have been as blind as a bat."

He descended a steep place, and so came to the wall and channel that ran about the valley, near where the latter spouted out its surplus contents into the deeps of the gorge in a thin and wavering thread of cascade. He could now see a number of men and women resting on piled heaps of grass, as if taking a siesta, in the remoter part of the meadow, and nearer the village a number of recumbent children, and then nearer at hand three men carrying pails on yokes along a little path that ran from the encircling wall towards the houses. These latter were clad in garments of llama cloth and boots and belts of leather, and they wore caps of cloth with back and ear flaps. They followed one another in single file, walking slowly and yawning as they walked, like men who have been up all night. There was something so reassuringly prosperous and respectable in their bearing that after a moment's hesitation Nunez stood forward as conspicuously as possible upon his rock, and gave vent to a mighty shout that echoed round the valley.

The three men stopped, and moved their heads as though they were looking about them. They turned their faces this way and that, and Nunez gesticulated with freedom. But they did not appear to see him for all his gestures, and after a time, directing themselves towards the mountains far away to the right, they shouted as if in answer. Nunez bawled again, and then once more, and as he gestured ineffectually the word "blind" came up to the top of his thoughts. "The fools must be blind," he said.

When at last, after much shouting and wrath, Nunez crossed the stream by a little bridge, came through a gate in the wall, and approached them, he was sure that they were blind. He was sure that this was the Country of the Blind of which the legends told. Conviction had sprung upon him, and a sense of great and rather enviable adventure. The three stood side by side, not looking at him, but with their ears directed towards him, judging him by his unfamiliar steps. They stood close together like men a little afraid, and he could see their eyelids closed and sunken, as though the very balls beneath had shrunk away. There was an expression near awe on their faces.

"A man," one said, in hardly recognisable Spanish—"a man it is—a man or a spirit—coming down from the rocks."

But Nunez advanced with the confident steps of a youth who enters upon life. All the old stories of the lost valley and the Country of the Blind had come back to his mind, and through his thoughts ran this old proverb, as if it were a refrain—

"In the Country of the Blind the One-eyed Man is King."

"In the Country of the Blind the One-eyed Man is King."

And very civilly he gave them greeting. He talked to them and used his eyes.

"Where does he come from, brother Pedro?" asked one.

"Down out of the rocks."

"Over the mountains I come," said Nunez, "out of the country beyond there—where men can see. From near Bogota, where there are a hundred thousands of people, and where the city passes out of sight."

"Sight?" muttered Pedro. "Sight?"

"He comes," said the second blind man, "out of the rocks."

The cloth of their coats Nunez saw was curiously fashioned, each with a different sort of stitching.

They startled him by a simultaneous movement towards him, each with a hand outstretched. He stepped back from the advance of these spread fingers.

"Come hither," said the third blind man, following his motion and clutching him neatly.

And they held Nunez and felt him over, saying no word further until they had done so.

"Carefully," he cried, with a finger in his eye, and found they thought that organ, with its fluttering lids, a queer thing in him. They went over it again.

"A strange creature, Correa," said the one called Pedro. "Feel the coarseness of his hair. Like a llama's hair."

"Rough he is as the rocks that begot him," said Correa, investigating Nunez's unshaven chin with a soft and slightly moist hand. "Perhaps he will grow finer." Nunez struggled a little under their examination, but they gripped him firm.

"Carefully," he said again.

"He speaks," said the third man. "Certainly he is a man."

"Ugh!" said Pedro, at the roughness of his coat.

"And you have come into the world?" asked Pedro.

"Out of the world. Over mountains and glaciers; right over above there, half-way to the sun. Out of the great big world that goes down, twelve days' journey to the sea."

They scarcely seemed to heed him. "Our fathers have told us men may be made by the forces of Nature," said Correa. "It is the warmth of things and moisture, and rottenness—rottenness."

"Let us lead him to the elders," said Pedro.

"Shout first," said Correa, "lest the children be afraid. This is a marvellous occasion."

So they shouted, and Pedro went first and took Nunez by the hand to lead him to the houses.

He drew his hand away. "I can see," he said.

"See?" said Correa.

"Yes, see," said Nunez, turning towards him, and stumbled against Pedro's pail.

"His senses are still imperfect," said the third blind man. "He stumbles, and talks unmeaning words. Lead him by the hand."

"As you will," said Nunez, and was led along, laughing.

It seemed they knew nothing of sight.

Well, all in good time, he would teach them.

He heard people shouting, and saw a number of figures gathering together in the middle roadway of the village.

He found it tax his nerve and patience more than he had anticipated, that first encounter with the population of the Country of the Blind. The place seemed larger as he drew near to it, and the smeared plasterings queerer, and a crowd of children and men and women (the women and girls, he was pleased to note, had some of them quite sweet faces, for all that their eyes were shut and sunken) came about him, holding on to him, touching him with soft, sensitive hands, smelling at him, and listening at every word he spoke. Some of the maidens and children, however, kept aloof as if afraid, and indeed his voice seemed coarse and rude beside their softer notes. They mobbed him. His three guides kept close to him with an effect of proprietorship, and said again and again, "A wild man out of the rocks."

"Bogota," he said. "Bogota. Over the mountain crests."

"A wild man—using wild words," said Pedro. "Did you hear that— *Bogota?* His mind is hardly formed yet. He has only the beginnings of speech."

A little boy nipped his hand. "Bogota!" he said mockingly.

"Ay! A city to your village. I come from the great world—where men have eyes and see."

"His name's Bogota," they said.

"He stumbled," said Correa, "stumbled twice as we came hither."

"Bring him to the elders."

And they thrust him suddenly through a doorway into a room as black as pitch, save at the end there faintly glowed a fire. The crowd closed in behind him and shut out all but the faintest glimmer of day, and before he could arrest himself he had fallen headlong over the feet of a seated man. His arm, outflung, struck the face of someone else as he went down; he felt the soft impact of features and heard a cry of anger, and for a moment he struggled against a number of hands that clutched him. It was a one-sided fight. An inkling of the situation came to him, and he lay quiet.

"I fell down," he said; "I couldn't see in this pitchy darkness."

There was a pause as if the unseen persons about him tried to understand his words. Then the voice of Correa said: "He is but newly formed. He stumbles as he walks and mingles words that mean nothing with his speech."

Others also said things about him that he heard or understood imperfectly.

"May I sit up?" he asked, in a pause. "I will not struggle against you again."

They consulted and let him rise.

The voice of an older man began to question him, and Nunez found himself trying to explain the great world out of which he had fallen, and the sky and mountains and sight and such-like marvels, to these elders who sat in darkness in the Country of the Blind. And they would believe and understand nothing whatever he told them, a thing quite outside his expectation. They would not even understand many of his words. For fourteen generations these people had been blind and cut off from all the seeing world; the names for all the things of sight had faded and changed; the story of the outer world was faded and changed to a child's story; and they had ceased to concern themselves with anything beyond the rocky slopes above their circling wall. Blind men of genius had arisen among them and questioned the shreds of belief and tradition they had brought with them from their seeing days, and had dismissed all these things as idle fancies, and replaced them with new and saner explanations. Much of their imagination had shrivelled with their eyes, and they had made for themselves new imaginations with their ever more sensitive ears and finger-tips. Slowly Nunez realised this; that his expectation of wonder and reverence at his origin and his gifts was not to be borne out; and after his poor attempt to explain sight to them had been set aside as the confused version of a new-made being describing the marvels of his incoherent sensations, he subsided, a little dashed, into listening to their instruction. And the eldest of the blind men explained to him life and philosophy and religion, how that the world (meaning their valley) had been first an empty hollow in the rocks, and then had come, first, inanimate things without the gift of touch, and llamas and a few other creatures that had little sense, and then men, and at last angels, whom one could hear singing and making fluttering sounds, but whom no one could touch at all, which puzzled Nunez greatly until he thought of the birds.

He went on to tell Nunez how this time had been divided into the warm and the cold, which are the blind equivalents of day and night, and how it was good to sleep in the warm and work during the cold, so that now, but for his advent, the whole town of the blind would have been asleep. He said Nunez must have been specially created to learn and serve the wisdom they had acquired, and for that all his mental incoherency and stumbling behaviour he must have courage, and do his best to learn, and at that all the people in the doorway murmured encouragingly. He said the night—for the blind call their day night—was now far gone, and it behooved every one to go back to sleep. He asked Nunez if he knew how to sleep, and Nunez said he did, but that before sleep he wanted food.

They brought him food—llama's milk in a bowl, and rough salted bread—and led him into a lonely place to eat out of their hearing, and afterwards to slumber until the chill of the mountain evening roused them to begin their day again. But Nunez slumbered not at all.

Instead, he sat up in the place where they had left him, resting his limbs and turning the unanticipated circumstances of his arrival over and over in his mind.

Every now and then he laughed, sometimes with amusement, and sometimes with indignation.

"Unformed mind!" he said. "Got no senses yet! They little know they've been insulting their heaven-sent king and master. I see I must bring them to reason. Let me think—let me think."

He was still thinking when the sun set.

Nunez had an eye for all beautiful things, and it seemed to him that the glow upon the snowfields and glaciers that rose about the valley on every side was the most beautiful thing he had ever seen. His eyes went from that inaccessible glory to the village and irrigated fields, fast sinking into the twilight, and suddenly a wave of emotion took him, and he thanked God from the bottom of his heart that the power of sight had been given him.

He heard a voice calling to him from out of the village.

"Ya ho there, Bogota! Come hither!"

At that he stood up smiling. He would show these people once and for all what sight would do for a man. They would seek him, but not find him.

"You move not, Bogota," said the voice.

He laughed noiselessly, and made two stealthy steps aside from the path.

"Trample not on the grass, Bogota; that is not allowed."

Nunez had scarcely heard the sound he made himself. He stopped amazed.

The owner of the voice came running up the piebald path towards him.

He stepped back into the pathway. "Here I am," he said.

"Why did you not come when I called you?" said the blind man. "Must you be led like a child? Cannot you hear the path as you walk?"

Nunez laughed. "I can see it," he said.

"There is no such word as *see*," said the blind man, after a pause. "Cease this folly, and follow the sound of my feet."

Nunez followed, a little annoyed.

"My time will come," he said.

"You'll learn," the blind man answered. "There is much to learn in the world."

"Has no one told you, 'In the Country of the Blind the One-eyed Man is King'?"

"What is blind?" asked the blind man carelessly over his shoulder.

Four days passed, and the fifth found the King of the Blind still incognito, as a clumsy and useless stranger among his subjects.

It was, he found, much more difficult to proclaim himself than he had supposed, and in the meantime, while he meditated his *coup d'état,* he did what he was told and learned the manners and customs of the Country of the Blind. He found working and going about at night a particularly irksome thing, and he decided that that should be the first thing he would change.

They led a simple, laborious life, these people, with all the elements of virtue and happiness, as these things can be understood by men. They toiled, but not oppressively; they had food and clothing sufficient for their needs; they had days and seasons of rest; they made much of music and singing, and there was love among them, and little children.

It was marvellous with what confidence and precision they went about their ordered world. Everything, you see, had been made to fit their needs; each of the radiating paths of the valley area had a constant angle to the others, and was distinguished by a special notch upon its kerbing; all obstacles and irregularities of path or meadow had long since been cleared away; all their methods and procedure arose naturally from their special needs. Their senses had become marvellously acute; they could hear and judge the slightest gesture of a man a dozen paces away—could hear the very beating of his heart. Intonation had long replaced expression with them, and touches gesture, and their work with hoe and spade and fork was as free and confident as garden work can be. Their sense of smell was extraordinarily fine; they could distinguish individual differences as readily as a dog can, and they went about the tending of the llamas, who lived among the rocks above and came to the wall for food and shelter, with ease and confidence. It was only when at last Nunez sought to assert himself that he found how easy and confident their movements could be.

He rebelled only after he had tried persuasion.

He tried at first on several occasions to tell them of sight. "Look you here, you people," he said. "There are things you do not understand in me."

Once or twice one or two of them attended to him; they sat with faces downcast and ears turned intelligently towards him, and he did his best to tell them what it was to see. Among his hearers was a girl, with eyelids less red and sunken than the others, so that one could almost fancy she was hiding eyes, whom especially he hoped to persuade. He spoke of the beauties of sight, of watching the mountains, of the sky and the sunrise, and they heard him with amused incredulity that presently became condemnatory. They told him there were indeed no mountains at all, but that the end of the rocks where the llamas grazed was indeed the end of the world; thence sprang a cavernous roof of the universe, from which the dew and the avalanches fell; and when he maintained stoutly the world had neither end nor roof such as they supposed, they said his thoughts were wicked. So far as he could describe sky and clouds and stars to them it seemed to them a hideous void, a terrible blankness in the place of the smooth roof to things in which they believed—it was an article of faith with them that the cavern roof was exquisitely smooth to the touch. He saw that in some manner he shocked them, and gave up that aspect of the matter altogether, and tried to show them the practical value of sight. One morning he saw Pedro in the path called Seventeen and coming towards the central houses, but still too far off for hearing or scent, and he told them as much. "In a little while," he prophesied, "Pedro will be here." An old man remarked that Pedro had no business on path Seventeen, and then, as if in confirmation, that individual as he drew near turned and went transversely into Path Ten, and so back with nimble paces towards the outer wall. They mocked Nunez when Pedro did not arrive, and afterwards, when he asked Pedro questions to clear his character, Pedro denied and outfaced him, and was afterwards hostile to him.

Then he induced them to let him go a long way up the sloping meadows towards the wall with one complacent individual, and to him he promised to describe all that happened among the houses. He noted certain goings and comings, but the things that really seemed to signify to these people happened inside of or behind the windowless houses —the only things they took note of to test him by—and of these he could see or tell nothing; and it was after the failure of this attempt, and the ridicule they could not repress, that he resorted to force. He thought of seizing a spade and suddenly smiting one or two of them to earth, and so in fair combat showing the advantage of eyes. He went so far with that resolution as to seize his spade, and then he discovered a new thing about himself, and that was that it was impossible for him to hit a blind man in cold blood.

He hesitated, and found them all aware that he snatched up the spade. They stood alert, with their heads on one side, and bent ears towards him for what he would do next.

"Put that spade down," said one, and he felt a sort of helpless horror. He came near obedience.

Then he thrust one backwards against a house wall, and fled past him and out of the village.

He went athwart one of their meadows, leaving a track of trampled grass behind his feet, and presently sat down by the side of one of their ways. He felt something of the buoyancy that comes to all men in the beginning of a fight, but more perplexity. He began to realise that you cannot even fight happily with creatures who stand upon a different mental basis to yourself. Far away he saw a number of men carrying spades and sticks come out of the street of houses, and advance in a spreading line along the several paths towards him. They advanced slowly, speaking frequently to one another, and ever and again the whole cordon would halt and sniff the air and listen.

The first time they did this Nunez laughed. But afterwards he did not laugh.

One struck his trail in the meadow grass, and came stooping and feeling his way along it.

For five minutes he watched the slow extension of the cordon, and then his vague disposition to do something forthwith became frantic. He stood up, went a pace or so towards the circumferential wall, turned, and went back a little way. There they all stood in a crescent, still and listening.

He also stood still, gripping his spade very tightly in both hands. Should he charge them?

The pulse in his ears ran into the rhythm of "In the Country of the Blind the One-eyed Man is King!"

Should he charge them?

He looked back at the high and unclimbable wall behind—unclimbable because of its smooth plastering, but withal pierced with many little doors, and at the approaching line of seekers. Behind these, others were now coming out of the street of houses.

Should he charge them?

"Bogota!" called one. "Bogota! where are you?"

He gripped his spade still tighter, and advanced down the meadows towards the place of habitations, and directly he moved they converged upon him. "I'll hit them if they touch me," he swore; "by Heaven, I will. I'll hit." He called aloud, "Look here, I'm going to do what I like in this valley. Do you hear? I'm going to do what I like and go where I like!"

They were moving in upon him quickly, groping, yet moving rapidly. It was like playing blind man's buff, with everyone blindfolded except one. "Get hold of him!" cried one. He found himself in the arc of a loose curve of pursuers. He felt suddenly he must be active and resolute.

"You don't understand," he cried in a voice that was meant to be great and resolute, and which broke. "You are blind, and I can see. Leave me alone!"

"Bogota! Put down that spade, and come off the grass!"

The last order, grotesque in its urban familiarity, produced a gust of anger.

"I'll hurt you," he said, sobbing with emotion. "By Heaven, I'll hurt you. Leave me alone!"

He began to run, not knowing clearly where to run. He ran from the nearest blind man, because it was a horror to hit him. He stopped, and then made a dash to escape from their closing ranks. He made for where a gap was wide, and the men on either side, with a quick perception of the approach of his paces, rushed in on one another. He sprang forward, and then saw he must be caught, and *swish!* the spade had struck. He felt the soft thud of hand and arm, and the man was down with a yell of pain, and he was through.

Through! And then he was close to the street of houses again, and blind men, whirling spades and stakes, were running with a sort of reasoned swiftness hither and thither.

He heard steps behind him just in time, and found a tall man rushing forward and swiping at the sound of him. He lost his nerve, hurled his spade a yard wide at his antagonist, and whirled about and fled, fairly yelling as he dodged another.

He was panic-stricken. He ran furiously to and fro, dodging when there was no need to dodge, and in his anxiety to see on every side of him at once, stumbling. For a moment he was down and they heard his fall. Far away in the circumferential wall a little doorway looked like heaven, and he set off in a wild rush for it. He did not even look round at his pursuers until it was gained, and he had stumbled across the bridge, clambered a little way among the rocks, to the surprise and dismay of a young llama, who went leaping out of sight, and lay down sobbing for breath.

And so his *coup d'état* came to an end.

He stayed outside the wall of the valley of the Blind for two nights and days without food or shelter, and meditated upon the unexpected. During these meditations he repeated very frequently and always with a profounder note of derision the exploded proverb: "In the Country of the Blind the One-Eyed Man is King." He thought chiefly of ways of fighting and conquering these people, and it grew clear that for him no practicable way was possible. He had no weapons, and now it would be hard to get one.

The canker of civilisation had got to him even in Bogota, and he could not find it in himself to go down and assassinate a blind man. Of course, if he did that, he might then dictate terms on the threat of assassinating them all. But—sooner or later he must sleep! . . .

He tried also to find food among the pine trees, to be comfortable under pine boughs while the frost fell at night, and—with less confidence—to catch a llama by artifice in order to try to kill it—perhaps by hammering it with a stone—and so finally, perhaps, to eat some of it. But the llamas had a doubt of him and regarded him with distrustful brown eyes, and spat when he drew near. Fear came on him the second day and fits of shivering. Finally he crawled down to the wall of the Country of the Blind and tried to make terms. He crawled along by the stream, shouting, until two blind men came out to the gate and talked to him.

"I was mad," he said. "But I was only newly made."

They said that was better.

He told them he was wiser now, and repented of all he had done.

Then he wept without intention, for he was very weak and ill now, and they took that as a favourable sign.

They asked him if he still thought he could "see."

"No," he said. "That was folly. The word means nothing—less than nothing!"

They asked him what was overhead.

"About ten times ten the height of a man there is a roof above the world—of rock—and very, very smooth." . . . He burst again into hysterical tears. "Before you ask me any more, give me some food or I shall die."

He expected dire punishments, but these blind people were capable of toleration. They regarded his rebellion as but one more proof of his general idiocy and inferority; and after they had whipped him they appointed him to do the simplest and heaviest work they had for anyone to do, and he, seeing no other way of living, did submissively what he was told.

He was ill for some days, and they nursed him kindly. That refined his submission. But they insisted on his lying in the dark, and that was a great misery. And blind philosophers came and talked to him of the wicked levity of his mind, and reproved him so impressively for his doubts about the lid of rock that covered their cosmic casserole that he almost doubted whether indeed he was not the victim of hallucination in not seeing it overhead.

So Nunez became a citizen of the Country of the Blind, and these people ceased to be a generalised people and became individualities and familiar to him, while the world beyond the mountains became more and more remote and unreal. There was Yacob, his master, a kindly man when not annoyed; there was Pedro, Yacob's nephew; and there was Medina-saroté, who was the youngest daughter of Yacob. She was little esteemed in the world of the blind, because she had a clear-cut face, and lacked that satisfying, glossy smoothness that is the blind man's ideal of feminine beauty; but Nunez thought her beautiful at first, and presently the most beautiful thing in the whole creation. Her closed eyelids were not sunken and red after the common way of the valley, but lay as though they might open again at any moment; and she had long eyelashes, which were considered a grave disfigurement. And her voice was strong, and did not satisfy the acute hearing of the valley swains. So that she had no lover.

There came a time when Nunez thought that, could he win her, he would be resigned to live in the valley for all the rest of his days.

He watched her; he sought opportunities of doing her little services, and presently he found that she observed him. Once at a rest-day gathering they sat side by side in the dim starlight, and the music was sweet. His hand came upon hers and he dared to clasp it. Then very tenderly she returned his pressure. And one day, as they were at their meal in the darkness, he felt her hand very softly seeking him, and as it chanced the fire leaped then and he saw the tenderness of her face.

He sought to speak to her.

He went to her one day when she was sitting in the summer moonlight spinning. The light made her a thing of silver and mystery. He sat down at her feet and told her he loved her, and told her how beautiful she seemed to him. He had a lover's voice, he spoke with a tender reverence that came near to awe, and she had never before been touched by adoration. She made him no definite answer, but it was clear his words pleased her.

After that he talked to her whenever he could make an opportunity. The valley became the world for him, and the world beyond the mountains where men lived in sunlight seemed no more than a fairy tale he would some day pour into her ears. Very tentatively and timidly he spoke to her of sight.

Sight seemed to her the most poetical of fancies, and she listened to his description of the stars and the mountains and her own sweet white-lit beauty as though it was a guilty indulgence. She did not believe, she could only half understand, but she was mysteriously delighted, and it seemed to him that she completely understood.

His love lost its awe and took courage. Presently he was for demanding her of Yacob and the elders in marriage, but she became fearful and delayed. And it was one of her elder sisters who first told Yacob that Medina-saroté and Nunez were in love.

There was from the first very great opposition to the marriage of Nunez and Medina-saroté; not so much because they valued her as because they held him as a being apart, an idiot, an incompetent thing below the permissible level of a man. Her sisters opposed it bitterly as bringing discredit on them all; and old Yacob, though he had formed a sort of liking for his clumsy, obedient serf, shook his head and said the thing could not be. The young men were all angry at the idea of corrupting the race, and one went so far as to revile and strike Nunez. He struck back. Then for the first time he found an advantage in seeing, even by twilight, and after that fight was over no one was disposed to raise a hand against him. But they still found his marriage impossible.

Old Yacob had a tenderness for his last little daughter, and was grieved to have her weep upon his shoulder.

"You see, my dear, he's an idiot. He has delusions; he can't do anything right."

"I know," wept Medina-saroté. "But he's better than he was. He's getting better. And he's strong, dear father, and kind—stronger and kinder than any other man in the world. And he loves me—and, father, I love him."

Old Yacob was greatly distressed to find her inconsolable, and, besides —what made it more distressing—he liked Nunez for many things. So he went and sat in the windowless council-chamber with the other elders and watched the trend of the talk, and said, at the proper time, "He's better than he was. Very likely, some day, we shall find him as sane as ourselves."

Then afterwards one of the elders, who thought deeply, had an idea. He was the great doctor among these people, their medicine-man, and he had a very philosophical and inventive mind, and the idea of curing Nunez of his peculiarities appealed to him. One day when Yacob was present he returned to the topic of Nunez.

"I have examined Bogota," he said, "and the case is clearer to me. I think very probably he might be cured."

"That is what I have always hoped," said old Yacob.

"His brain is affected," said the blind doctor.

The elders murmured assent.

"Now, *what* affects it?"

"Ah!" said old Yacob.

"*This*," said the doctor, answering his own question. "Those queer things that are called the eyes, and which exist to make an agreeable soft depression in the face, are diseased, in the case of Bogota, in such a way as to affect his brain. They are greatly distended, he has eyelashes, and his eyelids move, and consequently his brain is in a state of constant irritation and distraction."

"Yes?" said old Yacob. "Yes?"

"And I think I may say with reasonable certainty that, in order to cure him completely, all that we need do is a simple and easy surgical operation—namely, to remove these irritant bodies."

"And then he will be sane?"

"Then he will be perfectly sane, and a quite admirable citizen."

"Thank Heaven for science!" said old Yacob, and went forth at once to tell Nunez of his happy hopes.

But Nunez's manner of receiving the good news struck him as being cold and disappointing.

"One might think," he said, "from the tone you take, that you did not care for my daughter."

It was Medina-saroté who persuaded Nunez to face the blind surgeons.

"*You* do not want me," he said, "to lose my gift of sight?"

She shook her head.

"My world is sight."

Her head drooped lower.

"There are the beautiful things, the beautiful little things—the flowers, the lichens among the rocks, the lightness and softness on a piece of fur, the far sky with its drifting down of clouds, the sunsets and the stars. And there is *you*. For you alone it is good to have sight, to see your sweet, serene face, your kindly lips, your dear, beautiful hands folded together. . . . It is these eyes of mine you won, these eyes that hold me to you, that these idiots seek. Instead, I must touch you, hear you, and never see you again. I must come under that roof of rock and stone and darkness, that horrible roof under which your imagination stoops. . . . No; you would not have me do that?"

A disagreeable doubt had risen in him. He stopped, and left the thing a question.

"I wish," she said, "sometimes——" She paused.

"Yes?" said he, a little apprehensively.

"I wish sometimes—you would not talk like that."

"Like what?"

"I know it's pretty—it's your imagination. I love it, but *now*——"

He felt cold. "*Now?*" he said faintly.

She sat quite still.

"You mean—you think—I should be better, better perhaps——"

He was realising things very swiftly. He felt anger, indeed, anger at the dull course of fate, but also sympathy for her lack of understanding —a sympathy near akin to pity.

"Dear," he said, and he could see by her whiteness how intensely her spirit pressed against the things she could not say. He put his arms about her, he kissed her ear, and they sat for a time in silence.

"If I were to consent to this?" he said at last, in a voice that was very gentle.

She flung her arms about him, weeping wildly. "Oh, if you would," she sobbed, "if only you would!"

For a week before the operation that was to raise him from the servitude and inferiority to the level of a blind citizen, Nunez knew nothing of sleep, and all through the warm sunlit hours, while the others slumbered happily, he sat brooding or wandered aimlessly, trying to bring his mind to bear on his dilemma. He had given his answer, he had given his consent, and still he was not sure. And at last work-time was over, the sun rose in splendour over the golden crests, and his last day of vision began for him. He had a few minutes with Medina-saroté before she went apart to sleep.

"To-morrow," he said, "I shall see no more."

"Dear heart!" she answered, and pressed his hands with all her strength.

"They will hurt you but little," she said; "and you are going through this pain—you are going through it, dear lover, for *me*. . . . Dear, if a woman's heart and life can do it, I will repay you. My dearest one, my dearest with the tender voice, I will repay."

He was drenched in pity for himself and her.

He held her in his arms, and pressed his lips to hers, and looked on her sweet face for the last time. "Good-bye!" he whispered at that dear sight, "good-bye!"

And then in silence he turned away from her.

She could hear his slow retreating footsteps, and something in the rhythm of them threw her into a passion of weeping.

He had fully meant to go to a lonely place where the meadows were beautiful with white narcissus, and there remain until the hour of his sacrifice should come, but as he went he lifted up his eyes and saw the morning, the morning like an angel in golden armour, marching down the steeps. . . .

It seemed to him that before this splendour he, and this blind world in the valley, and his love, and all, were no more than a pit of sin.

He did not turn aside as he had meant to do, but went on, and passed through the wall of the circumference and out upon the rocks, and his eyes were always upon the sunlit ice and snow.

He saw their infinite beauty, and his imagination soared over them to the things beyond he was now to resign for ever.

He thought of that great free world he was parted from, the world that was his own, and he had a vision of those further slopes, distance beyond distance, with Bogota, a place of multitudinous stirring beauty, a glory by day, a luminous mystery by night, a place of palaces and fountains and statues and white houses, lying beautifully in the middle distance. He thought how for a day or so one might come down through passes, drawing ever nearer and nearer to its busy streets and ways. He thought of the river journey, day by day, from great Bogota to the still vaster world beyond, through towns and villages, forest and desert places, the rushing river day by day, until its banks receded and the big steamers came splashing by, and one had reached the sea—the limitless sea, with its thousand islands, its thousands of islands, and its ships seen dimly far away in their incessant journeyings round and about that greater world. And there, unpent by mountains, one saw the sky—the sky, not such a disc as one saw it here, but an arch of immeasurable blue, a deep of deeps in which the circling stars were floating. . . .

His eyes scrutinised the great curtain of the mountains with a keener inquiry.

For example, if one went so, up that gully and to that chimney there, then one might come out high among those stunted pines that ran round in a sort of shelf and rose still higher and higher as it passed above the gorge. And then? That talus might be managed. Thence perhaps a climb might be found to take him up to the precipice that came below the snow; and if that chimney failed, then another farther to the east might serve his purpose better. And then? Then one would be out upon the amber-lit snow there, and halfway up to the crest of those beautiful desolations.

He glanced back at the village, then turned right round and regarded it steadfastly.

He thought of Medina-saroté, and she had become small and remote.

He turned again towards the mountain wall, down which the day had come to him.

Then very circumspectly he began to climb.

When sunset came he was no longer climbing, but he was far and high. He had been higher, but he was still very high. His clothes were torn, his limbs were blood-stained, he was bruised in many places, but he lay as if he were at his ease, and there was a smile on his face.

From where he rested the valley seemed as if it were in a pit and nearly a mile below. Already it was dim with haze and shadow, though the mountain summits around him were things of light and fire. The little details of the rocks near at hand were drenched with subtle beauty —a vein of green mineral piercing the grey, the flash of crystal faces here and there, a minute, minutely beautiful orange lichen close beside his face. There were deep mysterious shadows in the gorge, blue deepening into purple, and purple into a luminous darkness, and overhead was the illimitable vastness of the sky. But he heeded these things no longer, but lay quite inactive there, smiling as if he were satisfied merely to have escaped from the valley of the Blind in which he had thought to be King.

The glow of the sunset passed, and the night came, and still he lay peacefully contented under the cold stars.

42

Mary with the High Hand

BY ARNOLD BENNETT

IN the front bedroom of Edward Beechinor's small house in Trafalgar Road the two primary social forces of action and reaction—those forces which under a thousand names and disguises have alternately ruled the world since the invention of politics—were pitted against each other in a struggle rendered futile by the equality of the combatants. Edward Beechinor had his money, his superior age, and the possible advantage of being a dying man; Mark Beechinor had his youth and his devotion to an ideal. Near the window, aloof and apart, stood the strange, silent girl whose aroused individuality was to intervene with such effectiveness on behalf of one of the antagonists. It was early dusk on an autumn day.

"Tell me what it is you want, Edward," said Mark quietly. "Let us come to the point."

"Aye," said the sufferer, lifting his pale hand from the counterpane, "I'll tell thee."

He moistened his lips as if in preparation, and pushed back a tuft of spare gray hair, damp with sweat.

The physical and moral contrast between these two brothers was complete. Edward was forty-nine, a small, thin, stunted man, with a look of narrow cunning, of petty shrewdness working without imagination. He had been clerk to Lawyer Ford for thirty-five years, and had also furtively practised for himself. During this period his mode of life had never varied, save once, and that only a year ago. At the age of fourteen he sat in a grimy room with an old man on one side of him, a copying-press on the other, and a law-stationer's almanac in front, and he earned half a crown a·week. At the age of forty-eight he still sat in the same grimy room (of which the ceiling had meanwhile been whitened three times), with the same copying-press and the almanac of the same law-stationer's, and he earned thirty shillings a week. But now he, Edward Beechinor, was the old man, and the indispensable lad of fourteen, who had once been himself, was another lad, perhaps thirtieth of the dynasty of office-boys. Through this interminable and sterile desert of time he had drawn the same deeds, issued the same writs, written the same letters, kept the same accounts, lied the same lies, and thought the same thoughts. He had learned nothing except craft, and forgotten nothing except happiness. He had never married, never loved, never been a rake, never deviated from respectability. He was a success because he had conceived an object, and by sheer persistence attained it. In the eyes of Bursley people he was a very decent fellow, a steady fellow, a confirmed bachelor, a close 'un, a knowing customer, a curmudgeon, an excellent clerk, a narrow-minded ass, a good Wesleyan, a thrifty individual, and an intelligent burgess—according to the point of view. The lifelong operation of vigorous habit had sunk him into a groove as deep as the cañon of some American river. His ideas on every subject were eternally and immutably fixed, and, without being altogether aware of it, he was part of the solid foundation of England's greatness. In 1892, when the whole of the Five Towns was agitated by the great probate case of Wilbraham, in which Mr. Ford acted for the defendants, Beechinor, then aged forty-eight, was torn from his stool and sent out to Rio de Janeiro as part of a commission to take the evidence of an important witness who had declined all offers to come home.

The old clerk was full of pride and self-importance at being thus selected, but secretly he shrank from the journey, the mere idea of which filled him with a vague apprehension and alarm. His nature had lost all its adaptability; he trembled like a young girl at the prospect of new experiences. On the return voyage the vessel was quarantined at Liverpool for a fortnight, and Beechinor had an attack of fever. Eight months afterwards he was ill again. Beechinor went to bed for the last time, cursing Providence, Wilbraham v. Wilbraham, and Rio.

Mark Beechinor was thirty, just nineteen years younger than his brother. Tall, uncouth, big-boned, he had a rather ferocious and forbidding aspect; yet all women seemed to like him, despite the fact that he seldom could open his mouth to them. There must have been something in his wild and liquid dark eyes which mutely appealed for their protective sympathy, something about him of shy and wistful romance that atoned for the huge awkwardness of this taciturn elephant. Mark was at present the manager of a small china manufactory at Longshaw, the farthest of the Five Towns in Staffordshire, and five miles from Bursley. He was an exceptionally clever potter, but he never made money. He had the dreamy temperament of the inventor. He was a man of ideas, the kind of man who is capable of forgetting that he has not had his dinner, and who can live apparently content amid the grossest domestic neglect. He had once spoiled a hundred and fifty pounds' worth of ware by firing it in a new kiln of his own contrivance; it cost him three years of atrocious parsimony to pay for the ware and the building of the kiln. He was impulsively and recklessly charitable, and his Saturday afternoons and Sundays were chiefly devoted to the passionate propagandism of the theories of liberty, equality, and fraternity.

"Is it true as thou'rt for marrying Sammy Mellor's daughter over at Hanbridge?" Edward Beechinor asked, in the feeble, tremulous voice of one agonized by continual pain.

Among relatives and acquaintances he commonly spoke the Five Towns dialect, reserving the other English for official use.

Mark stood at the foot of the bed, leaning with his elbows on the brass rail. Like most men, he always felt extremely nervous and foolish in a sick-room, and the delicacy of this question, so bluntly put, added to his embarrassment. He looked round timidly in the direction of the girl at the window; her back was towards him.

"It's possible," he replied; "I haven't asked her yet."

"Her'll have no money?"

"No."

"Thou'lt want some vrass to set up with. Look thee here, Mark; I made my will seven years ago i' thy favour."

"Thank ye," said Mark gratefully.

"But that," the dying man continued with a frown—"that was afore thou'dst taken up with these socialistic doctrines o' thine. I've heard as thou'rt going to be th' secretary o' the Hanbridge Labour Church, as they call it."

Hanbridge is the metropolis of the Five Towns, and its Labour Church is the most audacious and influential of all the local activities, half secret, but relentlessly determined, whose aim is to establish the new democratic heaven and the new democratic earth by means of a gradual and bloodless revolution. Edward Beechinor uttered its abhorred name with a bitter and scornful hatred characteristic of the Toryism of a man who, having climbed high up out of the crowd, fiercely resents any widening or smoothing of the difficult path which he himself has conquered.

"They've asked me to take the post," Mark answered.

"What's the wages?" the older man asked, with exasperated sarcasm.

"Nothing."

"Mark, lad," the other said, softening, "I'm worth seven hundred pounds and this freehold house. What dost think o' that?"

Even in that moment, with the world and its riches slipping away from his dying grasp, the contemplation of this great achievement of thrift filled Edward Beechinor with a sublime satisfaction. That sum of seven hundred pounds, which many men would dissipate in a single night, and forget the next morning that they had done so, seemed vast and almost incredible to him.

"I know you've always been very careful," said Mark politely.

"Give up this old Labour Church"—again old Beechinor laid a withering emphasis on the phrase—"give up this Labour Church, and it's all thine—house and all."

Mark shook his head.

"Think twice," the sick man ordered angrily. "I tell thee thou'rt standing to lose every shilling."

"I must manage without it, then."

A silence fell.

Each brother was absolutely immovable in his decision, and the other knew it. Edward might have said: "I am a dying man; give up this thing to oblige me." And Mark could have pleaded: "At such a moment I would do anything to oblige you—except this, and this I really can't do. Forgive me." Such amenities would possibly have eased the cord which was about to snap; but the idea of regarding Edward's condition as a factor in the case did not suggest itself favourably to the grim Beechinor stock, so stern, harsh, and rude. The sick man wiped from his sunken features the sweat which continually gathered there. Then he turned upon his side with a grunt.

"Thou must fetch th' lawyer," he said at length, "for I'll cut thee off."

It was a strange request—like ordering a condemned man to go out and search for his executioner; but Mark answered with perfect naturalness.

"Yes. Mr. Ford, I suppose?"

"Ford? No! Dost think I want him meddling i' my affairs? Go to young Baines up th' road. Tell him to come at once. He's sure to be at home, as it's Saturday night."

"Very well."

Mark turned to leave the room.

"And, young 'un, I've done with thee. Never pass my door again till thou know'st I'm i' my coffin. Understand?"

Mark hesitated a moment, and then went out, quietly closing the door. No sooner had he done so than the girl, hitherto so passive at the window, flew after him.

There are some women whose calm, enigmatic faces seem always to suggest the infinite. It is given to few to know them so rare as they are, and their lives usually so withdrawn; but sometimes they pass in the street, or sit like sphinxes in the church or the theatre, and then the memory of their features, persistently recurring, troubles us for days. They are peculiar to no class, these women; you may find them in a print gown or in diamonds. Often they have thin, rather long lips and deep rounded chins; but it is the fine upward curve of the nostrils and the fall of the eyelids which most surely mark them. Their glances and their faint smiles are beneficent, yet with a subtle shade of half-malicious superiority. When they look at you from under those apparently fatigued eyelids, you feel that they have an inward and concealed existence far beyond the ordinary—that they are aware of many things which you can never know. It is as though their souls, during former incarnations, had trafficked with the secret forces of nature, and so acquired a mysterious and nameless quality above all the transient attributes of beauty, wit, and talent. They exist: that is enough; that is their genius. Whether they control, or are at the mercy of, those secret forces; whether they have in fact learned, but may not speak, the true answer to the eternal Why; whether they are not perhaps a riddle even to their own simple selves: these are points which can never be decided.

Everyone who knew Mary Beechinor, in her cousin's home, or at chapel, or in Titus Price's earthenware manufactory, where she worked, said or thought that "there was something about her . . ." and left the phrase unachieved. She was twenty-five, and she had lived under the same roof with Edward Beechinor for seven years, since the sudden death of her parents. The arrangement then made was that Edward should keep her, while she conducted his household. She insisted on permission to follow her own occupation, and in order that she might be at liberty to do so she personally paid eighteenpence a week to a little girl who came in to perform sundry necessary duties every day at noon. Mary Beechinor was a paintress by trade. As a class the paintresses of the Five Towns are somewhat similar to the more famous mill-girls of Lancashire and Yorkshire—fiercely independent by reason of good wages earned, loving finery and brillant colours, loud-tongued and aggressive, perhaps, and for the rest neither more nor less kindly, passionate, faithful, than any other Saxon women anywhere. The paintresses, however, have some slight advantage over the mill-girls in the outward reticence of demeanour, due, no doubt, to the fact that their ancient craft demands a higher skill, and is pursued under more humane and tranquil conditions. Mary Beechinor worked in the "band-and-line" department of the painting-shop at Price's. You may have observed the geometrical exactitude of the broad and thin coloured lines round the edges of a common cup and saucer, and speculated upon the means by which it was arrived at. A girl drew those lines, a girl with a hand as sure as Giotto's, and no better tools than a couple of brushes and a small revolving table called a whirler. Forty-eight hours a week Mary Beechinor sat before her whirler. Actuating the treadle, she placed a piece of ware on the flying disc, and with a single unerring flip of the finger pushed it precisely to the centre; then she held the full brush firmly against the ware, and in three seconds the band encircled it truly; another brush taken up, and the line below the band also stood complete. And this process was repeated, with miraculous swiftness, hour after hour, week after week, year after year. Mary could decorate over thirty dozen cups and saucers in a day, at three halfpence the dozen. "Doesn't she ever do anything else?" some visitor might curiously inquire, whom Titus Price was showing over his ramshackle manufactory. "No, always the same thing," Titus would answer, made proud for the moment of this phenomenon of stupendous monotony. "I wonder how she can stand it—she has a refined face," the visitor might remark; and Mary Beechinor was left alone again. The idea that her work was monotonous probably never occurred to the girl. It was her work—as natural as sleep, or the knitting which she always did in the dinner-hour. The calm and silent regularity of it had become part of her, deepening her original quiescence, and setting its seal upon her inmost spirit. She was not in the fellowship of the other girls in the painting-shop. She seldom joined their more boisterous diversions, nor talked their talk, and she never maneuvered for their men. But they liked her, and their attitude showed a certain respect, forced from them by they knew not what. The powers in the office spoke of Mary Beechinor as "a very superior girl."

She ran downstairs after Mark, and he waited in the narrow hall, where there was scarcely room for two people to pass. Mark looked at her inquiringly. Rather thin, and by no means tall, she seemed the merest morsel by his side. She was wearing her second-best crimson merino frock, partly to receive the doctor and partly because it was Saturday night; over this a plain bibless apron. Her cold gray eyes faintly sparkled in anger above the cheeks white with watching, and the dropped corners of her mouth showed a contemptuous indignation. Mary Beechinor was ominously roused from the accustomed calm of years. Yet Mark at first had no suspicion that she was disturbed. To him that pale and inviolate face, even while it cast a spell over him, gave no sign of the fires within.

She took him by the coat-sleeve and silently directed him into the gloomy little parlour crowded with mahogany and horsehair furniture, and white antimacassars, wax flowers under glass, and ponderous gilt-clasped Bibles.

"It's a cruel shame!" she whispered, as though afraid of being overheard by the dying man upstairs.

"Do you think I ought to have given way?" he questioned, reddening.

"You mistake me," she said quickly; and with a sudden movement she went up to him and put her hand on his shoulder. The caress, so innocent, unpremeditated, and instinctive, ran through him like a voltaic shock. These two were almost strangers; they had scarcely met till within the past week, Mark being seldom in Bursley. "You mistake me —it is a shame of *him!* I'm fearfully angry."

"Angry?" he repeated, astonished.

"Yes, angry." She walked to the window, and, twitching at the blindcord, gazed into the dim street. It was beginning to grow dark. "Shall you fetch the lawyer? I shouldn't, if I were you. I won't."

"I must fetch him," Mark said.

She turned round and admired him. "What will he do with his precious money?" she murmured.

"Leave it to you, probably."

"Not he. I wouldn't touch it—not now; it's yours by rights. Perhaps you don't know that when I came here it was distinctly understood I wasn't to expect anything under his will. Besides, I have my own money. . . . Oh, dear! If he wasn't in such pain, wouldn't I talk to him —for the first and last time in my life!"

"You must please not say a word to him. I don't really want the money."

"But you ought to have it. If he takes it away from you he's *unjust.*"

"What did the doctor say this afternoon?" asked Mark, wishing to change the subject.

"He said the crisis would come on Monday, and when it did Edward would be dead all in a minute. He said it would be just like taking prussic acid."

"Not earlier than Monday?"

"He said he thought on Monday."

"Of course, I shall take no notice of what Edward said to me—I shall call tomorrow morning—and stay. Perhaps he won't mind seeing me. And then you can tell me what happens tonight."

"I'm sure I shall send that lawyer man about his business," she threatened.

"Look here," said Mark timorously as he was leaving the house, "I've told you I don't want the money—I would give it away to some charity; but do you think I ought to pretend to yield, just to humour him, and let him die quiet and peaceful? I shouldn't like him to die hating——"

"Never—never!" she exclaimed.

"What have you and Mark been talking about?" asked Edward Beechinor apprehensively as Mary re-entered the bedroom.

"Nothing," she replied with a grave and soothing kindliness of tone.
"Because, miss, if you think——"

"You must have your medicine now, Edward."

But before giving the patient his medicine she peeped through the
curtain and watched Mark's figure till it disappeared up the hill towards Bleakridge. He, on his part, walked with her image always before him. He thought hers was the strongest, most righteous soul he
had ever encountered; it seemed as if she had a perfect passion for truth
and justice. And a week ago he had deemed her a capable girl, certainly
—but lackadaisical!

The clock had struck ten before Mr. Baines, the solicitor, knocked at
the door. Mary hesitated, and then took him upstairs in silence while
he suavely explained to her why he had been unable to come earlier.
This lawyer was a young Scotsman who had descended upon the town
from nowhere, bought a small decayed practice, and within two years
had transformed it into a large and flourishing business by one of those
feats of energy, audacity, and tact, combined, of which some Scotsmen
seem to possess the secret.

"Here is Mr. Baines, Edward," Mary said quietly; then, having rear-
ranged the sick man's pillows, she vanished out of the room and went
into the kitchen.

The gas-jet there showed only a point of blue, but she did not turn
it up. Dragging an old oak rush-seated rocking-chair near to the range,
where a scrap of fire still glowed, she rocked herself gently in the darkness.

After about half an hour Mr. Baines's voice sounded at the head of
the stairs:

"Miss Beechinor, will ye kindly step up? We shall want some as-
seestance."

She obeyed, but not instantly.

In the bedroom Mr. Baines, a fountain-pen between his fine white
teeth, was putting some coal on the fire. He stood up as she entered.

"Mr. Beechinor is about to make a new will," he said, without removing the pen from his mouth, "and ye will kindly witness it."

The small room appeared to be full of Baines—he was so large and
fleshy and assertive. The furniture, even the chest of drawers, was
dwarfed into toy-furniture, and Beechinor, slight and shrunken-up,
seemed like a cadaverous manikin in the bed.

"Now, Mr. Beechinor." Dusting his hands, the lawyer took a newly-
written document from the dressing-table, and, spreading it on the lid
of a cardboard box, held it before the dying man. "Here's the pen.
There! I'll help ye to hold it."

Beechinor clutched the pen. His wrinkled and yellow face, flushed in irregular patches as though the cheeks had been badly rouged, was covered with perspiration, and each difficult movement, even to the slightest lifting of the head, showed extreme exhaustion. He cast at Mary a long sinister glance of mistrust and apprehension.

"What is there in this will?"

Mr. Baines looked sharply up at the girl, who now stood at the side of the bed opposite him. Mechanically she smoothed the tumbled bed-clothes.

"That's nowt to do wi' thee, lass," said Beechinor resentfully.

"It isn't necessary that a witness to a will should be aware of its contents," said Baines. "In fact, it's quite unusual."

"I sign nothing in the dark," she said, smiling. Through their half-closed lids her eyes glimmered at Baines.

"Ha! Legal caution acquired from your cousin, I presume." Baines smiled at her. "But let me assure ye, Miss Beechinor, this is a mere matter of form. A will must be signed in the presence of two witnesses, both present at the same time; and there's only yeself and me for it."

Mary looked at the dying man, whose features were writhed in pain, and shook her head.

"Tell her," he murmured with bitter despair, and sank down into the pillows, dropping the fountain-pen, which had left a stain of ink on the sheet before Baines could pick it up.

"Well, then, Miss Beechinor, if ye must know," Baines began with sarcasm, "the will is as follows: The testator—that's Mr. Beechinor—leaves twenty guineas to his brother Mark to show that he bears him no ill-will and forgives him. The rest of his estate is to be realized, and the proceeds given to the North Staffordshire Infirmary, to found a bed, which is to be called the Beechinor Bed. If there is any surplus, it is to go to the Law Clerks' Provident Society. That is all."

"I shall have nothing to do with it," said Mary coldly.

"Young lady, we don't want ye to have anything to do with it. We only desire ye to witness the signature."

"I won't witness the signature, and I won't see it signed."

"Damn thee, Mary; thou'rt a wicked wench," Beechinor whispered in hoarse, feeble tones. He saw himself robbed of the legitimate fruit of all those interminable years of toilsome thrift. This girl by a trick would prevent him from disposing of his own. He, Edward Beechinor, shrewd and wealthy, was being treated like a child. He was too weak to rave, but from his aggrieved and furious heart he piled silent curses on her. "Go, fetch another witness," he added to the lawyer.

"Wait a moment," said Baines. "Miss Beechinor, do ye mean to say that ye will cross the solemn wish of a dying man."

"I mean to say I won't help a dying man to commit a crime."

"A crime?"

"Yes," she answered, "a crime. Seven years ago, Mr. Beechinor willed everything to his brother Mark, and Mark ought to have everything. Mark is his only brother—his only relation except me. And Edward knows it isn't me wants any of his money. North Staffordshire Infirmary, indeed! It's a crime! . . . What business have you," she went on to Edward Beechinor, "to punish Mark just because his politics aren't ——"

"That's beside the point," the lawyer interrupted. "A testator has a perfect right to leave his property as he chooses, without giving reasons. Now, Miss Beechinor, I must ask ye to be judeecious."

Mary shut her lips.

"Her'll never do it. I tell thee, fetch another witness."

The old man sprang up in a sort of frenzy as he uttered the words, and then fell back in a brief swoon.

Mary wiped his brow, and pushed away the wet and matted hair. Presently he opened his eyes, moaning. Mr. Baines folded up the will, put it in his pocket, and left the room with quick steps. Mary heard him open the front-door and then return to the foot of the stairs.

"Miss Beechinor," he called, "I'll speak with ye a moment."

She went down.

"Do you mind coming into the kitchen?" she said, preceding him and turning up the gas; "there's no light in the front-room."

He leaned up against the high mantelpiece; his frock-coat hung to the level of the oven-knob. She had one hand on the white deal table. Between them a tortoiseshell cat purred on the red-tiled floor.

"Ye're doing a verra serious thing, Miss Beechinor. As Mr. Beechinor's solicitor, I should just like to be acquaint with the real reasons for this conduct."

"I've told you." She had a slightly quizzical look.

"Now, as to Mark," the lawyer continued blandly, "Mr. Beechinor explained the whole circumstances to me. Mark as good as defied his brother."

"That's nothing to do with it."

"By the way, it appears that Mark is practically engaged to be married. May I ask if the lady is yeself?" She hesitated.

"If so," he proceeded, "I may tell ye informally that I admire the pluck of ye. But, nevertheless, that will has got to be executed."

"The young lady is a Miss Mellor of Hanbridge."

"I'm going to fetch my clerk," he said shortly. "I can see ye're an obstinate and unfathomable woman. I'll be back in half an hour."

When he departed she bolted the front-door top and bottom, and went upstairs to the dying man.

Nearly an hour elapsed before she heard a knock. Mr. Baines had had to arouse his clerk from sleep. Instead of going down to the front-door, Mary threw up the bedroom window, and looked out. It was a mild but starless night. Trafalgar Road was silent save for the steam car, which, with its load of revellers returning from Hanbridge—that centre of gaiety—slipped rumbling down the hill towards Bursley.

"What do you want—disturbing a respectable house at this time of night?" she called in a loud whisper when the car passed. "The door's bolted, and I can't come down. You must come in the morning."

"Miss Beechinor, ye will let us in—I charge ye."

"It's useless, Mr. Baines."

"I'll break the door down. I'm a strong man, and a determined. Ye are carrying things too far."

In another moment the two men heard the creak of the bolts. Mary stood before them vaguely discernible, but a forbidding figure.

"If you must—come upstairs," she said coldly.

"Stay here in the passage, Arthur," said Mr. Baines; "I'll call ye when I want ye," and he followed Mary up the stairs.

Edward Beechinor lay on his back, and his sunken eyes stared glassily at the ceiling. The skin of his emaciated face, stretched tightly over the protruding bones, had lost all its crimson, and was green, white, yellow. The mouth was wide open. His drawn features wore a terribly sardonic look—a purely physical effect of the disease; but it seemed to the two spectators that this mean and disappointed slave of a miserly habit had by one superb imaginative effort realized the full vanity of all human wishes and pretensions.

"Ye can go; I shan't want ye," said Mr. Baines, returning to the clerk.

The lawyer never spoke of that night's business. Why should he? To what end? Mark Beechinor, under the old will, inherited the seven hundred pounds and the house. Miss Mellor of Hanbridge is still Miss Mellor, her hand not having been formally sought. But Mark, secretary of the Labour Church, is married. Miss Mellor, with a quite pardonable air of tolerant superiority, refers to his wife as "a strange, timid little creature—she couldn't say 'boo' to a goose."

43

The Apple-Tree

The Apple-tree, the singing, and the gold.
MURRAY, *Hippolytus of Euripides*

BY JOHN GALSWORTHY

ON THEIR silver-wedding day Ashurst and his wife were motoring along the outskirts of the moor, intending to crown the festival by stopping the night at Torquay, where they had first met. This was the idea of Stella Ashurst, whose character contained a streak of sentiment. If she had long lost the blue-eyed, flower-like charm, the cool slim purity of face and form, the apple-blossom coloring, which had so swiftly and so oddly affected Ashurst twenty-six years ago, she was still at forty-three a comely and faithful companion, whose cheeks were faintly mottled, and whose grey-blue eyes had acquired a certain fullness.

It was she who had stopped the car where the common rose steeply to the left, and a narrow strip of larch and beech, with here and there a pine, stretched out towards the valley between the road and the first long high hill of the full moor. She was looking for a place where they might lunch, for Ashurst never looked for anything; and this, between the golden furze and the feathery green larches smelling of lemons in the last sun of April—this, with a view into the deep valley and up to the long moor heights, seemed fitting to the decisive nature of one who sketched in water-colors, and loved romantic spots. Grasping her paint box, she got out.

"Won't this do, Frank?"

Ashurst, rather like a bearded Schiller, grey in the wings, tall, long-legged, with large remote grey eyes which sometimes filled with meaning and became almost beautiful, with nose a little to one side, and bearded lips just open—Ashurst, forty-eight, and silent, grasped the luncheon basket, and got out too.

"Oh! Look, Frank! A grave!"

By the side of the road, where the track from the top of the common crossed it at right angles and ran through a gate past the narrow wood, was a thin mound of turf, six feet by one, with a moorstone to the west, and on it someone had thrown a blackthorn spray and a handful of blue-bells. Ashurst looked, and the poet in him moved. At cross-roads—a suicide's grave! Poor mortals with their superstitions! Whoever lay there, though, had the best of it, no clammy sepulchre among other hide-ous graves carved with futilities—just a rough stone, the wide sky, and wayside blessings! And, without comment, for he had learned not to be a philosopher in the bosom of his family, he strode away up on to the common, dropped the luncheon basket under a wall, spread a rug for his wife to sit on—she would turn up from her sketching when she was hungry—and took from his pocket Murray's translation of the *Hip-polytus*. He had soon finished reading of "The Cyprian" and her re-venge, and looked at the sky instead. And watching the white clouds so bright against the intense blue, Ashurst, on his silver-wedding day, longed for—he knew not what. Mal-adjusted to life—man's organism! One's mode of life might be high and scrupulous, but there was always an undercurrent of greediness, a hankering, and sense of waste. Did women have it too? Who could tell? And yet, men who gave vent to their appetites for novelty, their riotous longings for new adventures, new risks, new pleasures, these suffered, no doubt, from the reverse side of starvation, from surfeit. No getting out of it—a mal-adjusted animal, civilised man! There could be no garden of his choosing, of "the Apple-tree, the singing, and the gold," in the words of that lovely Greek chorus, no achievable elysium in life, or lasting haven of happiness for any man with a sense of beauty—nothing which could compare with the captured loveliness in a work of art, set down for ever, so that to look on it or read was always to have the same precious sense of exalta-tion and restful inebriety. Life no doubt had moments with that quality of beauty, of unbidden flying rapture, but the trouble was, they lasted no longer than the span of a cloud's flight over the sun; impossible to keep them with you, as Art caught beauty and held it fast. They were fleeting as one of the glimmering or golden visions one had of the soul in nature, glimpses of its remote and brooding spirit. Here, with the sun hot on his face, a cuckoo calling from a thorn tree, and in the air the honey savour of gorse—here among the little fronds of the young fern, the starry blackthorn, while the bright clouds drifted by high above the hills and dreamy valleys—here and now was such a glimpse. But in a moment it would pass—as the face of Pan, which looks round the corner of a rock, vanishes at your stare. And suddenly he sat up. Surely there was something familiar about this view, this bit of common, that ribbon of road, the old wall behind him. While they were driving he had not been taking notice—never did; thinking of far things or of nothing—but now he saw! Twenty-six years ago, just at this time of year, from the farmhouse within half a mile of this very spot he had started for that day in Torquay whence it might be said he had never returned. And a sudden ache beset his heart; he had stumbled on just one of those past moments in his life, whose beauty and rapture he had failed to arrest, whose wings had fluttered away into the unknown; he had stumbled on a buried memory, a wild sweet time, swiftly choked and ended. And, turning on his face, he rested his chin on his hands, and stared at the short grass where the little blue milkwort was growing. . . .

And this is what he remembered.

On the first of May, after their last year together at college, Frank Ashurst and his friend Robert Garton were on a tramp. They had walked that day from Brent, intending to make Chagford, but Ashurst's football knee had given out, and according to their map they had still some seven miles to go. They were sitting on a bank beside the road, where a track crossed alongside a wood, resting the knee and talking of the universe, as young men will. Both were over six feet, and thin as rails; Ashurst pale, idealistic, full of absence; Garton queer, round-the-corner, knotted, curly, like some primeval beast. Both had a literary bent; neither wore a hat. Ashurst's hair was smooth, pale, wavy, and had a way of rising on either side of his brow, as if always being flung back; Garton's was a kind of dark unfathomed mop. They had not met a soul for miles.

"My dear fellow," Garton was saying, "pity's only an effect of self-consciousness; it's a disease of the last five thousand years. The world was happier without."

Ashurst, following the clouds with his eyes, answered:

"It's the pearl in the oyster, anyway."

"My dear chap, all our modern unhappiness comes from pity. Look at animals, and Red Indians, limited to feeling their own occasional misfortunes; then look at ourselves—never free from feeling the toothaches of others. Let's get back to feeling for nobody, and have a better time."

"You'll never practise that."

Garton pensively stirred the hotch-potch of his hair.

"To attain full growth, one mustn't be squeamish. To starve oneself emotionally's a mistake. All emotion is to the good—enriches life."

"Yes, and when it runs up against chivalry?"

"Ah! That's so English! If you speak of emotion the English always think you want something physical, and are shocked. They're afraid of passion, but not of lust—oh, no!—so long as they can keep it secret."

Ashurst did not answer; he had plucked a blue floweret, and was twiddling it against the sky. A cuckoo began calling from a thorn tree. The sky, the flowers, the songs of birds! Robert was talking through his hat! And he said:

"Well, let's go on, and find some farm where we can put up." In uttering those words, he was conscious of a girl coming down from the common just above them. She was outlined against the sky, carrying a basket, and you could see that sky through the crook of her arm. And Ashurst, who saw beauty without wondering how it could advantage him, thought: "How pretty!" The wind, blowing her dark frieze skirt against her legs, lifted her battered peacock tam-o'-shanter; her greyish blouse was worn and old, her shoes were split, her little hands rough and red, her neck browned. Her dark hair waved untidy across her broad forehead, her face was short, her upper lip short, showing a glint of teeth, her brows were straight and dark, her lashes long and dark, her nose straight; but her grey eyes were the wonder—dewy as if opened for the first time that day. She looked at Ashurst—perhaps he struck her as strange, limping along without a hat, with his large eyes on her, and his hair flung back. He could not take off what was not on his head, but put up his hand in a salute, and said:

"Can you tell us if there's a farm near here where we could stay the night? I've gone lame."

"There's only our farm near, sir." She spoke without shyness, in a pretty, soft, crisp voice.

"And where is that?"

"Down here, sir."

"Would you put us up?"

"Oh! I think we would."

"Will you show us the way?"

"Yes, sir."

He limped on, silent, and Garton took up the catechism.

"Are you a Devonshire girl?"

"No, sir."

"What then?"

"From Wales."

"Ah! I *thought* you were a Celt; so it's not your farm?"

"My aunt's, sir."

"And your uncle's?"

"He is dead."

"Who farms it, then?"

"My aunt, and my three cousins."

"But your uncle was a Devonshire man?"

"Yes, sir."

"Have you lived here long?"

"Seven years."

"And how d'you like it after Wales?"

"I don't know, sir."

"I suppose you don't remember?"

"Oh, yes! But it is different."

"I believe you!"

Ashurst broke in suddenly:

"How old are you?"

"Seventeen, sir."

"And what's your name?"

"Megan David."

"This is Robert Garton, and I am Frank Ashurst. We wanted to get on to Chagford."

"It is a pity your leg is hurting you."

Ashurst smiled, and when he smiled his face was rather beautiful.

Descending past the narrow wood, they came on the farm suddenly— a long, low, stone-built dwelling with casement windows, in a farmyard where pigs and fowls and an old mare were straying. A short steep-up grass hill behind was crowned with a few Scotch firs, and in front, an old orchard of apple-trees, just breaking into flower, stretched down to a stream and a long wild meadow. A little boy with oblique dark eyes was shepherding a pig, and by the house door stood a woman, who came towards them. The girl said:

"It is Mrs. Narracombe, my aunt."

"Mrs. Narracombe, my aunt," had a quick, dark eye, like a mother wild-duck's, and something of the same snaky turn about her neck.

"We met your niece on the road," said Ashurst; "she thought you might perhaps put us up for the night."

Mrs. Narracombe, taking them in from head to heel, answered:

"Well, I can, if you don't mind one room. Megan, get the spare room ready, and a bowl of cream. You'll be wanting tea, I suppose."

Passing through a sort of porch made by two yew trees and some flowering-currant bushes, the girl disappeared into the house, her pea-cock tam-o'-shanter bright athwart that rosy-pink and the dark green of the yews.

"Will you come into the parlour and rest your leg? You'll be from college, perhaps?"

"We were, but we've gone down now."

Mrs. Narracombe nodded sagely.

The parlour, brick-floored, with bare table and shiny chairs and sofa stuffed with horsehair, seemed never to have been used, it was so terribly clean. Ashurst sat down at once on the sofa, holding his lame knee between his hands, and Mrs. Narracombe gazed at him. He was the only son of a late professor of chemistry, but people found a certain lordliness in one who was often so sublimely unconscious of them.

"Is there a stream where we could bathe?"

"There's the strame at the bottom of the orchard, but sittin' down you'll not be covered!"

"How deep?"

"Well, 'tis about a foot and a half, maybe."

"Oh! That'll do fine. Which way?"

"Down the lane, through the second gate on the right, an' the pool's by the big apple tree that stands by itself. There's trout there, if you can tickle them."

"They're more likely to tickle us!"

Mrs. Narracombe smiled. "There'll be the tea ready when you come back."

The pool, formed by the damming of a rock, had a sandy bottom; and the big apple tree, lowest in the orchard, grew so close that its boughs almost overhung the water; it was in leaf, and all but in flower—its crimson buds just bursting. There was not room for more than one at a time in that narrow bath, and Ashurst waited his turn, rubbing his knee and gazing at the wild meadow, all rocks and thorn trees and field flowers, with a grove of beeches beyond, raised up on a flat mound. Every bough was swinging in the wind, every spring bird calling, and a slanting sunlight dappled the grass. He thought of Theocritus, and the river Cherwell, of the moon, and the maiden with the dewy eyes; of so many things that he seemed to think of nothing; and he felt absurdly happy.

During a late and sumptuous tea with eggs to it, cream and jam, and thin, fresh cakes touched with saffron, Garton descanted on the Celts. It was about the period of the Celtic awakening, and the discovery that there was Celtic blood about this family had excited one who believed that he was a Celt himself. Sprawling on a horsehair chair, with a handmade cigarette dribbling from the corner of his curly lips, he had been plunging his cold pin-points of eyes into Ashurst's and praising the refinement of the Welsh. To come out of Wales into England was like the change from china to earthenware! Frank, as a d——d Englishman, had not of course perceived the exquisite refinement and emotional capacity of that Welsh girl! And, delicately stirring in the dark mat of his still wet hair, he explained how exactly she illustrated the writings of the Welsh bard Morgan-ap-Something in the twelfth century.

Ashurst, full length on the horsehair sofa, and jutting far beyond its end, smoked a deeply-coloured pipe, and did not listen, thinking of the girl's face when she brought in a relay of cakes. It had been exactly like looking at a flower, or some other pretty sight in Nature—till, with a funny little shiver, she had lowered her glance and gone out, quiet as a mouse.

"Let's go to the kitchen," said Garton, "and see some more of her."

The kitchen was a white-washed room with rafters, to which were attached smoked hams; there were flower-pots on the window-sill, and guns hanging on nails, queer mugs, china and pewter, and portraits of Queen Victoria. A long, narrow table of plain wood was set with bowls and spoons, under a string of high-hung onions; two sheep-dogs and three cats lay here and there. On one side of the recessed fireplace sat two small boys, idle, and good as gold; on the other sat a stout, light-eyed, red-faced youth with hair and lashes the colour of the tow he was running through the barrel of a gun; between them Mrs. Narracombe dreamily stirred some savoury-scented stew in a large pot. Two other youths, oblique-eyed, dark-haired, rather sly-faced, like the two little boys, were talking together and lolling against the wall; and a short, elderly, clean-shaven man in corduroys, seated in the window, was conning a battered journal. The girl Megan seemed the only active creature —drawing cider and passing with the jugs from cask to table. Seeing them thus about to eat, Garton said:

"Ah! If you'll let us, we'll come back when supper's over," and without waiting for an answer they withdrew again to the parlour. But the colour in the kitchen, the warmth, the scents, and all those faces, heightened the bleakness of their shiny room, and they resumed their seats moodily.

"Regular gipsy type, those boys. There was only one Saxon—the fellow cleaning the gun. That girl is a very subtle study psychologically."

Ashurst's lips twitched. Garton seemed to him an ass just then. Subtle study! She was a wild flower. A creature it did you good to look at. Study!

Garton went on:

"Emotionally she would be wonderful. She wants awakening."

"Are you going to awaken her?"

Garton looked at him and smiled. "How coarse and English you are!" that curly smile seemed saying.

And Ashurst puffed his pipe. Awaken her! This fool had the best opinion of himself! He threw up the window and leaned out. Dusk had gathered thick. The farm buildings and the wheel-house were all dim and bluish, the apple trees but a blurred wilderness; the air smelled of wood smoke from the kitchen fire. One bird going to bed later than the others was uttering a half-hearted twitter, as though surprised at the darkness. From the stable came the snuffle and stamp of a feeding horse. And away over there was the loom of the moor, and away and away the shy stars which had not as yet full light, pricking white through the deep blue heavens. A quavering owl hooted. Ashurst drew a deep breath. What a night to wander out in! A padding of unshod hoofs came up the lane, and three dim, dark shapes passed—ponies on an evening march. Their heads, black and fuzzy, showed above the gate. At the tap of his pipe, and a shower of little sparks, they shied round and scampered. A bat went fluttering past, uttering its almost inaudible "chip, chip." Ashurst held out his hand; on the upturned palm he could feel the dew. Suddenly from overhead he heard little burring boys' voices, little thumps of boots thrown down, and another voice, crisp and soft—the girl's putting them to bed, no doubt; and nine clear words: "No, Rick, you can't have the cat in bed"; then came a skirmish of giggles and gurgles, a soft slap, a laugh so low and pretty that it made him shiver a little. A blowing sound, and the glim of the candle which was fingering the dusk above, went out; silence reigned. Ashurst withdrew into the room and sat down; his knee pained him, and his soul felt gloomy.

"You go to the kitchen," he said; "I'm going to bed."

For Ashurst the wheel of slumber was wont to turn noiseless and slick and swift, but though he seemed sunk in sleep when his companion came up, he was really wide awake; and long after Garton, smothered in the other bed of that low-roofed room, was worshipping darkness with his upturned nose, he heard the owls. Barring the discomfort of his knee, it was not unpleasant—the cares of life did not loom large in night watches for this young man. In fact he had none; just enrolled a barrister, with literary aspirations, the world before him, no father or mother, and four hundred a year of his own. Did it matter where he went, what he did, or when he did it? His bed, too, was hard, and this preserved him from fever. He lay, sniffing the scent of the night which drifted into the low room through the open casement close to his head. Except for a definite irritation with his friend, natural when you have tramped with a man for three days, Ashurst's memories and visions that sleepless night were kindly and wistful and exciting. One vision, specially clear and unreasonable, for he had not even been conscious of noting it, was the face of the youth cleaning the gun; intent, stolid, yet startled uplook at the kitchen doorway, quickly shifted to the girl carrying the cider jug. This red, blue-eyed, light-lashed, tow-haired face stuck as firmly in his memory as the girl's own face, so dewy and simple. But at last, in the square of darkness through the uncurtained casement, he saw day coming, and heard one hoarse and sleepy caw. Then followed silence, dead as ever, till the song of a blackbird, not properly awake, adventured into the hush. And, from staring at the framed brightening light, Ashurst fell asleep.

Next day his knee was badly swollen; the walking tour was obviously over. Garton, due back in London on the morrow, departed at midday with an ironical smile left a scar of irritation—healed the moment his loping figure vanished round the corner of the steep lane. All day Ashurst rested his knee, in a green-painted wooden chair on the patch of grass by the yew-tree porch, where the sunlight distilled the scent of stocks and gillyflowers, and a ghost of scent from the flowering-currant bushes. Beatifically he smoked, dreamed, watched.

A farm in spring is all birth—young things coming out of bud and shell, and human beings watching over the process with faint excitement feeding and tending what has been born. So still the young man sat, that a mother-goose, with stately cross-footed waddle, brought her six yellow-necked, grey-backed goslings to strop their little beaks against the grass blades at his feet. Now and again Mrs. Narracombe or the girl Megan would come and ask if he wanted anything, and he would smile and say: "Nothing, thanks. It's splendid here." Towards tea-time they came out together, bearing a long poultice of some dark stuff in a bowl, and after a long and solemn scrutiny of his swollen knee, bound it on. When they were gone, he thought of the girl's soft "Oh!"—of her pitying eyes, and the little wrinkle in her brow. And again he felt that unreasoning irritation against his departed friend, who talked such rot about her. When she brought out his tea, he said:

"How did you like my friend, Megan?"

She forced down her upper lip, as if afraid that to smile was not polite. "He was a funny gentleman; he made us laugh. I think he is very clever."

"What did he say to make you laugh?"

"He said I was a daughter of the bards. What are they?"

"Welsh poets, who lived hundreds of years ago."

"Why am I their daughter, please?"

"He meant that you were the sort of girl they sang about."

She wrinkled her brows. "I think he likes to joke. Am I?"

"Would you believe me, if I told you?"

"Oh, yes."

"Well, I think he was right."

She smiled.

And Ashurst thought: "You *are* a pretty thing!"

"He said, too, that Joe was a Saxon type. What would that be?"

"Which is Joe? With the blue eyes and red face?"

"Yes. My uncle's nephew."

"Not your cousin, then?"

"No."

"Well, he meant that Joe was like the men who came over to England about fourteen hundred years ago, and conquered it."

"Oh! I know about them; but is he?"

"Garton's crazy about that sort of thing; but I must say Joe does look a bit Early Saxon."

"Yes."

That "Yes" tickled Ashurst. It was so crisp and graceful, so conclusive, and politely aquiescent in what was evidently Greek to her.

"He said that all the other boys were regular gipsies. He should not have said that. My aunt laughed, but she didn't like it, of course, and my cousins were angry. Uncle was a farmer—farmers are not gipsies. It is wrong to hurt people."

Ashurst wanted to take her hand and give it a squeeze, but he only answered:

"Quite right, Megan. By the way, I heard you putting the little ones to bed last night."

She flushed a little. "Please to drink your tea—it is getting cold. Shall I get you some fresh?"

"Do you ever have time to do anything for yourself?"

"Oh, yes."

"I've been watching, but I haven't seen it yet."

She wrinkled her brows in a puzzled frown, and her colour deepened.

When she was gone, Ashurst thought: "Did she think I was chaffing her? I wouldn't for the world!" He was at that age when to some men "Beauty's a flower," as the poet says, and inspires in them the thoughts of chivalry. Never very conscious of his surroundings, it was some time before he was aware that the youth whom Garton had called "a Saxon type" was standing outside the stable door; and a fine bit of colour he made in his soiled brown velvetcords, muddy gaiters, and blue shirt; red-armed, red-faced, the sun turning his hair from tow to flax; immovably stolid, persistent, unsmiling he stood. Then, seeing Ashurst looking at him, he crossed the yard at that gait of the young countryman always ashamed not to be slow and heavy-dwelling on each leg, and disappeared round the end of the house towards the kitchen entrance. A chill came over Ashurst's mood. Clods! With all the good will in the world, how impossible to get on terms with them! And yet—see that girl! Her shoes were split, her hands rough; but—what was it? Was it really her

Celtic blood, as Garton had said?—she was a lady born, a jewel, though probably she could do no more than just read and write!

The elderly, clean-shaven man he had seen last night in the kitchen had come into the yard with a dog, driving the cows to their milking. Ashurst saw that he was lame.

"You've got some good ones there!"

The lame man's face brightened. He had the upward look in his eyes which prolonged suffering often brings.

"Yeas; they'm praaper buties; gude milkers tu."

"I bet they are."

" 'Ope as yure leg's better, zurr."

"Thank you, it's getting on."

The lame man touched his own: "I know what 'tes, meself; 'tes a main worritin' thing, the knee. I've a 'ad mine bad this ten year."

Ashurst made the sound of sympathy which comes so readily from those who have an independent income, and the lame man smiled again.

"Mustn't complain, though—they mighty near 'ad it off."

"Ho!"

"Yeas; an' compared with what 'twas, 'tes almost so gude as nu."

"They've put a bandage of splendid stuff on mine."

"The maid she picks et. She'm a gude maid wi' the flowers. There's folks zeem to know the healin' in things. My mother was a rare one for that. 'Ope as yu'll zune be better, zurr. Goo ahn, therr!"

Ashurst smiled. "Wi' the flowers!" A flower herself.

That evening, after his supper of cold duck, junket, and cider, the girl came in.

"Please, auntie says—will you try a piece of our Mayday cake?"

"If I may come to the kitchen for it."

"Oh, yes! You'll be missing your friend."

"Not I. But are you sure no one minds?"

"Who would mind? We shall be very pleased."

Ashurst rose too suddenly for his stiff knee, staggered, and subsided. The girl gave a little gasp, and held out her hands. Ashurst took them, small, rough, brown; checked his impulse to put them to his lips, and let her pull him up. She came close beside him, offering her shoulder. And leaning on her he walked across the room. That shoulder seemed quite the pleasantest thing he had ever touched. But he had presence of mind enough to catch his stick out of the rack, and withdraw his hand before arriving at the kitchen.

That night he slept like a top, and woke with his knee of almost normal size. He again spent the morning in his chair on the grass patch, scribbling down verses; but in the afternoon he wandered about with the two little boys Nick and Rick. It was Saturday, so they were early home from school; quick, shy, dark little rascals of seven and six, soon talkative, for Ashurst had a way with children. By four o'clock they had shown him all their methods of destroying life, except the tickling of trout; and with breeches tucked up, lay on their stomachs over the trout stream, pretending they had this accomplishment also. They tickled nothing, of course, for their giggling and shouting scared every spotted thing away. Ashurst, on a rock at the edge of the beech clump, watched them, and listened to the cuckoos, till Nick, the elder and less persevering, came up and stood beside him.

"The gipsy bogle zets on that stone," he said.

"What gipsy bogle?"

"Dunno; never zeen 'e. Megan zays 'e zets there; an' old Jim zeed 'e once. 'E was zettin' there naight afore our pony kicked-in father's 'ead. 'E plays the viddle."

"What tune does he play?"

"Dunno."

"What's he like?"

" 'E's black. Old Jim zays 'e's all over 'air. 'E's a praaper bogle. 'E don' come only at naight." The little boy's oblique dark eyes slid round. "D'y'u think 'e might want to take me away? Megan's feared of 'e."

"Has she seen him?"

"No. She's not afeared o' yu."

"I should think not. Why should she be?"

"She zays a prayer for yu."

"How do you know that, you little rascal?"

"When I was asleep, she said: 'God bless us all, an' Mr. Ashes.' I yeard 'er whisperin'."

"You're a little ruffian to tell what you hear when you're not meant to hear it!"

The little boy was silent. Then he said aggressively:

"I can skin rabbits. Megan, she can't bear skinnin' 'em. I like blood."

"Oh! you do; you little monster!"

"What's that?"

"A creature that likes hurting others."

The little boy scowled. "They'm only dead rabbits, what us eats."

"Quite right, Nick. I beg your pardon."

"I can skin frogs, tu."

But Ashurst had become absent. "God bless us all, and Mr. Ashes!" And puzzled by that sudden inaccessibility, Nick ran back to the stream where the giggling and shouts again uprose at once.

When Megan brought his tea, he said:

"What's the gipsy bogle, Megan?"

She looked up, startled.

"He brings bad things."

"Surely you don't believe in ghosts?"

"I hope I will never see him."

"Of course you won't. There aren't such things. What old Jim saw was a pony."

"No! There are bogles in the rocks; they are the men who lived long ago."

"They aren't gipsies, anyway; those old men were dead long before gipsies came."

She said simply: "They are all bad."

"Why? If there are any, they're only wild, like the rabbits. The flowers aren't bad for being wild; the thorn trees were never planted—and you don't mind them. I shall go down at night and look for your bogle, and have a talk with him."

"Oh, no! Oh, no!"

"Oh, yes! I shall go and sit on his rock."

She clasped her hands together: "Oh, please!"

"Why! What does it matter if anything happens to me?"

She did not answer; and in a sort of pet he added:

"Well, I daresay I shan't see him, because I suppose I must be off soon."

"Soon?"

"Your aunt won't want to keep me here."

"Oh, yes! We always let lodgings in summer."

Fixing his eyes on her face, he asked:

"Would you like me to stay?"

"Yes."

"I'm going to say a prayer for *you* to-night!"

She flushed crimson, frowned, and went out of the room. He sat cursing himself, till his tea was stewed. It was as if he had hacked with his thick boots at a clump of bluebells. Why had he said such a silly thing? Was he just a towny college ass like Robert Garton, as far from understanding this girl?

Ashurst spent the next week confirming the restoration of his leg, by exploration of the country within easy reach. Spring was a revelation to him this year. In a kind of intoxication he would watch the pink-white buds of some backward beech tree sprayed up in the sunlight against the deep blue sky, or the trunks and limbs of the few Scotch firs, tawny in violent light, or again on the moor, the gale-bent larches which had such a look of life when the wind streamed in their young green, above the rusty black underboughs. Or he would lie on the banks, gazing at the clusters of dog-violets, or up in the dead bracken, fingering the pink, transparent buds of the dewberry, while the cuckoos called and yaffles laughed, or a lark, from very high, dripped its beads of song. It was certainly different from any spring he had ever known, for spring was within him, not without. In the daytime he hardly saw the family; and when Megan brought in his meals she always seemed too busy in the house or among the young things in the yard to stay talking long. But in the evenings he installed himself in the window seat in the kitchen, smoking and chatting with the lame man, Jim, or Mrs. Narracombe, while the girl sewed, or moved about, clearing the supper things away. And sometimes with the sensation a cat must feel when it purrs, he would become conscious that Megan's eyes—those dew-grey eyes—were fixed on him with a sort of lingering soft look which was strangely flattering.

It was on Sunday week in the evening, when he was lying in the orchard listening to a blackbird and composing a love poem, that he heard the gate swing to, and saw the girl come running among the trees, with the red-cheeked, stolid Joe in swift pursuit. About twenty yards away the chase ended, and the two stood fronting each other, not noticing the stranger in the grass—the boy pressing on, the girl fending him off. Ashurst could see her face, angry, disturbed; and the youth's—who would have thought that red-faced yokel could look so distraught! And painfully affected by that sight, he jumped up. They saw him then. Megan dropped her hands, and shrank behind a tree-trunk; the boy gave an angry grunt, rushed at the bank, scrambled over and vanished. Ashurst went slowly up to her. She was standing quite still, biting her lip— very pretty, with her fine, dark hair blown loose about her face, and her eyes cast down.

"I beg your pardon," he said.

She gave him one upward look, from eyes much dilated; then, catching her breath, turned away. Ashurst followed.

"Megan!"

But she went on; and taking hold of her arm, he turned her gently round to him.

"Stop and speak to me."

"Why do you beg my pardon? It is not to me you should do that."

"Well, then, to Joe."

"How dare he come after me?"

"In love with you, I suppose."

She stamped her foot.

Ashurst uttered a short laugh. "Would you like me to punch his head?"

She cried with sudden passion:

"You laugh at me—you laugh at us!"

He caught hold of her hands, but she shrank back, till her passionate little face and loose dark hair were caught among the pink clusters of the apple blossom. Ashurst raised one of her imprisoned hands and put his lips to it. He felt how chivalrous he was, and superior to that clod Joe—just brushing that small, rough hand with his mouth! Her shrinking ceased suddenly; she seemed to tremble towards him. A sweet warmth overtook Ashurst from top to toe. This slim maiden, so simple and fine and pretty, was pleased, then, at the touch of his lips! And, yielding to a swift impulse, he put his arms round her, pressed her to him, and kissed her forehead. Then he was frightened—she went so pale, closing her eyes, so that the long dark lashes lay on her pale cheeks; her hands, too, lay inert at her sides. The touch of her breast sent a shiver through him. "Megan!" he sighed out, and let her go. In the utter silence a blackbird shouted. Then the girl seized his hand, put it to her cheek, her heart, her lips, kissed it passionately, and fled away among the mossy trunks of the apple trees, till they hid her from him.

Ashurst sat down on a twisted old tree growing almost along the ground, and, all throbbing and bewildered, gazed vacantly at the blossom which had crowned her hair—those pink buds with one white open apple star. What had he done? How had he let himself be thus stampeded by beauty—or—just the spring! He felt curiously happy, all the same; happy and triumphant, with shivers running through his limbs, and a vague alarm. This was the beginning of—what? The midges bit him, the dancing gnats tried to fly into his mouth, and all the spring around him seemed to grow more lovely and alive; the songs of the cuckoos and the blackbirds, the laughter of the yaffles, the level-slanting sunlight, the apple blossom which had crowned her head—! He got up from the old trunk and strode out of the orchard, wanting space, an open sky, to get on terms with these new sensations. He made for the moor, and from an ash tree in the hedge a magpie flew out to herald him.

Of man—at any age from five years on—who can say he has never been in love? Ashurst had loved his partners at his dancing class; loved his nursery governess; girls in school-holidays; perhaps never been quite out of love, cherishing always some more or less remote admiration. But this was different, not remote at all. Quite a new sensation; terribly delightful, bringing a sense of completed manhood. To be holding in his fingers such a wild flower, to be able to put it to his lips, and feel it tremble with delight against them! What intoxication, and—embarrassment! What to do with it—how meet her next time? His first caress had been cool, pitiful; but the next could not be, now that, by her burning little kiss on his hand, by her pressure of it to her heart, he knew that she loved him. Some natures are coarsened by love bestowed on them;

others, like Ashurst's, are swayed and drawn, warmed and softened, almost exalted, by what they feel to be a sort of miracle.

And up there among the tors he was racked between the passionate desire to revel in this new sensation of spring fulfilled within him, and a vague but very real uneasiness. At one moment he gave himself up completely to his pride at having captured this pretty, trustful, dewy-eyed thing! At the next he thought with factitious solemnity: "Yes, my boy! But look out what you're doing! You know what comes of it!"

Dusk dropped down without his noticing—dusk on the carved, Assyrian-looking masses of the rocks. And the voice of Nature said: "This is a new world for you!" As when a man gets up at four o'clock and goes out into a summer morning, and beasts, birds, trees stare at him and he feels as if all had been made new.

He stayed up there for hours, till it grew cold, then groped his way down the stones and heather roots to the road, back into the lane, and came again past the wild meadow to the orchard. There he struck a match and looked at his watch. Nearly twelve! It was black and unstirring in there now, very different from the lingering, bird-befriended brightness of six hours ago! And suddenly he saw this idyll of his with the eyes of the outer world—had mental vision of Mrs. Narracombe's snake-like neck turned, her quick dark glance taking it all in, her shrewd face hardening; saw the gipsy-like cousins coarsely mocking and distrustful; Joe stolid and furious; only the lame man, Jim, with the suffering eyes, seemed tolerable to his mind. And the village pub!—the gossiping matrons he passed on his walks; and then—his own friends—Robert Garton's smile when he went off that morning ten days ago; so ironical and knowing! Disgusting! For a minute he literally hated this earthly, cynical world to which one belonged, willy-nilly. The gate where he was leaning grew grey, a sort of shimmer passed before him and spread into the bluish darkness. The moon! He could just see it over the bank behind; red, nearly round—a strange moon! And turning away, he went up the lane which smelled of the night and cow-dung and young leaves. In the straw-yard he could see the dark shapes of cattle, broken by the pale sickles of their horns, like so many thin moons, fallen ends-up. He unlatched the farm gate stealthily. All was dark in the house. Muffling his footsteps, he gained the porch, and, blotted against one of the yew trees, looked up at Megan's window. It was open. Was she sleeping, or lying awake perhaps disturbed—unhappy at his absence? An owl hooted while he stood there peering up, and the sound seemed to fill the whole night, so quiet was all else, save for the never-ending murmur of the stream running below the orchard. The cuckoos by day, and now the owls—how wonderfully they voiced this troubled ecstasy within him! And suddenly he saw her at her window, looking out. He moved a little from the yew tree, and whispered: "Megan!" She drew back, vanished, reappeared, leaning far down. He stole forward on the grass patch, hit his shin against the green-painted chair, and held his breath at the sound. The pale blur of her stretched-down arm and face did not stir; he moved the chair, and noiselessly mounted it. By stretching up his arm he could just reach. Her hand held the huge key of the front door, and he clasped that burning hand with the cold key in it. He could just see her face, the glint of teeth between her lips, her tumbled hair. She was still dressed—poor child, sitting up for him, no doubt! "Pretty Megan!" Her hot, roughened fingers clung to his; her face had a strange, lost look. To have been able to reach it—even with his hand! The owl hooted, a scent of sweetbriar crept into his nostrils. Then one of the farm dogs barked; her grasp relaxed, she shrank back.

"Good-night, Megan!"

"Good-night, sir!" She was gone! With a sigh he dropped back to earth, and sitting on that chair, took off his boots. Nothing for it but to creep in and go to bed; yet for a long while he sat unmoving, his feet chilly in the dew, drunk on the memory of her lost, half-smiling face, and the clinging grip of her burning fingers, pressing the cold key into his hand.

He awoke feeling as if he had eaten heavily overnight, instead of having eaten nothing. And far off, unreal, seemed yesterday's romance! Yet it was a golden morning. Full spring had burst at last—in one night the "goldiecups," as the little boys called them, seemed to have made the field their own, and from his window he could see apple blossoms covering the orchard as with a rose and white quilt. He went down almost dreading to see Megan; and yet, when not she but Mrs. Narracombe brought in his breakfast, he felt vexed and disappointed. The woman's quick eye and snaky neck seemed to have a new alacrity this morning. Had she noticed?

"So you an' the moon went walkin' last night, Mr. Ashurst! Did ye have your supper anywheres?"

Ashurst shook his head.

"We kept it for you, but I suppose you was too busy in your brain to think o' such a thing as that?"

Was she mocking him, in that voice of hers, which still kept some Welsh crispness against the invading burr of the West Country? If she knew! And at that moment he thought: "No, no; I'll clear out. I won't put myself in such a beastly false position."

But, after breakfast, the longing to see Megan began and increased with every minute, together with fear lest something should have been said to her which had spoiled everything. Sinister that she had not appeared, not given him even a glimpse of her! And the love poem, whose manufacture had been so important and absorbing yesterday afternoon under the apple trees, now seemed so paltry that he tore it up and rolled it into pipe spills. What had he known of love, till she seized his hand and kissed it! And now—what did he not know? But to write of it seemed mere insipidity! He went up to his bedroom to get a book, and his heart began to beat violently, for she was in there making the bed. He stood in the doorway watching; and suddenly, with turbulent joy, he saw her stoop and kiss his pillow, just at the hollow made by his head last night. How let her know he had seen that pretty act of devotion? And yet if she heard him stealing away, it would be even worse. She took the pillow up, holding it as if reluctant to shake out the impress of his cheek, dropped it, and turned round.

"Megan!"

She put her hands up to her cheeks, but her eyes seemed to look right into him. He had never before realised the depth and purity and touching faithfulness in those dew-bright eyes, and he stammered:

"It was sweet of you to wait up for me last night."

She still said nothing, and he stammered on:

"I was wandering about on the moor; it was such a jolly night. I—I've just come up for a book."

Then, the kiss he had seen her give the pillow afflicted him with sudden headiness, and he went up to her. Touching her eyes with his lips, he thought with queer excitement: "I've done it! Yesterday all was sudden—anyhow; but now—I've done it!" The girl let her forehead rest against his lips, which moved downwards till they reached hers. That first real lover's kiss—strange, wonderful, still almost innocent—in which heart did it make the most disturbance?

"Come to the big apple tree to-night, after they've gone to bed. Megan —promise!"

She whispered back: "I promise!"

Then, scared at her white face, scared at everything, he let her go, and went downstairs again. Yes! he had done it now! Accepted her love, declared his own! He went out to the green chair as devoid of a book as ever; and there he sat staring vacantly before him, triumphant and remorseful, while under his nose and behind his back the work of the farm went on. How long he had been sitting in that curious state of vacancy he had no notion when he saw Joe standing a little behind him to the right. The youth had evidently come from hard work in the fields, and stood shifting his feet, breathing loudly, his face coloured like a setting sun, and his arms, below the rolled-up sleeves of his blue shirt, showing the hue and furry sheen of ripe peaches. His red lips were open, his blue eyes with their flaxen lashes stared fixedly at Ashurst, who said ironically:

"Well, Joe, anything I can do for you?"

"Yeas."

"What, then?"

"Yu can goo away from yere. Us don' want yu."

Ashurst's face, never too humble, assumed its most lordly look.

"Very good of you, but, do you know, I prefer the others should speak for themselves."

The youth moved a pace or two nearer, and the scent of his honest heat afflicted Ashurst's nostrils.

"What d'yu stay yere for?"

"Because it pleases me."

" 'Twon't please yu when I've bashed yure head in!"

"Indeed! When would you like to begin that?"

Joe answered only with the loudness of his breathing, but his eyes looked like those of a young and angry bull. Then a sort of spasm seemed to convulse his face.

"Megan don' want yu."

A rush of jealousy, of contempt, and anger with this thick, loud-breathing rustic got the better of Ashurst's self-possession; he jumped up and pushed back his chair.

"You can go to the devil!"

And as he said those simple words, he saw Megan in the doorway with a tiny brown spaniel puppy in her arms. She came up to him quickly:

"It's eyes are blue!" she said.

Joe turned away; the back of his neck was literally crimson.

Ashurst put his finger to the mouth of the little brown bull-frog of a creature in her arms. How cosy it looked against her!

"It's fond of you already. Ah! Megan, everything is fond of *you*."

"What was Joe saying to you, please?"

"Telling me to go away, because you didn't want me here."

She stamped her foot; then looked up at Ashurst. At that adoring look he felt his nerves quiver, just as if he had seen a moth scorching its wings.

"To-night!" he said. "Don't forget!"

"No." And smothering her face against the puppy's little fat, brown body, she slipped back into the house.

Ashurst wandered down the lane. At the gate of the wild meadow he came on the lame man and his cows.

"Beautiful day, Jim!"

"Ah! 'Tes brave weather for the grass. The ashes be later than th' oaks this year. 'When th' oak before th' ash——.' "

Ashurst said idly: "Where were you standing when you saw the gipsy bogle, Jim?"

"It might be under that big apple tree, as you might say."

"And you really do think it was there?"

The lame man answered cautiously:

"I shouldn't like to say rightly that 't *was* there. 'Twas in my mind as 'twas there."

"What do you make of it?"

The lame man lowered his voice.

"They du zay old master, Mist' Narracombe, come o' gipsy stock. But that's tellin'. They'm a wonderful people, yu know, for claimin' their own. Maybe they knu 'e was goin', and sent this feller along for company. That's what I've a-thought about it."

"What was he like?"

" 'E 'ad 'air all over 'is face, an' goin' like this, he was, zame as if 'e 'ad a viddle. They zay there's no such thing as bogles, but I've a-zeen the 'air on this dog standin' up of a dark naight, when I couldn' zee nothin', meself."

"Was there a moon?"

"Yeas, very near full, but 'twas on'y just risen, gold-like be'ind them trees."

"And you think a ghost means trouble, do you?"

The lame man pushed his hat up; his aspiring eyes looked at Ashurst more earnestly than ever.

" 'Tes not for me to zay that—but 'tes they ben' so unrestin'-like. There's things us don' understand, that's zartin, for zure. There's people that zee things, tu, an' others that don't never zee nothin'. Now, our Joe—yu might putt anything under 'is eyes an' 'e'd never see it; and them other boys, tu, they'm rattlin' fellers. But yu take an' putt our Megan where there's suthin', she'll zee it, an' more tu, or I'm mistaken."

"She's sensitive, that's why."

"What's that?"

"I mean, she feels everything."

"Ah! She'm very lovin'-'earted."

Ashurst, who felt colour coming into his cheeks, held out his tobacco pouch.

"Have a fill, Jim?"

"Thank 'ee, sir. She'm one in an 'underd, I think."

"I expect so," said Ashurst shortly, and folding up his pouch, walked on.

"Lovin'-'earted!" Yes! And what was he doing? What were his intentions—as they say—towards this loving-hearted girl? The thought dogged him, wandering through fields bright with buttercups, where the little red calves were feeding, and the swallows flying high. Yes, the oaks were before the ashes, brown-gold already; every tree in different stage and hue. The cuckoos and a thousand birds were singing; the little streams were very bright. The ancients believed in a golden age, in the garden of the Hesperides! . . . A queen wasp settled on his sleeve. Each queen wasp killed meant two thousand fewer wasps to thieve the apples which would grow from that blossom in the orchard; but who, with love in his heart, could kill anything on a day like this? He entered a field where a young red bull was feeding. It seemed to Ashurst that he looked like Joe. But the young bull took no notice of this visitor, a little drunk himself, perhaps, on the singing and the glamour of the golden pasture, under his short legs. Ashurst crossed out unchallenged to the hillside above the stream. From that slope a tor mounted to its crown of rocks. The ground there was covered with a mist of bluebells, and nearly a score of crab-apple trees were in full bloom. He threw himself down on the grass. The change from the buttercup glory and oak-goldened glamour of the fields to this ethereal beauty under the grey tor filled him with a sort of wonder; nothing the same, save the sound of running water and the songs of the cuckoos. He lay there a long time, watching the sunlight wheel till the crab-trees threw shadows over the bluebells, his only companions a few wild bees. He was not quite sane, thinking of that morning's kiss, and of to-night under the apple tree. In such a spot as this, fauns and dryads surely lived; nymphs, white as the crab-apple blossoms, retired within those trees; fauns, brown as the dead bracken, with pointed ears, lay in wait for them. The cuckoos were still calling when he woke, there was the sound of running water; but the sun had couched behind the tor, the hillside was cool, and some rabbits had come out. "To-night!" he thought. Just as from the earth every-thing was pushing up, unfolding under the soft insistent fingers of an unseen hand, so were his heart and senses being pushed, unfolded. He got up and broke off a spray from a crab-apple tree. The buds were like Megan—shell-like, rose-pink, wild, and fresh; and so, too, the opening flowers, white, and wild, and touching. He put the spray into his coat. And all the rush of the spring within him escaped in a triumphant sigh. But the rabbits scurried away.

It was nearly eleven that night when Ashurst put down the pocket *Odyssey* which for half an hour he had held in his hands without reading, and slipped through the yard down to the orchard. The moon had just risen, very golden, over the hill, and like a bright, powerful, watching spirit peered through the bars of an ash tree's half-naked boughs. In among the apple trees it was still dark, and he stood making sure of his direction, feeling the rough grass with his feet. A black mass close behind him stirred with a heavy grunting sound, and three large pigs settled down again close to each other, under the wall. He listened. There was no wind, but the stream's burbling whispering chuckle had gained twice its daytime strength. One bird, he could not tell what, cried "Pip—pip," "Pip—pip," with perfect monotony; he could hear a nightjar spinning very far off; an owl hooting. Ashurst moved a step or two, and again halted, aware of a dim living whiteness all round his head. On the dark unstirring trees innumerable flowers and buds all soft and blurred were being bewitched to life by the creeping moonlight. He had the oddest feeling of actual companionship, as if a million white moths or spirits had floated in and settled between dark sky and darker ground, and were opening and shutting their wings on a level with his eyes. In the bewildering, still, scentless beauty of that moment he almost lost memory of why he had come to the orchard. The flying glamour which had clothed the earth all day had not gone now that night had fallen, but only changed into this new form. He moved on through the thicket of stems and boughs covered with that live powdering whiteness, till he reached the big apple tree. No mistaking that, even in the dark, nearly twice the height and size of any other, and leaning out towards the open meadows and the stream. Under the thick branches he stood still again, to listen. The same sounds exactly, and a faint grunting from the sleepy pigs. He put his hands on the dry, almost warm tree trunk, whose rough mossy surface gave forth a peaty scent at his touch. Would she come—would she? And among these quivering, haunted, moon-witched trees he was seized with doubts of everything! All was unearthly here, fit for no earthly lovers; fit only for god and goddess, faun and nymph—not for him and this little country girl. Would it not be almost a relief if she did not come? But all the time he was listening. And still that unknown bird went "Pip—pip," "Pip—pip" and there rose the busy chatter of the little trout stream, whereon the moon was flinging glances through the bars of her tree-prison. The blossom on a level with his eyes seemed to grow more living every moment, seemed with its mysterious white beauty more and more a part of his suspense. He plucked a fragment and held it close—three blossoms. Sacrilege to pluck fruit-tree blossom—soft, sacred, young blossom—and throw it away! Then suddenly he heard the gate close, the pigs stirring again and grunting; and leaning against the trunk, he pressed his hands to its mossy sides behind him, and held his breath. She might have been a spirit threading the trees, for all the noise she made! Then he saw her quite close—her dark form part of a little tree, her white face part of its blossom; so still, and peering towards him. He whispered: "Megan!" and held out his hands. She ran forward, straight to his breast. When he felt her heart beating against him, Ashurst knew to the full the sensations of chivalry and passion. Because she was not of his world, because she was so simple and young and headlong, adoring and defenceless, how could he be other than her protector, in the dark! Because she was all simple Nature and beauty, as much a part of this spring night as was the living blossom, how should he not take all that she would give him—how not fulfil the spring in her heart and his! And torn between these two emotions he clasped her close, and kissed her hair. How long they stood there without speaking he knew not. The stream went on chattering, the owls hooting, the moon kept stealing up and growing whiter; the blossom all round them and above brightened in suspense of living beauty. Their lips had sought each other's, and they did not speak. The moment speech began all would be unreal! Spring has no speech, nothing but rustling and whispering. Spring has so much more than speech in its unfolding flowers and leaves, and the coursing of its streams, and in its sweet restless seeking! And sometimes spring will come alive, and, like a mysterious Presence, stand, encircling lovers with its arms, laying on them the fingers of enchantment, so that, standing lips to lips, they forget everything but just a kiss. While her heart beat against him, and her lips quivered on his, Ashurst felt nothing but simple rapture—Destiny meant her for his arms, Love could not be flouted! But when their lips parted for breath, division began again at once. Only, passion now was so much the stronger, and he sighed:

"Oh! Megan! Why did you come?"

She looked up, hurt, amazed.

"Sir, you asked me to."

"Don't call me 'sir,' my pretty sweet."

"What should I be callin' you?"

"Frank."

"I could not. Oh, no!"

"But you love me—don't you?"

"I could not help lovin' you. I want to be with you—that's all."

"All!"

So faint that he hardly heard, she whispered:

"I shall die if I can't be with you."

Ashurst took a mighty breath.

"Come and be with me, then!"

"Oh!"

Intoxicated by the awe and rapture in that "Oh!" he went on, whispering:

"We'll go to London. I'll show you the world. And I *will* take care of you, I promise, Megan. I'll never be a brute to you!"

"If I can be with you—that is all."

He stroked her hair, and whispered on:

"To-morrow I'll go to Torquay and get some money, and get you some clothes that won't be noticed, and then we'll steal away. And when we get to London, soon perhaps, if you love me well enough, we'll be married."

He could feel her hair shiver with the shake of her head.

"Oh, no! I could not, I only want to be with you!"

Drunk on his own chivalry, Ashurst went on murmuring:

"It's I who am not good enough for you. Oh! Megan, when did you begin to love me?"

"When I saw you in the road, and you looked at me. The first night I loved you; but I never thought you would want me."

She slipped down suddenly to her knees, trying to kiss his feet.

A shiver of horror went through Ashurst; he lifted her up bodily and held her fast—too upset to speak.

She whispered: "Why won't you let me?"

"It's I who will kiss your feet!"

Her smile brought tears into his eyes. The whiteness of her moonlit face so close to his, the faint pink of her opened lips, had the living unearthly beauty of the apple blossom.

And then, suddenly, her eyes widened and stared past him painfully; she writhed out of his arms, and whispered: "Look!"

Ashurst saw nothing but the brightened stream, the furze faintly gilded, the beech trees glistening, and behind them all the wide loom of the moonlit hill. Behind him came her frozen whisper: "The gipsy bogle!"

"Where?"

"There—by the stone—under the trees!"

Exasperated, he leapt the stream, and strode towards the beech clump. Prank of the moonlight! Nothing! In and out of the boulders and thorn trees, muttering and cursing, yet with a kind of terror, he rushed and stumbled. Absurd! Silly! Then he went back to the apple-tree. But she was gone; he could hear a rustle, the grunting of the pigs, the sound of a gate closing. Instead of her, only this old apple-tree! He flung his arms round the trunk. What a substitute for her soft body; the rough moss against his face—what a substitute for her soft cheek; only the scent, as of the woods, a little the same! And above him, and around, the blossoms, more living, more moonlit than ever, seemed to glow and breathe.

Descending from the train at Torquay station, Ashurst wandered uncertainly along the front, for he did not know this particular queen of English watering places. Having little sense of what he had on, he was quite unconscious of being remarkable among its inhabitants, and strode along in his rough Norfolk jacket, dusty boots, and battered hat, without observing that people gazed at him rather blankly. He was seeking a branch of his London bank, and having found one, found also the first obstacle to his mood. Did he know anyone in Torquay? No. In that case, if he would wire to his bank in London, they would be happy to oblige him on receipt of the reply. That suspicious breath from the matter-of-fact world somewhat tarnished the brightness of his visions. But he sent the telegram.

Nearly opposite to the post office he saw a shop full of ladies' garments, and examined the window with strange sensations. To have to undertake the clothing of his rustic love was more than a little disturbing. He went in. A young woman came forward; she had blue eyes and a faintly puzzled forehead. Ashurst stared at her in silence.

"Yes, sir?"

"I want a dress for a young lady."

The young woman smiled. Ashurst frowned—the peculiarity of his request struck him with sudden force.

The young woman added hastily:

"What style would you like—something modish?"

"No. Simple."

"What figure would the young lady be?"

"I don't know; about two inches shorter than you, I should say."

"Could you give me her waist measurement?"

Megan's waist!

"Oh! anything usual!"

"Quite!"

While she was gone he stood disconsolately eyeing the models in the window, and suddenly it seemed to him incredible that Megan—his Megan—could ever be dressed save in the rough tweed skirt, coarse blouse, and tam-o'-shanter cap he was wont to see her in. The young woman had come back with several dresses in her arms, and Ashurst eyed her laying them against her own modish figure. There was one whose colour he liked, a dove-grey, but to imagine Megan clothed in it was beyond him. The young woman went away, and brought some more. But on Ashurst there had now come a feeling of paralysis. How choose? She would want a hat too, and shoes, and gloves; and, suppose, when he had got them all, they commonised her, as Sunday clothes always commonised village folk! Why should she not travel as she was? Ah! But conspicuousness would matter; this was a serious elopement. And, staring at the young woman, he thought: "I wonder if she guesses, and thinks me a blackguard?"

"Do you mind putting aside that grey one for me?" he said desperately at last. "I can't decide now; I'll come in again this afternoon."

The young woman sighed.

"Oh! certainly. It's a very tasteful costume. I don't think you'll get anything that will suit your purpose better."

"I expect not," Ashurst murmured, and went out.

Freed again from the suspicious matter-of-factness of the world, he took a long breath, and went back to visions. In fancy he saw the trustful pretty creature who was going to join her life to his; saw himself and her stealing forth at night, walking over the moor under the moon, he with his arm around her, and carrying her new garments, till, in some far-off wood, when dawn was coming, she would slip off her old things and put on these, and an early train at a distant station would bear them away on their honeymoon journey, till London swallowed them up, and the dreams of love came true.

"Frank Ashurst! Haven't seen you since Rugby, old chap!"

Ashurst's frown dissolved; the face, close to his own, was blue-eyed, suffused with sun—one of those faces where sun from within and without join in a sort of lustre. And he answered:

"Phil Halliday, by Jove!"

"What are you doing here?"

"Oh! nothing. Just looking round, and getting some money. I'm staying on the moor."

"Are you lunching anywhere? Come and lunch with us; I'm here with my young sisters. They've had measles."

Hooked in by that friendly arm Ashurst went along, up a hill, down a hill, away out of the town, while the voice of Halliday, redolent of optimism as his face was of sun, explained how "in this mouldy place the only decent things were the bathing and boating," and so on, till presently they came to a crescent of houses a little above and back from the sea, and into the centre one—an hotel—made their way.

"Come up to my room and have a wash. Lunch'll be ready in a jiffy."

Ashurst contemplated his visage in a looking-glass. After his farmhouse bedroom, the comb and one spare shirt *régime* of the last fortnight, this room littered with clothes and brushes was a sort of Capua; and he thought: "Queer—one doesn't realise——" But what—he did not quite know.

When he followed Halliday into the sitting-room for lunch, three faces, very fair and blue-eyed, were turned suddenly at the words: "This is Frank Ashurst—my young sisters."

Two were indeed young, about eleven and ten. The third was perhaps seventeen, tall and fair-haired too, with pink-and-white cheeks just touched by the sun, and eyebrows, rather darker than the hair, running a little upwards from her nose to their outer points. The voices of all three were like Halliday's, high and cheerful; they stood up straight, shook hands with a quick movement, looked at Ashurst critically, away again at once, and began to talk of what they were going to do in the afternoon. A regular Diana and attendant nymphs! After the farm this crisp, slangy, eager talk, this cool, clean, off-hand refinement, was queer at first, and then so natural that what he had come from became suddenly remote. The names of the two little ones seemed to be Sabina and Freda; of the eldest, Stella.

Presently the one called Sabina turned to him and said:

"I say, will you come shrimping with us?—it's awful fun!"

Surprised by this unexpected friendliness, Ashurst murmured:

"I'm afraid I've got to get back this afternoon."

"Oh!"

"Can't you put it off?"

Ashurst turned to the new speaker, Stella, shook his head, and smiled. She was very pretty! Sabina said regretfully: "You might!" Then the talk switched off to caves and swimming.

"Can you swim far?"

"About two miles."

"Oh!"

"I say!"

"How jolly!"

The three pairs of blue eyes, fixed on him, made him conscious of his new importance. The sensation was agreeable. Halliday said:

"I say, you simply must stop and have a bathe. You'd better stay the night."

"Yes, do!"

But again Ashurst smiled and shook his head. Then suddenly he found himself being catechised about his physical achievements. He had rowed—it seemed—in his college boat, played in his college football team, won his college mile and he rose from table a sort of hero. The two little girls insisted that he must see "their" cave, and they set forth chattering like magpies, Ashurst between them, Stella and her brother a little behind. In the cave, damp and darkish like any other cave, the great feature was a pool with possibility of creatures which might be caught and put into bottles. Sabina and Freda, who wore no stockings on their shapely brown legs, exhorted Ashurst to join them in the middle of it, and help sieve the water. He too was soon bootless and sockless. Time goes fast for one who has a sense of beauty, when there are pretty children in a pool and a young Diana on the edge, to receive with wonder anything you can catch! Ashurst never had much sense of time. It was a shock when, pulling out his watch, he saw it was well past three. No cashing his cheque to-day—the bank would be closed before he could get there. Watching his expression, the little girls cried out at once:

"Hurrah! Now you'll have to stay!"

Ashurst did not answer. He was seeing again Megan's face, when at breakfast he had whispered: "I'm going to Torquay, darling, to get everything; I shall be back this evening. If it's fine we can go to-night. Be ready." He was seeing again how she quivered and hung on his words. What would she think? Then he pulled himself together, conscious suddenly of the calm scrutiny of this other young girl, so tall and fair and Diana-like, at the edge of the pool, of her wondering blue eyes under those brows which slanted up a little. If they knew what was in his mind—if they knew that this very night he had meant——! Well, there would be a little sound of disgust, and he would be alone in the cave. And with a curious mixture of anger, chagrin, and shame, he put his watch back into his pocket and said abruptly:

"Yes; I'm dished for to-day."

"Hurrah! Now you can bathe with us."

It was impossible not to succumb a little to the contentment of these pretty children, to the smile on Stella's lips, to Halliday's "Ripping, old chap! I can lend you things for the night!" But again a spasm of longing and remorse throbbed through Ashurst, and he said moodily:

"I must send a wire!"

The attractions of the pool palling, they went back to the hotel. Ashurst sent his wire, addressing it to Mrs. Narracombe: "Sorry, detained for the night, back to-morrow." Surely Megan would understand that he had too much to do; and his heart grew lighter. It was a lovely afternoon, warm, the sea calm and blue, and swimming his great passion; the favour of these pretty children flattered him, the pleasure of looking at them, at Stella, at Halliday's sunny face; the slight unreality, yet extreme naturalness of it all—as of a last peep at normality before he took this plunge with Megan! He got his borrowed bathing dress, and they all set forth. Halliday and he undressed behind one rock, the three girls behind another. He was first into the sea, and at once swam out with the bravado of justifying his self-given reputation. When he turned he could see Halliday swimming along shore, and the girls flopping and dipping, and riding the little waves, in the way he was accustomed to despise, but now thought pretty and sensible, since it gave him the distinction of the only deep-water fish. But drawing near, he wondered if they would like him, a stranger, to come into their splashing group; he felt shy, approaching that slim nymph. Then Sabina summoned him to teach her to float, and between them the little girls kept him so busy that he had no time even to notice whether Stella was accustomed to his presence, till suddenly he heard a startled sound from her. She was standing submerged to the waist, leaning a little forward, her slim white arms stretched out and pointing, her wet face puckered by the sun and an expression of fear.

"Look at Phil! Is he all right? Oh, look!"

Ashurst saw at once that Phil was not all right. He was splashing and struggling out of his depth, perhaps a hundred yards away; suddenly he gave up a cry, threw up his arms, and went down. Ashurst saw the girl launch herself towards him, and crying out: "Go back, Stella! Go back!" he dashed out. He had never swum so fast, and reached Halliday just as he was coming up a second time. It was a case of cramp, but to get him in was not difficult, for he did not struggle. The girl, who had stopped when Ashurst told her to, helped as soon as he was in his depth, and once on the beach they sat down one on each side of him to rub his limbs, while the little ones stood by with scared faces. Halliday was soon smiling. It was—he said—rotten of him, absolutely rotten! If Frank would give him an arm, he could get to his clothes all right now. Ashurst gave him the arm, and as he did so caught sight of Stella's face, wet and flushed and tearful, all broken up out of its calm; and he thought: "I called her Stella! Wonder if she minded?"

While they were dressing, Halliday said quietly:

"You saved my life, old chap!"

"Rot!"

Clothed, but not quite in their right minds, they went up all together to the hotel and sat down to tea, except Halliday, who was lying down in his room. After some slices of bread and jam, Sabina said:

"I say, you know, you *are* a brick!" And Freda chimed in: "Rather!"

Ashurst saw Stella looking down; he got up in confusion, and went to the window. From there he heard Sabina mutter: "I say, let's swear blood bond. Where's your knife, Freda?" and out of the corner of his eye could see each of them solemnly prick herself, squeeze out a drop of blood and dabble on a bit of paper. He turned and made for the door.

"Don't be a stoat! Come back!" His arms were seized; imprisoned between the little girls he was brought back to the table. On it lay a piece of paper with an effigy drawn in blood, and the three names Stella Halliday, Sabina Halliday, Freda Halliday—also in blood, running towards it like the rays of a star. Sabina said:

"That's you. We shall have to kiss you, you know."

And Freda echoed:

"Oh! Blow—Yes!"

Before Ashurst could escape, some wettish hair dangled against his face, something like a bite descended on his nose, he felt his left arm pinched, and other teeth softly searching his cheek. Then he was released, and Freda said:

"Now, Stella."

Ashurst, red and rigid, looked across the table at a red and rigid Stella. Sabina giggled; Freda cried:

"Buck up—it spoils everything!"

A queer, ashamed eagerness shot through Ashurst: then he said quietly:

"Shut up, you little demons!"

Again Sabina giggled.

"Well, then, she can kiss her hand, and you can put it against your nose. It *is* on one side!"

To his amazement the girl did kiss her hand and stretch it out. Solemnly he took that cool, slim hand and laid it to his cheek. The two little girls broke into clapping, and Freda said:

"Now, then, we shall have to save your life at any time; that's settled. Can I have another cup, Stella, not so beastly weak?"

Tea was resumed, and Ashurst, folding up the paper, put it in his pocket. The talk turned on the advantages of measles, tangerine oranges, honey in a spoon, no lessons, and so forth. Ashurst listened, silent, exchanging friendly looks with Stella, whose face was again of its normal sun-touched pink and white. It was soothing to be so taken to the heart of this jolly family, fascinating to watch their faces. And after tea, while the two little girls pressed seaweed, he talked to Stella in the window seat and looked at her water-colour sketches. The whole thing was like a pleasurable dream; time and incident hung up, importance and reality suspended. To-morrow he would go back to Megan, with nothing of all this left save the paper with the blood of these children, in his pocket. Children! Stella was not quite that—as old as Megan! Her talk—quick, rather hard and shy, yet friendly—seemed to flourish on his silences, and about her there was something cool and virginal—a maiden in a bower. At dinner, to which Halliday, who had swallowed too much seawater, did not come, Sabina said:

"I'm going to call you Frank."

Freda echoed:

"Frank, Frank, Franky."

Ashurst grinned and bowed.

"Every time Stella calls you Mr. Ashurst, she's got to pay a forfeit. It's ridiculous."

Ashurst looked at Stella, who grew slowly red. Sabina giggled; Freda cried:

"She's 'smoking'—'smoking!'—Yah!"

Ashurst reached out to right and left, and grasped some fair hair in each hand.

"Look here, you two! Leave Stella alone, or I'll tie you together!" Freda gurgled:

"Ouch! You *are* a beast!"

Sabina murmured cautiously:

"*You* call *her* Stella, you see!"

"Why shouldn't I? It's a jolly name!"

"All right; we give you leave to!"

Ashurst released the hair. Stella! What would she call him—after this? But she called him nothing; till at bedtime he said, deliberately:

"Good-night, Stella!"

"Good-night, Mr. —— Good-night, Frank! It *was* jolly of you, you know!"

"Oh—that! Bosh!"

Her quick, straight handshake tightened suddenly, and as suddenly, became slack.

Ashurst stood motionless in the empty sitting-room. Only last night, under the apple-tree and the living blossom, he had held Megan to him, kissing her eyes and lips. And he gasped, swept by that rush of remembrance. To-night it should have begun—his life with her who only wanted to be with him! And now, twenty-four hours and more must pass, because—of not looking at his watch! Why had he made friends with this family of innocents just when he was saying good-bye to innocence, and all the rest of it? "But I mean to marry her," he thought; "I told her so!"

He took a candle, lighted it, and went to his bedroom, which was next to Halliday's. His friend's voice called as he was passing:

"Is that you, old chap? I say, come in."

He was sitting up in bed, smoking a pipe and reading.

"Sit down a bit."

Ashurst sat down by the open window.

"I've been thinking about this afternoon, you know," said Halliday rather suddenly. "They say you go through all your past. I didn't. I suppose I wasn't far enough gone."

"What did you think of?"

Halliday was silent for a little, then said quietly:

"Well, I did think of one thing—rather odd—of a girl at Cambridge that I might have—you know; I was glad I hadn't got her on my mind. Anyhow, old chap, I owe it to you that I'm here; I should have been in the big dark by now. No more bed, or baccy; no more anything. I say, what d'you suppose happens to us?"

Ashurst murmured:

"Go out like flames, I expect."

"Phew!"

"We may flicker, and cling about a bit, perhaps."

"H'm! I think that's rather gloomy. I say, I hope my young sisters have been decent to you?"

"Awfully decent."

Halliday put his pipe down, crossed his hands behind his neck, and turned his face towards the window.

"They're not bad kids!" he said.

Watching his friend, lying there, with that smile, and the candle-light on his face, Ashurst shuddered. Quite true! He might have been lying there with no smile, with all that sunny look gone out for ever! He might not have been lying there at all, but "sanded" at the bottom of the sea, waiting for resurrection on the—ninth day, was it? And that smile of Halliday's seemed to him suddenly something wonderful, as if in it were all the difference between life and death—the little flame— the all! He got up, and said softly:

"Well, you ought to sleep, I expect. Shall I blow out?"

Halliday caught his hand.

"I can't say it, you know; but it must be rotten to be dead. Good-night, old boy!"

Stirred and moved, Ashurst squeezed the hand, and went downstairs. The hall door was still open, and he passed out on to the lawn before the Crescent. The stars were bright in a very dark blue sky, and by their light some lilacs had that mysterious colour of flowers by night which no one can describe. Ashurst pressed his face against a spray; and before his closed eyes Megan started up, with the tiny brown spaniel pup against her breast. "I thought of a girl that I might have—you know. I was glad I hadn't got her on my mind!" He jerked his head away from the lilac, and began pacing up and down over the grass, a grey phantom coming to substance for a moment in the light from the lamp at either end. He was with her again under the living, breathing whiteness of the blossom, the stream chattering by, the moon glinting steel-blue on the bathing-pool; back in the rapture of his kisses on her upturned face of innocence and humble passion, back in the suspense and beauty of that pagan night. He stood still once more in the shadow of the lilacs. Here the sea, not the stream, was Night's voice; the sea with its sigh and rustle; no little bird, no owl, no nightjar called or spun; but a piano tinkled, and the white houses cut the sky with solid curve, and the scent from the lilacs filled the air. A window of the hotel, high up, was lighted; he saw a shadow move across the blind. And most queer sensations stirred within him, a sort of churning, and twining, and turning of a single emotion on itself, as though spring and love, bewildered and confused, seeking the way, were baffled. This girl, who had called him Frank, whose hand had given his that sudden little clutch, this girl so cool and pure—what would *she* think of such wild, unlawful loving? He sank down on the grass, sitting there cross-legged, with his back to the house, motionless as some carved Buddha. Was he really going to break through innocence, and steal? Sniff the scent out of a wild flower, and—perhaps—throw it away? "Of a girl at Cambridge that I might have—you know!" He put his hands to the grass, one on each side, palms downwards, and pressed; it was just warm still—the grass, barely moist, soft and firm and friendly. "What am I going to do?" he thought. Perhaps Megan was at her window, looking out at the blossom, thinking of him! Poor little Megan! "Why not?" he thought. "I love her! But do I—really love her? or do I only want her because she is so pretty, and loves me? What am I going to do?" The piano tinkled on, the stars winked; and Ashurst gazed out before him at the dark sea, as if spellbound. He got up at last, cramped and rather chilly. There was no longer light in any window. And he went in to bed.

Out of a deep and dreamless sleep he was awakened by the sound of thumping on the door. A shrill voice called:

"Hi! Breakfast's ready."

He jumped up. Where was he——? Ah!

He found them already eating marmalade, and sat down in the empty place between Stella and Sabina, who, after watching him a little, said: "I say, do buck up; we're going to start at half-past nine."

"We're going to Berry Head, old chap; you *must* come!"

Ashurst thought: "Come! Impossible. I shall be getting things and going back." He looked at Stella. She said quickly:

"Do come!"

Sabina chimed in:

"It'll be no fun without you."

Freda got up and stood behind his chair.

"You've got to come, or else I'll pull your hair!"

Ashurst thought: "Well—one day more—to think it over! One day more!" And he said:

"All right! You needn't tweak my mane!"

"Hurrah!"

At the station he wrote a second telegram to the farm, and then—tore it up; he could not have explained why. From Brixham they drove in a very little wagonette. There, squeezed between Sabina and Freda, with his knees touching Stella's, they played "Up Jenkins"; and the gloom he was feeling gave way to frolic. In this one day more to think it over, he did not want to think! They ran races, wrestled, paddled—for to-day nobody wanted to bathe—they sang catches, played games, and ate all they had brought. The little girls fell asleep against him on the way back, and his knees still touched Stella's in the wagonette. It seemed incredible that thirty hours ago he had never set eyes on any of those three flaxen heads. In the train he talked to Stella of poetry, discovering her favourites, and telling her his own with a pleasing sense of superiority; till suddenly she said, rather low:

"Phil says you don't believe in a future life, Frank. I think that's dreadful."

Disconcerted, Ashurst muttered:

"I don't either believe or not believe—I simply don't know."

She said quickly:

"I couldn't bear that. What would be the use of living?"

Watching the frown of those pretty oblique brows, Ashurst answered:

"I don't believe in believing things because one wants to."

"But why should one *wish* to live again, if one isn't going to?"

And she looked full at him.

He did not want to hurt her, but an itch to dominate pushed him on to say:

"While one's alive one naturally wants to go on living for ever; that's part of being alive. But it probably isn't anything more."

"Don't you believe in the Bible at all, then?"

Ashurst thought: "Now I shall really hurt her!"

"I believe in the Sermon on the Mount, because it's beautiful and good for all time."

"But don't you believe Christ was divine?"

He shook his head.

She turned her face quickly to the window, and there sprang into his mind Megan's prayer, repeated by little Nick: "God bless us all, and Mr. Ashes!" Who else would ever say a prayer for him, like her who at this moment must be waiting—waiting to see him come down the lane? And he thought suddenly: "What a scoundrel I am!"

All that evening this thought kept coming back: but, as is not unusual, each time with less poignancy, till it seemed almost a matter of course to be a scoundrel. And—strange!—he did not know whether he was a scoundrel if he meant to go back to Megan, or if he did not mean to go back to her.

They played cards till the children were sent off to bed; then Stella went to the piano. From over on the window seat, where it was nearly dark, Ashurst watched her between the candles—that fair head on the long, white neck bending to the movement of her hands. She played fluently, without much expression; but what a picture she made, the faint golden radiance, a sort of angelic atmosphere—hovering about her! Who could have passionate thoughts or wild desires in the presence of that swaying, white-clothed girl with the seraphic head? She played a thing of Schumann's called *"Warum?"* Then Halliday brought out a flute, and the spell was broken. After this they made Ashurst sing, Stella playing him accompaniments from a book of Schumann songs, till, in the middle of *"Ich grolle nicht,"* two small figures clad in blue dressing-gowns crept in and tried to conceal themselves beneath the piano. The evening broke up in confusion, and what Sabina called "a splendid rag."

That night Ashurst hardly slept at all. He was thinking, tossing and turning. The intense domestic intimacy of these last two days, the strength of this Halliday atmosphere, seemed to ring him round, and make the farm and Megan—even Megan—seem unreal. Had he really made love to her—really promised to take her away to live with him? He must have been bewitched by the spring, the night, the apple blossom! The notion that he was going to make her his mistress—that simple child not yet eighteen—now filled him with a sort of horror, even while it still stung and whipped his blood. He muttered to himself: "It's awful, what I've done—awful!" And the sound of Schumann's music throbbed and mingled with his fevered thoughts, and he saw again Stella's cool, white, fair-haired figure and bending neck, the queer, angelic radiance about her. "I must have been—I must be—mad!" he thought. "What came into me? Poor little Megan!" "God bless us all, and Mr. Ashes!" "I want to be with you—only to be with you!" And burying his face in his pillow, he smothered down a fit of sobbing. Not to go back was awful! To go back—more awful still!

Emotion, when you are young, and give real vent to it, loses its power of torture. And he fell asleep, thinking: "What was it—a few kisses—all forgotten in a month!"

Next morning he got his cheque cashed, but avoided the shop of the dove-grey dress like the plague; and, instead, bought himself some necessaries. He spent the whole day in a queer mood, cherishing a kind of sullenness against himself. Instead of the hankering of the last two days, he felt nothing but a blank—all passionate longing gone, as if quenched in that outburst of tears. After tea Stella put a book down beside him, and said shyly:

"Have you read that, Frank?"

It was Farrar's *Life of Christ*. Ashurst smiled. Her anxiety about his beliefs seemed to him comic, but touching. Infectious, too, perhaps, for he began to have an itch to justify himself, if not to convert her.

And in the evening, when the children and Halliday were mending their shrimping nets, he said:

"At the back of orthodox religion, so far as I can see, there's always the idea of reward—what you can get for being good; a kind of begging for favours. I think it all starts in fear."

She was sitting on the sofa making reefer knots with a bit of string. She looked up quickly:

"I think it's much deeper than that."

Ashurst felt again that wish to dominate.

"You think so," he said; "but wanting the *quid pro quo* is about the deepest thing in all of us! It's jolly hard to get to the bottom of it!"

She wrinkled her brows in a puzzled frown.

"I don't think I understand."

He went on obstinately:

"Well, think, and see if the most religious people aren't those who feel that this life doesn't give them all they want. I believe in being good because to be good is good in itself."

"Then you do believe in being good?"

How pretty she looked now—it was easy to be good with her! And he nodded and said:

"I say, show me how to make that knot!"

With her fingers touching his, in manœuvring the bit of string he felt soothed and happy. And when he went to bed he wilfully kept his thoughts on her, wrapping himself in her fair, cool, sisterly radiance, as in some garment of protection.

Next day he found they had arranged to go by train to Totnes, and picnic at Berry Pomeroy Castle. Still in that resolute oblivion of the past, he took his place with them in the landau beside Halliday, back to the horses. And, then, along the sea front, nearly at the turning to the railway station, his heart almost leaped into his mouth. Megan—Megan herself!—was walking on the far pathway, in her old skirt and jacket and her tam-o'-shanter, looking up into the faces of the passers-by. Instinctively he threw his hand up for cover, then made a feint of clearing dust out of his eyes; but between his fingers he could see her still, moving, not with her free country step, but wavering, lost-looking, pitiful—like some little dog which has missed its master and does not know whether to run on, to run back—where to run. How had she come like this?—what excuse had she found to get away?—what did she hope for? But with every turn of the wheels bearing him away from her, his heart revolted and cried to him to stop them, to get out and go to her. When the landau turned the corner to the station he could stand it no more, and opening the carriage door, muttered: "I've forgotten something! Go on—don't wait for me! I'll join you at the castle by the next train!" He jumped, stumbled, spun round, recovered his balance, and walked forward, while the carriage with the astonished Hallidays rolled on.

From the corner he could only just see Megan, a long way ahead now. He ran a few steps, checked himself, and dropped into a walk. With each step nearer to her, further from the Hallidays, he walked more and more slowly. How did it alter anything—this sight of her? How make the going to her, and that which must come of it, less ugly? For there was no hiding it—since he had met the Hallidays he had become gradually sure that he would not marry Megan. It would only be a wild love-time, a troubled, remorseful, difficult time—and then —well, then he would get tired, just because she gave him everything, was so simple, and so trustful, so dewy. And dew—wears off! The little spot of faded colour, her tam-o'-shanter cap, wavered on far in front of him; she was looking up into every face, and at the house windows. Had any man ever such a cruel moment to go through? Whatever he did, he felt he would be a beast. And he uttered a groan which made a nursemaid turn and stare. He saw Megan stop and lean against the sea-wall, looking at the sea; and he too stopped. Quite likely she had never seen the sea before, and even in her distress could not resist that sight. "Yes—she's seen nothing," he thought; "everything's before her. And just for a few weeks' passion, I shall be cutting her life to ribbons. I'd better go and hang myself rather than do it!" And suddenly he seemed to see Stella's calm eyes looking into his, the wave of fluffy hair on her forehead stirred by the wind. Ah! it would be madness, would mean giving up all that he respected, and his own self-respect. He turned and walked quickly back towards the station. But memory of that poor, bewildered little figure, those anxious eyes searching the passers-by, smote him too hard again, and once more he turned towards the sea. The cap was no longer visible; that little spot of colour had vanished in the stream of the noon promenaders. And impelled by the passion of longing, the dearth which comes on one when life seems to be whiling something out of reach, he hurried forward. She was nowhere to be seen; for half an hour he looked for her; then on the beach flung himself face downward in the sand. To find her again he knew he had only to go to the station and wait till she returned from her fruitless quest, to take her train home; or to take train himself and go back to the farm, so that she found him there when she returned. But he lay inert in the sand, among the indifferent groups of children with their spades and buckets. Pity at her little figure wandering, seeking, was well-nigh merged in the spring-running of his blood; for it was all wild feeling now—the chivalrous part, what there had been of it, was gone. He wanted her again, wanted her kisses, her soft, little body, her abandonment, all her quick, warm, pagan emotion; wanted the wonderful feeling of that night under the moon-lit apple boughs; wanted it all with a horrible intensity, as the faun wants the nymph. The quick chatter of the little bright trout-stream, the dazzle of the buttercups, the rocks of the old "wild men"; the calling of the cuckoos and yaffles, the hooting of the owls; and the red moon peeping out of the velvet dark at the living whiteness of the blossom; and her face just out of reach at the window, lost in its love-look; and her heart against his, her lips answering his, under the apple tree—all this besieged him. Yet he lay inert. What was it which struggled against pity and this feverish longing, and kept him there paralysed in the warm sand? Three flaxen heads—a fair face with friendly blue-grey eyes, a slim hand pressing his, a quick voice speaking his name—"So you do believe in being good?" Yes, and a sort of atmosphere as of some old walled-in English garden, with pinks, and corn-flowers, and roses, and scents of lavender and lilac—cool and fair, untouched, almost holy—all that he had been brought up to feel was clean and good. And suddenly he thought: "She might come along the front again and see me!" and he got up and made his way to the rock at the far end of the beach. There, with the spray biting into his face, he could think more coolly. To go back to the farm and love Megan out in the woods, among the rocks, with everything around wild and fitting—that, he knew, was impossible, utterly. To transplant her to a great town, to keep, in some little flat or rooms, one who belonged so wholly to Nature —the poet in him shrank from it. His passion would be a mere sensuous revel, soon gone; in London, her very simplicity, her lack of all intellectual quality, would make her his secret plaything—nothing else. The longer he sat on the rock, with his feet dangling over a greenish pool from which the sea was ebbing, the more clearly he saw this; but it was as if her arms and all of her were slipping slowly, slowly down from him, into the pool, to be carried out to sea; and her face looking up, her lost face with beseeching eyes, and dark, wet hair—possessed, haunted, tortured him! He got up at last, scaled the low rock-cliff, and made his way down into a sheltered cove. Perhaps in the sea he could get back his control—lose this fever! And stripping off his clothes, he swam out. He wanted to tire himself so that nothing mattered, and swam recklessly, fast and far; then suddenly, for no reason, felt afraid. Suppose he could not reach shore again—suppose the current set him out—or he got cramp, like Halliday! He turned to swim in. The red cliffs looked a long way off. If he were drowned they would find his clothes. The Hallidays would know; but Megan perhaps never—they took no newspaper at the farm. And Phil Halliday's words came back to him again: "A girl at Cambridge I might have——Glad I haven't got her on my mind!" And in that moment of unreasoning fear he vowed he would not have her on his mind. Then his fear left him; he swam in easily enough, dried himself in the sun, and put on his clothes. His heart felt sore, but no longer ached; his body cool and refreshed.

When one is as young as Ashurst, pity is not a violent emotion. And, back in the Halliday's sitting-room, eating a ravenous tea, he felt much like a man recovered from fever. Everything seemed new and clear; the tea, the buttered toast and jam tasted absurdly good; tobacco had never smelt so nice. And walking up and down the empty room, he stopped here and there to touch or look. He took up Stella's work-basket, fingered the cotton reels and a gaily-coloured plait of sewing silks, smelt at the little bag filled with woodroffe she kept among them. He sat down at the piano, playing tunes with one finger, thinking: "To-night she'll play; I shall watch her while she's playing; it does me good to watch her." He took up the book, which still lay where she had placed it beside him, and tried to read. But Megan's little, sad figure began to come back at once, and he got up and leaned in the window, listening to the thrushes in the Crescent gardens, gazing at the sea, dreamy and blue below the trees. A servant came in and cleared the tea away, and he still stood, inhaling the evening air, trying not to think. Then he saw the Hallidays coming through the gate of the Crescent, Stella a little in front of Phil and the children, with their baskets, and instinctively he drew back. His heart, too sore and discomfited, shrank from this encounter, yet wanted its friendly solace—bore a grudge a-gainst this influence, yet craved its cool innocence, and the pleasure of watching Stella's face. From against the wall behind the piano he saw her come in and stand looking a little blank as though disappointed; then she saw him and smiled, a swift, brilliant smile which warmed yet irritated Ashurst.

"You never came after us, Frank."

"No; I found I couldn't."

"Look! We picked such lovely late violets!" She held out a bunch. Ashurst put his nose to them, and there stirred within him vague long-ings, chilled instantly by a vision of Megan's anxious face lifted to the faces of the passers-by.

He said shortly: "How jolly!" and turned away. He went up to his room, and, avoiding the children, who were coming up the stairs, threw himself on his bed, and lay there with his arms crossed over his face. Now that he felt the die really cast, and Megan given up, he hated him-self, and almost hated the Hallidays and their atmosphere of healthy, happy English homes. Why should they have chanced here, to drive away first love—to show him that he was going to be no better than a common seducer? What right had Stella, with her fair, shy beauty, to make him know for certain that he would never marry Megan; and, tarnishing it all, bring him such bitterness of regretful longing and such pity? Megan would be back by now, worn out by her miserable seeking—poor little thing!—expecting, perhaps, to find him there when she reached home. Ashurst bit at his sleeve, to stifle a groan of remorseful longing. He went to dinner glum and silent, and his mood threw a dinge even over the children. It was a melancholy, rather ill-tempered evening, for they were all tired; several times he caught Stella looking at him with a hurt, puzzled expression, and this pleased his evil mood. He slept miserably; got up quite early, and wandered out. He went down to the beach. Alone there with the serene, the blue, the sunlit sea, his heart relaxed a little. Conceited fool—to think that Megan would take it so hard! In a week or two she would almost have forgotten! And he—well, he would have the reward of virtue! A good young man! If Stella knew, she would give him her blessing for resisting that devil she believed in; and he uttered a hard laugh. But slowly the peace and beauty of sea and sky, the flight of the lonely seagulls, made him feel ashamed. He bathed, and turned homewards.

In the Crescent gardens Stella herself was sitting on a camp stool, sketching. He stole up close behind. How fair and pretty she was, bent diligently, holding up her brush, measuring, wrinkling her brows.

He said gently:

"Sorry I was such a beast last night, Stella."

She turned round, startled, flushed very pink, and said in her quick way:

"It's all right. I knew there was something. Between friends it doesn't matter, does it?"

Ashurst answered:

"Between friends—and we are, aren't we?"

She looked up at him, nodded vehemently, and her upper teeth gleamed again in that swift, brilliant smile.

Three days later he went back to London, traveling with the Hallidays. He had not written to the farm. What was there he could say?

On the last day of April in the following year he and Stella were married. . . .

Such were Ashurst's memories, sitting against the wall among the gorse, on his silver-wedding day. At this very spot, where he had laid out the lunch, Megan must have stood outlined against the sky when he had first caught sight of her. Of all queer coincidences! And there moved in him a longing to go down and see again the farm and the orchard, and the meadow of the gipsy bogle. It would not take long; Stella would be an hour yet, perhaps.

How well he remembered it all—the little crowning group of pine trees, the steep-up grass hill behind! He paused at the farm gate. The low stone house, the yew-tree porch, the flowering currants—not changed a bit; even the old green chair was out there on the grass under the window, where he had reached up to her that night to take the key. Then he turned down the lane, and stood leaning on the orchard gate —grey skeleton of a gate, as then. A black pig even was wandering in there among the trees. Was it true that twenty-six years had passed, or had he dreamed and awakened to find Megan waiting for him by the big apple-tree? Unconsciously he put up his hand to his grizzled beard and brought himself back to reality. Opening the gate, he made his way down through the docks and nettles till he came to the edge, and the old apple-tree itself. Unchanged! A little more of the grey-green lichen, a dead branch or two, and for the rest it might have been only last night that he had embraced that mossy trunk after Megan's flight and inhaled its woody savour, while above his head the moonlit blossom had seemed to breathe and live. In that early spring a few buds were showing already; the blackbirds shouting their songs, a cuckoo calling, the sunlight bright and warm. Incredibly the same—the chattering trout-stream, the narrow pool he had lain in every morning, splashing the water over his flanks and chest; and out there in the wild meadow the beech clump and the stone where the gipsy bogle was supposed to sit. And an ache for lost youth, a hankering, a sense of wasted love and sweetness, gripped Ashurst by the throat. Surely, on this earth of such wild beauty, one was meant to hold rapture to one's heart, as this earth and sky held it! And yet, one could not!

He went to the edge of the stream, and looking down at the little pool, thought: "Youth and spring! What has become of them all, I wonder?" And then, in sudden fear of having this memory jarred by human encounter, he went back to the lane, and pensively retraced his steps to the cross-roads.

Beside the car an old, grey-bearded labourer was leaning on a stick, talking to the chauffeur. He broke off at once, as though guilty of disrespect, and touching his hat, prepared to limp on down the lane.

Ashurst pointed to the narrow green mound. "Can you tell me what this is?"

The old fellow stopped; on his face had come a look as though he were thinking: "You've come to the right shop, Mister!"

" 'Tes a grave," he said.

"But why out here?"

The old man smiled. "That's a tale, as yu may say. An' not the first time as I've a-told et—there's plenty folks asks 'bout that bit o' turf. 'Maid's Grave' us calls et, 'ereabouts."

Ashurst held out his pouch. "Have a fill?"

The old man touched his hat again, and slowly filled an old clay pipe. His eyes, looking upward out of the mass of wrinkles and hair, were still quite bright.

"If yu don' mind, zurr, I'll zet down—my leg's 'urtin' a bit to-day." And he sat down on the mound of turf.

"There's always a vlower on this grave. An' 'tain't so very lonesome, neither; brave lot o' folks goes by now, in they new motor cars an' things—not as 'twas in th' old days. She've a-got company up 'ere. 'Twas a poor soul killed 'erself."

"I see!" said Ashurst. "Cross-roads burial. I didn't know that custom was kept up."

"Ah! but 'twas a main long time ago. Us 'ad a parson as was very God-fearin' then. Let me see, I've 'ad my pension six year come Michaelmas, an' I were just on fifty when t'appened. There's none livin' knows more about et than what I du. She belonged close 'ere; same farm as where I used to work along o' Mrs. Narracombe—'tes Nick Narracombe's now; I dus a bit for 'im still, odd times."

Ashurst, who was leaning against the gate, lighting his pipe, left his curved hands before his face for long after the flame of the match had gone out.

"Yes?" he said, and to himself his voice sounded hoarse and queer.

"She was one in an 'undred, poor maid! I puts a vlower 'ere every time I passes. Pretty maid an' gude maid she was, though they wouldn't burry 'er up tu th' church, nor where she wanted to be burried neither." The old labourer paused, and put his hairy, twisted hand flat down on the turf beside the bluebells.

"Yes?" said Ashurst.

"In a manner of speakin'," the old man went on, "I think as 'twas a love-story—though there's no one never knu for zartin. Yu can't tell what's in a maid's 'ead—but that's wot I think about it." He drew his hand along the turf. "I was fond o' that maid—don' know as there was anyone as wasn' fond of 'er. But she was tu lovin'-'earted—that's where 'twas, I think." He looked up. And Ashurst, whose lips were trembling in the cover of his beard, murmured again: "Yes?"

"'Twas in the spring, 'bout now as't might be, or a little later—blossom time—an' we 'ad one o' they young college gentlemen stayin' at the farm—nice feller tu, with 'is 'ead in the air. I liked 'e very well, an' I never see nothin' between 'em, but to my thinkin' e' turned the maid's fancy." The old man took the pipe out of his mouth, spat, and went on:

"Yu see, 'e went away sudden one day, an' never come back. They got 'is knapsack and bits o' things down there still. That's what stuck in my mind—'is never sendin' for 'em. 'Is name was Ashes, or somethin' like that."

"Yes?" said Ashurst once more.

The old man licked his lips.

"'Er never said nothin', but from that day 'er went kind of dazed lukin'; didn' seem rightly therr at all. I never knu a 'uman creature so changed in me life—never. There was another young feller at the farm —Joe Biddaford 'is name wer', that was praaperly sweet on 'er, tu; I guess 'e used to plague 'er wi' 'is attentions. She got to luke quite wild. I'd zee her sometimes of an avenin' when I was bringin' up the calves; ther' she'd stand in th' orchard, under the big apple tree, lukin' straight before 'er. 'Well,' I used t'think, 'I dunno what 'tes that's the matter wi' yu, but yu'm lukin' pittiful, that yu be!'"

The old man relit his pipe, and sucked at it reflectively.

"Yes?" said Ashurst.

"I remembers one day I said to 'er; 'What's the matter, Megan?'— 'er name was Megan David, she come from Wales same as 'er aunt, ol' Missis Narracombe. 'Yu'm frettin' about something,' I says. 'No, Jim,' she says, 'I'm not frettin'.' 'Yes, yu be!' I says. 'No,' she says, and tu tears cam' rollin' out. 'Yu'm cryin'—what's that, then?' I says. She putts 'er 'and over 'er 'eart: 'It 'urts me,' she says; 'but 'twill sune be better,' she says. 'But if anything shude 'appen to me, Jim, I wants to be burried under this 'ere apple-tree.' I laughed. 'What's goin' to 'appen to you?' I says: 'don't 'ee be fulish.' 'No,' she says, 'I won't be fulish.' Well, I know what maids are, an' I never thought no more about et, till tu days arter that, 'bout six in the avenin' I was comin' up wi' the calves, when I see somethin' dark lyin' in the strame, close to that big apple-tree. I says to meself: 'Is that a pig—funny place for a pig to get to!' an' I goes up to et, an' I see what 'twas."

The old man stopped: his eyes, turned upward, had a bright, suffering look.

"'Twas the maid, in a little narrer pool ther' that's made by the stoppin' of a rock—where I see the young gentleman bathin' once or twice. 'Er was lyin' on 'er face in the watter. There was a plant o' goldie-cups growin' out o' the stone just above 'er 'ead. An' when I come to luke at 'er face, 'twas luvly, butiful, so calm's a baby's—wonderful butiful et was. When the doctor saw 'er, 'e said: ''Er culdn' never a-done it in that little bit o' watter ef 'er 'adn't a-been in an extarsy.' Ah! an' judgin' from 'er face, that was just 'ow she was. Et made me cry praaper—butiful et was! 'Twas June then, but she'd a-found a little bit of apple-blossom left over somewheres, and stuck et in 'er 'air. That's why I thinks 'er must a-been in an extarsy, to go to et gay, like that. Why! there wasn't more than a fute and 'arf o' watter. But I tell 'ee one thing—that meadder's 'arnted; I knu et, an' she knu et; an' no one'll persuade me as 'tesn't. I told 'em what she said to me 'bout bein' buried under th' apple-tree. But I think that turned 'em—made et luke tu much 's ef she'd 'ad it in 'er mind deliberate; an' so they buried 'er up 'ere. Parson we 'ad then was very particular, 'e was."

Again the old man drew his hand over the turf.

" 'Tes wonderful, et seems," he added slowly, "what maids'll du for love. She 'ad a lovin' 'eart; I guess 'twas broken. But us never *knu* nothin'!"

He looked up as if for approval of his story, but Ashurst had walked past him as if he were not there.

Up on the top of the hill, beyond where he had spread the lunch, over, out of sight, he lay down on his face. So had his virtue been rewarded, and "the Cyprian," goddess of love, taken her revenge! And before his eyes, dim with tears, came Megan's face with the sprig of apple blossoms in her dark, wet hair. "What did I do that was wrong?" he thought. "What did I do?" But he could not answer. Spring, with its rush of passion, its flowers and song—the spring in his heart and Megan's! Was it just Love seeking a victim! The Greek was right, then—the words of the *Hippolytus* as true to-day!

> For mad is the heart of Love,
> And gold the gleam of his wing;
> And all to the spell thereof
> Bend when he makes his spring.
> All life that is wild and young
> In mountain and wave and stream,
> All that of earth is sprung,
> Or breathes in the red sunbeam;
> Yea, and Mankind. O'er all a royal throne
> Cyprian, Cyprian, is thine alone!

The Greek was right! Megan! Poor little Megan—coming over the hill! Megan under the old apple tree waiting and looking! Megan dead, with beauty printed on her! . . .

A voice said:

"Oh, there you are! Look."

Ashurst rose, took his wife's sketch, and stared at it in silence.

"Is the foreground right, Frank?"

"Yes."

"But there's something wanting, isn't there?"

Ashurst nodded. Wanting? The apple-tree, the singing, and the gold!

44

Action

BY C. E. MONTAGUE

WHEN Christopher Bell was just fifty-two he woke up one September morning to feel a slight numbness all down his right side. Some of the numbness was in his right arm; a good deal of it in his right thigh, along its outside, rather less in his right foot; and just a little in his head—all over the hinterland of his right ear.

It seemed a big percentage of a man to "go to sleep" at one time. He lay still for a minute, to let it pass off. But it didn't. So he began to speculate. When he got up, would he be able to stand? And to walk straight? Would his head go on working all right, with that bit of it stiff? Just how hard a punch would it turn out to be, that some god or devil had given him in the night?

He tried. Yes, he could stand, walk, dress and shave. No portion of him was absolutely on strike. But the numbness went on. And somehow he couldn't feel sure that some part of the right flank of his body or brain would not give way, without notice, and give him a cropper. You never know how deliciously sure you have been of yourself, of every scrap of yourself, all the days of your health, till some small gadget inside you is put out of action: Bell made this deep reflection while going downstairs to his solitary breakfast. He kept one hand on the banisters.

Christopher Bell was the reigning sovereign of a respectable dynasty of "merchant princes" in Manchester. For several generations his clan had embraced the higher civilisation so far as English Public schools and universities lead to such embraces. He had read with understanding and relish, and he had travelled with open eyes. He could value the great things in the arts and in science—indeed, in the whole ampler

624

life of the race. And always, till now, his blood had pretty well bubbled with health. He had rowed, run, swum and ridden well. To his body, at forty years old, the War had brought a second boyhood of happy absorption in efforts merely physical.

Half-way through the war, the wife he had loved in every tissue of body and soul had died of something brought on by too passionate overwork for the cause. The news came to Bell in a hospital where he had just begun to grow a new skin on a face and hands well flayed and charred by chemical warfare. He could not see at the time, so a nurse read the telegram out. His face was buried deep in a canary-coloured mask of wadding stained with picric acid, so the nurse could not see how he took it—only knew that he thanked her very civilly through the little blow-hole left for his mouth. I fancy Bell was hanging on hard to the thought that he still had two children, a boy and a girl, both in their teens. Soldiers, even educated ones, are apt to grow sentimental, especially when wounded. Bell, the war widower, lay, week by week, behind his fancy-dress mask, staying his mind on an ingenuous vision of an improved world, to come after the war. He saw it as a young man and a young woman standing in summer twilight, under the stars, with their eyes all a-shine at the loveliness of the life which it had taken so much pain and shame to make possible for them.

Many soldiers hugged these quaint fancies, in their bad times. They helped, for the moment. It was afterwards that they had to be paid for. In the foul enervatory air that filled England and Europe just after the war Bell's boy and girl drifted feebly into failure. Both were married lovelessly now, each to another small waste product of that waste-producing time. Somewhere out of Bell's sight these forfeited objects of his pride and joy were shuffling punily through life. He gathered that they were rather ashamed of him as an old slow-coach provincial.

Bell was not given to wallowing in self-pity. Still, as you see, he had had his losses, like another.

Your merchant prince, in these days, is prone to lose heart, get himself up as an owner of land and beeves, and melt weakly into the common herd of squires who know not, poor fellows, what it is to go on 'Change. Bell was different. He had pride. He stuck, as his father had done, to his post among the garrison of the smutty city that had done well by them. He lived where he could hear the Town Hall clock strike twelve when the traffic was quiet at night, and a North wind blowing. He liked the sound, he was so oddly civic a person.

To this old-fashioned hobby Bell added some cheap habits less rare in rich men. He stood on guard against his wealth, lest it should cut him off from the sight and sound of ordinary and unprincely men, for whom his regard had been re-doubled by four years of living with them in the war. Because of this fad he nearly always went in to the city by tram. This morning he walked the three hundred yards from his house to the tram's stopping-place with deliberate caution. He could not be sure of that sleepy right leg. He was still distrusting it temperately when he had taken his seat and was tendering his fare to town.

The conductor rejected the tender, at sight. "We doan't taäke boottons," he said with civil composure.

Bell examined the bright disc that he had offered as a sixpence.

Behold! a silvery trouser-button. Last night it had come off and he had slipped it into a pocket. He put his finger-tips ruefully up to his eyes. "I'm sorry," he said to the man, as he gave the right coin.

"It's aal reet, Sir," the conductor said quietly. Once he saw that no pulling of legs had been intended, his tact and sympathy were perfect.

He passed on to collect other fares. But a new care remained in Bell's mind. Sight, too? Was that going? Sight, touch, the whole sensory business, losing precision, entering on the long slope to decay—the silver cord going loose and the golden bowl cracking? When a man who has known how to read feels the first clap of the hand of Time on his shoulder, he has plenty of ready prompters to ruefulness; so many excellent poets have found handsome words for the mists and mellow poignancy of man's autumn, the lapse from old vigour and vision into mere drug-takers' dreams while we are led down the avenue lined with overblown roses, to lie in the dust at its end.

Bell kept his head. But his memory was beginning to bulge with lovely quotations not conducive to high spirits—"Bare ruined choirs where late the sweet birds sang," and all that lot.

The morning's office work did him good, while it lasted. He had more than most men of the gift of forgetting himself in the excitement of getting a job to come right—any old job, the dictating of letters, anything. And just now the affairs of his firm were of quite stirring interest. Like many others it had been making large losses for several years. Bell's game was to keep these losses as low as he could without stopping the work and wages of a moorland village-ful of people who spun and wove cotton for Bell to sell for less than it cost to make it. This unacquisitive practice brought Bell into great infamy. Most of his fellow-employers wanted to close all the factories down, or half close them down, and leave the work-people to live on their fat. So Bell was an arrant traitor to them. Still, he was an employer: and so, to ardent Socialist eyes, he was a sucker of blood, *ex officio*. This lively crossfire of censures braced Bell. If it had to be woe unto you when all men spoke well of you, it might be safer when everyone slated you hard. Anyhow it livened you up, like a good stinging wind that has blown across snow. While he schemed to find some not quite ruinous sale for the stuff that piled itself up at the mills, Bell could forget the thing that had clawed him in its clutch during the night.

But the clouds return after the rain: luncheon-time set his mind free to worry, the way your sore tongue returns and returns to the amusement of hurting itself on the sharp point of a tooth lately broken. He lunched at the club; and twice in the one hour it took him, his mind accused younger members of paying him the pestilential kind of unarguing deference which is really the civil refusal of youth to keep its communications open with age. Could they have noticed the way he walked down the stairs—a canny way, like a horse's when it is afraid on a slippery slope? One younger man opened the door of the billiard-room for him. Damn these good manners that ain't good at all.

Going home at twilight, in the tram, Bell thought over all this so absorbedly that he kept his legs crossed the whole way. So, when he stood up, to get off, his right leg had gone clean asleep. It was only asleep in the common and blameless way. Still he couldn't know that, at first. For all he could tell, a second stroke might have fallen, and this time a real knock-out. Of course he kept his fears dark; still, he stepped off the car with such unconcealable care that the conductor slipped a friendly hand under his arm and led him slowly to the safety of the footpath, like a blind man or a drunk.

When Bell had walked a few yards by himself the extra numbness was gone. But the other numbness remained. And so did the feel of that patiently guarding hand under his arm. Of course he had not needed it. Still, perhaps he would, presently. *Mene, mene, etc.*—every wall seemed to be covered with sinister shreds of writing. An object for everybody's protection, a call on everyone's forbearance—that was the kind of pest that he might become. Soon, too, perhaps. This kind of plague crept on and on. It never turned back. Five years might bring an invalid-chair and a male nurse to put him to bed and to see that he was carted securely about from place to place, to sprawl in the sun—Mentone, the Canaries, Egypt, all the places to which the *passés* butterflies of our commonwealth were brought to lie out and doze in the warmth when too much eating and idling had brought them back all the way to the status of larvae. Disgusting!

Bell gazed steadily into this smiling future, while eating his dinner alone. From the table he went straight, like a man who knew what he needed, to that shelf in his study on which there were all his pet Alpine books. No other sport had ever so wholly ravished his soul as mountaineering. On the high snows it seemed as if magical fires were lit in your blood; the flame of life burned amazingly; something was added unto a man as divine as whatever it is that makes its way into the vapid juice of a fruit and turns it to wine. Nowhere else in the world was the taste of success so wholly and indefeasibly sweet as it was on the tip of some spire of granite and ice that had all but turned you back in despair by the Daphnean rigour of its resistance. There, uplifted on the swell of the round earth, you could see how men had come to dream Gardens of Eden and Ages of Gold.

He took from the shelf a great climber's narratives of his greatest adventures. Two of these, in especial, could always entrance Bell as soon as he had read a few lines: their vividness gave him an almost physical sense of what they described. Each was a case of cutting steps up a long and extremely steep slope of ice. And in each case the slope had, at one point, ceased even to slope. For just a few feet of its height it had become as vertical as the wall of a house: each man of the party had had to hold himself in to the perpendicular wall by sheer strength and good hand-hold, against gravitation.

In each case the party had come safely through. But with how big a margin of safety, as engineers say? Bell wondered. A pretty big one, he fancied. Few good climbers slipped in really difficult places; all their faculties were bent up too intently for that, with danger about; they were above their own everyday form. But what if such a party were to try paring and paring away at that pretty wide margin? Something like an experiment, that! To what untold heights of achievement might not the party attain before all the margin was gone! And of course the party might be a party of one.

Bell had once had a holiday dream of climbing a crag that grew steeper and steeper till it was vertical first, and then overhung, more and more, but still he climbed on and on because the crag beetled out over a warm summer sea, so that, when he lost hold in the end, he would only fall from one pleasure into another, out of a mountaineer's paradise into a swimmer's. Cut out the old fear of death in that way, or some other, and—why, you could do anything.

As he sat back with the open book on his knees, a light wind stirred the trees in the garden. It may have been this that called up another old notion of his. This one had visited him in a wood close to Arras, in 1916. During some dark windless weeks of that autumn the unfallen leaves had been fading inertly from green to a dull rusty red, and so down to a dead russet brown; the whole burning heart of the year was collapsing into shabby ashes. Then a night of frost came and then a gale on a day of broken sunshine thrown wildly about between clouds. As the gale stripped the trees it had seemed almost to blow them aflame; sparks of brave yellow flew in the air; the dun beech-leaves took light and fell lustrously. Somehow the sight had filled Bell, at the time, with a wish that, when he had to go, he might do it like that—all a-stir and a-glow, by one of the "violent" deaths, as most of the easy ones seemed to be called. Anything but to lie on a bed in a hushed room, with the lights low and life's jolly noises shut out, and people whispering among the shadows. One wrench for the undecayed body, and then unbreakable sleep—what end could equal it?

Now, almost suddenly, these several notions ran into one, as raindrops do on a newly wet window. Here was the moment to put into practice that old and sound choice of his between the long decrepitude of the flesh and the one clean cut and summary pang that save you it all. Suicide? Oh! no. But just to carry on, right to the end, the piquant experiment of paring and paring away that limiting and restraining margin of safety which mountaineers, even the boldest, keep in reserve. Had not all things conspired to free him from too much love of remaining alive—bereavement and baulked hope and now this first lick of fire from heaven, soon to blast the whole of him by degrees? Why, fate had brought him the fulfilment of his old dream. No precipice in the world would now have an abhorred death waiting at its foot—merely a warm quiet sea of painless forgetfulness.

Only—he must be quick, before the accursed thing that was setting to work on him could pith so much of the vigour out of his body that he could not make his own way to a place—already he had a good place in his mind—where he might try the thing out.

At the end of September a savoursome blend of jollity and melancholy pervades the little Val d'Anniviers. The summer hotels of Zinal, at the head of the valley, are closing. Down the bridle-path, through forests of fir, the hotel staffs stream along joyously, laden with the year's vintage of tips, to their snug winter homes in the Rhone Valley below. Reconverted, after four months of restraint and disguise, into young, natural Swiss men and women, they caper like Alpine cows let out in the spring. Shouting, chaffing and singing, they seem to flout with their merriment Nature's yearly menace to marmots and men. And Nature answers them back. Almost hour by hour the new snow creeps down the forested slopes of the valley and grizzles more of its firs; the morning dew lies late, and even at noon the weakening sun hangs lazily low above the main chain of the Alps. You feel, all about you, a big closing-in, the rustle of a heavy curtain falling upon a good time that is played out at last.

As Bell walked the six miles up from Vissoye to Zinal, he breasted that jovial current of waiters and chamber-maids thawed and re-human-ised. Jove! they were good to see and to hear, with their jokes and catches and bold, friendly, unobsequious looks at any man and brother they met. But everything was good in this place. Even the smell of Vissoye and its pigs, as he passed, had been the smell of the best holiday of his boyhood. How he had liked life—every bit of it, coloured or plain, the high lights and the low! Even the jars had been part of the makings of the incomparable adventure. He wondered whether the mere feel of things—common things, all sorts of things—could ever have given anyone else such raptures of secret contentment as they had given to him.

He had made sure of a room at Zinal. He dined by the light of one lamp in a corner of the hotel's dining-room, now empty and shadowy. An elderly woman waited upon him; everyone else in the house had gone down the valley; she had been left for a week or two more, to cook, wait, make a bed and draw out a bill for anyone mad enough to turn up so belatedly. Bell had known her for thirty years—ever since her marriage to an old guide of his, recently killed on the Meije. She told him how their son Pierre was now a guide too, rather to her alarm. She seemed amazingly glad to see Bell, as if he were a bit of some good old world that had been slipping away. And he——? she asked. Was he making a *grande course,* as always? Surely not, at this time of year?

He fenced with her apt, friendly questions. He felt like a liar. Indeed, he was one, pretty well; for he fully meant to deceive. He would go for a walk by himself, he said, after breakfast to-morrow—perhaps to the Arpitetta Alp only, perhaps rather further.

She looked at him sadly, with peasant directness. "All alone now!" she said simply. "And once it was you and Madame—and Gaspard and me. Ah! the good times." She had all humanity's fate in her face, like an old woman drawn by Rembrandt—hopes and happy love and then the dust of the day, dimming the roses, and then great loneliness and unconsolable tears. Would Monsieur have coffee she asked.

Bell could face her no longer. It was too treacherous. No, he said, he would want nothing more. Let her go to bed early, like all the good marmots. So would he too, when he had smoked a little end of tobacco.

When she was gone, he sat by a fire of logs she had lit for him in the small smoking-room. To his surprise he found he had nothing to do. There could be no saying good-bye, no specious last letter to write, no will to be made, no manifesto of any sort to be left. People do not do such things just before unforeseen accidents—for the wood must look raw at the break. A real good tip for the widow of Gaspard would have to be left in an obvious place: that was all.

It went beyond having nothing to do. There was nothing to think.

He had no fear of *post mortem* torture to busy his brain, for the God of his faith was no fiend. He was equally void of covetous hopes of a sensational "good time" when the breath should be out of his body. So far he might have expected his mind to be free. The strange thing was to find how much of one's usual matter for thought is taken away if, in twenty hours or so, one will have nothing whatever to fix up or to see to, no house or business to run, no social beat to patrol, no arts or letters to care for, nor "public duties" to mind. It was a release. But it was a queer one—a kind of vacuous and disquieting freedom, such as a man might attain who was suddenly let off the pressure of gravitation, so that he needn't keep his feet down to the earth any more—in fact couldn't press on it hard if he tried, and so couldn't get any purchase for putting forth his strength upon anything at all. Bell's released mind did its best to think firmly of what he was going to do the next day. But no firmness came: the levers of thought could not find any fulcrum; they worked at a loss feebly and fumblingly.

He brought over the lamp to review the Inn's tiny library—two shelves freakishly peopled with the printed leavings of guests lettered, half-lettered, unlettered, conventional, independent and odd. There was the common aphrodisiac novel of commerce; there was *The Vicar of Wakefield,* all golden sunshine and wit; there were Nat Gould and the wise, humane book of the great William James on the incessant endeavour of men to find or to imagine some larger life on which to rest the frail and soon-tired figure of their own. Yes, that was it: something to lean against: something sure not to give when you put your whole weight on it, in any state of yourself: that was where peace and strength were to be had; nowhere else. So he fancied, at least: he could not be sure: he was still in that vacuum where his thought had no pivot to work on: the wheels did not bite on the road; the cogs would not engage; he thought and he felt, but gropingly, not with the sure and eager drive of a mind and heart that have found themselves by forgetting themselves.

The place that Bell had picked for his purpose was on the West side of the Schallijoch. The Schallijoch, as you may know, is a dip in the ridge that joins the Weisshorn to the Schallihorn. Even the lowest point of the dip is more than 12,000 feet high. The last part of the rise to the ridge from the West is up one of the steepest slopes of ice that are climbed. That is if you mount it where it is least steep. At some other points it is steeper than any slope that is climbed, or thought to be climbable. The surface of this wall of ice undulates like a sheet of hammered copper—here a concave patch and there a convex one. Though the wall, at its steepest, leans back from the straight, as a whole, it has parts—the upper halves of these hollows and lower of these bulges—at which it is vertical for some feet at a time; and at two or three parts it even overhangs slightly. These last, avoided by climbers happily wedded to life, were what Bell had in mind. He would start up the wall at the steepest part he could find; as he went on, he would make, at each stage, for the point where there seemed to be most an overhang. He would do the thing honestly—try all that was in him to bring the climb off, reach the ridge and prove that, in this small matter, man could do more than he knew. With careful timing he would be up, if up at all, about dusk. In that unlikely event he would carry the test a step further and try to come down his ice ladder by feel, in the dark, instead of descending the gentle snow slopes on the Eastern side of the pass.

He worked out a time-table. Three hours' walk up to the Arpitetta Alp from Zinal. Three more up from the Alp to the foot of the final icewall. Half an hour for eating; another half hour for sundries and lateage. Four for the ultimate work on the wall. Eleven hours in all. Tomorrow's evening dusk would be over by seven. He would push off at eight in the morning.

Probably you would have thought him rather a pleasant sight as he quitted Zinal—the outward figure of a hale, fit mountaineer; just a little stricken with years, but vigorous; brindled but not at all bald; leanly and brownly good-looking, turning out by himself, with his axe under his arm and a little luncheon in his pocket, for a walk among the feet of sporting old friends like the Weisshorn and Roth-horn. How can you tell by the looks of a man that he would not feel the point of a pin if you ran it into his thigh, or that this exemption from pain is causing any disturbance of his spirits?

Nobody was to be seen at the emerald Alp of Arpitetta. Like the almost deserted Zinal, like yesterday's valley path streaming with walkers carrying bundles, the empty hovels on the Alp recalled the sight of a whole countryside in flight before the army of an invader. The ashes left from the cheesemaker's fire were wet with drippings from the roof; the rough wooden crane used for swinging the cauldron over the flames flapped in a draught from the door. Outside, the intoxicant beauty of gentian and orchis was over for the year; the rich grass had spread back over the trodden mud of the milking-place; but snow was lying a few hundred feet higher up. The invader was near.

Bell's legs were liking the work. The numb one was numb, but it did not give out: it would not let him down. By one o'clock he had reached the tail end—some would call it the snout—of the big Weisshorn Glacier, eaten his rations and set a first foot on the rough convex swell of honey-combed ice with water flushing out its millions of cells; for the sun was on it. He pawed the stuff tenderly with his axe. Perdition catch his soul but he did love it—strong as iron, carvable as cheese; what genius could have conceived so delicious a union of opposites if, by some disaster, no glaciers had been made?

By three o'clock he was through the freak shapes of the ice-fall, across the snowfield above it and close to the wall that he sought. Yes, its great width and height had the wavy surface that he remembered. It showed like a vast relief map of some low rolling downland, modelled in ice and then set up to stand on its edge. Off to his right, as he looked up, the general angle was easiest. That was the regular way—very steep but quite practicable. That was of no use for his purpose. Far away to his left the slope looked ferocious enough. But down it an almost continuous fall of stones of all sizes, broken away from the sun-warmed rocks of the Weisshorn, came sliding and hissing, or bounding and smashing explosively. That was no use either. That way would be suicide, not experiment.

He soon saw what he wanted—almost directly above him. There, nearly all the way up to the ridge, the ice was steep and bare and blue, and the face of it waved more at this place than anywhere else. Several broad bosses of rocks must have underlain the smooth surface. Over these the close-fitting ice swelled like a stocking upon a bent knee. Up to the centre of each of these bosses it bulged out overhangingly; just above each centre it would recede at a more merciful angle; but nowhere in the whole thousand feet of ascent would a man have a foothold to stand on, unless he made it.

Bell conscientiously tightened each boot-lace and puttee-string. Then he set off for the point where he had descried the best overhangs. It was half-way, as he judged, to the top of the wall. If he should conquer that one, then he would look for another, more bulgy.

He cut his steps with almost fanatical care. He had a disagreeable sense of doing something furtive: he couldn't help asking himself, against his own will, "What if somebody saw?" Damn somebody, another part of him said. Still, he cut every step as if he defied the whole solar system to say that it was not the work of a good craftsman bent upon keeping alive. So he rose slowly. It took a good two hours' work to mount a third of the way to the ridge. But then he was close to what mattered more—the great bulge that he was making for.

The bulge stood out like a gigantic blister upon the face of the ice. It must have been forty feet in diameter and it jutted so much that a stone dropped from its outermost point would only have touched the slope again some fifty feet lower. So the climax had come. To reach that outermost point he would have to climb for about twenty feet as you climb up the under side of a ladder that leans against a wall. And he would have to make the ladder, rung by rung, as he climbed it—fashion each rung out of the ice with his axe, held in one hand, while with the other hand and both feet he clung to three of the rungs made already, and held up the body against the drag of its weight. Every rung would have to be made like a letter-box in a door, big enough for the toe of a boot to go in, but so shaped that, when a hand entered, the fingers could bend down inside and grip as you grip the top of a fence. The grand, the crucial question was how long one hand and one arm could hold the body in to the projecting ice-wall. For what part of the two hours or so that the other labouring hand might require to cut that fantastical staircase? Of course, if his axe should slip out of his hand, or if one step should break, that would end the affair. But away with the thought of any such bungling.

The moment the overhang started Bell discovered the theory of gravitation to be exceedingly true. The work was amazingly hard. When he had carved five letter-boxes, and used them, an hour had gone. He carved five more and observed that daylight was failing. Behind his back an unsensational sunset was going on at its ease. His left hand was chilled almost dead with all the ice it had gripped; his right wrist was swollen and sore with the intensity of the axe-work; his right knee had begun to shake as uncontrollably as chattering teeth; he heard his breath as if it were somebody else's: it made a dry rustling noise, like a bird struggling silently in the hand.

The centre of the boss was now, he reckoned, some eight feet above his head. Beyond it he could see nothing as yet, but a tranquil sky with a rose-coloured flush dying out of it. Five letter-boxes more, he thought, might take him up to the nipple of this frozen breast and bring the receding slope of its upper half into his sight. It was just at this point that it struck him as a clear, sober matter of fact that he could not get up those eight feet. His strength was running out fast: one more good letter-box was all that he could conceive himself able to make. He made it, hacking away with slow, painful strokes, his axe-handle slippery with his sweat. He reached up his left hand to grab the new hold and dragged a foot up to its new place below. Then, just to go down fighting, he went through the movements of starting to chip out yet another step. Second by second the effort held out; his strokes were the taps of a child; his wrist felt like breaking; yet somehow he finished the hole and forced his left hand to rise up to it: then he even hauled up in its turn a right foot of infinite weight: the poor quivering knee had to straighten out next, and did it, after a long, doubtful struggle. But that was the end, he felt, of all possible effort.

By this time all his senses had the morbid exultation that will sometimes come of fierce physical effort. His mind was at leisure, after a fashion. He was fully aware of the sunset; he did not miss the charm of its sabbatical calm: the majesty and mystery of mountains were still there, all right. A verse he had liked as a boy came into his head, as beautiful things that have built themselves into your mind are apt to do at a crisis —as people who once went to church will cry out "Oh! God!" when a smash comes.

> *And here indeed might death be fair*
> *If death be dying into air*
> *And souls evanished mix with the*
> *Illumined sky, eternal sea.*

But no pretty dying for him, if death could be still headed off. He started desperately to try again, sweating and straining. No good: the feeble strokes of his axe scarcely scratched the bare ice; his left hand was frost-bitten now, past feeling anything. Only five feet to relative safety, but five more than any spur worn by his will could drive the spent body. "I'm done," he said, and ceased to struggle upwards.

Some innate impulse to take the thing well and not let human dignity down at a pinch kept him resolved to hold on, foot and hand, to the last moment possible.

While he clung so, the sun left him. A high Alpine sunset is sudden, like tropical ones. A cold, sharp-edged shadow raced up from the valley, chasing the sunlight before it. Pursuer and fugitive scudded up over the tops of the firs and across the bright green of the Alp Bell had passed, and then up the ice-fall and on up the wall till the shadow came down like a great frigid hand on the sweaty back of his neck. Next moment the last warmth and light fleeted up out of sight, over the bulge. As his gaze followed, his cheeks felt the sting of a few falling granules of ice; little chips of it, rather; even a few rather big ones. A trickle of ice scraps seemed to be sliding down the upper half of the bulge, to dive into space on reaching its centre—most of them clear of his back.

Queer! Was an ice avalanche coming? No need to suppose it, though. Glaciers, crushed and huddled things, always heaving and cracking, played curious tricks and ground out all sorts of freak rubbish. Oh! let the ice do what it liked, all his business with it was done; all that he could now attend to was a kind of dream noise, big, muted and almost asleep, that the torrent was making, enormously far off, down in the blackening trench of the valley—that and a kind of emotional dream of himself, the dying man doing his best to take leave as was meet—a figure at which he could look, as it were, from outside, and dreamily feel it to be rather touching.

Into this semi-dream there managed to enter, also, a sound more abrupt—a little noise like the low startled cry that some women give when they see a horse fall or a big window is smashed. The cry worked itself into his dream, but also it roused him. "Getting light-headed," he thought. But he wasn't. Almost as quick as that thought, a new sound, a light hissing rub, rushed down to his ears and an ice-axe slid over the bulge overhead and out into the air: it whizzed past the back of his head.

To anyone versed in high mountains an ice-axe loose and falling in any such place is a portent of horror, like a child's pony galloping riderless home or a boat adrift, bottom uppermost in a Thames lasher. It means that somebody may have just lost the power to move, without help, at a place where a man unable to move will soon be unable to live. Suddenly Bell's mind took eyes to itself; it saw a party of some sort above him, trying to cut its way down the ice wall, straight towards the deadly bulge that now beetled over himself. At this hour! And by such a route! They must be mad; so he thought—forgetting himself. And now one of them was disabled—perhaps had disabled the whole of his party—tethered it to the ice-wall. The idea was frightful to Bell.

Another sound came. From somewhere not far overhead there broke, like an explosion, the singular cry that Swiss peasants and some mountaineers employ as a long-distance hail. No other noise of purely human production will carry so far. Harsh, wild and long, it starts, as the noise of a rocket does, at its maximum loudness, and then wails itself out in a dying fall that has an effect of collapse into despair. Though commonly uttered on quite cheerful occasions, it might be the passionate scream of some wretched animal terrified by the solitude of a desolate place and trying to empty into one impetuous lamentation all its burden of loneliness and desire.

Bell held his breath as the sinking shriek thinned away into silence. Then he counted off the seconds half-aloud, by guess work, as bombthrowers learnt how to do in the war. The count ran to seven—eight—nine—and, just as Bell was muttering "Ten," the great yell smashed into the silence again. Yes: he had expected that. Someone above was in the last extremity of danger—was trying the last shift of all, the most all-but-hopeless of all—was sending out the Alpine signal of distress into this stone and snow desert where autumn and night had joined to make it utterly certain that no answer could come. It was like praying to God, for dear life, that a well of fresh water might open itself in the dry middle of the Sahara.

Up to that point of time, as you have seen, Bell had been the kind of dual creature that most of us are for nearly the whole of our days. Part of him had toiled, sweated and ached, and another part of him had been sorry for that one. But, from the moment the second yell came, this two-fold arrangement was somehow abolished. All craving or need for any part of himself to be troubled about any other was over; now there was nothing at all to work out any more, no next move to be consciously planned, nor hesitant will to be coaxed or hustled, nor any plaguey choice to be made. All of the man was one unit at last, and it lived intently and intensely, moved by some force which it had no more desire to question than flames have to ask "Why burn upward?"

The next mystery was that out of the mind so suddenly lightened there seemed, as it were, to overflow lightness into Bell's body of lead. Strangely empowered, his left foot was rising already to thrust itself into the next letter-box; almost gaily his right arm, freed from its preoccupation with pain, was beginning to hack a new hand-hold above. How long it took him to make he could not have told, then or after. For time, too, was abolished; long trains of executive, practical thought could run on to their end instantaneously; courses, whole courses, of study of relevant things—of the state of the ice, minute changes of gradient, the swift re-gelation following sundown—were carried out without any sense of duration. One of the revelatory trances had come, in which even a plain man sees for once that an eternity need not be long and that in a single moment he may have everlasting life.

A minor, but still a piquant, discovery was that he had never really known till now what it was to cut a good sizable strip off that old margin of safety which he had imagined himself to have all but used up. His new letter-boxes were marvels of sketchy adequacy; they were high art in the skimpiness of the means that they took to their end; triumphs of confident "cheek" to Nature, they bluffed that august power quite wittily. Almost before the vocalist overhead had completed the long S.O.S. of the mountains—it takes three minutes in all—Bell had his chest up to the dead centre of the bulge and saw what he had come for.

Some thirty feet higher up, a woman in mountain kit, with no axe and no hold for hand or foot, was dangling at a long rope's end. Her body revolved a little as it hung against the steep ice, but she was making no voluntary movement. The rope constricting her chest was held with one straining hand by a man perched eighty feet higher up. He was clearly unable to move, hand or foot, without being dragged off his stance by the weight of the woman. He stood on one foot—his right: it seemed to be firmly placed, on a tiny step; and a little above his hand, he had the pick of his axe driven well into the ice. To the steel bracket thus formed by the axe-head the man was holding on stoutly with his right hand.

The sorry sight explained itself. The woman must have been cutting steps down the slope; she must have slipped from a step, and dropped her axe with the shock. The man had checked her fall well, but both were hung up as immovably as a couple of stoats nailed to a gamekeeper's door. And now the rope must be slowly killing the woman. Just as Bell's head topped the bulge she called out in a strangled voice to the man, "Can you cut the rope, Teddy? I'm done, anyhow. Think of the kiddies. You *must*." The man held on.

Bell gave tongue as loud as the dry brown fur lining his mouth would allow. "Well held, Sir," he roared. "It's all right, I'm coming."

Not once in a long and respectable Alpine career had Bell thought he would ever entrust his person to ledges quite so narrow as those on which he made the rest of his way up to that pendant woman. And yet he had never, in any hard place, felt such absolute freedom from any uneasiness. As he romped up, he sang out, at intervals "There in three minutes," "Just two minutes more," "Only one minute more," "Half a shake—I'm just there." Then he arrived. He cut a big step close to where the woman's feet hung, planted his own firmly on it, and then stooping and straightening up again, took the weight of her, sitting, on his right shoulder. Lest she be fainting he put up his right hand behind her, to hold her in place.

She was no fainter, though she was white, yellow, greenish all the bad colours that beauty itself may have to put on in bad times. "She's a good 'un," Bell thought, as she sat quiet, panting.

"*You're* a great sportsman," she gasped, when she had breath enough.

Feeling all the weight off the rope of a sudden, the man above shouted down thickly, "Sure you have got her, Sir?"

"Right as rain," she called up from her perch.

Bell added, "Leave the rope slack, and dig in. We'll come up when you're comfy."

The man gave a tuneless yodel of joy and was plying his axe the same instant; chips and wedges of ice came pelting down from the great step that he must be cutting, from which to make the whole caravan fast. In five minutes he ceased hacking, braced himself, drew in the slack of the rope and announced that now he could hold up a cow for a day.

Bell let the woman cannily down till her feet found a trim ledge that he had managed to scratch out while holding her up. But some four or five feet of smooth ledgeless ice intervened between this and the lowest step the woman had cut, coming down, before she slipped off. Some new ones had to be made. "Care to cut 'em?" Bell asked. "Or shall I?"

She ruefully opened the hands in which no axe was now held. "I dropped it," she said, "like a mug. I feel sick with shame."

"Have mine," he said holding it out.

Her open boy face shone with joyous relief, as if at a gift of free absolution from sin. Even now their lives hung on this axe that he was entrusting to her, the convicted axe-dropper. She took it. "You are a very generous person," she said. "Now I'll unrope, and go up by myself, and you shall tie on."

He shook his head firmly. "You mustn't unrope."

Her eyes broke out in a quick sparkle of anger. "You've *got* to rope up," she said, flushing. "I know that I've done a dud thing and can't preach. But what about you? Climbing alone! coming up out of nowhere, almost at night. Up a worse slope than this beast! Think it bears looking into? Eh? Well, do you mean to rope up, or shall both of us climb in this way that you seem to think right?"

Bell fairly funked the scrutiny of the young woman's spirited simplicity. When once simplicity sets out to inquire, what else is so penetrating? "Well, you tie on in the middle," he said, "and I at the end."

"That's fair," she agreed. A few feet of spare rope were let down by her husband. In two or three minutes, at most, the man who would have shuffled off the mortal coil was securely girt with the most delectable of its loops, the cheerfullest symbol of human determination not to withdraw from the banquet of life—only to salt a dish now and then with a few little hazards.

The last daylight was gone when the three stood safe on the level roof of the ridge, scrunching its gritty granular snow somewhat shyly, though partly kept in countenance by the dark, which is itself a shy, friendly thing. Bell, now a mere dual creature again, had been wondering, all the way up the last flight of ice stairs, how he should give these married lovers a chance to re-assert their lately threatened right to possession of each other's lips. Best, he thought, just to turn his back on them when he got up, and try to look busy, coiling the rope.

But they also seemed to have some sort of plan. The man was waiting above the last step, to shake Bell by the hand—really to shake him—and mumbling something which Bell did not desire to make out more clearly. The cup of his consternation was filled when the lady raised his disengaged hand to her lips, a gesture for which he had not been prepared by her vivacity lower down.

Then, with one silent consent, they all stampeded away from the key of emotion. "You travel light, Sir," said Bell, just to say something trivial. The other two seemed to carry not so much as a prune or a biscuit between them.

"Well——" said the man, and then Bell imagined the man must be having a quiet laugh in the dark.

"Oh! I know I can't talk," Bell admitted. "The fact is I didn't expect to be coming right over the Pass."

"Same here," said the man. "We just walked up from Randa—meant to go only as far as the hut for the Weisshorn, eat our sandwiches there and go back to dinner. Then—it *was* rather mad, but the snow was so toppingly good—we thought we might just rush the Schallijoch before dark, sleep at Zinal and come back to-morrow."

"Gosh! it was rash!" exclaimed Bell, off his guard. He felt sure the next instant, the man was quite seeing the humour of such a rebuke from such a sinner. Hastily trying to cover the slip, Bell made another. He asked, "How on earth did you miss the way down?"

The man didn't exactly say, "How did *you* miss the way up?" but he did say, "Yes, it was stupid, but—well you know how it isn't so easy to see a way down from above as it is from below?"

"Hadn't we better push off?" said Bell rather hurriedly. "We'll be getting friz, up here." But it was not the cold that he minded. It was the heat. It felt as if he couldn't move his tongue without burning his fingers.

The three truants had luck. Just such a full moon as they needed, not having a lantern, was on the point of rising from behind the snowy mass of the Mischabel, beyond the forest glen of the Visp. The mounting light could no longer contain itself. Its bright animation was pulsing up the dark violet of the sky in tremulous waves. It would be easy, by such a light as was coming, to follow the downward track left by the couple, on their way up, almost to the door of the old Weisshorn hut, a refuge squat, squalid, flea-haunted and cramped, but divinely rich in raw materials for manufacturing heat, against a long night of hard frost.

At any time it is rather exciting to walk in the dark, and in silence, with anyone whom you like but don't yet know very well. What is he thinking about? You? And, if so, in what way? Barring you? Liking you? Wanting to throw down the conventional fence and talk frankly? An hour or two of this blindfold contact between mind and mind may so work on them both that when their eyes meet under a lamp at the end of the walk it may feel as if they had had a long and intimate conversation, leaving each of them just slightly anxious to know that the other has taken nothing amiss. Even thus, with friendly and deprecatory looks, did Bell and the strangers regard each other by candle-light two hours later, among the strong shadows and smells of the hut.

In ten minutes more the man's wife, who had walked like a true Joan of Arc, was exercising the blessed privilege of healthy and tired young people of thirty or so. While she slept like a prosperous babe, her man and Bell smoked as they lay in the hay at the big sleeping-shelf's other end. Smoking helps to keep talk good. A man can puff at his pipe between each thing he really wants to say and the next. No gap-filling rubble is required.

Bell ascertained first that the man's name was Gollen and that he was a doctor—the Harley Street species of doctor. Bell gave in return his own name and description. Then they enjoyed one of those unembarrassing pauses. Then Bell said, somewhat brusquely, "There's one thing we have to get straight."

"Go it," said Gollen.

"You seem to imagine you're under some sort of obligation to me."

"Well, you see, we're alive. And, before you appeared, our number was up."

"So was mine."

"Oh! everyone's is, in a sense. 'All condemned to death,' doesn't somebody say, 'with an indefinite reprieve.' But ours wasn't indefinite. We were booked to go West in five minutes."

"I was to do it in one. In less. I should have dropped off my holds in ten seconds if you people hadn't blown in."

"Hullo?"

"Sure thing. I was done. I had never known until then how far doneness could go. That's how it felt, anyhow. Then your wife's axe came along. That by itself held me on for a jiffy or two. And then you hollered—gad! you *can* holler—and everything changed. There was something new in me, or round me, at work on me somehow. Every bit of soreness and worry and funk was taken right off me—nothing was left in the world but one energy—just an enveloping, mastering sort of a push. It went up like a flame and it took me along—it made everything easy and light. And it wasn't only a thing in the mind. Old brother body himself was roped into the movement: some of the waft of this impulse seemed to get itself into my muscles. D'you follow these ravings?"

"Rather. Physicians aren't the fools that they were. We don't go on missing out what the mind—or the soul, if you like—has to say to all the dynamic affairs of the body."

Bell puffed his pipe for a while. Then he said "See? That's how you two preserved me. So if thanking is what we're about, thanky kindly."

Gollen, too, smoked in silence for the next minute or two, before asking "The ice overhung where you were when I first caterwauled?"

"Can't tell you the angle. Hadn't got a clinometer thing. Of course it wasn't a motoring road."

Gollen laughed. Bell liked Gollen's face when he laughed, so far as it could be seen among the tangle of dry shadows thrown about the hut by a small flame that still leapt in the stove. Gollen's face made Bell think of a trade term—"good ordinary." He had blunt goodish features, strong and good-tempered. A straight, friendly man, you would say, and easily amused; a good man to be in a hole with. Bell enjoyed such men. They made the world go round. As he was thinking so, Gollen suddenly asked, "I say—why did you do it?"

As Bell did not answer at once, Gollen added, "Of course, it's cheek—asking. Tell me to go to Hell, if you like, and I'll warmly approve. Only, well—I'm a doctor."

Bell cut the thing short. He answered at once what Gollen might go on to ask in another few minutes. "Yes—the spring's running dry. The salt losing its savour, you know—the wine going flat. And worse coming."

Again Gollen did the bold thing. "Any particular evil?" he said.

Bell liked the man. And when two men would both have been dead a few hours ago if either had failed at a pinch, they may soon get on terms. Bell avowed the whole business—his symptoms, his surmises and disgusts and his specious experiment.

Gollen listened as wise doctors do. "Did that numbness cramp you to-day?" he asked at the end.

"No. But it was there all the day—except just the time—ten minutes or so, I suppose—when——" Bell hesitated for a moment.

"When you were in action?" said Gollen.

"Action?"

"Oh! I don't mean just doing violent things out of doors—pressing triggers or lassoing cows. I mean getting every Jack fibre there is in your nature alive and utterly turned on to something outside you—absorbed in it, lost in it—every bit of your consciousness taken up into some ecstasy of endeavour that's passion and peace."

Bell nodded, and Gollen went on. "I guess the great artists—all sorts of 'em—know how to bring the fit on, or it comes when they're at the top of their form—they seem to get further and further above 'emselves —hold the note out in a way that we can't—bring every tissue they have in their being to bear on the effort to get a wee touch to come right. Saints, too, I suppose—the pukka ones, like Francis, the man at Assisi: they have the knack too: they can get more alive; they've found how to exist at a sort of top pressure. I fancy all of us get just a glimpse of the thing now and then—of what living might be, you know—at a great turn in a game, or when we're in love, or if some beautiful thing in a book bowls us over. Only, we can't hold the note, or we can't do it yet: the pitch is too high for our reach; so we flop back into flatness. But we shall get there. I do believe that. What we've done since we started as jelly-fish is to get more and more of ourselves into action, and we shall go on until we are as much more in action—real true action—than now, as we are now than when we were jelly-fish. Why, in a few thousand years we may all be able to live half our time as you lived to-day for ten minutes."

"Something in that," Bell assented.

Gollen apologised meekly. "Sorry to verge upon 'uplift'. Still, one can't always bother about the convention that talk has got to be pessimist piffle."

Bell nodded. Reigning conventions had few less dutiful followers than he.

They smoked again for a while. Presently Gollen said, "How goes the weather?" He rose and opened the door of the hut very quietly. Bell followed him out to the hut's tiny terrace.

Nothing at all was wrong with that night. Beyond the queenly white shape of Mont Rose the moon rode gloriously high, burnished and flashing with frost, above sleeping Lombardy. Gowned in new snow and bejewelled with sparkles of light, the Weisshorn, the greatest great lady in Nature, looked as lovely to Bell as when the first sight of that pale supreme grace had taken his breath away in his youth. At the height where they stood the frost had silenced every trickle of water, leaving all space to be filled with subtler challenges to the ear. The air almost crackled with crispness: it was alive with the massed animation of millions of infinitesimal crystallisations. The Schalliberg Glacier, a little away to their right, had its own living whisper, the sum of the innumerable tiny creaks and fractures of its jostling molecules of ice. Up here, where the quiet of night was suffused with this audible stir of the forces fashioning the earth, it felt as if some murmurous joint voice of all existence were abroad and life itself were trying to make its high urgency felt.

"Pretty good!" Gollen said presently.

"Yes, it's all right," answered Bell.

Gollen waited a minute or two. Then he asked, "Is it all right—enough?"

"Oh! yes," said Bell. "I'm sticking on."

45

The Valley of the Beasts

BY ALGERNON BLACKWOOD

As they emerged suddenly from the dense forest the Indian halted, and Grimwood, his employer, stood beside him, gazing into the beautiful wooded valley that lay spread below them in the blaze of a golden sunset. Both men leaned upon their rifles, caught by the enchantment of the unexpected scene.

"We camp here," said Tooshalli abruptly, after a careful survey. "Tomorrow we make a plan."

He spoke excellent English. The note of decision, almost of authority, in his voice was noticeable, but Grimwood set it down to the natural excitement of the moment. Every track they had followed during the last two days, but one track in particular as well, had headed straight for this remote and hidden valley, and the sport promised to be unusual.

"That's so," he replied, in the tone of one giving an order. "You can make camp ready at once." And he sat down on a fallen hemlock tree to take off his moccasin boots and grease feet that ached from the arduous day now drawing to a close. Though under ordinary circumstances he would have pushed on for another hour or two, he was not averse to a night here, for exhaustion had come upon him during the last bit of rough going, his eye and muscles were no longer steady, and it was doubtful if he could have shot straight enough to kill. He did not mean to miss a second time.

With his Canadian friend, Iredale, the latter's half-breed, and his own Indian, Tooshalli, the party had set out three weeks ago to find the "wonderful big moose" the Indians reported were traveling in the Snow River country. They soon found that the tale was true; tracks were abundant; they saw fine animals nearly every day. These carried good heads, but the hunters expected better still and left them alone. Pushing up the river to a chain of small lakes near its source, they then separated into two parties, each with its nine-foot bark canoe, and packed in for three days after the yet bigger animals the Indians agreed would be found in the deeper woods beyond. Excitement was keen, expectation keener still. The day before they separated, Iredale shot the biggest moose of his life, and its head, bigger even than the grand Alaskan heads, hangs in his house today. Grimwood's hunting blood was fairly up. His blood was of the fiery, not to say ferocious, quality. It almost seemed he liked killing for its own sake.

Four days after the party broke into two he came upon a gigantic track, whose measurements and length of stride keyed every nerve he possessed to its highest tension.

Tooshalli examined the tracks for some minutes with care. "It is the biggest moose in the world," he said at length, a new expression on his inscrutable red visage.

Following it all that day, they yet got no sight of the big fellow that seemed to be frequenting a little marshy dip of country, too small to be called valley, where willow and undergrowth abounded. He had not yet scented his pursuers. They were after him again at dawn. Toward the evening of the second day Grimwood caught a sudden glimpse of the monster among a thick clump of willows, and the sight of the magnificent head that easily beat all records set his heart beating like a hammer with excitement. He aimed and fired. But the moose, instead of crashing, went thundering away through the further scrub and disappeared, the sound of his plunging canter presently dying away. Grimwood had missed, even if he had wounded.

They camped, and all next day, leaving the canoe behind, they followed the huge track, but though finding signs of blood, these were not plentiful, and the shot had evidently only grazed the big beast. The traveling was of the hardest. Toward evening, utterly exhausted, the spoor led them to the ridge they now stood upon, gazing down into the enchanting valley that opened at their feet. The giant moose had gone down into this valley. He would consider himself safe there. Grimwood agreed with the Indian's judgment. They would camp for the night and continue at dawn the wild hunt after "the biggest moose in the world."

Supper was over, the small fire used for cooking dying down, when Grimwood became first aware that the Indian was not behaving quite as usual. What particular detail drew his attention is hard to say. He was a slow-witted, heavy man, full-blooded, unobservant; a fact had to hurt him through his comfort, through his pleasure, before he noticed it. Yet anyone else must have observed the changed mood of the Redskin long ago. Tooshalli had made the fire, fried the bacon, served the tea, and was arranging the blankets, his own and his employer's, before the latter remarked upon his—silence. Tooshalli had not uttered a word for over an hour and a half, since he had first set eyes upon the new valley, to be exact. And his employer now noticed the unaccustomed silence, because after food he liked to listen to wood talk and hunting lore.

"Tired out, aren't you?" said big Grimwood, looking into the dark face across the firelight. He resented the absence of conversation, now that he noticed it. He was over-weary himself, he felt more irritable than usual, though his temper was always vile.

"Lost your tongue, eh?" he went on with a growl, as the Indian returned his stare with solemn, expressionless face. That dark inscrutable look got on his nerves a bit. "Speak up, man!" he exclaimed sharply. "What's it all about?"

The Englishman had at last realized that there was something to "speak up" about. The discovery, in his present state, annoyed him further. Tooshalli stared gravely, but made no reply. The silence was prolonged almost into minutes. Presently the head turned sideways, as though the man listened. The other watched him very closely, anger growing in him.

But it was the way the Redskin turned his head, body rigid, that gave the jerk to Grimwood's nerves, providing him with a sensation he had never known in his life before—it gave him what is generally called "the goose-flesh." It seemed to jangle his entire system, yet at the same time made him cautious. He did not like it, these emotions puzzled him.

"Say something, I tell you," he repeated in a harsher tone, raising his voice. He sat up, drawing his great body closer to the fire. "Say something, damn it!"

His only voice fell dead against the wall of surrounding trees, making the silence of the forest unpleasantly noticeable. Very still the great woods stood about them; there was no wind, no stir of branches; only the crackle of a snapping twig was audible from time to time, as the night-life moved unwarily sometimes watching the humans round their little fire. The October air had a frosty touch that nipped.

The Redskin did not answer. No muscle of his neck nor of his stiffened body moved. He seemed all ears.

"Well?" repeated the Englishman, lowering his voice this time instinctively. "What d'you hear, God damn it!" The touch of odd nervousness that made his anger grow betrayed itself in his language.

Tooshalli slowly turned his head back again to its normal position, the body rigid as before.

"I hear nothing, Mr. Grimwood," he said, gazing with quiet dignity into his employer's eyes.

This was too much for the other, a man of savage temper at the best of times. He was the type of Englishman who held strong views as to the right way of treating "inferior" races.

"That's a lie, Tooshalli, and I won't have you lie to me. Now what was it? Tell me at once!"

"I hear nothing," repeated the other. "I only think."

"And what is it you're pleased to think?" Impatience made a nasty expression round the mouth.

"I go not," was the abrupt reply, unalterable decision in the voice.

The man's rejoinder was so unexpected that Grimwood found nothing to say at first. For a moment he did not take its meaning; his mind, always slow, was confused by impatience, also by what he considered the foolishness of the little scene. Then in a flash he understood; but he also understood the immovable obstinacy of the race he had to deal with. Tooshalli was informing him that he refused to go into the valley where the big moose had vanished. And his astonishment was so great at first that he merely sat and stared. No words came to him.

"It is——" said the Indian, but used a native term.

"What's that mean?" Grimwood found his tongue, but his quiet tone was ominous.

"Mr. Grimwood, it mean the 'Valley of the Beasts'," was the reply in a tone quieter still.

The Englishman made a great, a genuine effort at self-control. He was dealing, he forced himself to remember, with a superstitious Redskin. He knew the stubbornness of the type. If the man left him, his sport was irretrievably spoiled, for he could not hunt in this wilderness alone, and even if he got the coveted head, he could never, never get it out alone. His native selfishness seconded his effort. Persuasion, if only he could keep back his rising anger, was his rôle to play.

"The Valley of the Beasts," he said, a smile on his lips rather than in his darkening eyes; "but that's just what we want. It's beasts we're after, isn't it?" His voice had a false cheery ring that could not have deceived a child. "But what d'you mean, anyhow—the Valley of the Beasts?" He asked it with a dull attempt at sympathy.

"It belong to Ishtot, Mr. Grimwood." The man looked him full in the face, no flinching in the eyes.

"My—our—big moose is there," said the other, who recognized the name of the Indian Hunting God, and understanding better, felt confident he would soon persuade his man. Tooshalli, he remembered, too, was nominally a Christian. "We'll follow him at dawn and get the biggest head the world has ever seen. You will be famous," he added, his temper better in hand again. "Your tribe will honor you. And the white hunters will pay you much money."

"He go there to save himself. I go not."

The other's anger revived with a leap at this stupid obstinacy. But, in spite of it, he noticed the odd choice of words. He began to realize that nothing now would move the man. At the same time he also realized that violence on his part must prove worse than useless. Yet violence was natural to his "dominant" type. "That brute Grimwood" was the way most men spoke of him.

"Back at the settlement you're a Christian, remember," he tried, in his clumsy way, another line. "And disobedience means hell-fire. You know that!"

"I a Christian—at the post," was the reply, "but out here the Red God rule. Ishtot keep that valley for himself. No Indian hunt there." It was as though a granite boulder spoke.

The savage temper of the Englishman, enforced by the long difficult suppression, rose wickedly into sudden flame. He stood up, kicking his blankets aside. He strode across the dying fire to the Indian's side. Too-shalli also rose. They faced each other, two humans alone in the wilderness, watched by countless invisible forest eyes.

Tooshalli stood motionless, yet as though he expected violence from the foolish, ignorant white-face. "You go alone, Mr. Grimwood." There was no fear in him.

Grimwood choked with rage. His words came forth with difficulty, though he roared them into the silence of the forest:

"I pay you, don't I? You'll do what *I* say, not what *you* say!" His voice woke the echoes.

The Indian, arms hanging by his side, gave the old reply.

"I go not," he repeated firmly.

It stung the other into uncontrollable fury.

The beast then came uppermost. "You've said that once too often, Tooshalli!" and he struck him brutally in the face. The Indian fell, rose to his knees again, collapsed sideways beside the fire, then struggled back into a sitting position. He never once took his eyes from the white man's face.

Beside himself with anger, Grimwood stood over him. "Is that enough? Will you obey me now?" he shouted.

"I go not," came the thick reply, blood streaming from his mouth. The eyes had no flinching in them. "That valley Ishtot keep. Ishtot see us now. *He see you.*" The last words he uttered with strange, almost uncanny emphasis.

Grimwood, arm raised, fist clenched, about to repeat his terrible assault, paused suddenly. His arm sank to his side. What exactly stopped him he could never say. For one thing, he feared his own anger, feared that if he let himself go he would not stop till he had killed—committed murder. He knew his own fearful temper and stood afraid of it. Yet it was not only that. The calm firmness of the Redskin, his courage under pain, and something in the fixed and burning eyes arrested him. Was it also something in the words he had used—"Ishtot see *you*"—that stung him into a queer caution midway in his violence?

He could not say. He only knew that a momentary sense of awe came over him. He became unpleasantly aware of the enveloping forest, so still, listening in a kind of impenetrable, remorseless silence. This lonely wilderness, looking silently upon what might easily prove murder, laid a faint, inexplicable chill upon his raging blood. The hand dropped slowly to his side again, the fist unclenched itself, his breath came more evenly.

"Look you here," he said, adopting without knowing it the local way of speech. "I ain't a bad man, though your going-on do make a man damned tired. I'll give you another chance." His voice was sullen, but a new note in it surprised even himself. "I'll do that. You can have the night to think it over, Tooshalli—see? Talk it over with your——"

He did not finish the sentence. Somehow the name of the Redskin God refused to pass his lips. He turned away, flung himself into his blankets, and in less than ten minutes, exhausted as much by his anger as by the day's hard going, he was sound asleep.

The Indian, crouching beside the dying fire, had said nothing.

Night held the woods, the sky was thick with stars, the life of the forest went about its business quietly, with that wondrous skill which millions of years have perfected. The Redskin, so close to this skill that he instinctively used and borrowed from it, was silent, alert and wise, his outline as inconspicuous as though he merged, like his four-footed teachers, into the mass of the surrounding bush.

He moved perhaps, yet nothing knew he moved. His wisdom, derived from that eternal, ancient mother who from infinite experience makes no mistakes, did not fail him. His soft tread made no sound; his breathing, as his weight, was calculated. The stars observed him, but they did not tell; the light air knew his whereabouts, yet without betrayal. . . .

The chill dawn gleamed at length between the trees, lighting the pale ashes of an extinguished fire, also of a bulky obvious form beneath a blanket. The form moved clumsily. The cold was penetrating.

And that bulky form now moved because a dream had come to trouble it. A dark figure stole across its confused field of vision. The form started, but it did not wake. The figure spoke: "Take this," it whispered, handing a little stick, curiously carved. "It is the totem of great Ishtot. In the valley all memory of the White Gods will leave you. Call upon Ishtot. . . . Call on Him if you dare"; and the dark figure glided away out of the dream and out of all remembrance. . . .

The first thing Grimwood noticed when he woke was that Tooshalli was not there. No fire burned, no tea was ready. He felt exceedingly annoyed. He glared about him, then got up with a curse to make the fire. His mind seemed confused and troubled. At first he only realized one thing clearly—his guide had left him in the night.

It was very cold. He lit the wood with difficulty and made his tea, and the actual world came gradually back to him. The Red Indian had gone; perhaps the blow, perhaps the superstitious terror, perhaps both, had driven him away. He was alone, that was the outstanding fact. For anything beyond outstanding facts, Grimwood felt little interest. Imaginative speculation was beyond his compass. Close to the brute creation, it seemed, his nature lay.

It was while packing his blankets—he did it automatically, a dull, vicious resentment in him—that his fingers struck a bit of wood that he was about to throw away when its unusual shape caught his attention suddenly. His odd dream came back then. But was it a dream? The bit of wood was undoubtedly a totem stick. He examined it. He paid it more attention than he meant to, wished to. Yes, it was unquestionably a totem stick. The dream, then, was not a dream. Tooshalli had quit, but, following with Redskin faithfulness some code of his own, had left him the means of safety. He chuckled sourly, but thrust the stick inside his belt. "One never knows," he mumbled to himself.

He faced the situation squarely. He was alone in the wilderness. His capable, experienced woodsman had deserted him. The situation was serious. What should he do? A weakling would certainly retrace his steps, following the track they had made, afraid to be left alone in the vast hinterland of pathless forest. But Grimwood was of yet another build. Alarmed he might be, but he would not give in. He had the defects of his own qualities. The brutality of his nature argued force. He was determined and a sportsman. He would go on. And ten minutes after breakfast, having first made a *cache* of what provisions were left over, he was on his way—down across the ridge and into the mysterious valley, the Valley of the Beasts.

It looked, in the morning sunlight, entrancing. The trees closed in behind him, but he did not notice. It led him on. . . .

He followed the track of the gigantic moose he meant to kill, and the sweet, delicious sunshine helped him. The air was like wine, the seductive spoor of the great beast, with here and there a faint splash of blood on leaves or ground, lay forever just before his eyes. He found the valley, though the actual word did not occur to him, enticing; more and more he noticed the beauty, the desolate grandeur of the mighty spruce and hemlock, the splendor of the granite bluffs which in places rose above the forest and caught the sun. . . . The valley was deeper, vaster than he had imagined. He felt safe, at home in it, though, again these actual terms did not occur to him. . . . Here he could hide for ever and find peace. . . . He became aware of a new quality in the deep loneliness. The scenery for the first time in his life appealed to him, and the form of the appeal was curious—he felt the comfort of it.

For a man of his habit, this was odd, yet the new sensations stole over him so gently, their approach so gradual, that they were first recognized by his consciousness indirectly. They had already established themselves in him before he noticed them; and the indirectness took this form—that the passion of the chase gave place to an interest in the valley itself. The lust of the hunt, the fierce desire to find and kill, the keen wish, in a word, to see his quarry within range, to aim, to fire, to witness the natural consummation of the long expedition—these had all become measurably less, while the effect of the valley upon him had increased in strength. There was a welcome about it that he did not understand.

The change was singular, yet it did not occur to him as singular; it was unnatural, yet it did not strike him so. To a mind of his unobservant, unanalytical type, a change had to be marked and dramatic before he noticed it; something in the nature of a shock must accompany it for him to recognize it had happened. And there had been no shock. The spoor of the great moose was much cleaner, now that he caught up with the animal that made it; the blood more frequent; he had noticed the spot where it had rested, its huge body leaving a marked imprint on the soft ground; where it had reached up to eat the leaves of saplings here and there was also visible; he had come undoubtedly very near to it, and any minute now might see its great bulk within range of an easy shot. Yet his ardor had somehow lessened.

He first realized this change in himself when it suddenly occurred to him that the animal itself had grown less cautious. It must scent him easily now, since a moose, its sight being indifferent, depends chiefly for its safety upon its unusually keen sense of smell, and the wind came from behind him. This now struck him as decidedly uncommon: the moose itself was obviously careless of his close approach. It felt no fear.

It was this inexplicable alteration in the animal's behavior that made him recognize, at last, the alteration in his own. He had followed it now for a couple of hours and had descended some eight hundred to a thousand feet; the trees were thinner and more sparsely placed; there were open, park-like places where silver birch, sumach and maple splashed their blazing colors; and a crystal stream, broken by many waterfalls, foamed past toward the bed of the great valley, yet another thousand feet below. By a quiet pool against some over-arching rocks, the moose

had evidently paused to drink, paused at its leisure, moreover. Grimwood, rising from a close examination of the direction the creature had
taken after drinking—the hoof-marks were fresh and very distinct in
the marshy ground about the pool—looked suddenly straight into the
great creature's eyes. It was not twenty yards from where he stood, yet
he had been standing on that spot for at least ten minutes, caught by
the wonder and loneliness of the scene. The moose, therefore, had been
close beside him all this time. It had been calmly drinking, undisturbed
by his presence, unafraid.

The shock came now, the shock that woke his heavy nature into realization. For some seconds, probably for minutes, he stood rooted to the
ground, motionless, hardly breathing. He stared as though he saw a vision. The animal's head was lowered, but turned obliquely somewhat,
so that the eyes, placed sideways in its great head, could see him properly; its immense proboscis hung as though stuffed upon an English wall;
he saw the forefeet planted wide apart, the slope of the enormous shoulders dropping back toward the fine hind-quarters and lean flanks. It
was a magnificent bull. The horns and head justified his wildest expectations, they were superb, a record specimen, and a phrase—where had
he heard it?—ran vaguely, as from far distance, through his mind: "the
biggest moose in the world."

There was the extraordinary fact, however, that he did not shoot; nor
feel the wish to shoot. The familiar instinct, so strong hitherto in his
blood, made no sign; the desire to kill apparently had left him. To raise
his rifle, aim and fire had become suddenly an absolute impossibility.

He did not move. The animal and the human stared into each other's
eyes for a length of time whose interval he could not measure. Then
came a soft noise close beside him: the rifle had slipped from his grasp
and fallen with a thud into the mossy earth at his feet. And the moose
for the first time now was moving. With slow, easy stride, its great
weight causing a squelching sound as the feet drew out of the moist
ground, it came toward him, the bulk of the shoulders giving it an appearance of swaying like a ship at sea. It reached his side, it almost
touched him, the magnificent head bent low, the spread of the gigantic
horns lay beneath his very eyes. He could have patted, stroked it. He
saw, with a touch of pity, that blood trickled from a sore in its left
shoulder, matting the thick hair. It sniffed the rifle.

Then, lifting its head and shoulders again, it sniffed the air, this time
with an audible sound that shook from Grimwood's mind the last possibility that he witnessed a vision or dreamed a dream. One moment
it gazed into his face, its big brown eyes shining and unafraid, then
turned abruptly, and swung away at a speed ever rapidly increasing
across the park-like spaces till it was lost finally among the dark tangle

of undergrowth beyond. And the Englishman's muscles turned to paper, his paralysis passed, his legs refused to support his weight, and he sank heavily to the ground. . . .

It seems he slept, slept long and heavily; he sat up, stretched himself, yawned and rubbed his eyes. The sun had moved across the sky, for the shadows, he saw, now ran from west to east, and they were long shadows. He had slept evidently for hours, and evening was drawing in. He was aware that he felt hungry. In his pouch-like pockets he had dried meat, sugar, matches, tea, and the little billy that never left him. He would make a fire, boil some tea and eat.

But he took no steps to carry out his purpose, he felt disinclined to move, he sat thinking, thinking. . . . What was he thinking about? He did not know, he could not say exactly; it was more like fugitive pictures that passed across his mind. Who, and where, was he? This was the Valley of the Beasts, that he knew; he felt sure of nothing else. How long had he been here, and where had he come from, and why? The questions did not linger for their answers, almost as though his interest in them was merely automatic. He felt happy, peaceful, unafraid.

He looked about him, and the spell of this virgin forest came upon him like a charm; only the sound of falling water, the murmur of wind sighing among innumerable branches, broke the enveloping silence. Overhead, beyond the crests of the towering trees, a cloudless evening sky was paling into transparent orange, opal, mother of pearl. He saw buzzards soaring lazily. A scarlet tanager flashed by. Soon would the owls begin to call and the darkness fall like a sweet black veil and hide all detail, while the stars sparkled in their countless thousands. . . .

A glint of something that shone upon the ground caught his eye—a smooth, polished strip of rounded metal: his rifle. And he started to his feet impulsively, yet not knowing exactly what he meant to do. At the sight of the weapon, something had leaped to life in him, then faded out, died down, and was gone again.

"I'm—I'm——" he began muttering to himself, but could not finish what he was about to say. His name had disappeared completely. "I'm in the Valley of the Beasts," he repeated in place of what he sought but could not find.

This fact, that he was in the Valley of the Beasts, seemed the only positive item of knowledge that he had. About the name something known and familiar clung, though the sequence that led up to it he could not trace. Presently, nevertheless, he rose to his feet, advanced a few steps, stooped and picked up the shining metal thing, his rifle. He examined it a moment, a feeling of dread and loathing rising in him, a sensation of almost horror that made him tremble, then, with a convulsive movement that betrayed an intense reaction of some sort he could not comprehend, he flung the thing far from him into the foaming torrent.

He saw the great white splash it made, he also saw that same instant a large grizzly bear swing heavily along the bank not a dozen yards from where he stood. It, too, heard the splash, for it started, turned, paused a second, then changed its direction and came toward him. It came up close. Its fur brushed his body. It examined him leisurely, as the moose had done, sniffed, half rose upon its terrible hind legs, opened its mouth so that red tongue and gleaming teeth were plainly visible, then flopped back upon all fours again with a deep growling that yet had no anger in it, and swung off at a quick trot back to the bank of the torrent. He had felt its hot breath upon his face, but he had felt no fear. The monster was puzzled but not hostile. It disappeared.

"They know not——" he sought for the word "man," but could not find it. "They have never been hunted."

The words ran through his mind again and again if perhaps he was not entirely certain of their meaning; they rose, as it were, automatically; a familiar sound lay in them somewhere. At the same time there rose feelings in him that were equally, though in another way, familiar and quite natural, feelings he had once known intimately but long since laid aside.

What were they? What was their origin? They seemed distant as the stars, yet were actually in his body, in his blood and nerves, part and parcel of his flesh. Long, long ago. . . . Oh, how long, how long?

Thinking was difficult; feeling was what he most easily and naturally managed. He could not think for long; feeling rose up and drowned the effort quickly.

That huge and awful bear—not a nerve, not a muscle quivered in him as its acrid smell rose to his nostrils, its fur brushed down his legs. Yet he was aware that somewhere there was danger, though not here. Somewhere there was attack, hostility, wicked and calculated plans against him—as against that splendid, roaming animal that had sniffed, examined, then gone its own way, satisfied. Yes, active attack, hostility and careful, cruel plans against his safety, but—not here. Here he was safe, secure, at peace; here he was happy; here he could roam at will, no eye cast sideways into forest depths, no ear pricked high to catch sounds not explained, no nostrils quivering to scent alarm. He felt this, but he did not think of it. He felt hungry, thirsty too.

Something prompted him now at last to act. His billy lay at his feet, and he picked it up; the matches—he carried them in a metal case whose screw top kept out all moisture—were in his hand. Gathering a few dry twigs, he stooped to light them, then suddenly drew back with the first touch of fear he had yet known.

Fire! What *was* fire? The idea was repugnant to him, it was impossible, he was afraid of fire. He flung the metal case after the rifle and saw it gleam in the last rays of sunset, then sink with a little splash beneath the water. Glancing down at his billy, he realized next that he could not make use of it either, nor of the dark dry dusty stuff he had meant to boil in water. He felt no repugnance, certainly no fear, in connection with these things, only he could not handle them, he did not need them, he had forgotten, yes, "forgotten," what they meant exactly. This strange forgetfulness was increasing in him rapidly, becoming more and more complete with every minute. Yet his thirst must be quenched.

The next moment he found himself at the water's edge; he stooped to fill his billy; paused, hesitated, examined the rushing water, then abruptly moved a few feet higher up the stream, leaving the metal can behind him. His handling of it had been oddly clumsy, his gestures awkward, even unnatural. He now flung himself down with an easy, simple motion of his entire body, lowered his face to a quiet pool he had found, and drank his fill of the cool, refreshing liquid. But, though unaware of the fact, he did not drink. He lapped.

Then, crouching where he was, he ate the meat and sugar from his pockets, lapped more water, moved back a short distance again into the dry ground beneath the trees, but moved this time without rising to his feet, curled his body into a comfortable position and closed his eyes again to sleep. . . . No single question now raised its head in him. He felt contentment, satisfaction only. . . .

He stirred, shook himself, opened half an eye and saw, as he had felt already in slumber, that he was not alone. In the park-like spaces in front of him, as in the shadowed fringe of the trees at his back, there was sound and movement, the sound of stealthy feet, the movement of innumerable dark bodies. There was the pad and tread of animals, the stir of backs, of smooth and shaggy beasts in countless numbers. Upon this host fell the light of a half moon sailing high in a cloudless sky; the gleam of stars, sparkling in the clear night air like diamonds, shone reflected in hundreds of ever-shifting eyes, most of them but a few feet above the ground. The whole valley was alive.

He sat upon his haunches, staring, staring, but staring in wonder, not in fear, though the foremost of the great host were so near that he could have stretched an arm and touched them. It was an ever-moving, ever-shifting throng he gazed at, spell-bound, in the pale light of moon and stars, now fading slowly towards the approaching dawn. And the smell of the forest itself was not sweeter to him in that moment than the mingled perfume, raw, pungent, acrid, of this furry host of beautiful wild animals that moved like a sea, with a strange murmuring, too, like sea, as the myriad feet and bodies passed to and fro together. Nor was the gleam of the starry, phosphorescent eyes less pleasantly friendly than those happy lamps that light home-lost wanderers to cosy rooms and safety. Through the wild army, in a word, poured to him the deep comfort of the entire valley, a comfort which held both the sweetness of invitation and the welcome of some magical home-coming.

No thoughts came to him, but feeling rose in a tide of wonder and acceptance. He was in his rightful place. His nature had come home. There was this dim, vague consciousness in him that after long, futile straying in another place where uncongenial conditions had forced him to be unnatural and therefore terrible, he had returned at last where he belonged. Here, in the Valley of the Beasts, he had found peace, security and happiness. He would be—he was at last—himself.

It was a marvelous scene he watched, his nerves at highest tension yet quite steady, his senses exquisitely alert, yet no uneasiness in the full, accurate reports they furnished. Strong as some deep flood-tide, yet dim, as with untold time and distance, rose over him the spell of long-forgotten memory of a state where he was content and happy, where he was natural. The outlines, as it were, of mighty, primitive pictures, flashed before him, yet were gone again before the detail was filled in.

He watched the great army of the animals, they were all about him now; he crouched upon his haunches in the center of an ever-moving circle of wild forest life. Great timber wolves he saw pass to and fro, loping past him with long stride and graceful swing; their red tongues lolling out; they swarmed in hundreds. Behind, yet mingling freely with them, rolled the huge grizzlies, not clumsy as their uncouth bodies promised, but swiftly, lightly, easily, their half-tumbling gait masking agility and speed. They gamboled, sometimes they rose and stood half upright, they were comely in their mass and power, they rolled past him so close that he could touch them. And the black bear and the brown went with them, bears beyond counting, monsters and little ones, a splendid multitude. Beyond them, yet only a little further back, where the park-like spaces made free movement easier, rose a sea of horns and antlers like a miniature forest in the silvery moonlight. The immense tribe of deer gathered in vast throngs beneath the starlit sky. Moose and caribou, he saw, the mighty wapiti, and the smaller deer in their crowding thousands. He heard the sound of meeting horns, the tread of innumerable hoofs, the occasional pawing of the ground as the bigger creatures maneuvered for more space about them. A wolf, he saw, was licking gently at the shoulder of a great bull-moose that had been injured. And the tide receded, advanced again, once more receded, rising and falling like a living sea whose waves were animal shapes, the inhabitants of the Valley of the Beasts.

Beneath the quiet moonlight they swayed to and fro before him. They watched him, knew him, recognized him. They made him welcome.

He was aware, moreover, of a world of smaller life that formed an under-sea, as it were, numerous under-currents rather, running in and out between the great upright legs of the larger creatures. These, though he could not see them clearly, covered the earth, he was aware, in enormous numbers, darting hither and thither, now hiding, now reappearing, too intent upon their busy purposes to pay him attention like their huger comrades, yet ever and anon tumbling against his back, cannoning from his sides, scampering across his legs even, then gone again with a scuttering sound of rapid little feet, and rushing back into the general host beyond. And with this smaller world also he felt at home.

How long he sat gazing, happy in himself, secure, satisfied, contented, natural, he could not say, but it was long enough for the desire to mingle with what he saw, to know closer contact, to become one with them all—long enough for this deep blind desire to assert itself, so that at length he began to move from his mossy seat toward them, to move, moreover, as they moved, and not upright on two feet.

The moon was lower now, just sinking behind a towering cedar whose ragged crest broke its light into silvery spray. The stars were a little paler, too. A line of faint red was visible beyond the heights at the valley's eastern end.

He paused and looked about him, as he advanced slowly, aware that the host already made an opening in their ranks and that the bear even nosed the earth in front, as though to show the way that was easiest for him to follow. Then, suddenly, a lynx leaped past him into the low branches of a hemlock, and he lifted his head to admire its perfect poise. He saw in the same instant the arrival of the birds, the army of the eagles, hawks and buzzards, birds of prey—the awakening flight that just precedes the dawn. He saw the flocks and streaming lines, hiding the whitening stars a moment as they passed with a prodigious whirr of wings. There came the hooting of an owl from the tree immediately overhead where the lynx now crouched, but not maliciously, along its branch.

He started. He half rose to an upright position. He knew not why he did so, knew not exactly why he started. But in the attempt to find his new, and, as it now seemed, his unaccustomed balance, one hand fell against his side and came in contact with a hard, straight thing that projected awkwardly from his clothing. He pulled it out, feeling it all over with his fingers. It was a little stick. He raised it nearer to his eyes, examined it in the light of dawn now growing swiftly, remembered, or half remembered what it was—and stood stock still.

"The totem stick," he mumbled to himself, yet audibly, finding his speech, and finding another thing—a glint of peering memory—for the first time since entering the valley.

A shock like fire ran through his body; he straightened himself, aware that a moment before he had been crawling upon his hands and knees; it seemed that something broke in his brain, lifting a veil, flinging a shutter free. And Memory peered dreadfully through the widening gap. "I'm—I'm Grimwood," his voice uttered, though below his breath. "Tooshalli's left me. I'm alone. . . .!"

He was aware of a sudden change in the animals surrounding him. A big, grey wolf sat three feet away, glaring into his face; at its side an enormous grizzly swayed itself from one foot to the other; behind it, as if looking over its shoulder, loomed a gigantic wapiti. But dawn was nearer, the sun already close to the horizon. He saw details with sharp distinctness now. The great bear rose, balancing a moment on its massive hind-quarters, then took a step toward him, its front paws spread like arms. A huge bull-moose, lowering its horns as if about to charge, joined it. A sudden excitement ran quivering over the entire host; the distant ranks moved in a new, unpleasant way; a thousand heads were lifted, ears were pricked, a forest of muzzles pointed to the wind.

And the Englishman, beside himself suddenly with a sense of ultimate terror that saw no possible escape, stiffened and stood rigid. The horror of his position petrified him. Motionless and silent he faced the awful army of his enemies, while the white light of breaking day added fresh ghastliness to the scene which was the setting for his death in the Valley of the Beasts.

Above him crouched the hideous lynx, ready to spring the instant he sought safety in the tree; above it again, he was aware of a thousand talons of steel, fierce hooked beaks of iron, and the angry beating of prodigious wings.

He reeled, for the grizzly touched his body with its outstretched paw; the wolf crouched just before its deadly spring; in another second he would have been torn to pieces, crushed, devoured, when terror, operating naturally as ever, released the muscles of his throat and tongue. He shouted with what he believed was his last breath on earth. It was a prayer to whatever gods there be, an anguished cry for help to heaven.

"Ishtot! Great Ishtot, help me!" his voice rang out, while his hand still clutched the forgotten totem stick.

And the Red Heaven heard him.

Grimwood that same instant was aware of a presence that, but for his terror of the beasts, must have frightened him into sheer unconsciousness. A gigantic Red Indian stood before him. Yet, while the figure rose close in front of him, causing the birds to settle and the wild animals to crouch quietly where they stood, it rose also from a great distance, for it seemed to fill the entire valley with its influence, its power, its amazing majesty. In some way, moreover, that he could not understand, its vast appearance included the actual valley itself with all its trees, its running streams, its open spaces and its rocky bluffs. These marked its outline, as it were, the outline of a superhuman shape. There was a mighty bow, there was a quiver of enormous arrows, there was this Redskin to whom they belonged.

Yet the appearance, the outline, the face and figure too—these were the valley; and when the voice became audible it was the valley itself that uttered the appalling words. It was the voice of trees and wind, and of running, falling water that woke the echoes in the Valley of the Beasts, as, in that same moment, the sun topped the ridge and filled the scene, the outline of the majestic figure too, with a flood of dazzling light:

"You have shed blood in this my valley. . . . *I will not save*. . . .!"

The figure melted away into the sunlit forest, merging with the new-born day. But Grimwood saw close against his face the shining teeth, hot fetid breath passed over his cheeks, a power enveloped his whole body as though a mountain crushed him. He closed his eyes. He fell. A sharp, crackling sound passed through his brain, but already unconscious, he did not hear it.

His eyes opened again, and the first thing they took in was—fire. He shrank back instinctively.

"It's all right, old man. We'll bring you round. Nothing to be frightened about." He saw the face of Iredale looking down into his own. And behind Iredale stood Tooshalli. His face was swollen. Grimwood remembered the blow. The big man began to cry.

"Painful still, is it?" Iredale said sympathetically. "Here, swallow a little of this. It'll set you right in no time."

Grimwood gulped down the spirit. He made a violent effort to control himself, but was unable to keep the tears back. He felt no pain. It was his heart that ached, though why or wherefore, he had no idea.

"I'm all to pieces," he mumbled, ashamed yet somehow not ashamed. "My nerves are rotten. What's happened?" There was no memory in him.

"You've been hugged by a bear, old man. But no bones broken. Tooshalli saved you. He fired in the nick of time—a brave shot, for he might easily have hit you instead of the brute."

"The other brute," whispered Grimwood, as the whiskey worked in him and memory came slowly back.

He saw a lake, canoes drawn up on the shore, two tents, and figures moving. Iredale explained matters briefly, then left him to sleep a bit. Tooshalli, it appeared, traveling without rest, had reached Iredale's camping ground twenty-four hours after leaving his employer. He found it deserted, Iredale and his Indian being on the hunt. When they returned at nightfall, he had explained his presence in his brief native fashion: "He struck me and I quit. He hunt now alone in Ishtot's Valley of the Beasts. He is dead, I think."

Iredale and his guide, with Tooshalli as leader, started off then and there, but Grimwood had covered a considerable distance, though leaving an easy track to follow. It was the moose tracks and the blood that guided them. They came up with him suddenly enough—in the grip of an enormous bear. It was Tooshalli that fired.

The Indian lives now in easy circumstances, all his needs cared for, while Grimwood, his benefactor but no longer his employer, has given up hunting. He is a quiet, easy-tempered, almost gentle sort of fellow, and people wonder rather why he hasn't married. "Just the fellow to make a good father," is what they say; "so kind, good-natured and affectionate." Over the mantelpiece hangs a totem stick. He declares it saved his soul, but what he means by the expression he has never quite explained.

46

Mrs. Packletide's Tiger

BY SAKI

IT was Mrs. Packletide's pleasure and intention that she should shoot a tiger. Not that the lust to kill had suddenly descended on her, or that she felt that she would leave India safer and more wholesome than she had found it, with one fraction less of wild beast per million of inhabitants. The compelling motive for her sudden deviation towards the foot-steps of Nimrod was the fact that Loona Bimberton had recently been carried eleven miles in an aeroplane by an Algerian aviator, and talked of nothing else; only a personally procured tiger-skin and a heavy harvest of Press photographs could successfully counter that sort of thing. Mrs. Packletide had already arranged in her mind the lunch she would give at her house in Curzon Street, ostensibly in Loona Bimberton's honour, with a tiger-skin rug occupying most of the foreground and all of the conversation. She had also already designed in her mind the tiger-claw brooch that she was going to give Loona Bimberton on her next birthday. In a world that is supposed to be chiefly swayed by hunger and by love Mrs. Packletide was an exception; her movements and motives were largely governed by dislike of Loona Bimberton.

Circumstances proved propitious. Mrs. Packletide had offered a thousand rupees for the opportunity of shooting a tiger without overmuch risk or exertion, and it so happened that a neighbouring village could boast of being the favoured rendezvous of an animal of respectable antecedents, which had been driven by the increasing infirmities of age to abandon game-killing and confine its appetite to the smaller domestic animals. The prospect of earning the thousand rupees had stimulated the sporting and commercial instinct of the villagers; children were posted night and day on the outskirts of the local jungle to head the tiger back in the unlikely event of his attempting to roam away to fresh hunting-grounds, and the cheaper kinds of goats were left about with elaborate carelessness to keep him satisfied with his present quarters. The one great anxiety was lest he should die of old age before the date appointed for the memsahib's shoot. Mothers carrying their babies home through the jungle after the day's work in the fields hushed their singing lest they might curtail the restful sleep of the venerable herd-robber.

The great night duly arrived, moonlit and cloudless. A platform had been constructed in a comfortable and conveniently placed tree, and thereon crouched Mrs. Packletide and her paid companion, Miss Mebbin. A goat, gifted with a particularly persistent bleat, such as even a partially deaf tiger might be reasonably expected to hear on a still night, was tethered at the correct distance. With an accurately sighted rifle and a thumb-nail pack of patience cards the sportswoman awaited the coming of the quarry.

"I suppose we are in some danger?" said Miss Mebbin.

She was not actually nervous about the wild beast, but she had a morbid dread of performing an atom more service than she had been paid for.

"Nonsense," said Mrs. Packletide; "it's a very old tiger. It couldn't spring up here even if it wanted to."

"If it's an old tiger I think you ought to get it cheaper. A thousand rupees is a lot of money."

Louisa Mebbin adopted a protective elder-sister attitude towards money in general, irrespective of nationality or denomination. Her energetic intervention had saved many a rouble from dissipating itself in tips in some Moscow hotel, and francs and centimes clung to her instinctively under circumstances which would have driven them headlong from less sympathetic hands. Her speculations as to the market depreciation of tiger remnants were cut short by the appearance on the scene of the animal itself. As soon as it caught sight of the tethered goat it lay flat on the earth, seemingly less from a desire to take advantage of all available cover than for the purpose of snatching a short rest before commencing the grand attack.

"I believe it's ill," said Louisa Mebbin, loudly in Hindustani, for the benefit of the village headman, who was in ambush in a neighbouring tree.

"Hush!" said Mrs. Packletide, and at that moment the tiger commenced ambling towards his victim.

"Now, now!" urged Miss Mebbin with some excitement; "if he doesn't touch the goat we needn't pay for it." (The bait was an extra.)

The rifle flashed out with a loud report, and the great tawny beast sprang to one side and then rolled over in the stillness of death. In a moment a crowd of excited natives had swarmed on to the scene, and their shouting speedily carried the glad news to the village, where a thumping of tom-toms took up the chorus of triumph. And their triumph and rejoicing found a ready echo in the heart of Mrs. Packletide; already that luncheon-party in Curzon Street seemed immeasurably nearer.

It was Louisa Mebbin who drew attention to the fact that the goat was in death-throes from a mortal bullet-wound, while no trace of the rifle's deadly work could be found on the tiger. Evidently the wrong animal had been hit, and the beast of prey had succumbed to heart-failure, caused by the sudden report of the rifle, accelerated by senile decay. Mrs. Packletide was pardonably annoyed at the discovery; but, at any rate, she was the possessor of a dead tiger, and the villagers, anxious for their thousand rupees, gladly connived at the fiction that she had shot the beast. And Miss Mebbin was a paid companion. Therefore did Mrs. Packletide face the cameras with a light heart, and her pictured fame reached from the pages of the *Texas Weekly Snapshot* to the illustrated Monday supplement of the *Novoe Vremya*. As for Loona Bimberton, she refused to look at an illustrated paper for weeks, and her letter of thanks for the gift of a tiger-claw brooch was a model of repressed emotions. The luncheon-party she declined; there are limits beyond which repressed emotions become dangerous.

From Curzon Street the tiger-skin rug travelled down to the Manor House, and was duly inspected and admired by the county, and it seemed a fitting and appropriate thing when Mrs. Packletide went to the County Costume Ball in the character of Diana. She refused to fall in, however, with Clovis's tempting suggestion of a primeval dance party, at which every one should wear the skins of beasts they had recently slain. "I should be in rather a Baby Bunting condition," confessed Clovis, "with a miserable rabbit-skin or two to wrap up in, but then," he added, with a rather malicious glance at Diana's proportions, "my figure is quite as good as that Russian dancing boy's."

"How amused every one would be if they knew what really happened," said Louisa Mebbin a few days after the ball.

"What do you mean?" asked Mrs. Packletide quickly.

"How you shot the goat and frightened the tiger to death," said Miss Mebbin, with her disagreeably pleasant laugh.

"No one would believe it," said Mrs. Packletide, her face changing colour as rapidly as though it were going through a book of patterns before post-time.

"Loona Bimberton would," said Miss Mebbin. Mrs. Packletide's face settled on an unbecoming shade of greenish white.

"You surely wouldn't give me away?" she asked.

"I've seen a week-end cottage near Dorking that I should rather like to buy," said Miss Mebbin with seeming irrelevance. "Six hundred and eighty, freehold. Quite a bargain, only I don't happen to have the money."

Louisa Mebbin's pretty week-end cottage, christened by her *Les Fauves,* and gay in summer-time with its garden borders of tiger-lilies, is the wonder and admiration of her friends.

"It is a marvel how Louisa manages to do it," is the general verdict. Mrs. Packletide indulges in no more big-game shooting.

"The incidental expenses are so heavy," she confides to inquiring friends.

47

The Happy Hypocrite

BY MAX BEERBOHM

NONE, it is said, of all who revelled with the Regent, was half so wicked as Lord George Hell. I will not trouble my little readers with a long recital of his great naughtiness. But it were well they should know that he was greedy, destructive, and disobedient. I am afraid there is no doubt that he often sat up at Carlton House until long after bed-time, playing at games, and that he generally ate and drank more than was good for him. His fondness for fine clothes was such that he used to dress on weekdays quite as gorgeously as good people dress on Sundays. He was thirty-five years old and a great grief to his parents.

And the worst of it was that he set such a bad example to others. Never, never did he try to conceal his wrong-doing; so that, in time, every one knew how horrid he was. In fact, I think he was proud of being horrid. Captain Tarleton, in his account of *Contemporary Bucks,* suggested that his lordship's great candour was a virtue and should incline us to forgive some of his abominable faults. But, painful as it is to me to dissent from any opinion expressed by one who is now dead, I hold that candour is good only when it reveals good actions or good sentiments, and that, when it reveals evil, itself is evil, even also.

Lord George Hell did, at last, atone for all his faults, in a way that was never revealed to the world during his life-time. The reason of his strange and sudden disappearance from that social sphere, in which he had so long moved and never moved again, I will unfold. My little readers will then, I think, acknowledge that any angry judgment they may have passed upon him must be reconsidered and, it may be, withdrawn. I will leave his lordship in their hands. But my plea for him will not be based upon that candour of his, which some of his friends so much admired. There were, yes! some so weak and so wayward as to think it a fine thing to have an historic title and no scruples. "Here comes George Hell," they would say, "How wicked my lord is looking!" *Noblesse oblige,* you see, and so an aristocrat should be very careful of his good name. Anonymous naughtiness does little harm.

It is pleasant to record that many persons were inobnoxious to the magic of his title and disapproved of him so strongly that, whenever he entered a room where they happened to be, they would make straight for the door and watch him very severely through the key-hole. Every morning when he strolled up Piccadilly they crossed over to the other side in a compact body, leaving him to the companionship of his bad companions on that which is still called the "shady" side. Lord George—σχετλιος—was quite indifferent to this demonstration. Indeed, he seemed wholly hardened, and when ladies gathered up their skirts as they passed him he would lightly appraise their ankles.

I am glad I never saw his lordship. They say he was rather like Caligula, with a dash of Sir John Falstaff, and that sometimes on wintry mornings in St. James's Street young children would hush their prattle and cling in disconsolate terror to their nurses' skirts as they saw him come (that vast and fearful gentleman!) with the east wind ruffling the rotund surface of his beaver, ruffling the fur about his neck and wrists, and striking the purple complexion of his cheeks to a still deeper purple. "King Bogey" they called him in the nurseries. In the hours when they too were naughty, their nurses would predict his advent down the chimney or from the linen-press, and then they always "behaved." So that, you see, even the unrighteous are a power for good, in the hands of nurses.

It is true that his lordship was a non-smoker—a negative virtue, certainly, and due, even that, I fear, to the fashion of the day—but there the list of his good qualities comes to an abrupt conclusion. He loved with an insatiable love the town and the pleasures of the town, whilst the ennobling influences of our English lakes were quite unknown to him. He used to boast that he had not seen a buttercup for twenty years, and once he called the country "a Fool's Paradise." London was the only place marked on the map of his mind. London gave him all he wished for. Is it not extraordinary to think that he had never spent a happy day nor a day of any kind in Follard Chase, that desirable mansion in Herts, which he had won from Sir Follard Follard, by a chuck of the dice, at Boodle's, on his seventeenth birthday? Always cynical and unkind, he had refused to give the broken baronet his "revenge." Always unkind and insolent, he had offered to instal him in the lodge—an offer which was, after a little hesitation, accepted. "On my soul, the man's place is a sinecure," Lord George would say; "he never has to open the gate for me."[1] So rust had covered the great iron gates of Follard Chase, and moss had covered its paths. The deer browsed upon its terraces. There were only wild flowers anywhere. Deep down among the weeds and water-lilies of the little stone-rimmed pond he had looked down upon, lay the marble faun, as he had fallen.

Of all the sins of his lordship's life surely not one was more wanton than his neglect of Follard Chase. Some whispered (nor did he ever trouble to deny) that he had won it by foul means, by loaded dice. Indeed no card-player in St. James's cheated more persistently than he. As he was rich and had no wife and family to support, and as his luck was always capital, I can offer no excuse for his conduct. At Carlton House, in the presence of many bishops and cabinet ministers, he once dunned the Regent most arrogantly for 5000 guineas out of which he had cheated him some months before, and went so far as to declare that he would not leave the house till he got it; whereupon His Royal Highness, with that unfailing tact for which he was ever famous, invited him to stay there as a guest, which, in fact, Lord George did, for several months. After this, we can hardly be surprised when we read that he "seldom sat down to the fashionable game of Limbo with less than four, and sometimes with *as many as seven aces* up his sleeve."[2] We can only wonder that he was tolerated at all.

At Garble's, that nightly resort of titled rips and roysterers, he usually spent the early part of his evenings. Round the illuminated garden, with La Gambogi, the dancer, on his arm and a Bacchic retinue at his heels, he would amble leisurely, clad in Georgian costume, which was not then, of course, fancy dress, as it is now.[3] Now and again, in the midst of his noisy talk, he would crack a joke of the period, or break into a sentimental ballad, dance a little or pick a quarrel. When he tired of such fooling, he would proceed to his box in the tiny *al fresco* theatre and patronize the jugglers, pugilists, play-actors and whatever eccentric persons happened to be performing there.

The stars were splendid and the moon as beautiful as a great camellia one night in May, as his lordship laid his arms upon the cushioned ledge of his box and watched the antics of the Merry Dwarf, a little, curly-headed creature, whose *début* it was. Certainly Garble had found a novelty. Lord George led the applause, and the Dwarf finished his frisking with a pretty song about lovers. Nor was this all. Feats of archery were to follow. In a moment the Dwarf reappeared with a small,

---

[1] *Lord Coleraine's Correspondence*, p. 101.

[2] *Contemporary Bucks*, vol. 1, p. 73.

[3] It would seem, however, that, on special occasions, his lordship indulged in odd costumes. "I have seen him," says Captain Tarleton (vol. 1, p. 69), "attired as a French clown, as a sailor, or in the crimson hose of a Sicilian grandee—*peu beau spectacle*. He never disguised his face, whatever his costume, however."

gilded bow in his hand and a quiverful of arrows slung at his shoulder. Hither and thither he shot these vibrant arrows, very precisely, several into the bark of the acacias that grew about the overt stage, several into the fluted columns of the boxes, two or three to the stars. The audience was delighted. *"Bravo! Bravo Saggitario!"* murmured Lord George, in the language of La Gambogi, who was at his side. Finally, the waxen figure of a man was carried on by an assistant and propped against the trunk of a tree. A scarf was tied across the eyes of the Merry Dwarf, who stood in a remote corner of the stage. *Bravo* indeed! For the shaft had pierced the waxen figure through the heart or just where the heart would have been, if the figure had been human and not waxen.

Lord George called for port and champagne, and beckoned the bowing homuncle to his box, that he might compliment him on his skill and pledge him in a bumper of the grape.

"On my soul, you have a genius for the bow," his lordship cried with florid condescension. "Come and sit by me, but first let me present you to my divine companion the Signora Gambogi—Virgo and Sagittarius, egad! You may have met on the Zodiac."

"Indeed, I met the Signora many years ago," the Dwarf replied, with a low bow. "But not on the Zodiac, and the Signora perhaps forgets me."

At this speech the Signora flushed angrily, for she was indeed no longer young, and the Dwarf had a childish face. She thought he mocked her; her eyes flashed. Lord George's twinkled rather maliciously.

"Great is the experience of youth," he laughed. "Pray, are you stricken with more than twenty summers?" "With more than I can count," said the Dwarf. "To the health of your lordship!" and he drained his long glass of wine. Lord George replenished it, and asked by what means or miracle he had acquired his mastery of the bow.

"By long practice," the little thing rejoined; "long practice on human creatures." And he nodded his curls mysteriously.

"On my heart, you are a dangerous box-mate."

"Your lordship were certainly a good target."

Little liking this joke at his bulk, which really rivalled the Regent's, Lord George turned brusquely in his chair and fixed his eyes upon the stage. This time it was the Gambogi who laughed.

A new operette, *The Fair Captive of Samarcand,* was being enacted, and the frequenters of Garble's were all curious to behold the new *débutante,* Jenny Mere, who was said to be both pretty and talented. These predictions were surely fulfilled, when the captive peeped from the window of her wooden turret. She looked so pale under her blue turban. Her eyes were dark with fear; her parted lips did not seem capable of speech. "Is it that she is frightened of us?" the audience wondered. "Or of the flashing scimitar of Aphoschaz, the cruel father who holds her captive?" So they gave her loud applause, and when at length she jumped down, to be caught in the arms of her gallant lover, Nissarah, and, throwing aside her Eastern draperies, did a simple dance, in the convention of Columbine, their delight was quite unbounded. She was very young and did not dance very well, it is true, but they forgave her that. And when she turned in the dance and saw her father with his scimitar, their hearts beat swiftly for her. Nor were all eyes tearless when she pleaded with him for her life.

Strangely absorbed, quite callous of his two companions, Lord George gazed over the footlights. He seemed as one who was in a trance. Of a sudden, something shot sharp into his heart. In pain he sprang to his feet and, as he turned, he seemed to see a winged and laughing child, in whose hand was a bow, fly swiftly away into the darkness. At his side was the Dwarf's chair. It was empty. Only La Gambogi was with him, and her dark face was like the face of a fury.

Presently he sank back into his chair, holding one hand to his heart, that still throbbed from the strange transfixion. He breathed very painfully and seemed scarce conscious of his surroundings. But La Gambogi knew he would pay no more homage to her now, for that the love of Jenny Mere had come into his heart.

When the operette was over, his love-sick lordship snatched up his cloak and went away without one word to the lady at his side. Rudely he brushed aside Count Karoloff and Mr. FitzClarence, with whom he had arranged to play hazard. Of his comrades, his cynicism, his reckless scorn—of all the material of his existence—he was oblivious now. He had no time for penitence or diffident delay. He only knew that he must kneel at the feet of Jenny Mere and ask her to be his wife.

"Miss Mere," said Garble, "is in her room, resuming her ordinary attire. If your lordship deign to await the conclusion of her humble toilet, it shall be my privilege to present her to your lordship. Even now, indeed, I hear her footfall on the stair."

Lord George uncovered his head and with one hand nervously smoothed his rebellious wig.

"Miss Mere, come hither," said Garble. "This is my Lord George Hell, that you have pleased who by your poor efforts this night will ever be the prime gratification of your passage through the roseate realms of art."

Little Miss Mere who had never seen a lord, except in fancy or in dreams, curtseyed shyly and hung her head. With a loud crash Lord George fell on his knees. The manager was greatly surprised, the girl greatly embarrassed. Yet neither of them laughed, for sincerity dignified his posture and sent eloquence from its lips.

"Miss Mere," he cried, "give ear, I pray you, to my poor words, nor spurn me in misprision from the pedestal of your beauty, genius, and virtue. All too conscious, alas! of my presumption in the same, I yet abase myself before you as a suitor for your adorable hand. I grope under the shadow of your raven locks. I am dazzled in the light of those translucent orbs, your eyes. In the intolerable whirlwind of your fame I faint and am afraid."

"Sir——" the girl began, simply.

"Say 'My Lord,'" said Garble, solemnly.

"My lord, I thank you for your words. They are beautiful. But indeed, indeed, I can never be your bride."

Lord George hid his face in his hands.

"Child,' said Mr. Garble, "let not the sun rise e'er you have retracted those wicked words."

"My wealth, my rank, my irremediable love for you, I throw them at your feet," Lord George cried, piteously. "I would wait an hour, a week, a lustre, even a decade, did you but bid me hope!"

"I can never be your wife," she said, slowly. "I can never be the wife of any man whose face is not saintly. Your face, my lord, mirrors, it may be, true love for me, but it is even as a mirror long tarnished by the reflection of this world's vanity. It is even as a tarnished mirror. Do not kneel to me, for I am poor and humble. I was not made for such impetuous wooing. Kneel, if you please, to some greater, gayer lady. As for my love, it is my own, nor can it ever be torn from me, but given, as true love needs be given, freely. Ah, rise from your knees. That man, whose face is wonderful as the faces of the saints, to him I will give my true love."

Miss Mere, though visibly affected, had spoken this speech with a gesture and elocution so superb, that Mr. Garble could not help applauding, deeply though he regretted her attitude towards his honoured patron. As for Lord George, he was immobile, a stricken oak. With a sweet look of pity, Miss Mere went her way, and Mr. Garble, with some solicitude, helped his lordship to rise from his knees. Out into the night, without a word, his lordship went. Above him the stars were still splendid. They seemed to mock the festoons of little lamps, dim now and guttering in the garden of Garble's. What should he do? No thoughts came; only his heart burnt hotly. He stood on the brim of Garble's lake, shallow and artificial as his past life had been. Two swans slept on its surface. The moon shone strangely upon their white, twisted necks. Should he drown himself? There was no one in the garden to prevent him, and in the morning they would find him floating there, one of the noblest of love's victims. The garden would be closed in the evening. There would be no performance in the little theatre. It might be that Jenny Mere would mourn him. "Life is a prison, without bars," he murmured, as he walked away.

All night long he strode, knowing not whither, through the mysterious streets and squares of London. The watchmen, to whom his figure was most familiar, gripped their staves at his approach, for they had old reason to fear his wild and riotous habits. He did not heed them. Through that dim conflict between darkness and day, which is ever waged silently over our sleep, Lord George strode on in the deep absorption of his love and of his despair. At dawn he found himself on the outskirts of a little wood in Kensington. A rabbit rushed past him through the dew. Birds were fluttering in the branches. The leaves were tremulous with the presage of day, and the air was full of the sweet scent of hyacinths.

How cool the country was! It seemed to cure the feverish maladies of his soul and consecrate his love. In the fair light of the dawn he began to shape the means of winning Jenny Mere, that he had conceived in the desperate hours of the night. Soon an old woodman passed by, and, with rough courtesy, showed him the path that would lead him quickest to the town. He was loth to leave the wood. With Jenny, he thought, he would live always in the country. And he picked a posy of wild flowers for her.

His *rentrée* into the still silent town strengthened his Aracadian resolves. He, who had seen the town so often in its hours of sleep, had never noticed how sinister its whole aspect was. In its narrow streets the white houses rose on either side of him like cliffs of chalk. He hurried swiftly along the unswept pavement. How had he loved this city of evil secrets?

At last he came to St. James's Square, to the hateful door of his own house. Shadows lay like memories in every corner of the dim hall. Through the window of his room a sunbeam slanted across his smooth, white bed, and fell ghastly on the ashen grate.

It was a bright morning in Old Bond Street, and fat little Mr. Aeneas, the fashionable mask-maker, was sunning himself at the door of his shop. His window was lined as usual with all kinds of masks—beautiful masks with pink cheeks, and absurd masks with protuberant chins; curious πρόσωπα copied from old tragic models; masks of paper for children, of fine silk for ladies, and of leather for working men; bearded or beardless, gilded or waxen (most of them, indeed were waxen), big or little masks. And in the middle of this vain galaxy hung the presentment of a Cyclop's face, carved cunningly of gold, with a great sapphire in its brow.

The sun gleamed brightly on the window and on the bald head and varnished shoes of fat little Mr. Aeneas. It was too early for any customers to come and Mr. Aeneas seemed to be greatly enjoying his leisure in the fresh air. He smiled complacently as he stood there, and well he might, for he was a great artist, and was patronized by several crowned heads and not a few of the nobility. Only the evening before, Mr. Brummell had come into his shop and ordered a light summer mask, wishing to evade for a time the jealous vigilance of Lady Otterton. It pleased Mr. Aeneas to think that his art made him the recipient of so many high secrets. He smiled as he thought of the titled spendthrifts, who, at this moment, *perdus* behind his masterpieces, passed unscathed among their creditors. He was the secular confessor of his day, always able to give absolution. An unique position!

The street was as quiet as a village street. At an open window over the way, a handsome lady, wrapped in a muslin *peignoir,* sat sipping her cup of chocolate. It was La Signora Gambogi, and Mr. Aeneas made her many elaborate bows. This morning, however, her thoughts seemed far away, and she did not notice the little man's polite efforts. Nettled at her negligence, Mr. Aeneas was on the point of retiring into his shop, when he saw Lord George Hell hastening up the street, with a posy of wild flowers in his hand.

"His lordship is up betimes!" he said to himself. "An early visit to La Signora, I suppose."

Not so, however. His lordship came straight towards the mask-shop. Once he glanced up at the Signora's window and looked deeply annoyed when he saw her sitting there. He came quickly into the shop.

"I want the mask of a saint," he said.

"Mask of a saint, my lord? Certainly!" said Mr. Aeneas, briskly. "With or without halo? His Grace the Bishop of St. Aldreds always wears his with a halo. Your lordship does not wish for a halo? Certainly! If your lordship will allow me to take the measurement——"

"I must have the mask to-day," Lord George said. "Have you none ready-made?"

"Ah, I see. Required for immediate wear," murmured Mr. Aeneas, dubiously. "You see, your lordship takes a rather large size." And he looked at the floor.

"Julius!" he cried suddenly to his assistant, who was putting finishing touches to a mask of Barbarossa which the young king of Zürremburg was to wear at his coronation the following week. "Julius! Do you remember the saint's mask we made for Mr. Ripsby, a couple of years ago?"

"Yes, sir," said the boy. "It's stored upstairs."

"I thought so," replied Mr. Aeneas. "Mr. Ripsby only had it on hire.

Step upstairs, Julius, and bring it down. I fancy it is just what your lordship would wish. Spiritual, yet handsome."

"Is it a mask that is even as a mirror of true love?" Lord George asked gravely.

"It was made precisely as such," the mask-maker answered. "In fact it was made for Mr. Ripsby to wear at his silver wedding, and was very highly praised by the relatives of Mrs. Ripsby. Will your lordship step into my little room?"

So Mr. Aeneas led the way to his parlour behind the shop. He was elated by the distinguished acquisition to his *clientèle,* for hitherto Lord George had never patronized his business. He bustled round his parlour and insisted that his lordship should take a chair and a pinch from his snuff-box, while the saint's mask was being found.

Lord George's eye travelled along the rows of framed letters from great personages, which lined the walls. He did not see them though, for he was calculating the chances that La Gambogi had not observed him, as he entered the mask-shop. He had come down so early that he thought she would be still abed. That sinister old proverb, *La jalouse se lève de bonne heure,* rose in his memory. His eye fell unconsciously on a large, round mask made of dull silver, with the features of a human face traced over its surface in faint filigree.

"Your lordship wonders what mask that is!" chirped Mr. Aeneas, tapping the thing with one of his little finger nails.

"What is that mask?" Lord George murmured, absently.

"I ought not to divulge, my lord," said the mask-maker. "But I know your lordship would respect a professional secret, a secret of which I am pardonably proud. This," he said, "is a mask for the sun-god, Apollo, whom heaven bless!"

"You astound me," said Lord George.

"Of no less a person, I do assure you. When Jupiter, his father, made him lord of the day, Apollo craved that he might sometimes see the doings of mankind in the hours of night time. Jupiter granted so reasonable a request, and when next Apollo had passed over the sky and hidden in the sea, and darkness had fallen on all the world, he raised his head above the waters that he might watch the doings of mankind in the hours of night time. But," Mr. Aeneas added, with a smile, "his bright countenance made light all the darkness. Men rose from their couches or from their revels, wondering that day was so soon come, and went to their work. And Apollo sank weeping into the sea. 'Surely,' he cried, 'it is a bitter thing that I alone, of all the gods, may not watch the world in the hours of night time. For in those hours, as I am told, men are even as gods are. They spill the wine and are wreathed with roses. Their daughters dance in the light of torches. They laugh to the sound of flutes. On their long couches they lie down at last and sleep comes to kiss their eyelids. None of these things may I see. Wherefore the brightness of my beauty is even as a curse to me and I would put it from me.' And as he wept, Vulcan said to him, 'I am not the least cunning of the gods, nor the least pitiful. Do not weep, for I will give you that which shall end your sorrow. Nor need you put from you the brightness of your beauty.' And Vulcan made a mask of dull silver and fastened it across his brother's face. And that night, thus masked, the sun-god rose from the sea and watched the doings of mankind in the night time. Nor any longer were men abashed by his bright beauty, for it was hidden by the mask of silver. Those whom he had so often seen haggard over their daily tasks, he saw feasting now and wreathed with red roses. He heard them laugh to the sound of flutes, as their daughters danced in the red light of torches. And when at length they lay down upon their soft couches and sleep kissed their eyelids, he sank back into the sea and hid his mask under a little rock in the bed of the sea. Nor have men ever known that Apollo watches them often in the night time, but fancied it to be some pale goddess."

"I myself have always thought it was Diana," said Lord George Hell.

"An error, my lord!" said Mr. Aeneas, with a smile. "*Ecce signum!*" And he tapped the mask of dull silver.

"Strange!" said his lordship. "And pray how comes it that Apollo has ordered of *you* this new mask?"

"He has always worn twelve new masks every year, inasmuch as no mask can endure for many nights the near brightness of his face, before which even a mask of the best and purest silver soon tarnishes, and wears away. Centuries ago, Vulcan tired of making so very many masks. And so Apollo sent Mercury down to Athens, to the shop of Phoron, a Phoenician mask-maker of great skill. Phoron made Apollo's masks for many years, and every month Mercury came to his shop for a new one. When Phoron died, another artist was chosen, and, when he died, another, and so on through all the ages of the world. Conceive, my lord, my pride and pleasure when Mercury flew into my shop, one night last year, and made me Apollo's warrant-holder. It is the highest privilege that any mask-maker can desire. And when I die," said Mr. Aeneas, with some emotion, "Mercury will confer my post upon another."

"And do they pay you for your labour?" Lord George asked.

Mr. Aeneas drew himself up to his full height, such as it was. "In Olympus, my lord," he said, "they have no currency. For any maskmaker, so high a privilege is its own reward. Yet the sun-god is generous. He shines more brightly into my shop than into any other. Nor does he suffer his rays to melt any waxen mask made by me, until its wearer doff it and it be done with." At this moment Julius came in with the Ripsby mask. "I must ask your lordship's pardon, for having kept you so long," pleaded Mr. Aeneas. "But I have a large store of old masks and they are imperfectly catalogued."

It certainly was a beautiful mask, with its smooth, pink cheeks and devotional brows. It was made of the finest wax. Lord George took it gingerly in his hands and tried it on his face. It fitted *à merveille*.

"Is the expression exactly as your lordship would wish?" asked Mr. Aeneas.

Lord George laid it on the table and studied it intently. "I wish it were more as a perfect mirror of true love," he said at length. "It is too calm, too contemplative."

"Easily remedied!" said Mr. Aeneas. Selecting a fine pencil, he deftly drew the eyebrows closer to each other. With a brush steeped in some scarlet pigment, he put a fuller curve upon the lips. And, behold! it was the mask of a saint who loves dearly. Lord George's heart throbbed with pleasure.

"And for how long does your lordship wish to wear it?" asked Mr. Aeneas.

"I must wear it until I die," replied Lord George.

"Kindly be seated then, I pray," rejoined the little man. "For I must apply the mask with great care. Julius, you will assist me!"

So, while Julius heated the inner side of the waxen mask over a little lamp, Mr. Aeneas stood over Lord George gently smearing his features with some sweet-scented pomade. Then he took the mask and powdered its inner side, quite soft and warm now, with a fluffy puff. "Keep quite still, for one instant," he said, and clapped the mask firmly on his lordship's upturned face. So soon as he was sure of its perfect adhesion, he took from his assistant's hand a silver file and a little wooden spatula, with which he proceeded to pare down the edge of the mask, where it joined the neck and ears. At length, all traces of the "join" were obliterated. It remained only to arrange the curls of the lordly wig over the waxen brow.

The disguise was done. When Lord George looked through the eyelets of his mask into the mirror that was placed in his hand, he saw a face that was saintly, itself a mirror of true love. How wonderful it was! He felt his past was a dream. He felt he was a new man indeed. His voice went strangely through the mask's parted lips, as he thanked Mr. Aeneas.

"Proud to have served your lordship," said that little worthy, pocketing his fee of fifty guineas, while he bowed his customer out.

When he reached the street, Lord George nearly uttered a curse through those sainted lips of his. For there, right in his way, stood La Gambogi, with a small, pink parasol. She laid her hand upon his sleeve and called him softly by his name. He passed her by without a word. Again she confronted him.

"I cannot let go so handsome a lover," she laughed, "even though he spurn me! Do not spurn me, George. Give me your posy of wild flowers. Why, you never looked so lovingly at me in all your life!"

"Madam," said Lord George, sternly, "I have not the honour to know you." And he passed on.

The lady gazed after her lost lover with the blackest hatred in her eyes. Presently she beckoned across the road to a certain spy.

And the spy followed him.

Lord George, greatly agitated, had turned into Piccadilly. It was horrible to have met this garish embodiment of his past on the very threshold of his fair future. The mask-maker's elevating talk about the gods, followed by the initiative ceremony of his saintly mask, had driven all discordant memories from his love-thoughts of Jenny Mere. And then to be met by La Gambogi! It might be that, after his stern words, she would not seek to cross his path again. Surely she would not seek to mar his sacred love. Yet, he knew her dark, Italian nature, her passion for revenge. What was the line in Virgil? *Spretaeque*—something. Who knew but that somehow, sooner or later, she might come between him and his love?

He was about to pass Lord Barrymore's mansion. Count Karoloff and Mr. FitzClarence were lounging in one of the lower windows. Would they know him under his mask? Thank God! they did not. They merely laughed as he went by, and Mr. FitzClarence cried in a mocking voice, "Sing us a hymn, Mr. What-ever-your-saint's-name-is!" The mask, then, at least, was perfect. Jenny Mere would not know him. He need fear no one but La Gambogi. But would not she betray his secret? He sighed.

That night he was going to visit Garble's and to declare his love to the little actress. He never doubted that she would love him for his saintly face. Had she not said, "That man whose face is wonderful as are the faces of the saints, to him I will give my true love?" She could not say now that his face was as a tarnished mirror of love. She would smile on him. She would be his bride. But would La Gambogi be at Garble's?

The operette would not be over before ten that night. The clock in Hyde Park Gate told him it was not yet ten—ten of the morning. Twelve whole hours to wait, before he could fall at Jenny's feet! "I cannot spend that time in this place of memories," he thought. So he hailed a yellow cabriolet and bade the jarvey drive him out to the village of Kensington.

When they came to the little wood where he had been but a few hours ago, Lord George dismissed the jarvey. The sun, that had risen as he stood there thinking of Jenny, shone down on his altered face, but, though it shone very fiercely, it did not melt his waxen features. The old woodman, who had shown him his way, passed by under a load of faggots and did not know him. He wandered among the trees. It was a lovely wood.

Presently he came to the bank of that tiny stream, the Ken, which still flowed there in those days. On the moss of its bank he lay down and let its water ripple over his hand. Some bright pebble glistened under the surface, and, as he peered down at it, he saw in the stream the reflection of his mask. A great shame filled him that he should so cheat the girl he loved. Behind that fair mask there would still be the evil face that had repelled her. Could he be so base as to decoy her into love of that most ingenious deception? He was filled with a great pity for her, with a hatred of himself. And yet, he argued, was the mask indeed a mean trick? Surely it was a secret symbol of his true repentance and of his true love. His face was evil, because his life had been evil. He had seen a gracious girl, and of a sudden his very soul had changed. His face alone was the same as it had been. It was not just that his face should be evil still.

There was the faint sound of some one sighing. Lord George looked up, and there, on the further bank, stood Jenny Mere, watching him. As their eyes met, she blushed and hung her head. She looked like nothing but a tall child, as she stood there, with her straight, limp frock of lilac cotton and her sunburnt straw bonnet. He dared not speak; he could only gaze at her. Suddenly there perched astride the bough of a tree, at her side, that winged and laughing child, in whose hand was a bow. Before Lord George could warn her, an arrow had flashed down and vanished in her heart, and Cupid had flown away.

No cry of pain did she utter, but stretched out her arms to her lover, with a glad smile. He leapt quite lightly over the little stream and knelt at her feet. It seemed more fitting that he should kneel before the gracious thing he was unworthy of. But she, knowing only that his face was as the face of a great saint, bent over him and touched him with her hand.

"Surely," she said, "you are that good man for whom I have waited. Therefore do not kneel to me, but rise and suffer me to kiss your hand. For my love of you is lowly, and my heart is all yours."

But he answered, looking up into her fond eyes, "Nay, you are a queen, and I must needs kneel in your presence."

And she shook her head wistfully, and she knelt down, also, in her tremulous ecstasy, before him. And as they knelt, the one to the other, the tears came into her eyes, and he kissed her. Though the lips that he pressed to her lips were only waxen, he thrilled with happiness, in that mimic kiss. He held her close to him in his arms, and they were silent in the sacredness of their love.

From his breast he took the posy of wild flowers that he had gathered. "They are for you," he whispered, "I gathered them for you, hours ago, in this wood. See! They are not withered."

But she was perplexed by his words and said to him, blushing, "How was it for me that you gathered them, though you had never seen me?"

"I gathered them for you," he answered, "knowing I should soon see you. How was it that you, who had never seen me, yet waited for me?"

"I waited, knowing I should see you at last." And she kissed the posy and put it at her breast.

And they rose from their knees and went into the wood, walking hand in hand. As they went, he asked the names of the flowers that grew under their feet. "These are primroses," she would say. "Did you not know? And these are ladies' feet, and these forget-me-nots. And that white flower, climbing up the trunks of the trees and trailing down so prettily from the branches, is called Astyanax. These little yellow things are buttercups. Did you not know?" And she laughed.

"I know the names of none of the flowers," he said.

She looked up into his face and said timidly, "Is it worldly and wrong of me to have loved the flowers? Ought I to have thought more of those higher things that are unseen?"

His heart smote him. He could not answer her simplicity.

"Surely the flowers are good, and did not you gather this posy for me?" she pleaded. "But if you do not love them, I must not. And I will try to forget their names. For I must try to be like you in all things."

"Love the flowers always," he said. "And teach me to love them."

So she told him all about the flowers, how some grew very slowly and others bloomed in a night; how clever the convolvulus was at climbing, and how shy violets were, and why honeycups had folded petals. She told him of the birds, too, that sang in the wood, how she knew them all by their voices. "That is a chaffinch singing. Listen!" she said. And she tried to imitate its note, that her lover might remember. All the birds, according to her, were good, except the cuckoo, and whenever she heard him sing she would stop her ears, lest she should forgive him for robbing the nests. "Every day," she said, "I have come to the wood, because I was lonely, and it seemed to pity me. But now I have you. And it is glad."

She clung closer to his arm, and he kissed her. She pushed back her straw bonnet, so that it dangled from her neck by its ribands, and laid her little head against his shoulder. For a while he forgot his treachery to her, thinking only of his love and her love. Suddenly she said to him, "Will you try not to be angry with me, if I tell you something? It is something that will seem dreadful to you."

"*Pauvrette,*" he answered, "you cannot have anything very dreadful to tell."

"I am very poor," she said, "and every night I dance in a theatre. It is the only thing I can do to earn my bread. Do you despise me because I dance?" She looked up shyly at him and saw that his face was full of love for her and not angry.

"Do you like dancing?" he asked.

"I hate it," she answered, quickly. "I hate it indeed. Yet—to-night, alas! I must dance again in the theatre."

"You need never dance again," said her lover. "I am rich and I will pay them to release you. You shall dance only for me. Sweetheart, it cannot be much more than noon. Let us go into the town, while there is time, and you shall be made my bride, and I your bridegroom, this very day. Why should you and I be lonely?"

"I do not know," she said.

So they walked back through the wood, taking a narrow path which Jenny said would lead them quickest to the village. And, as they went, they came to a tiny cottage, with a garden that was full of flowers. The old woodman was leaning over its paling, and he nodded to them as they passed.

"I often used to envy the woodman," said Jenny, "living in that dear little cottage."

"Let us live there, then," said Lord George. And he went back and asked the old man if he were not unhappy, living there alone.

"'Tis a poor life here for me," the old man answered. "No folk come to the wood, except little children, now and again, to play, or lovers like you. But they seldom notice me. And in winter I am alone with Jack Frost. Old men love merrier company than that. Oh! I shall die in the snow with my faggots on my back. A poor life here!"

"I will give you gold for your cottage and whatever is in it, and then you can go and live happily in the town," Lord George said. And he took from his coat a note for two hundred guineas, and held it across the palings.

"Lovers are poor, foolish derry-docks," the old man muttered. "But I thank you kindly, sir. This little sum will keep me cosy, as long as I last. Come into the cottage as soon as can be. It's a lonely place and does my heart good to depart from it."

"We are going to be married this afternoon, in the town," said Lord George. "We will come straight back to our home."

"May you be happy!" replied the woodman. "You'll find me gone when you come."

And the lovers thanked him and went their way.

"Are you very rich?" Jenny asked. "Ought you to have bought the cottage for that great price?"

"Would you love me as much if I were quite poor, little Jenny?" he asked her after a pause.

"I did not know you were rich when I saw you across the stream," she said.

And in his heart Lord George made a good resolve. He would put away from him all his worldly possessions. All the money that he had won at the clubs, fairly or foully, all that hideous accretion of gold guineas, he would distribute among the comrades he had impoverished. As he walked, with the sweet and trustful girl at his side, the vague record of his infamy assailed him, and a look of pain shot behind his smooth mask. He would atone. He would shun no sacrifice that might cleanse his soul. All his fortune he would put from him. Follard Chase he would give back to Sir Follard. He would sell his house in St. James's Square. He would keep some little part of his patrimony, enough for him in the wood, with Jenny, but no more.

"I shall be quite poor, Jenny," he said.

And they talked of the things that lovers love to talk of, how happy they would be together and how economical. As they were passing Herbert's pastry shop, which as my little readers know, still stands in Kensington, Jenny looked up rather wistfully into her lover's ascetic face.

"Should you think me greedy," she asked him, "if I wanted a bun? They have beautiful buns here!"

Buns! The simple word started latent memories of his childhood. Jenny was only a child, after all. Buns! He had forgotten what they were like. And as they looked at the piles of variegated cakes in the window, he said to her, "Which are buns, Jenny? I should like to have one, too."

"I am almost afraid of you," she said. "You must despise me so. Are you so good that you deny yourself all the vanity and pleasure that most people love? It is wonderful not to know what buns are! The round, brown, shiny cakes, with little raisins in them, are buns."

So he bought two beautiful buns, and they sat together in the shop, eating them. Jenny bit hers rather diffidently, but was reassured when he said that they must have buns very often in the cottage. Yes! he, the famous toper and *gourmet* of St. James's, relished this homely fare, as it passed through the insensible lips of his mask to his palate. He seemed to rise, from the consumption of his bun, a better man.

But there was no time to lose now. It was already past two o'clock. So he got a chaise from the inn opposite the pastry-shop, and they were

swiftly driven to Doctors' Commons. There he purchased a special
license. When the clerk asked him to write his name upon it, he hesitated. What name should he assume? Under a mask he had wooed this
girl, under an unreal name he must make her his bride. He loathed
himself for a trickster. He had vilely stolen from her the love she would
not give him. Even now, should he not confess himself the man whose
face had frightened her, and go his way? And yet, surely, it was not
just that he, whose soul was transfigured, should bear his old name.
Surely George Hell was dead, and his name had died with him. So
he dipped a pen in the ink and wrote "George Heaven," for want of
a better name. And Jenny wrote "Jenny Mere" beneath it.

An hour later they were married according to the simple rites of a
dear little registry office in Covent Garden.

And in the cool evening they went home.

In the cottage that had been the woodman's they had a wonderful
honeymoon. No king and queen in any palace of gold were happier
than they. For them their tiny cottage was a palace, and the flowers that
filled the garden were their couriers. Long and careless and full of
kisses were the days of their reign.

Sometimes, indeed, strange dreams troubled Lord George's sleep.
Once he dreamt that he stood knocking and knocking at the great door
of a castle. It was a bitter night. The frost enveloped him. No one
came. Presently he heard a footstep in the hall beyond, and a pair of
frightened eyes peered at him through the grill. Jenny was scanning
his face. She would not open to him. With tears and wild words he
beseeched her, but she would not open to him. Then, very stealthily,
he crept round the castle and found a small casement in the wall. It
was open. He climbed swiftly, quietly through it. In the darkness
of the room some one ran to him and kissed him gladly. It was Jenny.
With a cry of joy and shame he awoke. By his side lay Jenny, sleeping
like a little child.

After all, what was a dream to him? It could not mar the reality
of his daily happiness. He cherished his true penitence for the evil
he had done in the past. The past! That was indeed the only unreal
thing that lingered in his life. Every day its substance dwindled, grew
fainter yet, as he lived his rustic honeymoon. Had he not utterly put it
from him? Had he not, a few hours after his marriage, written to his
lawyer, declaring solemnly that he, Lord George Hell, had forsworn the
world, that he was where no man would find him, that he desired all his
worldly goods to be distributed, thus and thus, among these and those
of his companions? By this testament he had verily atoned for the
wrong he had done, had made himself dead indeed to the world.

No address had he written upon this document. Though its injunctions were final and binding, it could betray no clue of his hiding-place. For the rest, no one would care to seek him out. He, who had done no good to human creature, would pass unmourned out of memory. The clubs, doubtless, would laugh and puzzle over his strange recantations, envious of whomever he enriched. They would say 'twas a good riddance of a rogue and soon forget him.[1] But she, whose prime patron he had been, who had loved him in her vile fashion, La Gambogi, would she forget him easily, like the rest? As the sweet days went by, her spectre, also, grew fainter and less formidable. She knew his mask indeed, but how should she find him in the cottage near Kensington? *Devia dulcedo latebrarum!* He was safe hidden with his bride. As for the Italian, she might search and search—or had forgotten him, in the arms of another lover.

Yes! Few and faint became the blemishes of his honeymoon. At first, he had felt that his waxen mask, though it had been the means of his happiness, was rather a barrier 'twixt him and his bride. Though it was sweet to kiss her through it, to look at her through it with loving eyes, yet there were times when it incommoded him with its mockery. Could he but put it from him! yet, that, of course, could not be. He must wear it all his life. And so, as days went by he grew reconciled to his mask. No longer did he feel it jarring on his face. It seemed to become an integral part of him, and, for all its rigid material, it did forsooth express the one emotion that filled him, true love. The face, for whose sake Jenny gave him her heart, could not but be dear to this George Heaven, also.

Every day chastened him with its joy. They lived a very simple life, he and Jenny. They rose betimes, like the birds, for whose goodness

---

[1] I would refer my little readers once more to the pages of *Contemporary Bucks,* where Captain Tarleton speculates upon the sudden disappearance of Lord George Hell and describes its effect on the town. "Not even the shrewdest," says he, "even gave a guess that would throw a ray of revealing light on the *disparition* of this profligate man. It was supposed that he carried off with him a little dancer from Garble's, at which *haunt of pleasantry* he was certainly on the night he vanished, and whither the young lady never returned again. Garble declared he had been compensated for her perfidy, but that he was sure she had not succumbed to his lordship, having in fact rejected him soundly. Did his lordship, say the cronies, take his life—and hers? *Il n'y a pas d'épreuve.*

"The most astonishing matter is that the runaway should have written out a complete will, restoring all money he had won at cards, etc., etc. This certainly corroborates the opinion that he was seized with a sudden repentance and fled over the seas to a foreign monastery, where he died at last in *religious silence.* That's as it may, but many a spendthrift found his pocket clinking with guineas, a not unpleasant sound, I declare. The Regent himself was benefited by the odd will, and old Sir Follard Follard found himself once more in the ancestral home he had forfeited. As for Lord George's mansion in St. James's Square, that was sold with all its appurtenances, and the money fetched by the sale, no bagatelle, was given to various good objects, according to my lord's stated wishes. Well, many of us blessed his name—we had cursed it often enough. Peace to his ashes, in whatever urn they may be resting, on the billows of whatever ocean they float!"

they both had so sincere a love. Bread and honey and little strawberries were their morning fare, and in the evening they had seed cake and dewberry wine. Jenny herself made the wine and her husband drank it, in strict moderation, never more than two glasses. He thought it tasted far better than the Regent's cherry brandy, or the Tokay at Brooks's. Of these treasured topes he had, indeed, nearly forgotten the taste. The wine made from wild berries by his little bride was august enough for his palate. Sometimes, after they had dined thus, he would play the flute to her upon the moonlit lawn, or tell her of the great daisy-chain he was going to make for her on the morrow, or sit silently by her side, listening to the nightingale, till bedtime. So admirably simple were their days.

One morning, as he was helping Jenny to water the flowers, he said to her suddenly, "Sweetheart, we had forgotten!"

"What was there we should forget?" asked Jenny, looking up from her task.

" 'Tis the mensiversary of our wedding," her husband answered gravely. "We must not let it pass without some celebration."

"No, indeed," she said, "we must not. What shall we do?"

Between them they decided upon an unusual feast. They would go into the village and buy a bag of beautiful buns and eat them in the afternoon. So soon, then, as all the flowers were watered, they set forth to Herbert's shop, bought the buns and returned home in very high spirits, George bearing a paper bag that held no less than twelve of the wholesome delicacies. Under the plane tree on the lawn Jenny sat her down, and George stretched himself at her feet. They were loth to enjoy their feast too soon. They dallied in childish anticipation. On the little rustic table Jenny built up the buns, one above the other, till they looked like a tall pagoda. When, very gingerly, she had crowned the structure with the twelfth bun, her husband looking on with admiration, she clapped her hands and danced about it. She laughed so loudly (for, though she was only sixteen years old, she had a great sense of humour), that the table shook, and alas! the pagoda tottered and fell to the lawn. Swift as a kitten, Jenny chased the buns, as they rolled, hither and thither, over the grass, catching them deftly with her hand. Then she came back, flushed and merry under her tumbled hair, with her arm full of buns. She began to put them back in the paper bag.

"Dear husband," she said, looking down to him, "why do not you smile too at my folly? Your grave face rebukes me. Smile, or I shall think I vex you. Please smile a little."

But the mask could not smile, of course. It was made for a mirror of true love, and it was grave and immobile. "I am very much amused, dear," he said, "at the fall of the buns, but my lips will not curve to a smile. Love of you has bound them in spell."

"But I can laugh, though I love you. I do not understand." And she wondered. He took her hand in his and stroked it gently, wishing it were possible to smile. Some day, perhaps, she would tire of this monotonous gravity, this rigid sweetness. It was not strange that she should long for a little facile expression. They sat silently.

"Jenny, what is it?" he whispered suddenly. For Jenny, with wide-open eyes, was gazing over his head, across the lawn. "Why do you look frightened?"

"There is a strange woman smiling at me across the palings," she said. "I do not know her."

Her husband's heart sank. Somehow, he dared not turn his head to the intruder. He dreaded who she might be.

"She is nodding to me," said Jenny. "I think she is foreign, for she has an evil face."

"Do not notice her," he whispered. "Does she look evil?"

"Very evil and very dark. She has a pink parasol. Her teeth are like ivory."

"Do not notice her. Think! It is the mensiversary of our wedding, dear!"

"I wish she would not smile at me. Her eyes are like bright blots of ink."

"Let us eat our beautiful buns!"

"Oh, she is coming in!" George heard the latch of the gate jar. "Forbid her to come in!" whispered Jenny, "I am afraid!" He heard the jar of heels on the gravel path. Yet he dared not turn. Only he clasped Jenny's hand more tightly, as he waited for the voice. It was La Gambogi's.

"Pray, pray, pardon me! I could not mistake the back of so old a friend."

With the courage of despair, George turned and faced the woman.

"Even," she smiled, "though his face has changed marvellously."

"Madam," he said, rising to his full height and stepping between her and his bride, "begone, I command you, from the garden. I do not see what good is to be served by the renewal of our acquaintance."

"Acquaintance!" murmured La Gambogi, with an arch of her beetle-brows. "Surely we were friends, rather, nor is my esteem for you so dead that I would crave estrangement."

"Madam," rejoined Lord George, with a tremor in his voice, "you see me happy, living very peacefully with my bride——"

"To whom, I beseech you, old friend, present me."

"I would not," he said hotly, "desecrate her sweet name by speaking it with so infamous a name as yours."

"Your choler hurts me, old friend," said La Gambogi, sinking composedly upon the garden-seat and smoothing the silk of her skirts.

"Jenny," said George, "then do you retire, pending this lady's departure, to the cottage." But Jenny clung to his arm. "I were less frightened at your side," she whispered. "Do not send me away!"

"Suffer her pretty presence," said La Gambogi. "Indeed I am come this long way from the heart of the town, that I may see her, no less than you, George. My wish is only to befriend her. Why should she not set you a mannerly example, giving me welcome? Come and sit by me, little bride, for I have things to tell you. Though you reject my friendship, give me, at least, the slight courtesy of audience. I will not detain you overlong, will be gone very soon. Are you expecting guests, George? *On dirait une masque champêtre!*" She eyed the couple critically. "Your wife's mask," she said, "is even better than yours."

"What does she mean?" whispered Jenny. "Oh, send her away!"

"Serpent," was all George could say, "crawl from our Eden, ere you poison with your venom its fairest denizen."

La Gambogi rose. "Even *my* pride," she cried passionately, "knows certain bounds. I have been forbearing, but even in *my* zeal for friendship I will not be called 'serpent.' I will indeed begone from this rude place. Yet, ere I go, there is a boon I will deign to beg. Show me, oh show me but once again, the dear face I have so often caressed, the lips that were dear to me!"

George started back.

"What does she mean?" whispered Jenny.

"In memory of our old friendship," continued La Gambogi, "grant me this piteous favour. Show me your own face but for one instant, and I vow I will never again remind you that I live. Intercede for me, little bride. Bid him unmask for me. You have more authority over him than I. Doff his mask with your own uxorious fingers."

"What does she mean?" was the refrain of poor Jenny.

"If," said George, gazing sternly at his traitress, "you do not go now, of your own will, I must drive you, man though I am, violently from the garden."

"Doff your mask and I am gone."

George made a step of menace towards her.

"False saint!" she shrieked, "then *I* will unmask you."

Like a panther she sprang upon him and clawed at his waxen cheeks. Jenny fell back, mute with terror. Vainly did George try to free himself from the hideous assailant, who writhed round and round him, clawing, clawing at what Jenny fancied to be his face. With a wild cry, Jenny fell upon the furious creature and tried, with all her childish strength, to release her dear one. The combatives swayed to and fro, a revulsive trinity. There was a loud pop, as though some great cork had been withdrawn, and La Gambogi recoiled. She had torn away the mask. It lay before her upon the lawn, upturned to the sky.

George stood motionless. La Gambogi stared up into his face, and her dark flush died swiftly away. For there, staring back at her, was the man she had unmasked, but, lo! his face was even as his mask had been. Line for line, feature for feature, it was the same. 'Twas a saint's face.

"Madam," he said, in the calm voice of despair, "your cheek may well blanch, when you regard the ruin you have brought upon me. Nevertheless do I pardon you. The gods have avenged, through you, the imposture I wrought upon one who was dear to me. For that unpardonable sin I am punished. As for my poor bride, whose love I stole by the means of that waxen semblance, of her I cannot ask pardon. Ah, Jenny, Jenny, do not look at me. Turn your eyes from the foul reality that I dissembled." He shuddered and hid his face in his hands. "Do not look at me. I will go from the garden. Nor will I ever curse you with the odious spectacle of my face. Forget me, forget me."

But, as he turned to go, Jenny laid her hands upon his wrists and besought him that he would look at her. "For indeed," she said, "I am bewildered by your strange words. Why did you woo me under a mask? And why do you imagine I could love you less dearly, seeing your own face?"

He looked into her eyes. On their violet surface he saw the tiny reflection of his own face. He was filled with joy and wonder.

"Surely," said Jenny, "your face is even dearer to me, even fairer, than the semblance that hid it and deceived me. I am not angry. 'Twas well that you veiled from me the full glory of your face, for indeed I was not worthy to behold it too soon. But I am your wife now. Let me look always at your own face. Let the time of my probation be over. Kiss me with your own lips."

So he took her in his arms, as though she had been a little child, and kissed her with his own lips. She put her arms round his neck, and he was happier than he had ever been. They were alone in the garden now. Nor lay the mask any longer upon the lawn, for the sun had melted it.

48

The Derelict

BY H. M. TOMLINSON

IN a tramp steamer, which was overloaded, and in midwinter, I had crossed to America for the first time. What we experienced of the western ocean during that passage gave me so much respect for it that the prospect of the return journey, three thousand miles of those seas between me and home, was already a dismal foreboding.

The shipping posters of New York, showing stately liners too lofty even to notice the Atlantic, were arguments good enough for steerage passengers, who do, I know, reckon a steamer's worth by the number of its funnels; but the pictures did nothing to lessen my regard for that dark outer world I knew. And having no experience of ships installed with racquet courts, Parisian cafes, swimming baths, and pergolas, I was naturally puzzled by the inconsequential behavior of the first-class passengers at the hotel. They were leaving by the liner which was to take me, and, I gathered, were going to cross a bridge to England in the morning. Of course, this might have been merely the innocent profanity of the simple-minded.

Embarking at the quay next day, I could not see that our ship had either a beginning or an end. There was a blank wall which ran out of sight to the right and left. How far it went, and what it enclosed, were beyond me. Hundreds of us in a slow procession mounted stairs to the upper floor of a warehouse, and from thence a bridge led us to a door in the wall half-way in its height. No funnels could be seen. Looking straight up from the embarkation gangway, along what seemed the parapet of the wall was a row of far-off indistinguishable faces peering straight down at us. There was no evidence that this building we were entering, of which the high black wall was a part, was not an important and permanent feature of the city. It was in keeping with the magnitude of New York's skyscrapers, which this planet's occasionally non-irritant skin permits to stand there to afford man an apparent reason to be gratified with his own capacity and daring.

But with the knowledge that this wall must be afloat there came no sense of security when, going through that little opening in its altitude, I found myself in a spacious decorated interior which hinted nothing of a ship, for I was puzzled as to direction. My last ship could be surveyed in two glances; she looked, and was, a comprehensible ship, no more than a manageable handful for an able master. In that ship you could see at once where you were and what to do. But in this liner you could not see where you were, and would never know which way to take unless you had a good memory. No understanding came to me in that hall of a measured and shapely body, designed with a cunning informed by ages of sea-lore to move buoyantly and surely among the raging seas, to balance delicately, a quick and sensitive being, to every precarious slope, to recover a lost poise easily and with the grace natural to a quick creature controlled by an alert mind.

There was no shape at all to this structure. I could see no line the run of which gave me warrant that it was comprised in the rondure of a ship. The lines were all of straight corridors, which, for all I knew, might have ended blindly on open space, as streets which traverse a city and are bare in vacancy beyond the dwellings. It was possible we were encompassed by walls, but only one wall was visible. There we idled, all strangers, in a large hall roofed by a dome of colored glass. Quite properly, palms stood beneath. There were offices and doors everywhere. On a broad staircase a multitude of us wandered aimlessly up and down. Each side of the stairway were electric lifts, intermittent and brilliant apparitions. I began to understand why the saloon passengers thought nothing of the voyage. They were encountering nothing unfamiliar. They had but come to another hotel for a few days.

I attempted to find my cabin, but failed. A uniformed guide took care of me. But my cabin, curtained, upholstered, and warm, with mirrors and plated ware, sunk somewhere deeply among carpeted and silent streets down each of which the perspective of glow-lamps looked interminable, left me still questioning. The long walk had given me a fear that I was remote from important affairs which might be happening beyond. My address was 323. The street door—I was down a side turning, though—bore that number. A visitor could make no mistake, supposing he could find the street and my side turning. That was it. There was a very great deal in this place for everybody to remember, and most of us were strangers. No doubt, however, we were afloat, if the lifebelts in the rack meant anything. Yet the cabin, insulated from all noise, was not soothing, but disturbing. I had been used to a ship in which you could guess all that was happening even when in your bunk; a sensitive and communicative ship.

A steward appeared at my door, a stranger out of nowhere, and asked whether I had seen a bag not mine in the cabin. He might have been created merely to put that question, for I never saw him again on the voyage. This liner was a large province having irregular and shifting bounds, permitting incontinent entrance and disappearance. All this should have inspired me with an idea of our vastness and importance, but it did not. I felt I was one of a multitude included in a nebulous mass too vague to hold together unless we were constantly wary.

In the saloon there was the solid furniture of rare woods, the ornate decorations, and the light and shadows making vague its limits and giving it an appearance of immensity, to keep the mind from the thought of our real circumstances. At dinner we had valentine music, dreamy stuff to accord with the shaded lamps which displayed the tables in a lower rosy light. It helped to extend the mysterious and romantic shadows. The pale, disembodied masks of the waiters swam in the dusk above the tinted light. I had for a companion a vivacious American lady from the Middle West, and she looked round that prospect we had of an expensive café, and said, "Well, but I am disappointed. Why, I've been looking forward to seeing the ocean, you know. And it isn't here."

"Smooth passage," remarked a man on the other side. "No sea at all worth mentioning." Actually, I know there was a heavy beam sea running before a half-gale. I could guess the officer in charge somewhere on the exposed roof might have another mind about it; but it made no difference to us in our circle of rosy intimate light bound by those vague shadows which were alive with ready servitude.

"And I've been reading *Captains Courageous* with this voyage in view. Isn't this the month when the forties roar? I want to hear them roar, just once, you know, and as gently as any sucking dove." We all laughed. "We can't even tell we're in a ship."

She began to discuss Kipling's book. "There's some fine seas in that. Have you read it? But I'd like to know where that ocean is he pretends to have seen. I do believe the realists are no more reliable than the romanticists. Here we are a thousand miles out, and none of us has seen the sea yet. Tell me, does not a realist have to magnify his awful billows just to get them into his reader's view?"

I murmured something feeble and sociable. I saw then why sailors never talk directly of the sea. I, for instance, could not find my key at that moment—it was in another pocket somewhere—so I had no iron to touch. Talking largely of the sea is something like the knowing talk of young men about women; and what is a simple sailor man that he should open his mouth on mysteries?

Only on the liner's boat-deck, where you could watch her four funnels against the sky, could you see to what extent the liner was rolling. The arc seemed to be considerable then, but slowly described. But the roll made little difference to the promenaders below. Sometimes they walked a short distance on the edges of their boots, leaning over as they did so, and swerving from the straight, as though they had turned giddy. The shadows formed by the weak sunlight moved slowly out of ambush across the white deck, but often moved indecisively, as though uncertain of a need to go; and then slowly went into hiding again. The sea whirling and leaping past was far below our wall side. It was like peering dizzily over a precipice when watching those green and white cataracts.

The passengers, wrapped and comfortable on the lee deck, chatted as blithely as at a garden-party, while the band played medleys of national airs to suit our varied complexions. The stewards came round with loaded trays. A diminutive and wrinkled dame in costly furs frowned through her golden spectacles at her book, while her maid sat attentively by. An American actress was the center of an eager group of grinning young men; she was unseen, but her voice was distinct. The two Vanderbilts took their brisk constitutional among us as though the liner had but two real passengers though many invisible nobodies. The children, who had not ceased laughing and playing since we left New York, waited for the slope of the deck to reach its greatest, and then ran down toward the bulwarks precipitously. The children, happy and innocent, completed for us the feeling of comfortable indifference and security which we found when we saw there was more ship than ocean. The liner's deck canted slowly to leeward, went over more and more, beyond what it had done yet, and a pretty little girl with dark curls riotous from under her red tam-o'shanter, ran down, and brought up against us violently with both hands, laughing heartily. We laughed too. Looking seaward, I saw receding the broad green hill, snow-capped, which had lifted us and let us down. The sea was getting up.

Near sunset, when the billows were mounting express along our run, sometimes to leap and snatch at our upper structure, and were rocking us with some ease, there was a commotion forward. Books and shawls went anywhere as the passengers ran. Something strange was to be seen upon the waters.

It looked like a big log out there ahead, over the starboard bow. It was not easy to make out. The light was failing. We overhauled it rapidly, and it began to shape as a ship's boat. "Oh, it's gone," exclaimed some one then. But the forlorn object lifted high again, and sank once more. Whenever it was glimpsed it was set in a patch of foam.

That flotsam, whatever it was, was of man. As we watched it intently, and before it was quite plain, we knew intuitively that hope was not there, that we were watching something past its doom. It drew abeam, and we saw what it was, a derelict sailing ship, mastless and awash. The alien wilderness was around us now, and we saw a sky that was overcast and driven, and seas that were uplifted, which had grown incredibly huge, swift, and perilous, and they had colder and more somber hues.

The derelict was a schooner, a lifeless and soddened hulk, so heavy and uncontesting that its foundering seemed at hand. The waters poured back and forth at her waist, as though holding her body captive for the assaults of the active seas which came over her broken bulwarks, and plunged ruthlessly about. There was something ironic in the indifference of her defenseless body to these unending attacks. It mocked this white and raging post-mortem brutality, and gave her a dignity that was cold and superior to all the eternal powers could now do. She pitched helplessly head first into a hollow, and a door flew open under the break of her poop; it surprised and shocked us, for the dead might have signed to us then. She went astern of us fast, and a great comber ran at her, as if it had but just spied her, and thought she was escaping. There was a high white flash, and a concussion we heard. She had gone. But she appeared again far away, on a summit in desolation, black against the sunset. The stump of her bowsprit, the accusatory finger of the dead, pointed at the sky.

I turned, and there beside me was the lady who had wanted to find the sea. She was gazing at the place where the wreck was last seen, her eyes fixed, her mouth a little open in awe and horror.

49

Red

BY W. SOMERSET MAUGHAM

THE skipper thrust his hand into one of his trouser pockets and with difficulty, for they were not at the sides but in front and he was a portly man, pulled out a large silver watch. He looked at it and then looked again at the declining sun. The Kanaka at the wheel gave him a glance, but did not speak. The skipper's eyes rested on the island they were approaching. A white line of foam marked the reef. He knew there was an opening large enough to get his ship through, and when they came a little nearer he counted on seeing it. They had nearly an hour of daylight still before them. In the lagoon the water was deep and they could anchor comfortably. The chief of the village which he could already see among the coconut trees was a friend of the mate's, and it would be pleasant to go ashore for the night. The mate came forward at that minute and the skipper turned to him.

"We'll take a bottle of booze along with us and get some girls in to dance," he said.

"I don't see the opening," said the mate.

He was a Kanaka, a handsome, swarthy fellow, with somewhat the look of a later Roman emperor, inclined to stoutness; but his face was fine and clean-cut.

"I'm dead sure there's one right here," said the captain, looking through his glasses. "I can't understand why I can't pick it up. Send one of the boys up the mast to have a look."

The mate called one of the crew and gave him the order. The captain watched the Kanaka climb and waited for him to speak. But the Kanaka shouted down that he could see nothing but the unbroken line of foam. The captain spoke Samoan like a native, and he cursed him freely.

"Shall he stay up there?" asked the mate.

"What the hell good does that do?" answered the captain. "The blame fool can't see worth a cent. You bet your sweet life I'd find the opening if I was up there."

He looked at the slender mast with anger. It was all very well for a native who had been used to climbing up coconut trees all his life. He was fat and heavy.

"Come down," he shouted. "You're no more use than a dead dog. We'll just have to go along the reef till we find the opening."

It was a seventy-ton schooner with paraffin auxiliary, and it ran, when there was no head wind, between four and five knots an hour. It was a bedraggled object; it had been painted white a very long time ago, but it was now dirty, dingy, and mottled. It smelt strongly of paraffin and of the copra which was its usual cargo. They were within a hundred feet of the reef now and the captain told the steersman to run along it till they came to the opening. But when they had gone a couple of miles he realised that they had missed it. He went about and slowly worked back again. The white foam of the reef continued without interruption and now the sun was setting. With a curse at the stupidity of the crew the skipper resigned himself to waiting till next morning.

"Put her about," he said. "I can't anchor here."

They went out to sea a little and presently it was quite dark. They anchored. When the sail was furled the ship began to roll a good deal. They said in Apia that one day she would roll right over; and the owner, a German-American who managed one of the largest stores, said that no money was big enough to induce him to go out in her. The cook, a Chinese in white trousers, very dirty and ragged, and a thin white tunic, came to say that supper was ready, and when the skipper went into the cabin he found the engineer already seated at table. The engineer was a long, lean man with a scraggy neck. He was dressed in blue overalls and a sleeveless jersey which showed his thin arms tattooed from elbow to wrist.

"Hell, having to spend the night outside," said the skipper.

The engineer did not answer, and they ate their supper in silence. The cabin was lit by a dim oil lamp. When they had eaten the canned apricots with which the meal finished the Chink brought them a cup of tea. The skipper lit a cigar and went on the upper deck. The island now was only a darker mass against the night. The stars were very bright. The only sound was the ceaseless breaking of the surf. The skipper sank into a deck-chair and smoked idly. Presently three or four members of the crew came up and sat down. One of them had a banjo and another a concertina. They began to play, and one of them sang. The native song sounded strange on these instruments. Then to the singing a couple began to dance. It was a barbaric dance, savage and primeval, rapid, with quick movements of the hands and feet and contortions of the body; it was sensual, sexual even, but sexual without passion. It was very animal, direct, weird without mystery, natural in short, and one might almost say childlike. At last they grew tired. They stretched themselves on the deck and slept, and all was silent. The skipper lifted himself heavily out of his chair and clambered down the companion. He went into his cabin and got out of his clothes. He climbed into his bunk and lay there. He panted a little in the heat of the night.

But next morning, when the dawn crept over the tranquil sea, the opening in the reef which had eluded them the night before was seen a little to the east of where they lay. The schooner entered the lagoon. There was not a ripple on the surface of the water. Deep down among the coral rocks you saw little coloured fish swim. When he had anchored his ship the skipper ate his breakfast and went on deck. The sun shone from an unclouded sky, but in the early morning the air was grateful and cool. It was Sunday, and there was a feeling of quietness, a silence as though nature were at rest, which gave him a peculiar sense of comfort. He sat, looking at the wooded coast, and felt lazy and well at ease. Presently a slow smile moved his lips and he threw the stump of his cigar into the water.

"I guess I'll go ashore," he said. "Get the boat out."

He climbed stiffly down the ladder and was rowed to a little cove. The coconut trees came down to the water's edge, not in rows, but spaced out with an ordered formality. They were like a ballet of spinsters, elderly but flippant, standing in affected attitudes with the simpering graces of a bygone age. He sauntered idly through them, along a path that could be just seen winding its tortuous way, and it led him presently to a broad creek. There was a bridge across it, but a bridge constructed of single trunks of coconut trees, a dozen of them, placed end to end and supported where they met by a forked branch driven into the bed of the creek. You walked on a smooth, round surface, narrow and slippery, and there was no support for the hand. To cross such a bridge required sure feet and a stout heart. The skipper hesitated. But he saw on the other side, nestling among the trees, a white man's house; he made up his mind and, rather gingerly, began to walk. He watched his feet carefully, and where one trunk joined on to the next and there was a difference of level, he tottered a little. It was with a gasp of relief that he reached the last tree and finally set his feet on the firm ground of the other side. He had been so intent on the difficult crossing that he never noticed anyone was watching him, and it was with surprise that he heard himself spoken to.

"It takes a bit of nerve to cross these bridges when you're not used to them."

He looked up and saw a man standing in front of him. He had evidently come out of the house which he had seen.

"I saw you hesitate," the man continued, with a smile on his lips, "and I was watching to see you fall in."

"Not on your life," said the captain, who had now recovered his confidence.

"I've fallen in myself before now. I remember, one evening I came back from shooting, and I fell in, gun and all. Now I get a boy to carry my gun for me."

He was a man no longer young, with a small beard, now somewhat grey, and a thin face. He was dressed in a singlet, without arms, and a pair of duck trousers. He wore neither shoes nor socks. He spoke English with a slight accent.

"Are you Neilson?" asked the skipper.

"I am."

"I've heard about you. I thought you lived somewheres round here."

The skipper followed his host into the little bungalow and sat down heavily in the chair which the other motioned him to take. While Neilson went out to fetch whisky and glasses he took a look round the room. It filled him with amazement. He had never seen so many books. The shelves reached from floor to ceiling on all four walls, and they were closely packed. There was a grand piano littered with music, and a large table on which books and magazines lay in disorder. The room made him feel embarrassed. He remembered that Neilson was a queer fellow. No one knew very much about him, although he had been in the islands for so many years, but those who knew him agreed that he was queer. He was a Swede.

"You've got one big heap of books here," he said, when Neilson returned.

"They do no harm," answered Neilson with a smile.

"Have you read them all?" asked the skipper.

"Most of them."

"I'm a bit of a reader myself. I have the *Saturday Evening Post* sent me regler."

Neilson poured his visitor a good stiff glass of whisky and gave him a cigar. The skipper volunteered a little information.

"I got in last night, but I couldn't find the opening, so I had to anchor outside. I never been this run before, but my people had some stuff they wanted to bring over here. Gray, d'you know him?"

"Yes, he's got a store a little way along."

"Well, there was a lot of canned stuff that he wanted over, an' he's got some copra. They thought I might just as well come over as lie idle at Apia. I run between Apia and Pago-Pago mostly, but they've got smallpox there just now, and there's nothing stirring."

He took a drink of his whisky and lit a cigar. He was a taciturn man, but there was something in Neilson that made him nervous, and his nervousness made him talk. The Swede was looking at him with large dark eyes in which there was an expression of faint amusement.

"This is a tidy little place you've got here."

"I've done my best with it."

"You must do pretty well with your trees. They look fine. With copra at the price it is now. I had a bit of a plantation myself once, in Upolu it was, but I had to sell it."

He looked round the room again, where all those books gave him a feeling of something incomprehensible and hostile.

"I guess you must find it a bit lonesome here though," he said.

"I've got used to it. I've been here for twenty-five years."

Now the captain could think of nothing more to say, and he smoked in silence. Neilson had apparently no wish to break it. He looked at his guest with a meditative eye. He was a tall man, more than six feet high, and very stout. His face was red and blotchy, with a network of little purple veins on the cheeks, and his features were sunk into its fatness. His eyes were bloodshot. His neck was buried in rolls of fat. But for a fringe of long curly hair, nearly white, at the back of his head, he was quite bald; and that immense, shiny surface of forehead, which might have given him a false look of intelligence, on the contrary gave him one of peculiar imbecility. He wore a blue flannel shirt, open at the neck and showing his fat chest covered with a mat of reddish hair, and a very old pair of blue serge trousers. He sat in his chair in a heavy ungainly attitude, his great belly thrust forward and his fat legs uncrossed. All elasticity had gone from his limbs. Neilson wondered idly what sort of man he had been in his youth. It was almost impossible to imagine that this creature of vast bulk had ever been a boy who ran about. The skipper finished his whisky, and Neilson pushed the bottle towards him.

"Help yourself."

The skipper leaned forward and with his great hand seized it.

"And how come you in these parts anyways?" he said.

"Oh, I came out to the islands for my health. My lungs were bad and they said I hadn't a year to live. You see they were wrong."

"I meant, how come you to settle down right here?"

"I am a sentimentalist."

"Oh!"

Neilson knew that the skipper had not an idea what he meant, and he looked at him with an ironical twinkle in his dark eyes. Perhaps just because the skipper was so gross and dull a man the whim seized him to talk further.

"You were too busy keeping your balance to notice, when you crossed the bridge, but this spot is generally considered rather pretty."

"It's a cute little house you've got here."

"Ah, that wasn't here when I first came. There was a native hut, with its beehive roof and its pillars, overshadowed by a great tree with red flowers; and the croton bushes, their leaves yellow and red and golden, made a pied fence around it. And then all about were the coconut trees, as fanciful as women, and as vain. They stood at the water's edge and spent all day looking at their reflections. I was a young man then—Good Heavens, it's a quarter of a century ago—and I wanted to enjoy all the loveliness of the world in the short time allotted to me before I passed into the darkness. I thought it was the most beautiful spot I had ever seen. The first time I saw it I had a catch at my heart, and I was afraid I was going to cry. I wasn't more than twenty-five, and though I put the best face I could on it, I didn't want to die. And somehow it seemed to me that the very beauty of this place made it easier for me to accept my fate. I felt when I came here that all my past life had fallen away, Stockholm and its University, and then Bonn: it all seemed the life of somebody else, as though now at last I had achieved the reality which our doctors of philosophy—I am one myself, you know—had discussed so much. 'A year,' I cried to myself. 'I have a year. I will spend it here and then I am content to die.'

"We are foolish and sentimental and melodramatic at twenty-five, but if we weren't perhaps we should be less wise at fifty."

"Now drink, my friend. Don't let the nonsense I talk interfere with you."

He waved his thin hand towards the bottle, and the skipper finished what remained in his glass.

"You ain't drinking nothin'," he said, reaching for the whisky.

"I am of a sober habit," smiled the Swede. "I intoxicate myself in ways which I fancy are more subtle. But perhaps that is only vanity. Anyhow, the effects are more lasting and the results less deleterious."

"They say there's a deal of cocaine taken in the States now," said the captain.

Neilson chuckled.

"But I do not see a white man often," he continued, "and for once I don't think a drop of whisky can do me any harm."

He poured himself out a little, added some soda, and took a sip.

"And presently I found out why the spot had such an unearthly loveliness. Here love had tarried for a moment like a migrant bird that happens on a ship in mid-ocean and for a little while folds its tired wings. The fragrance of a beautiful passion hovered over it like the fragrance of hawthorn in May in the meadows of my home. It seems to me that the places where men have loved or suffered keep about them always some faint aroma of something that has not wholly died. It is as though they had acquired a spiritual significance which mysteriously affects those who pass. I wish I could make myself clear." He smiled a little. "Though I cannot imagine that if I did you would understand."

He paused.

"I think this place was beautiful because here I had been loved beautifully." And now he shrugged his shoulders. "But perhaps it is only that my æsthetic sense is gratified by the happy conjunction of young love and a suitable setting."

Even a man less thick-witted than the skipper might have been forgiven if he were bewildered by Neilson's words. For he seemed faintly to laugh at what he said. It was as though he spoke from emotion which his intellect found ridiculous. He had said himself that he was a sentimentalist, and when sentimentality is joined with scepticism there is often the devil to pay.

He was silent for an instant and looked at the captain with eyes in which there was a sudden perplexity.

"You know, I can't help thinking that I've seen you before somewhere or other," he said.

"I couldn't say as I remember you," returned the skipper.

"I have a curious feeling as though your face were familiar to me. It's been puzzling me for some time. But I can't situate my recollection in any place or at any time."

The skipper massively shrugged his heavy shoulders.

"It's thirty years since I first come to the islands. A man can't figure on remembering all the folk he meets in a while like that."

The Swede shook his head.

"You know how one sometimes has the feeling that a place one has never been to before is strangely familiar. That's how I seem to see you." He gave a whimsical smile. "Perhaps I knew you in some past existence. Perhaps, perhaps you were the master of a galley in ancient Rome and I was a slave at the oar. Thirty years have you been here?"

"Every bit of thirty years."

"I wonder if you knew a man called Red?"

"Red?"

"That is the only name I've ever known him by. I never knew him personally. I never even set eyes on him. And yet I seem to see him more clearly than many men, my brothers, for instance, with whom I passed my daily life for many years. He lives in my imagination with the dis-

tinctness of a Paolo Malatesta or a Romeo. But I daresay you have never
read Dante or Shakespeare?"

"I can't say as I have," said the captain.

Neilson, smoking a cigar, leaned back in his chair and looked vacantly
at the ring of smoke which floated in the still air. A smile played on his
lips, but his eyes were grave. Then he looked at the captain. There was
in his gross obesity something extraordinarily repellent. He had the ple-
thoric self-satisfaction of the very fat. It was an outrage. It set Neilson's
nerves on edge. But the contrast between the man before him and the
man he had in mind was pleasant.

"It appears that Red was the most comely thing you ever saw. I've
talked to quite a number of people who knew him in those days, white
men, and they all agree that the first time you saw him his beauty
just took your breath away. They called him Red on account of his
flaming hair. It had a natural wave and he wore it long. It must have
been of that wonderful colour that the pre-Raphaelites raved over. I
don't think he was vain of it, he was much too ingenuous for that, but
no one could have blamed him if he had been. He was tall, six feet and
an inch or two—in the native house that used to stand here was the
mark of his height cut with a knife on the central trunk that supported
the roof—and he was made like a Greek god, broad in the shoulders
and thin in the flanks; he was like Apollo, with just that soft roundness
which Praxiteles gave him, and that suave, feminine grace which has
in it something troubling and mysterious. His skin was dazzling white,
milky, like satin; his skin was like a woman's."

"I had kind of a white skin myself when I was a kiddie," said the
skipper, with a twinkle in his bloodshot eyes.

But Neilson paid no attention to him. He was telling his story now
and interruption made him impatient.

"And his face was just as beautiful as his body. He had large blue
eyes, very dark, so that some say they were black, and unlike most red-
haired people he had dark eyebrows and long dark lashes. His features
were perfectly regular and his mouth was like a scarlet wound. He was
twenty."

On these words the Swede stopped with a certain sense of the dramatic. He took a sip of whisky.

"He was unique. There never was anyone more beautiful. There was
no more reason for him than for a wonderful blossom to flower on a
wild plant. He was a happy accident of nature.

"One day he landed at that cove into which you must have put this
morning. He was an American sailor, and he had deserted from a man-
of-war in Apia. He had induced some good-humoured native to give
him a passage on a cutter that happened to be sailing from Apia to Safo-

to, and he had been put ashore here in a dugout. I do not know why he deserted. Perhaps life on a man-of-war with its restrictions irked him, perhaps he was in trouble, and perhaps it was the South Seas and these romantic islands that got into his bones. Every now and then they take a man strangely, and he finds himself like a fly in a spider's web. It may be that there was a softness of fibre in him, and these green hills with their soft airs, this blue sea, took the northern strength from him as Delilah took the Nazarite's. Anyhow, he wanted to hide himself, and he thought he would be safe in this secluded nook till his ship had sailed from Samoa.

"There was a native hut at the cove and as he stood there, wondering where exactly he should turn his steps, a young girl came out and invited him to enter. He knew scarcely two words of the native tongue and she as little English. But he understood well enough what her smiles meant, and her pretty gestures, and he followed her. He sat down on a mat and she gave him slices of pineapple to eat. I can speak of Red only from hearsay, but I saw the girl three years after he first met her, and she was scarcely nineteen then. You cannot imagine how exquisite she was. She had the passionate grace of the hibiscus and the rich colour. She was rather tall, slim, with the delicate features of her race, and large eyes like pools of still water under the palm trees; her hair, black and curling, fell down her back, and she wore a wreath of scented flowers. Her hands were lovely. They were so small, so exquisitely formed, they gave your heart-strings a wrench. And in those days she laughed easily. Her smile was so delightful that it made your knees shake. Her skin was like a field of ripe corn on a summer day. Good Heavens, how can I describe her? She was too beautiful to be real.

"And these two young things, she was sixteen and he was twenty, fell in love with one another at first sight. That is the real love, not the love that comes from sympathy, common interests, or intellectual community, but love pure and simple. That is the love that Adam felt for Eve when he awoke and found her in the garden gazing at him with dewy eyes. That is the love that draws the beasts to one another, and the Gods. That is the love that makes the world a miracle. That is the love which gives life its pregnant meaning. You have never heard of the wise, cynical French duke who said that with two lovers there is always one who loves and one who lets himself be loved; it is a bitter truth to which most of us have to resign ourselves; but now and then there are two who love and two who let themselves be loved. Then one might fancy that the sun stands still as it stood when Joshua prayed to the God of Israel.

"And even now after all these years, when I think of these two, so young, so fair, so simple, and of their love, I feel a pang. It tears my heart just as my heart is torn when on certain nights I watch the full moon shining on the lagoon from an unclouded sky. There is always pain in the contemplation of perfect beauty.

"They were children. She was good and sweet and kind. I know nothing of him, and I like to think that then at all events he was ingenuous and frank. I like to think that his soul was as comely as his body. But I daresay he had no more soul than the creatures of the woods and forests who made pipes from reeds and bathed in the mountain streams when the world was young, and you might catch sight of little fawns galloping through the glade on the back of a bearded centaur. A soul is a troublesome possession and when man developed it he lost the Garden of Eden.

"Well, when Red came to the island it had recently been visited by one of those epidemics which the white man has brought to the South Seas, and one third of the inhabitants had died. It seems that the girl had lost all her near kin and she lived now in the house of distant cousins. The household consisted of two ancient crones, bowed and wrinkled, two younger women, and a man and a boy. For a few days he stayed there. But perhaps he felt himself too near the shore, with the possibility that he might fall in with white men who would reveal his hiding-place; perhaps the lovers could not bear that the company of others should rob them for an instant of the delight of being together. One morning they set out, the pair of them, with the few things that belonged to the girl, and walked along a grassy path under the coconuts, till they came to the creek you see. They had to cross the bridge you crossed, and the girl laughed gleefully because he was afraid. She held his hand till they came to the end of the first tree, and then his courage failed him and he had to go back. He was obliged to take off all his clothes before he could risk it, and she carried them over for him on her head. They settled down in the empty hut that stood here. Whether she had any rights over it (land tenure is a complicated business in the islands), or whether the owner had died during the epidemic, I do not know, but anyhow no one questioned them, and they took possession. Their furniture consisted of a couple of grass-mats on which they slept, a fragment of looking-glass, and a bowl or two. In this pleasant land that is enough to start housekeeping on.

"They say that happy people have no history, and certainly a happy love has none. They did nothing all day long and yet the days seemed all too short. The girl had a native name, but Red called her Sally. He picked up the easy language very quickly, and he used to lie on the mat for hours while she chattered gaily to him. He was a silent fellow, and perhaps his mind was lethargic. He smoked incessantly the cigarettes which she made him out of the native tobacco and pandanus leaf, and he watched her while with deft fingers she made grass mats. Often natives would come in and tell long stories of the old days when the island was disturbed by tribal wars. Sometimes he would go fishing on the reef, and bring home a basket full of coloured fish. Sometimes at night he would go out with a lantern to catch lobster. There were plantains round the hut and Sally would roast them for their frugal meal. She knew how to make delicious messes from coconuts, and the breadfruit tree by the side of the creek gave them its fruit. On feast-days they killed a little pig and cooked it on hot stones. They bathed together in the creek; and in the evening they went down to the lagoon and paddled about in a dugout, with its great outrigger. The sea was deep blue, wine-coloured at sundown, like the sea of Homeric Greece; but in the lagoon the colour had an infinite variety, aquamarine and amethyst and emerald; and the setting sun turned it for a short moment to liquid gold. Then there was the colour of the coral, brown, white, pink, red, purple; and the shapes it took were marvellous. It was like a magic garden, and the hurrying fish were like butterflies. It strangely lacked reality. Among the coral were pools with a floor of white sand and here, where the water was dazzling clear, it was very good to bathe. Then, cool and happy, they wandered back in the gloaming over the soft grass road to the creek, walking hand in hand, and now the mynah birds filled the coconut trees with their clamour. And then the night, with that great sky shining with gold, that seemed to stretch more widely than the skies of Europe, and the soft airs that blew gently through the open hut, the long night again was all too short. She was sixteen and he was barely twenty. The dawn crept in among the wooden pillars of the hut and looked at those lovely children sleeping in one another's arms. The sun hid behind the great tattered leaves of the plantains so that it might not disturb them, and then, with playful malice, shot a golden ray, like the outstretched paw of a Persian cat, on their faces. They opened their sleepy eyes and they smiled to welcome another day. The weeks lengthened into months, and a year passed. They seemed to love one another as—I hesitate to say passionately, for passion has in it always a shade of sadness, a touch of bitterness or anguish, but as whole heartedly, as simply and naturally as on that first day on which, meeting, they had recognised that a god was in them.

"If you had asked them I have no doubt that they would have thought it impossible to suppose their love could ever cease. Do we not know that the essential element of love is a belief in its own eternity? And yet perhaps in Red there was already a very little seed, unknown to himself and unsuspected by the girl, which would in time have grown to weariness. For one day one of the natives from the cove told them that some way down the coast at the anchorage was a British whaling-ship.

" 'Gee,' he said, 'I wonder if I could make a trade of some nuts and plantains for a pound or two of tobacco.'

"The pandanus cigarettes that Sally made him with untiring hands were strong and pleasant enough to smoke, but they left him unsatisfied; and he yearned on a sudden for real tobacco, hard, rank, and pungent. He had not smoked a pipe for many months. His mouth watered at the thought of it. One would have thought some premonition of harm would have made Sally seek to dissuade him, but love possessed her so completely that it never occurred to her any power on earth could take him from her. They went up into the hills together and gathered a great basket of wild oranges, green, but sweet and juicy; and they picked plantains from around the hut, and coconuts from their trees, and breadfruit and mangoes; and they carried them down to the cove. They loaded the unstable canoe with them, and Red and the native boy who had brought them the news of the ship paddled along outside the reef.

"It was the last time she ever saw him.

"Next day the boy came back alone. He was all in tears. This is the story he told. When after their long paddle they reached the ship and Red hailed it, a white man looked over the side and told them to come on board. They took the fruit they had brought with them and Red piled it up on the deck. The white man and he began to talk, and they seemed to come to some agreement. One of them went below and brought up tobacco. Red took some at once and lit a pipe. The boy imitated the zest with which he blew a great cloud of smoke from his mouth. Then they said something to him and he went into the cabin. Through the open door the boy, watching curiously, saw a bottle brought out and glasses. Red drank and smoked. They seemed to ask him something, for he shook his head and laughed. The man, the first man who had spoken to them, laughed too, and he filled Red's glass once more. They went on talking and drinking, and presently, growing tired of watching a sight that meant nothing to him, the boy curled himself up on the deck and slept. He was awakened by a kick; and, jumping to his feet, he saw that the ship was slowly sailing out of the lagoon. He caught sight of Red seated at the table, with his head resting heavily on his arms, fast asleep. He made a movement towards him, intending to wake him, but a rough hand seized his arm, and a man, with a scowl and words which he did not understand, pointed to the side. He shouted to Red, but in a moment he was seized and flung overboard. Helpless, he swam round to his canoe which was drifting a little way off, and pushed it on to the reef. He climbed in and, sobbing all the way, paddled back to shore.

"What had happened was obvious enough. The whaler, by desertion or sickness, was short of hands, and the captain when Red came aboard had asked him to sign on; on his refusal he had made him drunk and kidnapped him.

"Sally was beside herself with grief. For three days she screamed and cried. The natives did what they could to comfort her, but she would not be comforted. She would not eat. And then, exhausted, she sank into a sullen apathy. She spent long days at the cove, watching the lagoon, in the vain hope that Red somehow or other would manage to escape. She sat on the white sand, hour after hour, with the tears running down her cheeks, and at night dragged herself wearily back across the creek to the little hut where she had been happy. The people with whom she had lived before Red came to the island wished her to return to them, but she would not; she was convinced that Red would come back, and she wanted him to find her where he had left her. Four months later she was delivered of a still-born child, and the old woman who had come to help her through her confinement remained with her in the hut. All joy was taken from her life. If her anguish with time became less intolerable it was replaced by a settled melancholy. You would not have thought that among these people, whose emotions, though so violent, are very transient, a woman could be found capable of so enduring a passion. She never lost the profound conviction that sooner or later Red would come back. She watched for him, and every time someone crossed this slender little bridge of coconut trees she looked. It might at last be he."

Neilson stopped talking and gave a faint sigh.

"And what happened to her in the end?" asked the skipper.

Neilson smiled bitterly.

"Oh, three years afterwards she took up with another white man."

The skipper gave a fat, cynical chuckle.

"That's generally what happens to them," he said.

The Swede shot him a look of hatred. He did not know why that gross, obese man excited in him so violent a repulsion. But his thoughts wandered and he found his mind filled with memories of the past. He went back five and twenty years. It was when he first came to the island, weary of Apia, with its heavy drinking, its gambling and coarse sensuality, a sick man, trying to resign himself to the loss of the career which had fired his imagination with ambitious thoughts. He set behind him resolutely all his hopes of making a great name for himself and strove to content himself with the few poor months of careful life which was all that he could count on. He was boarding with a half-caste trader who had a store a couple of miles along the coast at the edge of a native village; and one day, wandering aimlessly along the grassy paths of the coconut groves, he had come upon the hut in which Sally lived. The beauty of the spot had filled him with a rapture so great that it was almost painful, and then he had seen Sally. She was the loveliest creature he had ever seen, and the sadness in those dark, magnificent eyes of hers affected him strangely. The Kanakas were a handsome race, and beauty was not rare among them, but it was the beauty of shapely animals. It was empty. But those tragic eyes were dark with mystery, and you felt in them the bitter complexity of the groping, human soul. The trader told him the story and it moved him.

"Do you think he'll ever come back?" asked Neilson.

"No fear. Why, it'll be a couple of years before the ship is paid off, and by then he'll have forgotten all about her. I bet he was pretty mad when he woke up and found he'd been shanghaied, and I shouldn't wonder but he wanted to fight somebody. But he'd got to grin and bear it, and I guess in a month he was thinking it the best thing that had ever happened to him that he got way from the island."

But Neilson could not get the story out of his head. Perhaps because he was sick and weakly, the radiant health of Red appealed to his imagination. Himself an ugly man, insignificant of appearance, he prized very highly comeliness in others. He had never been passionately in love, and certainly he had never been passionately loved. The mutual attraction of those two young things gave him a singular delight. It had the ineffable beauty of the Absolute. He went again to the little hut by the creek. He had a gift for languages and an energetic mind, accustomed to work, and he had already given much time to the study of the local tongue. Old habit was strong in him and he was gathering together material for a paper on the Samoan speech. The old crone who shared the hut with Sally invited him to come in and sit down. She gave him *kava* to drink and cigarettes to smoke. She was glad to have someone to chat with and while she talked he looked at Sally. She reminded him of the Psyche in the museum at Naples. Her features had the same clear purity of line, and though she had borne a child she had still a virginal aspect.

It was not till he had seen her two or three times that he induced her to speak. Then it was only to ask him if he had seen in Apia a man called Red. Two years had passed since his disappearance, but it was plain that she still thought of him incessantly.

It did not take Neilson long to discover that he was in love with her. It was only by an effort of will now that he prevented himself from going every day to the creek, and when he was not with Sally his thoughts were. At first, looking upon himself as a dying man, he asked only to look at her, and occasionally hear her speak, and his love gave him a wonderful happiness. He exulted in its purity. He wanted nothing from her but the opportunity to weave around her graceful person a web of beautiful fancies. But the open air, the equable temperature, the rest, the simple fare, began to have an unexpected effect on his health. His temperature did not soar at night to such alarming heights, he coughed less and began to put on weight; six months passed without his having a hæmorrhage; and on a sudden he saw the possibility that he might live. He had studied his disease carefully, and the hope dawned upon him that with great care he might arrest its course. It exhilarated him to look forward once more to the future. He made plans. It was evident that any active life was out of the question, but he could live on the islands, and the small income he had, insufficient elsewhere, would be ample to keep him. He could grow coconuts; that would give him an occupation; and he would send for his books and a piano; but his quick mind saw that in all this he was merely trying to conceal from himself the desire which obsessed him.

He wanted Sally. He loved not only her beauty, but that dim soul which he divined behind her suffering eyes. He would intoxicate her with his passion. In the end he would make her forget. And in an ecstasy of surrender he fancied himself giving her too the happiness which he had thought never to know again, but had now so miraculously achieved.

He asked her to live with him. She refused. He had expected that and did not let it depress him, for he was sure that sooner or later she would yield. His love was irresistible. He told the old woman of his wishes, and found somewhat to his surprise that she and the neighbours, long aware of them, were strongly urging Sally to accept his offer. After all, every native was glad to keep house for a white man, and Neilson according to the standards of the island was a rich one. The trader with whom he boarded went to her and told her not to be a fool; such an opportunity would not come again, and after so long she could not still believe that Red would ever return. The girl's resistance only increased Neilson's desire, and what had been a very pure love now became an agonising passion. He was determined that nothing should stand in his way. He gave Sally no peace. At last, worn out by his persistence and the persuasions, by turns pleading and angry, of everyone around her, she consented. But the day after when, exultant, he went to see her he found that in the night she had burnt down the hut in which she and Red had lived together. The old crone ran towards him full of angry abuse of Sally, but he waved her aside; it did not matter; they would build a bungalow on the place where the hut had stood. A European house would really be more convenient if he wanted to bring out a piano and a vast number of books.

And so the little wooden house was built in which he had now lived for many years, and Sally became his wife. But after the first few weeks of rapture, during which he was satisfied with what she gave him he had known little happiness. She had yielded to him, through weariness, but she had only yielded what she set no store on. The soul which he had dimly glimpsed escaped him. He knew that she cared nothing for him. She still loved Red, and all the time she was waiting for his return. At a sign from him, Neilson knew that, notwithstanding his love, his tenderness, his sympathy, his generosity, she would leave him without a moment's hesitation. She would never give a thought to his distress. Anguish seized him and he battered at that impenetrable self of hers which sullenly resisted him. His love became bitter. He tried to melt her heart with kindness, but it remained as hard as before; he feigned indifference, but she did not notice it. Sometimes he lost his temper and abused her, and then she wept silently. Sometimes he thought she was nothing but a fraud, and that soul simply an invention of his own, and that he could not get into the sanctuary of her heart because there was no sanctuary there. His love became a prison from which he longed to escape, but he had not the strength merely to open the door—that was all it needed—and walk out into the open air. It was torture and at last he became numb and hopeless. In the end the fire burnt itself out and, when he saw her eyes rest for an instant on the slender bridge, it was no longer rage that filled his heart but impatience. For many years now they had lived together bound by the ties of habit and convenience, and it was with a smile that he looked back on his old passion. She was an old woman, for the women on the islands age quickly, and if he had no love for her any more he had tolerance. She left him alone. He was contented with his piano and his books.

His thoughts led him to a desire for words.

"When I look back now and reflect on that brief passionate love of Red and Sally, I think that perhaps they should thank the ruthless fate that separated them when their love seemed still to be at its height. They suffered, but they suffered in beauty. They were spared the real tragedy of love."

"I don't know exactly as I get you," said the skipper.

"The tragedy of love is not death or separation. How long do you think it would have been before one or other of them ceased to care? Oh, it is dreadfully bitter to look at a woman whom you have loved with all your heart and soul, so that you felt you could not bear to let her out of your sight, and realise that you would not mind if you never saw her again. The tragedy of love is indifference."

But while he was speaking a very extraordinary thing happened. Though he had been addressing the skipper he had not been talking to him, he had been putting his thoughts into words for himself, and with his eyes fixed on the man in front of him he had not seen him. But now an image presented itself to them, an image not of the man he saw, but of another man. It was as though he were looking into one of those distorting mirrors that make you extraordinarily squat or outrageously elongate, but here exactly the opposite took place, and in the obese, ugly old man he caught the shadowy glimpse of a stripling. He gave him now a quick, searching scrutiny. Why had a haphazard stroll brought him just to this place? A sudden tremor of his heart made him slightly breathless. An absurd suspicion seized him. What had occurred to him was impossible, and yet it might be a fact.

"What is your name?" he asked abruptly.

The skipper's face puckered and he gave a cunning chuckle. He looked then malicious and horribly vulgar.

"It's such a damned long time since I heard it that I almost forget it myself. But for thirty years now in the islands they've always called me Red."

His huge form shook as he gave a low, almost silent laugh. It was obscene. Neilson shuddered. Red was hugely amused, and from his bloodshot eyes tears ran down his cheeks.

Neilson gave a gasp, for at that moment a woman came in. She was a native, a woman of somewhat commanding presence, stout without being corpulent, dark, for the natives grow darker with age, with very grey hair. She wore a black Mother Hubbard, and its thinness showed her heavy breasts. The moment had come.

She made an observation to Neilson about some household matter and he answered. He wondered if his voice sounded as unnatural to her as it did to himself. She gave the man who was sitting in the chair by the window an indifferent glance, and went out of the room. The moment had come and gone.

Neilson for a moment could not speak. He was strangely shaken. Then he said:

"I'd be very glad if you'd stay and have a bit of dinner with me. Pot luck."

"I don't think I will," said Red. "I must go after this fellow Gray. I'll give him his stuff and then I'll get away. I want to be back in Apia tomorrow."

"I'll send a boy along with you to show you the way."

"That'll be fine."

Red heaved himself out of his chair, while the Swede called one of the boys who worked on the plantation. He told him where the skipper wanted to go, and the boy stepped along the bridge. Red prepared to follow him.

"Don't fall in," said Neilson.

"Not on your life."

Neilson watched him make his way across and when he had disappeared among the coconuts he looked still. Then he sank heavily in his chair. Was that the man who had prevented him from being happy? Was that the man whom Sally had loved all these years and for whom she had waited so desperately? It was grotesque. A sudden fury seized him so that he had an instinct to spring up and smash everything around him. He had been cheated. They had seen each other at last and had not known it. He began to laugh, mirthlessly, and his laughter grew till it became hysterical. The Gods had played him a cruel trick. And he was old now.

At last Sally came in to tell him dinner was ready. He sat down in front of her and tried to eat. He wondered what she would say if he told her now that the fat old man sitting in the chair was the lover whom she remembered still with the passionate abandonment of her youth. Years ago, when he hated her because she made him so unhappy, he would have been glad to tell her. He wanted to hurt her then as she hurt him, because his hatred was only love. But now he did not care. He shrugged his shoulders listlessly.

"What did that man want?" she asked presently.

He did not answer at once. She was old too, a fat old native woman. He wondered why he had ever loved her so madly. He had laid at her feet all the treasures of his soul, and she had cared nothing for them. Waste, what waste! And now, when he looked at her, he felt only contempt. His patience was at last exhausted. He answered her question.

"He's the captain of a schooner. He's come from Apia."

"Yes."

"He brought me news from home. My eldest brother is very ill and I must go back."

"Will you be gone long?"

He shrugged his shoulders.

50

The Hammer of God

BY G. K. CHESTERTON

THE little village of Bohun Beacon was perched on a hill so steep that the tall spire of its church seemed only like the peak of a small mountain. At the foot of the church stood a smithy, generally red with fires and always littered with hammers and scraps of iron; opposite to this, over a rude cross of cobbled paths, was "The Blue Boar," the only inn of the place. It was upon this crossway, in the lifting of a leaden and silver daybreak, that two brothers met in the street and spoke; though one was beginning the day and the other finishing it. The Rev. and Hon. Wilfred Bohun was very devout, and was making his way to some austere exercises of prayer or contemplation at dawn. Colonel the Hon. Norman Bohun, his elder brother, was by no means devout, and was sitting in evening dress on the bench outside "The Blue Boar," drinking what the philosophic observer was free to regard either as his last glass on Tuesday or his first on Wednesday. The colonel was not particular.

The Bohuns were one of the very few aristocratic families really dating from the Middle Ages, and their pennon had actually seen Palestine. But it is a great mistake to suppose that such houses stand high in chivalric tradition. Few except the poor preserve traditions. Aristocrats live not in traditions but in fashions. The Bohuns had been Mohocks under Queen Anne and Mashers under Queen Victoria. But like more than one of the really ancient houses, they had rotted in the last two centuries into mere drunkards and dandy degenerates, till there had even come a whisper of insanity. Certainly there was something hardly human about the colonel's wolfish pursuit of pleasure, and his chronic resolution not to go home till morning had a touch of the hideous clarity of insomnia. He was a tall, fine animal, elderly, but with hair still startlingly yellow. He would have looked merely blond and leonine, but his blue eyes were sunk so deep in his face that they looked black. They were a little too close together. He had very long yellow moustaches; on each side of them a fold or furrow from nostril to jaw, so that a sneer seemed cut into his face. Over his evening clothes he wore a curious pale yellow coat that looked more like a very light dressing-gown than an overcoat, and on the back of his head was stuck an extraordinary broad-brimmed hat of a bright green colour, evidently some oriental curiosity caught up at random. He was proud of appearing in such incongruous attires —proud of the fact that he always made them look congruous.

His brother the curate had also the yellow hair and the elegance, but he was buttoned up to the chin in black, and his face was clean-shaven, cultivated, and a little nervous. He seemed to live for nothing but his religion; but there were some who said (notably the blacksmith, who was a Presbyterian) that it was a love of Gothic architecture rather than of God, and that his haunting of the church like a ghost was only another and purer turn of the almost morbid thirst for beauty which sent his brother raging after women and wine. This charge was doubtful, while the man's practical piety was indubitable. Indeed, the charge was mostly an ignorant misunderstanding of the love of solitude and secret prayer, and was founded on his being often found kneeling, not before the altar, but in peculiar places, in the crypts or gallery, or even in the belfry. He was at the moment about to enter the church through the yard of the smithy, but stopped and frowned a little as he saw his brother's cavernous eyes staring in the same direction. On the hypothesis that the colonel was interested in the church he did not waste any speculations. There only remained the blacksmith's shop, and though the blacksmith was a Puritan and none of his people, Wilfred Bohun had heard some scandals about a beautiful and rather celebrated wife. He flung a suspicious look across the shed, and the colonel stood up laughing to speak to him.

"Good morning, Wilfred," he said. "Like a good landlord I am watching sleeplessly over my people. I am going to call on the blacksmith."

Wilfred looked at the ground, and said: "The blacksmith is out. He is over at Greenford."

"I know," answered the other with silent laughter; "that is why I am calling on him."

"Norman," said the cleric, with his eye on a pebble in the road, "are you ever afraid of thunderbolts?"

"What do you mean?" asked the colonel. "Is your hobby meteorology?"

"I mean," said Wilfred, without looking up, "do you ever think that God might strike you in the street?"

"I beg your pardon," said the colonel; "I see your hobby is folk-lore."

"I know your hobby is blasphemy," retorted the religious man, stung in the one live place of his nature. "But if you do not fear God, you have good reason to fear man."

The elder raised his eyebrows politely. "Fear man?" he said.

"Barnes the blacksmith is the biggest and strongest man for forty miles round," said the clergyman sternly. "I know you are no coward or weakling, but he could throw you over the wall."

This struck home, being true, and the lowering line by mouth and nostril darkened and deepened. For a moment he stood with the heavy sneer on his face. But in an instant Colonel Bohun had recovered his own cruel good humour and laughed, showing two dog-like front teeth under his yellow moustache. "In that case, my dear Wilfred," he said quite carelessly, "it was wise for the last of the Bohuns to come out partially in armour."

And he took off the queer round hat covered with green, showing that it was lined within with steel. Wilfred recognised it indeed as a light Japanese or Chinese helmet torn down from a trophy that hung in the old family hall.

"It was the first hat to hand," explained his brother airily; "always the nearest hat—and the nearest woman."

"The blacksmith is away at Greenford," said Wilfred quietly; "the time of his return is unsettled."

And with that he turned and went into the church with bowed head, crossing himself like one who wishes to be quit of an unclean spirit. He was anxious to forget such grossness in the cool twilight of his tall Gothic cloisters; but on that morning it was fated that his still round of religious exercises should be everywhere arrested by small shocks. As he entered the church, hitherto always empty at that hour, a kneeling figure rose hastily to its feet and came towards the full daylight of the doorway. When the curate saw it he stood still with surprise. For the early worshipper was none other than the village idiot, a nephew of the blacksmith, one who neither would nor could care for the church or for anything else. He was always called "Mad Joe," and seemed to have no other name; he was a dark, strong, slouching lad, with a heavy white face, dark straight hair, and a mouth always open. As he passed the priest, his moon-calf countenance gave no hint of what he had been doing or thinking of. He had never been known to pray before. What sort of prayers was he saying now? Extraordinary prayers surely.

Wilfred Bohun stood rooted to the spot long enough to see the idiot go out into the sunshine, and even to see his dissolute brother hail him with a sort of avuncular jocularity. The last thing he saw was the colonel throwing pennies at the open mouth of Joe, with the serious appearance of trying to hit it.

This ugly sunlight picture of the stupidity and cruelty of the earth sent the ascetic finally to his prayers for purification and new thoughts. He went up to a pew in the gallery, which brought him under a coloured window which he loved and always quieted his spirit; a blue window with an angel carrying lilies. There he began to think less about the half-wit, with his livid face and mouth like a fish. He began to think less of his evil brother, pacing like a lean lion in his horrible hunger. He sank deeper and deeper into those cold and sweet colours of silver blossoms and sapphire sky.

In this place half an hour afterwards he was found by Gibbs, the village cobbler, who had been sent for him in some haste. He got to his feet with promptitude, for he knew that no small matter would have brought Gibbs into such a place at all. The cobbler was, as in many villages, an atheist, and his appearance in church was a shade more extraordinary than Mad Joe's. It was a morning of theological enigmas.

"What is it?" asked Wilfred Bohun rather stiffly, but putting out a trembling hand for his hat.

The atheist spoke in a tone that, coming from him, was quite startlingly respectful, and even, as it were, huskily sympathetic.

"You must excuse me, sir," he said in a hoarse whisper, "but we didn't think it right not to let you know at once. I'm afraid a rather dreadful thing has happened, sir. I'm afraid your brother——"

Wilfred clenched his frail hands. "What devilry has he done now?" he cried in involuntary passion.

"Why, sir," said the cobbler, coughing, "I'm afraid he's done nothing, and won't do anything. I'm afraid he's done for. You had really better come down, sir."

The curate followed the cobbler down a short winding stair, which brought them out at an entrance rather higher than the street. Bohun saw the tragedy in one glance, flat underneath him like a plan. In the yard of the smithy were standing five or six men mostly in black, one in an inspector's uniform. They included the doctor, the Presbyterian minister, and the priest from the Roman Catholic chapel, to which the blacksmith's wife belonged. The latter was speaking to her, indeed, very rapidly, in an undertone, as she, a magnificent woman with red-gold hair, was sobbing blindly on a bench. Between these two groups, and just clear of the main heap of hammers, lay a man in evening dress, spreadeagled and flat on his face. From the height above Wilfred could have sworn to every item of his costume and appearance, down to the Bohun rings upon his fingers; but the skull was only a hideous splash, like a star of blackness and blood.

Wilfred Bohun gave but one glance, and ran down the steps into the yard. The doctor, who was the family physician, saluted him, but he scarcely took any notice. He could only stammer out: "My brother is dead. What does it mean? What is this horrible mystery?" There was an unhappy silence; and then the cobbler, the most outspoken man present, answered: "Plenty of horror, sir," he said, "but not much mystery."

"What do you mean?" asked Wilfred, with a white face.

"It's plain enough," answered Gibbs. "There is only one man for forty miles round that could have struck such a blow as that, and he's the man that had most reason to."

"We must not prejudge anything," put in the doctor, a tall, black-bearded man, rather nervously; "but it is competent for me to corroborate what Mr. Gibbs says about the nature of the blow, sir; it is an incredible blow. Mr. Gibbs says that only one man in this district could have done it. I should have said myself that nobody could have done it."

A shudder of superstition went through the slight figure of the curate. "I can hardly understand," he said.

"Mr. Bohun," said the doctor in a low voice, "metaphors literally fail me. It is inadequate to say that the skull was smashed to bits like an eggshell. Fragments of bone were driven into the body and the ground like bullets into a mud wall. It was the hand of a giant."

He was silent a moment, looking grimly through his glasses; then he added: "The thing has one advantage—that it clears most people of suspicion at one stroke. If you or I or any normally made man in the country were accused of this crime, we should be acquitted as an infant would be acquitted of stealing the Nelson Column."

"That's what I say," repeated the cobbler obstinately; "there's only one man that could have done it, and he's the man that would have done it. Where's Simeon Barnes, the blacksmith?"

"He's over at Greenford," faltered the curate.

"More likely over in France," muttered the cobbler.

"No; he is in neither of those places," said a small and colourless voice, which came from the little Roman priest who had joined the group. "As a matter of fact, he is coming up the road at this moment."

The little priest was not an interesting man to look at, having stubbly brown hair and a round and stolid face. But if he had been as splendid as Apollo no one would have looked at him at that moment. Everyone turned round and peered at the pathway which wound across the plain below, along which was indeed walking, at his own huge stride and with a hammer on his shoulder, Simeon the smith. He was a bony and gigantic man, with deep, dark, sinister eyes and a dark chin beard. He was walking and talking quietly with two other men; and though he was never specially cheerful, he seemed quite at his ease.

"My God!" cried the atheistic cobbler, "and there's the hammer he did it with."

"No," said the inspector, a sensible-looking man with a sandy moustache, speaking for the first time. "There's the hammer he did it with over there by the church wall. We have left it and the body exactly as they are."

All glanced round, and the short priest went across and looked down in silence at the tool where it lay. It was one of the smallest and the lightest of the hammers, and would not have caught the eye among the rest; but on the iron edge of it were blood and yellow hair.

After a silence the short priest spoke without looking up, and there was a new note in his dull voice. "Mr. Gibbs was hardly right," he said, "in saying that there is no mystery. There is at least the mystery of why so big a man should attempt so big a blow with so little a hammer."

"Oh, never mind that," cried Gibbs, in a fever. "What are we to do with Simeon Barnes?"

"Leave him alone," said the priest quietly. "He is coming here of himself. I know those two men with him. They are very good fellows from Greenford, and they have come over about the Presbyterian chapel."

Even as he spoke the tall smith swung round the corner of the church, and strode into his own yard. Then he stood there quite still, and the hammer fell from his hand. The inspector, who had preserved impenetrable propriety, immediately went up to him.

"I won't ask you, Mr. Barnes," he said, "whether you know anything about what has happened here. You are not bound to say. I hope you don't know, and that you will be able to prove it. But I must go through the form of arresting you in the King's name for the murder of Colonel Norman Bohun."

"You are not bound to say anything," said the cobbler in officious excitement. "They've got to prove everything. They haven't proved yet that it is Colonel Bohun, with the head all smashed up like that."

"That won't wash," said the doctor aside to the priest. "That's out of the detective stories. I was the colonel's medical man, and I knew his body better than he did. He had very fine hands, but quite peculiar ones. The second and third fingers were the same in length. Oh, that's the colonel right enough."

As he glanced at the brained corpse upon the ground the iron eyes of the motionless blacksmith followed them and rested there also.

"Is Colonel Bohun dead?" said the smith quite calmly. "Then he's damned."

"Don't say anything! Oh, don't say anything," cried the atheist cobbler, dancing about in an ecstasy of admiration of the English legal system. For no man is such a legalist as the good secularist.

The blacksmith turned on him over his shoulder the august face of a fanatic.

"It's well for you infidels to dodge like foxes because the world's law favours you," he said; "but God guards His own in His pocket, as you shall see this day."

Then he pointed to the colonel and said: "When did this dog die in his sins?"

"Moderate your language," said the doctor.

"Moderate the Bible's language, and I'll moderate mine. When did he die?"

"I saw him alive at six o'clock this morning," stammered Wilfred Bohun.

"God is good," said the smith. "Mr. Inspector, I have not the slightest objection to being arrested. It is you who may object to arresting me. I don't mind leaving the court without a stain on my character. You do mind, perhaps, leaving the court with a bad set-back in your career."

The solid inspector for the first time looked at the blacksmith with a lively eye; as did everybody else, except the short, strange priest, who was still looking down at the little hammer that had dealt the dreadful blow.

"There are two men standing outside this shop," went on the blacksmith with ponderous lucidity, "good tradesmen in Greenford whom you all know, who will swear that they saw me from before midnight till daybreak and long after in the committee-room of our Revival Mission, which sits all night, we save souls so fast. In Greenford itself twenty people could swear to me for all that time. If I were a heathen, Mr. Inspector, I would let you walk on to your downfall. But as a Christian man I feel bound to give you your chance, and ask you whether you will hear my alibi now or in court."

The inspector seemed for the first time disturbed, and said, "Of course I should be glad to clear you altogether now."

The smith walked out of his yard with the same long and easy stride, and returned to his two friends from Greenford, who were indeed friends of nearly everyone present. Each of them said a few words which no one ever thought of disbelieving. When they had spoken, the innocence of Simeon stood up as solid as the great church above them.

One of those silences struck the group which are more strange and insufferable than any speech. Madly, in order to make conversation, the curate said to the Catholic priest:

"You seem very much interested in that hammer, Father Brown."

"Yes, I am," said Father Brown; "why is it such a small hammer?"

The doctor swung round on him.

"By George, that's true," he cried; "who would use a little hammer with ten larger hammers lying about?"

Then he lowered his voice in the curate's ear and said: "Only the kind of person that can't lift a large hammer. It is not a question of force or courage between the sexes. It's a question of lifting power in the shoulders. A bold woman could commit ten murders with a light hammer and never turn a hair. She could not kill a beetle with a heavy one."

Wilfred Bohun was staring at him with a sort of hypnotized horror, while Father Brown listened with his head a little on one side, really interested and attentive. The doctor went on with more hissing emphasis:

"Why do these idiots always assume that the only person who hates the wife's lover is the wife's husband? Nine times out of ten the person who most hates the wife's lover is the wife. Who knows what insolence or treachery he had shown her—look there?"

He made a momentary gesture towards the red-haired woman on the bench. She had lifted her head at last and the tears were drying on her splendid face. But the eyes were fixed on the corpse with an electric glare that had in it something of idiocy.

The Rev. Wilfred Bohun made a limp gesture as if waving away all desire to know; but Father Brown, dusting off his sleeve some ashes blown from the furnace, spoke in his indifferent way.

"You are like so many doctors," he said; "your mental science is really suggestive. It is your physical science that is utterly impossible. I agree that the woman wants to kill the co-respondent much more than the petitioner does. And I agree that a woman will always pick up a small hammer instead of a big one. But the difficulty is one of physical impossibility. No woman ever born could have smashed a man's skull flat like that." Then he added reflectively, after a pause: "These people haven't grasped the whole of it. The man was actually wearing an iron helmet, and the blow scattered it like broken glass. Look at that woman. Look at her arms."

Silence held them all up again, and then the doctor said rather sulkily: "Well, I may be wrong; there are objections to everything. But I stick to the main point. No man but an idiot would pick up that little hammer if he could use a big hammer."

With that the lean and quivering hands of Wilfred Bohun went up to his head and seemed to clutch his scanty yellow hair. After an instant they dropped, and he cried: "That was the word I wanted; you have said the word."

Then he continued, mastering his discomposure: "The words you said were, 'No man but an idiot would pick up the small hammer.'"

"Yes," said the doctor. "Well?"

"Well," said the curate, "no man but an idiot did." The rest stared at him with eyes arrested and riveted, and he went on in a febrile and feminine agitation.

"I am a priest," he cried unsteadily, "and a priest should be no shedder of blood. I—I mean that he should bring no one to the gallows. And I thank God that I see the criminal clearly now—because he is a criminal who cannot be brought to the gallows."

"You will not denounce him?" enquired the doctor.

"He would not be hanged if I did denounce him," answered Wilfred with a wild but curiously happy smile. "When I went into the church this morning I found a madman praying there—that poor Joe, who has been wrong all his life. God knows what he prayed; but with such strange folk it is not incredible to suppose that their prayers are all upside down. Very likely a lunatic would pray before killing a man. When I last saw poor Joe he was with my brother. My brother was mocking him."

"By Jove!" cried the doctor, "this is talking at last. But how do you explain——"

The Rev. Wilfred was almost trembling with the excitement of his own glimpse of the truth. "Don't you see; don't you see," he cried feverishly; "that is the only theory that covers both the queer things, that answers both the riddles. The two riddles are the little hammer and the big blow. The smith might have struck the big blow, but would not have chosen the little hammer. His wife would have chosen the little hammer, but she could not have struck the big blow. But the madman might have done both. As for the little hammer—why, he was mad and might have picked up anything. And for the big blow, have you never heard, doctor, that a maniac in his paroxysm may have the strength of ten men?"

The doctor drew a deep breath and then said, "By golly, I believe you've got it."

Father Brown had fixed his eyes on the speaker so long and steadily as to prove that his large grey, ox-like eyes were not quite so insignificant as the rest of his face. When silence had fallen he said with marked respect: "Mr. Bohun, yours is the only theory yet propounded which holds water every way and is essentially unassailable. I think, therefore, that you deserve to be told, on my positive knowledge, that it is not the true one." And with that the old little man walked away and stared again at the hammer.

"That fellow seems to know more than he ought to," whispered the doctor peevishly to Wilfred. "Those popish priests are deucedly sly."

"No, no," said Bohun, with a sort of wild fatigue. "It was the lunatic. It was the lunatic."

The group of the two clerics and the doctor had fallen away from the more official group containing the inspector and the man he had arrested. Now, however, that their own party had broken up, they heard voices from the others. The priest looked up quietly and then looked down again as he heard the blacksmith say in a loud voice:

"I hope I've convinced you, Mr. Inspector. I'm a strong man, as you say, but I couldn't have flung my hammer bang here from Greenford. My hammer hasn't any wings that it should come flying half a mile over hedges and fields."

The inspector laughed amicably and said: "No, I think you can be considered out of it, though it's one of the rummiest coincidences I ever saw. I can only ask you to give us all the assistance you can in finding a man as big and strong as yourself. By George! you might be useful, if only to hold him! I suppose you yourself have no guess at the man?"

"I may have a guess," said the pale smith, "but it is not at a man." Then, seeing the scared eyes turn towards his wife on the bench, he put his huge hand on her shoulder and said: "Nor a woman either."

"What do you mean?" asked the inspector jocularly. "You don't think cows use hammers, do you?"

"I think no thing of flesh held that hammer," said the blacksmith in a stifled voice; "mortally speaking, I think the man died alone."

Wilfred made a sudden forward movement and peered at him with burning eyes.

"Do you mean to say, Barnes," came the sharp voice of the cobbler, "that the hammer jumped up of itself and knocked the man down?"

"Oh, you gentlemen may stare and snigger," cried Simeon; "you clergymen who tell us on Sunday in what a stillness the Lord smote Sennacherib. I believe that One who walks invisible in every house defended the honour of mine, and laid the defiler dead before the door of it. I believe the force in that blow was just the force there is in earthquakes, and no force less."

Wilfred said, with a voice utterly undescribable: "I told Norman myself to beware of the thunderbolt."

"That agent is outside my jurisdiction," said the inspector with a slight smile.

"You are not outside His," answered the smith; "see you to it," and, turning his broad back, he went into the house.

The shaken Wilfred was led away by Father Brown, who had an easy and friendly way with him. "Let us get out of this horrid place, Mr. Bohun," he said. "May I look inside your church? I hear it's one of the oldest in England. We take some interest, you know," he added with a comical grimace, "in old English churches."

Wilfred Bohun did not smile, for humour was never his strong point. But he nodded rather eagerly, being only too ready to explain the Gothic splendours to someone more likely to be sympathetic than the Presbyterian blacksmith or the atheist cobbler.

"By all means," he said; "let us go in at this side." And he led the way into the high side entrance at the top of the flight of steps. Father Brown was mounting the first step to follow him when he felt a hand on his shoulder, and turned to behold the dark, thin figure of the doctor, his face darker yet with suspicion.

"Sir," said the physician harshly, "you appear to know some secrets in this black business. May I ask if you are going to keep them to yourself?"

"Why, doctor," answered the priest, smiling quite pleasantly, "there is one very good reason why a man of my trade should keep things to himself when he is not sure of them, and that is that it is so constantly his duty to keep them to himself when he is sure of them. But if you think I have been discourteously reticent with you or anyone, I will go to the extreme limit of my custom. I will give you two very large hints."

"Well, sir?" said the doctor gloomily.

"First," said Father Brown quietly, "the thing is quite in your own province. It is a matter of physical science. The blacksmith is mistaken, not perhaps in saying that the blow was divine, but certainly in saying that it came by a miracle. It was no miracle, doctor, except in so far as a man is himself a miracle, with his strange and wicked and yet half-heroic heart. The force that smashed that skull was a force well known to scientists—one of the most frequently debated of the laws of nature."

The doctor, who was looking at him with frowning intentness, only said: "And the other hint!"

"The other hint is this," said the priest. "Do you remember the blacksmith, though he believes in miracles, talking scornfully of the impossible fairy tale that his hammer had wings and flew half a mile across country?"

"Yes," said the doctor, "I remember that."

"Well," added Father Brown, with a broad smile, "that fairy tale was the nearest thing to the real truth that has been said to-day." And with that he turned his back and stumped up the steps after the curate.

The Reverend Wilfred, who had been waiting for him, pale and impatient, as if this little delay were the last straw for his nerves, led him immediately to his favourite corner of the church, that part of the gallery closest to the carved roof and lit by the wonderful window with the angel. The little Latin priest explored and admired everything exhaustively, talking cheerfully but in a low voice all the time. When in the course of his investigation he found the side exit and the winding stair down which Wilfred had rushed to find his brother dead, Father Brown ran not down but up, with the agility of a monkey, and his clear voice came from an outer platform above.

"Come up here, Mr. Bohun," he called. "The air will do you good."

Bohun followed him, and came out on a kind of stone gallery or balcony outside the building, from which one could see the illimitable plain in which their small hill stood, wooded away to the purple horizon and dotted with villages and farms. Clear and square, but quite small beneath them, was the blacksmith's yard, where the inspector still stood taking notes and the corpse still lay like a smashed fly.

"Might be the map of the world, mightn't it?" said Father Brown.

"Yes," said Bohun very gravely, and nodded his head.

Immediately beneath and about them the lines of the Gothic building plunged outwards into the void with a sickening swiftness akin to suicide. There is that element of Titan energy in the architecture of the Middle Ages that, from whatever aspect it be seen, it always seems to be rushing away, like the strong back of some maddened horse. This church was hewn out of ancient and silent stone, bearded with old fungoids and stained with the nests of birds. And yet, when they saw it from below, it sprang like a fountain at the stars; and when they saw it, as now, from above, it poured like a cataract into a voiceless pit. For these two men on the tower were left alone with the most terrible aspect of the Gothic; the monstrous foreshortening and disproportion, the dizzy perspectives, the glimpses of great things small and small things great; a topsy-turvydom of stone in the mid-air. Details of stone, enormous by their proximity, were relieved against a pattern of fields and farms, pygmy in their distance. A carved bird or beast at a corner seemed like some vast walking or flying dragon wasting the pastures and villages below. The whole atmosphere was dizzy and dangerous, as if men were upheld in air amid the gyrating wings of colossal genii; and the whole of that old church, as tall and rich as a cathedral, seemed to sit upon the sunlit country like a cloud-burst.

' I think there is something rather dangerous about standing on these high places even to pray," said Father Brown. "Heights were made to be looked at, not to be looked from."

"Do you mean that one may fall over?" asked Wilfred.

"I mean that one's soul may fall if one's body doesn't," said the other priest.

"I scarcely understand you," remarked Bohun indistinctly.

"Look at that blacksmith, for instance," went on Father Brown calmly; "a good man, but not a Christian—hard, imperious, unforgiving. Well, his Scotch religion was made up by men who prayed on hills and high crags, and learnt to look down on the world more than to look up at heaven. Humility is the mother of giants. One sees great things from the valley; only small things from the peak."

"But he—he didn't do it," said Bohun tremulously.

"No," said the other in an odd voice; "we know he didn't do it." After a moment he resumed, looking tranquilly out over the plain with his pale grey eyes. "I knew a man," he said, "who began by worshipping with others before the altar, but who grew fond of high and lonely places to pray from, corners or niches in the belfry or the spire. And once in one of those dizzy places, where the whole world seemed to turn under him like a wheel, his brain turned also, and he fancied he was God. So that though he was a good man, he committed a great crime."

Wilfred's face was turned away, but his bony hands turned blue and white as they tightened on the parapet of stone.

"He thought it was given to *him* to judge the world and strike down the sinner. He would never have had such a thought if he had been kneeling with other men upon a floor. But he saw all men walking about like insects. He saw one especially strutting just below him, insolent and evident by the bright green hat—a poisonous insect."

Rooks cawed round the corners of the belfry; but there was no other sound till Father Brown went on.

"This also tempted him, that he had in his hand one of the most awful engines of nature; I mean gravitation, that mad and quickening rush by which all earth's creatures fly back to her heart when released. See, the inspector is strutting just below us in the smithy. If I were to toss a pebble over this parapet it would be something like a bullet by the time it struck him. If I were to drop a hammer—even a small hammer——"

Wilfred Bohun threw one leg over the parapet, and Father Brown had him in a minute by the collar.

"Not by that door," he said quite gently; "that door leads to hell."

Bohun staggered back against the wall, and stared at him with frightful eyes.

"How do you know all this?" he cried. "Are you a devil?"

"I am a man,'" answered Father Brown gravely; "and therefore have all devils in my heart. Listen to me," he said after a short pause. "I know what you did—at least, I can guess the great part of it. When you left your brother you were racked with no unrighteous rage to the extent even that you snatched up a small hammer, half inclined to kill him with his foulness on his mouth. Recoiling, you thrust it under your buttoned coat instead, and rushed into the church. You pray wildly in many places, under the angel window, upon the platform above, and on a higher platform still, from which you could see the colonel's Eastern hat like the back of a green beetle crawling about. Then something snapped in your soul, and you let God's thunderbolt fall."

Wilfred put a weak hand to his head, and asked in a low voice: "How did you know that his hat looked like a green beetle?"

"Oh, that," said the other with the shadow of a smile, "that was common sense. But hear me further. I say I know all this; but no one else shall know it. The next step is for you; I shall take no more steps; I will seal this with the seal of confession. If you ask me why, there are many reasons, and only one that concerns you. I leave things to you because you have not yet gone very far wrong, as assassins go. You did not help to fix the crime on the smith when it was easy; or on his wife, when that was easy. You tried to fix it on the imbecile because you knew that he could not suffer. That was one of the gleams that it is my business to find in assassins. And now come down into the village, and go your own way as free as the wind; for I have said my last word."

They went down the winding stairs in utter silence, and came out into the sunlight by the smithy. Wilfred Bohun carefully unlatched the wooden gate of the yard, and going up to the inspector, said: "I wish to give myself up; I have killed my brother."

51

The Kings of Orion

BY JOHN BUCHAN

"An ape and a lion lie side by side in the heart of a man."
                                        Persian Proverb.

SPRING-FISHING in the North is a cold game for a man whose blood has become thin in gentler climates. All afternoon I had failed to stir a fish, and the wan streams of the Laver, swirling between bare grey banks, were as icy to the eye as the sharp gusts of hail from the north-east were to the fingers. I cast mechanically till I grew weary, and then with an empty creel and a villainous temper set myself to trudge the two miles of bent to the inn. Some distant ridges of hill stood out snow-clad against the dun sky, and half in anger, half in a dismal satisfaction, I told myself that fishing to-morrow would be as barren as to-day.

At the inn door a tall man was stamping his feet and watching a servant lifting rod-cases from a dog-cart. Hooded and wrapped though he was, my friend Thirlstone was an unmistakable figure in any landscape. The long, haggard, brown face, with the skin drawn tightly over the cheek-bones, the keen blue eyes finely wrinkled round the corners with staring at many suns, the scar which gave his mouth a humorous droop to the right, made up a whole which was not easily forgotten. I had last seen him on the quay at Funchal bargaining with some rascally boatman to take him after mythical wild goats in the Desertas. Before that we had met at an embassy ball in Vienna, and still earlier at a hill station in Persia to which I had been sent post-haste by an anxious and embarrassed government. Also I had been at school with him, in those far-away days when we rode nine stone and dreamed of cricket averages. He was a soldier of note, who had taken part in two little wars and one big one; had himself conducted a political mission through a hard country with some success, and was habitually chosen by his superiors to keep his eyes open as a foreign attaché in our neighbours' wars. But his fame as a hunter had gone abroad into places where even the name of the British army is unknown. He was the hungriest shikari I have ever seen, and I have seen many. If you are wise you will go forth-with to some library and procure a little book entitled *Three Hunting Expeditions,* by A. W. T. It is a modest work, and the style is that of a leading article, but all the lore and passion of the Red Gods are in its pages.

The sitting-room at the inn is a place of comfort, and while Thirlstone warmed his long back at the fire I sank contentedly into one of the well-rubbed leather arm-chairs. The company of a friend made the weather and the scarcity of salmon less the intolerable grievance they had seemed an hour ago than a joke to be laughed at. The landlord came in with whisky, and banked up the peats till they glowed beneath a pall of blue smoke.

"I hope to goodness we are alone," said Thirlstone, and he turned to the retreating landlord and asked the question.

"There's naebody bidin' the nicht forbye yoursels," he said, "but the morn there's a gentleman comin'. I got a letter frae him the day. Maister Wiston, they ca' him. Maybe ye ken him?"

I started at the name, which I knew very well. Thirlstone, who knew it better, stopped warming himself and walked to the window, where he stood pulling his moustache and staring at the snow. When the man had left the room, he turned to me with the face of one whose mind is made up on a course but uncertain of the best method.

"Do you know this sort of weather looks infernally unpromising? I've half a mind to chuck it and go back to town."

I gave him no encouragement, finding amusement in his difficulties. "Oh, it's not so bad," I said, "and it won't last. To-morrow we may have the day of our lives."

He was silent for a little, staring at the fire. "Anyhow," he said at last, "we were fools to be so far up the valley. Why shouldn't we go down to the Forest Lodge? They'll take us in, and we should be deucedly comfortable, and the water's better."

"There's not a pool on the river to touch the stretch here," I said. "I know, for I've fished every inch of it."

He had no reply to this, so he lit a pipe and held his peace for a time. Then, with some embarrassment but the air of having made a discovery, he announced that his conscience was troubling him about his work, and he thought he ought to get back to it at once. "There are several things I have forgotten to see to, and they're rather important. I feel a beast behaving like this, but you won't mind, will you?"

"My dear Thirlstone," I said, "what is the good of hedging? Why can't you say you won't meet Wiston?"

His face cleared. "Well, that's the fact—I won't. It would be too infernally unpleasant. You see, I was once by way of being his friend, and he was in my regiment. I couldn't do it."

The landlord came in at the moment with a basket of peats. "How long is Capt—Mr. Wiston staying here?" I asked.

"He's no bidin' ony time. He's just comin' here in the middle o' the day for his denner, and then drivin' up the water to Altbreac. He has the fishin' there."

Thirlstone's face showed profound relief. "Thank God!" I heard him mutter under his breath, and when the landlord had gone he fell to talking of salmon with enthusiasm. "We must make a big day of it to-morrow, dark to dark, you know. Thank Heaven, our beat's downstream, too." And thereafter he made frequent excursions to the door, and bulletins on the weather were issued regularly.

Dinner over, we drew our chairs to the hearth, and fell to talk and the slow consumption of tobacco. When two men from the ends of the earth meet by a winter fire, their thoughts are certain to drift overseas. We spoke of the racing tides off Vancouver, and the lonely pine-clad ridges running up to the snow peaks of the Selkirks, to which we had both travelled once upon a time in search of sport. Thirlstone on his own account had gone wandering to Alaska, and brought back some bear-skins and a frost-bitten toe as trophies, and from his tales had consorted with the finest band of rogues which survived unhanged on this planet. Then some casual word took our thoughts to the south, and our memories dallied with Africa. Thirlstone had hunted in Somaliland and done mighty slaughter; while I had spent some never-to-be-forgotten weeks long ago in the hinterland of Zanzibar, in the days before railways and game preserves. I had gone through life with a keen eye for the discovery of earthly paradises, to which I intend to retire when my work is over, and the fairest I thought I had found above the Rift valley, where you have a hundred miles of blue horizon and the weather of Scotland. Thirlstone, not having been there, naturally differed, and urged the claim of a certain glen in Kashmir, where you may hunt two varieties of bear and three of buck in thickets of rhododendron, and see the mightiest mountain-wall on earth from your tent door. The mention of the Indian frontier brought us back to our professions, and for a little we talked "shop," with the unblushing confidence of those who know each other's work and approve it. As a very young soldier Thirlstone had gone shooting in the Pamirs, and had blundered into a Russian party of exploration which contained Kuropatkin. He had in consequence grossly outstayed his leave, having been detained for a fortnight by an arbitrary hospitality; but he had learned many things, and the experience had given him strong views on frontier questions. Half an hour was devoted to a masterly survey of the East, until a word pulled us up.

"I went there in '99," Thirlstone was saying,—"the time Wiston and I were sent——" and then he stopped, and his eager face clouded. Wiston's name cast a shadow over our reminiscences.

"What did he actually do?" I asked after a short silence.

"Pretty bad! He seemed a commonplace, good sort of fellow, popular, fairly competent, a little bad-tempered perhaps. And then suddenly he did something so extremely blackguardly that everything was at an end. It's no good repeating details, and I hate to think about it. We know little about our neighbours, and I'm not sure that we know much about ourselves. There may be appalling depths of iniquity in every one of us, only most people are fortunate enough to go through the world without meeting anything to wake the devil in them. I don't believe Wiston was bad in the ordinary sense. Only there was something else in him—*somebody else,* if you like,—and in a moment it came uppermost, and he was a branded man. Ugh! it's a gruesome thought."

Thirlstone had let his pipe go out, and was staring moodily into the fire.

"How do you explain things like that?" he asked. "I have an idea of my own about them. We talk glibly of ourselves and our personality and our conscience, as if every man's nature were a smooth, round, white thing, like a chuckiestone. But I believe there are two men— perhaps more—in every one of us. There's our ordinary self, generally rather humdrum; and then there's a bit of something else, good, bad, but never indifferent—and it is that something else which may make a man a saint or a great villain."

" 'The Kings of Orion have come to earth,' " I quoted.

Something in the words struck Thirlstone, and he asked me what was the yarn I spoke of.

"It's an old legend," I explained. "When the kings were driven out of Orion, they were sent to this planet and given each his habitation in some mortal soul. There were differences of character in that royal family, and so the *alter ego* which dwells alongside of us may be virtuous or very much the reverse. But the point is that he is always greater than ourselves, for he has been a king. It's a foolish story, but very widely believed. There is something of the sort in Celtic folk-lore, and there's a reference to it in Ausonius. Also the bandits in the Bakhtiari have a version of it in a very excellent ballad."

"Kings of Orion," said Thirlstone musingly. "I like that idea. Good or bad, but always great! After all, we show a kind of belief in it in our daily practice. Every man is always making fancies about himself; but it is never his workaday self, but something else. The bank clerk who pictures himself as a financial Napoleon knows that his own thin little soul is incapable of it; but he knows, too, that it is possible enough for that other bigger thing which is not his soul, but yet in some odd way is bound up with it. I fancy myself a field-marshal in a European war; but I know perfectly well that if the job were offered me, I should realise my incompetence and decline. I expect you rather picture yourself now and then as a sort of Julius Cæsar and empire-maker, and yet, with all respect, my dear chap, I think it would be rather too much for you."

"There was once a man," I said, "an early Victorian Whig, whose chief ambitions were to reform the criminal law and abolish slavery. Well, this dull, estimable man in his leisure moments was Emperor of Byzantium. He fought great wars and built palaces, and then, when the time for fancy was past, went into the House of Commons and railed against militarism and Tory extravagance. That particular king from Orion had a rather odd sort of earthly tenement."

Thirlstone was all interest. "A philosophic Whig and the throne of Byzantium. A pretty rum mixture! And yet—yet," and his eyes became abstracted. "Did you ever know Tommy Lacelles?"

"The man who once governed Deira? Retired now, and lives somewhere in Kent? Yes, I've met him once or twice. But why?"

"Because," said Thirlstone solemnly, "unless I'm greatly mistaken, Tommy was another such case, though no man ever guessed it except myself. I don't mind telling you the story, now that he is retired and vegetating in his ancestral pastures. Besides, the facts are all to his credit, and the explanation is our own business. . . .

"His wife was my cousin, and when she died Tommy was left a very withered, disconsolate man, with no particular object in life. We all thought he would give up the service, for he was hideously well off; and then one fine day, to our amazement, he was offered Deira, and accepted it. I was short of a job at the time, for my battalion was at home, and there was nothing going on anywhere, so I thought I should like to see what the East Coast of Africa was like, and wrote to Tommy about it. He jumped at me, cabled offering me what he called his Military Secretaryship, and I got seconded, and set off. I had never known him very well, but what I had seen I had liked; and I suppose he was glad to have one of Maggie's family with him, for he was still very low about her loss. I was in pretty good spirits, for it meant new experiences, and I had hopes of big game.

"You've never been to Deira? Well, there's no good trying to describe it, for it's the only place in the world like itself. God made it and left it to its own devices. The town is pretty enough, with its palms and green headland, and little scrubby islands in the river's mouth. It has the usual half-Arab, half-Portugee look—white green-shuttered houses, flat roofs, sallow little men in duck, and every type of nigger from the Somali to the Shangaan. There are some good buildings, and Government House was the mansion of some old Portugee seigneur, and was built when people in Africa were not in such a hurry as to-day. Inland there's a rolling forest country, beginning with decent trees and ending in mimosa-thorn, when the land begins to rise to the stony hills of the interior; and that poisonous yellow river rolls through it all, with a denser native population along its banks than you will find anywhere else north of the Zambesi. For about two months in the year the climate is Paradise, and for the rest you live in a Turkish bath, with every known kind of fever hanging about. We cleaned out the town and improved the sanitation, so there were few epidemics, but there was enough ordinary malaria to sicken a crocodile.

"The place was no special use to us. It had been annexed in spite of a tremendous Radical outcry, and, upon my soul, it was one of the few cases where the Radicals had something to say for themselves. All we got by it was half a dozen of the nastiest problems an unfortunate governor can have to face. Ten years before it had been a decaying strip of coast, with a few trading firms in the town, and a small export of ivory and timber. But some years before Tommy took it up there had been a huge discovery of copper in the hills inland, a railway had been built, and there were several biggish mining settlements at the end of it. Deira itself was filled with offices of European firms, it had got a Stock Exchange of its own, and it was becoming the usual cosmopolitan playground. It had a knack, too, of getting the very worst breed of adventurer. I know something of your South African and Australian mining towns, and with all their faults they are run by white men. If they haven't much morals, they have a kind of decency which keeps them fairly straight. But for our sins we got a brand of Levantine Jew who was fit for nothing but making money and making trouble. They were always defying the law, and then, when they got into a hole, they squealed to Government for help, and started a racket in the home papers about the weakness of the Imperial power. The crux of the whole difficulty was the natives, who lived along the river and in the foothills. They were a hardy race of Kaffirs, sort of far-away cousins to the Zulu, and till the mines were opened they had behaved well enough. They had arms, which we had never dared to take away, but they kept quiet and paid their hut-taxes like men. I got to know many of the chiefs, and liked them, for they were upstanding fellows to look at and heaven-born shikaris. However, when the Jews came along they wanted labour, and, since we did not see our way to allow them to add to the imported coolie population, they had to fall back upon the Labonga. At first things went smoothly. The chiefs were willing to let their men work for good wages, and for a time there was enough labour for everybody. But as the mines extended, and the natives, after making a few pounds, wanted to get back to their kraals, there came a shortage; and since the work could not be allowed to slacken, the owners tried other methods. They made promises which they never intended to keep, and they stood on the letter of a law which the natives did not understand, and they employed touts who were little better than slave-dealers. They got the labour, of course, but soon they had put the Labonga into a state of unrest which a very little would turn into a rising.

"Into this kettle of fish Tommy was pitchforked, and when I arrived he was just beginning to understand how unpleasant it was. As I said before, I did not know him very well, and I was amazed to find how bad he was at his job. A more curiously incompetent person I never met. He was a long, thin man, with a grizzled moustache, and a mild sleepy eye—not an impressive figure, except on a horse; and he had an odd lisp which made even a shrewd remark sound foolish. He was the most industrious creature in the world, and a model of official decorum. His papers were always in order, his dispatches always neat and correct, and I don't believe anyone ever caught him tripping in office work. But he had no more conception than a child of the kind of trouble that was brewing. He never knew an honest man from a rogue, and the result was that he received all unofficial communications with a polite disbelief. I used to force him to see people—miners, prospectors, traders, anyone who had something to say worth listening to, but it all glided smoothly off his mind. He was simply the most incompetent being ever created, living in the world as not being of it, or rather creating a little official world of his own, where all events happened on lines laid down by the Colonial Office, and men were like papers, to be rolled into packets and properly docketed. He had an Executive Council of people like himself, competent officials and blind bats at anything else. Then there was a precious Legislative Council, intended to represent the different classes of the population. There were several good men on it—one old trader called Mackay, for instance, who had been thirty years in the country—but most were nominees of the mining firms, and very seedy rascals at that. They were always talking about the rights of the white man, and demanding popular control of the government, and similar twaddle. The leader was a man who hailed from Hamburg, and called himself Le Foy—descended from a Crusader of the name of Levi—who was a jackal of one of the chief copper firms. He overflowed with Imperialist sentiment, and when he was not waving the flag he used to gush about the beauties of English country life and the grandeur of the English tradition. He hated me from the start, for when he talked of going 'home' I thought he meant Hamburg, and said so; and then a thing happened which made him hate me worse. He was infernally rude to Tommy, who, like the dear sheep he was, never saw it, and, if he had, wouldn't have minded. But one day I chanced to overhear some of his impertinences, so I hunted out my biggest sjambok and lay in wait for Mr. Le Foy. I told him that he was a representative of the sovereign people, that I was a member of an effete bureaucracy, and that it would be most painful if unpleasantness arose between us. But, I added, I was prepared, if necessary, to sacrifice my official career to my private feelings, and if he dared to use such language again to his Majesty's representative I would give him a hiding he would remember till he found himself in Abraham's bosom. Not liking my sjambok, he became soap and butter at once, and held his tongue for a month or two.

"But though Tommy was no good at his job, he was a tremendous swell at other things. He was an uncommonly good linguist, and had always about a dozen hobbies which he slaved at; and when he found himself at Deira with a good deal of leisure, he became a bigger crank than ever. He had a lot of books which used to follow him about the world in zinc-lined boxes—your big paper-backed German books which mean research—and he was a Fellow of the Royal Society, and corresponded with half a dozen foreign shows. India was his great subject, but he had been in the Sudan and knew a good deal about African races. When I went out to him, his pet hobby was the Bantu, and he had acquired an amazing amount of miscellaneous learning. He knew all about their immigration from the North, and the Arab and Phœnician trade-routes, and the Portuguese occupation, and the rest of the history of that unpromising seaboard. The way he behaved in his researches showed the man. He worked hard at the Labonga language—which, I believe, is a linguistic curiosity of the first water—from missionary books and the conversation of tame Kaffirs. But he never thought of paying them a visit in their native haunts. I was constantly begging him to do it, but it was not Tommy's way. He did not care a straw about political expedience, and he liked to look at things through the medium of paper and ink. Then there were the Phœnician remains in the foothills where the copper was mined—old workings, and things which might have been forts or temples. He knew all that was to be known about them, but he had never seen them, and never wanted to. Once only he went to the hills, to open some new reservoirs and make the ordinary Governor's speech; but he went in a special train and stayed two hours, most of which was spent in lunching and being played to by brass bands.

"But, oddly enough, there was one thing which stirred him with an interest that was not academic. I discovered it by accident one day when I went into his study and found him struggling with a map of Central Asia. Instead of the mild, benevolent smile with which he usually greeted my interruptions, he looked positively furtive, and, I could have sworn, tried to shuffle the map under some papers. Now it happens that Central Asia is the part of the globe that I know better than most men, and I could not help picking up the map and looking at it. It was a wretched thing, and had got the Oxus two hundred miles out of its course. I pointed this out to Tommy, and to my amazement he became quite excited. 'Nonsense,' he said. 'You don't mean to say it goes south of that desert. Why, I meant to——' and then he stammered and stopped. I wondered what on earth he had meant to do, but I merely observed that I had been there, and knew. That brought Tommy out of his chair in real excitement. 'What!' he cried, 'you! You never told me,' and he started to fire off a round of questions, which showed that if he knew very little about the place, he had it a good deal in his mind. I drew some sketch-plans for him, and left him brooding over them.

"That was the first hint I got. The second was a few nights later, when we were smoking in the billiard-room. I had been reading Marco Polo, and the talk got on to Persia and drifted all over the north side of the Himalaya. Tommy, with an abstracted eye, talked of Alexander and Timour and Genghis Khan, and particularly of Prester John, who was a character that took his fancy. I had told him that the natives in the Pamirs were true Persian stock, and this interested him greatly. 'Why was there never a great state built up in those valleys?' he asked. 'You get nothing but a few wild conquerors rushing east and west, and then some squalid khanates. And yet all the materials were there—the stuff for a strong race, a rich land, the traditions of an old civilisation, and natural barriers against invasion.'

" 'I suppose they never found the man,' I said.

"He agreed. 'Their princes were sots, or they were barbarians of genius who could devastate to the gates of Peking or Constantinople, but could never build. They did not recognise their limits, and so they went out in a whirlwind. But if there had been a man of solid genius he might have built up the strongest nation on the globe. In time he could have annexed Persia and nibbled at China. He would have been rich, for he could tap all the inland trade-routes of Asia. He would have had to be a conqueror, for his people would be a race of warriors, but first and foremost he must have been a statesman. Think of such a civ--

ilisation, *the* Asian civilisation, growing up mysteriously behind the deserts and the ranges! That's my idea of Prester John. Russia would have been confined to the line of the Urals. China would have been absorbed. There would have been no Japan. The whole history of the world for the last few hundred years would have been different. It is the greatest of all the lost chances in history.' Tommy waxed pathetic over the loss.

"I was a little surprised at his eloquence, especially when he seemed to remember himself and stopped all of a sudden. But for the next week I got no peace with his questions. I told him all I knew of Bokhara, and Samarkand, and Tashkend, and Yarkand. I showed him the passes in the Pamirs and the Hindu Kush. I traced out the rivers, and I calculated distances; we talked over imaginary campaigns, and set up fanciful constitutions. It was a childish game, but I found it interesting enough. He spoke of it all with a curious personal tone which puzzled me, till one day when we were amusing ourselves with a fight on the Zarafshan, and I put in a modest claim to be allowed to win once in a while. For a second he looked at me in blank surprise. 'You can't,' he said; 'I've got to enter Samarkand before I can' . . . and he stopped again, with a glimmering sense in his face that he was giving himself away. And then I knew that I had surprised Tommy's secret. While he was muddling his own job, he was salving his pride with fancies of some wild career in Asia, where Tommy, disguised as the lord knows what Mussulman grandee, was hammering the little states into an empire.

"I did not think then as I think now, and I was amused to find so odd a trait in a dull man. I had known something of the kind before. I had met fellows who after their tenth peg would begin to swagger about some ridiculous fancy of their own—their little private corner of soul showing for a moment when the drink had blown aside their common sense. True, I had never known the thing appear in cold blood and everyday life, but I assumed the case to be the same. I thought of it only as a harmless fancy, never imagining that it had anything to do with character. I put it down to that kindly imagination which is the old opiate for failures. So I played up to Tommy with all my might, and though he became very discreet after the first betrayal, having hit upon the clue, I knew what to look for, and I found it. When I told him that the Labonga were in a devil of a mess, he would look at me with an empty face and change the subject; but once among the Turcomans his eye would kindle, and he would slave at his confounded folly with sufficient energy to reform the whole East Coast. It was the spark that kept the man alive. Otherwise he would have been as limp as a rag, but this craziness put life into him, and made him carry his head in the air and walk like a free man. I remember he was very keen about any kind of martial poetry. He used to go about crooning Scott and Macaulay to himself, and when we went for a walk or a ride he wouldn't speak for miles, but keep smiling to himself and humming bits of songs. I dare say he was very happy—far happier than your stolid, competent man, who sees only the one thing to do, and does it. Tommy was muddling his particular duty, but building glorious palaces in the air.

"One day Mackay, the old trader, came to me after a sitting of the precious Legislative Council. We were very friendly, and I had done all I could to get the Government to listen to his views. He was a dour, ill-tempered Scotsman, very anxious for the safety of his property, but perfectly careless about any danger to himself.

" 'Captain Thirlstone,' he said, 'that Governor of yours is a damned fool.'

"Of course I shut him up very brusquely, but he paid no attention. 'He just sits and grins, and lets yon Pentecostal crowd we've gotten here as a judgment for our sins do what they like wi' him. God kens what'll happen. I would go home to-morrow, if I could realise without an immoderate loss. For the day of reckoning is at hand. Maark my words, Captain—at hand.'

"I said I agreed with him about the approach of trouble, but that the Governor would rise to the occasion. I told him that people like Tommy were only seen at their best in a crisis, and that he might be perfectly confident that when it arrived he would get a new idea of the man. I said this, but of course I did not believe a word of it. I thought Tommy was only a dreamer, who had rotted any grit he ever possessed by his mental opiates. At that time I did not understand about the Kings from Orion.

"And then came the thing we had all been waiting for—a Labonga rising. A week before I had got leave and had gone up country, partly to shoot, but mainly to see for myself what trouble was brewing. I kept away from the river, and therefore missed the main native centres, but such kraals as I passed had a look I did not like. The chiefs were almost always invisible, and the young bloods were swaggering about and bukking to each other, while the women were grinding maize as if for some big festival. However, after a bit the country seemed to grow more normal, and I went into the foothills to shoot, fairly easy in my mind. I had got up to a place called Shimonwe, on the Pathi River, where I had ordered letters to be sent, and one night coming in from a hard day after kudu I found a post-runner half-dead of fatigue with a chit from Utterson, who commanded a police district twenty miles nearer the coast. It said simply that all the young men round about him had cleared out and appeared to be moving towards Deira, that he was in a devil of a quandary, and that, since the police were under the Governor, he would take his orders from me.

"It looked as if the heather were fairly on fire at last, so I set off early next morning to trek back. About midday I met Utterson, a very badly scared little man, who had come to look for me. It seemed that his policemen had bolted in the night and gone to join the rising, leaving him with two white sergeants, barely fifty rounds of ammunition, and no neighbour for a hundred miles. He said that the Labonga chiefs were not marching to the coast, as he had thought, but north along the eastern foothills in the direction of the mines. This was better news, for it meant that in all probability the railway would remain open. It was my business to get somehow to my chief, and I was in the deuce of a stew how to manage it. It was no good following the line of the natives' march, for they would have been between me and my goal, and the only way was to try and outflank them by going due east, in the Deira direction, and then turning north, so as to strike the railway about halfway to the mines. I told Utterson we had better scatter, otherwise we should have no chance of getting through a densely populated native country. So, about five in the afternoon, I set off with my chief shikari, who, by good luck, was not a Labonga, and dived into the jungly bush which skirts the hills.

"For three days I had a baddish time. We steered by the stars, travelling chiefly by night, and we showed extraordinary skill in missing the water-holes. I had a touch of fever and got light-headed, and it was all I could do to struggle through the thick grass and wait-a-bit thorns. My clothes were torn to rags, and I grew so footsore that it was agony to move. All the same we travelled fast, and there was no chance of our missing the road, for any route due north was bound to cut the railway. I had the most sickening uncertainty about what was to come next. Hely, who was in command at Deira, was a good enough man, but he had only three companies of white troops, and the black troops were as likely as not to be on their way to join the rebels. It looked as if we should have a Cawnpore business on a small scale, though I thanked Heaven there were no women in the case. As for Tommy, he would probably be repeating platitudes in Deira and composing an intelligent dispatch on the whole subject.

"About four in the afternoon of the third day I struck the line near a little station called Palala. I saw by the look of the rails that trains were still running, and my hopes revived. At Palala there was a coolie stationmaster, who gave me a drink and a little food, after which I slept heavily in his office till wakened by the arrival of an up train. It contained one of the white companies and a man Davidson, of the

101st, who was Hely's second in command. From him I had news that took away my breath. The Governor had gone up the line two days before with an A.D.C. and old Mackay. 'The sportsman has got a move on him at last,' said Davidson, 'but what he means to do Heaven only knows. The Labonga are at the mines, and a kind of mine-guard has been formed for defence. The joke of it is that most of the magnates are treed up there, for the railway is cut and they can't get away. I don't envy your chief the job of schooling that nervous crowd.'

"I went on with Davidson, and very early next morning we came to a broken culvert and had to stop. There we stuck for three hours till the down train arrived, and with it Hely. He was for ordinary a stolid soul, but I never saw a man in such a fever of excitement. He gripped me by the arm and fairly shook me. 'That old man of yours is a hero,' he cried. 'The Lord forgive me! and I have always crabbed him.'

"I implored him in Heaven's name to tell me what was up, but he would say nothing till he had had his pow-wow with Davidson. It seemed that he was bringing all his white troops up the line for some great demonstration that Tommy had conceived. Davidson went back to Deira, while we mended the culvert and got the men transferred to the other train. Then I screwed the truth out of Hely. Tommy had got up to the mines before the rebels arrived, and had found as fine a chaos as can be imagined. He did not seem to have had any doubts what to do. There were a certain number of white workmen, hard fellows from Cornwall mostly, with a few Australians, and these he got together with Mackay's help and organised into a pretty useful corps. He set them to guard the offices, and gave them strict orders to shoot at sight anyone attempting to leave. Then he collected the bosses and talked to them like a father. What he said Hely did not know, except that he had damned their eyes pretty heartily, and told them what a set of swine they were, making trouble which they had not the pluck to face. Whether from Mackay, or from his own intelligence, or from a memory of my neglected warnings, he seemed to have got a tight grip on the facts at last. Meanwhile, the Labonga were at the doors, chanting their battle-songs half a mile away, and shots were heard from the far pickets. If they had tried to rush the place then, all would have been over, but, luckily, that was never their way of fighting. They sat down in camp to make their sacrifices and consult their witch-doctors, and presently Hely arrived with the first troops, having come in on the northern flank when he found the line cut. He had been in time to hear the tail-end of Tommy's final address to the mine-owners. He told them, in words which Hely said he could never have imagined coming from his lips, that they would be well served if the Labonga cleaned the whole place out. Only, he said, that would be against the will of Britain, and it was his business, as a loyal servant, to prevent it. Then, after giving Hely his instructions, he had put on his uniform, gold lace and all, and every scrap of bunting he possessed—all the orders and 'Golden Stars' of half a dozen Oriental States where he had served. He made Ashurst, the A.D.C., put on his best Hussar's kit, and Mackay rigged himself out in a frock-coat and a topper; and the three set out on horseback for the Labonga. 'I believe he'll bring it off,' said Hely, with wild eyes, 'and, by Heaven, if he does, it'll be the best thing since John Nicholson!'

"For the rest of the way I sat hugging myself with excitement. The miracle of miracles seemed to have come. The old, slack, incompetent soul in Tommy seemed to have been driven out by that other spirit, which had hitherto been content to dream of crazy victories on the Oxus. I cursed my folly in having missed it all, for I would have given my right hand to be with him among the Labonga. I envied that young fool Ashurst his luck in being present at that queer transformation scene. I had not a doubt that Tommy would bring it off all right. The Kings from Orion don't go into action without coming out on top. As we got near the mines I kept my ears open for the sound of shots; but all was still—not even the kind of hubbub a native force makes when it is on the move. Something had happened, but what it was no man could guess. When we got to where the line was up, we made very good time over the five miles to the mines. No one interfered with us, and the nearer we got the greater grew my certainty. Soon we were at the pickets, who had nothing to tell us; and then we were racing up the long sandy street to the offices, and there, sitting smoking on the doorstep of the hotel, surrounded by everybody who was not on duty, were Mackay and Ashurst.

"They were an odd pair. Ashurst still wore his uniform; but he seemed to have been rolling about in it on the ground; his sleek hair was wildly ruffled, and he was poking holes in the dust with his sword. Mackay had lost his topper, and wore a disreputable cap, his ancient frock-coat was without buttons, and his tie had worked itself up behind his ears. They talked excitedly to each other, now and then vouchsafing a scrap of information to an equally excited audience. When they saw me they rose and rushed for me, and dragged me between them up the street, while the crowd tailed at our heels.

" 'Ye're a true prophet, Captain Thirlstone,' Mackay began, 'and I ask your pardon for doubting you. Ye said the Governor only needed a crisis to behave like a man. Well, the crisis has come; and if there's a man alive in this sinful world, it's that chief o' yours.' And then his emotion overcame him, and, hard-bitten devil as he was, he sat down on the ground and gasped with hysterical laughter, while Ashurst, with a very red face, kept putting the wrong end of a cigarette in his mouth and swearing profanely.

"I never remember a madder sight. There was the brassy blue sky and reddish granite rock and acres of thick red dust. The scrub had that metallic greenness which you find in all copper places. Pretty unwholesome it looked, and the crowd, which had got round us again, was more unwholesome still. Fat Jew boys, with diamond rings on dirty fingers and greasy linen cuffs, kept staring at us with twitching lips; and one or two smarter fellows in riding-breeches, mine managers and suchlike, tried to show their pluck by nervous jokes. And in the middle was Mackay, with his damaged frocker, drawling out his story in broad Scots.

" 'He made this laddie put on his braws, and he commandeered this iniquitous garment for me. I've raxed its seams, and it'll never look again on the man that owns it. Syne he arrayed himself in purple and fine linen till he was like the king's daughter, all glorious without; and says he to me, "Mackay," he says, "we'll go and talk to these uncovenanted deevils in their own tongue. We'll visit them at home, Mackay," he says. "They're none such bad fellows, but they want a little humouring from men like you and me." So we got on our horses and started the procession—the Governor with his head in the air, and the laddie endeavouring to look calm and collected, and me praying to the God of Israel and trying to keep my breeks from working up above my knees. I've been in Kaffir wars afore, but I never thought I would ride without weapon of any kind into such a black Armageddon. I am a peaceable man for ordinair', and a canny one, but I wasna myself in that hour. Man, Thirlstone, I was that overcome by the spirit of your chief, that if he had bidden me gang alone on the same errand, I wouldna say but what I would have gone.

" 'We hadna ridden half a mile before we saw the indunas and their men, ten thousand if there was one, and terrible as an army with banners. I speak feeguratively, for they hadna the scrap of a flag among them. They were beating the war-drums, and the young men were dancing with their big skin-shields and wagging their ostrich feathers, so I saw they were out for business. I'll no' say but what my blood ran cold, but the Governor's eye got brighter and his back stiffer. "Kings may be blest," I says to myself, "but thou art glorious."

" 'We rode straight for the centre of the crowd, where the young men were thickest and the big war-drums lay. As soon as they saw us a dozen lifted their spears and ran out to meet us. But they stopped after six steps. The sun glinted on the Governor's gold lace and my lum hat, and no doubt they thought we were heathen deities descended from the heavens. Down they went on their faces, and then back like rabbits to the rest, while the drums stopped, and the whole body awaited our coming in a silence like the tomb.

" 'Never a word we spoke, but just jogged on with our chins cocked up till we were forent the big drum, where yon old scoundrel Umgazi was standing with his young men looking as black as sin. For a moment their spears were shaking in their hands, and I heard the click of a breech-bolt. If we had winked an eye we would have become pincushions that instant. But some unearthly power upheld us. Even the laddie kept a stiff face, and for me I forgot my breeks in watching the Governor. He looked as solemn as an archangel, and comes to a halt opposite Umgazi, where he glowers at the old man for maybe three minutes, while we formed up behind him. Their eyes fell before his, and by and by their spears dropped to their sides. "The father has come to his children," says he in their own tongue. "What do the children seek from their father?"

" 'Ye see the cleverness of the thing. The man's past folly came to help him. The natives had never seen the Governor before till they beheld him in gold lace and a cocked hat on a muckle horse, speaking their own tongue and looking like a destroying angel. I tell you the Labonga's knees were loosed under them. They durstna speak a word until the Governor repeated the question in the same quiet, steely voice. "You seek something," he said, "else you had not come out to meet me in your numbers. The father waits to hear the children's desires."

" 'Then Umgazi found his tongue and began an uneasy speech. The mines, he said, truly enough, were the abode of devils, who compelled the people to work under the ground. The crops were unreaped and the buck went unspeared, because there were no young men left to him. Their father had been away or asleep, they thought, for no help had come from him; therefore it had seemed good to them, being freemen and warriors, to seek help for themselves.

" 'The Governor listened to it all with a set face. Then he smiled at them with supernatural assurance. They were fools, he said, and people of little wit, and he flung the better part of the Book of Job at their heads. The Lord kens where the man got his uncanny knowledge of the Labonga. He had all their heathen customs by heart, and he played with them like a cat with a mouse. He told them they were damned rascals to make such a stramash, and damned fools to think they could frighten the white man by their demonstrations. There was no brag about his words, just a calm statement of fact. At the same time, he said, he had no mind to let anyone wrong his children, and if any wrong had been done it should be righted. It was not meet, he said, that the young men should be taken from the villages unless by their own consent, though it was his desire that such young men as could be spared should have a chance of earning an honest penny. And then he fired at them some stuff about the British Empire and the King, and you could see the Labonga imbibing it like water. The man in a cocked hat might have told them that the sky was yellow, and they would have swallowed it.

" ' "I have spoken," he says at last, and there was a great shout from the young men, and old Umgazi looked pretty foolish. They were coming round our horses to touch our stirrups with their noses, but the Governor stopped them.

" ' "My children will pile their weapons in front of me," says he, "to show me how they have armed themselves, and likewise to prove that their folly is at an end. All except a dozen," says he, "whom I select as a bodyguard." And there and then he picked twelve lusty savages for his guard, while the rest without a cheep stacked their spears and guns forenent the big drum.

" 'Then he turned to us and spoke in English. "Get back to the mines hell-for-leather, and tell them what's happening, and see that you get up some kind of a show for to-morrow at noon. I will bring the chiefs, and we'll feast them. Get all the bands you can, and let them play me in. Tell the mines fellows to look active, for it's the chance of their lives." Then he says to the Labonga, "My men will return," he says, "but as for me I will spend the night with my children. Make ready food, but let no beer be made, for it is a solemn occasion."

" 'And so we left him. I will not describe how I spent last night mysel', but I have something to say about this remarkable phenomenon. I could enlarge on the triumph of mind over matter. . . .'

"Mackay did not enlarge. He stopped, cocked his ears, and looked down the road, from which came the strains of *Annie Laurie,* played with much spirit but grievously out of tune. Followed *The British Grenadiers,* and then an attempt at *The March of the Priests.* Mackay rose in excitement and began to crane his disreputable neck, while the band —a fine scratch collection of instruments—took up their stand at the end of the street, flanked by a piper in khaki who performed when their breath failed. Mackay chuckled with satisfaction. 'The deevils have entered into the spirit of my instructions,' he said. 'In a wee bit the place will be like Falkirk Tryst for din.'

"Punctually at twelve there came a great hullabaloo up the road, the beating of drums and the yelling of natives, and presently the procession hove in sight. There was Tommy on his horse, and on each side of him six savages with feather head-dress, and shields and war-paint complete. After him trooped about thirty of the great chiefs, walking two by two, for all the world like an Aldershot parade. They carried no arms, but the bodyguard shook their spears, and let yells out of them that would have scared Julius Cæsar. Then the band started in, and the piper blew up, and the mines people commenced to cheer, and I thought the heavens would fall. Long before Tommy came abreast of me I knew what I should see. His uniform looked as if it had been slept in, and his orders were all awry. But he had his head flung back, and his eyes very bright and his jaw set square. He never looked to right or left, never recognised me or anybody, for he was seeing something quite different from the red road and the white shanties and the hot sky."

The fire had almost died out. Thirlstone stooped for a moment and stirred the peats.

"Yes," he said, "I knew that in his fool's ear the trumpets of all Asia were ringing, and the King of Bokhara was entering Samarkand."

52

The Stranger in the Village

BY SIR PHILIP GIBBS

THE people of Lubimovka—those few who survived the famine which ravaged the Volga region of Russia in 1920 and 1921—believe firmly to this day that Nicholas, Tsar of All the Russias, was not murdered by Bolsheviks, according to newspaper stories which professed to give full and lurid details of that historic tragedy, but actually came to their village more than a year after he was supposed to be dead, lived among them with humility and love, and left behind him a relic worshipfully reverenced as proof of his identity.

It is an extraordinary story, and I confess when I heard it first from those Russian peasants and one young poet there, I regarded it merely as a variation of a myth which had been told me in Moscow, and once in a railway train on the way to Kazan, by highly educated Russians. They did not believe that the Tsar was dead. Some of them were convinced, without any evidence that seemed good to me, that he had escaped, or been allowed to escape, from his Bolshevik guards and had become a monk in some remote monastery in Asiatic Russia. Others believed that he was wandering about in peasant garb from one district to another, begging his way, and only revealing himself to trusted friends, most of them in misery or in hiding like himself.

It seemed to me the beginning of one of those fantastic traditions which spring up in popular imagination when some great personality disappears suddenly from the drama of life in which he played important parts. In the Middle Ages English kings murdered by their enemies, like Richard II or Edward II, were supposed to be alive long after their poor bodies had been buried secretly, and now and again a pretender took advantage of this popular belief. Even in England during the Great War there were thousands of people who refused to believe that Kitchener had been really drowned on the *Hampshire,* and asserted that he was a prisoner in the hands of the Germans. It is no wonder, therefore, that in Russia, with its credulous and simple peasants, there should be a widespread belief that the Tsar, their Little Father as they called him before the revolution, should be still alive.

What is remarkable about the tale of this stranger who came to Lubimovka is the unshakable faith of a young man like the poet Sacha—a sceptic and intellectual—and the apparent self-delusion of the man himself. From everything Sacha tells me it seems probable that this Nicholas Alexandrovitch, as he called himself, confessed that he was the Tsar, or at least did not deny that title, although he had nothing to gain except hunger and death, apart from a mystical power over a few starving peasants. He may have been mad, though his conversation was full of wisdom and sweetness. Certainly he could not have been a common charlatan, for that kind of man does not behave as this man did with simple charity. On the other hand, he may have been—well, I will tell you the story just as it happened and as it was told to me by Sacha the poet, by Sonia the schoolmistress, and by Michael and his wife, Anna.

It was in the autumn of 1920, when the first snow had fallen, but before the Volga had frozen up. In the village of Lubimovka, as in all other villages along the Volga valley, there were hunger and disease and death and fear. Worse than death was that great fear of the agony ahead and of inescapable doom, as it seemed. Strong peasant men, unafraid of death for themselves—many of them had fought against the Germans in the Great War with a simple and stubborn heroism in the midst of slaughter—trembled and felt their hearts turn to water when they saw their women weak with hunger and their children withering, and could see no hope at all of getting fresh supplies of food when their scanty stores had gone. They could not fight against this death which crept into Lubimovka like a grey wolf, hungry for the little ones and the old people.

It was in the afternoon of a day in middle October that the stranger came to the village. No one saw him enter through the gate in the stockade which surrounded the village according to the old custom of putting up a high fence to keep in the cattle and keep out the wolves. Now in Lubimovka no barrier could keep the wolf from the door—the invisible hunger-wolf—and most of the cattle had already been killed because there was no fodder left to keep the cows alive. The stranger entered by the gate which opens on the road towards Tetiushi. His footsteps made black smudges in the snow that had newly fallen. A peasant girl, staring through the window of a little wooden house facing the village pump—she was praying that death might come quickly to her mother, who lay stricken with typhus on the bed above the stove—saw the man's tall figure walking up the street towards the schoolhouse. He was a bearded man with deep-set eyes which looked very sad, as this girl told Sacha. He wore a sheepskin coat and military boots, broken at the toes, and he walked like a soldier, with a straight back, but very slowly, as though exhausted after a long march.

The girl was startled by the sight of him, because it was a long time since any stranger had come to Lubimovka, and instead of men coming to the village many had gone away after the summer when blackened crops stood in the burning sun which that year as well as last had utterly destroyed all hopes of harvest. They had gone away with their wives and children in boats down the Volga, hoping to reach districts where some food was left for winter months. Others had fought to get places on railway trains going towards Moscow, where there was always food according to the old proverb that "all things roll down to Moscow." But dreadful stories had come back of those refugee trains and those boatloads of people escaping from famine. It was months before the trains reached Moscow, and many died on the way. On the boats typhus broke out, and people who fled from famine found death in fever. It was better, perhaps, to stay in Lubimovka, and wait for death quietly at home.

But it was strange that an unknown man should come to the village, walking like this in the snow which fell in thick flakes on his sheepskin coat and his ragged fur cap. That peasant girl, Maria, who was the daughter of the blacksmith, Boris Markovitch, had a stupid idea, which she told Sacha, that it was Death himself coming to Lubimovka. She was afraid and yet glad when the man turned his head towards the window from which she was staring out, and looked at her with his sad, kind eyes. "It is Death calling on me," she thought, and crossed herself. But he passed on, and she still lived.

It was a hundred yards farther on that the black smudges of his footsteps in the snow came to an end, and it was the peasant Michael who was the next to see this stranger.

Michael had gone out into his yard to see his little cow, which was dying for lack of fodder. He had kept it alive by feeding it on cabbage stalks, which he had hidden in his cellar under a pile of sacks. His neighbours were angry with him because he kept it alive. They said: "Michael feeds his cow while our children die. He will burn in the next world because he cares more for his little cow than for our beautiful innocents who are withering like flowers. He has sold himself to the Devil."

Michael was afraid of that. Perhaps this love he had for his little cow was unholy and devilish. Perhaps God would punish him because he had given its milk to his own children and not a drop to his neighbours for their starving babes. But how could he share such a little milk with the whole village? He could at least keep his own family alive while the little cow was fed. Better that they should live than that all should die, and as for himself, he did not let a drop pass his lips, but munched only small morsels of bread made of leaves and straw and a few husks. Now there would be no more milk for his wife, and the little ones. He had come to the end of his secret hoard of cabbage stalks. It was three days since the little cow had been fed. Its eyes were glazing. He could not bear its pitiful gaze, so full of reproach that he had not the heart to kill it.

It was when he came out of its shed cursing himself because he had not the strength to kill it—it had licked his hand with a hot tongue— that he saw the stranger outside his house in the falling snow, and the long trail of black footsteps behind him. The stranger stood looking up the street, and his lips moved as though he were speaking, but suddenly he lurched sideways like a drunken man, and fell in a heap face downwards in the snow.

Michael stared at him stupidly. Then a kind of anger crept into his brain. What business had this man to die outside his house? Why not stay and die decently in his own home without troubling his neighbours? It was probably that foolish brute, Boris, the blacksmith, who had boasted so often of his great strength until typhus made him as weak as a maiden. The silly boaster! Michael was as strong as he was now, and still alive, though no blacksmith with arms like twisted wire.

Michael strode towards him sullenly, and then saw that it was not his old enemy the blacksmith, but some stranger. He could see that by the shape and colour of the man's hands. They were not hands that belonged to men of Lubimovka. They were queer-looking hands for any man, not gnarled and blunt by honest work in fields and sheds, with axe and spade and pick, but like the hands of some fine lady, or like those of Sonia, the schoolmistress.

Michael turned over the man's body as he lay crumpled up in the snow, and peered into his face. He seemed to have seen that bearded face before, those deep-set eyes, now closed, that straight nose. It was familiar to him in some vague way, like the memory of a face seen in a dream, or some picture. This man was dressed as a peasant. His sheepskin coat was torn. His soldier's boots were broken at the toes like the boots of all those men who had come back from the war. But this was no peasant's face. Even Michael, who was a stupid man, could see that. Lying there unconscious, grey as though the hand of death had touched it, it had a strange, noble look that was startling.

"He is like a saint," thought Michael. "He is even a little like the good Christ."

He had a sense of fear. There was something uncommon in the look of this senseless man who had come to a village from which other men fled, and where everyone waited for death. How had he come? There were no more boats on the Volga because of the floating ice. There were no sledges from Tetiushi, or any other place, because the horses had all dropped dead on the roadsides. This man with hands like a woman and face like a saint had come in a miraculous way, suddenly, just as one heard in old Russian tales which old women told about the stove on winter nights.

Michael called out to his wife:

"Anna! Anna!"

The fear in his voice brought her quickly to the door.

"Have you killed the little cow?" she asked, and then saw her man leaning over the body in the snow.

She crossed herself, and then leaned back, faint, against the doorpost.

"May his soul know peace!" she said.

Michael was angry with her because he was afraid.

"Can't you see his soul is still inside his body?" he growled. "Help me carry the wretch indoors. Snow makes a bad bed."

"You're mad," said Anna, drawing a shawl closer about her face. "If it's typhus he'll die better in the snow. And if it's hunger, we have enough mouths to feed and no food."

"I'll kill the little cow," said Michael. "There will be meat to eat for a month or two. God will curse us if we leave this fool to die at our threshold. Take hold of his legs, or I'll beat you."

Anna came from her doorway and peered at the senseless man, and touched his forehead.

"It's not the typhus," she said. "He's as cold as the snow beneath him."

"Look at his hands," said Michael.

Anna looked at the hands lying limp on the snow, and then at the face above the sheepskin coat.

"He is like a saint in a picture-book," she said, and put both hands on her bosom.

The man and woman took hold of the senseless body. In the old days Michael and his wife could have lifted him as easily as a sack of potatoes, but hunger had weakened them. They dragged the stranger across their threshold, and then stood in their room, breathing heavily. Their little girl Katinka climbed down from the bed above the stove, and stood with bare feet on the boards, clasping her mother's hand. The baby was whimpering in its sleep in a cradle near the stove.

It was the little girl who first made the astounding revelation which afterwards was believed by all the people of Lubimovka, except Vladimir, the Soviet agent, and Braunberg, the Jew, and Sara, his daughter.

"He is like the Little Father," she said, and looked up at a mark on the wall opposite the ikon. It was a mark made by a picture-frame which had hung there for years, as in all Russian cottages before the revolution, where a portrait of the Tsar, cut from some newspaper or magazine, or reproduced in colour by German printers, had always hung opposite the holy ikon. It was strange that this child should have remembered, for it was more than a year since the picture had been taken down by orders of the local Soviet, which had prohibited all portraits of the last of the Romanovs. With her bare feet she pattered to a cupboard on the other side of the stove, and dragged out a coloured print in a wooden frame, and held it up.

They were astounded and dismayed.

"The child is an idiot," said Michael sullenly. "Hunger has made her a little imbecile."

"It is a wonder we don't all go mad," said his wife.

They stood there, staring first at the portrait, and then at the man stretched out at their feet.

The portrait of the Tsar showed him in his uniform, with the star of St. Stanislaus at his breast. His beard was well trimmed. He smiled out of his deep-set eyes. This man lying senseless on their bare boards had a ragged beard, and there was no smile on his face and no star at his breast. And yet, now that Katinka had spoken her words, there could be no avoiding the amazing likeness of the stranger to that picture of the Emperor. Feature by feature it was the same face. The wide nostrils were the same, the low, broad forehead, the deep-set eye sockets.

The two peasants, husband and wife, stood silent, with their hands clasped and their mouths gaping.

It was the husband who spoke first.

"There are many Russians like the dead Tsar," he said, but his voice trembled uncertainly.

Anna, his wife, suddenly went down on her knees beside the stranger's senseless body, and thrust her hand beneath his sheepskin coat, as though about to choke him. Her poor, claw-like hands, skinny with hunger, trembled feverishly. There was a thin silver chain round the man's neck. She tugged at it, and with a jerk pulled something out from below a ragged vest. It was a jewel in the shape of a star, which lay now above the shaggy sheepskin. In that cottage of Lubimovka there was no light except the dusk of an October afternoon, with the white snow outside, but where the jewel lay it seemed to these peasants as though a real star had fallen from the sky, and was twinkling in their poor bare room.

Katinka clasped her thin little hands, and gave a cry of joy, as always she did when her father brought in a little milk from the cow.

"Truly," she said, "it is the Little Father!"

Michael went down on his knees beside his wife, and stared at the star so closely that his straw-coloured beard almost touched it. He raised a trembling hand, and tried to take hold of the jewel; but something withheld him, and he shrank back fearfully with a queer, strangled cry.

Anna swayed to and fro like a woman crooning to the dead.

"Christ Jesus!" she cried. "It is a miracle of God!"

At that moment the man who had been senseless opened his eyes, and stirred with a little groan.

As though trying to hide some dangerous and deadly secret, Anna put her claw-like hands at his throat again, and thrust the star out of sight below his ragged vest.

The man flung an arm over his head, and cried out in a faint, agonising voice:

"Oh, Death!"

Michael and his wife stayed there stiffly on their knees, staring at him in a dazed, frightened way. It was little Katinka who seemed to have most sense. She brought a jug of water from a shelf, and, wetting her little thin hand, moistened the man's forehead, and put some drops on his lips and beard. Presently he turned his head slightly, and smiled at her.

"Am I dead at last?" he asked very faintly. "Are you one of my little daughters?"

"You are my Little Father," said Katinka.

"Why, yes," said the man, "I am the Little Father of all my dear people."

He spoke only in a whisper, but his words were heard clearly by Michael and his wife, kneeling on either side of him.

"*Gospodin!*" said Michael, meaning Sir or Lord, "who are you, in God's name?"

The stranger heard the words and looked puzzled. For quite a long time he did not answer. Then he struggled up a little so that he leaned on one elbow, and stared round the dim room and into the faces of the peasant and his wife. Presently he spoke in a stronger voice, though still very gently.

"I am Nicholas Alexandrovitch, a wandering beggar. I think I am dying, so that I shall not trouble you long. What is the name of this village?"

It was Katinka who answered. The child's father and mother seemed speechless and stricken by fear.

"It is Lubimovka. We are all dying. Soon there will be no food for anyone. Then we shall die quickly."

"My poor people!" said the man, with a pitiful groan. "My poor Russia! My poor little ones!"

Tears came into his eyes and rolled slowly down his haggard cheeks until they touched his beard.

"If we are very careful," said Katinka, "we have enough bread to keep us alive for three or four weeks. And father is going to kill the little cow so that we shall have meat until the winter. After that, of course, we shall have to die."

She spoke simply, with the gravity of a child to a grown-up friend who understands. Then she went to the cupboard again and brought out the piece of bread which had been put aside for her evening meal. It was the bread made of straw and leaves and husks which I saw in that village in the year of famine.

"Eat, Little Father," she said to the stranger.

He shook his head and smiled.

"I have come here to die, not to eat your bread, my little one."

"If you do not eat it I shall cry," said Katinka.

He shook his head again, and said: "No, no, I am not hungry."

But when Katinka burst into tears he took a small portion of her bread and ate it, and said: "If men were as kind as little children, this world would be like heaven."

"*Gospodin,*" said Michael, moistening his lips and speaking hoarsely, "all that we have, which is little, we shall be glad to share with you."

"I thank you, *Tavarish,*" answered the man, using that word which means "comrade," and replaces all other titles in Russia, by order of the Bolsheviks.

That was the beginning of this legend or myth about the coming of the Tsar to Lubimovka. It was that evening after dark, when the man who called himself Nicholas Alexandrovitch was sleeping on the floor beside the stove, stirring sometimes in his dreams, that Michael took his lantern and walked through the falling snow to the house where young Sacha the poet lived with his mother and his crippled sister Lydia. Before the revolution, this family had been rich, with a house in Moscow; but Sacha's father, who was an officer of the old army, had been killed in the war, and the house in Moscow and all their wealth had been taken by the Bolsheviks, and now Sacha and his mother and his crippled sister were as poor as all the others in Lubimovka. But Sacha was a great reader of books, and wrote poetry; and, although no more than nineteen years of age, played a man's part in the village, and was the only one who was not afraid of Vladimir, the Soviet agent, or of Braunberg the Jew. He was the secretary of the village council, and had been put in prison for a time for resisting the requisition of grain and potatoes by the Red Army after the failure of the harvest. There was not a peasant in Lubimovka who did not regard this young man with hero-worship, because he had defied the Red soldiers for their sake. It was partly for that reason that Michael went round to his house to tell him of the stranger who had come. But it was also because Sacha had once lived in Moscow. Assuredly he must have seen the Tsar, the Little Father, as he was called then. He would be able to say whether this man who wore a flaming star under his vest was, or was not, the Emperor of all the Russias. Michael had hardly a doubt about it. But Sacha would know.

The young man was reading aloud by the dim light of a wax candle when Michael stood inside the door, with his fur cap in his hand and a thin mantle of snow on his leather tunic. Lydia, the crippled sister, lay on a couch by the stove, and Michael could see her shining eyes in a white face, though the candle-light hardly reached her. Sacha's mother sat with bowed head and her hands in her lap on the other side of the room—a black figure.

Sacha was reading something from a big book. It was something about passing from death to life, where there would be no hunger, but eternal joy and beauty. Then he raised his head as Michael opened the door, and the cold wind made his candle gutter.

"I wish to speak with you, Sacha," said Michael.

Sacha pushed back a lock of hair that had fallen over his forehead, and shielded the candle with his hands.

"What is it, Michael? Is it bad news you bring through the snow?"

"It is strange news," said Michael. "It is hard to believe one's own eyes."

"What have you seen?" asked Sacha.

Michael was slow in answering. He was a shy man, and perhaps these people would laugh at him if he told them something which was hard to believe. Perhaps also it would not be safe to tell anyone but Sacha. Women could not keep a secret. And this was a secret which might lead to trouble. They might all be shot by the Soviet Government if it leaked out.

"Pardon me," said Michael, "but I wish to tell you alone, Sacha. If you will step outside the door——"

"No, no," said Sacha, "it is better in this warm room. You need not be afraid of my mother and sister."

"I am afraid of what I have to tell you," said Michael.

It was some time before he could bring himself to tell these people. Sacha thought his cow had died. And little Lydia, the crippled girl, prayed that typhus had not stricken his household. There was no sound in the room except a kind of gasp when at last he told his tale.

"A stranger has come to the village. He fell with weakness at my door. It was my little girl who saw his likeness, and my wife who found a jewelled star beneath his vest. He is no common man. I verily believe, as God hears me, that it is the man whom we used to call our Little Father. The Tsar of Russia, whom all men believe to be dead."

The people in the room did not laugh at him. He was glad of that. But they stared at him silently. He could see their eyes upon him beyond the radiance of the candlelight.

It was Sacha who spoke first.

"Have you gone mad, Michael Michaelovitch?"

Michael answered with humility.

"It is possible that I have gone a little mad, Sacha. In this time of hunger and death it is hard to keep one's wits. But I believe that the Tsar Nicholas is now sleeping on the floor below my stove, and that my wife Anna is on her knees beside him, and that my little daughter Katinka was led by God to see his likeness."

They would not believe him. And yet they did not laugh at him. It seemed to Michael that they were a little frightened, as people who listen to a tale of ghosts, not believing, but afraid when the wind howls outside, and when the door blows open. Sacha's face had gone very white, and his crippled sister sat up on her couch with burning eyes.

"Do not tell this tale to others in the village," said Sacha. "Vladimir will report it to Moscow. You will be shot if they hear it there, Michael."

It was on the next morning that Sacha went round to Michael's house. The stranger was sitting by the stove with Katinka on his lap. He was telling her a story of old Russian history, and she had her arm about his neck, and her thin little face against his bearded cheek. Michael stood watching them from the doorway of the inner room, and Anna, his wife, was scrubbing the floor, and muttering prayers as she worked.

Sacha stood on the threshold and called out to Michael, while his eyes rested on the stranger's face.

"Have you killed the little cow, Michael?"

"I shall kill it directly," said Michael.

The stranger looked at Sacha and smiled, and said: "Good morning, comrade. You see, I have found a friend in Lubimovka."

"From what part do you come?" asked Sacha.

"I have been wandering," answered the man. "In spite of the famine people have given me a share of their bread. After all, the charity of man is greater than cruelty. That is the hope of the world—our only hope."

"Here," said Sacha, "we wait for certain death. There is no hope this side of the grave."

"I shall be glad to die here," answered the stranger; "perhaps I have reached the end of my journey!"

"I am young," said Sacha; "I do not wish to die."

He spoke harshly, and all the time his eyes were fixed on the stranger's face.

"It is hard for youth," said the stranger, very gently. "The old men of the world have betrayed them. It was the wickedness of the old men that made the war, and led to the agony and evil that followed in the wake of war. The sins of the fathers are visited on the children. How sad and pitiful is that! I am one of the old men whose ignorance and folly must be paid for by the sacrifice of youth. And yet Katinka here forgives me. Perhaps God will forgive, knowing my weakness and how I was betrayed."

Sacha stood there with a grave face, and one lock of hair falling over his forehead. Suddenly, as though something had broken in his spirit, he turned his head away and wept, and then stumbled forward and went down on one knee before the stranger, and took his hand, and said: "My Lord, my Lord!"

The man who called himself Nicholas Alexandrovitch was startled, and perhaps frightened, by this homage of the boy. He put little Katinka off his lap and stood up, leaning against the tall stove because of his weakness, and touched Sacha's head with his right hand.

"Do not call me that!" he said. "I am your comrade. I am a poor beggar living on the charity of starving folk. I am the lowest of the low in this Empire of misery and hunger and death. I am less lucky than those who have died more quickly. I am the scapegoat laden with the sins of Russia."

It must be remembered that this boy, Sacha, was weakened by hunger, like all men in the villages of the Volga Valley, and who, before then, had lived through the terror of the revolution, and had seen Russia brought to ruin and anarchy, and all its old civilisation overthrown. I think that is one explanation why not only Sacha, but other people in Lubimovka, found it easy to believe that the bearded stranger who had come among them was the man who had been their Tsar. They were in an emotional, overwrought state. The womenfolk, and even many of the men, had been praying for some miracle to happen by God's grace to save them from starvation. There were some who believed that war, famine and pestilence which had come upon the world was a presage of the second coming of Christ. Mingled with the Christian faith and most wonderful resignation of these peasants, all sorts of fanaticisms, credulities, superstitions, cropped up in those villages in the famine belt and beyond. The presence, therefore, of a man bearing a remarkable likeness—no doubt—to the Tsar Nicholas, and speaking in terms of mysticism and allegory, and certainly of the old noble rank, whoever he was, did not need more than a suggestion—which the child Katinka had supplied—to convince these people that he was truly the former ruler of Russia, who had come among them in the guise of a beggar. That is my theory, though I confess Sacha ridicules it and swears that he recognised beyond all doubt the Tsar himself, whom he had seen as a child in the palace of the Kremlin.

"How beyond all doubt?" I asked him, and he said: "Because below his left ear there was a little mole which I had remarked when my father took me to the palace and held me up for the Tsar to bless."

After that first meeting Sacha went round often to Michael's house, in order to gaze at the stranger with reverent eyes and listen to his tales to Katinka—he knew all the legends of Russian history—and his simple talk to the child's parents. He had a habit of sighing deeply in the midst of his tales about the old saints and heroes, and sometimes fell into a kind of trancelike silence, when the tears dropped slowly from his eyes and fell in his beard. At those times no one dared to interrupt his thoughts, and presently he would seem to wake with a start and smile at Katinka, and say: "Where was I in that tale?"

Always at meal times he would eat only the tiniest morsel of that poor bread which they made out of apple leaves and straw, and even when the little cow was killed at last, he would eat none of its meat, but only dipped his bread in the gravy. It was wonderful that he could keep alive on such little food, and although the weakness of his body was visible, he still had strength enough to walk a little, unlike other men in the village—the blacksmith among them—who lay on their beds above the stoves hardly able to lift a hand because of their long hunger.

Sacha's visits to Michael's house became a mystery to Sonia the school-mistress, and it was her dear jealousy which caused this boy to break the secrecy which he had imposed upon his own lips as well as upon his mother and sister. How could he keep this secret from her when they had none other in the world?

It was six months before the famine that they had discovered their love, and found it gave them not only joy, so that all the misery of Russia under Bolshevik rule did not touch them any more, but also courage to face all else that might happen, and even death itself. All Sacha's poetry was written for Sonia. All the knowledge she had from the books she read after her drudgery in the little school house was poured into the letters she wrote him every day, though they were never posted, but slipped into his pocket between their embraces. Together they discussed all the problems of life and death and eternity, and because of the time in which they lived, the philosophy of this boy and girl was touched with the grim knowledge of man's cruelty, and the failure of all men's dreams of liberty and progress. Yet with the faith and hope of youth they believed in the future of Russia after this time of agony, in its regeneration and greatness.

"We shan't live to see it, my dear," said Sacha many times, but was comforted when Sonia touched his hand and said: "Not in the body, but in the spirit, my comrade."

When the famine began, Sacha tightened his belt and hoarded up some of his own rations so that Sonia might not starve. But then he found that she was already starving herself by saving her rations for him. Only by entreaties and quarrels could they agree to eat enough to keep themselves alive so long as any food remained. This love story in the heart of the famine seemed to me one of the most touching and pitiful tales I have heard, and it was Sacha himself who told me, with that lack of self-consciousness and that simplicity which are the source of charm in Russian character.

It was after the fourth night that Sonia came round to Sacha's house. They met in the street, there, with a slight snow falling on them so that their fur caps were whitened.

He saw by her face that the girl had been weeping, and his heart felt a stab of guiltiness. Yet she smiled at him and spoke lightly.

"You look older since I last saw you, Sacha. Is it four nights or four years since we met?"

He stared down at his feet in the snow, afraid to meet her candid eyes. Yet after that moment of thought he knew that he must tell her the secret that had kept him away from her, or be unloyal to their love.

"Sonia," he said, "it is dangerous to know what I am going to tell you. It is the most perilous secret in Russia to-day, though its secrets are full of terror for those who keep them."

"Do not tell me that you have lost your love for me," she answered. "I could bear any secret but that."

He put his arm round her shoulder.

"Not that. That is impossible. But what I have to tell you is hardly less incredible. So unbelievable that even now I dare not tell you lest you should think me mad."

"What you tell me, I believe," she said, simply and gravely.

He told her then.

"A stranger has come to this village. He is a man whom all of us believed to be dead. A man betrayed by all his friends, and hated by all the world. He would be killed like a rat if they found him now, though he is innocent of all evil, I am certain."

"Is it Christ that has risen again?" asked Sonia, with a strange look at Sacha.

He was profoundly startled by those words. He, too, had wondered if Christ would come to Lubimovka before the ending of the world.

"Not that," he said. "But the stranger who has come was the ruler of all our people, and loved them, though he was powerless to help them. In Michael's house, lying on the boards, half dead with hunger, is he who was the Tsar. I have seen him and talked with him. I have no doubt."

"And you are not mad?" asked Sonia.

"No, I am not mad."

"Then I believe," she said.

Sacha led her into his house, and took off her shawl after the door was closed, and spoke to his mother and sister.

"I have told Sonia, and she believes."

"Then there is one more to be hanged when the Soviet knows," said Lydia, his crippled sister, and her voice had a sharp fear in it.

While they were talking in the darkness, without even one candle, because there was no more fat or oil, there was a knock at the door.

"Who is there?" called Sacha sharply, and from outside a quiet voice answered:

"Nicholas Alexandrovitch, the beggar."

Sacha opened the door, and across the threshold came the bearded man who wore a hidden star under his ragged vest. He carried Michael's lantern, and swayed a little as he stood on the threshold.

"My dear friends," he said, "I come for the sake of my little comrade, Katinka. She is stricken with typhus, and her mother asks for Sonia the schoolmistress, who saved the child of Boris the blacksmith."

Sonia moved across the room until she was touched with the rays of the lantern shining across the threshold.

"I am Sonia," she said. "I will go to the child."

"It is brave of you," said the man with the lantern. "The women of Russia have the spirit of Christ in their hearts. God will forgive the sins of their men after this time of punishment."

Sacha's mother, who had once been a lady of the Imperial Court in Moscow, though now she was like a gipsy, with dirty hands because she did rough work and there was no soap in Lubimovka, rose from her chair and faltered across the room, with her dark eyes staring at the man with the lantern. Then she uttered a shrill cry and fell to her knees before the stranger, and clasped his hands and wept over them.

"Do not kneel before me," he said. "I am Nicholas the beggar. An outcast and a sinner."

He beckoned to Sonia, and said: "Come, for my little comrade, Katinka, is very ill."

He held the lantern while she put on her shawl again, and led her out into the snow.

Sacha bent over his mother, and raised her from the floor.

"It is true, then?" he asked, and she said: "It is his face and voice."

It was through Anna, the wife of Michael, that the story was spread in Lubimovka. In her distraction because of Katinka's fever she talked wildly to her neighbours, and from cottage to cottage there passed the whisper that the stranger in the village was the man whom the world believed to be dead. Little groups of peasants gathered outside Michael's house, where Katinka lay tossing in her little bed by the stove, and they peered through the windows for a glimpse of the stranger who sat by the side of the child whom he called his little comrade. They whispered together, and one old woman said: "Perhaps he has come to rescue us from famine. God will listen to his prayers."

Another said: "He has but to touch the child, and she will be well."

Others said: "It is certainly the Little Father. But he will be taken and killed if we do not keep his secret."

It was a bad way of keeping a secret, this gathering outside Michael's house. Vladimir, the Soviet agent, saw them there and questioned them. One toothless old woman who hated him spat on the ground, and said: "All you Bolshevik devils will soon be hanged as you deserve. Our Tsar is back again."

"What does the old fool say?" asked Vladimir, with a black look. He was not haggard and thin like the other men in Lubimovka. As the Soviet agent he had first share of food sent down from Moscow at the beginning of the famine. It was believed that he had hoarded many sacks of potatoes which belonged to the commune. He was feared as well as hated, because he was in the pay of the *Cheka*—the secret police—and could send people to their death if he had a grudge against them.

Now they tried to cover up the words of the old woman, Kakoshka. "She has lost her wits with her last tooth!"

"She is the mother of imbeciles!"

But another woman in the crowd shouted at Vladimir:

"It is true what she says. Our Little Father has come to Lubimovka. Lenin had better look out for himself, and all his murderers."

Vladimir scowled round on the peasants.

"You people have all gone daft. If you weren't all starving to death, I would have you sent to the prisons in Moscow."

He strode away down the village, but he must have made it his business to find out more about the story, for that night he came to Michael's house with Braunberg, the Jew, and the girl, Sara. They were the only Communists in Lubimovka, where the peasants had no love for that philosophy.

Sonia was there, mixing some medicine for the child Katinka, whose thin little face was scarlet as she lay unconscious. Michael and his wife were sitting at their bare board weeping, with their heads on their arms, because their child was very near death. At the side of the stove the bearded stranger sat with his hands clasped on his knees and pity in his eyes as he watched Katinka.

Vladimir and his two companions came in noisily, without knocking at the door.

Michael raised his head and said: "What do you want, *Tavarish?*"

"I want to see the stranger in your house," said Vladimir.

"I am here," said the man who called himself Nicholas Alexandrovitch.

Vladimir stared at him and spoke roughly:

"What's your name? Who are you?"

"I am Nicholas, a wandering beggar."

"Where do you come from?"

The bearded man smiled, and raised his hand towards the west.

"I have been through many villages of Russia, always wandering in search of death. But I have not found it yet."

Vladimir laughed harshly.

"It's easy to find in Russia, to most men. Death! This village stinks with it."

"And this house," said Sara, the daughter of the Jew. "I do not like the smell of typhus. Let's get out of here, Vladimir. There is no harm in this man."

Vladimir stared at the stranger again.

"You had better get on with your wandering, old father," he said. "The sooner you're out of Lubimkova the better for you, or you'll find death sooner than you expect. There are crazy folk here who take you for the dead Tsar. It is not good to be taken for a ghost. It leads to trouble."

"That is true," said the man. "I will go away. I do not wish to lead the people into trouble. They have had enough."

Vladimir spoke less harshly.

"Well, I will give you a day or two. It's not your fault, old man, that the people here are daft with hunger and misery. Not their fault either, poor wretches."

Suddenly Sonia drew back from Katinka's bedside and gave a little cry. But a louder cry came from Anna, the mother of the child. She sprang up from her chair by the table and raised both hands above her head, and then fell with a piercing cry by the side of Katinka's little bed.

Nicholas the beggar, rose also from his chair and crossed himself. Then he put his hand on the shoulder of Michael and said: "It is well with the child. She is dead. God is merciful."

"Let us get out of here," said Sara the Jewess.

Vladimir and Braunberg and the woman were quick to get away from this house into which death had come so suddenly.

That evening when Sacha came round to take Sonia back to her house, he found only Nicholas the beggar in the front room. Little Katinka had been carried into the inner room, and Michael and Anna were praying with Sonia the schoolmistress.

The stranger was pacing up and down with his hands clasped behind his back. When he saw Sacha cross the threshold he smiled, and put his fingers to his lips for silence.

"My little comrade has gone ahead of me," he said in a quiet voice. "So many of my comrades have gone before me! I feel lonely as I wander."

"My Lord," said Sacha, "when is there going to be an end of all this misery? When are you coming back again so that Russia may be saved?"

"It is not through me that Russia can be saved," said the man. "Russia must save herself, after much agony and punishment for sin. We are being punished. Our poor Russia is suffering for the sins of our fathers. But her soul lives in these peasant folk. It is by their faith and charity that Russia will be saved."

"One day you will come back," said Sacha, with a kind of sob.

The bearded man shook his head.

"My end is near at hand. The end of my journey is close upon me. I shall be glad to rest at last."

Sacha has not told me all that was spoken between them that night. There are some things that he keeps secret still, but it seems that the stranger spoke in a kind of vision of the future that would come to Russia, and of a splendid destiny. Then, later, he put his hand below his ragged vest and pulled out the jewelled star, and slipped the silver chain over his head and gave the star to Sacha.

"This is all the wealth I have left in the world," he said. "I kept it as a holy relic, for it belonged to my ancestors and to one dear saint. But it is better to buy some food with it for these poor people here. If you can get as far as Moscow, it is likely that you could sell it for some grain. There are people still who covet such glittering stones."

"Moscow is a world away," said Sacha. "I could not get there or come back again."

"Then my star is worthless," said Nicholas, and his head drooped a little.

But he would not take it back again, and that night, when Sacha went back with Sonia, he carried the star in his breast pocket and it seemed to burn above his heart.

There was heavy snow next day, and Sacha bent his head to the storm when early in the morning he trudged round to Michael's house. All through the night he had lain awake, thinking of the star which lay under his pillow and of the man who had given it into his keeping. He had determined to make the journey to Moscow for the sake of the people of Lubimovka. If he could sell the star he might bring back food enough to save many lives. But before going he wanted to see its owner again, so that he might take a message from him to people in Moscow who believed him to be dead. The boy was on fire with faith and hope, so that he did not feel the coldness of the snow as it fell in flakes upon his face. He had an absolute faith that this man in Michael's house was he who had been Tsar of All the Russias, and Sacha was persuaded that it was a miracle which might lead Russia out of the depths and save her people.

On the threshold of Michael's house he saw the little coffin of Katinka being carried out on her father's shoulders. Behind, with her shawl over her face and shoulders, walked the poor wife Anna, and some peasant women who were wailing with her. Last of all came Sonia, weeping.

Sacha went up to the girl whom he loved before any in the world, and touched her on the arm.

"Where is the stranger?" he asked.

"He has gone," said Sonia. "He went way just now, after kissing Katinka before her coffin was closed. See, there are his footsteps in the snow."

Sacha gave a queer cry.

"I must follow him! I must speak with him again."

"The snow will hide his footsteps," said Sonia. "You will never follow his track."

But Sacha left her and hurried over the snow, where, very clearly at first, were the footmarks in the snow of a man with a long stride. They led up the village street to the gate in the stockade on the northern side, and then beyond to the flat, open country, until they disappeared beneath the snow which was falling thickly now. Sacha stumbled forward through the snow, which a light wind blew upon his breast and cap. He could hardly see a yard ahead, and he called out many times:

"My Lord! My Lord!" But no voice answered him. The stranger had disappeared into that white world of swirling flakes. Presently Sacha stood still, and then retraced his steps with his head bent.

Nicholas Alexandrovitch had gone on his journey again in search of death, and in Lubimovka he was not seen again.

Sacha kept the star, which was the only proof of a visit which otherwise might have seemed a dream. There was no need to go to Moscow to barter it for bread and potatoes, because the world had heard at last the cry of a starving people, and help came from England and the United States after many had died in Lubimovka, and all the villages of the Volga valley. It was at that time, and with some American relief officers, that I met Sacha and Sonia and heard their strange tale of the man with the star. It was Sonia the schoolmistress who was put in charge of the first soup kitchen, and it was good to see her joy when the children were fed.

"If only little Katinka could be here!" she murmured, and then said some words which I could not understand.

"It was the Little Father who brought us this good luck. God heard his prayers for the Russian people."

"Whom do you call the Little Father?" I asked, and it was then, from this girl and from Sacha, who spoke good English, that I heard the story I have now written. It seemed to me then as it seems to me now—utterly fantastic. Not for a moment do I believe that it was the Tsar of All the Russias who came to Lubimovka as a wandering beggar. Doubtless it was some Russian gentleman of the old *régime,* perhaps with some distant touch of kinship with the Tsar which would account for his likeness.

But neither Sacha nor Sonia, nor any of the people of Lubimovka, will listen to any theory of that kind. It was the Tsar himself, they say, and perhaps a hundred years hence this legend will still be believed in the Volga Valley, where already the jewelled star is kept as a relic and a proof of what is unbelievable.

53

The Higgler

BY A. E. COPPARD

ON a cold April afternoon a higgler was driving across Shag Moor in a two-wheeled cart.

H. WITLOW
Dealer in Poultry
DINNOP

was painted on the hood; the horse was of mean appearance but notorious ancestry. A high upland common was this moor, two miles from end to end, and full of furze and bracken. There were no trees and not a house, nothing but a line of telegraph poles following the road, sweeping with rigidity from north to south; nailed upon one of them a small scarlet notice to stone-throwers was prominent as a wound. On so high and wide a region as Shag Moor the wind always blew, or if it did not quite blow there was a cool activity in the air. The furze was always green and growing, and, taking no account of seasons, often golden. Here in summer solitude lounged and snoozed; at other times, as now, it shivered and looked sinister.

Higglers in general are ugly and shrewd, old and hard, crafty and callous, but Harvey Witlow, though shrewd, was not ugly; he was hard but not old, crafty but not at all unkind. If you had eggs to sell he would buy them, by the score he would, or by the long hundred. Other odds and ends he would buy or do, paying good bright silver, bartering a bag of apples, carrying your little pig to market, or fetching a tree from the nurseries. But the season was backward, eggs were scarce, trade was bad—by crumps, it was indeed!—and as he crossed the moor Harvey could not help discussing the situation with himself.

"If things don't change, and change for the better, and change

761

soon, I can't last and I can't endure it; I'll be damned and done and I'll have to sell," he said, prodding the animal with the butt of his whip, "this cob. And," he said, as if in afterthought, prodding the footboard, "this cart, and go back to the land. And I'll have lost my fifty pounds. Well, that's what war does for you. It does it for you, sir," he announced sharply to the vacant moor, "and it does it for me. Fifty pounds! I was better off in the war. I was better off working for farmers—much. But it's no good chattering about it, it's the trick of life; when you get so far, then you can go and order your funeral. Get along, Dodger!"

The horse responded briskly for a few moments.

"I tell ye," said Harvey adjuring the ambient air, "you can go and order your funeral. Get along Dodger!"

Again Dodger got along.

"Then there's Sophy, what about Sophy and me?"

He was not engaged to Sophy Daws, not exactly, but he was keeping company with her. He was not pledged or affianced, he was just keeping company with her. But Sophy, as he knew, not only desired a marriage with Mr. Witlow, she expected it, and expected it soon. So did her parents, her friends, and everybody in the village, including the postman who didn't live in it but wished he did, and the parson who did live in it but wished he didn't.

"Well, that's damned and done, fair damned and done now, unless things take a turn, and soon, so it's no good chattering about it."

And just then and there things did take a turn. He had never been across the moor before; he was prospecting for trade. At the end of Shag Moor he saw standing back on the common, fifty yards from the road, a neat square house set in a little farm. Twenty acres, perhaps. The house was girded by some white palings; beside it was a snug orchard in a hedge covered with blackthorn bloom. It was very green and pleasant in front of the house. The turf was cleared and closely cropped, some ewes were grazing and under the blackthorn, out of the wind, lay half a dozen lambs, but what chiefly moved the imagination of Harvey Witlow was a field on the far side of the house. It had a small rickyard with a few small stacks in it; everything here seemed on the small scale, but snug, very snug; and in that field and yard were hundreds of fowls, hundreds, of good breed, and mostly white. Leaving his horse to sniff the greensward, the higgler entered a white wicket gateway and passed to the back of the house, noting as he did so a yellow waggon inscribed *Elizabeth Sadgrove, Prattle Corner*.

At the kitchen door he was confronted by a tall gaunt woman of middle age with a teapot in her hands.

"Afternoon, ma'am. Have you anything to sell?" began Harvey Witlow, tilting his hat with a confident, affable air. The tall woman was cleanly dressed, a superior person; her hair was grey. She gazed at him.

"It's cold," he continued. She looked at him as uncomprehendingly as a mouse might look at a gravestone.

"I'll buy any mottal thing, ma'am. Except trouble; I'm full up wi' that already. Eggs? Fowls?"

"I've not seen you before," commented Mrs. Sadgrove a little bleakly, in a deep husky voice.

"No, 'tis the first time as ever I drove in this part. To tell you the truth, ma'am, I'm new to the business. Six months. I was in the war a year ago. Now I'm trying to knock up a connection. Difficult work. Things are very quiet."

Mrs. Sadgrove silently removed the lid of the teapot, inspected the interior of the pot with an intent glance, and then replaced the lid as if she had seen a blackbeetle there.

"Ah, well," sighed the higgler. "You've a neat little farm here, ma'am."

"It's quiet enough," said she.

"Sure it is, ma'am. Very lonely."

"And it's difficult work, too." Mrs. Sadgrove almost smiled.

"Sure it is, ma'am; but you does it well, I can see. Oh, you've some nice little ricks of corn, eh! I does well enough at the dealing now and again, but it's teasy work, and mostly I don't earn enough to keep my horse in shoe leather."

"I've a few eggs, perhaps," said she.

"I could do with a score or two, ma'am, if you could let me have 'em."

"You'll have to come all my way if I do."

"Name your own price, ma'am, if you don't mind trading with me."

"Mind! Your money's as good as my own, isn't it?"

"It must be, ma'am. That's meaning no disrespects to you," the young higgler assured her hastily, and was thereupon invited to enter the kitchen.

A stone floor with two or three mats; open hearth with burning logs; a big dresser painted brown, carrying a row of white cups on brass hooks and shelves of plates overlapping each other like the scales of fish. A dark settle half hid the flight of stairs with a small gate at the top. Under the window a black sofa, deeply indented, invited you a little repellingly, and in the middle of the room stood a large table, exquisitely scrubbed, with one end of it laid for tea. Evidently a living-room as well as kitchen. A girl, making toast at the fire, turned as the higgler entered. Beautiful she was: red hair, a complexion like the inside of a nut, blue eyes, and the hands of a lady. He saw it all at once, jacket of bright green wool, black dress, grey stockings and shoes, and forgot his errand, her mother, his fifty pounds, Sophy—momentarily he forgot everything. The girl stared strangely at him. He was tall, clean-shaven, with a loop of black hair curling handsomely over one side of his brow.

"Good afternoon," said Harvey Witlow, as softly as if he had entered a church.

"Some eggs, Mary," Mrs. Sadgrove explained. The girl laid down her toasting-fork. She was less tall than her mother, whom she resembled only enough for the relationship to be noted. Silently she crossed the kitchen and opened a door that led into a dairy. Two pans of milk were creaming on a bench there. and on the flags were two great baskets filled with eggs.

"How many are there?" asked Mrs. Sadgrove, and the girl replied: "Fifteen score, I think."

"Take the lot, higgler?"

"Yes, ma'am," he cried eagerly, and ran out to his cart and fetched a number of trays. In them he packed the eggs as the girl handed them to him from the baskets. Mrs. Sadgrove left them together. For a time the higgler was silent.

"No," at length he murmured, "I've never been this road before."

There was no reply from Mary. Sometimes their fingers touched, and often, as they bent over the eggs, her bright hair almost brushed his face.

"It is a loneish spot," he ventured again.

"Yes," said Mary Sadgrove.

When the eggs were all transferred her mother came in again.

"Would you buy a few pullets, higgler?"

"Any number, ma'am," he declared quickly. Any number; by crumps, the tide was turning! He followed the mother into the yard, and there again she left him, waiting. He mused about the girl and wondered about the trade. If they offered him ten thousand chicken, he'd buy them, somehow, he would! She had stopped in the kitchen. Just in there she was, just behind him, a few feet away. Over the low wall of the yard a fat black pony was strolling in a field of bright greensward. In the yard, watching him, was a young gander, and on a stone staddle beside it lay a dead thrush on its back, its legs stiff in the air. The girl stayed in the kitchen; she was moving about, though, he could hear her; perhaps she was spying at him through the window. Twenty million eggs he would buy if Mrs. Sadgrove had got them. She was gone a long time. It was very quiet. The gander began to comb its white breast with its beak. Its three-toed feet were a most tender pink, shaped like wide diamonds, and at each of the three forward points there was a toe like a small blanched nut. It lifted one foot, holding the webs, and hid it under its wing and sank into a resigned meditation on one leg. It had a blue eye that was meek—it had two, but you could only see one at a time—a meek blue eye, set in a pink rim that gave it a dissolute air, and its beak had raw red nostrils as if it suffered from the damp. Altogether a beautiful bird. And in some absurd way it resembled Mrs. Sadgrove.

"Would you sell that young gollan, ma'am?" Harvey inquired when the mother returned.

Yes, she would sell him, and she also sold him two dozen pullets. Harvey packed the fowls in a crate.

"Come on," he cried, cuddling the squawking gander in his arms, "you needn't be afeared of me, I never kills anything afore Saturdays."

He roped it by its leg to a hook inside his cart. Then he took out his bag of money, paid Mrs. Sadgrove her dues, said "Good day, ma'am, good day," and drove off without seeing another sign or stitch of that fine young girl.

"Get along, Dodger, get along wi' you." They went bowling along for nearly an hour, and then he could see the landmark on Dan'el Green's Hill, a windmill that never turned, though it looked a fine competent piece of architecture, just beyond Dinnop.

Soon he reached his cottage and was chaffing his mother, a hearty buxom dame, who stayed at home and higgled with any chance callers. At this business she was perhaps more enlightened than her son. It was almost a misfortune to get into her clutches.

"How much you give for this?" he cried, eyeing with humorous contempt an object in a coop that was neither flesh nor rude red herring.

"O crumps," he declared, when she told him, "I am damned and done!"

"Go on with you, that's a good bird, I tell you, with a full heart, as will lay in a month."

"I doubt it's a hen at all," he protested. "Oh, what a ravenous beak! Damned and done I am."

Mrs. Witlow's voice began indignantly to rise.

"Oh, well," mused her son, "it's thrifty perhaps. It ain't quite right, but it's not so wrong as to make a fuss about, especially as I be pretty sharp set. And if it's hens you want," he continued triumphantly, dropping the crate of huddled fowls before her, "there's hens for you; and a gander! There's a gander for you, if it's a gander you want."

Leaving them all in his cottage yard he went and stalled the horse and cart at the inn, for he had no stable of his own. After supper he told his mother about the Sadgroves of Prattle Corner. "Prettiest girl you ever seen, but the shyest mottal alive. Hair like a squirrel, lovey."

"Ain't you got to go over and see Sophy to-night?" inquired his mother, lighting the lamp.

"Oh, lord, if I ain't clean forgot that! Well, I'm tired, shan't go to-night. See her to-morrow."

Mrs. Sadgrove had been a widow for ten years—and she was glad of it. Prattle Corner was her property, she owned it and farmed it with the aid of a little old man and a large lad. The older this old man grew, and the less wages he received (for Elizabeth Sadgrove was reputed a "grinder"), the more ardently he worked; the older the lad grew the less he laboured and the more he swore. She was thriving. She was worth money, was Mrs. Sadgrove. Ah! And her daughter Mary, it was clear, had received an education fit for a lord's lady; she had been at a seminary for gentlefolks' females until she was seventeen. Well, whether or no, a clock must run as you time it; but it wronged her for the work of a farm, it spoiled her, it completely deranged her for the work of a farm; and this was a pity and foolish, because some day the farm was coming to her as didn't know hay from a bull's foot.

All this, and more, the young higgler quickly learned, and plenty more he soon divined. Business began to flourish with him now; his despair was gone, he was established, he could look forward, to whatever it was he wanted to look forward, with equanimity and such pleasurable anticipation as the chances and charges of life might engender. Every week, and twice a week, he would call at the farm, and though these occasions had their superior business inducements they often borrowed a less formal tone and intention.

"Take a cup of tea, higgler?" Mrs. Sadgrove would abruptly invite him; and he would drink tea and discourse with her for half an hour on barndoor ornithology, on harness, and markets, the treatment of swine, the wear and tear of gear. Mary, always present, was always silent, seldom uttering a word to the higgler; yet a certain grace emanated from her to him, an interest, a light, a favour, circumscribed indeed by some modesty, shyness, some inhibition, that neither of them had the wit or the opportunity to overcome.

One evening he pulled up at the white palings of Prattle Corner. It was a calm evening in May, the sun was on its down-going, chaffinches and wrens sung ceaselessly. Mary in the orchard was heavily veiled; he could see her over the hedge, holding a brush in her gloved hands, and a bee skep. A swarm was clustered like a great gnarl on the limb of an apple tree. Bloom was thickly covering the twigs. She made several timid attempts to brush the bees into the skep, but they resented this.

"They knows if you be afraid of 'em," bawled Harvey; "I better come and give you a hand."

When he took the skep and brush from her she stood like one helpless, released by fate from a task ill-understood and gracelessly waived. But he liked her shyness, her almost uncouth immobility.

"Never mind about that," said Harvey, as she unfastened her veil, scattering the white petals that had collected upon it; "when they kicks they hurts, but I've been stung so often that I'm 'nocolated against 'em. They knows if you be afraid of 'em."

Wearing neither veil nor gloves he went confidently to the tree, and collected the swarm without mishap.

"Don't want to show no fear of them," said Harvey. "Nor of anything else, come to that," he added with a guffaw, "nor anybody."

At that she blushed and thanked him very softly, and she did look straight and clearly at him.

Never anything beyond a blush and a thank-you. When, in the kitchen, or the parlour, Mrs. Sadgrove sometimes left them alone together Harvey would try a lot of talk, blarneying talk or sensible talk, or talk about events in the world that was neither the one nor the other. No good. The girl's responses were ever brief and confused. Why was this? Again and again he asked himself that question. Was there anything the matter with her? Nothing that you could see; she was a bright and beautiful being. And it was not contempt, either, for despite her fright, her voicelessness, her timid eyes, he devined her friendly feeling for himself; and he would discourse to his own mother about her and her mother:

"They are well-up people, you know, well-off, plenty of money and nothing to do with it. The farm's their own, freehold. A whole row of cottages she's got, too, in Smoorton Confrey, so I heard; good cottages, well let. She's worth a few thousands, I warrant. Mary's beautiful. I took a fancy to that girl the first moment I see her. But she's very highly cultivated—and, of course, there's Sophy."

To this enigmatic statement Mrs. Whitlow offered no response; but mothers are inscrutable beings to their sons, always.

Once he bought some trees of cherries from Mrs. Sadgrove, and went on a July morning to pick the fruit. Under the trees Mary was walking slowly to and fro, twirling a clapper to scare away the birds. He stood watching her from the gateway. Among the bejewelled trees she passed, turning the rattle with a listless air, as if beating time to a sad music that only she could hear. The man knew that he was deeply fond of her. He passed into the orchard, bade her Good-morning, and, lifting his ladder into one of the trees nearest the hedge, began to pluck cherries. Mary moved slimly in her white frock up and down a shady avenue in the orchard waving the clapper. The brightness of sun and sky was almost harsh; there was a little wind that feebly lifted the despondent leaves. He had doffed his coat; his shirt was white and clean. The lock of dark hair drooped over one side of his forehead; his face was brown and pleasant, his bare arms brown and powerful. From his high perch among the leaves Witlow watched for the girl to draw near to him in her perambulation. Knavish birds would scatter at her approach, only to drop again into the trees she had passed. His soul had an immensity of longing for her, but she never spoke a word to him. She would come from the shade of the little avenue, through the dumb trees that could only bend to greet her, into the sunlight whose dazzle gilded her own triumphant bloom. Fine! Fine! And always as she passed his mind refused to register a single thought he could offer her, or else his tongue would refuse to utter it. But his glance never left her face until she had passed out of sight again, and then he would lean against the ladder in the tree, staring down at the ground, seeing nothing or less than nothing, except a field mouse climbing to the top of a conventry bush in the hedge below him, nipping off one thick leaf and descending with the leaf in its mouth. Sometimes Mary rested at the other end of the avenue; the clapper would be silent and she would not appear for —oh, hours! She never rested near the trees Witlow was denuding. The mouse went on ascending and descending, and Witlow filled his basket and shifted his stand, and wondered.

At noon he got down and sat on the hedge bank to eat a snack of lunch. Mary had gone indoors for hers, and he was alone for a while. Capriciously enough, his thoughts dwelt upon Sophy Daws. Sophy was a fine girl, too; not such as lady as Mary Sadgrove—oh, lord, no! Her father was a gamekeeper!—but she was jolly and ample. She had been a little captious lately, said he was neglecting her. That wasn't true; hadn't he been busy? Besides, he wasn't bound to her in any sort of way, and, of course, he couldn't afford any marriage yet awhile. Sophy hadn't got any money, never had any. What she did with her wages—she was a parlourmaid—was a teaser! Harvey grunted a little, and said "Well!" And that is all he said, and all he thought, about Sophy Daws, then, for he could hear Mary's clapper begin again in a corner of the orchard. He went back to his work. There at the foot of the tree were the baskets full of cherries, and those yet to be filled.

"Phew, but that's hot!" commented the man, "I'm as dry as a rattle."

A few cherries had spilled from one basket and lay on the ground. The little furry mouse had found them and was industriously nibbling at one. The higgler nonchalantly stamped his foot upon it, and kept it so for a moment or two. Then he looked at the dead mouse. A tangle of entrails had gushed from its whiskered muzzle.

He resumed his work and the clapper rattled on throughout the afternoon, for there were other cherry trees that other buyers would come to strip in a day or two. At four o'clock he was finished. Never a word had he spoken with Mary, or she with him. When he went over to the house to pay Mrs. Sadgrove, Mary stopped in the orchard scaring the birds.

"Take a cup of tea, Mr. Witlow," said Mrs. Sadgrove; and then she surprisingly added, "Where's Mary?"

"Still a-frightening the birds, and pretty well tired of that, I should think, ma'am."

The mother had poured out three cups of tea.

"Shall I go and call her in?" he asked rising.

"You might," said she.

In the orchard the clappering had ceased. He walked all round, and in among the trees, but saw no sign of Mary; nor on the common, nor in the yard. But when he went back to the house Mary was there already, chatting at the table with her mother. She did not greet him, though she ceased talking to her mother as he sat down. After drinking his tea he went off briskly to load the baskets into the cart. As he climbed up to drive off, Mrs. Sadgrove came out and stood beside the horse.

"You're off now?" said she.

"Yes, ma'am; all loaded, and thank you."

She glanced vaguely along the road he had to travel. The afternoon was as clear as wine, the greensward itself dazzled him; lonely Shag Moor stretched away, humped with sweet yellow furze and pilastered with its telegraph poles. No life there, no life at all. Harvey sat on his driving board, musingly brushing the flank of the horse with the trailing whip.

"Ever round this way on Sundays?" inquired the woman, peering up at him.

"Well, not in a manner of speaking, I'm not, ma'am," he answered her.

The widow laid her hand on the horse's back, patting vaguely. The horse pricked up its ears, as if it were listening.

"If you are, at all, ever, you must look in and have a bit of dinner with us."

"I will, ma'am, I will."

"Next Sunday?" she went on.

"I will, ma'am, yes, I will," he repeated, "and thank you."

"One o'clock?" The widow smiled up at him.

"At one o'clock, ma'am; next Sunday; I will, and thank you," he said.

She stood away from the horse and waved her hand. The first tangible thought that floated mutely out of the higgler's mind as he drove away was: "I'm damned if I ain't a-going it, Sophy!"

He told his mother of Mrs. Sadgrove's invitation with an air of curbed triumph. "Come round—she says. Yes—I says—I 'ull. That's right—she says—so do!"

On the Sunday morn he dressed himself gallantly. It was again a sweet unclouded day. The church bell at Dinnop had begun to ring. From his window, as he fastened his most ornate tie, Harvey could observe his neighbour's two small children in the next garden, a boy and girl clad for church-going and each carrying a clerical book. The tiny boy placed his sister in front of a hen-roost and, opening his book, began to pace to and fro before her, shrilly intoning: "Jesus is the shepherd, ring the bell. Oh lord, ring the bell, am I a good boy? Amen. Oh lord, ring the bell." The little girl bowed her head piously over her book. The lad then picked up from the ground a dish which had contained the dog's food, and presented it momentarily before the lilac bush, the rabbit in a hutch, the axe fixed in a chopping block, and then before his sister. Without lifting her peering gaze from her book she meekly dropped two pebbles in the plate, and the boy passed on, lightly moaning, to the clothes-line post and a cock scooping in some dust.

"Ah, the little impets!" cried Harvey Witlow. "Here Toby! Here, Margaret!" He took two pennies from his pocket and lobbed them from the window to the astonished children. As they stooped to pick up the coins Harvey heard the hoarse voice of neighbour Nathan, their father, bawl from his kitchen: "Come on in, and shut that bloody door, d'y'ear!"

Harnessing his moody horse to the gig, Harvey was soon bowling away to Shag Moor, and as he drove along he sung loudly. He had a pink rose in his buttonhole. Mrs. Sadgrove received him almost affably, and though Mary was more shy than ever before, Harvey had determined to make an impression. During the dinner he fired off his bucolic jokes, and pleasant tattle of a more respectful and sober nature; but after dinner Mary sat like Patience, not upon a monument, but as if upon a rocking-horse, shy and fearful, and her mother made no effort to inspire her as the higgler did, unsuccessful though he was. They went to the pens to look at the pigs, and as they leaned against the low walls and poked the maudlin inhabitants, Harvey began: "Reminds me, when I was in the war . . ."

"Were you in the war!" interrupted Mrs. Sadgrove.

"Oh, yes, I was in that war, ah, and there was a pig. . . . Danger? Oh lord, bless me, it was a bit dangerous, but you never knew where it was or what it 'ud be at next; it was like the sword of Damockels. There was a bullet once come 'ithin a foot of my head, and it went through a board an inch thick, slap through that board." Both women gazed at him apprehendingly. "Why I might 'a been killed, you know," said Harvey, cocking his eye musingly at the weather-vane on the barn. "We was in billets at St. Gratien, and one day a chasseur came up—a French yoossar, you know—and he began talking to our sergeant. That was Hubert Luxter, the butcher: died a month or two ago of measles. But this yoossar couldn't speak English at all, and none of us chaps could make sense of him. I never could understand that lingo somehow, never; and though there was half a dozen of us chaps, there, none of us were man enough for it neither. 'Nil compree,' we says, 'non compos.' I told him straight: 'You ought to learn English,' I said, 'it's much easier than your kind of bally chatter.' So he kept shaping up as if he was holding a rifle, and then he'd say 'Fusee —bang!' and then he'd say 'cushion'—kept on saying 'cushion.' Then he gets a bit of chalk and draws on the wall something that looks like a horrible dog, and says 'cushion' again."

"Pig," interjected Mary Sadgrove softly.

"Yes, yes!" ejaculated Harvey, "so 'twas! Do you know any French lingo?"

"Oh, yes," declared her mother, "Mary knows it very well."

"Ah," sighed the higgler. "I don't, although I been to France. And I couldn't do it now, not for luck nor love. You learnt it, I suppose. Well, this yoossar wants to borrow my rifle, but of course I can't lend him. So he taps on this horrible pig he'd drawn, and then he taps on his own head, and rolls his eyes about dreadful. 'Mad?' I says. And that was it, that was it. He'd got a pig on his little farm there what had gone mad, and he wanted us to come and shoot it; he was on leave and he hadn't got any ammunition. So Hubert Luxter he says, 'Come on, some of you,' and we all goes with the yoossar and shot the pig for him. Ah, that was a pig! And when it died it jumped a somersault just like a rabbit. It had got the mange, and was mad as anything I ever see in my life; it was full of madness. Couldn't hit him at all at first, and it kicked up bobs-a-dying. 'Ready, present, fire!' Hubert Luxter says, and bang goes the six of us, and every time we missed him he spotted us and we had to run for our lives."

As Harvey looked up he caught a glance of the girl fixed on him. She dropped her gaze at once, and, turning away, walked off to the house.

"Come and take a look at the meadow," said Mrs. Sadgrove to him, and they went into the soft smooth meadow where the black pony was grazing. Very bright and green it was, and very blue the sky. He sniffed at the pink rose in his buttonhole, and determined that come what might he would give it to Mary if he could get a nice quiet chance to offer it. And just then, while he and Mrs. Sadgrove were strolling alone in the soft smooth meadow, quite alone, she suddenly, startlingly, asked him: "Are you courting anybody?"

"Beg pardon, ma'am?" he exclaimed.

"You haven't got a sweetheart, have you?" she asked, most deliberately.

Harvey grinned sheepishly: "Ha, ha, ha," and then he said, "No."

"I want to see my daughter married," the widow went on, significantly.

"Miss Mary!" he cried.

"Yes," said she; and something in the higgler's veins began to pound rapidly. His breast might have been a revolving cage and his heart a demon squirrel. "I can't live for ever," said Mrs. Sadgrove, almost with levity, "in fact, not for long, and so I'd like to see her settled soon with some decent understanding young man, one that could carry on here, and not make a mess of things."

"But, but," stuttered the understanding young man, "I'm no scholar, and she's a lady. I'm a poor chap, rough, and no scholar, ma'am. But mind you . . ."

"That doesn't matter at all," the widow interrupted, "not as things are. You want a scholar for learning, but for the land . . ."

"Ah, that's right, Mrs. Sadgrove, but . . ."

"I want to see her settled. This farm, you know, with the stock and things are worth nigh upon three thousand pounds."

"You want a farmer for farming, that's true, Mrs. Sadgrove, but when you come to marriage, well, with her learning and French and all that . . .!"

"A sensible woman will take a man rather than a box of tricks any day of the week," the widow retorted. "Education may be a fine thing, but it often costs a lot of foolish money."

"It do, it do. You want to see her settled?"

"I want to see her settled and secure. When she is twenty-five she comes into five hundred pounds of her own right."

The distracted higgler hummed and haa-ed in his bewilderment as if he had just been offered the purchase of a dubious duck. "How old is she, ma'am?" he at last huskily inquired.

"Two-and-twenty nearly. She's a good healthy girl, for I've never spent a pound on a doctor for her, and very quiet she is, and very sensible; but she's got a strong will of her own, though you might not think it or believe it."

"She's a fine creature, Mrs. Sadgrove, and I'm very fond of her, I don't mind owning up to that, very fond of her I am."

"Well, think it over, take your time, and see what you think. There's no hurry I hope, please God."

"I shan't want much time," he declared with a laugh, "but I doubt I'm the fair right sort for her."

"Oh, fair days, fair doings!" said she inscrutably. "I'm not a long liver, I'm afraid."

"God forbid, ma'am!" His ejaculation was intoned with deep gravity.

"No, I'm not a long-living woman." She surveyed him with her calm eyes, and he returned her gaze. Hers was a long sallow face, with heavy lips. Sometimes she would stretch her features (as if to keep them from petrifying) in an elastic grin, and display her dazzling teeth; the lips would curl thickly, no longer crimson, but blue. He wondered if there were any sign of a doom registered upon her gaunt face. She might die, and die soon.

"You couldn't do better than think it over, then, eh?" She had a queer frown as she regarded him.

"I couldn't do worse than not, Mrs. Sadgrove," he said gaily.

They left it at that. He had no reason for hurrying away, and he couldn't have explained his desire to do so, but he hurried away. Driving along past the end of the moor, and peering back at the lonely farm where they dwelled amid the thick furze snoozing in the heat, he remembered that he had not asked if Mary was willing to marry him! Perhaps the widow took her agreement for granted. That would be good fortune, for otherwise how the devil was he to get round a girl who had never spoken half a dozen words to him! And never would! She was a lady, a girl of fortune, knew her French; but there it was, the girl's own mother was asking him to wed her. Strange, very strange! He dimly feared something, but he did not know what it was he feared. He had still got the pink rose in his buttonhole.

At first his mother was incredulous; when he told her of the astonishing proposal she declared he was a joker; but she was soon as convinced of his sincerity as she was amazed at his hesitation. And even vexed: "Was there anything the matter with this Mary?"

"No, no, no! She's quiet, very quiet, indeed, I tell you, but a fine young woman, and a beautiful young woman. Oh, she's all right, right as rain, right as a trivet, right as ninepence. But there's a catch in it somewhere, I fear. I can't see through it yet, but I shall afore long, or I'd have the girl, like a shot I would. 'Tain't the girl, mother, it's the money, if you understand me."

"Well, I don't understand you, certainly I don't. What about Sophy?"

"Oh lord!" He scratched his head ruefully.

"You wouldn't think of giving this the go-by for Sophy, Harvey, would you! A girl as you ain't even engaged to, Harvey, would you!"

"We don't want to chatter about that," declared her son. "I got to think it over, and it's going to tie my wool, I can tell you, for there's a bit of craft somewhere, I'll take my oath. If there ain't, there ought to be!"

Over the alluring project his decision wavered for days until his mother became mortified at his inexplicable vacillation.

"I tell you," he cried, "I can't make tops or bottoms of it all. I like the girl well enough, but I like Sophy, too, and it's no good beating about the bush. I like Sophy, she's the girl I love; but Mary's a fine creature, and money like that wants looking at before you throw it away, love or no love. Three thousand pounds! I'd be a made man."

And as if in sheer spite to his mother; as if a bushel of money lay on the doorstep for him to kick over whenever the fancy seized him; in short (as Mrs. Witlow very clearly intimated) as if in contempt of Providence, he began to pursue Sophy Daws with a new fervour, and walked with that young girl more than he was accustomed to, more than ever before; in fact, as his mother bemoaned, more than he had need to. It was unreasonable, it was a shame, a foolishness; it wasn't decent and it wasn't safe.

On his weekly visits to the farm his mind still wavered. Mrs. Sadgrove let him alone; she was very good, she did not pester him with questions and entreaties. There was Mary with her white dress and her red hair and her silence; a girl with a great fortune, walking about the yard, or sitting in the room, and casting not a glance upon him. Not that he would have known it if she did, for now he was just as shy as she. Mrs. Sadgrove often left them alone, but when they were alone he could not dish up a word for the pretty maid; he was dumb as a statue. If either she or her mother had lifted so much as a finger then there would have been an end to his hesitations or suspicions, for in Mary's presence the fine glory of the girl seized him incontinently; he was again full of a longing to press her lips, to lay down his doubts, to touch her bosom—though he could not think she would ever allow that! Not an atom of doubt about *her* ever visited him; she was unaware of her mother's queer project. Rather, if she became aware he was sure it would be the end of him. Too beautiful she was, too learned, and too rich. Decidedly it was his native cunning, and no want of love, that inhibited him. Folks with property did not often come along and bid you help yourself. Not very often! And throw in a grand bright girl, just for good measure as you might say. Not very often!

For weeks the higgler made his customary calls, and each time the outcome was the same; no more, no less. "Some dodge," he mused, "something the girl don't know and the mother does." Were they going bankrupt, or were they mortgaged up to the neck, or was there anything the matter with the girl, or was it just the mother wanted to get hold of him? He knew his own value if he didn't know his own mind, and his value couldn't match that girl any more than his mind could. So what *did* they want him for? Whatever it was, Harvey Witlow was ready for it whenever he was in Mary's presence, but once away from her his own craftiness asserted itself: it was a snare, they were trying to make a mock of him!

But nothing could prevent his own mother mocking him, and her treatment of Sophy was so unbearable that if the heart of that dusky beauty had not been proof against all impediments, Harvey might have had to whistle for her favour. But whenever he was with Sophy he had only one heart, undivided and true, and certain as time itself. "I love Sophy best. It's true enough I love Mary, too, but I love Sophy better. I know it; Sophy's the girl I must wed. It might not be so if I weren't all dashed and doddered about the money; I don't know. But I do know that Mary's innocent of all this craftiness; it's her mother trying to mogue me into it."

Later he would be wishing he could only forget Sophy and do it. Without the hindrance of conscience he could do it, catch or no catch.

He went on calling at the farm, with nothing said or settled until October. Then Harvey made up his mind, and without a word to the Sadgroves he went and married Sophy Daws and gave up calling at the farm altogether. This gave him some feeling of dishonesty, some qualm, and a vague unhappiness; likewise he feared the cold hostility of Mrs. Sadgrove. She would be terribly vexed. As for Mary, he was nothing to her, poor girl; it was a shame. The last time he drove that way he did not call at the farm. Autumn was advancing, and the apples were down, the bracken dying, the furze out of bloom, and the farm on the moor looked more and more lonely, and most cold, though it lodged a flame-haired silent woman, fit for a nobleman, whom they wanted to mate with a common higgler. Crafty, you know, too crafty!

The marriage was a gay little occasion, but they did not go away for a honeymoon. Sophy's grandmother from a distant village, Cassandra Fundy, who had a deafness and a speckled skin, brought her third husband, Amos, whom the family had never seen before. Not a very wise man, indeed he was a common man, stooping like a decayed tree, he was so old. But he shaved every day and his hairless skull was yellow. Cassandra, who was yellow too, had long since turned into a fool; she did not shave, though she ought to have done. She was like to die soon, but everybody said old Amos would live to be a hundred; it was expected of him, and he, too, was determined. The guests declared that a storm was threatening, but Amos Fundy denied it and scorned it.

"Thunder p'raps, but 'twill clear; 'tis only de pride o' der morning."

"Don't you be a fool," remarked his wife enigmatically, "you'll die soon enough."

"You must behold der moon," continued the octogenarian; "de closer it is to der wheel, de closer der rain; de furder away it is, de furder der rain."

"You could pour that man's brains into a thimble," declared Cassandra of her spouse, "and they wouldn't fill it—he's deaf."

Fundy was right; the day did clear. The marriage was made and the guests returned with the man and his bride to their home. But Fundy was also wrong, for storm came soon after and rain set in. The guests stayed on for tea, and then, as it was no better, they feasted and stayed till night. And Harvey began to think they never would go, but of course they couldn't and so there they were. Sophy was looking wonderful in white stockings and shiny shoes and a red frock with a tiny white apron. A big girl she seemed, with her shaken dark hair and flushed face. Grandmother Fundy spoke seriously, but not secretly to her.

"I've had my fourteen touch of children," said Grandmother Fundy. "Yes, they were flung on the mercy of God—poor little devils. I've followed most of 'em to the churchyard. You go slow, Sophia."

"Yes, Granny."

"Why," continued Cassandra, embracing the whole company, as it were, with her disclosure, "my mother had me by some gentleman!"

The announcement aroused no response except sympathetic, and perhaps encouraging, nods from the women.

"She had me by some gentleman—she ought to ha' had a twal' month, she did!"

"Wasn't she ever married?" Sophy inquired of her grandmother.

"Married? Yes, of course she was," replied the old dame, "of course. But marriage ain't everything. Twice she was, but not to he, she wasn't."

"Not to the gentleman?"

"No! Oh, no! He'd got money—bushels! Marriage ain't much, not with these gentry."

"Ho, ho, that's a tidy come-up!" laughed Harvey.

"Who was that gentleman?" Sophia's interest was deeply engaged. But Cassandra Fundy was silent, pondering like a china image. Her gaze was towards the mantelpiece, where there were four lamps— but only one usable—and two clocks—but only one going—and a col- oured greeting card a foot long with large letters *KEEP SMILING* adorned with lithographic honeysuckle.

"She's hard of hearing," interpolated Grandfather Amos, "very hard, gets worse. She've a horn at home, big as that . . ." His eyes roved the room for an object of comparison, and he seized upon the fire shovel that lay in the fender. "Big as that shovel. Crown silver it is, and solid, a beautiful horn, but"—he brandished the shovel before them— "her won't use 'en."

"Granny, who was that gentleman?" shouted Sophy. "Did you know him?"

"No! no!" declared the indignant dame. "I dunno ever his name, nor I don't want to. He took hisself off to Ameriky, and now he's in the land of heaven. I never seen him. If I had, I'd a given it to him properly; oh, my dear, not blay-guarding him, you know, but just plain language! Where's your seven commandments?"

At last the rain abated. Peeping into the dark garden you could see the fugitive moonlight hung in a million raindrops in the black twigs of all sorts of bushes and trees, while along the cantle of the porch a line of raindrops hung, even and regular, as if they were nailheads made of glass. So all the guests departed, in one long, staggering, struggling, giggling and guffawing body, into the village street. The bride and her man stood in the porch, watching and waving hands. Sophy was momentarily grieving: what a lot of trouble and fuss when you announced that henceforward you were going to sleep with a man because you loved him true! She had said good-bye to her grand- mother Cassandra, to her father and her little sister. She had hung on her mother's breast, sighing an almost intolerable farewell to innocence—never treasured until it is gone, and thenceforward a pretty sorrow cherished more deeply than wilder joys.

Into Harvey's mind, as they stood there at last alone, momentarily stole an image of a bright-haired girl, lovely, silent, sad, whom he felt he had deeply wronged. And he was sorry. He had escaped the snare, but if there had been no snare he might this night have been sleeping with a different bride. And it would have been just as well. Sophy looked but a girl with her blown hair and wet face. She was wiping her tears on the tiny apron. But she had the breasts of a woman and decoying eyes.

"Sophy, Sophy!" breathed Harvey, wooing her in the darkness.

"It blows and it rains, and it rains and it blows," chattered the crumpled bride, "and I'm all so bescambled I can't tell wet from windy."

"Come, my love," whispered the bridegroom, "come in, to home."

Four or five months later the higgler's affairs had again taken a rude turn. Marriage, alas, was not all it might be; his wife and his mother quarreled unendingly. Sometimes he sided with the one and sometimes with the other. He could not yet afford to install his mother in a separate cottage, and therefore even Sophy had to admit that her mother-in-law had a right to be living there with them, the home being hers. Harvey hadn't bought much of it; and though he was welcome to it all now, and it would be exclusively his as soon as she died, still, it was her furniture, and you couldn't drive any woman (even your mother) off her own property. Sophy, who wanted a home of her own, was vexed and moody, and antagonistic to her man. Business, too, had gone down sadly of late. He had thrown up the Shag Moor round months ago; he could not bring himself to go there again, and he had not been able to square up the loss by any substantial new connections. On top of it all his horse died. It stumbled on a hill one day and fell, and it couldn't get up, or it wouldn't—at any rate, it didn't. Harvey thrashed it and coaxed it, then he cursed it and kicked it; after that he sent for a veterinary man, and the veterinary man ordered it to be shot. And it was shot. A great blow to Harvey Witlow was that. He had no money to buy another horse; money was tight with him, very tight; and so he had to hire at fabulous cost a decrepit nag that ate like a good one. It ate—well, it would have astonished you to see what that creature disposed of, with hay the price it was and corn gone up to heaven nearly. In fact Harvey found that he couldn't stand the racket much longer, and as he could not possibly buy another it looked very much as if he was in queer street once more, unless he could borrow the money from some friendly

person. Of course there were plenty of friendly persons, but they had
no money, just as there were many persons who had the money but
were not what you might call friendly; and so the higgler began to
reiterate twenty times a day, and forty times a day, that he was entirely
and absolutely damned and done. Things were thus very bad with
him, they were at their worst—for he had a wife to keep now, as
well as a mother, and a horse that ate like Satan, and worked like
a gnat—when it suddenly came into his mind that Mrs. Sadgrove
was reputed to have a lot of money, and had no call to be unfriendly
to him. He had his grave doubts about the size of her purse, but there
could be no harm in trying so long as you approached her in a right
reasonable manner.

For a week or two he held off from this appeal, but the grim spectre
of destitution gave him no rest, and so, near the close of a wild March
day, he took his desperate courage and his cart and the decrepit nag
to Shag Moor. Wild it was, though dry, and the wind against them,
a vast turmoil of icy air strident and baffling. The nag threw up its
head and declined to trot. Evening was but an hour away, the fury of
the wind did not retard it, nor the clouds hasten it. Low down the
sun was quitting the wrack of storm, exposing a jolly orb of magnify-
ing fire that shone flush under eaves and through the casements of
cottages, casting a pattern of lattice and tossing boughs upon the interior walls, lovelier than dreamed-of pictures. The heads of mothers
and old dames were also imaged there, recognizable in their black
shadows; and little children held up their hands between window and
wall to make five-fingered shapes upon the golden screen. To drive
on the moor then was to drive into blasts more dire. Darkness began
to fall, and bitter cold it was. No birds to be seen, neither beast nor
man; empty of everything it was except sound and a marvel of dying
light, and Harvey Witlow of Dinnop with a sour old nag driving
from end to end of it. At Prattle Corner dusk was already abroad:
there was just one shaft of light that broached a sharp angled stack
in the rickyard, an ark of darkness, along whose top the gads and
wooden pins and tilted straws were miraculously fringed in the last
glare. Hitching his nag to the palings he knocked at the door, and
knew in the gloom that it was Mary who opened it and stood peering
forth at him.

"Good-evening," he said, touching his hat.

"Oh!" the girl uttered a cry. "Higgler! What do you come for?" It
was the longest sentence she had ever spoken to him; a sad frightened
voice.

"I thought," he began, "I'd call—and see Mrs. Sadgrove. I wondered . . ."

"Mother's dead," said the girl. She drew the door farther back, as if inviting him, and he entered. The door was shut behind him, and they were alone in the darkness, together. The girl was deeply grieving. Trembling, he asked the question: "What is it you tell me, Mary?"

"Mother's dead," repeated the girl, "all day, all day, all day." They were close to each other, but he could not see her. All round the house the wind roved lamentingly, shuddering at doors and windows. "She died in the night. The doctor was to have come, but he has not come all day," Mary whispered, "all day, all day. I don't understand; I have waited for him, and he has not come. She died, she was dead in her bed this morning, and I've been alone all day, all day, and I don't know what is to be done."

"I'll go for the doctor," he said hastily, but she took him by the hand and drew him into the kitchen. There was no candle lit; a fire was burning there, richly glowing embers, that laid a gaunt shadow of the table across a corner of the ceiling. Every dish on the dresser gleamed, the stone floor was rosy, and each smooth curve on the dark settle was shining like ice. Without invitation he sat down.

"No," said the girl, in a tremulous voice, "you must help me." She lit a candle: her face was white as the moon, her lips were sharply red, and her eyes were wild. "Come," she said, and he followed her behind the settle and up the stairs to a room where there was a disordered bed, and what might be a body lying under the quilt. The higgler stood still staring at the form under the quilt. The girl, too, was still and staring. Wind dashed upon the ivy at the window and hallooed like a grieving multitude. A crumpled gown hid the body's head, but thrust from under it, almost as if to greet him, was her naked lean arm, the palm of the hand lying uppermost. At the foot of the bed was a large washing-bowl, with sponge and towels.

"You've been laying her out! Yourself!" exclaimed Witlow. The pale girl set down the candle on a chest of drawers. "Help me now," she said, and moving to the bed she lifted the crumpled gown from off the face of the dead woman, at the same time smoothing the quilt closely up to the body's chin. "I cannot put the gown on, because of her arm, it has gone stiff." She shuddered and stood holding the gown as if offering it to the man. He lifted that dead naked arm and tried to place it down at the body's side, but it resisted and he let go his hold. The arm swung back to its former outstretched position as if it still lived and resented that pressure. The girl retreated from the bed with a timorous cry.

"Get me a bandage," he said, "or something we can tear up."

She gave him some pieces of linen.

"I'll finish this for you," he brusquely whispered. "You get along downstairs and take a swig of brandy. Got any brandy?"

She did not move. He put his arm around her and gently urged her to the door.

"Brandy," he repeated, "and light your candles."

He watched her go heavily down the stairs before he shut the door. Returning to the bed he lifted the quilt. The dead body was naked and smelt of soap. Dropping the quilt he lifted the outstretched arm again, like cold wax to the touch and unpliant as a sturdy sapling, and tried once more to bend it to the body's side. As he did so the bedroom door blew open with a crash. It was only a draught of the wind, and a loose latch—Mary had opened a door downstairs, perhaps— but it awed him as if some invisible looker were there resenting his presence. He went and closed the door; the latch had a loose hasp, and tip-toeing nervously back he seized the dreadful arm with a sudden brutal energy, and bent it by thrusting his knee violently into the hollow of the elbow. Hurriedly he slipped the gown over the head and inserted the arm in the sleeve. A strange impulse of modesty stayed him for a moment: should he call the girl and let her complete the robing of the naked body under the quilt. That preposterous pause seemed to add a new anger to the wind, and again the door sprang open. He delayed no longer, but letting it remain open, he uncovered the dead woman. As he lifted the chill body the long outstretched arm moved and tilted like the boom of a sail, but crushing it to its side he bound the limb fast with the strips of linen. So Mrs. Sadgrove was made ready for her coffin. Drawing the quilt back to her neck, with a gush of relief he glanced about the room. It was a very ordinary bedroom: bed, washstand, chest of drawers, chair, and two pictures— one of deeply religious import, and the other a little pink print, in a gilded frame, of a bouncing nude nymph recumbent upon a cloud. It was queer: a lot of people, people whom you wouldn't think it of, had that sort of picture in their bedrooms.

Mary was now coming up the stairs again, with a glass half full of liquid. She brought it to him.

"No, you drink it," he urged, and Mary sipped the brandy.

"I've finished—I've finished," he said as he watched her, "she's quite comfortable now."

The girl looked her silent thanks at him, again holding out the glass. "No, sup it yourself," he said; but as she stood in the dim light, regarding him with her strange gaze, and still offering the drink, he took it from her, drained it at a gulp and put the glass upon the chest, beside the candle. "She's quite comfortable now. I'm very grieved,

Mary," he said with awkward kindness, "about all this trouble that's come on you."

She was motionless as a wax image, as if she had died in her steps, her hand still extended as when he took the glass from it. So piercing was her gaze that his own drifted from her face and took in again the objects in the room; the washstand, the candle on the chest, the little pink picture. The wind beat upon the ivy outside the window as if a monstrous whip were lashing its slaves.

"You must notify the registrar," he began again, "but you must see the doctor first."

"I've waited for him all day," Mary whispered, "all day. The nurse will come again soon. She went home to rest in the night." She turned towards the bed. "She has only been ill a week."

"Yes?" he lamely said. "Dear me, it is sudden."

"I must see the doctor," she continued.

"I'll drive you over to him in my gig." He was eager to do that.

"I don't know," said Mary slowly.

"Yes, I'll do that, soon's you're ready. Mary," he fumbled with his speech, "I'm not wanting to pry into your affairs, or anything as don't concern me, but how are you going to get along now? Have you got any relations?"

"No," the girl shook her head. "No."

"That's bad. What was you thinking of doing? How has she left you—things were in a baddish way, weren't they?"

"Oh, no," Mary looked up quickly. "She has left me very well-off. I shall go on with the farm; there's the old man and the boy—they've gone to a wedding to-day; I shall go on with it. She was so thoughtful for me, and I would not care to leave all this, I love it."

"But you can't do it by yourself, alone?"

"No. I'm to get a man to superintend, a working bailiff," she said.

"Oh!" And again they were silent. The girl went to the bed and lifted the covering. She saw the bound arm and then drew the quilt tenderly over the dead face. Witlow picked up his hat and found himself staring again at the pink picture. Mary took the candle preparatory to descending the stairs. Suddenly the higgler turned to her and ventured: "Did you know as she once asked me to marry you?" he blurted.

Her eyes turned from him, but he guessed—he could feel that she *had* known.

"I've often wondered why," he murmured, "why she wanted that."

"She didn't," said the girl.

That gave pause to the man; he felt stupid at once and roved his fingers in a silly way along the roughened nap of his hat.

"Well, she asked me to," he bluntly protested.

"She knew," Mary's voice was no louder than a sigh, "that you were courting another girl, the one you married."

"But, but," stuttered the honest higgler, "if she knew that why did she want for me to marry you?"

"She didn't," said Mary again; and again, in the pause, he did silly things to his hat. How shy this girl was, how lovely in her modesty and grief!

"I can't make tops or bottoms of it," he said; "but she asked me, as sure as God's my maker."

"I know. It was me, I wanted it."

"You!" he cried, "you wanted to marry me!"

The girl bowed her head, lovely in her grief and modesty: "She was against it, but I made her ask you."

"And I hadn't an idea that you cast a thought on me," he murmured. "I feared it was a sort of trick she was playing on me. I didn't understand, I had no idea that you knew about it even. And so I didn't ever ask you."

"Oh, why not, why not? I was fond of you then," whispered she. "Mother tried to persuade me against it, but I was fond of you—then."

He was in a queer distress and confusion: "Oh, if you'd only tipped me a word, or given me a sort of look," he sighed. "Oh, Mary!"

She said no more, but went downstairs. He followed her and immediately fetched the lamps from his gig. As he lit the candles: "How strange," Mary said, "that you should come back just as I most needed help. I am very grateful."

"Mary, I'll drive you to the doctor's now."

She shook her head; she was smiling.

"Then I'll stay till the nurse comes."

"No, you must go. Go at once."

He picked up the two lamps, and turning at the door said: "I'll come again to-morrow." Then the wind rushed into the room: "Good-bye," she cried, shutting the door quickly behind him.

He drove away into deep darkness, the wind howling, his thoughts strange and bitter. He had thrown away a love, a love that was dumb and hid itself. By God, he had thrown away a fortune, too! And he had forgotten all about his real errand until now, forgotten all about the loan! Well, let it go; give it up. He would give up higgling he would take on some other job; a bailiff, a working bailiff, that was the job that would suit him, a working bailiff. Of course there was Sophy; but still—Sophy!

54

The Western Islands

BY JOHN MASEFIELD

"ONCE there were two sailors; and one of them was Joe, and the other one was Jerry, and they were fishermen. And they'd a young apprentice-feller, and his name was Jim. And Joe was a great one for his pot, and Jerry was a wonder at his pipe; and Jim did all the work, and both of them banged him. So one time Joe and Jerry were in the beer-house, and there was a young parson there, telling the folks about foreign things, about plants and that. 'Ah,' he says, 'what wonders there are in the west.'

" 'What sort of wonders, begging your pardon, sir,' says Joe. 'What sort of wonders might them be?'

" 'Why, all sorts of wonders,' says the parson. 'Why, in the west,' he says, 'there's things you wouldn't believe. No, you wouldn't believe; not till you'd seen them,' he says. 'There's diamonds growing on the trees. And great, golden, glittering pearls as common as peastraw. And there's islands in the west. Ah, I could tell you of them. Islands? I rather guess there's islands. None of your Isles of Man. None of your Alderney and Sark. Not in them seas.'

" 'What sort of islands might they be, begging your pardon, sir?' says Jerry.

" 'Why,' he says (the parson feller says), 'ISLANDS. Islands as big as Spain. Islands with rivers of rum and streams of sarsaparilla. And none of your roses. Rubies and ame-thynes is all the roses grows in them parts. With golden stalks to them, and big diamond sticks to them, and the taste of pork-crackling if you eat them. They're the sort of roses to have in your area,' he says.

" 'And what else might there be in them parts, begging your pardon, sir?' says Joe.

" 'Why,' he says, this parson says, 'there's wonders. There's not only wonders but miracles. And not only miracles, but sperrits.'

" 'What sort of sperrits might they be, begging your pardon?' says Jerry. 'Are they rum and that?'

" 'When I says sperrits,' says the parson feller, 'I mean ghosts.'

" 'Of course ye do,' says Joe.

" 'Yes, ghosts,' says the parson. 'And by ghosts I mean sperrits. And by sperrits I mean white things. And by white things I mean things as turn your hair white. And there's red devils there, and blue devils there, and a great gold queen a-waiting for a man to kiss her. And the first man as dares to kiss that queen, why he becomes king, and all her sacks of gold become his.'

" 'Begging your pardon, sir,' said Jerry, 'but whereabouts might these here islands be?'

" 'Why, in the west,' says the parson. 'In the west, where the sun sets.'

" 'Ah,' said Joe and Jerry. 'What wonders there are in the world.'

"Now, after that, neither one of them could think of anything but these here western islands. So at last they take their smack, and off they go in search of them. And Joe had a barrel of beer in the bows, and Jerry had a box of twist in the waist, and pore little Jim stood and steered abaft all. And in the evenings Jerry and Joe would bang their pannikins together, and sing of the great times they meant to have when they were married to the queen. Then they would clump pore little Jim across the head, and tell him to watch out, and keep her to her course, or they'd ride him down like you would a main tack. And he'd better mind his eye, they told him, or they'd make him long to be boiled and salted. And he'd better put more sugar in the tea, they said, or they'd cut him up for cod-bait. And who was he, they asked, to be wanting meat for dinner, when there was that much weevilly biscuit in the bread-barge? And boys was going to the dogs, they said, when limbs the like of him had the heaven-born insolence to want to sleep. And a nice pass things was coming to, they said, when a lad as they'd done everything for, and saved, so to speak, from the workhouse, should go for to snivel when they hit him a clip. If they'd said a word, when they was hit, when they was boys, they told him, they'd have had their bloods drawed, and been stood in the wind to cool. But let him take heed, they said, and be a good lad, and do the work of five, and they wouldn't half wonder, they used to say, as he'd be a man before his mother. So the sun shone, and the stars came out golden, and all the sea was a sparkle of gold with them. Blue was the sea, and the wind blew, too, and it blew Joe and Jerry west as fast as a cat can eat sardines.

"And one fine morning the wind fell calm, and a pleasant smell came over the water, like nutmegs on a rum-milk-punch. Presently the dawn broke. And, lo and behold, a rousing great wonderful island, all scarlet with coral and with rubies. The surf that was beating on her sands went shattering into silver coins, into dimes; and pesetas, and francs, and fourpenny bits. And the flowers on the cliffs was all one gleam and glitter. And the beauty of that island was a beauty beyond the beauty of Sally Brown, the lady as kept the beer-house. And on the beach of that island, on a golden throne, like, sat a woman so lovely that to look at her was as good as a church-service for one.

" 'That's the party I got to kiss,' said Jerry. 'Steady, and beach her, Jim, boy,' he says. 'Run her ashore, lad. That's the party is to be my queen.'

" 'You've got a neck on you, all of a sudden,' said Joe. 'You ain't the admiral of this fleet. Not by a wide road you ain't. I'll do all the kissing as there's any call for. You keep clear, my son.'

"Here the boat ran her nose into the sand, and the voyagers went ashore.

" 'Keep clear, is it?' said Jerry. 'You tell me to keep clear? You tell me again, and I'll put a head on you—'ll make you sing like a kettle. Who are you to tell me to keep clear?'

" 'I tell you who I am,' said Joe. 'I'm a better man than you are. That's what I am. I'm Joe the Tank, from Limehouse Basin, and there's no tinker's donkey-boy'll make me stand from under. Who are you to go kissing queens? Who are you that talk so proud and so mighty? You've a face on you would make a Dago tired. You look like a sea-sick Kanaka that's boxed seven rounds with a buzz-saw. You've no more manners than a hog, and you've a lip on you would fetch the enamel off a cup.'

" 'If it comes to calling names,' said Jerry, 'you ain't the only pebble on the beach. Whatever you might think, I tell you you ain't. You're the round turn and two-half hitches of a figure of fun as makes the angels weep. That's what you are. And you're the right-hand strand, and the left-hand strand, and the centre strand, and the core, and the serving, and the marling, of a three-stranded, left-handed, poorly worked junk of a half begun and never finished odds and ends of a Port Mahon soldier. You look like a Portuguese drummer. You've a whelky red nose that shines like a port side-light. You've a face like a muddy field where they've been playing football in the rain. Your hair is an insult and a shame. I blush when I look at you. You give me a turn like the first day out to a first voyager. Kiss, will you? Kiss? Man, I tell you you'd paralyze a shark if you kissed him. Paralyze him, strike him cold. That's what a kiss of yours'd do.'

"'You ought to 'a' been a parson,' said Joe, 'that's what you'd ought. There's many would 'a' paid you for talk like that. But for all your fine talk, and for all your dandy language, you'll not come the old soldier over me. No, nor ten of you. *You* talk of kissing, when there's a handsome young man, the likes of me, around. Neither you nor ten of you. To hear you talk one'd think you was a Emperor or a Admiral. One would think you was a Bishop or a King. One might mistake you for a General or a Member of Parliament. You might. Straight, you might. A General or a Bishop or a King. And what are you? What are you? I ask you plain. What are you?—I'll tell you what you are.

"'You're him as hired himself out as a scarecrow, acos no one'd take you as a fo'c's'le hand. You're him as give the colic to a weather-cock. You're him as turned old Mother Bomby's beer. You're him as drowned the duck and stole the monkey. You're him as got the medal give him for having a face that made the bull tame. You're——'

"'Now don't you cast no more to me,' said Jerry. 'For I won't take no lip from a twelve-a-shilling, cent-a-corner, the likes of you are. You're the clippings of old junk, what the Dagoes smoke in cigarettes. A swab, and a-wash-deck-broom, and the half of a pint of paint'd make a handsomer figger of a man than what you are. I've seen a coir whisk, what they grooms a mule with, as had a sweeter face than you got. So stand aside, before you're put aside. I'm the king of this here island. You can go chase yourself for another. Stand clear, I say, or I'll give you a jog'll make your bells ring.'

"Now, while they were argufying, young Jim, the young apprentice feller, he creeps up to the queen upon the throne. She was beautiful, she was, and she shone in the sun, and she looked straight ahead of her like a wax-work in a show. And in her hand she had a sack full of jewels, and at her feet she had a sack full of gold, and by her side was an empty throne ready for the king she married. But round her right hand there was a red snake, and round her left hand there was a blue snake, and the snakes hissed and twisted, and they showed their teeth full of poison. So Jim looked at the snakes, and he hit them a welt, right and left, and he kissed the lady.

"And immediately all the bells and the birds of the world burst out a-ringing and a-singing. The lady awoke from her sleep, and Jim's old clothes were changed to cloth of gold. And there he was, a king, on the throne beside the lady.

"But the red snake turned to a big red devil who took a-hold of Joe, and the blue snake turned to a big blue devil, who took a-hold of Jerry.

And 'Come you here, you brawling pugs,' they said, 'come and shovel sand.' And Joe and Jerry took the spades that were given to them. And 'Dig, now,' said the devils. 'Heave round. Let's see you dig. Dig, you scarecrows. And tell us when you've dug to London.' "

55

The Sword of Welleran

BY LORD DUNSANY

WHERE the great plain of Tarphet runs up, as the sea in estuaries, among the Cyresian mountains, there stood long since the city of Merimna well-nigh among the shadows of the crags. I have never seen a city in the world so beautiful as Merimna seemed to me when first I dreamed of it. It was a marvel of spires and figures of bronze, and marble fountains, and trophies of fabulous wars, and broad streets given over wholly to the beautiful. Right through the centre of the city there went an avenue fifty strides in width, and along each side of it stood likenesses in bronze of the kings of all the countries that the people of Merimna had ever known. At the end of that avenue was a colossal chariot with three bronze horses driven by the winged figure of Fame, and behind her in the chariot the huge form of Welleran, Merimna's ancient hero, standing with extended sword. So urgent was the mien and attitude of Fame, and so swift the pose of the horses, that you had sworn that the chariot was instantly upon you, and that its dust already veiled the faces of the kings. And in the city was a mighty hall wherein were stored the trophies of Merimna's heroes. Sculptured it was, and domed, the glory of the art of masons a long while dead, and on the summit of the dome the image of Rollory sat gazing across the Cyresian mountains toward the wide lands beyond, the lands that knew his sword. And beside Rollory, like an old nurse, the figure of Victory sat, hammering into a golden wreath of laurels for his head the crowns of fallen kings.

Such was Merimna, a city of sculptured Victories and warriors of bronze. Yet in the time of which I write the art of war had been forgotten in Merimna, and the people almost slept. To and fro and up and down they would walk through the marble streets, gazing at memorials of the things achieved by their country's swords in the hands of those that long ago had loved Merimna well. Almost they slept, and dreamed of Welleran, Soorenard, Mommolek, Rollory, Akanax, and young Irain. Of the lands beyond the mountains that lay all round about them they knew nothing, save that they were the theatre of the terrible deeds of Welleran, that he had done with his sword. Long since these lands had fallen back into the possession of the nations that had been scourged by Merimna's armies. Nothing now remained to Merimna's men save their inviolate city and the glory of the remembrance of their ancient fame. At night they would place sentinels far out in the desert, but these always slept at their posts dreaming of Rollory, and three times every night a guard would march around the city, clad in purple, bearing lights, and singing songs of Welleran. Always the guard went unarmed; but, as the sound of their song went echoing across the plain towards the looming mountains, the desert robbers would hear the name of Welleran and steal away to their haunts. Often dawn would come across the plain, shimmering marvellously upon Merimna's spires, abashing all the stars, and find the guard still singing songs of Welleran, and would change the colour of their purple robes and pale the lights they bore. But the guard would go back leaving the ramparts safe, and one by one the sentinels in the plain would awake from dreaming of Rollory and shuffle back into the city quite cold. Then something of the menace would pass away from the faces of the Cyresian mountains, that from the north and the west and the south lowered upon Merimna, and clear in the morning the statues and the pillars would arise in the old inviolate city. You would wonder that an unarmed guard and sentinels that slept could defend a city that was stored with all the glories of art, that was rich in gold and bronze, a haughty city that had erst oppressed its neighbours, whose people had forgotten the art of war. Now this is the reason that, though all her other lands had long been taken from her, Merimna's city was safe.

A strange thing was believed or feared by the fierce tribes beyond the mountains, and it was credited among them that at certain stations round Merimna's ramparts there still rode Welleran, Soorenard, Mommolek, Rollory, Akanax, and young Irain. Yet it was close on a hundred years since Irain, the youngest of Merimna's heroes, fought his last battle with the tribes.

Sometimes indeed there arose among the tribes young men who doubted and said: "How may a man forever escape death?"

But graver men answered them: "Hear us, ye whose wisdom has discerned so much, and discern for us how a man may escape death when two score horsemen assail him with their swords, all of them sworn to kill him, and all of them sworn upon their country's gods; as often Welleran hath. Or discern for us how two men alone may enter a walled city by night, and bring away from it that city's king, as did Soorenard and Mommolek. Surely men that have escaped so many swords and so many sleety arrows shall escape the years and Time."

And the young men were humbled and became silent. Still, the suspicion grew. And often when the sun set on the Cyresian mountains, men in Merimna discerned the forms of savage tribesmen black against the light, peering towards the city.

All knew in Merimna that the figures round the ramparts were only statues of stone, yet even there a hope lingered among a few that some day their old heroes would come again, for certainly none had ever seen them die. Now it had been the wont of these six warriors of old, as each received his last wound and knew it to be mortal, to ride away to a certain deep ravine and cast his body in, as somewhere I have read great elephants do, hiding their bones away from lesser beasts. It was a ravine steep and narrow even at the ends, a great cleft into which no man could come by any path. There rode Welleran alone, panting hard; and there later rode Soorenard and Mommolek, Mommolek with a mortal wound upon him not to return, but Soorenard was unwounded and rode back alone from leaving his dear friend resting among the mighty bones of Welleran. And there rode Soorenard, when his day was come, with Rollory and Akanax, and Rollory rode in the middle and Soorenard and Akanax on either side. And the long ride was a hard and weary thing for Soorenard and Akanax, for they both had mortal wounds; but the long ride was easy for Rollory, for he was dead. So the bones of these five heroes whitened in an enemy's land, and very still they were, though they had troubled cities, and none knew where they lay saving only Irain, the young captain, who was but twenty-five when Mommolek, Rollory, Akanax rode away. And among them were strewn their saddles and their bridles, and all the accoutrements of their horses, lest any man should ever find them afterwards and say in some foreign city: "Lo, the bridles or the saddles of Merimna's captains, taken in war," but their beloved trusty horses they turned free.

Forty years afterwards, in the hour of a great victory, his last wound came upon Irain, and the wound was terrible and would not close. And Irain was the last of the captains, and rode away alone. It was a long way to the dark ravine, and Irain feared that he would never come to the resting place of the old heroes, and he urged his horse on swiftly, and clung to the saddle with his hands. And often as he rode he fell asleep, and dreamed of earlier days, and of the times when he first rode forth to the great wars of Welleran, and of the time when Welleran first spake to him, and of the faces of Welleran's comrades when they led charges in the battle. And ever as he awoke a great longing arose in his soul as it hovered on his body's brink, a-longing to lie among the bones of the old heroes. At last when he saw the dark ravine making a scar across the plain, the soul of Irain slipped out through his great wound and spread its wings, and pain departed from the poor hacked body, and, still urging his horse forward, Irain died. But the old true horse cantered on, till suddenly he saw before him the dark ravine, and put his forefeet out on the very edge of it and stopped. Then the body of Irain came toppling forward over the right shoulder of the horse, and his bones mingle and rest as the years go by with the bones of Merimna's heroes.

Now there was a little boy in Merimna named Rold. I saw him first; I, the dreamer, that sit before my fire asleep; I saw him first as his mother led him through the great hall where stand the trophies of Merimna's heroes. He was five years old, and they stood before the great glass casket wherein lay the sword of Welleran, and his mother said: "The sword of Welleran." And Rold said: "What should a man do with the sword of Welleran?" And his mother answered: "Men look at the sword and remember Welleran." And they went on and stood before the great red cloak of Welleran, and the child said: "Why did Welleran wear this great red cloak?" And his mother answered: "It was the way of Welleran."

When Rold was a little older he stole out of his mother's house quite in the middle of the night when all the world was still, and Merimna asleep, dreaming of Welleran, Soorenard, Mommolek, Rollory, Akanax, and young Irain. And he went down to the ramparts to hear the purple guard go by, singing of Welleran. And the purple guard came by with lights, all singing in the stillness, and dark shapes out in the desert turned and fled. And Rold went back again to his mother's house with a great yearning towards the name of Welleran, such as men feel for very holy things.

And in time Rold grew to know the pathway all round the ramparts, and the six equestrian statues that were there, guarding Merimna still. These statues were not like other statues; they were so cunningly wrought of many-coloured marbles that none might be quite sure until very close that they were not living men. There was a horse of dappled marble, the horse of Akanax. The horse of Rollory was of alabaster, pure white, his armour was wrought out of a stone that shone, and his horseman's cloak was made of a blue stone, very precious. He looked northward.

But the marble horse of Welleran was pure black, and there sat Welleran upon him looking solemnly westwards. His horse it was whose cold neck Rold most loved to stroke, and it was Welleran whom the watchers at sunset on the mountains the most clearly saw as they peered towards the city. And Rold loved the red nostrils of the great black horse and his rider's jasper cloak.

Now beyond the Cyresians the suspicion grew that Merimna's heroes were dead, and a plan was devised that a man should go by night and come close to the figures upon the ramparts and see whether they were Welleran, Soorenard, Mommolek, Rollory, Akanax, and young Irain. And all were agreed upon the plan, and many names were mentioned of those who should go,.and the plan matured for many years. It was during these years that watchers clustered often at sunset upon the mountains, but came no nearer. Finally a better plan was made, and it was decided that two men who had been by chance condemned to death should be given a pardon if they went down into the plain by night and discovered whether or not Merimna's heroes lived. At first the two prisoners dared not go, but after a while one of them, Seejar, said to his companion, Sajar-Ho: "See, now, when the King's axe-man smites a man upon the neck that man dies."

And the other said that this was so. Then said Seejar: "And even though Welleran smite a man with his sword no more befalleth him than death."

Then Sajar-Ho thought for a while. Presently he said: "Yet the eye of the King's axeman might err at the moment of his stroke or his arm fail him, and the eye of Welleran hath never erred nor his arm failed. It were better to bide here."

Then said Seejar: "Maybe that Welleran is dead and that some other holds his place upon the ramparts, or even a statue of stone."

But Sajar-Ho made answer: "How can Welleran be dead when he even escaped from two score horsemen with swords that were sworn to slay him, and all sworn upon our country's gods?"

And Seejar said: "This story his father told my grandfather concerning Welleran. On the day that the fight was lost on the plains of Kurlistan he saw a dying horse near to the river, and the horse looked piteously toward the water but could not reach it. And the father of my grandfather saw Welleran go down to the river's brink and bring water from it with his own hand and give it to the horse. Now we are in as sore a plight as was that horse, and as near to death; it may be that Welleran will pity us, while the King's axeman cannot because of the commands of the King."

Then said Sajar-Ho: "Thou wast ever a cunning arguer. Thou broughtest us into this trouble with thy cunning and thy devices; we will see if thou canst bring us out of it. We will go."

So news was brought to the King that the two prisoners would go down to Merimna.

That evening the watchers led them to the mountain's edge, and Seejar and Sajar-Ho went down towards the plain by the way of a deep ravine, and the watchers watched them go. Presently their figures were wholly hid in the dusk. Then night came up, huge and holy, out of waste marshes to the eastwards and low lands and the sea; and the angels that watched over all men through the day closed their great eyes and slept, and the angels that watched over all men through the night awoke and ruffled their deep blue feathers and stood up and watched. But the plain became a thing of mystery filled with fears. So the two spies went down the deep ravine, and coming to the plain sped stealthily across it. Soon they came to the line of sentinels asleep upon the sand, and one stirred in his sleep calling on Rollory, and a great dread seized upon the spies, and they whispered "Rollory lives," but they remembered the King's axeman and went on. And next they came to the great bronze statue of Fear, carved by some sculptor of the old glorious years in the attitude of flight towards the mountains, calling to her children as she fled. And the children of Fear were carved in the likeness of the armies of all the trans-Cyresian tribes, with their backs towards Merimna, flocking after Fear. And, from where he sat on his horse behind the ramparts, the sword of Welleran was stretched out over their heads as ever it was wont. And the two spies kneeled down in the sand and kissed the huge bronze foot of the statue of Fear, saying: "O Fear, Fear." And as they knelt they saw lights far off along the ramparts coming nearer and nearer, and heard men singing of Welleran. And the purple guard came nearer and went by with their lights, and passed on into the distance round the ramparts, still singing of Welleran. And all the while the two spies clung to the foot of the statue, muttering: "O Fear, Fear." But when they could hear the name of Welleran no more they arose and came to the ramparts and climbed over them and came at once upon the figure of Welleran, and they bowed low to the ground, and Seejar said: "O Welleran, we came to see whether thou didst yet live." And for a long while they waited with their faces to the earth. At last Seejar looked up towards Welleran's terrible sword, and it was still sretched out pointing to the carved armies that followed after Fear. And Seejar bowed to the ground again and touched the horse's hoof, and it seemed cold to him. And he moved his hand higher and touched the leg of the horse, and it seemed quite cold. At last he touched Welleran's foot, and the armour on it seemed hard and stiff. Then as Welleran moved not and spake not, Seejar climbed up at last and touched his hand, the terrible hand of Welleran, and it was marble. Then Seejar laughed aloud, and he and Sajar-Ho sped down the empty pathway and found Rollory, and he was marble too. Then they climbed down over the ramparts and went back across the plain, walking contemptuously past the figure of Fear, and heard the guard returning round the ramparts for the third time, singing of Welleran; and Seejar said: "Ay, you may sing of Welleran, but Welleran is dead and a doom is on your city."

And they passed on and found the sentinel still restless in the night and calling on Rollory. And Sajar-Ho muttered: "Ay, you may call on Rollory, but Rollory is dead and naught can save your city."

And the two spies went back alive to their mountains again, and as they reached them the first ray of the sun came up red over the desert behind Merimna and lit Merimna's spires. It was the hour when the purple guard were wont to go back into the city with their tapers pale and their robes a brighter colour, when the cold sentinels came shuffling in from dreaming in the desert; it was the hour when the desert robbers hid themselves away, going back to their mountain caves; it was the hour when gauze-winged insects are born that only live for a day; it was the hour when men die that are condemned to death; in this hour a great peril, new and terrible, arose for Merimna and Merimna knew it not.

Then Seejar turning, said: "See how red the dawn is and how red the spires of Merimna. They are angry with Merimna in Paradise and they bode its doom."

So the two spies went back and brought the news to their king, and for a few days the kings of those countries were gathering their armies together; and one evening the armies of four kings were massed together at the top of the deep ravine, all crouching below the summit waiting for the sun to set. All wore resolute and fearless faces, yet inwardly every man was praying to his gods, unto each one in turn.

Then the sun set, and it was the hour when the bats and the dark creatures are abroad and the lions come down from their lairs, and the desert robbers go into the plains again, and fevers rise up winged and hot out of chill marshes, and it was the hour when safety leaves the thrones of kings, the hour when dynasties change. But in the desert the purple guard came swinging out of Merimna with their lights to sing of Welleran, and the sentinels lay down to sleep.

Now into Paradise no sorrow may ever come, but may only beat like rain against its crystal walls; yet the souls of Merimna's heroes were half aware of some sorrow far away, as some sleeper feels that someone is chilled and cold yet knows not in his sleep that it is he. And they fretted a little in their starry home. Then unseen there drifted earthward across the setting sun the souls of Welleran, Soorenard, Mommolek, Rollory, Akanax, and young Irain. Already when they reached Merimna's ramparts it was just dark, already the armies of the four kings had begun to move, jingling, down the deep ravine. But when the six warriors saw their city again, so little changed after so many years, they looked towards her with a longing that was nearer to tears than any that their souls had known before, crying to her:

"O Merimna, our city: Merimna, our walled city.

"How beautiful thou art with all thy spires, Merimna. For thee we left the earth, its kingdom and little flowers, for thee we have come away for a while from Paradise.

"It is very difficult to draw away from the face of God—it is like a warm fire, it is like dear sleep, it is like a great anthem, yet there is a stillness all about it, a stillness full of lights.

"We have left Paradise for a while for thee, Merimna.

"Many women have we loved, Merimna, but only one city.

"Behold now all the people dream, all our loved people. How beautiful are dreams! In dreams the dead may live, even the long dead and the very silent. Thy lights are all sunk low, they have all gone out, no sound is in thy streets. Hush! Thou art like a maiden that shutteth up her eyes and is asleep, that draweth her breath softly and is quite still, being at ease and untroubled.

"Behold now the battlements, the old battlements. Do men defend them still as we defended them? They are worn a little, the battlements." And drifting nearer they peered anxiously. "It is not by the hand of man that they are worn, our battlements. Only the years have done it and indomitable Time. Thy battlements are like the girdle of a maiden, a girdle that is round about her. See now the dew upon them, they are like a jewelled girdle.

"Thou art in great danger, Merimna, because thou art so beautiful. Must thou perish to-night because we no more defend thee, because we cry out and none hear us, as the bruised lilies cry out and none have known their voices?"

Thus spake those strong-voiced, battle-ordering captains, calling to their dear city, and their voices came no louder than the whispers of little bats that drift across the twilight in the evening. Then the purple guard came near, going round the ramparts for the first time in the night, and the old warriors called to them: "Merimna is in danger! Already her enemies gather in the darkness." But their voices were never heard, because they were only wandering ghosts. And the guard went by and passed unheeding away, still singing of Welleran.

Then said Welleran to his comrades: "Our hands can hold swords no more, our voices cannot be heard, we are stalwart men no longer. We are but dreams, let us go among dreams. Go all of you, and thou too, young Irain, and trouble the dreams of all the men that sleep, and urge them to take the old swords of their grandsires that hang upon the walls, and to gather at the mouth of the ravine; and I will find a leader and make him take my sword."

Then they passed up over the ramparts and into their dear city. And the wind blew about, this way and that as he went, the soul of Welleran who had upon his day withstood the charges of tempestuous armies. And the souls of his comrades, and with them young Irain, passed up into the city and troubled the dreams of every man who slept, and to every man the souls said in their dreams: "It is hot and still in the city. Go out now into the desert, into the cool under the mountains, but take with thee the old sword that hangs upon the wall, for fear of the desert robbers."

And the god of that city sent up a fever over it, and the fever brooded over it and the streets were hot; and all that slept awoke from dreaming that it would be cool and pleasant where the breezes came down the ravine out of the mountains; and they took the old swords that their grandsires had, according to their dreams, for fear of the desert robbers. And in and out of dreams passed the souls of Welleran's comrades, and with them young Irain, in great haste as the night wore on; and one by one they troubled the dreams of all Merimna's men and caused them to arise and go out armed, all save the purple guard, who, heedless of danger, sang of Welleran still, for waking men cannot hear the souls of the dead.

But Welleran drifted over the roofs of the city till he came to the form of Rold lying fast asleep. Now Rold was grown strong and was eighteen years of age, and he was fair of hair and tall like Welleran, and the soul of Welleran hovered over him and went into his dreams as a butterfly flits through trellis-work into a garden of flowers, and the soul of Welleran said to Rold in his dreams: "Thou wouldst go and see again the sword of Welleran, the great curved sword of Welleran. Thou wouldst go and look at it in the night with the moonlight shining upon it."

And the longing of Rold in his dreams to see the sword caused him to walk still sleeping from his mother's house to the hall wherein were the trophies of the heroes. And the soul of Welleran urging the dreams of Rold caused him to pause before the great red cloak, and there the soul said among the dreams: "Thou art cold in the night; fling now a cloak around thee."

And Rold drew round about him the huge red cloak of Welleran. Then Rold's dreams took him to the sword, and the soul said to the dreams: "Thou hast a longing to hold the sword of Welleran: take up the sword in thy hand."

But Rold said: "What should a man do with the sword of Welleran?"

And the soul of the old captain said to the dreams: "It is a good sword to hold: take up the sword of Welleran."

And Rold, still sleeping, and speaking aloud, said: "It is not lawful; none may touch the sword."

And Rold turned to go. Then a great and terrible cry arose in the soul of Welleran, all the more bitter for that he could not utter it, and it went round and round his soul finding no utterance, like a cry evoked long since by some murderous deed in some old haunted chamber, that whispers through the ages heard by none.

And the soul of Welleran cried out to the dreams of Rold: "Thy knees are tied! Thou art fallen in a marsh! Thou canst not move."

And the dreams of Rold said to him: "Thy knees are tied, thou art fallen in a marsh." And Rold stood still before the sword. Then the soul of the warrior wailed among Rold's dreams, as Rold stood before the sword:

"Welleran is crying for his sword, his wonderful curved sword. Poor Welleran, that once fought for Merimna, is crying for his sword in the night. Thou wouldst not keep Welleran without his beautiful sword when he is dead and cannot come for it, poor Welleran who fought for Merimna."

And Rold broke the glass casket with his hand and took the sword, the great curved sword of Welleran; and the soul of the warrior said among Rold's dreams: "Welleran is waiting in the deep ravine that runs into the mountains, crying for his sword."

And Rold went down through the city and climbed over the ramparts, and walked, with his eyes wide open but still sleeping, over the desert to the mountains.

Already a great multitude of Merimna's citizens were gathered in the desert before the deep ravine with old swords in their hands, and Rold passed through them as he slept, holding the sword of Welleran, and the people cried in amaze to one another as he passed: "Rold hath the sword of Welleran!"

And Rold came to the mouth of the ravine, and there the voices of the people woke him. And Rold knew nothing that he had done in his sleep, and looked in amazement at the sword in his hand, and said: "What art thou, thou beautiful thing? Lights shimmer in thee, thou art restless. It is the sword of Welleran, the curved sword of Welleran!"

And Rold kissed the hilt of it, and it was salt upon his lips with the battle-sweat of Welleran. And Rold said: "What should a man do with the sword of Welleran?"

And all the people wondered at Rold as he sat there with the sword in his hand, muttering: "What should a man do with the sword of Welleran?"

Presently there came to the ears of Rold the noise of a jingling up in the ravine, and all the people, the people that knew naught of war, heard the jingling coming nearer in the night; for the four armies were moving on Merimna and not yet expecting an enemy. And Rold gripped upon the hilt of the great curved sword, and the sword seemed to lift a little. And a new thought came into the hearts of Merimna's people as they gripped their grandsires' swords. Nearer and nearer came the heedless armies of the four kings, and old ancestral memories began to arise in the minds of Merimna's people in the desert with their swords in their hands, sitting behind Rold. And all the sentinels were awake holding their spears, for Rollory had put their dreams to flight, Rollory that once could put to flight armies and now was but a dream struggling with other dreams.

And now the armies had come very near. Suddenly Rold leaped up, crying: "Welleran! And the sword of Welleran!" And the savage, lusting sword that had thirsted for a hundred years went up with the hand of Rold and swept through a tribesman's ribs. And with the warm blood all about it there came a joy into the curved soul of that mighty sword, like to the joy of a swimmer coming up dripping out of warm seas after living for long in a dry land. When they saw the red cloak and that terrible sword a cry ran through the tribal armies: "Welleran lives!" And there arose the sounds of the exulting of victorious men, and the panting of those that fled, and the sword singing softly to itself as it whirled dripping through the air. And the last that I saw of the battle as it poured into the depth and darkness of the ravine was the sword of Welleran sweeping up and falling, gleaming blue in the moonlight whenever it arose and afterwards gleaming red, and so disappearing into the darkness.

But in the dawn Merimna's men came back, and the sun arising to give new life to the world, shone instead upon the hideous things that the sword of Welleran had done. And Rold said: "O sword, sword! How horrible thou art! Thou art a terrible thing to have come among men. How many eyes shall look upon gardens no more because of thee? How many fields must go empty that might have been fair with cottages, white cottages with children all about them? How many valleys must go desolate that might have nursed warm hamlets, because thou hast slain long since the men that might have built them? I hear the wind crying against thee, thou sword! It comes from the empty valleys. It comes over the bare fields. There are children's voices in it. They were never born. Death brings an end to crying for those that had life once, but these must cry for ever. O sword, sword, why did the gods send thee among men?" And the tears of Rold fell down upon the proud sword, but could not wash it clean.

800 LORD DUNSANY

And now that the ardour of battle had passed away, the spirits of Merimna's people began to gloom a little, like their leader's, with their fatigue and with the cold of the morning; and they looked at the sword of Welleran in Rold's hand and said: "Not any more, not any more forever will Welleran now return, for his sword is in the hand of another. Now we know indeed that he is dead. O Welleran, thou wast our sun and moon and all our stars. Now is the sun fallen down and the moon broken, and all the stars are scattered, as the diamonds of a necklace that is snapped of one who is slain by violence."

Thus wept the people of Merimna in the hour of their great victory, for men have strange moods, while beside them their old inviolate city slumbered safe. But back from the ramparts and beyond the mountains, and over the lands that they had conquered of old, beyond the world and back again to Paradise, went the souls of Welleran, Soorenard, Mommolek, Rollary, Akanax, and young Irain.

56

The Celestial Omnibus

BY E. M. FORSTER

THE boy who resided at Aga-
thox Lodge, 28, Buckingham Park Road, Surbiton, had often been
puzzled by the old sign-post that stood almost opposite. He asked his
mother about it, and she replied that it was a joke, and not a very nice
one, which had been made many years back by some naughty young
men, and that the police ought to remove it. For there were two strange
things about this sign-post: firstly, it pointed up a blank alley, and,
secondly, it had painted on it, in faded characters, the words, "To
Heaven."

"What kind of young men were they?" he asked.

"I think your father told me that one of them wrote verses, and was
expelled from the University and came to grief in other ways. Still, it
was a long time ago. You must ask your father about it. He will say the
same as I do, that it was put up as a joke."

"So it doesn't mean anything at all?"

She sent him up-stairs to put on his best things, for the Bonses were
coming to tea, and he was to hand the cake-stand.

It struck him, as he wrenched on his tightening trousers, that he
might do worse than ask Mr. Bons about the sign-post. His father,
though very kind, always laughed at him—shrieked with laughter
whenever he or any other child asked a question or spoke. But Mr. Bons
was serious as well as kind. He had a beautiful house and lent one books,
he was a churchwarden, and a candidate for the County Council; he
had donated to the Free Library enormously, he presided over the Literary Society, and had Members of Parliament to stop with him—in
short, he was probably the wisest person alive.

Yet even Mr. Bons could only say that the sign-post was a joke—the
joke of a person named Shelley.

"Of course!" cried the mother; "I told you so, dear. That was the name."

"Had you never heard of Shelley?" asked Mr. Bons.

"No," said the boy, and hung his head.

"But is there no Shelley in the house?"

"Why, yes!" exclaimed the lady, in much agitation. "Dear Mr. Bons, we aren't such Philistines as that. Two at the least. One a wedding present, and the other, smaller print, in one of the spare rooms."

"I believe we have seven Shelleys," said Mr. Bons, with a slow smile. Then he brushed the cake crumbs off his stomach, and, together with his daughter, rose to go.

The boy, obeying a wink from his mother, saw them all the way to the garden gate, and when they had gone he did not at once return to the house, but gazed for a little up and down Buckingham Park Road.

His parents lived at the right end of it. After No. 39 the quality of the houses dropped very suddenly, and 64 had not even a separate servants' entrance. But at the present moment the whole road looked rather pretty, for the sun had just set in splendour, and the inequalities of rent were drowned in a saffron afterglow. Small birds twittered, and the breadwinners' train shrieked musically down through the cutting—that wonderful cutting which has drawn to itself the whole beauty out of Surbiton, and clad itself, like any Alpine valley, with the glory of the fir and the silver birch and the primrose. It was this cutting that had first stirred desires within the boy—desires for something just a little different, he knew not what, desires that would return whenever things were sunlit, as they were this evening, running up and down inside him, up and down, up and down, till he would feel quite unusual all over, and as likely as not would want to cry. This evening he was even sillier, for he slipped across the road towards the sign-post and began to run up the blank alley.

The alley runs between high walls—the walls of the gardens of "Ivanhoe" and "Belle Vista" respectively. It smells a little all the way, and is scarcely twenty yards long, including the turn at the end. So not unnaturally the boy soon came to a standstill. "I'd like to kick that Shelley," he exclaimed, and glanced idly at a piece of paper which was pasted on the wall. Rather an odd piece of paper, and he read it carefully before he turned back. This is what he read:

S. AND C. R. C. C.
Alteration in Service

Owing to lack of patronage the Company are regretfully compelled to suspend the hourly service, and to retain only the

Sunrise and Sunset Omnibuses,

which will run as usual. It is to be hoped that the public will patronize an arrangement which is intended for their convenience. As an extra inducement, the Company will, for the first time, now issue

Return Tickets!
(available one day only), which may be obtained of the driver. Passengers are again reminded that no tickets are issued at the other end, and that no complaints in this connection will receive consideration from the Company. Nor will the Company be responsible for any negligence or stupidity on the part of Passengers, nor for Hailstorms, Lightning, Loss of Tickets, nor for any Act of God.

§ *For the Direction.*

Now he had never seen this notice before, nor could he imagine where the omnibus went to. S. of course was for Surbiton, and R.C.C. meant Road Car Company. But what was the meaning of the other C.? Coombe and Malden, perhaps, or possibly "City." Yet it could not hope to compete with the South-Western. The whole thing, the boy reflected, was run on hopelessly unbusiness-like lines. Why not tickets from the other end? And what an hour to start! Then he realized that unless the notice was a hoax, an omnibus must have been starting just as he was wishing the Bonses good-bye. He peered at the ground through the gathering dusk, and there he saw what might or might not be the marks of wheels. Yet nothing had come out of the alley. And he had never seen an omnibus at any time in the Buckingham Park Road. No: it must be a hoax, like the sign-posts, like the fairy tales, like the dreams upon which he would wake suddenly in the night. And with a sigh he stepped from the alley—right into the arms of his father.

Oh, how his father laughed! "Poor, poor Popsey!" he cried. "Diddums! Diddums! Diddums think he'd walky-palky up to Evvink!" And his mother, also convulsed with laughter, appeared on the steps of Agathox Lodge. "Don't, Bob!" she gasped. "Don't be so naughty! Oh, you'll kill me! Oh, leave the boy alone!"

But all that evening the joke was kept up. The father implored to be taken too. Was it a very tiring walk? Need one wipe one's shoes on the door-mat? And the boy went to bed feeling faint and sore, and thankful for only one thing—that he had not said a word about the omnibus. It was a hoax, yet through his dreams it grew more and more real, and the streets of Surbiton, through which he saw it driving, seemed instead to become hoaxes and shadows. And very early in the morning he woke with a cry, for he had had a glimpse of its destination.

He struck a match, and its light fell not only on his watch but also on his calendar, so that he knew it to be half-an-hour to sunrise. It was pitch dark, for the fog had come down from London in the night, and all Surbiton was wrapped in its embrace. Yet he sprang out and dressed himself, for he was determined to settle once for all which was real: the omnibus or the streets. "I shall be a fool one way or the other," he thought, "until I know." Soon he was shivering in the road under the gas lamp that guarded the entrance to the alley.

To enter the alley itself required some courage. Not only was it horribly dark, but he now realized that it was an impossible terminus for an omnibus. If it had not been for a policeman, whom he heard approaching through the fog, he would never have made the attempt. The next moment he had made the attempt and failed. Nothing. Nothing but a blank alley and a very silly boy gaping at its dirty floor. It *was* a hoax. "I'll tell papa and mamma," he decided. "I deserve it. I deserve that they should know. I am too silly to be alive." And he went back to the gate of Agathox Lodge.

There he remembered that his watch was fast. The sun was not risen; it would not rise for two minutes. "Give the bus every chance," he thought cynically, and returned into the alley.

But the omnibus was there.

It had two horses, whose sides were still smoking from their journey, and its two great lamps shone through the fog against the alley's walls, changing their cobwebs and moss into tissues of fairyland. The driver was huddled up in a cape. He faced the blank wall, and how he had managed to drive in so neatly and so silently was one of the many things that the boy never discovered. Nor could he imagine how ever he would drive out.

"Please," his voice quavered through the foul brown air, "Please, is that an omnibus?"

"Omnibus est," said the driver, without turning round. There was a moment's silence. The policeman passed, coughing, by the entrance of the alley. The boy crouched in the shadow, for he did not want to be found out. He was pretty sure, too, that it was a Pirate; nothing else, he reasoned, would go from such odd places and at such odd hours.

"About when do you start?" He tried to sound nonchalant.

"At sunrise."

"How far do you go?"

"The whole way."

"And can I have a return ticket which will bring me all the way back?"

"You can."

"Do you know, I half think I'll come." The driver made no answer. The sun must have risen, for he unhitched the brake. And scarcely had the boy jumped in before the omnibus was off.

How? Did it turn? There was no room. Did it go forward? There was a blank wall. Yet it was moving—moving at a stately pace through the fog, which had turned from brown to yellow. The thought of warm bed and warmer breakfast made the boy feel faint. He wished he had not come. His parents would not have approved. He would have gone back to them if the weather had not made it impossible. The solitude was terrible; he was the only passenger. And the omnibus, though well-built, was cold and somewhat musty. He drew his coat round him, and in so doing chanced to feel his pocket. It was empty. He had forgotten his purse.

"Stop!" he shouted. "Stop!" And then, being of a polite disposition, he glanced up at the painted notice-board so that he might call the driver by name. "Mr. Browne! stop; O, do please stop!"

Mr. Browne did not stop, but he opened a little window and looked in at the boy. His face was a surprise, so kind it was and modest.

"Mr. Browne, I've left my purse behind. I've not got a penny. I can't pay for the ticket. Will you take my watch, please? I am in the most awful hole."

"Tickets on this line," said the driver, "whether single or return, can be purchased by coinage from no terrene mint. And a chronometer, though it had solaced the vigils of Charlemagne, or measured the slumbers of Laura, can acquire by no mutation the double-cake that charms the fangless Cerberus of Heaven!" So saying, he handed in the necessary ticket, and, while the boy said "Thank you," continued: "Titular pretensions, I know it well, are vanity. Yet they merit no censure when uttered on a laughing lip, and in an homonymous world are in some sort useful, since they do serve to distinguish one Jack from his fellow. Remember me, therefore, as Sir Thomas Browne."

"Are you a Sir? Oh, sorry!" He had heard of these gentlemen drivers. "It *is* good of you about the ticket. But if you go on at this rate, however does your bus pay?"

"It does not pay. It was not intended to pay. Many are the faults of my equipage; it is compounded too curiously of foreign woods; its cushions tickle erudition rather than promote repose; and my horses are nourished not on the evergreen pastures of the moment, but on the dried bents and clovers of Latinity. But that it pays!—that error at all events was never intended and never attained."

"Sorry again," said the boy rather hopelessly. Sir Thomas looked sad, fearing that, even for a moment, he had been the cause of sadness. He invited the boy to come up and sit beside him on the box, and together they journeyed on through the fog, which was now changing from yellow to white. There were no houses by the road; so it must be either Putney Heath or Wimbledon Common.

"Have you been a driver always?"

"I was a physician once."

"But why did you stop? Weren't you good?"

"As a healer of bodies I had scant success, and several score of my patients preceded me. But as a healer of the spirit I have succeeded beyond my hopes and my deserts. For though my draughts were not better nor subtler than those of other men, yet, by reason of the cunning goblets wherein I offered them, the queasy soul was ofttimes tempted to sip and be refreshed."

"The queasy soul," he murmured; "if the sun sets with trees in front of it, and you suddenly come strange all over, is that a queasy soul?"

"Have you felt that?"

"Why yes."

After a pause he told the boy a little, a very little, about the journey's end. But they did not chatter much, for the boy, when he liked a person, would as soon sit silent in his company as speak, and this, he discovered, was also the mind of Sir Thomas Browne and of many others with whom he was to be acquainted. He heard, however, about the young man Shelley, who was now quite a famous person, with a carriage of his own, and about some of the other drivers who are in the service of the Company. Meanwhile the light grew stronger, though the fog did not disperse. It was now more like mist than fog, and at times would travel quickly across them, as if it was part of a cloud. They had been ascending, too, in a most puzzling way; for over two hours the horses had been pulling against the collar, and even if it were Richmond Hill they ought to have been at the top long ago. Perhaps it was Epsom, or even the North Downs; yet the air seemed keener than that which blows on either. And as to the name of their destination, Sir Thomas Browne was silent.

Crash!

"Thunder, by Jove!" said the boy, "and not so far off either. Listen to the echoes! It's more like mountains."

He thought, not very vividly, of his father and mother. He saw them sitting down to sausages and listening to the storm. He saw his own empty place. Then there would be questions, alarms, theories, jokes, consolations. They would expect him back at lunch. To lunch he would not come, nor to tea, but he would be in for dinner, and so his day's truancy would be over. If he had had his purse he would have bought them presents—not that he should have known what to get them.

Crash!

The peal and the lightning came together. The cloud quivered as if it were alive, and torn streamers of mist rushed past. "Are you afraid?" asked Sir Thomas Browne.

"What is there to be afraid of? Is it much farther?"

The horses of the omnibus stopped just as a ball of fire burst up and exploded with a ringing noise that was deafening but clear, like the noise of a blacksmith's forge. All the cloud was shattered.

"Oh, listen, Sir Thomas Browne! No, I mean look; we shall get a view at last. No, I mean listen; that sounds like a rainbow!"

The noise had died into the faintest murmur, beneath which another murmur grew, spreading stealthily, steadily, in a curve that widened but did not vary. And in widening curves a rainbow was spreading from the horses' feet into the dissolving mists.

"But how beautiful! What colours! Where will it stop? It is more like the rainbows you can tread on. More like dreams."

The colour and the sound grew together. The rainbow spanned an enormous gulf. Clouds rushed under it and were pierced by it, and still it grew, reaching forward, conquering the darkness, until it touched something that seemed more solid than a cloud.

The boy stood up. "What is that out there?" he called. "What does it rest on, out at that other end?"

In the morning sunshine a precipice shone forth beyond the gulf. A precipice—or was it a castle? The horses moved. They set their feet upon the rainbow.

"Oh, look!" the boy shouted. "Oh, listen! Those caves—or are they gateways? Oh, look between those cliffs at those ledges. I see people! I see trees!"

"Look also below," whispered Sir Thomas. "Neglect not the diviner Acheron."

The boy looked below, past the flames of the rainbow that licked against their wheels. The gulf also had cleared, and in its depths there flowed an everlasting river. One sunbeam entered and struck a green pool, and as they passed over he saw three maidens rise to the surface of the pool, singing, and playing with something that glistened like a ring.

"You down in the water——" he called.

They answered, "You up on the bridge——" There was a burst of music. "You up on the bridge, good luck to you. Truth in the depth, truth on the height."

"You down in the water, what are you doing?"

Sir Thomas Browne replied: "They sport in the mancipiary possession of their gold"; and the omnibus arrived.

The boy was in disgrace. He sat locked up in the nursery of Agathox Lodge, learning poetry for a punishment. His father had said, "My boy! I can pardon anything but untruthfulness," and had caned him, saying at each stroke, "There is *no* omnibus, *no* driver, *no* bridge, *no* mountain; you are a *truant,* a *guttersnipe, a liar."* His father could be very stern at times. His mother had begged him to say he was sorry. But he could not say that. It was the greatest day of his life, in spite of the caning and the poetry at the end of it.

He had returned punctually at sunset—driven not by Sir Thomas Browne, but by a maiden lady who was full of quiet fun. They had talked of omnibuses and also of barouche landaus. How far away her gentle voice seemed now! Yet it was scarcely three hours since he had left her up the alley.

His mother called through the door. "Dear, you are to come down and to bring your poetry with you."

He came down, and found that Mr. Bons was in the smoking-room with his father. It had been a dinner party.

"Here is the great traveller!" said his father grimly. "Here is the young gentleman who drives in an omnibus over rainbows, while young ladies sing to him." Pleased with his wit, he laughed.

"After all," said Mr. Bons, smiling, "there is something a little like it in Wagner. It is odd how, in quite illiterate minds, you will find glimmers of Artistic Truth. The case interests me. Let me plead for the culprit. We have all romanced in our time, haven't we?"

"Hear how kind Mr. Bons is," said his mother, while his father said, "Very well. Let him say his poem, and that will do. He is going away to my sister on Tuesday, and *she* will cure him of this alley-slopering." (Laughter.) "Say your poem."

The boy began. " 'Standing aloof in giant ignorance.' "

His father laughed again—roared. "One for you, my son! 'Standing aloof in giant ignorance!' I never knew these poets talked sense. Just describes you. Here, Bons, you go in for poetry. Put him through it, will you, while I fetch up the whisky?"

"Yes, give me the Keats," said Mr. Bons. "Let him say his Keats to me."

So for a few moments the wise man and the ignorant boy were left alone in the smoking-room.

" 'Standing aloof in giant ignorance, of thee I dream and of the Cyclades, as one who sits ashore and longs perchance to visit——' "

"Quite right. To visit what?"

" 'To visit dolphin coral in deep seas,' " said the boy, and burst into tears.

"Come, come! why do you cry?"

"Because—because all these words that only rhymed before, now that I've come back they're me."

Mr. Bons laid the Keats down. The case was more interesting than he had expected. *"You?"* he exclaimed. "This sonnet, *you?*"

"Yes—and look further on: 'Aye, on the shores of darkness there is light, and precipices show untrodden green.' It *is* so, sir. All these things are true."

"I never doubted it," said Mr. Bons, with closed eyes.

"You—then you believe me? You believe in the omnibus and the driver and the storm and that return ticket I got for nothing and——"

"Tut, tut! No more of your yarns, my boy. I meant that I never doubted the essential truth of poetry. Some day, when you have read more, you will understand what I mean."

"But Mr. Bons, it *is* so. There *is* light upon the shores of darkness. I have seen it coming. Light and a wind."

"Nonsense," said Mr. Bons.

"If I had stopped! They tempted me. They told me to give up my ticket—for you cannot come back if you lose your ticket. They called from the river for it, and indeed I was tempted, for I have never been so happy as among those precipices. But I thought of my mother and father, and that I must fetch them. Yet they will not come, though the road starts opposite our house. It has all happened as the people up there warned me, and Mr. Bons has disbelieved me like every one else. I have been caned. I shall never see that mountain again."

"What's that about me?" said Mr. Bons, sitting up in his chair very suddenly.

"I told them about you, and how clever you were, and how many books you had, and they said, 'Mr. Bons will certainly disbelieve you.' "

"Stuff and nonsense, my young friend. You grow impertinent. I—well—I will settle the matter. Not a word to your father. I will cure you. To-morrow evening I will myself call here to take you for a walk, and at sunset we will go up this alley opposite and hunt for your omnibus, you silly little boy."

His face grew serious, for the boy was not disconcerted, but leapt about the room singing, "Joy! joy! I told them you would believe me. We will drive together over the rainbow. I told them that you would come." After all, could there be anything in the story? Wagner? Keats? Shelley? Sir Thomas Browne? Certainly the case was interesting.

And on the morrow evening, though it was pouring with rain, Mr. Bons did not omit to call at Agathox Lodge.

The boy was ready, bubbling with excitement, and skipping about in a way that rather vexed the President of the Literary Society. They took a turn down Buckingham Park Road, and then—having seen that no one was watching them—slippped up the alley. Naturally enough (for the sun was setting) they ran straight against the omnibus.

"Good heavens!" exclaimed Mr. Bons. "Good gracious heavens!"

It was not the omnibus in which the boy had driven first, nor yet that in which he had returned. There were three horses—black, gray, and white, the gray being the finest. The driver, who turned round at the mention of goodness and of heaven, was a sallow man with terrifying jaws and sunken eyes. Mr. Bons, on seeing him, gave a cry as if of recognition, and began to tremble violently.

The boy jumped in.

"Is it possible?" cried Mr. Bons. "Is the impossible possible?"

"Sir; come in, sir. It is such a fine omnibus. Oh, here is his name—Dan some one."

Mr. Bons sprang in too. A blast of wind immediately slammed the omnibus door, and the shock jerked down all the omnibus blinds, which were very weak on their springs.

"Dan . . . Show me. Good gracious heavens! we're moving."

"Hooray!" said the boy.

Mr. Bons became flustered. He had not intended to be kidnapped. He could not find the door-handle, nor push up the blinds. The omnibus was quite dark, and by the time he had struck a match, night had come on outside also. They were moving rapidly."

"A strange, a memorable adventure," he said, surveying the interior of the omnibus, which was large, roomy, and constructed with extreme regularity, every part exactly answering to every other part. Over the door (the handle of which was outside) was written, _Lasciate ogni baldanza voi che entrate_—at least, that was what was written, but Mr. Bons said that it was Lashy arty something, and that _baldanza_ was a mistake for _speranza_. His voice sounded as if he was in church. Meanwhile, the boy called to the cadaverous driver for two return tickets. They were handed in without a word. Mr. Bons covered his face with his hand and again trembled. "Do you know who that is!" he whispered, when the little window had shut upon them. "It is the impossible."

"Well, I don't like him as much as Sir Thomas Browne, though I shouldn't be surprised if he had even more in him."

"More in him?" He stamped irritably. "By accident you have made the greatest discovery of the century, and all you can say is that there is more in this man. Do you remember those vellum books in my library, stamped with red lilies? This—sit still, I bring you stupendous news! —*this is the man who wrote them.*"

The boy sat quite still. "I wonder if we shall see Mrs. Gamp?" he asked, after a civil pause.

"Mrs.——?"

"Mrs. Gamp and Mrs. Harris. I like Mrs. Harris. I came upon them quite suddenly. Mrs. Gamp's bandboxes have moved over the rainbow so badly. All the bottoms have fallen out, and two of the pippins off her bedstead tumbled into the stream."

"Out there sits the man who wrote my vellum books!" thundered Mr. Bons, "and you talk to me of Dickens and of Mrs. Gamp?"

"I know Mrs. Gamp so well," he apologized. "I could not help being glad to see her. I recognized her voice. She was telling Mrs. Harris about Mrs. Prig."

"Did you spend the whole day in her elevating company?"

"Oh, no. I raced. I met a man who took me out beyond to a race-course. You run, and there are dolphins out at sea."

"Indeed. Do you remember the man's name?"

"Achilles. No; he was later. Tom Jones."

Mr. Bons sighed heavily. "Well, my lad, you have made a miserable mess of it. Think of a cultured person with your opportunities! A cultured person would have known all these characters and known what to have said to each. He would not have wasted his time with a Mrs. Gamp or a Tom Jones. The creations of Homer, of Shakespeare, and of Him who drives us now, would alone have contented him. He would not have raced. He would have asked intelligent questions."

"But, Mr. Bons," said the boy humbly, "you will be a cultured person. I told them so."

"True, true, and I beg you not to disgrace me when we arrive. No gossiping. No running. Keep close to my side, and never speak to these Immortals unless they speak to you. Yes, and give me the return tickets. You will be losing them."

The boy surrendered the tickets, but felt a little sore. After all, he had found the way to this place. It was hard first to be disbelieved and then to be lectured. Meanwhile, the rain had stopped, and moonlight crept into the omnibus through the cracks in the blinds.

"But how is there to be a rainbow?" cried the boy.

"You distract me," snapped Mr. Bons. "I wish to meditate on beauty. I wish to goodness I was with a reverent and sympathetic person."

The lad bit his lip. He made a hundred good resolutions. He would imitate Mr. Bons all the visit. He would not laugh, or run, or sing, or do any of the vulgar things that must have disgusted his new friends last time. He would be very careful to pronounce their names properly, and to remember who knew whom. Achilles did not know Tom Jones— at least, so Mr. Bons said. The Duchess of Malfi was older than Mrs. Gamp—at least, so Mr. Bons said. He would be self-conscious, reticent, and prim. He would never say he liked any one. Yet, when the blind flew up at a chance touch of his head, all these good resolutions went to the winds, for the omnibus had reached the summit of a moonlit hill, and there was the chasm, and there, across it, stood the old precipices, dreaming, with their feet in the everlasting river. He exclaimed, "The mountain! Listen to the new tune in the water! Look at the camp fires in the ravines," and Mr. Bons, after a hasty glance, retorted, "Water? Camp fires? Ridiculous rubbish. Hold your tongue. There is nothing at all."

Yet, under his eyes, a rainbow formed, compounded not of sunlight and storm, but of moonlight and the spray of the river. The three horses put their feet upon it. He thought it the finest rainbow he had seen, but did not dare to say so, since Mr. Bons said that nothing was there. He leant out—the window had opened—and sang the tune that rose from the sleeping waters.

"The prelude to *Rhinegold?*" said Mr. Bons suddenly. "Who taught you these *leit motifs?*" He, too, looked out of the window. Then he behaved very oddly. He gave a choking cry, and fell back on to the omnibus floor. He writhed and kicked. His face was green.

"Does the bridge make you dizzy?" the boy asked.

"Dizzy!" gasped Mr. Bons. "I want to go back. Tell the driver."

But the driver shook his head.

"We are nearly there," said the boy. "They are asleep. Shall I call? They will be so pleased to see you, for I have prepared them."

Mr. Bons moaned. They moved over the lunar rainbow, which ever and ever broke away behind their wheels. How still the night was! Who would be sentry at the Gate?

"I am coming," he shouted, again forgetting the hundred resolutions. "I am returning—I, the boy."

"The boy is returning," cried a voice to other voices, who repeated, "The boy is returning."

"I am bringing Mr. Bons with me."

Silence.

"I should have said Mr. Bons is bringing me with him."

Profound silence.

"Who stands sentry?"

"Achilles."

And on the rocky causeway, close to the springing of the rainbow bridge, he saw a young man who carried a wonderful shield.

"Mr. Bons, it is Achilles, armed."

"I want to go back," said Mr. Bons.

The last fragment of the rainbow melted, the wheels sang upon the living rock, the door of the omnibus burst open. Out leapt the boy—he could not resist—and sprang to meet the warrior, who, stooping suddenly, caught him on his shield.

"Achilles!" he cried, "let me get down, for I am ignorant and vulgar, and I must wait for that Mr. Bons of whom I told you yesterday."

But Achilles raised him aloft. He crouched on the wonderful shield, on heroes and burning cities, on vineyards graven in gold, on every dear passion, every joy, on the entire image of the Mountain that he had discovered, encircled, like it, with an everlasting stream. "No, no," he protested, "I am not worthy. It is Mr. Bons who must be up here."

But Mr. Bons was whimpering, and Achilles trumpeted and cried, "Stand upright upon my shield!"

"Sir, I did not mean to stand! something made me stand. Sir, why do you delay? Here is only the great Achilles, whom you knew."

Mr. Bons screamed, "I see no one. I see nothing. I want to go back." Then he cried to the driver, "Save me! Let me stop in your chariot. I have honoured you. I have quoted you. I have bound you in vellum. Take me back to my world."

The driver replied, "I am the means and not the end. I am the food and not the life. Stand by yourself, as that boy has stood. I cannot save you. For poetry is a spirit; and they that would worship it must worship in spirit and in truth."

Mr. Bons—he could not resist—crawled out of the beautiful omnibus. His face appeared, gaping horribly. His hands followed, one gripping the step, the other beating the air. Now his shoulders emerged, his chest, his stomach. With a shriek of "I see London," he fell—fell against the hard, moonlit rock, fell into it as if it were water, fell through it, vanished, and was seen by the boy no more.

"Where have you fallen to, Mr. Bons? Here is a procession arriving to honour you with music and torches. Here come the men and women whose names you know. The mountain is awake, the river is awake, over the race-course the sea is awaking those dolphins, and it is all for you. They want you——"

There was the touch of fresh leaves on his forehead. Some one had crowned him.

ΤΕΛΟΣ

From the *Kingston Gazette, Surbiton Times,* and *Raynes Park Observer.*

The body of Mr. Septimus Bons has been found in a shockingly mutilated condition in the vicinity of the Bermondsey gas-works. The deceased's pockets contained a sovereign-purse, a silver cigar-case, a bijou pronouncing dictionary, and a couple of omnibus tickets. The unfortunate gentleman had apparently been hurled from a considerable height. Foul play is suspected, and a thorough investigation is pending by the authorities.

57

The Log of the "Evening Star"

BY ALFRED NOYES

WE were sitting in the porch of a low white bungalow with masses of purple bougainvillea embowering its eaves. A ruby-throated humming-bird, with green wings, flickered around it. The tall palms and the sea were whispering together. Over the water, the West was beginning to fill with that Californian sunset which is the most mysterious in the world, for one is conscious that it is the fringe of what Europeans call the East, and that, looking westward across the Pacific, our faces are turned towards the dusky myriads of Asia. All along the Californian coast there is a touch of incense in the air, as befits that silent orchard of the gods where dawn and sunset meet and intermingle; and though it is probably caused by some gardener burning the dead leaves of the eucalyptus trees, one might well believe that one breathed the scent of the joss-sticks, wafted across the Pacific from the land of paper lanterns.

A Japanese servant, in a white duck suit, marched like a ghostly little soldier across the lawn. The great hills behind us quietly turned to amethysts. The lights of Los Angeles, ten miles away to the north, began to spring out like stars in that amazing air beloved of the astronomer; and the evening star itself, over the huge, slow breakers crumbling into lilac-coloured foam, looked bright enough to be a companion of the city lights.

"I should like to show you the log of the *Evening Star*," said my visitor, who was none other than Moreton Fitch, president of the Insurance Company of San Francisco. "I think it may interest you as evidence that our business is not without its touches of romance. I don't mean what you mean," he added cheerfully, as I looked up smiling. "The *Evening Star* was a schoooner running between San Francisco and Tahiti and other places in the South Seas. She was insured in our Company. One April she was reported overdue. After search had been made, she was posted as lost in the maritime exchanges. There was no clue to what had happened, and we paid the insurance money, believing she had foundered with all hands.

"Two months later we got word from Tahiti that the *Evening Star* had been found drifting about in a dead calm, with all sails set, but not a soul aboard. Everything was in perfect order, except that the ship's cat was lying dead in the bows, baked to a bit of seaweed by the sun. Otherwise, there wasn't the slightest trace of any trouble. The tables below were laid for a meal, and there was plenty of water aboard."

"Were any of the boats missing?"

"No; she only carried three boats, and all were there. When she was discovered two of the boats were on deck as usual, and the third was towing astern. None of the men has been heard of from that day to this. The amazing part of it was not only the absence of anything that would account for the disappearance of the crew, but the clear evidence that they had been intending to stay, in the fact that the tables were laid for a meal and then abandoned. Besides, where had they gone, and how? There are no magic carpets, even in the South Seas. And this wasn't in wartime, remember.

"The best brains of our Company puzzled over the mystery for a year or more; but at the end of the time nothing had turned up and we had come out by the same door by which we had entered. No theory, even, seemed to fit the case at all; and in most mysteries there is room for a hundred theories. There were twelve persons aboard, and we investigated the history of them all. There were three American seamen, all of the domesticated kind, with respectable old mothers in gold-rimmed spectacles at home. There were five Kanakas of the mildest type, as easy to handle as an infant-school. There was a Japanese cook, who was something of an artist, used to spend his spare time in painting things to palm off on the unsuspecting connoisseur as the work of an obscure pupil of Hokusai, which I suppose he might have been in a way. I am told he was scrupulously careful never to tell a direct lie about it.

"Then there was Harper, the mate, rather an interesting young fellow, with the *wanderlust*. He had been pretty well educated. I believe he had spent a year or two at one of the Californian colleges. Altogether, about the most harmless kind of a ship's family that you could pick up anywhere between the Golden Gate and the Baltic. Then there was Captain Burgess, who was the most domesticated of them all, for he had his wife with him on this voyage. They had only been married about three months. She was the widow of the former captain of the

Evening Star, a fellow named Dayrell, and she had often been on the ship before. In fact, they were all old friends of the ship. Except one or two of the Kanakas, all the men had sailed on the *Evening Star* for something like two years under Captain Dayrell. Burgess himself had been his mate. Dayrell had only been dead about six months, and the only criticism we ever heard against anybody aboard was made by some of Dayrell's relatives, who thought the widow might have waited more than three months before marrying the newly promoted Burgess. They suggested, of course, that there must have been something between them before Dayrell was out of the way. But I hardly believed it. In any case, it threw no light on the mystery."

"What sort of a man was Burgess?"

"Big, burly fellow, with a fat, white face and curious little black eyes, like huckleberries in a lump of dough. He was very silent and inclined to be religious. He used to read Emerson and Carlyle, quite an unusual sort of sea captain. There was a *Sartor Resartus* in the cabin, with a lot of the queerest passages marked in pencil. What can you make of it?"

"Nothing at all, except that there was a woman aboard. What was she like?"

"She was one of our special Californian mixtures, touch of Italian, touch of Irish, touch of American, but Italian predominated, I think. She was a good deal younger than Burgess; and one of the clerks in our office who had seen her described her as a 'peach,' which, as you know, means a pretty woman, or if you prefer the description of her own lady friends, 'vurry attractive.'

"She had the dusky Italian beauty, black hair and eyes like black diamonds, but her face was very pale, the kind of pallor that makes you think of magnolia blossoms at dusk. She was obviously fond of bright colours, tawny reds and yellows, but they suited her. If I had to give you my impression of her in a single word, I should say that she looked like a gipsy. You know the song, 'Down the World with Marna,' don't you? Well, I could imagine a romantic vagabond singing it about her. By the by, she had rather a fine voice herself. Used to sing sentimental songs to Dayrell and his friends in Frisco—'Love's Old Sweet Song,' and that sort of stuff. Apparently they took it very seriously. Several of them told me that if she had been trained—well, you know the old story—every prima donna would have had to retire from business. I fancy they were all a little in love with her. The curious thing was that after Dayrell's death she gave up her singing altogether. Now, I think I have told you all the facts about the ship's company."

"Didn't you say there was a log you wanted to show me?"

"There were no ship's papers of any kind, and no log was found on the derelict; but a week or two ago we had a visit from the brother of the Japanese cook, who made us all feel like fifteen cents before the wisdom of the East. I have to go over and see him to-morrow after-noon. He is a fisherman, lives on the coast, not far from here. I'd like you to see what I call the log of the *Evening Star*. I won't say any more about it now. It isn't quite worked out yet; but it looks as if it's going to be interesting. Will you come—to-morrow afternoon? I'll call for you at a quarter after two. It won't take us long in the automobile. This is where he lives, see."

I switched on the electric light in the porch, while Fitch spread out a road-map, and pointed to our destination on the morrow. The Califor-nian night comes quickly, and the tree-toads that make it musical were chirruping and purr-ing all around us as we walked through the palms and the red-tasselled pepper trees to his car. Somewhere among the funeral clouds and poplar-like spires of the eucalyptus a mocking-bird began to whistle one of his many parts, and a delicious whiff of orange blossom blew on the cool night wind across a ranch of a thousand acres, mostly in fruit, but with a few trees yet in blossom, on the road to the Sunset Inn.

I watched his red rear lamp dwindling down that well-oiled road, and let the *Evening Star* go with it until the morrow, for I could make little of his yarn, except that Fitch was not a man to get excited over trifles.

Promptly at the time appointed on the following afternoon Fitch called for me, and a minute later we were gliding through orange groves along one of those broad, smooth roads that amaze the European whose impressions of California have been obtained from tales of the forty-niners. The keen scent of the orange blossom yielded to a tang of new incense as we turned into the Sunset boulevard and ran down the long vista of tall eucalyptus trees that stand out so darkly and distinctly against the lilac-coloured ranges of the Sierra Madre in the distance, and remind one of the poplar-bordered roads in France. Once we passed a swarthy cluster of Mexicans under a wayside palm. Big frag-ments, gnawed half-moons, of the blood-red, black-pipped water-melon they had been eating gleamed on the dark, oiled surface of the road, as a splash of the sunset is reflected in a dark river. Then we ran along the coast for a little way between the palms and the low white-pillared houses, all crimson poinsettias and marble, that looked as if they were meant for the gods and goddesses of Greece, but were only the homes of a few score lotus-eating millionaires. In another minute we had turned off the good highway, and were running along a narrow, sandy road. On one side, rising from the road, were great desert hills, covered with grey-green sage-brush, tinged at the tips with rusty brown; and on the other there was a strip of sandy beach where the big slow breakers tumbled, and the unmolested pelicans waddled and brooded like goblin sentries.

In three minutes more we sighted a cluster of tiny wooden houses ahead of us, and pulled up on the outskirts of a little Japanese fishing village built along the fringe of the beach itself. It was a single minia-ture street, nestling under the hill on one side of the narrow road, and built along the sand on the other. Japanese signs stood over quaint little stores, with here and there a curious tinge of Americanism. "Rice cakes and Candies" were advertised by one black-haired and boyish-looking gentleman, who sat at the door of his hut playing with three brown children, one of whom squinted at us gleefully with bright sloe-black eyes. Every tiny house, even when it stood on the beach, had its own little festoon of flowers. Wistaria drooped from the jutting eaves, and —perhaps only the Japanese could explain the miracle—tall and well-nourished red geraniums rose out of the salt seasand around their doors. A few had foregone their miracles and were content with window-boxes, but all were in blossom. In the centre of the village, on the sea-ward side, there was a miniature mission-house. A beautifully shaped bell swung over the roof, and there was a miniature notice-board at the door. The announcements upon it were in Japanese, but it looked as if East and West had certainly met and kissed each other there. Some of the huts had little oblong letter-boxes of grey tin, perched on stumps of bamboo fishing-poles, in front of their doors. It is a common device to help the postman in country places, where you sometimes see a letter-box on a broomstick standing half a mile from the owner's house. But here they looked curiously Japanese, perhaps because of the names in-scribed upon them, or through some trick of arrangement; for a Jap-anese hand no sooner touches a dead staff than it breaks into cherry blossom. We stopped before one that bore the name of Y. Kato. His un-painted wooden shack was the most Japanese of all in appearance; for the yellow placard underneath the window advertising "Sweet Caporal" was balanced by a single tall pole, planted in the sand a few feet to the right, and lifting a beautiful little bird-house high above the roof.

Moreton Fitch knocked at the door. It was opened at once by a dainty creature, a piece of animated porcelain, four feet high, with a black-eyed baby on her back; and we were ushered, with smiles, in a very bare living-room, to be greeted by the polished mahogany countenance of Kato himself, and the shell-spectacled intellectual pallor of Howard Knight, professor in the University of California.

"Amazing, amazing, perfectly amazing," said Knight, who was wearing two elderly tea-roses in his cheeks now from excitement. "I have just finished it. Sit down and listen."

"Wait a moment," said Fitch, "I want our friend here to see the original log of the *Evening Star*."

"Of course," said Knight, "a human document of the utmost value." Then, to my surprise, he took me by the arm and led me in front of a large *kakemono*, which was the only decoration on the walls of the room.

"This is what Mr. Fitch calls the log of the *Evening Star*," he said. "It was found among the effects of Mr. Kato's brother on the schooner; and, fortunately, it was claimed by Mr. Kato himself. Take it to the light and examine it."

I took it to the window and looked at it with curiosity, though I did not quite see its bearing on the mystery of the *Evening Star*. It was a fine piece of work, one of those weird night pictures in which the Japanese are masters; for they know how to give you the single point of light that tells you of the unseen life around the lamp of the household or the temple. This was a picture of a little dark house, with jutting eaves, and a tiny rose light in one window, overlooking the sea. At the brink of the sea rose a ghostly figure that might only be a drift of mist, for the curve of the vague body suggested that the off-shore wind was blowing it out to sea, while the great gleaming eyes were fixed on the lamp, and the shadowy arms outstretched towards it in hopeless longing. Sea and ghost and house were suggested in a very few strokes of the brush. All the rest, the peace and the tragic desire and a thousand other suggestions, according to the mood of the beholder, were concentrated into that single pinpoint of warm light in the window.

"Turn it over," said Fitch.

I obeyed him, and saw that the whole back of the *kakemono*, which measured about four feet by two, was covered with a fine scroll of Japanese characters in purple copying-pencil. I had overlooked it at first, or accepted it, with the eye of ignorance, as a mere piece of Oriental decoration.

"That is what we all did," said Fitch. "We all overlooked the simple fact that Japanese words have a meaning. We didn't trouble about it— you know how vaguely one's eye travels over a three-foot sign on a Japanese tea-house—we didn't even think about it till Mr. Kato turned up in our office a week or two ago. You can't read it. No more can I. But we got Mr. Knight here to handle it for us."

"It turns out to be a message from Harper," said Knight. "Apparently he was lying helpless in his berth, and told the Japanese to write it down. A few sentences here and there are unintelligible, owing to the refraction of the Oriental mind. Fortunately, it is Harper's own message. I have made two versions, one a perfectly literal one, which requires a certain amount of retranslation. The other is an attempt to give as nearly as possible what Harper himself dictated. This is the version which I had better read to you now. The original has various repetitions, and shows that Harper's mind occasionally wandered, for he goes into trivial detail sometimes. But he seems to have been possessed with the idea of getting his account through to the owners; and, whenever he got an opportunity, he made Kato take up his pencil and write, so that we have a very full account."

Knight took out a note-book, adjusted his glasses, and began to read, while the ghostly original fluttered in my hand, as the night wind blew from the sea.

"A terrible thing has happened, and I think it my duty to write this, in the hope that it may fall into the hands of friends at home. I am not likely to live another twenty-four hours. The first hint that I had of anything wrong was on the night of March the fifteenth, when Mrs. Burgess came up to me on deck, looking worried, and said, 'Mr. Harper, I am in great trouble. I want to ask you a question, and I want you to give me an honest answer.' She looked round nervously, and her hands were fidgeting with her handkerchief, as if she were frightened to death. 'Whatever your answer may be,' she said, 'you'll not mention what I've said to you.' I promised her. She laid her hand on my arm and said, with the most piteous look in her face I have ever seen, 'I have no other friends to go to, and I want you to tell me. Mr. Harper, is my husband sane?'

"I had never doubted the sanity of Burgess till that moment. But there was something in the dreadfulness of that question from a woman who had only been married a few months that seemed like a door opening into the bottomless pit.

"It seemed to explain many things that hadn't occurred to me before. I asked her what she meant, and she told me that last night Burgess had come into the cabin and waked her up. His eyes were starting out of his head, and he told her that he had seen Captain Dayrell walking on deck. She told him it was nothing but imagination, and he laid his head on his arms and sobbed like a child. He said he thought it was one of the deck hands that had just come out of the fo'c'sle, but all the men were short and smallish, and this was a big burly figure. It went ahead of him like his own shadow, and disappeared in the bows. But he knew it was Dayrell, and there was a curse on him. To-night, she said, half an hour ago, Burgess had come down to her, taking her by the throat, and sworn he would kill her if she didn't confess that Dayrell was still alive. She told him he must be crazy. 'My mind may be going,' he said, 'but you shan't kill my soul.' And he called her a name which she didn't repeat, but began to cry when she remembered it. He said he had seen Dayrell standing in the bows with the light of the moon full on his face, and he looked so brave and upright that he knew he must have been bitterly wronged. He looked like a soldier facing the enemy, he said.

"While she was telling me this she was looking around her in a very nervous kind of way, and we both heard someone coming up behind us very quietly. We turned round, and there—as God lives—stood the living image of Captain Dayrell looking at us in the shadow of the mast. Mrs. Burgess gave a shriek that paralysed me for the moment, then she ran like a wild thing into the bows, and before anyone could stop her she climbed up and threw herself overboard. Evans and Barron were only a few yards away from her when she did it, and they both went overboard after her immediately, one of them throwing a lifebelt over ahead of him as he went. They were both good swimmers, and as the moon was bright, I thought we had only to launch a boat to pick them all up. I shouted to the Kanakas, and they all came up running. Two of the men and myself got into one of the starboard boats; and we were within three feet of the water when I heard the crack of a revolver from somewhere in the bows of the *Evening Star*. The men, who were lowering away, let us down with a rush that nearly capsized us. There were four more shots while we were getting our oars out. I called to the men on deck, asking them who was shooting, but got no reply. I believe they were panic-stricken and had bolted into cover. We pulled round the bows, and could see nothing. There was not a sign of the woman or the two men in the water.

"We could make nobody hear us on the ship, and all this while we had seen nothing of Captain Burgess. It must have been nearly an hour before we gave up our search and tried to get aboard again. We were still unable to get any reply from the ship, and we were about to try to climb on board by the boat's falls. The men were backing her in, stern first, and we were about ten yards from the ship when the figure of Captain Dayrell appeared, leaning over the side of the *Evening Star*. He stood there against the moonlight with his face in the shadow; but we all of us recognised him, and I heard the teeth of the Kanakas chattering. They had stopped backing, and we all stared at one another. Then, as casually as if it were a joke, Captain Dayrell stretched out his arm, and I saw the moonlight glint on his revolver. He fired at us deliberately, as if he were shooting at clay pigeons. I felt the wind of the first shot going past my head, and the two men at once began to pull hard to get out of range. The second shot missed also. At the third shot he got the man in the bows full in the face. He fell over backwards, and lay there in the bottom of the boat. He must have been killed instantaneously. At the fourth shot I felt a stinging pain on the left side of my body, but hardly realised I had been wounded at the moment. A cloud passed over the moon just then, and the way we had got on the boat carried us too far for Dayrell to aim very accurately, so that I was able to get to the oars and pull out of range. The other man must have been wounded also, for he was lying in the bottom of the boat groaning, but I do not remember seeing him hit. I managed to pull fifty yards or so and then fainted, for I was bleeding very badly.

"When I recovered consciousness I found that the bleeding had stopped, and I was able to look at the two men. Both of them were dead and quite cold, so that I must have been unconscious for some time.

"The *Evening Star* was about a hundred yards away in the full light of the moon, but I could see nobody on deck. I sat watching her till daybreak, wondering what I should do, for there was no water or food in the boat, and I was unarmed. Unless Captain Burgess and the other men aboard could disarm Dayrell, I was quite helpless. Perhaps my wound had dulled my wits, for I was unable to think out any plan, and I sat there aimlessly for more than an hour.

"It was broad daylight, and I had drifted within fifty yards of the ship, when, to my surprise, Captain Burgess appeared on deck and nailed me. 'All right, Harper,' he said, 'come aboard.'

"I was able to scull the boat alongside, and Burgess got down into her without a word and helped me aboard. He took me down to my berth, with his arm around me, for I almost collapsed again with the effort, and he brought me some brandy. As soon as I could speak, I asked him what it all meant, and he said, 'The ship is his, Harper; we've got to give it up to him. That's what it means. I am not afraid of him by daylight, but what we shall do to-night, God only knows.' Then, just as Mrs. Burgess had told me, he put his head down on his arms, and began to sob like a child.

"'Where are the other men?' I asked him.

"'There's only you and I and Kato,' he said, 'to face it out aboard this ship.'

"With that he got up and left me, saying that he would send Kato to me with some food, if I thought I could eat. But I knew by this time that I was a dying man.

"There was only one thing I had to do, and that was to try to get this account written, and hide it somehow in the hope of someone finding it later, for I felt sure that neither Burgess nor myself would live to tell it. There was no paper in my berth, and it was Kato that thought of writing it down in this way.

"*About an hour later.*—Burgess has just been down to see me. He said that he had buried the two men who were shot in the boat. I wanted to ask him some questions, but he became so excited, it seemed useless. Neither he nor Kato seemed to have any idea where Dayrell was hiding. Kato believes, in fact, in ghosts; so that it is no use questioning him.

"I must have lost consciousness or slept very heavily since the above was written, for I remembered nothing more till nightfall, when I woke up in the pitch darkness. Kato was sitting by me, and gave me another drink of brandy. The ship was dead still, but I felt that something had gone wrong again.

"I do not know whether my own mind is going, but we have just heard the voice of Mrs. Burgess singing one of those sentimental songs that Captain Dayrell used to be so fond of. It seemed to be down in the cabin, and when she came to the end of it I heard Dayrell's voice calling out, 'Encore! Encore!' just as he used to do. Then I heard someone running down the deck like mad, and Captain Burgess came tumbling down to us with the whites of his eyes showing. 'Did you hear it?' he said. 'Harper, you'll admit you heard it. Don't tell me I'm mad. They're in the cabin together now. Come and look at them.' Then he looked at me with a curious, cunning look, and said, 'No, you'd better stay where you are, Harper. You're not strong enough.' And he crept up on the deck like a cat.

"Something urged me to follow him, even if it took the last drop of my strength. Kato tried to dissuade me, but I drained the brandy flask, and managed to get out of my berth on to the deck by going very slowly, though the sweat broke out on me with every step. Burgess had disappeared, and there was nobody on deck. It was not so difficult to get to the skylight of the cabin. God knows what I had expected to see, but there I did see the figure of Captain Dayrell, dressed as I had seen him in life, with a big scarf round his throat and the big peaked cap. There was an open sea-chest in the corner, with a good many clothes scattered about as if by someone who had been dressing in a hurry. It was an old chest belonging to Dayrell in the old days, and I often wondered why Burgess had left it lying there. The revolver lay on the table, and as Dayrell picked it up to load it the scarf unwound itself a little around his throat and the lower part of the face. Then, to my amazement, I recognised him."

"There," said Knight, "the log of the *Evening Star* ends, except for a brief sentence by Kato himself, which I will not read to you now."

"I wonder if the poor devil did really see," said Moreton Fitch. "And what do you suppose he did when he saw who it was?"

"Crept back to his own berth, barricaded himself in with Kato's help, finished his account, died in the night with Dayrell tapping on the door, and was neatly buried by Burgess in the morning, I suppose."

"And Burgess?"

"Tidied everything up and then jumped overboard."

"Probably—in his own clothes; for it's quite true that we did find a lot of Dayrell's old clothes in a sea-chest in the cabin. Funny idea, isn't it, a man ghosting himself like that?"

"Yes; but what did Harper mean by saying he heard Mrs. Burgess singing in the cabin that night?"

"Ah, that's another section of the log, recorded in a different way."

Moreton Fitch made a sign to the little Japanese, and told him to get a package out of his car. He returned in a moment and laid it at our feet on the floor.

"Dayrell was very proud of his wife's voice," said Fitch as he took the covers off the package. "Just before he was taken ill he conceived the idea of getting some records made of her songs to take with him on board ship. The gramophone was found amongst the old clothes. The usual sentimental stuff, you know. Like to hear it? She had rather a fine voice."

He turned a handle and, floating out into the stillness of the California night, we heard the full rich voice of the dead woman:

> *Just a song at twilight, when the lights are low*
> *And the flickering shadows softly come and go.*

At the end of the stanza a deep bass voice broke in with, "Encore! Encore!"

Then Fitch stopped it.

When we were in the car on our way home, I asked if there were any clue to the fate of the Japanese cook in the last sentence of the log of the *Evening Star*.

"I didn't want to bring it up before his brother," said Knight; "they are a sensitive folk; but the last sentence was to the effect that the *Evening Star* had now been claimed by the spirit of Captain Dayrell, and that the writer respectfully begged to commit hara-kiri."

Our road turned inland here, and I looked back toward the fishing village. The night was falling, but the sea was lilac-coloured with the afterglow. I could see the hut and the little bird-house, black against the water. On a sand-dune just beyond them the fisherman Kato and his wife were sitting on their heels and still watching us. They must have been nearly a mile away by this time; but in that clear air they were carved out sharp and black as minute ebony images against the fading light of the Pacific.

58

Jeeves and the Song of Songs

BY P. G. WODEHOUSE

ANOTHER day dawned all hot and fresh and, in pursuance of my unswerving policy at that time, I was singing "Sonny Boy" in my bath, when Jeeves's voice filtered through the woodwork.

"I beg your pardon, sir."

I had just got to that bit about the angels being lonely, where you need every ounce of concentration in order to make the spectacular finish, but I signed off courteously.

"Yes, Jeeves? Say on."

"Mr. Glossop, sir."

"What about him?"

"He is in the sitting room, sir."

"Young Tuppy Glossop?"

"Yes, sir," Jeeves answered in his monosyllabic way.

"You say that he is in the sitting room?" I asked.

"Yes, sir."

"Desiring speech with me?"

"Yes, sir."

"H'm!"

"Sir?"

"I only said 'H'm.'"

And I'll tell you why I said "H'm." It was because the man's story had interested me strangely. And I'll tell you why the man's story had interested me strangely. Owing to a certain episode that had occurred one night at the Drones' Club, there had sprung up recently a coolness, as you might describe it, between this Glossop and myself. The news, therefore, that he was visiting me at my flat, especially at an hour when he must have known that I would be in my bath and consequently in a strong strategic position to heave a wet sponge at him, surprised me considerably.

I hopped out with some briskness and, slipping a couple of towels about the torso, made for the sitting room. I found young Tuppy at the piano, playing "Sonny Boy" with one finger.

"What ho!" I said, not without hauteur.

"Oh, hullo, Bertie," said Tuppy. "I say, Bertie, I want to see you about something important."

It seemed to me that the bloke was embarrassed. He had moved to the mantelpiece, and now he broke a vase in a constrained way.

"The fact is, Bertie, I'm engaged."

"Engaged?"

"Engaged," said young Tuppy, coyly dropping a photograph frame upon the fender. "Practically, that is."

"Practically?"

"Yes. You'll like her, Bertie. Her name is Cora Bellinger. She's studying for opera. Wonderful voice she has. Also dark, flashing eyes and a great soul."

"How do you mean, 'practically'?"

"Well, it's this way. Before ordering the trousseau there is one little point she wants cleared up. You see, what with her great soul and all that, she has a rather serious outlook on life, and the one thing she absolutely bars is anything in the shape of hearty humour. You know, practical joking and so forth.

"She said if she thought I was a practical joker she would never speak to me again. And unfortunately she appears to have heard about that little affair at the Drones'. . . . I expect you have forgotten all about that, Bertie?"

"I have not!"

"No, no, not forgotten exactly. What I mean is, nobody laughs more heartily at the recollection than you. And what I want you to do, old man, is to seize an early opportunity of taking Cora aside and categorically denying that there is any truth in the story. My happiness, Bertie, is in your hands, if you know what I mean."

Well, of course, if he put it like that, what could I do? We Woosters have our code.

"Oh, all right," I said, but far from brightly.

"Splendid fellow!"

"When do I meet this blighted female?" I asked.

"Don't call her 'this blighted female,' Bertie, old man. I have planned all that out. I will bring her around here to-day for a spot of lunch."

"What!"

"At one-thirty. Right. Good. Fine. Thanks. I knew I could rely on you."

He pushed off, and I turned to Jeeves, who had shimmered in with the morning meal.

"Lunch for three to-day, Jeeves," I said.

"Very good, sir."

"You know, Jeeves, it's a bit thick. You remember my telling you about what Mr. Glossop did to me that night at the Drones'?"

"Yes, sir."

"For months I have been cherishing dreams of a hideous vengeance. And now, so far from crushing him into the dust, I've got to fill him and fiancée with rich food, and generally rally round and be the good angel."

"Life is like that, sir."

"True, Jeeves. What have we here?" I asked, inspecting the tray.

"Kippered herrings, sir."

"And I shouldn't wonder," I said, for I was in thoughtful mood, "if even herrings haven't troubles of their own."

"Quite possibly, sir."

"I mean, apart from getting kippered."

"Yes, sir."

"And so it goes on, Jeeves, so it goes on."

I can't say I saw exactly eye to eye with young Tuppy in his admiration for the Bellinger female. Delivered on the mat at one-twenty-five, she proved to be an upstanding light-heavyweight of some thirty summers with a commanding eye and a square chin which I, personally, would have steered clear of.

She seemed to me a good deal like what Cleopatra would have been after going in too freely for the starches and cereals. I don't know why it is, but women who have anything to do with opera, even if they're only studying for it, always appear to run to surplus poundage.

Tuppy, however, was obviously all for her. His whole demeanour, both before and during luncheon, was that of one striving to be worthy of a noble soul. When Jeeves offered him a cocktail he practically recoiled as from a serpent. It was terrible to see the change which love had effected in the man. The spectacle put me off my food.

At half-past two the Bellinger left to go to a singing lesson. Tuppy trotted after her to the door, bleating and frisking a goodish bit, and then came back and looked at me in a marked manner.

"Well, Bertie?"

"Well, what?"

"I mean, isn't she?"

"Oh, rather," I said, humouring the poor fish.

"Wonderful eyes?"

"Oh, rather."

"Wonderful figure?"

"Oh, quite."

"Wonderful voice?"

Here I was able to intone the response with a little more heartiness. The Bellinger, at Tuppy's request, had sung us a few songs before digging in at the trough, and nobody could have denied that her pipes were in great shape. The plaster was still falling from the ceiling.

"Terrific," I said.

Tuppy sighed, and, having helped himself to about four inches of whisky and one of soda, took a deep, refreshing draft.

"Ah!" he said. "I needed that."

"Why didn't you have it at lunch?"

"Well, it's this way," said Tuppy. "I have not actually ascertained what Cora's opinions are on the subject of the taking of slight snorts from time to time, but I thought it more prudent to lay off. The view I took was that laying off would seem to indicate the serious mind. It is touch and go, as you might say, at the moment, and the smallest thing may turn the scale."

"What beats me is how on earth you expect to make her think you've got a mind at all—let alone a serious one."

"Well, I have my own methods, Bertie, old man."

"I bet they're rotten, Tuppy."

"You do, do you?" said Tuppy warmly. "Well, let me tell you, my lad, that that's exactly what they're anything but. I am handling this affair with consummate generalship. Do you remember Beefy Bingham who was at Oxford with us?"

"I ran into him only the other day. He's a parson now."

"Yes. Down in the East End. Well, he runs a lads' club for the local toughs—you know the sort of thing—cocoa and backgammon in the reading room and occasional clean, bright entertainments in the Oddfellows' Hall; and I've been helping him. I don't suppose I've passed an evening away from the backgammon board for weeks.

"Cora is extremely pleased. I've got her to promise to sing on Tuesday at Beefy's next clean, bright entertainment."

"You have?"

"I absolutely have. And now mark my devilish ingenuity, Bertie. I'm going to sing, too."

"Why do you suppose that's going to get you anywhere?"

"Because the way I intend to sing the song I intend to sing will prove to her that there are great deeps in my nature, whose existence she has not suspected. She will see that rough, unlettered audience wiping the tears out of its bally eyes and she will say to herself, 'What ho! The old egg really has a soul!'

"For it is not one of your mouldy comic songs, Bertie. No low buffoonery of that sort for me. It is all about angels being lonely and what not."

I uttered a sharp cry. "You can't mean you're going to sing 'Sonny Boy'?"

"I jolly well do."

I was shocked. Yes, dash it, I was shocked. You see, I held strong views on "Sonny Boy." I considered it a song only to be attempted by a few of the elect in the privacy of the bathroom. And the thought of its being murdered in open Oddfellows' Hall by a bloke who could treat a pal as young Tuppy had treated me that night at the Drones' sickened me. Yes, sickened me.

I hadn't time, however, to express my horror and disgust, for at this juncture Jeeves came in.

"Mrs. Travers has just rung up on the telephone, sir. She desired me to say that she will be calling to see you in a few minutes."

"Contents noted, Jeeves," I said. "Now listen, Tuppy——" I began.

I stopped. The fellow wasn't there.

"Mr. Glossop has left, sir."

"Left? How can he have left? He was sitting there."

"That is the front door closing now, sir."

"But what made him shoot off like that?"

"Possibly Mr. Glossop did not wish to meet Mrs. Travers, sir."

"Why not?"

"I could not say, sir. But undoubtedly at the mention of Mrs. Travers's name he rose very swiftly.

"Strange, Jeeves."

"Yes, sir."

I turned to a subject of more moment.

"Jeeves," I said, "Mr. Glossop proposes to sing 'Sonny Boy' at an entertainment down in the East End next Tuesday before an audience consisting mainly of costermongers, with a sprinkling of whelk-stall owners, purveyors of blood oranges, and minor pugilists."

"Indeed, sir?"

"Make a note to remind me to be there. He will infallibly get the bird, and I want to witness his downfall."

"Very good, sir."

"And when Mrs. Travers arrives I shall be in the sitting room."

Those who know Bertram Wooster best are aware that in his journey through life he is impeded and generally snookered by about as scaly a collection of aunts as was ever assembled. But there is one exception to the general ghastliness—viz. my aunt Dahlia. She married old Tom Travers the year Bluebottle won the Cambridgeshire, and is one of the best. It is always a pleasure to me to chat with her, and it was with a courtly geniality that I rose to receive her as she sailed over the threshold at about two-fifty-five.

She seemed somewhat perturbed, and plunged into the agenda without delay. Aunt Dahlia is one of those big, hearty women. She used to go in a lot for hunting, and she generally speaks as if she had just sighted a fox on a hillside half a mile away.

"Bertie," she cried, in the manner of one encouraging a platoon of hounds to renewed efforts, "I want your help."

"And you shall have it, Aunt Dahlia," I replied suavely. "I can honestly say that there is no one to whom I would more readily do a good turn, no one to whom I am more delighted to be——"

"Less of it," she begged; "less of it. You know that friend of yours, young Glossop?"

"He's just been lunching here."

"He has, has he? Well, I wish you'd poisoned his soup."

"We didn't have soup. And when you describe him as a 'friend of mine,' I wouldn't quite say the term absolutely squared with the facts. Some time ago, one night when we had been dining together at the Drones'——"

At this point Aunt Dahlia—a little brusquely, it seemed to me—said that she would rather wait for the story of my life till she could get it in book form. I could see now that she was definitely not her usual sunny self, so I shelved my personal grievances and asked what was biting her.

"It's that young hound Glossop," she said.

"What's he been doing?"

"Breaking Angela's heart."

(Angela. Daughter of above. My cousin. Quite a good egg.)

"What!"

"I say he's—breaking—Angela's—*heart!*"

"You say he's breaking Angela's heart?"

She begged me to suspend the vaudeville cross-talk stuff.

"How's he doing that?" I asked.

"With his neglect. With his low, callous, double-crossing duplicity."

" 'Duplicity' is the word, Aunt Dahlia," I said. "In treating of young Tuppy Glossop, it springs naturally to the lips. Let me tell you what he did to me one night at the Drones'. We had finished dinner——"

"Ever since the beginning of the season, up to about three weeks ago, he was all over Angela. The sort of thing which, when I was a girl, we should have described as courting."

"Or wooing?"

"Wooing or courting, whichever you like."

"Whichever *you* like, Aunt Dahlia," I said courteously.

"Well, anyway, he haunted the house, lapped up daily lunches, took her out dancing half the night, and so on, till naturally the poor kid, who's quite off her oats about him, took it for granted that it was only a question of time before he suggested that they should feed for life out of the same crib. And now he's gone and dropped her like a hot brick, and I hear he's infatuated with some girl he met at a Chelsea tea party—a girl named—now, what was it?"

"Cora Bellinger."

"How do you know?"

"She was lunching here to-day."

"He brought her?"

"Yes."

"What's she like?"

"Pretty massive. In shape, a bit on the lines of the Albert Hall."

"Did he seem very fond of her?"

"Couldn't take his eyes off the chassis."

"The modern young man," said Aunt Dahlia, "is a pot of poison and wants a nurse to lead him by the hand and some strong attendant to kick him regularly at intervals of a quarter of an hour."

I tried to point out the silver lining.

"If you ask me, Aunt Dahlia," I said, "I think Angela is well out of it. This Glossop is a tough baby. One of London's toughest. I was trying to tell you just now what he did to me one night at the Drones'.

"First, having got me in sporting mood with a bottle of the ripest, he bet me that I wouldn't swing myself across the swimming pool by the ropes and rings. I knew I could do it on my head, so I took him on, exulting in the fun, so to speak. And when I'd done half the trip, and was going strong, I found he had looped the last rope back against the rail, leaving me no alternative but to drop into the depths and swim ashore in correct evening costume."

"He did?"

"He certainly did. It was months ago, and I haven't got really dry yet. You wouldn't want your daughter to marry a man capable of a thing like that!"

"On the contrary, you restore my faith in the young hound. I see that there must be lots of good in him, after all. And I want this Bellinger business broken up, Bertie."

"How?"

"I don't care how. Any way you please."

"But what can I do?"

"Do? Why, put the whole thing before your man Jeeves. Jeeves will find a way. One of the most capable fellers I ever met. Put the thing squarely up to Jeeves and let Nature take its course."

"There may be something in what you say, Aunt Dahlia," I said thoughtfully.

"Of course there is," said Aunt Dahlia. "A little thing like this will be child's play to Jeeves. Get him working on it right away, and I'll look in to-morrow to hear the result."

With which, she biffed off, and I summoned Jeeves to the presence.

"Jeeves," I said, "you have heard all?"

"Yes, sir."

"I thought you would. Aunt Dahlia has what you might call a carrying voice. Has it ever occurred to you that, if all other sources of income failed, she could make a good living calling the cattle home across the sands of Dee?"

"I had not considered the point, sir, but no doubt you are right."

"Well, how do we go? What is your reaction? I think we should do our best to help and assist."

"Yes, sir."

"I am fond of Aunt Dahlia, and I am fond of Angela. Fond of them both, if you get my drift. What the misguided girl finds to attract her in young Tuppy, I cannot say, Jeeves, and you cannot say. But apparently she loves the man—which shows it can be done, a thing I wouldn't have believed myself—and is pining away like——"

"Patience on a monument, sir."

"Like Patience, as you very shrewdly remark, on a monument. So we must cluster round. Bend your brain to the problem, Jeeves. It is one that will tax you to the uttermost."

Aunt Dahlia blew in on the morrow, and I rang the bell for Jeeves. He appeared, looking brainier than one could have believed possible—sheer intellect shining from every feature—and I could see at once that the engine had been turning over.

"Speak, Jeeves," I said.

"Very good, sir."

"You have brooded?"

"Yes, sir."

"With what success?"

"I have a plan, sir, which I fancy may produce satisfactory results."

"Let's have it," said Aunt Dahlia.

"In affairs of this description, madam, the first essential is to study the psychology of the individual."

"The what?"

"The psychology, madam."

"He means the psychology," I said.

"Oh, ah," said Aunt Dahlia.

"And by psychology, Jeeves," I went on, to help the thing along, "you imply——?"

"The natures and dispositions of the principals in the matter, sir."

"You mean, what they're like?"

"Precisely, sir."

"Does he talk like this when you're alone, Bertie?" asked Aunt Dahlia.

"Sometimes. Occasionally. And on the other hand, sometimes not. Proceed, Jeeves."

"Well, sir, if I may say so, the thing that struck me most forcibly about Miss Bellinger when she was under my observation was that hers was a somewhat imperious nature. I could envisage Miss Bellinger applauding success. I could not so easily see her pitying and sympathizing with failure.

"Possibly you will recall, sir, her attitude when Mr. Glossop endeavoured to light her cigarette with his automatic lighter? I thought I detected a certain impatience at his inability to produce the necessary flame."

"True, Jeeves. She ticked him off."

"Precisely, sir."

"Let me get this straight," said Aunt Dahlia. "You think if he goes on trying to light her cigarette with his automatic lighter long enough, she will eventually get fed up and hand him the mitten?"

"I merely mentioned the episode, madam, as an indication of Miss Bellinger's somewhat ruthless nature."

"Ruthless," I said, "is right. The Bellinger is hard-boiled. Those eyes. That chin. I could read them. A vicious specimen, if ever there was one."

"Precisely, sir. I think, therefore, that, should Miss Bellinger be a witness of Mr. Glossop's appearing to disadvantage in public, she would cease to entertain affection for him. In the event, for instance, of his failing to entertain the audience on Tuesday with his singing——"

I saw daylight.

"By Jove, Jeeves! You mean if he gets the bird all will be off?"

"I shall be greatly surprised if such is not the case, sir."

I shook my head.

"We cannot leave this thing to chance, Jeeves. Young Tuppy singing

'Sonny Boy' is the likeliest prospect for the bird that I can think of—but no . . . You see for yourself that we must do more than simply trust to luck."

"We need not trust to luck, sir. I would suggest that you approach your friend Mr. Bingham and volunteer your services at his forthcoming entertainment. It could readily be arranged to have you sing immediately before Mr. Glossop. I fancy, sir, that if Mr. Glossop were to sing 'Sonny Boy' directly after you had sung 'Sonny Boy' the audience would respond satisfactorily. By the time Mr. Glossop began to sing they would have lost their taste for that particular song and would express their feelings warmly."

"Jeeves," said Aunt Dahlia, "you're a marvel!"

"Thank you, madam."

"Jeeves," I said, "you're an ass!"

"What do you mean, he's an 'ass'?" said Aunt Dahlia hotly. "I think it's the greatest scheme I ever heard."

"Me sing 'Sonny Boy' at Beefy Bingham's clean, bright entertainment? I can see myself!"

"You sing it daily in your bath, sir. Mr. Wooster," said Jeeves, turning to Aunt Dahlia, "has a pleasant, light barytone."

"I bet he has," said Aunt Dahlia.

I checked the man with one of my looks.

"Between singing 'Sonny Boy' in one's bath, Jeeves, and singing it before a hall full of assorted blood-orange merchants and their young, there is a substantial difference."

"Bertie," said Aunt Dahlia, "you'll sing, and like it!"

"I will not."

"Bertie!"

"Nothing will induce——"

"Bertie," said Aunt Dahlia firmly, "you will sing 'Sonny Boy' on Tuesday, the third *prox.*, or may an aunt's curse——"

"I won't!"

"Think of Angela!"

"Dash Angela!"

"Bertie!"

"No, I mean, hang it all!"

"You won't?"

"No, I won't."

"That is your last word, is it?"

"It is. Once and for all, Aunt Dahlia, nothing will induce me to let out so much as a single note."

And so that afternoon I sent a prepaid wire to Beefy Bingham, offering my services in the cause, and by nightfall the thing was fixed up. I was billed to perform next but one after the intermission. Following me, came Tuppy. And immediately after him, Miss Cora Bellinger, the well-known operatic soprano.

How these things happen, I couldn't say. The chivalry of the Woosters, I suppose.

"Jeeves," I said that evening, and I said it coldly, "I shall be glad if you will pop round to the nearest music shop and procure me a copy of 'Sonny Boy.' It will now be necessary for me to learn both verse and refrain. Of the trouble and nervous strain which this will involve, I say nothing."

"Very good, sir."

"But this I do say——"

"I had better be starting immediately, sir, or the shop will be closed."

"Ha!" I said.

And I meant it to sting.

Although I had steeled myself to the ordeal before me and had set out full of the calm, quiet courage which makes men do desperate deeds with proud, set faces, I must admit that there was a moment, just after I had entered the Oddfellows' Hall at Bermondsey East and run an eye over the assembled pleasure seekers, when it needed all the bulldog pluck of the Woosters to keep me from calling it a day and taking a cab back to civilization.

The clean, bright entertainment was in full swing when I arrived, and somebody who looked as if he might be the local undertaker was reciting "Gunga Din." And the audience, though not actually chiyiking in the full technical sense of the term, had a grim look which I didn't like at all.

As I scanned the multitude it seemed to me that they were for the nonce suspending judgment. Did you ever tap on the door of one of those New York speakeasy places and see the grille snap back and a Face appear? There is one long, silent moment when its eyes are fixed on yours and all your past life seems to rise up before you. Then you say that you are a friend of Mr. Zinzinheimer and he told you they would treat you right if you mentioned his name, and the strain relaxes.

Well, these costermongers and whelk stallers appeared to me to be looking just like that Face. Start something, they seemed to say, and they would know what to do about it. And I couldn't help feeling that my singing "Sonny Boy" would come, in their opinion, under the head of Starting Something.

"A nice, full house, sir," said a voice at my elbow.

It was Jeeves, watching the proceedings with an indulgent eye.

"You here, Jeeves?" I said coldly.

"Yes, sir. I have been present since the commencement."

"Oh?" I said. "Any casualties yet?"

"Sir?"

"You know what I mean, Jeeves," I said sternly, "and don't pretend you don't. Anybody got the bird yet?"

"Oh, no, sir."

"I shall be the first, you think?"

"No, sir, I see no reason to expect such a misfortune. I anticipate that you will be well received."

A sudden thought struck me. "And you think everything will go according to plan?"

"Yes, sir."

"Well, I don't," I said. "I've spotted a flaw in your beastly scheme."

"A flaw, sir?"

"Yes. Do you suppose for a moment that when Mr. Glossop hears me singing that dashed song he'll come calmly on a minute after me and sing it, too? Use your intelligence, Jeeves. He will perceive the chasm in his path and pause in time. He will back out and refuse to go on at all."

"Mr. Glossop will not hear you sing, sir. At my advice he has stepped across the road to the Jug and Bottle, an establishment immediately opposite the hall, and he intends to remain there until it is time for him to appear on the platform."

"Oh!" I said.

"If I might suggest it, sir, there is another house named the Goat and Grapes only a short distance down the street. I think it might be a judicious move——"

"If I were to put a bit of custom in their way?"

"It would ease the nervous strain of waiting, sir."

I had not been feeling any too pleased with the man for having let me in for this ghastly binge, but at these words I'm bound to say my austerity softened a trifle. He was undoubtedly right.

He had studied the psychology of the individual, if you see what I mean, and it had not led him astray. A quiet ten minutes at the Goat and Grapes was exactly what my system required. To buzz off there and inhale a couple of swift whisky-and-sodas was with Bertram Wooster the work of a moment.

The treatment worked like magic. What they had put into the stuff, besides vitriol, I could not have said; but it completely altered my outlook on life. That curious, gulpy feeling passed. I was no longer conscious of the sagging sensation at the knees. The limbs ceased to quiver gently, the tongue became loosened in its socket, and the backbone stiffened.

Pausing merely to order and swallow another of the same, I made the barmaid a cheery good-night, nodded affably to one or two fellows in the bar whose faces I liked, and came prancing back to the hall, ready for anything.

And shortly afterward I was on the platform with about a million bulging eyes goggling up at me. There was a rummy sort of buzzing in my ears, and then through the buzzing I heard the sound of a piano starting to tinkle; and, commending my soul to God, I took a good long breath and charged in.

Well, it was a close thing. If ever my grandchildren cluster about my knee and want to know what I did in the Great War, I shall say, "Never mind about the Great War. Ask me about the time I sang 'Sonny Boy' at the Oddfellows' Hall at Bermondsey East."

The whole incident is a bit blurred, but I seem to recollect a kind of murmur as I hit the refrain. I thought at the time it was an attempt on the part of the many-headed to join in the chorus, and at the moment it rather encouraged me.

I passed the thing over the larynx with all the vim at my disposal, hit the high note, and went off gracefully into the wings. I didn't come on again to take a bow. I just receded and oiled round to where Jeeves awaited me among the standees at the back.

"Well, Jeeves," I said, anchoring myself at his side and brushing the honest perspiration from the brow. "They didn't rush the platform."

"No, sir."

"But you can spread it about that that's the last time I perform outside my bath. My "swan song," Jeeves. Anybody who wants to hear me in future must present himself at the bathroom door and shove his ear against the keyhole. I may be wrong, but it seemed to me that toward the end they were hotting up a trifle. The bird was hovering in the air. I could hear the beating of its wings."

"I did detect a certain restlessness, sir, in the audience. I fancy they had lost their taste for that particular melody. I should have informed you earlier, sir, that the song had already been sung twice before you arrived."

"What!"

"Yes, sir. Once by a lady and once by a gentleman. It is a very popular song, sir."

I gaped at the man. That, with this knowledge, he could calmly have allowed the young master to step straight into the jaws of death, so to speak, paralyzed me. It seemed to show that the old feudal spirit had passed away altogether. I was about to give him my views on the matter in no uncertain fashion, when I was stopped by the spectacle of young Tuppy lurching onto the platform.

Young Tuppy had the unmistakable air of a man who has recently been round to the Jug and Bottle. A few cheery cries of welcome, presumably from some of his backgammon-playing pals who felt that blood was thicker than water, had the effect of causing the genial smile on his face to widen till it nearly met at the back.

He was plainly feeling about as good as a man can feel and still remain on his feet. He waved a kindly hand to his supporters and bowed in a regal sort of manner, rather like an Eastern monarch acknowledging the plaudits of the mob.

Then the female at the piano struck up the opening bars of "Sonny Boy," and Tuppy swelled like a balloon, clasped his hands together, rolled his eyes up at the ceiling in a manner denoting Soul, and began.

I think the populace was too stunned for the moment to take immediate steps. It may seem incredible, but I give you my word that young Tuppy got right through the verse without so much as a murmur. Then they seemed to pull themselves together.

A costermonger roused is a terrible thing. I have never seen the proletariat really stirred before, and I'm bound to say it rather awed me. I mean, it gave you some idea of what it must have been like during the French Revolution.

From every corner of the hall there proceeded simultaneously the sort of noise you hear at one of those East End boxing places when the referee disqualifies the popular favourite and makes the quick dash for life. And then they passed beyond mere words and began to introduce the vegetable motif.

I don't know why, but somehow I had got it into my head that the first thing thrown at Tuppy would be a potato. One gets these fancies. It was, however, as a matter of fact, a banana, and I saw in an instant that the choice had been made by wiser heads than mine. These blokes who have grown up from childhood in the knowledge of how to treat a dramatic entertainment that doesn't please them are aware by a sort of instinct just what is best to do, and the moment I saw that banana splash on Tuppy's shirt front I realized how infinitely more effective and artistic it was than any potato could have been.

Not that the potato school of thought had not also its supporters. As the proceedings warmed up I noticed several intelligent-looking fellows who threw nothing else.

The effect on young Tuppy was rather remarkable. His eyes bulged and his hair seemed to stand up, and yet his mouth went on opening and shutting, and you could see that in a dazed, automatic way he was still singing "Sonny Boy."

Then, coming out of his trance, he began to pull for the shore with some rapidity. The last seen of him, he was beating a tomato to the exit by a short head.

Presently the tumult and the shouting died. I turned to Jeeves.

"Painful, Jeeves," I said. "But what would you?"

"Yes, sir."

"The surgeon's knife, what?"

"Precisely, sir."

"Well, with this happening beneath her eyes, I think that we may definitely consider the Glossop-Bellinger romance off."

"Yes, sir."

At this point old Beefy Bingham came out upon the platform.

I supposed that he was about to rebuke his flock for the recent expression of feeling. But such was not the case. No doubt he was accustomed by now to the wholesome give-and-take of these clean, bright entertainments and had ceased to think it worth while to make any comment when there was a certain liveliness.

"Ladies and gentlemen," said old Beefy. "The next item on the program was to have been songs by Miss Cora Bellinger, the well-known operatic soprano. I have just received a telephone message from Miss Bellinger, saying that her car has broken down. She is, however, on her way here in a cab and will arrive shortly. Meanwhile, our friend Mr. Enoch Simpson will recite 'The Charge of the Light Brigade.'"

I clutched at Jeeves. "Jeeves! You heard?"

"Yes, sir."

"She wasn't here!"

"No, sir."

"She saw nothing of Tuppy's Waterloo."

"No, sir."

"The whole bally scheme has blown a fuse."

"Yes, sir."

"Come, Jeeves," I said, and those standing by wondered, no doubt, what had caused that clean-cut face to grow so pale and set. "I have been subjected to a nervous strain unparalleled since the days of the early martyrs. I have lost pounds in weight and permanently injured my entire system. I have gone through an ordeal which will make me wake up screaming in the night for months to come. And all for nothing. Let us go."

"If you have no objection, sir, I would like to witness the remainder of the entertainment."

"Suit yourself, Jeeves," I said moodily. "Personally, my heart is dead and I am going to look in at the Goat and Grapes for another of their cyanide specials and then home."

It must have been about half-past ten, and I was in the old sitting room sombrely sucking down a more or less final restorative, when the front doorbell rang, and there on the mat was young Tuppy. He looked like a man who has passed through some great experience and stood face to face with his soul. He had the beginnings of a black eye.

"Oh, hullo, Bertie," said young Tuppy.

He came in and hovered about the mantelpiece, as if he were looking for things to fiddle with and break.

"I've just been singing at Beefy Bingham's entertainment," he said after a pause. "You weren't there, by any chance?"

"Oh, no," I said. "How did you go?"

"Like a breeze," said young Tuppy. "Held them spellbound."

"Knocked 'em, eh?"

"Cold," said young Tuppy. "Not a dry eye."

And this, mark you, a man who had had a good upbringing and had, no doubt, spent years at his mother's knee being taught to tell the truth.

"I suppose Miss Bellinger is pleased?" I said.

"Oh, yes. Delighted."

"So now everything's all right?"

"Oh, quite." Tuppy paused. "On the other hand, Bertie——"

"Yes?"

"Well, I've been thinking things over. Somehow, I don't believe Miss Bellinger is the mate for me, after all."

"What!"

"No, I don't."

"What makes you think that?"

"Oh, I don't know. These things sort of flash on you. I respect Miss Bellinger, Bertie. I admire her. But—er—well, I can't help feeling now that a sweet, gentle girl—er—like your cousin Angela, Bertie—would —er—in fact—— Well, what I came round for was to ask if you would phone Angela and find out how she reacts to the idea of coming out with me to-night to the Berkeley for a bit of supper and a spot of dancing."

"Go ahead. There's the phone."

"No; I'd rather you asked her, Bertie. What with one thing and another, if you paved the way—— You see, there's just a chance that she may be—I mean, you know how misunderstandings occur—and—— Well, what I'm driving at, Bertie, old man, is that I'd rather you surged round and did a bit of paving, if you don't mind."

I went to the phone and called up Angela.

"She says come right round," I said.

"Tell her," said Tuppy, in a devout sort of voice, "that I will be with her in something under a couple of ticks."

He had barely biffed when I heard a click in the keyhole and a soft padding in the passage without.

"Jeeves," I called.

"Sir," said Jeeves, manifesting himself.

"Jeeves, a remarkably rummy thing has happened. Mr. Glossop has just been here. He tells me all is off between him and Miss Bellinger."

"Yes, sir."

"You don't seem surprised."

"No, sir. I confess I had anticipated some such eventuality."

"Eh? What gave you that idea?"

"It came to me, sir, when I observed Miss Bellinger strike Mr. Glossop in the eye."

"Strike him!"

"Yes, sir."

"In the eye?"

"The right eye, sir."

I clutched the brow. "What on earth made her do that?"

"I fancy she was a little upset, sir, at the reception accorded her singing."

"Great Scott! Don't tell me she got the bird, too?"

"Yes, sir."

"But why? She's got a red-hot voice."

"Yes, sir. But I think the audience resented her choice of a song."

"Jeeves!" Reason was beginning to do a bit of tottering on its throne. "You aren't going to stand there and tell me that Miss Bellinger sang 'Sonny Boy,' too!"

"Yes, sir. And—mistakenly, in my opinion—brought a large doll onto the platform to sing it to. The audience affected to mistake it for a ventriloquist's dummy, and there was some little disturbance."

"But Jeeves, what a coincidence!"

"Not altogether, sir. I ventured to take the liberty of accosting Miss Bellinger on her arrival at the hall and recalling myself to her recollection. I then said that Mr. Glossop had asked me to request her that as a particular favour to him—the song being a favourite of his—she would sing 'Sonny Boy.'

"And when she found that you and Mr. Glossop had also sung the song immediately before her, I rather fancy that she supposed that she had been made a victim of a practical pleasantry by Mr. Glossop. Will there by anything further, sir?"

"No, thanks."

"Good-night, sir."

"Good-night, Jeeves," I said reverently.

59

Three Lovers Who Lost

BY JAMES STEPHENS

YOUNG Mr. O'Grady was in love. It was the first time he had been in love, and it was all sufficiently startling. He seemed to have leaped from boyhood to manhood at a stroke, and the things which had pretended to be of moment yesterday were to-day discovered to have only the very meanest importance. Different affairs now occupied him. A little while ago his cogitations had included, where he would walk to on the next Sunday, whether his aunt in Meath Street would lend him the price of a ticket for the coming Bank Holiday excursion, whether his brother would be using his bicycle on Saturday afternoon, and whether the packet of cigarettes which he was momently smoking contained as many cigarettes as could be got elsewhere for two pence.

These things were no longer noteworthy. Clothing had assumed an importance he could scarcely have believed in. Boots, neckties, the conduct of one's hat and of one's head, the progress of one's moustache, one's bearing towards people in the street and in the house, this and that social observance—all these things took on a new and important dignity. He bought a walking-stick, a card-case, a purse, a pipe with a glass bottom wherein one could observe one's own nicotine inexorably accumulating.—He bought a book on etiquette and a pot of paste for making moustaches grow in spite of providence, and one day he insisted on himself drinking a half glass of whisky—it tasted sadly, but he drank it without a grimace. Etiquette and whisky! these things have to be done, and one might as well do them with an air. He was in love, he was grown up, he was a man, and he lived fearlessly up to his razor and his lady.

From the book on etiquette he exhumed a miscellany of useful and peculiar wisdom. Following information about the portage of knives

843

and forks at incredible dinners he discovered that a well-bred person always speaks to the young lady's parents before he speaks to the young lady. He straightened his shoulders.—It would be almost as bad, he thought, as having to drink whisky, but if it had to be done why he would not shrink from this any more than he had from that. He set forth on the tingling errand.

Mr. O'Reilly was a scrivener, a husband and a father. He made copies of all kinds of documents for a living. He also copied maps. It has been said that scriveners have to get drunk at least twice a week in order to preserve their sanity; but the person whose miserable employment is to draw copies of maps is more desperately environed than an ordinary scrivener. It was Mr. O'Reilly's misfortune that he was unable to get drunk. He disliked liquor, and, moreover, it disagreed with him. He had, to paraphrase Lamb, toiled after liquor as other people toil after virtue, but the nearer he got the less did he like it. As a consequence of this enforced decency the ill-temper, which is the normal state of scriveners, had surged and buzzed around him so long that he had quite forgotten what a good temper was like.—It might be said that he hated every one, not excepting his wife and daughter. He could avoid other people, but these he could never escape from. They wanted to talk to him when he wanted to be let alone. They worried him with this and that domestic question or uproar. He would gladly have sold them both as slaves to the Barbadoes or presented them to the seraglio of any eastern potentate. There they were! and he often gnashed his teeth and grinned at them in amazement because they were there.

On the evening when young Mr. O'Grady sallied forth to ask him for the hand of his daughter in marriage he was sitting at supper with his consort—

Mr. O'Reilly took the last slice of bread from under his wife's hand. It was loot, so he ate it with an extra relish and his good lady waddled away to get more bread from cupboard—

"Everything's a trouble," said she, as she cut the loaf. "Doesn't it make you think of the hymn 'I'm but a stranger here, heaven is my home'?"

"No, ma'm," said her husband, "it does not. Where is Julia Elizabeth?" and he daringly and skilfully abstracted the next slice of bread while his wife was laying down the butter knife.

"I wish," said she, as she reached for the knife again, "I wish you would give me a chance, O'Reilly: you eat much quicker than I do, God help me!"

"I wish," rapped her husband fiercely, "that you would give a plain answer to a plain question. Now then, ma'm, in two words, where is that girl? My whole life seems to be occupied in asking that question, and yours seems to be spent in dodging the answer to it."

"I don't know," replied his wife severely, "and that's three words."

"You don't know!" he looked around in helpless appeal and condemnation. "What sort of an answer is that for a mother to give about her daughter?" and under cover of his wrath he stole the next slice of bread.

His wife also became angry—she put her plate in her lap and sat up at him—

"Don't barge me, man," said she. "A nice daughter to have to give such an answer about. Leave me alone now for I'm not well, I say, on the head of her. I never know where she does be. One night it's (she endeavoured to reproduce her daughter's soprano) 'I am going to a dance, mother, at the Durkins'——' "

"Ha'penny hops!" said her husband fiercely. "Can't you cut me a bit of bread!"

"And another night, 'she wants to go out to see Mary Durkan.' "

"I know her well, a big hat and no morals, a bankrupt's baggage."

"And the night after she 'wants to go to the theatre, ma.' "

"Dens of infamy," said he. "If I had my way I'd shut them all up and put the actors in gaol, with their hamleting and gamyacting and ha-ha'ing out of them."

"I can't keep her in," said his wife, wringing her hands, "and I won't try to any longer. I get a headache when I talk to her, so I do. Last night when I mentioned about her going out with that Rorke man she turned round as cool as you please and told me 'to shut up.' Her own mother!" and she surveyed Providence with a condemnatory eye—

At this point her husband swung his long arm and arrested the slice of bread in his wife's lap—

"If she spoke to me that way," he grinned, "I'll bet I'd astonish her."

His wife looked in amazement from her lap to his plate, but she had ability for only one quarrel at a time—

"And doesn't she talk to you like that? You never say a word to her but she has a look in her eye that's next door to calling you a fool.—I don't know where she is at all to-day."

"What time did she go out?"

"After breakfast this morning."

"And now it's supper-time—ha! that's good! Can't you give me a bit of bread, or do you want to eat the whole loaf yourself? Try to remember that I do pay for my food."

With an angry shake of the head his wife began to cut the loaf, and continued speaking—

" 'Where are you going to, Julia Elizabeth?' said I. 'Out,' said she, and not another word could I get from her. Her own mother, mind you, and her best clothes——"

Mr. O'Reilly ate the last slice of bread and arose from the table.

"I suppose," said he, "she is loafing about the streets with some young puppy who has nothing of his own but a cigarette and a walking-stick, and they both borrowed. I'll have a talk with her when she comes in, and we'll see if she tells me to shut up."

The door banged, the room shook, and Mrs. O'Reilly settled to her frustrated tea, but her thoughts still ran on her daughter.

It was at this point that, directed by love and etiquette, Mr. O'Grady knocked at the door. Mrs. O'Reilly was again cutting the loaf in an exasperation which was partly hunger and partly maternal, and, as she cut, she communed with herself—

"As if," said she, "I haven't enough trouble trying to keep a cranky man like her pa in good humour, without being plagued by Julia Elizabeth"—she paused, for there was a knock at the door.—"If," said she to the door, "you are a woman with ferns in a pot I don't want you, and I don't want Dublin Bay herrings, or boot-laces either, so you can go away.—The crankiness of that man is more than tongue can tell. As Miss Carty says, I shouldn't stand it for an hour—Come in, can't you—and well she may say it, and she a spinster without a worry under heaven but her suspicious nature and her hair falling out. And then to be treated the way I am by that girl! It'd make a saint waxy so it would.—Good heavens! can't you come in, or are you deaf or lame or what?" and in some exasperation she arose and went to the door. She looked in perplexity for one moment from her food to her visitor, but as good manners and a lady are never separate she welcomed and drew the young man inside—

"Come in, Mr. O'Grady," said she. "How are you now at all? Why it's nearly a week since you were here. Your mother's well I hope (sit down there now and rest yourself). Some people are always well, but I'm not—it's (sit there beside the window, like a good boy) it's hard to have poor health and a crotchety husband, but we all have our trials. Is your father well too? but what's the use of asking, every one's well but me. Did your aunt get the pot of jam I sent her last Tuesday? Raspberry is supposed to be good for the throat, but her throat's all right. Maybe she threw it out: I'm not blaming her if she did. God knows she can buy jam if she wants it without being beholden to any one for presents and her husband in the Post Office.—Well, well, well, I'm real glad to see you—and now, tell me all the news?"

The young man was a little embarrassed by this flood of language and its multiplicity of direction, but the interval gave him time to collect himself and get into the atmosphere.—He replied—

"I don't think there is any news to tell, ma'm. Father and mother are quite well, thank you, and Aunt Jane got the jam all right, but she didn't eat it, because——"

"I knew she didn't," said Mrs. O'Reilly with pained humility, "we all have our troubles and jam doesn't matter. Give her my love all the same, but maybe she doesn't want it either."

"You see," said the young man, "the children got at the jam before she could, and they cleaned the pot. Aunt Jane was very angry about it."

"Was she now?" said the instantly interested lady. "It's real bad for a stout person to be angry. Apoplexy or something might ensue and death would be instantaneous and cemeteries the price they are in Glasnevin and all: but the children shouldn't have eaten all the jam at once, it's bad for the stomach that way: still, God is good and maybe they'll recover."

"They don't seem much the worse for it," said he, laughing; "they said it was fine jam."

"Well they might," replied his hostess, with suppressed indignation, "and raspberries eightpence the pound in Grafton Street, and the best preserving sugar twopence three-farthings, and coal the way it is.—Ah, no matter, God is good, and we can't live for ever."

The four seconds of silence which followed was broken by the lover—

"Is Julia Elizabeth in, ma'm?" said he timidly.

"She's not, then," was the reply. "We all have our trials, Mr. O'Grady, and she's mine. I don't complain, but I don't deserve it, for a harder working woman never lived, but there you are."

"I'm rather glad she's out," said the youth hastily, "for I wanted to speak to yourself and your husband before I said anything to her."

Mrs. O'Reilly wheeled slowly to face him—

"Did you now?" said she, "and is it about Julia Elizabeth you came over? Well, well, well, just to think of it! But I guessed it long ago, when you bought the yellow boots. She's a real good girl, Mr. O'Grady. There's many and many's the young man, and they in good positions, mind you—but maybe you don't mean that at all. Is it a message from your Aunt Jane or your mother? Your Aunt Jane does send messages, God help her!"

"It's not, Mrs. O'Reilly: it's, if I may presume to say so, about myself."

"I knew it," was the rapid and enthusiastic reply. "She's a fine cook, Mr. O'Grady, and a head of hair that reaches down to her waist, and won prizes at school for composition. I'll call himself—he'll be delighted. He's in the next room making faces at a map. Maps are a terrible occupation, Mr. O'Grady, they spoil his eyesight and make him curse——"

She ambled to the door and called urgently—

"O'Reilly, here's young Mr. O'Grady wants to see you."

Her husband entered with a pen in his mouth and looked very severely at his visitor—

"What brought you round, young man?" said he.

The youth became very nervous. He stood up stammering—

"It's a delicate subject, sir," said he, "and I thought it would only be right to come to you first."

Here the lady broke in rapturously—

"Isn't it splendid, O'Reilly! You and me sitting here growing old and contented, and this young gentleman talking to us the way he is. Doesn't it make you think of the song 'John Anderson, my Jo, John'?"

Her husband turned a bewildered but savage eye on his spouse—

"It does not, ma'm," said he. "Well," he barked at Mr. O'Grady, "what do you want?"

"I want to speak about your daughter, sir."

"She's not a delicate subject."

"No indeed," said his wife. "Never a day's illness in her life except the measles, and they're wholesome when you're young, and an appetite worth cooking for, two eggs every morning and more if she got it."

Her husband turned on her with hands of frenzy—

"Oh——!" said he, and then to their visitor, "What have you to say about my daughter?"

"The fact is, sir," he stammered, "I'm in love with her."

"I see, you are the delicate subject, and what then?"

"And I want to marry her, sir."

"That's not delicacy, that's disease, young man. Have you spoken to Julia Elizabeth about this?"

"No, sir, I wanted first to obtain your and Mrs. O'Reilly's permission to approach her."

"And quite right, too," said the lady warmly. "Isn't it delightful," she continued, "to see a young, bashful youth telling of his love for our dear child? Doesn't it make you think of Moore's beautiful song, 'Love's Young Dream,' O'Reilly?"

"It does not," her husband snapped, "I never heard of the song I tell you, and I never want to."

He turned again to the youth—

"If you are in earnest about this, you have my permission to court Julia Elizabeth as much as she'll let you. But don't blame me if she marries you. People who take risks must expect accidents. Don't go about lamenting that I hooked you in, or led you on, or anything like that.—I tell you, here and now, that she has a rotten temper——"

His wife was aghast—

"For shame, O'Reilly," said she.

Her husband continued, looking steadily at her—

"A rotten temper," said he, "she gives back answers."

"Never," was Mrs. O'Reilly's wild exclamation.

"She scratches like a cat," said her husband.

"It's a falsehood," cried the lady, almost in tears.

"She is obstinate, sulky, stubborn and cantankerous."

"A tissue," said his wife. "An absolute tissue," she repeated with the firmness which masks hysteria.

Her husband continued inexorably—

"She's a gad-about, a pavement-hopper, and when she has the tooth-ache she curses like a carman. Now, young man, marry her if you like."

These extraordinary accusations were powerless against love and etiquette—the young man stood up: his voice rang—

"I will, sir," said he steadily, "and I'll be proud to be her husband."

In a very frenzy of enthusiasm, Mrs. O'Reilly arose—

"Good boy," said she. "Tell your Aunt Jane I'll send her another pot of jam." She turned to her husband, "Isn't it delightful, O'Reilly, doesn't it make you think of the song, 'True, True Till Death'?"

Mr. O'Reilly replied grimly—

"It does not, ma'm.—I'm going back to my work."

"Be a gentleman, O'Reilly," said his wife pleadingly. "Won't you offer Mr. O'Grady a bottle of stout or a drop of spirits?"

The youth intervened hastily, for it is well to hide one's vices from one's family—

"Oh no, ma'm, not at all," said he, "I never drink intoxicating liquors."

"Splendid," said the beaming lady. "You're better without it. If you knew the happy homes it has ruined, and the things the clergy say about it you'd be astonished. I only take it myself for the rheumatism, but I never did like it, did I, O'Reilly?"

"Never, ma'm," was his reply. "I only take it myself because my hearing is bad. Now, listen to me, young man. You want to marry Julia Elizabeth, and I'll be glad to see her married to a sensible, sober, industrious husband.—When I spoke about her a minute ago I was only joking."

"I knew it all the time," said his wife. "Do you remember, Mr. O'Grady, I winked at you?"

"The girl is a good girl," said her husband, "and well brought up."

"Yes," said his wife, "her hair reaches down to her waist, and she won a prize for composition—*Jessica's First Prayer,* all about a girl with——"

Mr. O'Reilly continued—

"She brings me up a cup of tea every morning before I get up."

"She never wore spectacles in her life," said Mrs. O'Reilly, "and she got a prize for freehand drawing."

"She did so," said Mr. O'Reilly.

His wife continued—

"*The Schoolboy Baronet* it was; all about a young man that broke his leg down a coal mine and it never got well again until he met the girl of his heart."

"Tell me," said Mr. O'Reilly, "how are you young people going to live, and where?"

His wife interpolated—

"Your Aunt Jane told me that you had seventeen shillings and sixpence a week.—Take my advice and live on the south side—two rooms easily and most salubrious."

The young man coughed guardedly, he had received a rise of wages since that information passed, but candour belongs to childhood, and one must live these frailties down—

"Seventeen and six isn't very much, of course," said he, "but I am young and strong——"

"It's more than I had," said his host, "when I was your age. Hello, there's the post!"

Mrs. O'Reilly went to the door and returned instantly with a letter in her hand. She presented it to her husband—

"It's addressed to you, O'Reilly," said she plaintively. "Maybe it's a bill, but God's good and maybe it's a cheque."

Her husband nodded at the company and tore his letter open. He read it, and, at once as it appeared, he went mad, he raved, he stuttered, now slapping the letter with his forefinger and, anon, shaking his fist at his wife—

"Here's your daughter, ma'm," he stammered. "Here's your daughter, I say."

"Where?" cried the amazed lady. "What is it, O'Reilly?" She arose hastily and rolled towards him.

Mr. O'Reilly repelled her fiercely—

"A good riddance," he shouted.

"Tell me, O'Reilly, I command you," cried his wife.

"A minx, a jade," snarled the man.

"I insist," said she. "I must be told. I'm not well, I tell you. My head's going round. Give me the letter."

Mr. O'Reilly drew about him a sudden and terrible calmness—

"Listen, woman," said he, "and you too, young man, and be thankful for your escape."

"DEAR PA," he read, "*this is to tell you that I got married to-day to Christie Rorke. We are going to open a little fried-fish shop near Amiens Street. Hoping this finds you as it leaves me at present, your loving daughter,*

"JULIA ELIZABETH.

"*P.S.—Give Christie's love to Ma.*"

Mrs. O'Reilly sank again to her chair. Her mouth was partly open. She breathed with difficulty. Her eyes were fixed on space, and she seemed to be communing with the guardians of Chaos—

"Married!" said she in a musing whisper. "Christie!" said she. She turned to her husband—"What an amazing thing. Doesn't it make you think, O'Reilly, of the poem, 'The World Recedes, it Disappears'?"

"It does not, ma'm," said her husband savagely.

"And what is this young gentleman going to do?" she continued, gazing tearfully at the suitor.

"He's going to go home," replied her husband fiercely. "He ought to be in bed long ago."

"A broken heart," said his wife, "is a sad companion to go home with. Doesn't it make you think of the song——?"

"It does not, ma'm," roared her husband. "I'm going back to my work," and once again the door banged and the room shook.

Young Mr. O'Grady arose timidly. The world was swimming about him. Love had deserted him, and etiquette was now his sole anchor; he shook hands with Mrs. O'Reilly—

"I think I had better be going now," said he. "Good-bye, Mrs. O'Reilly."

"Must you really go?" said that lady with the smile of a maniac.

"I'm afraid so," and he moved towards the door.

"Well," said she, "give my love to your mother and your Aunt Jane."

"I will," was his reply, "and," with firm politeness, "thank you for a very pleasant evening."

"Don't mention it, Mr. O'Grady. Good-bye."

Mrs. O'Reilly closed the door and walked back towards the table smiling madly. She sank into a chair. Her eye fell on the butter-knife—

"I haven't had a bit to eat this day," said she in a loud and threatening voice, and once again she pulled the loaf towards her.

His mother finished reading the story of the Beautiful Princess, and it was surely the saddest story he had ever heard. He could not bear to think of that lovely and delicate lady all alone in the great, black forest waiting until the giant came back from killing her seven brothers. He would return with their seven heads swinging pitifully from his girdle, and, when he reached the castle gates, he would gnash his teeth through the keyhole with a noise like the grinding together of great rocks, and would poke his head through the fanlight of the door, and say, fee-faw-fum in a voice of such exceeding loudness that the castle would be shaken to its foundation.

Thinking of this made his throat grow painful with emotion, and then his heart swelled to the most uncomfortable dimensions, and he resolved to devote his whole life to the rescue of the Princess, and, if necessary, die in her defence.

Such was his impatience that he could not wait for anything more than his dinner, and this he ate so speedily that his father called him a Perfect-Young-Glutton, and a Disgrace-To-Any-Table. He bore these insults in a meek and heroic spirit, whereupon his mother said that he must be ill, and it was only by a violent and sustained outcry that he escaped being sent to bed.

Immediately after dinner he set out in search of the giant's castle. Now there is scarcely anything in the world more difficult to find than a giant's castle, for it is so large that one can only see it through the wrong end of a telescope; and, furthermore, he did not even know this giant's name. He might never had found the place if he had not met a certain old woman on the common.

She was a very nice old woman. She had three teeth, a red shawl, an umbrella with groceries inside it; so he told her of the difficulty he was in.

She replied that he was in luck's way, and that she was the only person in the world who could assist him. She said her name was Really-and-Truly, and that she had a magic head, and that if he cut her head off it would answer any questions he asked it. So he stropped his penknife on his boot, and said he was ready if she was.

The old woman then informed him that in all affairs of this delicate nature it was customary to take the will for the deed, and that he might now ask her head anything he wanted to know—so he asked the head what was the way to the nearest giant, and the head replied that if he took the first turning to the left, the second to the right, and then the first to the left again, and if he then knocked at the fifth door on the right-hand side, he would see the giant.

He thanked the old woman very much for the use of her head, and she permitted him to lend her one threepenny-piece, one pocket-handkerchief, one gun-metal watch, one cap, and one boot-lace. She said that she never took two of anything, because that was not fair, and that she wanted these for a very particular, secret purpose, about which she dare not speak, and, as to which she trusted he would not press her, and then she took a most affectionate leave of him and went away.

He followed her directions with the utmost fidelity, and soon found himself opposite a house which, to the eyes of any one over seven years of age, looked very like any other house, but which, to the searching eye of six and three quarters, was patently and palpably a giant's castle.

He tried the door, but it was locked, as, indeed, he had expected it would be. Then he crept very cautiously, and peeped through the first floor window. He could see in quite plainly. There was a polar bear crouching on the floor, and the head looked at him so directly and vindictively that if he had not been a hero he would have fled. The unexpected is always terrible, and when one goes forth to kill a giant it is unkind of Providence to complicate one's adventure with a gratuitous and wholly unnecessary polar bear. He was, however, reassured by the sight of a heavy chair standing on the polar bear's stomach, and in the chair there sat the most beautiful woman in the world.

An ordinary person would not have understood so instantly that she was the most beautiful woman in the world, because she looked very stout, and much older than is customary with princesses—but that was owing to the fact that she was under an enchantment, and she would become quite young again when the giant was slain and three drops of his blood had been sprinkled on her brow.

She was leaning forward in the chair, staring into the fire, and she was so motionless that it was quite plain she must be under an enchantment. From the very first instant he saw the princess he loved her, and his heart swelled with pity to think that so beautiful a damsel should be subjected to the tyranny of a giant. These twin passions of pity and love grew to so furious a strength within him that he could no longer contain himself. He wept in a loud and very sudden voice which lifted the damsel out of her enchantment and her chair, and hurled her across the room as though she had been propelled by a powerful spring.

He was so overjoyed at seeing her move that he pressed his face against the glass and wept with great strength, and, in a few moments, the princess came timidly to the window and looked out. She looked right over his head at first, and then she looked down and saw him, and her eyebrows went far up on her forehead, and her mouth opened; and so he knew that she was delighted to see him. He nodded to give her courage, and shouted three times, "Open Sesame, Open Sesame, Open Sesame," and then she opened the window and he climbed in.

The princess tried to push him out again, but she was not able, and he bade her put all her jewels in the heel of her boot and fly with him. But she was evidently the victim of a very powerful enchantment, for she struggled violently, and said incomprehensible things to him, such as "Is it a fire, or were you chased?" and "Where *is* the cook?"

But after a little time she listened to the voice of reason, and recognised that these were legitimate and heroic embraces from which she could not honourably disentangle herself.

When her first transports of joy were somewhat abated she assured him that excessive haste had often undone great schemes, and that one should always look before one leaped, and that one should never be rescued all at once, but gradually, in order that one might become accustomed to the severe air of freedom—and he was overjoyed to find that she was as wise as she was beautiful.

He told her that he loved her dearly, and she admitted, after some persuasion, that she was not insensible to the charms of his heart and intellect, but she confessed that her love was given to another.

At these tidings his heart withered away within him, and when the princess admitted she loved the giant his amazement became profound and complicated. There was a rushing sound in his ears. The débris of his well-known world was crashing about him, and he was staring upon a new planet, the name of which was Incredulity. He looked round with a queer feeling of insecurity. At any moment the floor might stand up on one of its corners, or the walls might begin to flap and waggle. But none of these things happened. Before him sat the princess in an attitude of deep dejection, and her lily-white hands rested helplessly on her lap. She told him in a voice that trembled that she would have married him if he had asked her ten years earlier, and urged that she could not fly with him now, because, in the first place, she had six children, and, in the second place, it would be against the law, and, in the third place, his mother might object. She admitted that she was unworthy of his love, and that she should have waited, and she bore his reproaches with a meekness which finally disarmed him.

He stropped his penknife on his boot, and said that there was nothing left but to kill the giant, and that she had better leave the room while he did so, because it would not be a sight for a weak woman, and he wondered audibly how much hasty-pudding would fall out of the giant if he stabbed him right to the heart. The princess begged him not to kill her husband, and assured him that this giant had not got any hasty-pudding in his heart at all, and that he was really the nicest giant that ever lived, and, further, that he had not killed her seven brothers, but the seven brothers of quite another person entirely, which was only a reasonable thing to do when one looked at it properly, and she continued in a strain which proved to him that this unnatural woman really loved the giant.

It was more in pity than in anger that he recognised the impossibility of rescuing this person. He saw at last that she was unworthy of being rescued, and told her so. He said bitterly that he had grave doubts of her being a princess at all, and that if she was married to a giant it was no more than she deserved, and further he had a good mind to rescue the giant from her, and he would do so in a minute, only that it was against his principles to rescue giants.—And, saying so, he placed his penknife between his teeth and climbed out through the window again.

He stood for a moment outside the window with his right hand extended to the sky and the moonlight blazing on his penknife—a truly formidable figure, and one which the princess never forgot; and then he walked slowly away, hiding behind a cold and impassive demeanour a mind that was tortured and a heart that had plumbed most of the depths of human suffering.

Aloysius Murphy went a-courting when the woods were green. There were grapes in the air and birds in the river. A voice and a song went everywhere, and the voice said, "Where is my beloved?" and the song replied, "Thy beloved is awaiting thee, and she stretches her hands abroad and laughs for thy coming; bind then the feather of a bird to thy heel and a red rose upon thy hair, and go quickly."

So he took his hat from behind the door and his stick from beside the bed and went out into the evening.

He had been engaged to Miss Nora MacMahon for two ecstatic months, and held the opinion that the earth and the heavens were aware of the intensity of his passion, and applauded the unique justice of his choice.

By day he sat humbly in a solicitor's office, or scurried through the thousand offices of the Four Courts, but with night came freedom, and he felt himself to be of the kindred of the gods and marched in pomp. By what subterranean workings had he become familiar with the lady? Suffice it that the impossible is possible to a lover. Everything can be achieved in time. The man who wishes to put a mountain in his pocket can do so if his pocket and his wish be of the requisite magnitude.

Now the lady towards whom the raging torrent of his affections had been directed was the daughter of his employer, and this, while it notated romance, pointed also to tragedy. Further, while this fact was well within his knowledge, it was far from the cognizance of the lady. He would have enlightened her on the point, but the longer he delayed the revelation, the more difficult did it become. Perpetually his tongue ached to utter the truth. When he might be squeezing her hand or plunging his glance into the depths of her eyes, consciousness would touch him on the shoulder with a bony hand and say, "That is the boss's daughter you are hugging"—a reminder which was provocative sometimes of an almost unholy delight, when to sing and dance and go mad was but natural; but at other times it brought with it moods of woe, abysses of blackness.

In the solitude of the room wherein he lodged he sometimes indulged in a small drama, wherein, as the hero, he would smile a slightly sad and quizzical smile, and say gently, "Child, you are Mr. MacMahon's daughter, I am but his clerk"—here the smile became more sadly quizzical—"how can I ask you to forsake the luxury of a residence in Clontarf for the uncongenial, nay, bleak surroundings of a South Circular Road habitation?" And she, ah me! She vowed that a hut and a crust and the love of her heart. . . ! No matter!

So, nightly, Aloysius Murphy took the tram to Clontarf, and there, wide-coated and sombreroed like a mediæval conspirator, he trod delicately beside his cloaked and hooded inamorata, whispering of the spice of the wind and the great stretches of the sea.

Now a lover who comes with the shades of night, harbinger of the moon, and hand in glove with the stars, must be a very romantic person indeed, and, even if he is not, a lady whose years are tender can easily supply the necessary gauze to tone down his too-rigorous projections. But the bird that flies by night must adduce for our curiosity substantial reason why his flight has deserted the whiteness of the daytime; else we may be tempted to believe that his advent in darkness is thus shrouded for even duskier purposes.—Miss MacMahon had begun to inquire who Mr. Murphy was, and he had, accordingly, begun to explain who he was not. This explanation had wrapped his identity in the most labyrinthine mystery, but Miss MacMahon detected in the rapid, incomprehensible fluctuations of his story a heart torn by unmerited misfortune, and whose agony could only be alleviated by laying her own dear head against its turmoil.

To a young girl a confidant is almost as necessary as a lover, and when the rendezvous is clandestine, the youth mysterious, and his hat broad-leafed and flapping, then the necessity for a confidant becomes imperative.

Miss MacMahon confided the knowledge of all her happiness to the thrilled ear of her younger sister, who at once hugged her, and bubbled query, conjecture, and admonishment. " . . . Long or short? . . . Dark or fair?" " . . . and slender . . . with eyes . . . dove . . . lightning . . . hair . . . and so gentle . . . and then I said . . . and then he said . . . !" "Oh, sweet!" sighed the younger sister, and she stretched her arms wide and crushed the absent excellences of Mr. Murphy to her youthful breast.

On returning next day from church, having listened awe-stricken to a sermon on filial obediance, the little sister bound her mother to secrecy, told the story, and said she wished she were dead. Subsequently the father of Clann MacMahon was informed, and he said "Hum" and "Ha," and rolled a fierce, hard eye, and many times during the progress of the narrative he interjected with furious energy these words, "Don't be a fool, Jane," and Mrs. MacMahon responded meekly, "Yes, dear," and Mr. MacMahon then said "Hum" and "Ha" and "Gr-r-r-up" in a truly terrible and ogreish manner; and in her distant chamber Miss MacMahon heard the reverberation of that sonorous grunt, and whispered to her little sister, "Pa's in a wax," and the little sister pretended to be asleep.

The spectacle of an elderly gentleman, side-whiskered, precise and grey, disguising himself with mufflers and a squash hat, and stalking with sombre fortitude the erratic wanderings of a pair of young featherheads, is one which mirth may be pleased to linger upon. Such a spectacle was now to be observed in the semi-rural outskirts of Clontarf. Mr. MacMahon tracked his daughter with considerable stealth, adopting unconsciously the elongated and nervous stride of a theatrical villain. He saw her meet a young man wearing a broad-brimmed hat, whose clothing was mysteriously theatrical, and whose general shape, when it could be glimpsed, was oddly familiar.

"I have seen that fellow somewhere," said he.

The lovers met and kissed, and the glaring father spoke rapidly but softly to himself for a few moments. He was not accustomed to walking, and it appeared as if these two intended to walk for ever, but he kept them in sight, and when the time came for parting he was close at hand.

The parting was prolonged, and renewed, and rehearsed again with amendments and additions: he could not have believed that saying good-bye to a person could be turned into so complicated and symbolic a ceremony: but, at last, his daughter, with many a backward look and wave of hand, departed in one direction, and the gentleman, after similar signals, moved towards the tramway.

"I know that fellow, whoever he is," said Mr. MacMahon.

Passing a lamp-post, Mr. Aloysius Murphy stayed for a moment to light his pipe, and Mr. MacMahon stared, he ground his teeth, he foamed at the mouth, and his already prominent eyes bulged still further and rounder—

"Well, I'm——!" said he.

He turned and walked homewards slowly, murmuring often to himself and to the night, "All right! wait, though! Hum! Ha! Gr-r-r-up!"

That night he repeatedly entreated his wife "not to be a fool, Jane," and she as repeatedly replied, "Yes, dear." Long after midnight he awoke her by roaring violently from the very interior depths of a dream, "Cheek of the fellow! Pup! Gr-r-r-up!"

At breakfast on the following morning he suggested to his wife and elder daughter that they should visit his office later on in the day—

"You have never seen it, Nora," said he, "and you ought to have a look at the den where your poor old daddy spends his time grinding dress material for his family from the faces of the poor. I've got some funny clerks, too: one of them is a curiosity." Here, growing suddenly furious, he gave an egg a clout.

His daughter giggled—

"Oh, Pa," said she, "you are not breaking that egg, you are murdering it."

He looked at her gloomily—

"It wasn't the egg I was hitting," said he. "Gr-r-r-up," said he suddenly, and he stabbed a piece of butter, squashed it to death on a slice of bread, and tore it to pieces with his teeth.

The young lady looked at him with some amazement, but she said nothing, for she believed, as most ladies do, that men are a little mad sometimes, and are foolish always.

Her father intercepted that glance, and instantly snarled—

"Can you cook, young woman?" said he.

"Of course, father," replied the perplexed maiden.

He laid aside his spoon and gave her his full attention.

"Can you cook potatoes?" said he. "Can you mash 'em, eh? Can you mash 'em? What! You can. They call them Murphies in this country, girl. Can you mash Murphys, eh? I can. There's a Murphy I know, and, although it's been mashed already, by the Lord Harry, I'll mash it again. Did you ever know that potatoes had eyes, miss? Did you ever notice it when you were cooking them? Did you ever look into the eyes of a Murphy, eh? When you mashed it, what? Don't answer me, girl."

"I don't know what you are talking about, Pa," said the young lady.

"Don't you, now?" grinned the furious gentleman, and his bulging eyes looked like little round balls of glass. "Who said you did, miss? Gr-r-r-up," said he, and the poor girl jumped as though she had been prodded with a pin.

Mr. Aloysius Murphy's activities began at ten o'clock in the morning by opening the office letters with an ivory instrument and handing them to his employer; then, as each letter was read, he entered its receipt and date in a book kept for that purpose.

When Mr. MacMahon came in on the morning following the occurrences I have detailed he neglected, for the first time in many years, to respond to his clerk's respectfully-cordial salutation. To the discreet "Good-morning, sir," he vouchsafed no reply. Mr. Murphy was a trifle indignant and a good deal perturbed, for to an unquiet conscience a word or the lack of it is a goad. Once or twice, looking up from his book, he discovered his employer's hard eyes fixed upon him with a regard too particular to be pleasant.

An employer seldom does more than glance at his clerk, just the sideward glint of a look which remarks his presence without admitting his necessity, and in return the clerk slants a hurried eye on his employer, notes swiftly if his aspect be sulky or benign, and stays his vision at that. But, now, Mr. Murphy, with sudden trepidation, with a frightful sinking in the pit of his stomach, became aware that his employer was looking at him stealthily; and, little by little, he took to sneaking glances at his employer. After a few moments neither seemed to be able to keep his eyes from straying—they created opportunities in connection with the letters; the one looking intent, wide-eyed, and with a cold, frigid, rigid, hard stare, and the other scurrying and furtive, in-and-away, hit-and-miss-and-try-again, wink, blink, and twitter.

Mr. MacMahon spoke—

"Murphy!"

"Yes, sir."

"Have you anything in Court to-day?"

"Yes, sir, an ex parte application, Donald and Cluggs."

"Let O'Neill attend to it. I shall want you to draft a deed for some ladies who will call here at noon. You can come down at ten minutes after twelve."

"Yes, sir," said Murphy.

He grabbed his share of the letters and got to the door bathed in perspiration and forebodings. He closed the door softly behind him, and stood for a few seconds staring at the handle. "Blow you!" said he viciously to nothing in particular, and he went slowly upstairs.

"He can't know," said he on the first landing. On the second floor he thought, "She couldn't have told for she didn't know herself." He reached his desk. "I wish I had a half of whisky," said the young man to himself.

Before, however, twelve o'clock arrived he had journeyed on the hopeful pinions of youth from the dogmatic "could not be" to the equally immovable "is not," and his mind resumed its interrupted equilibrium.

At twelve o'clock Mrs. and Miss MacMahon arrived, and were at once shown into the private office. At ten minutes past, Mr. Murphy's respectful tap was heard. "Don't, Eddie," said Mrs. MacMahon in a queer, flurried voice. "Come in," said her husband. Nora was examining some judicial cartoons pinned over the mantelpiece. Mr. Murphy opened the door a few inches, slid through the aperture, and was at once caught and held by his employer's eye, which, like a hand, guided him to the table with his note-book. Under the almost physical pressure of that authoritative glare he did not dare to look who was in the room, but the rim of his eye saw the movement of a skirt like the far-away, shadowy canter of a ghost's robe. He fixed his attention on his note-book.

Mr. MacMahon began to dictate a Deed of Conveyance from a precedent deed in his hand. After dictating for some few minutes—

"Murphy," said he, and at the word the young lady studying the cartoons stiffened, "I've rather lost the thread of that clause; please read what you have down."

Murphy began to read, and, at the first word, the girl made a tiny, shrill, mouse's noise, and then stood stock-still, tightened up and frightened, with her two wild eyes trying to peep around her ears.

Mr. Murphy heard the noise and faltered—he knew instinctively. Something told him with the bellowing assurance of a cannon who was there. He must look. He forced his slack face past the granite image that was his employer, saw a serge-clad figure that he knew, one ear and the curve of a cheek. Then a cascade broke inside his head. It buzzed and chattered and crashed, with now and again the blank brutality of thunder bashing through the noise. The serge-clad figure swelled suddenly to a tremendous magnitude, and then it receded just as swiftly, and the vast earth spun minutely on a pin's point ten million miles away, and she was behind it, her eyes piercing with scorn. . . . Through the furious winds that whirled about his brain he heard a whisper, thin and cold, and insistent as a razor's edge, "Go on, Murphy; go on, Murphy." He strove to fix his attention on his shorthand notes— To fight it down, to stand the shock like a man, and then crawl into a hole somewhere and die; but his mind would not grip, nor his eyes focus. The only words which his empty brain could pump up were these, irrelevant and idiotic, " 'A frog he would a-wooing go, heigho,' said Rowley"; and they must not be said. "It is a bit difficult, perhaps," said the whispering voice that crept through the tumult of winds and waters in his head. "Never mind, take down the rest of it," and the far-away whisper began to say things all about nothing, making queer little noises and pauses, running for a moment into a ripple of sound, and eddying and dying away and coming back again—buz-z-z! His note-book lying on the table was as small as a postage stamp, while the pencil in his hand was as big as an elephant's leg. How can a man write on a microscopic blur with the stump of a fir tree? He poked and prodded, and Mr. MacMahon watched for a few moments his clerk poking his note-book with the wrong end of a pencil. He silently pulled his daughter forward and made her look. After a little—

"That will do, Murphy," said he, and Mr. Murphy, before he got out, made two severe attempts to walk through a wall.

For half an hour he sat at his desk in a trance, with his eyes fixed upon an ink-bottle. At last, nodding his head slowly—

"I'll bet you a shilling," said he to the ink-bottle, "that I get the sack to-night."

And the ink-bottle lost the wager.

60

The Dead

BY JAMES JOYCE

LILY, the caretaker's daughter, was literally run off her feet. Hardly had she brought one gentleman into the little pantry behind the office on the ground floor and helped him off with his overcoat, than the wheezy hall-door bell clanged again and she had to scamper along the bare hallway to let in another guest. It was well for her she had not to attend to the ladies also. But Miss Kate and Miss Julia had thought of that and had converted the bathroom upstairs into a ladies' dressing-room. Miss Kate and Miss Julia were there, gossiping and laughing and fussing, walking after each other to the head of the stairs, peering down over the banisters and calling down to Lily to ask her who had come.

It was always a great affair, the Misses Morkan's annual dance. Everybody who knew them came to it, members of the family, old friends of the family, the members of Julia's choir, any of Kate's pupils that were grown up enough, and even some of Mary Jane's pupils too. Never once had it fallen flat. For years and years it had gone off in splendid style, as long as anyone could remember: ever since Kate and Julia, after the death of their brother Pat, had left the house in Stoney Batter and taken Mary Jane, their only niece, to live with them in the dark, gaunt house on Usher's Island, the upper part of which they had rented from Mr. Fulham, the corn-factor on the ground floor. That was a good thirty years ago if it was a day. Mary Jane, who was then a little girl in short clothes, was now the main prop of the household, for she had the organ in Haddington Road. She had been through the Academy and gave a pupils' concert every year in the upper room of the Antient Concert Rooms. Many of her pupils belonged to the better-class families on the Kingstown and Dalkey line. Old as they were, her aunts also did their share. Julia, though she was quite grey, was still the leading soprano in Adam and Eve's, and Kate, being too feeble to go about much, gave music lessons to beginners on the old square piano in the back room. Lily, the caretaker's daughter, did housemaid's work for them. Though their life was modest, they believed in eating well; the best of everything: diamond-bone sirloins, three-shilling tea and the best bottled stout. But Lily seldom made a mistake in the orders, so that she got on well with her three mistresses. They were fussy, that was all. But the only thing they would not stand was back answers.

Of course, they had good reason to be fussy on such a night. And then it was long after ten o'clock and yet there was no sign of Gabriel and his wife. Besides they were dreadfully afraid that Freddy Malins might turn up screwed. They would not wish for worlds that any of Mary Jane's pupils should see him under the influence; and when he was like that it was sometimes very hard to manage him. Freddy Malins always came late, but they wondered what could be keeping Gabriel: and that was what brought them every two minutes to the banisters to ask Lily had Gabriel or Freddy come.

"Oh, Mr. Conroy," said Lily to Gabriel when she opened the door for him, "Miss Kate and Miss Julia thought you were never coming. Good night, Mrs. Conroy."

"I'll engage they did," said Gabriel, "but they forget that my wife here takes three mortal hours to dress herself."

He stood on the mat, scraping the snow from his goloshes, while Lily led his wife to the foot of the stairs and called out:

"Miss Kate, here's Mrs. Conroy."

Kate and Julia came toddling down the dark stairs at once. Both of them kissed Gabriel's wife, said she must be perished alive, and asked was Gabriel with her.

"Here I am as right as the mail, Aunt Kate! Go on up. I'll follow," called out Gabriel from the dark.

He continued scraping his feet vigorously while the three women went upstairs, laughing, to the ladies' dressing-room. A light fringe of snow lay like a cape on the shoulders of his overcoat and like toecaps on the toes of his goloshes; and, as the buttons of his overcoat slipped with a squeaking noise through the snow-stiffened frieze, a cold, fragrant air from out-of-doors escaped from crevices and folds.

"Is it snowing again, Mr. Conroy?" asked Lily.

She had preceded him into the pantry to help him off with his overcoat. Gabriel smiled at the three syllables she had given his surname and glanced at her. She was a slim, growing girl, pale in complexion and with hay-coloured hair. The gas in the pantry made her look still paler. Gabriel had known her when she was a child and used to sit on the lowest step nursing a rag doll.

"Yes, Lily," he answered, "and I think we're in for a night of it."

He looked up at the pantry ceiling, which was shaking with the stamping and shuffling of feet on the floor above, listened for a moment to the piano and then glanced at the girl, who was folding his overcoat carefully at the end of a shelf.

"Tell me, Lily," he said in a friendly tone, "do you still go to school?"

"Oh no, sir," she answered. "I'm done schooling this year and more."

"Oh, then," said Gabriel gaily, "I suppose we'll be going to your wedding one of these fine days with your young man, eh?"

The girl glanced back at him over her shoulder and said with great bitterness:

"The men that is now is only all palaver and what they can get out of you."

Gabriel coloured, as if he felt he had made a mistake and, without looking at her, kicked off his goloshes and flicked actively with his muffler at his patent-leather shoes.

He was a stout, tallish young man. The high colour of his cheeks pushed upwards even to his forehead, where it scattered itself in a few formless patches of pale red; and on his hairless face there scintillated restlessly the polished lenses and the bright gilt rims of the glasses which screened his delicate and restless eyes. His glossy black hair was parted in the middle and brushed in a long curve behind his ears where it curled slightly beneath the groove left by his hat.

When he had flicked lustre into his shoes he stood up and pulled his waistcoat down more tightly on his plump body. Then he took a coin rapidly from his pocket.

"O Lily," he said, thrusting it into her hands, "it's Christmas-time, isn't it? Just . . . here's a little. . . ."

He walked rapidly towards the door.

"O no, sir!" cried the girl, following him. "Really, sir, I wouldn't take it."

"Christmas-time! Christmas-time!" said Gabriel, almost trotting to the stairs and waving his hand to her in deprecation.

The girl, seeing that he had gained the stairs, called out after him: "Well, thank you, sir."

He waited outside the drawing-room door until the waltz should finish, listening to the skirts that swept against it and to the shuffling of feet. He was still discomposed by the girl's bitter and sudden retort. It had cast a gloom over him which he tried to dispel by arranging his cuffs and the bows of his tie. He then took from his waistcoat pocket a little paper and glanced at the headings he had made for his speech. He was undecided about the lines from Robert Browning, for he feared they would be above the heads of his hearers. Some quotation that they would recognize from Shakespeare or from the Melodies would be better. The indelicate clacking of the men's heels and the shuffling of their soles reminded him that their grade of culture differed from his. He would only make himself ridiculous by quoting poetry to them which they could not understand. They would think that he was airing his superior education. He would fail with them just as he had failed with the girl in the pantry. He had taken up a wrong tone. His whole speech was a mistake from first to last, an utter failure.

Just then his aunts and his wife came out of the ladies' dressing-room. His aunts were two small, plainly dressed old women. Aunt Julia was an inch or so the taller. Her hair, drawn low over the tops of her ears, was grey; and grey also, with darker shadows, was her large flaccid face. Though she was stout in build and stood erect, her slow eyes and parted lips gave her the appearance of a woman who did not know where she was or where she was going. Aunt Kate was more vivacious. Her face, healthier than her sister's, was all puckers and creases, like a shrivelled red apple, and her hair, braided in the same old-fashioned way, had not lost its ripe nut colour.

They both kissed Gabriel frankly. He was their favourite nephew, the son of their dead elder sister, Ellen, who had married T. J. Conroy of the Port and Docks.

"Gretta tells me you're not going to take a cab back to Monkstown to-night, Gabriel," said Aunt Kate.

"No," said Gabriel, turning to his wife, "we had quite enough of that last year, hadn't we? Don't you remember, Aunt Kate, what a cold Gretta got out of it? Cab windows rattling all the way, and the east wind blowing in after we passed Merrion. Very jolly it was. Gretta caught a dreadful cold."

Aunt Kate frowned severely and nodded her head at every word.

"Quite right, Gabriel, quite right," she said. "You can't be too careful."

"But as for Gretta there," said Gabriel, "she'd walk home in the snow if she were let."

Mrs. Conroy laughed.

"Don't mind him, Aunt Kate," she said. "He's really an awful bother, what with green shades for Tom's eyes at night and making him do the dumb-bells, and forcing Eva to eat the stirabout. The poor child! And she simply hates the sight of it! . . . Oh, but you'll never guess what he makes me wear now!"

She broke out into a peal of laughter and glanced at her husband, whose admiring and happy eyes had been wandering from her dress to her face and hair. The two aunts laughed heartily, too, for Gabriel's solicitude was a standing joke with them.

"Goloshes!" said Mrs. Conroy. "That's the latest. Whenever it's wet underfoot I must put on my goloshes. To-night even, he wanted me to put them on, but I wouldn't. The next thing he'll buy me will be a diving suit.

Gabriel laughed nervously and patted his tie reassuringly, while Aunt Kate nearly doubled herself, so heartily did she enjoy the joke. The smile soon faded from Aunt Julia's face and her mirthless eyes were directed towards her nephew's face. After a pause she asked:

"And what are goloshes, Gabriel?"

"Goloshes, Julia!" exclaimed her sister. "Goodness me, don't you know what goloshes are? You wear them over your . . . over your boots, Gretta, isn't it?"

"Yes," said Mrs. Conroy. "Gutta-percha things. We both have a pair now. Gabriel says everyone wears them on the Continent."

"Oh, on the Continent," murmured Aunt Julia, nodding her head slowly.

Gabriel knitted his brows and said, as if he were slightly angered:

"It's nothing very wonderful, but Gretta thinks it very funny, because she says the word reminds her of Christy Minstrels."

"But tell me, Gabriel," said Aunt Kate, with brisk tact. "Of course, you've seen about the room. Gretta was saying . . ."

"Oh, the room is all right," replied Gabriel. "I've taken one in the Gresham."

"To be sure," said Aunt Kate, "by far the best thing to do. And the children, Gretta, you're not anxious about them?"

"Oh, for one night," said Mrs. Conroy. "Besides, Bessie will look after them."

"To be sure," said Aunt Kate again. "What a comfort it is to have a girl like that, one you can depend on! There's that Lily, I'm sure I don't know what has come over her lately. She's not the girl she was at all."

Gabriel was about to ask his aunt some questions on this point, but she broke off suddenly to gaze after her sister, who had wandered down the stairs and was craning her neck over the banisters.

"Now, I ask you," she said almost testily, "where is Julia going? Julia! Julia! Where are you going?"

Julia, who had gone half-way down one flight, came back and announced blandly:

"Here's Freddy."

At the same moment a clapping of hands and a final flourish of the pianist told that the waltz had ended. The drawing-room door was opened from within and some couples came out. Aunt Kate drew Gabriel aside hurriedly and whispered into his ear:

"Slip down, Gabriel, like a good fellow and see if he's all right, and don't let him up if he's screwed. I'm sure he's screwed. I'm sure he is."

Gabriel went to the stairs and listened over the banisters. He could hear two persons talking in the pantry. Then he recognized Freddy Malin's laugh. He went down the stairs noisily.

"It's such a relief," said Aunt Kate to Mrs. Conroy, "that Gabriel is here. I always feel easier in my mind when he's here . . . Julia, there's Miss Daly and Miss Power will take some refreshment. Thanks for your beautiful waltz, Miss Daly. It made lovely time."

A tall wizen-faced man, with a stiff grizzled moustache and swarthy skin, who was passing out with his partner, said:

"And may we have some refreshment, too, Miss Morkan?"

"Julia," said Aunt Kate summarily, "and here's Mr. Browne and Miss Furlong. Take them in, Julia, with Miss Daly and Miss Power."

"I'm the man for the ladies," said Mr. Browne, pursing his lips until his moustache bristled and smiling in all his wrinkles. "You know, Miss Morkan, the reason they are so fond of me is . . ."

He did not finish his sentence, but, seeing that Aunt Kate was out of earshot, at once led the three young ladies into the back room. The middle of the room was occupied by two square tables placed end to end, and on these Aunt Julia and the caretaker were straightening and smoothing a large cloth. On the sideboard were arrayed dishes and plates, and glasses and bundles of knives and forks and spoons. The top of the closed square piano served also as a sideboard for viands and sweets. At a smaller sideboard in one corner two young men were standing, drinking hop-bitters.

Mr. Browne led his charges thither and invited them all, in jest, to some ladies' punch, hot, strong and sweet. As they said they never took anything strong, he opened three bottles of lemonade for them. Then he asked one of the young men to move aside, and, taking hold of the decanter, filled out for himself a goodly measure of whisky. The young men eyed him respectfully while he took a trial sip.

"God help me," he said, smiling, "it's the doctor's orders."

His wizened face broke into a broader smile, and the three young ladies laughed in musical echo to his pleasantry, swaying their bodies to and fro, with nervous jerks of their shoulders. The boldest said:

"Oh, now, Mr. Browne, I'm sure the doctor never ordered anything of the kind."

Mr. Browne took another sip of his whisky and said, with sidling mimicry:

"Well, you see, I'm like the famous Mrs. Cassidy, who is reported to have said: 'Now, Mary Grimes, if I don't take it, make me take it, for I feel I want it.'"

His hot face had leaned forward a little too confidentially and he had assumed a very low Dublin accent, so that the young ladies, with one instinct, received his speech in silence. Miss Furlong, who was one of Mary Jane's pupils, asked Miss Daly what was the name of the pretty waltz she had played; and Mr. Browne, seeing that he was ignored, turned promptly to the two young men, who were more appreciative.

A red-faced young woman, dressed in pansy, came into the room, excitedly clapping her hands and crying:

"Quadrilles! Quadrilles!"

Close on her heels came Aunt Kate, crying:

"Two gentlemen and three ladies, Mary Jane!"

"Oh, here's Mr. Bergin and Mr. Kerrigan," said Mary Jane. "Mr. Kerrigan, will you take Miss Power? Miss Furlong, may I get you a partner, Mr. Bergin. Oh, that'll just do now."

"Three ladies, Mary Jane," said Aunt Kate.

The two young gentlemen asked the ladies if they might have the pleasure, and Mary Jane turned to Miss Daly.

"Oh, Miss Daly, you're really awful good, after playing for the last two dances, but really we're so short of ladies to-night."

"I don't mind in the least, Miss Morkan."

"But I've a nice partner for you, Mr. Bartell D'Arcy, the tenor. I'll get him to sing later on. All Dublin is raving about him."

"Lovely voice, lovely voice!" said Aunt Kate.

As the piano had twice begun the prelude to the first figure Mary Jane led her recruits quickly from the room. They had hardly gone when Aunt Julia wandered slowly into the room, looking behind her at something.

"What is the matter, Julia?" asked Aunt Kate anxiously. "Who is it!"

Julia, who was carrying in a column of table-napkins, turned to her sister and said, simply, as if the question had surprised her:

"It's only Freddy, Kate, and Gabriel with him."

In fact, right behind her Gabriel could be seen piloting Freddy Malins across the landing. The latter, a young man of about forty, was of Gabriel's size and build, with very round shoulders. His face was fleshy and pallid, touched with colour only at the thick hanging lobes of his ears and at the wide wings of his nose. He had coarse features, a blunt nose, a convex and receding brow, tumid and protruded lips. His heavy-lidded eyes and the disorder of his scanty hair made him look sleepy. He was laughing heartily in a high key at a story which he had been telling Gabriel on the stairs and at the same time rubbing the knuckles of his left fist backwards and forwards into his left eye.

"Good evening, Freddy," said Aunt Julia.

Freddy Malins bade the Misses Morkan good evening in what seemed an offhand fashion by reason of the habitual catch in his voice and then, seeing that Mr. Browne was grinning at him from the sideboard, crossed the room on rather shaky legs and began to repeat in an undertone the story he had just told to Gabriel.

"He's not so bad, is he?" said Aunt Kate to Gabriel.

Gabriel's brows were dark, but he raised them quickly and answered: "Oh, no, hardly noticeable."

"Now, isn't he a terrible fellow!" she said. "And his poor mother made him take the pledge on New Year's Eve. But come on, Gabriel, into the drawing-room."

Before leaving the room with Gabriel she signalled to Mr. Browne by frowning and shaking her forefinger in warning to and fro. Mr. Browne nodded in answer and, when she had gone, said to Freddy Malins:

"Now, then, Teddy, I'm going to fill you out a good glass of lemonade just to buck you up."

Freddy Malins, who was nearing the climax of his story, waved the offer aside impatiently, but Mr. Browne, having first called Freddy Malins' attention to a disarray in his dress, filled out and handed him a full glass of lemonade. Freddy Malins' left hand accepted the glass mechanically, his right hand being engaged in the mechanical readjustment of his dress. Mr. Browne, whose face was once more wrinkling with mirth, poured out for himself a glass of whisky while Freddy Malins exploded, before he had well reached the climax of his story, in a kink of high-pitched bronchitic laughter and, setting down his untasted and overflowing glass, began to rub the knuckles of his left fist backwards and forwards into his left eye, repeating words of his last phrase as well as his fit of laughter would allow him.

Gabriel could not listen while Mary Jane was playing her Academy piece, full of runs and difficult passages, to the hushed drawing-room. He liked music, but the piece she was playing had no melody for him and he doubted whether it had any melody for the other listeners, though they had begged Mary Jane to play something. Four young men, who had come from the refreshment-room to stand in the doorway at the sound of the piano, had gone away quietly in couples after a few minutes. The only persons who seemed to follow the music were Mary Jane herself, her hands racing along the keyboard or lifted from it at the pauses like those of a priestess in momentary imprecation, and Aunt Kate standing at her elbow to turn the page.

Gabriel's eyes, irritated by the floor, which glittered with beeswax under the heavy chandelier, wandered to the wall above the piano. A picture of the balcony scene in *Romeo and Juliet* hung there and beside it was a picture of the two murdered princes in the Tower which Aunt Julia had worked in red, blue and brown wools when she was a girl. Probably in the school they had gone to as girls that kind of work had been taught for one year. His mother had worked for him as a birthday present a waistcoat of purple tabinet, with little foxes' heads upon it, lined with brown satin and having round mulberry buttons. It was strange that his mother had had no musical talent, though Aunt Kate used to call her the brains carrier of the Morkan family. Both she and Julia had always seemed a little proud of their serious and matronly sister. Her photograph stood before the pierglass. She held an open book on her knees and was pointing out something in it to Constantine who, dressed in a man-o'-war suit, lay at her feet. It was she who had chosen the names of her sons for she was very sensible of the dignity of family life. Thanks to her, Constantine was now senior curate in Balbriggan and, thanks to her, Gabriel himself had taken his degree in the Royal University. A shadow passed over his face as he remembered her sullen opposition to his marriage. Some slighting phrases she had used still rankled in his memory; she had once spoken of Gretta as being country cute and that was not true of Gretta at all. It was Gretta who had nursed her during all her last long illness in their house at Monkstown.

He knew that Mary Jane must be near the end of her piece, for she was playing again the opening melody with runs of scales after every bar, and while he waited for the end the resentment died down in his heart. The piece ended with a trill of octaves in the treble and a final deep octave in the bass. Great applause greeted Mary Jane as, blushing and rolling up her music nervously, she escaped from the room. The most vigorous clapping came from the four young men in the doorway who had gone away to the refreshment-room at the beginning of the piece but had come back when the piano had stopped.

Lancers were arranged. Gabriel found himself partnered with Miss Ivors. She was a frank-mannered, talkative young lady, with a freckled face and prominent brown eyes. She did not wear a low-cut bodice, and the large brooch which was fixed in the front of her collar bore on it an Irish device and motto.

When they had taken their places she said abruptly:

"I have a crow to pluck with you."

"With me?" said Gabriel.

She nodded her head gravely.

"What is it?" asked Gabriel, smiling at her solemn manner.

"Who is G. C.?" answered Miss Ivors, turning her eyes upon him.

Gabriel coloured and was about to knit his brows, as if he did not understand, when she said bluntly:

"Oh, innocent Amy! I have found out that you write for the *Daily Express*. Now, aren't you ashamed of yourself?"

"Why should I be ashamed of myself?" asked Gabriel, blinking his eyes and trying to smile.

"Well, I'm ashamed of you," said Miss Ivors frankly. "To say you'd write for a paper like that. I didn't think you were a West Briton."

A look of perplexity appeared on Gabriel's face. It was true that he wrote a literary column every Wednesday in the *Daily Express,* for which he was paid fifteen shillings. But that did not make him a West Briton surely. The books he received for review were almost more welcome than the paltry cheque. He loved to feel the covers and turn over the pages of newly printed books. Nearly every day when his teaching in the college was ended he used to wander down the quays to the second-hand booksellers, to Hickey's on Bachelor's Walk, to Webb's or Massey's on Aston's Quay, or to O'Clohissey's in the by-street. He did not know how to meet her charge. He wanted to say that literature was above politics. But they were friends of many years' standing and their careers had been parallel, first at the University and then as teachers: he could not risk a grandiose phrase with her. He continued blinking his eyes and trying to smile and murmured lamely that he saw nothing political in writing reviews of books.

When their turn to cross had come he was still perplexed and inattentive. Miss Ivors promptly took his hand in a warm grasp and said in a soft friendly tone:

"Of course, I was only joking. Come, we cross now."

When they were together again she spoke of the University question and Gabriel felt more at ease. A friend of hers had shown her his review of Browning's poems. That was how she had found out the secret: but she liked the review immensely. Then she said suddenly:

"Oh, Mr. Conroy, will you come for an excursion to the Aran Isles this summer? We're going to stay there a whole month. It will be splendid out in the Atlantic. You ought to come. Mr. Clancy is coming, and Mr. Kilkelly and Kathleen Kearney. It would be splendid for Gretta too if she'd come. She's from Connacht, isn't she?"

"Her people are," said Gabriel shortly.

"But you will come, won't you?" said Miss Ivors, laying her warm hand eagerly on his arm.

"The fact is," said Gabriel, "I have just arranged to go . . ."

"Go where?" asked Miss Ivors.

"Well, you know, every year I go for a cycling tour with some fellows and so . . ."

"But where?" asked Miss Ivors.

"Well, we usually go to France or Belgium or perhaps Germany," said Gabriel awkwardly.

"And why do you go to France and Belgium," said Miss Ivors, "instead of visiting your own land?"

"Well," said Gabriel, "it's partly to keep in touch with the languages and partly for a change."

"And haven't you your own language to keep in touch with—Irish?" asked Miss Ivors.

"Well," said Gabriel, "if it comes to that, you know, Irish is not my language."

Their neighbours had turned to listen to the cross-examination. Gabriel glanced right and left nervously and tried to keep his good humour under the ordeal, which was making a blush invade his forehead.

"And haven't you your own land to visit," continued Miss Ivors, "that you know nothing of, your own people, and your own country?"

"Oh, to tell you the truth," retorted Gabriel suddenly, "I'm sick of my own country, sick of it!"

"Why?" asked Miss Ivors.

Gabriel did not answer, for his retort had heated him.

"Why?" repeated Miss Ivors.

They had to go visiting together and, as he had not answered her, Miss Ivors said warmly:

"Of course, you've no answer."

Gabriel tried to cover his agitation by taking part in the dance with great energy. He avoided her eyes, for he had seen a sour expression on her face. But when they met in the long chain he was surprised to feel his hand firmly pressed. She looked at him from under her brows for a moment quizzically until he smiled. Then, just as the chain was about to start again, she stood on tiptoe and whispered into his ear:

"West Briton!"

When the lancers were over Gabriel went away to a remote corner of the room where Freddy Malins' mother was sitting. She was a stout, feeble old woman with white hair. Her voice had a catch in it like her son's and she stuttered slightly. She had been told that Freddy had come and that he was nearly all right. Gabriel asked her whether she had had a good crossing. She lived with her married daughter in Glasgow and came to Dublin on a visit once a year. She answered placidly that she had had a beautiful crossing and that the captain had been most attentive to her. She spoke also of the beautiful house her daughter kept in Glasgow, and of all the friends they had there. While her tongue rambled on Gabriel tried to banish from his mind all memory of the unpleasant incident with Miss Ivors. Of course the girl, or woman, or whatever she was, was an enthusiast, but there was a time for all things. Perhaps he ought not to have answered her like that. But she had no right to call him a West Briton before people, even in joke. She had tried to make him ridiculous before people, heckling him and staring at him with her rabbit's eyes.

He saw his wife making her way towards him through the waltzing couples. When she reached him she said into his ear:

"Gabriel, Aunt Kate wants to know won't you carve the goose as usual. Miss Daly will carve the ham and I'll do the pudding."

"All right," said Gabriel.

"She's sending in the younger ones first as soon as this waltz is over so that we'll have the table to ourselves."

"Were you dancing?" asked Gabriel.

"Of course I was. Didn't you see me? What row had you with Molly Ivors?"

"No row. Why? Did she say so?"

"Something like that. I'm trying to get that Mr. D'Arcy to sing. He's full of conceit, I think."

"There was no row," said Gabriel moodily, "only she wanted me to go for a trip to the west of Ireland and I said I wouldn't."

His wife clasped her hands excitedly and gave a little jump.

"Oh, do go, Gabriel," she cried. "I'd love to see Galway again."

"You can go if you like," said Gabriel coldly.

She looked at him for a moment, then turned to Mrs. Malins and said: "There's a nice husband for you, Mrs. Malins."

While she was threading her way back across the room Mrs. Malins, without adverting to the interruption, went on to tell Gabriel what beautiful places there were in Scotland and beautiful scenery. Her son-in-law brought them every year to the lakes and they used to go fishing. Her son-in-law was a splendid fisher. One day he caught a beautiful big fish and the man in the hotel cooked it for their dinner.

Gabriel hardly heard what she said. Now that supper was coming near he began to think again about his speech and about the quotation. When he saw Freddy Malins coming across the room to visit his mother Gabriel left the chair free for him and retired into the embrasure of the window. The room had already cleared and from the back room came the clatter of plates and knives. Those who still remained in the drawing-room seemed tired of dancing and were conversing quietly in little groups. Gabriel's warm, trembling fingers tapped the cold pane of the window. How cool it must be outside! How pleasant it would be to walk out alone, first along by the river and then through the park!

The snow would be lying on the branches of the trees and forming a bright cap on the top of the Wellington Monument. How much more pleasant it would be there than at the supper-table!

He ran over the headings of his speech: Irish hospitality, sad memories, the Three Graces, Paris, the quotation from Browning. He repeated to himself a phrase he had written in his review: "One feels that one is listening to a thought-tormented music." Miss Ivors had praised the review. Was she sincere? Had she really any life of her own behind all her propagandism? There had never been any ill-feeling between them until that night. It unnerved him to think that she would be at the supper-table, looking up at him while he spoke with her critical quizzing eyes. Perhaps she would not be sorry to see him fail in his speech. An idea came into his mind and gave him courage. He would say, alluding to Aunt Kate and Aunt Julia: "Ladies and Gentlemen, the generation which is now on the wane among us may have had its faults, but for my part I think it had certain qualities of hospitality, of humour, of humanity, which the new and very serious and hypereducated generation that is growing up around us seems to me to lack." Very good: that was one for Miss Ivors. What did he care that his aunts were only two ignorant old women?

A murmur in the room attracted his attention. Mr. Browne was advancing from the door, gallantly escorting Aunt Julia, who leaned upon his arm, smiling and hanging her head. An irregular musketry of applause escorted her also as far as the piano and then, as Mary Jane seated herself on the stool, and Aunt Julia, no longer smiling, half turned so as to pitch her voice fairly into the room, gradually ceased. Gabriel recognized the prelude. It was that of an old song of Aunt Julia's—"Arrayed for the Bridal." Her voice, strong and clear in tone, attacked with great spirit the runs which embellish the air, and though she sang very rapidly she did not miss even the smallest of the grace notes. To follow the voice, without looking at the singer's face, was to feel and share the excitement of swift and secure flight. Gabriel applauded loudly with all the others at the close of the song, and loud applause was borne in from the invisible supper-table. It sounded so genuine that a little colour struggled into Aunt Julia's face as she bent to replace in the music-stand the old leather-bound song-book that had her initials on the cover. Freddy Malins, who had listened with his head perched sideways to hear her better, was still applauding when everyone else had ceased and talking animatedly to his mother, who nodded her head gravely and slowly in acquiescence. At last, when he could clap no more, he stood up suddenly and hurried across the room to Aunt Julia whose hand he seized and held in both his hands, shaking it when words failed him or the catch in his voice proved too much for him.

"I was just telling my mother," he said, "I never heard you sing so well, never. No, I never heard your voice so good as it is to-night. Now! Would you believe that now? That's the truth. Upon my word and honour that's the truth. I never heard your voice sound so fresh and so. . . so clear and fresh, never."

Aunt Julia smiled broadly and murmured something about compliments as she released her hand from his grasp. Mr. Browne extended his open hand towards her and said to those who were near him in the manner of a showman introducing a prodigy to an audience:

"Miss Julia Morkan, my latest discovery!"

He was laughing very heartily at this himself when Freddy Malins turned to him and said:

"Well, Browne, if you're serious you might make a worse discovery. All I can say is I never heard her sing half so well as long as I am coming here. And that's the honest truth."

"Neither did I," said Mr. Browne. "I think her voice has greatly improved."

Aunt Julia shrugged her shoulders and said with meek pride:

"Thirty years ago I hadn't a bad voice as voices go."

"I often told Julia," said Aunt Kate emphatically, "that she was simply thrown away in that choir. But she never would be said by me."

She turned as if to appeal to the good sense of the others against a refractory child, while Aunt Julia gazed in front of her, a vague smile of reminiscence playing on her face.

"No," continued Aunt Kate, "she wouldn't be said or led by anyone, slaving there in that choir night and day, night and day. Six o'clock on Christmas morning! And all for what?"

"Well, isn't it for the honour of God, Aunt Kate?" asked Mary Jane, twisting round on the piano-stool and smiling.

Aunt Kate turned fiercely on her niece and said:

"I know all about the honour of God, Mary Jane, but I think it's not at all honourable for the pope to turn out the women out of the choirs that have slaved there all their lives and put little whipper-snappers of boys over their heads. I suppose it is for the good of the Church, if the pope does it. But it's not just, Mary Jane, and it's not right."

She had worked herself into a passion and would have continued in defence of her sister, for it was a sore subject with her, but Mary Jane, seeing that all the dancers had come back, intervened pacifically.

"Now, Aunt Kate, you're giving scandal to Mr. Browne, who is of the other persuasion."

Aunt Kate turned to Mr. Browne, who was grinning at this allusion to his religion, and said hastily:

"Oh, I don't question the pope's being right. I'm only a stupid old woman and I wouldn't presume to do such a thing. But there's such a thing as common everyday politeness and gratitude. And if I were in Julia's place I'd tell that Father Healey straight up to his face . . ."

"And besides, Aunt Kate," said Mary Jane, "we really are all hungry and when we are hungry we are all very quarrelsome."

"And when we are thirsty we are also quarrelsome," added Mr. Browne.

"So that we had better go to supper," said Mary Jane, "and finish the discussion afterwards."

On the landing outside the drawing-room Gabriel found his wife and Mary Jane trying to persuade Miss Ivors to stay for supper. But Miss Ivors, who had put on her hat and was buttoning her cloak, would not stay. She did not feel in the least hungry and she had already over-stayed her time.

"But only for ten minutes, Molly," said Mrs. Conroy. "That won't delay you."

"To take a pick itself," said Mary Jane, "after all your dancing."

"I really couldn't," said Miss Ivors.

"I am afraid you didn't enjoy yourself at all," said Mary Jane hope-lessly.

"Ever so much I assure you," said Miss Ivors, "but you really must let me run off now."

"But how can you get home?" asked Mrs. Conroy.

"Oh, it's only two steps up the quay?"

Gabriel hesitated a moment and said:

"If you will allow me, Miss Ivors, I'll see you home if you are really obliged to go."

But Miss Ivors broke away from them.

"I won't hear of it," she cried. "For goodness' sake go in to your sup-pers and don't mind me. I'm quite well able to take care of myself."

"Well, you're the comical girl, Molly," said Mrs. Conroy frankly.

"*Beannacht libh*," cried Miss Ivors, with a laugh, as she ran down the staircase.

Mary Jane gazed after her, a moody puzzled expression on her face, while Mrs. Conroy leaned over the banisters to listen for the hall-door. Gabriel asked himself was he the cause of her abrupt departure. But she did not seem to be in ill humour—she had gone away laughing. He stared blankly down the staircase.

At the moment Aunt Kate came toddling out of the supper-room, almost wringing her hands in despair.

"Where is Gabriel!" she cried. "Where on earth is Gabriel? There's every one waiting in there, stage to let, and nobody to carve the goose!"

"Here I am, Aunt Kate!" cried Gabriel, with sudden animation, "ready to carve a flock of geese, if necessary."

A fat brown goose lay at one end of the table, and at the other end, on a bed of creased paper strewn with sprigs of parsley, lay a great ham, stripped of its outer skin and peppered over with crust crumbs, a neat paper frill round its shin, and beside this was a round of spiced beef. Between these rival ends ran parallel lines of side-dishes: two little minsters of jelly, red and yellow; a shallow dish full of blocks of blancmange and red jam, a large green leaf-shaped dish with a stalk-shaped handle, on which lay bunches of purple raisins and peeled almonds, a companion dish on which lay a solid rectangle of Smyrna figs, a dish of custard topped with grated nutmeg, a small bowl full of chocolates and sweets wrapped in gold and silver papers and a glass vase in which stood some tall celery stalks. In the centre of the table there stood, as sentries to a fruit-stand which upheld a pyramid of oranges and American apples, two squat old-fashioned decanters of cut glass, one containing port and the other dark sherry. On the closed square piano a pudding in a huge yellow dish lay in waiting, and behind it were three squads of bottles of stout and ale and minerals, drawn up according to the colours of their uniforms, the first two black, with brown and red labels, the third and smallest squad white, with transverse green sashes.

Gabriel took his seat boldly at the head of the table and, having looked to the edge of the carver, plunged his fork firmly into the goose. He felt quite at ease now, for he was an expert carver and liked nothing better than to find himself at the head of a well-laden table.

"Miss Furlong, what shall I send you?" he asked. "A wing or a slice of the breast?"

"Just a small slice of the breast."

"Miss Higgins, what for you?"

"Oh, anything at all, Mr. Conroy."

While Gabriel and Miss Daly exchanged plates of goose and plates of ham and spiced beef, Lily went from guest to guest with a dish of hot floury potatoes wrapped in a white napkin. This was Mary Jane's idea and she had also suggested apple sauce for the goose, but Aunt Kate had said that plain roast goose without any apple sauce had always been good enough for her and she hoped she might never eat worse. Mary Jane waited on her pupils and saw that they got the best slices, and Aunt Kate and Aunt Julia opened and carried across from the piano bottles of stout and ale for the gentlemen and bottles of minerals for the ladies. There was a great deal of confusion and laughter and noise, the noise of orders and counter-orders, of knives and forks, of corks and glass-stoppers. Gabriel began to carve second helpings as soon as he had finished the first round without serving himself. Everyone protested loudly, so that he compromised by taking a long draught of stout, for he had found the carving hot work. Mary Jane settled down quietly to her supper, but Aunt Kate and Aunt Julia were still toddling round the table, walking on each other's heels, getting in each other's way and giving each other unheeded orders. Mr. Browne begged of them to sit down and eat their suppers and so did Gabriel, but they said there was time enough, so that at last Freddy Malins stood up and, capturing Aunt Kate, plumped her down on her chair amid general laughter.

When everyone had been well served Gabriel said, smiling:

"Now, if anyone wants a little more of what vulgar people call stuffing let him or her speak."

A chorus of voices invited him to begin his own supper, and Lily came forward with three potatoes which she had reserved for him.

"Very well," said Gabriel amiably, as he took another preparatory draught, "kindly forget my existence, ladies and gentlemen, for a few minutes."

He set to his supper and took no part in the conversation with which the table covered Lily's removal of the plates. The subject of talk was the opera company which was then at the Theatre Royal. Mr. Bartell D'Arcy, the tenor, a dark-complexioned young man with a smart moustache, praised very highly the leading contralto of the company, but Miss Furlong thought she had a rather vulgar style of production. Freddy Malins said there was a negro chieftain singing in the second part of the Gaiety pantomime who had one of the finest tenor voices he had ever heard.

"Have you heard him?" he asked Mr. Bartell D'Arcy across the table.

"No," answered Mr. Bartell D'Arcy carelessly.

"Because," Freddy Malins explained, "now I'd be curious to hear your opinion of him. I think he has a grand voice."

"It takes Teddy to find out the really good things," said Mr. Browne familiarly to the table.

"And why couldn't he have a voice too?" asked Freddy Malins sharply. "Is it because he's only a black?"

Nobody answered this question and Mary Jane led the table back to the legitimate opera. One of her pupils had given her a pass for *Mignon*. Of course it was very fine, she said, but it made her think of poor Georgina Burns. Mr. Browne could go back farther still, to the old Italian companies that used to come to Dublin—Tietjens, Ilma de Murzka, Campanini, the great Trebelli, Giuglini, Ravelli, Aramburo.

Those were the days, he said, when there was something like singing to be heard in Dublin. He told too of how the top gallery of the old Royal used to be packed night after night, of how one night an Italian tenor had sung five encores to "Let me like a Soldier fall," introducing a high C every time, and of how the gallery boys would sometimes in their enthusiasm unyoke the horses from the carriage of some great *prima donna* and pull her themselves through the streets to her hotel. "Why did they never play the grand old operas now," he asked, *"Dinorah, Lucrezia Borgia?* Because they could not get the voices to sing them: that was why."

"Oh, well," said Mr. Bartell D'Arcy, "I presume there are as good singers to-day as there were then."

"Where are they?" asked Mr. Browne defiantly.

"In London, Paris, Milan," said Mr. Bartell D'Arcy warmly. "I suppose Caruso, for example, is quite as good, if not better than any of the men you have mentioned."

"Maybe so," said Mr. Browne. "But I may tell you I doubt it strongly."

"Oh, I'd give anything to hear Caruso sing," said Mary Jane.

"For me," said Aunt Kate, who had been picking a bone, "there was only one tenor. To please me, I mean. But I suppose none of you ever heard of him."

"Who was he, Miss Morkan?" asked Mr. Bartell D'Arcy politely.

"His name," said Aunt Kate, "was Parkinson. I heard him when he was in his prime and I think he had then the purest tenor voice that was ever put into a man's throat."

"Strange," said Mr. Bartell D'Arcy. "I never even heard of him."

"Yes, yes, Miss Morkan is right," said Mr. Browne. "I remember hearing of old Parkinson, but he's too far back for me."

"A beautiful, pure, sweet, mellow English tenor," said Aunt Kate with enthusiasm.

Gabriel having finished, the huge pudding was transferred to the table. The clatter of forks and spoons began again. Gabriel's wife served out spoonfuls of the pudding and passed the plates down the table. Midway down they were held up by Mary Jane, who replenished them with raspberry or orange jelly or with blancmange and jam. The pudding was of Aunt Julia's making, and she received praises for it from all quarters. She herself said that it was not quite brown enough.

"Well, I hope, Miss Morkan," said Mr. Browne, "that I'm brown enough for you because, you know, I'm all brown."

All the gentlemen, except Gabriel, ate some of the pudding out of compliment to Aunt Julia. As Gabriel never ate sweets the celery had been left for him. Freddy Malins also took a stalk of celery and ate it with his pudding. He had been told that celery was a capital thing for the blood and he was just then under the doctor's care. Mrs. Malins who had been silent all through the supper, said that her son was going down to Mount Melleray in a week or so. The table then spoke of Mount Melleray, how bracing the air was down there, how hospitable the monks were and how they never asked for a penny-piece from their guests.

"And do you mean to say," asked Mr. Browne incredulously, "that a chap can go down there and put up there as if it were an hotel and live on the fat of the land and then come away without paying anything?"

"Oh, most people give some donation to the monastery when they leave," said Mary Jane.

"I wish we had an institution like that in our Church," said Mr. Browne candidly.

He was astonished to hear that the monks never spoke, got up at two in the morning and slept in their coffins. He asked what they did it for.

"That's the rule of the order," said Aunt Kate firmly.

"Yes, but why?" asked Mr. Browne.

Aunt Kate repeated that it was the rule, that was all. Mr. Browne still seemed not to understand. Freddy Malins explained to him, as best he could, that the monks were trying to make up for the sins committed by all the sinners in the outside world. The explanation was not very clear, for Mr. Browne grinned and said:

"I like that idea very much, but wouldn't a comfortable spring bed do them as well as a coffin?"

"The coffin," said Mary Jane, "is to remind them of their last end."

As the subject had grown lugubrious it was buried in a silence of the table, during which Mrs. Malins could be heard saying to her neighbour in an indistinct undertone:

"They are very good men, the monks, very pious men."

The raisins and almonds and figs and apples and oranges and chocolates and sweets were now passed about the table, and Aunt Julia invited all the guests to have either port or sherry. At first Mr. Bartell D'Arcy refused to take either, but one of his neighbours nudged him and whispered something to him, upon which he allowed his glass to be filled. Gradually as the last glasses were being filled the conversation ceased. A pause followed, broken only by the noise of the wine and by unsettlings of chairs. The Misses Morkan, all three, looked down at the table-cloth. Someone coughed once or twice, and then a few gentlemen patted the table gently as a signal for silence. The silence came and Gabriel pushed back his chair and stood up.

The patting at once grew louder in encouragement and then ceased altogether. Gabriel leaned his ten trembling fingers on the table-cloth and smiled nervously at the company. Meeting a row of upturned faces he raised his eyes to the chandelier. The piano was playing a waltz tune and he could hear the skirts sweeping against the drawing-room door. People, perhaps, were standing in the snow on the quay outside, gazing up at the lighted windows and listening to the waltz music. The air was pure there. In the distance lay the park, where the trees were weighted with snow. The Wellington Monument wore a gleaming cap of snow that flashed westward over the white field of Fifteen Acres.

He began:

"Ladies and Gentlemen,

"It has fallen to my lot this evening, as in years past, to perform a very pleasing task, but a task for which I am afraid my poor powers as a speaker are all too inadequate."

"No, no!" said Mr. Browne.

"But, however that may be, I can only ask you to-night to take the will for the deed, and to lend me your attention for a few moments while I endeavour to express to you in words what my feelings are on this occasion.

"Ladies and Gentlemen, it is not the first time that we have gathered together under this hospitable roof, around this hospitable board. It is not the first time that we have been the recipients—or perhaps, I had better say, the victims—of the hospitality of certain good ladies."

He made a circle in the air with his arm and paused. Every one laughed or smiled at Aunt Kate and Aunt Julia and Mary Jane, who all turned crimson with pleasure. Gabriel went on more boldly:

"I feel more strongly with every recurring year that our country had no tradition which does it so much honour and which it should guard so jealously as that of its hospitality. It is a tradition that is unique as far as my experience goes (and I have visited not a few places abroad) among the modern nations. Some would say, perhaps, that with us it is rather a failing than anything to be boasted of. But granted even that, it is, to my mind, a princely failing, and one that I trust will long be cultivated among us. Of one thing, at least, I am sure. As long as this one roof shelters the good ladies aforesaid—and I wish from my heart it may do so for many and many a long year to come—the tradition of genuine warm-hearted courteous Irish hospitality, which our fore-fathers have handed down to us and which we in turn must hand down to our descendants, is still alive among us."

A hearty murmur of assent ran round the table. It shot through Gabriel's mind that Miss Ivors was not there and that she had gone away discourteously: and he said with confidence in himself:

"Ladies and Gentlemen,

"A new generation is growing up in our midst, a generation actuated by new ideas and new principles. It is serious and enthusiastic, for these new ideas and its enthusiasm, even when it is misdirected, is, I believe, in the main sincere. But we are living in a sceptical and, if I may use the phrase, a thought-tormented age: and sometimes I fear that this new generation, educated or hyper-educated as it is, will lack those qualities of humanity, of hospitality, of kindly humour which belonged to an older day. Listening to-night to the names of all those great singers of the past it seemed to me, I must confess, that we were living in a less spacious age. Those days might, without exaggeration, be called spacious days: and if they are gone beyond recall, let us hope, at least, that in gatherings such as this we shall still speak of them with pride and affection, still cherish in our hearts the memory of those dead and gone great ones whose fame the world will not willingly let die."

"Hear, hear!" said Mr. Browne loudly.

"But yet," continued Gabriel, his voice falling into a softer inflection, "there are always in gatherings such as this sadder thoughts that will recur to our minds: thoughts of the past, of youth, of changes, of absent faces that we miss here to-night. Our path through life is strewn with many such sad memories: and were we to brood upon them always we could not find the heart to go on bravely with our work among the living. We have all of us living duties and living affections which claim, and rightly claim, our strenuous endeavours.

"Therefore, I will not linger on the past, I will not let any gloomy moralizing intrude upon us here to-night. Here we are gathered to-gether for a brief moment from the bustle and rush of our everyday rou-tine. We are met here as friends, in the spirit of good-fellowship, as col-leagues, also, to a certain extent, in the true spirit of *camaraderie,* and as the guests of—what shall I call them?—the Three Graces of the Dublin musical world."

The table burst into applause and laughter at this allusion. Aunt Julia vainly asked each of her neighbours in turn to tell her what Gabriel had said.

"He says we are the Three Graces, Aunt Julia," said Mary Jane.

Aunt Julia did not understand, but she looked up, smiling, at Gabriel, who continued in the same vein:

"Ladies and Gentlemen,

"I will not attempt to play to-night the part that Paris played on an other occasion. I will not attempt to choose between them. The task would be an invidious one and one beyond my poor powers. For when I view them in turn, whether it be our chief hostess herself, whose good heart, whose too good heart, has become a byword with all who know her; or her sister, who seems to be gifted with perennial youth and whose singing must have been a surprise and a revelation to us all to-night; or, last but not least, when I consider our youngest hostess, talented, cheerful, hard-working and the best of nieces, I confess, Ladies and Gentlemen, that I do not know to which of them I should award the prize."

Gabriel glanced down at his aunts and, seeing the large smile on Aunt Julia's face and the tears which had risen to Aunt Kate's eyes, hastened to his close. He raised his glass of port gallantly, while every member of the company fingered a glass expectantly, and said loudly:

"Let us toast them all three together. Let us drink to their health, wealth, long life, happiness and prosperity, and may they long continue to hold the proud and self-won position which they hold in their profession and the position of honour and affection which they hold in our hearts."

All the guests stood up, glass in hand, and turning towards the three seated ladies, sang in unison, with Mr. Browne as leader:

> *For they are jolly gay fellows,*
> *For they are jolly gay fellows,*
> *For they are jolly gay fellows,*
> *Which nobody can deny.*

Aunt Kate was making frank use of her handkerchief and even Aunt Julia seemed moved. Freddy Malins beat time with his pudding-fork and the singers turned towards one another, as if in melodious conference, while they sang with emphasis:

> *Unless he tells a lie,*
> *Unless he tells a lie,*

Then, turning once more towards their hostesses, they sang:

> *For they are jolly gay fellows,*
> *For they are jolly gay fellows,*
> *For they are jolly gay fellows,*
> *Which nobody can deny.*

The acclamation which followed was taken up beyond the door of the supper-room by many of the other guests and renewed time after time, Freddy Malins acting as officer with his fork on high.

The piercing morning air came into the hall where they were standing so that Aunt Kate said:

"Close the door, somebody. Mrs. Malins will get her death of cold."

"Browne is out there, Aunt Kate," said Mary Jane.

"Browne is everywhere," said Aunt Kate, lowering her voice.

Mary Jane laughed at her tone.

"Really," she said archly, "he is very attentive."

"He has been laid on here like the gas," said Aunt Kate in the same tone, "all during the Christmas."

She laughed herself this time good-humouredly and then added quickly:

"But tell him to come in, Mary Jane, and close the door. I hope to goodness he didn't hear me."

At that moment the hall-door was opened and Mr. Browne came in from the doorstep, laughing as if his heart would break. He was dressed in a long green overcoat with mock Astrakhan cuffs and collar and wore on his head an oval fur cap. He pointed down the snow-covered quay from where the sound of shrill prolonged whistling was borne in.

"Teddy will have all the cabs in Dublin out," he said.

Gabriel advanced from the little pantry behind the office, struggling into his overcoat and, looking round the hall, said:

"Gretta not down yet?"

"She's getting on her things, Gabriel," said Aunt Kate.

"Who's playing up there?" asked Gabriel.

"Nobody. They're all gone."

"Oh, no, Aunt Kate," said Mary Jane. "Bartell D'Arcy and Miss O'Callaghan aren't gone yet."

"Someone is fooling at the piano anyhow," said Gabriel.

Mary Jane glanced at Gabriel and Mr. Browne and said with a shiver:

"It makes me feel cold to look at you two gentlemen muffled up like that. I wouldn't like to face your journey home at this hour."

"I'd like nothing better this minute," said Mr. Browne stoutly, "than a rattling fine walk in the country or a fast drive with a good spanking goer between the shafts."

"We used to have a very good horse and trap at home," said Aunt Julia, sadly.

"The never-to-be-forgotten Johnny," said Mary Jane, laughing.

Aunt Kate and Gabriel laughed too.

"Why, what was wonderful about Johnny?" asked Mr. Browne.

"The late lamented Patrick Morkan, our grandfather, that is," explained Gabriel, "commonly known in his later years as the old gentleman, was a glue-boiler."

"Oh, now, Gabriel," said Aunt Kate, laughing, "he had a starch mill."

"Well, glue or starch," said Gabriel, "the old gentleman had a horse by the name of Johnny. And Johnny used to work in the old gentleman's mill, walking round and round in order to drive the mill. That was all very well; but now comes the tragic part about Johnny. One fine day the old gentleman thought he'd like to drive out with the quality to a military review in the park."

"The Lord have mercy on his soul," said Aunt Kate compassionately.

"Amen," said Gabriel. "So the old gentleman, as I said, harnessed Johnny and put on his very best tall hat and his very best stock collar and drove out in grand style from his ancestral mansion somewhere near Back Lane, I think."

Every one laughed, even Mrs. Malins, at Gabriel's manner, and Aunt Kate said:

"Oh, now, Gabriel, he didn't live in Back Lane, really. Only the mill was there."

"Out from the mansion of his forefathers," continued Gabriel, "he drove with Johnny. And everything went on beautifully until Johnny came in sight of King Billy's statue: and whether he fell in love with the horse King Billy sits on or whether he thought he was back again in the mill, anyhow he began to walk round the statue."

Gabriel paced in a circle round the hall in his goloshes amid the laughter of the others.

"Round and round he went," said Gabriel, "and the old gentleman, who was a very pompous old gentleman, was highly indignant. 'Go on, sir! What do you mean, sir? Johnny! Johnny! Most extraordinary conduct! Can't understand the horse!'"

The peals of laughter which followed Gabriel's imitation of the incident was interrupted by a resounding knock at the hall door. Mary Jane ran to open it and let in Freddy Malins. Freddy Malins, with his hat well back on his head and his shoulders humped with cold, was puffing and steaming after his exertions.

"I could only get one cab," he said.

"Oh, we'll find another along the quay," said Gabriel.

"Yes," said Aunt Kate. "Better not keep Mrs. Malins standing in the draught."

Mrs. Malins was helped down the front steps by her son and Mr. Browne and, after many manœuvres, hoisted into the cab. Freddy Malins clambered in after her and spent a long time settling her on the seat, Mr. Browne helping him with advice. At last she was settled comfortably and Freddy Malins invited Mr. Browne into the cab. There was a good deal of confused talk, and then Mr. Browne got into the cab. The cabman settled his rug over his knees, and bent down for the address. The confusion grew greater and the cabman was directed differently by Freddy Malins and Mr. Browne, each of whom had his head out through a window of the cab. The difficulty was to know where to drop Mr. Browne along the route, and Aunt Kate, Aunt Julia and Mary Jane helped the discussion from the doorstep with cross-directions and contradictions and abundance of laughter. As for Freddy Malins he was speechless with laughter. He popped his head in and out of the window every moment to the great danger of his hat, and told his mother how the discussion was progressing, till at last Mr. Browne shouted to the bewildered cabman above the din of everybody's laughter:

"Do you know Trinity College?"

"Yes, sir," said the cabman.

"Well, drive bang up against Trinity College gates," said Mr. Browne, "and then we'll tell you where to go. You understand now?"

"Yes, sir," said the cabman.

"Make like a bird for Trinity College."

"Right, sir," said the cabman.

The horse was whipped up and the cab rattled off along the quay amid a chorus of laughter and adieux.

Gabriel had not gone to the door with the others. He was in a dark part of the hall gazing up the staircase. A woman was standing near the top of the first flight, in the shadow also. He could not see her face but he could see the terra-cotta and salmon-pink panels of her skirt which the shadow made appear black and white. It was his wife. She was leaning on the banisters, listening to something. Gabriel was surprised at her stillness and strained his ear to listen also. But he could hear little save the noise of laughter and dispute on the front steps, a few chords struck on the piano and a few notes of a man's voice singing.

He stood still in the gloom of the hall, trying to catch the air that the voice was singing and gazing up at his wife. There was grace and mystery in her attitude as if she were a symbol of something. He asked himself what is a woman standing on the stairs in the shadow, listening to distant music, a symbol of. If he were a painter he would paint her in that attitude. Her blue felt hat would show off the bronze of her hair against the darkness and the dark panels of her skirt would show off the light ones. "Distant Music" he would call the picture if he were a painter.

The hall-door was closed, and Aunt Kate, Aunt Julia and Mary Jane came down the hall, still laughing.

"Well, isn't Freddy terrible?" said Mary Jane. "He's really terrible."

Gabriel said nothing, but pointed up the stairs towards where his wife was standing. Now that the hall-door was closed the voice and the piano could be heard more clearly. Gabriel held up his hand for them to be silent. The song seemed to be in the old Irish tonality and the singer seemed uncertain both of his words and of his voice. The voice, made plaintive by distance and by the singer's hoarseness, faintly illuminated the cadence of the air with words expressing grief:

> *O, the rain falls on my heavy locks*
> *And the dew wets my skin,*
> *My babe lies cold . . .*

"Oh," exclaimed Mary Jane. "It's Bartell D'Arcy singing, and he wouldn't sing all the night. Oh, I'll get him to sing a song before he goes."

"Oh, do, Mary Jane," said Aunt Kate.

Mary Jane brushed past the others and ran to the staircase, but before she reached it the singing stopped and the piano was closed abruptly.

"Oh, what a pity!" she cried. "Is he coming down, Gretta?"

Gabriel heard his wife answer yes and saw her come down towards them. A few steps behind her were Mr. Bartell D'Arcy and Miss O'Callaghan.

"Oh, Mr. D'Arcy," cried Mary Jane, "it's downright mean of you to break off like that when we were all in raptures listening to you."

"I have been at him all the evening," said Miss O'Callaghan, "and Mrs. Conroy, too, and he told us he had a dreadful cold and couldn't sing."

"Oh, Mr. D'Arcy," said Aunt Kate, "now that was a great fib to tell."

"Can't you see that I'm as hoarse as a crow?" said Mr. D'Arcy roughly.

He went into the pantry hastily and put on his overcoat. The others, taken back by his rude speech, could find nothing to say. Aunt Kate wrinkled her brows and made signs to the others to drop the subject. Mr. D'Arcy stood swathing his neck carefully and frowning.

"It's the weather," said Aunt Julia, after a pause.

"Yes, everybody has colds," said Aunt Kate readily, "everybody."

"They say," said Mary Jane, "we haven't had snow like it for thirty years, and I read this morning in the newspapers that the snow is general all over Ireland."

"I love the look of snow," said Aunt Julia sadly.

"So do I," said Miss O'Callaghan. "I think Christmas is never really Christmas unless we have the snow on the ground."

"But poor Mr. D'Arcy doesn't like the snow," said Aunt Kate, smiling.

Mr. D'Arcy came from the pantry, fully swathed and buttoned, and in a repentant tone told them the history of his cold. Everyone gave him advice and said it was a great pity and urged him to be very careful of his throat in the night air. Gabriel watched his wife, who did not join in the conversation. She was standing right under the dusty fanlight and the flame of the gas lit up the rich bronze of her hair, which he had seen her drying at the fire a few days before. She was in the same attitude and seemed unaware of the talk about her. At last she turned towards them and Gabriel saw that there was colour on her cheeks and that her eyes were shining. A sudden tide of joy went leaping out of his heart.

"Mr. D'Arcy," she said, "what is the name of that song you were singing?"

"It's called 'The Lass of Aughrim'," said Mr. D'Arcy, "but I couldn't remember it properly. Why? Do you know it?"

"'The Lass of Aughrim,'" she repeated. "I couldn't think of the name."

"It's a very nice air," said Mary Jane. "I'm sorry you were not in voice to-night."

"Now, Mary Jane," said Aunt Kate, "don't annoy Mr. D'Arcy. I won't have him annoyed."

Seeing that all were ready to start she shepherded them to the door, where good night was said:

"Well, good night, Aunt Kate, and thanks for the pleasant evening."

"Good night, Gabriel. Good night, Gretta!"

"Good night, Aunt Kate, and thanks ever so much. Good night, Aunt Julia."

"Oh, good night, Gretta, I didn't see you."

"Good night, Mr. D'Arcy. Good night, Miss O'Callaghan."

"Good night, Miss Morkan."

"Good night, again."

"Good night, all. Safe home."

"Good night. Good night."

The morning was still dark. A dull, yellow light brooded over the houses and the river; and the sky seemed to be descending. It was slushy underfoot, and only streaks and patches of snow lay on the roofs, on the parapets of the quay and on the area railings. The lamps were still burning redly in the murky air, and, across the river, the palace of the Four Courts stood out menacingly against the heavy sky.

She was walking on before him with Mr. Bartell D'Arcy, her shoes in a brown parcel tucked under one arm and her hands holding her skirt up from the slush. She had no longer any grace of attitude, but Gabriel's eyes were still bright with happiness. The blood went bounding along his veins and the thoughts went rioting through his brain, proud, joyful, tender, valorous.

She was walking on before him so lightly and so erect that he longed to run after her noiselessly, catch her by the shoulders and say something foolish and affectionate into her ear. She seemed to him so frail that he longed to defend her against something and then to be alone with her. Moments of their secret life together burst like stars upon his memory. A heliotrope envelope was lying beside his breakfast cup and he was caressing it with his hand. Birds were twittering in the ivy and the sunny web of the curtain was shimmering along the floor: he could not eat for happiness. They were standing on the crowded platform and he was placing a ticket inside the warm palm of her glove. He was standing with her in the cold, looking in through a grated window at a man making bottles in a roaring furnace. It was very cold. Her face, fragrant in the cold air, was quite close to his, and suddenly he called out to the man at the furnace:

"Is the fire hot, sir?"

But the man could not hear with the noise of the furnace. It was just as well. He might have answered rudely.

A wave of yet more tender joy escaped from his heart and went coursing in warm flood along his arteries. Like the tender fire of stars moments of their life together, that no one knew of or would ever know of, broke upon and illumined his memory. He longed to recall to her those moments, to make her forget the years of their dull existence together and remember only their moments of ecstasy. For the years, he felt, had not quenched his soul or hers. Their children, his writing, her household cares had not quenched all their souls' tender fire. In one letter that he had written to her then he had said: "Why is it that words like these seem to me so dull and cold? Is it because there is no word tender enough to be your name?"

Like distant music these words that he had written years before were borne towards him from the past. He longed to be alone with her. When the others had gone away, when he and she were in the room in the hotel, then they would be alone together. He would call her softly:

"Gretta!"

Perhaps she would not hear at once: she would be undressing. Then something in his voice would strike her. She would turn and look at him. . . .

At the corner of Winetavern Street they met a cab. He was glad of its rattling noise as it saved him from conversation. She was looking out of the window and seemed tired. The others spoke only a few words, pointing out some building or street. The horse galloped along wearily under the murky morning sky, dragging his old rattling box after his heels, and Gabriel was again in a cab with her, galloping to catch the boat, galloping to their honeymoon.

As the cab drove across O'Connell Bridge Miss O'Callaghan said:

"They say you never cross O'Connell Bridge without seeing a white horse."

"I see a white man this time," said Gabriel.

"Where?" asked Mr. Bartell D'Arcy.

Gabriel pointed to the statue, on which lay patches of snow. Then he nodded familiarly to it and waved his hand.

"Good night, Dan," he said gaily.

When the cab drew up before the hotel, Gabriel jumped out and, in spite of Mr. Bartell D'Arcy's protest, paid the driver. He gave the man a shilling over his fare. The man saluted and said:

"A prosperous New Year to you, sir."

"The same to you," said Gabriel cordially.

She leaned for a moment on his arm in getting out of the cab and while standing at the kerbstone, bidding the others good night. She leaned lightly on his arm, as lightly as when she had danced with him a few hours before. He had felt proud and happy then, happy that she was his, proud of her grace and wifely carriage. But now, after the kindling again of so many memories, the first touch of her body, musical and strange and perfumed, sent through him a keen pang of lust. Under cover of her silence he pressed her arm closely to his side, and, as they stood at the hotel door, he felt that they had escaped from their lives and duties, escaped from home and friends and run away together with wild and radiant hearts to a new adventure.

An old man was dozing in a great hooded chair in the hall. He lit a candle in the office and went before them to the stairs. They followed him in silence, their feet falling in soft thuds on the thickly carpeted stairs. She mounted the stairs behind the porter, her head bowed in the ascent, her frail shoulders curved as with a burden, her skirt girt tightly about her. He could have flung his arms about her hips and held her still, for his arms were trembling with desire to seize her and only the stress of his nails against the palms of his hands held the wild impulse of his body in check. The porter halted on the stairs to settle his guttering candle. They halted, too, on the steps below him. In the silence Gabriel could hear the falling of the molten wax into the tray and the thumping of his own heart against his ribs.

The porter led them along a corridor and opened a door. Then he set his unstable candle down on a toilet-table and asked at what hour they were to be called in the morning.

"Eight," said Gabriel.

The porter pointed to the switch of the electric-light and began a muttered apology, but Gabriel cut him short.

"We don't want any light. We have light enough from the street. And I say," he added, pointing to the candle, "you might remove that handsome article, like a good man."

The porter took up his candle again, but slowly, for he was surprised by such a novel idea. Then he mumbled good night and went out. Gabriel shot the lock to.

A ghastly light from the street lamp lay in a long shaft from one window to the door. Gabriel threw his overcoat and hat on a couch and crossed the room towards the window. He looked down into the street in order that his emotion might calm a little. Then he turned and leaned against a chest of drawers with his back to the light. She had taken off her hat and cloak and was standing before a large swinging mirror, unhooking her waist. Gabriel paused for a few moments, watching her, and then said:

"Gretta!"

She turned away from the mirror slowly and walked along the shaft of light towards him. Her face looked so serious and weary that the words would not pass Gabriel's lips. No, it was not the moment yet.

"You looked tired." he said.

"I am a little," she answered.

"You don't feel ill or weak?"

"No, tired: that's all."

She went on to the window and stood there, looking out. Gabriel waited again and then, fearing that diffidence was about to conquer him, he said abruptly:

"By the way, Gretta!"

"What is it?"

"You know that poor fellow Malins?" he said quickly.

"Yes. What about him?"

"Well, poor fellow, he's a decent sort of chap, after all," continued Gabriel in a false voice. "He gave me back that sovereign I lent him, and I didn't expect it, really. It's a pity he wouldn't keep away from that Browne, because he's not a bad fellow, really."

He was trembling now with annoyance. Why did she seem so abstracted? He did not know how he could begin. Was she annoyed, too, about something? If she would only turn to him or come to him of her own accord! To take her as she was would be brutal. No, he must see some ardour in her eyes first. He longed to be master of her strange mood.

"When did you lend him the pound?" she asked, after a pause.

Gabriel strove to restrain himself from breaking out into brutal language about the sottish Malins and his pound. He longed to cry to her from his soul, to crush her body against his, to overmaster her. But he said:

"Oh, at Christmas, when he opened that little Christmas-card shop, in Henry Street."

He was in such a fever of rage and desire that he did not hear her come from the window. She stood before him for an instant, looking at him strangely. Then, suddenly raising herself on tiptoe and resting her hands lightly on his shoulders, she kissed him.

"You are a very generous person, Gabriel," she said.

Gabriel, trembling with delight at her sudden kiss and at the quaintness of her phrase, put his hands on her hair and began smoothing it

back, scarcely touching it with his fingers. The washing had made it
fine and brilliant. His heart was brimming over with happiness. Just
when he was wishing for it she had come to him of her own accord.
Perhaps her thoughts had been running with his. Perhaps she had felt
the impetuous desire that was in him, and then, the yielding mood had
come upon her. Now that she had fallen to him so easily, he wondered
why he had been so diffident.

He stood, holding her head between his hands. Then, slipping one
arm swiftly about her body and drawing her towards him, he said softly:
"Gretta, dear, what are you thinking about?"

She did not answer nor yield wholly to his arm. He said again, softly:
"Tell me what it is, Gretta. I think I know what is the matter. Do I
know?"

She did not answer at once. Then she said in an outburst of tears:
"Oh, I am thinking about that song, 'The Lass of Aughrim'."

She broke loose from him and ran to the bed and, throwing her arms
across the bed-rail, hid her face. Gabriel stood stock-still for a moment
in astonishment and then followed her. As he passed in the way of the
cheval-glass he caught sight of himself in full length, his broad, well-
filled shirt-front, the face whose expression always puzzled him when
he saw it in a mirror, and his glimmering gilt-rimmed eye-glasses. He
halted a few paces from her and said:

"What about the song? Why does that make you cry?"

She raised her head from her arms and dried her eyes with the back
of her hand like a child. A kinder note than he had intended went into
his voice.

"Why, Gretta?" he asked.

"I am thinking about a person long ago who used to sing that song."

"And who was the person long ago?" asked Gabriel, smiling.

"It was a person I used to know in Galway when I was living with
my grandmother," she said.

The smile passed away from Gabriel's face. A dull anger began to
gather again at the back of his mind and the dull fires of his lust began
to glow angrily in his veins.

"Someone you were in love with?" he asked ironically.

"It was a young boy I used to know," she answered, "named Michael
Furey. He used to sing that song, 'The Lass of Aughrim.' He was very
delicate."

Gabriel was silent. He did not wish her to think that he was interested in this delicate boy.

"I can see him so plainly," she said, after a moment. "Such eyes as he
had: big, dark eyes! And such an expression in them—an expression!"

"Oh, then, you are in love with him?" said Gabriel.

husband, had played in her life. He watched her while she slept, as though he and she had never lived together as man and wife. His curious eyes rested long upon her face and on her hair: and, as he thought of what she must have been then, in that time of her first girlish beauty, a strange, friendly pity for her entered his soul. He did not like to say even to himself that her face was no longer beautiful, but he knew that it was no longer the face for which Michael Furey had braved death.

Perhaps she had not told him all the story. His eyes moved to the chair over which she had thrown some of her clothes. A petticoat string dangled to the floor. One boot stood upright, its limp upper fallen down: the fellow of it lay upon its side. He wondered at his riot of emotions of an hour before. From what had it proceeded? From his aunt's supper, from his own foolish speech, from the wine and dancing, the merrymaking when saying good night in the hall, the pleasure of the walk along the river in the snow. Poor Aunt Julia! She, too, would soon be a shade with the shade of Patrick Morkan and his horse. He had caught that haggard look upon her face for a moment when she was singing "Arrayed for the Bride." Soon, perhaps, he would be sitting in that same drawing-room, dressed in black, his silk hat on his knees. The blinds would be drawn down and Aunt Kate would be sitting beside him, crying and blowing her nose and telling him how Julia had died. He would cast about in his mind for some words that might console her, and would find only lame and useless ones. Yes, yes: that would happen very soon.

The air of the room chilled his shoulders. He stretched himself cautiously along under the sheets and lay down beside his wife. One by one, they were all becoming shades. Better pass boldly into that other world, in the full glory of some passion, than fade and wither dismally with age. He thought of how she who lay beside him had locked in her heart for so many years that image of her lover's eyes when he had told her that he did not wish to live.

Generous tears filled Gabriel's eyes. He had never felt like that himself towards any woman, but he knew that such a feeling must be love. The tears gathered more thickly in his eyes and in the partial darkness he imagined he saw the form of a young man standing under a dripping tree. Other forms were near. His soul had approached that region where dwell the vast hosts of the dead. He was conscious of, but could not apprehend, their wayward and flickering existence. His own identity was fading out into a grey impalpable world: the solid world itself, which these dead had one time reared and lived in, was dissolving and dwindling.

A few light taps upon the pane made him turn to the window. It had begun to snow again. He watched sleepily the flakes, silver and dark, falling obliquely against the lamp-light. The time had come for him to set out on his journey westward. Yes, the newspapers were right: snow was general all over Ireland. It was falling on every part of the dark central plain, on the treeless hills, falling softly upon the Bog of Allen, and farther westward, softly falling into the dark mutinous Shannon waves. It was falling, too, upon every part of the lonely churchyard on the hill where Michael Furey lay buried. It lay thickly drifted on the crooked crosses and headstones, on the spears of the little gate, on the barren thorns. His soul swooned slowly as he heard the snow falling faintly through the universe and faintly falling, like the descent of their last end, upon all the living and the dead.

61

Purple and Fine Linen

BY MAY EDGINTON

THE woman with the black hair that had a kind of blue bloom upon it like the bloom on grapes, watched every one who went by. She watched intently. She was walking up one side of the Haymarket and down the other, and then along Piccadilly, and then cutting down into Pall Mall and Clubland, most of the dull, dark afternoon. Her clothes, which had probably been good, were in hopeless ruins, and over the bloomy black hair was pulled a weary black hat. But her eyes were not weary. They were alive and burning, though her face was tired and dim and vague, and her lips were more blue than red. She had a naturally lithe and beautiful figure at which, had her clothes not been such wrecks, every passing man would have looked, yet she dragged her feet. Her feet were heavy like the feet of a very tired person.

She was begging.

She was begging cautiously, surreptitiously, with an eye sharply open for the police. For she was begging in a manner contrary to the manner ordained by law. She held no tray of trumpery, or box of matches, or dying flowers in her hands; she could not pass as a vendor of goods so pitiful that the charitable would not take them from her in exchange for their coppers.

She was just begging.

She begged mostly of men, especially when she sauntered in the heart of rich Clubland. It was a cold day and the men who went by looked mostly so warm and well fed. Sometimes some one paused and gave her something.

She observed them carefully, telling them different stories.

"Please help me buy a little food for my children . . . Please, sir, I am just out of hospital . . . Please, sir, excuse me, sir, I have lost my job and I have eaten nothing to-day . . . Pardon me, sir, my husband is coming out of prison to-morrow, and I want to buy a little coal and food for our room . . . I am down and out, sir, and my mother is dying down in the country; the fare is ten shillings and eightpence, and I want to raise it before the seven o'clock train leaves Waterloo . . . Thank you very, very much, sir. . . ."

Opposite two big clubs, to the doors of which cars and taxicabs drove incessantly, she paused and looked across the street. She crossed the street, braving the club commissionaires, very watchful for the likes of her, and accosted a fat member who was waddling in, warmly coated. Another member she followed a few steps down the street as he emerged from the famous portal; and she pleaded with him in a hurried undertone. He was good-humoured and gave her a shilling.

On the steps of the same famous club, a man stood observing the famous street. He was fairly tall and very broad, and there was no doubt about his prosperity. He had been standing there for quite a minute observing London, observing the traffic, the cars, the cabs, the pedestrians, the police, and the woman who begged.

He saw her raven hair and white face and drab condition, and lithe figure and manner of begging, just as he saw and noted any other incidents of the streets of the great city. For he was a visitor to London, and a temporary member of the ancient and honourable club on whose steps he stood on that dull, dark afternoon.

"No, I don't want a taxi," he answered the commissionaire.

He glanced after the woman who begged, until she turned back, retracing her steps slowly. She looked about her stealthily, wistfully, desperately, seeking the next probable almsgiver; and her eyes lighted on him, standing there.

She said to herself: "A Colonial, most likely; and rich."

For she was used to summing up men at a glance, and taking her chances.

The man came down the steps, walking with the free swing of the athlete and open-air man, his overcoat slung over his arm, and began to walk leisurely towards the Carlton.

The woman quickened her steps and came alongside.

She spoke.

"Please, sir, help me with a trifle . . . so near Christmas."

"Go away!" he said in a hard voice, "don't come troubling me."

As he answered her, it happened that he glanced round; and he caught the queerest look in her eyes as they flashed at him under the black hat. Almost he put his hand in his pocket to find a coin to reward her for that flash of the eyes. For they were beautiful eyes. In fact, his hand hovered in the edge of his pocket for an appreciable second, but he withdrew it again.

He was a Colonial; and rich. She had spotted him. All beggars spotted rich Colonials. Every one with a hard-luck story, every confidence trick man, made a bee line for his sort. He was used to it. He was tired of it. He had nothing for her. He was not easy money.

Big and burly, masterfully he went on. He arrived on the fringe of a crowd gathered about the victim of a street accident. Policemen were hurrying to the spot to disperse the crowd. He was in no haste. He paused interestedly to observe the demeanour of all these strangers, and the methods of the police—to draw comparisons between the old world and the new. Pausing there on the edge of the inquisitive crowd he lighted a cigarette.

People crowded up against him, behind and before, jostling him.

"Move on!" the police were ordering.

He began to elbow his way through, a rough business, for traffic piled up along the street, and the ghoulish sightseers, profiting by the difficulties of the police, still pushed forward. But he made his way masterfully. He gained the farther edge of the swaying crowd, and freed a hand to get at the left side of his coat.

His leather note-case no longer bulged the inside breast pocket.

"God! What a darn fool!" he said aloud. "Now," he thought, "do I go to the nearest police station or to this Scotland Yard place they admire so?"

Then, hesitating a second, he saw, walking quietly and swiftly along the pavement before him, free from the crowd as he was, the woman who had begged.

She walked so swiftly.

As swiftly, he went after her. She slipped between the bonnets of cars and cabs and omnibuses across the street, and he dived through them in pursuit. She turned to the left and was in the Haymarket, signalling to a crawling taxicab. Just as he rounded the corner of the Carlton Restaurant, he saw her jump in.

He signalled a second cab from the rank, and leapt into it.

"Follow that taxi there, see! That one! Hang on to it, and don't lose sight, or——"

They were off. His driver had an intelligent face. The man inside the cab thought: "He'll do it. And who knows? I may be going to see something really worth seeing this afternoon. I may be going into some den of crime—get among some crooks who'll show me more of London than I've seen already. I'd like to see the underworld of this old city. And I'll bet I'll get my money back at the end, too."

He loved money, because he had sweated to make it. He had toiled and fought and suffered to make it. "Yes," he thought, as the taxicab sped up Regent Street, and his big mouth took a grimmer line, "I'll get it back all right from that slut. Near Christmas, eh? Well, I reckon I know where she'll spend the festive day."

He had the number of his notes duly checked. He reverenced money and guarded it, even while he spent it freely.

"Where are we going?"

The cab slowed, drew to the kerb, and stopped. He saw the blazing, lighted windows of a fashionable women's shop. He leaned out of the window, and saw another cab that had drawn up immediately before them; and as he looked, he saw the lithe figure of a woman in sorry clothes alight from it. She hurried into the shop.

Her taxicab drew off slowly to the adjacent rank and waited, flag still down. She was keeping it. Her driver alighted and stood beside his cab, watchful gaze fixed upon the shop door.

"Doesn't trust her not to bilk him," said the man in the second cab sardonically to himself. "And if he knew what I knew, he'd know himself right." Aloud he asked his driver, "You saw that? Wait as near him as you can. I'm waiting at this door."

For a full half hour or more he stood near the lighted windows, slightly drawn aside from them, waiting. He had nothing else to do, after all, in the idle hours that stretched between him and a good dinner somewhere, save hunt down his quarry. And he was a stolid man, patient in pursuit of what he wanted. He had never yet tired in hunting down either man or woman who injured him.

He waited. He lighted a cigar from his handsome case. "It's a foul day," he said to himself, looking at the fog that seemed to fall particle by particle until it promised, presently, to envelope London.

There emerged among other women, a woman. Any man's eyes would have flown to her. She wore a slim outfit of black satin, fur edged. Her shoes were of black satin, with sparkling straps; her stockings were of sheerest silk the colour of flesh. First of all, it was only by her old hat pulled low over her black hair that he recognised her.

She *was* the woman.

She had a natural flush like geranium petals in her white cheeks, and her murky eyes shone like the street lamps shone out on the fog.

"My God!" said the watcher, with a grim, twisted smile. But he did not lay a hand on her arm and threaten her with the nearest policeman; he followed her quite quietly across to the taxicab rank where their two vehicles waited.

She entered hers first, not observing him, and gave her instructions.

"I bet I'll see some fun before I've finished to-night," he said to himself, as his cab moved away, following hers. "Where next?"

He looked at his wrist-watch. Five o'clock. . . .

Her cab curved down Conduit Street, entered Bond Street, and drew up before a jewellers! She went in:

She came out again.

The chase went on, to a beauty parlour higher up. Here she paid off her taxicab, before she went in. And after she had gone in he sat and thought a moment, and then paid off his. He was not altogether ignorant of the ways of women in beauty parlours. This would take time, possibly. And he went into the ground floor department of the shop, and looked around, and could not see her. But he was in time to see the gilded lift vanishing upward, and the glimpse of black satin shoe strapped with sparkling fire.

"Sir?" murmured an engaging attendant.

He looked around.

He saw in the background a cushioned seat or two beyond all the perfumes and creams and powders and the pretty women buying them. "Thanks," he replied urbanely, "I am waiting for a lady who has just gone upstairs."

So he sat down, and no one troubled him more.

The establishment would close at six; that was certain. It was almost equally certain that she would not emerge before six. She was bent upon beautifying herself to the utmost in the time that was hers. And she had —or rather, she had before the black satin and jewellers' business—some two hundred pounds of his in her possession. A wholly masculine curiosity entertained him for a while, keeping him wondering what she would look like when she came down again in the gilded lift. He was not softening; oh, no, his mood towards her remained entirely and sardonically hard. He knew her kind. He would deliver her up to justice just so soon as she came out this time, recover the balance of his cash, return the jewels—if any—to the jewellers—and——

But, no. He might let her keep that black satin outfit. Or he might not. It would rather depend on what the hussy looked like when the gilded lift disgorged her.

Two hundred pounds was nothing to him; only, after all, property was property. Money was money; sacred.

He thought about her.

"Why didn't she buy a hat too?" he thought. "A whole-hogger like her—why not the hat too?"

And he thought: "I wonder whom she hoped she was going to mash to-night?"

The full hour, as he had expected, he sat in that dreamy, odorous atmosphere, and then the lift bell, which had sounded many times for many clients, tinkled again. The lift shot upward and came down.

She stepped out.

Now he saw why she hadn't bought a hat, and why she had left the hat she had somewhere upstairs, behind her. She was in evening dress. The long, satin coat, thickly fur edged, was slightly open, and he caught the gleam of a diamond earring between the upstanding collar and her neck. Her raven hair bloomed blue-black. The grey-white of her tired face was now the cream-white of skilfully laid cosmetics. The hectic geranium flush had merged into the faintest painting of rouge. Her lips were no longer bluish, but richly red. And while they had massaged her face and dressed her hair, evidently a manicurist had been at work. The hand that held her slim coat round her slim figure had received its toilet too. She was a beautiful woman.

For a moment he sat forward, hands on his knees, feet planted square, staring. It seemed a pity; what a pity! A woman like that! But he was not soft-hearted, and he jumped up and followed her over the threshold.

"Cab, sir?" said the commissionaire of the beauty shop, seeing him in such close attendance.

He nodded; the commissionaire whistled; a taxicab came up. And then, with a sardonic smile, as she stood slightly in front of him, a woman in a dream, waiting her turn to be served, he took her arm very firmly in his hand.

She started and shuddered so violently that he felt her heart beating as his hand pressed between her arm and her side.

She turned and saw him, the man who had stood on the steps of the rich club awhile before; from whom she had begged. If she had screamed, bluffed, argued, protested, complained, or pleaded, it would have seemed natural to him. But, as if life had taken from her the faculty of surprise, she just stood there dumb, resigned, looking at him.

"Spent it all?" he smiled.

There was a rasp to his voice, a bitter hardness to his smile. He was not sorry for the thief, though, as he looked her up and down, he knew his sheer masculinity would allow her to keep the black satin, though she should hand back the change from his treasury notes; and the jewels. But, for her beauty, she should keep the black satin frock and coat that fitted her so sleekly. They were like a mould into which the figure of a woman, in perfect lines, had been poured.

She gave a long sigh and for a moment faltered against his hand as if all strength went out of her. He looked at her sharply. Her face, overlaid with that cream-white and rose tinting, might have showed the grey of starvation . . . But his look remained grim. He was not sorry for her, nor for any one. He had fought the world himself, and come within sight, a few times, of the ultimate wall against which sank the beaten and the weary; but he had not fallen exhausted under the shadow of that wall. If she did so, it was her affair. All must fight; men; and women too.

He was not soft.

"Well?" he asked.

The taxicab waited, with the commissionaire holding open the door.

"Give me a little time," she gasped.

"Get in," he said.

He seemed to be helping her in, with that hard hand on her arm. He got in closely after her. The commissionaire paused for orders at the open door.

The rich man looked at the beggar woman, sidelong.

"I'll tell him the nearest police station!" he whispered, "have you anything to say against that?"

She looked full in his eyes, "God!" he said to himself, "she's desperate." She answered him in a swift whisper:

"Yes. I have. Give me a little time."

It might be interesting; amusing even. One lived and could always learn. Scowling slightly he ordered the commissionaire, "Oh, tell him to drive through the park, and then we'll see."

He felt in his pocket, and handed the commissionaire a shilling. With his other hand he retained his grip of the woman's arm. She was a beautiful woman. It might have been affection that made him hold her so.

The taxicab started. They drove through the evening streets towards Park Lane.

"Well," he said, "I've watched you. I've followed you for more than an hour and a half since you stole my note case in that crowd. How did you do it? Come along! Out with it! I'd like to know."

She was looking intently into his face.

"It would amuse you?"

"It would amuse me."

She started: "When you refused me, I followed you——"

"Knowing I was a stranger and prosperous——"

"Yes; knowing that. I'd put you down as South African, or—or perhaps Australian——"

"I'm Australian."

"I was right then," she said in a voice extraordinarily even, the voice of one who does not so much think of what she is saying, as talk to gain time. "Well, I followed you, hoping for some sort of development; hoping that I'd get something out of you. Then—that heaven-sent accident, and the crowd. I pushed in close to you. I was at your shoulder the whole time, but you never saw me. Once in the crowd, you patted your left inside breast pocket. You weren't wearing your overcoat. You were pushing about. You're a big man—rather fat. Your coat bulged a little as you struggled. You put your arm up and held your hat for quite half a minute. It was foggy. I put my arm under yours, across your chest; I —I had the pocket book out in a moment. It was wonderful!"

"But you've done it so often that the thrill's surely gone."

"It was the first time."

He burst out laughing, coarsely.

She sat there taut, listening to the tune of his laughter, glad that he laughed. The taxicab entered the park at the Hyde Park Corner gates. Now solitude and dusk encompassed them.

"I'll tell him now, the nearest police station."

Then suddenly that tense withheld woman woke up. She was across his breast, in his arms, her mouth close to his, pleading.

"No! No! Mercy! Give me three hours! Three hours! And then, what you like. I beg you, just as one human creature to another, for three hours!"

He put her back forcibly into her corner. There was some scent they had sprayed on her hair. . . .

He held her back in her corner.

"I won't let you off."

"No! No! Anything you like—after three hours. Please——"

She sobbed.

"You'll spoil that fine make-up on your face."

She stopped.

"If I gave you three hours I'd want to keep you in sight all the time. For I won't let you go. And that'd spoil your game, eh?"

"You can keep me in sight all the time."

"Eh?"

"I will be your prisoner. But please, three hours. . . ."

"You want till nine o'clock."

"Nine-thirty, please. Please!"

"I'd a dull evening before me," he remarked thoughtfully. "Very well. I'll give you three hours and not let you out of my sight. What do you want to do with your last minutes, eh?"

"At nine o'clock I want to go to a house in Chesham Crescent and see —some one. That's all. I must—I must see some one at nine o'clock at Chesham Crescent. I'm so near—so near now! After all these years! Fate couldn't be so cruel as to prevent me!"

"Nine o'clock. At nine o'clock you have to be in Chesham Crescent. Very well, if I take you there. And listen! You'll dine with me first. This is a bully fine evening, giving dinner to a thief who's just pinched my wallet with two hundred pounds. It may make me laugh."

"I hope it does—if you need a laugh."

He sat forward looking at her closely.

"When did you last laugh, eh?"

"Oh," she said, "I laugh often. I can't help it. Life is so funny."

"You're a funny woman," he said slowly, suspiciously. She was clever, the creature! With her control of voice, her moods, her subtleties, her pathos, her bravado—she was clever!

"I must beware of you," he said surlily.

"You need not, I am in your power completely."

Then for a teeming minute they sat in silence, while the taxicab sped on, approaching the Bayswater side of the great park.

"If I'm to take you out to dinner," he said suddenly, with a hint of mockery in his tone, "I must change my clothes. I don't always. I'm a rough man. But since you're got up regardless," his sidelong look in the half dark added, 'at my expense'—"why, I must do you credit." And taking her hand in a firm grip, as if to assure himself that she should not escape while his head was turned, he leaned from the window.

"Fourteen Cheylsmore Mansions," he called to the taximan.

"Where's that?" she asked apprehensively, when his head came in again.

"My flat. The place I've taken temporarily while I'm in London. You can wait there while I change."

She did not reply, but sat in total silence, submissive, shrinking in repugnance; but resigned. He saw what she thought. It was a natural thought. But he did not undeceive her. She had put herself into this position, hadn't she? She deserved her loathing anticipation.

"Hateful fellow, aren't I?" he asked pleasantly.

"I don't know," she said, with a sigh.

"I shan't let you off anything. You've asked for it."

"Very well," she said, "but for God's sake—the three hours!"

"That's a bargain," he answered. "You have your three hours." The taxicab drew up.

It was the first time the man from Australia had ushered a woman of such appearance into that flat. When he opened the door with his latchkey, her demeanour made him stand aside quickly, and she walked in before him with a natural air of expecting surface courtesies and amenities at least, whatever was to follow. His eyebrows went up as he gazed at her suave back. Her effrontery made him smile. He followed her.

A manservant appeared in the background beyond them.

"Show this lady into the sitting-room, William," said the man from Australia, "and bring her a cocktail while she waits for me. My things ready?"

"All ready, sir."

The manservant opened the door of a warm red room, and the woman walked in. As if a sense of her tiredness were upon her under the expectations that buoyed her up, she sank, wilted into a couch by the fire. She seemed to lose herself by the fire in the warm red room. Instantly she travelled to another land than the land where he had met her. For a moment the man from Australia stood gazing in upon her, puzzled again; and then he went out sturdily, shut the door, and spoke to the servant.

"William. That lady. She's to stay where she is until I'm ready. No hanky-panky. Savvy?"

"Very good, sir."

He went to his warm bath and his change of raiment, listening keenly —though the man William was an astute and reliable servant—for some sound of the front door latch gently clicking. She would try to run, wouldn't she? William would see to it, of course; but still, there was little doubt but that she would make the effort. She was a desperate woman if ever there was one, and she would plan for escape. But though he listened all the while that, rapidly, he bathed and dressed, he did not hear the click of the front-door latch, nor any sound at all in the quiet flat.

She was going to try to play him?

That was another solution, of course. The lonely rich man, the beautiful woman, the hard-luck story, the forgiveness; favours and continued favours. She was no fool, this woman. She too counted upon it all.

Only, he was no fool either.

In a quarter of an hour he was with her again. He opened the sitting-room door quickly and quietly, hovering, observant, before he went in. But she was still lost by the fire, inanimate upon the red couch. The only movement she had made was to take off her coat and lay it aside. He saw the grace of her thin, white throat and arms.

Beside her was an untouched cocktail.

He advanced.

"Don't you like your cocktail?"

She looked up at him. She was at bay, looking him over swiftly, wondering just when the kill would be made. His masculinity could have made him tender, though his worldly sense kept him hard. He picked up the glass and offered it to her.

"Got a little warm, perhaps. My fellow shall make another."

"I daren't drink it; thank you."

"Daren't drink it?"

"I haven't eaten to-day."

She was a liar, of course.

"I should have thought, with two hundred pounds on you, you'd have made a beeline for the nearest ham-and-beef, at least."

"I forgot."

"Forgot?" He ruminated. She was a liar. He smiled. "Well," he said in a tone of raillery, "you must do justice to your dinner. If you won't drink this——"

He tossed it off.

"Come along."

She rose with a languor that made him a trifle dubious. Suppose she really hadn't eaten that day? He had known what it was to go a day without food himself.

Anyhow that would soon be remedied.

He held out her coat.

"I'm glad you bought a good one," he jeered, handling the supple stuff, weighted with fur.

"I wanted good clothes to-night."

"Did you hope to get them by begging coppers?"

"One never knows."

"No," he jeered, "one never knows."

She took no notice of his jeers. She was not of this world at all. In a strange, uncomfortable way he felt that. He lifted the coat up over her shoulders.

There was a mirror facing them in which she could see herself.

"I look very nice," she said, in a dreaming voice. "You have been really very good to me."

He avoided her glance a little sulkily. He saw her idea. Some men might have behaved differently; and then have forgiven her for what she had done—if they could have afforded it, as he could. He turned away.

"You look damn nice," he said. "Come on."

So they went down, side by side, in the lift, and out into the vestibule. This time, when she came into the street again she saw that a limousine waited.

"My man rang up for it while I was dressing," her escort explained. "When one takes a lady to dine——"

His hand at her elbow—lightly touching it, yet ready to grip firm, she knew—she got in. She took the right-hand corner as one accustomed to drive in such cars. The chauffeur spread over them a supple rug of sleek skin, and they were off again.

He darted hard, curious looks at her.

"You look in your right place somehow."

She smiled. "It's many years since I had a car like this."

"Played your cards badly then, with a figure like yours. Where were your wits?"

"I suppose you are right," she said, "I played my cards very badly. I always have. I hate—selling."

"Woman's business, isn't it?" he returned gruffly.

"Very few women think so."

With a hard laugh he said: "I must have struck unlucky a good many times then."

"No doubt you have."

She looked out of her window at the passing throngs. London was alive and blazing. There was a look of peace and a great expectancy in her face, almost as if she didn't think or care about him and what he could do to her. It was strange. She might have been unafraid; and yet that a woman should be unafraid in such conditions was nearly impossible. While she looked out of the window on her side, he remained turned towards her, looking at her.

"My God! You're a cool customer!"

Now she smiled.

"No. I am not cool."

"You don't even ask where I'm taking you."

"It doesn't matter, so that the time passes."

"Doesn't it indeed? Well, madam, we are going to the Ritz. You're a nice-looking woman, and I'm going to show you off. I'm a lonely stranger here, and my female acquaintance so far isn't the kind I boast about."

And they drew up before the vast pillared portico.

She stood a moment just inside the vestibule, looking about her like a woman awaked from a long sleep.

"See many friends?" he asked sardonically at her elbow.

"Not friends," she answered; "not friends now. But I see the faces of people who used to be my friends. There—oh! there—that must be Cicely Dorset! There's her husband! Can that be her baby daughter—that tall thing? Isn't she lovely. Oh! I wonder. . . ."

"Go and recall yourself to their memory," he suggested.

She shrank. "Impossible! They wouldn't . . . I've been on the Continent for more than seventeen years; wandering from place to place——"

"What places?"

"Nice, Cannes, Rome, Paris, Vienna, Budapest . . ."

"You chose the high spots."

"Oh, my God! There's Lady Mars! She's aged—who hasn't? I have. But I'd know her anywhere——"

"You're very clever, madam, at picking out faces from what you remember of the illustrated papers. Come on in to dinner."

She hardly listened to his sneer. In her eyes was a whole garden of memories; on her thin cheek bones burned a red flush.

He repeated, with a hand on her elbow; "Come on in to dinner. Don't go into a cloakroom to leave that coat; I don't trust you out of my sight." He beckoned an attendant, and, pulling off his overcoat, thrust it, with his silk hat, on the man.

"You're a good actress, madam. I'll pay you all the compliments you deserve."

Hardly listening, she walked with him into the immense room. Their table was at the side, near a corner.

The Australian seemed disappointed.

"I'd have liked to show you off in the very middle of the room."

She shrank.

"This is better. Please!"

"We've got to have it, I suppose. The darn place is full."

So they sat down at the little table, in the intimacy of a dinner *à deux;* and she droppped her coat back over her chair, and looked about her, sitting very still.

"Always feed the condemned," he said to her under his breath when he had ordered caviare, bortsch, sole, turkey—"because I expect you'll get beef at Christmas where you're going, and tough at that," he exclaimed pleasantly—*salade à l'Americaine,* omelette *en surpris,* and champagne, and they were awaiting the first course.

It was as if she tore her attention from the sea of tables spread beyond them.

"The condemned?"

"You're going to a police station in—" he glanced at the watch on his wrist—"two hours and a half."

"So I am!" She laughed.

"Lightheaded?" he thought. "Here," he said aloud, "was that true about having eaten nothing to-day? Feel a bit lightheaded, eh?"

"It was true; but I'm not lightheaded, although I well might be."

"At least you're not morbid. Don't meet your troubles till you come to 'em, anyway."

All the same he marvelled. She was cool!

Of course, he knew that the chances were that she still hoped to play him, work on his pity. "Let him get at the champagne," she was think-

ing. She would see that he ordered a second bottle. In the flat she had
refused her cocktail, hadn't she? She was wise!

How daintily she ate her caviare!

His glance travelled over her with supreme contempt and supreme
appreciation.

"Frightened?" he whispered with a smile.

The omelette *en surpris* had just been served to them. Her cheeks had
taken on a beautiful flush under the cleverly slight make-up; her eyes
glistened; she had talked; she was making herself a fine companion;
yet was it possible that she was at ease; careless; reckless of what was
going to happen to her? Her attention, through all her attractive conversation, was not really focused on him; he felt that. And yet it was not
focused on the looming calamity either. Her soul seemed away on
wings in a country of its own. He was mystified and hated it, for he
liked to feel that he understood people in and out. He prided himself
on it. He filled up her glass and his own. She had not tried to tempt him
to excess, but had drunk glass for glass with him. His mystification
grew.

"Frightened?"

"Of what?" She asked, bringing her happy eyes to rest on him.

Yes, her eyes were happy. They had been wretched, anxious, earlier
in the afternoon; but now they were happy.

What did she hope for from him?

"Prison."

"Oh no," she said calmly, almost as if she brushed the word aside.
"What happens to me after my three hours' grace is up does not matter."

"Here," he said carefully. "What *is* all this about three hours' grace?
What do you want to do?"

She glanced at a tiny, square watch on her wrist, carried on a moiré
strap and set round with brilliants; a pleasing toy. That, too, she had
bought with his money. His eyes followed her almost humorously; she
was so graceless in her wrongdoing.

"In half an hour I want to be at Chesham Crescent; Number 10
Chesham Crescent."

"Yes, Chesham Crescent, Mayfair. Now tell me, what for?"

"To visit some one."

"Front door or kitchen entrance?" he inquired, with a twist of the lip.

"Front door. It is my old home. I went there as a bride."

"Where you go, I go."

She sighed. "I suppose it must be so."

"Look," he said, "tell me a story. It'll be all lies, no doubt, but I shan't object so long as you make it a good one. Tell me what you want me to believe you're going to do at 10 Chesham Crescent."

"Something I've waited and longed for, for seventeen years."

"Why, how old are you?"

"Thirty-six."

"That might be true," he commented. "Go on."

She asked timorously: "What do you want to know?"

"Who lives there?"

"My ex-husband."

"Ex-husband?"

"Lord Malvern. He divorced me seventeen years ago."

"Go on. That's a very pretty beginning."

She made a little gesture of resignation. "There is no reason why you shouldn't know what every one knows—and has forgotten—if it will placate you. I'm in your power. I ran away with a man—I was miserable with my husband, or thought I was——"

"You were a mere kid, as they usually say in these cases."

"I was even peculiarly childish. I thought my lover was a god and a Galahad rolled in one."

"You married him?"

"Oh no! Thank God, not that!"

"Then what——"

"I told you, I've been living on the Continent, as best I could, sometimes living softly, sometimes half starving, for years. I hadn't an old friend left; my family repudiated me. Lately I've tried to pull myself together; tried to remember that though the law separates us I still have some one to live for——"

"Who?"

Her eyes gleamed with tears, but her mouth, now red and fuller lipped after food and drink, tried to laugh.

"I've had bad luck; been very ill; lost my looks; was literally stranded in Paris, hardly hoping when the letter came."

"Be explicit."

"Lord Malvern's letter."

"He's written to you? Provision? Reconciliation? Eh?"

The man laughed. He disbelieved every word she said, but mockingly displayed his interest in the progress of her story. She answered gravely: "No. To grant my request. I'd made it every year just before my birthday. I'd written every year and begged and begged him to let me see my little girl for five minutes; just because it is Christmas, I used to say, every year. He never answered once, till this year. And this year he telegraphed as soon as he had my letter. I am to see her for five minutes to-night at 9 o'clock."

"You managed to scrape up your fare across?"

"Just managed. That was yesterday. I got the first train, the first boat, after I had that wire. I begged in the streets all to-day trying to get enough to make me presentable to my daughter."

"Well, madam," he said with a hard smile, "you certainly look presentable."

"Thanks to your forbearance, your patience. I will bless you all my life for these three hours."

He stared at her, all doubting. She was a fine actress.

"I'll see you through to the end," he stated. "I dare say you can explain me somehow to his lordship——"

"Oh, must you——"

"I'll love to see you extricate yourself from the position you've described to me so feelingly."

"You don't believe a word I say."

"That doesn't prevent my appreciation of your story, you've got a brain like a fiction writer."

She was unmoved. She didn't care. "Very well," she said, "come into the house with me if you insist. It doesn't matter. All that matters is that I'm going to see my Meggie for a moment; that she'll see her mother looking as I look now; that there'll be no pity and no shock in my baby's mind; that—that—— Oh! I'm happy!"

"Save your raptures," said the Australian. "They're wasted on me. I shall like to hear you explain yourself to me at 9.30. I'll call your bluff then; and off we'll go to a less splendiferous building than 10 Chesham Crescent."

She smiled at him happily. She was far off.

"You're some actress," he acknowledged, "and I would like to know the card you've got up your sleeve."

He signed to the waiter, who cleared the table swiftly.

"Two black coffees, waiter, and two brandies."

She was still smiling. And as the minutes passed her new beauty grew marvellous and more marvellous. She was lighted from within. When people looked at her they pointed her out to one another and their glances lingered.

The Australian looked at her deeply, surmisingly, consideringly, his amusement gone. "I damn well wish I knew what card you're hiding!"

And suddenly with a catch like a sob in her voice, looking at her little jewelled watch, she begged, "Oh, let us go! Take me away! Don't make me lose one precious moment!"

"What next?" he was debating within himself while they paused for a second outside, waiting for a taxicab.

A thought struck him. Holding her arm, he turned to the commissionaire. "Do you know Lord Malvern by sight?"

"Oh yes, sir. He's here frequently."

"Does he—er—live at 10 Chesham Crescent?"

"That's the address, sir."

The taxicab drew up.

"You told the truth there," he soliloquized aloud.

The woman did not trouble to answer. She got in, lifted by his wary hand on her elbow.

"Well, if he really does live there," said the Australian to himself, but aloud, "what next? You're not taking me into any gaming house or any sort of trap. What next?"

But she did not even hear him.

She was talking to herself, in the fashion of the very lonely.

"I wonder if it'll be changed. I wonder if he's still got that Bokhara rug Mummy gave me, in the hall. I suppose all my things have gone. That new ballroom has been made, I heard. And the music room—I should think that is Meggie's. It would be an adorable girl's room . . . I wonder if . . . I hope the Chinese god is still on the pedestal at the staircase. . . . It'll be queer, seeing all my things . . . the things I used to be able to think of as mine, like a wife can do . . . There's a lot in being a wife . . . I've been both, and I know . . . All I don't want to see the same is the servants . . . I want all new faces; all strange faces . . . Strange as I'll be to Meggie. Oh, what'll I say first? How explain? What'll she say? . . . He must have prepared her a little; *he must have*. He couldn't just leave us to meet . . . I wonder what she's thought all this time? Girls are kinder, broader minded nowadays . . . she may even have excuses for me in her heart . . . I pray God she will . . . Curzon Street . . . Only a minute now. Now I must be strong. I must! I must!"

The Australian sat upright, listening to her, his mouth half open. Light, from the lamps they shot by, fell upon him revealing to her his rugged face, deep, small, straight eyes, pugnacious nose and mouth, had she cared to look.

She turned to him suddenly.

"I must be strong!" she wailed.

Her hand was all at once in his. How thin! How hot! How fragile!

He did not reply, but maintained an imperturbable front, and she recovered herself.

"I *am* strong!" she said exultantly.

Even in the dim cab he could see the splendour of her eyes.

They drew up.

The Australian alighted, helped her out, kept his hold of her with one hand, and sought in his pocket for the fare with the other.

As they walked up the steps she was still talking—to herself, to him, to the air.

"I thought he'd never forgive me. He's a revengeful man. Very revengeful. But this is very dear, very sweet of him. As people get older they should get kinder, do you not think so? He's not revengeful any more. He's letting me see my Meggie at last, this Christmas. A Christmas of Christmases! . . . ."

The Australian pushed the bell with determination, and the door opened at once, letting out a flood of light. A youngish butler stood there, who showed no recognition of her. She hesitated awhile over her name, and then gave it derisively:

"Lady Malvern and——"

"Mr. Frampton," said the Australian.

He realised that she had not, of course, known his name.

"His Lordship is expecting you," said the butler, ushering them in. He was a very pallid man whose face betrayed nothing; and yet the Australian in some remote, keen way sensed atmospheric storm or stress or calamity. He sensed that something was about to happen.

As they stepped into the hall, there appeared suddenly from an open door on the left—as if this woman's coming had been avidly watched for—a tall man. His age might have been forty-five or fifty. His face, hair and bearing were all older. He was slim and grey and steely; and the Australian, after the habitually swift glance he flashed upon him, had her words in his mind like the undertone to a picture: "He is a revengeful man."

This was, indeed, primarily a most revengeful man.

The woman stepped forward, the epitome of grace and ease and well being. One thin hand clutched around her, in the approved manner of the temporary fashion, in a sort of delicate, fastidious way, the black satin coat. The satin was no glossier than her hair.

"Max," she began, "after all these years. . . ."

Her voice vibrated and faltered, smile as she might, play act as she might. On the face of the grey man appeared also a faint smile, terrible and delighted.

"You are looking wonderful," he said, with a little bow, and his look appraised her, her clothes and whole ensemble, "and I heard——"

"No wonder she wanted to look well," the Australian was thinking; confounded, shaken almost into belief in spite of himself.

She was answering, on a high hysterical note of expectation: "I am feeling wonderful, thank you. I always have, I always do. Repentance and sackcloth would never suit me, you know, Max. But please, my time's short. Mayn't I, at once. . . ."

"You are not alone," said Lord Malvern. "I expected you to come alone."

"May I introduce Mr. Frampton—Lord Malvern."

The men nodded.

Lord Malvern's look inquired Frampton's status. New husband, new lover? said the look. It was cold as ice and unbearably insulting.

The Australian swallowed it reluctantly.

"Is she here?" the woman cried.

Lord Malvern smiled again that faint smile of terrible delight. "Why, of course. I wouldn't bring you here on a fool's errand, after all those marvellously pathetic letters of yours, written year after year, which have melted my heart at last."

She moved forward. "Oh, let me see her!"

"You will find her looking beautiful!" said Lord Malvern.

"But——" he added, frowning towards the intruder.

She glanced at Frampton. His return glance answered stubbornly, "You are my prisoner. Where you go, I go." She pulled herself together and smiled once more.

"Mr. Frampton knows everything. I—I want to show him Meggie. He can hardly believe I have a grown-up daughter."

"You will hardly believe it yourself when you see her. This way."

"Where—the music-room?"

"Yes. You haven't forgotten your way. But still, give me the pleasure of showing you." He escorted her with an exaggeration of courtesy down a cool, tiled passage, and the Australian followed close, still wary, though confused and confounded.

"Does she know I'm coming? What has she been told of me? Oh, Max!"

"She knows nothing, as you will see for yourself."

He now threw open the door of the room they sought.

"Oh, my God!" the Australian thought he said, but his lips did not move. The only sound that tore the air was a dreadful one, a long scream.

The woman turned: "Who screamed? Who screamed? Don't scream!" And she ran forward and fell in a heap, half lying, half on her knees, not knowing, perhaps, that she moaned any more than she knew when her dried lips uttered that barren shriek.

The girl lay on a bier, candles around her; flowers; her hands crossed on her breast. Her mouth half smiled; she had been a pretty child, and in death was lovely.

Now in the great room there fell a complete silence; the mother raised herself and kissing those cold hands, not saying a word, not crying, not trembling. But she was just the ghost of the radiant woman who had come in.

Through the red mist of his sudden rage the Australian heard Lord Malvern speaking very quietly somewhere near him.

"It happened the day before yesterday, the day I received your annual request, dear lady. Under the circumstances I thought I would accede to it. It does no harm now."

He was a most revengeful man.

The Australian ran into the room and lifted the kneeling woman with one arm. She made no resistance, gave not so much as an inquiring look. In one arm he half lifted her to the threshold. And there, standing aside watching them both with his dreary, implacable smile, was Lord Malvern, like an image. The Australian lifted his free hand and struck the smile from the image's mouth.

He was out on the pavement outside with the silent woman still gripped in his arm. A taxicab slid up at his signal.

"Time's up," he said in her ear.

"Time? Ah, time? Ah, yes. I forgot I am your prisoner."

He lifted her in and got in too. "Drive," he ordered vaguely, yet surely. He bent his face to her cold one. "I won't add one to the revengeful men to-night," he said softly and slowly. "I'll spend my life trying to make you happy in prison. You must be sick of the Old World. But there's a New World down under and I want to show it you. Let's go."

62

Mr. Oddy

BY SIR HUGH WALPOLE

THIS may seem to many people
an old-fashioned story; it is perhaps for that reason that I tell it. I can
recover here, it may be, for myself something of the world that is already
romantic, already beyond one's reach, already precious for the things
that one might have got out of it and didn't.

London of but a few years before the war! What a commonplace to
point out its difference from the London of to-day and to emphasise the
tiny period of time that made that difference!

We were all young and hopeful then, we could all live on a shilling
a year and think ourselves well off, we could all sit in front of the lumbering horse 'buses and chat confidentially with the omniscient driver,
we could all see Dan Leno in pantomime and watch Farren dance at
the Empire, we could all rummage among those cobwebby streets at
the back of the Strand where Aldwych now flaunts her shining bosom
and imagine Pendennis and Warrington, Copperfield and Traddles
cheek by jowl with ourselves, we could all wait in the shilling queue
for hours to see Ellen Terry in *Captain Brassbound* and Forbes-Robert-
son in *Hamlet,* we could all cross the street without fear of imminent
death, and above all we could all sink ourselves into that untidy, higgledy-piggledy, smoky and beery and gas-lampy London gone utterly and
forever.

But I have no wish to be sentimental about it; there is a new London
which is just as interesting to its new citizens as the old London was to
myself. It is my age that is the matter; before the war one was so *very*
young.

I like, though, to try and recapture that time, and so, as a simple way
to do it, I seize upon a young man; Tommy Brown we will call him. I
don't know where Tommy Brown may be now; that Tommy Brown

917

who lived as I did in two very small rooms in Glebe Place, Chelsea, who enjoyed hugely the sparse but economical meals provided so elegantly by two charming ladies at "The Good Intent" down by the river, that charming hostelry whence looking through the bow windows you could see the tubby barges go floating down the river, and the thin outline of Whistler's Battersea Bridge, and in the small room itself were surrounded by who knows what geniuses in the lump, geniuses of Art and Letters, of the Stage and of the Law.

For Tommy Brown in those days life was paradisal.

He had come boldly from Cambridge to throw himself upon London's friendly bosom; despite all warnings to the contrary he was certain that it would be friendly; how could it be otherwise to so charming, so brilliant, so unusually attractive a young man? For Tommy was conceited beyond all that his youth warranted, conceited indeed without any reason at all.

He had, it is true, secured the post of reviewer to one of the London daily papers; this seemed to him when he looked back in later years a kind of miracle, but at the time no miracle at all, simply a just appreciation of his extraordinary talents. There was also reposing in one of the publishers' offices at that moment the manuscript of a novel, a novel that appeared to him of astonishing brilliance, written in the purest English, sparkling with wit, tense with drama.

These things were fine and reassuring enough, but there was more than that; he felt in himself the power to rise to the greatest heights; he could not see how anything could stop him, it was his destiny.

This pride of his might have suffered some severe shocks were it not that he spent all of his time with other young gentlemen quite as conceited as himself. I have heard talk of the present young generation and its agreeable consciousness of its own merits, but I doubt if it is anything in comparison with that little group of twenty-five years ago. After all, the war has intervened—however young we may be and however greatly we may pretend, this is an unstable world and for the moment heroics have departed from it. But for Tommy Brown and his friends the future was theirs and nobody could prevent it. Something pathetic in that as one looks back.

Tommy was not really so unpleasant a youth as I have described him —to his elders he must have appeared a baby, and his vitality at least they could envy. After all, why check his confidence? Life would do that heavily enough in its own good time.

Tommy, although he had no money and no prospects, was already engaged to a young woman, Miss Alice Smith. Alice Smith was an artist sharing with a girl friend a Chelsea studio, and she was as certain of her future as Tommy was of his.

They had met at a little Chelsea dance, and two days after their meeting they were engaged. She had no parents who mattered, and no money to speak of, so that the engagement was the easiest thing in the world.

Tommy, who had been in love before many times, was certain, as he told his friend Jack Robinson so often as to bore that gentleman severely, that this time at last he knew what love was. Alice ordered him about—with her at any rate his conceit fell away—she had read his novel and pronounced it old-fashioned, the severest criticism she could possibly have made, and she thought his reviews amateur. He suffered then a good deal in her company. When he was away from her he told himself and everybody else that her critical judgment was marvellous, her comprehension of all the Arts quite astounding, but he left her sometimes with a miserable suspicion that perhaps after all he was not going to do anything very wonderful and that he would have to work very hard indeed to rise to her astonishing standards.

It was in such a mood of wholesome depression that he came one beautiful April day from the A.B.C. shop where he had been giving his Alice luncheon, and found his way to an old bookshop on the riverside round the corner from Oakley Street. This shop was kept by a gentleman called Mr. Burdett Coutts, and the grand associations of his name gave him from the very first a sort of splendour.

It was one of those old shops of which there are, thank God, still many examples surviving in London, in which the room was so small and the books so many that to move a step was to imperil your safety. Books ran in thick, tight rows from floor to ceiling everywhere, were piled in stacks upon the ground and hung in perilous heaps over chairs and window ledges.

Mr. Burdett Coutts himself, a very stout and grizzled old man enveloped always in a grey shawl, crouched behind his spectacles in a far corner and took apparently no interest in anything save that he would snap the price at you if you brought him a volume and timorously enquired. He was not one of those old booksellers dear to the heart of Anatole France and other great men who would love to discourse to you of the beauties of *The Golden Ass,* the possibility of Homer being a lady, or the virtues of the second *Hyperion* over the first. Not at all; he ate biscuits which stuck in his grizzly beard, and wrote perpetually in a large worm-eaten ledger which was supposed by his customers to contain all the secrets of the universe.

It was just because Mr. Coutts never interfered with you that Tommy Brown loved his shop so dearly. If he had a true genuine passion that went far deeper than all his little superficial vanities and egotisms, it was his passion for books—books of any kind.

He had at this time no fine taste—all was fish that came to his net.

The bundles of Thackeray and Dickens, parts tied up carelessly in coarse string, the old broken-backed volumes of Radcliffe and Barham and Galt, the red and gold Colburn's Novelists, all these were exciting to him, just as exciting as though they had been a first Gray's *Elegy* or an original *Robinson Crusoe*.

He had, too, a touching weakness for the piles of fresh and neglected modern novels that lay in their discarded heaps on the dusty floor; young though he was, he was old enough to realise the pathos of these so short a time ago fresh from the bursting presses, so eagerly cherished through months of anxious watching by their fond authors, so swiftly forgotten, dead almost before they were born.

So he browsed, moving like a panting puppy with inquisitive nose from stack to stack with a gesture of excitement, tumbling a whole racket of books about his head, looking then anxiously to see whether the old man would be angry with him, and realising for the thousandth time that the old man never was.

It was on this day, then, rather sore from the arrogancies of his Alice, that he tried to restore his confidence among these friendly volumes. With a little thrill of excited pleasure he had just discovered a number of the volumes born of those romantic and tragedy-haunted "Nineties." Here in little thin volumes were the stories of Crackanthorpe, the poems of Dowson, the *Keynotes* of George Egerton, *The Bishop's Dilemma* of Ella d'Arcy, *The Happy Hypocrite* of Max Beerbohm.

Had he only been wise enough to give there and then for that last whatever the old man had asked him for it he would have been fortunate indeed, but the pennies in his pocket were few—he was not yet a book collector, but rather that less expensive but more precious thing, a book adorer. He had the tiny volume in his hand, when he was aware that someone had entered the shop and was standing looking over his shoulder.

He turned slowly and saw someone who at first sight seemed vaguely familiar, so familiar that he was plunged into confusion at once by the sense that he ought to say "How do you do?" but could not accurately place him. The gentleman also seemed to know him very well, for he said in a most friendly way, "Ah, yes, the 'Nineties,' a very fruitful period."

Tommy stammered something, put down the Max Beerbohm, moved a little, and pulled about him a sudden shower of volumes. The room was filled with the racket of their tumbling, and a cloud of dust thickened about them, creeping into eyes and mouth and nose.

"I'm terribly sorry," Tommy stammered, and then, looking up, was sorry the more when he saw how extremely neat and tidy the gentleman was and how terribly the little accident must distress him.

Tommy's friend must have been between sixty and seventy years of age, nearer seventy perhaps than sixty, but his black hair was thick and strong and stood up *en brosse* from a magnificent broad forehead. Indeed, so fine was the forehead and the turn of the head that the face itself was a little disappointing, being so round and chubby and amiable as to be almost babyish. It was not a weak face, however, the eyes being large and fine and the chin strong and determined.

The figure of this gentleman was short and thick-set and inclined to stoutness; he had the body of a prize-fighter now resting on his laurels. He was very beautifully clothed in a black coat and waistcoat, pepper-and-salt trousers, and he stood leaning a little on a thick ebony cane, his legs planted apart, his whole attitude that of one who was accustomed to authority. He had the look of a magistrate, or even of a judge, and had his face been less kindly Tommy would have said good day, nodded to Mr. Burdett Coutts, and departed, but that was a smile difficult to resist.

"Dear me," the gentleman said, "this is a very dusty shop. I have never been here before, but I gather by the way that you knock the books about that it's an old friend of yours."

Tommy giggled in a silly fashion, shifted from foot to foot, and then, desiring to seem very wise and learned, proved himself only very young and foolish.

"The 'Nineties' are becoming quite romantic," he said in his most authoritative voice, "now that we're getting a good distance from them."

"Ah, you think so!" said the gentleman courteously; "that's interesting. I'm getting to an age now, I'm afraid, when nothing seems romantic but one's own youth and, ah, dear me! that was a very long time ago."

This was exactly the way that kindly old gentlemen were supposed to talk, and Tommy listened with becoming attention.

"In my young day," his friend continued, "George Eliot seemed to everybody a magnificent writer: a little heavy in hand for these days, I'm afraid. Now who is the God of your generation, if it isn't impertinent to enquire?"

Tommy shifted again from foot to foot. Who was the God of his generation? If the truth must be told, in Tommy's set there were no Gods, only young men who might be Gods if they lived long enough.

"Well," said Tommy awkwardly, "Hardy, of course—er—it's difficult to say, isn't it?"

"Very difficult," said the gentleman.

There was a pause then, which Tommy concluded by hinting that he was afraid that he must move forward to a very important engagement.

"May I walk with you a little way?" asked the gentleman very courteously. "Such a very beautiful afternoon."

Once outside in the beautiful afternoon air everything was much easier; Tommy regained his self-confidence, and soon was talking with his accustomed ease and freedom. There was nothing very alarming in his friend after all, he seemed so very eager to hear everything that Tommy had to say. He was strangely ignorant too; he seemed to be interested in the Arts, but to know very little about them; certain names that were to Tommy household words were to this gentleman quite unknown. Tommy began to be a little patronising. They parted at the top of Oakley Street.

"I wonder if you'd mind," the gentleman said, "our meeting again? The fact is, that I have very little opportunity of making friends with your generation. There are so many things that you could tell me. I am afraid it may be tiresome for you to spend an hour or two with so ancient a duffer as myself, but it would be very kind of you."

Tommy was nothing if not generous; he said that he would enjoy another meeting very much. Of course he was very busy and his spare hours were not many, but a walk another afternoon could surely be managed. They made an appointment, they exchanged names; the gentleman's name was Mr. Alfred Oddy.

That evening, in the middle of a hilarious Chelsea party, Tommy suddenly discovered to his surprise that it would please him very much to see Mr. Oddy walk in through the door.

Although it was a hilarious party Tommy was not very happy; for one thing, Spencer Russell, the novelist, was there and showed quite clearly that he didn't think Tommy very interesting. Tommy had been led up and introduced to him, had said one or two things that seemed to himself very striking, but Spencer Russell had turned his back almost at once and entered into eager conversation with somebody else.

This wasn't very pleasant, and then his own beloved Alice was behaving strangely; she seemed to have no eyes nor ears for anyone in the room save Spencer Russell, and this was the stranger in that only a week or so before she had in public condemned Spencer Russell's novels, utterly and completely, stating that he was written out, had nothing to say, and was as good as dead. To-night, however, he was not dead at all, and Tommy had the agony of observing her edge her way into the group surrounding him and then listen to him not only as though he were the fount of all wisdom, but an Adonis as well, which last was absurd seeing that he was fat and unwieldy and bald on the top of his head.

After a while Tommy came up to her and suggested that they should go, and received then the shock of his life when she told him that he could go if he liked, but that he was not to bother her. And she told him this in a voice so loud that everybody heard and many people tittered.

He left in a fury and spent then a night that he imagined to be sleepless, although in truth he slept during most of it.

It was with an eagerness that surprised himself that he met Mr. Oddy on the second occasion. He had not seen Alice for two days. He did not intend to be the one to apologise first; besides, he had nothing to apologise for; and yet during these two days there was scarcely a moment that he had not to restrain himself from running round to her studio and making it up.

When he met Mr. Oddy at the corner of Oakley Street he was a very miserable young man. He was so miserable that in five minutes he was pouring out all his woes.

He told Mr. Oddy everything, of his youth, his wonderful promise, and the extraordinary lack of appreciation shown to him by his relatives, of the historical novels that he had written at the age of anything from ten to sixteen and found only the cook for an audience, of his going to Cambridge, and his development there so that he became Editor of *The Lion,* that remarkable but very short-lived literary journal, and the President of "The Bats," the most extraordinary Essay Club that Cambridge had ever known; of how, alas, he took only a third in History owing to the perverseness of examiners; and so on and so on, until he arrived in full flood at the whole history of his love for Alice, of her remarkable talents and beauty, but of her strange temper and arrogance and general feminine queerness.

Mr. Oddy listened to it all in the kindest way. There's no knowing where they walked that afternoon; they crossed the bridge and adventured into Battersea Park, and finally had tea in a small shop smelling of stale buns and liquorice drops. It was only as they turned homewards that it occurred to Tommy that he had been talking during the whole afternoon. He had the grace to see that an apology was necessary.

"I beg your pardon, sir," he said, flushing a little, "I'm afraid I have bored you dreadfully. The fact is, that this last quarrel with Alice has upset me very badly. What would you do if you were in my position?"

Mr. Oddy sighed. "The trouble is," he said, "that I realise only too clearly that I shall never be in your position again. My time for romance is over, or at least I get my romance now in other ways. It wasn't always so; there was a lady once beneath whose window I stood night after night merely for the pleasure of seeing her candle outlined behind the blind."

"And did she love you," Tommy asked, "as much as you loved her?"

"Nobody, my dear boy," Mr. Oddy replied, "loves you as much as you love them; either they love you more or they love you less. The first of these is often boring, the second always tragic. In the present case I should go and make it up; after all, happiness is always worth having, even at the sacrifice of one's pride. She seems to me a very charming young lady."

"Oh, she is," Tommy answered eagerly. "I'll take your advice, I'll go this very evening; in fact, if you don't mind, I think it would be rather a good time to find her in now."

Mr. Oddy smiled and agreed; they parted to meet another day.

On the third occasion of their meeting, which was only two days after the second, Tommy cared for his companion enough to wish to find out something about him.

His scene of reconciliation with his beautiful Alice had not been as satisfactory as he had hoped; she had forgiven him indeed, but given him quite clearly to understand that she would stand none of his nonsense either now or hereafter. The satisfactory thing would have been for Tommy there and then to have left her, never to see her again; he would thus have preserved both his pride and his independence; but, alas, he was in love, terribly in love, and her indignation made her appear only the more magnificent.

And so on this third meeting with his friend he was quite humble and longing for affection.

And then his curiosity was stirred. Who was this handsome old gentleman, with his touching desire for Tommy's companionship? There was an air about him that seemed to suggest that he was someone of importance in his own world; beyond this there was an odd sense that Tommy knew him in some way, had seen him somewhere; so on this third occasion Tommy came out with his questions.

Who was he? Was he married? What was his profession, or was he perhaps retired now? And another question that Tommy would have liked to have asked, and had not the impertinence, was as to why this so late interest in the Arts and combined with this interest this so complete ignorance.

Mr. Oddy seemed to know a great deal about everything else, but in this one direction his questions were childish. He seemed never to have heard of the great Spencer Russell at all (which secretly gave Tommy immense satisfaction), and as for geniuses like Mumpus and Peter Arrogance and Samuel Bird, even when Tommy explained how truly great these men were, Mr. Oddy appeared but little impressed.

"Well, at least," Tommy burst out indignantly, "I suppose you've read something by Henry Galleon? Of course he's a back number now, at least he is not modern if you know what I mean, but then he's been writing for centuries. Why, his first book came out when Trollope and

George Eliot were still alive. Of course, between ourselves I think *The Roads,* for instance, a pretty fine book, but you should hear Spencer Russell go for it."

No, Mr. Oddy had never heard of Henry Galleon.

But there followed a most enchanting description by Mr. Oddy of his life when he was a young man and how he once heard Dickens give a reading of *A Christmas Carol,* of how he saw an old lady in a sedan chair at Brighton (she was cracked, of course, and even then a hundred years after her time, but still he had seen it), of how London in his young day was as dark and dirty at night as it had been in Pepys' time, of how crinolines when he was young were so large that it was one of the sights to see a lady getting into a cab, of how in the music-halls there was a chairman who used to sit on the stage with a table in front of him, ring a bell and drink out of a mug of beer, of how he heard Jean de Reszke in *Siegfried* and Ternina in *Tristan,* and of how he had been at the first night when Ellen Terry and Irving had delighted the world with *The Vicar of Wakefield.*

Yes, not only had Mr. Oddy seen and done all these things, but he related the events in so enchanting a way, drew such odd little pictures of such unexpected things and made that old London live so vividly, that at last Tommy burst out in a volley of genuine enthusiasm: "Why, you ought to be a writer yourself! Why don't you write your reminiscences?"

But Mr. Oddy shook his head gently: there were too many reminiscences, everyone was always reminiscing; who wanted to hear these old men talk?

At last when they parted Mr. Oddy had a request—one thing above all things that he would like would be to attend one of these evening gatherings with his young friend to hear these young men and women talk. He promised to sit very quietly in a corner—he wouldn't be in anybody's way.

Of course Tommy consented to take him; there would be one next week, a really good one; but in his heart of hearts he was a little shy. He was shy not only for himself but also for his friend.

During these weeks a strange and most unexpected affection had grown up in his heart for this old man; he really did like him immensely, he was so kind and gentle and considerate.

But he would be rather out of place with Spencer Russell and the others; he would probably say something foolish, and then the others would laugh. They were on the whole a rather ruthless set and were no respecters of persons.

However, the meeting was arranged; the evening came and with it Mr. Oddy, looking just as he always did, quiet and gentle but rather impressive in some way or another. Tommy introduced him to his hostess, Miss Thelma Bennet, that well-known futuristic artist, and then carefully settled him down in a corner with Miss Bennet's aunt, an old lady who appeared occasionally on her niece's horizon but gave no trouble because she was stone deaf and cared only for knitting.

It was a lively evening; several of the brighter spirits were there, and there was a great deal of excellent talk about literature. Every writer over thirty was completely condemned save for those few remaining who had passed eighty years of age and ceased to produce.

Spencer Russell especially was at his best; reputations went down before his vigorous fist like ninepins. He was so scornful that his brilliance was, as Alice Smith everywhere proclaimed, "simply withering." Everyone came in for his lash, and especially Henry Galleon. There had been some article in some ancient monthly written by some ancient idiot suggesting that there was still something to be said for Galleon and that he had rendered some service to English literature. How Russell pulled that article to pieces! He even found a volume of Galleon's among Miss Bennet's books, took it down from the shelf and read extracts aloud to the laughing derision of the assembled company.

Then an odd thing occurred. Tommy, who loved to be in the intellectual swim, nevertheless stood up and defended Galleon. He defended him rather feebly, it is true, speaking of him as though he were an old man ready for the almshouse who nevertheless deserved a little consideration and pity. He flushed as he spoke, and the scorn with which they greeted his defence altogether silenced him. It silenced him the more because Alice Smith was the most scornful of them all; she told him that he knew nothing and never would know anything, and she imitated his piping excited treble, and then everyone joined in.

How he hated this to happen before Mr. Oddy! How humiliating after all the things that he had told his friend, the implication that he was generally considered to be one of England's most interesting young men, the implication above all that although she might be a little rough to him at times Alice really adored him, and was his warmest admirer. She did not apparently adore him to-night, and when he went out at last with Mr. Oddy into the wintry, rain-driven street it was all he could do to keep back tears of rage and indignation.

Mr. Oddy had, however, apparently enjoyed himself. He put his hand for a minute on the boy's shoulder.

"Good night, my dear boy," he said. "I thought it very gallant of you to stand up for that older writer as you did: that needed courage. I wonder," he went on, "whether you would allow me to come and take tea with you one day—just our two selves. It would be a great pleasure for me."

And then, having received Tommy's invitation, he vanished into the darkness.

On the day appointed, Mr. Oddy appeared punctually at Tommy's rooms. That was not a very grand house in Glebe Place where Tommy lived, and a very soiled and battered landlady let Mr. Oddy in. He stumbled up the dark staircase that smelt of all the cabbage and all the beef and all the mutton ever consumed by lodgers between these walls, up again two flights of stairs, until at last there was the weather-beaten door with Tommy's visiting-card nailed upon it. Inside was Tommy, a plate with little cakes, raspberry jam, and some very black-looking toast.

Mr. Oddy, however, was appreciative of everything; especially he looked at the books. "Why," he said, "you've got quite a number of the novels of that man you defended the other evening. I wonder you're not ashamed to have them if they're so out of date."

"To tell you the truth," said Tommy, speaking freely now that he was in his own castle, "I like Henry Galleon awfully. I'm afraid I pose a good deal when I'm with those other men; perhaps you've noticed it yourself. Of course Galleon is the greatest novelist we've got, with Hardy and Meredith, only he's getting old, and everything that's old is out of favour with our set."

"Naturally," said Mr. Oddy, quite approving, "of course it is."

"I have got a photograph of Galleon," said Tommy. "I cut it out of a publisher's advertisement, but it was taken years ago."

He went to his table, searched for a little and produced a small photograph of a very fierce-looking gentleman with a black beard.

"Dear me," said Mr. Oddy, "he does look alarming!"

"Oh, that's ever so old," said Tommy. "I expect he's mild and soft now, but he's a great man all the same; I'd like to see Spencer Russell write anything as fine as *The Roads* or *The Pattern in the Carpet.*"

They sat down to tea very happy and greatly pleased with one another.

"I do wish," said Tommy, "that you'd tell me something about yourself; we're such friends now, and I don't know anything about you at all."

"I'd rather you didn't," said Mr. Oddy. "You'd find it so uninteresting if you did; mystery's a great thing."

"Yes," said Tommy, "I don't want to seem impertinent, and of course if you don't want to tell me anything you needn't, but—I know it sounds silly, but, you see, I like you most awfully. I haven't liked anybody so much for ever so long, except Alice, of course. I don't feel as though you were of another generation or anything; it's just as though we were the same age!"

Mr. Oddy was enchanted. He put his hand on the boy's for a moment and was going to say something, when they were interrupted by a knock on the door, and the terrible-looking landlady appeared in the room. She apologised, but the afternoon post had come and she thought the young gentleman would like to see his letters. He took them, was about to put them down without opening them, when suddenly he blushed. "Oh, from Alice," he said. "Will you forgive me a moment?"

"Of course," said Mr. Oddy.

The boy opened the letter and read it. It fell from his hand on to the table. He got up gropingly as though he could not see his way, and went to the window and stood there with his back to the room. There was a long silence.

"Not bad news, I hope," said Mr. Oddy at last.

Tommy turned round. His face was grey and he was biting his lips. "Yes," he answered, "she's—gone off."

"Gone off?" said Mr. Oddy, rising from the table.

"Yes," said Tommy, "with Russell. They were married at a register office this morning."

He half turned round to the window, put out his hands as though he would shield himself from some blow, then crumpled up into a chair, his head falling between his arms on the table.

Mr. Oddy waited. At last he said: "Oh, I'm sorry: that's dreadful for you!"

The boy struggled, trying to raise his head and speak, but the words would not come. Mr. Oddy went behind him and put his hands on his shoulders.

"You know," he said, "you mustn't mind me. Of course, I'll go if you like, but if you could think of me for a moment as your oldest friend, old enough to be your father, you know."

Tommy clutched his sleeve, then, abandoning the struggle altogether, buried his head in Mr. Oddy's beautiful black waistcoat.

Later he poured his heart out. Alice was all that he had; he knew that he wasn't any good as a writer, he was a failure altogether; what he'd done he'd done for Alice, and now that she'd gone——

"Well, there's myself," said Mr. Oddy. "What I mean is that you're not without a friend; and as for writing, if you only write to please somebody else, that's no use; you've got to write because you can't help it. There are too many writers in the world already for you to dare to add to their number unless you're simply compelled to. But there—I'm preaching. If it's any comfort to you to know, I went through just this same experience myself once—the lady whose candle I watched behind the blind. If you cared to, would you come and have dinner with me to-night at my home? Only the two of us, you know; but don't if you'd rather be alone."

Tommy, clutching Mr. Oddy's hand, said he would come.

About half-past seven that evening he had beaten up his pride. Even in the depth of his misery he saw that they would never have got on together, he and Alice. He was quickly working himself into a fine state of hatred of the whole female race, and this helped him—he would be a bachelor all his days, a woman-hater; he would preserve a glorious independence. How much better this freedom than a houseful of children and a bagful of debts.

Only, as he walked to the address that Mr. Oddy had given him he held sharply away from him the memory of those hours that he had spent with Alice, those hours of their early friendship when the world had been so wonderful a place that it had seemed to be made entirely of golden sunlight. He felt that he was an old man indeed as he mounted the steps of Mr. Oddy's house.

It was a big house in Eaton Square. Mr. Oddy must be rich. He rang the bell, and a door was opened by a footman. He asked for Mr. Oddy.

The footman hesitated a little, and then, smiling, said: "Oh yes, sir, will you come in?"

He left his coat in the hall, mounted a broad staircase, and then was shown into the finest library that he had ever seen. Books! Shelf upon shelf of books, and glorious books, editions de luxe and, as he could see with half an eye, rare first editions and those lovely bindings in white parchment and vellum that he so longed one day himself to possess. On the broad writing-table there was a large photograph of Meredith; it was signed in sprawling letters, "George Meredith, 1887." What could this mean? Mr. Oddy, who knew nothing about literature, had been given a photograph by George Meredith and had this wonderful library! He stared bewildered about him.

A door at the far end of the library opened and an elegant young man appeared. "Mr. Galleon," he said, "will be with you in a moment. Won't you sit down?"

63

A Busman's Holiday

BY FRANCIS BRETT YOUNG

IF THERE was one thing that Doctor Malcolm detested and dreaded more than another it was a busman's holiday—in other words, the intrusion of medicine, that science to which his name had added so much luster, into those precious weeks when sea-trout were on the run.

When a celebrated lawyer or stockbroker goes away for a holiday and the man who is sitting next to him in the train reads his name on his baggage, edges up to him, slips gradually into polite conversation, then drops in a casual question about some hypothetical case of law or the future of International Nickels or General Motors, that lawyer or stockbroker is within his rights if he changes his seat or turns the subject in the direction of golf, cocktails or fishing-tackle.

Neither litigation nor speculation is a matter of life and death; neither the lawyer nor the stockbroker has a duty towards humanity. But a doctor has. Hence the nobility and some of the prime disadvantages of his profession. That was one of the reasons why Henry Malcolm had chosen this remote retreat, the "Forest Arms" at Felindre, on the Welsh border, for his summer holiday. And that was why he felt an acute and justifiable annoyance when, just as he was pulling on his waders after breakfast, the landlord announced a lady to see him.

"Miss Morgan of 'Bryntyrion'," he said. "She says that she knows you, sir."

"Miss Morgan? I don't remember anyone of that name. What does she want?"

"She wants to see you, sir. She didn't say why."

"Well, show her in, Jones," said Henry Malcolm resignedly. "No peace for the wicked!"

He pulled off his waders and put on his shoes again. Miss Morgan. . . . It was difficult for a physician with an extensive practice to remember the name of everyone who had consulted him. The remoteness of the "Forest Arms" had its disadvantages; in tiny places of this kind every stranger was conspicuous. The fact that he had been run to earth like this, within a few days of his arrival, might be taken as a compliment to his celebrity as a neurologist—but that was small consolation for the loss of a morning's sport.

"Miss Morgan," the landlord announced.

Miss Morgan entered. She came in with a nervous smile, an odd little woman of fifty or thereabouts, dressed primly, severely, in a fashion of twenty years since. In her face, in her smile, there was something vaguely familiar to Malcolm, half recalling a memory too remote to be fixed. When she spoke, her speech was, quite obviously, that of a lady.

"I'm afraid you don't remember me, doctor," she said. "It's hardly to be expected. Thirty years. . . . You were only a boy when last I saw you. But my sister Agatha and I have followed your wonderful career with the greatest interest and pride, and when I heard, last night, that you were staying in the village"—tears welled into her eyes—"it seemed like an act of Providence. Ah, I'm afraid you've forgotten."

Miss Morgan? Miss Agatha Morgan? And thirty years ago? At last he had it! Two old maids, the Miss Morgans! Of course, he remembered perfectly! They lived in a tiny house, as neat as a bird's nest, at the corner of the street where Malcolm had spent his childhood. Their father was a retired colonel, a Crimean veteran, who went stumping past the schoolroom window every afternoon on his constitutional—a precise, gray-whiskered figure with an Indian cheroot in his teeth.

He remembered, above all, the smell of the Miss Morgans' sitting-room, a chamber as small and orderly as a ship's cabin. It was a composite odor of furniture-polish, potpourri, and cigar-smoke, enveloping a confused and exotic collection of furniture: a spinet, tortured carvings of ebony, Benares brass. He remembered the red and gold of a Crown Derby tea-set, the richness of Miss Agatha's fruit cake, the flavor of the guava-jelly which the Colonel imported from Jamaica and which the Miss Morgans insisted on calling not "jam" but "preserve," and, even more awe-inspiring, their father's Crimean sword, which hung, in a place of honor, above the mantelpiece. Thirty years. . . .

"Why, of course I remember," he said. "You must be Miss Susan."

She flushed, almost prettily. "How clever of you to remember my name!"

"But what are you doing here, in Felindre?" he asked. "You must tell me all about it. And how is Miss Agatha?"

"She isn't Miss Agatha any longer; she's married—her name's Mrs. Peters. And she's not very well. That's why I have taken this . . . liberty."

"Liberty indeed!" He encouraged her. "Sit down and make yourself comfortable. Since I've settled in Harley Street, I rarely see old friends. I should never have forgiven you if you hadn't looked me up. I shall want to know everything that's happened since last I saw you."

She sat down nervously. "It's a very long story," she said. "If it weren't that your dear mother had been so kind to us in the old days I should almost hesitate . . ."

He shook his head smilingly; the poor little withered thing was pathetic. "I can see you're in trouble," he said. "Tell me all about it. First of all, how on earth did you get here?"

She smiled, with a wan, appealing gratitude. "Perhaps," she said, "I had better begin at the beginning." She straightened her back and composed her thin hands on her lap, but Malcolm could see, by the nervous twining of her fingers, that her mind was agitated.

"About fifteen years ago," she began, "long after you had gone to London, dear father died. He was a wonderful man, a true soldier and gentleman, and the best of fathers. We had always lived modestly, well within our income, as everybody should; but when father died, you see, his pension died with him, and Agatha and I were left in very reduced circumstances. If we hadn't been used to careful living I really don't know how we should have got on. But Agatha, of course, was a marvelous housekeeper—the very soul of thrift—so we managed to keep up appearances and go on living in accordance with dear father's station. It wasn't easy, though!" She shook her head slowly.

Malcolm could see what that meant; the little room, cozy no longer; the economies of fuel in winter; the diet, which verged on starvation, of bread and margarine, the makeshift dressmaking. How many spinsters of this kind were prepared to pay this price for their faded gentility!

"However," she went on cheerfully, "we managed to pull through. Of course, from time to time we had to sell little bits of furniture. Some of the most lovely things that father had brought from India fetched next to nothing. It was a crying shame that we had to part with them; but what could we do? If I had had my own way I should have tried to get a post as a lady's companion or governess; but Agatha would never consent to it. 'We may be poor, Susan,' she said, 'but we're proud. Nobody in our family has ever done a thing like that. I think father would turn in his grave,' she said, 'if we ever forgot that we are gentlewomen.' So there it was! Of course Agatha is much more strong-minded than I am. And, as I've said, we *did* manage to pull through, hard though it was, until Agatha came into the property."

"The property?" Malcolm repeated. "Come, that sounds better!" He felt a considerable relief to know that this harrowing tale of hardships would not be prolonged.

"Yes, it was most fortunate in a way," Miss Susan continued demurely, "and quite unexpected. You see," she explained, "our family is a very old one; the Morgans have been squires of Felindre for hundreds of years. When you go to church on Sunday you'll see all our ancestors' monuments."

"Shall I?" Malcolm thought grimly. "Not if I know it! I'm on a holiday!"

" 'Bryntyrion,' the family seat," Miss Susan went on, "had gone to dear father's cousin, Howell Morgan. He was very proud of it; and so, when he died, he left it to Agatha, who was his eldest living relative. Quite properly, too. It would have been dreadful to think of it going out of the family.

"Of course, it all came as a wonderful surprise to us. I'm afraid, if I had my own way—I mean, if it had been left to me—I should have wanted to sell it and settle down in some nice neighborhood where father's service reputation was known. But Agatha is extremely determined and has a high sense of duty. She said we were bound, out of respect for dear father's memory, to keep up the family tradition and go and live there, even though it *was* so dreadfully out of the way."

"The property is near here?"

"Just three miles from Felindre. Quite alone in the country, and over ten miles from a railway station. Please don't misunderstand me—the property is not very valuable. Cousin Howell had sold the greater part of the estate. Apart from the house there were only a couple of farms, which were let, at the time when Agatha inherited, to tenants who run sheep on them. My sister, who is terribly courageous, would like to have taken them over and set up farming herself. But really, you know, we had lived all our lives in town, and hadn't the necessary experience; besides which, the payment of the death-duties and the expense of moving into Wales left us with very little capital to spare for an adventure of that kind. Our lawyer, very wisely I think, dissuaded Agatha from embarking on it, but nothing and nobody could persuade her that it wasn't our duty to live at 'Bryntyrion'."

"So you came there, all alone?" Malcolm asked. The hues of romantic prosperity were already beginning to fade from the picture.

"Well, no. Not exactly alone," said Miss Susan nervously. She threw an anxious glance behind her, as though she suspected that somebody was listening, then continued in a voice that was almost lowered to a whisper:

"Not exactly alone," she repeated. "You see, it was like this. Our

lawyer, who was the soul of wisdom and kindness and consideration—
I cannot blame *him*—our lawyer impressed upon us most strongly the
necessity of *not* being alone. At first Agatha laughed at him—she's a
typical soldier's daughter, very different from me, I'm afraid—but
eventually even she was forced to admit that he was right. 'You can't
go out living in the wilds of Wales,' he told her, 'unless you have a
capable man in the house.' The mere mention of a man was enough to
make Agatha obstinate. Apart from one rather unfortunate love-affair,
nearly forty years ago, Agatha had never had anything to do with men.
She despised them, in fact, and was almost scornful whenever I made
any gentlemen friends; she said that dear father's society was surely
enough for us."

"How jealous these old maids are!" Malcolm thought, while Miss
Susan continued:

"At first she refused point blank to entertain the idea. She despised
me, you know, for my lack of self-reliance; but really the idea of living
right out in the country like that got so much on my nerves that I'm
afraid I was guilty of playing a trick on her. I told her that I was sure
it would be more in keeping with the family dignity if we had a butler
—not a *real* butler, of course, but a man of all work—the kind of man
who was used to good service, who could open the door and take messages when our new neighbors called."

"I think that was very wise of you and entirely reasonable," Malcolm
agreed.

"Yes, in principle I'm sure I was right. Of course I never dreamed.
. . ." She shook her head sadly. "I suggested that our lawyer should
find a suitable man," she went on, "but Agatha would not be beholden
to anybody. She said that she herself was a sufficiently good judge. So
she put an advertisement in the paper and interviewed all the applicants
personally. Mr. Peters was the last of the lot. From the moment when
he entered the room I could see that Agatha had made up her mind.
She engaged him at once.

"And really, I must confess," Miss Susan admitted, "I completely
agreed with her choice. To begin with, Peters was an extremely handsome man—the kind of figure who would lend dignity to any house.
You would have said at once that he was a man who knew his place.
We liked the way he said 'Madam' whenever he addressed us, and stood
with his feet together. In spite of his perfect manners there was nothing
servile about him. As Agatha said at the time, it almost seemed as
though he must have gentle blood in his veins. So different, in every
way, from the servant type!

"Indeed, though he had been a butler once, Peters had not been in
service for years. That was why he didn't bring any references with him.

He had been keeping a bicycle-shop ever since the war. It seemed just like fate when he told us he had served in father's old regiment. He was wearing cycling stockings on the day when he came to apply for the post, and really, as Agatha said—his limbs were most shapely! We felt sorry for him, too: he had lately lost his wife. He said he'd been born in the country and was handy with his fingers. He could knock up a hencoop or anything like that, you know; and it quite touched our hearts when he suggested bringing his fowls along with him to 'Bryntyrion.' There's nothing like having a hobby, Agatha said; and it would be such a change to have new-laid eggs for breakfast!"

Miss Susan sighed. Once more the tears came into her eyes. She dabbed them with her handkerchief.

"So I gather," said Malcolm encouragingly, "that this man Peters wasn't exactly a success?"

Miss Susan shook her head. "I must try," she said, "not to do him any injustice. In a sense, you see, I was responsible for him coming to us, although it was actually Agatha who chose him. At first, I must say, I thought he was marvelous. To begin with, even for such a fine man, he's exceptionally strong. All the work of moving the furniture—he made it seem just like child's play. Then again, having been brought up in the country, he knew far more than we did about farming and that sort of thing. And it was a relief, I can't deny it, to hear him whistling and singing about the place, even though the words he sang were sometimes excessively vulgar. He knew just how a house should be run, and 'bossed up' the other servants, as he used to call it. Indeed, I don't know what we should ever have done without him. As I've told you already, there was something superior about him that singled him out from the ordinary run of his class. You couldn't help thinking of him more as a bailiff than as a butler. He dealt with the tenants, collected the rents, and kept his accounts so exactly and in the most beautiful copperplate handwriting."

"Ah, now I begin to see," said Malcolm sympathetically.

"Oh, no, you don't," Miss Susan hurriedly interrupted him. "As far as money is concerned, Mr. Peters is the soul of honor. It was because of that—his reliability, I mean—that we became so dependent on him, and passed over little things that otherwise we might have objected to."

"You mean he became too familiar?"

"Well, so I thought at the time. . . ." She hesitated. "What I noticed first of all was that he seemed to have taken a dislike to me personally. I used to hear him saying terrible things about me behind my back. The other servants must have heard."

"Of course you told your sister?"

"Of course. Up till then we had always shared our confidence. It came as a great shock to me"—her lips trembled—"when Agatha appeared to be taking his side against me. So unlike her . . . and so humiliating!"

"So that's it!" Malcolm thought: "Persecution mania. Poor old thing!"

"But it's no good arguing with Agatha," Miss Susan went on pitifully, "she's so strong-minded. I felt—oh, so terribly isolated: Mr. Peters and Agatha on one side and me on the other! Do you know, if I'd had a penny of my own at that time, I really believe I should have left 'Bryntyrion.' But I hadn't even expectations. Of course, later on," she continued mysteriously, "I understood just what it meant . . ."

"Which was . . . ?"

"Let me tell you in my own way. Last autumn, you see, we both of us had influenza. I took it lightly—I'm very much stronger than I look—but Agatha was left with a sort of bronchitis. It always rains here, you know. That makes the house damp, and we hadn't enough money to repair it. Well, one night I woke up and thought I heard Agatha talking. I wondered if she were wandering—delirious, you know—so I lit a candle and put on my slippers and went out on to the landing; and I saw—oh, I hardly like to tell you! . . ." She put her hands to her eyes —"I saw Mr. Peters coming out of Agatha's room.

"That night I didn't sleep a wink, as you can imagine. Next morning, to my surprise, Agatha got up for breakfast. I felt so ashamed that I couldn't look at her. All through the meal she never spoke a word. Then, at the end of it, she got up, folded her napkin, and said, most terribly calmly: 'Susan, I have some news for you: I'm going to marry Mr. Peters.' "

"So she isn't mad after all," Henry Malcolm thought with relief. "Well, what did you say to that?" he asked encouragingly.

"Why, of course, I protested; I said it was quite impossible. I asked her what dear father, who was so exclusive, would have thought of a union of that kind; and that set poor Agatha off in a terrible rage: she said that she wasn't going to stand there and see her fiancé insulted. Outside of her presence, she said, I could say what I liked about Mr. Peters; but anyway he was a *Man*. Then Mr. Peters himself came in, and I had to stop."

"And she carried it through?"

"They were married three weeks later. Since that moment, Dr. Malcolm, my life has been one long agony. I can't even attempt to describe it. You see, poor Agatha lost her head completely; he could do no wrong; and Peters, who'd been bad enough before, became quite unbearable. All his beautiful manners—which, really, had been unexceptionable—were thrown to the wind. He went on with the housework, cleaning the silver and things like that; but when he sat down to table with us he was quite disgusting. He ate like a wolf, and when he had indigestion he made no attempt to conceal it. Indeed, he used to wink at me as though he took pride in it. And Agatha—poor dear Agatha— seemed quite blind to his disgusting coarseness. He ordered her about like a slave, and she'd only smile as if she thought it was a privilege. Why, would you believe it? She didn't even protest when he brought a big brass spittoon into the drawing-room! Although I always carefully called him Mr. Peters, he insisted on calling me 'Sue.' And he called her 'Aggie'—such a vulgar abbreviation! It got so much on my nerves—his vulgarity and the way in which Agatha seemed to delight in it—that I couldn't bear sitting with them. I used to go up to my bedroom and freeze there: you see, Mr. Peters wouldn't allow us to have fires upstairs. 'Coal costs money,' he said, 'and if you think I'm going to chop wood for you, you're damn well mistaken!' You must excuse the word, Dr. Malcolm, but that's what he said and that's nothing, *nothing* to the language he generally uses!"

"Well, people of that kind, you know . . ." Henry Malcolm began.

"Oh, of course; I know only too well; it's unbelievable. But where was I? Oh yes. The fires . . . that was part of his plan. Apart from his food—he's excessively particular about that—he thinks about nothing but money. He's so mean. You can have no idea of his meanness. In the very first week after the marriage he dismissed our maids. He said it was ridiculous to have two able-bodied women (he never calls us ladies) in the house just eating their heads off. So Agatha, if you please, just had to do the cooking and me the housework, and if anything isn't just to his liking, you should hear the language. You've only to look at my hands, Dr. Malcolm, to see what that means!"

And she held out her pitiful, toil-stained delicate fingers.

"So now that poor Agatha's ill in bed," she went on pathetically, "the whole of it falls on me. I'm no better than a slave, Dr. Malcolm; yet what can I do? I ask you, what can I do?" She wrung her hands helplessly. "It's not *that* I mind," she said, "it's just Agatha's illness. In spite of all her cruelty, she's still my sister, and I simply can't bear to see her wasting away like this!" Miss Susan composed her working features rapidly. "That's why," she went on, "I've slipped away without telling them, and dared to ask you, as an old friend of father's to come and see her. Will you come?" she entreated.

"Why, of course, I'll be glad to consult with your local doctor," Malcolm told her. "What does *he* say about her?"

She shook her head. "They won't even allow me to call him in. You see, Dr. Meredith, our nearest doctor, lives ten miles away. His visits would be expensive, and Mr. Peters has persuaded Agatha that we can't afford them. He's had some experience of nursing, he says—I think he was an attendant in an asylum at one time—and really, to do the man justice, he *is* most attentive. He prepares all her food, and washes her, and makes her bed. Agatha herself is quite satisfied; she thinks he's wonderful; but, after all, Dr. Malcolm, Peters is an ignorant man, and if you *would* be so kind . . ."

"Of course I'll come," Malcolm told her. "I'll walk up to 'Bryntyrion' this afternoon. You'd better warn them."

"Oh, I don't think I dare do that," said Miss Susan tremulously. He watched her, a poor little shrunken figure, as she went fluttering away.

The road to "Bryntyrion" ran upward through lanes so deep and suffocating, between banks of over-arching hazel and insurgent bracken, that Malcolm was only aware at intervals of the line of mountain which dominated the sky like a hanging thunder-cloud. The air was all dead and dense, the blank sky so white with heat, the torment of wood-flies so incessant, that it was with a sense of relief that he emerged on to a higher plateau, a shelf upon the mountain's flank, and saw before him the gloomy mass of stucco that the older Miss Morgan had inherited. It was a tall house, whose rectangular building had a low-pitched roof; an ugly, eerie-looking place, whose blank, uncurtained windows gave an impression of deadness and desolation. He approached it through an unkempt avenue of wind-tortured beeches that led to a sweep of moss-grown gravel skirting a pillared portico from which the plaster had fallen in flakes that gave it an aspect of disease. It was hard to imagine that any living soul inhabited it. The bell, which Malcolm rang, seemed to echo in utter emptiness.

For a long while his summons remained unanswered; then heavy hobnails rang on the stone flags, and the warped door was pulled open with a screech. The man who opened it and glowered at him with grudging, suspicious eyes, was obviously Mr. Peters.

From that first glance Malcolm took a dislike to him. He was, as Miss Susan had indicated, by certain standards, a fine figure of a man; six feet of bulky masculinity. But the eyes of the physician saw more than that. They saw the body of a strong man who had gone soft with idleness and indulgence; an unruly paunch; pouched eyes; cheeks above whose lax muscles a fine network of congested blood-vessels showed a ruddiness that was not that of health. It was the body of a man who slept too much, ate too much, drank too much. The small eyes, set like a pig's in shallow orbits, were suffused with angry red at the inner corners. They were full of resentment, obstinacy; prepared to bluff. And yet, behind all their suspicion, fear was lurking. "This man is a coward," Malcolm thought. "I have his measure."

"Well, what do you want?" Mr. Peters asked him gruffly. He stood in the doorway, blocking it with his bulk. He was not inviting.

"You are Mr. Peters?" Malcolm asked.

"Yes. That's my name. What is it?"

"I have come to call on your wife. My name is Malcolm. I knew her when she was Miss Morgan."

"You can't see her," said Peters stolidly. "She's ill in bed."

"I'm sorry to hear that," said Malcolm blandly. "However, I'm glad I came. You see, I'm a doctor."

"A doctor?" Peters repeated. ("Yes, he's afraid," Malcolm thought.) "That makes no difference," the man went on. "It's nothing serious. I'm a bit of a nurse myself," he continued, with a smile that was not meant to be ugly. "What's more, Mrs. Peters has a great dislike to doctors. She refuses to see one, though I've pressed her again and again. Besides, she's asleep just now, and that's what she needs. I'm not going to wake her for you or anyone!" he added obstinately.

"Don't you think it's a pity to miss this opportunity?" Malcolm urged. "You see, I'm a very old friend of the family's: I knew her father, Colonel Morgan. I'm leaving the district to-morrow, and I think both she and Miss Susan would be disappointed if I missed seeing them."

"I don't know where Susan is," Peters answered. "And as for my wife, I've told you I'm not going to wake her."

"And I tell you I'm going to see her," said Malcolm firmly.

"Look here, I'd have you know this is my house," Peters blustered.

"It is not your house . . . not yet. And I'm going to see her."

The gross man went red in the face. His shoulders went back. It looked, for one moment, as if he intended violence. Then his pig-eyelids fluttered, his protruded lips relaxed into an uneasy smile; his truculence vanished; he became, in one moment, that mixture of dignity and obsequiousness which is the well-trained manservant. With the manners of a perfect butler he bowed and stood aside for Malcolm to enter.

"Perhaps you are right, sir," he said. "It's not very often Mrs. Peters has the chance of seeing old friends. And to tell you the truth," he admitted, "I *am* a bit worried about her. Will you be so good as to wait here a minute?"

He showed Malcolm into a dank drawing-room, in which, among the relics of the Colonel's house, he recognized traces of Mr. Peters' occupation: the big brass spittoon, of which Miss Susan had told him; an odor of stale shag tobacco; a copy of the *Police Budget,* and a barrel of beer supported on an eighteenth-century love-seat. Within a few moments Peters lumbered in again.

"She's awake," he said, "and says she'll be pleased to see you. Only, if you'll take my advice, as one who knows her in and out, you'll be wise not to mention her illness. It only upsets her. All the same, I should take it as a great kindness on your part," he added, "if you'd just run your eye over her as a doctor, like, and give me any hints that come into your mind when you're alone with me afterwards. I don't say there's anything to worry about, but you never know. . . ."

"No, you never know," Malcolm agreed. "Perhaps it would be just as well if you told me her symptoms beforehand?"

"Well, you see," Mr. Peters confided, "it's this indigestion. It's been troubling her for months. It's what I should call the acidity. She can't peck no more than a bird; and, of course, that means she's lost flesh. Seeing the way she was, I've taken no risks. A milk diet, just slops, nothing solid to bring on the pain. And no morsel of food has passed her lips, sir, that I haven't prepared with my own hands. Then she's had some trouble with her nerves as well; but I think that's just the result of lying in bed. One thing I will say, though, I couldn't have paid her more attention if she'd been my own child. And she'll tell you the same."

"Well, she *is* your own wife, isn't she?" Malcolm suggested.

Mr. Peters preceded him upstairs; through their creaking progress Malcolm became more than ever oppressed by "Bryntyrion's" dank emptiness. He wondered wherever that poor little Miss Susan had got to; he pictured her trembling in her bedroom, aware of his presence. Mr. Peters, with admirable decorum, knocked at the door. They entered.

"Here's Dr. Malcolm, love," said Peters kindly.

"It's very good of him, I'm sure," a feeble voice answered.

Even Malcolm, who was used to such sights, was shocked by the woman's appearance. Instead of the Miss Agatha he remembered, a strong, dark creature with a certain grim hardness about her firm, handsome features, he saw a frail wisp of a woman with scanty gray hair, yellow and wasted. He took a seat at her bedside and pressed her thin hand. She gave a little gasp: "Oh, you hurt me!" she said. "My fingers are so tender I can scarcely bear any one to touch them. Edward"—she beamed wanly on her husband—"is always very gentle with me. I'm so glad you have met him."

Malcolm was curiously touched by the humble gratitude of the glance which she gave Mr. Peters. Her eyes dwelt on him tenderly; it was obvious that she wanted the visitor to see the best of him. If ever he had seen love, blind devotion in a woman's eyes, Malcolm thought, he could see it in those. And Peters himself seemed different, gentle, solicitous. He wondered if, after all, he had done the man an injustice. But that tenderness in the fingers . . . ? His medical mind was at work.

All through their talk, which was of old times, his boyhood, the Colonel, his mind kept on working, his eyes were never at rest. Miss

Agatha, as he still thought of her, went on talking with a gentle dreaminess, eagerly contriving to draw Mr. Peters into their conversation, displaying his unapparent virtues with the care of a mother showing off an uncomely child. Only when he happened to mention Miss Susan's name did her voice, her features, harden.

"I hardly like to tell you," she said, "but Susan has not behaved well. She objected to our marriage. You can see for yourself how unreasonably," she added, with a loving glance at Mr. Peters. Mr. Peters, embarrassed, smiled and cleared his throat.

That tenderness of the fingers . . . that history of dyspepsia . . . that queer pigmentation of the skin. . . .

Tactfully, almost without letting her know it, Malcolm diverted the conversation in the direction of Miss Agatha's illness. "She doesn't like to talk about it," Peters protested. "It always upsets her."

"Still, it does seem like missing an opportunity when the doctor's here," Miss Agatha replied.

Yes, for a long time she had been suffering from indigestion; she'd always had that tendency, but lately it had become much worse. Indeed, she couldn't imagine what she would have done without Edward. In times of sickness Susan was absolutely useless. But Edward—would he believe it?—was a perfect invalid cook. Such delicious, light, appetizing food he prepared for her. And all with his own hands! If she'd had a trained nurse in the house she couldn't have been more comfortable. Apart from the indigestion there wasn't much wrong with her—nothing except that queer tenderness which had made her jump when they shook hands. Oh, no, it wasn't only in the fingers, it was in the arms as well. And in her legs, too; she could scarcely bear the touch of the bedclothes. And an odd tingling and numbness—as if they had gone to sleep! But that wasn't anything serious, really, was it?

"If you'd let me examine you for a moment," Malcolm suggested, "I'll try to be just as gentle with you as your husband."

"I'm not going to have you upset, love," said Peters, with a flash of the old stubbornness.

"I'd like him to, Edward darling," his wife entreated. By this time, whether she liked it or no, Malcolm meant to have his way. A perfunctory examination was enough to confirm his conjectures. The case was quite simple—a general peripheral neuritis. Three causes—three only, for alcohol was out of question. Lead, antimony, chronic arsenical poisoning. How . . . why? The answer to both of these questions seemed fairly obvious.

"It isn't serious?" Miss Agatha was saying. "It will be a great comfort to my dear husband if you can tell him that."

Malcolm smiled. "It's not serious at all. If you follow my instructions religiously you'll be well in a month. I'm ready to promise you that, if you do what I tell you."

"You may be sure we'll do that," said Peters, with humble gratitude. "I'm sure we're much obliged to you. This is a great relief."

"I'll talk to you downstairs. There's no point in tiring her further," said Malcolm.

Mr. Peters had spoken truly when he said that the verdict was a great relief. He seemed almost boyish and excited as he led Malcolm into the drawing-room and offered him a glass of beer.

"You've taken a great weight off my mind, doctor," he said. "Now what shall we do? I'll drive into town this evening and fetch out the medicine."

He spoke boisterously, confidently; the fear had gone out of his eyes; he was the perfect picture of a relieved, a devoted husband.

Malcolm chose his words carefully:

"Mr. Peters, I've said that this case is not serious. Well, it isn't—it won't be—if you obey my prescription to the letter. The person I'm most concerned about is not your wife but yourself."

"Why, doctor, you're wrong. I was never better in my life."

"Ah, there you're mistaken, my friend. As a doctor I know better. I'm being quite candid when I tell you that your life is in danger. Wait a moment—let me go on. All this long anxiety, all this watching at your wife's bedside, all this delicate invalid cookery—unless we do something about it I won't answer for the consequences. Your obvious anxiety has been getting on the poor woman's nerves. You play on each other. You're having a bad effect on her. This isn't a matter of medicine, it's plain common sense. Now listen to me. There's no time to be lost. You must leave 'Bryntyrion' this evening. Go right away from here!"

"But, doctor!" Mr. Peters was pale as a sheet, his thick lips quivered.

"No doubt she will miss you," Malcolm continued smoothly. "But it's you who have to be considered, Mr. Peters. You leave 'Bryntyrion' this evening. If you don't come back I guarantee she'll be better in a month. Miss Susan will have to take up the invalid cookery; she's perfectly capable of doing so, don't you worry. Now remember," he went on sternly, "you are going away this evening. I advise you not to tell anyone when or where. If you don't come back—well, that will be even better for you. If you *do* come back, I shall know. Be quite sure of that! So I warn you, here and now, it's a matter of life and death. Understand?"

From the blanched terror in Peters's eyes Malcolm knew that he understood.

He left "Bryntyrion," that ghastly house, without another word. Midway on his journey homeward a frail black figure fluttered out of the hedge. It was little Miss Susan, who had run down the hill to intercept him.

"You've seen him . . . and her?" she gasped. "Oh, is it all right?"

"It's all right, Miss Susan," he told her. "You'll have to get busy. Your brother-in-law is going on a holiday."

"A holiday? Where?" she stammered.

"I haven't the least idea where. But he's going. That's all that matters. I want you to promise me one thing," he went on calmly. "I am returning to London to-morrow by the first train; I shan't see you again. Now if Mr. Peters has not left 'Bryntyrion' by then, or if he comes back—which I don't think he will—or if anything happens that you think I'd like to know—and I want to know everything—will you promise to send me a wire to my house in Harley Street? Number forty-seven. Be sure you remember."

"Yes, yes, I'll remember," she said eagerly. "But Agatha, doctor . . . ?"

"I promise you that Agatha will be as well as you are in a month."

"Oh, how can I thank you?" she cried.

"You needn't thank me," he laughed. "But don't forget what I've told you. Now run along home to your sister; she may be needing you."

Next evening, when Malcolm opened the door of his house in Harley Street, he found a telegram awaiting him in the hall. Although he guessed what was inside it he opened it eagerly.

"*Terrible accident,*" he read, "*Peters shot dead accidentally this evening while cleaning gun. Susan Morgan.*".

With a smile of satisfaction on his face he tore the telegram into fragments. The last day of his holiday, he reflected, had been the most profitable of all.

64

A Sleeping Draft

BY WESTON MARTYR

THE SHIP was pushing steadily through the solid blackness of a night as stifling and oppressive as only a night in the doldrums can be. It was time for me to turn in; but I stood in my pyjamas outside my cabin door and eyed the oven-like interior with loathing. Its steel walls blazed raw-white in the glare of the unshaded electrics, and I knew the engine-room bulkhead beside my bunk was hot enough to burn the naked hand. A multitude of fat but active cockroaches disported joyously in this salubrious environment; and a sour nauseating whiff from the gaping mouth of a hold ventilator bore witness that our cargo of sugar was heating. These things caused me to think regretfully of that clean and spacious liner's stateroom, with its whirring fans, the booking of which I had abandoned so recklessly at the bidding of my friend, the master of this unclean and ancient tramp. Across a gap of years we two had met again on the steps of the shipping office at Port Louis, and, after explanations, he had suddenly slapped me on the back and cried, "What! going Home in a gilded steam-hotel? Why, *we're* sailing for London River the first thing in the morning. Now, why not come with me?" He assured me that I should thereby see life, save money, and be some one for him to talk to; and I had accordingly saved my money, and was now seeing life—as it is lived aboard a strictly utilitarian and economical tramp upon the high seas. I was finding it a life chock-full of interest—and discomfort.

There were compensations, though. For instance, "Passengers are not allowed on this deck" is a notice which bars one from the most desirable portions of any passenger ship; but this *S.S. Wisby Hall* was mine own, all of her, to do as I liked with. So I turned from that distressful cabin and climbed the ladder to the lower bridge in search of a draft of air. A cane chair creaked, and out of the darkness came the Skipper's voice.

"Ah!" he said, "I can't sleep either. I think this is the coolest spot in the ship; but, if you want to get clear of the smell, the crow's-nest is the place."

"I'll never touch sugar again as long as I live," I grumbled. "It's making me feel sick, and I can't sleep. I only wish I'd known the ship was going to smell like this before I joined her. You ought to have told me, and then I shouldn't have come."

"Yes, it's pretty bad now it's started to sweat," said the Skipper. "It's a nasty cargo to live with is sugar—but I've known worse."

"I don't believe it," said I; and I fear the ill-humor caused by my bodily discomforts showed a little in my voice.

"Oh! You get used to sugar in time and don't notice it," said my host soothingly. "There are worse cargoes—dye wood, for instance. I loaded a cargo of logs once at Puerto Caballos, and they fairly crawled with scorpions and spiders—not to mention snakes. You'd find 'em in your bunk. It was nasty. But even that lot was better than a live cargo."

"Logwood sounds lively enough for me. But what do you mean by a live cargo. Cattle?"

"Well, cattle are bad, too. So are sheep. The smell from them's so bad sometimes it almost blinds you. Really blinds you, I mean. It's the ammonia in their droppings, I think."

"Lord!" said I, "I'm beginning to feel glad we've only got sugar aboard."

"Yes. But I wasn't thinking of cattle," went on the Skipper. "It's human cargoes I don't like. Passengers are bad enough, and I wouldn't command a liner for any money. But it's a cargo of coolies we once had aboard this ship that I'm talking about. Chinese they were—eight hundred of 'em—and they were the limit."

The Skipper paused for a little, and presently he surprised me by sighing profoundly in the darkness. I held my peace, and waited. But nothing happened, so I became diplomatic. "They must have been bad," said I, "if the thought of them makes you feel like that still."

"Bad!" said the Skipper, as if the adjective hurt him. "Bad. Why, they were, without a doubt, the very toughest gang of roughs on record. If you sweep up the scrapings from the jails of all China, it stands to reason you are going to get a precious collection of bad eggs. And if, on top of that, you go to work and sort out the worst specimens from your collection, you can then be certain you have achieved a most notable concentration of thugs. Well—that's how my cargo of devils was raked up."

"But how—it doesn't seem reasonable," I exclaimed.

"Maybe not; but it happened anyhow," said the Skipper. "Very reasonably and simply, too, if it comes to that. You see, the gold mines on the Rand ran short of labor, because the simple Kaffir is a wise man; and he won't work unless he has to. He'd work until he'd earned enough to buy a wife to work for him, and then he retired smiling. The mine owners were silly enough to offer higher wages, thinking they'd attract more labor that way, I suppose; but the result was, of course, that the unmarried boys came in and earned their wife-money in less time than ever, and then *they* retired happy. After that the mines were in the cart—until somebody thought of recruiting labor in China. They went to the Chinese authorities for permission to recruit, and, you can believe me, the authorities were delighted. You know what the beggars are. They jumped at the chance. 'Yes,' they said, 'You bet. And, what's more, *we* will supply the men. You send your ships and we'll fill 'em up with coolies'—at so many dollars a head. You note the graft? The result was that, when the ships turned up, they just emptied their jails into them, thus getting rid of their criminals, saving the expense of their keep, and making an honest penny or so for themselves at one sweep. You can't beat a Chinaman at that sort of game. Well, that's how the dregs of China came to be dumped into the Transvaal. I've heard they were fine workers, though. They'd drill two holes in a shift against a Kaffir's one, and the mine people were mighty pleased with 'em. They'd escape from their compounds every now and again, of course, and then there'd be murder, robbery, and rape round and about Johannesburg for a bit. I have heard, too, that it paid to be popular with 'em if you worked below ground, on account of a playful habit they had of signaling 'Man coming' on the engine-room bell, and then sending up your severed head in the skip. They were tough, all right, but they did put their backs into their jobs, and the miners were mighty sorry when they had to send them all back again.

"You remember that Chinese slavery fuss in the Home papers? I never quite got the true hang of it myself; but it seemed to me the mine people were happy, and so were the coolies. Apparently the Home politicians weren't, though; so those coolies had to be shipped back again. Some of them didn't want to go at all, and they made trouble. They were mostly men who knew they'd be shot into prison the moment they landed in China, so you can't very well blame them for kicking. And I must say I don't blame the Chinese authorities either for wanting to make sure of those birds as soon as they arrived, for they weren't the kind of lads any authorities, even Chinese ones, would care to have loose about the country. The Peking Government didn't want 'em back at any price, and I believe they said so officially. In any case, what with one thing and another, the worst bunch of the lot, about eight hundred of 'em, were kept back till the last ship-load; and then, my luck being out as usual, this ship was chartered to load that unholy gang at Durban and take them to Ching-Wan-Tau. That's how I got the most infernal mob of toughs on record loaded on to me. I told you that at first, and you didn't believe it; but, as I said, the explanation's simple."

"I see," said I. "They must have been a handful. Did you have much trouble?"

"I did," replied the Skipper. "And I didn't have long to wait for it either. In fact, it started the moment the charterers took over the ship at Durban. They had to fit her up, of course, and they played Old Harry with her. Will you believe it, they actually pierced the 'tween-deck plating in twenty-six different places—for latrine pipes! The terms of the charter-party allowed them to do pretty well as they liked with the ship, you see, and left me powerless to stop 'em. They fitted the after 'tween-decks solid with wooden bunks, and ran up four tiers of berths in Numbers Three and Four lower holds. They even built a hospital on top of the wheel-house aft; but, except for fixing a row of rice cookers the size of young donkey-boilers along both sides of Number Two hatch, they left the fore end of the ship alone. Then they filled the main hold with stores, and put the ship down six inches by the head, and I went to the Agent and protested. I raised Cain. I said they'd made the ship unseaworthy, and the beggar just laughed at me. He said that six inches out of trim wouldn't hurt, and, anyhow, I'd have to lump it, because the fore part of the ship had to be kept absolutely clear of all coolies. 'If we were to give 'em a free run of the deck,' says he, 'it wouldn't be long before they'd take charge of the ship. You'd find them roosting in your bunk, Captain, and they'd certainly make trouble with your Lascar crew. They're dangerous men,' says he. 'They aren't safe, and that's a fact. And that's the reason we mean to make the after end of your ship a sort of prison for 'em. We're going to fit an eight-foot iron grill right across your deck amidships, and if you take my advice you won't let any of them get forward of it once you're out at sea.' Then he finished off by telling me that, instead of making difficulties, I ought to be grateful to the charterers for thinking of my safety and comfort—so I got the worse of it. That was the first time I'd heard I was going to ship a dangerous cargo, and I remember I went straight out of that office and did something I'd never done in all my life before. I went and bought a revolver.

"When I got back aboard I had another surprise. I found the charterers had appointed a man to take charge of my cargo for me! That's just what it amounted to, and you can bet I didn't like it. And I knew, as soon as I saw the fellow they'd put in charge, that I couldn't like him either. He was the sort of man I haven't got any use for. Finch was his name. A great big bucko of a man, whose only qualification for the job, as far as I could see, was that he could talk Chinese. He seemed to think at first, too, he was going to run the ship, and I had to show him right away there was only one master aboard her—and that was me. He'd brought a dozen or so assorted Chinks along with him—cooks and 'orderlies' he called 'em,—and he comes along worrying me about where he was to stow them. So I told him to run away and ask the Mate, and I could see by the look he gave me that I'd surprised him.

"Next morning our cargo arrived alongside—a train-load full; and it took Finch all day to get those coolies aboard. It seems he wasn't taking any chances. He made the shore people march the beggars up our gang-way one by one, and as each man reached the deck, Finch and his boys went through him. They did the job properly, too. They stripped every one down pretty well naked, and searched 'em and looked through their bundles of duds and things. I could see those Chinks didn't like it a bit; and whenever Finch came across a knife or a bit of opium or something, they'd give him some mighty dirty looks. Not that Finch cared, bless you. He stood there looking as fierce and tough as he knew how, and every now and again he'd touch up any boy that showed signs of jib-bing with his sjambok. And a sjambok's a nasty thing to get hit with. It's a strip of dried rhino hide, and a smack with one on the bare skin will draw blood quick if you aren't careful. And Finch wasn't careful at all. I didn't like it; but that wasn't the time or the place to interfere—so I waited.

"The last man in the procession came up handcuffed between two Kaffir policemen. He was a big man, but he didn't look particularly dangerous to me. In fact, he had rather a fine-looking figure-head on him—sort of quiet and sad and gentle. But Finch gets into a great state about the beggar, and he comes bawling to me wanting to know where he is going to stow him. 'The swine's dangerous,' says he. 'He's mur-dered three men down the Rhineveldt Deep, and the only reason his neck isn't stretched for it is because they badly wanted him for some other devilment in Tientsin. He'll get *his* all right,' says he, 'when they get him ashore at the other end; but what I want to know is, what'll I do with him now?' 'Oh, put him in your bunk,' says I, 'and good luck to him.' And with that I laughed, and went up on the bridge and got the ship under way."

"You don't seem to have liked that man much," said I. "What did he do with his murderer eventually?"

"Oh, shackled him to a stanchion down Number One hold," went on the Skipper. "It was the Mate's idea, and the man was nice and snug down there, and well out of the way of everybody. And as for not liking Finch—well, he wasn't my style; but he had his points, and I have to ad-mit it. I had him up to my cabin the first night out, and went for him about the way he was manhandling the coolies. It was my idea to go easy with them and leave 'em alone and not stir up trouble, and I said so. I told him to take a close reef in that sjambok of his, or one night, as likely as not, he'd be getting his throat cut, to say nothing of the throats of the rest of us white men aboard. I gave him beans, I tell you.

"And then, when I'd quite done, *he* started. He told me some things that surprised me and made me feel mighty thoughtful. He said he mightn't know much about ships, but he did know how to handle coolies, and that if I thought we would ever get to Ching-Wan-Tau unless he put the fear of death into those Chinks and kept it there, then I was an old fool. Yes. That man sat there in my cabin and called me an old fool! And I sat and listened to him. I had to, for, you see, he was speaking the cold truth—and it frightened me. I knew we had a bad crowd aboard all right, and that if they wanted to scupper us they wouldn't have much trouble doing it; but I hadn't worried much, because I never seriously thought they'd *want* to scupper us. But according to Finch, that was just what they were almost sure to do. Says he, 'There's over eight hundred of 'em, and they're all bad; but there's one gang a darned sight worse than the rest. They're all due for the clink as soon as they get ashore; but some of them are due for more than that. They won't live long once their police get hold of them—and they know it. And if you were in their place, what would *you* do? Why, you'd get hold of the ship and run her in somewhere handy along the China coast and clear out. It stands to reason; and it's my firm belief that's what they'll try to do. And as for getting hold of this ship—it's easy. What does the crew amount to? There's you and me and your three Mates and the four engineers. That's only nine of us whites all told, not counting the Doc., who's a half-caste Macao Portuguese, as far as I can make out, and not to be relied on. And you know better than I do what your Lascar crew is worth; but I bet, if it comes to a scrap, that they'll lie low and try and save their skins—and I don't blame 'em.'

"Well, that was bad enough; but as soon as he had got me pretty near frightened to death with talk like that he started off again on a fresh tack. 'Now, here's another thing,' says he. 'These birds don't get paid their wages till they get to Ching-Wan-Tau. *That* was a little scheme arranged by our Repatriation people. When I was wangling this job out of them in Pretoria they tried to tell me this bally scheme of theirs was a better insurance against trouble aboard the ship than the armed guard I was asking for. According to them, the coolies were all going to be good boys, because they knew if they weren't they wouldn't draw their pay. That's why we haven't got a guard. Can you beat it? The Chink authorities jumped at the idea, of course. They get the handling of the cash that way, and a fat lot of it our coolies are likely to see. The trouble is, the beggars know it. They know they haven't a hope of ever touching a bean of their money. And d'you think that's going to make nice boys of 'em? You bet it isn't. Why, they're ripe for trouble. And the worst of it is that making trouble's worth while for some of them. Knowing what they know, each man must have drawn an advance before they left Jo'burg. Wanted to make sure of getting something, I guess. Anyway, when I was searching them I found nearly every man jack had from five to ten pounds stowed away on him. It doesn't sound much; but it means there's from six to eight thousand pounds loose aboard this ship; and what's more, it's all in round, yellow, golden sovereigns. Now, Cap., you can believe me or not, just as you like; but I know we've got men aboard here who'd cut every throat in the ship rather than let a sum like that get away from them. And yet you sit there and tell me to go slow and treat the beggars easy. Why, if I don't show 'em, right from the start, that I'm top dog, and mean to stay there, then you and I and the rest of us white men would be wise to step over the side now. We'd be a darned sight more comfortable there than if we stayed aboard.'

"Yes, that's just about the way that man talked to me. I was scared. And when I had more time to think about things I was more scared than ever. You say you can't sleep because of the smell of this sugar. Well, I tell you, with that cargo aboard, I *daren't* sleep! What worried me most was that I couldn't do anything about it. I knew, against that crowd of Chinamen, we nine whites were helpless. They could have knocked us on the head and thrown us all overboard any night they liked. That grill amidships the charterers were so proud about was really as much use as nothing, because it didn't prevent any one from climbing over the engine-room casing and dropping down on us from the top of the fiddley. Then the Indian Ocean's a lonely place. Ships didn't carry wireless then, remember, and there was no port I could run into. Even if there had been I didn't see what excuse I could give for calling in anywhere. It's a serious thing for a master to deviate out of his proper voyage. It means expense to the owners, waste of time and bunkers, with the insurance on the ship invalidated, and the Lord knows what else. You've got to have some mighty good reasons before you dare deviate—and what reasons could I give? I should have looked pretty blowing in somewhere, and saying I'd come because I was scared of what my cargo might get up to. No, I could see I'd got to get the ship to Ching-Wan-Tau or nowhere. You see, I was in a nasty fix—and no way out of it.

"For the first week things kept more or less quiet. There was a lot of grousing about the chow, of course, and a scrap or so at night in the 'tween-decks; but nothing much happened to amount to anything until two coolies died of beri-beri, and there was a riot because we dumped them over the side. It seems their friends wanted to keep 'em and bury them in China; but we couldn't keep any corpses aboard, of course, and Finch had to climb up on the after-hatch and tell 'em so. Things looked nasty for a bit, but when they burst out laughing at something he'd said, I knew Finch had managed to fix 'em. He told me afterwards what the joke was. 'I told 'em,' he says, 'we didn't feel like keeping any corpses about the place this hot weather, but the next man that died, his friends could have him—and welcome. And then I offered to bet ten dollars Mex. to a ticoy *they* wouldn't keep him for more than three days. They saw the sense of the thing then, and that settled it.' Finch said he didn't mind that kind of trouble, and how it was simple enough to settle just ordinary foolishness like that with nothing ugly behind it.

" 'What worries me,' he says, 'is this small knife outfit the beggars have started. How they smuggled the knives through beats me, especially when I think of the way I went through 'em as they came aboard. I could have sworn there wasn't a weapon of any sort on the lot, and now here's these damned small knives turned up. I don't know how many there are yet, or who's got them; but I reckon there's maybe a dozen or twenty coolies aboard each with a knife on him. And, Cap., these are the birds we've got to look out for. They'll get together; and, in fact, as far as I can make out, they've formed themselves into a sort of a gang already. It's in the nature of a Chinaman to do that sort of thing. A secret society's a regular institution with 'em, and a secret society's just what these swine with the knives have formed. It's secret all right, because I'll be hung if I can find out who's in it; but what they call themselves—to give you the English of it—is "Small Knife Society." I've managed to find that much out, anyway. I was anxious enough about this trip of ours right from the start; but now this thing's happened— well, I'm scared, and I'll admit it. It's all very well to say they've only got little pocket-knives, which is the only kind of a knife they could have hidden; but the point is, they *are* armed. "In the country of the blind the one-eyed man is boss," so twenty men with knives on 'em and working together are going to run the rest of this bunch. They'll run them like sheep. They'll run them and they'll rob them; and if anybody objects they'll cut him up in small bits. I know these birds, Cap. I've worked with Chinese most of my life, and I can see what's going to happen as plain as if I was sitting in a movie, with the picture running in front of my eyes and the man in the corner explaining it all through a megaphone. You mark what I say! Before we get to Ching-Wan-Tau the men who've got the knives will be the men who've got hold of most of the money too. They know, as well as we do, the minute this ship arrives she's going to be filled with police. Chinese police. And who'll collect that money then? Why, the police; and you can't tell me those Small

Knife blighters are going to wait for that. No, sir! As sure as my name's Bill Finch, they'll try to do us in and then pile this ship of ours up somewhere handy, and clear out with what they've got. That is, they will if I can't stop 'em. I don't know if I can; but I'm going to have a shot at it.'

"It was about then that I began to think a lot more of Finch than I did when I first saw him. I think, if he hadn't been rash, he might perhaps have managed to settle the trouble. But he was rash. His notion was to jump right into the middle of a mess and try and clean it up that way, instead of skirmishing about a bit, like a wise man, and then putting his smack in where it was likely to do the most good. One morning he didn't show up at breakfast. He didn't turn up at all, although I turned the ship inside out looking for him. He just vanished."

"Good Lord!" said I. "What do you mean? What happened?"

"I don't know," went on the Skipper. "But I can guess. He must have made too much of a nuisance of himself for those Small Knife people, and I suppose they just laid for him one night when he was going his rounds, and then slipped him over the side. I should think that was about what happened. However, there he was—gone; and it seemed to me at first that it put the lid on things properly. The job was up to me then—and I couldn't see how I was going to tackle it. The worse of it was, Finch was the only man in the ship who could talk Chinese, and I couldn't find one coolie out of the lot who understood English. So there we were, you see, with the ship a regular powder magazine, a sleeping volcano and a tower of Babel all rolled into one, and me tongue-tied and pretty well helpless.

"And I tell you, with Finch gone and out of the way, things didn't take long to warm up. The daytime wasn't so bad: just that crowd of yellow beggars squatting all over the after-deck and chattering a language that didn't sound human. I'd go and take a look at them through the bars of that grill, and I'd say to myself, 'There they are, my son. Just ordinary John Chinamen, taking it easy and doing nothing. No need to be scared of *them*.' And then I'd catch the glint of an eye maybe, or a sideways look from a face chock-full of evil; and I'd feel like you do when you go to the Zoo and look at the lions and tigers—specially the tigers. It was the nights, though that got on your nerves. There was hell to pay at night down those after-holds. You could hear it. I didn't know *what* was going on, you understand, because we never dared go aft in the dark at all. But you could hear things happening all night. Plenty of things, and it was awful. Those Small Knife devils were doing it all, just as Finch warned me they would. I had plain proof of it. Da Silva, our Doc., was a better man than I'd thought. He wouldn't face that hospital of his on top of the wheel-house at night; but each morning he'd go aft and attend to what would be waiting for him. And every day there'd be maybe six or a dozen poor devils, all cut about and bleeding, for him to sew up and bandage. I used to go aft too, and lend him a hand, and I noticed the wounds were all about the same—just slashes and long shallow cuts as if they'd been done with razors or small sharp knives. I don't remember that we ever had a real deep wound to deal with; but all the same we had some horrible-looking cases. And five of 'em died—from loss of blood, I guess, as there wasn't much whole skin left on any of 'em. That Small Knife lot was putting its trade-marks on the rest of the bunch all right.

"It was plain enough what they were up to: just robbing the rest, as Finch said they would, and if any one kicked or tried to make a fight of it, then they sliced him up, and Da Silva and me we'd have to fix up the results in the morning. At the rate they were working I could see it wouldn't be long before they'd have every coolie in the ship cleaned out, and then, as likely as not, it would be *our* turn. If I could only have talked the lingo I might have done something. Roused up the rest of the Chinks, perhaps, and made 'em set about those Small Knife birds. Or at least I might have found out who they were, and then we whites could have had a go at them. As it was, I was helpless; but I did what I could, of course. I got the engineers to connect up some flexible hose to the deck steampipes. We led the hoses up on the bridge, so that if steam was turned on they'd squirt straight down both bridge ladders. We reckoned to gather on the bridge if things got desperate, and give the beasts a dose of high-pressure live steam, and boil a few of them at any rate before they scuppered us.

"With all this worry and trouble on my mind I was a fine sample of a nervous wreck by the time we'd run across the Indian Ocean and raised Achin Head. One night, when we were about half-way down the Malacca Straits, I was standing up here trying to make up my mind whether or not to take the ship into Singapore—and chance getting fired for it,—when I caught sight of somebody leaning on the rail right up in the bows. It was dark, but I could make out the shape of the man against the sky, and I saw he was a Chinaman. It startled me, because the forepart of the ship wasn't a place where any coolie ought to have been. I could see the man wasn't one of the crew, for, even at night, it's easy to tell the difference between a Chinaman and a Lascar. It wasn't natural, anyhow, for any of the hands to be knocking about forward at that time of night; and you know our look-out man is stationed up in the crow's-nest and never on the fo'c'sle head. Well, things being in the state they were, I thought I'd better go forward and see what the fellow was up to. I had on my carpet slippers, so I sneaked quietly along the deck; and when I tell you I felt in my pocket to see if I had my gun on me, you'll understand the state of mind I'd got into during that last week or two.

"The chap was standing right up in the eyes of the ship, and I'd got about abreast of the windlass before he heard me. I startled him all right, and he jumped round and stared at me with his mouth open. And then it was my turn to jump. I recognized him at once. He was the bird who should have been ironed to a stanchion down Number One hold—the murderer, in fact, that Finch had made such a fuss about when he'd first come aboard. I'd clean forgotten all about him, and it gave my poor nerves an awful shock to run suddenly up against the beggar like that. I suppose I must have got rattled, because, though I don't remember pulling out my gun, I can still see myself jumping about behind the windlass like some fool in the movies and pointing my revolver in the general direction of that poor man. No wonder I scared him. He dodged about, too. Then, 'Don't shoot!' he sings out. 'It's all right. Don't shoot.' And I was so surprised at hearing English from him that I couldn't have stopped him if he'd come for me. However, he didn't show any signs of that, and when he'd got over his scare and I'd got over mine, we just stood there looking at each other and feeling sheepish—at least, I know I did. I think it struck both of us that a grown man can make a terrible ass of himself if he isn't careful.

" 'Well, John,' says I at last, 'it may be very funny and all that; but you're supposed to be a dangerous murderer, and what I want to know is how did you get on deck? And what d'you mean by talking English anyway?' He didn't speak for a bit; just hung his head and backed away to the rail and looked sulky, and I was pulling out my whistle to call the watch when he suddenly put out his hand to me and said, 'Don't.' Like that he said it; just 'Don't,' and there was something about the way he spoke that I—well, I didn't. I asked him again who he was and how he'd come by his English, and after a bit he went right ahead and told me his trouble. I can't remember his words, of course, but if you'll believe me, he talked better English than I do myself. It turns out he'd lived in London for seven years or so, learning to be a doctor, which accounted for things. He asked me if I was an officer, and when I told him who I was he opened out a lot. He said an Englishman would give him a square deal if any one would, and then he asked me to give him a chance. A few days after we'd started, it seems he'd discovered he could slip his wrist out of his handcuff. He was left quite alone down the hold, and the only time he saw anybody was when one of the cooks brought his chow down to him in the morning. He'd lie low all day, he said; but on some nights, when things were quiet on deck, he'd venture up for a bit and get some clean air. He said he'd made up his mind to wait and drop over the side one night and swim for it if we passed close enough to any land. It was a mighty slim chance; but the man was desperate, and I could see he meant to do what he said. I was the only soul aboard who knew he could slip his irons, and he begged me to say nothing and leave him to take his chance. In any case, he said he'd rather drown than be tortured to death, which was what he seemed to think he was due for if the Chinese officials got hold of him again.

"He didn't tell me exactly what it was he'd been up to in China to make himself so unpopular with the authorities; but as far as I could make out he'd been what we'd call an agitator or something like that, and that's a thing you know very well yourself the Chinese high muck-a-mucks won't stand for at any price. He must have had some sort of following, too, in Tientsin, which was where he'd been at work, because they started to riot one day and did in a mandarin or somebody, and then this chap had been arrested and tortured to make him give away his pals. He said he wouldn't do it, and he'd been waiting and hoping for a quick death, when they surprised him by putting him aboard ship and sending him off to South Africa. I think the man must just have been a natural born kicker. I mean, if he saw any dirty work going on he was the sort that couldn't rest unless he'd done his darnedest to clean things up. He even gets into trouble again on his mine. He found a gang there who were running and robbing the rest of the coolies and doing 'em in with a steel drill or a charge of dynamite if they objected. He said he couldn't stand it, so he got up a gang of his own. It was pretty much the same sort of thing he'd done before in Tientsin, and there'd been scrapping, of course, and some more men killed. He told me his lot had managed more or less to clean the other gang up; and then, with his usual luck, he ran foul of the Jo'burg C.I.D. They found out he had something to do with the business, but they got hold of the wrong end of the stick, because, instead of giving him credit for stopping the trouble they reckoned he was the cause of it and ran him in for murder.

"That was his yarn, or as much as I can remember of it. It was a hard luck tale anyhow, and I was sorry for him, and believed him. And his talk had set me thinking. I hadn't exactly a plan in my head; but what he'd said about that gang down the mine reminded me of my own troubles. 'If he managed to fix that lot,' thinks I to myself, 'then he might be able to settle these Small Knife beggars too.' That was a good thought, and when I'd got it clear in my head I put it to him flat. I told him the state of things aboard us, and what I was afraid might happen before the ship got in. I told him everything, and then I said straight out that, if he thought he could settle the business, I'd see he got his chance to get away.

" 'If you think you can do it,' I said, 'then go ahead. But you must understand I can't help you—openly at any rate. You were put aboard here as a murderer. You're in my charge, and my job is to hand you over to the police as soon as we arrive. But if you pull this thing off for me, then I'll give you every chance I can to get clear away from the ship before the police get hold of you. You'll have to trust me,' I said. 'Will you do it?' And 'I will,' says he, straight out like a man, and I knew from the way he spoke that I could trust him too. He held out his hand to me on the strength of our bargain, like a Christian, and we shook.

"And then, for the best part of an hour I should think, we two stood there behind the windlass and planned things out. I was hoping to goodness all the while that no one would see us, because if one single soul aboard the ship ever got to know I was hand in glove with the man like that, his escape would look too fishy and more than I'd care to risk. He saw that point, too; so we tried to settle things then and there, so as not to have to see each other again, that being too risky. We agreed he'd better stay down below in his irons during the daytime, and do what he had to do at night. He wouldn't tell me how he was going to set about the job; but he seemed fairly certain that if he could get into the after-part of the ship he'd be able to manage. I told him how he could do that by climbing over the fiddley and engine-room casing. 'If I can find friends aboard,' he said, 'it will be less difficult. But, Captain, I must have a weapon. There is only one way to stop those men now,' he says. 'Captain—you must let me have your pistol.'

"Now this was something I tell you I didn't like the thought of at all. Don't misunderstand me. I trusted that man, and I wasn't scared he'd turn my own gun on me. No. But I didn't like to think what else he might have to do with it. He was as good as a self-confessed murderer, remember—in a good cause, maybe; but, still—a murderer. And, believe me, it makes you think before you hand over a loaded automatic to a man like that. And I was thinking hard, and wondering what I'd better do, when he bent down and looked me close and straight between the eyes. 'It's either them or us, Captain,' he said, 'and you must face it.' And with that he took the thing gently out of my hand—and I let him take it. He balanced it in his hand for a little, and then he said, 'Good. When the matter is finished, you shall have proof of it. Then you must tell me how to escape.'

" 'If the ship ever gets to Ching-Wan-Tau,' I said, 'that's all the proof I'll need; and the best chance I can see for you is to swim for it, as you meant to before. What else can we do? You'll have to swim; but I'll see the ship gets in to Ching-Wan-Tau Roads at night and I'll anchor her as close as I dare to the land. I'll try and see the way's all clear for you— and the rest you'll have to do yourself. You'll be in your irons down the hold, and, as soon as we anchor, you must slip up on deck quickly and drop over the side and swim ashore. Will you be all right if you do get ashore?'

" 'If I can land without being seen,' he says, 'I've friends who'll hide me. But how shall I know when the time has come—to swim?'

" 'When the anchor's let go,' I said. 'Then's your time. You'll hear the chain running out all right. You'll hear that down the hold even if you're asleep. Well—that will be the signal.'

" 'Good,' says he again. 'But take the ship in very close to the shore, Captain. I can't swim far; but I'll trust you. You must trust me too, and when I've done what I've got to do, remember, I'll be waiting and listening for your signal.'

"After that we shook hands again on our bargain, and I left him. I went up on the bridge and he went down the hold. I didn't see him again."

The Skipper's long chair screeched as he sat up suddenly. For a while he said nothing at all; but when he spoke again his voice surprised me. "It's not wise," he said, "to put too much trust in any man. We trusted each other too much, and it isn't fair. We're only human—and things happen: things you can't foresee. And one forgets. Just for a second or two, perhaps; but one *does* forget—and then a trust is broken. No, it wasn't fair."

"Ah! I see," said I. "So your trusted murderer didn't fulfill his bargain? Well, I must say, I'm not surprised."

"Him?" went on the Skipper. "Don't you make any mistake, my friend. He didn't fail. No. He did all he said he would; although I don't know how he did it. I can only guess, and go by the facts—as they appeared. For instance, you take the facts we'd find each day inside Da Silva's hospital. The first few days after I'd made my bargain there'd be the usual crop of victims—twelve to twenty poor devils, that is, all slashed up and bleeding. And then one morning Da Silva comes along, smiling all over his face. 'They don't fight no more,' says he. 'Today there is no one cut.' But next morning he wasn't so happy. 'Bad, Captain, bad,' he says. 'Four men they bring me today. Four—all shot in the face and dead. It's bad for us, Captain, I think, now they begin shooting.'

" 'Maybe it's not so bad as you think, Doc.,' I told him. And that's all I'd say, for I guessed what had happened. And when I went aft and took a look at the corpses, I knew it was all right—for my partner wasn't one of 'em.

"The next fact to appear was an old gunny bag. It was shoved through the port-hole over my bunk that same night, and it fell on me with a bump and a rattle that scared me out of the first good sleep I'd had since we'd left Durban. I switched on my light in a hurry and picked the thing up. It was heavy, and the mouth of it was tied up with a piece of twine. For a little while I just sat there looking at the thing, and wondering who'd thrown it in and what was in it. But when I did open it and spilt the contents out on my blanket, I understood at once. It was a message—to tell me one side of the bargain had been fulfilled. It was proof, too, that tumbled out of that bag on to my lap. Nineteen small knives and my Colt automatic was proof enough for me. The knives were just ordinary folding pocket-knives, and the blades of four of them were broken; but all the rest were as sharp as razors. The barrel of the gun was fouled, and the magazine was short of four cartridges. It was good evidence; but I wasn't keen on anyone else seeing it, so I put the things into the bag again, and went out on deck and dropped the lot overboard. For a minute or two I thought of going forward and paying my friend a visit. I wanted to tell him I understood, and thank him, and try to make some better arrangement for getting him clear of the ship; but there was a bright moon shining full on the forward deck, and the officer on the bridge would have been certain to see me, so I turned in again—and slept.

"Next day at noon Cape Shantung was abeam, and we headed west to run through the Gulf of Pechili to Ching-Wan-Tau. That gave us two hundred seventy miles to go, and meant arriving about three o'clock the next afternoon. This wouldn't do, and I saw I'd have to slow the ship up if I was to carry out my part of the bargain and get her in after dark. Now, you can't go easing a ship down unless you've got good reasons for it. It all goes down in the log, of course, and when you get home they call you up to the office and want to know what you've been playing at. However, there it was, and I'd got to chance it. Slowed down the ship had got to be, office or no office, and I was trying hard to think of a good excuse, when the weather supplied me with the finest kind of a one I could have wished for. It came on thick. It started with some patches of fog closing down on us about four in the afternoon, and it got thicker and thicker, until by ten o'clock that night we were steaming dead slow, and you couldn't see the foremast from the bridge. The Gulf of Pechili's a horrible place to be drifting around in in thick weather. When a fog shuts in properly there it's apt to last for a long while, and the blessed tides run all over the place at the rate of knots, and you can't tell where or how far they're going to set you. By midnight I didn't like the look of things. We'd been dodging along dead slow for hours, and I wasn't sure within twenty miles or so where we'd got to. Cape Lai Lee Shan was somewhere ahead of us I hoped; but I didn't want to hit it, so I stopped the engine and sent the Second Mate aft to take a cast of the lead. I did it because it never pays to take chances at sea, especially in a fog; but as a matter of fact I felt pretty sure we'd got plenty of water under us. So you can understand when that young officer of mine came running up the bridge singing out he'd got bottom at eight fathoms, it gave me the deuce of a start. We'd been set to the devil and gone off our course, and there was only one thing to be done. I roused out the Mate to stand by forward, and then took another cast of the lead. This time we only got six fathoms, and I saw it was high time to bring the ship up and wait until we could see something. 'Stand by, forward,' I sang out, and 'All ready, sir,' answers the Mate. 'Let go, then,' I shouted, and 'Leggo, sir,' says he. Then there was a squeak from the windlass brake and our cable roared out through the hawse pipe, shaking the whole ship as it went. 'Give her thirty-five fathoms to the water's edge, mister,' I said, and then I walked to the binnacle to watch which way the tide would swing us. And the tide there must have been running like a race, for as soon as the ship brought up on her cable she swung round through nine points so quickly you'd have thought a tug had got hold of her head. I looked over the side and heard the tide regularly sluicing past us. 'Hear that?' said I to the Second. 'No wonder we've been set off to blazes.' And then, in a flash, I understood what I'd done. I feared it was too late; but it wasn't many seconds before I found myself on the fore deck, shouting down the hold to the man who'd been waiting there and listening for the signal I'd promised to give. I called and I kept on calling; but I got no answer. He'd heard the signal. He'd taken me at my word and gone overboard—with the ship somewhere in the middle of the Pechili Straits and a five-knot tide running past her straight out to sea."

The awning bellied out above us and came down again with a smack on the spreaders, and a warm brisk wind that I had not noticed before made my pyjamas flap about my legs. There are times when it is not well to talk, so I held my tongue and waited. In a little while the Skipper spoke again. "You go and turn in," he said. "There's a nice breeze now, and your berth's to wind'ard, so you ought to be able to sleep. And if you can't, you can spend your time nicely thanking God there's only the smell from sweating sugar to keep *you* awake."

65

The Prussian Officer

BY D. H. LAWRENCE

THEY HAD marched more than thirty kilometres since dawn, along the white, hot road where occasional thickets of trees threw a moment of shade, then out into the glare again. On either hand, the valley, wide and shallow, glittered with heat; dark green patches of rye, pale young corn, fallow and meadow and black pine woods spread in a dull, hot diagram under a glistening sky. But right in front the mountains ranged across, pale blue and very still, snow gleaming gently out of the deep atmosphere. And towards the mountains, on and on, the regiment marched between the rye-fields and the meadows, between the scraggy fruit trees set regularly on either side the highroad. The burnished, dark green rye threw off a suffocating heat, the mountains drew gradually nearer and more distinct. While the feet of the soldiers grew hotter, sweat ran through their hair under their helmets, and their knapsacks could burn no more in contact with their shoulders, but seemed instead to give off a cold, prickly sensation.

He walked on and on in silence, staring at the mountains ahead, that rose sheer out of the land, and stood fold behind fold, half earth, half heaven, the heaven, the barrier with slits of soft snow, in the pale, bluish peaks.

He could now walk almost without pain. At the start, he had determined not to limp. It had made him sick to take the first steps, and during the first mile or so, he had compressed his breath, and the cold drops of sweat had stood on his forehead. But he had walked it off. What were they after all but bruises! He had looked at them, as he was getting up: deep bruises on the backs of his thighs. And since he had made his first step in the morning, he had been conscious of them, till now he had a tight, hot place in his chest, with suppressing the pain and holding himself in. There seemed no air when he breathed. But he walked almost lightly.

The Captain's hand had trembled at taking his coffee at dawn: his orderly saw it again. And he saw the fine figure of the Captain wheeling on horseback at the farmhouse ahead, a handsome figure in pale blue uniform with facings of scarlet, and the metal gleaming on the black helmet and the sword-scabbard, and dark streaks of sweat coming on the silky bay horse. The orderly felt he was connected with that figure moving so suddenly on horseback: he followed it like a shadow, mute and inevitable and damned by it. And the officer was always aware of the tramp of the company behind, the march of his orderly among the men.

The Captain was a tall man of about forty, grey at the temples. He had a handsome, finely knit figure, and was one of the best horsemen in the West. His orderly, having to rub him down, admired the amazing riding-muscles of his loins.

For the rest, the orderly scarcely noticed the officer any more than he noticed himself. It was rarely he saw his master's face: he did not look at it. The Captain had reddish-brown, stiff hair, that he wore short upon his skull. His mustache was also cut short and bristly over a full, brutal mouth. His face was rather rugged, the cheeks thin. Perhaps the man was the more handsome for the deep lines in his face, the irritable tension of his brow, which gave him the look of a man who fights with life. His fair eyebrows stood bushy over light-blue eyes that were always flashing with cold fire.

He was a Prussian aristocrat, haughty and overbearing. But his mother had been a Polish Countess. Having made too many gambling debts when he was young, he had ruined his prospects in the Army, and remained an infantry captain. He had never married: his position did not allow of it, and no woman had ever moved him to it. His time he spent riding—occasionally he rode one of his own horses at the races—and at the officers' club. Now and then he took himself a mistress. But after such an event, he returned to duty with his brow still more tense, his eyes still more hostile and irritable. With the men, however, he was merely impersonal, though a devil when roused; so that, on the whole, they feared him, but had no great aversion from him. They accepted him as the inevitable.

To his orderly he was at first cold and just and indifferent: he did not fuss over trifles. So that his servant knew practically nothing about him, except just what orders he would give, and how he wanted them obeyed. That was quite simple. Then the change gradually came.

The orderly was a youth of about twenty-two, of medium height, and well built. He had strong, heavy limbs, was swarthy, with a soft, black, young moustache. There was something altogether warm and young about him. He had firmly marked eyebrows over dark, expressionless eyes, that seemed never to have thought, only to have received life direct through his senses, and acted straight from instinct.

Gradually the officer had become aware of his servant's young, vigorous, unconscious presence about him. He could not get away from the sense of the youth's person, while he was in attendance. It was like a warm flame upon the older man's tense, rigid body, that had become almost unliving, fixed. There was something so free and self-contained about him, and something in the young fellow's movement, that made the officer aware of him. And this irritated the Prussian. He did not choose to be touched into life by his servant. He might easily have changed his man, but he did not. He now very rarely looked direct at his orderly, but kept his face averted, as if to avoid seeing him. And yet as the young soldier moved unthinking about the apartment, the elder watched him, and would notice the movement of his strong young shoulders under the blue cloth, the bend of his neck. And it irritated him. To see the soldier's young, brown, shapely peasant's hand grasp the loaf or the wine bottle sent a flash of hate or of anger through the elder man's blood. It was not that the youth was clumsy; it was rather the blind, instinctive sureness of movement of an unhampered young animal that irritated the officer to such a degree.

Once, when a bottle of wine had gone over, and the red gushed out on the tablecloth, the officer had started up with an oath, and his eyes, bluey like fire, had held those of the confused youth for a moment. It was a shock to the young soldier. He felt something sink deeper, deeper into his soul, where nothing had ever gone before. It left him rather blank and wondering. Some of his natural completeness in himself was gone, a little uneasiness took its place. And from that time an undiscovered feeling had held between the two men.

Henceforward the orderly was afraid of really meeting his master. His subconsciousness remembered those steely blue eyes and the harsh brows, and did not intend to meet them again. So he always stared past his master, and avoided him. Also, in a little anxiety, he waited for the three months to have gone, when his time would be up. He began to feel a constraint in the Captain's presence, and the soldier even more than the officer wanted to be left alone, in his neutrality as servant.

He had served the Captain for more than a year, and knew his duty. This he performed easily, as if it were natural to him. The officer and his commands he took for granted, as he took the sun and the rain, and he served as a matter of course. It did not implicate him personally.

But now if he were going to be forced into a personal interchange with his master he would be like a wild thing caught, he felt he must get away.

But the influence of the young soldier's being had penetrated through the officer's stiffened discipline, and perturbed the man in him. He, however, was a gentleman, with long, fine hands and cultivated movements, and was not going to allow such a thing as the stirring of his innate self. He was a man of passionate temper, who had always kept himself suppressed. Occasionally there had been a duel, an outburst before the soldiers. He knew himself to be always on the point of breaking out. But he kept himself hard to the idea of the Service. Whereas the young soldier seemed to live out his warm, full nature, to give it off in his very movements, which had a certain zest, such as wild animals have in free movement. And this irritated the officer more and more.

In spite of himself, the Captain could not regain his neutrality of feeling towards his orderly. Nor could he leave the man alone. In spite of himself, he watched him, gave him sharp orders, tried to take up as much of his time as possible. Sometimes he flew into a rage with the young soldier, and bullied him. Then the orderly shut himself off, as it were, out of earshot, and waited, with sullen, flushed face, for the end of the noise. The words never pierced to his intelligence, he made himself, protectively, impervious to the feelings of his master.

He had a scar on his left thumb, a deep seam going across the knuckle. The officer had long suffered from it, and wanted to do something to it. Still it was there, ugly and brutal on the young, brown hand. At last the Captain's reserve gave way. One day as the orderly was smoothing out the tablecloth, the officer pinned down his thumb with a pencil, asking: "How did you come by that?"

The young man winced and drew back at attention.

"A wood axe, Herr Hauptmann," he answered.

The officer waited for further explanation. None came. The orderly went about his duties. The elder man was sullenly angry. His servant avoided him. And the next day he had to use all his will power to avoid seeing the scarred thumb. He wanted to get hold of it and—a hot flame ran in his blood.

He knew his servant would soon be free, and would be glad. As yet, the soldier had held himself off from the elder man. The Captain grew madly irritable. He could not rest when the soldier was away, and when he was present, he glared at him with tormented eyes. He hated those fine, black brows over the unmeaning, dark eyes, he was infuriated by the free movement of the handsome limbs, which no military discipline could make stiff. And he became harsh and cruelly bullying, using contempt and satire. The young soldier only grew more mute and expressionless.

"What cattle were you bred by, that you can't keep straight eyes? Look me in the eyes when I speak to you."

And the soldier turned his dark eyes to the other's face, but there was no sight in them: he stared with the slightest possible cast, holding back his sight, perceiving the blue of his master's eyes, but receiving no look from them. And the elder man went pale, and his reddish eyebrows twitched. He gave his order, barrenly.

Once he flung a heavy military glove into the young soldier's face. Then he had the satisfaction of seeing the black eyes flare up into his own, like a blaze when straw is thrown on a fire. And he had laughed with a little tremor and a sneer.

But there were only two months more. The youth instinctively tried to keep himself intact: he had tried to serve the officer as if the latter were an abstract authority and not a man. All his instinct was to avoid personal contact, even definite hate. But in spite of himself the hate grew, responsive to the officer's passion. However, he put it in the background. When he had left the Army he could dare acknowledge it. By nature he was active, and had many friends. He thought what amazing good fellows they were. But, without knowing it, he was alone. Now this solitariness was intensified. It would carry him through his term. But the officer seemed to be going irritably insane, and the youth was deeply frightened.

The soldier had a sweetheart, a girl from the mountains, independent and primitive. The two walked together, rather silently. He went with her, not to talk, but to have his arm round her, and for the physical contact. This eased him, made it easier for him to ignore the Captain, for he could rest with her held fast against his chest. And she, in some unspoken fashion, was there for him. They loved each other.

The Captain perceived it, and was mad with irritation. He kept the young man engaged all the evenings long, and took pleasure in the dark look that came on his face. Occasionally, the eyes of the two men met, those of the younger sullen and dark, doggedly unalterable, those of the elder sneering with restless contempt.

The officer tried hard not to admit the passion that had got hold of him. He would not know that his feeling for his orderly was anything but that of a man incensed by his stupid, perverse servant. So, keeping quite justified and conventional in his consciousness, he let the other thing run on. His nerves, however, were suffering. At last he slung the end of a belt in his servant's face. When he saw the youth start back, the pain-tears in his eyes and the blood on his mouth, he had felt at once a thrill of deep pleasure and of shame.

But this, he acknowledged to himself, was a thing he had never done before. The fellow was too exasperating. His own nerves must be going to pieces. He went away for some days with a woman.

It was a mockery of pleasure. He simply did not want the woman. But he stayed on for his time. At the end of it, he came back in an agony of irritation, torment, and misery. He rode all the evening, then came straight in to supper. His orderly was out. The officer sat with his long, fine hands lying on the table, perfectly still, and all his blood seemed to be corroding.

At last his servant entered. He watched the strong, easy young figure, the fine eyebrows, the thick black hair. In a week's time the youth had got back his old well-being. The hands of the officer twitched and seemed to be full of mad flame. The young man stood at attention, unmoving, shut off.

The meal went in silence. But the orderly seemed eager. He made a clatter with the dishes.

"Are you in a hurry?" asked the officer, watching the intent, warm face of his servant. The other did not reply.

"Will you answer my question?" said the Captain.

"Yes, sir," replied the orderly, standing with his pile of deep Army plates. The Captain waited, looked at him, then asked again:

"Are you in a hurry?"

"Yes, sir," came the answer, that sent a flash through the listener.

"For what?"

"I was going out, sir."

"I want you this evening."

There was a moment's hesitation. The officer had a curious stiffness of countenance.

"Yes, sir," replied the servant in his throat.

"I want you to-morrow evening also—in fact, you may consider your evenings occupied, unless I give you leave."

The mouth with the young moustache set close.

"Yes, sir," answered the orderly, loosening his lips for a moment. He again turned to the door.

"And why have you a piece of pencil in your ear?"

The orderly hesitated, then continued on his way without answering. He set the plates in a pile outside the door, took the stump of pencil from his ear, and put it in his pocket. He had been copying a verse for his sweetheart's birthday card. He returned to finish clearing the table. The officer's eyes were dancing, he had a little eager smile.

"Why have you a piece of pencil in your ear?" he asked.

The orderly took his hands full of dishes. His master was standing near the great green stove, a little smile on his face, his chin thrust forward. When the young soldier saw him his heart suddenly ran hot. He felt blind. Instead of answering, he turned dazedly to the door. As he was crouching to set down the dishes, he was pitched forward by a kick from behind. The pots went in a stream down the stairs, he clung to the pillar of the bannisters. And as he was rising he was kicked heavily again, and again, so that he clung sickly to the post for some moments. His master had gone swiftly into the room and closed the door. The maidservant downstairs looked up the staircase and made a mocking face at the crockery disaster.

The officer's heart was plunging. He poured himself a glass of wine, part of which he spilled on the floor, and gulped the remainder, leaning against the cool, green stove. He heard his man collecting the dishes from the stairs. Pale, as if intoxicated, he waited. The servant entered again. The Captain's heart gave a pang, as of pleasure, seeing the young fellow bewildered and uncertain on his feet, with pain.

"Schöner!" he said.

The soldier was a little slower in coming to attention.

"Yes, sir!"

The youth stood before him, with pathetic young moustache, and fine eyebrows very distinct on his forehead of dark marble.

"I asked you a question."

"Yes, sir."

The officer's tone bit like acid.

"Why had you a pencil in your ear?"

Again the servant's heart ran hot, and he could not breathe. With dark, strained eyes, he looked at the officer, as if fascinated. And he stood there sturdily planted, unconscious. The withered smile came into the Captain's eyes, and he lifted his foot.

"I—I forgot it—sir," panted the soldier, his dark eyes fixed on the other man's blue ones.

"What was it doing there?"

He saw the young man's breast heaving as he made an effort for words.

"I had been writing."

"Writing what?"

Again the soldier looked him up and down. The officer could hear him panting. The smile came into the blue eyes. The soldier worked his dry throat, but could not speak. Suddenly the smile lit like a flame on the officer's face, and a kick came heavily against the orderly's thigh. The youth moved a pace sideways. His face was dead, with two black, staring eyes.

"Well?" said the officer.

The orderly's mouth had gone dry, and his tongue rubbed in it as on dry brown-paper. He worked his throat. The officer raised his foot. The servant went stiff.

"Some poetry, sir," came the crackling, unrecognisable sound of his voice.

"Poetry, what poetry?" asked the Captain, with a sickly smile.

Again there was the working in the throat. The Captain's heart had suddenly gone down heavily, and he stood sick and tired.

"For my girl, sir," he heard the dry, inhuman sound.

"Oh!" he said, turning away. "Clear the table."

"Click!" went the soldier's throat; then again, "click!" and then the half-articulate:

"Yes, sir."

The young soldier was gone, looking old, and walking heavily.

The officer, left alone, held himself rigid, to prevent himself from thinking. His instinct warned him that he must not think. Deep inside him was the intense gratification of his passion, still working powerfully. Then there was a counter-action, a horrible breaking down of something inside him, a whole agony of reaction. He stood there for an hour motionless, a chaos of sensations, but rigid with a will to keep blank his consciousness, to prevent his mind grasping. And he held himself so until the worst of the stress had passed, when he began to drink, drank himself to an intoxication, till he slept obliterated. When he woke in the morning he was shaken to the base of his nature. But he had fought off the realisation of what he had done. He had prevented his mind from taking it in, had suppressed it along with his instincts, and the conscious man had nothing to do with it. He felt only as after a bout of intoxication, weak, but the affair itself all dim and not to be recovered. Of the drunkenness of his passion he successfully refused remembrance. And when his orderly appeared with coffee, the officer assumed the same self he had had the morning before. He refused the event of the past night—denied it had ever been—and was successful in his denial. He had not done any such thing—not he himself. Whatever there might be lay at the door of a stupid, insubordinate servant.

The orderly had gone about in a stupor all the evening. He drank some beer because he was parched, but not much; the alcohol made his feeling come back, and he could not bear it. He was dulled, as if nine-tenths of the ordinary man in him were inert. He crawled about disfigured. Still, when he thought of the kicks, he went sick, and when he thought of the threat of more kicking, in the room afterwards, his heart went hot and faint, and he panted, remembering the one that had come. He had been forced to say, "For my girl." He was much too done even to want to cry. His mouth hung slightly open, like an idiot's. He felt vacant, and wasted. So, he wandered at his work, painfully, and very slowly and clumsily, fumbling blindly with the brushes, and finding it difficult, when he sat down, to summon the energy to move again. His limbs, his jaw, were slack and nerveless. But he was very tired. He got to bed at last, and slept inert, relaxed, in a sleep that was rather stupor than slumber, a dead night of stupefaction, shot through with gleams of anguish.

In the morning were the manoeuvres. But he woke even before the bugle sounded. The painful ache in his chest, the dryness of his throat, the awful steady feeling of misery made his eyes come awake and dreary at once. He knew, without thinking, what had happened. And he knew that the day had come again when he must go on with this round. The last bit of darkness was being pushed out of the room. He would have to move his inert body and go on. He was so young, and had known so little trouble, that he was bewildered. He only wished it would stay night, so that he could lie still, covered up with the darkness. And yet nothing would prevent the day from coming, nothing would save him from having to get up and saddle the Captain's horse, and make the Captain's coffee. It was there, inevitable. And then, he thought, it was impossible. Yet they would not leave him free. He must go and take the coffee to the Captain. He was too stunned to understand it. He only knew it was inevitable—inevitable, however long he lay inert.

At last, after heaving at himself, for he seemed to be a mass of inertia, he got up. But he had to force every one of his movements from behind, with his will. He felt lost, and dazed, and helpless. Then he clutched hold of the bed, the pain was so keen. And looking at his thighs, he saw the darker bruises on his swarthy flesh and he knew that, if he pressed one of his fingers on one of the bruises, he should faint. But he did not want to faint—he did not want anybody to know. No one should ever know. It was between him and the Captain. There were only two people in the world now—himself and the Captain.

Slowly, economically, he got dressed and forced himself to walk. Everything was obscure, except just what he had his hands on. But he managed to get through his work. The very pain revived his dull senses. The worst remained yet. He took the tray and went up to the Captain's room. The officer, pale and heavy, sat at the table. The orderly, as he saluted, felt himself put out of existence. He stood still for a moment submitting to his own nullification—then he gathered himself, seemed to regain himself, and then the Captain began to grow vague, unreal, and the younger soldier's heart beat up. He clung to this situation—that the Captain did not exist—so that he himself might live. But when he saw his officer's hand tremble as he took the coffee, he felt everything falling shattered. And he went away, feeling as if he himself were coming to pieces, disintegrated. And when the Captain was there on horseback, giving orders, while he himself stood, with rifle and knapsack, sick with pain, he felt as if he must shut his eyes on everything. It was only the long agony of marching with a parched throat that filled him with one single, sleep-heavy intention: to save himself.

He was getting used even to his parched throat. That the snowy peaks were radiant among the sky, that the whity-green glacier-river twisted through its pale shoals, in the valley below, seemed almost supernatural. But he was going mad with fever and thirst. He plodded on uncomplaining. He did not want to speak, not to anybody. There were two gulls, like flakes of water and snow, over the river. The scent of green rye soaked in sunshine came like a sickness. And the march continued, monotonously, almost like a bad sleep.

At the next farmhouse, which stood low and broad near the high-road, tubs of water had been put out. The soldiers clustered round to drink. They took off their helmets, and the steam mounted from their wet hair. The Captain sat on horseback, watching. He needed to see his orderly. His helmet threw a dark shadow over his light, fierce eyes, but his moustache and mouth and chin were distinct in the sunshine. The orderly must move under the presence of the figure of the horseman. It was not that he was afraid, or cowed. It was as if he was disembowelled, made empty, like an empty shell. He felt himself a nothing, a shadow creeping under the sunshine. And, thirsty as he was, he could scarcely drink, feeling the Captain near him. He would not take off his helmet to wipe his wet hair. He wanted to stay in shadow, not to be forced into consciousness. Starting, he saw the light heel of the officer prick the belly of the horse; the Captain cantered away, and he himself could relapse into vacancy.

Nothing, however, could give him back his living place in the hot, bright morning. He felt like a gap among it all. Whereas the Captain was prouder, overriding. A hot flash went through the young servant's body. The Captain was firmer and prouder with life, he himself was empty as a shadow. Again the flash went through him, dazing him out. But his heart ran a little firmer.

The company turned up the hill, to make a loop for the return. Below, from among the trees, the farm-bell clanged. He saw the labourers, mowing barefoot at the thick grass, leave off their work and go downhill, their scythes hanging over their shoulders, like long, bright claws curving down behind them. They seemed like dream-people, as if they had no relation to himself. He felt as in a blackish dream: as if all the other things were there and had form, but he himself was only a consciousness, a gap that could think and perceive.

The soldiers were tramping silently up the glaring hillside. Gradually his head began to revolve, slowly, rhythmically. Sometimes it was dark before his eyes, as if he saw this world through a smoked glass, frail shadows and unreal. It gave him a pain in his head to walk.

The air was too scented, it gave no breath. All the lush green-stuff seemed to be issuing its sap, till the air was deathly, sickly with the smell of greenness. There was the perfume of clover, like pure honey and bees. Then there grew a faint acrid tang—they were near the beeches; and then a queer clattering noise, and a suffocating, hideous smell; they were passing a flock of sheep, a shepherd in a black smock, holding his crook. Why should the sheep huddle together under this fierce sun? He felt that the shepherd would not see him, though he could see the shepherd.

At last there was the halt. They stacked rifles in a conical stack, put down their kits in a scattered circle around it, and dispersed a little, sitting on a small knoll high on the hillside. The chatter began. The soldiers were steaming with heat, but were lively. He sat still, seeing the blue mountains rising upon the land, twenty kilometres away. There was a blue fold in the ranges, then out of that, at the foot, the broad, pale bed of the river, stretches of whity-green water between pinkish-grey shoals among the dark pine woods. There it was, spread out a long way off. And it seemed to come downhill, the river. There was a raft being steered, a mile away. It was a strange country. Nearer, a red-roofed, broad farm with white base and square dots of windows crouched beside the wall of beech foliage on the wood's edge. There were long strips of rye and clover and pale green corn. And just at his feet, below the knoll, was a darkish bog, where globe flowers stood breathless still on their slim stalks. And some of the pale gold bubbles were burst, and a broken fragment hung in the air. He thought he was going to sleep.

Suddenly something moved into this coloured mirage before his eyes. The Captain, a small, light-blue and scarlet figure, was trotting evenly between the strips of corn, along the level brow of the hill. And the man making flag-signals was coming on. Proud and sure moved the horseman's figure, the quick, bright thing, in which was concentrated all the light of this morning, which for the rest lay a fragile, shining shadow. Submissive, apathetic, the young soldier sat and stared. But as the horse slowed to a walk, coming up the last steep path, the great flash flared over the body and soul of the orderly. He sat waiting. The back of his head felt as if it were weighted with a heavy piece of fire. He did not want to eat. His hands trembled slightly as he moved them. Meanwhile the officer on horseback was approaching slowly and proudly. The tension grew in the orderly's soul. Then again, seeing the Captain ease himself on the saddle, the flash blazed through him.

The Captain looked at the patch of light-blue and scarlet, and dark heads, scattered closely on the hillside. It pleased him. The command pleased him. And he was feeling proud. His orderly was among them in common subjection. The officer rose a little in his stirrups to look. The young soldier sat with averted, dumb face. The Captain relaxed on his seat. His slim-legged, beautiful horse, brown as a beech-nut, walked proudly uphill. The Captain passed into the zone of the company's atmosphere: a hot smell of men, of sweat, of leather. He knew it very well. After a word with the lieutenant, he went a few paces higher, and sat there, a dominant figure, his sweat-marked horse swishing its tail, while he looked down on his men, on his orderly, a nonentity among the crowd.

The young soldier's heart was like fire in his chest, and he breathed with difficulty. The officer, looking downhill, saw three of the young soldiers, two pails of water between them, staggering across a sunny green field. A table had been set up under a tree, and there the slim lieutenant stood, importantly busy. Then the Captain summoned himself to an act of courage. He called his orderly.

The flame leaped into the young soldier's throat as he heard the command, and he rose blindly, stifled. He saluted, standing below the officer. He did not look up. But there was the flicker in the Captain's voice.

"Go to the inn and fetch me . . ." the officer gave his commands. "Quick!" he added.

At the last word, the heart of the servant leapt with a flash, and he felt the strength come over his body. But he turned in mechanical obedience, and set off at a heavy run downhill, looking almost like a bear, his trousers bagging over his military boots. And the officer watched this blind, plunging run all the way.

But it was only the outside of the orderly's body that was obeying so humbly and mechanically. Inside had gradually accumulated a core into which all the energy of that young life was compact and concentrated. He executed his commission, and plodded quickly back uphill. There was a pain in his head, as he walked, that made him twist his features unknowingly. But hard there in the centre of his chest was himself, himself, firm and not to be plucked to pieces.

The Captain had gone up into the wood. The orderly plodded through the hot, powerful smelling zone of the company's atmosphere. He had a curious mass of energy inside him now. The Captain was less real than himself. He approached the green entrance to the wood. There, in the half-shade, he saw the horse standing, the sunshine and the flickering shadow of leaves dancing over his brown body. There was a clearing where timber had lately been felled. Here, in the gold-green shade beside the brilliant cup of sunshine, stood two figures, blue and pink, the bits of pink showing out plainly. The Captain was talking to his lieutenant.

The orderly stood on the edge of the bright clearing, where great trunks of trees, stripped and glistening, lay stretched like naked, brown-skinned bodies. Chips of wood littered the trampled floor, like splashed light, and the bases of the felled trees stood here and there, with their raw, level tops. Beyond was the brilliant, sunlit green of a beech.

"Then I will ride forward," the orderly heard his Captain say. The lieutenant saluted and strode away. He himself went forward. A hot flash passed through his belly, as he tramped towards his officer.

The Captain watched the rather heavy figure of the young soldier stumble forward, and his veins, too, ran hot. This was to be man to man between them. He yielded before the solid, stumbling figure with bent head. The orderly stooped and put the food on a level-sawn tree-base. The Captain watched the glistening, sun-inflamed, naked hands. He wanted to speak to the young soldier, but could not. The servant propped a bottle against his thigh, pressed open the cork, and poured out the beer into the mug. He kept his head bent. The Captain accepted the mug.

"Hot!" he said, as if amiably.

The flame sprang out of the orderly's heart, nearly suffocating him.

"Yes, sir," he replied, between shut teeth.

And he heard the sound of the Captain's drinking, and he clenched his fists, such a strong torment came into his wrists. Then came the faint clang of the closing of the pot-lid. He looked up. The Captain was watching him. He glanced swiftly away. Then he saw the officer stoop and take a piece of bread from the tree-base. Again the flash of flame went through the young soldier, seeing the stiff body stoop beneath him, and his hands jerked. He looked away. He could feel the officer was nervous. The bread fell as it was being broken. The officer ate the other piece. The two men stood tense and still, the master laboriously chewing his bread, the servant staring with averted face, his fist clenched.

Then the young soldier started. The officer had pressed open the lid of the mug again. The orderly watched the lid of the mug, and the white hand that clenched the handle, as if he were fascinated. It was raised. The youth followed it with his eyes. And then he saw the thin, strong jaw working. And the instinct which had been jerking at the young man's wrists suddenly jerked free. He jumped, feeling as if it were rent in two by a strong flame.

The spur of the officer caught in a tree-root, he went down backwards with a crash, the middle of his back thudding sickeningly against a sharp-edged tree-base, the pot flying away. And in a second the orderly, with serious, earnest young face, and underlip between his teeth, had got his knee in the officer's chest and was pressing the chin backward over the farther edge of the tree-stump, pressing, with all his heart behind a passion of relief, the tension of his wrists exquisite with relief. And with the base of his palms he shoved at the chin, with all his might. And it was pleasant, too, to have that chin, that hard jaw already slightly rough with beard, in his hands. He did not relax one hair's breadth, but, all the force of all his blood exulting in his thrust, he shoved back the head of the other man, till there was a little "cluck" and a crunching sensation. Then he felt as if his head went to vapour. Heavy convulsions shook the body of the officer, frightening and horrifying the young soldier. Yet it pleased him, too, to repress them. It pleased him to keep his hands pressing back the chin, to feel the chest of the other man yield in expiration to the weight of his strong, young knees, to feel the hard twitchings of the prostrate body jerking his own whole frame, which was pressed down on it.

But it went still. He could look into the nostrils of the other man, the eyes he could scarcely see. How curiously the mouth was pushed out, exaggerating the full lips, and the moustache bristling up from them. Then, with a start, he noticed the nostrils gradually filled with blood. The red brimmed, hesitated, ran over, and went in thin trickle down the face to the eyes.

It shocked and distressed him. Slowly, he got up. The body twitched and sprawled there, inert. He stood and looked at it in silence. It was a pity *it* was broken. It represented more than the thing which had kicked and bullied him. He was afraid to look at the eyes. They were hideous now, only the whites showing, and the blood running to them. The face of the orderly was drawn with horror at the sight. Well, it was so. In his heart he was satisfied. He had hated the face of the Captain. It was extinguished now. There was a heavy relief in the orderly's military body lying broken over the tree-base, the fine fingers crisped. He wanted to hide it away.

Quickly, busily, he gathered it up and pushed it under the felled tree-trunks, which rested their beautiful, smooth length either end on logs. The face was horrible with blood. He covered it with the helmet. Then he pushed the limbs straight and decent, and brushed the dead leaves off the fine cloth of the uniform. So, it lay quite still in the shadow under there. A little strip of sunshine ran along the breast, from a chink between the logs. The orderly sat by it for a few moments. Here his own life also ended.

Then, through his daze, he heard the lieutenant, in a loud voice, explaining to the men outside the wood, that they were to suppose the bridge on the river below was held by the enemy. Now they were to march to the attack in such and such a manner. The lieutenant had no gift of expression. The orderly, listening from habit, got muddled. And when the lieutenant began it all again he ceased to hear.

He knew he must go. He stood up. It surprised him that the leaves were glittering in the sun, and the chips of wood reflecting white from the ground. For him a change had come over the world. But for the rest it had not—all seemed the same. Only he had left it. And he could not go back. It was his duty to return with the beer-pot and the bottle. He could not. He had left all that. The lieutenant was still hoarsely explaining. He must go, or they would overtake him. And he could not bear contact with anyone now.

He drew his fingers over his eyes, trying to find out where he was. Then he turned away. He saw the horse standing in the path. He went up to it and mounted. It hurt him to sit in the saddle. The pain of keeping his seat occupied him as they cantered through the wood. He would not have minded anything, but he could not get away from the sense of being divided from the others. The path led out of the trees. On the edge of the wood he pulled up and stood watching. There in the spacious sunshine of the valley soldiers were moving in a little swarm. Every now and then, a man harrowing on a strip of fallow shouted to his oxen, at the turn. The village and the white-towered church was small in the sunshine. And he no longer belonged to it—he sat there, beyond, like a man outside in the dark. He had gone out from everyday life into the unknown, and he could not, he even did not want to go back.

Turning from the sun-blazing valley, he rode deep into the wood. Tree-trunks, like people standing grey and still, took no notice as he went. A doe, herself a moving bit of sunshine and shadow, went running through the flecked shade. There were bright green rents in the foliage. Then it was all pine wood, dark and cool. And he was sick with pain, he had an intolerable great pulse in his head, and he was sick. He had never been ill in his life. He felt lost, quite dazed with all this.

Trying to get down from the horse, he fell, astonished at the pain and his lack of balance. The horse shifted uneasily. He jerked its bridle and sent it cantering jerkily away. It was his last connection with the rest of things.

But he only wanted to lie down and not be disturbed. Stumbling through the trees, he came on a quiet place where beeches and pine trees grew on a slope. Immediately he had lain down and closed his eyes, his consciousness went racing on without him. A big pulse of sickness beat in him as if it throbbed through the whole earth. He was burning with dry heat. But he was too busy, too tearingly active in the incoherent race of delirium to observe.

He came to with a start. His mouth was dry and hard, his heart beat heavily, but he had not the energy to get up. His heart beat heavily. Where was he?—the barracks—at home? There was something knocking. And, making an effort, he looked round—trees, and litter of greenery, and reddish, bright, still pieces of sunshine on the floor. He did not believe it was himself, he did not believe what he saw. Something was knocking. He made a struggle toward consciousness, but relapsed. Then he struggled again and gradually his surroundings fell into relationship with himself. He knew, and a great pang of fear went through his heart. Somebody was knocking. He could see the heavy, black rags of a fir tree overhead. Then everything went black. Yet he did not believe he had closed his eyes. He had not. Out of the blackness sight slowly emerged again. And someone was knocking. Quickly, he saw the blood-disfigured face of his Captain, which he hated. And he held himself still with horror. Yet, deep inside him, he knew that it was so, the Captain should be dead. But the physical delirium got hold of him. Someone was knocking. He lay perfectly still, as if dead, with fear. And he went unconscious.

When he opened his eyes again, he started, seeing something creeping swiftly up a tree-trunk. It was a little bird. And the bird was whistling overhead. Tap-tap-tap—it was the small, quick bird rapping the tree-trunk with its beak, as if its head were a little round hammer. He watched it curiously. It shifted sharply, in its creeping fashion. Then, like a mouse, it slid down the bare trunk. Its swift creeping sent a flash of revulsion through him. He raised his head. It felt a great weight. Then, the little bird ran out of the shadow across a still patch of sunshine, its little head bobbing swiftly, its white legs twinkling brightly for a moment. How neat it was in its build, so compact, with pieces of white on its wings. There were several of them. They were so pretty—but they crept like swift, erratic mice, running here and there among the beech-mast.

He lay down again exhausted, and his consciousness lapsed. He had a horror of the little creeping birds. All his blood seemed to be darting and creeping in his head. And yet he could not move.

He came to with a further ache of exhaustion. There was the pain in his head, and the horrible sickness, and his inability to move. He had never been ill in his life. He did not know where he was or what he was. Probably he had got sunstroke. Or what else?—he had silenced the Captain for ever—some time ago—oh, a long time ago. There had been blood on his face, and his eyes had turned upwards. It was all right, somehow. It was peace. But now he had got beyond himself. He had never been here before. Was it life, or not life? He was by himself. They were in a big bright place, those others, and he was outside. The town, all the country, a big, bright place of light: and he was outside, here, in the darkened open beyond, where each thing existed alone. But they would all have to come out there sometime, those others. Little, and left behind him, they all were. There had been father and mother and sweet-heart. What did they all matter? This was the open land.

He sat up. Something scuffled. It was a little, brown squirrel running in lovely, undulating bounds over the floor, its red tail completing the undulation of its body—and then, as it sat up, furling and unfurling. He watched it, pleased. It ran on again, friskily, enjoying itself. It flew wildly at another squirrel, and they were chasing each other, and mak-ing little scolding, chattering noises. The soldier wanted to speak to them. But only a hoarse sound came out of his throat. The squirrels burst away—they flew up the trees. And then he saw the one peeping round at him, half-way up a tree-trunk. A start of fear went through him, though, in so far as he was conscious, he was amused. It still stayed, its little, keen face staring at him half-way up the tree-trunk, its little ears pricked up, its clawy little hands clinging to the bark, its white breast reared. He started from it in panic.

Struggling to his feet, he lurched away. He went on walking, walk-ing, looking for something—for a drink. His brain felt hot and inflamed for want of water. He stumbled on. Then he did not know anything. He went unconscious as he walked. Yet he stumbled on, his mouth open.

When, to his dumb wonder, he opened his eyes on the world again, he no longer tried to remember what it was. There was thick, golden light behind golden-green glitterings, and tall, grey-purple shafts, and dark-nesses further off, surrounding him, growing deeper. He was conscious of a sense of arrival. He was amid the reality, on the real, dark bottom. But there was the thirst burning in his brain. He felt lighter, not so heavy. He supposed it was newness. The air was muttering with thun-der. He thought he was walking wonderfully swiftly and was coming straight to relief—or was it to water?

Suddenly he stood still with fear. There was a tremendous flare of gold, immense—just a few dark trunks like bars between him and it. All the young level wheat was burnished gold glaring on its silky green. A woman, full-skirted, a black cloth on her head for head-dress, was pass-ing like a block of shadow through the glistening, green corn, into the full glare. There was a farm, too, pale blue in shadow, and the timber black. And there was a church spire, nearly fused away in the gold. The woman moved on, away from him. He had no language with which to speak to her. She was the bright, solid unreality. She would make a noise of words that would confuse him, and her eyes would look at him with-out seeing him. She was crossing there to the other side. He stood against a tree.

When at last he turned, looking down the long, bare grove whose flat bed was already filling dark, he saw the mountains in a wonderlight, not far away, and radiant. Behind the soft, grey ridge of the nearest range the further mountains stood golden and pale grey, the snow all radiant like pure, soft gold. So still, gleaming in the sky, fashioned pure out of the ore of the sky, they shone in their silence. He stood and looked at them, his face illuminated. And like the golden, lustrous gleaming of the snow, he felt his own thirst bright in him. He stood and gazed, leaning against a tree. And then everything slid away into space.

During the night the lightning fluttered perpetually, making the whole sky white. He must have walked again. The world hung livid round him for moments, fields a level sheen of grey-green light, trees in dark bulk, and the range of clouds black across the white sky. Then the darkness fell like a shutter, and the night was whole. A faint flutter of a half-revealed world, that could not quite leap out of the darkness!— Then there again stood a sweep of pallor for the land, dark shapes looming, a range of clouds hanging overhead. The world was a ghostly shadow, thrown for a moment upon the pure darkness, which returned ever whole and complete.

And the mere delirium of sickness and fever went on inside him—his brain opening and shutting like the night—then sometimes convulsions of terror from something with great eyes that stared round a tree—then the long agony of the march, and the sun decomposing his blood—then the pang of hate for the Captain, followed by a pang of tenderness and ease. But everything was distorted, born of an ache and resolving into an ache.

In the morning he came definitely awake. Then his brain flamed with the sole horror of thirstiness! The sun was on his face, the dew was steaming from his wet clothes. Like one possessed, he got up. There, straight in front of him, blue and cool and tender, the mountains ranged across the pale edge of the morning sky. He wanted them—he wanted them alone—he wanted to leave himself and be identified with them. They did not move, they were still and soft, with white, gentle markings of snow. He stood still, mad with suffering, his hands crisping and clutching. Then he was twisting in a paroxysm on the grass.

He lay still, in a kind of dream of anguish. His thirst seemed to have separated itself from him, and to stand apart, a single demand. Then the pain he felt was another single self. Then there was the clog of his body, another separate thing. He was divided among all kinds of separate beings. There was some strange, agonised connection between them, but they were drawing further apart. Then they would all split. The sun, drilling down on him, was drilling through the bond. Then they would all fall, fall through the everlasting lapse of space. Then again, his consciousness reasserted itself. He roused on to his elbow and stared at the gleaming mountains. There they ranked, all still and wonderful between earth and heaven. He stared till his eyes went black, and the mountains, as they stood in their beauty, so clean and cool, seemed to have it, that which was lost in him.

When the soldiers found him, three hours later, he was lying with his face over his arm, his black hair giving off heat under the sun. But he was still alive. Seeing the open, black mouth the young soldiers dropped him in horror.

He died in the hospital at night, without having seen again.

The doctors saw the bruises on his legs, behind, and were silent.

The bodies of the two men lay together, side by side, in the mortuary, the one white and slender, but laid rigidly at rest, the other looking as if every moment it must rouse into life again, so young and unused, from a slumber.

66

Fish Are Such Liars

BY ROLAND PERTWEE

THERE HAD been a fuss in the pool beneath the alders, and the small rainbow trout, with a skitter of his tail, flashed upstream, a hurt and angry fish. For three consecutive mornings he had taken the rise in that pool, and it injured his pride to be jostled from his drift just when the Mayfly was coming up in numbers. If his opponent had been a half-pounder like himself, he would have stayed and fought, but when an old hen fish weighing fully three pounds, with a mouth like a rat hole and a carnivorous, cannibalistic eye rises from the reed beds and occupies the place, flight is the only effective argument.

But Rainbow was very much provoked. He had chosen his place with care. Now the Mayfly was up, the little French chalk stream was full of rising fish, and he knew by experience that strangers are unpopular in that season. To do one's self justice during a hatch, one must find a place where the fly drifts nicely overhead with the run of the stream, and natural drifts are scarce even in a chalk stream. He was not content to leap at the fly like an hysterical youngster who measured his weight in ounces and his wits in milligrams. He had reached that time of life which demanded that he should feed off the surface by suction rather than exertion. No living thing is more particular about his table manners than a trout, and Rainbow was no exception.

"It's a sickening thing," he said to himself, "and a hard shame." He added: "Get out of my way," to a couple of fat young chub with negroid mouths who were bubbling the surface in the silly, senseless fashion of their kind.

"Chub indeed!"

But even the chub had a home and he had none—and the life of a homeless river dweller is precarious.

979

"I will not and shall not be forced back to midstream," he said.

For, save at eventide or in very special circumstances, trout of personality do not frequent open water where they must compete for every insect with the wind, the lightning-swift sweep of swallows and martins and even the laborious pursuit of predatory dragon-flies with their bronze wings and bodies like rods of coloured glass. Even as he spoke he saw a three-ouncer leap at a dapping Mayfly which was scooped out of his jaws by a passing swallow. Rainbow heard the tiny click as the Mayfly's body cracked against the bird's beak. A single wing of yellowy gossamer floated downward and settled upon the water. Under the shelving banks to right and left, where the fly, discarding its nymph and still too damp for its virgin flight, drifted downstream, a dozen heavy trout were feeding thoughtfully and selectively.

"If only some angler would catch one of them, I might slip in and occupy the place before it gets known there's a vacancy."

But this uncharitable hope was not fulfilled, and with another whisk of his tail he propelled himself into the unknown waters upstream. A couple of strands of rusty barbed wire, relic of the War, spanned the shallows from bank to bank. Passing beneath them he came to a narrow reach shaded by willows, to the first of which was nailed a board bearing the words, *Pêche Reservée*. He had passed out of the communal into private water—water running languidly over manes of emerald weed between clumps of alder, willow herb, tall crimson sorrel and masses of yellow iris. Ahead, like an apple-green rampart, rose the wooded heights of a forest; on either side were flat meadows of yellowing hay. Overhead, the vast expanse of blue June sky was tufted with rambling clouds. "My scales!" said Rainbow. "Here's water!"

But it was vain to expect any of the best places in such a reach would be vacant, and to avoid a recurrence of his unhappy encounter earlier in the morning, Rainbow continued his journey until he came to a spot where the river took one of those unaccountable right-angle bends which result in a pool, shallow on the one side, but slanting into deeps on the other. Above it was a water break, a swirl, smoothing, as it reached the pool, into a sleek, swift run, with an eddy which bore all the lighter floating things of the river over the calm surface of the little backwater, sheltered from above by a high shelving bank and a tangle of bramble and herb. Here in this backwater the twig, the broken reed, the leaf, the cork, the fly floated in suspended activity for a few instants until drawn back by invisible magnetism to the main current.

Rainbow paused in admiration. At the tail of the pool two sound fish were rising with regularity, but in the backwater beyond the eddy the surface was still and unbroken. Watching open-eyed, Rainbow saw not one but a dozen Mayflies, fat, juicy and damp from the nymph, drift in, pause and carried away untouched. It was beyond the bounds of possibility that such a place could be vacant, but there was the evidence of his eyes to prove it; and nothing if not a trier, Rainbow darted across the stream and parked himself six inches below the water to await events.

It so happened that at the time of his arrival the hatch of fly was temporarily suspended, which gave Rainbow leisure to make a survey of his new abode. Beyond the eddy was a submerged snag—the branch of an apple tree borne there by heavy rains, water-logged, anchored and intricate—an excellent place to break an angler's line. The river bank on his right was riddled under water with old rat holes, than which there is no better sanctuary. Below him and to the left was a dense bed of weeds brushed flat by the flow of the stream.

"If it comes to the worst," said Rainbow, "a smart fish could do a getaway here with very little ingenuity, even from a cannibalistic old hen like—hullo!"

The exclamation was excited by the apparition of a gauzy shadow on the water, which is what a Mayfly seen from below looks like. Resisting a vulgar inclination to leap at it with the violence of a youngster, Rainbow backed into the correct position which would allow the stream to present the morsel, so to speak, upon a tray. Which it did—and scarcely a dimple on the surface to tell what had happened.

"Very nicely taken, if you will accept the praise of a complete stranger," said a low, soft voice, one inch behind his line of sight.

Without turning to see by whom he had been addressed, Rainbow flicked a yard upstream and came back with the current four feet away. In the spot he had occupied an instant before lay a great old trout of the most benign aspect, who could not have weighed less than four pounds.

"I beg your pardon," said Rainbow, "but I had no idea that any one —that is, I just dropped in en passant, and finding an empty house, I made so bold——"

"There is no occasion to apologize," said Old Trout seductively. "I did not come up from the bottom as early to-day as is my usual habit at this season. Yesterday's hatch was singularly bountiful and it is possible I did myself too liberally."

"Yes, but a gentleman of your weight and seniority can hardly fail to be offended at finding——"

"Not at all," Old Trout broke in. "I perceive you are a well-conducted fish who does not advertise his appetite in a loud and splashing fashion."

Overcome by the charm of Old Trout's manner and address, Rainbow reduced the distance separating them to a matter of inches.

"Then you do not want me to go?" he asked.

"On the contrary, dear young sir, stay by all means and take the rise.

You are, I perceive, of the rainbow or, as they say here in France, of the *Arc en ciel* family. As a youngster I had the impression that I should turn out a rainbow, but events proved it was no more than the bloom, the natural sheen of youth."

"To speak the truth, sir," said Rainbow, "unless you had told me to the contrary, I would surely have thought you one of us."

Old Trout shook his tail. "You are wrong," he said. "I am from Dulverton, an English trout farm on the Exe, of which you will have heard. You are doubtless surprised to find an English fish in French waters."

"I am indeed," Rainbow replied, sucking in a passing Mayfly with such excellent good manners that it was hard to believe he was feeding. "Then you, sir," he added, "must know all about the habits of men."

"I may justly admit that I do," Old Trout agreed. "Apart from being hand-reared, I have in my twelve years of life studied the species in moods of activity, passivity, duplicity, and violence."

Rainbow remarked that such must doubtless have proved of invaluable service. It did not, however, explain the mystery of his presence on a French river.

"For, sir," he added, "Dulverton, as once I heard when enjoying 'A Chat about Rivers' delivered by a much travelled sea trout, is situated in the West of England, and without crossing the Channel I am unable to explain how you arrived here. Had you belonged to the salmon family, with which, sir, it is evident you have no connection, the explanation would be simple, but in the circumstances it baffles my understanding."

Old Trout waved one of his fins airily. "Yet cross the Channel I certainly did," said he, "and at a period in history which I venture to state will not readily be forgotten. It was during the War, my dear young friend, and I was brought in a can, in company with a hundred yearlings, to this river, or rather the upper reaches of this river, by a young officer who wished to further an entente between English and French fish even as the War was doing with the mankind of these two nations."

Old Trout sighed a couple of bubbles and arched his body this way and that.

"There was a gentleman and sportsman," he said. "A man who was acquainted with our people as I dare to say very few are acquainted. Had it ever been my lot to fall victim to a lover of the rod, I could have done so without regret to his. If you will take a look at my tail, you will observe that the letter *W* is perforated on the upper side. He presented me with this distinguishing mark before committing me, with his blessing, to the water."

"I have seldom seen a tail more becomingly decorated," said Rainbow. "But what happened to your benefactor?"

Old Trout's expression became infinitely sad. "If I could answer that," said he, "I were indeed a happy trout. For many weeks after he put me into the river I used to watch him in what little spare time he was able to obtain, casting a dry fly with the most exquisite precision and likeness to nature in all the likely pools and runs and eddies near his battery position. Oh, minnows! It was a pleasure to watch that man, even as it was his pleasure to watch us. His bravery too! I call to mind a dozen times when he fished unmoved and unstartled while bullets from machine-guns were pecking at the waters like herons and thudding into the mud banks upon which he stood."

"An angler!" remarked Rainbow. "It would be no lie to say I like him the less on that account."

Old Trout became unexpectedly stern.

"Why so?" he retorted severely. "Have I not said he was also a gentleman and a sportsman? My officer was neither a pot-hunter nor a beast of prey. He was a purist—a man who took delight in pitting his knowledge of nature against the subtlest and most suspicious intellectual forces of the wild. Are you so young as not yet to have learned the exquisite enjoyment of escaping disaster and avoiding error by the exercise of personal ingenuity? Pray, do not reply, for I would hate to think so hard a thing of any trout. We, as a race, exist by virtue of our brilliant intellectuality and hypersensitive selectivity. In waters where there are no pike and only an occasional otter, but for the machinations of men, where should we turn to school our wits? Danger is our mainstay, for I tell you, Rainbow, that trout are composed of two senses—appetite, which makes of us fools, and suspicion, which teaches us to be wise."

Greatly chastened not alone by what Old Trout had said but by the forensic quality of his speech, Rainbow rose short and put a promising Mayfly on the wing.

"I am glad to observe," said Old Trout, "that you are not without conscience."

"To tell the truth, sir," Rainbow replied apologetically, "my nerve this morning has been rudely shaken, but for which I should not have shown such want of good sportsmanship."

And with becoming brevity he told the tale of his eviction from the pool downstream. Old Trout listened gravely, only once moving, and that to absorb a small blue dun, an insect which he keenly relished.

"A regrettable affair," he admitted, "but as I have often observed, women, who are the gentlest creatures under water in adversity, are a thought lacking in moderation in times of abundance. They are apt to snatch."

"But for a turn of speed she would certainly have snatched me," said Rainbow.

"Very shocking," said Old Trout. "Cannibals are disgusting. They destroy the social amenities of the river. We fish have but little family life and should therefore aim to cultivate a freemasonry of good fellowship among ourselves. For my part, I am happy to line up with other well-conducted trout and content myself with what happens along my own particular drift. Pardon me!" he added, breasting Rainbow to one side. "I invited you to take the rise of Mayfly, but I must ask you to leave the duns alone." Then, fearing this remark might be construed to reflect adversely upon his hospitality, he proceeded: "I have a reason which I will explain later. For the moment we are discussing the circumstances that led to my presence in this river."

"To be sure—your officer. He never succeeded in deluding you with his skill?"

"That would have been impossible," said Old Trout, "for I had taken up a position under the far bank where he could only have reached me with a fly by wading in a part of the river which was in view of a German sniper."

"Wily!" Rainbow chuckled. "Cunning work, sir."

"Perhaps," Old Trout admitted, "although I have since reproached myself with cowardice. However, I was at the time a very small fish and a certain amount of nervousness is forgivable in the young."

At this gracious acknowledgment the rose-coloured hue in Rainbow's rainbow increased noticeably—in short, he blushed.

"From where I lay," Old Trout went on, "I was able to observe the manœuvres of my officer and greatly profit thereby."

"But excuse me, sir," said Rainbow, "I have heard it said that an angler of the first class is invisible from the river."

"He is invisible to the fish he is trying to catch," Old Trout admitted, "but it must be obvious that he is not invisible to the fish who lie beside or below him. I would also remind you that during the War every tree, every scrap of vegetation, and every vestige of natural cover had been torn up, trampled down, razed. The river banks were as smooth as the top of your head. Even the buttercup, that very humorous flower that tangles up the back cast of so many industrious anglers, was absent. Those who fished on the Western Front had little help from nature."

Young Rainbow sighed, for, only a few days before, his tongue had been badly scratched by an artificial alder which had every appearance of reality.

"It would seem," he said, "that this war had its merits."

"My young friend," said Old Trout, "you never made a greater mistake. A desire on the part of our soldiery to vary a monotonous diet of bully beef and biscuit often drove them to resort to villainous methods of assault against our kind."

"Nets?" gasped Rainbow in horror.

"Worse than nets—bombs," Old Trout replied. "A small oval black thing called a Mills bomb, which the shameless fellows flung into deep pools."

"But surely the chances of being hit by such a——"

"You reveal a pathetic ignorance," said Old Trout. "There is no question of being hit. The wretched machine exploded under water and burst our people's insides or stunned us so that we floated dead to the surface. I well remember my officer coming upon such a group of marauders one evening—yes, and laying about him with his fists in defiance of King's Regulations and the Manual of Military Law. Two of them he seized by the collar and the pants and flung into the river. Spinning minnows, that was a sight worth seeing! 'You low swine,' I heard him say; 'you trash, you muck! Isn't there enough carnage without this sort of thing?' Afterward he sat on the bank with the two dripping men and talked to them for their souls' sake.

" 'Look ahead, boys. Ask yourselves what are we fighting for? Decent homes to live in at peace with one another, fields to till and forests and rivers to give us a day's sport and fun. It's our rotten job to massacre each other, but, by gosh, don't let's massacre the harmless rest of nature as well. At least, let's give 'em a running chance. Boys, in the years ahead, when all the mess is cleared up, I look forward to coming back to this old spot, when there is alder growing by the banks, and willow herb and tall reeds and the drone of insects instead of the rumble of those guns. I don't want to come back to a dead river that I helped to kill, but to a river ringed with rising fish—some of whom were old comrades of the War.' He went on to tell of us hundred Dulverton trout that he had marked with the letter *W*. 'Give 'em their chance,' he said, 'and in the years to come those beggars will reward us a hundred times over. They'll give us a finer thrill and put up a cleaner fight than old Jerry ever contrived.' Those were emotional times, and though you may be reluctant to believe me, one of those two very wet men dripped water from his eyes as well as his clothing.

" 'Many's the 'appy afternoon I've 'ad with a roach pole on Brentford Canal,' he sniffed, 'though I've never yet tried m' hand against a trout.' 'You shall do it now,' said my officer, and during the half-hour that was left of daylight that dripping soldier had his first lesson in the most delicate art in the world. I can see them now—the clumsy, wet fellow, and my officer timing him, timing him—'one and two, and one and two, and——' The action of my officer's wrist with its persuasive flick was the prettiest thing I have ever seen."

"Did he carry out his intention and come back after the War?" Rainbow asked.

"I shall never know," Old Trout replied. "I do not even know if he

survived it. There was a great battle—a German drive. For hours they
shelled the river front, and many falling short exploded in our midst
with terrible results. My own bank was torn to shreds and our people
suffered. How they suffered! About noon the infantry came over—
hordes in field grey. There were pontoons, rope bridges and hand-to-
hand fights on both banks and even in the stream itself."

"And your officer?"

"I saw him once, before the water was stamped dense into liquid mud
and dyed by the blood of men. He was in the thick of it, unarmed, and
a German officer called on him to surrender. For answer he struck him
in the face with a light cane. Ah, that wrist action! Then a shell burst,
smothering the water with clods of fallen earth and other things."

"Then you never knew?"

"I never knew, although that night I searched among the dead. Next
day I went downstream, for the water in that place was polluted with
death. The bottom of the pool in which I had my place was choked with
strange and mangled tenants that were not good to look upon. We
trout are a clean people that will not readily abide in dirty houses. I am
a Dulverton trout, where the water is filtered by the hills and runs cool
over stones."

"And you have stayed here ever since?"

Old Trout shrugged a fin. "I have moved with the times. Choosing a
place according to the needs of my weight."

"And you have never been caught, sir, by any other angler?"

"Am I not here?" Old Trout answered with dignity.

"Oh, quite, sir. I had only thought, perhaps, as a younger fish enthusiasm might have resulted to your disadvantage, but that, nevertheless,
you had been returned."

"Returned! Returned!" echoed Old Trout. "Returned to the frying
pan! Where on earth did you pick up that expression? We are in France,
my young friend; we are not on the Test, the Itchen, or the Kennet. In
this country it is not the practice of anglers to return anything, however
miserable in size."

"But nowadays," Rainbow protested, "there are Englishmen and
Americans on the river who show us more consideration."

"They may show you consideration," said Old Trout, "but I am of
an importance that neither asks for nor expects it. Oblige me by being
a little more discreet with your plurals. In the impossible event of my
being deceived and caught, I should be introduced to a glass case with
an appropriate background of rocks and weeds."

"But, sir, with respect, how can you be so confident of your unassail-
ability?" Rainbow demanded, edging into position to accept an at-

tractive Mayfly with yellow wings that was drifting downstream toward him.

"How?" Old Trout responded. "Because——" Then suddenly: "Leave it, you fool!"

Rainbow had just broken the surface when the warning came. The yellow-winged Mayfly was wrenched off the water with a wet squeak. A tangle of limp cast lapped itself round the upper branches of a willow far upstream and a raw voice exclaimed something venomous in French. By common consent the two fish went down.

"Well, really," expostulated Old Trout, "I hoped you were above that kind of thing! Nearly to fall victim to a downstream angler. It's a little too much! And think of the effect it will have on my prestige. Why, that incompetent fool will go about boasting that he rose me. Me!"

For some minutes Rainbow was too crestfallen even to apologize. At last:

"I am afraid," he said, "I was paying more heed to what you were saying than to my own conduct. I never expected to be fished from above. The fly was an uncommonly good imitation and it is a rare thing for a Frenchman to use Four-X gut."

"Rubbish," said Old Trout testily. "These are mere half-pound arguments. Four-X gut, when associated with a fourteen-stone shadow, should deceive nothing over two ounces. I saved your life, but it is all very provoking. If that is a sample of your general demeanour, it is improbable that you will ever reach a pound."

"At this season we are apt to be careless," Rainbow wailed. "And nowadays it is so hard, sir, to distinguish the artificial fly from the real."

"No one expects you to do so," was the answer, "but common prudence demands that you should pay some attention to the manner in which it is presented. A Mayfly does not hit the water with a splash, neither is it able to sustain itself in midstream against the current. Have you ever seen a natural insect leave a broadening wake of cutwater behind its tail? Never mind the fly, my dear boy, but watch the manner of its presentation. Failure to do that has cost many of our people their lives."

"You speak, sir," said Rainbow, a shade sulkily, "as though it were a disgrace for a trout ever to suffer defeat at the hands of an angler."

"Which indeed it is, save in exceptional circumstances," Old Trout answered. "I do not say that a perfect upstream cast from a well-concealed angler when the fly alights dry and cocked and dances at even speed with the current, may not deceive us to our fall. And I would be the last to say that a grasshopper skilfully dapped on the surface through the branches of an overhanging tree will not inevitably bring about our destruction. But I do most emphatically say that in such a spot as this, where the slightest defect in presentation is multiplied a hundredfold by the varying water speeds, a careless rise is unpardonable. There is only one spot—and that a matter of twelve yards downstream—from which a fly can be drifted over me with any semblance to nature. Even so, there is not one angler in a thousand who can make that cast with success, by reason of a willow which cramps the back cast and the manner on which these alders on our left sprawl across the pool."

Rainbow did not turn about to verify these statements because it is bad form for a trout to face downstream. He contented himself by replying, with a touch of acerbity:

"I should have thought, sir, with the feelings you expressed regarding sportsmanship, you would have found such a sanctuary too dull for your entertainment."

"Every remark you make serves to aggravate the impression of your ignorance," Old Trout replied. "Would you expect a trout of my intelligence to put myself in some place where I am exposed to the vulgar assaults of every amateur upon the bank? Of the green boy who lashes the water into foam, of the purblind peasant who slings his fly at me with a clod of earth or a tail of weed attached to the hook? In this place I invite attention from none but the best people—the expert, the purist."

"I understood you to say that there were none such in these parts," grumbled Rainbow.

"There are none who have succeeded in deceiving me," was the answer. "As a fact, for the last few days I have been vastly entranced by an angler who, by any standard, is deserving of praise. His presentation is flawless and the only fault I can detect in him is a tendency to overlook piscine psychology. He will be with us in a few minutes, since he knows it is my habit to lunch at noon."

"Pardon the interruption," said Rainbow, "but there is a gallant hatch of fly going down. I can hear your two neighbours at the tail of the pool rising steadily."

Old Trout assumed an indulgent air. "We will go up if you wish," said he, "but you will be well advised to observe my counsel before taking the rise, because if my angler keeps his appointment you will most assuredly be *meuniered* before nightfall."

At this unpleasant phophecy Rainbow shivered. "Let us keep to weed," he suggested.

But Old Trout only laughed, so that bubbles from the river bed rose and burst upon the surface.

"Courage," said he; "it will be an opportunity for you to learn the finer points of the game. If you are nervous, lie nearer to the bank. The natural fly does not drift there so abundantly, but you will be secure from the artificial. Presently I will treat you to an exhibition of playing with death you will not fail to appreciate." He broke off and pointed with his eyes. "Over you and to the left."

Rainbow made a neat double rise and drifted back into line. "Very mellow," he said—"very mellow and choice. Never tasted better. May I ask, sir, what you meant by piscine psychology?"

"I imply that my angler does not appreciate the subtle possibilities of our intellect. Now, my officer concerned himself as vitally with what we were thinking as with what we were feeding upon. This fellow, secure in the knowledge that his presentation is well-nigh perfect, is content to offer me the same variety of flies day after day, irrespective of the fact that I have learned them all by heart. I have, however, adopted the practice of rising every now and then to encourage him."

"Rising? At an artificial fly? I never heard such temerity in all my life," gasped Rainbow.

Old Trout moved his body luxuriously. "I should have said, appearing to rise," he amended. "You may have noticed that I have exhibited a predilection for small duns in preference to the larger *Ephemeridæ*. My procedure is as follows: I wait until a natural dun and his artificial Mayfly are drifting downstream with the smallest possible distance separating them. Then I rise and take the dun. Assuming I have risen to him, he strikes, misses, and is at once greatly flattered and greatly provoked. By this device I sometimes occupy his attention for over an hour and thus render a substantial service to others of my kind who would certainly have fallen victim to his skill."

"The river is greatly in your debt, sir," said Young Rainbow, with deliberate satire.

He knew by experience that fish as well as anglers are notorious liars, but the exploit his host recounted was a trifle too strong. Taking a sidelong glance, he was surprised to see that Old Trout did not appear to have appreciated the subtle ridicule of his remark. The long, lithe body had become almost rigid and the great round eyes were focussed upon the surface with an expression of fixed concentration.

Looking up Rainbow saw a small white-winged Mayfly with red legs and a body the colour of straw swing out from the main stream and describe a slow circle over the calm surface above Old Trout's head. Scarcely an inch away a tiny blue dun, its wings folded as closely as the pages of a book, floated attendant. An upward rush, a sucking kerr-rop, and when the broken water had calmed, the dun had disappeared and the Mayfly was dancing away downstream.

"Well," said Old Trout, "how's that, my youthful sceptic? Pretty work, eh?"

"I saw nothing in it," was the impertinent reply. "There is not a trout on the river who could not have done likewise."

"Even when one of those two flies was artificial?" Old Trout queried tolerantly.

"But neither of them was artificial," Rainbow retorted. "Had it been so the angler would have struck. They always do."

"Of course he struck," Old Trout replied.

"But he didn't," Rainbow protested. "I saw the Mayfly go down with the current."

"My poor fish!" Old Trout replied. "Do you presume to suggest that I am unable to distinguish an artificial from a natural fly? Are you so blind that you failed to see the prismatic colours in the water from the paraffin in which the fly had been dipped? Here you are! Here it is again!"

Once more the white-winged insect drifted across the backwater, but this time there was no attendant dun.

"If that's a fake I'll eat my tail," said Rainbow.

"If you question my judgment," Old Trout answered, "you are at liberty to rise. I dare say, in spite of a shortage of brain, that you would eat comparatively well."

But Rainbow, in common with his kind, was not disposed to take chances.

"We may expect two or three more casts from this fly and then he will change it for a bigger. It is the same programme every day without variation. How differently my officer would have acted. By now he would have discovered my little joke and turned the tables against me. Aye me, but some men will never learn! Your mental outfit, dear Rainbow, is singularly like a man's," he added. "It lacks elasticity."

Rainbow made no retort and was glad of his forbearance, for every word Old Trout had spoken was borne out by subsequent events. Four times the white-winged Mayfly described an arc over the backwater, but in the absence of duns Old Trout did not rise again. Then came a pause, during which, through a lull in the hatch, even the natural insect was absent from the river.

"He is changing his fly," said Old Trout, "but he will not float it until the hatch starts again. He is casting beautifully this morning and I hope circumstances will permit me to give him another rise."

"But suppose," said Rainbow breathlessly, "you played this game once too often and were foul hooked as a result?"

Old Trout expanded his gills broadly. "Why, then," he replied, "I should break him. Once round a limb of that submerged apple bough and the thing would be done. I should never allow myself to be caught and no angler could gather up the slack and haul me into midstream in time to prevent me reaching the bough. Stand by."

The shadow of a large, dark Mayfly floated cockily over the backwater and had almost returned to the main stream when a small iron-blue dun settled like a puff of thistledown in its wake.

The two insects were a foot nearer the fast water than the spot where Old Trout was accustomed to take the rise. But for the presence of a spectator, it is doubtful whether he would have done so, but Young Rainbow's want of appreciation had excited his vanity, and with a rolling swoop he swallowed the dun and bore it downward.

And then an amazing thing happened. Instead of drifting back to his place as was expected, Old Trout's head was jerked sideways by an invisible force. A thin translucent thread upcut the water's surface and tightened irresistibly. A second later Old Trout was fighting, fighting, fighting to reach the submerged apple bough with the full weight of the running water and the full strength of the finest Japanese gut strained against him.

Watching, wide-eyed and aghast, from one of the underwater rat holes into which he had hastily withdrawn, Rainbow saw the figure of a man rise out of a bed of irises downstream and scramble upon the bank. In his right hand, with the wrist well back, he held a light split-cane rod whose upper joint was curved to a half-circle. The man's left hand was detaching a collapsible landing net from the ring of his belt. Every attitude and movement was expressive of perfectly organized activity. His mouth was shut as tightly as a steel trap, but a light of happy excitement danced in his eyes.

"No, you don't, my fellar," Rainbow heard him say. "No, you don't. I knew all about that apple bough before ever I put a fly over your pool. And the weed bed on the right," he added, as Old Trout made a sudden swerve half down and half across stream.

Tucking the net under his arm, the man whipped up the slack with a lightning-like action. The manœuvre cost Old Trout dear, for when, despairing of reaching the weed and burrowing into it, he tried to regain his old position, he found himself six feet farther away from the apple bough than when the battle began.

Instinctively Old Trout knew it was useless to dash downstream, for a man who could take up slack with the speed his adversary had shown would profit by the expedient to come more quickly to terms with him. Besides, lower down there was broken water to knock the breath out of his lungs. Even where he lay straining and slugging this way and that, the water was pouring so fast into his open mouth as nearly to drown him. His only chance of effecting a smash was by a series of jumps, followed by quick dives. Once before, although he had not confessed it to Rainbow, Old Trout had saved his life by resorting to this expedient. It takes the strain off the line and returns it so quickly that even the finest gut is apt to sunder.

Meanwhile the man was slowly approaching, winding up as he came. Old Trout, boring in the depths, could hear the click of the check reel with increasing distinctness. Looking up, he saw that the cast was almost vertical above his head, which meant that the moment to make the attempt was at hand. The tension was appalling, for ever since the fight began his adversary had given him the butt unremittingly. Aware of his own weight and power, Old Trout was amazed that any tackle could stand the strain.

"Now's my time," he thought, and jumped.

It was no ordinary jump, but an aerial rush three feet out of the water, with a twist at its apex and a cutting lash of the tail designed to break the cast. But his adversary was no ordinary angler, and at the first hint of what was happening he dropped the point of the rod flush with the surface.

Once and once more Old Trout flung himself into the air, but after each attempt he found himself with diminishing strength and with less line to play with.

"It looks to me," said Rainbow mournfully, "as if my unhappy host will lose this battle and finish up in that glass case to which he was referring a few minutes ago." And greatly affected, he burrowed his nose in the mud and wondered, in the event of this dismal prophecy coming true, whether he would be able to take possession of the pool without molestation.

In consequence of these reflections he failed to witness the last phase of the battle, when, as will sometimes happen with big fish, all the fight went out of Old Trout, and rolling wearily over and over, he abandoned himself to the clinging embraces of the net. He never saw the big man proudly carry Old Trout back into the hayfield, where, before proceeding to remove the fly, he sat down beside a shallow dyke and lit a cigarette and smiled largely. Then, with an affectionate and professional touch, he picked up Old Trout by the back of the neck, his forefinger and thumb sunk firmly in the gills.

"You're a fine fellar," he said, extracting the fly, "a good sportsman and a funny fish. You fooled me properly for three days, but I think you'll own I outwitted you in the end."

Rummaging in his creel for a small rod of hard wood that he carried for the purpose of administering the quietus, he became aware of something that arrested the action. Leaning forward, he stared with open eyes at a tiny *W* perforated in the upper part of Old Trout's tail.

"Shades of the War! Dulverton!" he exclaimed. Then with a sudden warmth: "Old chap, old chap, is it really you? This is red-letter stuff. If you're not too far gone to take another lease of life, have it with me."

And with the tenderness of a woman, he slipped Old Trout into the dyke and in a tremble of excitement hurried off to the *auberge* where the fishermen lodged, to tell a tale no one even pretended to believe.

For the best part of an hour Old Trout lay in the shallow waters of the dyke before slowly cruising back to his own place beneath the overhanging bank. The alarming experience through which he had passed had made him a shade forgetful, and he was not prepared for the sight of Young Rainbow rising steadily at the hatch of fly.

"Pardon me, but a little more to your right," he said, with heavy courtesy.

"Diving otters!" cried Young Rainbow, leaping a foot clear of the water. "You, sir! You!"

"And why not?" Old Trout replied. "Your memory must be short if you have already forgotten that this is my place."

"Yes, but——" Rainbow began and stopped.

"You are referring to that little circus of a few minutes ago," said Old Trout. "Is it possible you failed to appreciate the significance of the affair? I knew at once it was my dear officer when he dropped the artificial dun behind the natural Mayfly. In the circumstances I could hardly do less than accept his invitation. Nothing is more delightful than a reunion of comrades of the war." He paused and added: "We had a charming talk, he and I, and I do not know which of us was the more affected. It is a tragedy that such friendship and such intellect as we share cannot exist in a common element."

And so great was his emotion that Old Trout dived and buried his head in the weeds. Whereby Rainbow did uncommonly well during the midday hatch.

67

A Source of Irritation

BY STACY AUMONIER

To LOOK at old Sam Gates you would never suspect him of having nerves. His sixty-nine years of close application to the needs of the soil had given him a certain earthy stolidity. To observe him hoeing, or thinning out a broad field of turnips, hardly attracted one's attention, he seemed so much part and parcel of the whole scheme. He blended into the soil like a glorified swede. Nevertheless, the half-dozen people who claimed his acquaintance knew him to be a man who suffered from little moods of irritability.

And on this glorious morning a little incident annoyed him unreasonably. It concerned his niece Aggie. She was a plump girl with clear, blue eyes, and a face as round and inexpressive as the dumplings for which the county was famous. She came slowly across the long sweep of the downland and, putting down the bundle wrapped in a red handkerchief which contained his breakfast and dinner, she said:

"Well, Uncle, is there any noos?"

Now, this may not appear to the casual reader to be a remark likely to cause irritation, but it affected old Sam Gates as a very silly and unnecessary question. It was, moreover, the constant repetition of it which was beginning to anger him. He met his niece twice a day. In the morning she brought his bundle of food at seven, and when he passed his sister's cottage on the way home to tea at five she was invariably hanging about the gate, and she always said in the same voice:

"Well, Uncle, is there any noos?"

Noos! What noos should there be? For sixty-nine years he had never lived farther than five miles from Halvesham. For nearly sixty of those years he had bent his back above the soil. There were, indeed, historic occasions. Once, for instance, when he had married Annie Hachet. And there was the birth of his daughter. There was also a famous occasion when he had visited London. Once he had been to a flower-show at Market Roughborough. He either went or didn't go to church on Sundays. He had many interesting chats with Mr. James at the Cowman, and three years ago had sold a pig to Mrs. Way. But he couldn't always have interesting noos of this sort up his sleeve. Didn't the silly zany know that for the last three weeks he had been hoeing and thinning out turnips for Mr. Hodge on this very same field? What noos could there be?

He blinked at his niece, and didn't answer. She undid the parcel and said:

"Mrs. Goping's fowl got out again last night."

"Ah," he replied in a non-committal manner and began to munch his bread and bacon. His niece picked up the handkerchief and, humming to herself, walked back across the field.

It was a glorious morning, and a white sea mist added to the promise of a hot day. He sat there munching, thinking of nothing in particular, but gradually subsiding into a mood of placid content. He noticed the back of Aggie disappear in the distance. It was a mile to the cottage and a mile and a half to Halvesham. Silly things, girls. They were all alike. One had to make allowances. He dismissed her from his thoughts, and took a long swig of tea out of a bottle. Insects buzzed lazily. He tapped his pocket to assure himself that his pouch of shag was there, and then he continued munching. When he had finished, he lighted his pipe and stretched himself comfortably. He looked along the line of turnips he had thinned and then across the adjoining field of swedes. Silver streaks appeared on the sea below the mist. In some dim way he felt happy in his solitude amidst this sweeping immensity of earth and sea and sky.

And then something else came to irritate him: it was one of "these dratted airyplanes." "Airyplanes" were his pet aversion. He could find nothing to be said in their favor. Nasty, noisy, disfiguring things that seared the heavens and made the earth dangerous. And every day there seemed to be more and more of them. Of course "this old war" was responsible for a lot of them, he knew. The war was a "plaguy noosance." They were short-handed on the farm, beer and tobacco were dear, and Mrs. Steven's nephew had been and got wounded in the foot.

He turned his attention once more to the turnips; but an "airyplane" has an annoying genius for gripping one's attention. When it appears on the scene, however much we dislike it, it has a way of taking the stage-center. We cannot help constantly looking at it. And so it was with old Sam Gates. He spat on his hands and blinked up at the sky. And suddenly the aeroplane behaved in a very extraordinary manner. It was well over the sea when it seemed to lurch drunkenly and skimmed the water. Then it shot up at a dangerous angle and zig-zagged. It started to go farther out, and then turned and made for the land. The engines were making a curious grating noise. It rose once more, and then suddenly dived downward, and came plump down right in the middle of Mr. Hodge's field of swedes.

And then, as if not content with this desecration, it ran along the ground, ripping and tearing up twenty-five yards of good swedes, and then came to a stop.

Old Sam Gates was in a terrible state. The aeroplane was more than a hundred yards away, but he waved his arms and called out:

"Hi, you there, you mustn't land in they swedes! They're Mister Hodge's."

The instant the aeroplane stopped, a man leaped out and gazed quickly round. He glanced at Sam Gates, and seemed uncertain whether to address him or whether to concentrate his attention on the flying-machine. The latter arrangement appeared to be his ultimate decision. He dived under the engine and became frantically busy. Sam had never seen any one work with such furious energy; but all the same it was not to be tolerated. It was disgraceful. Sam started out across the field, almost hurrying in his indignation. When he appeared within earshot of the aviator he cried out again:

"Hi! you mustn't rest your old airyplane here! You've kicked up all Mr. Hodge's swedes. A noice thing you've done!"

He was within five yards when suddenly the aviator turned and cov-ered him with a revolver! And speaking in a sharp, staccato voice, he said:

"Old Grandfather, you must sit down. I am very much occupied. If you interfere or attempt to go away, I shoot you. So!"

Sam gazed at the horrid, glittering little barrel and gasped. Well, he never! To be threatened with murder when you're doing your duty in your employer's private property! But, still, perhaps the man was mad. A man must be more or less mad to go up in one of those crazy things. And life was very sweet on that summer morning despite sixty-nine years. He sat down among the swedes.

The aviator was so busy with his cranks and machinery that he hardly deigned to pay him any attention except to keep the revolver handy. He worked feverishly, and Sam sat watching him. At the end of ten minutes he appeared to have solved his troubles with the ma-chine, but he still seemed very scared. He kept on glancing round and out to sea. When his repairs were complete he straightened his back and wiped the perspiration from his brow. He was apparently on the point of springing back into the machine and going off when a sudden mood of facetiousness, caused by relief from the strain he had endured, came to him. He turned to old Sam and smiled, at the same time remarking:

"Well, old Grandfather, and now we shall be all right, isn't it?"

He came close up to Sam, and then suddenly started back.

"*Gott!*" he cried, "Paul Jouperts!"

Bewildered, Sam gazed at him, and the madman started talking to him in some foreign tongue. Sam shook his head.

"You no right," he remarked, "to come bargin' through they swedes of Mr. Hodge's."

And then the aviator behaved in a most peculiar manner. He came up and examined Sam's face very closely, and gave a sudden tug at his beard and hair, as if to see whether they were real or false.

"What is your name, old man?" he said.

"Sam Gates."

The aviator muttered some words that sounded something like "mare vudish," and then turned to his machine. He appeared to be dazed and in a great state of doubt. He fumbled with some cranks, but kept glancing at old Sam. At last he got into the car and strapped himself in. Then he stopped, and sat there deep in thought. At last he suddenly unstrapped himself and sprang out again and, approaching Sam, said very deliberately:

"Old Grandfather, I shall require you to accompany me."

Sam gasped.

"Eh!" he said. "What be talkin' about? 'Company? I got these 'ere loines o' turnips—I be already behoind—" The disgusting little revolver once more flashed before his eyes.

"There must be no discussion," came the voice. "It is necessary that you mount the seat of the car without delay. Otherwise I shoot you like the dog you are. So!"

Old Sam was hale and hearty. He had no desire to die so ignominiously. The pleasant smell of the Norfolk downland was in his nostrils; his foot was on his native heath. He mounted the seat of the car, contenting himself with a mutter:

"Well, that be a noice thing, I must say! Flyin' about the country with all they turnips on'y half thinned!"

He found himself strapped in. The aviator was in a fever of anxiety to get away. The engines made a ghastly splutter and noise. The thing started running along the ground. Suddenly it shot upward, giving the swedes a last contemptuous kick. At twenty minutes to eight that morning old Sam found himself being borne right up above his fields and out to sea! His breath came quickly. He was a little frightened.

"God forgive me!" he murmured.

The thing was so fantastic and sudden that his mind could not grasp it. He only felt in some vague way that he was going to die, and he struggled to attune his mind to the change. He offered up a mild prayer to God, Who, he felt, must be very near, somewhere up in these clouds. Automatically he thought of the vicar at Halvesham, and a certain sense of comfort came to him at the reflection that on the previous day he had taken a "cooking of runner beans" to God's representative in that village. He felt calmer after that, but the horrid machine seemed to go higher and higher. He could not turn in his seat and he could see nothing but sea and sky. Of course the man was mad, mad as a March hare. Of what earthly use could *he* be to any one? Besides, he had talked pure gibberish, and called him Paul something, when he had already told him that his name was Sam. The thing would fall down into the sea soon, and they would both be drowned. Well, well, he had almost reached three-score years and ten. He was protected by a screen, but it seemed very cold. What on earth would Mr. Hodge say? There was no one left to work the land but a fool of a boy named Billy Whitehead at Dene's Cross. On, on, on they went at a furious pace. His thoughts danced disconnectedly from incidents of his youth, conversations with the vicar, hearty meals in the open, a frock his sister wore on the day of the postman's wedding, the drone of a psalm, the illness of some ewes belonging to Mr. Hodge. Everything seemed to be moving very rapidly, upsetting his sense of time. He felt outraged, and yet at moments there was something entrancing in the wild experience. He seemed to be living at an incredible pace. Perhaps he was really dead and on his way to the kingdom of God. Perhaps this was the way they took people.

After some indefinite period he suddenly caught sight of a long strip of land. Was this a foreign country, or were they returning? He had by this time lost all feeling of fear. He became interested and almost disappointed. The "airyplane" was not such a fool as it looked. It was very wonderful to be right up in the sky like this. His dreams were suddenly disturbed by a fearful noise. He thought the machine was blown to pieces. It dived and ducked through the air, and things were bursting all round it and making an awful din, and then it went up higher and higher. After a while these noises ceased, and he felt the machine gliding downward. They were really right above solid land— trees, fields, streams, and white villages. Down, down, down they glided. This was a foreign country. There were straight avenues of poplars and canals. This was not Halvesham. He felt the thing glide gently and bump into a field. Some men ran forward and approached them, and the mad aviator called out to them. They were mostly fat men in gray uniforms, and they all spoke this foreign gibberish. Some one came and unstrapped him. He was very stiff and could hardly move. An exceptionally gross-looking man punched him in the ribs and roared with laughter. They all stood round and laughed at him, while the mad aviator talked to them and kept pointing at him. Then he said:

"Old Grandfather, you must come with me."

He was led to an iron-roofed building and shut in a little room. There were guards outside with fixed bayonets. After a while the mad aviator appeared again, accompanied by two soldiers. He beckoned him to follow. They marched through a quadrangle and entered another building. They went straight into an office where a very important-looking man, covered with medals, sat in an easy-chair. There was a lot of saluting and clicking of heels. The aviator pointed at Sam and said something, and the man with the medals started at sight of him, and then came up and spoke to him in English.

"What is your name? Where do you come from? Your age? The name and birthplace of your parents?"

He seemed intensely interested, and also pulled his hair and beard to see if they came off. So well and naturally did he and the aviator speak English that after a voluble examination they drew apart, and continued the conversation in that language. And the extraordinary conversation was of this nature:

"It is a most remarkable resemblance," said the man with medals. *"Unglaublich!* But what do you want me to do with him, Hausemann?"

"The idea came to me suddenly, Excellency," replied the aviator, "and you may consider it worthless. It is just this. The resemblance is so amazing. Paul Jouperts has given us more valuable information than any one at present in our service, and the English know that. There is an award of five thousand francs on his head. Twice they have captured him, and each time he escaped. All the company commanders and their staff have his photograph. He is a serious thorn in their flesh."

"Well?" replied the man with the medals.

The aviator whispered confidentially:

"Suppose, your Excellency, that they found the dead body of Paul Jouperts?"

"Well?" replied the big man.

"My suggestion is this. To-morrow, as you know, the English are attacking Hill 701, which for tactical reasons we have decided to evacuate. If after the attack they find the dead body of Paul Jouperts in, say, the second line, they will take no further trouble in the matter. You know their lack of thoroughness. Pardon me, I was two years at Oxford University. And consequently Paul Jouperts will be able to prosecute his labors undisturbed."

The man with the medals twirled his mustache and looked thoughtfully at his colleague.

"Where is Paul at the moment?" he asked.

"He is acting as a gardener at the Convent of St. Eloise, at Mailleton-en-haut, which, as you know, is one hundred meters from the head-quarters of the British central army staff."

The man with the medals took two or three rapid turns up and down the room, then he said:

"Your plan is excellent, Hausemann. The only point of difficulty is that the attack started this morning."

"This morning?" exclaimed the other.

"Yes; the English attacked unexpectedly at dawn. We have already evacuated the first line. We shall evacuate the second line at eleven-fifty. It is now ten-fifteen. There may be just time."

He looked suddenly at old Sam in the way that a butcher might look at a prize heifer at an agricultural show and remarked casually:

"Yes, it is a remarkable resemblance. It seems a pity not to—do something with it."

Then, speaking in German, he added:

"It is worth trying. And if it succeeds the higher authorities shall hear of your lucky accident and inspiration, Herr Hausemann. Instruct *Ober-lieutenant* Schultz to send the old fool by two orderlies to the east extremity of Trench 38. Keep him there till the order of evacuation is given, then shoot him, but don't disfigure him, and lay him out face up-ward."

The aviator saluted and withdrew, accompanied by his victim. Old Sam had not understood the latter part of the conversation, and he did not catch quite all that was said in English; but he felt that somehow things were not becoming too promising, and it was time to assert him-self. So he remarked when they got outside:

"Now, look 'ee 'ere, Mister, when am I goin' to get back to my tur-nips?"

And the aviator replied, with a pleasant smile:

"Do not be disturbed, old Grandfather. You shall get back to the soil quite soon."

In a few moments he found himself in a large gray car, accompanied by four soldiers. The aviator left him. The country was barren and hor-rible, full of great pits and rents, and he could hear the roar of the artillery and the shriek of shells. Overhead, aeroplanes were buzzing angrily. He seemed to be suddenly transported from the kingdom of God to the pit of darkness. He wondered whether the vicar had enjoyed the runner beans. He could not imagine runner beans growing here; runner beans, aye, or anything else. If this was a foreign country, give him dear old England!

Gr-r-r! bang! Something exploded just at the rear of the car. The sol-diers ducked, and one of them pushed him in the stomach and swore.

"An ugly-looking lout," he thought. "If I wor twenty years younger, I'd give him a punch in the eye that 'u'd make him sit up."

The car came to a halt by a broken wall. The party hurried out and dived behind a mound. He was pulled down a kind of shaft, and found himself in a room buried right underground, where three officers were drinking and smoking. The soldiers saluted and handed them a type-written despatch. The officers looked at him drunkenly, and one came up and pulled his beard and spat in his face and called him "an old English swine." He then shouted out some instructions to the soldiers, and they led him out into the narrow trench. One walked behind him, and occasionally prodded him with the butt-end of a gun. The trenches were half full of water and reeked of gases, powder, and decaying mat-ter. Shells were constantly bursting overhead, and in places the trenches had crumbled and were nearly blocked up. They stumbled on, some-times falling, sometimes dodging moving masses, and occasionally crawling over the dead bodies of men. At last they reached a deserted-looking trench, and one of the soldiers pushed him into the corner of it and growled something, and then disappeared round the angle. Old Sam was exhausted. He leaned panting against the mud wall, expect-ing every minute to be blown to pieces by one of those infernal things that seemed to be getting more and more insistent. The din went on for nearly twenty minutes, and he was alone in the trench. He fancied he heard a whistle amidst the din. Suddenly one of the soldiers who had accompanied him came steathily round the corner, and there was a look in his eye old Sam did not like. When he was within five yards the soldier raised his rifle and pointed it at Sam's body. Some instinct im-pelled the old man at that instant to throw himself forward on his face. As he did so he was aware of a terrible explosion, and he had just time to observe the soldier falling in a heap near him, and then he lost con-sciousness.

His consciousness appeared to return to him with a snap. He was lying on a plank in a building, and he heard some one say:

"I believe the old boy's English."

He looked round. There were a lot of men lying there, and others in khaki and white overalls were busy among them. He sat up, rubbed his head, and said:

"Hi, Mister, where be I now?"

Some one laughed, and a young man came up and said:

"Well, old man, you were very nearly in hell. Who the devil are you?"

Some one came up, and two of them were discussing him. One of them said:

"He's quite all right. He was only knocked out. Better take him in to the colonel. He may be a spy."

The other came up, touched his shoulder, and remarked:

"Can you walk, Uncle?"

He replied:

"Aye, I can walk all roight."

"That's an old sport!"

The young man took his arm and helped him out of the room into a courtyard. They entered another room, where an elderly, kind-faced officer was seated at a desk. The officer looked up and exclaimed:

"Good God! Bradshaw, do you know who you've got there?"

The younger one said:

"No. Who, sir?"

"It's Paul Jouperts!" exclaimed the colonel.

"Paul Jouperts! Great Scott!"

The older officer addressed himself to Sam. He said:

"Well, we've got you once more, Paul. We shall have to be a little more careful this time."

The young officer said:

"Shall I detail a squad, sir?"

"We can't shoot him without a courtmartial," replied the kind-faced senior.

Then Sam interpolated:

"Look 'ee 'ere, sir, I'm fair' sick of all this. My name bean't Paul. My name's Sam. I was a-thinnin' a loine o' turnips——"

Both officers burst out laughing, and the younger one said:

"Good! damn good! Isn't it amazing, sir, the way they not only learn the language, but even take the trouble to learn a dialect!"

The older man busied himself with some papers.

"Well, Sam," he remarked, "you shall be given a chance to prove your identity. Our methods are less drastic than those of your *Boche* masters. What part of England are you supposed to come from? Let's see how much you can bluff us with your topographical knowledge."

"I was a-thinnin' a loine o' turnips this mornin' at 'alf-past seven on Mr. Hodge's farm at Halvesham when one o' these 'ere airyplanes came down among the swedes. I tells 'e to get clear o' that, when the feller what gets out o' the car 'e drahs a revowlver and 'e says, 'you must 'company I——' "

"Yes, yes," interrupted the senior officer, "that's all very good. Now tell me—where is Halvesham? What is the name of the local vicar? I'm sure you'd know that."

Old Sam rubbed his chin.

"I sits under the Reverend David Pryce, Mister, and a good, God-fearin' man he be. I took him a cookin' o' runner beans on'y yesterday.

I works for Mr. Hodge, what owns Greenway Manor and 'as a stud-farm at Newmarket, they say."

"Charles Hodge?" asked the young officer.

"Aye, Charlie Hodge. You write and ask un if he knows old Sam Gates."

The two officers looked at each other, and the older one looked at Sam more closely.

"It's very extraordinary," he remarked.

"Everybody knows Charlie Hodge," added the younger officer.

It was at that moment that a wave of genius swept over old Sam. He put his hand to his head and suddenly jerked out:

"What's more, I can tell 'ee where this yere Paul is. He's actin' a gardener in a convent——" He puckered up his brows, fumbled with his hat, and then got out, "Mighteno."

The older officer gasped.

"Mailleton-en-haut! Good God! what makes you say that, old man?"

Sam tried to give an account of his experience and the things he had heard said by the German officers; but he was getting tired, and he broke off in the middle to say:

"Ye haven't a bite o' somethin' to eat, I suppose, Mister; or a glass o' beer? I usually 'as my dinner at twelve o'clock."

Both the officers laughed, and the older said:

"Get him some food, Bradshaw, and a bottle of beer from the mess. We'll keep this old man here. He interests me."

While the younger man was doing this, the chief pressed a button and summoned another junior officer.

"Gateshead," he remarked, "ring up the G.H.Q. and instruct them to arrest the gardener in that convent at the top of the hill and then to report."

The officer saluted and went out, and in a few minutes a tray of hot food and a large bottle of beer were brought to the old man, and he was left alone in the corner of the room to negotiate his welcome compensation. And in the execution he did himself and his country credit. In the meanwhile the officers were very busy. People were coming and going and examining maps, and telephone bells were ringing furiously. They did not disturb old Sam's gastric operations. He cleaned up the mess tins and finished the last drop of beer. The senior officer found time to offer him a cigarette, but he replied:

"Thank 'ee kindly, sir, but I'd rather smoke my pipe."

The colonel smiled and said:

"Oh, all right; smoke away."

He lighted up, and the fumes of the shag permeated the room. Some one opened another window, and the young officer who had addressed him at first suddenly looked at him and exclaimed:

"Innocent, by God! You couldn't get shag like that anywhere but in Norfolk."

It must have been an hour later when another officer entered and saluted.

"Message from the G.H.Q., sir," he said.

"Well?"

"They have arrested the gardener at the convent of St. Eloise, and they have every reason to believe that he is the notorious Paul Jouperts."

The colonel stood up, and his eyes beamed. He came over to old Sam and shook his hand.

"Mr. Gates," he said, "you are an old brick. You will probably hear more of this. You have probably been the means of delivering something very useful into our hands. Your own honor is vindicated. A loving Government will probably award you five shillings or a Victoria Cross or something of that sort. In the meantime, what can I do for you?"

Old Sam scratched his chin.

"I want to get back 'ome," he said.

"Well, even that might be arranged."

"I want to get back 'ome in toime for tea."

"What time do you have tea?"

"Foive o'clock or thereabouts."

"I see."

A kindly smile came into the eyes of the colonel. He turned to another officer standing by the table and said:

"Raikes, is any one going across this afternoon with despatches?"

"Yes, sir," replied the other officer. "Commander Jennings is leaving at three o'clock."

"You might ask him if he could see me."

Within ten minutes a young man in a flight-commander's uniform entered.

"Ah, Jennings," said the colonel, "here is a little affair which concerns the honor of the British army. My friend here, Sam Gates, has come over from Halvesham, in Norfolk, in order to give us valuable information. I have promised him that he shall get home to tea at five o'clock. Can you take a passenger?"

The young man threw back his head and laughed.

"Lord!" he exclaimed, "what an old sport! Yes, I expect I can manage it. Where is the God-forsaken place?"

A large ordnance-map of Norfolk (which had been captured from a German officer) was produced, and the young man studied it closely.

At three o'clock precisely old Sam, finding himself something of a hero and quite glad to escape from the embarrassment which the position entailed upon him, once more sped skyward in a "dratted airyplane."

At twenty minutes to five he landed once more among Mr. Hodge's swedes. The breezy young airman shook hands with him and departed inland. Old Sam sat down and surveyed the familiar field of turnips.

"A noice thing, I must say!" he muttered to himself as he looked along the lines of unthinned turnips. He still had twenty minutes, and so he went slowly along and completed a line which he had begun in the morning. He then deliberately packed up his dinner-things and his tools and started out for home.

As he came round the corner of Stillway's meadow and the cottage came in view, his niece stepped out of the copse with a basket on her arm.

"Well, Uncle," she said, "is there any noos?"

It was then that old Sam really lost his temper.

"Noos!" he said. "Noos! Drat the girl! What noos should there be? Sixty-nine year' I live in these 'ere parts, hoein' and weedin' and thinnin', and mindin' Charlie Hodge's sheep. Am I one o' these 'ere storybook folk havin' noos 'appen to me all the time? Ain't it enough, ye silly, dab-faced zany, to earn enough to buy a bite o' some'at to eat and a glass o' beer and a place to rest a's head o' night without always wantin' noos, noos, noos! I tell 'ee it's this that leads 'ee to 'alf the troubles in the world. Devil take the noos!"

And turning his back on her, he went fuming up the hill.

68

The Chink and the Child

BY THOMAS BURKE

IT IS a tale of love and lovers that they tell in the low-lit Causeway that slinks from West India Dock Road to the dark waste of waters beyond. In Pennyfields, too, you may hear it; and I do not doubt that it is told in far-away Tai-Ping, in Singapore, in Tokio, in Shanghai, and those other gay-lamped haunts of wonder whither the wandering people of Limehouse go and whence they return so casually. It is a tale for tears, and should you hear it in the lilied tongue of the yellow men, it would awaken in you all your pity. In our bald speech it must, unhappily, lose its essential fragrance, that quality that will lift an affair of squalor into the loftier spheres of passion and imagination, beauty and sorrow. It will sound unconvincing, a little . . . you know . . . the kind of thing that is best forgotten. Perhaps . . .

But listen.

It is Battling Burrows, the lightning welterweight of Shadwell, the box o' tricks, the Tetrarch of the ring, who enters first. Battling Burrows, the pride of Ratcliff, Poplar and Limehouse, and the despair of his manager and backers. For he loved wine, woman and song; and the boxing world held that he couldn't last long on that. There was any amount of money in him for his parasites if only the damned women could be cut out; but again and again would he disappear from his training quarters on the eve of a big fight, to consort with Molly and Dolly, and to drink other things than barley-water and lemon-juice. Wherefore Chuck Lightfoot, his manager, forced him to fight on any and every occasion while he was good and a money-maker; for at any moment the collapse might come, and Chuck would be called upon by his creditors to strip off that "shirt" which at every contest he laid upon his man.

Battling was of a type that is too common in the eastern districts of London; a type that upsets all accepted classifications. He wouldn't be classed. He was a curious mixture of athleticism and degeneracy. He could run like a deer, leap like a greyhound, fight like a machine, and drink like a suction-hose. He was a bully; he had the courage of the high hero. He was an open-air sport; he had the vices of a French decadent.

It was one of his love adventures that properly begins this tale; for the girl had come to Battling one night with a recital of terrible happenings, of an angered parent, of a slammed door. . . . In her arms was a bundle of white rags. Now Battling, like so many sensualists, was also a sentimentalist. He took that bundle of white rags; he paid the girl money to get into the country; and the bundle of white rags had existed in and about his domicile in Pekin Street, Limehouse, for some eleven years. Her position was nondescript; to the casual observer it would seem that she was Battling's relief punch-ball—an unpleasant post for any human creature to occupy, especially if you are a little girl of twelve, and the place be the one-room household of the lightning welter-weight. When Battling was cross with his manager . . . well, it is indefensible to strike your manager or to throw chairs at him, if he is a good manager; but to use a dog-whip on a small child is permissible and quite as satisfying; at least, he found it so. On these occasions, then, when very cross with his sparring partners, or over-flushed with victory and juice of the grape, he would flog Lucy. But he was reputed by the boys to be a good fellow. He only whipped the child when he was drunk; and he was only drunk for eight months of the year.

For just over twelve years this bruised little body had crept about Poplar and Limehouse. Always the white face was scarred with red, or black-furrowed with tears; always in her steps and in her look was expectation of dread things. Night after night her sleep was broken by the cheerful Battling's brute voice and violent hands; and terrible were the lessons which life taught her in those few years. Yet, for all the starved face and the transfixed air, there was a lurking beauty about her, a something that called you in the soft curve of her cheek that cried for kisses and was fed with blows, and in the splendid mournfulness that grew in eyes and lips. The brown hair chimed against the pale face, like the rounding of a verse. The blue cotton frock and the broken shoes could not break the loveliness of her slender figure or the shy grace of her movements as she flitted about the squalid alleys of the docks; though in all that region of wasted life and toil and decay, there was not one that noticed her, until . . .

Now there lived in Chinatown, in one lousy room over Mr Tai Fu's store in Pennyfields, a wandering yellow man, named Cheng Huan.

Cheng Huan was a poet. He did not realise it. He had never been able to understand why he was unpopular; and he died without knowing. But a poet he was, tinged with the materialism of his race, and in his poor listening heart strange echoes would awake of which he himself was barely conscious. He regarded things differently from other sailors; he felt things more passionately, and things which they felt not at all; so he lived alone instead of at one of the lodging-houses. Every evening he would sit at his window and watch the street. Then, a little later, he would take a jolt of opium at the place at the corner of Formosa Street.

He had come to London by devious ways. He had loafed on the Bund at Shanghai. The fateful intervention of a crimp had landed him on a boat. He got to Cardiff, and sojourned in its Chinatown; thence to Liverpool, to Glasgow; thence, by a ticket from the Asiatics' Aid Society, to Limehouse, where he remained for two reasons—because it cost him nothing to live there, and because he was too lazy to find a boat to take him back to Shanghai.

So he would lounge and smoke cheap cigarettes, and sit at his window, from which point he had many times observed the lyrical Lucy. He noticed her casually. Another day, he observed her, not casually. Later, he looked long at her; later still, he began to watch for her and for that strangely provocative something about the toss of the head and the hang of the little blue skirt as it coyly kissed her knee.

Then that beauty which all Limehouse had missed smote Cheng. Straight to his heart it went, and cried itself into his very blood. Thereafter the spirit of poetry broke her blossoms all about his odorous chamber. Nothing was the same. Pennyfields became a happy-lanterned street, and the monotonous fiddle in the house opposite was the music of his fathers. Bits of old song floated through his mind: little sweet verses of Le Tai-pih, murmuring of plum blossom, rice-field and stream. Day by day he would moon at his window, or shuffle about the streets, lighting to a flame when Lucy would pass and gravely return his quiet regard; and night after night, too, he would dream of a pale, lily-lovely child.

And now the Fates moved swiftly various pieces on their sinister board, and all that followed happened with a speed and precision that showed direction from higher ways.

It was Wednesday night in Limehouse, and for once clear of mist. Out of the coloured darkness of the Causeway stole the muffled wail of reed instruments, and, though every window was closely shuttered, between the joints shot jets of light and stealthy voices, and you could hear the whisper of slippered feet, and the stuttering steps of the satyr and the sadist. It was to the café in the middle of the Causeway, lit by the pallid blue light that is the symbol of China throughout the world, that Cheng Huan came, to take a dish of noodle and some tea. Thence he moved to another house whose stairs ran straight to the street, and above whose doorway a lamp glowed like an evil eye. At this establishment he mostly took his pipe of "chandu" and a brief chat with the keeper of the house, for, although not popular, and very silent, he liked sometimes to be in the presence of his compatriots. Like a figure of a shadowgraph he slid through the door and up the stairs.

The chamber he entered was a bit of the Orient squatting at the portals of the West. It was a well-kept place where one might play a game of fan-tan, or take a shot or so of *li-un,* or purchase other varieties of Oriental delight. It was sunk in a purple dusk, though here and there a lantern stung the glooms. Low couches lay around the walls, and strange men decorated them: Chinese, Japs, Malays, Lascars, with one or two white girls; and sleek, noiseless attendants swam from couch to couch. Away in the far corner sprawled a lank figure in brown shirting, its nerveless fingers curled about the stem of a spent pipe. On one of the lounges a scorbutic nigger sat with a Jewess from Shadwell. Squatting on a table in the centre, beneath one of the lanterns, was a musician with a reed, blinking upon the company like a sly cat, and making his melody of six repeated notes.

The atmosphere churned. The dirt of years, tobacco of many growings, opium, betel nut, and moist flesh allied themselves in one grand assault against the nostrils.

As Cheng brooded on his insect-ridden cushion, of a sudden the lantern above the musician was caught by the ribbon of his reed. It danced and flung a hazy radiance on a divan in the shadow. He saw—started—half rose. His heart galloped, and the blood pounded in his quiet veins. Then he dropped again, crouched, and stared.

O lily-flowers and plum blossoms! O silver streams and dim-starred skies! O wine and roses, song and laughter! For there, kneeling on a mass of rugs, mazed and big-eyed, but understanding, was Lucy . . . his Lucy . . . his little maid. Through the dusk she must have felt his intent gaze upon her; for he crouched there, fascinated, staring into the now obscured corner where she knelt.

But the sickness which momentarily gripped him on finding in this place his snowy-breasted pearl passed and gave place to great joy. She was here; he would talk with her. Little English he had, but simple words, those with few gutturals, he had managed to pick up; so he rose, the masterful lover, and, with feline movements, crossed the nightmare chamber to claim his own.

If you wonder how Lucy came to be in this bagnio, the explanation is simple. Battling was in training. He had flogged her that day before starting work; he had then had a few brandies—not many; some eighteen or nineteen—and had locked the door of his room and taken the key. Lucy was, therefore, homeless, and a girl somewhat older than Lucy, so old and so wise, as girls are in that region, saw in her a possible source of revenue. So there they were, and to them appeared Cheng.

From what horrors he saved her that night cannot be told, for her ways were too audaciously childish to hold her long from harm in such a place. What he brought to her was love and death.

For he sat by her. He looked at her—reverently yet passionately. He touched her—wistfully yet eagerly. He locked a finger in her wondrous hair. She did not start away; she did not tremble. She knew well what she had to be afraid of in that place; but she was not afraid of Cheng. She pierced the mephitic gloom and scanned his face. No, she was not afraid. His yellow hands, his yellow face, his smooth black hair . . . well, he was the first thing that had ever spoken soft words to her; the first thing that had ever laid a hand upon her that was not brutal; the first thing that had deferred in manner towards her as though she, too, had a right to live. She knew his words were sweet, though she did not understand them. Nor can they be set down. Half that he spoke was in village Chinese; the rest in a mangling of English which no distorted spelling could possibly reproduce.

But he drew her back against the cushions and asked her name, and she told him; and he inquired her age, and she told him; and he had then two beautiful words which came easily to his tongue. He repeated them again and again:

"Lucia . . . li'l Lucia. . . . Twelve. . . . Twelve." Musical phrases they were, dropping from his lips, and to the child who heard her name pronounced so lovingly, they were the lost heights of melody. She clung to him, and he to her. She held his strong arm in both of hers as they crouched on the divan, and nestled her cheek against his coat.

Well . . . he took her home to his wretched room.

"Li'l Lucia, come-a-home . . . Lucia."

His heart was on fire. As they slipped out of the noisomeness into the night air and crossed the West India Dock Road into Pennyfields, they passed unnoticed. It was late, for one thing, and for another . . . well, nobody cared particularly. His blood rang with soft music and the solemnity of drums, for surely he had found now what for many years he had sought—his world's one flower. Wanderer he was, from Tuan-tsen to Shanghai, Shanghai to Glasgow . . . Cardiff . . . Liverpool . . . London. He had dreamed often of the women of his native land; perchance one of them should be his flower. Women, indeed, there had been. Swatow . . . he had recollections of certain rose-winged hours in coast cities. At many places to which chance had led him a little bird had perched itself upon his heart, but so lightly and for so brief a while as hardly to be felt. But now—now he had found her in this alabaster Cockney child. So that he was glad and had great joy of himself and the blue and silver night, and the harsh flares of the Poplar Hippodrome.

You will observe that he had claimed her, but had not asked himself whether she were of an age for love. The white perfection of the child had captivated every sense. It may be that he forgot that he was in London and not in Tuan-tsen. It may be that he did not care. Of that nothing can be told. All that is known is that his love was a pure and holy thing. Of that we may be sure, for his worst enemies have said it.

Slowly, softly they mounted the stairs to his room, and with almost an obeisance he entered and drew her in. A bank of cloud raced to the east and a full moon thrust a sharp sword of light upon them. Silence lay over all Pennyfields. With a bird-like movement, she looked up at him—her face alight, her tiny hands upon his coat—clinging, wondering, trusting. He took her hand and kissed it; repeated the kiss upon her cheek and lip and little bosom, twining his fingers in her hair. Docilely, and echoing the smile of his lemon lips in a way that thrilled him almost to laughter, she returned his kisses impetuously, gladly.

He clasped the nestling to him. Bruised, tearful, with the love of life almost thrashed out of her, she had fluttered to him out of the evil night.

"O li'l Lucia!" And he put soft hands upon her, and smoothed her and crooned over her many gracious things in his flowered speech. So they stood in the moonlight, while she told him the story of her father, of her beatings, and starvings, and unhappiness.

"O li'l Lucia. . . . White Blossom. . . . Twelve. . . . Twelve years old!"

As he spoke, the clock above the Milwall Docks shot twelve crashing notes across the night. When the last echo died, he moved to a cupboard, and from it he drew strange things . . . formless masses of blue and gold, magical things of silk, and a vessel that was surely Aladdin's lamp, and a box of spices. He took these robes, and, with tender, reverent fingers, removed from his White Blossom the besmirched rags that covered her, and robed her again, and led her then to the heap of stuff that was his bed, and bestowed her safely.

For himself, he squatted on the floor before her, holding one grubby little hand. There he crouched all night, under the lyric moon, sleepless, watchful; and sweet content was his. He had fallen into an uncomfortable posture, and his muscles ached intolerably. But she slept, and he dared not move nor release her hand lest he should awaken her. Weary and trustful, she slept, knowing that the yellow man was kind and that she might sleep with no fear of a steel hand smashing the delicate structure of her dreams.

In the morning, when she awoke, still wearing her blue and yellow silk, she gave a cry of amazement. Cheng had been about. Many times had he glided up and down the two flights of stairs, and now at last his room was prepared for his princess. It was swept and garnished, and was an apartment worthy a maid who is loved by a poet-prince. There was a bead curtain. There were muslins of pink and white. There were four bowls of flowers, clean, clear flowers to gladden the White Blossom and set off her sharp beauty. And there was a bowl of water, and a sweet lotion for the bruise on her cheek.

When she had risen, her prince ministered to her with rice and egg and tea. Cleansed and robed and calm, she sat before him, perched on the edge of many cushions as on a throne, with all the grace of the child princess in the story. She was a poem. The beauty hidden by neglect and fatigue shone out now more clearly and vividly, and from the head sunning over with curls to the small white feet, now bathed and sandalled, she seemed the living interpretation of a Chinese lyric. And she was his; her sweet self and her prattle, and her birdlike ways were all his own.

Oh, beautifully they loved. For two days he held her. Soft caresses from his yellow hands and long, devout kisses were all their demonstration. Each night he would tend her, as might mother to child; and each night he watched and sometimes slumbered at the foot of her couch.

But now there were those that ran to Battling at his training quarters across the river, with the news that his child had gone with a Chink— a yellow man. And Battling was angry. He discovered parental rights. He discovered indignation. A yellow man after his kid! He'd learn him. Battling did not like men who were not born in the same great country as himself. Particularly he disliked yellow men. His birth and education in Shadwell had taught him that of all creeping things that creep upon the earth the most insidious is the Oriental in the West. And a yellow man and a child. It was . . . as you might say . . . so . . . kind of . . . well, wasn't it? He bellowed that it was "unnacherel." The yeller man would go through it. Yeller! It was his supreme condemnation, his final epithet for all conduct of which he disapproved.

There was no doubt that he was extremely annoyed. He went to the Blue Lantern, in what was once Ratcliff Highway, and thumped the bar, and made all his world agree with him. And when they agreed with him he got angrier still. So that when, a few hours later, he climbed through the ropes at the Netherlands to meet Bud Tuffit for ten rounds, it was Bud's fight all the time, and to that bright boy's

ﾍtonishment he was the victor on points at the end of the ten. Battling slouched out of the ring, still more determined to let the Chink have it where the chicken had the axe. He left the house with two pals and a black man, and a number of really inspired curses from his manager.

On the evening of the third day, then, Cheng slipped sleepily down the stairs to procure more flowers and more rice. The genial Ho Ling, who keeps the Canton store, held him in talk some little while, and he was gone from his room perhaps half-an-hour. Then he glided back, and climbed with happy feet the forty stairs to his temple of wonder.

With a push of a finger he opened the door, and the blood froze on his cheek, the flowers fell from him. The temple was empty and desolate; White Blossom was gone. The muslin hangings were torn down and trampled underfoot. The flowers had been flung from their bowls about the floor, and the bowls lay in fifty fragments. The joss was smashed. The cupboard had been opened. Rice was scattered here and there. The little straight bed had been jumped upon by brute feet. Everything that could be smashed or violated had been so treated, and —horror of all—the blue and yellow silk robe had been rent in pieces, tied in grotesque knots, and slung derisively about the table legs.

I pray devoutly that you may never suffer what Cheng Huan suffered in that moment. The pangs of death, with no dying; the sickness of the soul which longs to escape and cannot; the imprisoned animal within the breast which struggles madly for a voice and finds none; all the agonies of all the ages—the agonies of every abandoned lover and lost woman, past and to come—all these things were his in that moment.

Then he found voice and gave a great cry, and men from below came up to him; and they told him how the man who boxed had been there with a black man; how he had torn the robes from his child, and dragged her down the stairs by her hair; and how he had shouted aloud for Cheng and had vowed to return and deal separately with him.

Now a terrible dignity came to Cheng, and the soul of his great fathers swept over him. He closed the door against them, and fell prostrate over what had been the resting-place of White Blossom. Those without heard strange sounds as of an animal in its last pains; and it was even so. Cheng was dying. The sacrament of his high and holy passion had been profaned; the last sanctuary of the Oriental—his soul dignity—had been assaulted. The love robes had been torn to ribbons; the veil of his temple cut down. Life was no longer possible; and life without his little lady, his White Blossom, was no longer desirable.

Prostrate he lay for the space of some five minutes. Then, in his face all the pride of accepted destiny, he arose. He drew together the little bed. With reverent hands he took the pieces of blue and yellow silk, kissing them and fondling them and placing them about the pillow. Silently he gathered up the flowers, and the broken earthenware, and burnt some prayer papers and prepared himself for death.

Now it is the custom among those of the sect of Cheng that the dying shall present love-gifts to their enemies; and when he had set all in order, he gathered his brown canvas coat about him, stole from the house, and set out to find Battling Burrows, bearing under the coat his love-gift to Battling. White Blossom he had no hope of finding. He had heard of Burrows many times; and he judged that, now that she was taken from him, never again would he hold those hands or touch that laughing hair. Nor, if he did, could it change things from what they were. Nothing that was not a dog could live in the face of this sacrilege.

As he came before the house in Pekin Street, where Battling lived, he murmured gracious prayers. Fortunately, it was a night of thick river mist, and through the enveloping velvet none could observe or challenge him. The main door was open, as are all doors in this district. He writhed across the step, and through to the back room, where again the door yielded to a touch.

Darkness. Darkness and silence, and a sense of frightful things. He peered through it. Then he fumbled under his jacket—found a match—struck it. An inch of candle stood on the mantelshelf. He lit it. He looked round. No sign of Burrows, but . . . Almost before he looked he knew what awaited him. But the sense of finality had kindly stunned him; he could suffer nothing more.

On the table lay a dog-whip. In the corner a belt had been flung. Half across the greasy couch lay White Blossom. A few rags of clothing were about her pale, slim body; her hair hung limp as her limbs; her eyes were closed. As Cheng drew nearer and saw the savage red rails that ran across and across the beloved body, he could not scream—he could not think. He dropped beside the couch. He laid gentle hands upon her, and called soft names. She was warm to the touch. The pulse was still.

Softly, oh, so softly, he bent over the little frame that had enclosed his friend-spirit, and his light kisses fell all about her. Then, with the undirected movements of a sleep-walker, he bestowed the rags decently about her, clasped her in strong arms, and crept silently into the night.

From Pekin Street to Pennyfields it is but a turn or two, and again he passed unobserved as he bore his tired bird back to her nest. He laid her upon the bed, and covered the lily limbs with the blue and yellow silks and strewed upon her a few of the trampled flowers. Then, with more kisses and prayers, he crouched beside her.

So, in the ghastly Limehouse morning, they were found—the dead child, and the Chink, kneeling beside her, with a sharp knife gripped in a vice-like hand, its blade far between his ribs.

Meantime, having vented his wrath on his prodigal daughter, Battling, still cross, had returned to the Blue Lantern, and there he stayed with a brandy tumbler in his fist, forgetful of an appointment at Premierland, whereby he should have been in the ring at ten o'clock sharp. For the space of an hour Chuck Lightfoot was going blasphemously to and fro in Poplar, seeking Battling and not finding him, and murmuring, in tearful tones: "Battling—you dammanblasted Battling—where are yeh?"

His opponent was in his corner sure enough, but there was no fight. For Battling lurched from the Blue Lantern to Pekin Street. He lurched into his happy home, and he cursed Lucy, and called for her. And finding no matches, he lurched to where he knew the couch should be, and flopped heavily down.

Now it is a peculiarity of the reptile tribe that its members are impatient of being flopped on without warning. So, when Battling flopped, eighteen inches of writhing gristle upreared itself on the couch, and got home on him as Bud Tuffit had done the night before—one to the ear, one to the throat, and another to the forearm.

Battling went down and out.

And he, too, was found in the morning, with Cheng Huan's love-gift coiled about his neck.

69

Life of Ma Parker

BY KATHERINE MANSFIELD

WHEN the literary gentleman, whose flat old Ma Parker cleaned every Tuesday, opened the door to her that morning, he asked after her grandson. Ma Parker stood on the doormat inside the dark little hall, and she stretched out her hand to help her gentleman shut the door before she replied. "We buried 'im yesterday, sir," she said quietly.

"Oh, dear me! I'm sorry to hear that," said the literary gentleman in a shocked tone. He was in the middle of his breakfast. He wore a very shabby dressing-gown and carried a crumpled newspaper in one hand. But he felt awkward. He could hardly go back to the warm sitting-room without saying something—something more. Then because these people set such store by funerals he said kindly, "I hope the funeral went off all right."

"Beg parding, sir?" said old Ma Parker huskily.

Poor old bird! She did look dashed. "I hope the funeral was a—a—success," said he. Ma Parker gave no answer. She bent her head and hobbled off to the kitchen, clasping the old fish bag that held her cleaning things and an apron and a pair of felt shoes. The literary gentleman raised his eyebrows and went back to his breakfast.

"Overcome, I suppose," he said aloud, helping himself to the marmalade.

Ma Parker drew the two jetty spears out of her toque and hung it behind the door. She unhooked her worn jacket and hung that up too. Then she tied her apron and sat down to take off her boots. To take off her boots or to put them on was an agony to her, but it had been an agony for years. In fact, she was so accustomed to the pain that her face was drawn and screwed up ready for the twinge before she'd so much

as untied the laces. That over, she sat back with a sigh and softly rubbed
her knees. . . .

"Gran! Gran!" Her little grandson stood on her lap in his button
boots. He'd just come in from playing in the street.

"Look what a state you've made your gran's skirt into—you wicked
boy!"

But he put his arms round her neck and rubbed his cheek against hers.

"Gran, gi' us a penny!" he coaxed.

"Be off with you; Gran ain't got no pennies."

"Yes, you 'ave."

"No, I ain't."

"Yes, you 'ave. Gi' us one!"

Already she was feeling for the old, squashed, black leather purse.

"Well, what'll you give your gran?"

He gave a shy little laugh and pressed closer. She felt his eyelid quivering against her cheek. "I ain't got nothing," he murmured. . . .

The old woman sprang up, seized the iron kettle off the gas stove and
took it over to the sink. The noise of the water drumming in the kettle
deadened her pain, it seemed. She filled the pail, too, and the washing-
up bowl.

It would take a whole book to describe the state of that kitchen. During the week the literary gentleman "did" for himself. That is to say,
he emptied the tea leaves now and again into a jam jar set aside for that
purpose, and if he ran out of clean forks he wiped over one or two on
the roller towel. Otherwise, as he explained to his friends, his "system"
was quite simple, and he couldn't understand why people make all this
fuss about housekeeping.

"You simply dirty everything you've got, get a hag in once a week
to clean up, and the thing's done."

The result looked like a gigantic dustbin. Even the floor was littered
with toast crusts, envelopes, cigarette ends. But Ma Parker bore him no
grudge. She pitied the poor young gentleman for having no one to look
after him. Out of the smudgy little window you could see an immense
expanse of sad-looking sky, and whenever there were clouds they looked
very worn, old clouds, frayed at the edges, with holes in them, or dark
stains like tea.

While the water was heating, Ma Parker began sweeping the floor.
"Yes," she thought, as the broom knocked, "what with one thing and
another I've had my share. I've had a hard life."

Even the neighbours said that of her. Many a time, hobbling home with her fish bag she heard them, waiting at the corner, or leaning over the area railings, say among themselves, "She's had a hard life, has Ma Parker." And it was so true she wasn't in the least proud of it. It was just as if you were to say she lived in the basement-back at Number 27. A hard life . . .

At sixteen she'd left Stratford and come up to London as kitching-maid. Yes, she was born in Stratford-on-Avon. Shakespeare, sir? No, people were always arsking her about him. But she'd never heard his name until she saw it on the theatres.

Nothing remained of Stratford except that "sitting in the fireplace of a evening you could see the stars through the chimley," and "Mother always 'ad 'er side of bacon 'anging from the ceiling." And there was something—a bush, there was—at the front door, that smelt ever so nice. But the bush was very vague. She'd only remembered it once or twice in the hospital, when she'd been taken bad.

That was a dreadful place—her first place. She was never allowed out. She never went upstairs except for prayers morning and evening. It was a fair cellar. And the cook was a cruel woman. She used to snatch away her letters from home before she'd read them, and throw them in the range because they made her dreamy. . . . And the beedles! Would you believe it?—until she came to London she'd never seen a black bee-dle. Here Ma always gave a little laugh, as though—not to have seen a black beedle! Well! It was as if to say you'd never seen your own feet.

When that family was sold up she went as "help" to a doctor's house, and after two years there, on the run from morning till night, she married her husband. He was a baker.

"A baker, Mrs. Parker!" the literary gentleman would say. For occasionally he laid aside his tomes and lent an ear, at least, to this product called Life. "It must be rather nice to be married to a baker!"

Mrs. Parker didn't look so sure.

"Such a clean trade," said the gentleman.

Mrs. Parker didn't look convinced.

"And didn't you like handing the new loaves to the customers?"

"Well, sir," said Mrs. Parker, "I wasn't in the shop above a great deal. We had thirteen little ones and buried seven of them. If it wasn't the 'ospital it was the infirmary, you might say!"

"You might, *indeed,* Mrs. Parker!" said the gentleman, shuddering, and taking up his pen again.

Yes, seven had gone, and while the six were still small her husband was taken ill with consumption. It was flour on the lungs, the doctor told her at the time. . . . Her husband sat up in bed with his shirt pulled over his head, and the doctor's finger drew a circle on his back.

"Now, if we were to cut him open *here,* Mrs. Parker," said the doctor, "you'd find his lungs chock-a-block with white powder. Breathe, my good fellow!" And Mrs. Parker never knew for certain whether she saw or whether she fancied she saw a great fan of white dust come out of her poor dead husband's lips. . . .

But the struggle she'd had to bring up those six little children and keep herself to herself. Terrible it had been! Then, just when they were old enough to go to school her husband's sister came to stop with them to help things along, and she hadn't been there more than two months when she fell down a flight of steps and hurt her spine. And for five years Ma Parker had another baby—and such a one for crying!—to look after. Then young Maudie went wrong and took her sister Alice with her; the two boys emigrimated, and young Jim went to India with the army, and Ethel, the youngest, married a good-for-nothing little waiter who died of ulcers the year little Lennie was born. And now little Lennie—my grandson. . . .

The piles of dirty cups, dirty dishes, were washed and dried. The ink-black knives were cleaned with a piece of potato and finished off with a piece of cork. The table was scrubbed, and the dresser and the sink that had sardine tails swimming in it. . . .

He'd never been a strong child—never from the first. He'd been one of those fair babies that everybody took for a girl. Silvery fair curls he had, blue eyes, and a little freckle like a diamond on one side of his nose. The trouble she and Ethel had had to rear that child! The things out of the newspapers they tried him with! Every Sunday morning Ethel would read aloud while Ma Parker did her washing.

"Dear Sir,—Just a line to let you know my little Myrtil was laid out for dead. . . . After four bottils . . . gained 8 lbs. in 9 weeks, *and is still putting it on.*"

And then the egg-cup of ink would come off the dresser and the letter would be written, and Ma would buy a postal order on her way to work next morning. But it was no use. Nothing made little Lennie put it on. Taking him to the cemetery, even, never gave him a colour; a nice shake-up in the bus never improved his appetite.

But he was gran's boy from the first. . . .

"Whose boy are you?" said old Ma Parker, straightening up from the stove and going over to the smudgy window. And a little voice, so warm, so close, it half stifled her—it seemed to be in her breast under her heart—laughed out, and said, "I'm gran's boy!"

At that moment there was a sound of steps, and the literary gentleman appeared, dressed for walking.

"Oh, Mrs. Parker, I'm going out."

"Very good, sir."

"And you'll find your half-crown in the tray of the ink-stand."

"Thank you, sir."

"Oh, by the way, Mrs. Parker," said the literary gentleman quickly, "you didn't throw away any cocoa last time you were here—did you?"

"No, sir."

"*Very* strange. I could have sworn I left a teaspoonful of cocoa in the tin." He broke off. He said softly and firmly, "You'll always tell me when you throw things away—won't you, Mrs. Parker?" And he walked off very well pleased with himself, convinced, in fact, he'd shown Mrs. Parker that under his apparent carelessness he was as vigilant as a woman.

The door banged. She took her brushes and cloths into the bedroom. But when she began to make the bed, smoothing, tucking, patting, the thought of little Lennie was unbearable. Why did he have to suffer so? That's what she couldn't understand. Why should a little angel child have to arsk for his breath and fight for it? There was no sense in making a child suffer like that.

. . . From Lennie's little box of a chest there came a sound as though something was boiling. There was a great lump of something bubbling in his chest that he couldn't get rid of. When he coughed the sweat sprang out on his head; his eyes bulged, his hands waved, and the great lump bubbled as a potato knocks in a saucepan. But what was more awful than all was when he didn't cough he sat against the pillow and never spoke or answered, or even made as if he heard. Only he looked offended.

"It's not your poor old gran's doing it, my lovey," said old Ma Parker, patting back the damp hair from his little scarlet ears. But Lennie moved his head and edged away. Dreadfully offended with her he looked—and solemn. He bent his head and looked at her sideways as though he couln't have believed it of his gran.

But at the last . . . Ma Parker threw the counterpane over the bed. No, she simply couldn't think about it. It was too much—she'd had too much in her life to bear. She'd borne it up till now, she'd kept herself to herself, and never once had she been seen to cry. Never by a living soul. Not even her own children had seen Ma break down. She'd kept a proud face always. But now! Lennie gone—what had she? She had nothing. He was all she'd got from life, and now he was took too. Why must it all have happened to me? she wondered. "What have I done?" said old Ma Parker. "What have I done?"

As she said those words she suddenly let fall her brush. She found herself in the kitchen. Her misery was so terrible that she pinned on her hat, put on her jacket and walked out of the flat like a person in a dream. She did not know what she was doing. She was like a person so dazed by the horror of what has happened that he walks away—anywhere, as though by walking away he could escape. . . .

It was cold in the street. There was a wind like ice. People went flitting by, very fast; the men walked like scissors; the women trod like cats. And nobody knew—nobody cared. Even if she broke down, if at last, after all these years, she were to cry, she'd find herself in the lock-up as like as not.

But at the thought of crying it was as though little Lennie leapt in his gran's arms. Ah, that's what she wants to do, my dove. Gran wants to cry. If she could only cry now, cry for a long time, over everything, beginning with her first place and the cruel cook, going on to the doctor's, and then the seven little ones, death of her husband, the children's leaving her, and all the years of misery that led up to Lennie. But to have a proper cry over all these things would take a long time. All the same, the time for it had come. She must do it. She couldn't put it off any longer; she couldn't wait any more. . . . Where could she go?

"She's had a hard life, has Ma Parker." Yes, a hard life, indeed! Her chin began to tremble; there was no time to lose. But where? Where?

She couldn't go home; Ethel was there. It would frighten Ethel out of her life. She couldn't sit on a bench anywhere; people would come arsking her questions. She couldn't possibly go back to the gentleman's flat; she had no right to cry in strangers' houses. If she sat on some steps a policeman would speak to her.

Oh, wasn't there anywhere where she could hide and keep herself to herself and stay as long as she liked, not disturbing anybody, and nobody worrying her? Wasn't there anywhere in the world where she could have her cry out—at last?

Ma Parker stood, looking up and down. The icy wind blew out her apron into a balloon. And now it began to rain. There was nowhere.

70

A Day in a Woman's Life

BY SHEILA KAYE-SMITH

I. MORNING

THE first colourless light of dawn crept slowly up from the east, over the meadows of Padgeham and Dorngate. It left the Rother Marshes in shadow, touching only the tops of the hills, making them stand out as pale islands above the valleys of the little streams. It shimmered on the windows of Pipsden, that cluster of tiny cottages on the road from Hawkhurst to Rye. The cottages were beginning to wake—blinds were drawn, windows opened, columns of blue, wood-scented smoke rose out of their chimneys into the windless air. It was time for the men to go to work—on the Tong Wood estate, or on the Manor Farm—and the women were busy preparing breakfast. Only a house rather larger than the rest, standing a little way back from the road among some barns, was still asleep.

For some time Joyce Armstrong had been conscious of the disturbing light. She had thrust her face into the pillow and tried to shut it away. But she was aware of it spilling itself about the room over her shoulders, into the mirror, and she knew when the moment came when it filled itself with sunshine and she could ignore it no longer.

She sat up in bed, shaking back the long hair from her face, stretching her arms slowly. She was a beautiful woman, of slow movement and heavy though not ungraceful build—in the middle of her thirties, but bearing their trace not in any ageing of her features or her skin so much as in an indefinite weight of character expressed in her sombre eyes. The first spring sun had tanned her slightly, and her extended throat and arms showed a warm yellowish brown against her white muslin nightdress.

She yawned . . . carelessly flinging the back of one large hand to her mouth . . . then a deep shiver went through her. . . .

Time to get up. It must be quite seven o'clock, and she had a lot to do before she started. Started . . . should she go? Why, of course, she'd go. She must know for certain—understand the meaning of all this. Anything would be better than the past week with its uncertainty, its hope deferred.

There might be a letter this morning. Of course it wasn't likely that he'd write at the last minute—unless he put her off. He'd done that before—put her off at the last minute. He probably did it like that to avoid any protest or entreaty from her. Bah! His little treacheries. But after three years one couldn't help it—if only one could help going on in spite of his faults. That was what humiliated her—forgive, forgive, forgive. Angry tears flowed into her eyes, and she jumped out of bed.

She pulled up the blind, and the sunshine filled the room. A soft blue sky lay over the fields, over the woods that roughened the piling ridges of Kent. Near at hand was the smoke of the Pipsden breakfast fires, the red roofs slanting to windward, the busyness of the little backyards, the stillness of a pond. Her throat tightened, and the tears of anger became tears of blinding sorrow. Oh, those soft blue and golden days that had been in the beginning, when every day some token of his love and tenderness came up to her from the Marsh—either a letter or a little gift, or he himself in his big Sunbeam car . . . she remembered how once she had heard its throbbing in her dreams, and woken at seven to find him already there. Those were the days before he was sure of her. She turned quickly from the window, back into the sun-filled room, and shrugged on a kimono which lay over a chair, thrusting at the same time her bare feet into mules. Clap, clap went her heels on the carpet of the room, and then a louder clap on the polished boards that surrounded it. It would wake Mother if she went clapping downstairs like that—mules were no good if your heels were slim—better have got moccasins. . . . But Laurie had loved the way they used to hang from her toes when she dangled her legs . . . she must not think of Laurie—already she could feel the tears coming back. She made a vow to herself not to think of Laurie till she had made the tea.

The kitchen was dark. The blinds were down and the sun was at the other side of the house. She hoped there were no black-beetles about. Oh, what was that?—Only Perkins the cat, rubbing against her legs in an ecstasy of joy. His tail waved like a pine tree above his arched back, his hair stood out, all his body quivered with the organ-music of his song. The lovely, lovely thing. She picked him up, and buried her face in the humming softness of his flank.

"Oh, Perkins, love me—don't kick—don't go away."

But Perkins was on the floor, still vibrant, but aloof. His love was strictly practical, with a view to the morning's milk—it was not to be squandered on anything merely human. He stepped daintily beside her to the door, as she went to take in the jug. Then he led the way back to his saucer. She filled it with new milk.

"You don't deserve it, you naughty Perkins. You don't really love me —it's only cupboard love."

"Lap-lap-lap-smack," said Perkins.

"After all why should you love me more disinterestedly than—no, I haven't made the tea."

She leaped to the stove. What a nuisance it was, being unable to get a girl to sleep in the house. One had to do all the morning's work one-self. In summer it wasn't so bad, but in winter. . . . Ugh! Thank heaven, winter was over. But next winter . . . what would that be like? —Not like last winter—no, it couldn't be. It must be different. But would it be?—She mustn't think of it. "If winter comes can spring be far behind?" . . . A tear fell hissing on the stove. "Some more milk, Perkins? Don't put your head in the jug."

A loud rat-tat sounded in the front of the house. Joyce jerked herself upright, and the blood ebbed out of her cheeks. That was the post. For a moment she felt as if she could not move. Was there a letter from him lying on the doormat, where she had so often seen it—his black, vigor-ous handwriting distinguishing it from other letters even at a distance. But if there was, it could mean nothing good—it would be putting her off, otherwise he'd never leave her ten days without a letter and then write on the morning he was expecting to see her. It would be better if there was no letter—and yet, would it? Would the fact that he had not written tell her anything? Wouldn't it leave her more hopeless in the dark than ever? At least if he wrote, she would know definitely if he expected to see her, and if he did not, why not. Lord! What a coward she was! She had it in her power to put an end to all this questioning by going to the door. But she could not move. Rat-tat! Again! That meant the postman was waiting. She would have to go.

"Good morning—a registered parcel to be signed for?" That must be from Laurie—who else? . . . No, it was her mother's tortoise-shell spec-tacles, sent back from repair. . . . "Thanks. And the letters? Thanks. Good morning."

A circular, her mother's weekly letter from her aunt—that was all.

Then suddenly she knew that she had wanted desperately to hear, even if it meant the destruction of her one faint hope of seeing him. Anything was better than this uncertainty. He had not written for ten days, not since their last meeting. He had never been so long before without writing—and she had written twice, the last letter imploring him to write to her, if it was only a line. What had happened? Something must have happened to account for his silence. Had he gone away suddenly and in his hurry forgotten to post the letter that told her of it —or had he given the letter to someone else who had forgotten to post it? All the explanations which could possibly leave her a good opinion of him rushed through her mind, and she took the kettle off the stove, filled the teapot, and set the bedroom tray. By the time she was carrying the tray upstairs, others more disquieting had arrived. Perhaps he was wanting to choke her off, and had chosen this way of doing it—perhaps he had found someone else he liked. . . . Oh, no, he had been so sweet when she had seen him last and they had planned this day. . . . He could not have changed—perhaps he was ill, too ill to write—perhaps he was dead.

"Good morning, Mother dear—I hope you had a good night."

She sat down the tray by her mother's bed, and kissed her.

"Here are your spectacles come back—and Aunt Milly's letter."

"I heard you go downstairs a great while ago."

"Yes—I'm afraid my heels flopped and woke you. I must get some new slippers."

"No, no, I was awake. I've been awake since five. I wish I could get someone to help you in the mornings, dear—it's a shame for you to have to get up and make my tea."

"Oh, I don't mind a bit. I like getting up early on these fine mornings."

So they prattled to each other—about the house and the weather and the tea and the cat; and all the time Joyce was saying to her mother in her heart—"Oh, Mother, I'm in anguish because my lover doesn't write to me, because he's getting casual about me, getting tired—soon he'll want a change, and I love him as much as I ever did, though I see all his faults as I never did. Oh, Mother, help me! But you can't!"

No, her mother couldn't help her, because her mother had never known anything like this. Love had come to her, as it seemed to have come to so many of her generation, as an expanding flower instead of a devouring flame. Love for her had meant marriage, protection, children . . . why must it mean something so different to her daughter, who needed all these things as much as she?—Oh, why, why, why? . . . "If Laurie really loved me he would marry me," she said in her heart— "it is all nonsense what he says about being unable to. He has a comfortable home and lots of money to spend on things like cars and trips to London. If he really loved me, he'd let the mortgage rip, and be poor with me. He doesn't really love me. Then why do I love him? Because I can't help it, I suppose."

As she was carrying the tray out of the door, a new thought flashed upon her—"I won't go." She suddenly made up her mind not to go to see him at Warehorne. If he was calmly expecting her to come, though he hadn't written to her since their last meeting, it would serve him right if she failed to appear, and perhaps make him appreciate her a little more. If he had been untrue to her, it would save her face—if he had merely gone away . . . it would be horrible turning up at the farm and having to ask: "Where is Mr. Holt?" and be answered: "He's not here, ma'am, he's in London." No, she had much better not to go, and for quite an hour she really thought she wouldn't.

During that hour she dressed, let in the daily girl who prepared the breakfast, helped her mother over the last stages of her toilet. Perkins came up, voluptuous with the thought of fish, rubbing against Joyce as she knelt to fasten her mother's frock, with little hoarse cries in his throat. Joyce thought: "If I don't go it will mean more uncertainty. To-day's Saturday—I can't hear from him till Monday—perhaps I shan't hear then. I can't bear this for another three days. I must go and find out what's happened, however bad it is."

"What are you doing to-day, my dear?" asked her mother, when they were at breakfast.

"I'm going over in the car to Warehorne to see the Holts—don't you remember my telling you?"

"Yes, of course I do—and Lilian Smith is coming to spend the day with me."

That was another reason why she must go—she'd ask Lilian Smith to come in and spend the day with her mother— "So good of you, Lilian dear; you know I can't leave Mother alone all day, and I simply must go to see some people at Warehorne." What a fool she'd look if she stayed at home!

"Has Mrs. Holt come back from Italy?" continued her mother.

"Yes, she came back last week"—no need to tell that Mrs. Holt had gone to stop with a sister at Brighton.

"Well, give her my very kind remembrances. Tell her I'm so sorry I'm not equal to calling upon her. Mr. Laurie Holt is at home, I suppose?"

"Yes, Mother," said Joyce, and blushed heavily. It was dreadful having to deceive Mother like this—Mother who was so understanding, and so young, in spite of her age—so much younger than her daughter. Mrs. Armstrong saw the blush and the droop of the head.

"Well, you be wise and careful, my dear. He's paid you a great deal of attention, but young men seem to be so queer nowadays. You mustn't let him play with you."

Joyce laughed.

"Darling, I'm not what you'd exactly call in my first youth, and if I'm not able to look after myself I ought to be."

That was true, anyhow.

When breakfast was over, she went out to get her car. It was kept in one of the sheds at the back of the house—sheds which did not belong to the Armstrongs, but to the smallholder who rented the steading. The car was a small Humber; she had bought it secondhand in a fit of extravagance and daring with some money left her by an uncle. Those were the days when the big Sunbeam could no longer be depended on as in the beginning to bridge the gulf between Pipsden and Warehorne, and she had become terribly conscious of the looping miles of the marsh road. Moreover, the lesson had given her a less plaintive excuse for her demands on Laurie's time and company. She would never be a good driver—she was not capable or resourceful enough—but she had the right amount of timidity, neither so much as to make her nervous, nor so little as to make her presumptuous, and had come through her first six months without any mishap, though her speedometer recorded over a thousand miles, most of which had been run to and fro between Hawkhurst and the Marsh.

The Humber was difficult to start. She flooded the carburettor, advanced the spark, cranked furiously and in vain. This was when one wanted a man—when one saw the preposterousness of a woman living alone. Living alone . . . and she and Laurie were what she supposed was called "living together" . . . living together fifteen miles apart.

There! It had started at last. Chug-chug-chug. She brought it round to the door, and ran in to fetch her hat and driving gloves and say goodbye to her mother.

"When will you be back, dear?"

"I don't know. They may ask me to stay to tea. But you'll be all right with Lilian, won't you?"

"Oh, perfectly. Enjoy yourself, my dear. You've got a lovely day."

Suppose Laurie wasn't there—what should she do about lunch? Suppose her conjectures were right as to his being away? She couldn't come home and tell them she'd found nobody at Warehorne. She'd have to get lunch at the inn—she must take enough money with her. Lord! What a fool she was, setting out on a wild-goose chase like this.

II. NOON

She backed out of the gate—a process she hated—and was on the great ridge road that flows like a ribbon from Hawkhurst to Rye. Craunch! —that was an ugly gear-change—how careless she was—craunch!—the second was just as bad. Now the little car was running smoothly, the speedometer climbing into the twenties. She leaned back, giving herself up to the soothing of speed. It soothed her thoughts into a queer rhythm —they no longer fluttered to and fro like the needle on the accumulator dial—but went resolutely and rhythmically forward like the wheels. They told her that she was a fool to make this journey, and just because she was a fool to make it, it must not be made in vain. When she came home some useful purpose must have been accomplished, she must somehow have retrieved her life out of this miserable uncertainty, either by a fresh start in happiness or by a decided end. Her journey would definitely show her what had happened and what was going to be. She dared not think of joy, so she thought of sorrow.

She was going to break off with Laurie. She could bear no more of his treatment, of his neglect, of the slow, selfish dying of his love. Better end it all, and find herself free again as she had been once. Free . . . it seemed a hundred years since she had been free, since she had worked in the morning feeling that the day belonged to her. Some words floated into her mind—"union libre" . . . that meant "free union"—free when you were bound in body, mind, and heart. . . . But soon she would be really free, so free that she would forget that once she had found her slavery sweet.

Free . . . She remembered some words she had read in a novel, about how at the beginning of a love affair, the man is the seeker, the maker of occasions, and how at the end it is the woman. That was true. At the beginning it had all been Laurie's pursuit, his delicious pursuit—now it was hers, her sorrowful, humiliating pursuit. Why, it was she who had fixed to-day's meeting—he would have trusted to something more fortuitous bringing them together. Why couldn't she let him go?—as he would have let her go at the beginning if she had run away faster than she had.

But now she would let him go—more, she would send him away. "Laurie, I have endured enough—I can endure no more." "Oh, Joyce," he would plead. But she would be firm—"No, I am going. You must learn that a woman can't be treated like this." Oh, she almost hoped that he would give her the opportunity—that he would not have a reasonable excuse for his conduct in . . . of course, he might. He might have gone away—he must have gone away—he couldn't have received both her last letters and not answered them. . . . Perhaps he had been away, and for some reason the letters had not been forwarded, and he had come back either last night or early this morning and had found them there, and was now waiting for her full of anxiety, full of regret and tenderness. . . . "Oh, my darling little Joyce—how dreadful for you. I'm so terribly sorry. But I was sent for suddenly up to town, and those idiots never forwarded anything. How can I make things up to you? It's difficult now, but when we are married . . ." The colour had mounted on her cheeks and her lips parted joyfully—she almost forgot it was a dream.

She came out of it the next moment, as a flock of sheep met her in Sandhurst. She stopped the car, and her thoughts seemed to stop with it. She saw only the dusty, panting sheep, and her heart was full of pity for the poor things—many of them had lambs running along beside them, bleating too, but in shriller voices. They were past now, and she set forward again, through the trim wide street of Sandhurst, quickening her pace towards Linkhill.

How well she knew the road—the sign of the running greyhound outside the inn, the throws where one road went into Sussex and the other into Kent. She had hardly ever been along that Kentish road, though she had often wanted to. She had used the car almost entirely for her visits to Warehorne. But when she was Free she would drive a lot about the country. She would take her mother out for drives—her mother had often seemed as if she wanted to come and wondered why her daughter drove off without her. She would make up to her mother for a lot of things when she was Free . . . she knew now that she would be free—that momentary softness of hope was but a dream. Laurie would have no reasonable excuse to offer, and short of a clear, convincing, reasonable excuse she would not forgive. If he had been unfaithful (she had forgiven him for that once) or remiss (she had forgiven him for that a hundred times), or had got into another of his queer, selfish muddles, her mind was made up as to what she would do. "I can bear no more. You don't really love me, or you couldn't treat me like this. No— it really is ended now."

> *Let us agree to give up love*
> *And root up the infernal grove,*
> *Then shall we return and see*
> *The worlds of happy Eternity——*

sang the car, as she ran across the Rother Marshes into Sussex—where the villages of Northiam and Beckley and Peasmarsh were threaded on the road like beads on a string.

Well, she had lived through three years of it, and only the first had been worth living. The others had been hell. However, they had done her this service in showing her the kind of husband he would have made —weak, selfish, unreliable—how dreadful it sounded!—but it was true. It was true, too, that she had loved him in spite of it all. He was so attractive. . . . But she was glad she had not married him . . . though she would never forget the day he had told her he could not marry her, bringing forward long strings of figures and talks of mortgages and his plans for the farm, and other things which she could not understand. What a fool she had been not to finish it all that day . . . that was when she ought to have broken with him, and spared herself all this. What had made her stick to him—love or hope? Had she hoped that her love would make him change his mind, change his fate, and marry her after all?—Hadn't she all along been hoping that he would marry her in the end?—didn't she hope it still? Oh, God!—what it is to have a patient, indestructible hope . . . and wouldn't it be degrading as well as foolish to marry him after all that had happened? . . . Hang it all, he had treated her badly from the start . . . a woman like herself, desirable, well-connected, who had been sought by others . . . to condemn her to this unutterable life, just so that he could be free and spend money and buy land . . . it was monstrous! She owed it to her dignity to end things at once.

And throughout all eternity
I forgive you, you forgive me—
As our dear Redeemer said,
This the wine and this the bread——

sang the car, taking her through Peasmarsh.

She would soon be in Rye. Already the fields were falling away to the southeast. She saw the blue line of the sea . . . and then the green vastness of the marsh spreading away into veiled distances. From the ridge it looked like a huge map, marked out with roads and water-courses, with dots of roofs and steeples. She saw the foot of the Isle of Oxney—she saw the abrupt hillock of Stone with its square church tower . . . when she was Free she would go to church again. . . . Now she was entering Rye, and for a few relieving moments her mind was fixed on manœuvring the car through the narrow streets. . . . Now she was out of the town, rushing along the Straight Mile—zip-zip . . . let her out . . . open the throttle wide . . . zip-zip . . . thirty coming round on the speedometer tape . . . thirty-five . . . oh, if only I can get her up to forty . . . if I can get her up to forty, Laurie will have a reasonable excuse that I can accept . . . zip-zip . . . Guldeford corner . . . I must slow down . . . and of course I won't accept any excuse. . . . I'm going to be Free.

Now she was nearing Warehorne she began to feel afraid. It would be a very terrible meeting—it would make her sick. And suppose he had taken the matter out of her hands and had decided to get rid of her—suppose she found a message from him telling her all was over . . . it would be a cruel way of doing things, but then men were often cruel when they were frightened . . . or angry . . . angry with themselves. Besides, what else could have happened?—What else could account for his silence, except a definite determination to break with her? . . . Unless he was dead. . . . Oh, God, Laurie dead!

Then a new fear attacked her. What would she say to the parlourmaid when she arrived? If he was away from home, she didn't want the girl to think that she had come to lunch. She must put on speed and arrive well before the luncheon hour—she must put on a careless and haphazard manner as if she'd called in on the chance. Yet if he was expecting her and had told the servants, it would look queer if she seemed undecided herself. . . .

Both these fears—the big that made her feel sick and the little that made her feel silly—went with her all the way to Warehorne. Her hand on the steering-wheel was clammy, her foot shook on the accelerator. What a pitiful spectacle is a woman driving a motor-car when she is in love!

By the time she had reached the house, she had made up her mind to be casual—better that the maid should think her foolish than disappointed. Agney House stood just outside the village—it was really a glorified farm, in the midst of its steading, a red, comfortable, seventeenth-century house, with staring, white-rimmed windows. It looked prosperous—exceedingly prosperous for a man who professed himself too poor to marry; but of course the prosperity was in the house only and the penury was in the land, the land which Laurie refused to give up for her sake.

She was on the doorstep—her tongue was thick and her mouth was dry. In a minute now she would know.

"Is Mr. Laurence Holt at Warehorne?"

"Yes, ma'am. But he's gone over to Brenzett on business."

"When will he be back?"

"He said about three o'clock."

"Then he's not lunching at home?"

"No, ma'am—he's lunching at Mr. Staple's."

"I see. But he'll be back at three."

"Yes, ma'am. Shall I give him any message?"

"No—that's to say—yes, tell him Miss Armstrong called, and that she'll call again later in the afternoon. Tell him it's on urgent business."

"Very well, ma'am."

The girl was a new importation—she suspected nothing. Joyce had saved her face, but nothing else.

She mechanically got into the car—as part of the programme of casualness she had left the engine running—and drove round the little sweep and out of the gate. Mechanically she turned to the right, into the village. Everything she did was mechanical. Her brain felt rigid, frozen—ossified—she could not think.

Then suddenly she began to feel, in furious throes. She felt anger, bewilderment, grief, despair—so violently that she had to bring the car to a standstill. She was trembling all over. This was worse than anything she had expected. Laurie was at home, but had gone out to lunch with someone else on the day he had invited her to come to him. He could not have forgotten their arrangement—no, that was impossible—he must have meant to slight her, to show her in this incredibly male, clumsy way that all was over between them. What should she do?—for nothing was certain. How should she act? For the first time she knew the meaning of the expression "at your wit's end."

Should she go home?—No, that was impossible. What explanation could she make to her mother or Lilian Smith? Besides, she would be condemning herself to long days of uncertainty. She could not endure that. Should she drive to Mr. Staple's and demand to see Laurie?—In her desperation she felt inclined to do that. She had a right to make a fuss, to make things hot for him—he mustn't expect her always to take everything lying down. But something at the bottom of her heart restrained her from exposing herself—better far wait till he came home, and see him there. She could manage to fill in the time somehow till three o'clock.

What should she do? Lunch was out of the question—she could not eat. Neither could she sit still. A terrible restlessness was in all her limbs —her anxiety translated into terms of motion. She would drive out somewhere in the car—drive really far and really fast—fill up all the hours with speed.

There was a wide space to turn in outside the church, and she swung round, the nose of her car pointing towards the sea. A long, white, flat road ran out into flat distances. It was the road to New Romney, so she was told by the signpost, and she set out along it, with the throttle well open. Oh, she was thankful she had got the car, that she could fill her waiting-time with fierce activity and the lull of motion, and yet was not required to support herself on legs that were weak and shaking. Her speedometer showed her that she had already come twenty-five miles, and there would of course be the twenty-five miles home. By driving out seawards she would probably add thirty miles to her day's tally, and fifty was quite enough for her unaccustomed driving. But she did not care. She must go—she could not live through time without the help of space.

She had never been out on the seaward side of the marsh, knowing only the road between Rye and Warehorne. Soon a toll-gate pulled her up.

"Sixpence . . . thank you" . . . craunch! Another noisy change— and how her leg was shaking as she put out the clutch!

How many miles to New Romney?
Scarcely more than ten.
Shall I get there by three o'clock?
Yes, and back again.

She mustn't be later than three, or he might have gone out again. She had better be there at a quarter to three. She could contrive to sit still for a quarter of an hour.

The marsh felt very huge lying there all round her, misty, flat, and green. It was foreign—unlike the country round Hawkhurst, which was all little hills covered with spinneys and fields, and farms with fairy names. Here the farms were set far apart among sheep-dotted miles of pasture—their roofs were immensely steep and high, and yellowed over with sea-lichen, and their ricks were thatched with osiers. She passed an enormous church standing between two farms—a few miles farther on she passed another, standing among some tiny cottages which could easily have been packed into its aisles. She thought of Brookland church, and the colour left her face.

It was in Brookland tower, all among the salt-riddled oak beams, that he had first told her that he loved her, holding her to him in the darkness. She had not been surprised—for several days she had been expecting, hoping he would speak, and now at last he had spoken . . . at least, he had not spoken—his lips had given her kisses instead of words. But she had understood—or rather she had not understood. She had thought he wanted to marry her—it was not till quite a week later that she discovered he did not.

O stop your ringing and let me be—
Let be, O Brooklands bells—
You'll ring Old Goodman out of the sea
Before I wed one else.

Old Goodman's farm is rank sea sand
And was this thousand year.
But it shall turn to rich plough land
Before I change my dear.

That was the way her little car, rushing and humming along, always set her thoughts to music. But this was a silly song—because she was going to change her dear that very evening. She had made up her mind. Weakness hitherto had been her fault, but now she would be firm. She could bear no more. How many times had she told herself that since the beginning? The first year had been beautiful, full of happiness, in spite of some twinges of conscience and the stinging of the lies she had to tell.

By the second year he had grown casual and remiss, but she had borne with him, knowing that it was his nature, and having always understood that men don't bother about little things the way women do. In the third year he had been unfaithful to her, but she had forgiven him, because she had always understood that men were liable to these attacks. Besides, she could not do without him. . . . What had happened that she could do without him now? A lot had happened—her heart was dead. He had slowly killed her heart. She did not love him any more. No, she didn't. She didn't, she didn't, she didn't!

The flat horizon was growing rough. A great shaggy wood spread across it, out of which a tower rose. Here was New Romney and the marsh's edge. Should she turn before going into the town? What time was it?—Nearly two. She had better turn. It would be too dreadful if she were late and missed him—she would turn at the next cross roads.

A signpost said: To New Romney: To Ivy-Church: To Lydd. She stopped the car and backed up the Lydd road. She did it clumsily and blocked the way. A little boy on a bicycle squeezed past. He turned round and smiled at her—not mockingly, but encouragingly and kindly. The smile at once comforted and melted her—she felt grateful for this unknown being's token of good will.

III. EVENING

Back again . . . back over the same road she had come. The bonnet of her car running before her was like the nose of a living thing—the cap of the radiator was like a funny little inquiring snout. If only her car was alive and loved her, how happy she would be! She was a big fool. . . . But, oh! she did want a little love—a little affectionate, tender love—love that never demanded anything. . . . She did not think she had ever had it. Of course there was her mother . . . but so many lies stood between her and her mother. She would love her mother when she was Free. Well, to-day wouldn't be wasted now, for all its anguish —at the end of it she would be Free. No longer would she have to tell lies, no longer would she have to wrestle with circumstances, no longer would she have to run after Laurie, either drawn by his whims or driven by her longings. Free . . . Free . . . he had set her Free at last— kicked her out, put her on the pavement—but she was Free. "There's no good, Laurie—it really is done—finished this time. You don't love me. You wouldn't treat me like this if you did. . . ."

Ah, here was the toll gate. How much quicker she seemed to have come back. Another sixpence . . . the girl said: "If I'd seen who it was, I'd have let you through. We're not supposed to, but——" Another kind creature. Joyce wanted to thank her, but instead she said in her heart to

Laurie: "No, this time I really will not pass it over. It's nothing to me if you care for this woman or not. You can take her, or nobody, you're not going to have me. Of course I will always be your friend."—No—she was done with him—for good—till she was fifty at any rate . . . then perhaps. . . . Not, even then. . . .

Lord! There he was on the road in front of her. She recognised his familiar step, his familiar grey suit, the way he flourished his stick instead of walking with it like other men. He must have left Mr. Staple's earlier than he had intended. What should she do? Pass him carelessly by? . . . That might hurt. . . . No, she must speak to him, otherwise the break would not be definite. She would leave no raw edges. She would cut—clean.

She sounded her horn as she drew even with him, ran on a few yards ahead, and then stopped. Without getting out of the car she turned and faced him—she saw the recognition dawn in his eyes, without reproach or fear.

"Dearest child . . ."

He came up to her, and was in the car beside her before she could speak.

"Laurie . . ." she said faintly.

"Start away, dear, and drive me home. You'll come in for a few minutes, won't you?"

"Laurie,—didn't you know I was coming to-day? Weren't you expecting me?—You asked me to lunch."

She saw his face grow blank—his brown, speckled eyes looked vacantly into hers. It was only for a second, but in that second such an agony of realization rushed over her as almost to deprive her of consciousness. She knew that he had forgotten. All her wild conjectures of unfaithfulness, urgent business, or determined slight were beside the mark. He had made no effort to shake her off, to break bad news, his absence had been no part of a plan either cruel or compassionate. He had simply forgotten all about her.

"My dear," he was saying—"how absolutely dreadful! How perfectly awful of me! But surely we didn't fix anything definite. I said I'd let you know."

"No, you didn't"—she spoke gruffly—"it was fixed. Don't you remember? You said your people would be away, and we'd have a whole lovely day together. We'd go over to St. Mary's . . ." Her voice broke.

"Yes—of course." . . . He was beginning to be embarrassed. "Mind the gatepost"—she nearly struck it as she swung the car into the sweep. . . . "I'm awfully sorry, Joyce, you came all this way and found me out. You make me feel dreadful."

He got out and opened the door for her. She followed him into the familiar room, half office, half study—she sank down in an armchair and burst into tears.

"Joyce—darling—don't! Don't be so upset about it—it's only a little thing."

"A little thing! . . . Oh! . . . and I've been thinking all sorts of things about you—that you'd thrown me over—that you were dead even —but this is worse than anything I'd imagined."

"Worse!—My dear girl, don't be hysterical."

He came over to her and tried to pull her hands down from her eyes.

"Don't—you don't love me, or you couldn't have forgotten me. And you haven't written, either—not for ten days."

"I'd nothing to write about . . . and I was waiting till I was sure about to-day." . . . . He was tying two lies together.

"Laurie, don't tell me you'd have forgotten about me, if you loved me as much as you used to."

"But I do love you just as much." Again he tried to pull away her hands.

"You don't."

"I do."

"You don't." This wasn't what she had meant to say, how she had intended the interview to go off. He slipped his arm round her, and in spite of her resistance, drew her head to his shoulder as he knelt beside her.

"Oh, Joyce darling, don't be angry. Don't let us quarrel over this. Surely we know each other well enough not to be upset by an accident."

"An accident! Oh, Laurie, if you knew what I've suffered—what I've thought. . . ."

"But it's all over now—oh, do be generous and forgive me."

"But it will happen again—something like it . . . Laurie, I can't bear any more . . . and I mean, what am I bearing it for?—where is all this leading us?"

"What do you mean, dear?"

"I mean—are—are we just going on like this until one of us marries someone else?"

"My dear child, I've told you that I can't marry you. Don't let us go over that all again."

"But I don't understand . . ."

He had risen and was walking about the room.

"Dearest, can't you let that alone? Can't we love each other as we used to do, without worrying about what may happen years ahead?"

"But we don't love each other as we used to do. Oh, Laurie, I won't say you love me less, but you love me differently. You forget me. I could bear it if I thought it was . . . I mean if we were going to be . . . but I have to bear it in vain."

"In vain? So this is 'in vain,' Joyce—all our love, all our friendship, all the heavenly moments we've had together?—It's all in vain, if you haven't something material to look forward to? Is that what you mean?"

"Oh, no, no!"

"Then what in God's name do you mean?"

She wished she knew. She wished she had said the things she had meant to say—done what she had meant to do. His sin against her was even worse than she had imagined, and yet . . . Free . . . the things she had meant to do when she was Free . . . But she would be Free— even the sight of him there before her in all his alert and lovely strength should not cheat her of her freedom. She sprang to her feet.

"Laurie . . . I'm not going on with it—I can't. . . . I can't bear . . . I'm going to be Free."

His arms were round her—her words were choked out against his breast . . . the smell of his tweed coat seemed to stifle her. She felt his warmth and strength, his arm upholding her. His lips were warm against her ear, murmuring tenderly and reproachfully—"Oh, you silly little thing—you don't know what you're saying. You're going to forgive me, and love me more than ever. Of course you are. You're upset with the heat."

Then her spirit fainted. She did not know whether she despaired more of him or of herself. He tilted back her unresisting head, and his lips came down upon hers, the seal of her bondage.

" 'Lord, how oft shall my brother sin against me and I forgive him— till seven times?'

" 'Not until seven times; but until seventy times seven' " . . . unto the bitter end. . . .

Tired . . . tired . . . That was the only refrain her car had for her on the journey home . . . no more furious thinking . . . no more furious rhymes . . . only tired . . . tired . . . exhausted, eighty-seven miles on the speedometer. . . . Tired . . . tired. . . .

Home at last.

"Well, dear, have you had a nice day?"

"Yes, Mother, thank you—a lovely day."

71

Rivers of Damascus

BY DONN BYRNE

"Sweeter to me are Albana and Parphar, rivers of Damascus, than all the waters of Israel."

NOW if he had been a white man, with his little spare body, his powerful hands, his light legs and wizened face, you might have taken him for what he was, a jockey. But as he was coloured, you would hardly think of that. One is apt to forget the black man's light, strong legs, his beautiful hands for a horse's mouth, his strange, caressing way with animals. Besides, one's experience of jockeys is that they are invariably well-dressed in that exaggerated mode that passes for smartness on Broadway and Piccadilly. But this one was dressed in a French suit, baggy trousers with gussets, waisted coat, and shoes that turned up at the toe like a Turk's slippers. His favourite seat was on the Promenade des Anglais at Nice, where he sat on a public wooden bench and sunned himself like a cat because there was nothing else for him to do. His name—none remembers it now—was Les Armstrong.

Now a Negro in Nice is not something to look and wonder at and perhaps shoot, if you have a spare cartridge, as he would be in Ireland. From Martinique, from Madagascar, from Algeria they come and are welcomed as free men and brothers. They dress like the smarter sort of Frenchman, and often are "princes in their own country." But this poor chap, sitting on the smartest promenade in the world, dressed in a suit of cheap French reach-me-downs, was Virginian American, and proud of it. To him a khan of India or a bey of Algiers was a nigger. He was an American. He did not proclaim it in an arrogant manner, for there was no arrogance in him. As he sat there on the Promenade des Anglais reading his Continental edition of an American paper, picking possible winners at Auteuil, and wondering which of the surreptitious French bookmakers he could trust with his ten or twenty francs, there was about him the dignity all small gentle people have. A Moor of Tunis in white burnous, with prayer carpets for sale, approached him. There was a quiet superiority in the little jockey's: "Nix, guy, nix!" that put him, who was a sheikh in his own country, as all Riviera Moors are, into his proper plane of colour.

And yet if he had not been so loyally American, as indeed it would have been to his advantage not to be, one could hardly have blamed him. For it was only two afternoons ago that paying his fifty centimes, or half a nickel, he had gone into the Jetty Casino, on the off-chance of picking up a little on *petits chevaux*. The throbbing drum and the moaning bassoon of the band playing the blues had drawn him in curiosity to the dancing floor. There they circled slowly around, English peer and demimondaine, American millionaire and shady countess, professional gambler and his female lure, Egyptian prince and fair, post-war Englishwoman, little Provençal shopkeepers who love to dance. And honeymooners from Scotland, or Birmingham perhaps, who are thrilled to the core at being one with the mad, bad life of France; and who will bore their grandchildren with descriptions of how wild grandpa and granny were when young. The little jockey looked on with pathetic face, for he loved dancing. A slim Creole instructress from Martinique, whom he had spoken to once, took pity on him.

"*Voulez-vous . . .?*"

"Why, dog-gone, I'd just love to. You sure are one decent girl!"

They had made a half circle when the band stopped. It would go on again in a second or two if the applause warranted. High above the clapping of hands, a woman's voice rang out abruptly.

"Look here, I'm not going on if this thing's allowed."

The little jockey turned around. A hard-faced, brittle woman was pointing at him. Les Armstrong didn't know her, but he knew her type. He had often seen it flash from limousine to baccarat rooms in furs and diamonds. He flushed and turned to the little instructress.

"You excusez me, mademoiselle. One moment."

He went toward the hard-faced woman, making up a little speech as he went: "Ma'am, if you want me to, I won't dance on this floor again. But, if you don't mind, I'll dance this dance, because this little professional girl asked me to. Ma'am, I'm sorry, I'm real sorry."

But he never got a word of it out, for the woman's escort, a burly man of six feet two, caught him a vicious crack with the right fist on the side of the head. It was a fat man's punch, untimed, all elbow; but it was heavy. It caught the little one-hundred-and-fifteen-pounder on neck and ear and smashed him to the floor as if he had been picked up and hurled. It stunned him. Attendants, detectives, what not, rushed over. In all the commotion Armstrong could hear the fat man's voice say:

"I'm an American, sir! and we don't stand for these guys dancing on the same floor as white women."

The little jockey knew that, American or not, if he had been a French Negro, by now the fat man would have been led off by police to be placed in jail, unbailed. The interpreter was bawling in his ear.

"You wish make no complaint? No, you no wish make complaint. No, he make no complaint."

"No," said Armstrong quietly, "I don't want to make no complaint."

He tottered up and away, leaving the little instructress, her blazing eyes filled with tears, her body crisp as a tiger's, without a word of farewell. Somebody pushed his hat into his hand. He slunk past the loud boule table, and out into the mellow sunset.

"I ain't ever going into that joint never any more."

He walked along the promenade blindly.

"I had no right to dance on that floor nohow. . . ."

"Dog-gone, what could I do, when that little girl asked me. . . ."

"Them black Frenchmen dance. Nobody says a word. . . ."

The worst of it was he had recognized the big man who struck him. He had seen him at the Longchamps races, and later outside Monte Carlo. A year before when the English hunter, Devon Pride, had won a big race with himself up, the fat man had pushed through the crowd when Armstrong was on his way to the scales with his saddle over his arm. "Attaboy!" he had shouted. "Attaboy! You showed them Frenchies what an American boy can do!"

"He ain't no American. . . ."

"Ain't I heard that guy outside the Café de Paris knocking America to a bunch of Englishmen and saying he was so sick of it he couldn't live there any more? Yes, boy, I did."

He stood and looked at the flaming Esterel. There were tears in his eyes. His heart was more hurt than his ear and neck were.

"He ain't no American. . . . No American would hit a little guy like me. . . ."

The truth of the matter was that he was ill—more ill than even he knew.

At times his face would take on a brownish grey colour and his knees tremble for no reason. But this would pass, and he would feel all right again.

Years of sweating down to keep his weight down had taken the vitality out of him; and homesickness, that thing that gnaws like a rat, had

eaten his heart. Because he had never accustomed himself to read anything but newspapers, and because that dingy little room of his in Old
Nice was so lonely, his nights would be passed in bars a little more sor-
did and less artificial than those of Paris.

Hither would come, when the tables of the Casino closed, women in
diamonds and men in evening clothes for a cocktail or a dance or a look
at the underworld. Once when some of them were present he keeled
over.

He came to in a second or so. A burly man with the red face of a
butcher, and wearing a white carnation in his dinner jacket, was holding his wrist. Little Armstrong didn't know it, but the beefy citizen
was Sir Michael O'Callaghan, the Dublin surgeon known to all Ireland
as "Big Mike."

He had come south "to cut the tripes out of some Grand Jook begob!"
but the coloured jockey was getting for nothing the thought and sympathy that had cost the Romanoff half an emerald mine.

"Boy, you're sick," he roared.

"Yes, sir. I knows."

"Do you? What's wrong with you?"

"No, sir. I don't."

"Why don't you go home?"

"Yes, sir. Why?"

"What do you do? Follow the races?"

"Yes, sir. I follows the races now. I was a good jockey once. Some
folks as knew," he added quietly, "said there was none better."

Big Mike thought an instant. Only those who knew him intimately,
knew how deeply religious he was, would have caught the meaning of
his next remark.

"Well, boy, there's a good time coming soon."

He dug his hand into his pocket where his baccarat winnings were;
pulled out a thousand franc note. The little jockey shook his head.

"I don't want to hurt your feelings, no, sir, but I ain't got as far as
that yet. It sure was good of you——"

"Well, you'll have a drink on me," said Big Mike. "Garsong," he
shouted in his abominable French, "apportez un poo brandy quicko!"
He patted the coloured boy on the shoulder and left him. There was
nothing else to do.

"If that big man had been home folks now," the jockey would talk
to himself afterwards on his seat on the promenade, "I sure could have
taken his money. I couldn't let no stranger say an American boy had
taken his money. No, sir. Dog-gone, that guy sure was a white man."

He had been born outside Norfolk, Virginia, and his early days had
been happy. His father he remembered as a cheery, fat, small man, al-

ways laughing; his mother had been a raw-boned Louisiana woman. But his father died when he was eleven, and the mother removed to New Orleans. There his mother went bad, taking to drink and a saturnine Jamaican who saw to it that she kept him in the state to which Jamaicans of the better sort are accustomed. The Jamaican, who bore the name of Horatio Wilson Jones, beat little Les on every possible occasion. Hence his dislike of New Orleans and his love for Virginia where he had been happy as a child. The only refuge was the race-track, where he made himself useful, running errands for grooms and handlers. One day, as a joke, he was given a leg-up at exercise on a five-year-old selling plater. He went around the track as if he had been cradled in pig-skin.

Now anybody can acquire a good seat on a horse, even—I have it on competent authority—a Knight of the British Empire; but hands are indubitably the gift of God. And hands little Les had. So in the course of a few years he was taken on as apprentice, and later on rose to the dignity of having a black plate with his name on it in white letters— Les Armstrong. Within a couple of years he had won two or three sound races. And then he began "pulling the hat trick," which means winning three races in one day. He did it two or three times a season, so his future was assured.

He went North to New York for the summer season at Empire and Jamaica and Tuxedo, where for various reasons he didn't do so well. There is a great deal more in racing than meets the eye. And wizened white jockeys cannot be blamed, if you look at the matter from the human standpoint, because they are not enthusiastic about a coloured jockey winning. In my own most sporting country, in a large field, I should be tremendously surprised to see an English jockey win a race, no matter how good his mount is. But that is for psychologists.

An owner gave him the chance to come to Paris for the season, to ride there and at the seaside courses, at Deauville. Armstrong had heard of the great Paris races, of the fine horses, and the flower of European society, the beautiful midinettes, the royalty on the lawn. "Dog-gone, I'll go," he laughed. "I sure wants to see this Paris."

He found out very soon that little interest was attached to the horses. They were an adjunct to the betting machines. For flat racing, few out of the multitude cared. Hurdles and steeplechases were the popular idea of what the racing should be, the jumps being thrown in to make the gambling a little more thrilling, as deuces are made wild in a poker game. Of how a horse was bred few cared. To whom the horse belonged mattered a lot. And owners' instructions were often very puzzling. One had the impression of them meeting the night before the race, in the Casino. "This poor Gaston," the Alphonses would say, "this poor Gaston, my old, has not won a race at the meeting. Impossible! But I, who speak to you! His pleasure here will be spoiled, utterly spoiled. Also his legitimate will say: 'I told you so! Why didn't you stick to politics?' Gaston must win to-morrow. No! No! Gaston, we insist!" All this may be untrue, but one got the impression. Also, Gaston won.

With the four and five-year-olds over the hurdles Armstrong was singularly successful. He seemed to know to an ounce what a horse could do. Warily, waiting for the exact second, he would nurse his mount along, that touch of the nervous, muscular hands telling the horse that he knew what he was doing, until the most nervous, fractious, ill-treated racer knew that it was in the hands of a comrade and a master. Owners might rave, bettors tear their beards and weep, as French bettors will, but until his moment arrived, Les never moved, and then, a touch of the little finger on the reins, a tightening of the knees, and his husky friendly: "Horse, let's go!" and he would sweep along to take his easy win or certain place, as the mount was worth. The sight of the fluttering silk, the black face and black hands pounding up from behind came to be a recognized feature of certain race-courses. *"Le noir, il gagne, il gagne encore,"* they would shout on the lawn, "the black wins, wins again." It was as though he were the colour on a roulette wheel. And at steeplechasing, too, he lifted three or four of the big plumes, and a host of minor ones. For some reason or other the horses took to the coloured American jockey. They liked his hand, they liked his confidence, they knew he was a master in his craft.

Then Armstrong's luck turned.

He was riding, for a French owner, a big brown gelding called Mistral, a son of Chimney Sweep, a fine fencer and a horse with a great heart; and coming to the last hurdle, he felt that little give in the stride that told him his mount had gone lame.

"Dog-gone!" he said. "This baby's gone and hurt himself."

His eyes shifted, pivoted in his still head, to the mounts beside him. He noticed the falter, the half-stride lost at the hurdle. From the lawn in front the crowds were shouting "Mistral! Mistral!" A big English grey beside him began to stretch. He leaned over and showed Mistral the whip. The big dun never quickened his stride.

"Dog-gone," Armstrong said, "he ain't got nothing no more."

The shouts came louder. *"Tuez-le! Tuez-le!* Kill him! Kill him!" And some voice was calling in English: "Beat him up, Les! Beat him up!" Armstrong slackened his reins.

"Another race another day, boy," he said to the big chaser.

He was half-way across the lawn when the owner accosted him, a huge, burly man with a huge, curling, black beard like that of an Assyrian king, oiled and perfumed. His black eyes were like snakes' eyes, alive with venom.

"Vat you do?" he shouted. "Vat you do?"

"I pulled up your horse, monsoo, because he'd gone lame."

"Vy you pull up, ha? Vy you pull up?"

"I said: because your horse had gone lame."

"Couldn't you get a place, ha? No? Yes, you get a place?" He leaned over half smothering the little jockey with his exquisite beard. People began to gather, chattering.

"I guess I could have, if I'd killed that horse, but I ain't going to kill no horse for no owner, no, sir."

The Frenchman's fingers contracted, like the claws of a hawk. They suddenly descended on Armstrong's shoulder, ripping the silk jacket from his back, leaving him a ridiculous figure in a sleeveless grey woollen shirt, with black arms like brittle sticks, among the concourse of chic women and men dressed in gray cutaways and black stocks with diamonds in them. The owner waved the torn jacket in the air.

"Ainsi aux caguins!" he bellowed. "Thus treat rascals." He might have been the chief executioner of an antique commonwealth holding up a bleeding head. "Thus perish traitors!" It was all ridiculous.

"I don't care," Armstrong said. "I ain't going to kill no horse for no man. A win is only a win," he said, "but a horse, well, a horse is a horse."

It was ridiculous, but——

Caesar's wife must be above suspicion, but what must Caesar's jockey be? The cold attitude of that righteousness is terrifying. To pull a horse, to slacken up, all this is right if the owner says it is. But, to be under the suspicion of not obeying the owner's orders is the chief sin of the racing world, the penalty for which is the chief penalty of the racing world—no mounts.

He may be all right and he may not, say owners; he's a nice fellow, he's a good rider, but this is a hard enough game as it is, without taking extra chances——

All the mounts he got now were rank outsiders with which he was expected to do miracles, but miracles are not done on race-courses unless the stage has been carefully set beforehand. The vanishing favourite of a race-course must be as carefully prepared as the Vanishing Lady in vaudeville. The other mounts he got were horses conditioning up, who hadn't a chance in the race, but were out for exercise. Added to this, his luck had definitely turned. Riderless mounts seemed to like getting in his way in preference to other jockeys'. And three times he took a toss trying to jam through at fences, where, had he had a decent horse, he would have waited his time. Little by little his name disappeared. That thing the French denote as luck, and which we more sensible folk call the phenomenon of the law of average, had left him. And when that thing leaves a man definitely, he is in a bad way.

There is something about French money, too, that lacks power. It hasn't the efficient look of a five dollar bill, nor the crisp solidity of a pound. It has a consumptive, appealing look that makes you extremely generous with it, so you part with it saying: after all, it's only francs. It is only when they are gone that one considers that those flimsy notes might not have been so anæmic after all. Also, if there is one person who is more foolish about money than a prize fighter, it is a jockey, for the fighter has usually sense enough not to bet on fights.

So after a while of barren racing and money given into that most heartless of all human contraptions, the totalisator, Armstrong felt himself poor.

"Dog-gone," he said, "I must ride me a winner."

He went South to Pau. The local papers greeted the Parisian jockey with a column of eulogy. But after he had been down the field three consecutive days, the papers were silent, if the public weren't.

"Dog-gone," he puzzled, "I must have passed a funeral, or a cross-eyed woman, or something."

At Marseilles it was the same story. No winners and plunging on the pari mutuel, until he discovered with a shock that he was down to his last thousand-franc note. A thousand francs is roughly fifty dollars; but fifty is a good masculine sum with which much can be done. A thousand francs—well, all you can do with it is spend it.

He had, as all men have, one song he was fond of singing. It was the only song a white man had written for Negroes that the Negroes love: "Carry me back to old Virginny." That was the song he whistled or sang as he tested girths and leathers:

> *Carry me back to old Virginny,*
> *That's where the cotton and the corn and taters grow.*
> *That's where the birds warble sweet in the Springtime,*
> *There's where this darky's heart am long'd to go.*

There never had been any one to work for, barring owners for whom one rode, and his only experience of cornfields was to see them as he passed in trains, but he would sing the little song as though the words translated a life of personal experience:

> *There's where I laboured so hard for old massa*
> *Day after day in the fields of yellow corn——*

But this he understood—

No place on earth do I love more sincerely
Than old Virginny, the place where I was born.

Night would steal over Marseilles, the last rays of the sun bless Notre
Dame de la Garde; along the ancient Prado the lights would come up
one by one, the Cannebière blaze suddenly, and he would feel that he
was in a strange city, stranger than any he had known. Here people
were interested in ships, not in horses.

He moved along the quays of the Vieux Port, and like an answer
from Heaven to a breathed prayer he saw on the counter of a freighter
the name *Elisha Hopkins,* Baltimore.

"Dog-gone," he said, "Baltimore, Maryland."

If it had occurred six weeks before, when he had money in his pocket,
and no sense that his luck was black out, he would have gone direct to
the master and bargained for a passage home, or made friends with the
doctor, as the ship's cook is familiarly called, who was probably one of
his own race. But bad luck brings timidity.

"I'll just sneak aboard and lay low, and when the boat's off, I'll come
out and tell the stewards I'm an American boy out of luck, and everything will be all right. Yes, boy!"

He did manage to slip up the gang-plank, and work into a lifeboat
under the tarpaulin. It had been raining, and the boat, for all its cover,
was half filled with glutinous water, in which he knelt shivering. But
the hawk-eyed mate noticed something amiss, and had the cover off.

"Come out o' that," he directed. He was a florid Scandinavian type.
Armstrong came out.

"Stowaway, hey?"

"Boss, I'm an American——"

"That's what they all are."

"I'm trying to get back home," he said. "I'm sure sick of this France."

"You'll be sicker before you're through, my lad." He motioned up
two policemen from the pier. Armstrong trembled.

"You ain't going to turn me over to the cops, boss," he pleaded.

"You didn't think I was going to give you flowers, did you?"

"Boss, you wouldn't do that to an American."

"I done it to fifty, kid. You're the fifty-first." The mate was cruel. He
was one of those men in whom cruelty is a vice, as drugs and drink are
in other men.

"I guess," Armstrong gave in, "I'm out of luck."

"Look-a-here," the mate gave him a baffled, wicked glance that made
him shiver. "You're in luck. That's what you are. What I does to stow-
aways, when I finds them aboard at sea, though I says it myself, it's a

shame. They don't exactly die, but they ain't any good after. You believe it, nigger. You're in luck."

So the police took him, speaking words to him he couldn't understand, and the judge, in a language he couldn't understand, gave him a month. They kept him sewing mail bags and coats for Moroccan soldiers, while he never spoke. Warders with beards and warders with fine moustaches saw to it he worked: *"Allez-houp!"* they would call, as to a broken down cab-horse. Occasionally his little song would come to his lips in a quavering nostalgia.

> *There's where the birds warble sweet in the Springtime,*
> *There's where this darky's heart am long'd to go.*

But *"Silence, le noir!"* they would shout, and he would bend over his sewing again, his eyes blinded.

They fed him on fish, which he could hardly eat, so nauseating did he find it. They gave him a cough, which can be cured, and a broken heart, which cannot. And on the thirtieth day they took him out and gave him his own clothes again. They led him to the door of the jail, where he stood blinking for an instant in the sunlight. They pushed him along. *"En route!"* they called, "off with you now," and they added, out of the kindness of their hearts, *"au revoir!"*

On leaving Marseilles he walked eastward toward Italy, not for the reason he needed car fare, but for this: that he feared that every one on the railroad carriage would know he had been in jail. For each of us, white, black or yellow, has his degradation point. It may be drink or drugs, or nobbling a horse, or cheating at cards. With the little jockey it was having been in jail. It put him in his own mind on the level with those of his race who used razors in brawls, of the travelling Negro hoboes who are accused of brutal crimes. His thought went back to the laughing father in Norfolk, whom he remembered so dimly, so affectionately.

"I'm glad the old man croaked," he said. "It sure would have hurt him bad, to know his boy was a bum."

"Yes, boy, that's all you is," tears came into his eyes. "You is a bum, a plain bum."

He trudged along the long road to Nice, a withered black speck of broken humanity, by the Mediterranean, bluest of all oceans, cat-like, indifferent. The sea which had seen Tyre and Sidon, the crowning cities, go; Greece crumble; Rome pass;—not one breath, or chime of sympathy came from that harsh Latin sea. Atlantic, our mother, would have breathed comfort. And the sullen, supercilious Alps, they had seen so many pass by. The greatest Caesar, gallant Eugene of Savoy, Napoleon. What did they care for the black speck on the road? Some ancient, hoary mountain may have blinked in its sleep, remembering how centuries ago the black folk were Lords of the Isles of Lerius and the scourge of the littoral, and thought: Have these bronze, supple men gone too? Have they come to this? Everything passes, everything grows tired, everything breaks. Only we, born of ice and fire abide—we and the stars.

He had an impression that in Nice his troubles would cease. There was a city with Americans; Nice was a city with races—some of the biggest stakes in France were run for there. It would be a month or more before the races began, but he would lie up and get well—get rid of this cough, dog-done!—and luck must change. There were two desires in his heart—to get back to Virginia, and to ride a great horse to victory before he went, for when he went back, he knew, it would be going from fair to fair with the trotters and pacers. He would never swing a leg over pig-skin any more.

Armstrong found Nice a pleasant town. Here and there were bars behind which were men who had been in America, French waiters who had picked up a good deal of the American language and a certain aptitude in mixing cocktails, and returning to France had been raised to the episcopal rank of bar-tender. Though few of these had been farther south than New York, yet it set the blood warm in his veins to talk about Empire race track, and Butler's horses, and Jamaica. And they had heard of Ral Parr's great string in Kentucky, and Man of War, whose immense stride was a miracle. To these ex-missionaries, now bishops, of the catering world, he would discourse on the temperament of the horse.

"There is something about a horse, dog-gone, look-a-here. If a horse is a mean horse, he's just naturally mean. If a man is mean, it may be his relatives, it may be his wife, it may be he ain't a well man. But a horse ain't got no relatives, ain't got no wife, and if a horse is sick, you call the vet. Then if it's proven to you that a horse is born mean, then you got to get around that some way. Look-a-here, a man may be yellow, and you never find that out in all your life. But if a horse is yellow, you find it out the first time you're in the home stretch and the favourite's creeping up on you. You says: Horse, here's where you pay for your oats, and if he lies down and dies, boy, you know he's a dog. A horse ain't no actor. Me, I knows horses, but I don't get men."

And then he would say, in a queer tone of voice, very different from his enthusiastic tone of before:

"Horses remember you!"

One day a piece of luck came his way. A fifty to one shot rolled home at Marseilles, on which he had ten francs. So he could still go around his accustomed haunts.

At all these places he was welcome, because at two o'clock in the morning he gave an air of disreputability to the place that was worth money. Most of the night bars were intensely respectable, the proprietor insisted on it, and his wife more so, for little Jean-Baptiste, or Pierre-Marie, when he grew a marshal like Petain, or a premier like Poincaré, mustn't be ashamed of his origin. So the pretty ladies were dragooned like a girls' school. If they wished to be rough, let them go outside. But they drew customers, and Armstrong's shiny black face made the bar look like a hell-hole out of some hack writer's novel. *Ex Africa semper aliquid novi.* Africa always provides a novelty.

They were very decent to him, by and large. The pretty ladies never bothered him, for they had wisdom enough to see he was a clean little cuss, and they liked him for it. Also they understood in a vague way that a man who is interested in horses is interested in little else. They bothered about his cough. And were vituperative on the subject. Why did he allow himself to be made a fool of? *Tiens, tiens!* It was a shame. Ah, those rascals!

And often they would ask him to sing his little song, and he would give it in his fair tenor, always preserving the rhythm but sometimes leaving out the body of the music to emphasise the words.

> *No place on earth do I love more sincerely*
> *Than old Virginny, the place where I was born.*
> *Carry me back to old Virginny,*
> *That's where the cotton and the corn and taters grow.*
> *There's where the birds warble sweet in the Springtime,*
> *There's where this darky's heart am long'd to go.*
>
> *Carry me back to old Virginny,*
> *There let me live till I wither and decay.*
> *Long by the old Dismal Swamp have I wandered,*
> *There's where this darky's life will pass away——*

And sometimes there his voice would take on a quaver, or sink into a whisper, and he would say: "I ain't feeling much like singing to-night, folks, if you don't mind." And the bar-keeper would nod, for he too in America had had his moments of nostalgia, and the pretty ladies would look sad, and not speak, but apply themselves to their grenadines or bocks, drinking daintily as birds.

Whenever one thinks of France in a far country as, for instance, in America or Ireland, one thinks of roulette wheels, and it comes as a distinct blow to know that roulette is not allowed. Roulette is gambling. *Petits chevaux* are allowed. But that is not gambling; that is piracy. Baccarat is allowed. But that is not gambling; that is just over the hills to the poorhouse. If you want the Royal and Ancient Game of Roulette you have to leave France and go to Monte Carlo.

He had looked forward to seeing this roulette, to seeing the strained faces of the players around the baize, to see the wheel a blaze of colour, and hear the whir of the ball, the hoarse cry of the croupier: *"Rien ne va plus!* No more bets!" or the announcement of the result: *"Quatorze gagne, rouge pair et manque!* Fourteen wins, red evens and below the line." The click of chips, the rustle of bank-notes, all the strain of the hot, crowded rooms, heavy with stale air, all this he wanted to see, for there are three things we all wish to know about in this life: Love, Death and Monte Carlo.

At the desk they refused him entry. An official who spoke English much better than he did, punched him all around the ring in machine-gun French. He kept smiling that insincere, chilly smile which tells you there is nothing doing.

"I guess there's worse 'n me comes in here, boss," Armstrong said. "I guess when all's said and done, I'm the honestest of the bunch."

His objurgation moved them not. Three men had cursed them that week, one as he jumped to death from the upper Corniche Road; one as he shot himself in a back room at Mentone, and one as he went overboard from a small row boat he had hired, into the black Mediterranean. All three had called God to witness their end, and yet no heaven had opened, nor had the Casino been consumed like the cities of the plain.

He was wandering into the sunshine, where the palms sighed and the pigeons drummed, and going toward the Café de Paris, where he wondered would they refuse to serve him, when a large hand descended on his shoulder.

"Ain't you Les Armstrong, the jock?"

"Yeh. I'm Armstrong."

"I thought I was right," a hearty, insincere voice roared. "Boy, I got something for you. Come right here."

Armstrong studied the red-faced, hearty-voiced man. He had once been an American, he was one no longer, which was one up to the Western Republic. For his voice was loud; his feet were not in his own house.

"Come right along, boy," Armstrong was encouraged. "I got something you'll love."

"Is it, is it a mount?"

"Yeh, it's a nice big horse for you to ride."

"I sure likes a nice horse," he said. "Is it a good horse?"

"Ain't no better."

"Is it a square ride?"

"Do I look like a guy," the ex-American demanded hotly, "who would want to pull some dirty trick? I ask you, do I?"

If he had asked you or me, who are six footers, and handy with the mitts, we would have answered: You sure do! and awaited the result with interest. But if you are a small, underfed jockey, out of luck, you don't have much *joie de coeur* in matching wallops. So Armstrong gave the soft answer that turneth away wrath.

"I ain't meant nothing, boss. Dog-gone, you know. In this horse business a jock has got to be careful."

"Kid, you're all right. You're the guy we want. Come right with me."

He brought him over to the striped awnings of the Café de Paris. A huge, dark, fat man was sitting before a glass of Perrier. He was not jollily fat, as many fat men are, but fat in a sinister way, like some adipose evil thing in the depths of the sea. He had small black eyes that seldom moved, but have the keen edge of knives. He was scrubbed to the perfection of cleanliness, his spatulate, grubby hands were beautifully manicured. On one hand shone a great diamond. The other held a cigar. He never moved. His eyes just shifted slightly.

"Well, Chief," his scout called, "I got the guy we want."

The Chief slowly pivoted his eyes, as a searchlight is pivoted, on the little jockey. He moved them away again.

"Yeh, Chief," the ex-American told him, "this is the kid. You can sit down, Armstrong," he condescended.

The little jockey was not very comfortable, for out of this immense fat man there exhaled an atmosphere of evil. It was not very hard to place him. You will see him, or one of the eleven or twelve like him, at various Casinos during the season, at Biarritz, at Deauville, at Hamburg, at Cannes. They are the ones who are called the professional gamblers. Whence they come God knows. They speak English and French well, almost perfectly if that were possible, but French or English or American they are not. This swarthy one will be an Egyptian, perhaps; and this one a Greek, perhaps. They always win.

They win for this reason—that gambling to them is a business, and they have toward money an attitude that is neither yours nor mine. When you or I bet a hundred pounds or a thousand dollars on a fine horse, we bet it because we like the horse. We know of no better horse in the race. We have confidence in the jockey. The course suits both of them. And when we lose, we have lost money. We have lost something that cost us work and effort. A little share of power is gone.

But to these men money is not money but a commodity, as fish is to a fishmonger. There are so many counters on a table. They are not money. They are counters. What they spend outside is money. What they lose or win at the tables is a commodity. They exchange the commodity for money to spend, or invest money in the commodity. But of risking big sums they are not afraid, as we would be, and as they know we are. Also they have developed a sense of luck. When their luck is going bad, they will leave the table where they are risking tens of thousands, and go to a small table where you risk ten francs. This is known as "running the bad luck out." They are not alone. They have ancient, vile old women who play for them at smaller tables. They have young girls, beautiful, perfectly groomed young girls to sit beside and encourage losers, suckers, that expressive term, whose vanity will not let them be quitters before the bright, sympathetic eyes of the young girl. If you will ask me, I believe they are virtuous, these girls, to use that sweet old-time word, but they have sold their souls to the devil. The Tribunal of Heaven, I make free to believe, prefers their sisters of the street. Such is the gambler.

"Baron Ganzoni here," the scout explained, "has a horse for the Grand Prix de la Ville de Nice, and he wants you to ride. He'll walk it."

"I don't know," said Armstrong, "any Baron Ganzoni racing. And about walking that course, I heard of four that'll do it."

"Well, this horse is by Spearmint out of Moyra's Pride. His name is Kilkenny Boy."

"But that horse," Armstrong stood aghast, "that horse belongs to a English dook."

"It did, kid, it did," the scout soothed him. The gambler leaned forward on the table. When he moved the slightest bit he breathed heavily, like some horrible animal coming at you in the dark of a hideous dream. "He don't no more. Listen, this horse is the goods."

"I know he's the goods," the jockey answered. "I don't see yet how he's your Chief's."

"Well, I'll tell you, kid. This English dook has no money, see, and he figures out he's had so much bad luck there's some good coming. So he sails into Monte for the baccarat with what dough he can collect, and right away he runs into the Chief.

"Well, you know baccarat. It makes an aeroplane look slow. In a while there's only the dook and the Chief in the game, and this dook's luck is certainly gone flooey. If it was raining, and the dook in the middle of the street, boy, if luck was rain, this guy would be bone dry. And before he knows anything he has nothing. He ain't the sort of guy to pull bum cheques or rough stuff like that. He gets up.

" 'What? No more?' says the Chief. And he smiles dirty. Boy, the Chief's smile would make a rabbit furious.

" 'I'm cleaned out,' says the Duke, 'but I've got a horse at Marseilles that ought to win the Grand Prix at Nice. That's worth a hundred and twenty-five thousand francs in stakes. He won at Marseilles easily and he got a very poor ride. I don't even know how good he is, and weight won't stop him!' The Chief looks at me and I tips my mitt that what the dook says is O.K.

" 'Supposing?' says the dook, 'I match his luck against yours. Between himself and stakes and bets he's worth three thousand pounds. If you care to, put that up in a bank and I'll go you. You take the horse or I take your money.'

"The Chief looks at me, and I nods, it's O.K. The Chief puts up a quarter of a million francs on the table.

" 'Bank of a quarter million francs,' says the croupier.

" 'Banco!' says the dook.

"So the Chief deals him two cards, and takes two. You know this game. The nearest to nine wins. You can draw a card if the other guy hasn't a eight or a nine.

" 'I'll have a card,' says the dook.

"The Chief turns up his cards and they's two picture cards, worth nothing. Boy, I nearly fainted. I'm standing behind the dook, and I sees he's got an ace and a two spot, making three, and the Chief chucks him a five.

" 'I've got *huit*,' says the dook. The money was won.

"The Chief pulls a card from the box, and looks at it for a moment before putting it down.

" '*Noof!*' says he. 'Nine!'

"And that's how we gets the horse!

"Now here's where we get a raw deal. We brings the horse from Marseilles and tries to get a trainer, but this dook, see, he may be short of jack but he's got a lot of friends. And all the trainers say: Sorry, but we ain't got no stalls. And all the jocks down here, Mitchell and Atkinson and Head, and the French guys and the Eyetalians, they all got mounts for the race. Kind o' cold and distant, just because the baron, see, he ain't in with the racing gang. Wouldn't that get your goat? So then I remembers you. And I says: Bo, what are you worrying about? Here's a guy will look back and laugh at 'em.

"What do you say, kid? What do you say?"

If he had not been so out of luck, he, too would have said: Sorry, but I got a mount for this race. But nobility, and contempt for sharp practice are perquisites of the reasonably rich. It is easy to be noble with a sound balance at your bankers. But try it on two-bits.

"Well," he thought, "the horse and me is on the square anyhow." And aloud he said: "I'll go it."

The ex-American pulled a wallet out of his pocket.

"Well," he said, "just to show you what I think of you, I'll pay you the winning jockey's fee now." And he handed him two hundred francs. "That's how I do things, see? And there'll be the same on for you with this pari mutuel, see?

"Now, look-a-here, kid, no cracks about this, see? If the gang thinks we can't get a regular jock, boy, they'll leave this horse alone on the machines. They'll hardly put a cent up. And guy, we'll just take their shoes off. So put it away in your dome, and forget it till the day of the race. We'll show these dooks and dooks' friends they can't be cold and haughty with us, see?"

Well, that was legitimate. That didn't come into the infernal region of pulling or doping a horse. That was with-holding stable information. There was nothing wrong about that.

Ganzoni, the gambler, spoke for the first time in the interview. His heavy, glucose voice rumbled out:

"Are you in good shape to ride this race?'

Armstrong's heart sank for a moment. Had they noticed he was ill? Were they going to take this mount from him? Had the man's infernal eye plumbed through clothes and flesh and bone to the stricken organs beneath? Those horrible coughing fits which shook him until he was covered with sweat, and had to lean against something for support— did they know of those? It was only that morning when he was tying a shoe lace he had fallen on his face, and lain there for an hour, unconscious.

But sick and all as he was, he knew he had a good race in him still. He was certain of that as of——

"I'm all right, boss. You needn't worry."

Now you may laugh at the Var race-course as much as you like. You may say it isn't a race-course, it's a motion picture. You may say put an Irish hunter at those jumps and he will take them in his stride. Barring the Act of God or the King's enemies, a half bred handy horse will walk it.

For the Act of God and the King's enemies seemed to have selected Nice race-course as their favourite winter resort. Here are hurdles a plough horse will take. Here is an Irish bank that the hunter Pelican would skim over with the Meath hounds. Here is a stone wall a green five-year-old will take. Here is a water jump that is a great test of jumping, for a cow. It is all tremendously simple.

Yet lying hidden beside each fence are two small, ghoul-like figures with a stretcher, small, wizened-faced men with cynical expressions and cigarettes, trolls, gnomes, the meaner sort of earth elementals, as a mystic might put it. And their stretchers are always in use. Of course every one laid on those stretchers, next day the papers will tell you, is in a fair way to recovery; but if you notice you don't see them racing again. The kind-hearted foreign customers might not come to the race-course again, if they heard a jockey was killed. So that in France jockeys never die.

For all that the jumps are low, they are narrow, real estate in Nice being what real estate in New York is in a minor way. The fields are big, fifteen or twenty horses starting in a steeplechase. There you will not find the beautiful timing of the Irish meets, the nursing of the horses, the course craft, the burst in the home stretch. The horses in a big race are there to win. Four abreast and six behind they take the narrow jumps together. So that the Act of God and the King's enemies figure largely in the French racing equation.

Apart from racing, barring sweet Leopardstown—Leopardstown of the Irish heart, green turf and soft brooding hills!—there is no prettier spot on earth for a race-course. Beside you, you can hear the Mediterranean chime on the pebbly shore. Back of you, the little Var drowses downward from the Alpine gorges. Eastward, the coast sweeps toward Monte Carlo in a bold, reckless line. The red sails of the fisher folk show daintily on the peacock blue sea. The higher Alps are furred with snow. It will be crimson for a minute when the sun drops westward back of the Esterel. The grey sleeping towns of Roman days dream, like an old sheep-dog by the fire, in the bluish hills. And somewhence chimes a sweet old bell in a monastery calling the Fathers to lauds.

The second race was over. The beautiful six-year-old mare, Carina, had carried off the La Turbie hurdle race from a field of sound starters. At the totalisators people were swarming to have their bets paid. On the lawns mannequins, with faces made up as in some exotic play about Arabia, pass to and fro in clothes that represent more value than their bodies and souls. Here passes an Indian rajah, dressed in European clothes, with a brown sealskin waistcoat and a huge watch chain, looking very much like a retired saloon keeper, but for his dark skin. He is entitled to a salute of twenty-one guns from His Majesty's government, as they will call it; but the meanest Frenchman here jostles him as if he were just "George." Here are two Egyptian princes, dressed in flaming oriental costume, that seem tawdry somehow, in bad taste in this setting. Here is an Irish marquess, dressed like a farmer, leaning on an ash plant and wishing that "he was in Dublin this minute, so!" Here is an ex-King of an European state, looking very much like a cad. Beside him is a great Second Avenue safe-blower, "resting," looking one's ideal of an Italian prince. Through and over and past them swarm the common or garden people. French folk, vivacious, excited, chattering, like small birds in a tree; English people, striding like male and female Juggernauts, happily unconscious of the comments of the trodden

French; Americans, notable by the huge frames of the men, and outwardly tolerant of and inwardly a little awed by this colour and glory. Nearby in the field a band plays a quick fox-trot.

A fat and not scrupulously clean man climbed a ladder by the starting board, and began clicking runners and jockeys up for the big race. Number One went, Velvet, Mark Baldwin's fast chaser, with Poivier up. So went Carbusy; so went Saint Nitouche, "Little Puritan" it would be in English, by Quaker out of Moralité; Viouret of the grey, and great, strain of Roi Hérode; Helicopter, that excellent fencer; so went Parakeet, who never looked much in a race, but was always in the running; so went Hans, who was to run in the Grand National in England, Daniele riding him—

Number Ten went up, Kilkenny Boy. There was a pause until the jockey's name was shown, "L. Armstrong" painted roughly in black letters on a piece of white planking. There was no glint of recognition in eyes that would have been charmed by it six months before. "Armstrong. *Connais pas!*" "Never heard of him!" A man went by selling the *"premier jaune!"*—the yellow slip that gives probable pari mutuel results. They turned from the board to rush on him. . . .

In the jockey's room Armstrong was received with coldness, while he worked into boots and breeches, and pulled on the flaming crimson silk jacket and cap that Ganzoni had chosen for his colours. Only Fred Rankin, the English jockey riding Viouret, an old enemy, came up and shook hands.

"I'm glad to see you up again," he said, "but I hate to see you on this job."

"I hate it myself, Fred, but, dog-gone, you know how it is, when you're out o' luck, boy, you got to take what you can get."

"I got the winner, myself," Rankin said. "I wish it was another race, and you had it."

"They tell me this horse is good."

"He's good for home—Listen, darky," Rankin's voice was sincere, "you're not looking well, why don't you go home to that place you're always singing about."

"Old Virginny. Believe me, Fred, when I gets me a good winner, you won't see my heels for dust. Oh, boy, and how!"

"Well, good luck, darky!"

"Good luck, Fred."

They went down to the scales, Armstrong carrying his heavily weighted saddle. Outside, the band had broken into the great hunting song:

> *D'ye ken John Peel, with his coat so gay,*
> *D'ye ken John Peel, when he's far away,*

D'ye ken John Peel, at the break of the day
With his hounds and his horn in the morning?
Yes, I ken John Peel, and Ruby, too——

Armstrong walked swiftly to the paddock. A French stable boy whipped the cloth from the big chestnut and took the saddle. The jockey took the snaffle and looked at the horse. His heart swelled.

"Dog-gone, boy," he said, "you'se a horse."

His eyes roved along the sweet line of body; the hind quarters, powerful as artillery; the legs delicate as a flower's; the pretty feet. The head was so small, so lovely. The nose could go in a cup. The eyes were a gentleman's eyes. They looked with wonder at the dark face above the crimson racing jacket. But the Irish chaser felt the masterly, knowing hands, and sensed everything was right. The jockey smiled with a dazzling show of white teeth.

"Boy," he said, "you'se a champeen horse. That's what you is, a champeen horse."

A burst of happiness came to him, and with it a flow of false strength. He tested girths and stirrups and sang as he tested them; not with any nostalgia now, but with happiness.

Carry me back to old Virginny,
That's where the cotton and the corn and taters grow.
There's where the birds warble sweet in the Springtime,
There's where this darky's heart am long'd to go——

The horse, knowing with the mystic sense animals have, that the merry heart is the good heart, turned and nuzzled him.

"Quit your kidding, horse," Armstrong rebuffed him with mock severity. "This ain't no picnic. This is a race."

No place on earth do I love more sincerely
Than old Virginny, the land where I was born.

He took the reins and slid his left foot into the iron. The stable boy caught his right knee and swung him into the saddle.

Ganzoni lumbered up.

"I know nothing about horses——"

"Yeh," Armstrong agreed.

"But it looks a good horse."

"What do you say, kid, what do you say," the ex-American boomed heartily.

"I says: Anything that beats this horse wins; and I says: I ain't seen anything like this horse."

"He's at tens," the scout whispered hoarsely. "And the Chief's put on some dough for you. There's some jack coming to you, kid, if you comes in first."

"It's finding money," Armstrong grinned.

He followed the other horses through the gate into the course. A thrill he had never known when he was popular and lucky ran through him as he passed the stand and lawn swarming with people. The buzz of comment, the white faces, the flash of field glasses, it was all a throbbing, swarming mass of excitement. He loosed the chestnut for a dash down the field. The big horse broke into his beautiful stretching canter. The wind whipped into Armstrong's silk jacket like a pleasantly cold shower. They skimmed a hurdle like a swallow.

"Dog-gone, boy," Armstrong grinned, "you're it." He pulled the horse in and returned to where the others were waiting. Velvet, the big black horse that Poivier was riding, vicious and eager; Saint Nitouche, quiet as a mouse. Viouret, quiet and watchful, with Rankin up. Immense Hans, with his Italian rider, stupid, relying on his great stride to carry him home. The silken jackets were a strange, mad jumble of colour in the Midi sunshine. Green and crimson, brown, blue with white spots, purple, orange—they shifted and mixed as the horses moved. A man in a slouch hat raised a white flag half a furlong away. Horses pranced, turned, curvetted. Riders cursed in English, French, Italian. Of a sudden, like a figure in a country dance, they turned their backs on the starter, and cantered downfield; and then, as if answering a command of some invisible master of ceremonies, they each turned again and came forward gently in a line that was at first a little ragged, gradually grew even as the horses stretched out. Their hooves thumped like drums on the sunburnt turf. They swept on, like a squadron on parade.

Then with an abrupt movement, the starter whipped the fluttering white flag to his feet. The crowd roared. On the lawn a bell rang madly. The crowd roared again. In a dozen languages they called the world-old cry.

"They're off!"

For an instant on the left hand side of the riders the stand appeared, an anthill of swarming folk, a flash of a thousand field glasses. And then it whipped out of sight like something seen from an aeroplane. The first hurdle showed; its white rails, its stiff, bristling bush. The horses took it leisurely, carefully. Back of them, the crowd cried:

"They're over."

They swept along the right hand course, fighting for position now. Américaine, the sweet little mare, galloped along, first of the field. Behind came Savvice, the huge Italian jumper. Parakeet and Hans raced together. Viouret lay easily on the rails. Back of the field Armstrong held his mount. The Irish chaser was fighting for his head, not understanding why this rush of mounts should take precedence of him. He was not yet the cunning old racer that appreciates a yard here, an effort saved there. He was still the wild, free hunter that loves horn and hounds.

But "Dog-gone, boy," Armstrong was soothing him, "take it easy. This ain't no waltz. This is work." And, "Easy baby, easy, I'll say when." And the big horse eased down, galloping sweetly, confidently. They took the second hurdle. Ahead the course forked to left and right. They swung to the right hand side. Américaine still led. Entente, an outsider, swirled along, in a mad rush. None paid any attention to him. The battle was not on yet. They swept toward the first water jump, a hedge with a treacherous dyke on the far side. The little mare skimmed it. The outsider faltered, took it clumsily, came down. He rolled over on his jockey. The jockey lay still. Carbusy's iron caught him on the head, where he lay. A woman near the rails screamed like a rabbit caught by a stoat. The field swept on.

But for the slow thunder of the hooves all was silence. The jockeys were still as clay figures set on moving platforms. Their eyes never left the ground ahead of them. Their eyes were half-closed, wary as eagles'. Their hands were still. Their peaked, wizened faces showed under the silk caps like creations of some artist with a morbid twist in his mind. They galloped on. Behind them the mountains rose, before them the sea chimed. About them, hemming them on all sides, were dark rings of people, on the rails, on the tops of motor cars, in trees. They paid no heed. They might have been riding between land and stars.

Big Hans, ugly-headed, splay-footed, with his clumsy, deceptive, dangerous stride came creeping up on the favourite. Rankin's voice came from the side of his mouth.

"If you cross me, you Wop, I'll cut your face off with the whip." But his eyes never moved. His hands never moved. They took the hurdle easily. The little American mare fell behind. Now the race began to quicken. Velvet and Viouret, Hans and Parakeet began duelling for position. The biggest of the hurdles rose before them. The leaders took it carefully. Armstrong heard the crash and thump behind him as more of the field came down.

Suddenly Parakeet began to slow up. They passed him. *"Estropié,"* his rider called. "He's gone lame."

They huddled the left hand side now, going toward the big bank with the hedge. As they went for it, each called on his horse. "Hip!" Rankin shouted, and brought his hand down sharply on his horse's ribs. "Ey-ah," shrilled the Italian jockey, and Hans rose like an aeroplane. The Frenchman sent Velvet over, with a vicious dig of the heel. Armstrong gathered Kilkenny Boy gently. The big horse slowed a little, then suddenly drove forward. He gathered his hind feet prettily in mid-air. They were over.

Now, the field had broken into three parts. Ahead were Hans and Viouret, with the big black, Velvet, sparring for mastery. Behind them a few lengths Armstrong lay, quietly biding his time. Back of him four lengths were the rest of the field. They scrambled over the earthen ditch. They swung toward the dyke. They took it easily, Velvet and Viouret gaining a little at each jump on Hans, but Hans regaining it each time with his powerful, deceptive stride. At the stone wall Viouret faltered and almost fell, regained, went ahead. The Irish jumper cleared without laying an iron on it. They swept toward the grand stand to take the water jump. Big Hans rushed forward. They could see Daniele try to steady him. The horse seemed to bolt forward through the air. There was a crash as he came on his knees. And for an instant, Daniele appeared in the air, shot out of his irons as from a catapult. He turned over in mid-air and came down on his head. There was a long moan of horror from the grand stand. Daniele, he was done!

From the corner of his eye Armstrong could see the Italian where he lay, limp on his back, his hands outstretched as on a cross, a froth of blood on his mouth and nostrils. Behind thundered the field. Ahead, riderless, big Hans loped. Velvet and Viouret galloped one behind the other on the rails, each awaiting the moment for the other to crack. They swept around to the right again to cross the line of hurdles the second time. They quickened a little. Armstrong let Kilkenny Boy out a little. He mustn't make the leaders suspicious, but he mustn't let them get too far away. The wind had been right behind him coming down the field, bellying his silk jacket out in front, and now as he turned the wind, the jacket whipped close to his body, and he had a feeling it was raining. He looked down. His jacket was wet with perspiration. His hands were wet. The reins where his hands held were wet.

"Dog-gone," he said, "that Italian guy, he must have made me sick."

He knew he was trembling in the saddle. His arms had no strength in them. He was afraid for an instant that the horse might feel there was something wrong.

"It's all right, boy," he said. "It's all right. Just a little weak, that's all."

They skimmed the hedge. He pulled himself together with a great effort as they came for the double fence, some inner reserve of strength giving his fingers the touch to steady the chaser, time him and send him over flying. They swept around again toward the ditch and hedge. Very hazily the leaders appeared to him, as though they were hazy horses in a hazy dream. Everything seemed furry. The landscape had an ethereal look, as though at any moment it might dissolve into nothingness. And queerly enough, the sea made a loud chiming in his ears, high above the thunder of the hooves and the shouting. For a fraction of an instant this would endure, then would come super-clear lucidity. Ahead of them was the last jump, the bank and hedge, and the stretch home. Viouret was slightly ahead of the black horse, Velvet. He saw Velvet's jockey loose his right hand. The whip would be going soon. Rankin's head moved slightly, ever so slightly, to the left. He sat down to ride Viouret home.

"Boy," Armstrong whispered, "now we go."

With the old cunning, the old craft, he swung out to the left. His knees gripped a little closer. He went down on the chestnut's neck as they thundered to the jump.

"Over, boy!" he called. And they were over like a rocket.

But the last effort seemed to have taken all out of him. He was empty, it seemed, empty of vitality, of everything. He could hear crack-crack-crack-crack of a whip before him, beside him, now behind him. He had passed Velvet. Now he was racing beside the favourite, now he passed him. Ahead of him loomed the black mass of the grand stand, the circle on top of the winning post. A great roar came to his ears, and curiously enough, above that the chime of the sea.

He heard the swish of Rankin's whip, the crack of it. The favourite crept up, crept, crept . . .

"Horse," he called in agony, "I'm done. You must win yourself." His fingers caught the mane to avoid falling off.

The big chestnut felt the favourite come along, come up to his forehand, come to his neck. With an immense burst of fighting speed, he hurled himself forward, the stand, the favourite, the winning post were passed in four gigantic strides. Armstrong faintly heard the roar of the crowd as he won, clearly heard the insistent chiming of the sea, of a sea.

With the wisdom all good horses have, the chestnut slowed up, cantered, walked. He stood for an instant to give the little jockey a chance to sit up. He turned toward the paddock. A stable boy ran up and led him into the weighing enclosure. Ganzoni's scout met him with a frown.

"You cut that a bit fine," he criticised.

"Did I?" Armstrong said dully.

"Yeh," he said. "The Chief's sore. You might have lost us our dough. He says you rode a bum race, and he ain't going to come through with no bonus for a bum race."

"No?" He turned to the stable boy. "Give us a hand down," he said. He tottered on his feet when he was on the ground. He managed to get the saddle off. He turned to the horse for a moment.

"Boy," he said—he probably didn't know what he was saying—"boy, I'll see you again."

He walked toward the chair, and sat down in it mechanically, his saddle in his lap. He tipped the scale down.

"All right," said the weightsman.

But Armstrong didn't hear.

"Get up."

But he didn't move.

"He's fainted," Rankin, who was waiting his turn, suggested. "That darky's sick."

They carried him off and laid him on a couch.

"He's cold and stiff," somebody remarked.

"He's dead."

Ganzoni bustled forward, roused out of his lethargy.

"But I win my race," he called excitedly. "Don't I win my race?"

"Yes, you win your race," the officials told him. "But what about your jockey?"

"Him! He's nothing to me," Ganzoni lifted his shoulders. "Besides I paid him in advance. But there's no objection?"

"What objection could there be?" they assured him. "He weighed in."

The gong rang. Everything was all right. The totalisator could pay. New jockeys appeared. New horses were brought out. The day merged into the short Mediterranean twilight. The moon that had just been a vague shape in the east became an immense silver penny while as yet the sun had not gone down. A little mistral sprang up, and the Mediterranean, sleek as a cat, turned like a cat, and struck back in small, vicious, snarling grey waves. The mountains became forbidding. The band, because there were so many Americans at Nice that year, played a medley of American songs, giving to them that faint twist of unbelief and cynicism with which French bands will always treat songs of sentiment.

> *Carry me back to old Virginny.*
> *There's where the cotton and the corn and taters grow.*
> *There's where the birds warble sweet in the Springtime,*
> *There's where this darky's heart am long'd to go.*

And two small ghouls, smoking cigarettes, removed the last of the jockey to an unseen place, where he would be kept until dark. Thence they would remove him to the house of the friendless dead. And lest his name should be forgotten, they had chucked on his chest the piece of plank from the starters' board with "L. Armstrong" on it in hasty, uncouth letters.

"No place on earth do I love more sincerely," the band seemed to sneer, "Than old Virginny, the place where I was born."

But the band might have saved its irony. He had ridden and won a great race. Also, he was in Virginny now.

72

The Gioconda Smile

BY ALDOUS HUXLEY

"Miss Spence will be down directly, sir."

"Thank you," said Mr. Hutton, without turning round. Janet Spence's parlourmaid was so ugly—ugly on purpose, it always seemed to him, malignantly, criminally ugly—that he could not bear to look at her more than was necessary. The door closed. Left to himself, Mr. Hutton got up and began to wander round the room, looking with meditative eyes at the familiar objects it contained.

Photographs of Greek statuary, photographs of the Roman Forum, coloured prints of Italian masterpieces, all very safe and well known. Poor, dear Janet, what a prig—what an intellectual snob! Her real taste was illustrated in that water-colour by the pavement artist, the one she had paid half a crown for (and thirty-five shillings for the frame). How often he had heard her tell the story, how often expatiate on the beauties of that skilful imitation of an oleograph! "A real Artist in the streets," and you could hear the capital A in Artist as she spoke the words. She made you feel that part of his glory had entered into Janet Spence when she tendered him that half-crown for the copy of the oleograph. She was implying a compliment to her own taste and penetration. A genuine Old Master for half a crown. Poor, dear Janet!

Mr. Hutton came to a pause in front of a small oblong mirror. Stooping a little to get a full view of his face, he passed a white, well-manicured finger over his moustache. It was as curly, as freshly auburn as it had been twenty years ago. His hair still retained its colour, and there was no sign of baldness yet—only a certain elevation of the brow. "Shakespearean," thought Mr. Hutton, with a smile, as he surveyed the smooth and polished expanse of his forehead.

Others abide our question, thou art free. . . . Footsteps in the sea . . .

Majesty. . . . Shakespeare, thou shouldst be living at this hour. No, that was Milton, wasn't it? Milton, the Lady of Christ's. There was no lady about him. He was what the women would call a manly man. That was why they liked him—for the curly auburn moustache and the discreet redolence of tobacco. Mr. Hutton smiled again; he enjoyed making fun of himself. Lady of Christ's? No, no. He was the Christ of Ladies. Very pretty, very pretty. The Christ of Ladies. Mr. Hutton wished there were somebody he could tell the joke to. Poor, dear Janet wouldn't appreciate it, alas!

He straightened himself up, parted his hair, and resumed his peregrination. Damn the Roman Forum; he hated those dreary photographs.

Suddenly he became aware that Janet Spence was in the room, standing near the door. Mr. Hutton started, as though he had been taken in some felonious act. To make these silent and spectral appearances was one of Janet Spence's peculiar talents. Perhaps she had been there all the time, and seen him looking at himself in the mirror. Impossible! But, still, it was disquieting.

"Oh, you gave me such a surprise," said Mr. Hutton, recovering his smile and advancing with outstretched hand to meet her.

Miss Spence was smiling too: her Gioconda smile, he had once called it in a moment of half-ironical flattery. Miss Spence had taken the compliment seriously, and always tried to live up to the Leonardo standard. She smiled on in silence while Mr. Hutton shook hands; that was part of the Gioconda business.

"I hope you're well," said Mr. Hutton. "You look it."

What a queer face she had! That small mouth pursed forward by the Gioconda expression into a little snout with a round hole in the middle as though for whistling—it was like a penholder seen from the front. Above the mouth a well-shaped nose, finely aquiline. Eyes large, lustrous, and dark, with the largeness, lustre, and darkness that seems to invite sties and an occasional bloodshot suffusion. They were fine eyes, but unchangingly grave. The penholder might do its Gioconda trick, but the eyes never altered in their earnestness. Above them, a pair of boldly arched, heavily pencilled black eyebrows lent a surprising air of power, as of a Roman matron, to the upper portion of the face. Her hair was dark and equally Roman; Agrippina from the brows upwards.

"I thought I'd just look in on my way home," Mr. Hutton went on. "Ah, it's good to be back here"—he indicated with a wave of his hand the flowers in the vases, the sunshine and greenery beyond the windows —"it's good to be back in the country after a stuffy day of business in town."

Miss Spence, who had sat down, pointed to a chair at her side.

"No, really, I can't sit down," Mr. Hutton protested. "I must get back to see how poor Emily is. She was rather seedy this morning." He sat down, nevertheless. "It's these wretched liver chills. She's always getting them. Women——" He broke off and coughed, so as to hide the fact that he had uttered. He was about to say that women with weak digestions ought not to marry; but the remark was too cruel, and he didn't really believe it. Janet Spence, moreover, was a believer in eternal flames and spiritual attachments. "She hopes to be well enough," he added, "to see you at luncheon to-morrow. Can you come? Do?" He smiled persuasively. "It's my invitation too, you know."

She dropped her eyes, and Mr. Hutton almost thought that he detected a certain reddening of the cheek. It was a tribute; he stroked his moustache.

"I should like to come if you think Emily's really well enough to have a visitor."

"Of course. You'll do her good. You'll do us both good. In married life three is often better company than two."

"Oh, you're cynical."

Mr. Hutton always had a desire to say "Bow-wow-wow" whenever that last word was spoken. It irritated him more than any other word in the language. But instead of barking he made haste to protest.

"No, no. I'm only speaking a melancholy truth. Reality doesn't always come up to the ideal, you know. But that doesn't make me believe any the less in the ideal. Indeed, I believe in it passionately—the ideal of a matrimony between two people in perfect accord. I think it's realizable. I'm sure it is."

He paused significantly and looked at her with an arch expression. A virgin of thirty-six, but still unwithered; she had her charms. And there was something really rather enigmatic about her. Miss Spence made no reply, but continued to smile. There were times when Mr. Hutton got rather bored with the Gioconda. He stood up.

"I must really be going now. Farewell, mysterious Gioconda." The smile grew intenser, focused itself, as it were, in a narrower snout. Mr. Hutton made a Cinquecento gesture, and kissed her extended hand. It was the first time he had done such a thing; the action seemed not to be resented. "I look forward to to-morrow."

"Do you?"

For answer Mr. Hutton once more kissed her hand, then turned to go. Miss Spence accompanied him to the porch.

"Where's your car?" she asked.

"I left it at the gate of the drive."

"I'll come and see you off."

"No, no." Mr. Hutton was playful, but determined. "You must do no such thing. I simply forbid you."

"But I should like to come," Miss Spence protested, throwing a rapid Gioconda at him.

Mr. Hutton held up his hand. "No," he repeated, and then, with a gesture that was almost the blowing of a kiss, he started to run down the drive, lightly, on his toes, with long, bounding strides like a boy's. He was proud of that run; it was quite marvellously youthful. Still, he was glad the drive was no longer. At the last bend, before passing out of sight of the house, he halted and turned round. Miss Spence was still standing on the steps, smiling her smile. He waved his hand, and this time quite definitely and overtly wafted a kiss in her direction. Then, breaking once more into his magnificent canter, he rounded the last dark promontory of trees. Once out of sight of the house he let his high paces decline to a trot, and finally to a walk. He took out his handkerchief and began wiping his neck inside his collar. What fools, what fools! Had there ever been such an ass as poor, dear Janet Spence? Never, unless it was himself. Decidedly he was the more malignant fool, since he, at least, was aware of his folly and still persisted in it. Why did he persist? Ah, the problem that was himself, the problem that was other people . . .

He had reached the gate. A large, prosperous-looking motor was standing at the side of the road.

"Home, M'Nab." The chauffeur touched his cap. "And stop at the cross-roads on the way, as usual," Mr. Hutton added, as he opened the door of the car. "Well?" he said, speaking into the obscurity that lurked within.

"Oh, Teddy Bear, what an age you've been!" It was a fresh and childish voice that spoke the words. There was the faintest hint of Cockney impurity about the vowel sounds.

Mr. Hutton bent his large form and darted into the car with the agility of an animal regaining his burrow.

"Have I?" he said, as he shut the door. The machine began to move. "You must have missed me a lot if you found the time so long." He sat back in the low seat; a cherishing warmth enveloped him.

"Teddy Bear . . ." and with a sigh of contentment a charming little head declined on to Mr. Hutton's shoulder. Ravished, he looked down sideways at the round, babyish face.

"Do you know, Doris, you look like the pictures of Louise de Kerouaille." He passed his fingers through a mass of curly hair.

"Who's Louise de Kera-whatever-it-is?" Doris spoke from remote distances.

"She was, alas! *Fuit*. We shall all be 'was' one of these days. Meanwhile . . ."

Mr. Hutton covered the babyish face with kisses. The car rushed smoothly along. M'Nab's back through the front window, was stonily impassive, the back of a statue.

"Your hands," Doris whispered. "Oh, you mustn't touch me. They give me electric shocks."

Mr. Hutton adored her for the virgin imbecility of the words. How late in one's existence one makes the discovery of one's body!

"The electricity isn't in me, it's in you." He kissed her again, whispering her name several times: Doris, Doris, Doris. The scientific appellation of the sea-mouse, he was thinking as he kissed the throat she offered him, white and extended like the throat of a victim awaiting the sacrificial knife. The sea-mouse was a sausage with iridescent fur: very peculiar. Or was Doris the sea-cucumber, which turns itself inside out in moments of alarm? He would really have to go to Naples again, just to see the aquarium. These sea creatures were fabulous, unbelievably fantastic.

"Oh, Teddy Bear!" (More zoology; but he was only a land animal. His poor little jokes!) "Teddy Bear, I'm so happy."

"So am I?" said Mr. Hutton. Was it true?

"But I wish I knew if it were right. Tell me, Teddy Bear, is it right or wrong?"

"Ah, my dear, that's just what I've been wondering for the last thirty years."

"Be serious, Teddy Bear. I want to know if this is right; if it's right that I should be here with you and that we should love one another, and that it should give me electric shocks when you touch me."

"Right? Well, it's certainly good that you should have electric shocks rather than sexual repressions. Read Freud; repressions are the devil."

"Oh, you don't help me. Why aren't you ever serious? If only you knew how miserable I am sometimes, thinking it's not right. Perhaps, you know, there is a hell, and all that. I don't know what to do. Sometimes I think I ought to stop loving you."

"But could you?" asked Mr. Hutton, confident in the powers of his seduction and his moustache.

"No, Teddy Bear, you know I couldn't. But I could run away, I could hide from you, I could lock myself up and force myself not to come to you."

"Silly little thing!" He tightened his embrace.

"Oh, dear. I hope it isn't wrong. And there are times when I don't care if it is."

Mr. Hutton was touched. He had a certain protective affection for this little creature. He laid his cheek against her hair and so, interlaced, they sat in silence, while the car, swaying and pitching a little as it hastened along, seemed to draw in the white road and the dusty hedges towards it devouringly.

"Good-bye, good-bye."

The car moved on, gathered speed, vanished round a curve, and Doris was left standing by the sign-post at the cross-roads, still dizzy and weak with the languor born of those kisses and the electrical touch of those gentle hands. She had to take a deep breath, to draw herself up deliberately, before she was strong enough to start her homeward walk. She had half a mile in which to invent the necessary lies.

Alone, Mr. Hutton suddenly found himself the prey of an appalling boredom.

Mrs. Hutton was lying on the sofa in her boudoir, playing Patience. In spite of the warmth of the July evening a wood fire was burning on the hearth. A black Pomeranian, extenuated by the heat and the fatigues of digestion, slept before the blaze.

"Phew! Isn't it rather hot in here?" Mr. Hutton asked as he entered the room.

"You know I have to keep warm, dear." The voice seemed breaking on the verge of tears. "I get so shivery."

"I hope you're better this evening."

"Not much, I'm afraid."

The conversation stagnated. Mr. Hutton stood leaning his back against the mantelpiece. He looked down at the Pomeranian lying at his feet, and with the toe of his right boot he rolled the little dog over and rubbed its white-flecked chest and belly. The creature lay in an inert ecstasy. Mrs. Hutton continued to play Patience. Arrived at an *impasse,* she altered the position of one card, took back another, and went on playing. Her Patiences always came out.

"Dr. Libbard thinks I ought to go to Llandrindod Wells this summer."

"Well, go, my dear—go, most certainly."

Mr. Hutton was thinking of the events of the afternoon: how they had driven, Doris and he, up to the hanging wood, had left the car to wait for them under the shade of the trees, and walked together out into the windless sunshine of the chalk down.

"I'm to drink the waters for my liver, and he thinks I ought to have massage and electric treatment, too."

Hat in hand, Doris had stalked four blue butterflies that were dancing together round a scabious flower with a motion that was like the flickering of blue fire. The blue fire burst and scattered into whirling sparks; she had given chase, laughing and shouting like a child.

"I'm sure it will do you good, my dear."

"I was wondering if you'd come with me, dear."

"But you know I'm going to Scotland at the end of the month."

Mrs. Hutton looked up at him entreatingly. "It's the journey," she said. "The thought of it is such a nightmare. I don't know if I can manage it. And you know I can't sleep in hotels. And then there's the luggage and all the worries. I can't go alone."

"But you won't be alone. You'll have your maid with you." He spoke impatiently. The sick woman was usurping the place of the healthy one. He was being dragged back from the memory of the sunlit down and the quick, laughing girl, back to this unhealthy, overheated room and its complaining occupant.

"I don't think I shall be able to go."

"But you must, my dear, if the doctor tells you to. And, besides, a change will do you good."

"I don't think so."

"But Libbard thinks so, and he knows what he's talking about."

"No, I can't face it. I'm too weak. I can't go alone." Mrs. Hutton pulled a handkerchief out of her black silk bag, and put it to her eyes.

"Nonsense, my dear, you must make the effort."

"I had rather be left in peace to die here." She was crying in earnest now.

"O Lord! Now do be reasonable. Listen now, please." Mrs. Hutton only sobbed more violently. "Oh, what is one to do?" He shrugged his shoulders and walked out of the room.

Mr. Hutton was aware that he had not behaved with proper patience; but he could not help it. Very early in his manhood he had discovered that not only did he not feel sympathy for the poor, the weak, the diseased, and deformed; he actually hated them. Once, as an undergraduate, he spent three days at a mission in the East End. He had returned, filled with a profound and ineradicable disgust. Instead of pitying, he loathed the unfortunate. It was not, he knew, a very comely emotion, and he had been ashamed of it at first. In the end he had decided that it was temperamental, inevitable, and had felt no further qualms. Emily had been healthy and beautiful when he married her. He had loved her then. But now—was it his fault that she was like this?

Mr. Hutton dined alone. Food and drink left him more benevolent than he had been before dinner. To make amends for his show of exasperation he went up to his wife's room and offered to read to her. She was touched, gratefully accepted the offer, and Mr. Hutton, who was particularly proud of his accent, suggested a little light reading in French.

"French? I am so fond of French." Mrs. Hutton spoke of the language of Racine as though it were a dish of green peas.

Mr. Hutton ran down to the library and returned with a yellow volume. He began reading. The effort of pronouncing perfectly absorbed his whole attention. But how good his accent was! The fact of its goodness seemed to improve the quality of the novel he was reading.

At the end of fifteen pages an unmistakable sound aroused him. He looked up; Mrs. Hutton had gone to sleep. He sat still for a little while, looking with a dispassionate curiosity at the sleeping face. Once it had been beautiful; once, long ago, the sight of it, the recollection of it, had moved him with an emotion profounder, perhaps, than any he had felt before or since. Now it was lined and cadaverous. The skin was stretched tightly over the cheekbones, across the bridge of the sharp, bird-like nose. The closed eyes were set in profound bone-rimmed sockets. The lamplight striking on the face from the side emphasised with light and shade its cavities and projections. It was the face of a dead Christ by Morales.

Le squelette était invisible
Au temps heureux de l'art païen.

He shivered a little, and tiptoed out of the room.

On the following day Mrs. Hutton came down to luncheon. She had had some unpleasant palpitations during the night, but she was feeling better now. Besides, she wanted to do honour to her guest. Miss Spence listened to her complaints about Llandrindod Wells, and was loud in sympathy, lavish with advice. Whatever she said was always said with intensity. She leaned forward, aimed, so to speak, like a gun, and fired her words. Bang! the charge in her soul was ignited, the words whizzed forth at the narrow barrel of her mouth. She was a machine-gun riddling her hostess with sympathy. Mr. Hutton had undergone similar bombardments, mostly of a literary or philosophic character—bombardments of Maeterlinck, of Mrs. Besant, of Bergson, of William James. To-day the missiles were medical. She talked about insomnia, she expatiated on the virtues of harmless drugs and beneficent specialists. Under the bombardment Mrs. Hutton opened out, like a flower in the sun.

Mr. Hutton looked on in silence. The spectacle of Janet Spence evoked in him an unfailing curiosity. He was not romantic enough to imagine that every face masked an interior physiognomy of beauty or strangeness, that every woman's small talk was like a vapour hanging over mysterious gulfs. His wife, for example, and Doris; they were nothing more than what they seemed to be. But with Janet Spence it was somehow different. Here one could be sure that there was some kind of a queer face behind the Gioconda smile and the Roman eyebrows. The only question was: What exactly was there? Mr. Hutton could never quite make out.

"But perhaps you won't have to go to Llandrindod after all," Miss Spence was saying. "If you get well quickly Dr. Libbard will let you off."

"I only hope so. Indeed, I do really feel rather better to-day."

Mr. Hutton felt ashamed. How much was it his own lack of sympathy that prevented her from feeling well every day? But he comforted himself by reflecting that it was only a case of feeling, not of being better. Sympathy does not mend a diseased liver or a weak heart.

"My dear, I wouldn't eat those red currants if I were you," he said, suddenly solicitous. "You know that Libbard has banned everything with skins and pips."

"But I am so fond of them," Mrs. Hutton protested, "and I feel so well to-day."

"Don't be a tyrant," said Miss Spence, looking first at him and then at his wife. "Let the poor invalid have what she fancies; it will do her good." She laid her hand on Mrs. Hutton's arm and patted it affectionately two or three times.

"Thank you, my dear." Mrs. Hutton helped herself to the stewed currants.

"Well, don't blame me if they make you ill again."

"Do I ever blame you, dear?"

"You have nothing to blame me for," Mr. Hutton answered playfully. "I am the perfect husband."

They sat in the garden after luncheon. From the island of shade under the old cypress tree they looked out across a flat expanse of lawn, in which the parterres of flowers shone with a metallic brilliance.

Mr. Hutton took a deep breath of the warm and fragrant air. "It's good to be alive," he said.

"Just to be alive," his wife echoed, stretching one pale, knot-jointed hand into the sunlight.

A maid brought the coffee; the silver pots and the little blue cups were set on a folding table near the group of chairs.

"Oh, my medicine!" exclaimed Mrs. Hutton. "Run in and fetch it, Clara, will you? The white bottle on the sideboard."

"I'll go," said Mr. Hutton. "I've got to go and fetch a cigar in any case."

He ran in towards the house. On the threshold he turned round for an instant. The maid was walking back across the lawn. His wife was sitting up in her deck-chair, engaged in opening her white parasol. Miss Spence was bending over the table, pouring out the coffee. He passed into the cool obscurity of the house.

"Do you like sugar in your coffee?" Miss Spence inquired.

"Yes, please. Give me rather a lot. I'll drink it after my medicine to take the taste away."

Mrs. Hutton leaned back in her chair, lowering the sunshade over her eyes, so as to shut out from her vision the burning sky.

Behind her, Miss Spence was making a delicate clinking among the coffee-cups.

"I've given you three large spoonfuls. That ought to take the taste away. And here comes the medicine."

Mr. Hutton had reappeared, carrying a wine-glass, half full of a pale liquid.

"It smells delicious," he said, as he handed it to his wife.

"That's only the flavouring." She drank it off at a gulp, shuddered, and made a grimace. "Ugh, it's so nasty. Give me my coffee."

Miss Spence gave her the cup; she sipped at it. "You've made it like syrup. But it's very nice, after that atrocious medicine."

At half-past three Mrs. Hutton complained that she did not feel as well as she had done, and went indoors to lie down. Her husband would have said something about the red currants, but checked himself; the triumph of an "I told you so" was too cheaply won. Instead, he was sympathetic, and gave her his arm to the house.

"A rest will do you good," he said. "By the way, I shan't be back till after dinner."

"But why? Where are you going?"

"I promised to go to Johnson's this evening. We have to discuss the war memorial, you know."

"Oh, I wish you weren't going." Mrs. Hutton was almost in tears. "Can't you stay? I don't like being alone in the house."

"But, my dear, I promised—weeks ago." It was a bother having to lie like this. "And now I must get back and look after Miss Spence."

He kissed her on the forehead and went out again into the garden. Miss Spence received him aimed and intense.

"Your wife is dreadfully ill," she fired off at him.

"I thought she cheered up so much when you came."

"That was purely nervous, purely nervous. I was watching her closely. With a heart in that condition and her digestion wrecked—yes, wrecked—anything might happen."

"Libbard doesn't take so gloomy a view of poor Emily's health." Mr. Hutton held open the gate that led from the garden into the drive; Miss Spence's car was standing by the front door.

"Libbard is only a country doctor. You ought to see a specialist."

He could not refrain from laughing. "You have a macabre passion for specialists."

Miss Spence held up her hand in protest. "I am serious. I think poor Emily is in a very bad state. Anything might happen—at any moment."

He handed her into the car and shut the door. The chauffeur started the engine and climbed into his place, ready to drive off.

"Shall I tell him to start?" He had no desire to continue the conversation.

Miss Spence leaned forward and shot a Gioconda in his direction. "Remember, I expect you to come and see me again soon."

Mechanically he grinned, made a polite noise, and, as the car moved forward, waved his hand. He was happy to be alone.

A few minutes afterwards Mr. Hutton himself drove away. Doris was waiting at the cross-roads. They dined together twenty miles from home, at a roadside hotel. It was one of those bad, expensive meals which are only cooked in country hotels frequented by motorists. It revolted Mr. Hutton, but Doris enjoyed it. She always enjoyed things. Mr. Hutton ordered a not very good brand of champagne. He was wishing he had spent the evening in his library.

When they started homewards Doris was a little tipsy and extremely affectionate. It was very dark inside the car, but looking forward, past the motionless form of M'Nab, they could see a bright and narrow universe of forms and colours scooped out of the night by the electric headlamps.

It was after eleven when Mr. Hutton reached home. Dr. Libbard met him in the hall. He was a small man with delicate hands and well-formed features that were almost feminine. His brown eyes were large and melancholy. He used to waste a great deal of time sitting at the bedside of his patients, looking sadness through those eyes and talking in a sad, low voice about nothing in particular. His person exhaled a pleasing odour, decidedly antiseptic but at the same time suave and discreetly delicious.

"Libbard?" said Mr. Hutton in surprise. "You here? Is my wife ill?"

"We tried to fetch you earlier," the soft, melancholy voice replied. "It was thought you were at Mr. Johnson's, but they had no news of you there."

"No, I was detained. I had a breakdown," Mr. Hutton answered irritably. It was tiresome to be caught out in a lie.

"Your wife wanted to see you urgently."

"Well, I can go now." Mr. Hutton moved towards the stairs.

Dr. Libbard laid a hand on his arm. "I am afraid it's too late."

"Too late?" He began fumbling with his watch; it wouldn't come out of the pocket.

"Mrs. Hutton passed away half an hour ago."

The voice remained even in its softness, the melancholy of the eyes did not deepen. Dr. Libbard spoke of death as he would speak of a local cricket match. All things were equally vain and equally deplorable.

Mr. Hutton found himself thinking of Janet Spence's words. At any moment—at any moment. She had been extraordinarily right.

"What happened?" he asked. "What was the cause?"

Dr. Libbard explained. It was heart failure brought out by a violent attack of nausea, caused in its turn by the eating of something of an irritant nature. Red currants? Mr. Hutton suggested. Very likely. It had been too much for the heart. There was chronic valvular disease: something had collapsed under the strain. It was all over; she could not have suffered much.

"It's a pity they should have chosen the day of the Eton and Harrow match for the funeral," old General Grego was saying as he stood, his top hat in his hand, under the shadow of the lych gate, wiping his face with his handkerchief.

Mr. Hutton overheard the remark and with difficulty restrained a desire to inflict grievous bodily pain on the General. He would have liked to hit the old brute in the middle of his big red face. Monstrous great mulberry, spotted with meal! Was there no respect for the dead? Did nobody care? In theory he didn't much care; let the dead bury their dead. But here, at the graveside, he had found himself actually sobbing. Poor Emily, they had been pretty happy once. Now she was lying at the bottom of a seven-foot hole. And here was Grego complaining that he couldn't go to the Eton and Harrow match.

Mr. Hutton looked round at the groups of black figures that were drifting slowly out of the churchyard towards the fleet of cabs and motors assembled in the road outside. Against the brilliant background of the July grass and flowers and foliage, they had a horribly alien and unnatural appearance. It pleased him to think that all these people would soon be dead too.

That evening Mr. Hutton sat up late in his library reading the life of Milton. There was no particular reason why he should have chosen Milton; it was the book that first came to hand, that was all. It was after midnight when he had finished. He got up from his armchair, unbolted the French windows, and stepped out on to the little paved terrace. The night was quiet and clear. Mr. Hutton looked at the stars and at the holes between them, dropped his eyes to the dim lawns and hueless flowers of the garden, and let them wander over the farther landscape, black and grey under the moon.

He began to think with a kind of confused violence. There were the stars, there was Milton. A man can be somehow the peer of stars and night. Greatness, nobility. But is there seriously a difference between

the noble and the ignoble? Milton, the stars, death, and himself—
himself. The soul, the body; the higher and the lower nature. Perhaps
there was something in it, after all. Milton had a god on his side and
righteousness. What had he? Nothing, nothing whatever. There were
only Doris's little breasts. What was the point of it all? Milton, the stars,
death, and Emily in her grave, Doris and himself—always himself . . .

　Oh, he was a futile and disgusting being. Everything convinced him
of it. It was a solemn moment. He spoke aloud: "I will, I will." The
sound of his own voice in the darkness was appalling; it seemed to him
that he had sworn that infernal oath which binds even the gods: "I will,
I will." There had been New Year's days and solemn anniversaries in
the past, when he had felt the same contritions and recorded similar resolutions. They had all thinned away, these resolutions, like smoke, into
nothingness. But this was a greater moment and he had pronounced a
more fearful oath. In the future it was to be different. Yes, he would
live by reason, he would be industrious, he would curb his appetites,
he would devote his life to some good purpose. It was resolved and it
would be so.

　In practice he saw himself spending his mornings in agricultural
pursuits, riding round with the bailiff, seeing that his land was farmed
in the best modern way—silos and artificial manures and continuous
cropping, and all that. The remainder of the day should be devoted to
serious study. There was that book he had been intending to write for
so long—*The Effect of Diseases on Civilisation*.

　Mr. Hutton went to bed humble and contrite, but with a sense that
grace had entered into him. He slept for seven and a half hours, and
woke to find the sun brilliantly shining. The emotions of the evening
before had been transformed by a good night's rest into his customary
cheerfulness. It was not until a good many seconds after his return to
conscious life that he remembered his resolution, his Stygian oath. Milton and death seemed somehow different in the sunlight. As for the
stars, they were not there. But the resolutions were good; even in the
daytime he could see that. He had his horse saddled after breakfast, and
rode round the farm with the bailiff. After luncheon he read Thucy-
dides on the plague at Athens. In the evening he made a few notes on
malaria in Southern Italy. While he was undressing he remembered
that there was a good anecdote in Skelton's jest-book about the Sweating Sickness. He would have made a note of it if only he could have
found a pencil.

　On the sixth morning of his new life Mr. Hutton found among his
correspondence an envelope addressed in that peculiarly vulgar handwriting which he knew to be Doris's. He opened it, and began to read.
She didn't know what to say, words were so inadequate. His wife dy-

ing like that, and so suddenly—it was too terrible. Mr. Hutton sighed, but his interest revived somewhat as he read on:

"Death is so frightening, I never think of it when I can help it. But when something like this happens, or when I am feeling ill or depressed, then I can't help remembering it is there so close, and I think about all the wicked things I have done and about you and me, and I wonder what will happen, and I am so frightened. I am so lonely, Teddy Bear, and so unhappy, and I don't know what to do. I can't get rid of the idea of dying, I am so wretched and helpless without you. I didn't mean to write to you; I meant to wait till you were out of mourning and could come and see me again, but I was so lonely and miserable, Teddy Bear, I had to write. I couldn't help it. Forgive me, I want you so much; I have nobody in the world but you. You are so good and gentle and understanding; there is nobody like you. I shall never forget how good and kind you have been to me, and you are so clever and know so much, I can't understand how you ever came to pay any attention to me, I am so dull and stupid, much less like me and love me, because you do love me a little, don't you, Teddy Bear?"

Mr. Hutton was touched with shame and remorse. To be thanked like this, worshipped for having seduced the girl—it was too much. It had just been a piece of imbecile wantonness. Imbecile, idiotic: there was no other way to describe it. For, when all was said, he had derived very little pleasure from it. Taking all things together, he had probably been more bored than amused. Once upon a time he had believed himself to be a hedonist. But to be a hedonist implies a certain process of reasoning, a deliberate choice of known pleasures, a rejection of known pains. This had been done without reason, against it. For he knew beforehand—so well, so well—that there was no interest or pleasure to be derived from these wretched affairs. And yet each time the vague itch came upon him he succumbed, involving himself once more in the old stupidity. There had been Maggie, his wife's maid, and Edith, the girl on the farm, and Mrs. Pringle, and the waitress in London, and others—there seemed to be dozens of them. It had all been so stale and boring. He knew it would be; he always knew. And yet, and yet . . . Experience doesn't teach.

Poor little Doris! He would write to her kindly, comfortingly, but he wouldn't see her again. A servant came to tell him that his horse was saddled and waiting. He mounted and rode off. That morning the old bailiff was more irritating than usual.

Five days later Doris and Mr. Hutton were sitting together on the pier at Southend; Doris, in white muslin with pink garnishings, radiated happiness; Mr. Hutton, legs outstretched and chair tilted, had pushed the panama back from his forehead, and was trying to feel like a tripper. That night, when Doris was asleep, breathing and warm by his side, he recaptured, in this moment of darkness and physical fatigue, the rather cosmic emotion which had possessed him that evening, not a fortnight ago, when he had made his great resolution. And so his solemn oath had already gone the way of so many other resolutions. Unreason had triumphed; at the first itch of desire he had given way. He was hopeless, hopeless.

For a long time he lay with closed eyes, ruminating his humiliation. The girl stirred in her sleep. Mr. Hutton turned over and looked in her direction. Enough faint light crept in between the half-drawn curtains to show her bare arm and shoulder, her neck, and the dark tangle of hair on the pillow. She was beautiful, desirable. Why did he lie there moaning over his sins? What did it matter? If he were hopeless, then so be it; he would make the best of his hopelessness. A glorious sense of irresponsibility suddenly filled him. He was free, magnificently free. In a kind of exaltation he drew the girl towards him. She woke, bewildered, almost frightened under his rough kisses.

The storm of his desire subsided into a kind of serene merriment. The whole atmosphere seemed to be quivering with enormous silent laughter.

"Could anyone love you as much as I do, Teddy Bear?" The question came faintly from distant worlds of love.

"I think I know somebody who does," Mr. Hutton replied. The submarine laughter was swelling, rising, ready to break the surface of silence and resound.

"Who? Tell me. What do you mean?" The voice had come very close; charged with suspicion, anguish, indignation, it belonged to this immediate world.

"A—ah!"

"Who?"

"You'll never guess." Mr. Hutton kept up the joke until it began to grow tedious, and then pronounced the name: "Janet Spence."

Doris was incredulous. "Miss Spence of the Manor? That old woman?" It was too ridiculous. Mr. Hutton laughed too.

"But it's quite true," he said. "She adores me." Oh, the vast joke! He would go and see her as soon as he returned—see and conquer. "I believe she wants to marry me," he added.

"But you wouldn't . . . you don't intend . . ."

The air was fairly crepitating with humour. Mr. Hutton laughed aloud. "I intend to marry you," he said. It seemed to him the best joke he had ever made in his life.

When Mr. Hutton left Southend he was once more a married man. It was agreed that, for the time being, the fact should be kept secret. In the autumn they would go abroad together, and the world should be informed. Meanwhile he was to go back to his own house and Doris to hers.

The day after his return he walked over in the afternoon to see Miss Spence. She received him with the old Gioconda.

"I was expecting you to come."

"I couldn't keep away," Mr. Hutton gallantly replied.

They sat in the summer-house. It was a pleasant place—a little old stucco temple bowered among dense bushes of evergreen. Miss Spence had left her mark on it by hanging up over the seat a blue-and-white Della Robbia plaque.

"I am thinking of going to Italy this autumn," said Mr. Hutton. He felt like a ginger-beer bottle, ready to pop with bubbling humorous excitement.

"Italy. . . ." Miss Spence closed her eyes ecstatically. "I feel drawn there too."

"Why not let yourself be drawn?"

"I don't know. One somehow hasn't the energy and initiative to set out alone."

"Alone. . . ." Ah, sound of guitars and throaty singing! "Yes, travelling alone isn't much fun."

Miss Spence lay back in her chair without speaking. Her eyes were still closed. Mr. Hutton stroked his moustache. The silence prolonged itself for what seemed a very long time.

Pressed to stay to dinner, Mr. Hutton did not refuse. The fun had hardly started. The table was laid in the loggia. Through its arches they looked out on to the sloping garden, to the valley below and the farther hills. Light ebbed away; the heat and silence were oppressive. A huge cloud was mounting up the sky, and there were distant breathings of thunder. The thunder drew nearer, a wind began to blow, and the first drops of rain fell. The table was cleared. Miss Spence and Mr. Hutton sat on in the growing darkness.

Miss Spence broke a long silence by saying meditatively:

"I think everyone has a right to a certain amount of happiness, don't you?"

"Most certainly." But what was she leading up to? Nobody makes generalisations about life unless they mean to talk about themselves.

Happiness: he looked back on his own life, and saw a cheerful, placid existence disturbed by no great griefs or discomforts or alarms. He had always had money and freedom; he had been able to do very much as he wanted. Yes, he supposed he had been happy—happier than most men. And now he was not merely happy; he had discovered in irresponsibility the secret of gaiety. He was about to say something about his happiness when Miss Spence went on speaking.

"People like you and me have a right to be happy some time in our lives."

"Me?" said Mr. Hutton, surprised.

"Poor Henry! Fate hasn't treated either of us very well."

"Oh, well, it might have treated me worse."

"You're being cheerful. That's brave of you. But don't think I can't see behind the mask."

Miss Spence spoke louder and louder as the rain came down more and more heavily. Periodically the thunder cut across her utterances. She talked on, shouting against the noise.

"I have understood you so well and for so long."

A flash revealed her, aimed and intent, leaning towards him. Her eyes were two profound and menacing gun-barrels. The darkness re-engulfed her.

"You were a lonely soul seeking a companion soul. I could sympathise with you in your solitude. Your marriage . . ."

The thunder cut short the sentence. Miss Spence's voice became audible once more with the words:

". . . could offer no companionship to a man of your stamp. You needed a soul mate."

A soul mate—he! a soul mate. It was incredibly fantastic. "Georgette Leblanc, the ex-soul mate of Maurice Maeterlinck." He had seen that in the paper a few days ago. So it was thus that Janet Spence had painted him in her imagination—as a soul-mater. And for Doris he was a picture of goodness and the cleverest man in the world. And actually, really, he was what?—Who knows?

"My heart went out to you. I could understand; I was lonely, too." Miss Spence laid her hand on his knee. "You were so patient." Another flash. She was still aimed, dangerously. "You never complained. But I could guess—I could guess."

"How wonderful of you!" So he was an *âme incomprise.* "Only a woman's intuition . . ."

The thunder crashed and rumbled, died away, and only the sound of the rain was left. The thunder was his laughter, magnified, externalised. Flash and crash, there it was again, right on top of them.

"Don't you feel that you have within you something that is akin to this storm?" He could imagine her leaning forward as she uttered the words. "Passion makes one the equal of the elements."

What was his gambit now? Why, obviously, he should have said, "Yes," and ventured on some unequivocal gesture. But Mr. Hutton suddenly took fright. The ginger beer in him had gone flat. The woman was serious—terribly serious. He was appalled.

Passion? "No," he desperately answered. "I am without passion."

But his remark was either unheard or unheeded, for Miss Spence went on with a growing exaltation, speaking so rapidly, however, and in such a burningly intimate whisper that Mr. Hutton found it very difficult to distinguish what she was saying. She was telling him, as far as he could make out, the story of her life. The lightning was less frequent now, and there were long intervals of darkness. But at each flash he saw her still aiming towards him, still yearning forward with a terrifying intensity. Darkness, the rain, and then flash! her face was there, close at hand. A pale mask, greenish white; the large eyes, the narrow barrel of the mouth, the heavy eyebrows. Agrippina, or wasn't it rather—yes, wasn't it rather George Robey?

He began devising absurd plans for escaping. He might suddenly jump up, pretending he had seen a burglar—Stop thief! stop thief!— and dash off into the night in pursuit. Or should he say that he felt faint, a heart attack? or that he had seen a ghost—Emily's ghost—in the garden? Absorbed in his childish plotting, he had ceased to pay any attention to Miss Spence's words. The spasmodic clutching of her hand recalled his thoughts.

"I honoured you for that, Henry," she was saying.

Honoured him for what?

"Marriage is a sacred tie, and your respect for it, even when the marriage was, as it was in your case, an unhappy one, made me respect you and admire you, and—shall I dare say the word?——"

Oh, the burglar, the ghost in the garden! But it was too late.

". . . yes, love you, Henry, all the more. But we're free now, Henry."

Free? There was a movement in the dark, and she was kneeling on the floor by his chair.

"Oh, Henry, Henry, I have been unhappy too."

Her arms embraced him, and by the shaking of her body he could feel that she was sobbing. She might have been a suppliant crying for mercy.

"You mustn't, Janet," he protested. Those tears were terrible, terrible. "Not now, not now! You must be calm; you must go to bed." He patted her shoulder, then got up, disengaging himself from her embrace.

He left her still crouching on the floor beside the chair on which he had been sitting.

Groping his way into the hall, and without waiting to look for his hat, he went out of the house, taking infinite pains to close the front door noiselessly behind him. The clouds had blown over, and the moon was shining from a clear sky. There were puddles all along the road, and a noise of running water rose from the gutters and ditches. Mr. Hutton splashed along, not caring if he got wet.

How heartrendingly she had sobbed! With the emotions of pity and remorse that the recollection evoked in him there was a certain resentment: why couldn't she have played the game that he was playing—the heartless, amusing game? Yes, but he had known all the time that she wouldn't, she couldn't, play that game; he had known and persisted.

What had she said about passion and the elements? Something absurdly stale, but true, true. There she was, a cloud black-bosomed and charged with thunder, and he, like some absurd little Benjamin Franklin, had sent up a kite into the heart of the menace. Now he was complaining that his toy had drawn the lightning.

She was probably still kneeling by that chair in the loggia, crying.

But why hadn't he been able to keep up the game? Why had his irresponsibility deserted him, leaving him suddenly sober in a cold world? There were no answers to any of his questions. One idea burned steady and luminous in his mind—the idea of flight. He must get away at once.

"What are you thinking about, Teddy Bear?"

"Nothing."

There was a silence. Mr. Hutton remained motionless, his elbows on the parapet of the terrace, his chin in his hands, looking down over Florence. He had taken a villa on one of the hilltops to the south of the city. From a little raised terrace at the end of the garden one looked down a long fertile valley on to the town and beyond it to the bleak mass of Monte Morello and, eastward of it, to the peopled hill of Fiesole, dotted with white houses. Everything was clear and luminous in the September sunshine.

"Are you worried about anything?"

"No, thank you."

"Tell me, Teddy Bear."

"But, my dear, there's nothing to tell." Mr. Hutton turned round, smiled, and patted the girl's hand. "I think you'd better go in and have your siesta. It's too hot for you here."

"Very well, Teddy Bear. Are you coming too?"

"When I've finished my cigar."

"All right. But do hurry up and finish it, Teddy Bear." Slowly, reluctantly, she descended the steps of the terrace and walked toward the house.

Mr. Hutton continued his contemplation of Florence. He had need to be alone. It was good sometimes to escape from Doris and the restless solicitude of her passion. He had never known the pains of loving hopelessly, but he was experiencing now the pains of being loved. These last weeks had been a period of growing discomfort. Doris was always with him, like an obsession, like a guilty conscience. Yes, it was good to be alone.

He pulled an envelope out of his pocket and opened it, not without reluctance. He hated letters; they always contained something unpleasant—nowadays, since his second marriage. This was from his sister. He began skimming through the insulting home-truths of which it was composed. The words "indecent haste," "social suicide," "scarcely cold in her grave," "person of the lower classes," all occurred. They were inevitable now in any communication from a well-meaning and right-thinking relative. Impatient, he was about to tear the stupid letter to pieces when his eye fell on a sentence at the bottom of the third page. His heart beat with uncomfortable violence as he read it. It was too monstrous! Janet Spence was going about telling everyone that he had poisoned his wife in order to marry Doris. What damnable malice! Ordinarily a man of the suavest temper, Mr. Hutton found himself trembling with rage. He took the childish satisfaction of calling names —he cursed the woman.

Then suddenly he saw the ridiculous side of the situation. The notion that he should have murdered anyone in order to marry Doris! If they only knew how miserably bored he was. Poor, dear Janet! She had tried to be malicious; she had only succeeded in being stupid.

A sound of footsteps aroused him; he looked round. In the garden below the little terrace the servant girl of the house was picking fruit. A Neapolitan, strayed somehow as far north as Florence, she was a specimen of the classical type—a little debased. Her profile might have been taken from a Sicilian coin of a bad period. Her features, carved floridly in the grand tradition, expressed an almost perfect stupidity. Her mouth was the most beautiful thing about her; the calligraphic hand of nature had richly curved it into an expression of mulish bad temper. . . . Under her hideous black clothes, Mr. Hutton divined a powerful body, firm and massive. He had looked at her before with a vague interest and curiosity. To-day the curiosity defined and focused itself into a desire. An idyll of Theocritus. Here was the woman; he, alas, was not precisely like a goatherd on the volcanic hills. He called to her.

"Armida!"

The smile with which she answered him was so provocative, attested so easy a virtue, that Mr. Hutton took fright. He was on the brink once more—on the brink. He must draw back, oh! quickly, quickly, before it was too late. The girl continued to look up at him.

"Ha chiamato?" she asked at last.

Stupidity or reason? Oh, there was no choice now. It was imbecility every time.

"Scendo," he called back to her. Twelve steps led from the garden to the terrace. Mr. Hutton counted them. Down, down, down, down. . . . He saw a vision of himself descending from one circle of the inferno to the next—from a darkness full of wind and hail to an abyss of stinking mud.

For a good many days the Hutton case had a place on the front page of every newspaper. There had been no more popular murder trial since George Smith had temporarily eclipsed the European War by drowning in a warm bath his seventh bride. The public imagination was stirred by this tale of a murder brought to light months after the date of the crime. Here, it was felt, was one of those incidents in human life, so notable because they are so rare, which do definitely justify the ways of God to man. A wicked man had been moved by an illicit passion to kill his wife. For months he had lived in sin and fancied security—only to be dashed at last more horribly into the pit he had prepared for himself. "Murder will out," and here was a case of it. The readers of the newspapers were in a position to follow every movement of the hand of God. There had been vague, but persistent rumours in the neighbourhood; the police had taken action at last. Then came the exhumation order, the post-mortem examination, the inquest, the evidence of the experts, the verdict of the coroner's jury, the trial, the condemnation. For once Providence had done its duty, obviously, grossly, didactically, as in a melodrama. The newspapers were right in making of the case the staple intellectual food of a whole season.

Mr. Hutton's first emotion when he was summoned from Italy to give evidence at the inquest was one of indignation. It was a monstrous, a scandalous thing that the police should take such idle, malicious gossip seriously. When the inquest was over he would bring an action for malicious prosecution against the Chief Constable; he would sue the Spence woman for slander.

The inquest was opened; the astonishing evidence unrolled itself. The experts had examined the body, and had found traces of arsenic; they were of opinion that the late Mrs. Hutton had died of arsenic poisoning.

Arsenic poisoning. . . . Emily had died of arsenic poisoning? After that, Mr. Hutton learned with surprise that there was enough arsenicated insecticide in his greenhouses to poison an army.

It was now, quite suddenly, that he saw it: there was a case against him. Fascinated, he watched it growing, growing, like some monstrous tropical plant. It was enveloping him, surrounding him; he was lost in a tangled forest.

When was the poison administered? The experts agreed that it must have been swallowed eight or nine hours before death. About lunch-time? Yes, about lunch-time. Clara, the parlour-maid, was called. Mrs. Hutton, she remembered, had asked her to go and fetch her medicine. Mr. Hutton had volunteered to go instead; he had gone alone. Miss Spence—ah, the memory of the storm, the white aimed face! the horror of it all!—Miss Spence confirmed Clara's statement, and added that Mr. Hutton had come back with the medicine already poured out in a wine-glass, not in the bottle.

Mr. Hutton's indignation evaporated. He was dismayed, frightened. It was all too fantastic to be taken seriously, and yet this nightmare was a fact—it was actually happening.

M'Nab had seen them kissing, often. He had taken them for a drive on the day of Mrs. Hutton's death. He could see them reflected in the wind-screen, sometimes out of the tail of his eye.

The inquest was adjourned. That evening Doris went to bed with a headache. When he went to her room after dinner, Mr. Hutton found her crying.

"What's the matter?" He sat down on the edge of her bed and began to stroke her hair. For a long time she did not answer, and he went on stroking her hair mechanically, almost unconsciously; sometimes, even, he bent down and kissed her bare shoulder. He had his own affairs, however, to think about. What had happened? How was it that the stupid gossip had actually come true? Emily had died of arsenic poisoning. It was absurd, impossible. The order of things had been broken, and he was at the mercy of an irresponsibility. What had happened, what was going to happen? He was interrupted in the midst of his thoughts.

"It's my fault—it's my fault!" Doris suddenly sobbed out. "I shouldn't have loved you; I oughtn't to have let you love me. Why was I ever born?"

Mr. Hutton didn't say anything, but looked down in silence at the abject figure of misery lying on the bed.

"If they do anything to you I shall kill myself."

She sat up, held him for a moment at arm's length, and looked at him with a kind of violence, as though she were never to see him again.

"I love you, I love you, I love you." She drew him, inert and passive, towards her, clasped him, pressed herself against him. "I didn't know you loved me as much as that, Teddy Bear. But why did you do it—why did you do it?"

Mr. Hutton undid her clasping arms and got up. His face became very red. "You seem to take it for granted that I murdered my wife," he said. "It's really too grotesque. What do you all take me for? A cinema hero?" He had begun to lose his temper. All the exasperation, all the fear and bewilderment of the day, was transformed into a violent anger against her. "It's all such damned stupidity. Haven't you any conception of a civilised man's mentality? Do I look the sort of man who'd go about slaughtering people? I suppose you imagined I was so insanely in love with you that I could commit any folly. When will you women understand that one isn't insanely in love? All one asks for is a quiet life, which you won't allow one to have. I don't know what the devil ever induced me to marry you. It was all a damned stupid, practical joke. And now you go about saying I'm a murderer. I won't stand it."

Mr. Hutton stamped towards the door. He had said horrible things, he knew—odious things that he ought speedily to unsay. But he wouldn't. He closed the door behind him.

"Teddy Bear!" He turned the handle; the latch clicked into place. "Teddy Bear!" The voice that came to him through the closed door was agonised. Should he go back? He ought to go back. He touched the handle, then withdrew his fingers and quickly walked away. When he was half-way down the stairs he halted. She might try to do something silly—throw herself out of the window or God knows what! He listened attentively; there was no sound. But he pictured her very clearly, tiptoeing across the room, lifting the sash as high as it would go, leaning out into the cold night air. It was raining a little. Under the window lay the paved terrace. How far below? Twenty-five or thirty feet? Once, when he was walking along Piccadilly, a dog had jumped out of a third-storey window of the Ritz. He had seen it fall; he had heard it strike the pavement. Should he go back? He was damned if he would; he hated her.

He sat for a long time in the library. What had happened? What was happening? He turned the question over and over in his mind and could find no answer. Suppose the nightmare dreamed itself out to its horrible conclusion. Death was waiting for him. His eyes filled with tears; he wanted so passionately to live. "Just to be alive." Poor Emily had wished it too, he remembered: "Just to be alive." There were still so many places in this astonishing world unvisited, so many queer delightful people still unknown, so many lovely women never so much as seen. The huge white oxen would still be dragging their wains along the Tuscan roads, the cypresses would still go up, straight as pillars, to the blue heaven; but he would not be there to see them. And the sweet southern wines—Tears of Christ and Blood of Judas—others would drink them, not he. Others would walk down the obscure and narrow lanes between the bookshelves in the London Library, sniffing the dusty perfume of good literature, peering at strange titles, discovering unknown names, exploring the fringes of vast domains of knowledge. He would be lying in a hole in the ground. And why, why? Confusedly he felt that some extraordinary kind of justice was being done. In the past he had been wanton and imbecile and irresponsible. Now Fate was playing as wantonly, as irresponsibly, with him. It was tit for tat, and God existed after all.

He felt that he would like to pray. Forty years ago he used to kneel by his bed every evening. The nightly formula of his childhood came to him almost unsought from some long unopened chamber of the memory. "God bless Father and Mother, Tom and Cissie and the Baby, Mademoiselle and Nurse, and everyone that I love, and make me a good boy. Amen." They were all dead now—all except Cissie.

His mind seemed to soften and dissolve; a great calm descended upon his spirit. He went upstairs to ask Doris's forgiveness. He found her lying on the couch at the foot of the bed. On the floor beside her stood a blue bottle of liniment, marked "Not to be taken"; she seemed to have drunk about half of it.

"You didn't love me," was all she said when she opened her eyes to find him bending over her.

Dr. Libbard arrived in time to prevent any very serious consequences. "You mustn't do this again," he said while Mr. Hutton was out of the room.

"What's to prevent me?" she asked defiantly.

Dr. Libbard looked at her with his large, sad eyes. "There's nothing to prevent you," he said. "Only yourself and your baby. Isn't it rather bad luck on your baby, not allowing it to come into the world because you want to go out of it?"

Doris was silent for a time. "All right," she whispered. "I won't."

Mr. Hutton sat by her bedside for the rest of the night. He felt himself now to be indeed a murderer. For a time he persuaded himself that he loved this pitiable child. Dozing in his chair, he woke up, stiff and cold, to find himself drained dry, as it were, of every emotion. He had become nothing but a tired and suffering carcase. At six o'clock he undressed and went to bed for a couple of hours' sleep. In the course of the same afternoon the coroner's jury brought in a verdict of "Wilful Murder," and Mr. Hutton was committed for trial.

Miss Spence was not at all well. She had found her public appearances in the witness-box very trying, and when it was all over she had something that was very nearly a breakdown. She slept badly, and suffered from nervous indigestion. Dr. Libbard used to call every other day. She talked to him a great deal—mostly about the Hutton case. . . . Her moral indignation was always on the boil. Wasn't it appalling to think that one had had a murderer in one's house? Wasn't it extraordinary that one could have been for so long mistaken about the man's character? (But she had had an inkling from the first.) And then the girl he had gone off with—so low class, so little better than a prostitute. The news that the second Mrs. Hutton was expecting a baby—the posthumous child of a condemned and executed criminal—revolted her; the thing was shocking—an obscenity. Dr. Libbard answered her gently and vaguely, and prescribed bromide.

One morning he interrupted her in the midst of her customary tirade. "By the way," he said in his soft, melancholy voice, "I suppose it was really you who poisoned Mrs. Hutton."

Miss Spence stared at him for two or three seconds with enormous eyes, and then quietly said, "Yes." After that she started to cry.

"In the coffee, I suppose."

She seemed to nod assent. Dr. Libbard took out his fountain-pen, and in his neat, meticulous calligraphy wrote out a prescription for a sleeping-draught.

73

The Cavalier of the Streets

BY MICHAEL ARLEN

IT would not have occurred to
you that Mrs. Avalon was a discontented woman. It would not even
have occurred to you that she could be, for what had she not? She was,
of course, the wife of John Avalon, K.C. But she was more than that,
she was Fay Avalon. Now of the lovely, the gracious Fay Avalon,
what shall be said that has not already been said? She was a figure of
the world, and in it most centrally situated. She had not pushed, but
she was *there*. More, she was a figure of legend, remote and courteous.
Every one knew about her, but of nothing against her, and this was so
because she was a lady who never by any means sought any publicity
but that which the love and respect of her wide acquaintance spread
for her. She was, in fact, a darling. It was the fashion to speak well
of Fay Avalon, and it is only shallow people who say that all fashions
are shallow because they change. There is nothing in the world that
does not change, and if fashions change oftener than most that is because—well, it is difficult to say exactly why that is, and anyway this is
not the place for it.

Now why are people like sheep? But perhaps it would be better to
ask: "Why, in nearly all novels and conversations, is there one law for
the rich and another for the poor?" For in nearly all novels and conversations there is a sort of asinine implication that among the rich, the
social, there is no real friendship, but that real friendship exists only
among the poor. For years and years and years England has been living
under a tyranny, a silly tyranny: it is called the middle-class, and it is
belauded by all because nearly all belong to it. Now if a writer writes
of the middle-class he is said to have a sense of the Reality of Life, but
if he writes of the poor wretches who continue to eke out a miserable
existence on their capital in Mayfair, it is said of him that he is writing

of people who do not matter, people who are not worth writing about, people among whom none of the real emotions exist, and so on. The patricians never protest, for a gentleman is one who can take abuse properly, the same, of course, applying to a lady. But the others, the Backbone of England! Oh, what a Backbone that is, and how swiftly it becomes a jawbone when it is scratched by a well-aimed bit of contumely! But what does all that matter, particularly when we were talking of Fay Avalon, and how charming she was. She had many real friends, and these confided much in her, but in them she did not confide. Fay Avalon was not capable of telling even the least of her troubles to any one, for she was shy. Beneath her polish, her wit, her grave courtesy—a rare enchantment, that—her supreme ability as a hostess at whose table enemies were notably changed to friends, she was as shy as a girl. Never, never, in all her brilliant life, and it really was a very brilliant life, had she been able to exclude the idea that she might very easily bore people, that, in fact, she was not nearly so clever and amusing as other people. That is why she never confided: she only seemed to. . . .

One of the many secrets that Fay Avalon hid within herself was that she was romantic, deeply. She had always been romantic. John Avalon, K.C. had never been romantic, and never knew anything of his wife's trouble. He loved his wife jealously, but being a great K.C. is, of course, a very tiring way of life, and so he spent most of his time with her in sleeping.

Romance came into the life of Fay Avalon at a time when she would sometimes say: "I am older than most women." She was thirty-eight years old, and so she was sorry for herself, and then romance came. It was Prince Nicholas Pavlovitch Shuvarov who brought it. He was, of course, a refugee from Bolshevy, and it was said that before the Revolution his people had owned half of Petrograd, as was only natural, for there are countless Russians of the old order in London and Paris whose people once owned halves of Petrograd, not to speak of the Grand Dukes who made such a mess of all of it. But Prince N. P. Shuvarov was charming, and he was an artist. You knew that because people went about saying he was charming and an artist. You were asked to respect him because he earned his living, and of course you did what you were asked, although you were not aware of any particular esteem instantly alight in the eyes of those to whom you volunteered the information that you worked in the City. But life is different for Russians, they look so tragic, even when drunk, and so one went on respecting old Shuvarov for earning his living. He did this amazing feat by going about doing ghastly drawings of his friends Lady This and Lady That, which he somehow sold to the illustrated journals of the week, where they appeared in all sorts of colours under headings like "The Third of Five Lovely Sisters" or "Popular Daughter of a Great American," and boldly signed "Shuvarov."

He was everywhere, in a quiet and pleasant way. Sometimes he was at Fay Avalon's, but only sometimes at Fay Avalon's. Superior people who had read Dostoeffsky called him Nicholas Pavlovitch, which is of course the proper way to address a Russian gentleman; while others just called him Shove-off, though not as though they meant it, for every one liked him. Women found him attractive. These Russians, they said, are so Sombre. Mrs. Mountjenkins said he had Magnetism. "One can feel it," she said, "when he comes into a room." Lady Carnal said he was charming and so *sound*.

In Prince Nicholas Pavlovitch Shuvarov, then, Mrs. Avalon found romance. No breath of scandal had ever been breathed against her, and no such breath was breathed now. Her purity and her lovely aloofness were landmarks of London society in the second decade of this century. Colonel Repington, you will remember, remarked them in particular. During the period of the war alone he sat beside her thirty-eight times for luncheon, twenty-eight times for dinner, not to speak of the innumerable times when he said "Good-evening" to her in such a way that she not only heard him but answered him. He reports a conversation in which Fay Avalon was distinctly heard to say to the Home Secretary that she detested all secret vices like drugs and love, especially middle-aged love.

"One should live in public," said Mrs. Avalon. "It is the private life that has ruined so many great lives and rotted so many good brains."

"Quite," said the Home Secretary. "Quite." But in a few days he had to resign owing to liver trouble—so it was said—and Mrs. Avalon fell in love with Prince N. P. Shuvarov. Her one lapse, you understand. All her life she had longed for this one thing, romance; and at last it had come, in the sombre eyes of a stranger.

Mrs. Avalon did not know much about that Kind of Thing—the "private life"—but she knew a good deal about her friends, and that was a good deal more than she intended they should know about her. She organised her life to suit her love. It sounds beastly, that, but then you do not know Fay Avalon and I do, and that is why I know that nothing she did could ever be so beastly as if any one else did it, for she was a darling. As for Prince Shuvarov, he was Russian all the way and could organise nothing. She adored that. . . .

Never, never, did they go anywhere together: neither to the play, nor to a restaurant, nor to a ball; and only very seldom was he at her house, a guest among many. But every afternoon Fay Avalon would steal to her lover's studio in a quiet street in Hampstead. Not, of course, in her car, but in a taxi.

And what a relief it was, to enter the dim, bare silence of that studio! The clatter of the voices of the luncheon-party she had just left faded instantly from her mind, a lovely mist came in between the unquiet delight of her heart and the usual labours of her life. She rested on a divan in a corner of that secret studio, while Shuvarov would pace about in his feverish way. It was a very bare studio, but it would not have remained so bare if she had had her way. Though, indeed, Fay Avalon, she who had so despised "the private life," would have been shocked, she simply could not have helped being shocked, if he had not impatiently dismissed her offer to make of the studio a pavilion worthy of Babylonian lovers. "I make just enough money not to starve," said Shuvarov. "And that is enough for any man."

They were, of course, quite often unhappy, for Russians are like that. There were scenes, introspective and bitter, there were accusations, quarrels, reconciliations. It was some time before Mrs. Avalon realised that it is in the Slav Temperament to make violent scenes about nothing and then to yield adorably to passionate reconciliations. It was rather wearing for the nerves, she protested. "You have lived smoothly for too long," he retorted in a harsh moment. "You have known no wretchedness, Fay, because you have *felt* nothing! God, you English-women! In Russia our women *live,* they *feel.* . . ."

But Fay Avalon only sighed at that, certain that no woman any-where could feel so much as she . . . and she was a little afraid for herself, the way this thing she had not known before, this thing called love, had taken hold of her.

One day their privacy suffered a shock. Mrs. Avalon had just left the studio, in the evening, and had turned the corner into a more fre-quented street in search for a taxi, when a tall, shabby young man confronted her. He stood before her so that she could not pass, and his face mocked her, a lean face made very sinister by his nose, perhaps a fine nose once but now broken so that it inclined noticeably to one side. He examined her with a sneer in his eyes. She did not at first know it for a sneer, for no man had ever sneered at Fay Avalon before. He swept off his hat, a sardonic gesture, and he replaced it. It was a soft, dirty, dilapidated hat of the rakish sort, such as has been worn by every pirate that has ever been heard of.

"Good-evening, Mrs. Avalon," said the shabby young man.

"I am afraid . . ." doubtfully began Fay Avalon.

"Not at all!" said the shabby young man. He smiled graciously.

"It is my misfortune," he said, "that we have not been introduced. I have not been going about very much in society lately, because of one thing and another. And I called you by your name merely to show you that I know who you are. I also know where you have been. I can't, of course, say that I know exactly what you have been doing, but I can't help thinking that your husband would have no doubt about it. Husbands are like that, madam. Juries are also like that. I wonder, Mrs. Avalon, if you will think me very boorish if I, well, insist on your lending me fifty pounds?"

The young man was very shabbily dressed, but he was so very unpleasant, so entirely and symmetrically unpleasant, that, she thought, he must once have been a gentleman. She stared at him, and she shivered a little. Perhaps, she thought, this is the first man I have ever met who has simply no desire to please me. Perhaps most men are only possible because they desire to please women. This one is unaffectedly foul. . . .

"You are blackmailing me, then?" she asked him: and her voice did not tremble more than ever so little.

"Yes," said the shabby young man. "And I am doing it as unpleasantly as I know how. I am sure, Mrs. Avalon, that you had rather I was unpleasant than that I made love, like the greasy blackmailers one meets in books. And, anyhow, I could not possibly compete with Prince Nicholas Pavlovitch Shuvarov. These foreigners, I am told, have the technique . . ."

She stared at him with unbelieving eyes. Could there be men such as this, so foul! To what awful depths of bitterness must this revolting man have sunk, that he could so wantonly and cruelly insult a stranger!

"I realise you dislike me very much," said the young man with the broken nose. "But, even so, I should prefer that that matter of the fifty pounds should engage your attention more or less immediately."

Mrs. Avalon shivered a little.

"Don't, please, speak any more!" she breathed at last. "You seem to know so much that I am sure you know the address of my house. The telephone-book will, however, provide you with any details that may have escaped your attention. If you will call at noon to-morrow you will be given an envelope at the door. May I pass now, please?"

"Why, of course!" said he, and stood aside.

But somehow she did not pass immediately. She stared into his face with very wide, childish eyes, and there was a queer sort of hurt smile crucified in their depths.

"I have never been spoken to like this before," she said. "Who are you?"

"I am the cavalier of the streets, madam," said the tall shabby man with the broken nose. She stared at him very thoughtfully.

"And is that a good thing to be?"

The cavalier of the streets smiled curiously.

"I had thought, Mrs. Avalon, that it was I who was detaining you. . . ."

"You see," said Mrs. Avalon gently, "you are the vilest man I have ever met. You are probably the vilest man in the world, and so I am curious. You will have your fifty pounds. Or would you not prefer a hundred?"

But the ice of Fay Avalon did not freeze the cavalier of the streets.

"I do not accept presents from ladies," he said. "Fifty is business, but the extra fifty is an insult to a gentleman." He smiled right into her face. "You may pass, Mrs. Avalon."

"You are a gentleman? You were, perhaps you mean?"

"A gentleman," said the shabby young man, "is a man who is never *unintentionally* rude to any one. I am a gentleman."

He stood aside, and swept off his dilapidated hat. She took one step, two, three. . . .

"I do hope," she murmured swiftly, "that I will never see you again."

The lean, weathered face with the fantastic nose mocked her. Fay Avalon had never been mocked before.

"Didn't I tell you," he said, "that I was the cavalier of the streets? I am alone, the solitary supporter of chivalry and all manner of outdoor manliness. Thus, it will be very difficult to resist the pleasure of seeing you again, Mrs. Avalon, for you are, without a doubt, a darling. But I will try to resist it, really I will. . . ."

"Please," said Mrs. Avalon, and went swiftly.

The next afternoon Mrs. Avalon had promised to appear at a charity matinée in a playful duologue between Cleopatra and a hearty gentleman alleged to be Mark Antony's valet; and as she had never gone to the trouble of acquiring a reputation as Unreliable—in fact, Fay Avalon was born with "careless habits of accuracy"—and though she was feeling less like Cleopatra than she had ever felt in her life, it was only after she had done her duty by the charity matinée that she set out for the quiet street in Hampstead.

She gave Nicholas Pavlovitch only the bald outline of the beastly happening. Blackmailer, money. He blushed furiously. Often she had seen him blush, but never as now. He was like a child who has just been smacked and knows he has not deserved it. He couldn't, he said, bear the indecency, the shame, of it . . . that, through loving him, she should have to endure this awful thing. There was only one thing to do. She must "cut him out," that's all! And how funnily tragic that slang sounded in his twisted Russian pronunciation.

She laughed at that. Not much, but just enough. "We do not," she said, "take our tragedies so tragically. But scratch a Russian and you find a baby . . ." She kissed him.

"It is easier than that," she explained. "You must move, dear. For weeks you have been complaining of the lighting in this studio—and now you have every excuse for taking steps about leaving it. Long steps are preferable, Nicholas. From Hampstead to Chelsea, in fact. . . ."

Shove-off took steps at once, and these lead him to a little studio in a little street off the King's Road, Chelsea. It was a little street like another, with a pillar-box at one end and the noise of buses at the other. Near the pillar-box was a lamp-post. And one autumn evening, as Mrs. Avalon walked from her lover's studio into Cheyne Walk, she saw a man leaning against the lamp-post, and under a soft dilapidated hat she saw the shape of a lean face and a broken nose. He was motionless, indifferent, and he was not looking at her but at the wind that blew the leaves about the little street. Her heart jumped, and then was as still as a cut flower.

"So!" she whispered bitterly. "Blackmailers are like history, then!"

The vile person made the courteous gesture.

"Mr. Beerbohm has it," the vile person said gravely, "that it is not history that repeats itself but historians who repeat one another. A charming writer, don't you think?"

"Oh, dear!" said Mrs. Avalon very miserably, "I thought you were vile! But I am disappointed in you. I actually thought you would leave me alone. You are even viler than I thought, you who call yourself the cavalier of the streets!"

"Perhaps," murmured the shabby young man. "Perhaps. It seems always to have been my fate to find out the indecencies of decent people, and so, of course, decent people do not take a very liberal view of me. You find me this evening, Mrs. Avalon, in a conversational vein."

There was a ghastly sort of subtlety in his neglect to mention why he was there, a thin, rakish hawk by the lamp-post. Impotent, she loathed him. And she passed him resolutely, with a very proud face, one step, two, three. . . . And then his voice fell harshly on her back:

"You are the kind of woman men dream about in lonely moments. My life is made of lonely moments, and I think this is the loneliest of all. Go away quickly, Fay Avalon!"

Bewilderment wheeled her round.

"*What* did you say?" she cried.

But he stood as when she had first seen him, the silhouette of a hawk with a broken nose, and he stared not at her but at the wind that blew the leaves about the little street.

"It is not worth repeating," he said sharply into the middle air.

"But to what I said, I added 'Go very quickly,' and meant it—for your sake. This is a lonely place, Mrs. Avalon, and the cavalier of the streets is as nearly an outlaw as any one outside a cinema. It is a long time since I kissed a lady, and the only thing that restrains me from doing it now is the fact that I have never in my life kissed any one who did not wish to be kissed by me. So you had better go quickly, Fay Avalon."

She went, as swiftly as a shadow.

Mrs. Avalon, after her first horrid experience, had had the forethought to keep in her jewel-safe a roll of Bank of England notes. That evening, having sent her maid from the room, she counted out five notes from the roll. She smiled wryly . . . "And so," she thought, "this is hell. And Fay Avalon is well in it, she is in a very ghastly hell." Very slowly, very absently, she recounted the five ten-pound notes. They were clean and crisp and delicious, marvellously above the funny stuff that passes for money in France and America. They were symbols of a spacious England, of splendid adventurers and gallant merchantmen, they were symbols of all the luxuries of *race* and manners, dead now except in the hearts of a few shy people. A Bank of England note is the cleanest expression money has ever acquired, it is more than money, it decorates money. Only one of the five notes that passed through Mrs. Avalon's fingers bore even a sign that other human hands had ever touched them, and that was but a little splash as of red ink on its back.

She put them in an envelope, wrote "To C. O. S." across it, and privily instructed the butler that he give it into the hands of the person who had already called once before and who *might* call again towards noon the following morning.

"The gentleman called, madam," said Smith the next morning, when she came in from a walk for luncheon.

"The gentleman, Smith?"

"He had that manner, madam."

"There will be ten for luncheon, not eight, Smith."

"Major Cypress and Mr. Trevor rang up to inquire if you expected them to luncheon, madam. They seemed, I think, disappointed that you did not."

"They rang up together?"

"Such was my impression, madam. They said that there must be some mistake about your not expecting them to luncheon as they had not been asked to luncheon anywhere else. On asking my opinion as to whether, if they called at about half-past one, you would or would not ask them to stay, I ventured to say, madam, that it was very probable. I gather that that will make twelve for luncheon, madam."

Mrs. Avalon smiled. "Very good, Smith."

"The gentleman who called left this letter, madam."

"Put it down over there. That will do, Smith, thank you."

When she was alone she gingerly touched the letter. It was not addressed. The expression on her face was as though she was breathing the air of a pest-house.

"I see," said the note, "that you think me even viler than I am. That is what I intended. By giving me money when I did not ask for it, you have made the profession of blackmailer an impossible one for a man of sensibility. Good-bye."

She did not tell Nicholas Pavlovitch of this second encounter. It would, she thought, be only disturbing him for nothing, for she was quite convinced that she had now seen the last of the cavalier of the streets. She couldn't help having a little private conceit about it. After all, not every woman would have managed that foul man so—certainly not those notoriously managing women who know How to deal with men. "Oh, dear!" she thought, "I am clever, I really am!" Even this man, so brutally undesirous to please, had been charmed back into the loathsome shades whence he had so horridly come—so impressed had he been by her original way of being blackmailed that he had been appalled into respectful invisibility. She had, after all, allowed herself to be blackmailed charmingly, she had been as charming as any woman being blackmailed could possibly be.

It was because of such thoughts that, eleven evenings later, she was so particularly angry: for the lamp-light near the pillar-box fell on the figure of the cavalier of the streets, the careless, rakish figure at his disgusting post. By the beating of her heart, she knew him yards and yards away. Still she stood for one long moment, to quiet her heart, and then, intolerantly, she swept on. She was humiliated in a most private conceit. She was angrier than she had ever been in her life.

Swiftly she pressed on, to pass him with inexpressible contempt; but the pavement was narrow, and wide the sweep of the bad man's hat. "Forgive me," said he. "I had not intended to worry you again, but——"

"You do not *worry* me," said a lady to an insect.

"In that case," said the cavalier of the streets, "I may spare you my apologies, which, I assure you, are quite dangerously insincere. I had intended not to sin against you again. But, this very afternoon, something has happened, something really rather awkward. I do not often lose money at poker, Mrs. Avalon—in fact I make a point of not losing money at poker, in so far, of course, as a man of honour may make a point about a hazard. But, whether it was the memory of your beauty, for I may not ever forget it, that came between me and my skill, or whether— Oh, what does it matter why it was, since the fact remains that I have lost money, and must pay what I owe or forfeit my honour. . . ."

"Your *honour!*" she gasped. "Oh, *commedia, commedia!*"

"I could wish I was as privileged as you to take a comical view of it. It is only a small debt, however. A matter of twenty pounds. I have still ten left of the fifty you so kindly lent to me the other day—I wonder, Mrs. Avalon, I wonder if you could by any chance help me with the rest? I should be so grateful."

So she had been right about him, after all! He would not have come again, in the ordinary way. She looked into his eyes, and they were as the eyes of other men. The cavalier of the streets was without his sneer.

"Yes," she said gravely. "A debt of honour—surely you must pay a debt of honour, O cavalier of the streets! It is very commendable in you to want to."

"It is merely good sense, madam. Like all matters of honour. If one does not pay, one does not get paid."

Her fingers were playing within her bag. They ceased.

"I'm so afraid," she murmured, "that I have only a few shillings . . ."

"Pity!" whispered the shabby young man; and he smiled curiously, as might a man whose horse has been beaten by a short head.

"I will go home," said Fay Avalon, "and get you the money."

"You will do nothing of the sort, Mrs. Avalon. Ridiculous to put you to that trouble for a mere ten pounds. Besides, it might cause comment if I showed myself at your door again."

"My butler thought you charming," she told him gravely.

"Therein he discerned your influence over me, Mrs. Avalon. No, I have a better idea! Go back to Prince Shuvarov and ask him to——"

"But he is so poor!"

"Heavens, those insufferable drawings of his must sometimes fetch some money! Try, please. It is only fair, after all, that he should contribute a little towards my support——"

"Your debt of honour, surely!"

"I am rebuked. A man's honour would be very adequately preserved by you, Mrs. Avalon. But please do as I suggest. I will abide by the weight of Shuvarov's pocket."

With a quick gesture, she left him. She found Shuvarov preparing to shave, for when he was dining out he always shaved twice, like all proper men. She did not give him time to voice his surprise at her reentrance.

"That wretch is here again," she explained swiftly. "I know you are poor, dear, but have you just a few pounds you could lend me? Ten, for instance?"

Shuvarov began furiously, his cheeks mantling. "That man . . ." He waved his shaving-brush.

"Never mind that now, dear. Have you or haven't you the money? Please, Nicholas?" She was always gentle with him. He was such a child.

Nicholas Pavlovitch shrugged his shoulders, and banged down the shaving-brush.

"You are encouraging him," he said fatalistically. "Lucky I sold a drawing for just that amount to-day. Lucky for that man, I mean." He fumbled in his waistcoat pocket, and gave her a banknote.

"Bless you, Nicholas!" she cried softly, and was going, when the light fell on the banknote in her hand so that there was visible on it a little splash as of red ink. . . .

Slowly, she looked up at Prince Nicholas Pavlovitch Shuvarov. Her lips did not move, but he understood, and his thin, handsome face went as white as a soiled handkerchief.

The cavalier of the streets saw her face as she approached. She flung the note at him, so that it fell from his jacket to his feet. She passed him. But fingers swiftly clutched her arm, so that it hurt.

"That," he said harshly, "will teach a lovely lady to love scum. I intended that it should. He and I arranged the *coup,* ages ago. But when I saw you the first time, in Hampstead, I sickened. That is why I was so beastly, that you should hate me as much as I hated myself. *Le coup est nul,* I told Shuvarov after that. Since then your face has haunted me. So I did this—to cure you of your silly infatuation for a man who would eat into your life like a foul little worm into a lovely fruit. God, how you could ever have liked that lousy, half-baked, professional Russian! I saw him to-day, and saw that he still had the note with the red mark on it—this!" And he ground his heel on the note on the pavement. Tighter he held her arm, and he scowled into her face. She thought of the wet-white she would have to use on her arm to hide the bruises of his fingers.

"You're hurting me!" she cried.

"I know. I have sinned against you," he said, "but you have done worse. You have sinned against yourself. Now go, and sin no more. And you'd better go damn quick else you'll be very late for dinner and the old K.C. will get cross."

"*You* to talk of sin!" she cried, and laughed.

"Naturally, Fay Avalon. For only Satan can rebuke sin with authority."

"Oh, pouf!" she laughed. "You are sentimental then!"

"Hell!" snapped the cavalier of the streets. "I am in love!" And as he swept off his dilapidated hat she could not help a thought that a plume would wave more becomingly from that particular hat than from any other hat she knew or would ever know. Romance. . . .

"Oh, dear!" sighed Mrs. Avalon. "Good-bye." But the cavalier was already only a distant shadow in the street.

74

The Old Hunter

BY LIAM O'FLAHERTY

$\mathbf{M}$R. STEPHEN MULLEN, the horse-dealer of Ballyhaggard, went to an auction one day. He was a tall, slim man with a red face and white eyebrows. Being a very popular man, on account of his dry wit and his good temper, he met many friends in the town where the auction was being held, and the result was that he spent the morning in the hotels drinking. Slightly intoxicated, he arrived at the auction when everything was sold except an old hunter called Morrissey.

Mr. Mullen went up to the auctioneer, a friend of his, and asked him, had he anything left. The auctioneer pointed to the old hunter.

"That's the lot," he said.

"What's that?" said Mr. Mullen, shutting one eye and cocking his head sideways.

"Pooh!" said the auctioneer, "there's enough iron in that old rascal to keep a factory going for a month. Tell you what, these bank-clerks and shopkeepers that are buying horses now with their ill-gotten gains don't know a——"

"Hech, hech," said Mr. Mullen, "let's have a look at him. I might give ye the price of a drink for him."

They walked over to the hunter. He was a finely built animal, but he looked like a man that had just left a nursing home after a serious nervous breakdown. His bones were sticking through his hide, and though he held his head proudly in the air, it was obvious that he did so out of respect for his ancestry and not because of any consciousness of his strength. He was of a bay colour, and somebody had fired his left hind leg, so clumsily and in such a cruel manner that it appeared to have been done with a red-hot crowbar. The pelt was quite naked of hair and the flesh was singed in streaks.

"Look at that," said Mr. Mullen, pointing to the leg. "Did ye get him from a tinker, or what?"

"Lord have mercy on yer soul," said the auctioneer, "that fellah has a pedigree as long as yer arm. Come here, I'll show ye."

"Ye needn't bother," said Mr. Mullen. "What good is a pedigree to a dying man? The Master o' the Hounds might give a few bob for him for the pack."

Mr. Mullen wrinkled up his face in a smile and he looked at the auctioneer with his mouth open. He really wanted the horse, because he liked the old fellow's head, but he wanted to get him for next to nothing. The auctioneer also wanted to get rid of him very badly, but still, he wanted to strike a good bargain.

"Now drop the coddin', Mr. Mullen," he said, "and buy the horse if ye want him. Sure I needn't tell you what a horse is, whether he is a horse or a mule. Man alive, sure a few square meals 'ud change that fellah so much ye wouldn't know him. Look at his——"

"Aye," said Mullen coldly, "let's have a look at them. I mean at his insides. I bet he's got a smoker's heart and a liver stitched together with the best silk thread. If I buy him, would ye get him carted home for me?"

"I can see it's out for coddin' me ye are," said the auctioneer, turning to go away.

"Very well," said Mr. Mullen, clearing his throat, "I'll make ye an offer for him."

"What's that?" said the auctioneer, halting abruptly and turning around to Mr. Mullen.

"I've got thirty bob on me," said Mullen, contracting his white eyebrows. "I'll give ye the lot, though it's good money wasted."

The auctioneer pursed up his lips and stared at Mr. Mullen for a few moments as if he were dumfounded.

"D'ye really mean it?" he said.

Mr. Mullen nodded.

"Take him home, for God's sake," said the auctioneer, waving his hands.

Mr. Mullen paid for the horse and took him home. He led him along beside his own horse, and it was the devil of a job to keep him in hand. My boy, he had his head in the wind and champed along, rearing and trying to break loose.

"Good Lord," thought Mr. Mullen, "that fellah is a corker only for his age."

Mr. Mullen went to a party that night and there was heavy drinking. In his cups he began to boast about the old hunter he had bought for thirty shillings. Everybody made fun of him about it, so Mr. Mullen boasted that he would ride the old horse to the meet of the Ballyhaggard hounds next day.

"Wait till you see," he cried. "I'll leave you all so far behind that I'll have the fox's skin dressed before you arrive."

Next day Mr. Mullen's head was as big as a pot, and when he remembered his boast he was disgusted with himself. But he was a man of his word and he ordered the old hunter to be saddled for him. He drank a considerable amount of raw whiskey and mounted him. Off he went to the meet.

Everybody in the district turns out with the hounds, from Lord Clonmore to Mr. Mulligan, the butcher of Murren. All sorts of ungainly beasts appear. In fact, Mr. Murchison, the new Protestant curate, once joined, mounted on a cart-horse, which a scoundrel called The Tiger Donnelly sold him as an Irish hunter. Since the war and the revolution all sorts of people have been thrown together in the district, so that, as Mr. Mullen says, "There's no class about anything nowadays." But when Mr. Mullen himself appeared that day on Morrissey, everybody agreed that such an extraordinary animal had never been seen before. It was like a mortally sick man appearing at a wedding, half drunk and insisting on being the most hilarious person present.

"Bravo, Mr. Mullen," said Lord Clonmore. "The dead have arisen. Eh?"

Everybody laughed and Mr. Mullen was mortally insulted, but when the cavalcade set off, by Jove, Morrissey behaved himself marvellously. Like a good thoroughbred of the old school, he showed every ounce that was in him. He cleared the ditches and fences as lightly as those wonderful horses for which the Galway Blazers were famous, fellows that could live for a week on a raw turnip and cross a bog without wetting their fetlocks. Mr. Mullen kept refreshing himself now and again with stimulants, and as a consequence rode even more daringly than was his custom; but the old hunter carried him all day without a single stumble, until at last, just before the finish, he arrived at the drain that flows from the workhouse, about a mile outside the town. There is no more filthy or evil-smelling drain in the world. There is no necessity to describe it.

But when Morrissey arrived at this drain at full speed, he stopped dead. Undoubtedly the animal was too well bred to face it. Mr. Mullen was pitched over the horse's head and he fell headlong into the stinking place. Several people pulled up, but Mr. Mullen crawled out, uninjured. Seeing him, everybody went into hysterics with laughter. He was indescribable, and in fact unrecognizable. Morrissey lowered his head, sniffed at Mr. Mullen and set off back at a mad canter.

"It must have turned his stomach," laughed a red-haired farmer.

"Yer a lot of scoundrels," shouted Mr. Mullen, struggling to his feet and holding out his dripping hands that were as black and sticky as if he had dipped them in tar.

Morrissey was found again and brought back to the stables. Mr. Mullen went home and had a bath, and by that time his anger had worn off and he himself was able to laugh at the joke. Next morning he went to look at Morrissey. The poor animal was quite stiff with his efforts of the previous day. But he still had his head in the air and he whinnied joyfully when he saw Mr. Mullen. That softened Mr. Mullen's heart toward him.

"Damn it," he said to the stable-boy, "he's a great old horse. I'll take him down to the shore and give him a dip in the salt water to soften his legs."

He rode Morrissey down to the strand. It was a fine day, but there was a rather heavy ground-swell and the waves broke on the sand with a thundering noise. This thundering noise and the menacing aspect of the dark green waves, rising suddenly within a few feet of the shore and falling with a thud, terrified the horse. It was impossible to get him to walk in the tide. At last Mr. Mullen managed to get him near the surf, when the tide had receded for a particularly long distance, as it does now and again, after a certain number of short waves have broken. Then as the horse was stamping about and snorting, trying to get away from the water, an enormous wave rose suddenly and almost enveloped him. Instead of trying to rush backward, he was so confused by the rush of water under his stomach that he plunged out to sea. Mr. Mullen tried to head him off, but it was no use. Presently another equally large wave arose, passed right over the horse and the rider, so that they both turned a somersault. Mr. Mullen was thrown from the saddle and he became entangled somehow in the horse's legs. When he came to the surface, after having saved himself, the horse was five yards away and Mr. Mullen was in deep water. He swam a few strokes, struck ground and then looked behind him. There was the horse, swimming mightily out toward the open sea.

"God Almighty!" cried Mr. Mullen. "With ten pounds worth of a saddle on him!"

Mr. Mullen dashed up on to the strand and began to call some boatmen that were there. They ran over to him.

"Hey," he cried, "if he drowns, will he sink or float?"

"God save us," they cried, "who are ye talkin' about?"

"My horse, damn it," cried Mr. Mullen; "he's gone out to sea. Don't ye see him? Look."

"Aw, snakes alive," they said, when they saw the dark object, heaving along sideways, like an unwieldy porpoise.

"He'll float sure enough," said one man, "with the water he'll swallow."

"All right, then," said Mr. Mullen, "get me a boat. I want to save the saddle. The horse isn't worth his keep, but the saddle is worth money. Get a boat for me."

They rushed down a boat and put to sea after the horse. When they had gone out almost half a mile, they met the horse swimming back toward them.

"There he is," cried one boatman.

"He's floatin' sure enough," said Mr. Mullen. "Get alongside him and get the saddle."

"It's not floatin' he is, but swimmin' like a warrior," said the boatman.

"God!" said Mr. Mullen.

They were all amazed and they lay on their oars, as Morrissey swept past them toward the beach, going at a terrific pace. They followed him, and when they reached the strand, Morrissey was standing there, shivering and exhausted. Mr. Mullen took off his hat and struck his forehead.

"Well, that horse beats all I ever saw," he said. "Here. I'll buy a bottle of whiskey over this. Come on, men."

After that Mr. Mullen and the horse that went to sea became quite famous in the district. So that Mr. Mullen grew fond of the horse and he kept him all that winter in his stables with plenty of food. But he made no attempt to ride him, and although the fame of the horse spread afar, still nobody made an offer for him. Because even though he was famous for having swum a mile out to sea and then swum back again, he was also famous for having thrown Mr. Mullen into the workhouse drain.

Then in the following April another extraordinary thing happened to the horse. I must say that he had improved considerably during the winter. He had fattened a great deal and his hide was becoming almost glossy. The mark on his hind leg was not so outrageous, and to an ordinary person he seemed a perfectly sound horse. But to a horseman he was still an old crock. One of those game old things, whether they are old colonels who insist on wearing tight waists in their seventieth year, or old horses or old battered fighting cocks that take a step ferociously and then glare, wagging their chaps aggressively as if they were in the prime of their lives,—I say he was one of those game old things that make a virtue of looking fit even when they might be excused drooping their heads and lying down to die. But all the buyers admired him and left him alone. Then Mr. Stanley Edwards came to the town.

Mr. Edwards might be called a crock as well as the old hunter. He spent a greater part of each year in a nursing home. The remainder of the year he spent in the pursuit of extravagant pleasures, not always very well considered. His money was tied up in this country, otherwise it is very probable that he would never spend a week in it. But when he had done a great bout in London, he always had to return to Ireland to get some more money. After one of those bouts and a month in hospital, he engaged a villa in Ballyhaggard to take the sea air. A few days after his arrival in the town he came to Mr. Mullen. Mr. Mullen looked him up and down, rather surprised that such a weakling should come to him for anything.

"Well," he said, "what could I do for you?"

"Look here," said Mr. Edwards, "I have to live for a few months in this ghastly place. I'm sick and I have very little money. I have been here three days and I'm quite fed up with walking up and down the shore and talking to the lunatics around here. I want a horse. Can you get me one?"

"Let me see," said Mr. Mullen, looking at him shrewdly, "you'd want a quiet horse, I suppose?"

"I want a horse," said Mr. Edwards pettishly. "It doesn't matter what he is. If he breaks my neck it might be a jolly good idea."

"I see," said Mr. Mullen. "I think I've got the very thing that'll suit you."

"Oh! Look here," said Mr. Edwards rather nervously. "I don't mean I want some—eh—crazy thing. You know—a—oh, well——"

"You leave it to me," said Mr. Mullen. "You can try him out before you buy him."

Morrissey was brought out and Mr. Edwards immediately mounted him and trotted off. Mr. Edwards looked a very poor figure on horseback. Some wit said that he was born to be a rag-picker, because his gaunt frame bent like a willow rod and his nose was so long that he could use it in the same way that an elephant uses the tip of his trunk. But such a slight weight suited the old horse, and he went off very gallantly indeed, with that twirl in his right hind leg, which is a sign of old age in a horse and which warns off the cunning buyer but which is very attractive; like the smart twirl of the spurred boot which tells the swagger cavalry officer.

Mr. Mullen looked after the horse, scratching his chin and thinking that he would be very glad to accept a five-pound note for him.

After an hour, Mr. Edwards returned, perspiring but looking very happy. A good hour's trotting on a well-bred horse on a fine spring morning would make a corpse almost come to life again.

"Go all right?" said Mr. Mullen, smiling his most engaging smile.

"Splendid," said Mr. Edwards, sitting the horse and wiping his forehead, as if he were loath to dismount. "How much do you want for him?"

"I'll take thirty pounds at a pinch," said Mr. Mullen, after a moment's apparent thought and looking at Mr. Edwards as if he were going to do him a favour, which, however, gave him a great deal of pain.

"Oh!" said Mr. Edwards, a little surprised.

Then he dismounted and looked curiously at Mr. Mullen.

"It's a lot," he said.

"Oh! Well," said Mr. Mullen, making a gesture with his hands, "a horse isn't a bicycle."

"Quite," said Mr. Edwards. "Now, let me see."

He walked around the horse and passed his hand over the horse's body in various places. Mr. Mullen was very glad to see that he touched the wrong places. Then Mr. Edwards stood at a distance from the horse and looked at him. He seemed very loath to leave him. Mr. Mullen began to feel very comfortable.

"Look here," said Mr. Edwards at length, "I'll come back to-morrow and have another ride. May I?"

"Why, certainly," said Mr. Mullen affably. "You can have a look at his pedigree now if you like."

"Oh, has he got a pedigree?" said Mr. Edwards.

"Lord, yes," said Mr. Mullen, "yards of it."

Here it must be stated, that although Mr. Edwards was a wealthy country gentleman, he kept motor-cars instead of horses and knew nothing about the animals except on race-courses. So that a pedigree seemed to him as good a guarantee of perfection as the maker's name on a Rolls-Royce.

"Let's have a look at it," he said.

Mr. Mullen produced the pedigree and Mr. Edwards inspected it.

"In that case," he said, "I'll buy the horse right away."

"It's like taking milk from a child," thought Mr. Mullen, as Mr. Edwards wrote out the cheque.

Everybody expected Mr. Edwards to break his neck, and some people said that Mr. Mullen played rather a scurvy trick on the poor fellow, but during the whole of that summer the horse was seen on the roads almost every day, trotting along in the pink of condition. And what was more, Mr. Edwards became quite a new man. Whether it was the sea air or the riding that did it, he regained his health to an extraordinary extent. He did not become robust, but he was no longer an invalid and he led a decent healthy life. In fact, just before he went away, he came to Mr. Mullen and said: "Look here, Mr. Mullen, you've saved my life."

"Glad to hear it," said Mr. Mullen, without winking an eye.

In September Mr. Edwards left the district, but instead of going to England, as was his custom, he returned to his property in County Kilkenny. Nothing more was heard of him or of the horse for two years. And then two months ago I met Mr. Mullen in Dublin. We were having a drink together and talking about various things, when he suddenly gripped my arm and said:

"D'ye remember that horse, Morrissey, I had, the fellah that threw me into the drain?"

I nodded.

"Ye remember I sold him to a chap called Edwards from Kilkenny. Well, I've just been down there to a show. Met him there. He's still got the horse, going as strong as a three-year-old and . . . d'ye know what I'm going to tell ye? That horse saved his life, as he said himself. When I asked him about the horse, he said: 'I wouldn't part with that horse for a thousand. I haven't left this district since I saw you last, and I can drink two bottles of port now after dinner without turning a hair.' "

So that, indeed, it seems that there is something in a pedigree.

75

The White Cottage

BY L. A. G. STRONG

AS SOON as they reached the lane running down to the loch, the two men were delivered abruptly from the pressure and leaping buffets of the wind. The relief was extraordinary. The young doctor, who had been labouring, head down, bent almost double, forcing each thigh forward as against a weight of water, suddenly felt his body become light and irresponsible. It wanted to leave the ground altogether. A single bound should have been enough to take him to the loch side. Then, in immediate reaction, his limbs felt shaky and weak. They were not properly under control. He took a couple of long, uncertain strides, and caught up on his companion: but he, his anxiety urging him on, plunged at a shambling run into the darkness.

"Hey! half a minute." The doctor stumbled and stopped. Even through the noise of the storm, he somehow heard the other man stop.

"Sorry," he called, "I can't see my way."

The other was silent for a moment.

"Stand for a minute. Your eyes will get accustomed to it."

I'm damned if they will, thought the doctor: but he was glad enough of a chance to get his breath. It was as if they had come into another world. The darkness was solid, rich as the smell of wet earth and dead leaves that came in breaths from the wood. Outside, on the moor, there had been light of a sort, which, penetrating the scud and lashing rain, enabled them to see one another and distinguish the road from the heather on either side. Here there was nothing but stillness and dark, while, overhead, and all around, came the crash of the gale and the threshing of trees in torment. It was like nothing the doctor had ever experienced. Looking up, he could now see, against a patch of sky, an agitated fringe of blackness. The tops of the trees were lashing wildly, while at the roots, where the two men were standing, there was peace.

His companion stirred impatiently, and the doctor, rousing himself, followed him. It was no use. The way grew darker as it ploughed deeper between the trees. The doctor could see nothing. He walked by faith for fifty yards or so, then tripped, and all but fell.

"It's no use," he called. Then, as the other, impatient, stopped again, "I'd better not break my leg, had I?"

He took a step forward, and almost bumped into his companion.

"Take hold of my coat." The voice was more friendly. "Then you'll be all right."

Meekly the doctor obeyed. A nice fool I must look, he reflected, as he walked along, holding on to his companion's coat tails: only, luckily, there was no one to see him, and it would be too dark, even if there were. He gave a chuckle, then cursed himself for want of consideration. Probably the man hadn't heard.

"You know," he said, over the noise of the trees, "this is a great change for me."

"I'm sure."

"I'm well accustomed to being called out at all times, of course, but it's along pavements, with plenty of lights, and a bobby to pass the time of night with at the street corner."

"It must be a change indeed."

The voice was courteous but constrained. I'm a brute to bother him, the doctor thought. All the same, he'll be the better for a talk. Sympathy lit in him, a small, warm flame.

"You mustn't worry," he said. "We'll be with her soon now."

"It is the crossing I am thinking of," the other said.

"You came over all right."

"Aye. But the wind was mostly at our back. We shall have it against us. And the boat will be heavier."

"I'd like to help," said the doctor. "But I oughtn't to do too much. I may want a steady hand, when we get there."

The other did not answer at once.

"Och, you could not help," he said. "There are two of us. It would upset the rowing."

The darkness seemed to part above them: the gap widened: and, with a last twist, the road arrived beside the loch. They felt the wind again, but it was not nearly so strong as on the moor.

"Why," the doctor exclaimed. "It's much calmer down here."

"Wait," said the other grimly. "We are sheltered."

"It's lighter, anyway," said the doctor, and, relieved from the pressure of gale and darkness, he walked along cheerfully beside his companion. "How far is it to the boat?"

"A quarter of a mile."

There was a silence. The doctor spoke again.

"Is yours the cottage one can see right across the other side of the loch, at the foot of the mountain?"

"Aye."

"I was looking at it the other day, when I was coming back from seeing to one of the children at the farm up on the hill there."

"John Mackenzie's."

"Yes, that's the place. I looked over, and I thought to myself, That's an out of the way place to live."

"It is so."

"Aren't you very lonely, all by yourselves?"

"We have one neighbour. He is waiting for us. He helped me row over."

"Is he married?"

"No, he is a single man."

The young doctor peered sideways at his companion. He judged him to be nearer forty than thirty. Well spoken, an educated voice; but then, all the people of this district spoke well and musically. What on earth could persuade a man to live in such a God-forsaken spot? The tiny white cottage, huddled at the foot of the huge green wall of mountain, seemed a very symbol of loneliness.

"You know," he said. "It would be better, when these events are coming on, to move your wife in to some more accessible place."

"Move my wife?" The voice was shocked. "*Move* her?"

"Yes. Bring her in to the village. To some neighbour's. Surely someone would be only too glad to give her a room."

"Och," said the other, recovering speech. "She would never go. She would never think of being anywhere but in her own house. And who would do the work?"

"Someone will have to do it now."

"Och, yes, but——"

Evidently I've put my foot in it, thought the doctor. Some local taboo, I suppose. It's all damned fine: but here have I got to go a wild goose chase, get soaked to the skin, drowned maybe. . . .

"You know," he said. "It might in certain circumstances be very dangerous to wait out there. You might be obliged to move her. In which case it would be more sensible to move her while she is well than afterwards."

The other was silent for a moment. When he spoke, his voice was distant.

"As I was telling you, doctor, it has come upon her suddenly. We were not expecting it for a week or ten days."

The doctor cursed his inexperience. Now he had gone and offended the poor chap. Frightened him too, most likely. He kicked at the road, trying to be angry with his companion, but succeeding only in being angrier with himself.

It was lighter. The scud overhead was vaguely luminous.

"The moon is trying to get through."

"Aye, maybe."

They turned a corner, and saw dim shapes ahead of them which emerged as a rock, a small tree, and a jetty. The waves of the loch were slapping and splashing against the rock. There was more wind. A figure rose from the gloom, and confronted them. A voice asked a question in Gaelic.

"Aye."

"Good evening," said the doctor, stepping forward. He felt the need to assert himself.

"Good evening."

The neighbour's voice suggested that the doctor was a regrettable necessity, something impersonal, like medicine or sheep dip, which had to be secured, but was otherwise negligible. Without further word, he turned and led the way down to the boat.

It was not so dark by the loch's edge, and the young doctor noted once more the uncanny power of water to collect more light than there appeared to be in the sky. Even as he thought it, a sudden gust of wind made him stagger, and a shower of drops was flung in his face.

"There's plenty of wind, after all," he said ruefully, to no one in particular.

"Aye. There is wind enough."

The man who had fetched him was in the boat, feeling for something. The other stood on the jetty.

"Where shall I sit?" The doctor was anxious to show that he was not altogether a novice. "In the bows?"

There was a brief exchange of Gaelic.

"No. The waves are too big. They would come inside the boat."

"As you like. You'll want some weight in the bows, though, won't you, if we are heading into it?"

There was a silence. They don't like being told their business, thought the doctor. I don't care. I'm not going to have them treating me as a child. He planted his feet firmly against the wind, and leaned back, tilting up his face to the rain. The drops came, not steadily, but like a series of sharp, indignant backhanders. He heard a scraping noise, stooped, peered, and saw that his companions were putting a large stone in the bows.

"Now, doctor. If you will be so kind."

With the rain in his face, it was not easy to judge distance. As he hesitated, a hand reached up and grasped his. Angrily, he leaped down. The boat bounced and swayed. He all but fell over sideways, but the hand held him firm.

"Steady. There you are."

The doctor sat on the wet thwart. He stowed his bag safely underneath, hunched up his shoulders, pulled the ends of his mackintosh down over his knees, and braced himself to endure worse discomfort. That the crossing could be actively dangerous he did not believe. He had all a townsman's faith in the inevitability of getting where he wanted. His job was the important thing: it had to be done. He could not really conceive of any valid obstacle. He had never before failed to reach a case, and he was not going to fail now.

The boat was away. The shore, a vague blackness, receded, became a blur, and was lost. They were adrift in a grey universe, troubled, faintly luminous. The boat bobbed and bounced, the water slapped and gurgled. It was not so bad.

Then the rain, which had eased, was suddenly intensified. A squall took the boat, spinning her round like a shell. The rain came in sheets; the doctor had to bend his head to breathe. Three separate cold rivulets ran down his chest. A moment later, they were no longer distinguishable. He was soaked to the skin. He gasped, and looked up. The huddled figures before him were fighting to get the boat straight on her course. Grimly, doggedly, they dug their oars deep into the water, and with short, chopping strokes brought her round. A wave came and sat in the doctor's lap. He noticed it, with faint surprise.

Then, suddenly, things were easier. They were pulling left, to correct the error in their course. The boat was steadier. The rowers took longer strokes. The doctor stirred from his cramped posture, and felt his clothes move cold and wet against him.

"That's better," he ventured.

"Aye. We are under the lee of the island."

Peering to his right, the doctor thought he could see, not so much a shape, as an obstruction to the prevailing luminous greyness. It spread, and grew darker. Indefinitely, but perceptibly, the wind leaned away from them, and was lost overhead. The dark blur was suddenly very near. There was a sharp word from the man in the bow, and the boat jerked away at an angle.

The water was almost calm here. All around, the wind could be heard, with a crash like that of a perpetually breaking wave, but here there was the illusion of stillness. For the first time, the doctor could hear the hiss and tingle of rain upon the water.

The gloom began to recede upon the right. It was getting lighter. Something happened in the air above their heads. The rain whispered and stopped.

"Are we clearing the point of the island?"

"Aye. And the squall is passing."

The doctor stared ahead. Light was growing in the sky, vague, sickly, like a mildewy stain. As it spread, the shape of the island darkened, and the figures in the boat took on firm outlines. Turning his head, the doctor saw that they were quite close to the island. As he stared, the dark outline metamorphosed into a rock, a streak of dirty whitish sand, a rising bank, and the stems of trees. All came to ghastly life as he watched. Upon the tree stems, the rocks, the dripping bushes appeared odd mucous-like patches of pallor, so shamefaced that he did not at first recognise them as light. Puzzled as to their cause, he looked up, and saw the weak shape of the moon, like a false florin, fleeing sideways through an unhealthy haze that thinned as he watched. His eyes upon the reeling disc, he saw it pale, blur, darken, reappear: there was suddenly a great torn hole in the sky to the right of it, pricked by a star: something glittered beyond the bows: and the moon leaped out, laughing in triumphant brilliance. The diseased nightmare island had vanished, and in its place stood shining rock, winking jewelled bushes, and pine stems splashed with silver.

But he was given no time to admire the island. Hastily the two pulled across a little bay to the further point, whence they could see the strip of water, three quarters of a mile wide, which they had yet to cross. The sky was open now, but it would not be so for long. Away to the northwest was a vague unheaved mass, like a sheep's fleece, its edges combed and fluffed to an incredible softness. It looked motionless: yet, even as one watched, it was larger, and higher up in the sky.

The doctor looked over at the mountain. The summit was drowned in cloud, lit on the top to woolly loveliness, but dark and forbidding underneath. The cloud reached to half way down. At the foot, tiny, forlorn, could just be seen the white face of the cottage.

Between it and them lay a belt of beaten silver. Close to them, where the water was moderately calm, its motion could be seen. Near at hand were ripples. Farther out, the water felt the edges of the wind, and a current streamed sideways, thoughtful, with dark stipplings, in shape like a partly opened fan. Beyond that, where the waves leaped, all appeared static, a frozen band of tumbled silver crests. Only by the closest peering could he detect that it was in angry movement.

"We must make a run for it."

"We will not get there before it, Allan," said the neighbour.

"We must try. The next squall may be longer."

And, looking, the doctor saw that the fleecy cloud had risen enormously, and its mass was darker.

Settling down, the two men rowed hard, and drove the boat through the brief stretch of quiet water. The trees on the lee side of the island had been still. Now, before the boat felt it, they caught the wind, rolling and tossing in an agitation that, from below, seemed meaningless. Another few seconds, and the first whiff caught the boat. The water ruffled, and came at them sideways. The doctor felt cold jets of air squirt down his neck, reminding him that his underclothes were a sodden mass. He shifted on his seat, and looked ahead. The wind stiffened at each second. They would have to bear to the right, he saw, in order to take the waves bow on, and not be carried out of their course. Then they might——

Bump! With a shock so sudden he thought they had run on a rock, the first wave butted them under the bows. Another, and another: the doctor's knees were jerked upwards, the breath was shot from his lungs. He caught at the gunwale, and leaned forward, to avoid being tilted over on his back.

At first, it seemed impossible that the boat should live, let alone that she should make progress. To row was like trying to force the boat over broken ice, or up the side of a cottage. Yet the two maniacs went on pulling. The boat did not go down. Buffeted, jolted, bumped, the doctor tried to protect himself, to keep his bottom on the seat, to learn a rhythm which would allow him to breathe. Grasping the gunwale on each side, he tensed his muscles, dug in his heels, and tried by main force to press his buttocks down on the leaping thwart. It was so fantastically difficult that he almost laughed. Ride her, cowboy! A second, professional thought warned him swiftly that, at this rate, when they got to the cottage, his arms would be shaking and aching, and he would be as weak as a cat. Perhaps it would be better to relax, and—a biff that made him bite his tongue supplied the answer, and he sat, in mingled alarm and rage, his eyes filled with tears of pain.

When they cleared, he forcibly detached his attention from the boat, and tried to look ahead. It was not easy, for the boat reared like a bucking horse, and, as soon as he caught sight of the silvery expanse, the bodies of the rowers were thrown up at the sky and blotted it out. In fragmentary glimpses, he managed to see that, till it came near the boat, the surface had the same stiff, immobile look as from the island. At a distance, the crests of the waves were like bright, silver cabbages. Then, nearer, they seemed, all together, to lean forward, till suddenly one would leave the rest, swell, and fling itself with disproportionate fury at the boat. Some broke ahead, were split by the bow's blackness, and creamed by in rushing magnificence. Others got underneath the boat, threw up their heads, and seemed to knock her right up into the air, so that it was with a bruised astonishment that he found himself still on the surface at all. It was all mad, too mad to think about. The doctor gave up trying, and was gradually buffeted into a trance. He was aware of his surroundings, but of little else. The violent motion ceased to be unpleasant. He was emptied of all emotion, all reflection. The dazzling belt of water leaped and fell, leaped and fell.

Abruptly he came to himself. There was a change, a new force. Something was pressing against his right side, against the whole boat. He looked around, feeling the clothes wet against his neck. The water ahead was not so bright: it seemed to frown as he watched. Wind— more wind—blowing hard. He looked up, and saw with consternation that the woolly cloud had grown inconceivably, and was towering above them. No longer did it look soft and innocent. Even its edge, where the moon caught it, was an angry blur, with a smudge of pallor. Then the boat started to leap madly from side to side, like a terrified beast on a tether. A wave, ugly, grey, seen only an instant before its attack, broke over and into the bows. The boat struggled, trembled, shook itself, and rose heavily. Before it could recover, it had shipped water from two lesser waves.

Steadying himself with one hand, the doctor leaned forward, and groped beneath the seat.

"To your right, man, Your *right*."

He nodded, fumbled on the other side, found a pan, and, wedging himself as best he could, began to bale. The next few minutes were a painful dream. Somehow he managed to hold on, and keep one hand free for baling. He baled frantically. The first thing that had really frightened him was that stunned, sluggish feel of the boat as she tried to recover from the weight of water. While she was buoyant, tossing up and down like a cork, she was distinct from the water, victimised, but capable. But that slow wounded rolling—although his arm felt red hot, as if it was coming off at the shoulder, he kept the pan flying. He saw, in a shaft of moonlight, the almost continuous stream of water splayed out in the air.

Next time he noticed anything, he had stopped baling. It was dark. It was raining. A sickly ghost of moonlight retreated softly on their left, and was sucked up in grey, deepening darkness. But the boat was steadier. The waves were lessening. The wild jolting was over.

He decided to speak. It was an effort to recall how one did it: what muscles one moved. He opened his mouth twice before words came.

"What has happened?"

A spent voice gasped an answer.

"We are nearly there. Under . . . the shelter . . . the mountain."

The doctor was a mere heap of limbs and clothes. He sat upright, because that was the position into which his body had subsided. As, with each tired stroke of the oars, the water grew calmer, his interest returned. He remembered who he was, and the errand on which he was bound. God, he thought, I hope it's an easy case. If it's a forc., I'm done. I couldn't take the tooth out of a baby.

They were nearing the shore. The rain was falling heavily. Once again he could hear the tingle of the drops upon the water. A few seconds more, and the bow bumped violently.

"Hullo."

"We are forgetting ourselves."

"It would not do to sink her now."

The shaken voices were trying to jest. The strain was over. All they knew was that they were safe. With each instant, sense was returning. The doctor felt for his bag. It was still there. He grasped it, but, as he tried to rise, the boat rocked violently, and he sat down again. Allan had jumped out, and could be heard stumbling off inland.

Cautiously, the doctor got up.

"He is very anxious," he said, as he took the other man's hand, and stepped out on what felt like a rough stone slip.

"He has good reason. His wife is not too young, and it is the first child."

"Is it, by damn," said the doctor, with a chill at the heart.

He followed his companion up the slip, and felt his feet strike soft upon grass.

"It is all most unfortunate, and Nurse Ferguson not free to come. Will you be able for it, do you think?" The neighbour had evidently not much confidence in a locum.

Somehow, the question restored the doctor's good humour.

"I hope so," he said. "I've had a good many."

"Humph," said the other, and added, "It is a misfortune, her to be taken like this. Dr. Macdonald expected to be back from his holiday in good time for her."

The doctor grinned in the darkness. He respected this dour loyalty.

"He's an old man," he said. "How does he like trips of this sort?"

"Och," said the other. "He is well used to them. He has lived his life here."

The doctor looked up, and saw a faint light ahead. It was almost at once obscured, and the figure of Allan emerged from the gloom and grasped his arm.

"God be praised," he cried. "She is well. Nothing has happened yet."

You must forgive me, doctor, for running away from you like that. I could not be easy in my mind till I had a word with her. I did not wait. I only looked in at the door to ask."

"Of course," said the doctor. He had already forgotten the crossing and his discomfort. Professional enthusiasm rose, a thin, intense warmth in his chilled body.

"Well." The neighbour halted. "I will be going now."

"Bless you, man." Allan grasped his arm. "Bless you."

"Och, it is nothing. I will stand by, in the morning, in case you want me."

"Bless you." They shook hands forcibly. "Now, doctor."

The doctor, plodding stiffly in his sodden clothes, followed Allan to the cottage. He squelched with every step. Allan opened the door, and plunged in first. When the doctor came in, put down his bag, and started to peel off his dripping macintosh, Allan was bending over the bed in the corner.

"How are you, my darling? What a fearsome long wait for you. Oh, I am so thankful!"

"Was it terrible rough?" murmured the woman's voice. Then, as she touched his sleeve, "Och, Allan, you are drenched! You are drenched to the skin. Take off your clothes this instant. Doctor——" she raised herself, peering past the lamp into the gloom. "Make him take off his wet clothes."

The doctor grinned.

"Why," said Allan, reprovingly, "the doctor is in no better case. Indeed, he is worse. We had the exercise of rowing to keep us warm. He must be perished."

"To be sure," she cried. "Doctor, what will you be thinking of me! Get the doctor a dram. Give him a g——" She lay back suddenly, and groaned.

"My love!"

Allan bent over her in agony.

"It is all right." Her face was shining with sweat in the lamplight. She forced a smile. "Go on, now. Pour the doctor a good dram, and take one yourself."

"All in good time," said the doctor good-humouredly. "Let's have a look first, to see how things are. Excuse my costume," he added, for he had peeled off coat and waistcoat. "I don't want to drip over you more than I can help."

"Can I be of any use?"

"You can hold the lamp."

Allan held it, with averted head, biting his lip. Once the doctor asked him to bring it nearer. There was silence, save for a gentle question or two, and the sound of the woman catching her breath. Once she moaned, causing Allan to tremble and shake the lamp.

The doctor stood up. A flood of relief and satisfaction warmed him.

"All is quite as it should be," he announced. "Your wife is a wonderful woman, Mr.—— By the way, I don't even know your name."

"M'Kechnie. Allan M'Kechnie. You think it will be all right, doctor?"

His eagerness was pathetic. Obviously a man of strong reserve, he was utterly beaten down by his wife's ordeal.

"I do," said the doctor. "And now—what was that I heard about a dram?"

"Is there time?"

"Time and to spare. Nothing will happen for three or four hours yet."

"Of course there's time, you silly man," scolded his wife affectionately.

"In any case," said the doctor. "I prescribe a dram for us both." He wriggled. "I suppose you haven't a change of clothes you could lend me?"

Even in the lamplight, he could see Allan flush.

"I have only the one besides this, doctor, and it got wet yesterday, going to kirk. I doubt it is dry yet."

"It is not dry," said his wife.

There was a silence.

"I can't stay in these," said the doctor, half to himself.

"Allan," said his wife: and, as he bent over her, a whispered argument followed.

"Och, no."

"Och, yes."

"My wife says, would you mind putting on one of my nightshirts? They are good warm flannel."

"The very thing," cried the doctor. "I'll put my things by the fire, and, by the time they're wanted, they'll be dry. Or dry enough."

He went over to the fire, turned his back on the bed, and began to pull off the wet, clinging garments. Allan, standing carefully between him and the bed, handed him the nightshirt. Made of thick flannel, it was large as a tent.

"Here is a blanket, in case you feel the cold."

"Good." The doctor draped it round his waist like a kilt. "Unprofessional," he declared, looking down himself, "but effective."

He turned to Allan, who had begun to strip.

"What will you do?"

"I have my nightshirt too."

"But no kilt?"

"No kilt."

"I've pinched the only one. That's not fair."

Allan hesitated. He flushed again. "I thought, for the present, as nothing is happening——"

"Yes?"

"I might get into the bed."

"An excellent idea. You get in and keep warm. I'll sit by the fire."

"Will you be warm enough?"

"Grand."

Without paying him any more attention, the doctor pulled a chair to the fire, and methodically spread out his dripping clothes upon the hearth. There was, he noted with approval, a large kettle beside the fire. Presently he heard a creaking noise. Allan was cautiously getting into bed.

A long silence followed. For the first time since he had come in, the doctor became aware of the gale. He could hear it high overhead, rushing over the mountain, swooping on the loch in thunderous gusts. Its noise was like a memory. The cottage was sheltered, under the huge shoulder of the mountain.

He glanced around the room. It seemed to be the only room in the cottage. It did not take long to see that the M'Kechnies were poor. The furniture was of the plainest. Even the chair on which he sat was rickety. There was not much crockery on the dresser. Poor devils, he thought; stuck out in this God-forsaken place, getting a living the best way they can. The place was clean, though. After some of the homes he had visited, it was a paradise.

He stirred, and shivered. In spite of fire and dram, he was not too warm. He had got thoroughly chilled in the boat. To avoid sitting still, he rose, fetched his bag, and began to get everything out. It was too soon yet to do any more. He straightened up, and swung his arms across his chest.

There was a whispering in the bed. It sounded as if the wife was saying something which shocked Allan. She persisted. There was a silence. Then she spoke.

"Doctor."

"Yes?"

"Why don't you come into the bed, and keep yourself warm? There is plenty of room there beside Allan."

The doctor hesitated only for a second.

"An excellent suggestion," he said. "Thank you, Mrs. M'Kechnie. I will."

He shed his improvised kilt, and climbed in beside Allan. There was a short, embarrassed silence, which the doctor determined to break.

"Hark at that wind," he said. "We are better off here than out on the loch, eh?"

"Indeed we are." Allan's deep voice rumbled, surprisingly close to his ear. "We shall always be grateful to you for coming, doctor."

"Nonsense. It's all a new experience to me, Mrs. M'Kechnie. I come from the town. My usual night-call is to take a bus or a tram and walk a mile among tenements and things."

"I could never live in the city," declared Mrs. M'Kechnie. The words came with an effort. The doctor raised himself on one elbow.

"Turn over on your side," he commanded. "And get your husband to rub your back. Can you get at her? Is there room? Or shall I get out?"

"No, there is room."

"Rub hard," said the doctor. "You won't hurt her."

He lay down again, making as much room as he could. Allan's back was pressed against his side and he felt it move in steady rhythmic effort. Presently Mrs. M'Kechnie whispered something, and the rubbing ceased. She and Allan lay on their backs again.

The doctor stared at the ceiling, which loomed a faint orange in the glow of the fire. The whiskey crawled in his brain. He felt light again, as if his body were rising from the bed. His mind, detached and alert, perceived thoughts and images with stereoscopic clearness. How simple life was, when one approached it sensibly! He remembered half a dozen obscene stories in which this was the central situation, husband, wife, and stranger in the same bed. From what deep springs of life those stories rose. How earthy, how sane and direct their laughter, based on the eternal verities of human nature. Yet how remote were they from the present situation. Remote, because the very place was remote. Here, in this lost cottage, cut off from the world by gale and raging waters, there were no conventions, no precedents. A situation existed by its own right, and was met on its own terms. They were not bound here by any of the rules that regulated ordinary human contact, because there was nothing to which the rules could refer. Nothing could be less scandalous than this situation, which would be so wildly scandalous once it was taken across to the other side of the water. He smiled into the darkness, feeling in his heart a great compassion for the follies of mankind. Cautious, idolatrous, they made rules, they tried to pin down and systematise the unique flying moment. Poor, labouring fools! Right living was not obedience to rule: it was a balance, renewed each instant, like a tight-rope walker's, a tension between opposites. Here, for a moment, in this bed, in this cottage, in this tiny focus of life, beneath storm and towering sky, was wisdom. Men did not possess wisdom. It possessed them. Like a light, it flickered here and there over the vast dark mass of humanity, illumining briefly every now and then a single understanding. Here, for the moment, it possessed him; and by its light he gave thanks, and loved all men.

Then he must have fallen asleep, for the next thing he knew was that Allan was shaking his arm. Startled, he sat upright, and in a flash remembered.

"Doctor. Doctor."

"Right."

He was out of bed with a bound. A minute later he was telling Allan to boil the kettle.

"Half a minute." The doctor stood, in the grey filtering daylight, wiping his hands upon a towel. He had just finished bathing the baby. Allan was on his knees by the hearth. "You'd better let me do that. I'm a great cook. You mightn't believe it, but I am."

"Och, doctor." Allan's hands were still shaking, and his voice not under proper control. "You have done your share of work. It is my turn now."

"I want my breakfast right," said the doctor, grinning at him. "It doesn't matter who cooks it."

The crofter looked up at him, with an answering smile.

"I feel useless enough, as it is," he said. "You must not humiliate me any more, doctor. At least, I can prepare breakfast for you in my own house."

"I'm not so sure that you can." They laughed at one another affectionately, like old friends. The doctor laid down the towel. "I'll help you, anyway."

He went to the cupboard, and rummaged.

"What have we here? Coffee essence, or I'm seeing cross-eyed. You know, M'Kechnie, you are a man of rare discernment. I made sure I should have to take tea for my breakfast: and, to be frank with you, I abominate tea for my breakfast."

Allan's face beamed with gratification.

"We always like to have the coffee, for a special occasion."

"Well, if this isn't a special occasion, I'd like to know what is. And, talking of that—as it's such a *very* special occasion—do you think I might have a spot of what killed Auntie, just to keep me going till breakfast is ready?"

"A spot of—what killed————?"

Suddenly comprehending, Allan scrambled to his feet.

"Och, what has come to me. I am forgetting myself altogether."

He poured out the whiskey with shaking hand, one tumbler for the doctor, another for himself.

"We'll both be the better of it," declared the doctor. "And—a much more important matter—we must drink his lordship's health."

"We must indeed. And his mother's."

"And his mother's. You know, you're a lucky man, M'Kechnie. She was grand. I'm not saying it to flatter you. She was grand."

Allan, his eyes wet, looked lovingly over at his wife. She lay asleep, the beatitude of her face visible even in that twilight.

He could not speak.

"Here's to her," said the doctor, raising his glass. They drank deeply. "And here's to her son. He will be worthy of her."

"He will."

Allan's faith shone in his eyes. He did not hope. He knew.

"He will grow up fine and strong, and be a credit to his parents."

"He will."

The doctor leaned back his head. He felt the whiskey seize on his empty stomach, and let his mind soar on the winds of prophecy.

"He will be clever," he declared, waving his glass, "clever and able-minded."

"Aye." Allan nodded hard. "I plan a great education for him. He shall have the best schooling."

"And carry all before him."

"He shall go to the University."

"And win scholarships by the bucketful. Oh, he'll be a great man."

They drank again.

"And here's to you, M'Kechnie. Health and prosperity."

"And here is to you, doctor. I wish I could say what I am feeling."

"Nonsense."

The doctor laid a hand on his shoulder, then put down the glass. A dim shadow moved on the window. Allan started forward.

"It is Donald. He has come to know——"

He stumbled to the door, and the doctor heard him outside telling his neighbour the good news.

"Come in, come in."

"Och, no. I could not disturb Mistress M'Kechnie. I will come in later on."

Yawning, the doctor stooped over the hearth, and began to prepare breakfast. He felt suddenly tired and sleepy.

"He would not come in," said Allan, returning and shutting the door. "He will come back presently."

"Breakfast," said the doctor sleepily: and, forgetful of his boast, he sat back. smiling and blinking, to watch the other get it ready.

Three hours later, they took leave of one another at the loch side.

Donald had come, and had been persuaded to take a peep at mother and child—he held his breath, and drew back, as if they might explode in his face. Now he was going to row the doctor back. The storm had gone. It was a lovely, sunny morning, with small, soft clouds flying high up in a clean sky. There was still some wind, and the loch, its ruffled surface straining away from them, was the colour of gunmetal.

"I'll send the nurse over to-day."

"Will she be free yet, do you think?"

"Oh yes. I'll take on, if she isn't. And I'll come over myself again to-morrow afternoon."

"Och, doctor, don't trouble yourself."

Courtesy struggled with natural solicitude in his voice.

"No trouble, man. It's a pleasure—besides being my plain duty. Mind you, she'll be right as rain. But I'll come."

"It is good of you, doctor. It is indeed."

"On one condition," said the doctor.

He yawned as he spoke.

"I beg your pardon?"

"I'll come on one condition."

"What is that?"

"That you give me at least two cups of that splendid coffee."

"Indeed, doctor, but you shall have a kettleful."

They stopped, and shook hands. Donald, his austere countenance a little relaxed, looked on.

"Well, doctor, good-bye, and God bless you."

"God bless you, old man."

They wrung one another's hands in silence. The doctor suddenly found his eyes full of tears. Hardly able to see where he was going, he clambered into the boat. Donald pulled away. The doctor screwed round to wave. Allan stood for a minute, waving, watching the boat. When the doctor looked again, he had turned, and was making his way quickly back towards the cottage. Its whitewashed face shone, small and innocent, in the morning sun.

76

The Trapper's Mates

BY HENRY WILLIAMSON

FOR the generations jackdaws that goister round the battlements of d'Essantville Castle have watched hounds leaving kennels four days a week in soft weather from November to April. The little viscounts of the House are blooded almost before they can walk; and they can ride long before they have learnt to talk (alternatively with the beautiful West Country dialect) the peculiar slang, which, changing with every generation, is curiously called King's English; and they die before they learn to spell, but that is nothing to do with the way they hunt the fox. The first thing a future Master learns after his personal servant has buttoned the fawn-coloured cloth gaiters up his baby legs, and set him in the wicker basket-chair on the back of a Shetland pony, is that the fox is hunted *as a gentleman*.

The term is both actual and metaphorical. The fox is permitted to live during eight months of the year under the patronage of the great landowner. Any extravagances of taste which would bring an ordinary man before the magistrates—such as the killing of another man's hens —is tolerated. The fox's gentlemen friends will pay the cost, and he goes free. Like all gentlemen, however, he has his obligations. Certain things are expected of him. He must show sport when called upon by his Lordship's huntsman to do so any time during the daylight, Sundays and Christmas Day excepted, between the beginning of November and the end of March. If, after a long hard chase, he can run no more, but grows stiff, so that hounds catch him and break him up, he is a "good fox." If he skulks in woods, if he won't run, if he hides behind badgers in the deep earths, or otherwise tries to survive, he is a "bad fox."

But what can be said of a fox who behaved as though the Hunt existed only for his own pleasure. A fox who, if a meet was fixed at Lashingcot Brake, would probably be there; as he attended the meets at

Doves Moor, Skilgate, Five Cross Ways, Smoky House, Hibbert's Folly, and Hanging Woman Spinney? That is what the bobtailed fox was wont to do. Naturally, he had a right to be in those places, and at any time, the Hunt Secretary told me, after my first day's hunting with the d'Essantville pack; but this fox had the damned impertinence to appear when another fox was being chased, and deliberately to draw hounds —unless the whipper-in happened to be well up with them—after himself. And when this fox had had, apparently, all the selfish enjoyment he wanted, he disappeared. Time after time he spoiled the huntin', declared the Secretary, interfering with the hounds' legitimate desire for blood, leading them after himself, and vanishing at a certain field, just inside the western boundary of the d'Essantville country, called Cockabells. There was a League for the Prohibition of Cruel Huntin', Fishin' and Shootin', but what about one for the Prevention of Cruelty to Hounds which needed Blood, what?

I concluded that the Secretary placed me among what he despised as the "sentimentalising public," and that his light humour was as a kindness to one who had been publicly roared at by the Master.

You may imagine how this fox interested me. How could he know when the hounds were meeting at these places? I spoke to many people about him. To some followers, particularly among the young and unworldly-wise, I gathered that he was a creature of charm and mystery, whose continued existence was regarded with affection and delight; to others, he was a bore and a nuisance, to be gotten rid of as quickly as possible—in the only way in which a fox should die, it must be understood. The reader may be able to decide which of the two types possesses the better mind for the governing of our great people. And if this makes you snort (as his Lordship snorted at me) the snort is your answer, and you will be unable to enjoy the story of this extraordinary fox, whose early history I learned after the first time I hunted him, when I was reclining, as flat as I could get, in an armchair in the parlour of an inn called *The Moon in the Mere.*

It was my third glass of bullace wine, and it appeared to me then to be the funniest thing I had seen, the wrath and snort on the Master's face because I had said that surely the fox deserved his life after such a fine run. Outside the winter sky was dull, before me a fire of beech logs burned, warming the soles of my boots from which ruddy steam arose as the mud dried on spur and leather. Delightful to stretch one's legs after the chase, holding one's fourth glass of bullace wine, while 'baccy smoke strays past the nostrils from the bowl of the old briar pipe held loosely in teeth and resting on crumpled stock. Blackie in stall wisped and feeding, a ten-mile hack home in the dark, a bath, change, and food afterwards. Lolling in the chair I watched the sluggish ruby flame flickering in my bullace wine—I swear that the best sloe-gin in the West Country is made by the landlord of *The Moon in the Mere*.

I was about to call for another glass when a man entered, and sat heavily on the settle, after bidding me good evening. Seeing my kit, he asked me if I had been out with his Lordship's hounds. I recognised him as a pig-farmer, a member of the Long White Lop-eared Pig Society, and a prizewinner at the last show. He was a big red-faced man, jovial like one of his clean beasts, of whom he was very fond and proud. I had noticed him during the run that morning, for he rode a piebald gelding 17 hands high that carried him with magnificent ease. "And I'm no ladybird neither, am I?" And he confessed, after a sorrowful tipping of the pewter pot, that he rode at "twelve score"—two hundred and forty pounds. "Too much, too much," he sighed. "But they say a man takes after the things he has most to do with. Ah, well. Landlord, another pint for me, and a pint for this gentleman."

"Yes, sir, I'll bring a lamp in a moment, gentlemen."

I asked the farmer if he knew why the fox had a tag instead of a brush. Perhaps he had been caught in a trap?

"No, it wasn't a trap," he said, leaning forward to stare at one of his boots. The girth of the leg seemed to depress him. He tapped it with the handle of his whip.

"Chopped off by a hound?" I suggested, when I had allowed him enough time to consider his enormous calf.

"No, one of my boars bit it off when he was a cub. He disappeared afterwards."

The grandfather clock ticked on. The drinks were brought, and when we had proposed and drunk each other's health, I ventured to ask him more questions; and he told me the circumstances of the cub's birth, and its early life history; and the pictures which his facts made in my mind, I will try and make in words, as now follow.

Bobtail's mother was the littlest vixen that ever leapt from shelf to shelf in the disused apple-cellar of George Cog, the gamekeeper. Indeed, she was so small that she was able to hide up the flue when they came to bag the foxes.

The country of the d'Essantville Hunt had many deep earths, both of badger and fox. When hounds drew the thick North Side wood there was never a screaming *Gone Away!* The foxes knew too much to break covert. They slunk about the wood, dozens of them. They preyed on the game birds in the coverts to such an extent that it was necessary to destroy them. Many were shot and trapped by George Cog, but more ran free; and the hunt agent made a bargain with the keeper, which was that he would pay the keeper half a guinea for every runnable fox or vixen dug out and handed over to him.

In turn the keeper made a bargain with Tom Cockerlegg, an elderly unmarried man who earned his living by wiring and trapping rabbits in the winter, the right of which he bought from several farmers by working for them in the summer without wages. Tom Cockerlegg agreed to receive from the keeper five shillings for every uninjured fox or vixen brought to the apple-cellar by the cottage in the wood.

There are hunting men in the d'Essantville country, and his lordship is one of the most emphatic, who declare that a fox has no sense of fear, because its limited intelligence cannot formulate the idea of death: that the terror of annihilation, of ceasing to be, is unknown by animals. But there are many fears, and the greatest fear of a wild animal is when it is trapped or caged. One evening there were nine foxes in the confined darkness of the apple-cellar. All night they sat on their haunches with restless sweeping of brushes, leaping upon the mildewed shelves, pacing the floor of trodden earth and cowdung. The smallest noise from outside quieted every movement. Ears were cocked, brushes stilled, breathing ceased, noses quivered. In one corner sat Fang-over-lip, a dog-fox with points of long upper canines showing over closed mouth. He was the most cunning fox in the West Country, the most experienced, and therefore he felt fear more than the others.

When footfalls of men sounded afar, he sprang up and leapt on the lowest shelf. A key was put into the padlock, and turned. The lock was lifted off the staple, the door opened a few inches, and the keeper looked in.

The rank taint of warm foxes, like hops drying in an outhouse, made him spit. Behind him stood Tom Cockerlegg, the trapper, with lantern, sacks, string, and thorning gloves. Cockerlegg spoke to a grey sheepdog, his constant companion. "Lie down, you." She sat down outside, obediently. Both men entered, and shut the door. The eye-pupils of the foxes were pale green slits glowing in the lantern light. Lips writhed back from teeth in silent snarls. They waited. Neither of the men lost his stolidity. While George Cog held the lantern and a sack Tom Cockerlegg grasped the brush of the nearest fox. It struggled and twisted and kicked while it was being pushed and shaken into the sack, which was tied up.

The keeper missed the ninth fox, and peering with the lantern he saw the white tag of her brush up the flue. She had scrambled there in terror. He pulled the brush, but could not shift her. He felt for her leg, lifted the pad off the stonework, and jerked. She yelped, and fell on the floor, trying to bite and lick the pain in the joint which was dislocated. Later in the morning the kennelman drove up with a cart and she was slung up with the others and taken a journey made painful with jolts. The journey ended at the kennels, where several hounds were singing while they waited for the two whippers-in who exercised them in the summer. Soon the corn would be cut in the fields, and woodland cub-hunting begin. The little vixen was only a cub, and she was spared a worry in the dewy morning, for Charlie Tarr gave her to the pig-farmer, who bound and bathed the injured limb, and made it sound again. He tended her with regular care and after a few weeks she grew tame and friendly, answering to the name of Judy. She slept at night in the garden, wearing a dog-collar to which a chain was hooked. Dur-ing the day he unfastened the chain, and she used to go into the house and curl up by the fire. Like many countrymen, the farmer rarely listened to the songs of birds wild in their native air, but the twitters of a goldfinch, caught and caged, his property, gave him pleasure. He had one in his sitting-room, and during the many hours that Judy played before the fire, or leapt upon his lap, the bird was filled with terror. The vixen watched it continually, and people coming in to see him on busi-ness or in friendship were usually treated to the sight of the finch fall-ing off its perch in a temporary paralysis of fright—the sweetest singers are always the most nervous.

It was a green winter that year, and one night in January, as he was getting into bed, the breeder of long white lop-eared pigs heard Judy hooting. The cry was unmistakable. Three barks, higher in tone than a terrier's, sharper, shorter, and joined. He listened again, but it was not repeated, and soon he fell asleep. The next night was lit by the moon, and he heard Judy hooting again. For some minutes he watched at the window, for he had heard the answer of a dog fox. He saw nothing. The next morning he moved the kennel nearer the house, and in the moonlight of the third night a lean grey thing stole down the orchard, and disappeared in the black shadow of an apple-tree. This was Fang-over-lip, who sat there a long time. He moved sufficiently to keep the shadow always upon himself. He sat there so long that the farmer grew tired of watching, and went to bed.

Fang-over-lip came soon after owl-light the next night, but he did not linger in any shadows, although the nearness of the house made him uneasy. As he crept nearer his nose sought the smells of danger. He sat outside Judy's kennel, but she would not come out. She lay down in the straw of the kennel, watching him. He suddenly fled, alarmed by the sight of the farmer moving at the window. He must have re-turned again, for the next morning when the farmer took her a bowl of food, he found plover's feathers in the kennel. Judy slept all that day; and the goldfinch twittered to the birds seen through the window. Early the next night Judy was outside the kennel, and hooting for Fang-over-lip. The farmer did not see him return, but in the morning he found one of his own hen's feet in the kennel.

"The cheek of it. Would you believe it, sir, but that fox had left my fowls alone until the night of his final visit!"

Clicketting time was long past when the daffodils peered in their beauty from the grass under the apple-trees. When the first white wild violets bloomed in the hedge, the farmer took a ferreting spade and dug a hole in the gravel pit in the meadow, and Judy scratched it deeper. One day he took off her dog collar, patted her affectionately, and turned her loose. Two days afterwards she scraped at the kitchen door, and jumped up at him, licking his hand. He knew that she was asking for food, and gave her a basin of porridge, with cream in it, which she ate hungrily. A cooked rabbit was next given her, she cracked it up, gave him a sly look, and with a sweep of her brush ran back to her cubs in the gravel pit.

Regularly she came for food, and for the first fortnight she returned after a meal. Then she began to loiter and even to curl herself by the fire, watching the goldfinch that could not accustom itself to her bright hard eyes. After the third week she seemed inclined to spend all the day from the cubs, and the farmer had to put her out of doors, bidding her return and nourish them. And one morning while she was eating he saw five cubs sitting in the long grass below the bank, where nettles grew over the wilted white violets. They were dark brown and furry, and their blue eyes peered at their mother. The farmer went slowly to them, and four turned into the nettles, and hid themselves. One remained, and tried to bite the hand that picked him up. It was carried to the scullery, and, given bread-and-milk, it tried to bite that instead of a hand.

Again the next morning the five cubs sat in a row before the nettles, wondering where their mother had gone. When the bold cub saw the farmer, it ran unsteadily to him, and was fed on porridge. On the third morning while the mother and cub were eating, and the pig-farmer was inside the house, a lumbering white animal trotted round the corner of the wall, so frightening Judy that she made off. The alarming animal was a boar, and at the scent of fox it snorted angrily. The cub went into a rabbit hole underneath a holly tree, but the boar bit the bone of his tail as he scrambled down. When the farmer returned the pig was goaded to its sty. Judy did not return that day, and when the next morning she did not come for her breakfast the farmer went to the gravel pit and dug out the earth. "It was empty, sir."

My companion in the fire-comforted parlour of *The Moon in the Mere* had aroused my curiosity about the disappearance of the vixen, when the door opened and a hand came into the room. Then a squeaky voice begged his honour's pardon, and the hand was withdrawn. I saw a single eye beyond it, in the gloom, staring straight like an owl's eye.

After a moment the hand returned, an earthy hand, knobbed, raw, and thick. The fingernail of the index finger was half an inch longer than the others, a repulsive pale length of chipped horn. Then came a felt hat, the band of which was rotted to tatters, and a face. The shaggy hair, the thick eyebrows, and the tangled moustache were like autumn bracken. The man wore a celluloid collar, worn and flaked, but I could see that when new it had been a striped affair of black and white and red lines. The man peered about until the wandering eyes fixed on me, then he squeaked again, "I beg your honour's pardon." I hastened to tell him that we were not having a private talk, and begged him to come by the hearth. He sat on the settle, and fingered a short clay pipe. His coat was faded to the hues of bark and earth and lichen, so were his trousers. After a wondering scrutiny of my form in the chair he said, "I beg your honour to excuse me, but have you had good sport, your honour?"

"Your friend the bobtailed fox, Tom," replied the farmer. Bracken-brows scowled.

"Wait till I catch that there beggar," he squeaked, staring at the ashes in his pipe bowl. "I'll give he a knock on the head, won't I now?"

He tried to light the ashes in his pipe, and shook his head when the match went out. Promptly he took the tobacco pouch I offered him. Perhaps he was waiting for someone, for he pulled out a large brass watch from his pocket, levered open the back with the nail, and continued to fill his pipe while holding the watch in the same hand.

"This be Tom Cockerlegg," explained the pig-farmer. "He doesn't seem over fond of Bobtail. For why," he added with a chuckle, "I can't imagine."

It was a curious sight, the angry and violent expression in the large hairy weather-roughed face of the trapper contrasted with the puling pipe of the squeaky voice. He stared at me while he declared that Bobtail followed him as he used his long net on windy moonlit nights, less than two hundred yards away. He would hear the cry of a caught rabbit, but before Bess or he could get there, the "varx would have'n out of the net."

"Bess here, her baint no good to catch'n," squeaked the wild man of the rabbit buries, pointing with the horrible nail of his lumpy forefinger. How many tons of earth and iron had the trapper handled?

"Her's runned after un many times."

"Bobtail's too fast without a brush," said the massive member of the Long White Lop-eared Pig Society.

"Darnee, if Bess baint no good, they varx dogs baint no good neither!" retorted Cockerlegg. He began to laugh, an absurd and feeble cackling, while he continued to fill his pipe. It seemed to take him a long time.

He saw me looking at it, and returned the pouch promptly. It was half empty, and it had been full. The farmer winked at me, and said,

"What be time, Tom Cockerlegg?"

"It baint closing time yet, midear," replied Tom, and fixed his owlish eyes on my pint pot.

"Will you have a drink?" I asked, when the watch had gone back into its pocket.

"Thank you, your honour," he replied immediately, and knocked loudly on the table for the landlord, who came, and returned with a quart of beer, which Tom had ordered almost before the door was opened.

Bess the sheepdog was a beautiful animal. She had long woolly grey hair, a noble head with contemplative eyes. She leaned against the trapper's legs, and he pushed her away with a hobnailed boot. I patted my knee, but she would not come to me, preferring to sit by the foot that had spurned her. She regarded her master's face with grave and watchful patience.

I wanted to hear what had become of the cub under the holly tree.

"You were saying just now that the earth in the gravel pit was deserted after the scare Judy had from the boar. Did she ever come back for food?"

The pig-farmer shook his head.

"What happened to the cubs?"

"They must have died without the mother. Two days afterwards she was found in a gin set by a rat-run in a cornfield. Died of lockjaw. Tom found her, and brought her to me. I've got her stuffed in a glass case: we put it on a table opposite the goldfinch. And you'll hardly believe this, but it's as true as I'm sitting here. The constant sight of a stuffed fox killed my singing bird. It died of fright, did that bird. I was very fond of it, too, as I'd had it from the nest. You'd hardly believe it, eh?"

I said something, but not what I thought. These good countryfolk, unimaginative . . . sad little sun-singer beating the bars.

Presently I asked, "Then is Bobtail the cub grown up, the cub that had hidden under the holly tree?"

"Ah, now your asking me one. You see, not knowing that Judy was dead, I didn't bother to dig it out, thinking that she would call it out in the evening. Perhaps she did call it out, and with the others went on the prowl—but I don't know, they were too small. Tiny creatures, like kittens, they were."

"Barbt'l baint much like a kitten to-day!" said the trapper in squeaking fury. "Wait till I clitch on to he!"

I imagined that the earthy creature was upset by the thought of sixpences he had lost. A ten-mile hack home awaited me. I rose, and

stretched my legs. Cockerlegg was peering at me through the dry ferns
of his eyebrows as though I were a being far superior to his humble
self. But he was only waiting to borrow my lighted match.

In the stable, Blackie, the soft-mouthed, greeted me with a whinney,
and the groom unstrapped the rug. We set out for home. There were
stars shining in the water of the ditches, and the wind passed in the
darkness.

Three days afterwards I walked and trotted Blackie to the meet at
Smoky House, a thatched inn at the joining of three roads. Charlie Tarr
the huntsman was going to draw Scythe Wood. His Lordship was heard
to exclaim to a friend that it *ought* to be a good scenting day, but of
course, one could never tell. The keen blue eye of the Master had noted
that no hound had rolled on the wayside grass, or bitten a blade. No
gossamer floated on the air, and no spider webs were yet spun on the
hedges. The paving stones of the courtyard had shown sweat that
morning, the air was clear and light, and, most significant of all, hounds
had smelled strongly as they trotted out of kennels. There was no wind.

Nimrod was out to-day, the pad of his near forepaw healed. It had
been cut by a broken glass bottle on Pippacott Common. He was the
best hound in the country. His puppies were famous in the Quorn and
the Pytchley, the V.W.H. and the Duke of Beaufort's. An American
sportsman had offered five thousand dollars for him, but no money
would buy Nimrod. His head was light and dignified, he had a long
clean neck, without looseness or throatiness, his ears were set low and
close to the head. His muscular back was straight and wide, his chest
was deep, his shoulders long and sloping, his forelegs white and straight
as mushroom stalks, his feet round and catlike. Strong and straight
hocks for tireless running, a stern carried gaily upwards, and a tongue
true as its music. Three young hounds were licking his head as he stood
on the triangle of sward before the inn, watching the eyes of the huntsman.

While I was looking at the faces above the gleaming coats of horses
around me, I heard a squeaky voice saying, "Good morning, your lordship's honour, and I hope you'm very well, midear." Turning round, I
saw Tom Cockerlegg grab his tattered hat from off his head, and with
the horny finger touch his brow to the Master above him.

"Mornin,' Tam, mornin,' " replied the Master, as he fingered his
bristly moustache. He was a short fierce tubby little man, and his intimate friends called him Seal.

The horny finger beckoned. The Master leant over.

"If your Lordship's honour will excuse me, but please to listen, my lord, there be a turrible lively varx (fox) in Smoky Wood, a monster girt varx I can't abear, for it steals all my rabbuts, my lord, and I were so near to un last dimmity (twilight) I could have dapped un on the head, surenuff, if your Lordship's honour will excuse me telling of ee."

"Us'll r-r-roll'n over for ee, one day!" cried the Seal on horseback, in a hearty voice. "Don't ee worry, midear."

Tom had taken his Lordship birdnesting when he was a boy, and they were good friends. Then the trapper beckoned, the Master leant down again, and Tom whispered, "Yurr, you! Yurr! Has your Lordship's honour a bit o' baccy? I haven't had a smoke for a week and more. Too poor, my lord, 'tis Bobtail, my lord, taking all my rabbuts."

Out came the pipe, and the big brass watch. Now I knew why the fingernail was kept so long. Cunningly it levered open the back of the watch; and his Lordship's tobacco, the expensive John Cotton, was pushed and rammed with amazing speed into the watch, which was empty of works, and but a hollow box.

"Thank ee my lord, thank ee midear," said Tom, giving back the oilskin pouch to the Master, and looking at the face of the watch. "It be half-past ten o'clock a'ready, my lord!" and he hurried away to the van of the rabbit agent, which was collecting rabbits from farm and cottage to take them to the station.

Huntsman Charlie blew a note on his horn. Whipper-in called names of hounds. We moved off down one of the roads, and up a lane. "Follow me," said the pig-farmer.

Just before eleven o'clock Nimrod entered Scythe Wood at the north-eastern end, followed by Thunderer, Doomsday, Firefly, Solway, Duchess, and Guardsman. The pig-farmer and I waited behind a cattle shed from where we could observe a gap in the western point of the Scythe, by a lightning-burned stump of an ash-tree. "The best place," he said. "If a fox is at home, he'll leave at this end. We must keep pretty quiet."

"Do you think Bobtail is here?" I asked.

"Tom Cockerlegg says he saw him last night, coming out."

I had to soothe Blackie, for the cries of huntsman and whip could be heard faintly in the wood. Immediately the pigeons flew out of the oaks. We waited. The last pigeon had clattered out and the wood had been silent for about a minute, when a jay started to scream, in the querulous and sustained manner which I recognised as the call to other birds when man is not the enemy. My companion looked at me significantly. "Quiet, Blackie, quiet," I whispered, pulling the ears of the restless horse. A family of longtailed tits flitted down the hedge, hanging upside down to search the bud-coverings for insects, and calling to each other with tiny cries which made a gossamer-link of sound in the winter morning. The jay kept up its scolding. Was a fox on his pads? A dead stick snapped in the woods, and I could hear a hound going through the undergrowth.

I whispered, "Have you any idea how the fox seems to know where hounds will meet?"

He shrugged his shoulders, meaning that he didn't know.

"Shsh!" he warned.

A hound whimpered in the wood. A blackbird scuttled away down the hedge, and dived into the leafy ditch.

"That was Nimrod speaking. Hark!"

Other hounds were whimpering.

"That's Bobtail. I know the line he'll take to get to Cockabells. He'll run the bottoms, where it's thick stuff, and boggy, and take a sweep round through Pippacott Wood, and come out by Turberville Common. You follow me."

He whispered this rapidly. Nimrod spoke again.

"Don't make a sound. He'll be out and away in a flash."

Blackie stood still. Sometimes his withers shivered. He who had been striving to shake the bits from his mouth, and half-playfully to rid himself of the irksome girths, saddle, and, perhaps, the two-legged encumbrance astride his back, now was taut from ears to cannons. A centaur stood under the hazels. Nimrod threw his tongue, the horn sang in the trees, the thrilling clamour of a find sent the blood faster. I felt light as the sunlight.

A brown leaf moved on the bank, and I was looking into the mask of a fox eight feet away from me. It looked boldly at me, without the least fear, and I had the extraordinary thought that the mind behind the glance was equal with my own. But whereas my knees trembled with excitement, the fox was calm, and a little amused. Then it turned to look over its shoulder, and listen to the hounds. I saw its eyes a moment later, and they were laughing. Yes, as a dog laughs in play with its master. The yellow eyes laughed, and blinked; and then it was gone, but not before I had time to notice that a leather collar, with brass studs on it, was fastened round its neck.

There was no time to wonder. The pig-farmer let out a series of bellowing "Tally Ho's." Hound music filled the wood. Then, among the trees, *Ton-ton-ton-tavern, Ton-ton-ton-tavern, Ton-ton-ton-ton-ton-ton-tavern!* The hill on our left turned back a faint echo of the Gone Away. Horsemen waiting on the higher ground moved down at a canter. The pack broke through the undergrowth, and streamed over the bank by the burnt ash, led by Nimrod. He jumped from the bank, his larger pads slurring the track of Bobtail. Blackie reared and neighed as I held him back. Hounds dropped over the bank. Blackie danced, pranced, and fought for his head. Quiet, Blackie, quiet! Let hounds go first.

When the last hound had left the wood, Charlie came over, his chestnut climbing like a cat and changing feet as it jumped. "It's Bobtail!" yelled the farmer, and added the weight of his "Yoi, yoi, on little dogs," to the marvellous and screaming cheer of Charlie Tarr. Blackie shot forward at a gallop—too much spirit for your heart, my dear, you must be held at a canter. He shook his head, the clods flew behind us, the hounds streamed before us, and two fields away went Bobtail. Hounds ran like a string of black and brown and white beads which had broken, but not scattered.

Bobtail leapt up the farther bank as Nimrod leapt down into the stubble of the field called Broadwall. He was going at nearly his fastest pace, but he did not fear. As he ran, many smells crossed his way. The smell of flat-poll cabbages, whose outer leaves were decaying, lay like an air-covering all around the field. Mingled in this still layer were the smells of rats, of tar, and of men. Squeezing under a gate he came into a field where two men were putting down tar into the the holes of rats. A terrier was watching the hole, with bent head. Bobtail ran quietly down the hedge, and then up, through a row of flat-polls a few yards south of the ratters. As he passed them they heard the hounds, and stood upright. Bobtail got to the opposite hedge without being seen, and he gained a field while the pace slackened among the cabbages, for the hounds were confused by the smell of tar, and (possibly) by the yapping of the terrier struggling in the arms of her master. Nimrod took them on, and down the next field to the impassable "bottom," where among thorns, bracken, brambles, and marsh rushes, we could not follow.

I followed the pig-farmer and the huntsman. We went through gates and down lanes and over meadows, splashing through watery gaps which the hooves of the field far behind would soon beat into yellow mud. We crossed the main road, and cantered across several fields, coming to a small track green with sward in a rough heathland of gorse and heather. This was an old Roman road, which was used now only by carters. Here we waited, and dismounted in order to save our horses as much as possible for what was coming.

The beams of the sun were not yet warm enough to dry the dew from the sere heads of the carline thistles, and scent would be thick for their following. I was lighting a cigarette when the tongueing of the pack floated up from below the common. Almost immediately I saw Bobtail again. He was racing across a stubble field about half a mile away. The huntsman vaulted in the saddle, and was galloping downhill before I could get my left foot into the iron. Blackie stamped and snorted, and was off at a canter and then a gallop while I was lying across his back. Somehow I got my seat, and with flying irons we thudded down the swarded track. A brook ran over stones at the bottom, and this we hurtled over, and turned right-handed round a big hawthorn that clawed face, hat, boot, and coat.

Other riders appeared over the brow of the common, and got between the pig-farmer and myself. The mud of their hooves fell on my face. The pack was running without a straggler—as Charlie said afterwards, you could almost have laid a rug over them as they crossed a root-field, and covered all except the muzzle of Nimrod and the flag of Juniper. They swam the wimpling waters of the Fawley brook, and crashed through a "bottom," and over a field where a white Minorca was kicking a crazy dance beside its head. (Another claim for the Hunt agent.) Bobtail ran the lane for six hundred yards, past a cottage where a woman was hanging out a washing on the hedge, along a ditch and through a row of elms, and so to the soft brown earth of the Big Wheatfield. As he raced up the southern hedge a fox rose and slunk away from his bed in the centre; and in the northern hedge he sat and watched the hunt go by; and when the last horseman had gone, he stole back to this bed, and slept, for he was Fang-over-lip.

Bobtail ran on, Nimrod three hundred yards behind him, and Juniper three hundred and eighty. Five of us galloping across Hangman's Mash half a mile behind—huntsman, whip, pig-farmer, a girl riding astride, and I—and the Master cantering on the high road over and below the ridge a mile behind, at the head of a straggling cavalcade of fifty men and women.

It was a glorious chase. Charlie Tarr led, then the pig-farmer, then the whipper-in, the girl, and I came last. Through a gate, over more stubble, driving up three partridges with a whirr of wings into the air. A great bullfinch; I rammed my hat down on my ears. Steady, Black, old boy! Two were over, and then the whip's chestnut refused.

He forced his head round, swung back again, banged his heels into its muddy flanks; it turned away, he cried curtly, held its head straight, and clapped his boots against its flanks. I saw its muscles ridge and tighten. The man held its head straight to the tall black ragged hedge, it gathered itself together, its forelegs threw themselves up, it seemed to hang still, then crash; he was through. The hound-music was far away. Then the girl was over—her horse down on its knees. It stumbled, recovered, blundered. Somehow she pulled up its head, and cantered away over the stubble. It was my turn. Give Blackie his head, I thought hotly, he knows his job, and needs no spur. A tremendous bullfinch, dark and thick and thorny, and I'm tall, and that branch of the crab-apple tree will smack my forehead, and perhaps catch my chin, and that will be the end of me, unless I'm dragged a mile or so first. Lord, I'm a funk. He who hesitates at the take-off is assuredly lost! Grip with the calves, tuck the toes in, and give Blackie his head. 'Ware that branch! Up! Reins across withers, throw yourself on his neck. . . . My eyes closed themselves, before the sudden-big thorns—crash, rip, bang! My topper was gone, but not my neck, thank God, and Blackie was sinking to his knees, so very gently, it seemed, and the grass rose slowly as I curled off his neck and rolled clear. A nice toss. Dear old Blackie-boy, I think I cried, as I picked myself up, and took the iron off my boot. Quaking and hot and happy, I fixed the strap along the safety-bar under the saddle-flap, hopped round on my right toes with my left leg up, and foot through iron, muttering, Stand, you swine, stand! to the excited and high-stepping hunter. He stood still for a moment, I threw my-self across the saddle, and he hurled himself round and was off at a gallop. I had to shake free my left foot while leaning on the seat of the saddle, while nearer and nearer the ditch and low white-thorn hedge of the next field approached. The easy and smooth motion of the gal-lop enabled me to throw my leg over and get my seat, just before we rose in the air and the loose swinging irons clanged dully against my boots. On, and on! I was only one field behind Charlie's holly-red coat. Blackie's heart and wind were splendid, and I shouted a sort of song to the beat of his hoofs. Lord, I was happy.

Soon the ground sloped up, and over another hedge was the Big Wheatfield, rising to the skyline. In this expanse of harrowed clods and flints stood an object wearing a broken bowler, a ragged tarpaulin, and split trousers. It barred the fox's way with open arms. Or it may have been welcoming him. It had a whitey-green face fixed in a ghastly grin. A claypipe was in its mouth. Its head was sprouting through the crown of its hat, in a thick yellow green curl. Its only companion hung upside down beside it, tied by a leg to a stick. Like itself, this companion was eyeless. It was a dead rook, beside a scarecrow. As Bobtail fled past, he disturbed three dying flies which had been sitting for warmth on the paper-white face of the shot bird. Straight the fox ran, through Crow-starver's Spinney on the ridge, and down the right-of-way to a field called Chowles Park. Over another field, in view of a cottage out of which ran half-a-dozen children.

"Marm! Marm!" one was still shouting to his mother as I passed. "Yurr be the varx-dogs! Come, yurr, marm, come yurr to once, marm!"

Mother had been salting-in half a pig, and she hurried to the threshold with salt on her raw hands and dragging Parson's wife's old brogue shoes on her smaller feet. She faded out of the tail of my eye. I could see the fox running along a hedge three fields in front. About two hun-dred yards separated Nimrod's nose and Bobtail's tag. Five and a half miles behind was Scythe Wood, where twenty-three minutes previously the notes of the Gone Away had glanced among the trees. Bobtail was about half a mile from Cockabells. Over a bank and into a by-lane, a scramble up another bank, and down into Latten's Close, a grazing field. Nice going. Quarter of a mile more, and then the chase would end. I urged Blackie on, hoping to be near enough to see where the fox concealed himself. I saw him nip over a bank, a tiny brownish object that disappeared at once.

The pack poured over a few moments later.

There was one more field. Nimrod threw his tongue and led them on, for he knew that unless he caught Bobtail in the next field, he would lose him. The hound's sense of smell was keener than his sight, and by this sense alone had he pursued Bobtail, covering the level ground at thirty miles an hour, tongue flacking and flakes of froth flying. Behind him thirty-five throats made a blended harmony as of bells in a tower brought down off their stays together. Bobtail leapt between two elms on the last bank, and dropped down. Twenty seconds later Nimrod followed, and after him came Nemesis and Starlight, Solway and Thunderer, Firefly, Neptune, and the milkwhite Chloe. They ran about fifty yards into the field called Cockabells, and hesitated, sniffing the air. Some ran with noses to the ground, some straggled. Nimrod roved round the field, mute and eager, but not with the stride of two minutes before. He ran as in a maze. There was a certain area of the field, roughly defined by the reluctance of all hounds to enter it, which seemed to hold confusion. And then a hoarse long screeching cry was heard over the sunken lane, and the huntsman cantering over Latten's Close saw a ragged dark hat held by a great earthy paw waved above the plashed ash-sapling hedge.

"Oi-oo-aa-aa-yaa-yaaoiegh!"

The effort must have torn the throat strings out of the viewer's throat. The huntsman's horn spoke to the hounds. Up went their feathery sterns. Crack! crack! the lash of whip's thong a few moments later. The pig-farmer, his big red face streaked with mud-splashes running down to his chin in sweat, hooked the iron gate-fastener off its staple with the stag's-horn handle of his whip and swung open the five-bars for the pack to pass. Led by huntsmen, they trotted down the sunken lane, to where Tom Cockerlegg was standing, ragged hat on ragged head. He was grinning. His grey sheepdog sat on a sack high up the bank. He held a sieve in one hand, for he was about to scatter earth over a gin he had tilled at the opening of a rabbit bury. Big leather pads, like the armour of a gigantic brown beetle, were tied round his knees; the bones of which would have rotted seasons before if he had not always worn them.

"Have ee got 'n?" he asked.

"Which way did'n go, Tam?" cried the huntsman, abruptly.

"Oo, I can't say for sure, Charlie. I seed un rinning in Cockabells, and 'twas all a'could do to hold Bess back from sparking after un. But they varx dogs don't welcome shipdogs (sheepdogs), and so a'gave Bess a dapp, and told'n tu lie down." A look of earnestness came into his face as he asked, "Have ee killed Bobtail at last, Charlie?"

"If ee didden view un, then why the devil did ee holle', ye old vule (fool), you?" shouted Charlie, in a rage, wheeling round his horse.

"Woll, Charlie, woll," said the trapper, blinking like a bewildered owl, "I didden see no huntsman and so I were just sparking on the varx-dogs, Charlie!"

Charlie muttered something about the trapper being mazed as a vuz-peg. Hounds were taken back to the field. Here stood one tree, the Icicle Oak, a sapless ruin nine centuries old, hollow, and half its bark shed. It stood in the centre of the area of confusion. Its five remaining branches, all dead, stretched to the sky like the charred wrists and hand of a giant thrust up through the turf. It had not dropped an acorn for a hundred years. Again Nimrod cast round the field, followed by the bewildered and listless pack. The bobtailed fox had vanished, exactly as in other years.

The four long-drawn notes of the recall, a melancholy sound, for it meant no more excitement at bullfinches and over banks, floated out of Charlie's horn. The pressure against the corner of his mouth, where the mouthpiece was held, wrinkled his forehead, on which three thorn-rips showed red. The whip's voice calling hounds could be heard across the field in the air so still that not one woodpecker's tinder fragment, hanging on spider-thread on the dry bark, shook or spun.

The hounds sat down, rolled, licked veteran heads, growled, and yawned. In twos and threes the field cantered up on sweating horses. The Master had taken a toss in the Fawley Brook, and was covered with weed. He and the rest of the field had thought that a fox out of Scythe Wood would run another direction. Under the Icicle Oak many dismounted, handing reins to grooms, while sandwich boxes were opened, and saddle flasks taken out of leather cases.

I heard the huntsman telling the Master and Secretary about the collar round the neck of the fox. "Wha'?" barked the Seal, immediately, and enquired the name of the man who had seen it. Charlie said my name. His Lordship exclaimed, "Pooh, that writin' fellar! He will be shakin' hands with the fox next, or writin' that he has. Same thing, perhaps!"

Then he realized that I was near. He laughed, and said in a hearty bantering voice, "It's time you got a pair of spectacles, young fellar! Have some port."

I thanked him, and took the long parsnip-shaped glass flask. As I was turning the silver stopper, I watched the dismounted huntsman kicking with the toe of his boot one of the big yellow fungi that grew in the hollow of the oak, near its base. For years the tough growths had clung there, each as big as a saddle, but thicker. As I looked idly at Charlie's cap, something glinted in the weak winter sunlight. A drop of moisture fell on his boot, and ran a couple of inches down the black leather of the calf where the stirrup leather had worn a smooth mark. Charlie sniffed, and drew his hand across his nose. But the drop had not fallen from it. When I held back my head and tipped back the flask between my teeth, I saw the head of the fox looking out of a hole near the top of the tree. I choked over my mouthful of wine, and kept my eyes on the ground, dreading to hear the shout that must surely follow my stupid gasp and stare. Then I realized that I was pouring the Master's wine, and hastily righted the flask, secured the stopper, and returned it with thanks. A moment later I realized that no one had noticed anything about me. I moved away, two feelings strong in me—elation at the honour of being invited to drink from the Master's flask, and dread at the thought of discovery, with immediate death, for Bobtail.

About twenty yards from the tree I stopped, and slowly lifted my gaze to where he was sitting, calm and at ease. He seemed to have found a natural seat within the tree, from where he could watch the men and women below him. His ears were cocked, as though listening to what was being said. He looked from one face to another, and at the hounds. His tongue hung over his teeth but there was too much noise—the jingle of bits, voices, laughter, caw of rooks overhead—for his panting to be heard.

While I was covertly watching him, I realized that someone was trying to persuade the huntsman to try a terrier at the base of the hollow tree. It was the girl who had ridden before me during the run. Charlie grinned, and shook his head: "He bant there, miss." I walked near to hear exactly what would be said when the famous, or infamous Bobtail was caught at last. But why had not Charlie thought of the tree before? It was an obvious place, and had occurred to me the first time I saw it.

"Yurr, Vic!" said the huntsman, cracking second finger and thumb for the terrier, which had been carried during the chase in a leather satchel slung on a groom's chest.

Hounds sometimes walked up to the tree, to leave it again with expressions of disgust on their faces that all who are accustomed to any dogs recognise at once. The older hounds sat about thirty yards away, by the whipper-in, the terrier with him. Victor ran to Charlie Tarr. The terrier was patted, spoken to in a fierce low bloodthirsty tone, held by the ribs, and its nose shoved into the hole. Immediately it refused. Charlie called it back. It refused again, and ran away.

"No varx there, miss!" laughed Charlie, while Bobtail looked down at him, with bright eyes. "It's my own opinion, miss, that he runs himself out of scent just about hereabouts, and goes on, but the scent ends at this field. Scent is carried most in the brush, and that there li'l tag don't carry very much to begin with."

The Master decided to draw Gardebone Wood after lunch, and with the pack trotting at Charlie's heels, and preceded by about a hundred motor-cars, the Hunt moved off. Tom Cockerlegg stood and held open the gate. In his squeaky voice he asked Charlie why the mask of Bobtail was not hanging to his saddle.

"A'cuodden hear no rattle o' worrying, or dogs barking, but ye've got un, surenuff?"

Charlie did not answer. The Hunt passed through the gate, a little girl on a pony led by a groom trotting in the rear. I turned off to the right, wanting to see the end. I hid myself round a corner, and dismounted, holding Blackie's reins while he pulled at the grass.

When the last shoe had ceased to clack in the lane, the trapper climbed the steep bank to the field. I watched Bess the sheepdog with him. At a squeak from him she ran away to the Icicle Oak. Tom was carrying a hammer in his right hand. I slung the reins on a stub of a cut hazel stole and walked to where man and dog were waiting by the cold growths of the fungi. I hurried, in a rage at the thought of the fox being hit with the hammer, and, in its tired state, worried by the sheepdog. When I reached the tree the tag of the fox showed as it climbed down hindfirst. I was amazed, and then I remembered the collar.

"Fetch un," whispered Tom, and Bess seized the tag, and pulled it, very gently. Bobtail came into daylight and licked the hand of Tom, who took off the collar and fastened it round the neck of Bess, where it had been when first I had met man and dog in the parlour of the *Moon in the Mere*. I watched the sheepdog playing with the fox, which she had loved, said Tom, ever since he had put the little dark brown cub with her own litter of puppies, years before, when the trapper had found it whimpering and shivering in the dewy grass behind the pig-breeder's orchard.

"He's been a good mate to me, your honour, and can snick a rabbut smarter nor a lurcher dog will. And he's smart enough to know that they varx-dogs can't abear the stink of Granfer's Saddles, as us calls they girt toadstools."

That was why hounds had faltered. The taint of the fungi must have lain in a belt far around the tree, and overpowered the scent of the fox as soon as he entered it. It had lain warm and still in the windless morning.

"Yurr, Bob, shake hands wi' his honour, for a gennulman will stand by a friendship when his hand be to it."

The fox held up his slender paw, and I shook it, and then Bess held up hers, and looked at me with her grave and beautiful eyes. Afterwards dog and fox played together, bounding and rolling and running. I took out my pipe. Owlish eyes behind hair watched me, and the high squeaky voice said,

"Yurr, smoke a pipe of my baccy, midear. Tis grand to burn, surenuff!"

It pleased me to think that he considered me his friend to the extent of revealing his secret store; but to my surprise he did not hand me the watch, but an old cocoa tin, filled with various tobaccos, mostly shag, including what looked like a chopped-up cigar. When I had filled my pipe (intending to tap it out again as soon as I was out of his sight) the cunning old fellow took out the brass watch, exclaiming that it was time to get back to work, and walked away over the hoof-marked turf, squeaking with laughter, to his gins in the sunken lane.

77

The Forty-Third Division

BY RALPH BATES

THE SNOW was harder and crunched under their feet above the granite outcrop and they rested, facing the Dome of the Aneto peak, screwing up their eyes against its brightness. The wind rising out of the valley beyond the peak was driving plumes of snowdust up into the intense blue sky. On their side, however, the air flurries were soft and warm from the granite blocks. Agustin, the younger of the two scouts of the 43rd, the "lost" Division, made several attempts to drive his axe shaft into the snow.

"How lovely," he exclaimed. "Pere, do you see? If you make a hole in the snow it seems to fill up with blue light. Oh, lovely; soft light, you can see it pour in like a liquid." He ran about the ridge jabbing holes. The black-bearded Pere laughed, but he was pleased with the boy's delight.

Pere advanced to the edge of the great cliff on their left. In the gloomy amphitheater below the peak were coils of mist, slowly rising. "Eh, Agustin, the Malibierna Pass is just the other side, in the direction of that cairn. Eh, blast you, listen. We must go down the East Ridge."

The boy came running toward him, shielding his eyes; sun-smitten ice glittered on the East Ridge. "Pere, the light in the holes is the same color as the snow lakes, amethysts, dissolved in . . ." A rifle cracked, thin and feeble in the rarefied air. "Oh, Pere," the boy choked, and twisted as he fell. He lay still upon his back.

Pere flung himself down and fired at the cairn. A bee droned by, blown up from the lush spring valley of the Ribagorzana. Quickly he raised himself and dropped as he saw the flicker of movement on the peak. The bullet swished over his head toward the Cursed Glacier. Lying upon the snow, he was out of sight, and he crawled back to the dead boy and turned him over. He had transferred the rations to his own sack when he heard a scrunch on the snow. Standing boldly, tall and slender, silhouetted against the sky, was the Enemy, lifting his rifle.

Both men fired and missed. The Enemy flung himself down behind the hump. Pere was dashing forward when he remembered, without conscious thought, that there were rocks beyond the snow hump. The Enemy would have cover. His own position was determined; on his right the snow plunged down five hundred feet to the blue-green crevasses.

He crawled back to the dead boy and took his ammunition, the binoculars, and the ice axe; and retreated three yards and stood up. Again the Enemy missed. Raging, Pere lifted his rifle, but the Enemy had already begun to drop. Slinging his rifle and lying flat, Pere pushed himself down the steep slope. As he shot down and his hissing snow-wake rose high, he turned on his side and lay upon the axe shaft and drove the point into the snow. As he stopped, the axe grated among the nodules of icy snow that preceded the naked ice.

Quickly he cut steps down and across the Dome's north face. He noted that the wind was blowing chill up the Esbarrans Valley. Gaining the foot of the great rock bluff of the Aneto North Ridge, he climbed swiftly to its summit and with the binoculars searched the peak and the knife-edge leading to it, staring past the black mark on the snow hump.

Pere waited four hours. The north wind from France pushed heavy, canvas-hued clouds over the frontier range. Tongues of mist stuck out of the gaps in the frontier crest. The shadows sponged out the glacier's brilliance and the peaks blackened. The Enemy never approached the dead boy.

A burst of hail rattled on the granite as Pere climbed down. His will had frozen round one determination.

He reached the moraines as snow, a few grey flakes, began to drift in the brusque eddies; by the time he had descended the last dirt shoots the snow was falling with a faint hissing sound. At other times this would have caused him to hasten, but now he dawdled along the Esbarrans torrent course—toward the Aygualluts pasture, below the Cursed Peaks, where they had left their blankets—brooding over the boy's death.

Agustin, a young graduate of Barcelona University, had been working with Pere for nearly a year, and latterly had become a kind of assistant to him. One night, during the retreat, the boy had been of inestimable service to Pere, then operating with a rear-guard harassing company. He had suggested a movement which had enabled Pere to withdraw two hundred and twenty men given up for lost, the remains of a bombed battalion. Until recently Agustin had never been happy in the army, having been in constant trouble with the brigade authorities. Pere believed that he had always desired to be with him because Pere himself was something of a problem to the authorities.

For a while, on account of natural combativity, Pere had been a brigade commissar, but his explosive temper had undone much of his work, which he disliked. His indiscipline had finally disqualified him and his party had removed him. He had joined that party soon after the outbreak of the rebellion, not because of philosophic conviction, but because he approved its general war policy. Pere, a solitary, violent man of about forty years, had little patience with the problems of morale and adjustment, with which a commissar must occupy himself. Following this, he had done some fine skirmishing with a picked force against the Moors on the Sierra de Alcubierre. Again, he had so resented the strategical control of his work by the Staff that he had been asked by his party to surrender his commission. He had done so after a stormy scene with the Commissar, whom he had threatened.

He had fought magnificently during the retreat, when organization had broken down; leading shock parties back against advanced enemy forces, often working within the enemy offensive itself. For this he had been given the rank of lieutenant by the Division; he affected to ignore the promotion.

During the past fortnight, since they had been driven into the high mountains, Pere had again done splendid work as a scout. His mountaineering skill fitted him for that lonely work. Operating with a small unit, largely self-supporting, he was tireless and full of iniative, and had given first-rate protection to the "lost" Division. In order to be with him Agustin had declared, falsely, that he was a skilled climber, though he had made but one ascent of a rock peak in the Beciberi range.

Pere now reached their last night's resting place, took Agustin's blanket, and was about to set out for the overhanging boulder on the Maladetta pastures where he intended to sleep when an idea struck him.

The Enemy above had been watching the Malibierna pass; what was he doing there? Were the fascists launching an attack on the 43rd from Benasque? It would be a good route to the Ribagorzana Valley; the southern slopes of the Cursed Mountains, running down into the Malibierna Valley, were already free from snow. He decided to warn the low-level scouts stationed in the valley before the Tonnelé Pass.

From Aygualluts to the pass by the Mulleres Valley was a three hours' journey, and there were three hours of daylight left; he set out at once. During the hour he was passing over the lower pastures of the valley he was thinking of Agustin, lying above on the white Dome, buried already under snow, heaping the snow up in a bank . . . the top of it would blow off into the spirals of falling snow. But he felt no deep sorrow; sorrow had disappeared before the clean danger of the snowstorm. Already, as he passed the last broad flats, speculation died out, for the gusts lifted serpents of snow before him. The ground was made treacherous by its thick, insubstantial covering of snow. There was a noise of wind above on the little Esbarrans peak on his right, like the banging of a vast cathedral door. The rumbling of the Mulleres stream on his left guided him; the snow shut out the view of the valley sides.

And then suddenly the wind sheared through the snow and the hundred peaks boomed into the blind night. Hour after hour Pere fought his way to the pass, where huge sails of snow raced across the gap and broke against the ridge. Again and again the wind beat him down into the heaving snow and at last, near exhaustion, he hacked his way to the shallow crevasse between the cliff base and the snow field and there fell asleep, with the gale storming above him.

When Pere awoke the full moon hung over the peaks he had left. He reached the pass with care and rested behind low rocks, startled by the beauty of the cordillera. Away to the west the sharp, sail-like peaks of the French frontier and the vast cliff of the Perdiguero stood clear but ghostly under the full moon. To the southwest was the snow desert of the Posets, where no one ever wandered; and nearer, the Cursed Range itself, sharply outlined above the dimly shining glacier. He drew the blanket round him, staring at that solemn loveliness. Range after range stretched away on three sides, now cloaked in nocturnal white; their scribbled crests traced the finest of lines across a background of yet more peaks. The moonlight in the valleys between them seemed to be a faint mist rising out of blackness. On the slab-littered wilderness of the Mulleres, now a white dome, a torrent was flashing brightly; he could see the water twisting in the moonlight, and its black course beyond the beam.

He turned and regarded the valley he must soon descend. It was black, utterly black. Above its black emptiness floated a snow-laced lower peak, like a white suspended island. Beyond, the sprawling Beciberi and the Comolo Forno were like strange countries, suddenly perceived, or white palaces in the sky. He wanted others . . . he wanted Agustin to see the cordillera now. "Pere, Pere," the boy had cried, "the light in the holes is the same color as the snowflakes." Savage hatred momentarily burned in him. How Agustin had delighted in the little snow-field lakes, amethyst-hued, turquoise where the floes had been pressed below the surface by the weight of snow slipping down the banks. Prussian-blue lakes with bergs floating upon them.

"Pere, Pere," the boy's voice had cried, "it's like amethyst dissolved in . . ." What had he been going to say? But that still landscape, so vast and solemn that it was neutral to man, gradually immobilized Pere's emotions. He turned and slid down the first moonlit slopes and was swallowed up in the black depths.

In the first greyness he found his comrades, challenging the sentry with a shout when within ten yards of him.

"That's bad, Carlos," he said, shaking his head and frowning angrily. The scout made no answer, his expression admitting guilt.

After a while the sentry said, "I saw you higher up, then I lost you. I could see it was you." The others, awakening one by one, questioned him about his return. He straightened up from his sack and placed his rifle against the wall.

"Agustin's dead," he said. "One of their scouts shot him yesterday on the Aneto." Everyone kept silence, thinking of Agustin. After a while, Pere said, "Where's the Division? Any report?"

"Same position; yes, there's a report. There's a column of ours going to attack from Seo de Urgell, over the sierras into the Pallaresa Valley."

"Ah, going to relieve us, I suppose."

"Yes, our telegraphers have got the field wireless going again."

"Hope they don't relieve us too soon."

"Why, Pere?" It was the undertone in Pere's voice which had prompted the question.

"I am going back." He nodded toward the pass. Jaime, the Madrid climber, asked, "Are you taking anyone with you?"

"No . . . but you'd better make a visit every other day to the Tonnelé Pass. Get there about ten in the morning. If I'm not there traverse the ridges, by the Mulleres and the Salenques peak to the Salenques Pass. Bring what you can of rations for me and keep your eyes open. They have their scouts; I reckon they're stationed at the Renclusa refuge on the Maladetta. They won't send a force over the Salenques Pass but they might try the Malibierna. You go as far as that valley for the future, Enrique. It'll be tough I know, but you must try."

Pere prepared his bed against the wall, while Jaime, pleased at being given high-level work, warmed soup for the leader. Others, getting ready for their day's patrol, spread their blankets down for him.

"When are you going to be back, Pere?" Carlos asked.

"When . . ." he began, "in a few days, I hope."

Jaime brought a billy can of soup over to Pere's bed, knelt down and placed it on his leader's lap. "What was it like, Pere, up there?" he said confidentially.

"I was a fool not to think," Pere answered. "I am to blame for it;

that peak will be their lookout center if they expect an attack or if they try one on us by that route."

"No, I meant the storm. I wish . . ."

"The storm! Fine . . . you wish for a nice, romantic death in a blizzard while saving the Republic, do you, young fellow?"

"Eh, Pere . . . steady," the young climber exclaimed, crestfallen at the rebuke.

"Soup's good, fetch me some more," Pere continued, knowing this would content the boy. "Who's on guard here?"

"I am," answered the man newly detailed.

"All right, wake up in three hours, and don't let me get shot, as Carlos would."

"I saw you higher up, Pere," grumbled Carlos.

"All right, clean my rifle," grunted Pere.

"But I did . . ." The leader drew the blankets over his head and was silent. "I saw you by the hillock where the ruined cabin is."

Pere sprang up and glared at the man. "Cullon! Clean all the rifles for three days—for three months," he shouted, striking Carlos a light blow. He lay down and covered himself, muttering.

Carlos protested no more but showed resentment at the blow, and more than this, wounded affection. Some belonging to another party violently rebuked Pere. A few of Pere's fellow party members began to murmur, and this restraint was only a sign of their greater hurt. One or two openly said that this behavior ill befitted Pere, himself ever chafing at discipline.

"But you're to blame, Carlos, as well," Jaime said. "If we take a different view of discipline you shouldn't abuse it."

The boy acknowledged his fault but unwittingly gave fresh life to the controversy by defending Pere. "He hit me because he'll never send a fellow before the Brigade," was his argument.

Two days later Pere traveled from the valley ridge above Benasque—having noted the presence in that town of three enemy battalions, to the Col Tonnelé—to await Jaime. Swiftly moving clouds were streaming over the highest ridges from the southwest; mists hid the valley floor. For a while he was hurrying along a corridor between the puffy grayness of the mist and the rafterlike clouds, from which fronds hung down, emaciated arms grasping through the clouds. Then as he pulled up the ruddle-colored slopes of the Malibierna peak the valley mists suddenly heaved and rose with stealthy speed and enveloped him. Silence settled over the mountain. The shell-like murmur of the air in the valley's huge diapason was filtered out by the mist. The roaring of the water, swelling and diminishing as the gusts blew, no longer rose from the slopes. The click of stones beneath his nailed boots lost the sharpness of impact. The only sound was of a gentle seeping and dripping of moisture. There was little purpose in ascending a peak blind with clouds; yet he made the height.

Nearing the final ramps, he heard the click of stones as if men were approaching. Quickly he lay down and released the safety catch of his rifle, which he always carried cocked. The mists swirled, cold puffs of air ran up the dripping slope. The clicking stopped, but he heard a soft drumming as if the invisible enemy were passing over grass.

Again the clicking began; he wriggled himself into a secure position from which he could both leap and shoot. Silence again. There was a short cough and a sighing, higher up the slope, and a rattle of spilling scree stones behind him. "They're going round me," he muttered. He thought he saw a black form looming through the mist, and his left arm jerked the foresight up, and then the form was gone.

The drumming was below him now, but nothing was visible. Again there was silence except for the whisper of seeping moisture. He allowed five minutes to pass and then took off his boots and put on *alpargatas,* estimating meanwhile the exact location of the pass.

Pere strode quickly in the direction of the pass and then, looking at the ground, quietly laughed. He slapped the butt of his rifle and put his head back and laughed roundly.

"Of course," he said aloud. "Izard, a herd of izard." The clicking had been caused by a herd of the Pyrenean ibex.

Pere had often seen izards during his summer climbs but never at close quarters. The beasts had been as much puzzled as he, no doubt. They had been forced to leave their lower feeding grounds earlier than usual on account of the war; they were going from the high slopes of Ribagorzana to the upper heights of the Esera Valley, by way of the Malibierna. He pictured them standing in the mists, nostrils distended, heads up, forefeet nervously treading the ground. The whole herd had halted, tense. Then as he had crouched down they had advanced, trembling, suspicious, across the dark slope. What had prompted them to avoid the spot where he crouched, dividing in two files? He himself had experienced such sensations as they must have felt, in approaching the evil area, the malignant spot. . . . Still thinking of the invisible herd he continued his way to the Col Tonnelé.

Well before ten o'clock Jaime, the Castilian, appeared, working sensibly. He threw his arms round the leader and hugged him. "It's good to see you, Pere. Hungry?"

"Cullon! What have you brought?" Pere ejaculated, regarding the great packet of food Jaime was pulling out of his sack.

"The boys took a vote to allow you a part of their rations, Pere . . . my Lieutenant." The boy saluted. "All the boys," he added.

"Cullon," grunted the older man. "But I've got plenty left." He was pleased that resentment of the blow was at an end, yet beneath his pleasure he bridled at the implied censure.

"You have?" Jaime was disappointed that he could not give pleasure to his chief. The debate among the patrol had ended with the proposal Jaime had related. An anarchist had proposed it, and Pere's party members had agreed.

"Where'd you sleep, Pere. . . . Oh, I forgot to say, your appointment has been confirmed by the war office, Lieutenant."

"Ah, ha," murmured Pere, running his fingers through his beard.

"Here's a letter for you from Esquinazo," continued Jaime. The men of the 43rd spoke thus of their colonel, calling him Antonio, or by his nickname: "Esquinazo," the "Dodger."

Pere opened the letter; it contained thanks for his good work and a request for fuller reports that savored of rebuke.

"Cullon, does he think there are copybooks and lakes of ink up here?" Pere growled. Yet he knew that Colonel Beltrán's request was within reason. The rebuke was limited to the absence of any except verbal reports, but the scout felt that it applied to his present activities also. "But why?" he thought. "I have ascertained that there are enemy in Benasque, I've wached the passes, and they need watching." *"Why* are you staying up here instead of superintending all the patrol routes?" his conscience asked, and was promptly silenced.

"Christ," he said angrily; "what's he think I am, one of these literary soldiers?" But the remark hurt him, for it brought the image of Agustin into a region of his mind which was sensitive to pain.

Attached to the letter was a request for topographical information. "By what routes in your territory could an enemy force, stationed in the Val de Aran, reach the village of Aneto and its environs?"

"Ha, I hadn't thought much about that!" Pere said, pursing his lips. "Listen, Jaime, I am going to give you this side to do. You'll have to stay up two days at a time."

"Oh, fine! I say, Pere, these hills are better than the Guadarrama."

He gave Jaime explicit directions—told him what passes to watch and where to bring more food in order that he, Pere, might remain on the heights. He spoke cheerfully but was in a stubborn mood; stubborn against a reproof which only he himself had administered. In his imagination he heard the Commissar's voice saying, "Pere's a good soldier; he'd be better if he'd accept discipline *at once."*

"To hell with it," he muttered, "I'm as good a soldier as any of them." He wished they would give him a hundred men and tell him to bury himself in the hills and make war his own way. With these speculations he whipped himself into anger against authority; and leaving

Jaime, he climbed the Unnamed Peak to stare, from just beneath the streaming clouds, at the Cursed Range, whose peaks were hidden from sight by the ceiling of cloud.

Toward three of the afternoon when Jaime returned to their meeting-place, he found Pere writing. "Is that the report?"

Pere imagined that Jaime was commenting on the scantiness of the report and answered, with instantly checked irascibility, "Can't a man sleep sometimes? Did you get a chance to see down the Toro before the rain came on?"

"Yes; nothing there. I shall go up to the ridge to-morrow; there's no need to go to the pass itself."

As soon as Jaime had returned to the patrol with his brief report and the new instructions for the scouts, Pere set out over the Unnamed Peak for the Salenques Pass.

Five days later, still brooding over a message from the Adjutant which Jaime had given him the day preceding, calling him to Divisional Headquarters, Pere was sitting in the shade, legs astride a rock, at the foot of the great Maladetta couloir. He was gazing idly down at the deep Prussian-blue stain of Lake Gregoño. In the midst of that wilderness of blazing stone the solemnity of the lake was startling. It was a black and malignant will, banished here and brooding. Tiny ripples, glittering like fish scales, seemed to lie motionless upon its surface. Not a tree nor a patch of grass was within sight, the lake lay concentrated and aloof. Above him the organ pipe of the couloir boomed in the wind.

Pere started, his attention jerked to a movement at the far end of the lake. He took out the binoculars and focused them. One, two, three—ah, the enemy—four, five. . . . There were fourteen or fifteen of the enemy filing round the lake. He fancied he heard the click of their boots. Quickly he made his plan; indeed, he saw no alternative.

On the north side of the Cursed Peaks are small crests of rock rising out of the glaciers; crests constantly bombed by thunder and swept by drenching storms, dreaded by the herdsmen of the valleys below. Facing the Midday, on the other side, there is little snow, but the cliffs are much bigger. Almost at their highest point, between the Punta de Astorga and the Eastern Maladetta, these cliffs are split by a vast chimney, a strictly perpendicular grove of fifteen hundred feet, the Maladetta couloir. A severe climb on good granite for anyone wishing to ascend from the quivering heat of Gregoño to the northern glaciers, and so by the sprawling north ridge of the Eastern Maladetta to the Renclusa refuge.

Pere's plan was simple. He would climb the couloir, station himself on the rocks below the Astorga, and wait for the enemy. Sweet Christ, if only the Enemy, Agustin's slayer, is leading! Ah, there was an impossible pitch in the couloir where one is forced to climb out on to the Great Tower wall by minute holds; there, helpless on those fierce rocks, the Enemy would be located above perpendicular death; spread-eagled before well-aimed extinction.

Tying his boot laces tightly and adjusting his rifle, sack, and ice axe, Pere laid his hands on the rock; there was affection in his fondling of the granite. He was bracing himself for the long tense effort ahead of him.

The first pitch was a ten-foot wall where the legs could do little pushing, a mere inelegant armpull. Above it lay an easy staircase, gaining a hundred feet of height and leading back into the cold depths of the couloir. Rapidly he mounted the staircase and came face to face with the first difficulty.

Before him the back of the chimney bulged outward, cold wet rock swelling outward for at least twenty feet ahead. The way past the obstacle was obvious but uninviting. The right wall was split by a crack which ran out toward the open face, gradually approaching a ledge which gave access to good holds by which he could climb above the bulge.

To start upon the crack was the problem; there were no holds within reach by which he could balance himself and pull over, and the last foothold of the staircase brought him so close to the bulge that he could not stand up without danger of toppling backward. Well, that's the problem, he considered, and without straining his nerve by waiting longer, put his left foot on the highest hold and slowly straightened his body. Gradually he could feel the poise of his stance diminishing as his head pressed against the bulge. Spreading his arm wide on the holdless rock, he strove to regulate his breathing; for the swelling of his chest threatened to throw him down. His left leg began to tremble; he had not dared to place more than the ball of his foot on the hold for fear of being too near the rock. He heard water dropping behind him, and the sound was ominous to his tense mind as slowly, slowly he straightened his body. Just as he felt himself overbalancing he thrust his right hand into the crack on the wall and clenched it within the fissure and rested. Safe now, he commented, and reached above his head with his left hand and found a wet hold.

Then, shifting his left foot toward the corner, he carefully jammed his right foot in the crack. "Hope the Enemy is really a good climber," he thought when well out on the crack.

Now he maneuvered to gain a broad ledge that ran back into the chimney wall above the bulge, and for a moment, groping above his head, his right hand emerged into the sun. The tiny sensation of warmth was grateful, but it broke his concentration by making him think of the Great Tower far above. The ledge was broad but he was forced to sidle along it; the rifle barrel, colliding with the wall, threatened to fling him down the two hundred feet of echoing well.

Again the mountain threatened to stop him. From the end of the ledge, with extreme difficulty, he balanced himself into a deep pulpit-like niche with a downward sloping floor of smooth ribs of stone. There seemed to be no exit from this niche, and he raged inwardly at his folly in being trapped.

But surely this could not be the classical route! He must have taken a wrong pitch in his haste to be out of the chimney. He hated the echoing couloir and the water dripping with faint noise of whirring wings. A man should climb out in the sun, upon dry rock, not in these threatening glooms.

Below the hold, well to the left, was a waterworn knob of rock, protruding perhaps half an inch from the face. Well, nothing for it. His brain squeezed tight, expelling even consciousness of the mountain as he placed his right hand on the hold, lodged the best nails of his boot on the slippery knob, and lifted his body, left hand running like a swift lizard over the wall. Yes . . . no, it is not deep enough . . . only the first joints of his fingers would rest on the tiny ledge; pulling on it would weaken his grasp on the jughandle.

Sweet Christ, his sweating fingers were slowly pulling off the ledge. No . . . desperately he clutched with his nails and fingerballs, *feeling* the chasm behind him like a black monster. He was doing it . . . yes. . . . He straightened upon the knob, and then as the new hold came in sight, just as his right hand was losing its security he slowly raised his other hand to another jughandle high on the left.

Within twenty seconds he was standing upon safe holds at the foot of a clean arête, with dozens of notched holds all the way up its sharp back. He waited while his heart ceased to pound and joyfully scaled the arête without a moment's halt for eighty feet of exhilarating climbing. "No nail marks on this pitch," he noted; "can't be the right route."

Taught by his mistake in accepting the invitation of the ledge, he considered a full minute before swarming up the blocklike crags that rested above the arête. There was no deception, however. The line of attack was continuous. Ah, there in the depth of the chimney was the chockstone everyone talked about! "Big enough for a whole party to rest on," he murmured and gained the stone.

Soon the chimney opened out and he climbed with pleasant ease for three hundred feet. He had forgotten the Enemy and was once more the coppersmith of Lérida, on holiday among the peaks to be seen from the tower of his own city.

Pere climbed out of the chimney on to the ample ledge on the left wall and walked out to the base of the Great Tower, in his heart a strange amalgam of elation and fear. Soaring upward for two hundred feet was the Tower, its rich-hued granite glowing in the sunlight, lovely to his eye. He touched the rock with his fingertips, its hard grains were good to feel; he rapped it with his knuckles, and struck it gently with the metal-shod toe of his boot. Solid, flawless granite, warm and blossoming in the sunlight.

He was before the crux of his climb. All that he had overcome before was but preparation. He was fit now, his body limber, controlled and springy, his mind alight with a keen desire for style and economy in the effort to come. He glanced at his bootlaces, adjusted the rifle and touched the rock again, and his will, content in its daring, quickly closed over the first beautiful problem of the Tower, a classical and austere crack ascent.

Pere slid his hands sideways into the crack, pressed with fingertips and the back of the hand against both sides of the crack, carefully twisted his left boot in the crack and lightly rose the first two feet. Left hand braced doubly firm while the right hand slid up the crack and expanded, and the left followed. Right foot came over left, felt for the crack, inserted itself and twisted, and his body rose again, not adhering to the vast wall by force of muscle, but by resting with perfection of balance on its minute holds: almost as if floating on that thousand feet of void below him. Right hand slid up the crack, left hand, left foot. . . . Right hand, left hand, right foot . . . his body soared upward lightly, with continuous flowing motions. He was filled with serenity, his mind concentrated, co-ordinating the rippling movement of his muscles, judging precisely when to change his burden from leg to leg and arm to arm.

At fifty feet the crack began to narrow and his will closed more tightly over the new problem, but there was no strain. He measured his fatigue, relaxed a few muscles whose effort was superfluous; and was certain, yes! he had more than enough in hand for the Great Tower. A sensation like the thrill of great music began to germinate within him.

Without haste he laid his left hand upon the edge of the rock leaf and knew from that contact how safely he was climbing. Had he been afraid he would have felt relief at grasping the jughandle hold. He did not; it was a passing feature of this lovely climb and no more. He jammed his foot in the crack and balanced springily upon it. Then, with no special resolution to do so, he leaned forward and looked down between his feet; to the dull-green ice at the foot of the mighty couloir. Above the leaf was a deep recess in the wall, from which he balanced himself by small but trustworthy holds, and so reached the ledge without holds for his hands, so that he was compelled to move with calculated steps, his feet on the very edge of the shelf. Yes, he was moving easily. He rejoiced in the knowledge, which the climber's censorship of his mind gently prevented from becoming too insistent, that behind him was the enormous whispering void.

There was an interruption to the sensation of music as he moved along the shelf, not because of strain, but because that rare emotion was the product of his clean and economic conquest of height. "Ah," he murmured, as the deep groove-like crack came into sight. His knees and arms raising his body again, the music welled up once more, clean, severe, like the theme of the contemplative "long" steps of a Sardana danced in a village square, overlooking a serene landscape far below. Now, ahead, he saw the crux of the Tower, and without pause gently launched himself upon it.

It was a roof, inclined at an angle of fifty degrees, of roughish granite, but completely without real holds after the first yard. A shallow crack, not half an inch deep, ran up to its sharp upper edge, beyond which rose a steep wall of some twenty feet. He could see no route up this wall, but boot-scratches told him other men had passed here. Arms straight out, almost parallel to his sides, palms downward, fingers turned back toward the abyss, a nail of his right boot biting stealthily at the shallow crack, resting his weight evenly upon the rough, clinging stone, he edged his body up the fearful slab. The music was an undertone now, a light perspiration was on his forehead. Upward, upward, not breathing when for ten seconds he must take his right foot out of that minute fissure. Ah, he saw the hold for his right hand a foot beyond his head, and instantly realized that he dare not lift his palm from the rock, and continued his infinitely cautious movement up the roof. "Ah!" he murmured, five minutes later, as his right palm edged over the hold and the nail of his boot re-bit the rock. Slowly, with a swimmer's stroke, he brought his left hand round and it settled calmly upon the edge of the slab. The roof was conquered.

Pere drew himself up and threw his leg over the edge of the slab, for between the roof and the wall there was a deep fissure. He had won! Sweet Jesus, he had won! The theme in his brain swelled and burst into exultation, into glory; the blood rushed through his body, refreshing him; he drew deep breaths and lifted his face to the light with closed eyes. Then, advancing along the roof crest, he rounded a corner by a swing on spikeholds, toed along an easy crack to the gap between the cliff and the Tower, and there sat astride a boulder. Seeing that the bed of the couloir offered no more serious obstacles, he shinned schoolboy fashion, abandoning style, to the top of the Tower and gazed down on the wilderness of Gregoño and its solemn lake.

He could see nothing of the enemy patrol; they would be already engaged on the first pitches of the couloir. He allowed his gaze to wander. Beyond the dazzling hills of the Cinca foreground were the vaporous, petal-crested ranges. Pale-green hills, pale-gray; hills faintly washed in with diluted sienna, ochre, and Venetian red; and on the remote, legendary horizon the Sierra de Guara, a transparent stain of palest violet, almost invisible against the cobalt band of the lower sky.

A cry far below stirred him to action and he moved swiftly into the couloir and climbed up through a draughty amphitheater, into which tumors of green-black ice dripped water, to the brilliance of the glacier. With few precautions he ran along the edge of the *rimaye* to a dip in the ridge, clambered across the easy southern rocks of the Midday Peak, and descended to a ledge behind a red granite spire, in order to get a clear vision of the Great Tower. Lovingly he observed every pitch of that face; it was really one long pitch, the purest of joys.

While he was still contemplating the Tower he heard a sharp ejaculation in the couloir and at once lifted his rifle to the level of his waist. Ah, he could wait till the enemy—Sweet Christ, let it be the Enemy—was at mid-height of the first crack and then he would call to him, and the Enemy would look over and see the rifle barrel lifting slowly, surely, to point motionless, straight at his neck. Sweet Christ, let it be the Enemy. Pere glanced at his safety catch and leaned against the spire. The voice shouted again in the couloir and then he heard the collision of an axe point against rock, and the voice said clearly, "This is the Tower." He crouched behind the spire as a figure appeared on the ledge leading to the base of the Tower. It was not the Enemy, but a shorter man. His vexation was tempered by the fact that a rope trailed behind the enemy. A roped party!

The leading enemy returned to the couloir and for a while the party held conference; their voices only reached him as a hollow rumbling. Again the leader advanced and this time two others followed him; the rope still trailed back to the couloir. A party of four. Pere watched the leader as he attacked the crack, and without grudging he mentally praised the enemy's technic. Not quite mature, not mellow enough, but good and very daring, he judged, watching the sure though jerky movements of the leader. As the rope slack paid out, Number Two started up the crack. Also good. Now the fourth man advanced diffidently along the ledge, his hands fumbling at the rock. "Ha, ha," murmured Pere, "beginner."

The beginner looked flinchingly down the sickening abyss and shouted in Italian, *"E pericoloso."*

Pere chuckled, "Oh, yes, it's dangerous, very dangerous to-day." A fierce glee entered him. "Ha!" he exclaimed softly, "there must be Italians in the party below too." All his hatred of the Italian enemy throbbed like a festering wound.

The party's tactical plan was obvious but mistaken. There was no belay in the couloir over which the rear man could pass the rope, thus safeguarding himself, and possibly Number Three. Therefore the party, with sufficient rope to cover the whole length of the Tower, had elected to accept the collective risk. Number One, they had reasoned, would reach the recess at the top of the roof slab and there, as Number Two would be on the ledge below the knee crack, he would be able to hold his Two and Three if the beginner fell. But if Two or Three failed at his problem before the leader reached safety . . .

That was the mistake into which the leader's inexperience had betrayed him. He should have climbed the Tower as far as the last ledge alone, drawing up the whole rope to that point so that its weight should not pull him off the roof; and then from the summit he could have brought up his whole party in absolute security, one at a time. Bad leadership, he commented, bad leadership will ruin everything. But today it makes no difference.

Number Three started up the first crack, tense, working desperately. "Tt, Tt," Pere clicked his tongue in surprise. "Well, señor leader, you're risking it anyway." Number One was on the terrible roof! "Now," whispered Pere and stood upright. *"Ascolti, fascisti . . . piacere,"* he called in the dog-Italian an exile volunteer had taught him.

Number Three ceased struggling in the crack; the man on the ledge sought the origin of the voice, his face twitching.

"Buon giorno," Pere said, lifting his rifle leisurely and aiming it at Number Two. Numbers Three and Four screamed harshly. Number Three stared down the precipice in an agony of terror. Number One was still edging up the roof slab.

Weakly the last man fumbled at his rifle strap. "No . . . *piacere,"* Pere commanded, lowering the muzzle toward him, and the man obeyed, standing, with distorted face, staring at the black-bearded, grinning figure across the couloir.

Slowly Pere raised his rifle muzzle and took leisurely aim at the neck of Number Two, who put up a hand against the bullet. Pere lingered with his finger on the trigger, then gently, equally, his right hand squeezed on butt and trigger. The couloir thundered.

Number Two crumpled, his head collided with the cliff, throwing him outward into the air. The rope coil sprang like a serpent, straightened, and Number One was whipped from the slab. He screamed chokingly as he soared out over the precipice. Number Three closed his eyes and crouched in the crack, screaming like a crushed beast. "Tang," sounded the rope softly, and he was hurled from the Tower. Number Four did not scream at all; he had already knelt upon the ledge and had lost consciousness. Whipping and revolving, the enemy plunged down the thousand feet of sunny precipice.

Horrified cries came from the party in the couloir as they saw the leading group hurtle downward. Then silence. After the silence a voice whimpered and then another. The first whimpering voice began to weep and howl; the man's nerve was utterly destroyed. The animal howling agitated the sounding pipe of the couloir and it gave out monstrous wails of fear. Pere crept along the ledge and tried to catch sight of the enemy, but could not.

"Go on, cry, little Italian, cry," he shouted and laughed loudly. The laughter echoed in the couloir, mingling with the wails. "Cry, little Italian. You came to make war."

Pere ran back to the pinnacle and gathered up his rope and tied one end to his waist. Then he returned toward the couloir and, belaying the line, leaned slowly out over the wall. Regaining the perpendicular, he tied the loosed end and again leaned out, ejecting the empty shell from his rifle breach.

"Where are you, little weeper?" he yelled. The rope he could see but an overhang hid the enemy. He fired and the report crashed like the bursting of an Italian bomb; the idiot wails cracked harshly. Round after round he sent crashing into the couloir. "Jump, little weeper, jump," he yelled between peals of laughter. "Jump," the huge echo repeated, between its wails. The abyss crashed and wailed and roared with glee.

As Pere turned away from the couloir he experienced a sensation of weakness that he had not felt for many years—the sensation of the beginner after a severe climb. His knees trembled and he was nervous in crossing the gully by which he had descended to the rocks of the Astorga. It was not the climb that had overstrung him, he knew, but emotion unleashed by the event in the couloir. For a moment he recoiled from it, as from a sudden revelation about himself. Then he heard shouting and these sensations vanished.

On the crest of the Midday Peak, above him but out of sight, an enemy was calling, "Round to the col; he can't get down here."

Cullon! There must have been other patrols on the Maladetta, and they had heard the firing. "But how did they know where I was?" he thought as he raced across the cliff by an easy belt of broken rock. The shouting continued on the summit.

There was no other way of escape than to climb down to the narrow band of ice and snow that fringed the cliff base, and there was only one way of doing that, to *abseil*. There was no time for choice, the chimney in front of him ran out on to the smooth gray face below the weather-worn blocks. He tied the rope to his waist, wedged his way with knees and back as far down the chimney as he could go, flung the line over a block and paid himself out. The rope finished when he was still six or seven feet above the *rimaye,* here four or five feet broad and fifteen or more feet deep. "No time to go back; besides, I couldn't," he thought, and began to swing himself sideways, pushing on the cliff face with his feet. At the third swing he reached a spike and with a violent effort pulled himself erect upon it. "Leave the rope," he muttered and, unty-ing it, let it swing back to the perpendicular. It cost him a minute of anxiety as he released his ice axe and then, without hesitation, he leaped.

He landed upon one knee, pitched forward, ramming his face against the snow; could not position himself for a blow with the ice axe, slid, delivered a blow but failed to get the weight of his body upon the axe before he slid off the snow layer on to the scabby ice, encrusted with stones. He shot down the slope, feet spread, ripping cloth and skin, frantically striving to bunch himself and cover his head for the shock. He managed to draw his legs together a moment before he struck, broadside on, against a reef of rock. He bounced a foot clear of the reef and fell sprawling, ice axe clattering a dozen yards away. Half dazed, he dashed to recover his axe, and bolted for a narrow snow gully, flung himself into it on his side, the rifle barrel rattling over small rocks, and shot down the gully, a curving plume of snow rising from the axe point behind him. Again he collided heavily with rocks; as he stag-gered to his feet, a bullet struck a boulder to his left and thrummed away like an æolian harp. He plunged through a pool, scrambled over a bank, dropped clumsily down a wall of ten feet; fell, tearing the palm of his hand, rose slowly, slightly sick, flung himself upon a snow slope, and slid down it under weakening control until he broke through its surface where rocks protruding through it had half melted the snow. A bullet whined overhead as he dashed into a chaos of boulders to tem-porary safety.

"Now come down," he gasped, head throbbing, the pain of his left knee and thigh almost unbearable. Swaying, he unslung his rifle and chose his position. Two men were standing a little to one side of the dip between the Midday and the Corona Peaks. From his height, he guessed one of them to be the Enemy—the slayer of Agustin. "Ah, fool," he thought. "What a fool I am; shall I never learn to think?"

His mistake had lain in supposing that every man in a patrol of fif-teen would be good enough for the Maladetta couloir. That was the route which inevitably suggested itself to a first-rate cragsman, but to no other. Half the enemy, under the Enemy's leadership, had gone by the easy little southern glacier to the boulder slopes between the two

Maladetta peaks. The Enemy must have been near by when Pere had opened fire. A near go! Angry with himself, he fired at the two men, who darted to the rocks at the base of the Corona ridge. They did not answer his fire. "Ah, fool," Pere exclaimed, "they've lost me; they'd have thought I was hit."

He crept through the boulders toward the breach on the Estats ridge. No bullets sought him. Wearily he climbed to the summit of the eminence, parched with thirst. "They won't try it," he reasoned, looking out from a natural rifle pit. Yet he stood vigilant for two hours, until the descending sun cast its shadow upon the recess. There was no movement on the ridges.

"They're afraid to come down among the blocks," he said aloud and felt great confidence in himself. He began searching for water, crawling over the warm blocks, many of them as large as a cottage. He heard the guttural sound of water in the hollows below them and at last he found a way down to the snowmelt, washed his abrasions in icy water, filled his flask, and climbed out, intending to rest for at least an hour.

At the end of half an hour of clambering among that wilderness he seated himself behind a pile and ate a meal of bread, sausage, and sugar knobs, and was immediately refreshed. Shortly afterward he came to a corridor of unbelievably green though sparse grass, leading to a greener clearing in the sea of broken rock. The dung of izards lay all around him.

"You're the other dwellers," he murmured, smiling a little bitterly, thinking of the herd that had passed him in the mist; there was a minute comfort in the thought. He sat down on a block and gave himself over to unhurried reverie. Perhaps the izards would come in the night. For all the harm he would do them they might come now, trooping along the corridor, the little ones skipping on the rocks or bunting their sniffing muzzles against the small udders. He imagined them, the agile voyagers of the snow, the soft-eyed, tender dwellers among the waste of stone, stepping lightly into this green oasis and grazing, ignoring him, as if he were invisible.

The sun dipped suddenly behind the Posets. Small clouds, yellow-tinged, slid over the crest of the Maladetta. "Must get on the move," he thought, "get out of this chaos before dark." His left leg had become exceedingly painful, but he decided to make his way to the rendezvous with Jaime by way of the Corona pass and down over the Aneto glacier. Always go toward the enemy. If he's waiting—and he won't be—you'll have an equal chance.

He was still clambering painfully from block to block when darkness was complete and the chaos expanded and became a world; he was lost in the midst of a planetary surface of granite blocks. While he was upon the summit of the blocks the starlight was sufficient to disclose the outlines of the immobilized storm of granite, but below in the labyrinth of caves and tunnels he felt his way in darkness. Near the edge of the chaos it rained for a few minutes; he sought shelter and slept near rumbling water, for two hours. When he awoke, shortly before midnight, the half-moon was leaping from cloud to cloud.

He squatted for a few moments in the Corona pass and then decided to eat again and walked over to the Corona ridge and took out his food. As he did so a rifle shot rang out from the ridge summit. He saw the tawny flash; the bullet flew many yards wide. He dropped on to the rocks and crawled to the foot of a wall and there took off his boots. He waited for a finger of cloud to poke out the moon, and then, leaving his sack and ice axe behind him, he climbed twenty feet up the easy rocks before the cloud slid by. As the light returned he lay motionless between two shark's-fin crags.

In the next darkness he did not move but listened, lifting himself clear of cover. Ah, he breathed, hearing a faint clicking higher up the ridge. In the next interval of shade he picked his way swiftly across the ridge to the tumbled confusion of rocks on its flank. In two successive darknesses he moved and in the third he distinctly heard the click of metal above. Had the Enemy guessed his maneuver? The click was from a different place, to his left, and near. He remained still for three shadows but heard nothing. When next the moon was covered he threw a stone toward the edge of the ridge on his right and waited. A minute later he heard the faint scratch of nailed boots, farther off. "He's going," he commented mentally.

He ventured to lift his head in the moonlight but saw nothing. As the cloud approached the moon he pitched a large stone, and again a rifle cracked; fifty yards away, it seemed, and a little below the crest.

Slowly he began to crawl toward the crest. There was no sound, then there was a tiny impact of stone well down the slope at Pere's level. The skin prickled on his head but he suppressed the start his body attempted to make.

For five minutes there was complete silence and he lay, trying to silence the sound of his breathing, a sharp stone interrupting the circulation of his left forearm. Again the click of metal sounded on the summit ridge and he swore in a whisper and said, "Fooled with my own trick," and ignored the next sound of striking stone below him.

The moon entered upon a cloud lane and there was no shade for ten minutes; he did not dare lift his head. When the shadow crept over the ridge there was no guiding sound and he ceased moving well before the light shone out. In the following darkness he did not move, but raised himself and listened.

There was no sound on the ridge. He shivered because of the chilling of the sweat on the small of his back, but waited another ten minutes and then crawled swiftly toward the ridge, slinging a cartridge ahead of him. The round fell with a metallic click, but there was no movement on the crest. In the next interval he laid his coat over a high rock and then, the moon shining upon the peak, he rapped the boulder with the rifle muzzle and drew the coat toward him. The Enemy did not fire.

Half an hour later, having crawled another fifty yards, Pere stood up and there was no shot.

"Gone," he ejaculated; "couldn't stand it." He felt sick.

He slept that night between two rocks. The following morning he was late at the breach near the Tonnelé pass, and to his alarm neither Jaime nor the bag of rations was in the breach. Hungry and worn from restless sleep, he dawdled along the Unnamed ridge to the col, where he saw Carlos sitting on a rock on the very skyline, an ideal target.

"Cullon, what in hell's name are you doing there?" he shouted, and the boy, abashed, made no answer. "Haven't I told you never to sit on a skyline, idiot? You haven't the sense of a donkey; and who in hell sent you here? Get out of it, get down out of it," Pere yelled and dragged the boy by the shoulder.

"The Adjutant sent me, Pere."

"The Adjutant be damned. . . . I gave you orders, do you hear?" Pere shouted. "What does *he* know about mountains? He never saw a mountain till a month ago."

"But, Pere . . . Pere, Jaime is dead."

"Dead . . . you say." It was not until his next words that Pere changed his tone. "You say he's dead. . . . Little Mother of God, how did it happen?"

"The Adjutant made a visit of inspection; he wanted to see the passes you named in your report. He brought me here with him. We found Jaime in the Aran pass." The boy was still afraid of the senior scout.

"Dead?"

"Yes. . . . The Adjutant said I was to watch Jaime's passes," continued the boy, "because . . ."

"No." Pere spoke abstractedly, "No, you can't do that; go back to your old patrol. I'll look after the high ground." He was moved by kindness to the inexperienced lad, as well as by his hate of the Enemy. That the Enemy had killed Jaime he never even questioned.

"The Adjutant wants you to report to the Division at once, Pere."

"The adjutant can go to hell," he answered coldly; "give me my rations."

"I . . . I . . ." the boy's mouth dried and it was only with effort that at last he said, "I haven't got them."

"You haven't!"

"No . . . the comrades thought you wouldn't obey. . . . You didn't report the first time . . ."

"So they thought they'd starve me out, eh! Christ Jesus . . . get out, get out. . . ." Pere spoke with ferocity and advanced on the boy, who flinched but stood his ground.

"Pere, don't. . . . The party cell took a decision . . ."

"About me, to starve me out, eh—the party . . ." The rage in Pere's gaze increased and he did not finish the sentence, but half-turned and, keeping cover behind the rocks, moved off toward the Mulleres. Carlos appealed to him in vain to return, and then, taking out his own ration of bread, ran after Pere and forced it upon him.

"Keep it, I can look after myself."

"No, Pere . . . please, comrade." There was such distress in the boy's eyes that Pere accepted the gift. With an effort he controlled his voice.

"Listen, Carlos, you keep off these passes, do you hear?"

"Aren't you going to report, Pere?"

Rebellion reinforced angry hate of the Enemy. Pere strode away, without further speech.

That night, driven by hunger, and the obsession which had taken hold of his mind, Pere visited the Renclusa refuge. There he killed the fascist sentry and boldly entered the dining room. Though the rest of the guard was sleeping in the warm kitchen, he helped himself to tins of preserves and a bagful of bread. In the chapel, dug into the solid rock of a ridge in front of the refuge, he found ammunition, two German submachine guns and six boxes of hand grenades. He carried all this to the foot of a small rock ledge and, having ascended to the summit of the escarpment, he withdrew the pin of a grenade and dropped it among the rest of the war material, and running a few paces, flung himself down. The explosion roared among the peaks. The Renclusa summit appeared and disappeared with the flash.

He lay all day on the summit, overlooking the enemy patrol's head-quarters, brooding over the Division, Agustin, Jaime; building up his obsession, fomenting the rebellion within him. The Enemy, who appeared not to be the commander of the patrol, was among them; sitting before the refuge, drawing maps, it appeared, all the morning and afternoon.

A week went by of hunger and joyless effort. Two attitudes toward the 43rd struggled within Pere. He tried to consider that he had broken with organized resistance to the enemy, and in long debates with himself sustained that he should never have joined a party that had been the principal instrument in creating the regular army. He knew, none the less, that the irregular waging of trench warfare was, by definition, impossible. The Italian and German invasion of Spain had changed the whole technical character of the war; the day of guerrillas seemed to have gone. When he considered this his hatred of the invaders flamed up within him. The mechanical aid to the rebels was violating the nature of the Spaniard, he felt. Man to man, valor against valor— that was the Spanish way of fighting. Not factory against factory, bald-headed engineer against a peasant, a coppersmith.

His trapping of the patrol in the Maladetta couloir had seemed to release something within him at which he himself was surprised. One of his most persistent memories during these days and nights was of the wailing couloir after the enemy patrol had fallen from the Tower. The incident both delighted and repelled him; sometimes, indeed, he felt sick in remembering the event. There were cavernous recesses within his own being, it seemed, through which echoed his own voice, both weeping and yelling in ferocious glee. "War poisons everything, makes you love killing," he said once or twice, but more often he savagely repeated, "Weep, little Italian, weep; you came to make war." He had no proof, but he invariably thought of the Enemy as an Italian. It was the Italian Enemy who was drawing him away from his comrades . . . and when he used that word in place of Division he was suddenly sick at heart as well as in mind.

He felt, and acutely, the contradiction in his position—that he should have broken with his unit now when the whole Division must make guerrillas. Yet it seemed that he was the Division's chief defense against sniping attack. It was justification for his conduct, he argued.

He was on the Llosas ridge when, placing his hand upon a boulder and leaping lightly into the gully, he almost ran down upon the izard.

She was sitting upon a ledge of the gully, her head toward the ridge. He stood, trying not to disturb the stones, smiling, delighted, and then cautiously sat down, astonished that the beast did not leap to her feet and escape. The izard was sick, he thought; she was shivering and there was appeal in her face. Her mouth was open slightly and she breathed quickly. "Don't be afraid, señora," he said, and then could not restrain a hasty movement which startled the izard. There was a little cry from beside the animal. The kid was half-hidden by her flank.

The izard must have given birth a few minutes before he had arrived in the gully, for the little one was still too weak to stand. It uttered a weak cry, bumping its head clumsily against the mother, and she licked it and at once turned back and regarded him.

The izard's winter coat of blackish gray had not yet entirely disappeared, though the brown summer hair was prominent; she was a young animal, he considered, and this must be her first giving birth. "You're at least a thousand feet too high, señora," he thought, and another part of his brain recorded the fact, "Something's driven you up here out of the woods where you should be just now. What will you eat?" There was so little grass at this height. Perhaps she had been on her way to the green oasis in the wilderness where he had seen the izard dung. Her shivering increased for a few minutes and then the kid bleated again and she made a sudden movement of her body, and resettling, pushed her face against the kid, disregarding him. The kid tried to stand up and after several efforts succeeded, planting its feet wide, its head hanging. It tottered one step and tumbled over her flank, and the mother, stretching herself, bleated also and the kid began to suck. At the end of five minutes it was asleep.

Once or twice the izard looked at him, but for half an hour she made no movement. Pere could sit in that position no longer and with great care essayed to move. The izard was frightened and scrambled to her feet and climbed one or two yards up the gully, but was too fatigued to leap the low obstacle of a smooth rock rib. She gave up the attempt to drive him away and returned to her awakened baby. The kid walked two or three steps to meet her, its legs already strong enough to stand securely. The mother bleated and the kid replied, and both lay down again, the little one pressing itself against the warm white belly; the mother ceased to be afraid and lowered her head upon her flank, partly covering the kid, which protested and scrambled out. The mother bleated her protest and pushed the little one with her head. For a moment it resisted and then fell with a comical suddenness so that Pere chuckled aloud. The mother was very much startled.

At the end of its first hour of life the kid scrambled to its feet, its weakness gone, and stepped away from its mother into the gully bed and sniffed at the rock. Then it descended the gully boldly, for four or five feet, its tiny hooves tapping nervously on the rock. For a while it stood gazing out over the waste of small stones, along the Llosas valley, as if attracted by the glittering tarns. Presently it returned to its mother and sucked. A little later the kid began to move about the gully again and this time attempted to climb on to the rocks of the ridge face.

The izard's toleration of him delighted Pere. He also felt what he could not define, that after three weeks in the wilderness this encounter was especially gracious to him. His pleasure was boundless when the kid trotted up to the gully and stared at him, tilting its head, sniffing. He encouraged it when it tried to cross the rock rib.

He was watching the kid's growth; it was visibly growing strong. The giddiness and helplessness in one hour had become sturdiness; and in two hours more, he knew from shepherds' talk, the kid would be able to follow its mother over any mountain hazard.

Suddenly the mother became startled and stood up, listening, staring at Pere. Again she moved to attack him, but though the rock rib would have been no obstacle, she did not do so. She did not take up her old position, however, but quickly and nervously descended the gully, going out of sight. The kid climbed down easily behind her. Ten minutes later he saw the izard out upon the stony wastes facing the gully, bleating to the kid, which he could not see.

Pere, forgetting the izard, suddenly became alert and released the safety catch of his rifle. Above, on the crest, he heard a shot, and he crouched, resting the barrel on the stones at the head of the gully. There was no answering shot and he was wondering whether it could have been a signal when he heard the kid bleat, and glancing down, saw it standing by the body of its mother. The white stomach was upturned, the head twisted and pressed against a stone.

There were quick steps on the ridge, of rope-shod feet. His hand adjusted itself to the butt. As the Enemy appeared Pere fired, in anger at the izard's death. Satisfaction surged through him, impelling the blood fiercely through his body, the recoiling impact of accomplished vengeance. Then quietness settled over him.

The Enemy was not dead, for Pere could hear groans upon the ridge. He descended the gully a little way, traversed the face of the mountain, and reached the crest behind the Enemy. There was no need for caution, the rifle had fallen from the Enemy's grasp. He strode up to the fallen man and shouted, "Why did you kill the izard?" The Enemy looked up; in his eyes hatred was more visible than pain.

"Why did you kill the izard?" Pere repeated, his voice sinking. "Where are you hit?" He knelt beside the man, who continued to stare in hatred until his eyes closed in pain.

Pere began to examine the Enemy, unbuttoning his tunic, at which the man opened his eyes, pain intensifying the hate in them. The long, intellectual, but undistinguished face was paling rapidly. Caution again prompted Pere and he crouched low beside the man. The Enemy's hand, stained with colored inks, moved feebly, and Pere, following the movement, removed the Luger pistol the Enemy was carrying. Glancing at the rifle, he saw that it was a Mannlicher-Cacano.

"Are you an Italian?" he demanded sharply, and the Enemy did not reply; he shook the man by his tunic. "Italian?" he demanded sharply, ignoring the sign of new pain.

"More Spaniard than you," the man said, through closed jaws, his eyes shut.

"Ah," Pere exclaimed softly, and began to search the Enemy's clothing. Wishing to avoid causing him pain, he attempted to remove the rucksack.

"I'm sorry," he said; "I don't want to hurt you. I'll make you comfortable." He knew the man could not live, for the bullet had penetrated the stomach in what the Division doctor called Zone 4, of maximum gravity. He took out his own blanket and laid it over the Enemy, who made attempts to reject this comfort. Pere had never seen such hatred as in that white face, with its sunken cheekbones and colorless eyes. He opened the Enemy's sack intending to make a pillow of his blanket.

"Leave it alone," burst from the wounded man's twisted mouth.

The sack contained a Zeiss short-base range finder, three sheets of the Schrader map of the Central Pyrenees, with recent corrections and fine lines drawn upon them; a pair of Leitz binoculars and drawing instruments. A map-maker or an artillery officer, Pere thought, but he didn't look like a professional.

"Are you thirsty?" he asked, and offered him water, the last contained in his flask. The Enemy deliberately spilled the water.

"*Hombre,*" Pere exclaimed softly and instinctively looked toward the nearest tarn. Picking up the Leitz glasses, he counted four of the enemy crossing the last visible slopes of the Llosas valley. He watched them sink below the curve of the slope, going toward Malibierna, apparently having marched from below the Tempest. A little later two men crossed the col in the ridge on which he was kneeling, not two hundred yards from him. They were carrying heavy burdens.

The passage of the six men and the presence of the wounded Enemy had confirmed the intuition which had sent Pere upon this patrol round. He had been staring dully at the Enemy's maps for several minutes when the significance of the fine lines burst upon him. He saw that they were not artillery plottings, but cones of parabolic machine-gun fire. Their range indicated that clearly. "Ah, very nice," he exclaimed, noting their points of origin. When the Division returns from the Aran heights toward the Aneto village . . . Would the fellow never die? He wanted to be off, across the uplands, to warn Beltrán. . . .

The Enemy remained in the same condition all the morning, until the rain began. Shortly afterward he became delirious. Pere, sullen and miserable, arranged the two sacks in order to keep the rain from the Enemy's head, but the driving rain streamed upon his face.

At last the dying man subsided into a restless stupor. Again Pere attended to his sack. He decided that despite its weight he would carry away the range finder, as well as his own glasses. As he was flinging the Luger into the sack the Enemy uttered a piercing scream and beat his hands against sharp stones.

"Oh, Christ," Pere gasped and pulled the pistol trigger. The Enemy lay still. "Poor devil, ah, poor devil . . . it was best," Pere murmured, and averting his gaze, felt in the dead man's breast and removed a few rain-soaked papers and flung them into the sack. He plunged down the gully.

Below, on the gravel-littered slabs, hearing the kid's bleat, he altered his direction. The kid was still standing by the white-bellied body, its light hair darkened by the drenching rain, shivering. As he approached the creature ran away bleating. Pere swore, but again pursued it, yet being heavily laden, could not get near it. "Damn you, you've learned to be afraid," he shouted, waving his arm furiously in the direction of the pasture to which he had meant to carry the animal. He made one more attempt to capture the kid, but it eluded him. It cost him ten minutes of blundering and shouting to drive the bewildered creature within sight of the grass. "I don't know whether the cursed thing can eat grass yet," he muttered, and struck out once more down the slope. There were hundreds of the enemy in the Malibierna, he found. He turned and began the long journey to the 43rd.

Hearing his shout, six of the patrol stumbled out to meet him; one of them, feeling him stagger, linked his arm and led him to a pile of stones. He sat, his head bowed, breathing deeply.

"Now then," Pere began, "you, Carlos, you'll get out on the slope by Peak Russell, you know the spot. You, Tomas, go to your emergency place, on the bluff by the tarn. Enrique, you . . ."

One of the men stepped forward and said, "I'm sorry, comrade, I have orders to arrest you. I am in command here."

"Arrest me, to hell, what do you mean!" But he did not continue to give orders, nor did he so much as peer into the face of the man to identify him.

The old members of the patrol remained silent, standing a few paces withdrawn, while the new Commander took a paper from a wallet and offered it to Pere, and said, "If you care to come over to the wall I'll strike a light."

"I don't need documents," Pere mumbled and then jumped to his feet. "Listen, you're Commander. Here's what you do. . . ." He explained his plan of vigilance against the rear attack, his successor listening with growing excitement.

"I'll go on to Headquarters," Pere concluded; "you take the men out."

"I'm sorry, comrade, you are under arrest." There was a note of stubbornness in the voice.

"Cullon, arrest! What does arrest matter! Go on, arrest me, then; I'm not resisting, but *get on with your work*. Sweet Christ! they'll be over in the morning and you're worrying about an arrest."

"I've got to send a file with you."

"All right, send Carlos."

"Very good, Carlos, take this comrade to the Hospice de Viella."

The boy hastened along the black valley by the side of the prisoner.

Two hours later, as they approached the hostel below the anciently used pass into the Aran valley and France, Carlos laid his hand upon the prisoner's arm.

"What's the matter? Hurry."

"Pere, I don't like saying this, but you're not supposed to be carrying a rifle."

"Take it then. Take the damn thing. . . . All right, boy, I'm sorry."

They were challenged a hundred yards before the Hospice, but the sentry did not know of the order for Pere's arrest and to the boy's relief allowed them to continue without larger escort.

Carlos pushed open the door and called for the sergeant of the guard. "I've brought Pere," he said desperately and lowered both rifles to the floor.

"You'll have to go into the back room, comrade," the sergeant said, ashamed.

"Where's Esquinazo?"

"He'll be in soon; in an hour's time."

"Alberto?"

"On the pass; there's been a battle, they tried a frontal attack."

"The Adjutant . . . tell me, how'd it go up there, all right?"

"Yes, we've lost about twenty. They say a shepherd from Bosost warned our outposts two hours before they came into range. I don't know, there was a hell of a racket up there this morning."

"Now listen, comrade, look. I'll hand all this over to you." Pere dumped the sack heavily on the floor and, cutting the swollen cord, took out the maps. "There's a Luger in there too and other stuff."

"Come into the light, Pere," the sergeant exclaimed, and leaving Carlos in the passage, they shut the door. Behind the door the boy heard them talking excitedly. Presently they came out.

"Eh, you can go back, comrade," the sergeant said and Carlos turned toward the door.

"I shan't have time to get out to my post, Pere." The scout spoke hesitantly.

"No, the best thing would be to go up to the Unnamed peak—but I can't give you the order."

"I'll tell the other . . ."

"He'll be out, at work. Can't you keep him here?" Pere said to the sergeant.

"Yes, perhaps you'd better go back to-morrow. Turn in with the guard."

It seemed to Pere that he waited hours in the lightless detention room and then there was a great noise of stamping in the corridor, and a series of orders. When the sergeant came again and asked him to follow him to Esquinazo's office he did so without a word.

Beltrán, "Esquinazo," stood behind the table, still wearing his sheep-skin coat over his uniform and the cowherd's leather hat. His symbols of rank were pinned to the lapel of his tunic.

"So they caught you," he exclaimed, with fierce anger. The Chief of Operations and a junior officer were standing by the shuttered window.

"I came down."

"So you came down. . . . You will go before the court-martial. Do you wish to be tried by the men or by the officers alone?"

"It's all the same."

"Yes. I'm not going to be at the judges' table, I've had to do that before with you. I've told the Adjutant to ask for severe punishment. Do you wish to know what?"

"Yes . . . sir."

"Ah, well, if you're found guilty, you'll be reduced to the ranks, for the time being."

"For the time being, comrade?" Pere did not amend the expression but regarded the Commander with troubled gaze.

"If we get out of this, back to our own territory, I hope you'll be dis-missed from the Division. You will be."

"Why, Esquinazo, I've done good work for you."

"You have—and bad work; that will do."

"Bad work, what do you mean?"

"I ordered you down to supervise the outposts on this side as well. We got word from a French comrade, a shepherd, about the attack up there. If it hadn't been for him . . ." Esquinazo began calmly, but his temper rose sharply as he spoke. He knew this was not a valid accusa-tion, however, for the outposts he himself had placed had come in with reports an hour after the Frenchman had warned the Chief of Staff. "You've seen enough trouble with us, you'd better transfer to another unit," he added, and the Lieutenant smiled, hearing this softening of the original formula. Then, throwing his gun and holster on the table and flinging his coat into a corner, Esquinazo ordered the Lieutenant to fetch the Quartermaster and the Chief of Staff who were outside with the column. He bent over the maps until the officers came in.

"Sit down, comrades," he began, and shouted for the sergeant to bring more chairs. "Now, this man reports preparations for an attack from below, a battalion of Navarros stationed at the Balneario near Benasque. They're coming over Malibierna. He proposes the following plan . . ."

For five minutes Esquinazo outlined the plan and then said, "What's your opinion, comrades, can the men outside march at once? We have only two hundred in rest."

"They'll go of course. They'll go better if you speak to them," the Major said.

"I'm going with them; you'll take over here," the Commander addressed the Chief of Staff; then, turning to the Quartermaster he said, "Get dry rations for the battalion outside for one day, and prepare for two more days. We're moving off in a quarter of an hour."

"Comrades, can't I go?" Pere interjected. The Chief of Staff gazed hesitantly from him to the Commander.

"You? Hostia, is that man still here! Sergeant, Sergeant, why is this man hanging about here? Lock him up at once."

For a moment Pere expected the Commissar to ask for leniency, but Alberto marched out of the room. The Commander jumped to his feet and rebelted his pistol and holster. Getting into his sheepskin, he thrust Pere aside with a lurch of his massive body, and strode out.

"Better come along, Pere," the sergeant said, and he walked listlessly along the corridor and entered the detention room.

Pere awoke at two in the afternoon, to find food by his side; outside it was raining torrentially. He banged on the door and asked the guard whether the Commander had returned.

"No, no one's returned, except the Quartermaster and he went away at once."

"Any news?"

"No. It's snowing up on the main ridge. The sergeant says they're going to bring the Division down."

Impatient for news, Pere could find nothing to occupy the time. Then, shortly before nightfall, the armorer brought him a machine gun, an old United States 1920 model, and asked him to examine and clean it, and he worked until ten o'clock. He had lain down for the night when the pounding of hooves brought him to his feet. Yes, it was the Staff! He banged on the door but no one came. Then came shouts and laughter and a Viva, and answering Vivas and then he heard Esquinazo blunder noisily into his office and yell for the telegrapher. Pere hammered again, but in the uproar of shouts and stamping of feet he supposed no one heard him. Then the door slammed and he gave up hope of being able to catch a word of the din proceeding in Esquinazo's office.

At two in the morning, he heard the "Internationale" being sung, far down the valley it seemed. It must be the battalions returning, he thought. The Hospice seemed to be full of blundering, hurrying men. The "Internationale" was suddenly nearer. They're coming up over the bank, Pere thought, excitedly. Still singing, the battalions wheeled round the Hospice.

Presently Alberto's voice was heard, thanking the troops. They would rest two days if the enemy permitted. Fall out by companies.

"Viva Esquinazo," someone yelled. "Viva," cried the battalion.

There were more voices and again the "Internationale." Pere hammered at the door once more. "Cullon, why don't you open! Esquinazo, damn you, I planned that battle."

Hours seemed to go by. There was a conference in the common dormitory upstairs, he knew. At times there was a chorus of approval above and sometimes emphatic interjections. After a while he heard the Operations Chief reciting in his level, boring voice.

Many times in the old days Pere had yarned and slept in the dormitory above, retelling the day's climb or listening to the Aran muleteers going down to Ribagorzana's lower markets, or absorbing some contrabandist's tale of adventure, for the sake of the mountain knowledge such men had. He was brooding over the old days when the door rattled and his name was called. He got up, put on his tunic and buttoned it carefully, and went out behind the guard.

"Stand over there, please," the Commissar said, and Pere took his place beside the Operations Chief, before whom the Schrader maps were spread out. The barred shadows of the hurricane lamp suspended from the beam shifted backward and forward across the Commander's face. The telegraphic apparatus was tapping continuously in the next room.

"It will be impossible to do more than fix general alternatives," Operations said, "but we shall have simple maps prepared. They will be without great detail, for we have no unused paper left. Now tell me," he continued, looking at Pere, "what's the population of this town, Gistain?"

"About five hundred. San Pedro de las Tabernas goes with it; say six hundred."

"Cattle town?"

"Yes, some. There's cobalt and lead mines."

"Ah." The officers commented quietly.

"We'll find help there," Camps said. In his youth the assistant commissar had been a miner. The Operations Chief wrote in the information against the town's name.

"Bielsa, what do you know about this place?"

"About five hundred. There are mines in the valley."

"I can't see any way over the mountains here. Do you have to go down the valley to this juncture and up again to continue along the chain?"

"No. It's hard going though. There's a difficult route over the Pineda range, then through the Passet breach, it's about here, and then down the Paso de Golis into the Soaso amphitheater. It's not for everybody, there's iron rungs in a low cliff there. There are other routes but you'd need someone who knew the place."

"Do you know the place?"

"Yes."

"All this is the Monte Perdido group?"

"Yes."

"*Caramba,*" exclaimed a young middle-class lieutenant, "the Lost Division in the Lost Mountains!"

Pere started and looked with excitement toward Alberto. The telegrapher shouted, "I've got it, it's coming through," and everyone was silent, heads turned toward the door. The operator slowly wrote down a message on a piece of crumpled paper. A full minute of tense silence passed and then the telegrapher took off his head-piece and forced his way through to the Commander, ignoring the outthrust hands.

Esquinazo read the message slowly and then gave it to his Chief of Staff. It was next handed to Alberto who, silently inquiring of the Colonel, received a nod for answer. He looked round and waited for silence.

"Ministry of War, Barcelona, Seo de Urgell, for 43rd Division, commanding officer, Señor Don Antonio Beltrán. Message received. Congratulations. Viva República."

"Viva!" Esquinazo exclaimed, and in low voices the officers answered, "Viva!"

"Relieving force recaptured Llavorsí yesterday. Held up, bad weather. Hold on. Heartfelt gratitude. Negrín."

"Llavorsí, where's Llavorsí?" Alberto demanded.

"In the Pallaresa valley, the other side of the Enchanted peaks," Pere answered.

"Where's that?" Torres intoned.

"Parallel valley to this, toward the coast."

"Well, they've retaken it; that's the best enchantment I know," Esquinazo said.

"You may as well read this," the Commissar said quietly, waiting for the Commander to object. Esquinazo kept silent. Alberto passed a slip of paper to Pere. "This is the message we sent out."

"Seo for Barcelona. Seo for Barcelona. Seo Barcelona. Met and totally destroyed two battalions enemy to-day. Captured quantity war material. Can hold out, have food, munitions. Beltrán 43rd Division. Seo for Barcelona, Seo . . . Barcelona. . . ."

"Comrade," Pere burst out and the paper shook in his hands. They waited for him to speak. "Viva la República," he concluded, unable to say more. "Viva," they answered again.

"What are the difficulties about establishing contact with the relief column?" Operations asked tapping the map.

"We'd have to cross the Beciberis and the Enchanted range. They're difficult to move over. Then take Espot and strike down into the Pallaresa, below Esterri."

"Difficult," the officer muttered, tracing a line on the map.

"You were talking about the Perdido region," Pere began, and drew himself erect and was silent.

The Commander lighted a cigarette and nodded to the Commissar who, after a pause, said, "Comrade Pere Cardona."

"Sir," Pere answered, standing to attention.

"The Staff has taken a decision about you. You are censured for the offense of disobedience and neglect of your duty as controlling officer of the west-side patrols. You are severely censured for striking a comrade. Do you accept that?"

"Yes, sir."

"Besides this censure, I must ask you to come to my room to-morrow at nine o'clock."

"Yes, comrade." He knew that he would have to face the party's directive committee; and he knew what to expect from them.

"In view of this, the commanding officer and the Divisional Commissar have decided, in consultation with senior officers, that your offense can go without further punishment."

"O Little Mother of God!" whispered Pere and put out his hands to Esquinazo. The Commander waved him back and he stood at attention beside the Operations Chief. Alberto glanced at Esquinazo who motioned that the Commissar should be silent.

"All right. We've decided that we can't undertake any more pitched battles like the one up yonder"—he jerked his head backwards toward the Aran heights—"or we shall run out of ammunition and have to take the trip over the frontier. So we're going to break up one half of the Division into three guerrilla forces; each working on its own, but keeping contact with me at Bielsa. You are to command the western force."

Pere stood facing Esquinazo, as if dazed.

"Esquinazo," he said at last, hoarsely, and saluted.

"You'll be working the farthest away from the base," the Commander continued, "and you'll have to live off the region, and do it with next to no munitions. Can you do that?"

"Yes."

Conversation broke out among the officers, but the Chief of Staff soon called the conference to order. "We shall meet to-morrow, at ten o'clock if possible, for discussion. You'll be here to lead it, Pere; we've got to study the maps. Comrades, you may go."

Pere left the Hospice and, though it was raining heavily again, he sat upon a shelf of rock just beside a shelter. For an hour he reflected upon the events of the last fortnight and the Malibierna battle.

At the end of the hour he remembered that he had put a piece of bread in his pocket and, feeling for it, was delighted to find it was much bigger than he had remembered. "What luck!" he exclaimed aloud, and settled himself more comfortably, drew his coat collar high, and hunched his shoulders, so that his head was protected. How good is bread, he thought, listening to the rain outside the retreat he had made. Contentedly he ate the bread, piece by small piece, relishing its wheaten flavor; happiness growing within him. When he had finished, thinking with merriment of the comradeship he would have, he returned to the Hospice. The sentry saluted wearily and he entered. He went to the detention room for his blankets, and climbed up the narrow stairs to the dormitory. He felt along the sleeping platform to find a space between booted feet.

"Cullon, that's the biggest pair of feet I've ever met," he whispered.

"You leave my feet alone," growled a sleepy voice, and Pere chuckled and edged himself between two snoring colleagues and slept soundly.

78

The Eyes

BY THOMAS OWEN BEACHCROFT

IT HAD been a long day at the hospital. Like arches in a cloister the grey hours stretched backwards, a succession of long, exhausting days. With quick nervous movements Dr. Sylvester sped down the corridor to the street door. His rapid step was on the verge of running, like a man escaping. He saw the green paint of the walls was moist with the rime of the November evening. Fog had entered the passage and each electric light bulb was surrounded by a nimbus of misty air. The cement floor resounded dully underneath his feet.

It was a double swing door which opened on to the street, green painted, with a brown worn streak on each side where impatient feet had pushed it open. Drawing on his gloves as he went, Dr. Sylvester jerked his shoulder against the swinging door. But as it gave to let him through he heard a voice calling down the passage.

"Doctor! Doctor Sylvester!"

"Oh, damn," he muttered, "what now, what now?"

A second later he would have been through the doors away from the hospital. For a moment he hesitated and let the doors swing to behind him, but a nurse came running up the passage and he was caught again.

"I'm so sorry, Doctor," she said. "Sister asked me to find you before you went."

"Well?"

"Dr. Sterndale isn't here yet; there's a case come in; in the receiving-room now—it's a——"

Dr. Sylvester turned abruptly and ran past her up the passage, without listening to the rest of her explanations. As he pushed by, making her step back against the wall with his sudden movement, she saw his face was white, almost grey, and very tired. His black keen eyes were sunk in his head, and the skin dark and discoloured underneath them. His lips were pale, nearly as pale as his face.

"Still," she thought, "it's no use being a doctor, or a nurse, if you expect to have your life to yourself. And Dr. Sylvester was lucky to have a home and a wife and baby; his life wasn't *all* hospital. And again, if a doctor likes to do a hospital job as well as a practice, of course he gets used up; it's his own choice." She was forgetting, or perhaps never knew, that Dr. Sylvester's work at the hospital was unpaid.

Sylvester burst into the receiving-room and closed the door sharply.

"Well?" he said.

The Sister was there: with her, sitting on the bench that ran down one side of the bare-boarded room, was a young woman; an old-looking young woman, unbecomingly and dingily dressed. Her sallow skin and pale lips were utterly untouched by lipstick or powder, as if she had patiently refused to take any interest in her own appearance.

Lying limply in her arms was a little girl of four or five. The child's body seemed stiff and resistant: as if the arms could no longer make her comfortable. Her head hung back across the crook; rather too far back. The face was flushed and the eyes suffused with blood. The breathing was deep and heavy. The child was in a stupor of feverish sleep, or perhaps quite unconscious.

For a second no one spoke.

Sylvester, turning his back on the two women, flung off his coat and gloves and threw them on the table.

"Well?" he said, as he did so.

"This little girl was brought in about a quarter of an hour ago . . ." began the Sister, not quite certain if she had his attention. "Dr. Sterndale seems to have been delayed, and the case . . ."

"How did it begin?" said Sylvester, interrupting her and turning to the mother with spasmodic swiftness.

She glanced up at the Sister, not quite certain if she was to speak.

"Yesterday," she said, and hesitated. Sylvester began to pace the room.

"Go on," he said.

"Yesterday morning, when she woke up she seemed a bit queer and heavy; and as soon as my husband looked at her he said: 'Oh, look at her eyes, whatever has the child done to her eyes?' I thought she must have caught a bad cold in her eyes. . . ."

The woman paused. She found it hard to talk to this pale, abrupt doctor, who spoke in rapid nervous jerks, or said nothing and scarcely seemed to be listening.

The brilliant electric light beat hard on them, turning their faces dead white. It shed a dream-like brightness and cast hard-edged shadows all round them: the white starched apron and tall figure of the Sister stood vivid and luminous against the dark clothes of the mother. With an effort she went on speaking.

"Then she seemed very heavy all yesterday, and she had a bad headache. She just seemed to be asleep all the time, but was quite quiet—I didn't like her being so quiet. I gave her a little soup, but she didn't seem to care for it, though she took it."

As she spoke Sylvester placed a thermometer under the child's arm. Then he began to take her pulse. He found the hand was very hot and dry and the pulse slow, yet strongly marked and irregular. He turned up one of the child's eyelids and gazed for a moment at the eye; the ball was discoloured and filled with blood. He let it go, and as the dark lashes sank again on the cheek, the child made no sign or movement.

"Go on," he said to the mother, "don't stop."

"When my husband came in," she went on, " 'I don't like her looks,' he said. 'We ought to have the doctor, if she don't look better in the morning.' So I told him, let's see how she sleeps. I only hope I was right to leave it."

She broke off, as Sylvester took the thermometer from the child's arm. She sat very still, not moving the child on her lap, though her arms were aching. Surely he would say something, would tell her something about the child now, would let her know what he was thinking or what he knew.

He scarcely glanced at the thermometer, and handed it straight back to the Sister. In fact, he scarcely needed to glance at it. He knew now the temperature would be a hundred and two or over.

"Well?" he said, his voice still sounding stern and impatient.

"She slept quite quiet," said the mother, gathering resolution in some way from his abruptness. "She slept so well I thought it must be all right, but she was no better nor worse this morning. Just lay quite listless—then this evening she got so that I couldn't rouse her at all. I couldn't do nothing till my husband was back, and I brought her straight round here."

"Did your husband come?"

"No," she said. "I have two others—she's the eldest."

He nodded, and turned to the Sister and spoke quickly in a low voice, at the same time seizing his coat from the table and beginning to put it on.

"Yes, Doctor," she heard the Sister answer, "of course. The small annexe of Ward B is quite empty. I'll see to it at once. . . ."

"No—I'll see to that," he said, "you see to the child—then I must really go."

He was at the door as he finished speaking. He pulled it open, then darted back into the room as the woman stood up with her child.

"Good-bye," he said, "good-bye," nodded quickly, and was gone without waiting for her to reply.

Five minutes later Dr. Sylvester was again in the passage hurrying towards the door that led to the outside world. Once that door closed behind him he would be shut off from the strain and overwork of the last few weeks. It had gone too far now. He must rest.

But as he walked his step slackened, then involuntarily he paused before the door and stood waiting: he bit the fingers of the gloves he carried, pulling them with jerks against his teeth.

He had done all that was necessary. Sterndale was already in the hospital; he could hear his hearty voice echoing in the stone-floored corridors behind him. It would be absurd to go back now to give him personal details of this one case: and he was too tired for Sterndale. Besides, it wasn't the child he was thinking of; she was going to die. She had meningitis; the fulminant type that killed quickly. Already her blood-stained eyes had reflected their last image of her mother— the last sight of this world she would ever see.

For a few moments he stood biting his glove, then impulsively he pushed the doors open and stepped out, taking the direction which led to his home.

After a few moments he turned and walked back again, treading gently as if he were breaking some private rule. He passed the swing doors and reached the main entrance to the hospital. Here he carefully filled and lit a pipe, and took his stand in the shadow watching the tobacco glow in the darkness. From time to time a short sigh escaped him.

He had to wait ten minutes: then he saw the mother come out.

"Perhaps I'm going your way," said Sylvester. "Let me take you to the corner."

The woman walked by his side in silence.

"Did the Sister tell you?" he said.

"Yes sir," she answered.

Again they walked in silence.

"She's not your only child, you said?"

"No, sir—I have two others."

"But she was your first."

"Yes, sir."

"Are the others perfectly well?"

"Perfectly, thank you, sir—*now*. But then so was she. Supposing one of them was to wake up with those eyes to-morrow. What am I to do? How can I be safe?"

She spoke rapidly, but very calmly.

"Can anyone be safe?"

He asked the question in sympathy, yet it sounded almost like a rebuke. They neither of them spoke again till they reached the end of the street.

"I must go here," said Sylvester. "Good-bye."

He watched her pass two or three street lamps and she was lost in the misty darkness. She never looked back.

Sylvester began to walk home at a fierce pace. He wished he had said more to her. But what was the object of dwelling on it? His duty was to rest his nerves and keep his judgment clear: why pick out this one case from a week of too much strain? It was his knowledge the hospital needed, not misplaced sensibility and exacerbated nerves.

She was beyond sympathy, too. For the moment the calamity, like a terrible wound, when it is first inflicted, gave her no anguish. "My first-born child is dying," she was saying to herself—and it filled her with strange exaltation and strength.

Sylvester began to share in this exaltation. He strode on down the long avenue of street lamps: they glowed, two or three in front of him, in the wreaths of mist, each one casting round it an exhalation of doubtful light: a wheel of yellow ringed with blue that slowly revolved as he approached.

Who can be certain? A doctor faces danger every day, from fevers, from contagion, breaths laden with death, and touches of putrefying flesh. Closing the swing doors cannot cut off the dangers which may follow him out of the hospital into his private life and his home. Another tread was following his now; he turned and in the fog could see no one, only the muffled steps went on and a man cleared his throat.

He turned from the lights, and vivid pictures of the day were painted on the darkness before his open eyes. He saw the mother on the seat with the child unmoving in her arms: and the bright light beating on the child's face and fevered eyes: now rose-hued, now filled with flames and rubies; now immeasurably extended and far away, like a red-eyed western sky where veins and arteries hang in the air.

Then he stopped; and turning, at once walked quickly back to the hospital and shouldered through the swing doors.

"Sylvester," said Sterndale an hour later in his deep, commanding voice, "I'm surprised to see you still here, I thought you'd gone home. Did you have any sleep last night?"

"Oh, an hour or two: I'm all right, just a bit tired."

"My dear fellow, your face is grey—your eyes look a mile away: and you're walking about like a man in a dream. Do go home and get to bed."

"I'm going to stay to-night. There's something I want to see."

"There's not the slightest need: I shall be here myself till midnight or after. What is it?"

"A meningitis case in B annexe."

"What, that child who came in this evening? There's nothing to do. I can give you full details. She's bound to die."

Sylvester looked hard at the floor as if he were talking to it.

"I know," he said with a sudden jerk. "That's why I'm going to stay."

"I don't understand."

"I want to watch the eyes just at the moment of death."

Sterndale shook his head.

"Listen," he said, "you can do that some other time: you'll drop in your tracks."

"I never drop in my tracks."

"Why do you want to?"

"Obviously," said Sylvester without raising his eyes, "because it's a particularly good opportunity. She will be unconscious from now till the time she dies: it will happen before the morning and then I can rest. Have you ever seen what I mean?"

"Can't say I have."

"Well, I have, but only once: and I want to see it again. I can promise you it's the only reason on earth that would make me stay to-night."

Sterndale took him by the arm.

"You ought to think of the infection," he said. "You'll be bending over that child's face for hours, Sylvester. The breath from the nostrils is so dangerous. I wish you'd listen to me, Sylvester . . . besides, you owe something to your wife and your own child: it's not safe; especially in the state you're in."

Sylvester gave a short high-pitched laugh. "I'm sorry not to take your advice." Then with galvanic swiftness he began to race up the stairs three at a time, and vanished.

Sterndale heard him calling on the floor above.

"Bring me an ophthalmascope in the B annexe."

Sylvester was alone in the room with the dying child. Save for the bright light at the head of the bed, the room was all in darkness. He paced steadily backwards and forwards, passing now into the light, now into the darkness again. Each time he turned, his shadow blotted out, then revealed again, the small unmoving body that lay propped on the pillows.

Sylvester's step was light and firm. He was no longer tired. He congratulated himself that he had stayed, and on his mounting exhilaration. Backwards and forwards he went, from wainscot to wainscot. In a steady rhythm of light and shade his shadow rose and fell, rose and fell. And the beam flashed in and out on the child's face as he passed now dark, now light, now dark, now light.

He paused and listened to the breathing just faintly audible in the stillness. A hesitation, the slightest flutter, and he was at the bedside, his face against the child's. For whole minutes he remained rigidly still, staring into the eye, feeling the faint whisper of breath against his forehead. It was now three in the morning, and Sylvester had lost all sense of time. The child seemed dead and yet not dead. Occasionally he paused and stared fixedly at her face from a distance.

There were three other empty beds round him. He rested on the bed farthest from the child, lost as it were in the shadowed distances of the room. He picked up a book and, holding it awkwardly so that some dim light fell on it, peered at the print. He turned one page: then put it down.

Perhaps the child would not die till the morning. Already he had been waiting longer than he had expected. Sterndale had warned him of infection. He might next morning see his own child wake and look round with the same blood-filled eyes. That's what the mother had seen first. "Look at the child's eyes," her husband had said, "whatever has the child been doing to her eyes?"

The breathing became more tremulous. Instantly Sylvester's shadow leapt across the room, and he was crouching over the bed. The eye was flooded with a bright light from the mirror of the ophthalmascope; the pupil had already been paralysed by atropine. Sylvester was looking into the depths of a motionless rose-red pool. The beam of light clarified the translucent outer tegument of the eye; it shone past the cornea and the aqueous humour, through the tense and vitreous body with its hyaloid membrane, and gently irradiated the crimson floor of the pool itself—the delicate retina.

This deep background of red was now his whole field of vision. As he gazed the glowing pool changed into a vault of dark roseate midnight, stretching unfathomable leagues above his head, while he, sole gazer, stood rapt and frozen in timeless watching.

Far off at one side there glimmered a pale nebula of wax-like yellow, marking the point where the optic nerve led to the brain behind. From here diverged the delicate and immense wanderings of the veins and arteries across his firmament: the veins deeper in colour and the measureless arteries gleaming like rubies. In those veins and arteries blood was steadily flowing, and would flow for a second more.

At the moment some purulent suffusion paralysed the brain, the blood paused in its steady passage, and the scene changed. A minute colourless point, a hiatus in the bloodstream, appeared in each channel and moved in slow pulsations across the vault: then another. The flow changed to single beads, the last weak pulses of the heart. Sluggishly one final drop moved—paused; moved; then stopped. And the rose colour at once began to fade—faster and paler till the whole vision was drained of colour, and died away, misty and sere.

Sylvester stood back from his instrument with a sudden gush of human tenderness. It was a strange way to die. No tears: no love: just nameless material for medical observation. He closed his eyes, and under the lids the darkness became crimson and patterned like a damask: slowly it turned to purple, then to deepest black. He rang the bell for the nurses, and walked quickly out of the hospital.

In the street it was intensely cold. The street lamps were still burning, but not a soul was about. Sylvester felt too tired almost to walk. A horde of confused terrors attacked him. He should have followed Sterndale's advice. Sterndale was always right. He had been shut up for hours with the child. He had wantonly exposed his own child to the danger of infection.

Like a dwarfed figure in a nightmare he walked on through a dark and endless colonnade of light and shadows, tortured by the incessantly repeated thought of infection. He was oppressed by an intolerable feeling of eternity. His feet hurried him on faster and faster till without knowing it he ran.

When he reached home the house was silent. He felt his way in the darkness, without turning on the lights. His wife and baby were both in a sleep so deep that they neither turned nor sighed. He flung down his clothes quickly, forgetting even to wind his watch, and lay in bed trembling.

Soon a warm tide of sleep crept over him; his limbs were borne out like fronds of weed in a gentle stream; he sank down through fathoms of deep green till he was lost in total blackness; his body was carried restlessly this way and that on whispering currents. Salt fingers fretted at him, dissolving his flesh till his bones shimmered green and naked in the depths.

Shortly before dawn Sylvester moaned in his sleep. He was lying on his back with one arm flung behind his head. His breathing became spasmodic and heavy. In vain he struggled with the monstrous horrors of a nightmare. Lewd and ghastly faces pressed round, and touched him with their wet mouths. Cold tendrils closed round him, paralysing every limb. His soul wept with unbearable loathing and dread—abandoned and lost in the darkest pit of terror.

He screamed, yet he knew he made no sound. His body lay like marble on the bed, and only deep sighs could escape the stifled penetralia of his bosom. He opened his eyes, and for many minutes lay awake, yet powerless to move. He sighed many times: and at last, with an effort of will, roused himself. The room was filled with cool grey winter light.

There was a rustle of movement from his wife's bed.

"What are you doing?" she asked.

"I must get up for a few moments," he said. "I've had a terrible nightmare."

She turned to look at him; then cried out immediately:

"Oh, your eyes! Whatever have you done to your eyes?"

"What?" said Sylvester, almost in a whisper.

"They're so terribly red and bloodshot."

"Give me a looking-glass."

He saw his eyes fevered and deep red, the whole ball suffused with blood.

Desperately calm, he told his wife what it meant. For a few moments they sat silent, each avoiding the other's glance.

"Quick," he said. "Ring up Sterndale's house; there's no time to lose. Ask him to help us. He'll do something."

He watched her pick up the telephone by his bedside with trembling hands, and as she spoke the strength drained from his body. She turned to him.

"He says he must speak to you."

He heard Sterndale's strong firm voice speaking in his ear.

"Is that you, Sylvester? You should have followed my advice. Your nerves are running away with you. It's a bare twelve hours since you first saw that child: only three or four hours since you were in any real danger of infection."

"Yes," said Sylvester, dully.

"Well?" came the voice.

"Good God!" cried Sylvester. "The incubation period! I must be going mad. It's absurd—how could I forget that?"

"You'll forget your own name if you aren't careful," said Sterndale. "Go back to bed and get about twelve hours' sleep. Good-bye, Sylvester."

"It's all right," he said, feeling his heart beating wildly, "it's all right. Good God, how could I forget! I must be going mad."

"But your eyes," said his wife. "Your eyes!"

"Nothing. Just some queer nervous reaction. It's what I've been seeing and thinking. And my being too tired. It's strange the symptoms your mind can produce when it runs away like this. Damned strange . . . rather frightening. . . ."

He flung himself on the bed and burst into a torrent of tears and laughter.

79

The Betting Scotchman

ANONYMOUS

THE colonel of the Red Hussars was an Irishman, who was as proud of his nationality as it is possible for an Irishman to be, and that is not saying a little by any means. He carried his patriotism so far as to aver that not only were the Irish the finest, the most courageous, the most gifted, of the four nationalities, but that nearly all the great Englishmen were really Irishmen. He justified this Hibernianism by a mode of reasoning that was highly original, but not wholly convincing. It would have provoked shouts of laughter in the mess if it had proceeded from the lips of a subaltern, but the colonel was an altogether different person to deal with. It would be dangerous to quarrel with him, and he was as peppery as a London fog, or an old maid who has been jilted by the curate. It was considered far more advisable "to give him his head," and let him exhaust himself by the violence of his own efforts.

When he launched out on his favorite topic, therefore, he was listened to in disrespectful silence by his subordinates; but in revenge it was the greatest delight of the wags of the regiment to mimic his voice and manner, and to represent him as uttering the most astounding Hibernian falsehoods, garnished with numerous expressions of a wholly unprintable character. This was called "doing Old Pat," and was a very popular amusement in every mess-room where the colonel's personality was known. His real name, of course, as the army list will tell you, was Colonel Dominick Sydney Power, but this is a trifling detail. He had been nicknamed Old Pat at a very early stage of his military career, and Old Pat of the Red Hussars was almost as well known throughout the service as Cox's Bank or the cold-meat train to Woking.*

* Army slang for the funeral train to the great cemetery at Woking, near London.

1186

Therefore, when the Red Hussars heard that Sir James Macleod had been gazetted from the Blues to their own regiment, conjecture ran very rife among the officers whether Sir John would contrive to hit it off amicably with Old Pat. It was generally felt that the stranger would probably prove a Scotchman of the deepest dye, with a very large allotment of Scotch pride and patriotism, while, no doubt, after his experiences in the Blues, he would be inclined to regard a mere colonel in a hussar regiment with more compassion than reverence. Under these circumstances, there seemed to be every prospect of some lively scenes when the colonel should deem it fitting to take the Scotch baronet into his confidence on the important subject of national distinctions.

"It will be great fun if he goes for Old Pat, and gives it him hot when he begins the usual rot," said young Fanshawe, with a broad grin, and it was generally agreed among the junior officers of the regiment that it would be great fun indeed.

While his subordinates were coming to this insubordinate decision, Colonel Dominick Power was engaged in reading a long letter from an old schoolfellow of his, and a former brother-officer of Sir James Macleod's, to whom he had written in order to make some inquiries with regard to the new importation into the mess-room of the Red Hussars, and the baronet's motives for effecting the exchange.

"A woman is at the bottom of it, as usual," wrote Captain Fletcher, of the Blues. "Macleod was very hard hit, and she threw him over for no reason that any one can divine. Pure deviltry, that is all. He knew that you were ordered abroad, and he wants to get out of the country without appearing to run away. That's the bait. He is a capital fellow; no nonsense about him in any way; is a good sportsman; A-one shot; and very popular in the regiment. There is only one point on which I had better caution you. *Don't bet with him*. He is a very devil at bets, and always wins."

"Is he, indeed?" mused Colonel Power; "and he may be the very divil himself for all he'll get out of me. It's meself that would like to see the colonel of the regiment betting with a mere whipper-snapper of a subaltern!"

Sir James Macleod proved to be a tall, fair young man, whose long features and high cheek-bones testified very clearly that the place of his birth lay beyond the Tweed. He was not remarkably good-looking, but he carried himself with such an air of distinction that it seemed wonderful, as young Fanshawe said, that any woman could throw over "such a dasher, and a real, live baronet to boot." His manner, however, was that of a man of the world; and it is not remarkable, under the circumstances, that he got on at once with the young men who were to be his companions for the future.

"We thought you would be no end of a heavy swell," said young Fanshawe, in a day or two, during which friendship had ripened into familiarity; "but you ain't a bit."

Whereat Sir James Macleod laughed good-humoredly.

"What shall you do when Old Pat begins his usual rot," continued Fanshawe, in a confidential tone, "about Ireland being the finest country in the universe, and everybody else being miserable scarecrows and outsiders? Shall you stick up for Auld Reekie?* I wish you would. It would make Pat so sick!"

Young Fanshawe explained his meaning at some length.

"And you think that he would be furious if any one contradicted him?" inquired Macleod, fixing a very wary grey eye on the other.

"Furious! He would have a fit."

Macleod deliberated for a moment with the same wary expression of eye, and then he said quietly:

"I should like to make a bet with you. I will lay you two ponies to a five-pound note that, if you will draw the colonel out on his favorite topic, I will contradict him on every point, we will have a most angry discussion, and at the end the colonel will be as good-humored and pleased as if—well, as if I had put a hundred pounds in his pocket."

"You don't know Old Pat," replied Fanshawe, shaking his head. "He'll make the regiment too hot to hold you in less than no time."

"Well, shall I book the bet?" suggested Macleod blandly.

"No; I won't bet on a certainty."

"*Are* you sure," inquired Macleod, with an air of doubt, "that it isn't that you don't feel—quite—up—to drawing Old Pat——"

"You may book the bet," cried Fanshawe haughtily, and his cheek flushed with anger. "And if you lose, you will have no one to thank but yourself."

"Quite so," said Macleod calmly, and he made the entry in his pocket-book in the most businesslike way. "And if I lose—well, at any rate I shall afford you some amusement."

And so it came about that that same evening, after dinner, when the wine was circulating pretty freely, and a mellow glow was beginning to make its appearance on the colonel's ripe visage, young Fanshawe, to the consternation of the mess, introduced the subject of a deceased Irish politician.

"What a scoundrel that fellow was!" said young Fanshawe, apropos of nothing, and dragging the dead leader into the conversation pre-

* Edinburgh.

cisely as Mr. Dick used to hoist King Charles's head into the "memorial."

The other subs looked at young Fanshawe with an expression of amazement. Had he gone out of his senses, or had the wine got into his head? Closer inspection, however, showed that he looked unnaturally sober and unusually intelligent. Then there must be some game on—some game at the colonel's expense. This would probably be good sport, and it would be well to be in at the death. Every eye was fixed on the colonel. Old Pat was not to be drawn by young Fanshawe. He snorted indignantly, but reserved his steel for worthier foes.

The circle of watchful eyes now turned to Fanshawe. What would be his next move?

"My *pater* has just bought a hogshead of the finest Scotch whisky," said the youth, coming up to time with commendable alacrity and a cheerful smile. He launched out into some details on the subject, concluding with the following significant remark:

"I hate Irish whisky. It is such sickening, soapy stuff. I think Scotch is much the best."

A joyful gleam shone in the attentive optics. This was getting interesting. Young Fanshawe was actually, of malice prepense, "going for" Old Pat. "Hooray! Yoicks! Tallyho! Go it, young Fanshawe!" were the sentiments reflected in the breasts of that hopeful youth's brother-subalterns; while even the major, who certainly ought to have known better, grinned with intense enjoyment.

"Don't you think so, Macleod?" said young Fanshawe to the Scotchman, who was cracking walnuts with the utmost insouciance.

"Don't I think what?" he replied.

"That Scotch whisky is better than Irish."

"Why, of course. Can there be any doubt? Does any one dispute it?"

This sally was too much for Old Pat. He plunged at once into the fray, and a heated discussion ensued. At least, it was heated on his side, for Macleod retained an appearance of judicial calm that would have put Job himself in a bad temper. Young Fanshawe, it may be added, at once seized the opportunity to retire from the forefront of the battle, and took up the safe position of an interested spectator.

In a comparatively short time a great deal of unpalatable information was shot upon the colonel. He was told that not only was Scotch whisky far more pleasing to the taste than Irish, but it was less injurious to the health, and there was less of illicit distillation in Scotland than in Ireland. Warming apparently to his subject, and totally regardless of Old Pat's passionate and profane defense, Macleod went on to enunciate the view that all that was really good and great in the Irish nation was English or Scotch in origin, that the Irish colonies in English towns formed the most criminal and degraded portion of the population, and that there was actually something in the climate or the soil of Ireland which deteriorated the physical and moral nature of the inhabitants. He said this with the calm utterance of a lecturer who demonstrates facts. There was even a softer undertone perceptible now and then, as if he pitied the advocate of so miserable a cause.

The colonel became almost incoherent with rage. His face assumed a deep purple hue. He manifested an inclination to foam at the mouth.

"For proof of this," continued Macleod, "it is quite enough to refer to a well-known and incontrovertible fact. Whether it is due to the potatoes that they eat or the bog-water that they drink, I don't know; but it is quite enough for my purpose that every Irishman of anything like ancient descent has a black roof to his mouth. You will bear me out in that, colonel, I am sure."

The mess in vain endeavored to preserve a dignified demeanor. They were nearly choking with suppressed laughter. Young Fanshawe contrived to upset a decanter in order to hide his emotion. Another young scapegrace was obliged to go to the sideboard, where he gurgled subterraneously for several minutes with his back to the company.

"It's a lie!" roared the colonel, whose eyes were nearly starting out of his head. "An infernal lie!"

"How? A lie, colonel? Do you mean to deny what I have stated?"

"I mean," shrieked Old Pat, "that the Powers of Ballycoran are one of the oldest families in Irreland; that they were on intimate terms with Brian Boru; and that whin the blissid St. Patrick came that way, 'twas me own ancestorr that gave him the *cead mille failthe* to Ballycoran; and if ye can find a single black roof in the mouths of the intirre family, may the divil fly off with the soul of the dirty varmin!"

And with these words the colonel struck the table a blow that made the glasses ring.

"This is very interesting, indeed," replied Macleod, gazing at the colonel as if that dignitary were the missing link, or a new form of butterfly. "I had no idea that any one—even an Irishman—would dispute it. Now, I dare say that you have never thought of examining your own mouth?"

The colonel's reply was of a nature that would have been an expensive one had he made it in the presence of a magistrate who enforced the penalties against swearing.

"Strange, very strange," said Macleod, who was still quite calm. "Now, I think I will lay you two to one in ten-pound notes that I am right."

A wolfish light shone in the colonel's eyes, but he held back with the most praiseworthy self-control. It would be undignified to bet with a mere sub—and on such a subject.

"I will make it five to one in twenty-pound notes," continued Macleod, with an air of great confidence, "that you have a black roof to your mouth."

"I will take that bet," spluttered the colonel, who was now in a white heat of rage. "By me soul, I will take that same, just to teach you not to bet on subjects of which you know nothing. It will be a useful lesson. And now, how do you propose to decide the bet?"

Sir James Macleod suggested that ocular inspection would be the quickest and most satisfactory method—ocular inspection by the senior officers of the mess. Their words would probably be sufficient for both parties.

The colonel demurred a little to this proposition. It seemed to him totally subversive of discipline. He was quite sure that the commander-in-chief would not approve of it. No other possible way of settling the question occurred to him, however, and, now that he had got so far, he was determined to win that hundred pounds at all hazards, and give the young Scotch jackanapes his much-needed lesson.

Candles were accordingly sent for at once, and a dead silence ensued. Every man looked at the other as if inquiring what would be the next act in this singular drama. Even young Fanshawe forgot to laugh. The colonel breathed heavily, and his eyes glared at his adversary, who still retained his unmoved demeanor.

At last the lights came. Armed each with a candlestick, the major, the captains, and the senior subaltern in turn examined the gaping orifice which the colonel revealed to their gaze, during which inspection young Fanshawe threw himself headlong on to a sofa and kicked like a person in mortal agony; while two subalterns expressed their feelings in a bear-fight behind the colonel's unconscious head.

The verdict of the judges was unanimous. They declared that the roof of the colonel's mouth was red, not black.

"Decidedly red," said the senior captain, with a curious chuckle that seemed fraught with a world of meaning. "Not a trace of black."

"Not black?" cried Sir James Macleod in tones of amazement. "Are you sure?"

"Quite sure," replied the major judicially.

"'Pon honor!" remarked the others in chorus.

"Well, gentlemen, you *have* surprised me," said Macleod, glancing from one to the other, as if he could scarcely believe his ears. "Of course I believe you, but—if the colonel will permit—I should like to look just to convince my own eyes."

"Look away, me boy," chuckled the colonel hoarsely. He was convulsed with delight at his complete triumph. "Ye'll have to pay for your peep!"

"Well, then, please open your mouth a little wider, colonel; and will one of you hold the light? Really, colonel, you must excuse me, but I can't see. You must really let me open your mouth a little wider."

With these words he actually laid one sacrilegious hand on the colonel's nose and the other on the colonel's chin, and pressed them gently in opposite directions. There was not a man among all the reckless crew that stood around but held his breath in anticipation of a terrible explosion.

The colonel did not rise and annihilate the audacious Scotchman. He bore this insult like a lamb. The indignity was, however, of the very shortest duration, for Macleod was satisfied with the briefest glance.

"I have lost," he said quite cheerfully. "And I owe you an apology, colonel. Luckily, I have the notes about me."

He produced his pocketbook, extracted two fifty-pound notes from it, and handed them to the colonel. The latter took them with the most portentous gravity. He was clearly puzzled and uncertain as to the right course of action. He puckered up his face in the most curious wrinkles. Then he rubbed his nose reflectively. The humorous side of the question, however, presented itself very forcibly to him, and he broke into a broad grin.

"Well," he said, with a loud roar of laughter, "you are an impudent rascal! But I didn't think that a Scotchman and his money were so easily parted."

And amid sympathetic roars from the entire mess, who thought the whole thing a capital joke all round, the colonel's indignation melted into intense enjoyment of his own success. The only person who was unsettled in his mind was young Fanshawe, who could not understand why Macleod should have risked a hundred pounds in so foolish a way.

"I don't think much of that Scotch chap you sent us," wrote the colonel, a few days later, to his old schoolfellow, Captain Fletcher, of the Blues. "Too much brag; too little bottom. He'll never set the Thames on fire. Only a few nights ago he actually bet me a hundred pounds to twenty that I had a black roof to my mouth—cheeky young devil! Well, I took the bet, just to give him a lesson. You ought to have seen his face when he lost. Really, I couldn't help roaring with laughter to see how confident he had been and how sold he was. You must be a dull lot in the Blues if he always wins from you. Anyhow, I have broken the record."

Captain Fletcher wrote by return of post to his old schoolfellow, Colonel Dominick Power:

Confound you! Didn't I caution you most pointedly not to bet with him? Couldn't you have known that there must be some deviltry on, or a man would not throw away his money in such preposterous fashion? Before he left us, Macleod laid me one hundred pounds to a thousand that he would pull your nose in the presence of the mess before he had been a week in the regiment, and without being courtmartialed or even placed under arrest for it, and I have just received a round-robin, signed by your mess, declaring that he has won the bet.

80

Bella Fleace Gave a Party

BY EVELYN WAUGH

BALLINGAR is four and a half hours from Dublin if you catch the early train from Broadstone Station and five and a quarter if you wait until the afternoon. It is the market town of a large and comparatively well-populated district. There is a pretty Protestant Church in 1820 Gothic on one side of the square and a vast, unfinished Catholic cathedral opposite it, conceived in that irresponsible medley of architectural orders that is so dear to the hearts of transmontane pietists. Celtic lettering of a sort is beginning to take the place of the Latin alphabet on the shop fronts that complete the square. These all deal in identical goods in varying degrees of dilapidation; Mulligan's Store, Flannigan's Store, Riley's Store, each sells thick black boots, hanging in bundles, soapy colonial cheese, hardware and haberdashery, oil and saddlery, and each is licensed to sell ale and porter for consumption on or off the premises. The shell of the barracks stands with empty window frames and blackened interior as a monument to emancipation. A typical Irish town.

Fleacetown is fifteen miles from Ballingar, on a direct uneven road through typical Irish country; vague purple hills in the far distance and towards them, on one side of the road, fitfully visible among drifting patches of white mist, unbroken miles of bog, dotted with occasional stacks of cut peat. On the other side the ground slopes up to the north, divided irregularly into spare fields by banks and stone walls over which the Ballingar hounds have some of their most eventful hunting. Moss lies on everything; in a rough green rug on the walls and banks, soft green velvet on the timber—blurring the transitions so that there is no knowing where the ground ends and trunk and masonry begin. All the way from Ballingar there is a succession of whitewashed cabins and a dozen or so fair-size farmhouses; but there is no gentleman's house, for all this was Fleace property in the days before the Land Commission. The demesne land is all that belongs to Fleacetown now, and this is let for pasture to neighbouring farmers. Only a few beds are cultivated in the walled kitchen garden; the rest has run to rot, thorned bushes barren of edible fruit spreading everywhere among weedy flowers reverting rankly to type. The hot-houses have been draughty skeletons for ten years. The great gates set in their Georgian arch are permanently padlocked, the lodges are derelict, and the line of the main drive is only just discernible through the meadows. Access to the house is half a mile further up through a farm gate, along a track befouled by cattle.

But the house itself, at the date with which we are dealing, was in a condition of comparatively good repair; compared, that is to say, with Ballingar House or Castle Boycott or Knode Hall. It did not, of course, set up to rival Gordontown, where the American Lady Gordon had installed electric light, central heating and a lift, or Mock House or Newhill, which were leased to sporting Englishmen, or Castle Mockstock, since Lord Mockstock married beneath him. These four houses with their neatly raked gravel, bathrooms and dynamos, were the wonder and ridicule of the country. But Fleacetown, in fair competition with the essentially Irish houses of the Free State, was unusually habitable.

Its roof was intact; and it is the roof which makes the difference between the second and third grade of Irish country houses. Once that goes you have moss in the bedrooms, ferns on the stairs and cows in the library, and in a very few years you have to move into the dairy or one of the lodges. But so long as he has, literally, a roof over his head, an Irishman's house is still his castle. There were weak bits in Fleacetown, but general opinion held that the leads were good for another twenty years and would certainly survive the present owner.

Miss Annabel Rochfort-Doyle-Fleace, to give her the full name under which she appeared in books of reference, though she was known to the entire countryside as Bella Fleace, was the last of her family. There had been Fleces and Fleysers living about Ballingar since the days of Strongbow, and farm buildings marked the spot where they had inhabited a stockaded fort two centuries before the immigration of the Boycotts or Gordons or Mockstocks. A family tree emblazed by a nineteenth-century genealogist, showing how the original stock had merged with the equally ancient Rochforts and the respectable though more recent Doyles, hung in the billiard-room. The present home had been built on extravagant lines in the middle of the eighteenth century, when the family, though enervated, was still wealthy and influential.

It would be tedious to trace its gradual decline from fortune; enough to say that it was due to no heroic debauchery. The Fleaces just got unobtrusively poorer in the way that families do who make no effort to help themselves. In the last generations, too, there had been marked traces of eccentricity. Bella Fleace's mother—an O'Hara of Newhill—had from the day of her marriage until her death suffered from the delusion that she was a Negress. Her brother, from whom she had inherited, devoted himself to oil painting; his mind ran on the simple subject of assassination and before his death he had executed pictures of practically every such incident in history from Julius Cæsar to General Wilson. He was at work on a painting, his own murder, at the time of the troubles, when he was, in fact, ambushed and done to death with a shot-gun on his own drive.

It was under one of her brother's paintings—Abraham Lincoln in his box at the theatre—that Miss Fleace was sitting one colourless morning in November when the idea came to her to give a Christmas party. It would be unnecessary to describe her appearance closely, and somewhat confusing, because it seemed in contradiction to much of her character. She was over eighty, very untidy and very red; streaky grey hair was twisted behind her head into a horsy bun, wisps hung round her cheeks; her nose was prominent and blue veined; her eyes pale blue, blank and mad; she had a lively smile and spoke with a marked Irish intonation. She walked with the aid of a stick, having been lamed many years back when her horse rolled her among loose stones late in a long day with the Ballingar Hounds; a tipsy sporting doctor had completed the mischief, and she had not been able to ride again. She would appear on foot when hounds drew the Fleacetown coverts and loudly criticise the conduct of the huntsman, but every year fewer of her old friends turned out; strange faces appeared.

They knew Bella, though she did not know them. She had become a by-word in the neighbourhood, a much-valued joke.

"A rotten day," they would report. "We found our fox, but lost again almost at once. But we saw Bella. Wonder how long the old girl will last. She must be nearly ninety. My father remembers when she used to hunt—went like smoke, too."

Indeed, Bella herself was becoming increasingly occupied with the prospect of death. In the winter before the one we are talking of, she had been extremely ill. She emerged in April, rosy cheeked as ever, but slower in her movements and mind. She gave instructions that better attention must be paid to her father's and brother's graves, and in June took the unprecedented step of inviting her heir to visit her. She had always refused to see this young man up till now. He was an Englishman, a very distant cousin, named Banks. He lived in South Kensington and occupied himself in the Museum. He arrived in August and wrote long and very amusing letters to all his friends describing his visit, and later translated his experiences into a short story for the *Spectator*. Bella disliked him from the moment he arrived. He had horn-rimmed spectacles and a B.B.C. voice. He spent most of his time photographing the Fleacetown chimney-pieces and the moulding of the doors. One day he came to Bella bearing a pile of calf-bound volumes from the library.

"I say, did you know you had these?" he asked.

"I did," Bella lied.

"All first editions. They must be extremely valuable."

"You put them back where you found them."

Later, when he wrote to thank her for his visit—enclosing prints of some of his photographs—he mentioned the books again. This set Bella thinking. Why should that young puppy go poking round the house putting a price on everything? She wasn't dead yet, Bella thought. And the more she thought of it, the more repugnant it became to think of Archie Banks carrying off her books to South Kensington and removing the chimney-pieces and, as he threatened, writing an essay about the house for the *Architectural Review*. She had often heard that the books were valuable. Well, there were plenty of books in the library and she did not see why Archie Banks should profit by them. So she wrote a letter to a Dublin bookseller. He came to look through the library, and after a while he offered her twelve hundred pounds for the lot, or a thousand for the six books which had attracted Archie Bank's attention. Bella was not sure that she had the right to sell things out of the house; a wholesale clearance would be noticed. So she kept the sermons and military history which made up most of the collection, the Dublin bookseller went off with the first editions, which eventually fetched rather less than he had given, and Bella was left with winter coming on and a thousand pounds in hand.

It was then that it occurred to her to give a party. There were always several parties given round Ballingar at Christmas time, but of late years Bella had not been invited to any, partly because many of her neighbours had never spoken to her, partly because they did not think she would want to come, and partly because they would not have known what to do with her if she had. As a matter of fact she loved parties. She liked sitting down to supper in a noisy room, she liked dance music and gossip about which of the girls was pretty and who was in love with them, and she liked drink and having things brought to her by men in pink evening coats. And though she tried to console herself with contemptuous reflections about the ancestry of the hostesses, it annoyed her very much whenever she heard of a party being given in the neighbourhood to which she was not asked.

And so it came about that, sitting with the *Irish Times* under the picture of Abraham Lincoln and gazing across the bare trees of the park to the hills beyond, Bella took it into her head to give a party. She rose immediately and hobbled across the room to the bell-rope. Presently her butler came into the morning room; he wore the green baize apron in which he cleaned the silver and in his hand he carried the plate brush to emphasise the irregularity of the summons.

"Was it yourself ringing?" he asked.

"It was, who else?"

"And I at the silver!"

"Riley," said Bella with some solemnity, "I propose to give a ball at Christmas."

"Indeed!" said her butler. "And for what would you want to be dancing at your age?" But as Bella adumbrated her idea, a sympathetic light began to glitter in Riley's eye.

"There's not been such a ball in the country for twenty-five years. It will cost a fortune."

"It will cost a thousand pounds," said Bella proudly.

The preparations were necessarily stupendous. Seven new servants were recruited in the village and set to work dusting and cleaning and polishing, clearing out furniture and pulling up carpets. Their industry served only to reveal fresh requirements; plaster mouldings, long rotten, crumbled under the feather brooms, worm-eaten mahogany floorboards came up with the tin tacks; bare brick was disclosed behind the cabinets in the great drawing-room. A second wave of the invasion brought painters, paperhangers and plumbers, and in a moment of enthusiasm Bella had the cornice and the capitals of the pillars in the hall regilded; windows were reglazed, banisters fitted into gaping sockets, and the stair carpet shifted so that the worn strips were less noticeable.

In all these works Bella was indefatigable. She trotted from drawing-room to hall, down the long gallery, up the staircase, admonishing the hireling servants, lending a hand with the lighter objects of furniture, sliding, when the time came, up and down the mahogany floor of the drawing-room to work in the French chalk. She unloaded chests of silver in the attics, found long-forgotten services of china, went down with Riley into the cellars to count the few remaining and now flat and acid bottles of champagne. And in the evenings when the manual labourers had retired exhausted to their gross recreations, Bella sat up far into the night turning the pages of cookery books, comparing the estimates of rival caterers, inditing long and detailed letters to the agents for dance bands and, most important of all, drawing up her list of guests and addressing the high double piles of engraved cards that stood in her escritoire.

Distance counts for little in Ireland. People will readily drive three hours to pay an afternoon call, and for a dance of such importance no journey was too great. Bella had her list painfully compiled from works of reference, Riley's more up-to-date social knowledge and her own suddenly animated memory. Cheerfully, in a steady childish handwriting, she transferred the names to the cards and addressed the envelopes. It was the work of several late sittings. Many of those whose names were transcribed were dead or bedridden; some whom she just remembered seeing as small children were reaching retiring age in remote corners of the globe; many of the houses she wrote down were blackened shells, burned during the troubles and never rebuilt; some had "no one living in them, only farmers." But at last, none too early, the last envelope was addressed. A final lap with the stamps and then later than usual she rose from the desk. Her limbs were stiff, her eyes dazzled, her tongue cloyed with the gum of the Free State post office; she felt a little dizzy, but she locked her desk that evening with the knowledge that the most serious part of the work of the party was over. There had been several notable and deliberate omissions from that list.

"What's all this I hear about Bella giving a party?" said Lady Gordon to Lady Mockstock. "I haven't had a card."

"Neither have I yet. I hope the old thing hasn't forgotten me. I certainly intend to go. I've never been inside the house. I believe she's got some lovely things."

With true English reserve the lady whose husband had leased Mock Hall never betrayed the knowledge that any party was in the air at all at Fleacetown.

As the last days approached Bella concentrated more upon her own appearance. She had bought few clothes of recent years, and the Dublin dressmaker with whom she used to deal had shut up shop. For a delirious instant she played with the idea of a journey to London and even Paris, and considerations of time alone obliged her to abandon it. In the end she discovered a shop to suit her, and purchased a very magnificent gown of crimson satin; to this she added long white gloves and satin shoes. There was no tiara, alas! among her jewels, but she unearthed large numbers of bright, nondescript Victorian rings, some chains and lockets, pearl brooches, turquoise earrings, and a collar of garnets. She ordered a coiffeur down from Dublin to dress her hair.

On the day of the ball she woke early, slightly feverish with nervous excitement, and wriggled in bed till she was called, restlessly rehearsing in her mind every detail of the arrangements. Before noon she had been to supervise the setting of hundreds of candles in the sconces round the ball-room and supper-room, and in the three great chandeliers of cut Waterford glass; she had seen the supper tables laid out with silver and glass and stood the massive wine coolers by the buffet; she had helped bank the staircase and hall with chrysanthemums. She had no luncheon that day, though Riley urged her with samples of the delicacies already arrived from the caterer's. She felt a little faint; lay down for a short time, but soon rallied to sew with her own hands the crested buttons on to the liveries of the hired servants.

The invitations were timed for eight o'clock. She wondered whether that would be too early—she had heard tales of parties that began very late—but as the afternoon dragged on unendurably, and rich twilight enveloped the house, Bella became glad that she had set a short term on this exhausting wait.

At six she went up to dress. The hairdresser was there with a bag full of tongs and combs. He brushed and coiled her hair and whiffed it up and generally manipulated it until it became orderly and formal and apparently far more copious. She put on all her jewellery and, standing before the cheval glass in her room, could not forbear a gasp of surprise. Then she limped downstairs.

The house looked magnificent in the candlelight. The band was there, the twelve hired footmen, Riley in knee breeches and black silk stockings.

It struck eight. Bella waited. Nobody came.

She sat down on a gilt chair at the head of the stairs, looked steadily before her with her blank, blue eyes. In the hall, in the cloakroom, in the supper-room, the hired footmen looked at one another with knowing winks. "What does the old girl expect? No one'll have finished dinner before ten."

The linkmen on the steps stamped and chafed their hands.

At half-past twelve Bella rose from her chair. Her face gave no indication of what she was thinking.

"Riley, I think I will have some supper. I am not feeling altogether well."

She hobbled slowly to the dining-room.

"Give me a stuffed quail and a glass of wine. Tell the band to start playing."

The *Blue Danube* waltz flooded the house. Bella smiled approval and swayed her head a little to the rhythm.

"Riley, I am really quite hungry. I've had nothing all day. Give me another quail and some more champagne."

Alone among the candles and the hired footmen, Riley served his mistress with an immense supper. She enjoyed every mouthful.

Presently she rose. "I am afraid there must be some mistake. No one seems to be coming to the ball. It is very disappointing after all our trouble. You may tell the band to go home."

But just as she was leaving the dining-room there was a stir in the hall. Guests were arriving. With wild resolution Bella swung herself up the stairs. She must get to the top before the guests were announced. One hand on the banister, one on her stick, pounding heart, two steps at a time. At last she reached the landing and turned to face the company. There was a mist before her eyes and a singing in her ears. She breathed with effort, but dimly she saw four figures advancing and saw Riley meet them and heard him announce

"Lord and Lady Mockstock, Sir Samuel and Lady Gordon."

Suddenly the daze in which she had been moving cleared. Here on the stairs were the two women she had not invited—Lady Mockstock the draper's daughter, Lady Gordon the American.

She drew herself up and fixed them with her blank, blue eyes.

"I had not expected this honour," she said. "Please forgive me if I am unable to entertain you."

The Mockstocks and the Gordons stood aghast; saw the mad blue eyes of their hostess, her crimson dress; the ball-room beyond, looking immense in its emptiness; heard the dance music echoing through the empty house. The air was charged with the scent of chrysanthemums. And then the drama and unreality of the scene were dispelled. Miss Fleace suddenly sat down, and holding out her hands to her butler, said, "I don't quite know what's happening."

He and two of the hired footmen carried the old lady to a sofa. She spoke only once more. Her mind was still on the same subject. "They came uninvited, those two . . . and nobody else."

A day later she died.

Mr. Banks arrived for the funeral and spent a week sorting out her effects. Among them he found in her escritoire, stamped, addressed, but unposted, the invitations to the ball.

Biographical Notes

★ *Biographical Notes* ★

GEOFFREY CHAUCER
(1340–1400)

THE SHORT STORY is a form of literature that has been developed in comparatively recent times, and even the best examples of earlier centuries would scarcely pass the test of present-day requirements. The editors believe that Chaucer and Sir Thomas Malory definitely qualify for inclusion in an anthology of British stories; after them there is a sheer lapse of two centuries before another worthy entry is to be found.

Geoffrey Chaucer was born in London. His writings betoken acquaintance with every branch of learning of his time, but there is no record of his attendance at a university. He saw military service with the English Army in France and was later appointed comptroller of petty customs of the Port in London. In 1373 he began his *Canterbury Tales,* of which *The Pardoner's Tale,* the first story in the present volume, is, of course, a part.

Chaucer died in 1400, and was buried in Westminster Abbey. He is generally known as the Father of English Poetry, but might be hailed just as aptly as the Father of the English Short Story.

The present version of *The Pardoner's Tale* is reprinted from Tatlock and MacKaye's *Modern Reader's Chaucer.*

SIR THOMAS MALORY
(1430?–F.F.1470)

SIR THOMAS MALORY is said to have been a Warwickshire gentleman, knighted in 1445, who was taken captive in the War of the Roses. *Le Morte D'Arthur* is a collection of tales about King Arthur, Launcelot, Galahad, Percival, Tristram and other Knights of the Round Table, their loves and adventures. It was compiled from French Romances, but Malory was more than a translator; he was one of the first great English story-tellers. Spenser, Tennyson, Swinburne, Morris and Arnold were all inspired to write great poems by *Le Morte D'Arthur.* Richard Garnett says: "The *Morte D'Arthur* of Sir Thomas Malory would have been a brilliant star in any century, and almost monopolizes the starless literary heaven of the fifteenth." *The Marvellous Adventure of the Sword* is here reprinted from a modern English edition.

DANIEL DEFOE
(1660–1731)

DANIEL DEFOE was born in the Parish of St. Giles, Cripplegate, London. His father was a Dissenter and Defoe was educated at the Noncon- formist College at Stoke, Newington. Before he settled down to his career as a writer, he engaged in various business enterprises, none of which was successful. In 1719 appeared the first volume of *Robinson Crusoe* which made him instantly famous. This was followed by *Moll Flanders, Memoirs of a Cavalier, The Journal of the Plague Year, His- tory of Colonel Jack, Captain Singleton* and *Roxana*. His stories are vivid pictures of English life in the reign of Queen Anne. *The Appari- tion of Mrs. Veal* appeared in a pamphlet, published in 1706.

JOSEPH ADDISON
(1672–1719)

JOSEPH ADDISON, the son of Lancelot Addison, later Dean of Lichfield, was born in the Rectory of Milston, in Wiltshire. He was educated at the Charter House and Queen's College, Oxford. After traveling on the continent he became a contributor to the *Tatler*, published by Steele in 1709. When the *Tatler* ceased in 1711, Addison started the *Spectator*. When the *Spectator*, which enjoyed a prodigious success, ceased, he contributed to the *Guardian*. The invention of Sir Roger De Coverley was probably a combined stroke of genius in which Steele and Addison had equal share. Addison was one of the most popular men of his day and his essays which appeared in the above periodicals are remarkable for their ease, grace and clarity. He died at Holland House, June 17th, 1719. He was buried in Westminster Abbey at the foot of the monument to his friend and patron, Charles Montague. *The Vision of Mirza* appeared in the *Spectator*, Number 159.

OLIVER GOLDSMITH
(1728–1774)

OLIVER GOLDSMITH, poet, essayist and dramatist, son of an Irish clergy- man, was born at Pallas, County Longford, Ireland. He was educated at Trinity College, Dublin. After studying medicine at Edinburgh, he started on a long walking tour through France, Germany, Switzerland and Italy. He returned to London in 1756 and became, in turn, an apothecary's assistant, an usher in a school, and a "physician in a humble way." His *Traveller* appeared in 1764, his *Essays* in 1765, *The Vicar of Wakefield* in 1766, *The Good-Natured Man* in 1767, *The Deserted Village* in 1770 and *She Stoops to Conquer* in 1773. Goldsmith was a greatly loved member of the famous literary club founded by Dr. Johnson. He died in his Temple Chambers in Brick Court on April 9th, 1774, and was buried in the Temple Churchyard. Thackeray said of him: "To be the most beloved of English writers, what a title for a man." His *Asem, An Eastern Tale,* is reprinted from his *Essays.*

SIR WALTER SCOTT
(1771–1832)

SIR WALTER SCOTT, the greatest of the Scottish poets and novelists, was born at Edinburgh. He was educated at the high school, Edinburgh, and Edinburgh University. He was called to the bar in 1792 but never practiced. His first work of importance, *The Minstrelsy of the Scottish Border,* appeared in 1802. Then followed those famous novels that made him one of the greatest of English writers, *Waverley, Guy Mannering, Rob Roy, The Heart of Midlothian, The Bride of Lammermoor, Ivanhoe, Kenilworth, Quentin Durward, Red Gauntlet* and *Woodstock.* Scott's place in literature is unchallengeable; he still remains the master story-teller. He was also the most admired poet of his day. *The Lay of the Last Minstrel, Marmion, The Lady of the Lake, Rokeby* and *Lord of the Hills* were widely read and loved. He died at Abbotsford on July 11th, 1832, and was buried in Dryburgh Abbey. *The Two Drovers,* a story of Scott's beloved Highlands, is reprinted from *The Chronicles of the Canongate.*

WILLIAM MUDFORD
(1792–1848)

WILLIAM MUDFORD was born in London. For a half a century he was a keen and successful journalist. He was, at various times in his career, parliamentary reporter for the *Chronicle,* editor of the *Courier,* editor of the *Kentish Observer,* and finally he replaced Theodore Hook as editor of *John Bull.* Mudford possessed a gift of writing weird, fantastic and horrible tales. His most important novel was *The Five Nights at St. Albans.* His best-known short story is *The Iron Shroud* which originally appeared in *Blackwood's Magazine* and suggests comparison with Poe's *The Pit and the Pendulum.*

SAMUEL LOVER
(1797–1868)

SAMUEL LOVER, poet, painter, musician, dramatist and novelist, was born in Dublin. At the age of seventeen he took up the study of art and three years later he began to win success as a painter of miniatures. An admirable miniature of Paganini excited so much attention in London that he was induced to go to the metropolis. His weak eyesight, however, compelled him to give up art and he turned to literature and music. His most popular novels are *Handy Andy* and *Rory O'More*. He wrote several successful plays and hundreds of songs, most of which he set to music. He died in Jersey on July 6th, 1868. *The Gridiron* was one of his first stories.

EDWARD BULWER-LYTTON
(1803–1873)

EDWARD BULWER-LYTTON, First Lord Lytton, was born in London. He was educated at Cambridge University. Early in life he contributed innumerable tales, essays and articles to reviews and magazines. In 1831 he entered Parliament but continued his literary labors unabated. Some of his most popular novels are, *Last Days of Pompeii, Rienzi, The Last of the Barons, Harold* and *The Caxtons*. To the drama he contributed two plays that still enjoy popularity, *The Lady of Lyons* and *Richelieu. The House and the Brain* has been called by many critics the most powerful and appalling story of the supernatural ever printed in the English language. The story as printed here gives the complete text precisely as it first appeared in *Blackwood's Magazine* in 1859.

CHARLES JAMES LEVER
(1806–1872)

CHARLES JAMES LEVER, physician and novelist, was born in Dublin. He was educated at Trinity College, Dublin, and at Gottingen and Louvain. He was a one-time editor of the *Dublin Magazine* and contributed many tales to *Blackwood's* and other leading periodicals. He is the most widely read of the Irish novelists. His most popular novels are *Charles O'Malley, Harry Lorrequer, Jack Hinton, Tom Burke of Ours, Arthur O'Leary* and *The Dodd Family Abroad*. He acted as British Consul in Italy and died on June 1st, 1872, at Trieste. *Con Cregan's Legacy or How Con Cregan's Father Left Himself a Bit of Land* is reprinted from *The Confessions of Con Cregan,* the Irish *Gil Blas*.

JOHN BROWN
(1810–1882)

DR. JOHN BROWN, physician and essayist, was born at Biggar, Scotland. He was educated at the University of Edinburgh. Most of his life was spent in his chosen calling of physician. He numbered among his cherished friends many of the great writers of his day including Thackeray. His works, among which appear *Rab and His Friends,* were collected and issued under the title *Horae Subsecivae* (*Leisure Hours*).

ELIZABETH CLEGHORN (STEVENSON) GASKELL
(1810–1865)

ELIZABETH CLEGHORN (STEVENSON) GASKELL, the daughter of a Unitarian minister, was born in Chelsea. She was brought up by her mother's sister, Mrs. Lamb, at Knutsford in Cheshire. She attended school at Stratford-on-Avon. Among her well-known novels are *Cranford, Mary Barton, Ruth, Sylvia's Lovers, Moorland Cottage* and *Cousin Phillis*. She also wrote a life of her friend Charlotte Brontë. Mrs. Gaskell, graceful, cultivated and entertaining, was much beloved by her friends. She died in Hants on the 12th of November, 1865, and was buried at Knutsford. *The Half Brothers* is reprinted from *Round the Sofa,* volume two, issued in 1859.

WILLIAM MAKEPEACE THACKERAY
(1811–1863)

WILLIAM MAKEPEACE THACKERAY, novelist, poet and essayist, was born in Calcutta. After the death of his father, Thackeray was sent to England and was educated at Charter House and Trinity College, Cambridge. He studied art for a time in Paris but in 1837 he returned to London and became a contributor to *Fraser's Magazine*. In 1846, he published *Vanity Fair,* on which Thackeray's larger fame rests. Among the best known of his other novels are *Pendennis, The Newcomes, The History of Henry Esmond, The Virginians* and *The Adventures of Philip*. He visited America in 1851 and 1855 and delivered his lectures on "The English Humorists of the Eighteenth Century and the Four Georges." *Sultan Stork,* a satire on the *Arabian Nights,* is reprinted from *Sultan Stork and Other Papers*.

CHARLES DICKENS
(1812-1870)

CHARLES DICKENS, the greatest of English novelists, was born at Landport, a suburb of Portsea. His father moved to London in 1821 and the year following was consigned to the debtor's prison, the Marshalsea. Dickens was a packer for some time in a blacking warehouse and later found employment as a solicitor's clerk. In 1834, he was a reporter on the *Morning Chronicle* and about this time he wrote his *Sketches by Boz*. These sketches were followed by *The Posthumous Papers of the Pickwick Club* and those other immortal tales that made Dickens a household name throughout the English speaking world. In 1843, just before Christmas, the first edition of *A Christmas Carol* was issued in a small volume with eight illustrations by John Leach. It received an ovation not easily paralleled in the annals of short stories. Today, it is difficult to think of an English Christmas without thinking of the Fezziwigs and the Cratchits, the pudding singing in the copper and the prize turkey twice the size of Tiny Tim. Thackeray joined his voice to the general symphony of praise declaring that "It seems to me a national benefit and to every man or woman who reads it a personal kindness." Worn out by his lectures in America and his many years of self-inflicted labors, he died on June 8th, 1870, at Gadshill Place, near Rochester, and was buried in Westminster Abbey. *A Christmas Carol* is reprinted from *Christmas Books* (1843-1848).

ANTHONY TROLLOPE
(1815-1882)

ANTHONY TROLLOPE was born in London. He was educated at Harrow and Winchester but did not attend college. He entered the English postal service and served in London and Ireland. In 1855 he published the first of his Barsetshire series, *The Warden,* which immediately made him famous. The rest of the series followed: *Barchester Towers, Dr. Thorne, Framley Parsonage, The Small House at Allington* and *The Last Chronicles of Barset.* He wrote in all about fifty novels. Trollope, since he was born to it, had inside knowledge of upper-class society in London as well as of the life, the very exclusive life, of English Cathedral towns. *Malachi's Cove* is reprinted from *Lotta Schmidt.*

GEORGE MEREDITH
(1828-1909)

GEORGE MEREDITH was born at Portsmouth. He was educated at the Moravian School at Neuwied on the Rhine. He early took up journalism and wrote poetry for various magazines. In 1856 he published *The Shaving of Shagpat,* of which George Eliot said, "A work of genius precious as an apple tree amongst the trees of the world." Meredith wrote continuously for fifty years. The best of his novels, *The Ordeal of Richard Feverel, The Egoist, Diana of the Crossways, Beauchamp's Career* and *The Adventures of Harry Richmond,* belong permanently to our literature. His nature songs in his volumes of poetry are exquisite. He died at Boxhill and was buried in Dorking Abbey. *The Punishment of Shahpesh, the Persian, on Khipil, the Builder,* is reprinted from *The Shaving of Shagpat.*

THOMAS HARDY
(1840-1928)

THOMAS HARDY was born at Upper Bockhampton, near Dorsetshire. He took up architecture first but later gave his entire time to literature. Mr. Hardy's poems and novels are founded on old Wessex which includes Wiltshire, Hampshire, Somersetshire and Oxfordshire. Among his novels which made him the greatest of modern novelists are *Tess of the D'Urbervilles, The Return of the Native, Far from the Madding Crowd, A Pair of Blue Eyes, The Mayor of Casterbridge, The Woodlanders,* and *Jude the Obscure.* In 1904-6 he published his great epic poem, *The Dynasts,* a drama of Wessex in the Napoleonic period. John Drinkwater writes, "A few villages were enough for Jane Austen, the lake country circumscribed without imprisoning Wordsworth, the Yorkshire moorlands enclosed but could not enchain the Brontës, Thomas Hardy has seen the kingdoms of the world, their glory and futility, from Egdon Heath." *The Three Strangers* is taken from *Wessex Tales.*

WILLIAM HENRY HUDSON
(1841-1922)

W. H. HUDSON, novelist and naturalist, was born in Rio De La Plata, Argentina. He came to England in 1869. In 1904 he published a striking romance, *Green Mansions* which, thirty-five years later, still ranks as one of the ten most popular books in the 270 volumes that comprise *The*

Modern Library series. His most popular nature books are *A Naturalist in La Plata, Idle Days in Patagonia, Birds and Man* and *A Hind in
Richmond Park*. Hampshire was Hudson's country and the old town of
Wells had first place in his affection. His descriptions of the countryside
are unsurpassed, while his love and knowledge of bird-life is com-
memorated in a bird sanctuary dedicated to him in Hyde Park, London.
Story of a Piebald Horse is reprinted from *Tales of the Pampas*.

ROBERT LOUIS STEVENSON
(1850–1894)

ROBERT LOUIS STEVENSON, novelist, poet and essayist, was born in Edinburgh. He was educated at Edinburgh University and called to the bar
in 1875 but never practiced. A trip in a canoe in 1876 led to the publication of his first book, *An Inland Voyage*. Stevenson's novels are of original quality and delicate artistic finish. His *Treasure Island, Kidnapped*
and *The Master of Ballantrae* established him as one of the greatest of
contemporary writers. Some of his short stories are masterpieces. Although Stevenson did not consider himself a poet his *Child's Garden
of Verses* is one of the best collections of its kind ever published. He
travelled extensively in search of health and finally settled in Apia,
Samoa, where he died. He was greatly beloved by the natives of Samoa
and was called by them, "Tusitala," Teller of Tales, a title he richly
deserved. *Sire de Malétroit's Door* and *A Lodging for the Night* are reprinted from *New Arabian Nights*.

JOHN WATSON (IAN MACLAREN)
(1850–1907)

REV. JOHN WATSON (Ian Maclaren) was born at Manningtree, Scotland. He was educated at Stirling and Edinburgh University. He served
as rector of Sefton Park Presbyterian Church, Liverpool, where he was
a very popular preacher. He wrote several novels and short-story collections including, *Beside the Bonnie Briar Bush* and *The Days of Auld
Lang Syne*. His best-known religious work is *The Mind of the Master*.
Beside the Bonnie Briar Bush concerns doings of Drumtochty, an out-
of-the-way hamlet under the shadow of the Grampian mountains. One
of the principal characters is Dr. Maclure, a kindly village doctor un-
selfishly devoted to his neighbors and patients. The passage reprinted
here is one that forms the climax of the book and is printed to give the
reader one of the finest examples of the "Kailyard School" of fiction.
Mr. Alexander Woollcott, "the town crier," avers that he has personally

given away an entire edition of *Beside the Bonnie Briar Bush* at Christmas time.

ROBERT BONTINE CUNNINGHAME-GRAHAM
(1852–1936)

ROBERT BONTINE CUNNINGHAME-GRAHAM, a descendent of one of the oldest families in Scotland, was born in London. He was educated at Harrow. He was a great traveler and wrote a mass of miscellaneous literature, fiction, travel and historical studies. Among his best-known works are, *Mogreb-El-Acksa, Success, Scottish Stories* and *The Horses of the Conquest*. He entered Parliament in 1886 and served until 1892. *Faith* is taken from *Thirty-One Tales and Sketches*.

GEORGE MOORE
(1853–1933)

GEORGE MOORE was born in County Mayo, Ireland. He was educated in Ireland but studied art in London and Paris. On returning to London he issued *A Mummer's Wife, The Confessions of a Young Man* and *Memoirs of My Dead Life*. He established his reputation with three novels, *Esther Waters, Evelyn Innes* and *Sister Theresa*. He later increased his fame by his trilogy of autobiographical revelations in *Hail and Farewell* and with *Brook Kerith* and *Letters of Heloise and Abelard*. As a poet Moore is best known for *Flowers of Passion* and *Pagan Poetry*. *The Clerk's Quest* is reprinted here from *Untilled Fields*.

OSCAR WILDE
(1856–1900)

OSCAR WILDE was born in Dublin, and educated at Trinity College, Dublin, and Magdalen College, Oxford. While at Oxford his unusual behavior and mode of attire became the pattern for an aesthetic cult that enjoyed a violent if short-lived vogue, and that is caricatured so tellingly in Gilbert and Sullivan's *Patience*. Wilde was a versatile genius. His poems, his fairy tales, his novel, *The Picture of Dorian Gray,* were in themselves enough to win him fame, and the wit and repartee in his plays, *Lady Windermere's Fan, A Woman of No Importance,* and *The Importance of Being Earnest* still burn brightly enough to ensure frequent revivals to this very day. Oscar Wilde's private life was the scandal of London, and in 1895, after a celebrated trial, he was committed to prison for two years. The experience wrecked his life, but also inspired his best-known works, *The Ballad of Reading Gaol* and *De Profundis*. *The Birthday of the Infanta* is the most popular of his fairy tales.

FEODORE JOSEF KONRAD KORZENIOWSKI
(JOSEPH CONRAD)
(1857-1924)

JOSEPH CONRAD was born at Berdichev in the Ukraine, of Polish parents. Though born in a country with no sea coast, he felt the call of the sea, and shipped as a sailor on the first vessel he could find. One of his voyages ultimately brought him to England, and here he settled in 1875, eventually becoming a British citizen.

His first novel, *Almayer's Folly,* appeared in 1895. Bear in mind that Conrad was already forty-two years old—and that English, after all, was an alien tongue to him. Yet with *Nostromo, Lord Jim, Victory* and a dozen other masterly novels, Joseph Conrad established himself indisputably as the greatest writer of sea stories in the English language. His books are particularly popular in America, and first editions of his early works fetch prohibitive prices. Conrad spent the last years of his life in Kent, and there he died in 1924. He is buried in Canterbury. *Youth* is the title story of a volume that also includes the memorable *Heart of Darkness.*

MORLEY ROBERTS
(1857-   )

MORLEY ROBERTS, novelist, short-story writer and journalist, was born in London. He was educated at Bedford School and Owens College, Manchester. He went to Australia in 1876 and worked in the Bush. Later he went to sea and served before the mast. He visited Canada and the United States. His works include stories of his travels, and a number of novels, the best known of which is *The Purification of Dolores Silva.* *The Captain of the "Ullswater"* is taken from *Salt of the Sea.*

SIR ARTHUR CONAN DOYLE
(1859-1930)

SIR ARTHUR CONAN DOYLE was born in Edinburgh. He was educated at Stonyhurst and Edinburgh University. He adopted the profession of medicine and practiced at Southsea from 1882-90. His principal works are divided into two classes, historical romances and detective stories.

Among his historical romances may be mentioned *The White Company, The Exploits of Brigadier Girard, Rodney Stone* and *Micah Clarke*. Sir Arthur Conan Doyle will always be remembered as the creator of one of the best-known characters in modern fiction, "Sherlock Holmes." The great detective—and his faithful if sometimes exasperating lieutenant, Dr. Watson—have become as much household words as Mr. Pickwick. In 1926 he wrote a *History of Spiritualism,* a subject in which he was very much interested in his later years. *The Adventure of the Speckled Band* is reprinted from the *Adventures of Sherlock Holmes*.

JAMES MATTHEW BARRIE
(1860–1937)

SIR JAMES MATTHEW BARRIE, novelist and playwright, was born in the little village of Kirriemuir, Scotland, which he afterward made immortal under the name Thrums. He was educated at Dumfries Academy and Edinburgh University. Early in life he came to London and wrote articles for the *British Weekly*. Among the best of his earlier works are *Auld Licht Idylls, A Window in Thrums* and a biography of his mother, *Margaret Ogilvy*. Later came *My Lady Nicotine, Sentimental Tommy, Tommy and Grizel, The Little White Bird* and the immortal *Peter Pan*. His plays, *The Professor's Love Story, The Little Minister, Peter Pan, Alice Sit by the Fire, Dear Brutus, What Every Woman Knows* and *Mary Rose* added greatly to his fame. John Drinkwater says: "His plays broke every law held sacred by the critics, but the spectators laughed and shook or in turn were touched to tears. The wizard had waved his wand and they were mesmerized." He was Rector of St. Andrews University from 1919 to 1922 and Chancellor of Edinburgh University in 1930. *The Courting of T'nowhead's Bell* is reprinted from *Auld Licht Idylls*.

RABINDRANATH TAGORE
(1861–   )

SIR RABINDRANATH TAGORE, was born in Calcutta. He early gave his time to managing his father's estates. In 1901, he founded a school which became an international institution, the Visva Bharata. Tagore writes both in Bengali and English. Among his best-known works are *The Crescent Moon, Gitanjali, Chitra, The King of Dark Chamber, Fruit Gathering* and *The Post Office*. He was knighted in 1915 and awarded the Nobel Prize for Literature in 1919. *The Babus of Nayanjore* is reprinted from *Hungry Stones and Other Stories*.

E. O. SOMERVILLE (1861–   )
MARTIN ROSS (1862–1915)

EDITH OENONE SOMERVILLE was born near Skibereen, County Cork, Ireland. Violet Florence Martin (Martin Ross) was born at Ross House, County Galway, Ireland. They were cousins and in their early twenties began to write a series of tales of Irish life. Their best-known books are, *Some Experiences of an Irish R.M., Further Experiences of an Irish R.M.* and *In Mr. Knox's Country.* Miss Martin died in 1915 but Miss Somerville continues to write. In 1917 she published *Irish Memories,* a memoir of her deceased collaborator. *Philippa's Fox-Hunt* is reprinted from *Some Experiences of an Irish R.M.*

MONTAGUE RHODES JAMES
(1862–1936)

MONTAGUE RHODES JAMES was appointed Provost of Eton College in 1918. He has edited a great number of bibliographical and paleographical works. In 1924 he translated *The Apocryphal New Testament.* Provost James, however, is best known to the general reading public as one of the greatest writers of ghost stories in modern times. *The Mezzotint* is reprinted from *The Collected Ghost Stories* of Montague Rhodes James.

EDEN PHILLPOTTS
(1862–   )

EDEN PHILLPOTTS was born at Mount Abu, Rasputana Province, India. He was sent to England when quite young and was educated at Plymouth. He started life as an insurance clerk but in 1890 he gave up this work to devote his entire time to literature. His novels of Devonshire life made his reputation. Among them are, *The Lying Prophets, The Good Green Earth* and *The Forest of the Hills.* His most successful play, *The Farmer's Wife,* was produced in 1917. The magic of Dartmoor in Devonshire laid hold of him at an early age and he still writes his best novels about its moor-folk. *"Hey Diddle Diddle, the Cat . . ."* is taken from *Up Hill, Down Dale.*

WILLIAM JOHN LOCKE
(1863–1930)

WILLIAM JOHN LOCKE was born in Barbados. He was educated at Queen's Royal College, Trinidad, and St. John's College, Cambridge.

He was secretary of the Royal Institute of British Architects from 1897 to 1907. In 1905 he published *The Morals of Marcus Ordeyne* and in 1906 *The Beloved Vagabond,* two novels which attained wide popularity. Other stories which added to his fame were *Simon the Jester* and *Stella Maris. The Adventure of the Kind Mr. Smith* is reprinted from *The Joyous Adventures of Aristide Pujol*.

SIR ARTHUR T. QUILLER-COUCH ("Q")
(1863–   )

SIR ARTHUR T. QUILLER-COUCH is a native of Cornwall, educated at Newton Abbott College, Clifton College, and Trinity in Oxford. Since 1912 he has been Professor of English Literature at Cambridge. Under the pseudonym of "Q" he has written a number of novels with Cornish setting, including *Dead Man's Rock, Troy Town* and *The Splendid Spur,* and in 1899 wrote the conclusion to Stevenson's unfinished *St. Ives.* He is the editor of *The Oxford Book of English Verse.*

ARTHUR MORRISON
(1863–   )

ARTHUR MORRISON is a product of Fleet Street, London, but deserted journalism when his early novels bounded to popularity, and has since devoted himself to literature and art. His collection of paintings by Chinese and Japanese masters is now in the British Museum. Most of his stories and novels are based on life in London's slum areas, the best known being *Tales of Mean Streets, Chronicles of Martin Hewitt, The Hole in the Wall* and *The Red Triangle. That Brute Simmons* is one of the outstanding stories in *Tales of Mean Streets.*

WILLIAM WYMARK JACOBS
(1863–   )

W. W. JACOBS was born and educated in London. (The reader of these notes may be as surprised as the editors to note how many prominent English authors were born in or near London. Contrast this fact with the relatively small number of leading American writers who were born in New York—or other large American cities!) Jacobs spent a number of years in the savings-bank department of the civil service. He is best known as a writer of humorous tales of dock-towns, ports and the sea, such as *Many Cargoes, The Lady of the Barge, Odd Craft* and *Captains All.* But one horror story, *The Monkey's Paw,* has made him more famous than all the rest of his work put together, and no anthologist would dare omit it from a volume that purported to be representative of the best in English literature. It is reprinted here from *The Lady of the Barge.*

LEONARD MERRICK
(1864–1939)

LEONARD MERRICK is another product of London. He was educated at Brighton College. His real name was Leonard Miller, but when he took up acting, he adopted the name of Merrick, which he later made legal. While still on the stage, he wrote a number of excellent novels and short stories, including *The Actor Manager, Conrad in Quest of His Youth* and *A Little Boy Laughed,* but his work was singularly neglected until a sudden vogue about ten years ago won him belated recognition both in England and America. Have you heard the expression, "There is no road back to Rouen?" You must read *Conrad in Quest of His Youth* to understand its ironic significance. *A Doll in a Pink Silk Dress* is a typical Merrick story, taken from *A Chair on the Boulevard.*

RUDYARD KIPLING
(1865–1936)

RUDYARD KIPLING, one of the most popular writers of all time, was born at Bombay, India. He was educated in England at United Service College, in North Devon, but returned to India and took up journalism. In 1886 appeared his *Departmental Ditties* and in the following year, his *Plain Tales from the Hills.* These two volumes blazed Kipling's trail into the hearts of English readers. His fame rests on his short stories of India, the sea, the jungle and the Army and Navy. His *Inclusive Verse* was published in 1919. Among his great successes are, *Soldiers Three, The Light That Failed, Life's Handicap, Under the Deodars, Kim, Captains Courageous, Just So Stories* and *The Jungle Books.* It has been said, "Kipling has secured a greater number and variety of admirers than any modern English writer." He was awarded the Nobel Prize for Literature in 1907 and was Rector of St. Andrews from 1922-1925. *The Drums of the Fore and Aft* is reprinted from *Wee Willie Winkie* and *The Man Who Would Be King* from *Under the Deodars.*

WILLIAM BUTLER YEATS
(1865-1939)

WILLIAM BUTLER YEATS, poet, essayist and playwright, was born in Dublin. He was educated at the Godolphin School, Hammersmith, and at the Erasmus Smith School, Dublin. He studied art for a time but adopted literature as a profession in 1886. He founded the Irish Literary Society and created the Irish National Theatre which finally took over the Abbey Theatre, in Dublin. Here the Irish players have added many a glorious page to drama history. Yeats was awarded the Nobel Prize for Literature in 1923. His plays include *The Countess Cathleen, Deirdre, The King's Threshold, The Wild Swans at Coole* and *The Winds Among the Reeds.* His *Earlier and Later Poems* and *The Celtic Twilight,* a collection of essays, added to his fame. *Red Hanrahan* is reprinted from *Early Poems and Stories.*

HERBERT GEORGE WELLS
(1866-   )

H. G. WELLS, one of the titans of modern English literature, was born in Bromley, Kent, and educated at the Royal College of Science at South Kensington. He began his career as a teacher, but became world famous as a writer with the publication of his magnificent novel, *Tono-Bungay,* in 1909. An indefatigable worker, Mr. Wells has produced a prodigious number of best-selling novels and stories. *The Time Machine, The War of the Worlds, Ann Veronica, The History of Mister Polly* and *Mr. Britling Sees It Through* are only a few of them. His *Outline of History,* first published in 1920, is still said to sell a hundred thousand copies a year. Wells' earlier stories, fantastic and imaginative, often laid centuries in the future, will probably be remembered longest; of these, *The Country of the Blind* is a noteworthy example.

ENOCH ARNOLD BENNETT
(1867-1931)

THE BULK of England's pottery industry is centered in a cluster of five towns in Staffordshire. One of them, Hanley, was the birthplace of Arnold Bennett, and it was his superlative stories of these five towns that first made him famous. *Clayhanger, Hilda Lessways* and *The Old Wives' Tale* are among the finest of these stories, although some readers may prefer his later success, *Imperial Palace,* the story of the Savoy Hotel in London. In the decade preceding his death, Arnold Bennett was in the center of social life in Mayfair, and many of his last books were frankly written for the best-seller trade. The most inconsequential of his books, however, were models of literary craftsmanship. The editors' favorite Bennett novel is *The Old Wives' Tale. Mary with the High Hand* is from *Stories of the Five Towns.*

JOHN GALSWORTHY
(1867–1933)

The Forsyte Saga, of course, towers far above any other of John Galsworthy's works, but he is also the author of many other fine novels and plays. His writings are possibly the clearest picture future generations will get of England in its heyday—the comfortable, secure, smug era that preceded the World War—and his most notable plays, *The Silver Box, Strife, Justice, The Skin Game* and *Loyalties,* throw a penetrating light on some of the evils and injustices that lurked just under the surface of those placid late Victorian and Edwardian days. John Galsworthy was born at Coombe, in Surrey, and educated at Harrow and New College, Oxford. He lived to enjoy a universal acclaim that is rarely bestowed on literary figures, and to see first editions of his novels selling for fantastic sums in the auction rooms. *The Apple-Tree* is reprinted from *Caravan.* Some day a genius in Hollywood is going to discover this beautiful story and make a couple of million dollars out of it.

CHARLES EDWARD MONTAGUE
(1867–1928)

Charles Edward Montague, novelist, journalist and dramatic critic, was born at Ealing. He was educated at the City of London School and at Balliol College, Oxford. After graduation he joined the staff of the *Manchester Guardian* and became a very successful journalist. He served in the World War, and when he returned, wrote a number of successful novels and short stories, including *Disenchantment, Fiery Particles, Rough Justice, Right Off the Map* and *Action and Other Stories.* His best-known volumes of essays are *Dramatic Values, The Right Place* and *A Writer's Notes on His Trade.* Montague was a great lover of adventure, a member of the Alpine Club and an enthusiastic mountain climber. *Action* is taken from *Action and Other Stories.*

ALGERNON BLACKWOOD
(1867–   )

ALGERNON BLACKWOOD was born in England. He was educated at the
Moravian School in the Black Forest, Germany, and Wellington Col-
lege, Cambridge. He came to the United States and worked for the
New York *Sun* and the New York *Times*. In 1906 his first book, *The
Empty House*, was published. Among his best-known works are *John
Silence, The Lost Valley, Incredible Adventures, Tongues of Fire* and
The Centaur. Blackwood specialized in novels and stories of terror and
the supernatural. His short stories are reminiscent of Poe's. *The Valley
of the Beasts* is reprinted from *The Wolves of God*.

HECTOR HUGH MUNRO ("SAKI")
(1870–1916)

Mrs. Packletide's Tiger is typical of over a hundred sparkling and delightful stories by one of the greatest English humorists of all time.
Munro, or "Saki" as he is universally known, was a native of Burma.
He began his literary career with the *Westminster Gazette,* later becoming a foreign correspondent in Russia and France. His brilliant
career was cut short by death on the field of battle in the Great War
in 1916.

MAX BEERBOHM
(1872–   )

MAX BEERBOHM is one of the fabulous figures in English literature, the
more so because, since his removal to Rapallo in 1910, he has resolutely
refrained from answering any and all communications, including frenzied entreaties from his editors and publishers. A native of London, and
product of Cambridge, this amazingly talented man won equal fame as
a caricaturist, drama critic, essayist, and novelist. His first work was
printed in the *Yellow Book;* his best-known book, *Zuleika Dobson,* did
not appear until 1911. *The Happy Hypocrite* is one of the stories in this
anthology that was originally published as a complete book.

HENRY MAJOR TOMLINSON
(1873–   )

H. M. TOMLINSON was born in London. He was self-educated. He acted
as a correspondent in the World War and later served as literary critic

of the *Nation* and *Athenaeum*. His first book, *The Sea and the Jungle,* issued in 1912, made his reputation. Among his later works are, *Tide Marks, Gallion's Reach, London River, Illusion, Old Junk* and *All Our Yesterdays,* a story of the World War. He has traveled a great deal in Africa, the East Indies and in America. He once said, "I never expected to write, it's all so accidental, it just happened in spite of me." *The Derelict* is reprinted from *Old Junk.*

WILLIAM SOMERSET MAUGHAM
(1874-   )

WILLIAM SOMERSET MAUGHAM was born in Paris, France. He was educated in King's School at Canterbury and the University of Heidelberg. He studied medicine and received his degree at St. Thomas's Hospital in London but never practiced. His first novel, *Liza of Lambert,* appeared in 1897. His reputation was made with *Of Human Bondage, The Moon and Sixpence, Cakes and Ale* and his very successful plays, *A Man of Honour, Lady Frederick, Home and Beauty, Our Betters, The Circle* and *East of Suez.* He has published some very well-known volumes of short stories, *The Trembling of a Leaf, On a Chinese Screen* and *Ashenden,* and two very excellent collections of poetry and prose, *The Traveller's Library* and *Tellers of Tales.* Somerset Maugham's clarity of style, perfection of form, subtlety of thought, veiled thinly behind a worldly cynicism, have made him an international figure. *Red* is here reprinted from *The Trembling of a Leaf.* From another story in this volume, *Rain,* one of the most successful plays of our generation, was fashioned.

GILBERT KEITH CHESTERTON
(1874-1936)

GILBERT KEITH CHESTERTON, novelist, essayist, poet and critic, was born in London. He was educated at St. Paul's School and the Slades School of Art. He took up literature in 1900 and contributed to a number of periodicals. Among his best-known novels are *The Napoleon of Nottingham Hill, The Man Who Was Thursday, The Flying Inn* and *The Ball and the Cross.* His short stories, *The Innocence of Father Brown* and *The Wisdom of Father Brown* originally begun as a mere diversion, have won him more readers than all his serious works put together. His essays, *Heretics* and *Orthodoxy,* his volumes of poetry, *The Ballad of the White Horse, Wine, Water and Song,* and his volumes on Dickens and Browning added to his reputation. *The Hammer of God* is reprinted from *The Innocence of Father Brown.*

JOHN BUCHAN, LORD TWEEDSMUIR
(1875–)

JOHN BUCHAN, LORD TWEEDSMUIR, was born in Perth, Scotland. He was educated at Glasgow University and Brasenose College, Oxford. He was called to the Bar in 1901. He was a correspondent for the London *Times* in the World War. He also saw service as an Intelligence Officer and was finally appointed Director of Information. In 1907 he became a partner in the Thomas Nelson Sons, publishing house. In 1935 he was appointed Governor General of Canada. Among his many successful novels are *The Thirty-Nine Steps, Greenmantle, Mr. Standfast, Prester John, Witchwood, The Dancing Floor, Castle Gay* and his omnibus, *The Adventures of Richard Hannay.* He also wrote a *History of the Great War* and studies of Julius Caesar, Oliver Cromwell, Montrose, Sir Walter Scott and Augustine. *The Kings of Orion* is taken from *The Moon Endureth.*

PHILIP HAMILTON GIBBS
(1877–)

SIR PHILIP HAMILTON GIBBS, Chevalier of the Legion D'Honneur, was educated privately. He was a war correspondent in France and Belgium during the World War. For his brilliant services as a journalist the English government conferred a title on him in 1920. He has served as literary editor of the *Daily Mail* and the *Daily Chronicle.* Among his best-known works are *The Street of Adventure, The Age of Reason, Beauty and Nick, The Soul of the War, Now It Can Be Told, Venetian Lovers, The Reckless Lady* and *Young Anarchy. The Stranger in the Village* is reprinted from *Little Novels of Nowadays.*

ALFRED EDGAR COPPARD
(1877–)

A. E. COPPARD was born at Folkstone, and educated at the Lewes Road Board School. His first book, published in 1921, entitled, *Adam and Eve and Pinch Me,* made his reputation. Coppard is a teller of unusual and fanciful tales. Among them are *Clorinda, Walks in Heaven, The Black Dog, The Fishmonger's Fiddle* and *The Field of Mustard.* His two volumes of verse, *Palagea* and *Yokohama Garland,* are well known. *The Higgler* is taken from *The Fishmonger's Fiddle.*

JOHN MASEFIELD
(1878-　　)

JOHN MASEFIELD was born in Ledbury, Herefordshire. He attended a local school and ran away to sea when he was fourteen. He worked a number of years in New York. In 1897, Masefield returned to England. During the World War he served with the Red Cross in France and on the Gallipoli Peninsula. His novels include *Jim Davis, Sard Harker, Captain Margaret* and *Odtaa*. Masefield is best known for his poetry. He was created Poet Laureate in 1930. His most notable volumes of poems are *Salt Water Ballads, Ballads and Poems, The Everlasting Mercy, The Widow of Bye Street, Dauber, Reynard the Fox* and *The Daffodil Fields. The Western Islands* is reprinted from *A Mainsail Haul.*

EDWARD JOHN MORETON DRAY PLUNCKETT (LORD DUNSANY)
(1878-　　)

TWENTY YEARS ago the plays and stories of Lord Dunsany were a great deal more popular in America than they are today. Stuart Walker's Portmanteau Players were doing his elaborate whimsies with resounding success, and his *Tales of Wonder* was one of the featured titles in that sounding board of popular taste, the Modern Library. If Dunsany, like Maeterlinck, was overrated then, he still has produced some first-rate material, *The Sword of Welleran* being typical of his best vein. Dunsany is the eighteenth in a long line of Irish baronets. He was graduated from Eton and enlisted for the South African War. In the World War he was a Captain in the Royal Fusiliers. His writings are greatly influenced by his study of the Bible and Greek mythology.

EDWARD MORGAN FORSTER
(1879-　　)

E. M. FORSTER was born in London, and educated at King's College, Cambridge, where he was appointed a Fellow of the college. He established a high literary reputation with *A Passage to India,* published in 1924. Among his best-known works are *Where Angels Fear to Tread, A Room with a View, The Longest Journey* and *The Aspects of the Novel. The Celestial Omnibus* is the title story of his celebrated volume of short stories.

BIOGRAPHICAL NOTES

1225

ALFRED NOYES
(1880-   )

ALFRED NOYES, poet and novelist, was born at Staffs, and educated at
Exeter College, Oxford. His first volume of poems, *The Loom of Years,*
was published in 1902. His *Tales of a Mermaid Tavern, Flower of Old
Japan* and *The Forest of Wild Thyme* made him famous. His novels
include *The Wine Press, The Hidden Player* and *The Sun Cure. The
Log of the "Evening Star"* is reprinted from *Walking Shadows.*

PELHAM GRENVILLE WODEHOUSE
(1881-   )

P. G. WODEHOUSE, one of the funniest men in all the world, is England's crushing rejoinder to anyone who insinuates that the British
sense of humor is slightly under par. Equally successful in fiction, on
the stage and in Hollywood, Wodehouse is beloved by everybody who
ever heard of him, with the possible exception of a couple of old meanies
from the United States Income Tax Bureau. Wodehouse was born at
Guilford, and began his career as a columnist. For his creation of Jeeves,
the perfect manservant, he deserves a place on high, and his *Blandings
Castle* series (particularly *Fish Preferred*) is required reading for anybody who likes to laugh. *Jeeves and the Song of Songs* is Wodehouse's
most famous story. His novels include *Piccadilly Jim* and *A Damsel in
Distress,* his plays (in collaboration with Guy Bolton and Jerome Kern)
Oh, Boy and *Leave It to Jane.*

JAMES STEPHENS
(1882-   )

JAMES STEPHENS, poet and story-teller, was born in Dublin. He was self-
educated. He became famous on the publication, in 1912, of his prose
fancy, *The Crock of Gold.* He later issued *Deirdre, In the Land of
Youth, The Demi-Gods, The Charwoman's Daughter, Irish Fairy Tales*
and two collections of short stories, *Etched in Moonlight* and *Here Are
Ladies.* His collected volume of poems was issued in 1926. Stephens has
always been interested in the old folk-tales of Ireland and is an authority
on Gaelic art. *The Three Lovers Who Lost* is taken from *Here Are
Ladies.*

BIOGRAPHICAL NOTES

JAMES JOYCE
(1882–   )

JAMES JOYCE, the author of the most controversial novel of the twentieth century, *Ulysses,* is a native of Dublin, and a graduate of the Royal University there. He spent some years after his graduation in Paris, where he studied medicine for a while. When he quit his native land in disgust with its lack of appreciation of his talents, it was to Paris he returned, this time permanently. His first book was published in 1907— a volume of poems entitled *Chamber Music. Dubliners* came in 1914, and *A Portrait of the Artist as a Young Man* in 1916. *Ulysses,* the first "stream of consciousness" novel, was completed in 1920, but it was not until a court decision legalized its publication in America in 1934 that the author received any substantial compensation for a truly monumental work. American royalties enabled Joyce to undergo a number of operations that cured his failing eyesight, and to finish his latest work in 1939. It is called *Finnegan's Wake,* and is unfortunately intelligible to only a handful of initiates.

MRS. FRANCIS EVANS BAILY (MAY EDGINTON)
(1883–   )

MRS. FRANCIS EVANS BAILY (May Edginton), novelist, dramatist and short-story writer, has been a frequent contributor of short stories and novels to leading British and American magazines. Among her best-known works are *Lonely Road, So This Is Love, Storm Over Youth, Wives Must Weep, Fleet Street Girl* and *African Nymph.* She was also part author of a number of successful plays, including *Secrets* and *His Lady Friend. Purple and Fine Linen* is reprinted from *They Were All in Love.*

SIR HUGH SEYMOUR WALPOLE
(1884–   )

HUGH WALPOLE, novelist, lecturer, publicist and indefatigable contributor of introductions to other men's books, was born in Auckland, New Zealand. He was sent to England at an early age and was educated at King's School, Canterbury, and at Cambridge. He served with the Russian Red Cross in the World War. His first novel, *The Wooden Horse,* was published in 1909. This was followed by a great number of novels that made him famous, *Fortitude, The Captives, The Cathedral, The Dark Forest, The Duchess of Wrexe, Jeremy, The Silver Thorn* and *Rogue Herries*. Many of his novels reflect his early background. He says, "I grew up in the shadow of an Anglican Cathedral (Durham), and it's pretty hard to break away from old ties." *Mr. Oddy* is taken from *All Souls Night*.

FRANCIS BRETT YOUNG
(1884–   )

FRANCIS BRETT YOUNG, novelist and physician, was born in Worcestershire. He was educated at Epsom College and Birmingham University. He practiced medicine in Brixham, Devon, and served in Africa with the Royal Army Medical Corps in the World War. He spends a great deal of his time writing on the Island of Capri. Among his most popular books are *Marching on Tanga, The Crescent Moon, Wood Smoke, The Tragic Bride, The Black Diamond, My Brother Jonathan* and *Redlakes*. He is grateful for his medical training. As he says, "There is no education in humanity to compare with a doctor's life." *A Busman's Holiday* is taken from *The Cage Bird and Other Stories*.

WESTON MARTYR
(1885–   )

WESTON MARTYR was born in Southampton. He ran away to sea at the age of fifteen and served in square-rigged vessels for a number of years. He later became a gold miner in South Africa and recruited labor in China for the Rand Mines. He has been at different times a steamship agent in Japan, a banker in Formosa and a South Sea trader. He served as Captain of the Sherwood Foresters in the World War. Among his best-known works are *Not Without Dust and Heat, The South Sea Man, A General Cargo, The Pipe Pushers,* and *Paradise Enow. A Sleeping Draft* is from *Not Without Dust and Heat*.

DAVID HERBERT LAWRENCE
(1885–1930)

D. H. LAWRENCE, dead, has been the subject of bitter controversy by his intimates and a score of petty writers bent on exploiting their memories of him. Alive, his tormented pilgrimage in the world was a constant quest for health and a feverish devotion to his writings. He was born in Nottingham, the son of an impoverished coal miner, and began life as a school teacher. His first venture as a novelist was *The White Pea-cock,* published in 1911. Two years later came his masterpiece, *Sons and Lovers. The Rainbow,* in 1915, was declared obscene, and an entire edition destroyed by court order. Harassed by illness and shortage of funds, Lawrence wandered through Europe, Australia and America, where he lived awhile at Taos, New Mexico. In 1928, the private pub-lication of *Lady Chatterley's Lover* provoked another storm. Law-rence's last years were devoted as much to painting as to writing. *The Prussian Officer* is the title story of his finest collection of shorter tales.

ROLAND PERTWEE
(1885-   )

ROLAND PERTWEE, actor, novelist and portrait painter, was born in Eng-land. He studied painting under John Sargent and histrionics under H. B. Irving. He gave up his career as a portrait painter because his brush could catch only those facial characteristics which the sitters wished to conceal. He wrote his first novel in a hospital bed during the World War. Among his most successful novels are *Gentlemen March, Royal Heritage* and *Princess by Proxy.* His play, *Interference,* was one of the first successful American "talkies." Pertwee is passionately fond of fishing; *Fish Are Such Liars,* besides being one of the most charm-ing stories in this volume, will give the reader ample evidence of his knowledge of the subject!

STACY AUMONIER
(1887-1928)

STACY AUMONIER'S stories are practically unknown in America, and that is a great pity, for many of them are in the very first rank and, furthermore, fulfil much more clearly American requirements for a good story than the writings of a number of English authors who are ten times better known here. Aumonier began his career as a decorative designer and landscape painter. After service in the World War, he became a society entertainer, giving recitals of his own character sketches. Some of his books are *The Querrils, Heartbeats, Miss Brace-girdle* and *Odd Fish. A Source of Irritation* is reprinted here from *The Golden Windmill.* If you enjoy it as much as the editors did, you may become a member of that small Aumonier cult that makes up in enthu-siasm what it lacks in numbers.

THOMAS BURKE
(1887–   )

THOMAS BURKE was born in London, and grew up very close to those unsavory sections of the city that he has chosen as the setting for his score and more novels and books of short stories. *Limehouse Nights* made him famous, and millions of Americans who had never even heard of Limehouse hummed the slumbrous song that was named after his book. The most popular and most striking story in this volume is *The Chink and the Child,* which was made into a memorable motion picture by D. W. Griffith, and released under the title of *Broken Blossoms.*

KATHLEEN BEAUCHAMP MURRY
(KATHERINE MANSFIELD)
(1888–1923)

KATHERINE MANSFIELD was born in Wellington, New Zealand. At an early age she was sent to England and was educated at Queen's College, London. Her first stories and sketches appeared in *The New Age.* She suffered during her life from poor health and visited different climates searching for relief. Only three of her books were published in her lifetime. Four came later with her letters and journals. Among her works the best known are *Bliss, The Garden Party, The Doves' Nest, The Little Girl, Aloe* and her *Letters and Journals.* Katherine Mansfield has taken her place as one of the greatest short-story writers of modern times. *Life of Ma Parker* is taken from *The Garden Party.*

MRS. T. P. FRY (SHEILA KAYE-SMITH)
(1888–   )

SHEILA KAYE-SMITH's homey stories of the Sussex fields and farms have made her one of the most popular—and prosperous—of modern English authors. Her first story was printed when she was twenty, and there followed a steady stream of "best sellers," including *Joanna Godden, Sussex-Gorse, The Village Doctor* and *Isle of Thorns. A Day in a Woman's Life* is one of the stories in *Joanna Godden Married.*

BRIAN OSWALD DONN-BYRNE
(DONN BYRNE)
(1889–1928)

DONN BYRNE was born in New York while his parents were on a visit to the United States, but three months after his birth he was taken to his parents' home in the Vale of Armagh, Ireland, where he spent his boyhood. He studied at Dublin University, the Sorbonne and the University of Leipzig. Byrne called himself "the last of the traditional Irish story-tellers," and indeed was so determinedly Irish on occasion that his books lost all their spontaneity and charm. *Messer Marco Polo*, however, published in 1921, is a minor classic, and other outstanding books by Donn Byrne include *Hangman's House, O'Malley of Shangonagh* and *Blind Raferty*. Byrne was killed in an accident near his Coolmain castle by the Irish Sea. *Rivers of Damascus* was originally published as a complete book.

ALDOUS LEONARD HUXLEY
(1894–)

ALDOUS HUXLEY, one of the most brilliant English novelists of all time, is descended from a famous family. His great grandfather was Thomas Huxley; his brother is Julian Huxley. Aldous Huxley was educated at Eton and Oxford, and then, strongly under the influence of D. H. Lawrence at first, produced a series of novels whose erudition and profundity amazed the critics and the reading public. *Crome Yellow, Antic Hay, Point Counter Point, Brave New World* and *Eyeless in Gaza* followed one another in close order, interspersed with volumes of essays and stories that included *Mortal Coils, Music at Night* and *On the Margin*. In 1939, Aldous Huxley was lured by the siren song of Hollywood, and at present occupies a cubicle in Metro-Goldwyn-Mayer's writers' building. His latest novel, *After Many a Summer*, is a study of a thinly disguised California newspaper tycoon.

MICHAEL ARLEN
(1895–)

THE MICHAEL ARLEN cult reached its hysterical height in 1925, when *The Green Hat* was the book of the year, and its unbelievable heroine, Iris March, was played by Katharine Cornell on the stage, and Greta Garbo on the screen. Its author, Armenian by heritage, Bulgarian by birth, was wined and dined by Mayfair and Park Avenue (Irvin S. Cobb once introduced him as "the only Armenian I've met who didn't try to sell me a rug!"). He is now a naturalized British subject. Mr. Arlen has never had such a success again, although he is still writing novels and stories. His best tales are in a volume called *These Charming People,* from which *The Cavalier of the Streets* has been taken.

LIAM O'FLAHERTY
(1896–   )

LIAM O'FLAHERTY's powerful Irish tales have long won him critical acclaim, but it took a prize-winning motion-picture version of his novel, *The Informer,* to make him famous. O'Flaherty was born in the Aran Islands and educated at the University of Dublin. He served in the Irish Guards in the World War, and then beat his way clear around the globe, charming all and sundry by an irresistible and flaming personality. He lived for some time in Hartford, Connecticut, and it was there, in fact, that he first started submitting stories to the magazines. His novels include *The Neighbor's Wife, The Puritan, Mr. Gilhooly* and *Famine.* He now lives in France, where he is working on a novel about Cuba. *The Old Hunter* is from his collected short stories.

LEONARD ALFRED GEORGE STRONG
(1896–   )

L. A. G. STRONG, poet, novelist and short story writer, was born at Plympton in Devon. In his youth he spent his summers in Ireland. He was educated at Brighton College and Wadham College, Oxford. For twelve years he was a schoolmaster, teaching at a famous Oxford school. His *Selected Poems* were issued in 1931. His best-known novels are, *Dewer Rides, The Jealous Ghost, The Garden, The Brothers* and *Sea Wall.* His collections of short stories include *Doyle's Rock, The English Captain, Don Juan and the Wheelbarrow* and *Tuesday Afternoon and Other Stories.* William Butler Yeats took a great interest in Leonard Strong and persuaded him to give his entire time to writing. *The White Cottage* is taken from *Tuesday Afternoon and Other Stories.*

HENRY WILLIAMSON
(1897–   )

HENRY WILLIAMSON, novelist and nature writer, was born at Bedfordshire. He served as a private in the World War. He said, "After the war, the scenes of my boyhood, the fields, the trees, the birds, all came back to me poignantly. I saw where my salvation lay, in nature." Williamson's literary career started with his novel, *The Beautiful Years*. Then followed, *Dandelion Days, Sun Brothers, The Lone Swallows, The Old Stag and Other Stories, Tarka, The Otter* and *The Village Book*. The *Manchester Guardian* says, "One can read a chapter, a page, even a sentence, of Williamson, and, laying it down, dream of buttercup fields in the sunshine, whispering white throats and the lark's nest in the burnt rose." *The Trapper's Mates* is reprinted from *The Old Stag and Other Stories*.

RALPH BATES
(1899–)

No AUTHOR represented in this volume has had so exciting a life as Ralph Bates. He was born in Swindon, England, and his formal education was cut short by the little problem of earning money for food and sustenance. He became a machinist in British factories, and began to understand the elements of the class struggle. Directly after the War, he went to Spain and became a dock laborer and labor organizer. At the outbreak of the Spanish Civil War he joined the ranks of the Loyalist defenders. He fought in the front lines and later became a ranking officer in the International Brigade. He now lives in New York. His best-known works are *Lean Men, The Olive Field, Rainbow Fish* and *Sirocco. The Forty-Third Division* is one of the superlative stories in the latter volume.

THOMAS OWEN BEACHCROFT
(1902–)

THOMAS OWEN BEACHCROFT, short-story writer, was born in Bristol, England. He was educated at Clifton College. He is a versatile young man. At college, he won prizes for boxing, running and poetry. After leaving college, he became an announcer for the British Broadcasting Company. He then took up journalism and subsequently made a success in advertising. Mr. Beachcroft elects to write short stories because they can be turned out at odd moments in a busy life. Most of his tales, he declares, were literally written on tops of London buses. Among his best-known works are *Just Cats, The Man Who Started Clean, You Must Break Out Sometimes* and *A Young Man in a Hurry*. *The Eyes* is taken from *A Young Man in a Hurry*.

EVELYN WAUGH
(1903–   )

EVELYN WAUGH is one of the very bright young men from Oxford whose brilliant satirical novels express so well the cynicism and disillusion of Britain's post-war generation. He was born in London, the son of Arthur Waugh, a well-known publisher, and the brother of the novelist, Alec Waugh. *Decline and Fall* and *Vile Bodies* are two of the most bitterly humorous novels of our day; his latest books, *A Handful of Dust* and *Scoop,* are in a slightly more serious vein. *Bella Fleace Gave a Party* is from a volume of stories called *Mr. Loveday's Little Outing.*

> *These biographical sketches were written in the Fall of 1939. As revisions become necessary, they will be made in future editions.*
>
> THE EDITORS